Felicia Dorothea Browne Hemans

# The Poetical Works of Felicia Hemans

Complete, with a Critical Preface

Felicia Dorothea Browne Hemans

**The Poetical Works of Felicia Hemans**
*Complete, with a Critical Preface*

ISBN/EAN: 9783744719872

Printed in Europe, USA, Canada, Australia, Japan

Cover: Foto ©Andreas Hilbeck / pixelio.de

More available books at **www.hansebooks.com**

THE

# POETICAL WORKS

OF

# FELICIA HEMANS,

COMPLETE,

## WITH A CRITICAL PREFACE.

———

NEW YORK:
AMERICAN BOOK EXCHANGE,
764 BROADWAY.
1881.

# PREFACE.

It has been said by a fine writer, that, although genius is the heir of fame, the loss of life is the condition on which the bright reversion must be earned; that fame is the recompense not of the living, but of the dead,—its temple standing over the grave, and the flame of its altar kindled from the ashes of the great. There is truth in the thought, as well as beauty in the expression of it, though, like most general remarks of the same description, it is open to both qualification and exception. It is true that fame is not popularity merely. It is not the shout of the multitude. It is not 'the idle buzz of fashion, the venal puff, the soothing flattery of favour or of friendship.' But is it alone, on the other hand, the spirit of a man *surviving himself*, as Hazlitt describes it, in the minds and thoughts of other men? Or, as he splendidly represents it again, is it only 'the sound which the stream of high thoughts, carried down to *future ages*, makes as it flows—deep, distant, murmuring evermore like the waters of the mighty ocean?' This is fame, indeed. No reputation can be called *such*, that will not endure that test. But may it not begin also in the life of him that earns it? May it not begin, and continue, coincident with the mere popularity which is so often mistaken for itself,—as the immortal soul disdains not the envelope of perishing humanity, which it is destined so soon to leave, and to outlive so long? May not the spirit of a man transfuse its influence into the spirits of other men, without the mythological transmigration which, according to this theory, death implies;—and the force of that influence be felt, and recognized, and acknowledged,—imperfectly and tardily we admit that it generally is,—ere yet the 'swift decay' of him that so works for the world, and for posterity, shall quite release him from his toils? It is truly a weary life'—

"A wasting task, and lone—"

as that of the diver, in Eastern Seas, for the gem that, gleam as it may, 'a star to all the festive ball',—

"—Not one 'midst throngs will say,
' A life has been, like a rain-drop, shed,
For that pale quivering ray ' "*

A weary life! And who will think, the mournful fancy adds,

"When the strain is sung,
Till a thousand hearts are stirr'd,
What life-drops, from the minstrel wrung,
Have gush'd with every word?"

"None! none!—his treasures live like thine,
*He* strives and dies like thee,—
Thou that hast been to the pearl's dark shrine,
O wrestler with the sea!"

And *this* also is doubtless true,—that, weary and wasting as it is,—this diving for the gems of thought,—the world, that is to wear the rich results, does not and cannot appreciate, or but slowly and slightly at the best, the exhausting effort which it costs That can be understood only by him who suffers it, and it is the province of the one party even to enjoy 'the price of the bitter tears' of the other. But it is enjoyed; and that is fame. It is the influence of mind upon mind, independently of every personal consideration; and that is fame,—however much those considerations, or some of them, were they known and felt, as they cannot be, might add to the interest of that influence, and even to its force.

The best confirmation, melancholy though it be, of the truth of these remarks, is furnished by the case of the gifted, accomplish ed, and amiable writer whose beautiful illustration of her own career—not to call it a prediction of her own destiny—we have borrowed, and whose works are now for the first time gathered together, in the following pages, we trust with something like a completeness corresponding to the exertion which has been made by the Publisher, as well as to the merit and charm of the works themselves. The mere popularity of these poems,—their cotemporaneous notoriety,—and especially as indicated by the notice of the periodical press,—has been perhaps entirely unexampled in the history of literature of this description. Such at least was the reputation of the larger portion of them, all her later productions included; for it is true, as critics have remarked, that not only the debût which she made in a juvenile volume, at Liverpool, while yet in her childhood, (a collection of little effusions written between the ages of eight and thirteen, to which she, who had the right of decision, did not herself subsequently choose to give a place among her mature 'works',) but even the much more elaborate compositions of many succeeding years, including the Restoration of the Works of Art to Italy, (published in 1817,) and other poems studded as richly with brilliant passages, did not have the effect to establish her reputation. In fact, the Records of Woman, which appeared only some eight years since, may be considered as having fairly laid its foundations. From that time, however, as we have said, the favour her poems met with was unexampled. But who will pretend that it was no more than 'favour;' that it was but a transient air of popular whim which sustained them, but gave no test nor pledge of an inherent and enduring buoyancy? Who will deny that Mrs. Hemans has enjoyed—or, if we use the term which is applicable to the personal effort and effect, that she has suffered,—in her own life-time, a true fame,—even the truest, dearest, best, of all its species,—though only as the dim beginning of the brightness which awaits her name? Even the extraordinary newspaper popularity (so to speak) of her later writings, is itself an indication, on the whole, of the fact. It shows the feeling of the people, which dictates the fashion of the press; and although there are many of the works of genius which may largely attract the attention and admiration of the world, for a time, and for various and obvious reasons, without leaving their *mark* on the minds or hearts of men, others there are, possessed of a vital spirit, that, once appreciated, they will not 'willingly let die.' The notoriety of such an auth r, as an author, is equivalent to his fame. It is as true of virtue, especially, as of vice, that it 'needs but *to be seen;*' and although that conventional corporation which has the name of 'the public,' merely, are not seldom deceived by false pretences, and dazzled by brilliant shows, the world at large is wiser than the public, (as much as it is wiser than any individual,) and *will see.* It will feel, too; and acknowledge what it feels. It will acknowledge it, not in the columns of the newspapers, to be sure, alone—though these certainly have their part to play — but as Scott's was acknowledged, when a traveller states that he found, in the remotest regions of Hungary, a volume of one of his delightful romances in a peasant's cabin; as Thomson's was, when a shabby, soiled copy of 'The Seasons' was noticed, by a man of genius, lying on the table of an obscure ale-house, in England. 'That,' said he, 'is true fame!' And it was, and is so. Such is the fame of the Vicar of Wakefield, and John Gilpin, and the Pilgrim, and poor Robinson Crusoe, and the Cotter's Saturday Night. It is seen not in the diamond editions that glitter on the centre-tables of genteel society, or crowd, with everything else, the bibliopole's multifarious collections of *rarities;* but the ragged volumes of every circulating library, grown old and illegible before their time by dint of reading—and the thumbed copies that lie on the window-ledge of the poor man's cottage, with the leaves turned down by the good woman to 'keep the place'—and the song, or the ode, which the milk-maid trolls on the hill-side, or a band of freemen (like the descendants of the Plymouth Pilgrims) adopt for the festal commemoration of their fathers glory,— these are the quick pulses that prove the existence of an author in his fame. Such has been already the success of Mrs. Hemans. She addressed herself not to passion, or fashion, or the public, or any class of the community or country she lived in, but to human beings, as such,—to their hearts, as well as their heads—with truth's transparent and glowing passport in her hand;—and it was an introduction that never yet failed to be effectual, nor ever will. Fashion will pass away, and passion subside in satiety; and the frivolous industry that ministered to the gratification of the one, and the false excitement that led the other to its own destruction, will be despised first, and then forgotten; but man remains the same, from first to last; and truth, which also remains, is mighty, and, worthily interpreted, must prevail. How long it may be in making its way, depends upon the circumstances of each particular case. It may address the head, or the heart, or both. It may be more or less a matter of necessity, or of luxury alone. It may be left to the recommendation only of its own modest merit, or be drawn into notice by fortunate crises, or casual accompaniments, well adapted to excite a seasonable sympathy as it were at the mere sight of its features, or the sound of its name, while its absolute character is yet unknown. Meanwhile

" The soul whence these high gifts are shed,
  *May* faint in solitude,"

exhausted by these same efforts, or borne down by circumstances which have little or no connexion with them; or it may thrive as the young tree that leans over running waters, and grow stronger as it gives more fruit, till it lives to feel, in the airs that reach it from many a far-off shore, the joy of its own blossomy breath returned to it, and to hear the blessing of the poor pilgrim who has paused in the dust of the way-side of a weary life, and the school-girl's glee, and the child's murmur of sweet delight, as they turn down from the heat of the day, to be refreshed and rejoice together in the gloom of its green repose.

So, we say, has it been already, and so, we venture to predict, it will be still, with much of the poetry of Mrs. Hemans. She strove to be the worthy interpreter of worthy truth, deeply concerning the happiness of her race; and the vital spirit of virtue has inspired her to be equal to the task. This is her praise; and it is praise enough; not that she has spent her strength in the rearing of dazzling fabrics of fancy, as brilliant and as useless as the ice-palaces of the northern Queen; not that she has chosen to indulge the impulse of a wayward temperament in the reckless expression of feeling without principle, and of sentiment without point; not that she has dealt only in the cold oracles of a selfish philosophy, more thoughtful of truth, and of proof, than of the use of either

in the wants of the world; not that she has indulged unholy passion in her own breast, or the breast of any living creature; not that she has dared to exaggerate, that at all events she might astonish, or deigned to be mean, in the miserable hope of amusing. No! She has neither failed to feel the high dignity of her profession, nor forgotten to observe it. She has made no vain displa of genius faithless to its trust. She has cultivated self as the means, not consulted it as the end. She has been ambitious less to gain honour, than to give pleasure, and do good.) She has not assumed to assert what is doubtful, or to deny what is not. She has not dogmatized, criticized, or theorized. She has not speculated. She has not trifled. She has not flattered, nor inflamed. But she did strive to ennoble virtue; to encourage exertion; to sustain hope; to increase the happiness of men, by increasing their capacity to be happy, and developing their taste for what is deserving of pursuit. She strove, in a word, as we began with saying, to be the worthy interpreter of worthy truth. And she was so.

This, we say, is her praise; and it is the greater for its rarity. There has been too much among us of extravagant excitement,— even from the master-minds of the times,— as if there were no way of avoiding the cold gorgeousness of the mere phantasmagoria of fancy, or the idle insipidity of a soulless sentimentalism, or any other of the deficient styles of the day, but by rushing headlong to the opposite extreme. Mrs. Hemans has taken the reasonable medium, which her native sense and sensibility alike approved. She has shown us that nature alone is strange enough, and strong enough, for all the purposes of interest and instruction which poetry demands: and that its true office is not to distort, but to describe; not to magnify, but to simplify; to do justice, strictly, to divinity, and to humanity, and to the universe around us, not by assuming to paint them as they should be, but by faithfully labouring to interpret them as they are.

No Delphic frenzy could aid in the discharge of such a service; it would have made it, as in so many other cases, (*not* heathen,) it has done, a worse than worthless labour. She wanted the powers of perception, and reflection, to appreciate the world without, and the world within; and these she had, and did; but not as if to know, and to think, only, were the life of the soul. She wanted sensibility,—the more exquisite the better,—and the more cultivated with all the faculties in due proportion, the better,—' for what is it to live, if it be not to love ?'* She wanted to be ready to feel, as only the good can do, ' at the sight of whatever is excellent, an emotion like that which the sweet remembrance of infancy causes ;'—an instinct to recognize the face of the beautiful, wherever it may be, and to rush, as it were, into its arms, as the Syrian pilgrim,† from all his wanderings returned to his mother's home again, into *hers.* She wanted enthusiasm even, in the exercise of these capacities,—enthusiasm to make the exercise a delight, and to inspire her to communicate to other bosoms the rejoicing of her own. But with all these, which she had, she needed no morbid disorder. She had none. She knew that " we preserve this precious faculty of the heart"—even *this*—' only in proportion as we cultivate truth, and guard against the exaggerated, affected, or factitious.' She kept herself calm even for the purpose of feeling—of feeling rightly—as much as of seeing clearly,—knowing also it is a fruitless torture we choose to suffer, ' to force ourselves to be false to ourselves, and to everything, that we may learn how to be true:' that the mind may faithfully mirror, only in a state of composure, the impressions which meet it ; that the knowledge, the knowledge of all nature, and especially of his own, which the poet pursues, flees from the rushing footstep of passion, even as the haste of the hunter startles his game. ' And why, after all,'—the philosopher we have cited so often, inquires,—' why should we be disturbed ? What should we gain by so much toil ? Why do we not allow ourselves time to breathe ? The good we follow'—and this is as true in poetry, as in philosophy—' is nearer to the soul than we think ; *it would come to us, if we only consented to be calm.'*

This calmness it is, which eminently characterizes the poetry of Mrs. Hemans, and which most distinguishes it from the revolutionary poetry of the revolutionary age we live in. It is a self-possession which never forsakes her in the heat of her highest enthusiasm of joy or sorrow. There is a divine dignity, unsurpassed even by the grandeur of Milton, in the rapture of an admiration

that seems almost to lift her in her song, as upon angels' pinions,—

> " To the breath
> Of Dorian flute, or lyre-note soft and slow :"*

and again, in the darkest mood of the ' tender gloom' which beautifully tinges the whole surface of her works, (like the dim religious light of an ancient forest, or of one of her own lonely fanes—

"A mighty minster, dim, and proud, and vast,)"

there is yet a more than wakeful,—a cheerful, —an inextinguishably cheerful spirit,—an immortal hope,—'a calmness of the just,'—as manifest and as majestic in herself as in her own ' Alvar's glorious mien,'† — and making its voice heard in the midst of its sorrow, like the martyr's

> " Sweet and solemn-breathing strain,
> Piercing the flames, untremulous and clear."

We have called it the vital spirit of virtue which sustains her. Let us say, in her own language, again,—

> " It is a fearful, yet a glorious thing,
> To hear that hymn of martyrdom, and know
> That its glad stream of melody could spring
> Up from the unsounded gulfs of human woe !
> Alvar! Theresa!—What is deep ? what strong ?
> *God's breath within the soul!* "

For *such* an exhaustless reservoir of resources, after all, is the secret of her inspiration. And this, too, is the inspiration of truth, deep-seated, but calm, as a lake of the hills, in the sun-bright silence of the breast.

This, then, we regard as the *principle* of the poetry of Mrs. Hemans,—its *truth.* It implies much, in detail. It implies perception, imagination, sensibility, self-control, and control over language ; and truth, and taste, in all ; for there is need to know, feel, reason, conceive, and describe, and all in their due proportion and season ; in other words, as truth requires,—since to feel too much (for example) is of course as false to Nature as to feel too little, or not at all ; and as regards the party to whom poetry is addressed, to be unable to command the means of conveying what is felt, by suitable language, is the same, so far as the deficiency exists, as if there were nothing to be conveyed, and no effort made to do it.

This characteristic implies, then, that what is attempted, is done. It does not imply, necessarily, the highest order of genius, in the popular sense of the term, or,—not to settle the precedence of the diversities of genius,—it does not imply every kind of it.

---

* Degerando.  † The Crusader's Return.

* League of the Alps  ‡ Forest Sanctuary.

In the Evening Prayer at a Girls' School, Mrs. Hemans may have exquisitely succeeded in doing justice to the truth of a beautiful subject (as we think she has) without evincing (as we think she has not) the universal power of Shakspeare to identify himself, intuitively, as it has been described with every character which he wished to represent, "and to pass from one to another like the same soul successively animating different bodies." This may be necessary to a perfect dramatic talent, but not to every species of composition; the writer himself, whose splendid sketch we refer to, admits that even the universality of his genius was ' perhaps *a disadvantage to his single works*,' the variety of his resources sometimes diverting him from applying them to the most effectual purpose.

Mrs. Hemans did not attempt everything, though her range certainly was wide enough to content the mere ambition of most authors. Nor did she equally succeed in everything she did undertake, especially in the earlier part of her career, while it remained yet to be decided by trial, to her own satisfaction, what she was best qualified to do. It is one of the traits she most deserves to be praised for, that she has not attempted some things, as much as that she succeeded so eminently in others. It were far better for the world, as well as for those who write for it, if they would exercise a good deal more of the mind they do possess, in the shape of a sound judgment and a nice tact, to determine what they cannot accomplish, and what they should not attempt. There would be far more work done,—and far worthier of being done, —and better done;—and far fewer of those abortive abuses which consist in the juggling torture, and end often in the sacrifice, of real poetical power, with only the reward of the open-mouthed gaze of the mob,—upturned for a moment,—who are silly enough to surround the stage which it plays its pranks on. There is no necessity of particularizing those portions of the works of our authoress, in which she has succeeded best, or least, upon this principle of following her bent. Suffice it to say that she made it a study —at the expense of experience, of course — a serious and conscientious study; and that she finally devoted herself, for the most part, with a sagacity and a self-denial equally worthy of all admiration, to the department she found herself to be fitted for.

Thus, too, did she follow out the principle of her genius, its truth. She was true to herself, as well as to nature; true to her own nature, we should rather say; and because she was so, in no small degree it is, that she achieved, in those departments, a success unrivalled in the history of the literature to which we allude.

It might be expected that poetry to which these remarks were applicable, should be strongly distinguished by its simplicity; and it is so. Truth is always simple, as every species of affectation necessarily is otherwise, and stands directly in its light. These compositions are as simple as they are calm and serene. They will please therefore, at least, when they do not surprise; nay, in the midst of all the whirl and turmoil of the machinery of the poetry-factory of these days, they will surprise, even, by their serene simplicity. They did so, especially at their first appearance; and it is only because Mrs. Hemans herself has accustomed the public to this rarest of the novelties, that the impression of its charm may have been in any degree even transiently disparaged, as by the charge, for example, of monotony. An accomplished writer, to whom we are probably more indebted in this country, than to any other individual, next to the authoress herself, for the early acquaintance we have made with her poems, has well illustrated her merit in this respect, as compared with the noisy and difficult jargon of many who have gone before her, by reference to the anecdote of Napoleon's coronation, as emperor, in the cathedral of Notre Dame. The fondness of the French for parade and effect, is well known, and this was the most brilliant era of the great man's career. The Parisians, to astonish everybody, filled the orchestra with eighty harps, which were struck together with unequalled skill. ' The whole world' was delighted. But presently entered the Pope. A few of his singers, who came with him from Rome, received him with the *Tu es Petrus* of Scarlatti. Not an instrument was heard; there were no fashionable flourishes; but the simple majesty of the old-fashioned air, ' annihilated at once the whole effect of the preceding fanfaronade.'* We have had a liberal allowance of *instrumental* in the poetry of our

* North American Review, for April, 1827. We need scarcely say, that allusion is made above to the editor of the Boston edition of the Earlier Poems of Mrs. Hemans.

times; and the Voice of Spring is worth the whole of it. What a strength is in its simplicity! What power from 'lips that seem to tremble, as

"They strive to speak,
Like a frail harp-string, shaken by the storm!"

So spake the Switzer's Wife, when the *Spells of Home* inspired her:—

"Ay, pale she stood, but with an eye of light,
And took her fair child to her holy breast,
And lifted her soft voice, that gather'd might
As it found language:—"Are we thus oppress'd?
Then must we rise upon our mountain-sod,
And man must arm, and woman call on God!"

"I know what thou wouldst do,—and be it done.
Thy soul is darken'd with its fears for me.
Trust me to Heaven, my husband! This, thy son,
The babe whom I have borne thee, must be free!
And the sweet memory of our pleasant hearth
May well give strength—if aught be strong on earth.

"Thou hast been brooding o'er the silent dread
Of my desponding tears; now lift once more,
My hunter of the hills, thy stately head,
And let thine eagle glance my joy restore!
I can bear all, but seeing *thee* subdued,—
Take to thee back thine own undaunted mood.

"Go forth beside the waters, and along
The chamois-paths, and through the forests go;
And tell, in burning words, thy tale of wrong
To the brave hearts that 'midst the hamlets glow.
God shall be with thee, my beloved!—Away!
Bless but thy child, and leave me,—I can pray!"
He sprang up like a warrior-youth awaking
To clarion-sounds upon the ringing air;
He caught her to his breast, while proud tears, breaking
From his dark eyes, fell o'er her braided hair,—
And "Worthy art thou," was his joyous cry,
"That man for thee should gird himself to die."

Here, it must be confessed, after all, is the *forte* of Mrs. Hemans,— the fireside; and we come now to say, in a word, that we consider her not only, as the Edinburgh Review pronounced her some six years since, '*The most touching and accomplished writer of occasional verses that our literature has yet to boast of,*'—splendid as that compliment is,—but as the model, in every respect, of what a female writer of poetry should be. Her poetry, itself, is the model of female poetry, so to speak. It has not simply a negative merit, of course, though that in our times is something to be distinguished by, if not to boast of; the merit of being free from the characteristic faults or foibles of men or women; of being perfectly amiable as well as decorous, and meek and modest in all the fervour of its earnestness. This fervour itself, pure as it is, is an exquisite quality which belongs, in its true fineness, only to a woman's heart. Mrs. Hemans had a generous share of it in her temperament; and she has poured and pour-ed it out, strong and fresh as the rushing waters of her own 'streams and founts' of the Spring, when they burst

"From their sparry caves,
And the earth resounds with the joy of waves"

What devotedness,—what fearless, uncal-culating, uncompromising confidence, —the confidence of the heart,—of a woman's heart —breathe, as with a living ardour of the warm lips themselves, in the agony of Inez at the Auto da Fé, when the 'breathless rider' found her by the gleam of the midnight fire,

"And dash'd off fiercely those who came to part,
And rush'd to that pale girl, and clasp'd her to his heart!

*   *   *   *   *   *

And for a moment all around gave way
To that full burst of passion!—on his breast,
Like a bird panting yet from fear, she lay,
But blest—in misery's very lap—yet blest!—
Oh love, love, strong as death!—from such an hour
Pressing out joy by thine immortal power,
Holy and fervent love! had earth but rest
For thee and thine, this world were all too fair!
How could we thence be wean'd to die without despair?

But she—as falls a willow from the storm,
O'er its own river streaming—thus reclined
On the youth's bosom hung her fragile form
And clasping arms, so passionately twined
Around his neck—with such a trusting fold,
A full deep sense of safety in their hold,
As if naught earthly might th' embrace unbind!
Alas! a child's fond faith, believing still
Its mother's breast beyond the lightning's reach to kill!

What a picture is this! How do we feel that only one who has herself a heart, and such a heart, can render such justice to

"The strife
Of love, faith, fear, and that vain dream of life,
*Within her woman's breast!*"

How do we seem to hear, as her hero 'woos *her* back to life,' in his frenzy, her '*soft voice in his soul!*' How do we see, again,

" Her large tears gush
Like blood-drops from a victim; *with swift rain
Bathing the bosom where she lean'd that hour,
As if her life would melt in that o'erswelling shower.*"

Not an 'inalienable trust' is this, alone; but what an exquisite tenderness is mingled with it; and how does that trait pervade this poetry everywhere, till it must melt the manhood even of the 'stoics of the wood,' the savages in sentiment, who would have been themselves ashamed — forsooth '— to 'stain' their Indian page 'with grief.' Yet have they wept with the Bride of the Greek Isle, when leaving the vine at her father's door, and the myrtle once called her own,

"She turn'd—and her mother's gaze brought back
Each hue of her childhood's faded track.
Oh! hush the song, and let her tears
Flow to the dream of her early years!
Holy and pure are the drops that fall
Wher the young bride goes from her fathers' hall

*She goes unto love yet untried and new,*
*She parts from love which hath still been true ;*
*Mute be the song and the choral strain,*
*Till her heart's deep well-spring is clear again !*
*She wept on her mother's faithful breast,*
*Like a babe that sobs itself to rest ;*
*She wept—yet laid her hand the while*
*In his that waited her dawning smile,*
*Her soul's affianced, nor cherish'd less*
*For the gush of nature's tenderness !"*

These, we say, are the fervour, and the trust. and the tenderness, of a woman's poetry. Shakspeare himself, perfect as even his female characters are,—as far as they are not female, but only human,—did not write thus, and could not, for though he was like all other men, excepting that he resembled nobody, as Hazlitt describes him, he was not like *woman*, and he could enter into the *feeling* of her character,—the female feeling,—in some respects perhaps but little better than Milton himself. It is no reproach to him that he could, not, any more than it is to Mrs. Hemans that she could not write like him. It may, however, occasion a dramatic deficiency,—more or less perceptible to the reader, as he or she is possessed more or less of the quality itself in question,—wherever the play moves over ground which does not belong to this genius of man: and hence Shakspeare appears best upon his own ground, and so far forth as he represents the influence, rather than the absolute existence, of the other sex. And the same is true of her, and of her heroes. If it be true to a greater extent, on one hand, she has gained and saved something, on the other, by the exercise, in this instance, again, of that excellent tact—itself almost a characteristic of the sex—which she has generally employed to so good purpose in the choice of subjects as well as of style, and not less in forbearance than in effort. She has avoided, almost entirely, mere masculine material, and has gradually abandoned even those topics of general interest, which do not actually require the exertion of her more peculiar power. If she leaves the fireside occasionally, she does not travel in male disguise,—still less does she cease to be what she is. Her household gods go with her wherever she goes,—and the sound of their parting footsteps is audible with her own. With the wreck and the treasures of the deep, 'mid gold and gems, and buried isles, and towers o'erthrown, we find

*"The lost and lovely !—those for whom*
*The place was kept at board and hearth so long !"*

She brings her 'flowers' for crowns to the *early dead*, and for

*" Brides to wear,—*
*They were born to blush in their shining hair !"*

She sends the Crusader to Syrian deserts, that he may find his way back again to 'some fond mother's glance,' that 'o'er *him*, too, brooded in his early years.' She makes the conqueror in his sleep, 'a child again.' The Traveller, at the source of the Nile, thinks of the wild sweet voices of the streams in

*" Haunts of play,*
*Where brightly through the beechen shade,*
*Their waters glanced away."*

Her trumpet sounds for the lover to quit his marriage altar, and

*"The mother on her first-born son,*
*Looks with a boding eye ;"*

and it is still 'woman on the field of battle' itself. She *felt* that here was her empire. She *knew* that it was the spells of home which inspired her, and she clung even to the forsaken hearth, and to the graves themselves, of the household. The element of her poetry was the warm air of the fireside. The faith, the trust, the fear, the love, even the anguish, of a woman's heart, sustained her,—and she revived with the 'taste of tears,'*—and again, and again, while yet she weeps, like the Bride of the Isle, till her voice seems lost with the choking swell, sweeter and clearer than ever do

*——" Her lovely thoughts from their cells find way,*
*In the sudden flow of the plaintive lay."*

We say, then, the distinctive character of her poetry is female—and in its being in that department just what it should be. It is *all* the records of woman ; *all*, the songs of the affections. It is the poetry of the household, the poetry of the heart.

Nor let us, in this connexion, lose sight altogether of the aid she derived from her personal experience, her experience as a wife and a mother, and still more, the lessons which circumstances, more individual, must have taught her. We will not go largely into these, but it is essential to a right appreciation of her poetical character, that as much of her history as a popular foreign writer has lately communicated, should be known.†

---

* *Forest Sanctuary.*

† " Felicia Dorothea Browne was born in Liverpool, in a small quaint-looking house in St. Anne street, now standing. old fashioned and desolate, in the midst of the newer buildings by which it is surrounded. Our abstaining from any attempt minutely to trace her history, requires no apology ; it is enough to say that when she

'They learn in suffering what they teach in song,' was Shelley's maxim; and Mrs. Hemans did more than to adopt it as a theme.* She lived it her life long; and, like her Valencian heroine, she took her toils nobly on her, knowing how

> " *Strength* is born
> In the deep silence of long-suffering hearts,
> Not amidst joy;"

though mourning, with the Sicilian, as she did,

> "That there should be
> Things, which we love with such deep tenderness,
> But, through that love, to learn *how much of woe*
> Dwells in one hour like this."

Yet loved she on, and learned on, till her poetry has been imbued with such a spirit of the heart, as could seem only, like the dying breath of the trampled violet, to have been crushed out of it in the act of its extinction. There was no need of affectation. She had in herself, again, the truth. She looked in her heart, and wrote.†

Much might be said of the perfect purity and dignity of the poetry of Mrs. Hemans; but these are inferable from the sketch we have given already, as general as it is. She has not been surpassed in these attributes by any writer of the severest school. It was the result with her, of an ambition of the highest order—a deep religious principle—no more than Milton's 'to be raised from the heat of youth or the vapours of wine;' 'nor to be obtained by the invocation of Dame Memory and her siren daughters; but by devout prayer to that eternal Spirit who can enrich with all utterance and knowledge, and sends out his seraphim with the hallowed fire of his altar, to touch and purify the lips of whom he pleases.' To such a mind there was a beauty in every thing which God has created; and although it was no error of hers, as it has been of so many before her, to search out the materials of poetry with such microscopic eyes as to degrade its noble office—describing the interior of a cottage, (as a witty critic remarked of Crabbe,)

like a person sent there to distrain for the lease, and recording a rent in a counterpane as an event in history—none could be more alive than she was to the respectability, so to speak, of all that reason discovers and religion reveals, of the spiritual meanings of the universe around us, in the least as well as the grandest of its parts. She has told us where we may trace these meanings in our daily paths. She had traced them herself. She had looked upon nature with eyes of love, that clothed it, in all its shapes, with the mind's mystery, like the 'faith, touching all things with hues of heaven.' No author has luxuriated in the beauties of the physical world with a keener relish than she has; and none has come nearer to raising them as it were into *life* itself, by the connexion with the lessons of life which she gives them. There is no little genius to be exercised in preserving the delicate relation between the dignity of humanity, of mind, time, eternity, virtue, truth, of God himself,—the highest themes of song, in a word,—on one hand, and that of the subordinate subject-matter, equally to be regarded in its way, on the other. This relation she has seen and respected. All her imagery, borrowed from nature, rich as it is, is made, like oriental flowers, to mean something, and to utter it in a language of its own. It is a sort of trellice-work, for thought and affection to climb upon. The Palm Tree, for example, is laden, as it were, with a moral, as with clusters of golden grapes.

In respect to the religious dignity which she attached to her profession, the late writer in the Athenæum, referred to above, quotes from a letter which lay before him:— 'I have now,' she says, 'passed through the feverish and somewhat *visionary* state of mind often connected with the passionate study of art in early life; deep affections and deep sorrows seem to have solemnized my whole being, and I now feel as if bound to higher and holier tasks, which, though I may occasionally lay aside, I could not long wander from without some sense of dereliction. I hope it is no self-delusion, but I cannot help sometimes feeling as if it were my true task to enlarge the sphere of sacred poetry, and extend its influence. When you receive my volume of 'Scenes and Hymns,' you will see what I mean by enlarging its sphere, though my plan as yet is very imperfectly developed.' How much she ac

---

was very young, her family removed from Liverpool to the neighbourhood of St. Asaph, in North Wales; that she married at a very early age—that her married life, after the birth of five sons, was clouded by the estrangement of her husband—that, on the death of her mother, with whom she had resided, she broke up her establishment in Wales, and removed to Wavertree, in the neighbourhood of Liverpool—from whence, after a residence of about three years, she again removed to Dublin—her last resting place."——*Athenæum.*

* See *The Diary.*

† Sir Phillip Sydney

complished in this noblest sphere of her labours, will be seen in the following pages. How much remained to be done, which she might have accomplished, is a reflection that must add a new poignancy to the sorrow her death has occasioned

She speaks here of the passionate study of art in early life. And this is not the least of her merits,—that she did study, early and late, her whole life long, making poetry, as it deserves, no less a subject of science than a gift of genius. She was above the miserable disparagement of labour, and learning, and practice, and the advice of the world. She profited continually by them all; and the critics have in no respect rendered her fuller justice, than in noticing the astonishing progress indicated by her successive productions. There are embryo traces, indeed, of her peculiar mind, and particularly of her fervid temperament and rich imagination, even in the juvenile volume alluded to above —and passages of the Sceptic are scarcely surpassed in strength by anything which has followed them—but, in general, the continuity of character, so to speak, from first to last, is little more than sufficient to show, at the same time with the identity of the intellect, the wonder-working effect of what Milton calls ' industrious and select reading, steady observation, insight into all seemly and generous arts and affairs.' A glance at her notes, mottoes, and translations alone, will convey the notion of a learning in the languages which would seem to be result enough, in itself, for the toil of a life like hers. Hence much of her glowing facility and felicity of language. Much of it, indeed, —the unrivalled elegance, (for there is nothing in English literature which exceeds her in this regard,) the exquisite grace, the indescribable tact of phraseology,—these were original with her, and were especially among the female traits of her genius. Even these, however, were improved with the rest, till by dint of discipline, added to native ability, she came at length to be mistress of an inimitable finishing-power,—a power of doing precise justice to the niceties of conception with which perhaps the mind of a woman only is conversant,—a miniature minuteness,—such as nothing short of the power itself would enable us properly to describe. The enthusiasm of Mrs. Hemans made even her industry indefatigable. Those who affect her more attractive qualities, will

do well to imitate this. It requires no small share, in the outset, to study her works attentively enough—especially as they are read cursorily with such eager interest—to appreciate the credit she deserves in this respect. It was the most difficult result of her labour that she succeeded in concealing the *effort*, while she proved the *effect*.

Thus, then, is her poetry distinguished. Others have possessed her imagination, her taste, her ambition, her art, her glowing feeling, her christian principle; but they did not all undertake, and they were not all competent if they had, to devote the exercise of every energy, effectually, to the one object of her labours,—the composition of a model which might perfectly represent what female poetry is and should be. This Mrs. Hemans has done. She had a genius worthy to be the representative of that of her sex,—and she sounded the depths of its capacities of exertion and suffering, and trained them, with every faculty, to do justice to herself, her sex, her race, her Creator, in the discharge of the true office of the profession she chose,—the illuminating or figuring forth of truth, (as Sydney describes it,) and especially of the truth most worthy of the work, —which it most concerns men, as such, to feel the force of,—and which, also, she was herself best qualified so to set forth—' *by the speaking picture of poetry.*' She wrote not only as none but a woman could write, but so wrote as that, in her department, neither her predecessors, or successors, of her own sex, have been, or will be, able to surpass her.

In introducing her works entire, for the first time, it may be proper to allude to the interest she has been frequently known to express in our peculiar institutions and prospects, and the gratification she derived from the evidence, to which she could not be blind, that her productions were nowhere more cordially welcomed, or more fully appreciated, than here. For the numerous compositions founded on American themes, such a reception was rather to be anticipated, as a mark of the pleasure we felt in the worthy illustration of our national topics, and especially by the talent of one who by no means deemed it necessary to be faithless to her own country, or to any thing else her own, that she might do justice to the world at large beside. But this was not her sole recommendation to us. Five years since an English authority of note suggested that ' her peculiar beauties were first pointed out to us by our trans-atlantic brethren.' There was great truth in the remark; and the fact is as creditable to one party, as the admission of it is to the other. She has lost nothing among us in later days, and her American fame was dear to the last. The feeling with which the Landing of the Pilgrim Fathers is regarded, was rightly represented to her during the last season, by a gentleman from New-England, who called on her at Dublin, and the enthusiasm of gratification she expressed to him, was such as the composition itself might lead us to expect. She had composed that poem in the glow of a burst of admiration, immediately awakened by the chance perusal of a part of some Plymouth Oration (as it seemed to be) which she found on a scrap of an old newspaper. 'And I can tell you the portion of it we like best,' our friend added,—

" And they *left* unstained, what there they *found* ;"—

' Ay, *freedom to worship God !* ' she quickly subjoined; ' the *truth* was the best part of it, I know :—I rejoice that it is so, and that you so understand it.'

We trust it will be so understood, as long as the old Rock itself shall stand. To tell the truth of that grand occasion, was praise enough for any poet; it was a truth stronger than fiction ever was, and which fiction could but degrade. But we know her more than as the poet of the Pilgrims. We shall cherish the fame which was born with us; she has trusted it safely to our hands. We shall remember her as she would herself have desired to be remembered, in *all* ' words that breathe, and thoughts that burn.' She asks,—let us hear her once more,—

" When will ye think of me, my friends ?
    When will ye think of me ?—
When the last red light, the farewell of day,
From the rock and the river is passing away—
When the air with a deep'ning hush is fraught,
And the heart grows burden'd with tender thought,
    Then let it be !

When will ye think of me, kind friends ?
    When will ye think of me ?
When the rose of the rich mid-summer time
Is fill'd with the hues of its glorious p ime—
When ye gather its bloom, as in bright hours fled,
From the walks where my footsteps no more may
    tread—
    Then let it be !

When will ye think of me, sweet friends ?
    When will ye think of me ?
When the sudden tears o'erflow your eye
At the sound of some olden melody,
When ye hear the voice of a mountain stream
When ye feel the charm of a poet's dream
    Then let it be !

Thus let my memory be with you, friends !
    Thus ever think of me !
Kindly and gently, but as of one
For whom 'tis well to be fled and gone—
As of a bird from a chain unbound,
As of a wanderer whose home is found—
    So let it be !"

Ay, and so *will* it be. It will be with the thousands of hearts which have been, like Sydney's, ' moved more than with a trumpet,' now by the soft sweetness that pleaded for room in the Pagan Heaven, 'mid all the ' nobler dead,' for the unknown ' most loved,'

" Of whom fame speaks not, with her clarion voice,
   In regal halls ;"

and now with the majestic spirit of the strain that gives a ' memory on the mountains,' to the brave bands who pledged their faith for freedom—

      " Where the light
Of day's last footstep bathes in burning gold
Great Righi's cliffs ; and where Mount Pilate's height
Casts o'er his starry lake the darkness of his might."

It will be, as long as the deep yearnings which she knew so well to express, and to address, shall remain with men. It will be, in the Hour of Prayer, and the Hour of Death ; and the Dreams of the Better Land will be lighted with hues of the haunting beauty of remembered visions of the song. It will be while yet the honour of heroic virtue shall live upon human lips, and till the holy love, in human hearts so sorely tried, shall find, after all its weary tossing upon time's waves, a home where it may rest

    ————" remembering not
    The moaning of the sea !"

# CONTENTS.

HYMNS FOR CHILDHOOD.

# THE

# RESTORATION

OF THE

# WORKS OF ART TO ITALY.

## A POEM.

2

"But the joy of discovery was short, and the triumph of taste transitory. The French, who in every invasion have been the scourge of Italy, and have rivalled or rather surpassed the rapacity of the Goths and Vandals, laid their sacrilegious hands on the unparalleled collection of the Vatican, tore its masterpieces from their pedestals, and dragging them from their temples of marble, transported them to Paris, and consigned them to the dull sullen halls, or rather stables, of the *Louvre.*"—*Eustace's Classical Tour through Italy,* vol. ii., p. 60.

---

Italia, Italia! O tu cui feo la Sorte
  Dono infelice di bellezza, onde hai
  Funesta dote d'infiniti guai,
  Che 'n fronte scritti per gran doglia porte;
Deh, fossi tu men bella, o almen piu forte.

*Filicaja.*

# RESTORATION OF THE WORKS OF ART TO ITALY.

LAND of departed fame! whose classic plains
Have proudly echoed to immortal strains;
Whose hallow'd soil hath given the great and
    brave.
Day-stars of life, a birth-place and a grave;
Home of the Arts! where glory's faded smile
Sheds lingering light o'er many a mouldering pile;
Proud wreck of vanish'd power, of splendour fled,
Majestic temple of the mighty dead!
Whose grandeur, yet contending with decay,
Gleams through the twilight of thy glorious day;
Though dimm'd thy brightness, riveted thy chain
Yet, fallen Italy! rejoice again!
Lost, lovely realm! once more 't is thine to gaze
On the rich relics of sublimer days.

Awake, ye Muses of Etrurian shades,
Or sacred Tivoli's romantic glades;
Wake, ye that slumber in the bowery gloom,
Where the wild ivy shadows Virgil's tomb;
Or ye, whose voice, by Sorga's lonely wave,
Swell'd the deep echoes of the fountain's cave,
Or thrill'd the soul in Tasso's numbers high,
Those magic strains of love and chivalry;
If yet by classic streams ye fondly rove,
Haunting the myrtle-vale, the laurel grove;
Oh rouse once more the daring soul of song,
Seize with bold hand the harp, forgot so long,
And hail, with wonted pride, those works revered
Hallow'd by time, by absence more endear'd.

And breathe to those the strain, whose warrior-
    might,
Each danger stemm'd, prevail'd in every fight,
Souls of unyielding power, to storms inured,
Sublimed by peril, and by toil matured.
Sing of that leader, whose ascendant mind
Could rouse the slumbering spirit of mankind;
Whose banners track'd the vanquish'd Eagle's flight
O'er many a plain, and dark sierra's height;
Who bade once more the wild, heroic lay
Record the deeds of Roncesvalles' day;
Who, through each mountain-pass of rock and
    snow,
An Alpine huntsman, chased the fear-struck foe;
Waved his proud standard to the balmy gales,
Rich Languedoc! that fan thy glowing vales,
And 'mid those scenes renew'd th' achievements
    high,
Bequeath'd to fame by England's ancestry.

Yet, when the storm seem'd hush'd, the conflict
    past,
One strife remain'd—the mightiest and the last!
Nerved for the struggle, in that fateful hour,
Untamed Ambition summon'd all his power;
Vengeance and Pride, to frenzy roused, were there,
And the stern might of resolute Despair.

Isle of the free! 't was then thy champions stood
Breasting unmoved the combat's wildest flood,
Sunbeam of Battle, then thy spirit shone,
Glow'd in each breast, and sunk with life alone.

Oh hearts devoted! whose illustrious doom,
Gave there at once your triumph and your tomb,
Ye, firm and faithful, in th' ordeal tried
Of that dread strife, by Freedom sanctified;
Shrined, not entomb'd, ye rest in sacred earth,
Hallow'd by deeds of more than mortal worth.
What though to mark where sleeps heroic dust,
No sculptured trophy rise, or breathing bust,
Yours, on the scene where valour's race was run
A prouder sepulchre—the field ye won!
There every mead, each cabin's lowly name,
Shall live a watch-word blended with your fame;
And well may flowers suffice those graves to crown,
That ask no urn to blazon their renown.
There shall the bard in future ages tread,
And bless each wreath that blossoms o'er the dead;
Revere each tree whose sheltering branches wave
O'er the low mounds, the altars of the brave;
Pause o'er each warrior's grass-grown bed, and
    hear,
In every breeze, some name to glory dear,
And as the shades of twilight close around,
With martial pageants people all the ground.
Thither unborn descendants of the slain
Shall throng, as pilgrims to some holy fane,
While as they trace each spot, whose records tell
Where fought their fathers, and prevail'd, and fell
Warm in their souls, shall loftiest feelings glow,
Claiming proud kindred with the dust below!
And many an age shall see the brave repair,
To learn the hero's bright devotion there.

And well, Ausonia! may that field of fame,
From thee one song of echoing triumph claim.
Land of the lyre! 'twas there the avenging sword
Won the bright treasures to thy fanes restored;
Those precious trophies o'er thy realms that throw
A veil of radiance, hiding half thy woe,
And bid the stranger for a while forget
How deep thy fall, and deem thee glorious yet.

Yes! fair creations, to perfection wrought,
Embodied visions of ascending thought!
Forms of sublimity! by Genius traced,
In tints that vindicate adoring taste;
Whose bright originals, to earth unknown,
Live in the spheres encircling Glory's throne;
Models of art, to deathless fame consign'd,
Stamp'd with the high-born majesty of mind;
Yes, matchless works! your presence shall restore
One beam of splendour to your native shore,
And her sad scenes of lost renown illume,
As the bright sunset gilds some hero's tomb

Oh! ne'er, in other climes, though many an eye
Dwelt on your charms in beaming ecstasy;
Ne'er was it yours to bid the soul expand
With thoughts so mighty, dreams so boldly grand,
As in that realm, where each faint breeze's moan
Seems a low dirge for glorious ages gone;
Where 'mid the ruin'd shrines of many a vale,
E'en Desolation tells a haughty tale,
And scarce a fountain flows, a rock ascends,
But its proud name with song eternal blends!

Yea! in those scenes, where every ancient stream
Bids memory kindle o'er some lofty theme;
Where every marble deeds of fame records,
Each ruin tells of Earth's departed lords;
And the deep tones of inspiration swell,
From each wild olive-wood and Alpine dell;
Where heroes slumber, on their battle plains,
'Mid prostrate altars, and deserted fanes,
And Fancy communes in each lonely spot,
With shades of those who ne'er shall be forgot;
There was your home, and there your power im
    prest,
With tenfold awe, the pilgrim's glowing breast;
And as the wind's deep thrills, and mystic sighs,
Wake the wild harp to loftiest harmonies,
Thus at your influence, starting from repose,
Thought, Feeling, Fancy, into grandeur rose.

Fair Florence! Queen of Arno's lovely vale!
Justice and Truth, indignant heard thy tale,
And sternly smiled in retribution's hour,
To wrest thy treasures from the Spoiler's power.
Too long the spirits of thy noble dead
Mourn'd o'er the domes they rear'd in ages fled,
Those classic scenes their pride so richly graced,
Temples of genius, palaces of taste,
Too long, with sad and desolated mien,
Reveal'd where conquest's lawless track had been;
Reft of each form with brighter life imbued,
Lonely they frown'd, a desert solitude.
  Florence! th' Oppressor's noon of pride is o'er,
  Rise in thy pomp again, and weep no more!
As one, who, starting at the dawn of day
From dark illusions, phantoms of dismay,
With transport heighten'd by those ills of night,
Hails the rich glories of expanding light;
E'en thus awakening from thy dreams of woe,
While Heaven's own hues in radiance round thee
    glow,
With warmer ecstasy 't is thine to trace
Each tint of beauty, and each line of grace;
More bright, more prized, more precious since de-
    plored
As loved, lost relics, ne'er to be restored,
Thy grief as hopeless as the tear-drop shed
By fond affection bending o'er the dead.

Athens of Italy! once more are thine
Those matchless gems of Art's exhaustless mine.
For thee bright Genius darts his living beam,
Warm o'er thy shrines the tints of Glory stream
And forms august as natives of the sky,
Rise round each fane in faultless majesty,
So chastely perfect, so serenely grand,
They seem creations of no mortal hand.

Ye, at whose voice fair Art, with eagle glance,
Burst in full splendour from her death-like trance;
Whose rallying call bade slumbering nations wake,
And daring Intellect his bondage break;
Beneath whose eye the Lords of song arose,
And snatch'd the Tuscan lyre from long repose;
And bade its pealing energies resound,
With power electric, through the realms around
Oh! high in thought, magnificent in soul!
Born to inspire, enlighten, and control;
Cosmo, Lorenzo! view your reign once more,
The shrine where nations mingle to adore!
Again th' Enthusiast there, with ardent gaze,
Shall hail the mighty of departed days:
Those sovereign spirits, whose commanding mind
Seems in the marble's breathing mould enshrined
Still, with ascendant power, the world to awe,
Still the deep homage of the heart to draw;

To breathe some spell of holiness around,
Bid all the scene be consecrated ground,
And from the stone, by inspiration wrought,
Dart the pure lightnings of exalted thought.

There thou, fair offspring of immortal Mind!
Love's radiant Goddess, Idol of Mankind!
Once the bright object of Devotion's vow,
Shalt claim from taste a kindred worship now.
Oh! who can tell what beams of heavenly light
Flash'd o'er the sculptor's intellectual sight,
How many a glimpse reveal'd to him alone,
Made brighter beings, nobler worlds his own:
Ere, like some vision sent the earth to bless,
Burst into life thy pomp of loveliness!

Young Genius there, while dwells his kindling
    eye
On forms, instinct with bright divinity,
While new-born powers, dilating in his heart,
Embrace the full magnificence of Art;
From scenes by Raphael's gifted hand array'd;
From dreams of heaven, by Angelo portray'd;
From each fair work of Grecian skill sublime,
Seal'd with perfection, " sanctified by time;"
Shall catch a kindred glow, and proudly feel
His spirit burn with emulative zeal,
Buoyant with loftier hopes his soul shall rise,
Imbued, at once, with nobler energies;
O'er life's dim scenes on rapid pinion soar,
And worlds of visionary grace explore,
Till his bold hand give glory's day-dreams birth,
And with new wonders charm admiring earth.

Venice, exult, and o'er thy moonlight seas,
Swell with gay strains each Adriatic breeze!
What though long fled those years of martial fame
That shed romantic lustre o'er thy name,
Though to the winds thy streamers idly play,
And the wild waves another Queen obey;
Though quench'd the spirit of thine ancient race,
And power and freedom scarce have left a trace ·
Yet still shall Art her splendours round thee cast.
And gild the wreck of years for ever past.
Again thy fanes may boast a Titian's dyes,
Whose clear, soft brilliance emulates thy skies,
And scenes that glow in colouring's richest bloom,
With life's warm flush Palladian halls illume.
From thy rich dome again the unrivall'd steed
Starts to existence, rushes into speed,
Still for Lysippus claims the wreath of fame,
Panting with ardour, vivified with flame.

Proud Racers of the Sun! to fancy's thought,
Burning with spirit' from his essence caught,
No mortal birth ye seem—but form'd to bear
Heaven's car of triumph through the realms of
    air;
To range uncurb'd the pathless fields of space,
The winds your rivals in the glorious race;
Traverse empyreal spheres with buoyant feet,
Free as the zephyr, as the shot star fleet;
And waft through worlds unknown the vital ray,
The flame that wakes creations into day,
Creatures of fire and ether! wing'd with light,
To track the regions of the Infinite!
From purer elements whose life was drawn,
Sprung from the sunbeam, offspring of the dawn
What years on years, in silence gliding by,
Have spared those forms of perfect symmetry!
Moulded by Art to dignify alone
Her own bright deity's resplendent throne.
Since first her skill their fiery grace bestow'd,
Meet for such lofty fate, such high abode,
How many a race, whose tales of glory seem
An echo's voice—the music of a dream,
Whose records feebly from oblivion save
A few bright traces of the wise and brave;
How many a state, whose pillar'd strength sublime
Defied the storms of war, the waves of time,
Towering o'er earth majestic and alone,
Fortress of power—has flourish'd and is gone!
And they, from clime to clime by conquest borne
Each fleeting triumph destined to adorn,

They, that of powers and kingdoms lost and won,
Have seen the noontide and the setting sun,
Consummate still in every grace remain,
As o'er *their* heads had ages roll'd in vain !
Ages, victorious, in their ceaseless flight,
O'er countless monuments of earthly might!
While she, from fair Byzantium's lost domain,
Who bore those treasures to her ocean-reign.
'Midst the blue deep, who rear'd her island throne,
And call'd th' infinitude of waves her own ;
Venice the proud, the regent of the sea,
Welcomes in chains the trophies of the free !

And thou, whose Eagle's towering plume un
   furl'd,
Once cast its shadow o'er a vassal world,
Eternal city ! round whose Curule throne
'I' lords of nations knelt in ages flown ;
Thou, whose Augustan years have left to time,
Immortal records of their glorious prime ;
When deathless bards, thine olive-shades among.
Swell'd the high raptures of heroic song;
Fair, fallen empress ! raise thy languid head
From the cold altars of th' illustrious dead,
And once again, with fond delight, survey
The proud memorials of thy noblest day.

Lo ! where thy sons, oh Rome ! a god-like train,
In imaged majesty return again !
Bards, chieftains, monarchs, tower with mien
   august,
O'er scenes that shrine their venerable dust.
Those forms, those features, luminous with soul,
Still o'er thy children seem to claim control ;
With awful grace arrest the pilgrim's glance,
Bind his rapt soul in elevating trance,
And bid the past, to fancy's ardent eyes,
From time's dim sepulchre in glory rise.

Souls of the lofty ! whose undying names,
Rouse the young bosom still to noblest aims ;
Oh ! with your images could fate restore
Your own high spirit to your sons once more !
Patriots and heroes ! could those flames return,
That bade your hearts with freedom's ardour burn
Then from the sacred ashes of the first,
Might a new Rome in phœnix-grandeur burst !
With one bright glance dispel the horizon's gloom,
With one loud call wake Empire from the tomb ;
Bind round her brows her own triumphal crown,
Lift her dread Ægis with majestic frown.
Unchain her Eagle's wing, and guide his flight,
To bathe its plumage in the fount of light.

Vain dream ! degraded Rome ! thy noon is o'er,
Once lost, thy spirit shall revive no more.
It sleeps with those, the sons of other days,
Who fix'd on thee the world's adoring gaze ;
Those, blest to live, while yet thy star was high,
More blest, ere darkness quench'd its beam, to die!

Yet, though thy faithless tutelary powers
Have fled thy shrines, left desolate thy towers,
Still, still to thee shall nations bend their way,
Revered in ruin, sovereign in decay!
Oh ! what can realms, in fame's full zenith, boast,
To match the relics of thy splendour lost !
By Tiber's waves, on each illustrious hill,
Genius and Taste shall love to wander still,
For there has Art survived an empire's doom,
And rear'd her throne o'er Latium's trophied tomb;
She from the dust recalls the brave and free,
Peopling each scene with beings worthy thee !

Oh ! ne'er again may War, with lightning-stroke,
Rend its last honours from the shatter'd oak !
Long be those works, revered by ages, thine,
To lend one triumph to thy dim decline.

Bright with stern beauty, breathing wrathful
   fire
In all the grandeur of celestial ire,
Once more thine own, th' immortal Archer's form,
Sheds radiance round, with more than Being warm,
Oh ! who could view, nor deem that perfect frame,
A living temple of ethereal flame ?

Lord of the day-star ! how may words portray
Of thy chaste glory one reflected ray ?
Whate'er the soul could dream, the hand could
   trace,
Of regal dignity, and heavenly grace ;
Each purer effluence of the fair and bright,
Whose fitful gleams have broke on mortal sight ;
Each bold idea, borrow'd from the sky,
To vest th' embodied form of deity ;
All, all in the ennobled and refined,
Breathe and enchant, transcendently combined !
Son of Elysium ! years and ages gone .
Have bow'd in speechless homage, at thy throne ;
And days unborn, and nations yet to be,
Shall gaze, absorb'd in ecstasy, on thee !

And thou triumphant wreck, (1) e'en yet sublime
Disputed trophy, claim'd by Art and Time,
Hail to that scene again, where Genius caught
From thee its fervours of diviner thought !
Where He, th' inspired one, whose gigantic mind
Lived in some sphere, to him alone assign'd ;
Who from the past, the future, and th' unseen,
Could call up forms of more than earthly mien ;
Unrivall'd Angelo on thee would gaze,
Till his full soul imbibed perfection's blaze !
And who but he, that Prince of Art, might dare
Thy sovereign greatness view without despair ?
Emblem of Rome ! from power's meridian hurl'd,
Yet claiming still the homage of the world.

What hadst thou been, ere barbarous hand de-
   faced
The work of wonder, idolized by taste ?
Oh ! worthy still of some divine abode,
Mould of a conqueror ! (2) ruin of a god !
Still, like some broken gem, whose quenchless
   beam
From each bright fragment pours its vital stream
'Tis thine, by fate unconquer'd, to dispense
From every part, some ray of excellence !
E'en yet, inform'd with essence from on high,
Thine is no trace of frail mortality !
Within that frame a purer being glows,
Through viewless veins a brighter current flows ;
Fill'd with immortal life, each muscle swells,
In every line supernal grandeur dwells.

Consummate work ! the noblest and the last,
Of Grecian Freedom, (3) ere her reign was past.
Nurse of the mighty, she, while lingering still
Her mantle flow'd o'er many a classic hill,
Ere yet her voice its parting accents breathed,
A Hero's image to the world bequeathed ;
Enshrined in thee th' imperishable ray
Of high-soul'd Genius, foster'd by her sway,
And bade thee teach, to ages yet unborn,
What lofty dreams were hers—who never shall
   return !

And mark yon group, transfix'd with many a
   throe
Seal'd with the image of eternal woe :
With fearful truth, terrific power, exprest,
Thy pangs, Laocoon, agonize the breast,
And the stern combat picture to mankind,
Of suffering nature, and enduring mind.
Oh, mighty conflict ! though his pains intense
Distend each nerve, and dart through every sense
Though fix'd on him, his children's suppliant eyes
Implore the aid avenging fate denies ;
Though, with the giant-snake in fruitless strife
Heaves every muscle with convulsive life,
And in each limb Existence writhes, enroll'd
'Mid the dread circles of the venom'd fold ;
Yet the strong spirit lives—and not a cry
Shall own the might of Nature's agony !
That furrow'd brow unconquer'd soul reveals,
That patient eye to angry Heaven appeals,
That struggling bosom concentrates its breath
Nor yields one moan to torture or to death !(4)

Sublimest triumph of intrepid Art !
With speechless horror to congeal the heart,
To freeze each pulse, and dart through every vein
Cold thrills of fear, keen sympathies of pain ,

Yet teach the spirit how its lofty power
May brave the pangs of fate's severest hour.

Turn from such conflicts, and enraptured gaze
On scenes where Painting all her skill displays:
Landscapes, by colouring drest in richer dyes,
More mellow'd sunshine, more unclouded skies;
Or dreams of bliss, to dying Martyrs given,
Descending Seraphs robed in beams of heaven.

Oh! sovereign Masters of the Pencil's might,
Its depth of shadow, and its blaze of light,
Ye, whose bold thought, disdaining every bound,
Explored the worlds above, below, around,
Children of Italy! who stand alone,
And unapproach'd, 'midst regions all your own;
What scenes, what beings blest your favour'd sight
Severely grand, unutterably bright!
Triumphant spirits! your exulting eye
Could meet the noontide of eternity,
And gaze untired, undaunted, uncontroll'd,
On all that Fancy trembles to behold.

Bright on your view such forms their splendour
        shed,
As burst on Prophet-bards in ages fled:
Forms that to trace, no hand but yours might dare,
Darkly sublime, or exquisitely fair.
These o'er the walls your magic skill array'd,
Glow in rich sunshine, gleam through melting
        shade,
Float in light grace, in awful greatness tower,
And breathe and move, the records of your power.
Inspired of Heaven! what heighten'd pomp ye cast,
O'er all the deathless trophies of the past!
Round many a marble fane and classic dome,
Asserting still the majesty of Rome;
Round many a work that bids the world believe
What Grecian Art could image and achieve;
Again, creative minds, your visions throw
Life's chasten'd warmth, and Beauty's mellowest
        glow,
And when the morn's bright beams and mantling
        dyes
Pour the rich lustre of Ausonian skies,
Or evening suns illume, with purple smile,
The Parian altar, and the pillar'd aisle.
Then, as the full, or soften'd radiance falls,
On Angel-groups that hover o'er the walls,
Well may those Temples, where your hand has
        shed
Light o'er the tomb, existence round the dead,
Seem like some world, so perfect and so fair,
That naught of earth should find admittance there,
Some sphere, where Beings, to mankind unknown,
Dwell in the brightness of their pomp, alone!

Hence, ye vain fictions, fancy's erring theme,
Gods of illusion! phantoms of a dream!
Frail, powerless idols of departed time,
Fables of song, delusive, though sublime!
To loftier tasks has Roman Art assign'd
Her matchless pencil, and her mighty mind!
From brighter streams her vast ideas flow'd,
With purer fire her ardent spirit glow'd.
To her 'twas given in fancy to explore
The land of miracles, the holiest shore;
That realm where first the light of life was sent,
The loved, the punish'd, of th' Omnipotent!
O'er Judah's hills her thoughts inspired would stray,
Through Jordan's valleys trace their lonely way;
By Siloa's brook, or Almotana's (5) deep,
Chain'd in dead silence, and unbroken sleep;
Scenes whose cleft rocks, and blasted deserts, tell
Where pass'd th' Eternal, where his anger fell!
Where oft his voice the words of fate reveal'd,
Swell'd in the whirlwind, in the thunder peal'd,
Or heard by prophets in some palmy vale,
Breath'd 'still small' whispers on the midnight gale.
There dwelt her spirit—there her hand portray'd,

'Mid the lone wilderness or cedar-shade,
Ethereal forms, with awful missions fraught,
Or Patriarch-seers, absorb'd in sacred thought,
Bards, in high converse with the world of rest,
Saints of the earth, and spirits of the blest.
But chief to Him, the Conqueror of the grave,
Who lived to guide us, and who died to save;
Him, at whose glance the powers of evil fled,
And soul return'd to animate the dead;
Whom the waves own'd—and sunk beneath his eye,
Awed by one accent of Divinity;
To Him she gave her meditative hours,
Hallow'd her thoughts, and sanctified her powers.
O'er her bright scenes sublime repose she threw,
As all around the Godhead's presence knew,
And robed the Holy One's benignant mien
In beaming mercy, majesty serene.

Oh! mark, where Raphael's pure and perfect line
Portrays that form ineffably divine! (6)
Where with transcendent skill his hand has shed
Diffusive sunbeams round the Saviour's head;
Each heaven-illumined lineament imbued
With all the fullness of beatitude,
And traced the sainted group, whose mortal sight
Sinks overpower'd by th' excess of light!

Gaze on that scene, and own the might of Art,
By truth inspired to elevate the heart!
To bid the soul exultingly possess,
Of all her powers, a heighten'd consciousness,
And strong in hope, anticipate the day,
The last of life, the first of freedom's ray;
To realize, in some unclouded sphere,
Those pictured glories feebly imaged here!
Dim, cold reflections from her native sky,
Faint effluence of "the Day-spring from on high!"

## NOTES.

### NOTE 1.

The Belvidera Torso, the favourite study of Michael Angelo, and of many other distinguished artists.

### NOTE 2.

" Quoique cette statue d'Hercule ait ete maltraitee et mutilee d'une maniere etrange, se trouvant sans tete, sans bras, et sans jambes, elle est cependant encore un chef-dœuvre aux yeux des connoisseurs ; et ceux qui savent percer dans les mysteres de l'art, se la representent dans toute sa beaute. L'artiste, en voulant representer Hercule, a forme un corps ideal au-dessus de la nature. * * * Cet Hercule paroit donc ici tel qu'il dut etre, lorsque, purifie par le feu des foiblesses de l'humanite, il obtint l'immortalite, et prit place aupres des dieux. Il est represente sans aucun besoin de nourriture et de reparation de forces. Les veines y sont toutes invisibles."—*Winchelmann, Histoire de l'Art chez les Anciens,* tom. ii. p. 248.

### NOTE 3.

" Le Torso d'Hercule paroit un des derniers ouvrages parfaits que l'art ait produit en Grece, avant la perte de sa liberte. Car apres que la Grece fut reduite en province Romaine, l'histoire ne fait mention d'aucun artiste celebre de cette nation, jusqu'aux temps du Triumvirat Romain."—*Winchelmann, ibid.* tom. ii. p. 250.

### NOTE 4.

" It is not, in the same manner, in the agonised limbs, or in the convulsed muscles of the Laocoon, that the secret grace of its composition resides. It is in the majestic air of the head, which has not *yielded in suffering,* and in the deep serenity of the forehead, which seems to be still *superior* to all its *afflictions,* and significant of a mind that cannot be subdued."—*Alison's Essays,* vol. ii. p. 400.

" Laocoon nous offre le spectacle de la nature humaine dans la plus grande douleur dont elle soit susceptible, sous l'image d'homme qui tache de rassembler contre elle toute la force de l'esprit. Tandis que l'exces de la souffrance enfle les muscles, et tire violemment les nerfs, le courage se montre sur le front gonfle : la poitrine s'eleve avec peine par la necessite de la respiration, qui est egalement contrainte par le silence que la force de l'ame impose a la douleur qu'elle voudroit etouffer. * * * Son * * est plaintif, et non criard."—*Winchelmann, ibid.* tom. ii. p

### NOTE 5.

Almotana. The name given by the Arabs to the Dead Sea.

### NOTE 6.

The Transfiguration is thought to be so perfect a specimen of art, that, in honour of Raphael, it was carried before his body to the grave.

# TALES,

## AND

# HISTORIC SCENES.

Le Maure ne se venge pas parce que sa colere dure encore, mais parce que la vengeance seule peut
ecarter de sa tete le poids d'infamie dont il est accable.—Il se venge, parce qu'a ses yeux il n'y
a qu'une ame basse qui puisse pardonner les affronts; et il nourrit sa rancune, parce que s'il la
sentoit s'eteindre, il croiroit avec elle, avoir perdu une vertu.—*Sismondi.*

The events with which the following tale is interwoven, are related in the "Historia de las
Guerras Civiles de Granada." They occurred in the reign of Abu Abdeli or Abdali, the last Moorish
king of that city, called by the Spaniards *El Rey Chico.* The conquest of Granada, by Ferdinand
and Isabella, is said, by some historians, to have been greatly facilitated by the Abencerrages, whose
defection was the result of the repeated injuries they had received from the king at the instigation
of the Zegris. One of the most beautiful halls of the Alhambra is pointed out as the scene where
so many of the former celebrated tribe were massacred; and it still retains their name, being called
the "Sala de los Abencerrages." Many of the most interesting old Spanish ballads relate to the
events of this chivalrous and romantic period.

# THE ABENCERRAGE.

---

### CANTO I.

LONELY and still are now thy marble halls,
  Thou fair Alhambra! there the feast is o'er,
And with the murmur of thy fountain-falls,
  Blend the wild notes of minstrelsy no more.

Hush'd are the voices, that, in years gone by,
  Have mourn'd exulted, menaced, through thy towers;
Within thy pillar'd courts the grass waves high,
  And all uncultured bloom thy fairy bowers.

Unheeded there the flowering myrtle blows,
  Through tall arcades unmark'd the sunbeam smiles.
And many a tint of soften'd brilliance throws,
  O'er fretted walls, and shining peristyles.

And well might Fancy deem thy fabrics lone,
  So vast, so silent, and so wildly fair,
Some charm'd abode of beings all unknown,
  Powerful and viewless, children of the air.

For there no footstep treads the enchanted ground,
  There not a sound the deep repose pervades,
Save winds and founts diffusing freshness round,
  Through the light domes and graceful colonnades.

Far other tones have swell'd those courts along,
  In days romance yet fondly loves to trace;
The clash of arms, the voice of choral song,
  The revels, combats, of a vanish'd race.

And yet awhile, at Fancy's potent call,
  Shall rise that race, the chivalrous, the bold!
Peopling once more each fair, forsaken hall,
  With stately forms, the knights and chiefs of ol

—The sun declines—upon Nevada's height
There dwells a mellow flush of rosy light;
Each soaring pinnacle of mountain snow
Smiles in the richness of that parting glow,
And Darro's wave reflects each passing dye
That melts and mingles in th' empurpled sky.
Fragrance, exhaled from rose and citron bower,
Blends with the dewy freshness of the hour:
Hush'd are the winds, and Nature seems to sleep.
In light and stillness; wood, and tower, and steep,
Are dyed with tints of glory, only given
To the rich evening of a southern heaven;
Tints of the sun, whose bright farewell is fraught,
With all that art hath dreamt, but never caught
—Yes, Nature sleeps; but not with her at rest
The fiery passions of the human breast.
Hark! from the Alhambra's towers what stormy sound,
Each moment deepening, wildly swells around?
Those are no tumults of a festal throng,
Not the light zambra, (1) nor the choral song;
The combat rages—'tis the shout of war,
'Tis the loud clash of shield and scymetar.
Within the Hall of Lions, (2) where the rays
Of eve, yet lingering, on the fountain blaze;
There, girt and guarded by his Zegri bands,
And stern in wrath, the Moorish monarch stands
There the strife centres—swords around him wave
There bleed the fallen, there contend the brave,
While echoing domes return the battle-cry,
"Revenge and Freedom!—let the tyrant die!"
And onward rushing, and prevailing still,
Court, hall, and tower the fierce avengers fill.

But first and bravest of that gallant train,
Where foes are mightiest, charging ne'er in vain
In his red hand the sabre glancing bright,
His dark eye flashing with a fiercer light.
Ardent, untired, scarce conscious that he bleeds,
His Aben-Zurrahs (3) there young Hamet leads;
While swells his voice that wild acclaim on high,
"Revenge and freedom!—let the tyrant die!"

Yes, trace the footsteps of the warrior's wrath,
By helm and corslet shatter'd in his path;
And by the thickest harvest of the slain,
And by the marble's deepest crimson stain:
Search through the serried fight, where loudest cries
From triumph, anguish, or despair arise;
And brightest where the shivering falchions glare,
And where the ground is reddest—he is there.
Yes, that young arm, amidst the Zegri host,
Hath well avenged a sire, a brother, lost.
They perish'd—not as heroes should have died,
On the red field in victory's hour of pride,
In all the glow and sunshine of their fame,
And proudly smiling, as the death-pang came;
Oh! had they *thus* expired, a warrior's tear
Had flow'd almost in triumph, o'er their bier.
For thus alone the brave should weep for those
Who brightly pass in glory to repose.
—Not such their fate—a tyrant's stern command
Doom'd them to fall by some ignoble hand,
As, with the flower of all their high-born race,
Summon'd Abdallah's royal feast to grace,
Fearless in heart, no dream of danger nigh,
They sought the banquet's gilded hall—to die.
Betray'd, unarm'd, they fell—the fountain wave
Flow'd crimson with the life-blood of the brave,
Till far the fearful tidings of their fate
Through the wide city rung from gate to gate,
And of that lineage each surviving son
Rush'd to the scene where vengeance might be won.

For this young Hamet mingles in the strife,
Leader of battle, prodigal of life,
Urging his followers, till their foes, beset,
Stand faint and breathless, but undaunted yet.
Brave Aben-Zurrahs, on! one effort more,
Yours is the triumph, and the conflict o'er

But lo! descending o'er the darken'd hall,
The twilight shadows fast and deeply fall,
Nor yet the strife hath ceased—tho' scarce they
    know.
Through that thick gloom, the brother from the foe;
Till the moon rises with her cloudless ray,
The peaceful moon, and gives them light to slay.

Where lurks Abdallah?—'midst his yielding
    train
They seek the guilty monarch, but in vain:
He lies not number'd with the valiant dead,
His champions round him have not vainly bled;
But when the twilight spread her shadowy veil,
And his last warriors found each effort fail,
In wild despair he fled—a trusted few,
Kindred in crime, are still in danger true;
And o'er the scene of many a martial deed,
The Vega's (4) green expanse, his flying footsteps
    lead.
He pass'd th' Alhambra's calm and lovely bowers,
Where slept the glistening leaves and folded flow-
    ers
In dew and starlight—there from grot and cave,
Gush'd in wild music many a sparkling wave;
There, on each breeze, the breath of fragrance rose,
And all was freshness, beauty, and repose.

But thou, dark monarch! in thy bosom reign
Storms that, once roused, shall never sleep again.
Oh! vainly bright is nature in the course
Of him who flies from terror or remorse!
A spell is round him which obscures her bloom,
And dims her skies with shadows of the tomb;
There smiles no Paradise on earth so fair,
But guilt will raise avenging phantoms there.
Abdallah heeds not though the light gale roves
Fraught with rich odour, stolen from orange-
    groves,
Hears not the sounds from wood and brook that
    rise,
Wild notes of nature's vesper melodies;
Marks not, how lovely, on the mountain's head,
Moonlight and snow their mingling lustre spread·
But urges onward, till his weary band,
Worn with their toil, a moment's pause demand.
He stops, and turning on Granada's fanes
In silence gazing, fix'd awhile remains;
In stern, deep silence—o'er his feverish brow,
And burning cheek, pure breezes freshly flow,
But waft, in fitful murmurs from afar,
Sounds, indistinctly fearful—as of war.
What meteor bursts, with sudden blaze, on high,
O'er the blue clearness of the starry sky?
Awful it rises like some Genie-form,
Seen 'midst the redness of the desert storm, (5)
Magnificently dread—above, below,
Spreads the wild splendour of its deepening glow
Lo! from the Alhambra's towers the vivid glare
Streams through the still transparence of the air;
Avenging crowds have lit the mighty pyre,
Which feeds that waving pyramid of fire;
And dome and minaret, river, wood, and height,
From dim perspective start to ruddy light.

Oh Heaven! the anguish of Abdallah's soul,
The rage, though fruitless, yet beyond control!
Yet must he cease to gaze, and raving fly
For life—such life as makes it bliss to die!
On yon green height, the mosque, but half reveal'd
Through cypress-groves, a safe retreat may yield.
Thither his steps are bent— yet oft he turns,
Watching that fearful beacon as it burns.
But paler grow the sinking flames at last,
Flickering they fade, their crimson light is past.
And spiry vapours rising o'er the scene,
Mark where the terrors of their wrath have been.
And now his feet have reach'd that lonely pile,
Where grief and terror may repose awhile;
Embower'd it stands, 'midst wood and cliff on high,
Through the gray rocks a torrent sparkling nigh;
He hails the scene where every care should cease,
And all—except the heart he brings—is peace.

There is deep stillness in those halls of state,
Where the loud cries of conflict rung so late!
Stillness like that, when fierce the Kamsin's blast
Hath o'er the dwellings of the desert pass'd. (6)

Fearful the calm—nor voice, nor step, nor breath
Disturbs that scene of beauty and of death:
Those vaulted roofs re-echo not a sound,
Save the wild gush of waters—murmuring round
In ceaseless melodies of plaintive tone,
Through chambers peopled by the dead alone.
O'er the mosaic floors, with carnage red,
Breastplate and shield, and cloven helm are spread
In mingled fragments—glittering to the light
Of yon still moon, whose rays, yet softly bright,
Their streaming lustre tremulously shed,
And smile, in placid beauty, o'er the dead;
O'er features, where the fiery spirit's trace,
E'en death itself is powerless to efface,
O'er those who, flush'd with ardent youth, awoke
When glowing morn in bloom and radiance broke,
Nor dreamt how near the dark and frozen sleep,
Which hears not Glory call, nor Anguish weep,
In the low silent house, the narrow spot,
Home of forgetfulness, and soon forgot.

But slowly fade the stars—the night is o'er—
Morn beams on those who hail her light no more
Slumberers, who ne'er shall wake on earth again
Mourners, who call'd the loved, the lost, in vai.
Yet smiles the day—Oh! not for mortal tear
Doth nature deviate from her calm career,
Nor is the earth less laughing or less fair,
Though breaking hearts her gladness may not
    share.
O'er the cold urn the beam of summer glows,
O er fields of blood the zephyr freshly blows;
Bright shines the sun, though all be dark below,
And skies arch cloudless o'er a world of woe,
And flowers renew'd in spring's green pathway
    bloom,
Alike to grace the banquet and the tomb.

Within Granada's walls the funeral rite
Attends that day of loveliness and light;
And many a chief, with dirges and with tears,
Is gather'd to the brave of other years;
And Hamet, as beneath the cypress shade
His martyr'd brother and his sire are laid,
Feels every deep resolve, and burning thought
Of ampler vengeance, e'en to passion wrought;
Yet is the hour afar—and he must brood
O'er those dark dreams awhile in solitude.
Tumult and rage are hush'd—another day
In still solemnity hath pass'd away,
In that deep slumber of exhausted wrath,
The calm that follows in the tempest's path.

And now Abdallah leaves yon peaceful fane,
His ravaged city traversing again.
No sound of gladness his approach precedes,
No splendid pageant the procession leads;
Where'er he moves the silent streets along,
Broods a stern quiet o'er the sullen throng;
No voice is heard—but in each alter'd eye,
Once brightly beaming when his steps were nigh
And in each look of those whose love hath fled
From all on earth, to slumber with the dead,
Those, by his guilt made desolate, and thrown
On the bleak wilderness of life alone,
In youth's quick glance of scarce dissembled rage
And the pale mien of calmly mournful age,
May well be read a dark and fearful tale
Of thought that ill th' indignant heart can veil,
And passion, like the hush'd volcano's power,
That waits in stillness its appointed hour.

No more the clarion, from Granada's walls
Heard o'er the Vega, to the tourney calls;
No more her graceful daughters, throned on high
Bend o'er the lists the darkly radiant eye;
Silence and gloom her palaces o'erspread,
And song is hush'd, and pageantry is fled.
—Weep, fated city! o'er thy heroes weep—
Low in the dust the sons of glory sleep;
Furl'd are their banners in the lonely hall,
Their trophied shields hang mouldering on the wall
Wildly their chargers range the pastures o'er,
Their voice in battle shall be heard no more;
And they, who still thy tyrant's wrath survive,
Whom he hath wrong'd too deeply to forgive,

That race, of lineage high, of worth approved,
The chivalrous, the princely, the beloved;
Thine Aben-Zurrahs—they no more shall wield
In thy proud cause, the conquering lance and shield.
Condemn'd to bid the cherish'd scenes farewell
Where the loved ashes of their fathers dwell,
And far o'er foreign plains, as exiles, roam,
Their land the desert, and the grave their home.
Yet there is one shall see that race depart,
In deep, though silent, agony of heart;
One whose dark fate must be to mourn alone,
Unseen her sorrows, and their cause unknown,
And veil her heart, and teach her cheek to wear
That smile, in which the spirit hath no share;
Like the bright beams that shed their fruitless glow
O'er the cold solitude of Alpine snow.

Soft, fresh, and silent, is the midnight hour,
And the young Zayda seeks her lonely bower;
That Zegri maid within whose gentle mind
One name is deeply, secretly enshrined.
That name in vain stern reason would efface,
Hamet! 'tis thine, thou foe to all her race!

And yet not hers in bitterness to prove
The sleepless pangs of unrequited love;
Pangs, which the rose of wasted youth consume,
And make the heart of all delight the tomb,
Check the free spirit in its eagle-flight,
And the spring-morn of early genius blight;
Not such her grief—though now she wakes to weep,
While tearless eyes enjoy the honey-dews of
    sleep. (7)

A step treads lightly through the citron-shade,
Lightly, but by the rustling leaves betray'd—
Doth her young hero seek that well-known spot,
Scene of past hours that ne'er may be forgot?
'Tis he—but changed that eye, whose glance of fire
Could, like a sunbeam, hope and joy inspire,
As, luminous with youth, with ardour fraught,
It spoke of glory to the inmost thought;
Thence the bright spirit's eloquence hath fled,
And in its wild expression may be read
Stern thoughts and fierce resolves—now veil'd in
    shade,
And now in characters of fire portray'd.
Changed e'en his voice—as thus its mournful tone
Wakes in her heart each feeling of his own.

"Zayda, my doom is fix'd—another day,
And the wrong'd exile shall be far away;
Far from the scenes where still his heart must be,
His home of youth, and, more than all—from thee.
Oh! what a cloud hath gather'd o'er my lot,
Since last we met on this fair tranquil spot!
Lovely as then, the soft and silent hour,
And not a rose hath faded from thy bower;
But I—my hopes the tempest hath o'erthrown,
And changed my heart, to all but thee alone.
Farewell, high thoughts! inspiring hopes of praise,
Heroic visions of my early days!
In me the glories of my race must end,
The exile hath no country to defend!
E'en in life's morn, my dreams of pride are o'er,
Youth's buoyant spirit wakes for me no more,
And one wild feeling in my alter'd breast
Broods darkly o'er the ruins of the rest.
Yet fear not thou—to thee, in good or ill,
The heart, so sternly tried, is faithful still!
But when my steps are distant, and my name
Thou hear'st no longer in the song of fame,
When Time steals on, in silence to efface
Of early love each pure and sacred trace,
Causing our sorrows and our hopes to seem
But as the moonlight pictures of a dream,
Still shall thy soul be with me in the truth,
And all the fervour of affection's youth?
—If such thy love, one beam of heaven shall play
In lonely beauty, o'er thy wanderer's way."

"Ask not, if such my love! oh! trust the mind
To grief so long, so silently resign'd!
Let the light spirit, ne'er by sorrow taught
The pure and lofty constancy of thought,
Its fleeting trials eager to forget,
Rise with elastic power o'er each regret!

Foster'd in tears, our young affection grew,
And I have learn'd to suffer and be true.
Deem not my love a frail ephemeral flower,
Nursed by soft sunshine and the balmy shower;
No! 'tis the child of tempests, and defies,
And meets unchanged, the anger of the skies!
Too well I feel, with grief's prophetic heart,
That ne'er to meet in happier days, we part.
We part! and e'en this agonizing hour,
When Love first feels his own o'erwhelming power
Shall soon to Memory's fix'd and tearful eye
Seem almost happiness—for thou wert nigh!
Yes! when this heart in solitude shall bleed,
As days to days all wearily succeed,
When doom'd to weep in loneliness, 't will be
Almost like rapture to have wept with thee.

"But thou, my Hamet, thou canst yet bestow
All that of joy my blighted lot can know.
Oh! be thou still the high-soul'd and the brave,
To whom my first and fondest vows I gave,
In thy proud fame's untarnish'd beauty, still
The lofty visions of my youth fulfil,
So shall it soothe me 'midst my heart's despair,
To hold undimm'd one glorious image there!"

"Zayda, my best-beloved! my words too well,
Too soon, thy bright illusions must dispel;
Yet must my soul to thee unveil'd be shown,
And all its dreams and all its passions known.
Thou shalt not be deceived—for pure as heaven
Is thy young love, in faith and fervour given,
I said my heart was changed—and would thy
    thought
Explore the ruin by thy kindred wrought,
In fancy trace the land whose towers and fanes,
Crush'd by the earthquake, strew its ravaged plains,
And such that heart—where desolation's hand
Hath blighted all that once was fair or grand!
But Vengeance, fix'd upon her burning throne,
Sits 'midst the wreck in silence and alone,
And I, in stern devotion at her shrine,
Each softer feeling, but my love, resign.
—Yes! they whose spirits all my thoughts control,
Who hold dread converse with my thrilling soul;
They, the betray'd, the sacrificed, the brave,
Who fill a blood-stain'd and untimely grave,
Must be avenged! and pity and remorse,
In that stern cause, are banish'd from my course
Zayda, thou tremblest—and thy gentle breast
Shrinks from the passions that destroy my rest;
Yet shall thy form, in many a stormy hour,
Pass brightly o'er my soul with softening power,
And, oft recall'd, thy voice beguile my lot,
Like some sweet lay, once heard, and ne'er forgot

"But the night wanes—the hours too swiftly fly,
The bitter moment of farewell draws nigh;
Yet, loved one! weep not thus—in joy or pain,
Oh! trust thy Hamet, we shall meet again!
Yes, we shall meet! and haply smile at last
On all the clouds and conflicts of the past.
On that fair vision teach thy thoughts to dwell,
Nor deem these mingling tears our last farewell!"

Is the voice hush'd, whose loved, expressive tone
Thrill'd to her heart, and doth she weep alone?
Alone she weeps—that hour of parting o'er—
When shall the pang it leaves be felt no more?
The gale breathes light, and fans her bosom fair
Showering the dewy rose-leaves o'er her hair;
But ne'er for her shall dwell reviving power,
In balmy dew, soft breeze, or fragrant flower,
To wake once more, that calm, serene delight,
The soul's young bloom, which passion's breath
    could blight;
The smiling stillness of life's morning-hour,
Ere yet the day-star burns in all his power.
Meanwhile through groves of deep luxuriant shade
In the rich foliage of the south array'd,
Hamet, ere dawns the earliest blush of day,
Bends to the vale of tombs his pensive way.
Fair is that scene where palm and cypress wave
On high o'er many an Aben-Zurrah's grave,
Lonely and fair—its fresh and glittering leaves,
With the young myrtle there the laurel weaves,

To canopy the dead—nor wanting there
Flowers to the turf, nor fragrance to the air,
Nor wood-bird's note, nor fall of plaintive stream,
Wild music, soothing to the mourner's dream.
There sleep the chiefs of old—their combats o'er,
The voice of glory thrills their hearts no more !
Unheard by them th' awakening clarion blows ;
The sons of war at length in peace repose.
No martial note is in the gale that sighs,
Where proud their trophied sepulchres arise,
'Mid founts, and shades, and flowers of brightest
  bloom,
As, in his native vale, some shepherd's tomb.

There, where the trees their thickest foliage
  spread
Dark o'er that silent valley of the dead,
Where two fair pillars rise, embower'd and lone,
Not yet with ivy clad, with moss o'ergrown,
Young Hamet kneels—while thus his vows are
  pour'd,
The fearful vows that consecrate his sword.
—"Spirit of him, who first within my mind
Each loftier aim, each nobler thought enshrined,
And taught my steps the line of light to trace,
Left by the glorious fathers of my race,
Hear thou my voice—for thine is with me still,
In every dream its tones my bosom thrill,
In the deep calm of midnight they are near,
'Midst busy throngs they vibrate on my ear,
Still murmuring " vengeance !"—nor in vain the
  call,
Few, few shall triumph in a hero's fall !
Cold as thine own to glory and to fame,
Within my heart there lives one only aim ;
There, till th' oppressor for thy fate atone, .
Concentring every thought, it reigns alone.
I will not weep—revenge, not grief, must be,
And blood, not tears, an offering meet for thee ;
But the dark hour of stern delight will come,
And thou shalt triumph, warrior ! in thy tomb.

" Thou, too, my brother ! thou art pass'd away,
Without thy fame, in life's fair dawning day :
Son of the brave ! of thee no trace will shine
In the proud annals of thy lofty line,
Nor shall thy deeds be deathless in the lays,
That hold communion with the after-days.
Yet by the wreaths thou might'st have nobly won
Hadst thou but lived till rose thy noontide sun,
By glory lost, I swear, by hope betray'd,
Thy fate shall amply, dearly, be repaid ;
War with thy foes I deem a holy strife,
And to avenge thy death, devote my life.

" Hear ye my vows, oh spirits of the slain !
Hear and be with me on the battle-plain '
At noon, at midnight, still around me bide,
Rise on my dreams, and tell me how ye died !"

## CANTO II.

——Oh ! ben provvide il Cielo,
Ch' uom per delitti mai lieto non sia.
                              *Alfieri.*

Fair land ! of chivalry the old domain,
Land of the vine and olive, lovely Spain !
Though not for thee with classic shores to vie
In charms that fix'd the enthusiast's pensive eye,
Yet hast thou scenes of beauty richly fraught
With all that wakes the glow of lofty thought ;
Fountains and vales, and rocks, whose ancient
  name
High deeds have raised to mingle with their fame,
Those scenes are peaceful now : the citron blows,
Wild spreads the myrtle, where the brave repose.
No sound of battle swells on Douro's shore
And banners wave on Ebro's banks no more.
But who, unmoved, unawed, shall coldly tread
Thy fields that sepulchre the mighty dead ?

Blest be that soil ! where England's heroes share
The grave of chiefs, for ages slumbering there ;
Whose names are glorious in romantic lays,
The wild sweet chronicles of elder days.
By goatherd lone, and rude serrana sung,
Thy cypress dells, and vine-clad rocks among.
How oft those rocks have echo'd to the tale
Of knights who fell in Roncesvalles' vale ;
Of him, renown'd in old heroic lore,
First of the brave, the gallant Campeador ;
Of those the famed in song, who proudly died,
When " Rio Verde" roll'd a crimson tide :
Or that high name, by Garcilaso's might,
On the green Vega won in single fight. (8)

Round fair Granada, deepening from afar,
O'er that green Vega rose the din of war.
At morn or eve no more the sunbeams shone
O'er a calm scene in pastoral beauty lone ;
On helm and corslet tremulous they glanced,
On shield and spear in quivering lustre danced
Far as the sight by clear Xenil could rove,
Tents rose around, and banners glanced above,
And steeds in gorgeous trappings, armour bright
With gold reflecting every tint of light,
And many a floating plume, and blazon'd shield
Diffused romantic splendour o'er the field.

There swell those sounds that bid the life-blood
  start
Swift to the mantling cheek, and beating heart.
The clang of echoing steel, the charger's neigh,
The measured tread of hosts in war's array ;
And oh ! that music, whose exulting breath
Speaks but of glory on the road to death ;
In whose wild voice there dwells inspiring power
To wake the stormy joy of danger's hour,
To nerve the arm, the spirit to sustain,
Rouse from despondence, and support in pain,
And, 'midst the deepening tumults of the strife,
Teach every pulse to thrill with more than life.

High o'er the camp, in many a broider'd fold,
Floats to the wind a standard rich with gold :
There imaged on the cross, *his* form appears,
Who drank for man the bitter cup of tears. (9)
*His* form, whose word recall'd the spirit, fled,
Now borne by hosts to guide them o'er the dead
(O'er yon fair walls to plant the cross on high,
Spain hath sent forth her flower of chivalry.
Fired with that ardour, which, in days of yore,
To Syrian plains the bold Crusaders bore ;
Elate with lofty hope, with martial zeal,
They come, the gallant children of Castile ;
The proud, the calmly dignified :—and there
Ebro's dark sons with haughty mien repair,
And those who guide the fiery steed of war
From you rich province of the western star. (10)

But thou, conspicuous 'midst the glittering scene,
Stern grandeur stamp'd upon thy princely mien ;
Known by the foreign garb, the silvery vest,
The snow-white charger, and the azure crest, (11)
Young Aben-Zurrah ! 'midst that host of foes,
Why shines thy helm, thy Moorish lance ? Disclose !
Why rise the tents where dwell thy kindred train,
Oh son of Afric, 'midst the sons of Spain ?
Hast thou with these thy nation's fall conspired,
Apostate chief ! by hope of vengeance fired ?
How art thou changed ! Still first in every fight,
Hamet, the Moor ! Castile's devoted knight !
There dwells a fiery lustre in thine eye,
But not the light that shone in days gone by ;
There is wild ardour in thy look and tone,
But not the soul's expression once thine own,
Nor aught like peace within. Yet who shall say
What secret thoughts thine inmost heart may
  away ?
No eye but Heaven's may pierce that curtain'd
  breast,
Whose joys and griefs alike are unexprest.

There hath been combat on the tented plain ;
The Vega's turf is red with many a stain,
And rent and trampled, banner, crest, and shield
Tell of a fierce and well-contested field :

But all is peaceful now—the west is bright
With the rich splendour of departing light;
Mulhacen's peak, half lost amidst the sky,
Glows like a purple evening-cloud on high,
And tints, that mock the pencil's art, o'erspread
Th' eternal snow that crowns Veleta's head. (12)
While the warm sunset o'er the landscape throws
A solemn beauty, and a deep repose.
Closed are the toils and tumults of the day,
And Hamet wanders from the camp away,
In silent musings rapt:—the slaughter'd brave
Lie thickly strewn by Darro's rippling wave.
Soft fall the dews—but other drops have dyed
The scented shrubs that fringe the river-side,
Beneath whose shade, as ebbing life retired,
The wounded sought a shelter—and expired. (13)
Lonely, and lost in thoughts of other days,
By the bright windings of the stream he strays,
Till, more remote from battle's ravaged scene,
All is repose, and solitude serene.
There, 'neath an olive's ancient shade reclined,
Whose rustling foliage waves in evening's wind,
The harass'd warrior, yielding to the power,
The mild, sweet influence of the tranquil hour,
Feels, by degrees, a long-forgotten calm
Shed o'er his troubled soul unwonted balm;
His wrongs, his woes, his dark and dubious lot,
The past, the future, are awhile forgot;
And Hope, scarce own'd, yet stealing o'er his
    breast,
Half dares to whisper, "Thou shalt yet be blest!"

Such his vague musings—but a plaintive sound
Breaks on the deep and solemn stillness round;
A low half-stifled moan, that seems to rise
From life and death's contending agonies.
He turns: Who shares with him that lonely shade?
—A youthful warrior on his death-bed laid,
All rent and stain'd his broider'd Moorish vest,
The corslet shatter'd on his bleeding breast!
In his cold hand the broken falchion strain'd
With life's last force convulsively retain'd;
His plumage soil'd with dust, with crimson dyed,
And the red lance, in fragments, by his side;
He lies forsaken—pillow'd on his shield,
His helmet raised, his lineaments reveal'd.
Pale is that quivering lip, and vanish'd now
The light once throned on that commanding brow;
And o'er that fading eye, still upward cast,
The shades of death are gathering dark and fast.
Yet, as yon rising moon her light serene
Sheds the pale olive's waving boughs between,
Too well can Hamet's conscious heart retrace,
Though changed thus fearfully that pallid face,
Whose every feature to his soul conveys
Some bitter thought of long-departed days.

"Oh! is it thus," he cries, "we meet at last?
Friend of my soul, in years for ever past!
Hath fate but led me hither to behold
The last dread struggle ere that heart is cold,
Receive thy latest agonizing breath,
And, with vain pity, soothe the pangs of death?
Yet let me bear thee hence—while life remains,
E'en though thus feebly circling through thy veins,
Some healing balm thy sense may still revive,
Hope is not lost,—and Osmyn yet may live!
And blest were he, whose timely care should save
A heart so noble, e'en from glory's grave."

Roused by those accents, from his lowly bed
The dying warrior faintly lifts his head;
O'er Hamet's mien, with vague, uncertain gaze,
His doubtful glance awhile bewilder'd strays;
Till, by degrees, a smile of proud disdain
Lights up those features late convulsed with pain;
A quivering radiance flashes from his eye,
That seems too pure, too full of soul, to die;
And the mind's grandeur in its parting hour
Looks from that brow with more than wonted
    power.

"Away!" he cries, in accents of command,
And proudly waves his cold and trembling hand,
"Apostate, hence! my soul shall soon be free,
E'en now it soars, disdaining aid from thee:

'T is not for thee to close the fading eyes
Of him who faithful to his country dies;
Not for thy hand to raise the drooping head
Of him who sinks to rest on glory's bed.
Soon shall these pangs be closed, this conflict o'er
And worlds be mine where thou canst never soar.
Be thine existence with a blighted name,
Mine the bright death which seals a warrior's
    fame!"

The glow hath vanish'd from his cheek—his eye
Hath lost that beam of parting energy;
Frozen and fix'd it seems—his brow is chill;
One struggle more,—that noble heart is still.
Departed warrior! were thy mortal throes,
Were thy last pangs, ere nature found repose,
More keen, more bitter, than th' envenom'd dart
Thy dying words have left in Hamet's heart!
Thy pangs were transient; his shall sleep no more
'Till life's delirious dream itself is o'er;
But thou shalt rest in glory, and thy grave
Be the pure altar of the patriot brave.
Oh, what a change that little hour hath wrought
In the high spirit and unbending thought!
Yet, from himself each keen regret to hide,
Still Hamet struggles with indignant pride;
While his soul rises gathering all its force,
To meet the fearful conflict with remorse.

To thee, at length, whose artless love hath been
His own, unchanged, through many a stormy
    scene;
Zayda! to thee his heart for refuge flies;
Thou still art faithful to affection's ties.
Yes! let the world upbraid, let foes contemn,
Thy gentle breast the tide will firmly stem;
And soon thy smile, and soft consoling voice,
Shall bid his troubled soul again rejoice.

Within Granada's walls are hearts and hands,
Whose aid in secret Hamet yet commands;
Nor hard the task at some propitious hour,
To win his silent way to Zayda's bower,
When night and peace are brooding o'er the world
When mute the clarions, and the banners furl'd.
'That hour is come—and o'er the arms he bears
A wandering fakir's garb the chieftain wears:
Disguise that ill from piercing eye could hide
The lofty port, and glance of martial pride;
But night befriends — through paths obscure he
    pass'd,
And hail'd the lone and lovely scene at last;
Young Zayda's chosen haunt, the fair alcove,
The sparkling fountain, and the orange-grove;
Calm in the moonlight smiles the still retreat,
As form'd alone for happy hearts to meet.
For happy hearts?—not such is hers, who there
Bends o'er her lute, with dark, unbraided hair;
That maid of Zegri race, whose eye, whose mien,
Tell that despair her bosom's guest hath been.
So lost in thought she seems, the warrior's feet
Unheard approach her solitary seat,
Till his known accents every sense restore—
"My own loved Zayda! do we meet once more?"

She starts, she turns—the lightning of surprise,
Of sudden rapture, flashes from her eyes:
But that is fleeting—it is past—and now
Far other meaning darkens o'er her brow;
Changed is her aspect, and her tone severe—
"Hence, Aben Zurrah! death surrounds thee here!"

"Zayda! what means that glance, unlike thine
    own?
What mean those words, and that unwonted tone,
I will not deem thee changed—but in thy face,
It is not joy, it is not love, I trace!
It was not thus in other days we met;
Hath time, hath absence taught thee to forget?
Oh! speak once more—these rising doubts dispel,
One smile of tenderness, and all is well!"

"Not thus we met in other days! —oh no!
Thou wert not, warrior, then thy country's foe?
Those days are past—we ne'er shall meet again
With hearts all warmth, all confidence, as then

But thy dark soul no gentler feelings sway!
Leader of hostile bands! away, away!
On in thy path of triumph and of power,
Nor pause to raise from earth a blighted flower."

"And thou too changed! thine early vow forgot!
This, this alone, was wanting to my lot!
Exiled and scorn'd, of every tie bereft,
Thy love, the desert's lonely fount, was left;
And thou, my soul's last hope, its lingering beam,
Thou, the good angel of each brighter dream,
Wert all the barrenness of life possest,
To wake one soft affection in my breast!
That vision ended— faith hath naught in store,
Of joy or sorrow, e'er to touch me more.
Go, Zegri maid! to scenes of sunshine fly,
From the stern pupil of adversity!
And now to hope, to confidence adieu!
If thou art faithless, who shall e'er be true?"

"Hamet! oh wrong me not!—I too could speak
Of sorrows—trace them on my faded cheek,
In the sunk eye, and in the wasted form,
That tell the heart hath nursed a canker-worm!
But words were idle—read my sufferings there,
Where grief is stamp'd on all that once was fair.

"Oh, wert thou still what once I fondly deem'd,
All that thy mien express'd, thy spirit seem'd,
My love had been devotion—till in death
Thy name had trembled on my latest breath.
But not the chief who leads a lawless band,
To crush the altars of his native land;
Th' apostate son of heroes, whose disgrace
Hath stain'd the trophies of a glorious race;
Not him I loved—but one whose youthful name
Was pure and radiant in unsullied fame.
Hadst thou but died, ere yet dishonour's cloud
O'er that young name had gather'd as a shroud,
I then had mourn'd thee proudly—and my grief
In its own loftiness had found relief;
A noble sorrow, cherish'd to the last,
When every meaner woe had long been past.
Yes! let Affection weep—no common tear
She sheds, when bending o'er a hero's bier.
Let Nature mourn the dead—a grief like this,
To pangs that rend my bosom had been bliss!"

"High-minded maid! the time admits not now
To plead my cause, to vindicate my vow,
That vow, too dread, too solemn to recall,
Hath urged me onward, haply to my fall.
Yet this believe—no meaner aim inspires
My soul, no dream of poor ambition fires.
No! every hope of power, of triumph, fled,
Behold me but th' avenger of the dead!
One whose changed heart no tie, no kindred knows
And in thy love alone hath sought repose.
Zayda, wilt thou his stern accuser be?
False to his country, he is true to thee!
Oh, hear me yet!—if Hamet e'er was dear,
By our first vows, our young affection, hear!
Soon must this fair and royal city fall,
Soon shall the cross be planted on her wall!
Then who can tell what tides of blood may flow,
While her fanes echo to the shrieks of woe?
Fly, fly with me, and let me bear thee far
From horrors thronging in the path of war:
Fly! and repose in safety—till the blast
Hath made a desert in its course—and past."

"Thou that wilt triumph when the hour is come,
Hasten'd by thee, to seal thy country's doom,
With thee from scenes of death shall Zayda fly
To peace and safety?—Woman too can die!
And die exulting, though unknown to fame,
In all the stainless beauty of her name!
Be mine unmurmuring, undismay'd to share
The fate my kindred and my sire must bear.
And deem thou not my feeble heart shall fail,
When the clouds gather, and the blasts assail;
Thou hast but known me ere the trying hour
Call'd into life my spirit's latent power;
But I have energies that idly slept,
While withering o'er my silent woes I wept

And now, when hope and happiness are fled,
My soul is firm—for what remains to dread?
Who shall have power to suffer and to bear,
If strength and courage dwell not with Despair?

"Hamet, farewell!—retrace thy path again,
To join thy brethren on the tented plain.
There wave and wood, in mingled murmurs, tell,
How, in far other cause, thy fathers fell!
Yes! on that soil hath Glory's footstep been,
Names unforgotten consecrate the scene.
Dwell not the souls of heroes round thee there,
Whose voices call thee in the whispering air?
Unheard, in vain, they call—their fallen son
Hath stain'd the name those mighty spirits won,
And to the hatred of the brave and free
Bequeath'd his own, through ages yet to be!"

Still as she spoke, th' enthusiast's kindling eye
Was lighted up with inborn majesty,
While her fair form and youthful features caught
All the proud grandeur of heroic thought,
Severely beauteous! (14) awe-struck and amazed,
In silent trance awhile the warrior gazed
As on some lofty vision—for she seem'd
One all inspired—each look with glory beam'd,
While brightly bursting through its cloud of woes
Her soul at once in all its light arose.
Oh! ne'er had Hamet deem'd there dwelt enshrined
In form so fragile, that unconquer'd mind,
And fix'd, as by some high enchantment, there
He stood—till wonder yielded to despair.

"The dream is vanish'd—daughter of my foes!
Reft of each hope, the lonely wanderer goes.
Thy words have pierced his soul—yet deem thou
        not
Thou couldst be once adored, and e'er forgot!
O form'd for happier love! heroic maid!
In grief sublime, in danger undismay'd,
Farewell, and be thou blest!—all words were vain
For him who ne'er may view that form again,
Him, whose sole thought, resembling bliss, must be,
He hath been loved, once fondly loved, by thee!"

And is the warrior gone?—doth Zayda hear
His parting footstep, and without a tear?
Thou weep'st not, lofty maid?—yet who can tell
What secret pangs within thy heart may dwell?
They feel not least, the firm, the high in soul,
Who best each feeling's agony control.
Yes! we may judge the measure of the grief
Which finds in Misery's eloquence relief;
But who shall pierce those depths of silent woe,
Whence breathes no language, whence no tears
        may flow?
The pangs that many a noble breast hath proved,
Scorning itself that thus it could be moved?
He, He alone, the inmost heart who knows,
Views all its weakness, pities all its throes,
He who hath mercy when mankind contemn,
Beholding anguish—all unknown to them.

Fair city! thou, that 'midst thy stately fanes
And gilded minarets, towering o'er the plains,
In eastern grandeur proudly dost arise
Beneath thy canopy of deep-blue skies,
While streams that bear thee treasures in their
        wave, (15)
Thy citron-groves and myrtle-gardens lave;
Mourn! for thy doom is fix'd—the days of fear
Of chains, of wrath, of bitterness, are near!
Within, around thee are the trophied graves
Of kings and chiefs—their children shall be slaves
Fair are thy halls, thy domes majestic swell,
But there a race that rear'd them not shall dwell:
For 'midst thy counsels Discord still presides,
Degenerate fear thy wavering monarch guides,
Last of a line whose regal spirit flown
Hath to their offspring but bequeath'd a throne,
Without one generous thought, or feeling high,
To teach his soul how kings should live and die

A voice resounds within Granada's wall,
The hearts of warriors echo to its call. (16)
Whose are those tones with power electric fraught
To reach the source of pure, exalted thought?

See on a fortress-tower, with beckoning hand,
A form, majestic as a prophet, stand!
His mien is all impassion'd—and his eye
Fill'd with a light whose fountain is on high;
Wild on the gale his silvery tresses flow,
And inspiration beams upon his brow,
While, thronging round him, breathless thousands
    gaze,
As on some mighty seer of elder days.

"Saw ye the banners of Castile display'd,
The helmets glittering, and the line array'd?
Heard ye the march of steel-clad hosts? he cries,
"Children of conquerors! in your strength arise
O high-born tribes: oh names unstain'd by fear!
Azarques, Zegris, Almoradis, hear! (17)
Be every feud forgotten, and your hands
Dyed with no blood but that of hostile bands, (18)
Wake, princes of the land! the hour is come,
And the red sabre must decide your doom.
Where is that spirit which prevail'd of yore,
When Tarik's bands o'erspread the western
    shore? (19)
When the long combat raged on Xeres' plain, (20)
And Afric's techir swell'd thro' yielding Spain? (21)
Is the lance broken, is the shield decay'd,
The warrior's arm unstrung, his heart dismay'd?
Shall no high spirit of ascending worth
Arise to lead the sons of Islam forth?
To guard the regions where our fathers' blood
Hath bathed each plain, and mingled with each
    flood,
Where long their dust hath blended with the soil
Won by their swords, made fertile by their toil?

"O ye sierras of eternal snow!
Ye streams that by the tombs of heroes flow,
Woods, fountains, rocks, of Spain! ye saw their
    might
In many a fierce and unforgotten fight!
Shall ye behold their lost, degenerate race,
Dwell 'midst your scenes in fetters and disgrace?
With each memorial of the past around,
Each mighty monument of days renown'd?
May this indignant heart ere then be cold,
This frame be gather'd to its kindred mould!
And the last life-drop circling through my veins
Have tinged a soil untainted yet by chains!

"And yet one struggle ere our doom is seal'd,
One mighty effort, one deciding field!
If vain each hope, we still have choice to be,
In life the fetter'd, or in death the free!"

Still while he speaks, each gallant heart beats
    high,
And ardour flashes from each kindling eye;
Youth, manhood, age, as if inspired, have caught
The glow of lofty hope and daring thought,
And all is hush'd around—as every sense
Dwelt on the tones of that wild eloquence.

But when his voice hath ceased, th' impetuous cry
Of eager thousands burst at once on high;
Rampart, and rock, and fortress, ring around,
And fair Alhambra's inmost halls resound:
"Lead us, O chieftain! lead us to the strife,
To fame in death, or liberty in life!"
O zeal of noble hearts! in vain display'd!
High feeling wasted! generous hope betray'd!
Now, while the burning spirit of the brave
Is roused to energies that yet might save,
E'en now enthusiasts! while ye rush to claim
Your glorious trial on the field of fame,
Your king hath yielded! Valour's dream is o'er; (22)
Power, wealth, and freedom, are your own no
    more;
And for your children's portion, but remains
That bitter heritage—the stranger's chains.

## CANTO III.



HEROES of elder days! untaught to yield,
Who bled for Spain on many an ancient field,
Ye, that around the oaken cross of yore (23)
Stood firm and fearless on Asturia's shore,
And with your spirit, ne'er to be subdued,
Hallow'd the wild Cantabrian solitude;
Rejoice amidst your dwellings of repose,
In the last chastening of your Moslem foes!
Rejoice!—for Spain, arising in her strength,
Hath burst the remnant of their yoke at length
And they in turn the cup of woe must drain,
And bathe their fetters with their tears in vain
And thou, the warrior born in happy hour, (24)
Valencia's lord, whose name alone is power,
Theme of a thousand songs in days gone by,
Conquerer of Kings! exult, O Cid! on high.
For still 'twas thine to guard thy country's weal,
In life, in death, the watcher for Castile!

Thou, in that hour when Mauritania's bands
Rush'd from their palmy groves and burning lands
E'en in the realm of spirits didst retain
A patriot's vigilance, remembering Spain! (25)
Then, at deep midnight, rose the mighty sound,
By Leon heard, in shuddering awe profound,
As through her echoing streets in dread array,
Beings, once mortal, held their viewless way;
Voices from worlds we know not—and the tread
Of marching hosts, the armies of the dead,
Thou and thy buried chieftains—from the grave
Then did thy summons rouse a king to save,
And join thy warriors with unearthly might
To aid the rescue in Tolosa's fight.
Those days are past—the crescent on thy shore,
O realm of evening! sets, to rise no more. (26)
What banner streams afar from Vela's tower? (27)
The cross, bright ensign of Iberia's power!
What the glad shout of each exulting voice?
"Castile and Arragon! rejoice, rejoice!"
Yielding free entrance to victorious foes,
The Moorish city sees her gates unclose,
And Spain's proud host, with pennon, shield, and
    lance,
Through her long streets in knightly garb advance.

Oh! ne'er in lofty dreams hath Fancy's eye
Dwelt on a scene of statelier pageantry,
At joust or tourney, theme of poet's lore,
High masque, or solemn festival of yore.
The gilded cupolae, that proudly rise
O'erarch'd by cloudless and cerulean skies,
Tall minarets, shining mosques, barbaric towers,
Fountains, and palaces, and cypress bowers;
And they, the splendid and triumphant throng,
With helmets glittering as they move along,
With broider'd scarf, and gem-bestudded mail,
And graceful plumage streaming on the gale;
Shields gold-emboss'd, and pennons floating far,
And all the gorgeous blazonry of war,
All brighten'd by the rich transparent hues
That southern suns o'er heaven and earth diffuse,
Blend in one scene of glory, form'd to throw
O'er memory's page a never-fading glow.
And there too, foremost 'midst the conquering
    brave,
Your azure plumes, O Aben-Zurrahs! wave.
There Hamet moves; the chief whose lofty port
Seems nor approach to shun, nor praise to court,
Calm, stern, collected—yet within his breast
Is there no pang, no struggle unconfest?
If such there be, it still must dwell unseen,
Nor could a triumph with a sufferer's mien.

Hear'st thou the solemn, yet exulting sound,
Of the deep anthem floating far around?
The choral voices to the skies that raise
The full majestic harmony of praise?
Lo! where, surrounded by their princely train,
They come, the sovereigns of rejoicing Spain,
Borne on their trophied car—lo! bursting thence
A blaze of chivalrous magnificence!

Onward their slow and stately course they bend
To where th' Alhambra's ancient towers ascend
Rear'd and adorn'd by Moorish kings of yore,
Whose lost descendants there shall dwell no?

They reach those towers—irregularly vast,
And rude they seem, in mould barbaric cast: (28)
They enter—to their wondering sight is given
A genii palace—an Arabian heaven! (29)
A scene by magic raised, so strange, so fair,
Its forms and colours seem alike of air.
Here by sweet orange-boughs, half shaded o'er,
The deep clear bath reveals its marble floor,
Its margin fringed with flowers, whose glowing
      hues
The calm transparence of its wave suffuse.
There, round the court, where Moorish arches bend,
Aërial columns, richly deck'd, ascend;
Unlike the models of each classic race,
Of Doric grandeur, or Corinthian grace,
But answering well each vision that portrays
Arabian splendour to the poet's gaze:
Wild, wondrous, brilliant, all—a mingling glow
Of rainbow tints, above, around, below;
Bright-streaming from the many-tinctured veins
Of precious marble—and the vivid stains
Of rich mosaics o'er the light arcade,
In gay festoons and fairy knots display'd.

On through th' enchanted realm, that only seems
Meet for the radiant creatures of our dreams,
The royal conquerors pass—while still their sight
On some new wonder dwells with fresh delight.
Here the eye roves through slender colonnades,
O'er bowery terraces and myrtle shades,
Dark olive-woods beyond, and far on high
The vast sierra, mingling with the sky.
There, scattering far around their diamond spray,
Clear streams from founts of alabaster play,
Through pillar'd halls, where, exquisitely wrought,
Rich arabesques, with glittering foliage fraught,
Surmount each fretted arch, and lend the scene
A wild, romantic, oriental mien:
While many a verse from eastern bards of old,
Borders the wall in characters of gold. (30)
Here Moslem luxury, in her own domain,
Hath held for ages her voluptuous reign
'Midst gorgeous domes, where soon shall silence
      brood,
And all be lone—a splendid solitude.
Now wake their echoes to a thousand songs,
From mingling voices of exulting throngs;
Tambour, and flute, and atabal, are there, (31)
And joyous clarions pealing on the air,
While every hall resounds, " Granada won!
Granada! for Castile and Arragon!" (32)

'Tis night—from dome and tower, in dazzling
      maze,
The festal lamps innumerably blaze; (33)
Through long arcades their quivering lustre gleams,
From every lattice tremulously streams,
'Midst orange-gardens plays on fount and rill,
And gilds the waves of Darro and Xenil;
Red flame the torches on each minaret's height,
And shines each street an avenue of light;
And midnight feasts are held, and music's voice
Through the long night still summons to rejoice.

Yet there, while all would seem to heedless eye
One blaze of pomp, one burst of revelry,
Are hearts unsoothed by those delusive hours,
Gall'd by the chain, though deck'd awhile with
      flowers;
Stern passions working in th' indignant breast,
Deep pangs untold, high feelings unexprest,
Heroic spirits, unsubmitting yet.
Vengeance, and keen remorse, and vain regret.

From yon proud height, whose olive-shaded brow
Commands the wide luxuriant plains below,
Who lingering gazes o'er the lovely scene,
Anguish and shame contending in his mien?
He, who, of heroes and of kings the son,
Hath lived to lose whate'er his fathers won,
Whose doubts and fears his people's fate have
      seal'd—
Wavering alike in council and in field:
—A timid ruler of the wise and brave,
Still a fierce tyrant or a yielding slave.

Far from these vine-clad hills and azure skies,
To Afric's wilds the royal exile flies, (34)
Yet pauses on his way, to weep in vain,
O'er all he never must behold again.
Fair spreads the scene around—for him too fair,
Each glowing charm but deepens his despair.
The Vega's meads, the city's glittering spires,
The old majestic palace of his sires,
The gay pavilions, and retired alcoves,
Bosom'd in citron and pomegranate groves;
Tower-crested rocks, and streams that wind in
      light,
All in one moment bursting on his sight,
Speak to his soul of glory's vanish'd years,
And wake the source of unavailing tears
—Weep'st thou, Abdallah?—Thou dost
      weep,
O feeble heart! o'er all thou couldst not save·
Well do a woman's tears befit the eye
Of him who knew not, as a man, to die. (35)

The gale sighs mournfully through Zayda's
      bower,
The hand is gone that nursed each infant flower
No voice, no step, is in her father's halls,
Mute are the echoes of their marble walls
No stranger enters at the chieftain's gate,
But all is hush'd, and void, and desolate.

There, through each tower and solitary shade,
In vain doth Hamet seek the Zegri maid;
Her grove is silent, her pavilion lone,
Her lute forsaken, and her doom unknown;
And through the scene she loved, unheeded flows
The stream whose music lull'd her to repose.

But oh! to him whose self-accusing thought
Whispers 'twas he that desolation wrought:
He who his country and his faith betray'd,
And lent Castile revengeful, powerful aid;
A voice of sorrow swells in every gale,
Each wave, low rippling, tells a mournful tale;
And as the shrubs, untended, unconfined,
In wild exuberance rustle to the wind,
Each leaf hath language to his startled sense,
And seems to murmur—" Thou hast driven her
      hence!"
And well he feels to trace her flight were vain,
—Where hath lost love been once recall'd again?
In her pure breast, so long by anguish torn,
His name can rouse no feeling now but scorn.
O bitter hour! when first the shuddering heart
Wakes to behold the void within—and start!
To feel its own abandonment, and brood
O'er the chill bosom's depth of solitude.
The stormy passions that in Hamet's breast
Have sway'd so long, so fiercely, are at rest!
Th' avenger's task is closed: (36)—he finds too late,
It hath not changed his feelings, but his fate.
His was a lofty spirit, turned aside
From its bright path by woes, and wrongs, and
      pride,
And onward, in its new tumultuous course,
Borne with too rapid and intense a force
To pause one moment in the dread career,
And ask—if such could be its native sphere.
Now are those days of wild delirium o'er,
Their fears and hopes excite his soul no more;
The feverish energies of passion close,
And his heart sinks in desolate repose,
Turns sickening from the world, yet shrinks no
      less
From its own deep and utter loneliness.

There is a sound of voices on the air,
A flash of armour in the sunbeam's glare,

'Midst the wild Alpuxarras: (37)—there, on high
Where mountain-snows are mingled with the
    sky.
A few brave tribes, with spirit yet unbroke,
Have fled indignant from the Spaniard's yoke.

O ye dread scenes, where Nature dwells alone,
Severely glorious on her craggy throne;
Ye citadels of rock, gigantic forms,
Veil'd by the mists, and girdled by the storms;
Ravines, and glens, and deep resounding caves,
That hold communion with the torrent-waves;
And ye, the unstain'd and everlasting snows,
That dwell above in bright and still repose:
To you, in every clime, in every age,
Far from the tyrants or the conquror's rage,
Hath Freedom led her sons; untired to keep
Her fearless vigils on the barren steep
She like the mountain Eagle still delights
To gaze exulting from unconquer'd heights,
And build her erie in defiance proud,
To dare the wind and mingle with the cloud.

Now her deep voice, the soul's awakener, swells,
Wild Alpuxarras, through your inmost dells,
There, the dark glens and lonely rocks among,
As at the clarion's call, her children throng.
She with enduring strength hath nerved each frame,
And made each heart the temple of her flame,
Her own resisting spirit, which shall glow
Unquenchably, surviving all below.

    There high-born maids, that moved upon the
        earth.
More like bright creatures of aërial birth,
Nurslings of palaces, have fled to share
The fate of brothers and of sires ; to bear,
All undismav'd, privation and distress,
And smile, the roses of the wilderness.
And mothers with their infants, there to dwell
In the deep forest or the cavern cell,
And rear their offspring 'midst the rocks to be
If now no more the mighty, still the free.
    And 'midst that band of veterans, o'er whose
        head
Sorrows and years their mingled snow have shed :
They saw thy glory, they have wept thy fall,
O royal city! and the wreck of all
They loved and hallow'd most :—doth aught re-
    main
For these to prove of happiness or pain ?
Life's cup is drain'd—earth fades before their eye,
Their task is closing—they have but to die.
Ask ye, why fled they hither?—that their doom
Might be to sink unfetter'd to the tomb.
And youth, in all its pride of strength, is there;
And buoyancy of spirit, form'd to dare
And suffer all things,—fallen on evil days,
Yet darting o'er the world an ardent gaze,
As on th' arena, where its powers may find
Full scope to strive for glory with mankind.

    Such are the tenants of the mountain-hold,
The high in heart, unconquer'd, uncontroll'd ;
By day the huntsman of the wild—by night,
Unwearied guardians of the watch-fire's light.
They from their bleak, majestic home have caught
A sterner tone of unsubmitting thought,
While all around them hids the soul arise,
To blend with Nature's dread sublimities.
—But these are lofty dreams, and must not be
Where tyranny is near :—the bended knee,
The eye, whose glance no inborn grandeur fires,
And the tamed heart, are tributes she requires;
Nor must the dwellers of the rock look down
On regal conquerors and defy their frown.
What warrior-band is toiling to explore
The mountain-pass, with pine-wood shadow'd
        o'er ?
Startling with martial sound each rude recess.
Where the deep echo slept in loneliness.
These are the sons of Spain !—Your foes are near:
Oh, exiles of the wild sierra ! hear !
Hear! wake! arise! and from your inmost caves
Pour like the torrent in its might of waves!

3

Who leads th' invaders on ?—his features bear
The deep-worn traces of a calm despair;
Yet his dark brow is haughty—and his eye
Speaks of a soul that asks not sympathy.
'Tis he ! 'tis he again ! the apostate chief;
He comes in all the sternness of his grief.
He comes, but changed in heart, no more to wield
Falchion for proud Castile in battle-field,
Against his country's children—though he leads
Castilian bands again to hostile deeds:
His hope is but from ceaseless pangs to fly,
To rush upon the Moslem spears and die
So shall remorse and love the heart release,
Which dares not dream of joy, but sighs for peace
The mountain-echoes are awake—a sound
Of strife is rising through the rocks around.
Within the steep defile that winds between
Cliffs piled on cliffs, a dark, terrific scene.
There Moorish exile and Castilian knight
Are wildly mingled in the serried fight.
Red flows the foaming streamlet of the glen,
Whose bright transparence ne'er was stain'd
    till then;
While swell the war-notes and the clash of spears,
To the bleak dwellings of the mountaineers,
Wherh thy sad daughters, lost Grenada! wait
In dread suspense, the tidings of their fate.
But he—whose spirit panting for its rest,
Would fain each sword concentrate in his breast—
Who, where a spear is pointed, or a lance
Aim'd at another's breast, would still advance
Courts death in vain; each weapon glances by,
As if for him 't were bliss too great to die.
Yes! Aben-Zurrah! there are deeper woes;
Reserved for thee, ere Nature's last repose;
Thou know'st not yet what vengeance fate can
    wreak,
Nor all the heart can suffer ere it break.
Doubtful and long the strife, and bravely fell
The sons of battle in that narrow dell;
Youth in 'ts light of beauty there hath past,
And age, the weary, found repose at last:
Till few and faint the Moslem tribes recoil,
Borne down by numbers and o'erpower'd by toil.
Dispersed, dishcarten'd through the pass they fly,
Pierce the deep wood, or mount the cliff on high
While Hamet's band in wonder gaze, nor dare
Track o'er their dizzy path the footsteps of despair.

    Yet he to whom each danger hath become
A dark delight, and every wild a home,
Still urges onward—undismay'd to tread
Where life's fond lovers would recoil with dread,
But fear is for the happy—*they* may shrink
From the steep precipice, or torrent's brink ;
They to whom earth is paradise—their doom
Lends no stern courage to approach the tomb;
Not such his lot, who, school'd by fate severe,
Were but too bless'd if aught remain'd to fear. (38)
Up the rude crags, whose giant masses throw
Eternal shadows o'er the glen below ;
And by the fall whose many-tinctured spray
Half in a mist of radiance veils its way,
He holds his venturous track :—supported now
By some o'erhanging pine or ilex bough;
Now by some jutting stone that seems to dwell
Half in mid-air, as balanced by a spell :
Now hath his footsteps gain'd the summit's head,
A level span, with emerald verdure spread,
A fairy circle—there the heath-flowers rise,
And the rock-rose unnoticed blooms and dies;
And brightly plays the stream, ere yet its tide
In foam and thunder cleave the mountain side;
But all is wild beyond—and Hamet's eye
Roves o'er a world of rude sublimity.
That dell beneath, where e'en at noon of day
Earth's charter'd guest, the sunbeam, scarce can
    stray;
Around, untrodden woods ; and far above,
Where mortal footstep ne'er may hope to rove,
Bare granite cliffs, whose fix'd, inherent dies
Rival the tints that float o'er summer skies ; (39)
And the pure glittering snow-realm, yet more high,
That seems a part of heaven's eternity.

There is no track of man where Hamet stands
Pathless the scene as Libya's desert sands;
Yet on the calm, still air, a sound is heard
Of distant voices, and the gathering-word
Of Islam's tribes, now faint and fainter grown,
Now but the lingering echo of a tone.

That sound, whose cadence dies upon his ear,
He follows, reckless if his bands are near.
On by the rushing stream his way he bends,
And through the mountain's forest zone ascends
Piercing the still and solitary shades
Of ancient pines, and dark, luxuriant glades,
Eternal twilight's reign:—those mazes past,
The glowing sunbeams meet his eyes at last,
And the lone wanderer now hath reach'd the source
Whence the wave gushes, foaming on its course.
But there he pauses—for the lonely scene
Towers in such dread magnificence of mien,
And, mingled oft with some wild eagle's cry,
From rock-built eyrie rushing to the sky,
So deep the solemn and majestic sound
Of forests, and of waters murmuring round,
That, rapt in wondering awe, his heart forgets
Its fleeting struggles, and its vain regrets.
—What earthly feeling unabash'd can dwell
In Nature's mighty presence ?—'midst the swell
Of everlasting hills, the roar of floods,
And frown of rocks, and pomp of waving woods?
These their own grandeur on the soul impress,
And bid each passion feel its nothingness.

'Midst the vast marble cliffs, a lofty cave
Rears its broad arch beside the rushing wave;
Shadow'd by giant oaks, and rude, and lone,
It seems the temple of some power unknown,
Where earthly being may not dare intrude
To pierce the secrets of the solitude.
Yet thence at intervals a voice of wail
Is rising, wild and solemn, on the gale.
Did thy heart thrill, O Hamet, at the tone?
Came it not o'er thee as a spirit's moan?
As some loved sound that long from earth had fled,
The unforgotten accents of the dead?
E'en thus it rose—and springing from his trance
His eager footsteps to the sound advance.
He mounts the cliffs, he gains the cavern floor;
Its dark green moss with blood is sprinkled o'er:
He rushes on—and lo! where Zayda rends
Her locks, as o'er her slaughter'd sire she bends,
Lost in despair;—yet as a step draws nigh,
Disturbing sorrow's lonely sanctity,
She lifts her head, and all subdued by grief,
Views, with a wild, sad smile, the once-loved chief;
While rove her thoughts, unconscious of the past,
And every woe forgetting—but the last.

"Com'st thou to weep with me ?—for I am left
Alone on earth, of every tie bereft.
Low lies the warrior on his blood-stain'd bier;
His child may call, but he no more shall hear!
He sleeps—but never shall those eyes unclose:
'Twas not my voice that lull'd him to repose,
Nor can it break his slumbers.—Dost thou mourn?
And is thy heart, like mine, with anguish torn?
Weep and my soul a joy in grief shall know,
That o'er his grave my tears with Hamet's flow!"

But scarce her voice had breathed that well-
        known name,
When, swiftly rushing o'er her spirit, came
Each dark remembrance ; by affliction's power
Awhile effaced in that o'erwhelming hour,
To wake with tenfold strength;—'twas then her
        eye
Resumed its light, her mien its majesty,
And o'er her wasted cheek a burning glow
Spreads, while her lip's indignant accents flow.

"Away! I dream—oh, how hath sorrow's might
Bow'd down my soul, and quench'd its native light,
That I should thus forget! and bid thy tear
With mine be mingled o'er a father's bier!
Did he not perish, haply by thy hand,
In the last combat with thy ruthless band?

The morn beheld that conflict of despair:—
'Twas then he fell—he fell!—and thou wert there!
Thou! who thy country's children hast pursued
To their last refuge 'midst these mountains rude.
Was it for this I loved thee ?—Thou hast taught
My soul all grief, all bitterness of thought!
'Twill soon be past—I bow to Heaven's decree,
Which bade each pang be minister'd by thee."

" I had not deem'd that aught remain'd below
For me to prove of yet untasted woe;
But thus to meet thee, Zayda! can impart
One more, one keener agony of heart.
Oh, hear me yet!—I would have died to save
My foe, but still thy father, from the grave;
But in the fierce confusion of the strife,
In my own stern despair and scorn of life,
Borne wildly on, I saw not, knew not aught,
Save that to perish there in vain I sought.
And let me share thy sorrows—hadst thou known
All I have felt in silence and alone,
E'en thou might'st then relent, and deem at last
A grief like mine might expiate all the past.

" But oh! for thee, the loved and precious flower,
So fondly rear'd in luxury's guarded bower,
From every danger, every storm secured,
How hast thou suffer'd! what hast thou endured
Daughter of palaces! and can it be
That this bleak desert is a home for thee?
These rocks thy dwelling! thou, who shouldst
        have known
Of life the sunbeam and the smile alone!
Oh, yet forgive!—be all my guilt forgot,
Nor bid me leave thee to so rude a lot!"

" That lot is fix'd ; 'twere fruitless to repine,
Still must a gulf divide my fate from thine.
I may forgive—but not at will the heart
Can bid its dark remembrances depart.
No, Hamet, no!—too deeply these are traced,
Yet the hour comes when all shall be effaced!
Not long on earth, not long, shall Zayda keep
Her lonely vigils o'er the grave to weep:
E'en now prophetic of my early doom,
Speaks to my soul a presage of the tomb;
And ne'er in vain did hopeless mourner feel
That deep foreboding o'er the bosom steal!
Soon shall I slumber calmly by the side
Of him for whom I lived and would have died:
Till then, one thought shall soothe my orphan lot
In pain and peril—I forsook him not.

"And now, farewell!—behold the summer-day
Is passing, like the dreams of life, away.
Soon will the tribe of him who sleeps draw nigh,
With the last rites his bier to sanctify.
Oh, yet in time, away!—'twere not my prayer
Could move their hearts a foe like thee to spare!
This hour they come—and dost thou scorn to fly?
Save me that one last pang—to see thee die!"

E'en while she speaks is heard their echoing
        tread;
Onward they move, the kindred of the dead.
They reach the cave—they enter—slow their pace,
And calm, deep sadness marks each mourner's face,
And all is hush'd—till he who seems to wait
In silent, stern devotedness, his fate,
Hath met their glance—then grief to fury turns
Each mien is changed, each eye indignant burns
And voices rise, and swords have left their sheath:
Blood must atone for blood, and death for death!
They close around him:—lofty still his mien,
His cheek unalter'd, and his brow serene.
Unheard, or heard in vain, is Zayda's cry;
Fruitless her prayer unmark'd her agony.
But as his foremost foes their weapons bend
Against the life he seeks not to defend,
Wildly she darts between—each feeling pas[s]
Save strong affection, which prevails at last
Oh! not in vain its daring—for the blow
Aim'd at his heart hath bade her life-blood [flow]  ·  ·
And she hath sunk a martyr on the breast,
Where, in that hour, her head may calmly re[st]

For he is saved:—behold the Zegri band,
Pale with dismay and grief, around her stand;
While, every thought of hate and vengeance o'er,
They weep for her who soon shall weep no more.
She, she alone is calm:—a fading smile,
Like sunset, passes o'er her cheek the while;
And in her eye, ere yet it closes, dwell
Those last faint rays, the parting soul's farewell.

" Now is the conflict past, and I have proved
How well, how deeply thou hast been beloved!
Yes! in an hour like this 't were vain to hide
The heart so long and so severely tried:
Still to thy name that heart hath fondly thrill'd,
But sterner duties call'd—and were fulfill'd:
And I am blest!—To every holier tie
My life was faithful,—and for thee I die!
Nor shall the love so purified be vain;
Sever'd on earth, we yet shall meet again.
Farewell!—And ye, at Zayda's dying prayer,
Spare him, my kindred tribe! forgive and spare!
Oh! be his guilt forgotten in his woes,
While I, beside my sire, in peace repose."

Now fades her cheek, her voice hath sunk, and death
Sits in her eye, and struggles in her breath.
One pang—'t is past—her task on earth is done,
And the pure spirit to its rest hath flown
But he for whom she died—Oh! who may paint
The grief, to which all other woes were faint?
There is no power in language to impart
The deeper pangs, th' ordeals of the heart,
By the dread Searcher of the soul survey'd;
These have no words—nor are by words portray'd.

A dirge is rising on the mountain-air,
Whose fitful swells its plaintive murmurs bear
Far o'er the Alpuxarras;—wild its tone,
And rocks and caverns echo "Thou art gone!"

" Daughter of heroes! thou art gone
    To share his tomb who gave thee birth;
Peace to the lovely spirit flown!
    It was not form'd for earth.
Thou wert a sunbeam in thy race,
Which brightly past, and left no trace.

" But calmly sleep!—for thou art free,
    And hands unchain'd thy tomb shall raise.
Sleep! they are closed at length for thee,
    Life's few and evil days!
Nor shalt thou watch, with tearful eye,
The lingering death of liberty.

" Flower of the desert! thou thy bloom
    Didst early to the storm resign:
We bear it still—and dark their doom
    Who cannot weep for thine!
For us, whose every hope is fled,
The time is past to mourn the dead.

"The days have been, when o'er thy bier
    Far other strains than these had flow'd;
Now, as a home from grief and fear,
    We hail thy dark abode!
We who but linger to bequeath
Our sons the choice of chains or death.

" Thou art with those, the free, the brave,
    The mighty of departed years;
And for the slumberers of the grave
    Our fate hath left no tears.
Though loved and lost, to weep were vain
For thee, who ne'er shalt weep again.

" Have we not seen, despoll'd by foes,
    The land our fathers won of yore?
And is there yet a pang for those
    Who gaze on this no more?
Oh, that like them 't were ours to rest!
Daughter of heroes! thou art blest!"

A few short years, and in the lonely cave
Where sleeps the Zegri maid, is Hamet's grave.
Sever'd in life, united in the tomb—
Such of the hearts that loved so well, the doom!

Their dirge, of woods and waves th eternal moan
Their sepulchre, the pine-clad rocks alone.
And oft beside the midnight watch-fire's blaze,
Amidst those rocks, in long departed days
(When Freedom fled, to hold, sequester'd there,
The stern and lofty councils of despair),
Some exiled Moor, a warrior of the wild,
Who the lone hours with mournful strains beguiled,
Hath taught his mountain-home the tale of those
Who thus have suffer'd, and who thus repose.

## NOTES.

—

### NOTE 1.

*Not the light zambra.*

Zambra, a Moorish dance.

### NOTE 2.

*Within the hall of Lions.*

The hall of Lions was the principal one of the Alhambra, and was so called from twelve sculptured lions, which supported an alabaster basin in the centre.

### NOTE 3.

*His Aben-Zurrahs there young Hamet leads.*

Aben-Zurrah; the name thus written is taken from the translation of an Arabic MS. given in the 3d volume of Bourgoanne's Travels through Spain.

### NOTE 4.

*The Vega's green expanse*

The Vega, the plain surrounding Granada, the scene of frequent actions between the Moors and Christians.

### NOTE 5.

*Seen 'midst the redness of the desert storm.*

An extreme redness in the sky is the presage of the Simoom.—See *Bruce's Travels.*

### NOTE 6.

*Stillness like that, when fierce the Kamsin's blast
Hath o'er the dwellings of the desert passed.*

Of the Kamsin, a hot south wind, common in Egypt, we have the following account in Volney's Travels: " These winds are known in Egypt by the general name of the winds of fifty days, because they prevail more frequently in the fifty days preceding and following the equinox. They are mentioned by travellers under the name of the poisonous winds, or hot winds of the desert: their heat is so excessive, that it is difficult to form any idea of its violence without having experienced it. When they begin to blow, the sky, at other times so clear in this climate, becomes dark and heavy; the sun loses his splendour, and appears of a violet colour; the air is not cloudy, but gray and thick, and is filled with a subtile dust, which penetrates every where: respiration becomes short and difficult, the skin parched and dry, the lungs are contracted and painful, and the body consumed with internal heat. In vain is coolness sought for; marble, iron, water, though the sun no longer appears, are hot; the streets are deserted, and a dead silence appears every where. The natives of town and villages shut themselves up in their houses, and those of the desert in tents, or holes dug in the earth, where they wait the termination of this heat, which generally lasts three days. Woe to the traveller whom it surprises remote from shelter: he must suffer all its dreadful effects, which are sometimes mortal."

### NOTE 7.

*While fearless eyes enjoy the honey-dews of sleep.*
" Enjoy the honey-heavy-dew of slumber."—*Shakspeare.*

### NOTE 8.

*On the green Vega won in single fight.*

Garcilaso de la Vega derived his surname from a single combat (in which he was the victor) with a Moor, on the Vega of Granada.

### NOTE 9.

*Who drank for man the bitter cup of tears.*

" El Rey D. Fernando bolvio a la Vega, y puso su Real a la vista de Huesca., a veynte y seys dias del mes de Abril, adonde fue fortificado de todo lo necessario; poniendo el Christiano toda su gente en esquadron, con todas sus vanderas tendidas, y su Real Estandarte, el qual llevava por divisa un Christo crucificado."—*Historia de la Guerras Civiles de Granada.*

### NOTE 10.

*From yon rich province of the western star.*

Andalusia signifies, in Arabic, the region of the evening or of the west; in a word, the *Hesperia* of the Greeks.—See *Casiri Biblioi Arabico-Hispana,* and *Gibbon's Decline and Fall,* &c

### NOTE 11.

*The snow-white charger, and the azure crest,*

" Los Abencerrages salieron con su acostumbrada librea azul y blanca, todos llenos de ricos texidos de plata, las plumas de la misma color; en sus adargas, su acostumbrada divisa, salvages que desquixalavan leones, y otros su mundo que lo deshazia un salvage con un baston."—*Guerras Civiles de Granada.*

### NOTE 12.
*Th' eternal snows that crown Veleta's head.*

The loftiest heights of the Sierra Nevada are those called Mulhacen and Picacho de Veleta.

### NOTE 13.
*The wounded sought a shelter—and expired.*

It is known to be a frequent circumstance in battle, that the dying and the wounded drag themselves, as it were mechanically, to the shelter afforded by any bush or thicket on the field.

### NOTE 14.
*Severely beauteous.*

"Severe in youthful beauty."—*Milton.*

### NOTE 15.
*While streams, that bear thee treasures in their waves.*

Granada stands upon two hills, separated by the Darro. The Genil runs under the walls. The Darro is said to carry with its stream small particles of gold, and the Genil, of silver. When Charles V. came to Granada with the Empress Isabella, the city presented him with a crown, made of gold which had been collected from the Darro.—*See Bourgoanne's and other Travels.*

### NOTE 16.
*The hearts of warriors echo to its call.*

"At this period, while the inhabitants of Granada were sunk in indolence, one of those men, whose natural and impassioned eloquence has sometimes aroused a people to deeds of heroism, raised his voice, in the midst of the city, and awakened the inhabitants from their lethargy. Twenty thousand enthusiasts, ranged under his banners, were prepared to sally forth, with the fury of desperation, to attack the besiegers, when Abo Abdeli, more afraid of his subjects than of the enemy, resolved immediately to capitulate, and made terms with the Christians, by which it was agreed that the Moors should be allowed the free exercise of their religion and laws; should be permitted, if they thought proper, to depart unmolested with their effects to Africa; and that he himself, if he remained in Spain, should retain an extensive estate, with houses and slaves, or be granted an equivalent in money if he preferred retiring to Barbary."—*See Jacob's Travels in Spain.*

### NOTE 17.
*Azarques, Zegris, Almoradis, hear!*

Azarques, Zegris, Almoradis, different tribes of the Moors of Granada, all of high distinction.

### NOTE 18.
*Dyed with no blood but that of hostile bands.*

The conquest of Granada was greatly facilitated by the civil dissensions which, at this period, prevailed in the city. Several of the Moorish tribes, influenced by private feuds, were fully prepared for submission to the Spaniards; others had embraced the cause of Muley el Zagal, the uncle and competitor for the throne of Abdallah (or Abo Abdeli), and all was jealousy and animosity.

### NOTE 19.
*When Tarik's bands o'erspread the western shore.*

Tarik, the first leader of the Arabs and Moors into Spain.—"The Saracens landed at the pillar or point of Europe: the corrupt and familiar appellation of Gibraltar (Gebel al Tarik) describes the mountain of Tarik, and the intrenchments of his camp were the first outline of those fortifications, which, in the hands of our countrymen, have resisted the art and power of the House of Bourbon. The adjacent governors informed the court of Toledo of the descent and progress of the Arabs; and the defeat of his lieutenant Edeco, who had been commanded to seize and bind the presumptuous strangers, first admonished Roderic of the magnitude of the danger. At the royal summons, the dukes and counts, the bishops and nobles of the Gothic monarchy, assembled at the head of their followers; and the title of king of the Romans, which is employed by an Arabic historian, may be excused by the close affinity of language, religion, and manners between the nations of Spain."—*Gibbon's Decline and Fall, &c.* vol. ix. pp. 472, 473.

### NOTE 20.
*When the long combat raged on Xeres' plain.*

"In the neighbourhood of Cadiz, the town of Xeres has been illustrated by the encounter which determined the fate of the kingdom; the stream of the Guadalete, which falls into the bay, divided the two camps, and marked the advancing and retreating skirmishes of three successive days. On the fourth day, the two armies joined a more serious and decisive issue." "Notwithstanding the valour of the Saracens, they fainted under the weight of multitudes, and the plain of Xeres was overspread with sixteen thousand of their dead bodies.—'My brethren,' said Tarik to his surviving companions, 'the enemy is before you, the sea is behind; whither would ye fly? Follow your general; I am resolved either to lose my life, or to trample on the prostrate king of the Romans.' Besides the resource of despair, he confided in the secret correspondence and nocturnal interviews of count Julian with the sons and the brother of Witiza. The two princes, and the archbishop of Toledo, occupied the most important post; their well-timed defection broke the ranks of the Christians; each warrior was prompted by fear or suspicion to consult his personal safety; and the remains of the Gothic army were scattered or destroyed in the flight and pursuit of the three following days."—*Gibbon's Decline and Fall, &c.* vol. ix. pp. 473, 474.

### NOTE 21.
*And Afric's tecbir mailed through yielding Spain.*

The tecbir, the shout of onset used by the Saracens in battle.

### NOTE 22.
*Your king hath yielded! Valour's dream is o'er.*

The terrors occasioned by this sudden excitement of popular feeling seem even to have accelerated Abo Abdeli's capitulation. "Aterrado Abo Abdeli con el alboroto, y temiendo no ser ya el Dueño de un pueblo amotinado, se apresuro a concluir una capitulacion, la menos dura que podia obtener en tan urgentes circunstancias, y ofrecio entregar á Granada el dia seis de Enero."—*Pasos en Granada,* vol. i. p. 272.

### NOTE 23.
*Ye, that around the oaken cross of yore.*

The oaken cross, carried by Pelagius in battle.

### NOTE 24.
*And thou, the warrior, born in happy hour.*

See Southey's Chronicle of the Cid, in which that warrior is frequently styled, "*he who was born in happy hour.*"

### NOTE 25.
*E'en in the realm of spirits didst retain*
*A patriot's vigilance, remembering Spain!*

"Moreover, when the Miramamolin brought over from Africa, against King Don Alfonso, the eighth of that name, the mightiest power of the misbelievers that had ever been brought against Spain, since the destruction of the kings of the Goths, the Cid Campeador remembered his country in that great danger; for the night before the battle was fought at the Navas de Tolosa, in the dead of the night, a mighty sound was heard in the whole city of Leon, as if it were the tramp of a great army passing through; and it passed on to the royal monastery of St. Isidro, and there was a great knocking at the gate thereof, and they called to a priest who was keeping vigils in the church, and told him, that the captains of the army whom he heard were the Cid Ruydiez, and Count Ferran Gonzalez, and that they came there to call up King Don Ferrando the Great, who lay buried in that church, that he might go with them to deliver Spain. And on the morrow that great battle of the Navas de Tolosa was fought, wherein sixty thousand of the misbelievers were slain, which was one of the greatest and noblest battles ever won over the Moors."—*Southey's Chronicle of the Cid.*

### NOTE 26.
*O realm of evening!*

The name of Andalusia, the region of evening or of the west, was applied by the Arabs, not only to the province so called, but to the whole peninsula.

### NOTE 27.
*What banner streams afar from Vela's tower?*

"En este dia, para siempre memorable, los estandartes de la Cruz de St. Iago, y el de los Reyes de Castilla se tremolaron sobre la torre mas alta, llamada de la Vela; y un exercito prosternado, inundandose en lagrimas de gozo y reconocimiento, asistio al mas glorioso de los espectaculos."—*Pasos en Granada,* vol. i. p. 292.

### NOTE 28.
*They reach those towers—irregularly vast*
*And rude they seem, in mould barbaric cast.*

Swinburne, after describing the noble palace built by Charles V in the precincts of the Alhambra, thus proceeds: "Adjoining (to the north (b) stands a huge heap of as ugly buildings as can well be seen, all huddled together, seemingly without the least intention of forming one habitation out of them. The walls are entirely unornamented, all gravel and pebbles, daubed over with plaster by a very coarse hand; yet this is the palace of the Moorish kings of Granada, indisputably the most curious place within that exists in Spain, perhaps in Europe. In many countries you may see excellent modern as well as ancient architecture, both entire and in ruins; but nothing to be met with anywhere else can convey an idea of this edifice, except you take it from the decorations of an opera, or the tales of the genii."—*Swinburne's Travels through Spain.*

### NOTE 29.
*A genii palace—an Arabian heaven.*

'Passing round the corner of the emperor's palace, you are admitted at a plain unornamented door, in a corner. On my first visit, I confess, I was struck with amazement as I stept over the threshold, to find myself on a sudden transported into a species of fairy land. The first place you come to is the court called the Communa, or *del Mesucar,* that is, the common baths: an oblong square, with a deep bason of clear water in the middle; two flights of marble steps leading down to the bottom; on each side a parterre of flowers, and a row of orange-trees. Round the court runs a peristyle paved with marble; the arches bear upon very slight pillars, in proportions and style different from all the regular orders of architecture. The ceilings and walls are incrustated with fretwork in stucco, so minute and intricate, that the most patient draughtsman would find it difficult to follow it, unless he made himself master of the general plan."—*Swinburne's Travels in Spain.*

### NOTE 30.
*Borders the walls in characters of gold*

The walls and cornices of the Alhambra are covered with inscriptions in Arabic characters. "In examining this abode of magnificence," says Bourgoanne, "the observer is every moment astonished at the new and interesting mixture of architecture and poetry. The palace of the Alhambra may be called a collection of fugitive pieces; and whatever duration these may have, time, with which everything passes away, has too much contributed to confirm to them that title."—*See Bourgoanne's Travels in Spain.*

### Note 31.

*Tambour, and flute, and atabal, are there.*

Atabal, a kind of Moorish drum.

### Note 32.

*Granada! for Castile and Arragon!*

'Y assi entraron en la ciudad, y subieron al Alhambra, y encima de la torre de Comares tan famosa se levantó la senal de la Santa Cruz, y luego el real estandarte de los dos Christianos reyes. Y al punto los reyes de armas, a grandes bozes dixeron, 'Granada! Granada! por su magestad, y por la reyna su muger.' La serenissima reyna D. Isabel que vió la senal de la Santa Cruz sobre la hermosa torre de Comares, y el su estandarte real con ella, se hinco de Rodillas, y dio infinitas gracias a Dios por la victoria que le avia dado contra aquella gran ciudad. La musica real de la capilla del rey luego a canto de organo canto Te Deum laudamus. Fue tan grande el plazer que todos lloravan. Luego del Alhambra sonaron mil instrumentos de musica de belicas trompetas. Los Moros amigos del rey, que querian ser Christianos, cuya cabeza era el valeroso Muca, tomaron mil dulzaynas y anafiles, sonando grande ruydo de atambores por toda la ciudad.'—*Historia de las Guerras Civiles de Granada.*

### Note 33.

*The festal lamps innumerably blaze.*

" Los cavalleros Moros que avemos dicho, aquella noche jugaron galanamente alcancelas y canas. Andava Granada aquella noche con tanta alegria, y con tantas luminarias, que parecia que se ardia la tierra "—*Historia de las Guerras Civiles de Granada.*

Swinburne, in his Travels through Spain, in the years 1775 and 1776, mentions that the anniversary of the surrender of Granada to Ferdinand and Isabella was still observed in the city as a great festival and day of rejoicing; and that the populace on that occasion paid an annual visit to the Moorish palace.

### Note 34.

*To Afric's wilds the royal exile flies.*

" Los Gomeles todos se passaron en Africa, y el Rey Chico con ellos, que no quiso estar en Espana, y en Africa le mataron lo Moros de aquellas partes, porque perdio á Granada."—*Guerras Civiles de Granada.*

### Note 35.

*Of him who knew not, as a man, to die.*

Abo Abdell, upon leaving Granada, after its conquest by Ferdinand and Isabella, stopped on the hill of Padul to take a last look of his city and palace. Overcome by the sight, he burst into tears, and was thus reproached by his mother, the Sultaness Ayza: " Thou dost well to weep, like a woman, over the loss of that kingdom which thou knewest not how to defend and die for like a man."

### Note 36.

*Th' avenger's lash is closed.*

" El rey mando, que si quedavan Zegris, que no viviessen en Granada, por la maldad que hizieron contra los Abencerrages."—*Guerras Civiles de Granada.*

### Note 37.

*'Midst the wild Alpuxarras.*

" The Alpuxarras are so lofty that the coast of Barbary, and the cities of Tangier and Ceuta, are discovered from their summits; they are about seventeen leagues in length, from Veles Malaga to Almeria, and eleven in breadth, and abound with fruit-trees of great beauty and prodigious size. In these mountains the wretched remains of the Moors took refuge."—*Bourgoanne's Travels in Spain.*

### Note 38.

*Were but too blest if aught remained to fear.*

" Plut a Dieu que je craignisse!"—*Andromaque.*

### Note 39.

*Rival the tints that float o'er summer skies.*

Mrs. Radcliffe, in her journey along the banks of the Rhine, thus describes the colours of the granite rocks in the mountains of the Bergstrasse. " The nearer we approached these mountains, the more we had occasion to admire the various tints of their granites. Sometimes the precipices were of a faint pink, then of a deep red, a dull purple, or a blush approaching to lilac, and sometimes gleams of a pale yellow mingled with the low shrubs that grew upon their sides. The day was cloudless and bright, and we were too near these heights to be deceived by the illusions of aerial colouring; the real hues of their features were as beautiful, as their magnitude was sublime "

# THE
# WIDOW OF CRESCENTIUS.

---

"L'orage peut briser en un moment les fleurs qui tiennent encore la tete levee."—*Mad. de Stael.*

# ADVERTISEMENT.

"In the reign of Otho III., Emperor of Germany, the Romans, excited by their Consul, Crescentius, who ardently desired to restore the ancient glory of the republic, made a bold attempt to shake off the Saxon yoke, and the authority of the Popes, whose vices rendered them objects of universal contempt. The Consul was besieged by Otho in the Mole of Hadrian, which, long afterward, continued to be called the Tower of Crescentius. Otho, after many unavailing attacks upon this fortress, at last entered into negotiations; and pledging his imperial word to respect the life of Crescentius, and the rights of the Roman citizens, the unfortunate leader was betrayed into his power, and immediately beheaded, with many of his partisans. Stephana, his widow, concealing her affliction and her resentment for the insults to which she had been exposed, secretly resolved to revenge her husband and herself. On the return of Otho from a pilgrimage to Mount Garganna, which perhaps a feeling of remorse had induced him to undertake, she found means to be introduced to him, and to gain his confidence; and a poison administered by her was soon afterward the cause of his painful death."—See *Sismondi History of the Italian Republics*, vol. I.

# THE

# WIDOW OF CRESCENTIUS.

---

### PART I.

Midst Tivoli's luxuriant glades,
Bright-foaming falls, and olive shades,
Where dwelt, in days departed long,
The sons of battle and of song,
No tree, no shrub its foliage rears,
But o'er the wrecks of other years,
Temples and domes, which long have been
The soil of that enchanted scene.

There the wild fig-tree and the vine
O'er Hadrian's mouldering villa twine; (1)
The cypress, in funereal grace,
Usurps the varnish'd column's place;
O'er fallen shrine, and ruin'd frieze,
The wall-flower rustles in the breeze;
Acanthus-leaves the marble hide,
They once adorn'd in sculptured pride;
And nature hath resumed her throne
O'er the vast works of ages flown.

Was it for this that many a pile
Pride of Ilissus and of Nile,
To Anio's banks the image lent
Of each imperial monument? (2)
Now Athens weeps her shatter'd fanes,
Thy temples, Egypt, strew thy plains;
And the proud fabrics Hadrian rear'd
From Tiber's vale have disappear'd.
We need no prescient sibyl there,
The doom of grandeur to declare,
Each stone, where weeds and ivy climb,
Reveals some oracle of Time:
Each relic utters Fate's decree,
The future as the past shall be.

Halls of the dead! in Tiber's vale,
Who now shall tell your lofty tale?
Who trace the high patrician's dome,
The bard's retreat, the hero's home?
When moss-clad wrecks alone record,
There dwelt the world's departed lord!
In scenes where verdure's rich array
Still sheds young beauty o'er decay,
And sunshine, on each glowing hill,
'Midst ruins finds a dwelling still.

Sunk is thy palace, but thy tomb,
Hadrian! hath shared a prouder doom, (3)
Though vanish'd with the days of old
Its pillars of Corinthian mould;
And the fair forms by sculpture wrought,
Each bodying some immortal thought,
Which o'er that temple of the dead,
Serene, but solemn beauty shed,
Have found, like glory's self, a grave
In time's abyss or Tiber's wave: (4)
Yet dreams more lofty, and more fair,
Than art's bold hand hath imaged e'er,
High thoughts of many a mighty mind,
Expanding when all else declined,

In twilight years, when only they
Recall'd the radiance pass'd away,
Have made that ancient pile their home,
Fortress of freedom and of Rome.

There he, who strove in evil days,
Again to kindle glory's rays,
Whose spirit sought a path of light,
For those dim ages far too bright,
Crescentius long maintain'd the strife,
Which closed but with its martyr's life,
And left the imperial tomb a name.
A heritage of holier fame.
There closed De Brescia's mission high,
From thence the patriot came to die; (5)
And thou, whose Roman soul the last,
Spoke with the voice of ages past, (6)
Whose thoughts so long from earth had fled,
To mingle with the glorious dead,
That 'midst the world's degenerate race,
They vainly sought a dwelling-place,
Within that house of death didst brood
O'er visions to thy ruin woo'd.
Yet worthy of a brighter lot,
Rienzi! be thy faults forgot!
For thou, when all around thee lay
Chain'd in the slumbers of decay;
So sunk each heart, that mortal eye
Had scarce a *tear* for liberty;
Alone, amidst the darkness there,
Could'st gaze on Rome—yet not despair! (7)

'Tis morn, and Nature's richest dyes
Are floating o'er Italian skies;
Tints of transparent lustre shine
Along the snow-clad Apennine;
The clouds have left Soracte's height,
And yellow Tiber winds in light,
Where tombs and fallen fanes have strew'd
The wild Campagna's solitude.
'Tis sad amidst that scene to trace
Those relics of a vanish'd race;
Yet o'er the ravaged path of time,
Such glory sheds that brilliant clime,
Where nature still, though Empires fall,
Holds her triumphant festival;
E'en desolation wears a smile,
Where skies and sunbeams laugh the while;
And Heaven's own light, Earth's richest bloom
Array the ruin and the tomb.

But she, who from yon convent tower
Breathes the pure freshness of the hour;
She, whose rich flow of raven hair
Streams wildly on the morning air;
Heeds not how fair the scene below,
Robed in Italia's brightest glow,
Though throned 'midst Latium's classic plains
Th' Eternal City's towers and fanes,
And they, the Pleiades of earth,
The seven proud hills of Empire's birth

(41)

Lie spread beneath: not now her glance
Roves o'er that vast, sublime expanse;
Inspired, and bright with hope, 'tis thrown
On Hadrian's massy tomb alone;
There, from the storm, when Freedom fled,
His faithful few Crescentius led!
While she, his anxious bride, who now
Bends o'er the scene her youthful brow,
Sought refuge in the hallow'd fane,
Which then could shelter, not in vain
But now the lofty strife is o'er,
And Liberty shall weep no more.
At length imperial Otho's voice
Bids her devoted sons rejoice;
And he, who battled to restore
The glories and the rights of yore,
Whose accents, like the clarion's sound,
Could burst the dead repose around,
Again his native Rome shall see,
The sceptred city of the free!
And young Stephania waits the hour
When leaves her lord his fortress-tower,
Her ardent heart with joy elate,
That seems beyond the reach of fate;
Her mien, like creature from above,
All vivified with hope and love.

Fair is her form, and in her eye
Lives all the soul of Italy!
A meaning lofty and inspired,
As by her native day-star fired;
Such wild and high expression, fraught
With glances of impassion'd thought,
As fancy sheds in visions bright
O'er priestess of the God of Light!
And the dark locks that lend her face
A youthful and luxuriant grace,
Wave o'er her cheek, whose kindling dyes
Seem from the fire within to rise;
But deepen'd by the burning heaven
To her own land of sunbeams given
Italian art that fervid glow
Would o'er ideal beauty throw,
And with such ardent life express
Her high-wrought dreams of loveliness;—
Dreams which, surviving Empire's fall,
The shade of glory still recall.

But see,—the banner of the brave
O'er Hadrian's tomb hath ceased to wave
'T is lower'd—and now Stephania's eye
Can well the martial train descry,
Who, issuing from that ancient dome,
Pour through the crowded streets of Rome.
Now from her watch-tower on the height,
With step as fabled wood-nymph's light,
She flies—and swift her way pursues
Through the lone convent's avenues.
Dark cypress-groves, and fields o'erspread
With records of the conquering dead,
And paths which track a glowing waste,
She traverses in breathless haste:
And by the tombs where dust is shrined,
Once tenanted by loftiest mind,
Still passing on, hath reach'd the gate
Of Rome, the proud, the desolate!
Throng'd are the streets, and still renew'd,
Rush on the gathering multitude.

Is it their high-soul'd chief to greet,
That thus the Roman thousands meet?
With names that bid their thoughts ascend,
Crescentius, thine in song to blend;
And of triumphal days gone by
Recall th' inspiring pageantry?
—There is an air of breathless dread,
An eager glance, a hurrying tread:
And now a fearful silence round,
And now a fitful murmuring sound,
Midst the pale crowds, that almost seem
Phantoms of some tumultuous dream.
Quick is each step, and wild each mien,
Portentous of some awful scene.
Bride of Crescentius! as the throng
Bore thee with whelming force along,

How did thine anxious heart beat high,
Till rose suspense to agony!
Too brief suspense, that soon shall close,
And leave thy heart to deeper woes.

Who 'midst yon guarded precinct stands,
With fearless mien, but fetter'd hands?
The ministers of death are nigh,
Yet a calm grandeur lights his eye;
And in his glance there lives a mind,
Which was not form'd for chains to bind,
But cast in such heroic mould
As theirs, th' ascendant ones of old.
Crescentius! freedom's daring son,
Is this the guerdon thou hast won?
O worthy to have lived and died
In the bright days of Latium's pride!
Thus must the beam of glory close,
O'er the seven hills again that rose,
When at thy voice to burst the yoke,
The soul of Rome indignant woke?
Vain dream! the sacred shields are gone, (8)
Sunk is the crowning city's throne: (9)
Th' illusions that around her cast
Their guardian spells have long been past. (10)
Thy life hath been a shot star's ray,
Shed o'er her midnight of decay;
Thy death at freedom's ruin'd shrine
Must rivet every chain—but thine.

Calm is his aspect, and his eye
Now fix'd upon the deep-blue sky,
Now on those wrecks of ages fled,
Around in desolation spread;
Arch, temple, column, worn and gray,
Recording triumphs pass'd away;
Works of the mighty and the free,
Whose steps on earth no more shall be,
Though their bright course hath left a trace
Nor years nor sorrows can efface.

Why changes now the patriot's mien,
Erewhile so loftily serene?
Thus can approaching death control
The might of that commanding soul?
No!—Heard ye not that thrilling cry
Which told of bitterest agony?
He heard it, and, at once subdued,
Hath sunk the hero's fortitude,
He heard it, and his heart too well
Whence rose that voice of woe can tell;
And 'midst the gazing throngs around
One well-known form his glance hath found
One fondly loving and beloved,
In grief, in peril, faithful proved.
Yes, in the wildness of despair,
She, his devoted bride, is there.
Pale, breathless, through the crowd she flies
The light of frenzy in her eyes:
But ere her arms can clasp the form,
Which life ere long must cease to warm;
Ere on his agonizing breast
Her heart can heave, her head can rest;
Check'd in her course by ruthless hands,
Mute, motionless, at once she stands;
With bloodless cheek and vacant glance,
Frozen and fix'd in horror's trance;
Spell-bound, as every sense were fled,
And thought o'erwhelm'd, and feeling dead.
And the light waving of her hair,
And veil, far floating on the air,
Alone, in that dread moment, show,
She is no sculptured form of woe.

The scene of grief and death is o'er,
The patriot's heart shall throb no more;
But hers—so vainly form'd to prove
The pure devotedness of love,
And draw from fond affection's eye
All thought sublime, all feeling high;
When consciousness again shall wake,
Hath now no refuge—but to break.
The spirit long inured to pain
May smile at fate in calm disdain;
Survive its darkest hour, and rise
In more majestic energies.

But in the glow of vernal pride,
If each warm hope at once hath died,
Then sinks the mind, a blighted flower,
Dead to the sunbeam and the shower;
A broken gem, whose inborn light
Is scatter'd—ne'er to reunite.

## PART II.

Hast thou a scene that is not spread
With records of thy glory fled?
A monument that doth not tell
The tale of liberty's farewell?
Italia! thou art but a grave
Where flowers luxuriate o'er the brave,
And Nature gives her treasures birth
O'er all that hath been great on earth.
Yet smile thy heavens as once they smiled,
When thou wert Freedom's favour'd child:
Though fane and tomb alike are low,
Time hath not dimm'd thy sunbeam's glow
And robed in that exulting ray,
Thou seem'st to triumph o'er decay;
O yet, though by thy sorrows bent,
In nature's pomp magnificent;
What marvel if, when all was lost,
Still on thy bright enchanted coast,
Though many an omen warn'd him thence,
Linger'd the lord of eloquence! (11)
Still gazing on the lovely sky,
Whose radiance woo'd him—but to die!
Like him, who would not linger there,
Where heaven, earth, ocean, all are fair?
Who 'midst thy glowing scenes could dwell,
Nor bid awhile his griefs farewell?
Hath not thy pure and genial air
Balm for all sadness but despair? (12)
No! there are pangs, whose deep-worn trace
Not all thy magic can efface!
Hearts, by unkindness wrung, may learn
The world and all its gifts to spurn;
Time may steal on with silent tread,
And dry the tear that mourns the dead;
May change fond love, subdue regret,
And teach e'en vengeance to forget!
But thou, Remorse! there is no charm
Thy sting, avenger, to disarm!
Vain are bright suns, and laughing skies,
To soothe thy victim's agonies:
The heart once made thy burning throne,
Still, while it beats, is thine alone.

In vain for Otho's joyless eye
Smile the fair scenes of Italy,
As through her landscapes' rich array
Th' imperial pilgrim bends his way.
Thy form, Crescentius, on his sight
Rises when nature laughs in light,
Glides round him at the midnight hour,
Is present in his festal bower,
With awful voice and frowning mien,
By all but him unheard, unseen.
Oh! thus to shadows of the grave
Be every tyrant still a slave!

Where through Gargano's woody dells,
O'er bending oaks the north-wind swells, (13)
A sainted hermit's lowly tomb
Is bosom'd in umbrageous gloom,
In shades that saw him live and die
Beneath their waving canopy.
'Twas his, as legends tell, to share
The converse of immortals there;
Around that dweller of the wild
There " bright appearances" have smiled, (14)
And angel-wings, at eve, have been,
Gleaming the shadowy boughs between.
And oft from that secluded bower
Hath breathed, at midnight's calmer hour,
A swell of viewless harps, a sound
Of warbled anthems pealing round.
Oh, none but voices of the sky
Might wake that thrilling harmony,
Whose tones, whose very echoes, made
An Eden of the lonely shade!

Years have gone by; the hermit sleeps
Amidst Gargano's woods and steeps!
Ivy and flowers have half o'ergrown
And veil'd his low, sepulchral stone:
Yet still the spot is holy, still
Celestial footsteps haunt the hill;
And oft the awe-struck mountaineer
Aërial vesper-hymns may hear
Around those forest-precincts float,
Soft, solemn, clear,—but still remote.
Oft will affliction breathe her plaint
To that rude shrine's departed saint,
And deem that spirits of the blest
There shed sweet influence o'er her breast.

And thither Otho now repairs,
To soothe his soul with vows and prayers,
And if for him, on holy ground,
The lost one, Peace, may yet be found,
'Midst rocks and forests, by the bed
Where calmly sleep the sainted dead,
She dwells, remote from heedless eye,
With Nature's lonely majesty.

Vain, vain the search—his troubled breast
Nor vow nor penance lulls to rest;
The weary pilgrimage is o'er,
The hopes that cheer'd it are no more.
Then sinks his soul, and day by day,
Youth's buoyant energies decay.
The light of health his eye hath flown,
The glow that tinged his cheek is gone.
Joyless as one on whom is laid
Some baleful spell that bids him fade,
Extending its mysterious power
O'er every scene, o'er every hour;
E'en thus he withers; and to him,
Italia's brilliant skies are dim.
He withers—in that glorious clime
Where Nature laughs in scorn of Time;
And suns, that shed on all below
Their full and vivifying glow,
From him alone their power withhold,
And leave his heart in darkness cold.
Earth blooms around him, heaven is fair,
He only seems to perish there.

Yet sometimes will a transient smile
Play o'er his faded cheek awhile,
When breathes his minstrel-boy a strain
Of power to lull all earthly pain;
So wildly sweet, its notes might seem
Th' ethereal music of a dream,
A spirit's voice from worlds unknown,
Deep thrilling power in every tone!
Sweet is that lay, and yet its flow
Hath language only given to woe;
And if at times its wakening swell
Some tale of glory seems to tell,
Soon the proud notes of triumph die,
Lost in a dirge's harmony:
Oh! many a pang the heart hath proved,
Hath deeply suffer'd, fondly loved,
Ere the sad strain could catch from thence
Such deep impassion'd eloquence!
Yes! gaze on him, that minstrel-boy—
He is no child of hope and joy;
Though few his years, yet have they been
Such as leave traces on the mien,
And o'er the roses of our prime
Breathe other blights than those of time.

Yet, seems his spirit wild and proud,
By grief unsoften'd and unbow'd.
Oh! there are sorrows which impart
A sternness foreign to the heart,
And rushing with an earthquake's power,
That makes a desert in an hour;
Rouse the dread passions in their course,
As tempests wake the billows' force!—
'Tis sad on youthful Guido's face,
The stamp of woes like these to trace.
Oh! where can ruins awe mankind
Dark as the ruins of the mind?

His mien is lofty but his gaze
Too well a wandering soul betrays;
His full, dark eye at times is bright
With strange and momentary light.

Whose quick uncertain flashes throw
O'er his pale cheek a hectic glow:
And oft his features and his air
A shade of troubled mystery wear,
A glance of hurried wildness, fraught
With some unfathomable thought.
Whate'er that thought, still, unexpress'd,
Dwells the sad secret in his breast;
The pride his haughty brow reveals,
All other passion well conceals.
He breathes each wounded feeling's tone
In music's eloquence alone;
His soul's deep voice is only pour'd
Through his full song and swelling chord.
He seeks no friend, but shuns the train
Of courtiers with a proud disdain;
And, save when Otho bids his lay
Its half unearthly power essay,
In hall or bower the heart to thrill,
His haunts are wild and lonely still.
Far distant from the heedless throng,
He roves old Tiber's banks along,
Where Empire's desolate remains
Lie scatter'd o'er the silent plains;
Or, lingering 'midst each ruin'd shrine
That strews the desert Palatine,
With mournful, yet commanding mien,
Like the sad Genius of the scene,
Entranced in awful thought appears
To commune with departed years.
Or at the dead of night, when Rome
Seems of heroic shades the home;
When Tiber's murmuring voice recalls
The mighty to their ancient halls;
When hush'd is every meaner sound,
And the deep moonlight-calm around
Leaves to the solemn scene alone
The majesty of ages flown;
A pilgrim to each hero's tomb,
He wanders through the sacred gloom;
And, 'midst those dwellings of decay,
At times will breathe so sad a lay,
So wild a grandeur in each tone,
'Tis like a dirge for empires gone!

Awake thy pealing harp again,
But breathe a more exulting strain,
Young Guido! for awhile forgot,
Be the dark secrets of thy lot,
And rouse th' inspiring soul of song
To speed the banquet's hour along!
The feast is spread; and music's call
Is echoing through the royal hall,
And banners wave, and trophies shine,
O'er stately guests in glittering line;
And Otho seeks awhile to chase
The thoughts he never can erase,
And bid the voice, whose murmurs deep
Rise like a spirit on his sleep,
The still small voice of conscience die,
Lost in the din of revelry.
On his pale brow dejection lowers,
But that shall yield to festal hours;
A gloom is in his faded eye,
But that from music's power shall fly:
His wasted cheek is wan with care,
But mirth shall spread fresh crimson there.
Wake, Guido! wake thy numbers high,
Strike the bold chord exultingly!
And pour upon th' enraptured ear
Such strains as warriors love to hear!
Let the rich mantling goblet flow,
And banish all resembling woe;
And, if a thought intrude, of power
To mar the bright convivial hour,
Still must its influence lurk unseen,
And cloud the heart—but not the mien!

Away, vain dream!—on Otho's brow
Still darker lowers the shadows now;
Changed are his features, now o'erspread
With the cold paleness of the dead;
Now crimson'd with a hectic dye,
The burning flush of agony!
His lip is quivering, and his breast
Heaves, with convulsive pangs oppress'd;
Now his dim eye seems fix'd and glazed,
And now to heaven in anguish raised;

And as, with unavailing aid,
Around him throng his guests dismay'd,
He sinks—while scarce his struggling breath
Hath power to falter—"This is death!"

Then rush'd that haughty child of song,
Dark Guido, through the awe-struck throng,
Fill'd with a strange delirious light,
His kindling eye shone wildly bright,
And on the sufferer's mien awhile
Gazing with stern vindictive smile,
A feverish glow of triumph dyed
His burning cheek, while thus he cried:—
"Yes! these are death-pangs—on thy brow
Is set the seal of vengeance now!
Oh! well was mix'd the deadly draught,
And long and deeply hast thou quaff'd;
And bitter as thy pangs may be,
They are but guerdons meet from me!
Yet, these are but a moment's throes,
Howe'er intense, they soon shall close.
Soon shalt thou yield thy fleeting breath,
My life hath been a lingering death;
Since one dark hour of woe and crime,
A blood-spot on the page of time!

'Deem'st thou my mind of reason void?
It is not phrenzied,—but destroy'd!
Ay! view the wreck with shuddering thought —
That work of ruin thou hast wrought!

"The secret of thy doom to tell,
My name alone suffices well!
Stephania! once a hero's bride!
Otho! thou know'st the rest—*he died.*
Yes! trusting to a monarch's word,
The Roman fell, untried, unheard!
And thou, whose every pledge was vain,
How couldst *thou* trust in aught again?

"He died, and I was changed—my soul,
A lonely wanderer, spurn'd control.
From peace, and light, and glory hurl'd,
The outcast of a purer world,
I saw each brighter hope o'erthrown,
And lived for one dread task alone.
The task is closed—fulfill'd the vow,
The hand of death is on thee now.
Betrayer! in thy turn betray'd,
The debt of blood shall soon be paid!
Thine hour is come—the time hath been
My heart had shrunk from such a scene;
*That* feeling long is past—my fate
Hath made me stern as desolate.

"Ye, that around me shuddering stand,
Ye chiefs and princes of the land!
Mourn ye a guilty monarch's doom?
—Ye wept not o'er the patriot's tomb?
*He* sleeps unhonour'd—yet be mine
To share his low, neglected shrine.
His soul with freedom finds a home,
His grave is that of glory—Rome!
Are not the great of old with her,
That city of the sepulchre?
Lead me to death! and let me share
The slumbers of the mighty there!"

The day departs—that fearful day
Fades in calm loveliness away;
From purple heavens its lingering beam
Seems melting into Tiber's stream,
And softly tints each Roman hill
With glowing light, as clear and still,
As if, unstain'd by crime or woe,
Its hours had pass'd in silent flow.
The day sets calmly—it hath been
Mark'd with a strange and awful scene;
One guilty bosom throbs no more,
And Otho's pangs and life are o'er.
And thou, ere yet another sun
His burning race hath brightly run,
Released from anguish by thy foes,
Daughter of Rome! shalt find repose.—
Yes! on thy country's lovely sky
Fix yet once more thy parting eye!
A few short hours—and all shall be
The silent and the past for thee.
Oh! thus with tempests of a day
We struggle, and we pass away

Like the wild billows as they sweep,
Leaving no vestige on the deep!
And o'er thy dark and lowly bed
The sons of future days shall tread,
The pangs, the conflicts, of thy lot,
By them unknown, by thee forgot.

---

# NOTES.

### Note 1.

*O'er Hadrian's mouldering villa twine.*

"J'étais allé passer quelques jours seul à Tivoli. Je parcourus les environs, et surtout celles de la Villa Adriana. Surpris par la pluie au milieu de ma course, je me réfugiai dans les Salles des *Thermes* voisins du *Pœcile* (monuments de la villa), sous un figuier qu'. avait renversé le pan d'un mur en s'élevant. Dans un petit salon octogone, couvert devant moi, une vigne vierge avait percé la voûte de l'édifice, et son gros cep lisse, rouge, et tortueux, montait le long du mur comme un serpent. Autour de moi, à travers les arcades des ruines, s'ouvraient des points de vue sur la Campagne Romaine. Des buissons de sureau remplissaient les salles désertes où venaient se réfugier quelques merles solitaires. Les fragmens de maçonnerie s'aient tapissés des feuilles de scolopendre, dont la verdure satinée se dessinait comme un travail en mosaïque sur la blancheur des marbres: ça et là de hauts cyprès remplaçaient les colonnes tombées dans ces palais de la Mort; l'acanthe sauvage rampait à leurs pieds, sur des débris, comme si la nature s'était plu à reproduire sur ces chefs-d'œuvre mutile d'architecture, l'ornement de leur beauté passée."—*Chateaubriand   Souvenirs d'Italie.*

### Note 2.

*Of each imperial monument.*

The gardens and buildings of Hadrian's villa were copies of the most celebrated scenes and edifices in his dominions; the Lyceum, the Academia, the Prytaneum of Athens, the Temple of Serapis at Alexandria, the Vale of Tempe, &c.

### Note 3.

*Sunk is thy palace, but thy tomb,*
*Hadrian! hath shared a prouder doom.*

The mausoleum of Hadrian, now the castle of St. Angelo, was first converted into a citadel by Belisarius, in his successful defence of Rome against the Goths. "The lover of the arts," says Gibbon, "must read with a sigh, that the works of Praxiteles and Lysippus were torn from their lofty pedestals, and hurled into the ditch on the heads of the besiegers." He adds, in a note, that the celebrated Sleeping Faun of the Barberini palace was found, in a mutilated state, when the ditch of St. Angelo was cleansed under Urban VIII. In the middle ages, the *moles Hadriani* was made a permanent fortress by the Roman government, and bastions, outworks, &c. were added to the original edifice, which had been stripped of its marble covering, its Corinthian pillars, and the brazen cone which crowned its summit.

### Note 4.

*Have found, like glory's self, a grave*
*In time's abyss, or Tiber's wave.*

"Les plus beaux monumens des arts, les plus admirables statues ont été jetées dans le Tibre, et sont cachées sous ses flots. Qui sait 'i. pour les chercher, on ne le détournera pas un jour de son lit? Mais quand on songe que les chef-d'œuvres du génie humain sont peut-être là devant nous, et qu'un œil plus perçant les verrait à travers les ondes, l'on éprouve je ne sais quelle émotion qui ramène à Rome même sous diverses formes, et fait trouver une société pour la pensée dans les objets physiques, muets partout ailleurs."—*Mad. de Staël.*

### Note 5.

*There closed De Brescia's mission high,*
*From thence the patriot came to die.*

Arnold de Brescia, the undaunted and eloquent champion of Roman liberty, after unremitting efforts to restore the ancient constitution of the republic, was put to death in the year 1155, by Adrian IV. This event is thus described by Sismondi, *Histoire des Républiques Italiennes*, vol. ii. pages 68 and 69. "Le préfet demeura dans le château Saint Ange avec son prisonnier; il le fit transporter un matin sur la place destinée aux exécutions, devant la Porte du People. Arnaud de Brescia, élevé sur un bucher, fut attaché à un poteau, en face du Corso. Il pouvoit mesurer des yeux les trois longues rues qui aboutissoient devant son échafaud; elles font presque une moitié de Rome. C'est là qu'habitoient les hommes qu'il avoit si souvent appelés à la liberté. Ils reportèrent encore en paix, ignorant le danger de leur législateur. Le tumulte de l'exécution et la flamme du bucher réveillèrent les Romains; ils s'armèrent, ils accoururent, mais trop tard; et les cohortes du pape repoussèrent, avec leur lances, ceux qui, n'ayant pu sauver Arnaud, vouloient du moins recueillir ses cendres comme de précieuses reliques."

### Note 6.

*Spoke with the voice of ages past.*

"Posterity will compare the virtues and failings of this extraordinary man; but in a long period of anarchy and servitude the name of Rienzi has often been celebrated as the deliverer of his country, and the last of the Roman patriots."—*Gibbon's Decline and Fall, &c. vol. xii. p. 362.*

### Note 7.

*Couldst gaze on Rome—yet not despair!*

"Le consul Terentius Varron avoit fui honteusement jusqu'à Venouse; cet homme de la plus basse naissance, n'avoit été élevé au consulat que pour mortifier la noblesse: mais le sénat ne voulut pas jouir de ce malheureux triomphe; il vit combien il étoit nécessaire qu'il s'attirât dans cette occasion la confiance du peuple, il alla au-devant Varron, et le remercia de ce qu'il n'avoit pas désespéré de la république."—*Montesquieu.   Grandeur et Décadence des Romains.*

### Note 8.

*Vain dream! the sacred shields are gone.*

Of the sacred bucklers, or ancilia of Rome, which were kept in the temple of Mars, Plutarch gives the following account. "In the eighth year of Numa's reign a pestilence prevailed in Italy; Rome also felt its ravages. While the people were greatly dejected, we are told that a brazen buckler fell from heaven into the hands of Numa. Of this he gave a very wonderful account, received from Egeria and the Muses: that the buckler was sent down for the preservation of the city, and should be kept with great care: that eleven others should be made as like it as possible in size and fashion, in order that if any person were disposed to steal it, he might not be able to distinguish that which fell from heaven from the rest. He further declared, that the place, and the meadows about it, where he frequently conversed with the Muses, should be consecrated to those divinities: and that the spring which watered the ground should be sacred to the use of the Vestal Virgins, daily to sprinkle and purify their temple. The immediate cessation of the pestilence is said to have confirmed the truth of this account."—*Life of Numa.*

### Note 9.

*Sunk is the crowning city's throne.*

"Who hath taken this counsel against Tyre, the crowning city, whose merchants are princes, whose traffickers are the honourable of the earth?"—*Isaiah*, chap. xxiii.

### Note 10.

*Their guardian spells have long been past.*

"Un mélange bizarre de grandeur d'ame, et de foiblesse entroit dans cette époque (l'onzième siècle) dans le caractère des Romains.— Un mouvement généreux vers les grandes choses faisoit place tout-à-coup à l'abaissement; ils passoient de la liberté la plus orageuse, à la servitude la plus avilissante. On auroit dit que les ruines et les portiques déserts de la capitale du monde, entretenoient ses habitans dans les sentimens de leur impuissance; au milieu de ces monumens de leur domination passée, les citoyens éprouvoient d'une manière trop décourageante leur propre foiblesse. Le nom des Romains qu'ils portoient ranimoit fréquemment leur enthousiasme, comme il le ranime encore aujourd'hui; mais bientôt la vue de Rome, du Forum désert, des sept collines de nouveau rendues au pâturage des troupeaux, des temples démolis, des monumens tombant en ruine, les ranimoit à sentir qu'ils n'étoient plus les Romains d'autrefois."—*Sismondi. Histoire des Républiques Italiennes*, vol. i. p. 172.

### Note 11.

*Lingered the lord of eloquence?*

"As for Cicero, he was carried to Astyra, where, finding a vessel, he immediately went on board, and coasted along to Circæum with a favourable wind. The pilots were preparing immediately to sail from thence, but whether it was that he feared the sea, or had not yet given up all his hopes in Cæsar, he disembarked, and travelled a hundred furlongs on foot, as if Rome had been the place of his destination. Repenting, however, afterwards, he left that road and made again for the sea. He passed the night in the most perplexing and horrid thoughts; insomuch, that he was sometimes inclined to go privately into Cæsar's house and stab himself upon the altar of his domestic gods, to bring the divine vengeance upon his betrayer. But he was deterred from this by the fear of torture. Other alternatives equally distressful presented themselves. At last he put himself in the hands of his servants, and ordered them to carry him by sea to Cajeta, where he had a delightful retreat in the summer, when the Etesian winds set in. There was a temple of Apollo on that coast, from which a flight of crows came with great noise towards Cicero's vessel as it was making land. They perched on both sides the sail-yard, where some sat croaking, and others pecking the ends of the ropes. All looked upon this as an ill omen; yet Cicero went on shore, and, entering his house, lay down to repose himself. In the mean time a number of crows settled in the chamber-window, and croaked in the most doleful manner. One of them even entered it, and alighting on the bed, attempted, with its beak, to draw off the clothes with which he had covered his face. On sight of this, the servants began to reproach themselves. 'Shall we,' said they, 'remain to be spectators of our master's murder? Shall we not protect him, so innocent and so great a sufferer as he is, when the brute creatures give him marks of their care and attention?' Then, partly by entreaty, partly by force, they got him into his litter, and carried him towards the sea."—*Plutarch. Life of Cicero.*

### Note 12.

*Balm for all sadness but despair?*

"Now purer air
Meets his approach, and to the heart inspires
Vernal delight and joy, able to drive
All sadness but despair."—*Milton.*

### Note 13.

*O'er bending oaks the north-wind swells.*

Mount Gargano. "This ridge of mountains forms a very large promontory advancing into the Adriatic, and separated from the

Apennines on the west by the plains of Lucera and San Severo. We took a ride into the heart of the mountains through shady dells and noble woods, which brought to our minds the venerable groves that in ancient times bent with the loud winds sweeping along the rugged sides of Garganus.

> ' Aquilonibus
> Querceta Gargani laborant,
> Et foliis viduantur orni.'—*Horace.*

There is a respectable forest of evergreen and common oak, pine, hornbeam, chestnut, and manna-ash. The sheltered valleys are industriously cultivated, and seem to be blest with luxuriant vegetation."—*Swinburne's Travels.*

### Note 14.

*These "bright appearances" have smiled.*

> " In yonder nether world where shall I seek
> His bright appearances, or footstep trace ?"—*Milton.*

# THE LAST BANQUET

OF

# ANTONY AND CLEOPATRA.

"Antony, concluding that he could not die more honourably than in battle, determined to attack Cæsar at the same time both by sea and land. The night preceding the execution of this design, he ordered his servants at supper to render him their best services that evening, and fill the wine round plentifully, for the day following they might belong to another master, whilst he lay extended on the ground, no longer of consequence either to them or to himself. His friends were affected, and wept to hear him talk thus; which when he perceived, he encouraged them by assurances that his expectations of a glorious victory were at least equal to those of an honourable death. At the dead of night, when universal silence reigned through the city, a silence that was deepened by the awful thought of the ensuing day, on a sudden was heard the sound of musical instruments, and a noise which resembled the exclamations of Bacchanals. This tumultuous procession seemed to pass through the whole city, and to go out at the gate which led to the enemy's camp. Those who reflected on this prodigy concluded that Bacchus, the god whom Antony affected to imitate, had then forsaken him."— *Langhorne's Plutarch.*

Thy foes had girt thee with their dread array,
  O stately Alexandria!—yet the sound
Of mirth and music, at the close of day,
  Swell'd from thy splendid fabrics far around
O'er camp and wave. Within the royal hall,
  In gay magnificence the feast was spread;
And brightly streaming from the pictured wall,
  A thousand lamps their trembling lustre shed
O'er many a column rich with trembling dyes,
That tinge the marble's vein, 'neath Afric's burn-
    ing skies.

And soft and clear that wavering radiance play'd
  O'er sculptured forms that round the pillar'd
    scene
Calm and majestic rose, by art array'd
  In god-like beauty, awfully serene.
Oh! how unlike the troubled guests, reclined
  Round that luxurious board!—in every face,
Some shadow from the tempest of the mind
  Rising by fits, the searching eye might trace
Though vainly mask'd in smiles which are not
    mirth,
But the proud spirit's veil thrown o'er the woes of
    earth.

Their brows are bound with wreaths whose tran-
    sient bloom
  May still survive the wearers—and the rose
Perchance may scarce be wither'd when the tomb
  Receives the mighty to its dark repose!
The day must dawn on battle—and may set
  In death—but fill the mantling wine-cup high!

Despair is fearless, and the Fates e'en yet
  Lend her one hour for parting revelry.
They who the empire of the world possess'd
  Would taste its joys again, ere all exchanged for
    rest.

Its joys! oh! mark yon proud triumvir's mien,
  And read their annals on that brow of care!
'Midst pleasure's lotus-bowers his steps have been
  Earth's brightest pathway led him to despair.
Trust not the glance that fain would yet inspire
  The buoyant energies of days gone by;
There is delusion in its meteor-fire,
  And all within is shame, is agony!
Away! the tear in bitterness may flow,
But there are smiles which bear a stamp of deeper
    woe.

Thy cheek is sunk, and faded as thy fame,
  O lost, devoted Roman! yet thy brow
To that ascendant and undying name,
  Pleads with stern loftiness thy right e'en now.
Thy glory is departed—but hath left
  A lingering light around thee—in decay
Not less than kingly, though of all bereft,
  Thou seem'st as empire had not pass'd away.
Supreme in ruin! teaching hearts elate,
A deep, prophetic dread of still mysterious fate!

But thou, enchantress-queen! whose love hath
    made
  His desolation—thou art by his side,
In all thy sovereignty of charms array'd,
  To meet the storm with still unconquer'd pride.
Imperial being! e'en though many a stain
  Of error be upon thee, there is power
In thy commanding nature, which shall reign
  O'er the stern genius of misfortune's hour;
And the dark beauty of thy troubled eye
E'en now is all illumined with wild sublimity.

Thine aspect all impassion'd wears a light
  Inspiring and inspired—thy cheek a dye,
Which rises not from joy, but yet is bright
  With the deep glow of feverish energy.
Proud siren of the Nile! thy glance is fraught
  With an immortal fire—in every beam
It darts, there kindles some heroic thought,
  But wild and awful as a sibyl's dream;
For thou with death hast communed, to attain
Dread knowledge of the pangs that ransom from
    the chain. (1)

And the stern courage by such musings lent,
  Daughter of Afric! o'er thy beauty throws
The grandeur of a regal spirit, blent
  With all the majesty of mighty woes!
While he so fondly, fatally adored,
  Thy fallen Roman, gazes on thee yet,
Till scarce the soul, that once exulting soar'd,
  Can deem the day-star of its glory set;

Scare his charm'd heart believes that power can be
In sovereign fate, o'er him, thus fond.y loved
        by thee.
But there is sadness in the eyes around,
    Which mark that ruin'd leader. and survey
His changeful mien, whence oft the gloom
        profound
    Strange triumph chases haughtily away.
"Fill the bright goblet, warrior guests!" he cries,
    "Quaff, ere we part, the generous nectar deep!
Ere sunset gi'd once more the western skies,
    Your chief in co'd forgetfulness may s'eep,
Whi'e sounds of reve' float o'er shore and sea,
And the red bowl again is crown'd—but not for me.

"Yet weep not thus—the struggle is not o'er,
    O victors of Philippi! many a field
Hath yielded pa'ms to us:—one effort more,
    By one stern conflict must our doom be seal'd!
Forget not, Romans! o'er a subject wor d
How roya'ly your eagle's wing hath spread,
Though from his eyrie of dominion hur.'d
    Now bursts the tempest on his crested head;
Yet sovereign sti l, if banished from the sky,
The sun's indignant bird, he must not droop
        —but die.

The feast is o'er.  'Tis night, the dead of night—
    Unbroken stillness broods o'er earth and deep:
From Egypt's heaven of soft and starry light
    The moon looks cloudless or a world of sleep:
For those who wait the morn's awakening beams,
    The battle signal to decide their doom,
Have sunk to feverish rest and troubled dreams;
    Rest, that shall soon be calmer in the tomb.
Dreams, dark and ominous, but *there* to cease,
When sleep the lords of war in solitude and peace.

Wake, slumberers, wake! Hark! heard ye not
        a sound
Of gathering tumult?—near and nearer still
Its murmur swells.  Above, below, around
    Bursts a strange chorus forth, confused and
        shrill.
Wake, Alexandria! through thy streets the tread
    Of steps unseen is hurrying, and the note
Of pipe, and lyre, and trumpet, wild and dread
Is heard upon the midnight air to float:
And voices clamerous as in frenzied mirth,
Mingle their thousand tones which are not of the
        earth.

These are no mortal sounds—their thrilling strain
    Hath more mysterious power, and birth more
        high:
And the deep horror chilling every vein
    Owns them of stern, terrific augury.
Beings of worlds unknown! ye pass away,
    O ye invisible and awful throng!
Your echoing footsteps and resounding lay
To Cæsar's camp exulting move along.
Thy gods forsake thee, Antony! the sky
By that dread sign reveals—thy doom—"Despair
        and die!" (2)

---

## NOTES.

### NOTE 1.

*Dread knowledge of the pangs that ransom from the chain.*

Cleopatra made a collection of poisonous drugs, and being desirous
to ascertain which was least painful in the operation, she tried
them on the capital convicts.  Such poisons as were quick in their
operation, she found to be attended with violent pain and convul-
sions ; such as were mildest were slow in their effect : she therefore
applied herself to the examination of venomous creatures ; at length
she found that the bite of the asp was the most eligible kind of death,
for it brought on a gradual kind of lethargy.—*See Plutarch.*

### NOTE 2.

*Despair and die!*

"To-morrow in the battle think on me,
And fall thy edgeless sword ; despair and die!"
        *Richard III.*

<br>

## Alaric in Italy.

---

After describing the conquest of Greece and Italy by the
German and Scythian hordes. united under the command of Alaric, the historian of "The Decline and
Fall of the Roman Empire," thus proceeds:—"Whether
fame, or conquest, or riches, were the object of Alaric,
he pursued that object with an indefatigable ardour,
which could neither be quelled by adversity, nor satiated by success.  No sooner had he reached the extreme
land of Italy, than he was attracted by the neighbouring prospect of a fair and peaceful island.  Yet even
the possession of Sicily he considered only as an inter-
mediate step to the important expedition which he already meditated against the continent of Africa.  The
straits of Rhegium and Messina are twelve miles in
length, and, in the narrowest passage, about one mile
and a half broad ; and the fabulous monsters of the deep,
the rocks of Scylla, and the whirlpool of Charybdis,
could terrify none but the most timid and unskilful
mariners ; yet, as soon as the first division of the Goths
had embarked a sudden tempest arose, which sunk or
scattered many of the transports; their courage was
daunted by the terrors of a new element; and the whole
design was defeated by the premature death of Alaric,
which fixed, after a short illness, the fatal term of his
conquests.  The ferocious character of the barbarians
was displayed in the funeral of a hero, whose valour
and fortune they celebrated with mournful applause.
By the labor of a captive multitude they forcibly di-
verted the course of the Busentinus, a small river that
washes the walls of Consentia.  The royal sepulchre,
adorned with the splendid spoils and trophies of Rome,
was constructed in the vacant bed ; the waters were
then restored to their natural channel, and the secret
spot, where the remains of Alaric had been deposited,
was forever concealed by the inhuman massacre of the
prisoners who had been employed to execute the work."
—See *The Decline and Fall of the Roman Empire*, vol. v.
p. 329.

---

Heard ye the Gothic trumpet's blast ?
The march of hosts, as Alaric pass'd ?
His steps have track'd that glorious clime,
'The birth-place of heroic time;
But he, in northern deserts bred,
Spared not the living for the dead. (1)
Nor heard the voice, whose pleading cries
From temple and from tomb arise.
He pass'd—the light of burning fanes
Hath been his torch o'er Grecian plains;
And woke they not—the brave. the free,
To guard their own Thermopylæ ?
And left they not their silent dwelling,
When Scythia's note of war was swelling ?
No! where the bold Three Hundred slept,
Sad Freedom battled not—but wept!
For nerveless then the Spartan's hand,
And Thebes could rouse no Sacred Band ?
Nor one high soul from slumber broke,
When Athens own'd the northern yoke

But was there none for *thee* to dare
The conflict, scorning to despair ?
O city of the seven proud hills !
Whose name e'en yet the spirit thrills,
As doth a clarion's battle-call,
Didst thou too, ancient empress, fall ?
Did not Camillus from the chain
Ransom thy Capitol again ?
Oh! who shall tell the days to be,
No patriot rose to bleed for thee ?

Heard ye the Gothic trumpet's blast?
The march of hosts, as Alaric pass'd?
That fearful sound, at midnight deep, (2)
Burst on th' eternal city's sleep:
How woke the mighty? She, whose will
So long had bid the world be still,
Her sword a sceptre, and her eye
Th' ascendant star of destiny!
She woke—to view the dread array
Of Scythians rushing to their prey,
To hear her streets resound the cries
Pour'd from a thousand agonies!
While the strange light of flames, that gave
A ruddy glow to Tiber's wave,
Bursting in that terrific hour
From fane and palace, dome and tower,
Reveal'd the throngs, for aid divine
Clinging to many a worshipp'd shrine;
Fierce, fitful radiance wildly shed
O'er spear and sword with carnage red,
Shone o'er the suppliant and the flying,
And kindled pyres for Romans dying.

Weep, Italy! alas! that e'er
Should tears alone thy wrongs declare!
The time hath been when thy distress
Had roused up empires for redress!
Now, her long race of glory run,
Without a combat Rome is won,
And from her plunder'd temples forth
Rush the fierce children of the north,
To share beneath more genial skies
Each joy their own rude clime denies.

Ye who on bright Campania's shore
Bade your fair villas rise of yore,
With all their graceful colonnades,
And crystal baths and myrtle shades,
Along the blue Hesperian deep,
Whose glassy waves in sunshine sleep;
Beneath your olive and your vine
Ar other inmates now recline
And the tall plane, whose roots ye fed
With rich libations duly shed, (3)
O'er guests, unlike your vanish'd friends,
Its bowery canopy extends:
For them the southern heaven is glowing,
The bright Falernian nectar flowing;
For them the marble halls unfold,
Where nobler beings dwelt of old,
Whose children for barbarian lords
Touch the sweet lyre's resounding chords,
Or wreaths of Persian roses twine,
To crown the sons of Elbe and Rhine.
Yet though luxurious they repose
Beneath Corinthian porticoes,
While round them into being start
The marvels of triumphant art;
Oh! not for them hath Genius given
To Parian stone the fire of heaven,
Enshrining in the forms he wrought
A bright eternity of thought.
In vain the natives of the skies
In breathing marble round them rise,
And sculptured nymphs, of fount or glade
People the dark-green laurel shade;
Cold is the conqueror's heart and eye
To visions of divinity;
And rude his hand which dares deface
The models of immortal grace.

Arouse ye from your soft delights!
Chieftains! the war-note's call invites;
And other lands must yet be won,
And other deeds of havoc done.
Warriors! your flowery bondage break,
Sons of the stormy north, awake!
The barks are launching from the steep,
Soon shall the Isle of Ceres weep, (4)
And Afric's burning winds afar
Waft the shrill sounds of Alaric's war.
Where shall his race of victory close?
When shall the ravaged earth repose?
But hark! what wildly mingling cries
From Scythia's camp tumultuous rise?

4

Why swells dread Alaric's name on air?
A sterner conqueror hath been there!
A conqueror—yet his paths are peace,
He comes to bring the world's release;
He of the sword that knows no sheath,
Th' avenger, the deliver—Death!

Is then that daring spirit fled?
Doth Alaric slumber with the dead?
Tamed are the warrior's pride and strength,
And he and earth are calm at length.
The land where heaven unclouded shines,
Where sleep the sunbeams on the vines;
The land by conquest made his own
Can yield him now—a grave alone.
But his—her lord from Alp to sea—
No common sepulchre shall he!
Oh, make his tomb where mortal eye
Its buried wealth may ne'er descry!
Where mortal foot may never tread
Above a victor-monarch's bed.
Let not his royal dust be hid
'Neath star-aspiring pyramid;
Nor bid the gather'd mound arise,
To bear his memory to the skies.
Years roll away—oblivion claims
Her triumph o'er heroic names;
And hands profane disturb the clay
That once was fired with glory's ray!
And Avarice, from their secret gloom,
Drags e'en the treasures of the tomb.
But thou, O leader of the free!
That general doom awaits not thee!
Thou, where no step may e'er intrude,
Shalt rest in regal solitude,
Till, bursting on thy sleep profound,
Th' Awakener's final trumpet sound.
Turn ye the waters from their course,
Bid Nature yield to human force,
And hollow in the torrent's bed
A chamber for the mighty dead.
The work is done—the captive's hand
Hath well obey'd his lord's command.

Within that royal tomb are cast
The richest trophies of the past,
The wealth of many a stately dome,
The gold and gems of plunder'd Rome:
And when the midnight stars are beaming
And ocean-waves in stillness gleaming,
Stern in their grief, his warriors bear
The Chastener of the Nations there;
To rest at length from victory's toil,
Alone, with all an empire's spoil!

Then the freed current's rushing wave
Rolls o'er the secret of the grave;
Then streams the martyr'd captives' blood
To crimson that sepulchral flood,
Whose conscious tide alone shall keep
The mystery in its bosom deep.
Time hath past on since then—and swept
From earth the urns where heroes slept;
Temples of gods, and domes of kings,
Are mouldering with forgotten things;
Yet shall not ages e'er molest
The viewless home of Alaric's rest:
Still rolls, like them, th' unfailing river,
The guardian of his dust for ever.

---

## NOTES.

### Note 1.

*Spared not the living for the dead.*

After the taking of Athens by Sylla, "though such numbers were put in the sword, there were as many who laid violent hands upon themselves in grief for their sinking country. What reduced the best men among them to this despair of finding any mercy or moderate terms for Athens, was the well-known cruelty of Sylla; yet partly by the intercession of Midias and Calliphon, and the exiles who threw themselves at his feet, partly by the entreaties of the senators who attended him in that expedition, and being himself satiated with blood besides, he was at last prevailed upon to stop his hand, and in compliment to the ancient Athenians, he said, "he forgave the many for the sake of the few, *the living for the dead.*"—*Plutarch.*

### NOTE 2.

*That fearful round, ol midnight deep.*

" At the hour of midnight, the Salarian gate was silently opened, and the inhabitants were awakened by the tremendous sound of the Gothic trumpet. Eleven hundred and sixty-three years after the foundation of Rome, the imperial city, which had subdued and civilized so considerable a portion of mankind, was delivered to the licentious fury of the tribes of Germany and Scythia."—*Decline and Fall of the Roman Empire*, vol. v. p. 311.

### NOTE 3.

*With rich libations duly shed.*

The plane-tree was much cultivated among the Romans, on account of its extraordinary shade; and they used to nourish it with wine instead of water, believing (as Sir W. Temple observes) that This tree loved that liquor as well as those who used to drink under its shade."—*See the notes to Melmoth's Pliny.*

### NOTE 4.

*Soon shall the isle of Ceres weep.*

Sicily was anciently considered as the favoured and peculiar dominion of Ceres.

---

## THE

## WIFE OF ASDRUBAL.

"This governor, who had braved death when it was at a distance, and protested that the sun should never see him survive Carthage, this fierce Asdrubal, was so mean-spirited, as to come alone, and privately throw himself at the conqueror's feet. The general, pleased to see his proud rival humbled, granted his life and kept him to grace his triumph. The Carthaginians in the citadel no sooner understood that their commander had abandoned the place, than they threw open the gates, and put the proconsul in possession of Byrsa. The Romans had now no enemy to contend with but the nine hundred deserters, who, being reduced to despair, retired into the temple of Esculapius, which was a second citadel within the first; there the proconsul attacked them; and these unhappy wretches, finding there was no way to escape, set fire to the temple. As the flames spread, they retreated from one part to another, till they got to the roof of the building; there Asdrubal's wife appeared in her best apparel, as if the day of her death had been a day of triumph; and after having uttered the most bitter imprecations against her husband, whom she saw standing below with Emilianus, — 'Base coward!' said she, 'the mean things thou hast done to save thy life shall not avail thee: thou shalt die this instant, at least in thy two children.' Having thus spoken, she drew out a dagger, stabbed them both, and while they were yet struggling for life, threw them from the top of the temple, and leaped down after them into the flames."—*Ancient Universal History.*

---

THE sun sets brightly—but a ruddier glow
O'er Afric's heaven the flames of Carthage throw
Her walls have sunk, and pyramids of fire
In lurid splendour from her domes aspire;
Sway'd by the wind, they wave—while glares the
    sky,
As when the desert's red Simoom is nigh:
The sculptured altar, and the pillar'd hall,
Shine out in dreadful brightness ere they fall;
Far o'er the seas the light of ruin streams,
Rock, wave, and isle are crimson'd by its beams;
While captive thousands, bound in Roman chains,
Gaze in mute horror on their burning fanes;
And shouts of triumph, echoing far around,
Swell from the victor's tents with ivy crown'd.[*]
But mark from yon fair temple's loftiest height
What towering form bursts wildly on the sight,
All regal in magnificent attire,
And sternly beauteous in terrific ire?
She might be deem'd a Pythia in the hour
Of dread communion and delirious power!
A being more than earthly, in whose eye
There dwells a strange and fierce ascendency.
The flames are gathering round—intensely bright
Full on her features glares their meteor-light,
But a wild courage sits triumphant there,
The stormy grandeur of a proud despair;
A daring spirit, in its woes elate,
Mightier than death, untameable by fate;
The dark profusion of her locks unbound,
Waves like a warrior's floating plumage round;
Flush'd is her cheek, inspired her haughty mien,
She seems the avenging goddess of the scene.

Are those her infants, that with suppliant cry,
Cling round her, shrinking as the flame draws nigh,
Clasp with their feeble hands her gorgeous vest,
And fain would rush for shelter to her breast?
Is that a mother's glance, where stern disdain,
And passion awfully vindictive, reign?

Fix'd is her eye on Asdrubal, who stands,
Ignobly safe, amidst the conquering bands:
On him who left her to that burning tomb,
Alone to share her children's martyrdom;
Who, when his country perish'd, fled the strife,
And knelt to win the worthless boon of life.
" Live, traitor, live!" she cries, "since dear to
    thee,
E'en in thy fetters, can existence be!
Scorn'd and dishonour'd live!—with blasted name,
The Roman's triumph not to grace, but shame.
O slave in spirit! bitter be thy chain,
With tenfold anguish to avenge my pain!
Still may the manes of thy children rise
To chase calm slumber from thy wearied eyes;
Still may their voices on the haunted air
In fearful whispers tell thee to despair,
Till vain remorse thy wither'd heart consume,
Scourged by relentless shadows of the tomb!
E'en now my sons shall die—and thou, their sire,
In bondage safe, shall yet in them expire.
Think'st thou I love them not?—'Twas thine to
    fly—
'Tis mine with these to suffer and to die.
Behold their fate! the arms that cannot save
Have been their cradle, and shall be their grave."

Bright in her hand the lifted dagger gleams,
Swift from her children's hearts the life-blood
    streams;
With frantic laugh she clasps them to her breast,
Whose woes and passions soon shall be at rest;
Lifts one appealing, frenzied glance on high,
Then deep 'midst rolling flames is lost to mortal
    eye.

---

[*] It was a Roman custom to adorn the tents of victors with ivy

## Heliodorus in the Temple.

From Maccabees, book 2. chapter iii. 21. "Then it would have pitied a man to see the falling-down of the multitude of all sorts, and the fear of the high-priest, being in such an agony.—22. They then called upon the Almighty Lord to keep the things committed of trust safe and sure, for those that had committed them.—23. Nevertheless, Heliodorus executed that which was decreed.—24. Now as he was there present himself with his guard about the treasury, the Lord of Spirits, and the Prince of all Power, caused a great apparition, so that all that presumed to come in in with him were astonished at the power of God, and fainted, and were sore afraid.—25. For there appeared unto them a horse with a terrible rider upon him, and adorned with a very fair covering, and he ran fiercely, and smote at Heliodorus with his fore-feet, and it seemed that he that sat upon the horse had a complete harness of gold.—26. Moreover, two other young men appeared before him, notable in strength, excellent in beauty, and comely in apparel, who stood by him on either side, and scourged him continually, and gave him many sore stripes.—27. And Heliodorus fell suddenly to the ground, and was compassed with great darkness; but they that were with him took him up and put him into a litter.—28. Thus him that lately came with great train, and with all his guard into the said treasury, they carried out, being unable to help himself with his weapons, and manifestly they acknowledged the power of God.—29. For he by the hand of God was cast down, and lay speechless, without all hope of life."

A sound of woe in Salem! mournful cries
    Rose from her dwellings—youthful cheeks were
        pale,
Tears flowing fast from dim and aged eyes,
    And voices mingling in tumultuous wail;
Hands raised to heaven in agony of prayer,
And powerless wrath, and terror, and despair.

Thy daughters, Judah! weeping, laid aside
    The regal splendour of their fair array,
With the rude sackcloth girt their beauty's pride,
    And throng'd the streets in hurrying, wild dis
        may;
While knelt thy priests before *his* awful shrine,
Who made, of old, renown and empire thine.

But on the spoiler moves—the temple's gate,
    The bright, the beautiful, his guards unfold
And all the scene reveals its solemn state,
    Its courts and pillars, rich with sculptured gold,
And man, with eye unhallow'd, views th' abode,
The sever'd spot, the dwelling place of God.

Where art thou, Mighty Presence! that of yore
    Wert wont between the cherubim to rest,
Veil'd in a cloud of glory, shadowing o'er
    Thy sanctuary the chosen and the blest?
Thou! that didst make fair Sion's ark thy throne,
And call the oracle's recess thine own!

Angel of God! that through th' Assyrian host,
    Clothed with the darkness of the midnight hour,
To tame the proud, to hush th' invader's boast,
    Didst pass triumphant in avenging power,
Till burst the day-spring on the silent scene,
And death alone reveal'd where thou hadst been

Bit thou not wake, O Chastener! in thy might,
    To guard thine ancient and majestic hill,
Where oft from heaven the full Shechinah's light
    Hath stream'd, the house of holiness to fill?
Oh! yet once more defend thy loved domain,
Eternal one! Deliverer! rise again

Fearless of thee, the plunderer, undismay'd,
    Hastes on, the sacred chambers to explore
Where the bright treasures of the fane are laid,
    The orphan's portion, and the widow's store;
What recks *his* heart though age unsuccour'd die
And want consume the cheek of infancy?

Away, intruders!—hark! a mighty sound!
    Behold a burst of light!—away, away!
A fearful glory fills the temple round,
    A vision bright in terrible array!
And lo! a steed of no terrestrial frame,
His path a whirlwind, and his breath a flame!

His neck is clothed with thunder*—and his mane
    Seems waving fire—the kindling of his eye
Is as a meteor—ardent with disdain
    His glance—his gesture, fierce in majesty!
Instinct with light he seems, and form'd to bear
Some dread archangel through the fields of air.

But who is he, in panoply of gold,
    Throned on that burning charger?—bright hi
        form,
Yet in its brightness awful to behold,
    And girt with all the terrors of the storm!
Lightning is on his helmet's crest—and fear
Shrinks from the splendour of his brow severe.

And by his side two radiant warriors stand
    All arm'd and kingly in commanding grace—
Oh! more than kingly, godlike! sternly grand!
    Their port indignant, and each dazzling face
Beams with the beauty to immortals given,
Magnificent in all the wrath of heaven.

Then sinks each gazer's heart—each knee is bow'd
    In trembling awe—but, as to fields of fight,
Th' unearthly war-steed, rushing through the
        crowd,
    Bursts on their leader with terrific might;
And the stern angels of that dread abode
Pursue its plunderer with the scourge of God.

Darkness—thick darkness! low on earth he lies,
    Rash Heliodorus—motionless and pale—
Bloodless his cheek, and o'er his shrouded eyes
    Mists, as of death, suspend their shadowy veil:
And thus th' oppressor, by his fear-struck train,
Is borne from that inviolable fane.

The light returns—the warriors of the sky
    Have pass'd, with all their dreadful pomp, away;
Then wakes the timbrel, swells the song on high
    Triumphant, as in Judah's elder day;
Rejoice, O city of the sacred hill!
Salem, exult! thy God is with thee still.

## NIGHT-SCENE IN GENOA

[*From Sismondi's "Republiques Italiennes"*]

En même temps que les Genois poursuivoient avec ar deur la guerre contre Pise ils etoient dechires eux-memes par une discorde civile. Les consuls de l'année 1160, pour etablir la paix dans leur patrie au milieu des factions sourdes a leur voix et plus puissantes qu'eux, furent obliges d'ourdir en quelque sorte une conspiration. Ils commencerent par s'assurer secretement des dispositions pacifiques de plusieurs des citoyens, qui cependant etoient entraines dans les emeutes par leur parente avec les chefs de faction; puis, se concertant avec le venerable vieillard, Hugues, leur archeveque, ils firent, long-temps avant le lever du soleil, appeler au son des cloches les citoyens au parle-

* "Hast thou given the horse strength? Hast thou clothed his neck with thunder?"—*Job*, xxxix. 19.

cette convocation inattendue, au milieu de l'obscu-
rite de la nuit rendroit l'assemblee et plus complete et
plus docile. Les citoyens, en accourant au parlement
general, virent, au milieu de la place publique, le vieil
archeveque, entoure de son clerge en habit de ceremonies, et portant des torches allumees, tandis que les reliques de Saint Jean Baptiste, le protecteur de Genes,
etoient exposees devant lui, et que les citoyens les
plus respectables portoient a leurs mains des croix sup-
pliantes. Des que l'assemblee fut formee, le vieillard se
leva, et de sa voix cassee il conjura les chefs de parti,
au nom du Dieu de paix au nom du salut de leurs
ames, au nom de leur patrie et de la liberte, dont leurs
discordes entraineroient la ruine, de jurer sur l'evangile l'oubli de leurs querelles, et la paix a venir.

' Les herauts, des qu'il eut fini de parler, s'avancerent
aussitot vers Roland Avogado, le chef de l'une des
factions, qui etoit present a l'assemblee, et, secondes
par les acclamations de tout le peuple, et par les prieres de ses parens eux-memes, ils le sommerent de se
conformer au vœu des consuls et de la nation.

" Roland, a leur approche, dechira ses habits, et, s'asse-
yant par terre en versant des larmes, il appela a haute
voix les morts qu'il avoit jure de venger, et qui ne lui
permettoient pas de pardonner leurs vieilles offenses.
Comme on ne pouvoit le determiner a s'avancer, les
consuls eux-memes, l'archeveque et le clerge s'ap-
procherent de lui, et, renouvelant leurs prieres, ils
l'entrainerent enfin, et lui firent jurer sur l'evangile
l'oubli de ses inimities passees.

" Les chefs du parti contraire, Foulques de Castro, et
Ingo de Volta, n'etoient pas presens a l'assemblee,
mais le peuple et le clerge se porterent en foule a
leurs maisons; ils les trouverent deja ebranles par ce
qu'ils venoient d'apprendre, et, profitant de leur emotion, ils leur firent jurer une reconciliation sincere, et
donner le baiser de paix aux chefs de la faction oppo-
see. Alors les cloches de la ville sonnerent en te-
moignage d'allegresse, et l'archeveque de retour sur
la place publique entonna un *Tu Deum* avec toute le
peuple, en honneur du Dieu de paix qui avoit sauve
.eur patrie."—*Histoire des Republiques Italiennes*
vol. ii. p. 149—150.

## NIGHT-SCENE IN GENOA.

In Genoa, when the sunset gave
Its last warm purple to the wave,
No sound of war, no voice of fear,
Was heard, announcing danger near:
Though deadliest foes were there, whose hate
But slumber'd till its hour of fate,
Yet calmly, at the twilight's close,
Sunk the wide city to repose,

But when deep midnight reign'd around,
All sudden woke the alarm-bell's sound,
Full swelling, while the hollow breeze
Bore its dread summons o'er the seas.
Then, Genoa, from their slumber started
Thy sons, the free, the fearless-hearted;
Then mingled with th' awakening peal
Voices, and steps, and clash of steel.
" Arm, warriors, arm! for danger calls:
Arise to guard your native walls!"
With breathless haste the gathering throng
Hurry the echoing streets along;
Through darkness rushing to the scene
Where their bold councils still convene.
—But there a blaze of torches bright
Pours its red radiance on the night,
O'er fane, and dome, and column playing,
With every fitful night-wind swaying,
Now floating o'er each tall arcade,
Around the pillar'd scene display'd,
In light reveal'd by depth of shade;
And now, with ruddy meteor-glare,
Full streaming on the silvery hair
And the bright cross of him who stands,
Rearing that sign with suppliant hands,

Girt with his consecrated train,
The hallow'd servants of the fane.
Of life's past woes the fading trace
Hath given that aged patriarch's face
Expression holy, deep, resign'd,
The calm sublimity of mind.
Years o'er his snowy head had pass'd,
And left him of his race the last;
Alone on earth—yet still his mien
Is bright with majesty serene;
And those high hopes, whose guiding-star
Shines from th' eternal worlds afar,
Have with that light illumed his eye,
Whose fount is immortality,
And o'er his features pour'd a ray
Of glory, not to pass away.
He seems a being who hath known
Communion with his God alone,
On earth by naught but pity's tie
Detain'd a moment from on high!
One to sublimer worlds allied,
One, from all passion purified.
E'en now half mingled with the sky,
And all prepared—oh! not to die—
But like the prophet, to aspire,
In heaven's triumphal car of fire.
He speaks—and from the throngs around
Is heard not e'en a whisper'd sound;
Awe-struck each heart, and fix'd each glance,
They stand as in a spell-bound trance;
He speaks—oh! who can hear nor own
The might of each prevailing tone?

" Chieftains and warriors! ye, so long
Aroused to strife by mutual wrong,
Whose fierce and far-transmitted hate
Hath made your country desolate;
Now by the love ye bear her name,
By that pure spark of holy flame
On freedom's altar brightly burning,
But, once extinguish'd—ne'er returning;
By all your hopes of bliss to come
When burst the bondage of the tomb;
By Him, the God who bade us live
To aid each other and forgive;
I call upon ye to resign
Your discords at your country's shrine,
Each ancient feud in peace atone,
Wield your keen swords for her alone,
And swear upon the cross to cast
Oblivion's mantle o'er the past."

No voice replies—the holy bands
Advance to where yon chieftain stands,
With folded arms and brow of gloom
O'ershadow'd by his floating plume.
To him they lift the cross—in vain.
He turns—oh! say not with disdain,
But with a mien of haughty grief,
That seeks not e'en from heaven relief.
He rends his robes—he sternly speaks—
Yet tears are on the warrior's cheeks.

" Father! not thus the wounds may close
Inflicted by eternal foes.
Deem'st thou *thy* mandate can efface
The dread volcano's burning trace?
Or bid the earthquake's ravaged scene
Be smiling, as it once hath been?
No!—for the deeds the sword hath done
Forgiveness is not lightly won;
The words, by hatred spoke, may not
Be, as a summer breeze, forgot!
'Tis vain—we deem the war-feud's rage
A portion of our heritage.
Leaders, now slumbering with their fame
Bequeath'd us that undying flame;
Hearts that have long been still and cold
Yet rule us from their silent mould,
And voices, heard on earth no more,
Speak to our spirits as of yore.
Talk not of mercy—blood alone
The stain of bloodshed may atone;
Naught else can pay that mighty debt
The dead forbid us to forget."

He pauses—from the patriarch's brow
There beams more lofty grandeur'now;
His reverend form, his aged hand,
Assume a gesture of command.
His voice is awful, and his eye
Fill'd with prophetic majesty.

" The dead!—and deem'st thou *they* retain
Aught of terrestrial passion's stain!
Of guilt incurr'd in days gone by,
Aught but the fearful penalty?
And say'st thou, mortal! blood alone
For deeds of slaughter may atone?
There *hath* been blood—by HIM 't was shed
To expiate every crime who bled;
Th' absolving God who died to save,
And rose in victory from the grave!
And by that stainless offering given
Alike from all on earth to heaven;
By that inevitable hour
When death shall vanquish pride and power,
And each departing passion's force
Concentrate all in late remorse:
And by the day when doom shall be
Pass'd on earth's millions, and on thee,
The doom that shall not be repeal'd,
Once utter'd and for ever seal'd;
I summon thee, O child of clay!
To cast thy darker thoughts away,
And meet thy foes in peace and love,
As thou wouldst join the blest above."

Still as he speaks unwonted feeling
Is o'er the chieftain's bosom stealing;
Oh! not in vain the pleading cries
Of anxious thousands round him rise.
He yields—devotion's mingled sense
Of faith, and fear, and penitence,
Pervading all his soul, he bows
To offer on the cross his vows.
And that best incense to the skies
Each evil passion's sacrifice.

Then tears from warriors' eyes were flowing.
High hearts with soft emotions glowing,
Stern foes as long-loved brothers greeting,
And ardent throngs in transport meeting,
And eager footsteps forward pressing,
And accents loud in joyous blessing;
And when their first wild tumults cease,
A thousand voices echo " Peace!"

Twilight's dim mist hath roll'd away,
And the rich Orient burns with day;
Then as to greet the sunbeam's birth,
Rises the choral hymn of earth;
Th' exulting strain through Genoa swelling,
Of peace and holy rapture telling.
Far float the sounds o'er vale and steep,
The sunbeam hears them on the deep,
So mellow'd by the gale they seem
As the wild music of a dream;
But not on mortal ear alone
Peals the triumphant anthem's tone,
For beings of a purer sphere
Bend with celestial joy to hear.

# THE TROUBADOUR

## AND

# RICHARD CŒUR DE LION.

" Not only the place of Richard's confinement" (when thrown into prison by the Duke of Austria,) if we believe the literary history of the times, but even the circumstance of his captivity, was carefully concealed by his vindictive enemies: and both might have remained unknown but for the grateful attachment of a Provencal bard, or minstrel, named Blondel, who had shared that prince's friendship and tasted his bounty. Having travelled over all the European continent to learn the destiny of his beloved patron, Blondel accidentally got intelligence of a certain castle in Germany, where a prisoner of distinction was confined and guarded with great vigilance. Persuaded by a secret impulse that this prisoner was the King of England, the minstrel repaired to the place; but the gates of the castle were shut against him, and he could obtain no information relative to the name or quality of the unhappy person it secured. In this extremity, he bethought himself of an expedient for making the desired discovery. He chanted with a loud voice, some verses of a song which had been composed partly by himself, partly by Richard: and, to his unspeakable joy, on making a pause, he heard it re-echoed, and continued by the royal captive."—(*Hist. Troubadours.*) To this discovery the English monarch is said to have eventually owed his release."—See *Russell's Modern Europe*, vol. i. p. 369.

THE Troubadour o'er many a plain
Hath roam'd unwearied, but in vain.
O'er many a rugged mountain-scene,
And forest wild, his track hath been;
Beneath Calabria's glowing sky
He hath sung the song of chivalry,
His voice hath swell'd on the Alpine breeze
And rung through the snowy Pyrenees;
From Ebro's banks to Danube's wave
He hath sought his prince, the loved, the brave
And yet, if still on earth thou art,
O monarch of the lion-heart!
The faithful spirit, which distress
But heightens to devotedness,
By toil and trial vanquish'd not.
Shall guide thy minstrel to the spot.

He hath reach'd a mountain hung with vine
And woods that wave o'er the lovely Rhine;
The feudal towers that crest its height
Frown in unconquerable might;
Dark is their aspect of sullen state,
No helmet hangs o'er the massy gate (1)
To bid the wearied pilgrim rest,
At the chieftain's board a welcome guest;
Vainly rich evening's parting smile
Would chase the gloom of the haughty pile,
That 'midst bright sunshine lowers or high,
Like a thunder cloud in a summer-sky.

Not these the halls where a child of song
Awhile may speed the hours along,
Their echoes should repeat alone
The tyrant's mandate, the prisoner's moan,
Or the wild huntsman's bugle-blast
When his phantom-train are hurrying past. (2)

The weary minstrel paused—his eye
Roved o'er the scene despondingly:
Within the lengthening shadow cast
By the fortress-towers and ramparts vast,
Lingering he gazed—the rocks around
Sublime in savage grandeur frown'd;
Proud guardians of the regal flood,
In giant strength the mountains stood;
By torrents cleft, by tempests riven,
Yet mingling with the calm blue heaven.
Their peaks were bright with a sunny glow,
But the Rhine all shadowy roll'd below;
In purple tints the vineyards smiled,
But the woods beyond waved dark and wild
Nor pastoral pipe, nor convent's bell,
Was heard on the sighing breeze to swell,
But all was lonely, silent, rude,
A stern, yet glorious solitude.

But hark! that solemn stillness breaking,
The Troubadour's wild song is waking.
Full oft that song, in days gone by,
Hath cheer'd the sons of chivalry;
It hath swell'd o'er Judah's mountains lone,
Hermon! thy echoes have learn'd its tone;
On the Great Plain (3) its notes have rung,
The leagued Crusaders' tents among;
'T was loved by the Lion-heart, who won
The palm in the field of Ascalon;
And now afar o'er the rocks of Rhine
Peals the bold strain of Palestine.

### THE TROUBADOUR'S SONG.

" Thine hour is come, and the stake is set,"
    The soldan cried to the captive knight,
" And the sons of the Prophet in throngs are met
    To gaze on the fearful sight.'

" But be our faith by thy lips profess'd,
    The faith of Mecca's shrine,
Cast down the red-cross that marks thy vest,
    And life shall yet be thine "

' I have seen the flow of my bosom's blood,
    And gazed with undaunted eye;
I have borne the bright cross through fire and flood,
    And think'st thou I fear to die?

" I have stood where thousands by Salem's towers,
    Have fallen for the name divine;
And the faith that cheer'd *their* closing hours
    Shall be the light of mine."

" Thus wilt thou die in the pride of health,
    And the glow of youth's fresh bloom?
Thou art offer'd life, and pomp, and wealth,
    Or torture and the tomb."

" I have been where the crown of thorns was twined
    For a dying Saviour's brow;
*He* spurn'd the treasures that lure mankind,
    And I reject them now!

" Art thou the son of a noble line
    In a land that is fair and blest?
And doth not thy spirit, proud captive! pine,
    Again on its shores to rest?

Thine own is the choice to hail once more
    The soil of thy fathers' birth,
Or to sleep when thy lingering pangs are o'er,
    Forgotten in foreign earth."

' Oh  fair are the vine-clad hills that rise
    In the country of my love;
But yet  though cloudless my native skies,
    There's a brighter clime above!"

The bard hath paused—for another tone
Blends with the music of his own;
And his heart beats high with hope again,
As a well-known voice prolongs the strain.

' Are there none within thy father's hall,
    Far o'er the wide blue main.
Young Christian! left to deplore thy fall,
    With sorrow deep and vain?"

" There are hearts that still, through all the past
    Unchanging have loved me well;
There are eyes whose tears were streaming fast
    When I bade my home farewell.

" Better they wept o'er the warrior's bier
    Than th' apostate's living stain;
There's a land where those who loved, when here,
    Shall meet to love again."

'T is he! thy prince—long sought, long lost,
The leader of the red-cross host!
'T is he!—to none thy joy betray,
Young Troubadour! away, away!
Away to the island of the brave,
The gem on the bosom of the wave, (4)
Arouse the sons of the noble soil,
To win their lion from the toil;
And free the wassail-cup shall flow,
Bright in each hall the hearth shall glow;
The festal board shall be richly crown'd,
While knights and chieftains revel round,
And a thousand harps with joy shall ring,
When merry England hails her king.

---

# NOTES.

### NOTE 1.

*No helmet hangs o'er the mossy gate.*

It was a custom in feudal times to hang out a helmet on a castle, as a token that strangers were invited to enter, and partake of hospitality.  So in the romance of ' Perceforest,' " ils faisoient mettre au plus hault de leur hostel un *heaulme,* en signe que tous les gentils hommes et gentilles femmes entrassent hardiment en leur hostal comme en leur propre."

### NOTE 2.

*Or the wild huntsman's bugle-blast,*
*When his phantom-train are hurrying past.*

Popular tradition has made several mountains in Germany the haunt of the *wild Jäger,* or supernatural huntsman—the superstitious tales relating to the Unterburg are recorded in Eustace's Classical Tour; and it is still believed in the romantic district of the Odenwald, that the knight of Rodenstein, issuing from his ruined castle, announces the approach of war by traversing the air with a noisy armament to the opposite castle of Schnellerts.—See the *Manuel pour les Voyageurs sur le Rhin,* and *Schreiber on the Rhine.*

### NOTE 3.

*On the Great Plain its notes have rung.*

The plain of Esdraelon, called by way of eminence the " Great Plain;" in Scripture, and elsewhere, the " Field of Megiddo,' the " Galilean Plain."  This plain, the most fertile of all the land of Canaan, has been the scene of many a memorable contest in the first ages of Jewish history, as well as during the Roman empire, the Crusades, and even in later times.  It has been a chosen place for encampment in every contest carried on in this country, from the days of Nabuchodonosor, king of the Assyrians, until the disastrous march of Bonaparte from Egypt into Syria. Warriors out of " every nation which is under heaven" have pitched their tents upon the Plain of Esdraelon, and have beheld the various banners of their nations wet with the dews of Hermon and Thabor.—*Dr. Clarke's Travels.*

### NOTE 4.

*The gem on the bosom of the wave.*

" This precious stone set in the silver sea."

VOL. I.—15                          *Shakspeare's Richard II*

# THE
# Death of Conradin.

[*From Sismondi's "Republiques Italiennes."*]

La defaite de Conradin ne devoit mettre uno terme ni a ses malheurs, ni aux vengeances du roi (Charles d'Anjou). L'amour du peuple pour l'heritier legitime du trone, avoit eclate d'une maniere effrayante; il pouvoit causer de nouvelles revolutions, si Conradin demeuroit en vie; et Charles, revetant sa defiance et sa cruaute des formes de la justice, resolut de faire perir sur l'echafaud le dernier rejeton de la Maison do Souabe, l'unique esperance de son parti. Un seul juge Provencal et sujet de Charles, dont les historiens n'ont pas voulu conserver le nom, osa voter pour la mort, d'autres se renfermerent dans un timide et coupable silence; et Charles, sur l'autorite de ce seul juge, fit pronouncer, par Robert de Buri, protonotaire du royaume, la sentence de mort contre Conradin et tous ses compagnons. Cette sentence fut communiquee a Conradin, comme il jouoit aux echecs; on lui laissa peu de temps pour se preparer a son execution, et le 26 d'Octobre il fut conduit, avec tous ses amis, sur la Place du Marche de Naples, le long du rivage de la mer. Charles etoit present, avec tout sa cour, et une foule immense entouroit le roi vainqueur et le roi condamne. Conradin etoit entre les mains des bourreaux; il detacha lui meme son manteau, et s'etant mis a genoux pour prier, il sereleva en s'ecriant: 'Oh, ma mere, quelle profonde douleur te causera la nouvelle qu on va te porter de moi!' Puis il tourna les yeux sur la foule qui l'entouroit; il vit les larmes, it entendit les sanglots de son peuple; alors, detachant son gant, il jeta au milieu de ses sujets ce gage d'un combat de vengeance, et rendit sa tete au bourreau. Apres lui, sur le meme echafaud, Charles fit trancher la tete au Duc d'Autriche, aux Comtes Gualferano et Bartolommeo Laucia, et aux Comtes Gerard de Galvano Donoratico de Pise. Par une rafinement de cruaute, Charles voulut que le premier, fils du second, precedat son pere, mourut entre ses bras. Les cadavres, d'apres ses ordres, furent exclus d'une terre sainte, et inhumes sans pompe sur le rivage de la mer. Charles II. cependant fit dans la suite batir, sur le meme lieu, une eglise de Carmelites, comme pour appaiser ces ombres irritees."

---

No cloud to dim the splendour of the day
Which breaks o'er Naples and her lovely bay,
And lights that brilliant sea and magic shore
With every tint that charm'd the great of yore;
Th' imperial ones of earth—who proudly bade
Their marble domes e'en ocean's realm invade.

That race is gone—but glorious nature here
Maintains unchanged her own sublime career,
And bids these regions of the sun display
Bright hues, surviving empires past away.

The beam of heaven expands — its kindling smile
Reveals each charm of many a fairy isle,
Whose image floats in softer colouring drest
With all its rocks and vines on ocean's breast.
Misenum's cape hath caught the vivid ray,
On Roman streamers there no more to play;
Still as of old, unalterably bright,
Lovely it sleeps on Posillippo's height,
With all Italia's sunshine to illume
The ilex canopy of Virgil's tomb.
Campania's plains rejoice in light, and spread
Their gay luxuriance o'er the mighty dead;
Fair glittering to thine own transparent skies,
Thy palaces, exulting Naples! rise;
While far on high, Vesuvius rears his peak,
Furrow'd and dark with many a lava streak.

O ye bright shores of Circe and the Muse!
Rich with all Nature's and all fiction's hues;
Who shall explore your regions, and declare
The poet err'd to paint Elysium there?
Call up his spirit, wanderer! bid him guide
Thy steps, those siren-haunted seas beside,
And all the scene a lovelier light shall wear,
And spells more potent shall pervade the air.
What though his dust be scatter'd, and his urn
Long from its sanctuary of slumber torn, (1)
Still dwell the beings of his verse around,
Hovering in beauty o'er the enchanted ground;
His lays are murmur'd in each breeze that roves
Soft o'er the sunny waves and orange-groves.
His memory's charm is spread o'er shore and sea,
The soul, the genius of Parthenope;
Shedding o'er myrtle-shade and vine-clad hill
The purple radiance of Elysium still.

Yet that fair soil and calm resplendent sky
Have witness'd many a dark reality.
Oft o'er those bright blue seas the gale hath borne
The sighs of exiles never to return. (2)
There with the whisper of Campania's gale
Hath mingled oft affection's funeral wail,
Mourning for buried heroes—while to her
That glowing land was but their sepulchre. (3)
And there, of old, the dread, mysterious moan
Swell'd from strange voices of no mortal tone;
And that wild trumpet, whose unearthly note
Was heard, at midnight, o'er the hills to float
Around the spot where Agrippina died,
Denouncing vengeance on the matricide. (4)

Past are those ages—yet another crime,
Another woe must stain the Elysian clime.
There stands a scaffold on the sunny shore—
It must be crimson'd ere the day is o'er!
There is a throne in regal pomp array'd,—
A scene of death from thence must be survey'd.
Mark'd ye the rushing throngs?—each mien is pale,
Each hurried glance reveals a fearful tale;
But the deep workings of th' indignant breast,
Wrath, hatred, pity, must be all suppress'd;
The burning tear awhile must check its course,
Th' avenging thought concentrate all its force,
For tyranny is near, and will not brook
Aught but submission in each guarded look.

Girt with his fierce Provençals, and with mien
Austere in triumph, gazing on the scene, (5)
And in his eye a keen suspicious glance
Of jealous pride and restless vigilance,
Behold the conqueror!—vainly in his face,
Of gentler feeling hope would seek a trace;
Cold, proud, severe, the spirit which hath lent
Its haughty stamp to each dark lineament;
And pleading mercy in the sternness there,
May read at once her sentence—to despair!

But thou, fair boy! the beautiful, the brave,
Thus passing from the dungeon to the grave,
While all is yet around thee which can give
A charm to earth, and make it bliss to live;
Thou, on whose form hath dwelt a mother's eye
'Till the deep love that not with thee shall die
Hath grown too full for utterance,—can it be?
And is this pomp of death prepared for *thee?*
Young, royal Conradin! who should'st have known
Of life as yet the sunny smile alone!
Oh! who can view thee, in the pride and bloom
Of youth, array'd thus richly for the tomb,
Nor feel, deep-swelling in his inmost soul,
Emotions tyranny may ne'er control?
Bright victim! to ambition's altar led,
Crown'd with all flowers that heaven on earth can shed,
Who, from th' oppressor towering in his pride,
May hope for mercy—if to thee denied?
There is dead silence on the breathless throng,—
Dead silence all the peopled shore along,
As on the captive moves—the only sound
To break that calm so fearfully profound,

The low sweet murmur of the rippling wave,
Soft as it glides the smiling shore to lave;
While on that shore, his own fair heritage,
The youthful martyr to a tyrant's rage
Is passing to his fate—the eyes are dim
Which gaze, through tears that dare not flow, on
 him :
He mounts the scaffold—doth his footstep fail ?
Doth his lip quiver ? doth his cheek turn pale ?
Oh ! it may be forgiven him, if a thought
Cling to that world, for him with beauty fraught
To all the hopes that promised Glory's meed,
And all th' affections that with him shall bleed !
If in his life's young day-spring, while the rose
Of boyhood on his cheek yet freshly glows,
One human fear convulse his parting breath,
And shrink from all the bitterness of death !

But no !—the spirit of his royal race
Sits brightly on his brow—that youthful face
Beams with heroic beauty—and his eye
Is eloquent with injured majesty.
He kneels—but not to man—his heart shall own
Such deep submission to his God alone !
A.... who can tell with what sustaining power
That God may visit him in fate's dread hour ?
How the still voice, which answers every moan,
May speak of hope,—when hope on earth is gone ?

That solemn pause is o'er—the youth hath given
One glance of parting love to earth and heaven ;
The sun rejoices in th' unclouded sky,
Life all around him glows—and he must die !
Yet 'midst his people, undismay'd, he throws
The gage of vengeance for a thousand woes ;
Vengeance, that like their own volcano's fire,
May sleep suppress'd awhile—but not expire.
One softer image rises o'er his breast,
One fond regret, and all shall be at rest !
"Alas, for thee, my mother ! who shall bear
To thy sad heart the tidings of despair,
'When thy lost child is gone ?"—that thought can
 thrill
His soul with pangs one moment more shall still

The lifted axe is glittering in the sun—
It falls—the race of Conradin is run !
Yet from the blood which flows that shore to stain,
A voice shall cry to heaven—and not in vain !
Gaze thou, triumphant from thy gorgeous throne,
In proud supremacy of guilt alone,
Charles of Anjou !—but that dread voice shall be
A fearful summoner e'en yet to thee !

The scene of death is closed—the throngs depart,
A deep stern lesson graved on every heart.
No pomp, no funeral rites, no streaming eyes,
High-minded boy ! may grace thine obsequies.
O vainly royal and beloved ! thy grave,
Unsanctified, is bathed by ocean's wave,
Mark'd by no stone, a rude, neglected spot,
Unhonour'd, unadorn'd—but *unforgot:*
For thy deep wrongs in tameless hearts shall live,
Now mutely suffering—never to forgive !

The sunset fades from purple heavens away,—
A bark hath anchor'd in th' unruffled bay ;
Thence on the beach descends a female form, (6)
Her mien with hope and tearful transport warm ;
But life hath left sad traces on her cheek,
And her soft eyes a chasten'd heart bespeak,
Inured to woes—yet what were all the past !
*She* sunk not feebly 'neath affliction's blast,
While one bright hope remain'd—who now shall
 tell
Th' uncrown'd, the widow'd, how her loved one
 fell ?
To clasp her child, to ransom and to save,
The mother came—and she hath found his grave !
And by that grave, transfix'd in speechless grief,
Whose death-like trance denies a tear's relief,
Awhile she kneels—till roused at length to know,
To feel the might, the fullness of her woe,
On the still air a voice of anguish wild,
A mother's cry is heard—"My Conradin ! my child !"



# NOTES.

## NOTE 1.

*Long from its sanctuary of slumber torn.*

The urn, supposed to contain the ashes of Virgil, has long since been lost

## NOTE 2.

*The sighs of exiles never to return.*

Many Romans of exalted rank were formerly banished to some of the small islands in the Mediterranean, on the coast of Italy. Julia, the daughter of Augustus, was confined many years in the isle of Pandataria, and her daughter, Agrippina, the widow of Germanicus, afterwards died in exile on the same desolate spot.

## NOTE 3.

*That glowing land was but their sepulchre.*

" Quelques souvenirs du cœur, quelques noms de femmes, reclament aussi vos pleurs. C'est a Misene, dans le lieu même ou nous sommes, que la veuve de Pompee, Cornelie, conserva jusqu'a la mort son noble deuil ; Agrippine pleura long-temps Germanicus sur ces bords. Un jour, le même assassin qui lui ravit son epoux la trouva digne de le suivre. L'ile de Nisida fut temoin des adieux de Brutus et de Porcie."—*Madame de Stael—Corinne.*

## NOTE 4.

*Denouncing vengeance on the matricide.*

The sight of that coast, and those shores where the crime had been perpetrated, filled Nero with continual horrors; besides, there were some who imagined they heard horrid shrieks and cries from Agrippina's tomb, and a mournful sound of trumpets from the neighbouring cliffs and hills. Nero, therefore, flying from such tragical scenes, withdrew to Naples.—See *Ancient Universal History*

## NOTE 5.

*Austere in triumph, gazing on the scene.*

" Ce Charles," dit Giovanni Villani, " fut sage et prudent dans ses conseils, preux dans les armes, apre et fort redoute de tous les rois du monde, magnanime et de hautes pensees qui l'egaloient aux plus grandes entreprises ; inebranlable dans l'adversite, ferme et fidele dans toutes ses promesses, parlant peu et agissant beaucoup, ne riant presqus jamais, decent comme un religieux, zele catholique, apre a rendre justice, feroce dans ses regards. Sa taille etoit grande et nerveuse, sa couleur olivatre, son nez fort grand. Il paroissoit plus fait qu'aucun autre chevalier pour la majeste royale. Il ne dormoit presque point. Jamais il ne prit de plaisir aux mimes, aux troubadours, et aux gens de cour."—*Sismondi. Republiques Italiennes,* vol. iii.

## NOTE 6.

*Thence on the beach descends a female form.*

" The Carmine (at Naples) calls to mind the bloody catastrophe of those royal youths, Conradin and Frederick of Austria, butchered before its door. Whenever I traversed that square, my heart yearned at the idea of their premature fate, and at the deep distress of Conradin's mother, who, landing on the beach with her son's ransom, found only a lifeless trunk to redeem from the fangs of his barbarous conqueror."—*Swinburne's Travels in the Two Sicilies.*

---

# 𝕿ranslations

## FROM

## CAMOENS AND OTHER POETS.

---

Siamo nati veramente in un secolo in cui gl'ingegni e gli studj degli uomini sono rivolti all' utilita. L'Agricoltura, le Arti, il Commercio acquistano tutto di novi lumi dalle ricerche de'Saggi ; e il voler farsi un nome *tentando di dilettare,* quand' altri v' aspira con piu giustizia giovando, sembra impresa dura e difficile.—*Savioli.*

---

## CAMOENS.—SONNET 70.

### Na metade do Ceo subido ardia.

High in the glowing heavens, with cloudless beam,
The sun had reach'd the zenith of his reign,
And for the living fount, the gelid stream,
Each flock forsook the herbage of the plain :

'Midst the dark foliage of the forest-shade,
The birds had shelter'd from the scorching ray ;
Hush'd were their melodies—and grove and glade
Resounded but the shrill cicada's lay ;

When through the glassy vale a lovelorn swain,
To seek the maid who but despised his pain,
Breathing vain sighs of fruitless passion, roved :
" Why pine for her," the slighted wanderer cried,
" By whom thou art not loved ?"—and thus replied
An echo's murmuring voice—" *Thou art not loved !*"

## CAMOENS.—SONNET 282.

### FROM PSALM CXXXVII.

*Na ribeira do Euphrates assentado.*

WRAPT in sad musings by Euphrates' stream
I sat, retracing days for ever flown,
While rose thine image on the exile's dream,
O much-loved Salem! and thy glories gone.

When they who caused the ceaseless tears I shed,
Thus to their captive spoke,—Why sleep thy lays?
Sing of thy treasures lost, thy splendour fled,
And all thy triumphs in departed days!

"Know'st thou not, Harmony's resistless charm
Can soothe each passion, and each grief disarm?
Sing then, and tears will vanish from thine eye."
With sighs I answer'd,—" When the cup of woe
Is fill'd, till misery's bitter draught o'erflow,
The mourner's cure is not to sing,—but die."

## CAMOENS.—PART OF ECLOGUE 15.

*Se la no assento da maior alteza.*

IF in thy glorious home above
Thou still recallest earthly love,
If yet retain'd a thought may be
Of him whose heart hath bled for thee;

Remember still how deeply shrined
Thine image in his joyless mind,
Each well-known scene, each former care,
Forgotten—thou alone art there!

Remember that thine eye-beam's light
Hath fled for ever from his sight,
And with that vanish'd sunshine, lost
Is every hope he cherish'd most.

Think that his life from thee apart,
Is all but weariness of heart,
Each stream whose music once was dear,
Now murmurs discords to his ear.

Through thee, the morn, whose cloudless rays
Woke him to joy in other days,
Now in the light of beauty drest,
Brings but new sorrows to his breast.

Through thee, the heavens are dark to him,
The sun's meridian blaze is dim;
And harsh were e'en the bird of eve,
But that her song still loves to grieve.

All it hath been, his heart forgets,
So alter'd by its long regrets;
Each wish is changed, each hope is o'er,
And joy's light spirit wakes no more.

## CAMOENS.—SONNET 271.

*A formosura desta fresca serra.*

THIS mountain scene, with sylvan grandeur
    crown'd;
These chestnut woods, in summer verdure bright;
These founts and rivulets, whose mingling sound
Lulls every bosom to serene delight;

Soft on these hills the sun's declining ray;
This clime where all is new; these murmuring
    seas;
Flocks to the fold that bend their lingering way
Light clouds contending with the genial breeze

And all that Nature's lavish hands dispense,
In gay luxuriance, charming every sen

Ne'er in thy absence, can delight my breast:
Naught without thee my weary soul beguiles;
And joy may beam, yet 'midst her brightest smiles
A secret grief is mine that will not rest.

## CAMOENS.—SONNET 186.

*Os olhos onde o casto Amor ardia.*

THOSE eyes, whence Love diffused his purest light,
Proud in such beaming orbs his reign to show;
That face, with tints of mingling lustre bright,
Where the rose mantled o'er the living snow;

The rich redundance of that golden hair,
Brighter than sunbeams of meridian day;
That form so graceful, and that hand so fair,
Where now those treasures?—mouldering into
    clay!

Thus, like some blossom prematurely torn,
Hath young Perfection wither'd in its morn,
Touch'd by the hand that gathers but to blight!
Oh! how could Love survive his bitter tears?
Shed, not for her who mounts to happier spheres,
But for his own sad fate, thus wrapt in starless
    night!

## CAMOENS.—SONNET 108.

*Brandas aguas do Tejo que passando.*

FAIR Tajo! thou, whose calmly-flowing tide
Bathes the fresh verdure of these lovely plains,
Enlivening all where'er thy waves may glide,
Flowers, herbage, flocks, and sylvan nymphs, and
    swains:

Sweet stream! I know not when my steps again
Shall tread thy shores; and while to part I mourn,
I have no hope to meliorate my pain,
No dream that whispers—I may yet return!

My frowning destiny, whose watchful care
Forbids me blessings, and ordains despair,
Commands me thus to leave thee and repine;
And I must vainly mourn the scenes I fly,
And breathe on other gales my plaintive sigh,
And blend my tears with other waves than thine!

## CAMOENS.—SONNET 33.

### TO A LADY WHO DIED AT SEA.

*Chara minha Inimiga, em cuja mao.*

THOU, to whose power my hopes, my joys, I gave,
O fondly loved! my bosom's dearest care!
Earth, which denied to lend thy form a grave,
Yields not one spell to soothe my deep despair!

Yes! the wild seas entomb those charms divine,
Dark o'er thy head th' eternal billows roll;
But while one ray of life or thought is mine,
Still shalt thou live, the inmate of my soul.

And if the tones of my uncultured song
Have power the sad remembrance to prolong,
Of love so ardent, and of faith so pure;
Still shall my verse thine epitaph remain,
Still shall thy charms be deathless in my strain,
While Time, and Love, and Memory shall endure
    VOL. I.—16

### CAMOENS.—SONNET 19.

*Alma minha gentil, que te partiste.*

SPIRIT beloved! whose wing so soon hath flown
The joyless precincts of this earthly sphere,
Now is yon heaven eternally thine own,
Whilst I deplore thy loss, a captive here.

Oh! if allow'd in thy divine abode
Of aught on earth an image to retain,
Remember still the fervent love which glow'd
In my fond bosom, pure from every stain.

And if thou deem that all my faithful grief,
Caused by thy loss, and hopeless of relief,
Can merit thee, sweet native of the skies!
Oh! ask of heaven, which call'd thee soon away,
That I may join thee in those realms of day,
Swiftly, as *thou* hast vanish'd from mine eyes.

### CAMOENS.

*Que estranho caso de amor!*

How strange a fate in love is mine!
How dearly prized the pains I feel!
Pangs that to rend my soul combine,
  With avarice I conceal;
For did the world the tale divine,
My lot would then be deeper woe,
And mine is grief that none must know.

To mortal ears I may not dare
Unfold the cause, the pain I prove;
'Twould plunge in ruin and despair,
  Or me, or her I love.
My soul delights alone to bear
Her silent, unsuspected woe,
And none shall pity, none shall know.

Thus buried in my bosom's urn,
Thus in my inmost heart conceal'd,
Let me alone the secret mourn,
In pangs unsoothed and unreveal'd
For whether happiness or woe,
Or life or death its power bestow,
It is what none on earth must know.

### CAMOENS.—SONNET 58.

*Se as penas com que Amor tao mal me trata.*

SHOULD Love, the tyrant of my suffering heart
Yet long enough protract his votary's days,
To see the lustre from those eyes depart,
The lode-stars now,[*] that fascinate my gaze,

To see rude Time the living roses blight,
That o'er thy cheek their loveliness unfold,
And all unpitying change thy tresses bright,
To silvery whiteness, from their native gold;

Oh! then my heart an equal change will prove,
And mourn the coldness that repell'd my love,
When tears and penitence will all be vain;
And I shall see thee weep for days gone by,
And in thy deep regret and fruitless sigh,
Find amplest vengeance for my former pain.

### CAMOENS.—SONNET 178.

*Ja cantei, ja chorei a dura guerra.*

OFT have I sung and mourn'd the bitter woes,
Which Love for years hath mingled with my fate,
While he the tale forbade me to disclose,
That taught his votaries their deluded state.

[*] " Your eyes are lode-stars."——*Shakspeare.*

Nymphs! who dispense Castalia's living stream,
Ye, who from Death oblivion's mantle steal
Grant me a strain in powerful tone supreme,
Each grief by love inflicted to reveal;

That those, whose ardent hearts adore his sway,
May hear experience breathe a warning lay,
How false his smiles, his promises how vain;
Then, if ye deign this effort to inspire,
When the sad task is o'er, my plaintive lyre,
For ever hush'd, shall slumber in your fane.

### CAMOENS.—SONNET 80.

*Como quando do mar tempestuoso*

SAVED from the perils of the stormy wave,
And faint with toil, the wanderer of the main,
But just escaped from shipwreck's billowy grave
Trembles to hear its horrors named again.

How warm his vow, that Ocean's fairest mien
No more shall lure him from the smiles of home;
Yet soon, forgetting each terrific scene,
Once more he turns, o'er boundless deeps to roam.

Lady! thus I, who vainly oft in flight
Seek refuge from the dangers of thy sight,
Make the firm vow, to shun thee and be free·
But my fond heart, devoted to its chain,
Still draws me back where countless perils reign
And grief and ruin spread their snares for me.

### CAMOENS.—SONNET 239.
#### FROM PSALM CXXXVII.

*Embabylonia sobre os rios, quando.*

BESIDE the streams of Babylon, in tears
Of vain desire, we sat; remembering thee,
O hallow'd Sion! and the vanish'd years,
When Israel's chosen sons were blest and free;

Our harps, neglected and untuned, we hung
Mute on the willows of the stranger's land;
When songs, like those that in thy fanes we sung
Our foes demanded from their captive-band.

How shall our voices, on a foreign shore,
(We answer'd those whose chains the exile wore '
The songs of God, our sacred songs, renew?
If I forget, 'midst grief and wasting toil,
Thee, O Jerusalem! my native soil!
*May my right hand forget its cunning too!*

### CAMOENS.—SONNET 128.

*Huma admiravel herva se conhece.*

THERE blooms a plant, whose gaze, from hour to
  hour,
Still to the sun with fond devotion turns,
Wakes when Creation hails his dawning power,
And most expands, when most her idol burns:

But when he seeks the bosom of the deep,
His faithful plant's reflected charms decay;
Then fade her flowers. her leaves discolour'd weep
Still fondly pining for the vanish'd ray.

Thou whom I love, the day-star of my sight!
When thy dear presence wakes me to delight,

Joy in my soul, unto, as her fairest flower;
But in thy heaven of smiles alone it blooms
And of their light deprived, in grief consumes,
Born but to live within thine eye-beam's power.

## CAMOENS.

*Polo seen apartamento.*

Amidst the bitter tears that fell
In anguish at my last farewell,
Oh! who would dream that joy could dwell,
   To make that moment bright?
Yet be my judge, each heart! and say,
Which then could most my bosom sway,
   Affliction, or delight?

It was, when Hope, oppress'd with woes,
Seem'd her dim eyes in death to close,
That rapture's brightest beam arose
   In sorrow's darkest night.
Thus if my soul survive that hour,
'T is that my fate o'ercame the power
   Of anguish with delight.

For oh! her love, so long unknown,
She *then* confest, was all my own,
And in that parting hour alone
   Reveal'd it to my sight.
And now what pangs will rend my soul,
Should fortune still, with stern control,
   Forbid me this delight.

I know not if my bliss were vain,
For all the force of parting pain
Forbade suspicious doubts to reign,
   When exiled from her sight;
Yet now what double woe for me,
Just at the close of eve, to see
   The day-spring of delight.

## CAMOENS.—SONNET 205

*Quem diz que Amor he falso, o enganoso.*

He who proclaims that Love is light and vain
Capricious, cruel, false in all his ways;
Ah! sure too well has merited his pain,
Too justly finds him all he thus portrays.

For Love is pitying, Love is soft and kind;
Believe not him who dares the tale oppose:
Oh! deem him one whom stormy passions blind,
One to whom earth and heaven may well be foes.

If Love bring evils, view them all in me!
Here let the world his utmost rigour see,
His utmost power exerted to annoy:
But all his ire is still the ire of Love!
And such delight in all his woes I prove,
I would not change their pangs for aught of other
   joy!

## CAMOENS.—SONNET 133

*Doces, e claras aguas do Mondego.*

Waves of Mondego! brilliant and serene,
Haunts of my thought, where memory fondly
   strays;
Where hope allured me with perfidious mien,
Witching my soul, in long-departed days;

Yes: I forsake your banks; but still my heart
Shall hid remembrance all your charms restore,
And, suffering not one image to depart,
Find lengthening distance but endear you more.

Let fortune's will, through many a future day,
To distant realms this mortal frame convey,

Sport of each wind, and tost on every wave.
Yet my fond soul, to pensive memory true,
On thought's light pinion still shall fly to you,
And still, bright waters in your current lave.

## CAMOENS.—SONNET 181.

*Onde acharei fagar tao apartado.*

Where shall I find some desert-scene so rude,
Where loneliness so undisturb'd may reign,
That not a step shall ever there intrude
Of roving man, or nature's savage train?

Some tangled thicket, desolate and drear,
Or deep wild forest, silent as the tomb,
Boasting no verduro bright, no fountain clear,
But darkly suited to my spirit's gloom?

That there 'midst frowning rocks, alone with
   grief
Entomb'd in life, and hopeless of relief,
In lonely freedom I may breathe my woes—
For oh! since naught my sorrows can allay,
There shall my sadness cloud no festal day,
And days of gloom shall soothe me to repose.

## CAMOENS.—SONNET 278.

*Eu vivia de lagrimas isento.*

Exempt from every grief, 't was mine to live
In dreams so sweet, enchantments so divine,
A thousand joys propitious Love can give,
Were scarcely worth one rapturous pain of mine

Bound by soft spells, in dear illusions blest,
I breathed no sigh for fortune or for power;
No care intruding to disturb my breast,
I dwelt entranced in Love's Elysian hower;

But Fate, such transports eager to destroy,
Soon rudely woke me from the dream of joy,
And bade the phantoms of delight begone!
Bade hope and happiness at once depart,
And left but memory to distract my heart,
Retracing every hour of bliss for ever flown

## CAMOENS.

*Mi nuovo y dulce querella.*

No searching eye can pierce the veil
That o'er my secret love is thrown;
No outward signs reveal its tale,
   But to my bosom known.
Thus like the spark, whose vivid light
In the dark flint is hid from sight,
   It dwells within, alone.

## METASTASIO.

*Donque si sfoga in pianto.*

In tears, the heart oppress'd with grief
   Gives language to its woes;
In tears, its fullness finds relief,
   When rapture's tide o'erflows!
Who then unclouded bliss would seek
   On this terrestrial sphere;
When e'en Delight can only speak,
   Like Sorrow—in a tear?

## VINCENZIO DA FILICAJA.

*Italia! Italia! O tu cui feo la sorte.*

ITALIA! thou by lavish Nature graced
With ill starr'd beauty, which to thee hath been
A fatal dowry, whose effects are traced
In the deep sorrows graven on thy mien;

Oh! that more strength, or fewer charms, were
     thine,
That those might fear thee more, or love thee less,
Who seem to worship at thy beauty's shrine,
Then leave thee to the death-pang's bitterness!

Not then the herds of Gaul would drain the tide
Of that Eridanus thy blood had dyed;
Nor from the Alps would legions, still renew'd,
Pour down; nor wouldst thou wield a foreign
     brand,
Nor fight thy battles with the stranger's hand,
Still doom'd to serve, subduing or subdued!

---

## PASTORINI.

*Genova mia, se con asciutto ciglie.*

IF thus thy fallen grandeur I behold,
My native Genoa! with a tearless eye,
Think not thy son's ungrateful heart is cold.
But know—I deem rebellious every sigh!

Thy glorious ruins proudly I survey,
Trophies of firm resolve, of patriot might!
And in each trace of devastation's way
Thy worth, thy courage, meet my wandering sight.

Triumphs far less than suffering virtue shine!
And on the spoilers high revenge is thine,
While thy strong spirit unsubdued remains.
And lo! fair Liberty rejoicing flies,
To kiss each noble relic, while she cries,
'Hail! though in ruins, thou wert ne'er in chains!'

---

## LOPE DE VEGA.

*Estese el cortesano.*

LET the vain courtier waste his days,
Lured by the charms that wealth displays,
Couch of down, the board of costly fare;
'E his to kiss th' ungrateful hand
That waves the sceptre of command,
And rear full many a palace in the air;
     Whilst I enjoy, all unconfined,
     The glowing sun, the genial wind,
And tranquil hours, to rustic toil assign'd;
     And prize far more, in peace and health,
Contented indigence, than joyless wealth.

     Not mine in Fortune's face to bend,
     At Grandeur's altar to attend,
Reflect his smile, and tremble at his frown;
     Nor ' ae a fond aspiring thought,
     A wish, a sigh, a vision, fraught
With Fame's bright phantom, Glory's deathless
     crown!
     Nectareous draughts and viands pure,
     Luxuriant Nature will insure;
     These the clear fount, and fertile field,
     Still to the wearied shepherd yield;
     And when repose and visions reign,
Then we are equals all, the monarch and the swain!

## FRANCISCO MANUEL.

### ON ASCENDING A HILL LEADING TO A CONVENT.

*No bares temeroso, o peregrine.*

PAUSE not with lingering foot, O pilgrim, here;
Pierce the deep shadows of the mountain-side;
Firm be thy step, thy heart unknown to fear,
To brighter worlds this thorny path will guide.

Soon shall thy feet approach the calm abode,
So near the mansions of supreme delight;
Pause not—but tread this consecrated road,
'T is the dark basis of the heavenly height.

Behold, to cheer thee on the toilsome way,
How many a fountain glitters down the hill!
Pure gales, inviting, softly round thee play,
Bright sunshine guides—and wilt thou linger still?
Oh! enter there, where, freed from human strife
Hope is reality, and time is life.

---

## DELLA CASA.

### VENICE.

*Questi palazzi, e questa logge or colta.*

THESE marble domes, by wealth and genius graced
With sculptured forms, bright hues, and Parian
     stone,
Were once rude cabins 'midst a lonely waste,
Wild shores of solitude, and isles unknown.

Pure from each vice, 'twas here a virtuous train
Fearless in fragile barks explored the sea;
Not theirs a wish to conquer or to reign,
They sought these island-precincts—to be free.

Ne'er in their souls ambition's flame arose,
No dream of avarice broke their calm repose;
Fraud, more than death abhorr'd each artless
     breast;
Oh! now, since Fortune gilds their brightening day,
Let not those virtues languish and decay,
O'erwhelm'd by luxury, and by wealth opprest!

---

## IL MARCHESE CORNELIO BENTIVOGLIO.

*L'anima bella, che dal vero Eliso.*

THE sainted spirit, which from bliss on high
Descends like day-spring to my favour'd sight,
Shines in such noontide radiance of the sky,
Scarce do I know that form, intensely bright!

But with the sweetness of her well-known smile
That smile of peace! she bids my doubts depart,
And takes my hand, and softly speaks the while,
And heaven's full glory pictures to my heart.

Beams of that heaven in *her* my eyes behold,
And now, e'en now, in thought my wings unfold
To soar with her, and mingle with the blest!
But ah! so swift her buoyant pinion flies,
That I, in vain aspiring to the skies,
Fall to my native sphere by earthly bonds deprest.

---

## METASTASIO.

*Al furor d'avversa sorte.*

HE shall not dread Misfortune's angry mien,
Nor feebly sink beneath her tempest rude,
Whose soul hath learn'd, through many a trying
     scene,
To smile at fate, and suffer unsubdued.

In the rough school of billows, clouds, and storms,
Nursed and matured, the pilot learns his art:
Thus Fate's dread ire, by many a conflict, forms
The lofty spirit and enduring heart!

## METASTASIO.

*Quella onda che ruina.*

The torrent-wave, that breaks with force
Impetuous down the Alpine height,
Complains and struggles in its course,
But sparkles, as the diamond bright.

The stream in shadowy valley deep
May slumber in its narrow bed;
But silent in unbroken sleep,
Its lustre and its life are fled.

## METASTASIO.

*Leggiadra rosa, le cui pure foglie.*

Sweet rose! whose tender foliage to expand,
Her fostering dews the morning lightly shed,
Whilst gales of balmy breath thy blossoms fann'd,
And o'er thy leaves the soft suffusion spread;

That hand whose care withdrew thee from the
    ground,
To brighter worlds thy favour'd charms hath borne;
Thy fairest buds, with grace perennial crown'd,
There breathe and bloom, released from every
    thorn.

Thus, far removed, and now, transplanted flower
Exposed no more to blast or tempest rude,
Shelter'd with tenderest care from frost or shower,
And each rough season's chill vicissitude,
Now may thy form in bowers of peace assume
Immortal fragrance, and unwithering bloom.

## METASTASIO.

*Che speri, instabil Dea, di sassi e spine.*

Fortune! why thus, where'er my footsteps tread,
Obstruct each path with rocks and thorns like
    these?
Think'st thou that *I* thy threatening mien shall
    dread,
Or toil and pant thy waving locks to seize?

Reserve the frown severe, the menace rude,
For vassal-spirits that confess thy sway!
*My* constant soul could triumph unsubdued,
Were the wide universe destruction's prey.

Am I to conflicts new, in toils untried?
No! I have long thine utmost power defied,
And drawn fresh energies from every fight.
Thus from rude strokes of hammers and the wheel,
With each successive shock the temper'd steel
More keenly piercing proves, more dazzling bright.

## METASTASIO.

*Parlagli d' un periglio.*

Wouldst thou to Love of danger speak?—
Veil'd are his eyes, to perils blind!
Wouldst thou from Love a reason seek?—
He is a child of wayward mind!

But with a doubt, a jealous fear,
Inspire him once—the task is o'er;
His mind is keen, his sight is clear,
No more an infant, blind no more.

## METASTASIO.

*Sprezza il furor del vento.*

Unbending 'midst the wintry skies,
Rears the firm oak his vigorous form,
And stern in rugged strength defies
    The rushing of the storm;

Then sever'd from his native shore,
O'er ocean worlds the sail to bear,
Still with those winds he braved before
    He proudly struggles there.

## METASTASIO.

*Sol può dir che sia contento.*

Oh! those alone, whose sever'd hearts
Have mourn'd through lingering years in vain,
Can tell what bliss fond love imparts,
When Fate unites them once again:

Sweet is the sigh, and blest the tear,
Whose language hails that moment bright,
When past afflictions but endear
The presence of delight!

## METASTASIO.

*Ah! frenate il pianto imbelle.*

Ah! cease—those fruitless tears restrain,
I go misfortune to defy,
To smile at fate with proud disdain,
To triumph—not to die!

I with fresh laurels go to crown
My closing days at last,
Securing all the bright renown
Acquired in dangers past.

## QUEVEDO.
### ROME BURIED IN HER OWN RUINS.

*Busca en Roma a Roma, o peregrino!*

Amidst these scenes, O pilgrim! seek'st thou
    Rome?
Vain is thy search—the pomp of Rome is fled;
Her silent Aventine is glory's tomb;
Her walls, her shrines, but relics of the dead.

That hill where Cæsars dwelt in other days
Forsaken mourns, where once it tower'd sublime·
Each mouldering medal now far less displays
The triumphs won by Latium, than by Time.

Tiber alone survives—the passing wave,
That bathed her towers, now murmurs by her
    grave,
Wailing, with plaintive sound, her fallen fanes.
Rome! of thine ancient grandeur all is past,
That seem'd for years eternal framed to last
Naught but the wave, a fugitive—remains.

## EL CONDE JUAN DE TARSIS.

*Tu, que la dulce vida en tiernos anos.*

THOU, who hast fled from Life's enchanted bowers,
In youth's gay spring, in beauty's glowing morn,
Leaving thy bright array, thy path of flowers,
For the rude convent-garb, and couch of thorn;

Thou that, escaping from a world of cares,
Hast found thy haven in devotion's fane,
As to the port the fearful bark repairs,
To shun the midnight perils of the main;

Now the glad hymn, the strain of rapture pour,
While on thy soul the beams of glory rise!
For if the pilot hail the welcome shore,
With shouts of triumph swelling to the skies;
Oh! how shouldst *thou* the exulting pæan raise,
Now heaven's bright harbour opens on thy gaze.

## TORQUATO TASSO.

*Negli anni acerbi tuoi, purpurea rosa.*

THOU in thy morn wert like a glowing rose,
To the mild sunshine only half display'd,
That shunned its bashful graces to disclose,
And in its vale of verdure sought a shade;

Or like Aurora did thy charms appear,
(Since mortal form ne'er vied with aught so
  bright,)
Aurora, smiling from her tranquil sphere,
O'er vale and mountain shedding dew and light;

Now riper years have doom'd no grace to fade,
Nor youthful charms, in all their pride array'd,
Excel, or equal, thy neglected form,
Thus, full expanded, lovelier is the flower,
And the bright day-star, in its noontide hour,
More briliant shines, in genial radiance warm.

## BERNARDO TASSO.

*Quest' ombra che giammai non vide il sole.*

THIS green recess, where through the bowery
  gloom
Ne'er e'en at noontide hours the sunbeam play'd,
Where violet-beds in soft luxuriance bloom,
'Midst the cool freshness of the myrtle-shade;

Where through the grass a sparkling fountain
  steals,
Whose murmuring wave, transparent as it flows,
No more its bed of yellow sand conceals,
Than the pure crystal hides the glowing rose;

This bower of peace, thou soother of our care,
God of soft slumbers, and of visions fair!
A lowly shepherd consecrates to thee!
Then breathe around some spell of deep repose,
And charm his eyes in balmy dew to close,
Those eyes, fatigued with grief, from tear-drops
  never free.

## PETRARCH.

*Chi vuol veder quantunque puo natura.*

THOU that wouldst mark, in form of human birth
All heaven and nature's perfect skill combined,
Come gaze on her, the day-star of the earth,
Dazzling, not me alone, but all mankind:

And haste, for Death, who spares the guilty long,
First calls the brightest and the best away;
And to her home, amidst the cherub-throng,
The angelic mortal flies, and will not stay!

Haste! and each outward charm, each mental
  grace,
In one consummate form thine eye shall trace,
Model of loveliness, for earth too fair!
Then thou shalt own, how faint my votive lays,
My spirit dazzled by perfection's blaze—
But if thou still delay, for long regret prepare.

## PETRARCH

*Se lamentar augelli, o verdi fronde.*

IF to the sighing breeze of summer-hours
Bend the green leaves; if mourns a plaintive bird;
Or from some fount's cold margin, fringed with
  flowers,
The soothing murmur of the wave is heard;

Her, whom the heavens reveal, the earth denies,
I see and hear: though dwelling far above,
Her spirit, still responsive to my sighs,
Visits the lone retreat of pensive love.

"Why thus in grief consume each fruitless day,"
(Her gentle accents thus divinely say,)
"While from thine eyes the tear unceasing flows?
Weep not for me, who, hastening on my flight,
Died, to be deathless; and on Heavenly light
Whose eyes but open'd, when they seem'd to
  close!"

## VERSI SPAGNUOLI DI PIETRO BEMBO.

*O Muerte! que estas mr.*

THOU, the stern monarch of dismay,
Whom Nature trembles to survey,
Oh Death! to me, the child of grief,
Thy welcome power would bring relief,
Changing to peaceful slumber many a care.
  And though thy stroke may thrill with pain
  Each throbbing pulse, each quivering vein;
  The pangs that bid existence close,
  Ah! sure are far less keen than those
Which cloud its lingering moments with despair

## FRANCESCO LORENZINI

*O Zefiretto, che movendo vai*

SYLPH of the breeze! whose dewy pinions light
Wave gently round the tree I planted here,
Sacred to her, whose soul hath wing'd its flight
To the pure ether of her lofty sphere;

Be it thy care, soft spirit of the gale!
To fan its leaves in summer's noontide hour;
Be it thy care, that wintry tempests fell
To rend its honors from the sylvan bower.

Then shall it spread, and rear th' aspiring form,
Pride of the wood, secure from every storm
Graced with her name, a consecrated tree!
So may thy lord, the monarch of the wind,
Ne'er with rude chains by tender pinions bind,
But grant thee still to rove, a wanderer wild and
  free!

## GESSNER.

### MCRNING SONG.

*Willkommen, fruhe morgensonn.*

Hall! morning sun, thus early bright;
Welcome, sweet dawn! thou younger day!
Through the dark woods that fringe the height
    Beams forth, e'en now, the ray.

Bright on the dew, it sparkles clear,
Bright on the water's glittering fall,
And life, and joy, and health appear,
    Sweet morning! at thy call.

Now thy fresh breezes lightly spring
From beds of fragrance, where they lay,
And roving wild on dewy wing,
    Drive slumber far away.

Fantastic dreams, in swift retreat,
Now from each mind withdraw their spell,
While the young loves delighted meet,
    On Rosa's cheek to dwell.

Speed, zephyr! kiss each opening flower,
Its fragrant spirit make thine own,
Then wing thy way to Rosa's bower,
    Ere her light sleep is flown.

Then o'er her downy pillow, fly,
Wake the sweet maid to life and day;
Breathe on her balmy lip a sigh,
    And o'er her bosom play;

And whisper when her eyes unveil,
That I, since morning's earliest call,
Have sigh'd her name to every gale,
    By the lone waterfall.

### GERMAN SONG.

*Madchen, lerne! Amor kennen.*

Listen, fair maid, my song shall tell
How Love may still be known full well,
    His looks the traitor prove;
Dost thou not see that absent smile,
That fiery glance replete with guile?
    Oh! doubt not then—'t is Love.

When varying still the sly disguise,
Child of caprice, he laughs and cries,
    Or with complaint would move:
To-day is bold, to-morrow shy,
Changing each hour he knows not why,
    Oh! doubt not then—'t is Love.

There's magic in his every wile,
His lips, well practised to beguile,
    Breathe roses when they move;
See now with sudden rage he burns,
Disdains, implores, commands, by turns!
    Oh! doubt not then—'t is Love.

He comes—without the bow and dart,
That spare not e'en the purest heart;
    His looks the traitor prove;
That glance is fire, that mien is guile,
Deceit is lurking in that smile,
    Oh! trust him not—'t is Love!

## CHAULIEU.

*Grotte, d'ou sort ce clair ruisseau.*

Thou grot, whence flows this limpid spring,
Its margin fringed with moss and flowers,
Still bid its voice of murmurs bring
    Peace to my musing hours.

Sweet Fontenay! where first for me
The day-spring of existence rose,
Soon shall my dust return to thee,
    And 'midst my sires repose.

Muses, that watch'd my childhood's morn,
'Midst these wild haunts, with guardian eye,
Fair trees, that there beheld me born,
    Soon shall ye see me die.

## GARCILASO DE LA VEGA

*Coged de vuestra alegre primavera.*

Enjoy the sweets of life's luxuriant May,
Ere envious Age is hastening on its way,
With snowy wreaths to crown the beauteous brow;
The rose will fade when storms assail the year,
And Time, who changeth not his swift career,
Constant in this, will change all else below!

## LINES

#### WRITTEN IN A HERMITAGE ON THE SEA-SHORE

O wanderer! would thy heart forget
Each earthly passion and regret,
And would thy wearied spirit rise
To commune with its native skies;
Pause for awhile, and deem it sweet
To linger in this calm retreat;
And give thy cares, thy griefs, a short suspense,
Amidst wild scenes of lone magnificence.

Unmix'd with aught of meaner tone,
Here nature's voice is heard alone:
When the loud storm, in wrathful hour,
Is rushing on its wing of power,
And spirits of the deep awake,
And surges foam, and billows break,
And rocks and ocean-caves around,
Reverberate each awful sound;
That mighty voice, with all its dread control,
To loftiest thought shall wake thy thrilling soul

But when no more the sea-winds rave,
When peace is brooding on the wave,
And from earth, air, and ocean, rise
No sounds but plaintive melodies;
Soothed by their softly mingling swell,
As daylight bids the world farewell,
The rustling wood, the dying breeze,
The faint, low rippling of the seas,
A tender calm shall steal upon thy breast,
A gleam reflected from the realms of rest.

Is thine a heart the world hath stung,
Friends have deceived, neglect hath wrung?
Hast thou some grief that none may know
Some lonely, secret, silent woe?

Or have thy fond affections fled
From earth, to slumber with the dead?
Oh! pause awhile—the world disown,
And dwell with Nature's self alone!
And though no more she bids arise
Thy soul's departed energies,
And though thy joy of life is o'er,
Beyond her magic to restore;
Yet shall her spells o'er every passion steal,
And soothe the wounded heart they cannot heal!

---

### DIRGE OF A CHILD.

No bitter tears for thee be shed,
Blossom of being! seen and gone!
With flowers alone we strew thy bed,
    O blest departed One!
Whose all of life, a rosy ray,
Blush'd into dawn, and pass'd away.

Yes! thou art fled, ere guilt had power
To stain thy cherub-soul and form,
Closed is the soft ephemeral flower,
    That never felt a storm!
The sunbeam's smile, the zephyr's breath,
All that it knew from birth to death.

Thou wert so like a form of light,
That Heaven benignly called thee hence,
Ere yet the world could breathe one blight
    O'er thy sweet innocence:
And thou, that brighter home to bless,
Art pass'd with all thy loveliness!

Oh! hadst thou still on earth remain'd,
Vision of beauty! fair, as brief!
How soon thy brightness had been stain'd
    With passion or with grief!
Now not a sullying breath can rise,
To dim thy glory in the skies.

We rear no marble o'er thy tomb,
No sculptured image there shall mourn;
Ah! fitter for the vernal bloom
    Such dwelling to adorn,
Fragrance, and flowers, and dews, must be
The only emblems meet for thee.

Thy grave shall be a blessed shrine,
Adorn'd with Nature's brightest wreath,
Each glowing season shall combine
    Its incense there to breathe;
And oft, upon the midnight air,
Shall viewless harps be murmuring there.

And oh! sometimes in visions blest,
Sweet spirit! visit our repose,
And bear from thine own world of rest,
    Some balm for human woes!
What form more lovely could be given
Than thine, to messenger of heaven?

---

### INVOCATION.

Hush'd is the world in night and sleep,
Earth, Sea, and Air, are still as death;
Too rude to break a calm so deep,
    Were music's faintest breath,
Descend, bright Visions! from aërial bowers,
Descend to gild your own soft, silent hours.

In hope or fear, in toil or pain,
The weary day have mortals past,
Now, dreams of bliss, be yours to reign,
And all your spells around them cast;
Steal from their hearts the pang, their eyes the tear,
And lift the veil that hides a brighter sphere.

Oh! bear your softest balm to those,
Who fondly, vainly, mourn the dead,
To them that world of peace disclose,
    Where the bright soul is fled:

Where Love, immortal in his native clime,
Shall fear no pang from fate, no blight from time.

Or to his loved, his distant land,
On your light wings the exile bear;
To feel once more his heart expand,
In his own genial mountain-air;
Hear the wild echoes well-known strains repeat,
And bless each note, as heaven's own music sweet.

But oh! with Fancy's brightest ray,
Blest dreams! the bard's repose illume;
Bid forms of heaven around him play,
    And bowers of Eden bloom!
And waft his spirit to its native skies,
Who finds no charm in life's realities.

No voice is on the air of night,
Through folded leaves no murmurs creep,
Nor star nor moonbeam's trembling light
Falls on the placid brow of sleep.
Descend, bright visions, from your airy bower,
Dark, silent, solemn, is your favourite hour.

---

### TO THE MEMORY OF

### GENERAL SIR EDWARD PACKENHAM.

Brave spirit! mourn'd with fond regret,
Lost in life's pride, in valour's noon,
Oh! who could deem *thy* star should set
    So darkly and so soon?

Fatal, though bright, the fire of mind,
Which mark'd and closed thy brief career,
And the fair wreath, by Hope entwined,
    Lies wither'd on thy bier.

The soldier's death hath been thy doom,
The soldier's tear thy meed shall be,
Yet, son of war! a prouder tomb
    Might Fate have rear'd for thee.

*Thou* shouldst have died, O high-soul'd chief
In those bright days of glory fled,
When triumph so prevail'd o'er grief,
    We scarce could mourn the dead.

Noontide of fame! each tear-drop then
Was worthy of a warrior's grave—
When shall affection weep again
    So proudly o'er the brave?

There, on the battle-fields of Spain,
'Midst Roncesvalles' mountain-scene,
Or on Vittoria's blood-red plain,
    Meet had thy death-bed been.

We mourn not that a hero's life,
Thus in its ardent prime should close;
Hadst thou but fallen in nobler strife,
    But died 'midst conquer'd foes!

Yet hast thou still (though victory's flame
In that last moment cheer'd thee not)
Left Glory's isle another name,
    That ne'er may be forgot:

And many a tale of triumph won
Shall breathe that name in Memory's ear
And long may England mourn a son
    *Without reproach or fear.*

---

### TO THE MEMORY OF

### SIR HENRY E—LL—S

#### WHO FELL IN THE BATTLE OF WATERLOO

Happy are they who die in their youth, when their renown<br>
    around them.'—Ossian.

Weep'st thou for him whose doom was seal'd
On England's proudest battle-field?
For him, the lion-heart, who died
In victory's full, resistless tide?
    Oh! mourn him not,

By deeds like his that field was won,
And Fate could yield to Valor's son
    No brighter lot.

He heard his band's exulting cry,
He saw the vanquish'd eagles fly;
And envied be his death of fame,
It shed a sunbeam o'er his name, ·
    That naught shall dim—
No cloud obscured his glory's day,
It saw no twilight of decay—
    Weep not for him!

And breathe no dirge's plaintive moan,
A hero claims far loftier tone!
Oh! proudly should the war-song swell,
Recording how the mighty fell
    In that dread hour,
When England, 'midst the battle-storm,
Th' avenging angel—rear'd her form
    In tenfold power.

Yet, gallant heart! to swell thy praise,
Vain were the minstrel's noblest lays;
Since he, the soldier's guiding-star,
The victor-chief, the lord of war,
    Has own'd thy fame!
And oh! like *his* approving word,
What trophied marble could record
    A warrior's name?

---

## GUERILLA SONG

Founded on the story related of the Spanish Patriot, Mina.

Oh! forget not the hour, when through forest and
    vale,
We return'd with our chief to his dear native halls;
Through the woody Sierra there sigh'd not a gale,
And the moonbeam was bright on his battlement-
    walls:
And Nature lay sleeping, in calmness and light,
Round the home of the valiant, that rose on our
    sight.

We enter'd that home—all was loneliness round,
The stillness, the darkness, the peace of the grave;
Not a voice, not a step, bade its echoes resound,
Ah. such was the welcome that waited the brave!
For the spoilers had pass'd, like the poison-wind's
    breath,
And the loved of his bosom lay silent in death.

Oh! forget not that hour—let its image be near,
In the light of our mirth, in the dreams of our rest,
Let its tale awake feelings too deep for a tear,
And rouse into vengeance each arm and each
    breast,
Till cloudless the day-spring of liberty shine
O'er the plains of the olive, and hills of the vine

---

## THE AGED INDIAN

WARRIORS! my noon of life is past,
The brightness of my spirit flown;
I crouch before the wintry blast,
Amidst my tribe I dwell alone:
The heroes of my youth are fled,
They rest among the warlike dead.

Ye slumberers of the narrow cave!
My kindred-chiefs in days of yore,
Ye fill an unremember'd grave,
Your fame, your deeds, are known no more
The records of your wars are gone,
Your names forgot by all but one.

Soon shall that one depart from earth,
To join the brethren of his prime;
Then will the memory of your birth
Sleep with the hidden things of time!
With him, ye sons of former days!
Fades the last glimmering of your praise.

His eyes, that hail'd your spirit's flame,
Still kindling in the combat's shock,
Have seen, since darkness veil'd your fame,
Sons of the desert and the rock!
Another, and another race,
Rise to the battle, and the chase.

Descendants of the mighty dead!
Fearless of heart, and firm of hand!
Oh! let me join their spirits fled,
Oh! send me to their shadowy land. ·
Age hath not tamed Ontara's heart,
He shrinks not from the friendly dart.

These feet no more can chase the deer,
The glory of this arm is flown—
Why should the feeble linger here,
When all the pride of life is gone?
Warriors! why still the stroke deny,
Think ye Ontara fears to die?

He fear'd not in his flower of days,
When strong to stem the torrent's force,
When through the desert's pathless maze
His way was as an eagle's course!
When war was sunshine to his sight,
And the wild hurricane, delight!

Shall then the warrior tremble *now*?
Now when his envied strength is o'er?
Hung on the pine his idle bow,
His pirogue useless on the shore?
When death hath dimm'd his failing eye,
Shall he, the joyless, fear to die?

Sons of the brave! delay no more,
The spirits of my kindred call!
'T is but one pang, and all is o'er!
Oh! bid the aged cedar fall!
To join the brethren of his prime,
The mighty of departed time.

## EVENING AMONGST THE ALPS.

---

SOFT skies of Italy! how richly drest,
Smile these wild scenes in your purpureal glow;
What glorious hues, reflected from the west,
Float o'er the dwellings of eternal snow!

Yon torrent, foaming down the granite steep,
Sparkles all brilliance in the setting beam;
Dark glens beneath in shadowy beauty sleep,
Where pipes the goat-herd by his mountain-stream

Now from yon peak departs the vivid ray,
That still at eve its lofty temple knows;
From rock and torrent fade the tints away,
And all is wrapt in twilight's deep repose;
While through the pine-wood gleams the vesper
    star,
And roves the Alpine gale o'er solitudes afar.

---

## DIRGE OF THE HIGHLAND CHIEF IN
## "WAVERLEY."

---

Son of the mighty and the free!
High-minded leader of the brave!
Was it for lofty chief like thee,
    To fill a nameless grave?
Oh! if, amidst the valiant slain,
The warrior's bier had been thy lot,
E'en though on red Culloden's plain,
    We then had mourn'd thee not

But darkly closed thy dawn of fame,
That dawn whose sunbeam rose so fair;
Vengeance alone may breathe thy name,
    The watchword of Despair!
Yet oh! if gallant spirit's power
Had e'er ennobled death like thine,
Then glory mark'd *thy* parting hour,
    Last of a mighty line!

O'er thy own towers the sunshine falls,
But cannot chase their silent gloom;
Those beams, that gild thy native walls,
　　Are sleeping on thy tomb;
Spring on thy mountains laughs the while,
Thy green woods wave in vernal air,
But the loved scenes may vainly smile—
　　Not e'en thy dust is there.

On thy blue hills no bugle-sound
Is mingling with the torrent's roar,
Unmark'd the wild deer sport around—
　　Thou lead'st the chase no more!
Thy gates are closed, thy halls are still,
Those halls where peal'd the choral strain,
They hear the wind's deep murmuring thrill—
　　And all is hush'd again.

No banner from the lonely tower
Shall wave its blazon'd folds on high;
There the tall grass and summer flower
　　Unmark'd shall spring and die.
No more thy bard, for other ear,
Shall wake the harp once loved by thine—
Hush'd be the strain thou canst not hear,
　　Last of a mighty line!

## THE CRUSADER'S WAR-SONG

Chieftains, lead on! our hearts beat high,
　　Lead on to Salem's towers!
Who would not deem it bliss to die,
　　Slain in a cause like ours?
The brave who sleep in soil of thine,
Lie not entomb'd, but shrined, O Palestine;

Souls of the slain in holy war!
　　Look from your sainted rest!
Tell us ye rose in Glory's car,
　　To mingle with the blest;
Tell us how short the death-pang's power,
How bright the joys of your immortal bower

Strike the loud harp, ye minstrel train!
　　Pour forth your loftiest lays;
Each heart shall echo to the strain
　　Breathed in the warrior's praise.
Bid every string triumphant swell
Th' inspiring sounds that heroes love so well,

Salem! amidst the fiercest hour
　　The wildest rage of fight,
Thy name shall lend our falchions power,
　　And nerve our hearts with might,
Envied be those for thee that fall,
Who find their graves beneath thy sacred wall.

For them no need that sculptured tomb
　　Should chronicle their fame,
Or Pyramid record their doom.
　　Or deathless verse their name;
It is enough that dust of thine
Should shroud their forms, O blessed Palestine!

Chieftains, lead on! our hearts beat high
　　For combat's glorious hour;
Soon shall the red-cross banner fly
　　On Salem's loftiest tower!
We burn to mingle in the strife,
Where but to die insures eternal life



It was in the battle of Sheriffmoor that young Clanronald fell, leading on the Highlanders of the right wing, His death dispirited the assailants, who began to waver. But Glengary, chief of a rival branch of the Clan Colla, started from the ranks, and, waving his bonnet round his head, cried out, "To-day for revenge and to-morrow for mourning!" The Highlanders received a new impulse from his words, and, charging with redoubled fury, bore down all before them.—See the Quarterly Review, article of "Culloden Papers."

On! ne'er be Clanronald the valiant forgot!
Still fearless and first in the combat, he fell;
But we paused not one tear-drop to shed o'er the
　　spot,
We spared not one moment to murmur "Farewell."
We heard but the battle-word given by the chief,
"To-day for revenge, and to-morrow for grief!"

And wildly, Clanronald! we echoed the vow,
With the tear on our cheek, and the sword in our
　　hand;
Young son of the brave! we may weep for thee
　　now,
For well has thy death been avenged by thy band,
When they join'd in wild chorus the cry of the
　　chief,
"To-day for revenge, and to-morrow for grief!"

Thy dirge in that hour, was the bugle's wild call,
The clash of the claymore, the shout of the brave
But now thy own bard may lament for thy fall,
And the soft voice of melody sigh o'er thy grave,
While Albyn remembers the words of the chief,
"To-day for revenge, and to-morrow for grief!"

Thou art fallen, O fearless one! flower of thy race
Descendant of heroes! thy glory is set!
But thy kindred, the sons of the battle and chase,
Have proved that thy spirit is bright in them yet!
Nor vainly have echoed the words of the chief,
"To-day for revenge, and to-morrow for grief!"

## TO THE EYE.

Throne of expression! whence the spirit's ray
Pours forth so oft the light of mental day,
Where fancy's fire, affection's melting beam,
Thought, genius, passion, reign in turn supreme,
And many a feeling, words can ne'er impart,
Finds its own language to pervade the heart;
Thy power, bright orb, what bosom hath not felt,
To thrill, to rouse, to fascinate, to melt?
And by some spell of undefined control,
With magnet-influence touch the secret soul!

Light of the features! in the morn of youth
Thy glance is nature, and thy language, truth;
And ere the world, with all-corrupting sway,
Hath taught e'en *thee* to flatter and betray,
Th' ingenuous heart forbids thee to reveal,
Or speak one thought that interest would conceal;
While yet thou seem'st the cloudless mirror, given
But to reflect the purity of heaven;
Oh! then how lovely, there unveil'd to trace
Th' unsullied brightness of each mental grace

When genius lends thee all his living light,
Where the full beams of intellect unite,
When love illumes thee with his varying ray,
Where trembling Hope and tearful Rapture play;
Or Pity's melting cloud thy beam subdues,
Tempering its lustre with a vale of dews;
Still does thy power, whose all-commanding spell
Can pierce the mazes of the soul so well,
Bid some new feeling to existence start,
From its deep slumbers in the inmost heart.

And oh! when thought, in ecstasy sublime,
That soars triumphant o'er the bounds of time,
Fires thy keen glance with inspiration's blaze,
The light of heaven, the hope of nobler days,
(As glorious dreams, for utterance far too high,
Flash through the mist of dim mortality;)
Who does not own, that through thy lightning
    beams
A flame unquenchable, unearthly, streams?
That pure, though captive effluence of the sky,
The vestal-ray, the spark that cannot die;

---

## THE HERO'S DEATH

Life's parting beams were in his eye,
Life's closing accents on his tongue,
When round him, pealing to the sky,
    The shout of victory rung!
Then, ere his gallant spirit fled,
A smile so bright illumed his face—
Oh! never, of the light it shed,
    Shall memory lose a trace!

His was a death, whose rapture high
Transcended all that life could yield;
His warmest prayer was so to die,
    On the red battle-field!
And they may feel, who loved him most,
A pride so holy and so pure—
Fate hath no power o'er those who boast
    A treasure thus secure!

## STANZAS

*On the late National Calamity, the Death of the
Princess Charlotte.*

"Helas! nous composions son histoire de tout ce
qu'on peut imaginer de plus glorieux——Le passe et le
present nous garantissoient l'avenir——T'elle etoit l'agre-
able histoire que nous fuisions; et pour achever ces
nobles projets, il n'y avoit que la duree de sa vie; dont
nous ne croyons pas devoir etre en peine, car, qui eut pu
seulement penser, que les annees eussent du manquer a
un jeunesse qui sembloit si vive?"——*Bossuet.*

---

### I.

Mark'd ye the mingling of the city's throng,
Each mien, each glance, with expectation bright?
Prepare the pageant and the choral song,
The pealing chimes, the blaze of festal light
And hark! what rumour's gathering sound is nigh?
Is it the voice of joy, that murmur deep?
Away, be hush'd! ye sounds of revelry!
Back to your homes, ye multitudes, to weep!
Weep! for the storm hath o'er us darkly past,
And England's royal flower is broken by the blast!

### II.

Was it a dream? so sudden and so dread
That awful fiat o'er our senses came!
So loved, so blest, is that young spirit fled,
Whose early grandeur promised years of fame?
Oh! when hath life possess'd, or death destroy'd,
More lovely hopes, more cloudlessly that smiled?
When hath the spoiler left so dark a void!
For all is lost—the mother and her child!
Our morning-star hath vanish'd, and the tomb
Throws its deep-lengthen'd shade o'er distant
    years to come.

### III.

Angel of Death! did no presaging sign
Announce thy coming, and thy way prepare?
No warning voice, no harbinger, was thine,
Danger and fear seem'd past—but thou wert there!
Prophetic sounds along the earthquake's path
Foretell the hour of Nature's awful throes;
And the volcano, ere it burst in wrath,
Sends forth some herald from its dread repose:
But *thou*, dark Spirit! swift and unforeseen,
Cam'st like the lightning's flash, when heaven is
    all serene.

### IV.

And she is gone—the royal and the young,
In soul commanding, and in heart benign;
Who, from a race of Kings and Heroes sprung,
Glow'd with a spirit lofty as her line.
Now may the voice she loved on earth so well,
Breathe forth her name, unheeded and in vain;
Nor can those eyes on which her own would dwell
Wake from the breast one sympathy again:
The ardent heart, the towering mind are fled,
Yet shall undying love still linger with the dead.

### V.

Oh! many a bright existence we have seen
Quench'd in the glow and fullness of its prime;
And many a cherish'd flower, ere now, hath been
Cropt, ere its leaves were breathed upon by time
We have lost Heroes in their noon of pride,
Whose fields of triumph gave them but a bier;
And we have wept when soaring Genius died,
Check'd in the glory of his mid career!
But here our hopes were centred—all is o'er,
All thought in this absorb'd—she was—and is no
    more!

### VI.

We watch'd her childhood from its earliest hour,
From every word and look blest omens caught;
While that young mind developed all its power,
An I rose to energies of loftiest thought.
On her was fix'd the Patriot's ardent eye,
One hope still bloom'd—one vista still was fair;
And when the tempest swept the troubled sky,
She was our day-spring—all was cloudless *there;*
And oh! how lovely broke on England's gaze,
E'en through the mist and storm, the light of dis-
    tant days.

### VII.

Now hath one moment darken'd future years,
And changed the track of ages yet to be!—
Yet, mortal! 'midst the bitterness of tears,
Kneel, and adore th' inscrutable decree!
Oh! while the clear perspective smiled in light,
Wisdom should *then* have temper'd hope's excess,
And, lost One! when we saw thy lot so bright,
We might have trembled at its loveliness,
Joy is no earthly flower—nor framed to bear,
In its exotic bloom, life's cold, ungenial air.

### VIII.

All smiled around thee—Youth, and Love, and
    Praise,
Hearts all devotion and all truth were thine!
On thee was riveted a nation's gaze,
As on some radiant and unsullied shrine.
Heiress of empires! thou art pass'd away,
Like some fair vision that arose to throw,
O'er one brief hour of life, a fleeting ray,
Then leave the rest to solitude and woe!
Oh! who shall dare to woo such dreams again!
Who hath not wept to know, that tears for thee
    were vain!

### IX.

Yet there is one who loved thee—and whose soul
With mild affections nature form'd to melt;
His mind hath bow'd beneath the stern control
Of many a grief—but *this* shall be unfelt!
Years have gone by—and given his honor'd head
A diadem of snow—his eye is dim—
Around him Heaven a solemn cloud hath spread,

The past, the future, are a dream to him!
Yet in the darkness of his fate, alone
He dwells on earth, while thou, in life's full pride,
    art gone!

### X.

The Chastener's hand is on us—we may weep,
But not repine—for many a storm hath past,
And, pillow'd on her own majestic deep,
Hath England slept, unshaken by the blast!
And war hath raged o'er many a distant plain,
Trampling the vine and olive in his path;
While she, that regal daughter of the main,
Smiled, in serene defiance of his wrath;
As some proud summit, mingling with the sky,
Hears calmly far below the thunders roll and die.

### XI.

Her voice hath been th' awakener—and her name,
The gathering-word of nations—in her might
And all the awful beauty of her fame,
Apart she dwelt, in solitary light.
High on her cliffs, alone and firm she stood,
Fixing the torch upon her beacon-tower;
That torch, whose flame, far streaming o'er the
    flood,
Hath guided Europe through her darkest hour!—
Away, vain dreams of glory! in the dust
Be humbled, ocean-queen! and own thy sentence
    just!

### XII.

Hark! 't was the death-bell's note! which full and
    deep,
Unmix'd with aught of less majestic tone,
While all the murmurs of existence sleep,
Swells on the stillness of the air alone!
Silent, the throngs that fill the darken'd street,
Silent, the slumbering Thames, the lonely mart;
And all is still, where countless thousands meet,
Save the full throbbing of the awe-struck heart!
All deeply, strangely, fearfully serene,
As in each ravaged home th' avenging one had
    been.

### XIII.

The sun goes down in beauty—his farewell,
Unlike the world he leaves, is calmly bright:
And his last mellow'd rays around us dwell,
Lingering, as if on scenes of young delight.
They smile and fade—but when the day is o'er,
What slow procession moves, with measured
    tread?—
Lo! those who weep, with her who weeps no more,
A solemn train—the mourners and the dead!
While, throned on high, the moon's untroubled ray
Looks down, as earthly hopes are passing thus
    away.

### XIV.

But other light is in that holy pile,
Where, in the house of silence, kings repose;
There, through the dim arcade, and pillar'd aisle,
The funeral-torch its deep-red radiance throws.
There pall, and canopy, and sacred strain,
And all around the stamp of woe may bear;
But Grief, to whose full heart those forms are vain,
Grief unexpress'd, unsoothed by them—is there.
No darker hour hath Fate for him who mourns,
Than when the all he loved, as dust to dust, re-
    turns.

### XV.

We mourn—but not thy fate, departed One!
We pity—but the living, not the dead;
A cloud hangs o'er us—" the bright day is done,"*
And with a father's hopes, a nation's fled,
And he, the chosen of thy youthful breast,
Whose soul with thine had mingled every thought,
He, with thine early, fond affections blest,
Lord of a mind with all things lovely fraught;
What but a desert to his eye, that earth,
Which but retains of thee, the memory of thy
    worth?

*" The bright day is done,
    And we are for the dark."——Shakspeare.

### XVI.

Oh! there are griefs for nature too intense,
Whose first rude shock but stupefies the soul;
Nor hath the fragile and o'erlabour'd sense
Strength e'en to feel at once their dread control.
But when 't is past, that still and speechless hour
Of the seal'd bosom, and the tearless eye,
Then the roused mind awakes, with tenfold power,
To grasp the fullness of its agony!
Its death-like torpor vanish'd—and its doom,
To cast its own dark hues o'er life and nature's
    bloom.

### XVII.

And such his lot, whom thou hast loved and left,
Spirit! thus early to thy home recall'd!
So sinks the heart, of hope and thee bereft,
A warrior's heart! by danger ne'er appall'd.
Years may pass on—and, as they roll along,
Mellow those pangs which now his bosom rend;
And he once more, with life's unheeding throng,
May, though alone in soul, in seeming blend;
Yet still, the guardian-angel of his mind,
Shall thy loved image dwell, in Memory's temple
    shrined.

### XVIII.

Yet must the days be long ere time shall steal
Aught from his grief, whose spirit dwells with
    thee;
Once deeply bruised, the heart at length may heal,
But all it was—oh! never more shall be—
The flower, the leaf, o'erwhelm'd by winter-snow,
Shall spring again, when beams and showers re-
    turn;
The faded cheek again with health may glow,
And the dim eye with life's warm radiance burn;
But the pure freshness of the mind's young bloom,
Once lost, revives alone in worlds beyond the
    tomb.

### XIX.

But thou—thine hour of agony is o'er,
And thy brief race in brilliance hath been run,
While Faith, that bids fond nature grieve no more,
Tells that thy crown—though not on earth—is
    won.
Thou, of the world so early left, hast known
Naught but the bloom and sunshine—and for thee
Child of propitious stars! for thee alone,
The course of love ran smooth,* and brightly free—
Not long such bliss to mortal could be given,
It is enough for earth, to catch one glimpse of
    heaven.

### XX.

What though, ere yet the noonday of thy fame
Rose in its glory on thine England's eye,
The grave's deep shadows o'er thy spirit came?
Ours is that loss—and thou wert blest to die!
Thou might'st have lived to dark and evil years,
To mourn thy people changed, thy skies o'ercast;
But thy spring-morn was all undimm'd by tears,
And thou wert loved and cherish'd to the last!
And thy young name, ne'er breathed in ruder tone,
Thus dying, thou hast left to love and grief alone.

### XXI.

Daughter of Kings! from that high sphere look
    down,
Where still in hope, affection's thoughts may rise,
Where dimly shines to thee that mortal crown,
Which earth display'd to claim thee from the skies.
Look down! and if thy spirit yet retain
Memory of aught that once was fondly dear,
Soothe, though unseen, the hearts that mourn in
    vain,
And, in their hours of loneliness—be near!
Blest was thy lot e'en here—and one faint sigh,
Oh! tell those hearts, hath made that bliss eternity!

*" The course of true love never did run smooth."——Shakspeare

# The Sceptic,

## A POEM.

---

*Leur raison, qu'ils prennent pour guide, ne présente à leur esprit que des conjectures et des embarras ; les absurdités où ils tombent en niant la Religion deviennent plus insoutenables que les vérités dont la hauteur les étonne ; et pour ne vouloir pas croire des mystères incompréhensibles, ils suivent l'une après l'autre d'incompréhensibles erreurs."—Bossuet, Oraisons Funèbres.*

When the young Eagle, with exulting eye,
Has learn'd to dare the splendour of the sky,
And leave the Alps beneath him in his course,
To bathe his crest in morn's empyreal source,
Will his free wing, from that majestic height,
Descend to follow some wild meteor's light,
Which far below, with evanescent fire,
Shines to delude, and dazzles to expire?

No! still through clouds he wins his upward way,
And proudly claims his heritage of day!
—And shall the spirit on whose ardent gaze,
The day-spring from on high hath pour'd its blaze,
Turn from that pure effulgence, to the beam
Of earth-born light, that sheds a treacherous
      gleam,
Luring the wanderer from a star of faith,
To the deep valley of the shades of death?
What bright exchange, what treasure shall be
      given,
For the high birth-right of its hope in Heaven?
If lost the gem which empires could not buy,
What yet remains?—a dark eternity!

Is earth still Eden!—might a seraph guest,
Still, 'midst its chosen bowers, delighted rest?
Is all so cloudless and so calm below,
We seek no fairer scenes than *life* can show?
That the cold Sceptic, in his pride elate,
Rejects the promise of a brighter state,
And leaves the rock, no tempest shall displace,
To rear his dwelling on the quicksand's base?

Votary of doubt! then join the festal throng,
Bask in the sunbeam, listen to the song,
Spread the rich hoard, and fill the wine-cup high,
And bind the wreath ere yet the roses die!
'Tis well, thine eye is yet undimm'd by time,
And thy heart bounds, exulting in its prime;
Smile then unmoved at Wisdom's warning voice,
And, in the glory of thy strength, rejoice!

But life hath sterner tasks; e'en youth's brief
      hours
Survive the beauty of their loveliest flowers;
The founts of joy, where pilgrims rest from toil,
Are few and distant on the desert soil:
The soul's pure flame the breath of storms must fan,
And pain and sorrow claim their nursling—Man!
Earth's noblest sons the bitter cup have shared—
Proud child of reason, how art *thou* prepared?
When years, with silent might, thy frame have
      bow'd,
And o'er thy spirit cast their wintry cloud,
Will Memory soothe thee on thy bed of pain,
With the bright images of pleasure's train?
Yes! as the sight of some far distant shore,
Whose well-known scenes his foot shall tread no
      more,
Would cheer the seaman, by the eddying wave
Drawn, vainly struggling, to th' unfathom'd grave!
Shall Hope, the faithful cherub, hear thy call,
She, who like heaven's own sunbeam, smiles for
      all?
Will *she* speak comfort?—Thou hast shorn her
      plume,
That might have raised thee far above the tomb,
And hush'd the only voice whose angel tone
Soothes when all melodies of joy are flown!

For she was born beyond the stars to soar,
And kindling at the source of life, adore;
Thou couldst not, mortal! rivet to the earth
Her eye, whose beam is of celestial birth:

She dwells with those who leave her pinion free,
And sheds the dews of heav'n on all but thee.

Yet few there are, so lonely, so bereft,
But some true heart, that beats to theirs, is left,
And, haply, one whose strong affection's power
Unchanged may triumph through misfortune's hour
Still with fond care supports thy languid head,
And keeps unwearied vigils by thy bed.

But thou! whose thoughts have no blest home
      above,
Captive of earth! and canst thou dare to *love?*
To nurse such feelings as delight to rest,
Within that hallow'd shrine—a parent's breast,
To fix each hope, concentrate every tie,
On one frail idol,—destined but to die,
Yet mock the faith that points to worlds of light,
Where sever'd souls, made perfect, reunite?
Then tremble! cling to every passing joy,
Twined with the life a moment may destroy!
If there be sorrow in a parting tear,
Still let "*for ever*" vibrate on thine ear!
If some bright hour on rapture's wing hath flown,
Find more than anguish in the thought—'t is gone
Go! to a voice such magic influence give,
Thou canst not lose its melody, and live;
And make an eye the lode-star of thy soul,
And let a glance the springs of thought control;
Gaze on a mortal form with fond delight,
Till the fair vision mingles with thy sight;
There seek thy blessings, there repose thy trust,
Lean on the willow, idolize the dust!
Then, when thy treasure best repays thy care,
Think on that dread "*for ever*"—and despair!

And oh! no strange, unwonted storm there
      needs,
To wreck at once thy fragile ark of reeds,
Watch well its course—explore with anxious eye
Each little cloud that floats along the sky—
Is the blue canopy serenely fair?
Yet may the thunderbolt unseen be there,
And the bark sink, when peace and sunshine
      sleep
On the smooth bosom of the waveless deep!
Yes! ere a sound, a sign, announce thy fate,
May the blow fall which makes thee desolate!
Not always Heaven's destroying angel shrouds
His awful form in tempests and in clouds;
He fills the summer-air with latent power,
He hides his venom in the scented flower,
He steals upon thee, in the Zephyr's breath,
And festal garlands veil the shafts of death!

Where art thou *then*, who thus didst rashly cast
Thine all upon the mercy of the blast,
And vainly hope the tree of life to find
Rooted in sands that flit before the wind?
Is not that earth thy spirit loved so well,
It would not in a brighter sphere to dwell,
Become a desert *now*, a veil of gloom,
O'ershadow'd with the midnight of the tomb?
Where shalt thou turn?—it is not thine to raise
To you pure heaven thy calm confiding gaze.
No gleam reflected from that realm of rest
Steals on the darkness of thy troubled breast,
Not for thine eye shall faith divinely shed
Her glory round the image of the dead;
And if, when slumber's lonely couch is prest,
The form departed be thy spirit's guest,
It bears no light from purer worlds to this;
The future lends not e'en a dream of bliss.

But who shall dare the Gate of Life to close,
Or say, *thus far* the stream of mercy flows?
That fount unseal'd, whose boundless waves em-
      brace
Each distant isle, and visit every race,
Pours from the Throne of God its current free,
Nor yet denies th' immortal draught to thee.
Oh! while the doom impends, nor yet decreed,
While yet th' Atoner hath not ceased to plead,
While still, suspended by a single hair,
The sharp bright sword hangs quivering in the air,
Bow down thy heart to Him, who will not break
The bruised reed; e'en yet, awake, awake!

Patient, because Eternal, (1) He may hear
Thy prayer of agony with pitying ear,
And send his chastening spirit from above,
O'er the deep chaos of thy soul to move.

But seek thou mercy through His name alone,
To whose unequall'd sorrows none was shown,
Through Him, who here in mortal garb abode,
As man to suffer, and to heal as God!
And, born the sons of utmost time to bless,
Endured all scorn, and aided all distress.

Call thou on Him—for He, in human form,
Hath walk'd the waves of Life, and still'd the
	storm,
He, when her hour of lingering grace was past,
O'er Salem wept, relenting to the last,
Wept with such tears as Judah's monarch pour'd
O'er his lost child, ungrateful, yet deplored;
And, offering guiltless blood that guilt might live,
Taught from his Cross the lesson—to forgive!

Call thou on Him—his prayer e'en then arose,
Breathed in unpitied anguish, for his foes.
And haste!—ere bursts the lightning from on high
Fly to the City of thy refuge, fly! (2)
So shall the Avenger turn his steps away,
And sheathe his falchion, baffled of its prey.

Yet must long days roll on, ere peace shall brood,
As the soft Halcyon, o'er thy heart subdued;
Ere yet the dove of Heaven descend, to shed
Inspiring influence o'er thy fallen head.
—He who hath pined in dungeons, 'midst the shade
Of such deep night as man for man hath made,
Through lingering years; if call'd at length to be
Once more, by nature's boundless charter, free,
Shrinks feebly back, the blaze of noon to shun,
Fainting at day, and blasted by the sun!
Thus, when the captive soul hath long remain'd
In its own dread abyss of darkness chain'd,
If the Deliverer, in his might at last,
Its fetters, born of earth, to earth should cast,
The beam of truth o'erpowers its dazzled sight,
Trembling it sinks, and finds no joy in light.
But this will pass away—that spark of mind,
Within thy frame unquenchably enshrined,
Shall live to triumph in its brightening ray,
Born to be foster'd with ethereal day.
Then wilt thou bless the hour, when o'er thee
	pass'd,
On wing of flame, the purifying blast,
And sorrow's voice, through paths before untrod,
Like Sinai's trumpet, call'd thee to thy God!

But hop'st thou, in thy panoply of pride,
Heaven's messenger, affliction, to deride?
In thine own strength unaided to defy,
With Stoic smile, the arrows of the sky?
Torn by the vulture, fetter'd to the rock,
Still, Demigod! the tempest wilt thou mock?
Alas! the tower that crests the mountain's brow
A thousand years may awe the vale below,
Yet not the less be shatter'd on its height,
By one dread moment of the earthquake's might!
A thousand pangs thy bosom may have borne,
In silent fortitude, or haughty scorn,
Till comes the one, the master-anguish, sent
To break the mighty heart that ne'er was bent.

Oh! what is nature's strength? the vacant eye,
By mind deserted, hath a dread reply!
The wild delirious laughter of despair,
The mirth of frenzy—seek an answer there!
Turn not away, though pity's cheek grow pale,
Close not thine ear against their awful tale.
They tell thee, reason, wandering from the ray
Of Faith, the blazing pillar of her way,
In the mid-darkness of the stormy wave,
Forsook the struggling soul she could not save!
Weep not, sad moralist! o'er desert plains,
Strew'd with the wrecks of grandeur—mouldering
	fanes,
Arches of triumph, long with weeds o'ergrown,
And regal cities, now the serpent's own:
Earth has more awful ruins—one lost mind,
Whose star is quench'd, hath lessons for mankind

Of deeper import than each prostrate dome,
Mingling its marble with the dust of Rome.

But who with eye unshrinking shall explore
That waste, illumed by reason's beam no more?
Who pierce the deep, mysterious clouds that roll
Around the shatter'd temple of the soul,
Curtain'd with midnight?—low its columns lie,
And dark the chambers of its imag'ry, (3)
Sunk are its idols now—and God alone
May rear the fabric by their fall o'erthrown!
Yet from its inmost shrine, by storms laid bare,
Is heard an oracle that cries—" Beware!
Child of the dust! but ransom'd of the skies!
One breath of Heaven—and thus thy glory dies!
Haste, ere the hour of doom, draw nigh to Him
Who dwells above between the cherubim!"

Spirit dethroned! and check'd in mid career,
Son of the morning! exiled from thy sphere,
Tell us thy tale!—Perchance thy race was run
With science, in the chariot of the sun;
Free as the winds the paths of space to sweep,
Traverse the untrodden kingdoms of the deep,
And search the laws that Nature's springs control
There tracing all—save Him who guides the whole.

Haply thine eye its ardent glance had cast
Through the dim shades, the portals of the past;
By the bright lamp of thought thy care had fed
From the far beacon-lights of ages fled,
The depth of time exploring, to retrace
The glorious march of many a vanish'd race.

Or did thy power pervade the living lyre,
Till its deep chords became instinct with fire,
Silenced all meaner notes, and swell'd on high,
Full and alone, their mighty harmony,
While woke each passion from its cell profound,
And nations started at th' electric sound?

Lord of th' Ascendant! what avails it now,
Though bright the laurels waved upon thy brow?
What, though thy name, through distant empires
	heard,
Bade the heart bound as doth a battle-word?
Was it for this thy still unwearied eye
Kept vigil with the watch-fires of the sky,
To make the secrets of all ages thine,
And commune with majestic thoughts that shine
O'er Time's long shadowy pathway?—hath thy
	mind
Sever'd its lone dominions from mankind,
For *this* to woo their homage?—Thou hast sought
All, save the wisdom with salvation fraught,
Won every wreath—but that which will not die,
Nor aught neglected—save eternity!

And did all fail thee, in the hour of wrath,
When burst th' o'erwhelming vials on thy path?
Could not the voice of Fame inspire thee then,
O spirit! sceptred by the sons of men,
With an Immortal's courage to sustain
The transient agonies of earthly pain?

—One, one there was, all-powerful to have saved
When the loud fury of the billow raved;
But Him thou knew'st not—and the light he lent
Hath vanish'd from its ruin'd tenement,
But left thee breathing, moving, lingering yet,
A thing we shrink from—vainly to forget;
Lift the dread veil no further—hide, oh! hide
The bleeding form, the couch of suicide!
The dagger grasp'd in death—the brow, the eye,
Lifeless, yet stamp'd with rage and agony;
The soul's dark traces left in many a line
Graved on *his* mien, who died,—" and made no
	sign!"
Approach not, gaze not—lest thy fever'd brain
Too deep that image of despair retain;
Angels of slumber! o'er the midnight hour,
Let not such visions claim unhallow'd power,
Lest the mind sink with terror, and above
See but th' Avenger's arm, forgot th' Atoner's love!

O Thou ! th' unseen, th' all-seeing !—Thou whose
 ways
Mantled with darkness, mock all finite gaze,
Before whose eyes the creatures of Thy hand,
Seraph and man, alike in weakness stand,
And countless ages, trampling into clay
Earth's empires on their march, are but a day ;
Father of worlds unknown, unnumber'd—Thou,
With whom all time is one eternal *now*,
Who know'st no past, nor future—Thou whose
 breath
Goes forth, and bears to myriads, life or death !
Look on us, guide us !—wanderers of a sea
Wild and obscure, what are we, reft of Thee !
A thousand rocks, deep-hid, elude our sight,
A star may set—and we are lost in night ;
A breeze may waft us to the whirlpool's brink,
A treach'rous song allure us—and we sink !

Oh ! by *His* love, who, veiling Godhead's light,
To moments circumscribed the Infinite,
And Heaven and Earth disdain'd not to ally
By that dread union—Man with Deity ;
Immortal tears o'er mortal woes who shed,
And, ere he raised them, wept above the dead ;
Save, or we perish !—let Thy word control
The earthquakes of that universe—the soul ;
Pervade the depths of passion—speak once more
The mighty mandate, guard of every shore,
"Here shall thy waves be stay'd"—in grief, in pain,
The fearful poise of reason's sphere maintain,
Thou, by whom suns are balanced !—thus secure
In Thee shall Faith and Fortitude endure ;
Conscious of Thee, unfaltering shall the just
Look upward still, in high and holy trust,
And, by affliction guided to Thy shrine,
The first, last thought of suffering hearts be Thine.

And oh ! be near, when clothed with conquering
 power,
The King of Terrors claims his own dread hour :
When on the edge of that unknown abyss,
Which darkly parts us from the realm of bliss,
Awe-struck alike the timid and the brave,
Alike subdued the monarch and the slave,
Must drink the cup of trembling (4)—when we see
Naught in the universe but death and Thee,
Forsake us not ;—if still, when life was young,
Faith to Thy bosom, as her home, hath sprung,
If Hope's retreat hath been, through all the past,
The shadow by the Rock of Ages cast,
Father, forsake us not !—when tortures urge
The shrinking soul to that mysterious verge,
When from Thy justice to Thy love we fly,
On Nature's conflict look with pitying eye,
Bid the strong wind, the fire, the earthquake cease,
Come in the still small voice, and whisper—
 peace ! (5)

For oh ! 'tis awful—He that hath beheld
The parting spirit, by its fears repell'd,
Cling in weak terror to its earthly chain,
And from the dizzy brink recoil, in vain ;
He that hath seen the last convulsive throe
Dissolve the union form'd and closed in woe,
Well knows, that hour is awful.—In the pride
Of youth and health, by sufferings yet untried,
We talk of Death, as something, which 'twere
 sweet
In Glory's arms exultingly to meet,
A closing triumph, a majestic scene,
Where gazing nations watch the hero's mien,
As, undismay'd amidst the tears of all,
He folds his mantle, regally to fall !

Hush, fond enthusiast !—still, obscure, and lone,
Yet not less terrible because unknown,
Is the last hour of thousands—they retire
From life's throng'd path, unnoticed to expire.
As the light leaf, whose fall to ruin bears
Some trembling insect's little world of cares
Descends in silence—while around waves on,
The mighty forest, reckless what is gone !
Such is man's doom—and, ere an hour be flown,
—Start not, thou trifler !—such may be thine own

But as life's current in its ebb draws near
The shadowy gulf, there wakes a thought of fear
A thrilling thought, which, haply mock'd before,
We fain would stifle—but it sleeps no more !
There are, who fly its murmurs 'midst the throng,
That join the masque of revelry and song,
Yet still Death's image, by its power restored,
Frowns 'midst the roses of the festal board,
And, when deep shades o'er earth and ocean brood,
And the heart owns the might of solitude,
Is its low whisper heard—a note profound,
But wild and startling as the trumpet-sound ·
That bursts, with sudden blast, the dead repose
Of some proud city, storm'd by midnight foes !

Oh ! vainly reason's scornful voice would prove
That life hath naught to claim such lingering love,
And ask, if ere the captive, half unchain'd,
Clung to the links which yet his step restrain'd
In vain philosophy, with tranquil pride,
Would mock the feelings she perchance can hide,
Call up the countless armies of the dead.
Point to the pathway beaten by their tread,
And say—" What wouldst thou ? Shall the fix'd
 decree,
Made for creation, be reversed for *thee* ?"
—Poor, feeble aid !—proud Stoic ! ask not why,
It is enough, that nature shrinks to die !
Enough, *that* horror, which thy words upbraid,
Is her dread penalty, and must be paid !
—Search thy deep wisdom, solve the scarce defined
And mystic questions of the parting mind.
Half check'd, half utter'd—tell her, what shall
 burst,
In whelming grandeur, on her vision first,
When freed from mortal films ?—what viewless
 world
Shall first receive her wing, but half unfurl'd !
What awful and unbodied beings guide
Her timid flight through regions yet untried ?
Say if at once, her final doom to hear,
Before her God the trembler must appear,
Or wait that day of terror, when the sea
Shall yield its hidden dead, and heaven and earth
 shall flee ?
Hast thou no answer ?—then deride no more
The thoughts that shrink, yet cease not to explore
Th' unknown, th' unseen, the future—though the
 heart,
As at unearthly sounds, before them start,
Though the frame shudder, and the spirit sigh,
They have their source in immortality !
Whence, then, shall strength, which reason's aid
 denies,
An equal to the mortal conflict rise ?
When, on the swift pale horse, whose lightning
 pace,
Where'er we fly, still wins the dreadful race,
The mighty rider comes—oh ! whence shall aid
Be drawn, to meet his rushing, undismay'd ?
—Whence, but from thee, Messiah !—thou hast
 drain'd
The bitter cup, till not the dregs remain'd ;
To thee the struggle and the pang were known
The mystic horror all became thine own !

But did no hand celestial succour bring,
Till scorn and anguish haply lost their sting ?
Came not th' Archangel, in the final hour,
To arm thee with invulnerable power ?
No, Son of God ! upon thy sacred head,
The shafts of wrath their tenfold fury shed,
From man averted—and thy path on high
Pass'd through the strait of fiercest agony ;
For thus th' Eternal, with propitious eyes,
Received the last, th' almighty sacrifice !

But wake ! be glad, ye nations ! from the tomb
Is won the victory, and is fled the gloom !
The vale of death in conquest hath been trod,
Break forth in joy, ye ransom'd ! saith your God
Swell ye the raptures of the song afar,
And hail with harps your bright and morning star

He rose ! the everlasting gates of day
Receiv'd the King of Glory on his way !

The hope, the comforter of those who wept,
And the first fruits of them, in him that slept.
He rose, he triumph'd! he will yet sustain
Frail nature sinking in the strife of pain.
Aided by Him, around the martyr's frame
When fiercely blazed a living shroud of flame,
Hath the firm soul exulted, and the voice
Raised the victorious hymn, and cried, "Rejoice!"
Aided by Him, though none the bed attend,
Where the lone sufferer dies without a friend,
He, whom the busy world shall miss no more
Than morn one dew-drop from her countless store,
Earth's most neglected child, with trusting heart
Call'd to the hope of glory shall depart!

And say, cold Sophist! if by thee bereft
Of that high hope, to misery what were left?
But for the vision of the days to be,
But for the Comforter, despised by thee,
Should we not wither at the Chastener's look,
Should we not sink beneath our God's rebuke,
When o'er our heads the desolating blast,
Fraught with inscrutable decrees, hath pass'd,
And the stern power who seeks the noblest prey,
Hath call'd our fairest and our best away?
Should we not madden, when our eyes behold
All that we loved in marble stillness cold,
No more responsive to our smile or sigh,
Fix'd—frozen—silent—all mortality?
But for the promise, all shall yet be well,
Would not the spirit in its pangs rebel,
Beneath such clouds as darken'd, when the hand
Of wrath lay heavy on our prostrate land,
And thou, just lent thy gladden'd isles to bless,
Then snatch'd from earth with all thy loveliness,
With all a nation's blessings on thy head,
O England's flower! wert gather'd to the dead?
But thou didst teach us. Thou to every heart,
Faith's lofty lesson didst thyself impart!
When fled the hope through all thy pangs which
smiled,
When thy young bosom, o'er the lifeless child,
Yearn'd with vain longing—still thy patient eye,
To its last light, beam'd holy constancy!
Torn from a lot in cloudless sunshine cast,
Amidst those agonies—thy first and last,
Thy pale lip, quivering with convulsive throes,
Breathed not a plaint—and settled in repose;
While bow'd thy royal head to Him, whose power
Spoke in 'be fiat of that midnight hour,
Who from the brightest vision of a throne,
Love, glory, empire claim'd thee for his own,
And spread such terror o'er the sea-girt coast,
As blasted Israel, when her ark was lost!

"It is the will of God!"—yet, yet we hear
The words that closed thy beautiful career,
Yet should we mourn thee in thy blest abode,
But for that thought—"It is the will of God!"
Who shall arraign th' Eternal's dark decree,
If not one murmur then escaped from thee?
Oh! still, though vanishing without a trace,
Thou hast not left one scion of thy race,
Still may thy memory bloom our vales among,
Hallow'd by freedom, and enshrined in song!
Still may thy pure, majestic spirit dwell,
Bright on the isles which loved thy name so well,
E'en as an angel, with presiding care,
To wake and guard thine own high virtues there.

For lo! the hour when storm-presaging skies
Call on the watchers of the land to rise,
To set the sign of fire on every height, (6)
And o'er the mountains rear, with patriot might,
Prepared, if summon'd, in its cause to die,
The banner of our faith, the Cross of Victory!

By this hath England conquer'd—field and flood
Have own'd her sovereignty—alone she stood,
When chains o'er all the sceptred earth were
thrown,
In high and holy singleness, alone,
But mighty in her God—and shall she now
Forget before th' Omnipotent to bow?
From the bright fountain of her glory turn,
Or bid strange fire upon his altars burn?
No! sever'd land, midst rocks and billows rude,
Throned in thy majesty of solitude

Still in the deep asylum of thy breast
Shall the pure elements of greatness rest,
Virtue and faith, the tutelary powers,
Thy hearths that hallow, and defend thy towers!

Still, where thy hamlet-vales, O chosen isle!
In the soft beauty of their verdure smile,
Where yew and elm o'ershade the lowly fanes,
That guard the peasant's records and remains,
May the blest echoes of the Sabbath-bell
Sweet on the quiet of the woodlands swell,
And from each cottage-dwelling of thy glades,
When starlight glimmers through the deepening
shades,
Devotion's voice in choral hymns arise,
And bear the Land's warm incense to the skies.

There may the mother, as with anxious joy
To Heaven her lessons consecrate her boy,
Teach his young accents still the immortal lays
Of Zion's bards, in inspiration's days,
When Angels, whispering through a cedar's shade
Prophetic tones to Judah's harp convey'd;
And as, her soul all glistening in her eyes,
She bids the prayer of infancy arise,
Tell of his name, who left his throne on high,
Earth's lowliest lot to bear and sanctify,
His love divine, by keenest anguish tried,
And fondly say—"My child, for thee Ile died!"

---

# NOTES.

### Note 1.

*Patient, because Eternal.*

"He is patient, because he is eternal."——*St. Augustine.*

### Note 2.

*Fly to the City of thy Refuge, fly*

"Then ye shall appoint you cities, to be cities of refuge for you, that the slayer may flee thither which killeth any person at unawares.—And they shall be unto you cities for refuge from the avenger."——*Numbers,* chap. xxxv.

### Note 3.

*And dark the chambers of its imag'ry.*

"Every man in the chambers of his imagery."—*Ezekiel,* chap. viii.

### Note 4.

*Must drink the cup of trembling.*

"Thou hast drunken the dregs of the cup of trembling, and wrung them out."——*Isaiah,* chap. li.

### Note 5.

*Come in the still small voice, and whisper—peace.*

"And behold, the Lord passed by, and a great and strong wind rent the mountains, and brake in pieces the rocks before the Lord; but the Lord was not in the wind: and after the wind, an earthquake; but the Lord was not in the earthquake: and after the earthquake a fire; but the Lord was not in the fire: and after the fire a still small voice."——*1 Kings,* chap. xix.

### Note 6.

*To set the sign of fire on every height.*

"And set up a sign of fire."——*Jeremiah,* chap. vi.

---

# STANZAS

## TO THE

## MEMORY OF THE LATE KING.

---

"Among many nations there was no king like him."—*Nehemiah*

"Know ye not that there is a prince and a great man fallen this day in Israel?"——*Samuel.*

---

ANOTHER warning sound! the funeral bell,
Startling the cities of the isle once more,
With measured tones of melancholy swell,
Strike on th' awaken'd heart from shore to shore.
He, at whose coming monarchs sink to dust,
The chambers of our palaces hath trod,
And the long-suffering spirit of the just,
Pure from its ruins, hath return'd to God!
Yet may not England o'er her Father weep,
Thoughts to her bosom crowd, too many, and too
deep.

Vain voice of Reason, hush!—they yet must flow
  Th... strain'd, involuntary tears:
A thousand feelings sanctify the woe,
  Roused by the glorious shades of vanish'd years.
Tell us no more 't is not the time for grief,
  Now that the exile of the soul is past,
And Death blest messenger of Heaven's relief,
  Hath led the wanderer to his rest at last;
For him, Eternity hath tenfold day,
We feel, we know, 't is thus—yet Nature will
    have way.

What thou wert amidst us, like a blasted oak,
  Saddening the scene where once it nobly reign'd
A dread memorial of the lightning-stroke,
  Stamp'd with its fiery record, he remain'd;
Around that shatter'd tree still fondly clung
  Th' undying tendrils of our love, which drew
Fresh nurture from its deep decay, and sprung
  Luxuriant thence, to Glory's ruin true:
While England hung her trophies on the stem,
That desolately stood, unconscious e'en of *them*.

Of *them* unconscious! Oh mysterious doom!
  Who shall unfold the counsels of the skies!
His was the voice, which roused, as from the
    tomb
  The realm's high soul to loftiest energies!
His was the spirit, o'er the isles which threw
  The mantle of its fortitude; and wrought
In every bosom, powerful to renew
  Each dying spark of pure and generous thought:
The star of tempest beaming on the mast,*
The seamen's torch of Hope, 'midst perils deepen-
    ing fast.

Then from th' unslumbering influence of his worth
  Strength as of inspiration, fill'd the land;
A young, but quenchless, flame went brightly forth,
  Kindled by him—who saw it not expand!
Such was the will of Heaven,—the gifted seer,
  Who with his God had communed, face to face,
And from the house of bondage, and of fear,
  In faith victorious, led the chosen race;
He, through the desert and the waste their guide,
Saw dimly from afar the promised land—and died.

O full of days and virtues! on thy head
  Centred the woes of many a bitter lot;
Fathers have sorrow'd o'er their beauteous dead,
  Eyes, quench'd in night, the sun-beams have for-
    got;
Minds have striven buoyantly with evil years,
  And sunk beneath their glittering weight at
    length;
But Pain for thee had fill'd a cup of tears,
  Where every anguish mingled all its strength;
By thy lost child we saw thee weeping stand,
And shadows deep around fell from the Eternal's
    hand.

Then came the noon of glory, which thy dreams,
  Perchance of yore, had faintly prophesied;
But what to *thee* the splendour of its beams?
  The ice-rock glows not 'midst the summer's
    pride!
Nations leap'd up to joy—as streams that burst,
  At the warm touch of spring, their frozen chain;
And o'er the plains, whose verdure once they
    nursed,
  Roll in exulting melody again;
And bright o'er earth the long majestic line
Of England's triumphs swept, to rouse all hearts
    —but thine.

Oh! what a dazzling vision, by the veil
  That o'er thy spirit hung, was shut from thee,
When sceptred chieftains throng'd, with pinions, to
    hail
  The crowning isle, the anointed of the sea!
Within thy palaces the lords of earth
  Met to rejoice,—rich pageants glitter'd by
And stately revels imaged, in their mirth,
  The old magnificence of chivalry.

---

* The glittering meteor, like a star, which often appears about a
ship during tempests, if seen upon the mainmast, is considered by
the sailors as an omen of good weather.——See *Dampier's Voyages*

They reach'd not thee,—amidst them, yet alone
Stillness and gloom begirt one dim and shadowy
    throne.

Yet was there mercy still—if joy no more
  Within that blasted circle might intrude,
Earth had no grief whose footstep might pass o'er
  The silent limits of its solitude!
If all unheard the bridal song awoke
  Our hearts' full echoes, as it swell'd on high;
Alike unheard the sudden dirge, that broke
  On the glad strain, with dread solemnity!
If the land's rose unheeded wore its bloom,
Alike unfelt the storm, that swept it to the tomb.

And she, who, tried through all the stormy past,
  Severely, deeply proved, in many an hour,
Watch'd o'er thee, firm and faithful to the last,
  Sustain'd, inspired, by strong affection's power;
If to thy soul her voice no music bore,
  If thy closed eye, and wandering spirit caught
No light from looks, that fondly would explore
  Thy mien, for traces of responsive thought;
Oh! thou wert spared the pang that would have
    thrill'd
Thine inmost heart, when Death that anxious
    bosom still'd.

Thy loved ones fell around thee—manhood's prime,
  Youth, with its glory, in its fullness, Age,
All at the gates of their eternal clime
  Lay down, and closed their mortal pilgrimage;
The land wore ashes for its perish'd flowers,
  The grave's imperial harvest. Thou, meanwhile,
Didst walk unconscious through thy royal towers,
  The one that wept not in the tearful isle!
As a tired warrior, on his battle-plain,
Breathes deep in dreams amidst the mourners and
    the slain.

And who can tell what visions might be thine?
  The stream of thought, though broken, still was
    pure!
Still o'er that wave the stars of heaven might
    shine,
  Where earthly image would no more endure!
Though many a step, of once familiar sound,
  Came as a stranger's o'er thy closing ear,
And voices breathed forgotten tones around,
  Which that paternal heart once thrill'd to hear,
The mind hath senses of its own, and powers
To people boundless worlds, in its most wander
    ing hours.

Nor might the phantoms to thy spirit known
  Be dark or wild, creations of remorse;
Unstain'd by thee, the blameless past had thrown
  No fearful shadows o'er the future's course;
For thee no cloud, from memory's dread abyss,
  Might shape such forms as haunt the tyrant's
    eye;
And closing up each avenue of bliss,
  Murmur their summons, to " despair and die!"
No! e'en though joy depart, though reason cease,
Still virtue's ruin'd home is redolent of peace.

They might be with thee still—the loved, the tried,
  The fair, the lost—they might be with thee still!
More softly seen, in radiance purified
  From each dim vapour of terrestrial ill;
Long after earth received them, and the note
  Of the last requiem o'er their dust was pour'd,
As passing sunbeams o'er thy soul might float
    Those forms, from us withdrawn—to thee re-
    stored!
Spirits of holiness, in light reveal'd,
To commune with a mind whose source of tears
    was seal'd.

Came they with tidings from the worlds above,
  Those viewless regions, where the weary rest?
Sever'd from earth, estranged from mortal love,
  Was thy mysterious converse with the blest?
Or shone their visionary presence bright
  With human beauty?—did their smiles renew
Those days of sacred and serene delight,
  When fairest beings in thy pathway grew?

Oh! Heaven hath balm for every wound it makes,
Healing the broken heart; it smites—but ne'er
  forsakes.

These may be phantasies—and this alone,
  Of all we picture in our dreams, is sure;
That rest, made perfect, is at length thine own,
  Rest, in thy God immortally secure!
Enough for tranquil faith; released from all
  The woes that graved Heaven's lessons on thy
    brow,
No cloud to dim, no fetter to enthral,
  Haply thine eye is on thy people now;
Whose love around thee still its offerings shed,
Though vainly sweet as flowers, grief's tribute to
  the dead.

But if th' ascending, disembodied mind,
  Borne on the wings of Morning, to the skies,
May cast one glance of tenderness behind,
  On scenes, once hallow'd by its mortal ties,
How much hast thou to gaze on! all that lay
  By the dark mantle of thy soul conceal'd,
The might, the majesty, the proud array
  Of England's march o'er many a noble field,
All spread beneath thee, in a blaze of light,
Shine like some glorious land, view'd from an Al-
  pine-height.

Away presumptuous thought!—departed saint!
  To thy freed vision what can earth display
Of pomp, of royalty, that is not faint,
  Seen from the birth-place of celestial day?
Oh! pale and weak the sun's reflected rays,
  E'en in their fervour of meridian heat,
To him, who in the sanctuary may gaze
  On the bright cloud that fills the mercy-seat!
And thou mayest view, from thy divine abode,
The dust of empires flit, before a breath of God.

And yet we mourn thee! yes! thy place is void
  Within our hearts—there veil'd thine image
    dwelt,
But cherish'd still; and o'er that tie destroy'd,
  Though Faith rejoice, fond Nature still must
    melt.
Beneath the long-loved sceptre of thy sway,
  Thousands were born, who now in dust repose,
And many a head, with years and sorrows gray,
  Wore youth's bright tresses, when thy star arose;
And many a glorious mind, since that fair dawn,
Hath fill'd our sphere with light, now to its source
  withdrawn.

Earthquakes have rock'd the nations:—things re-
  vered,
  Th' ancestral fabrics of the world, went down
In ruins, from whose stones Ambition rear'd
  His lonely pyramid of dread renown.
But when the fires, that long had slumber'd, pent
  Deep in men's bosoms, with volcanic force,
Bursting their prison-house, each bulwark rent,
  And swept each holy barrier from their course,
Firm and unmoved, amidst that lava-flood,
Still, by thine arm upheld, our ancient landmarks
  stood.

Be they eternal!—Be thy children found
  Still, to their country's altars, true like thee;
And, while "the name of Briton" is a sound
  Of rallying music to the brave and free,
With the high feelings at the word which swell,
  To make the breast a shrine for Freedom's flame,
Be mingled thoughts of him, who loved so well,
  Who left so pure, its heritage of fame!
Let earth with trophies guard the conqueror's dust,
Heaven in our souls embalms the memory of the
  just.

All else shall pass away—the thrones of kings,
  The very traces of their *tombs* depart;
But number not with perishable things
  The holy records Virtue leaves the heart,
Heir-looms from race to race!—and oh! in days,
  When, by the yet unborn, thy deeds are blest,

When our sons learn, " as household words," thy
  praise,
  Still on thine offspring may thy spirit rest!
And many a name of that imperial line,
Father and patriot! blend, in England's songs,
  with thine!

---

# Modern Greece.

## A POEM.

O Greece! thou saplent nurse of finer arts,
  Which to bright Science blooming Fancy bore,
  Be this thy praise, that thou, and thou alone,
  In these hast led the way, in these excell'd,
  Crown'd with the laurel of assenting Time.
                *Thomson's Liberty.*

### I.

Oh! who hath trod thy consecrated clime,
  Fair land of Phidias! theme of lofty strains!
  And traced each scene, that 'midst the wrecks
    of time,
The print of Glory's parting step retains;
  Nor for awhile, in high-wrought dreams, forgot,
Musing on years gone by in brightness there,
  The hopes, the fears, the sorrows of his lot,
  The hues his fate hath worn, or yet may wear;
As when from mountain-heights his ardent eye
Of sea and heaven hath track'd the blue infinity

### II.

Is there who views with cold, unalter'd mien,
  His frozen heart with proud indifference fraught,
Each sacred haunt, each unforgotten scene,
  Where Freedom triumph'd, or where Wisdom
    taught?
Souls that too deeply feel, oh, envy not
  The sullen calm your fate hath never known;
Through the dull twilight of that wintry lot
  Genius ne'er pierced, nor Fancy's sunbeam
    shone,
Nor those high thoughts, that, hailing Glory's trace
Glow with the generous flames of every age and
  race.

### III.

But blest the wanderer, whose enthusiast mind
  Each muse of ancient days hath deep imbued
With lofty lore! and all his thoughts refined
  In the calm school of silent solitude;
Pour'd on his ear, 'midst groves and glens retired,
  The mighty strains of each illustrious clime,
All that hath lived, while empires have expired,
  To float for ever on the winds of Time;
And on his soul indelibly portray'd
Fair visionary forms, to fill each classic shade

### IV.

Is not his mind, to meaner thoughts unknown,
  A sanctuary of beauty and of light?
There he may dwell, in regions all his own,
  A world of dreams, where all is pure and bright.
For him the scenes of old renown possess
  Romantic charms, all veil'd from other eyes!
There every form of nature's loveliness
  Wakes in his breast a thousand sympathies;
As music's voice, in some lone mountain-dell,
From rocks and caves around calls forth each echo's
  swell.

### V.

For him Italia's brilliant skies illume
  The bard's lone haunts, the warrior's combat-
    plains,
And the wild-rose yet lives to breathe and bloom,
Round Doric Pæstum's solitary fanes. (1)

But most, fair Greece! on thy majestic shore
He feels the fervours of his spirit rise;
Thou birth-place of the Muse! whose voice, of
    yore,
Breathed in thy groves immortal harmonies;
And lingers still around the well-known coast,
Murmuring a wild farewell to fame and freedom
    lost

### VI.

By seas, that flow in brightness as they lave
Thy rocks, th' enthusiast, rapt in thought, may
    stray,
While roves his eye o'er that deserted wave,
Once the proud scene of battle's dread array.
—O ye blue waters! ye of old that bore
The free, the conquering, hymn'd by choral
    strains,
How sleep ye now around the silent shore,
The lonely realm of ruins and of chains!
How are the mighty vanish'd in their pride!
E'en as their barks have left no traces on your
    tide.

### VII.

Hush'd are the Pæans whose exulting tone
Swell'd o'er that tide (2)—the sons of battle
    sleep—
The wind's wild sigh, the halcyon's voice, alone
Blend with the plaintive murmurs of the deep.
Yet when those waves have caught the splendid
    hues
Of morn's rich firmament, serenely bright,
Or setting suns the lovely shores suffuse
With all their purple mellowness of light,
Oh! who could view the scene, so calmly fair,
Nor dream that peace, and joy, and liberty were
    there?

### VIII.

Where soft the sunbeams play, the zephyrs blow,
'T is hard to deem that misery can be nigh;
Where the clear heavens in blue transparence
    glow,
Life should be calm and cloudless as the sky:
—Yet o'er the low, dark dwellings of the dead
Verdure and flowers in summer-bloom may smile,
And ivy-boughs their graceful drapery spread
In green luxuriance o'er the ruin'd pile;
And mantling woodbine veils the wither'd tree,—
And thus it is, fair land, forsaken Greece! with
    thee.

### IX.

For all the loveliness, and light, and bloom,
That yet are thine, surviving many a storm,
Are but as heaven's warm radiance on the tomb,
The rose's blush that masks the canker-worm:—
And thou art desolate—thy morn hath pass'd
So dazzling in the splendour of its way,
That the dark shades the night hath o'er thee
    cast
Throw ten'old gloom around thy deep decay.
Once proud in freedom, still in ruin fair,
Thy fate hath been unmatch'd—in glory and des-
    pair.

### X.

For thee, lost .and! the hero's blood hath flow'd,
The high in soul have brightly lived and died;
For thee the light of soaring genius glow'd
O'er the fair arts it form'd and glorified.
Thine were the minds, whose energies sublime
So distanced ages in their lightning-race,
The task they left the sons of later time
Was but to follow their illumined trace.
—Now, bow'd to earth, thy children, to be free,
Must break each link that binds their filial hearts
    to thee

### XI.

Lo! to the scenes of fiction's wildest tales,
Her own bright East, thy son, Morea! flies, (3)
To seek repose 'midst rich, romantic vales,
Whose incense mounts to Asia's vivid skies.
There shall he rest?—Alas! his hopes in vain
Guide to the sun-clad regions of the palm,
Peace dwells not now on oriental plain,
Though earth is fruitfulness, and air is balm;
And the sad wanderer finds but lawless foes,
Where patriarchs reign'd of old in pastoral repose.

### XII.

Where Syria's mountains rise, or Yemen's
    groves,
Or Tigris rolls his genii-haunted wave,
Life to his eye, as wearily it roves,
Wears but two forms—the tyrant and the slave!
There the fierce Arab leads his daring horde,
Where sweeps the sand-storm o'er the burning
    wild,
There stern Oppression waves the wasting
    sword,
O'er plains that smile, as ancient Eden smiled;
And the vale's bosom, and the desert's gloom,
Yield to the injured there no shelter save the tomb.

### XIII.

But thou, fair world! whose fresh, unsullied
    charms
Welcom'd Columbus from the western wave,
Wilt thou receive the wanderer to thine arms, (4
The lost descendant of the immortal brave?
Amidst the wild magnificence of shades
That o'er thy floods their twilight-grandeur cast,
In the green depth of thine untrodden glades,
Shall he not rear his bower of peace at last?
Yes! thou hast many a lone, majestic scene,
Shrined in primeval woods, where despot ne'er
    hath been.

### XIV.

There, by some lake, whose blue, expansive
    breast
Bright from afar, an inland-ocean, gleams,
Girt with vast solitudes, profusely dress'd
In tints like those that float o'er poet's dreams;
Or where some flood from pine-clad mountain
    pours
Its might of waters, glittering in their foam,
'Midst the rich verdure of its wooded shores,
The exiled Greek hath fix'd his sylvan home,
So deeply lone, that round the wild retreat
Scarce have the paths been trod by Indian hunts-
    man's feet.

### XV.

The forests are around him in their pride,
The green savannas, and the mighty waves;
And isles of flowers, bright-floating o'er the
    tide, (5)
That images the fairy worlds it laves,
And stillness, and luxuriance—o'er his head
The ancient cedars wave their peopled bowers,
On high the palms their graceful foliage spread,
Cinctured with roses the magnolia towers,
And from those green arcades a thousand tones
Wake with each breeze, whose voice through Na-
    ture's temple moans.

### XVI.

And there, no traces left by brighter days,
For glory lost may wake a sigh of grief,
Some grassy mound perchance may meet his
    gaze,
The lone memorial of an Indian chief.
There man not yet hath mark'd the boundless
    plain
With marble records of his fame and power;
The forest is his everlasting fane,
The palm his monument, the rock his tower
Th' eternal torrent, and the giant tree,
Remind him but that they, like him, are wildly
    free.

### XVII.

But doth the exile's heart serenely there
In sunshine dwell?—Ah! when was exile blest?
When did bright scenes, clear heavens, or sum-
    mer-air,
Chase from his soul the fever of unrest?
—There is a heart-sick weariness of mood,
That like slow poison wastes the vital glow,
And shrines itself in mental solitude,
An uncomplaining and a nameless woe,
That coldly similes 'midst pleasure's brightest ray,
As the chill glacier's peak reflects the flush of day.

### XVIII.

Such grief, is theirs, who, fix'd on foreign shore,
Sigh for the spirit of their native gales,
As pines the seaman, 'midst the ocean's roar,
For the green earth, with all its woods and vales.
Thus feels thy child, whose memory dwells with
    thee,
Loved Greece! all sunk and blighted as thou art
Though thought and step in western wilds be
    free,
Yet thine are still the day-dreams of his heart;
The deserts spread between, the billows foam,
Thou, distant and in chains, art yet his spirit's
    home.

### XIX.

In vain for him the gay liannes entwine,
Or the green fire fly sparkles through the brakes,
Or summer-winds waft odours from the pine,
As eve's last blush is dying on the lakes.
Through thy fair vales his fancy roves the while,
Or breathes the freshness of Cithæron's height,
Or dreams how softly Athens' towers would
    smile,
Or Sunium's ruins, in the fading light;
On Corinth's cliffs what sunset hues may sleep,
Or, at that placid hour, how calm th' Egean deep;

### XX.

What scenes, what sunbeams, are to him like
    thine?
(The all of thine no tyrant could destroy!)
E'en to the stranger's roving eye they shine,
Soft as a vision of remember'd joy,
And he who comes, the pilgrim of a day,
A passing wanderer o'er each Attic hill,
Sighs as his footsteps turn from thy decay,
To laughing climes, where all is splendour still,
And views with fond regret thy lessening shore,
As he would watch a star that sets to rise no more.

### XXI.

Realm of sad beauty! thou art as a shrine
That Fancy visits with Devotion's zeal,
To catch high thoughts and impulses divine,
And all the glow of soul enthusiasts feel
Amidst the tombs of heroes—for the brave
Whose dust, so many an age, hath been thy soil,
Foremost in honour's phalanx, died to save
The land redeem'd and hallow'd by their toil;
And there is language in thy lightest gale,
That o'er the plains they won seems murmuring
    yet their tale.

### XXII.

And he, whose heart is weary of the strife
Of meaner spirits, and whose mental gaze
Would shun the dull, cold littleness of life,
Awhile to dwell amidst sublimer days,
Must turn to thee, whose every valley teems
With proud remembrances that cannot die.
Thy glens are peopled with inspiring dreams,
Thy winds, the voice of oracles gone by;
And 'midst thy laurel shades the wanderer hears
The sound of mighty names, the hymns of vanish-
    ed years

### XXIII.

Through that deep solitude he bis to stray,
By Faun and Oread loved in ages past,
Where clear Peneus winds his rapid way
Through the cleft heights, in antique grandeur
    vast.
Romantic Tempe! thou art yet the same—
Wild, as when sung by bards of elder time:(6)
Years, that have changed thy river's classic
    name, (7)
Have left thee still in savage pomp sublime;
And from thine Alpine clefts, and marble caves,
In living lustre still break forth the fountain-waves.

### XXIV.

Beneath thy mountain battlements and towers,
Where the rich arbute's coral berries glow, (8)
Or 'midst th' exuberance of thy forest bowers,
Casting deep shadows o'er the current's flow,
Oft shall the pilgrim pause, in lone recess,
As rock and stream some glancing light have
    caught,
And gaze, till Nature's mighty forms impress
His soul with deep sublimity of thought;
And linger oft, recalling many a tale,
That breeze, and wave, and wood, seem whisper
    ing through thy dale.

### XXV.

He, thought-entranced, may wander where of old
From Delphi's chasm the mystic vapour rose,
And trembling nations heard their doom foretold,
By the dread spirit throned 'midst rocks and
    snows.
Though its rich fanes be blended with the dust
And silence now the hallow'd haunt possess,
Still is the scene of ancient rites august,
Magnificent in mountain loneliness;
Still inspiration hovers o'er the ground,
Where Greece her councils held, (9) her Pythian
    victors crown'd.

### XXVI.

Or let his steps the rude, gray cliffs explore
Of that wild pass, once dyed with Spartan blood,
When by the waves that break on Œta's shore,
The few, the fearless, the devoted stood!
Or rove where, shadowing Mantinea's plain, ·
Bloom the wild laurels o'er the warlike dead, (10)
Or lone Platæa's ruins yet remain,
To mark the battle-field of ages fled;
Still o'er such scenes presides a sacred power,
Though Fiction's gods have fled from fountain,
    grot, and bower.

### XXVII.

Oh! still unblamed may fancy fondly deem
That, lingering yet, benignant genii dwell,
Where mortal worth has hallow'd grove or
    stream,
To sway the heart with some ennobling spell;
For mightiest minds have felt their blest control,
In the wood's murmur, in the zephyr's sigh,
And these are dreams that lend a voice and soul,
And a high power, to Nature's majesty!
And who can rove o'er Grecian shores, nor feel,
Soft o'er his inmost heart, their secret magic steal?

### XXVIII.

Yet many a sad reality is there,
That fancy's bright illusions cannot veil.
Pure laughs the light, and balmy breathes the
    air,
But Slavery's mien will tell its bitter tale;
And there not Peace, but Desolation, throws
Delusive quiet o'er full many a scene,
Deep as the brooding torpor of repose
That follows where the earthquake's track hath
    been;
Or solemn calm, on Ocean's breast that lies,
When sinks the storm, and death hath hush'd the
    seaman's cries.

### XXIX.

Hast thou beheld some sovereign spirit, hurl'd
By Fate's rude tempest from its radiant sphere,
Doom'd to resign the homage of a world,
For Pity's deepest sigh, and saddest tear?
Oh! hast thou watch'd the awful wreck of mind,
That weareth still a glory in decay?
Seen all that dazzles and delights mankind—
Thought, science, genius, to the storm a prey,
And o'er the blasted tree, the wither'd ground,
Despair's wild nightshade spread, and darkly
    flourish round?

### XXX.

So may'st thou gaze in sad and awe-struck
    thought,
On the deep fall of that yet lovely clime:
Such there the ruin Time and Fate have wrought,
So changed the bright, the splendid, the sublime!
There the proud monuments of Valour's name,
The mighty works Ambition piled on high,
The rich remains by Art bequeathed to Fame—
Grace, beauty, grandeur, strength, and sym-
    metry,
Blend in decay; while all that yet is fair
Seems only spared to tell how much hath perish'd
    here!

### XXXI.

There, while around lie mingling in the dust,
The column's graceful shaft with weeds o'er
    grown,
The mouldering torso, the forgotten bust,
The warrior's urn, the altar's mossy stone;
Amidst the loneliness of shatter'd fanes,
Still matchless monuments of other years,
O'er cypress groves, or solitary plains,
Its eastern form the minaret proudly rears;
As on some captive city's ruin'd wall
The victor's banner waves, exulting o'er its fall.

### XXXII.

Still, where that column of the mosque aspires,
Landmark of slavery, towering o'er the waste,
There science droops, the Muses hush their lyres
And o'er the blooms of fancy and of taste
Spreads the chill blight—as in that orient isle,
Where the dark upas taints the gale around, (11
Within its precincts not a flower may smile,
Nor dew nor sunshine fertilize the ground;
Nor wild bird's music float on zephyr's breath,
But all is silence round, and solitude, and death.

### XXXIII.

Far other influence pour'd the Crescent's light,
O'er conquer'd realms, in ages past away!
Full and alone it beam'd, intensely bright,
While distant climes in midnight darkness lay.
Then rose th' Alhambra, with its founts and
    shades,
Fair marble halls, alcoves, and orange bowers ·
Its sculptured lions, (12) richly wrought arcades,
Aerial pillars, and enchanted towers;
Light, splendid, wild as some Arabian tale
Would picture fairy domes, that fleet before the
    gale.

### XXXIV.

Then foster'd genius lent each Caliph's throne
Lustre barbaric pomp could ne'er attain;
And stars unnumber'd o'er the orient shone,
Bright as that Pleiad, shrined in Mecca's
    fane. (13)
From Bagdat's palaces, the choral strains
Rose and re-echoed to the desert's bound,
And Science, woo'd on Egypt's burning plains,
Rear'd her majestic head with glory crown'd;
And the wild Muses breathed romantic lore,
From Syria's palmy groves to Andalusia's shore.

### XXXV.

Those years have pass'd in radiance—they have
    pass'd,
As sinks the day-star in the tropic main;
His parting beams no soft reflection cast,
They burn—are quench'd—and deepest shadows
    reign,
And Fame and Science have not left a trace,
In the vast regions of the Moslem's power,—
Regions, to intellect a desert space,
A wild without a fountain or a flower,
Where towers oppression 'midst the deepening
    glooms,
As dark and lone ascends the cypress 'midst the
    tombs.

### XXXVI.

Alas for thee, fair Greece! when Asia pour'd
Her fierce fanatics to Byzantium's wall,
When Europe sheathed, in apathy, her sword
And heard unmoved the fated city's call,
No bold crusaders ranged their serried line
Of spears and banners round a falling throne;
And thou, O last and noblest Constantine! (14)
Didst meet the storm unshrinking and alone.
Oh! blest to die in freedom, though in vain,
Thine empire's proud exchange the grave, and
    not the chain.

### XXXVII.

Hush'd is Byzantium—'t is the dead of night—
The closing night of that imperial race! (15)
And all is vigil—but the eye of light
Shall soon unfold, a wilder scene to trace;
There is a murmuring stillness on the train,
Thronging the midnight streets, at morn to die;
And to the cross in fair Sophia's fane,
For the last time is raised Devotion's eye;
And, in his heart while faith's bright visions rise,
There kneels the high-soul'd prince, the summon'd
    of the skies.

### XXXVIII.

Day breaks in light and glory—'t is the hour,
Of conflict and of fate— the war-note calls—
Despair hath lent a stern, delirious power
To the brave few that guard the rampart walls
Far o'er Marmora's waves th' artillery's peal
Proclaims an empire's doom in every note;
Tambour and trumpet swell the clash of steel,
Round spire and dome the clouds of battle float,
From camp and wave rush on the crescent's host,
And the Seven Towers (16) are scaled, and all is
    won and lost.

### XXXIX.

Then, Greece! the tempest rose, that burst on
    thee,
Land of the bard, the warrior, and the sage!
Oh! where were then thy sons, the great, the free,
Whose deeds are guiding stars from age to age?
Though firm thy battlements of crags and snows,
And bright the memory of thy days of pride,
In mountain-might thro' Corinth's fortress rose.
On, unresisted, roll'd th' invading tide!
Oh! vain the rock, the rampart, and the tower,
If Freedom guard them not with Mind's uncon-
    quer'd power.

### XL.

Where were th' avengers then, whose viewless
    might
Preserved inviolate their awful fane, (17)
When through the steep defiles, to Delphi's
    height,
In martial splendour pour'd the Persian's train?
Then did those mighty and mysterious Powers,
Arm'd with the elements, to vengeance wake,
Call the dread storms to darken round their
    towers,
Hurl down the rocks, and bid the thunders break;
'Till far around, with deep and fearful clang,
Sounds of unearthly war through wild Parnassus
    rang

#### XLI.

Where was the spirit of the victor-throng,
Whose tombs are glorious by Scamander's tide,
Whose names are bright in everlasting song,
The lords of war, the praised, the deified?
Where he, the hero of a thousand lays,
Who from the dead at Marathon arose (18)
All arm'd; and beaming on th' Athenians' gaze,
A battle-meteor, guided to their foes?
Or they whose forms, to Alaric's awe-struck
 eye, (19)
Hovering o'er Athens, blazed, in airy panoply?

#### XLII.

Ye slept, oh heroes! chief ones of the earth! (20)
High demi-gods of ancient days! ye slept:
There lived no spark of your ascendant worth,
When o'er your land the victor Moslem swept;
No patriot then the sons of freedom led,
In mountain-pass devotedly to die;
The martyr-spirit of resolve was fled,
And the high soul's unconquer'd buoyancy;
And by your graves, and on your battle-plains,
Warriors! your children knelt, to wear the stran-
 ger's chains.

#### XLIII.

Now have your trophies vanish'd, and your homes
Are moulder'd from the earth, while scarce re-
 main
E'en the faint traces of the ancient tombs
That mark where sleep the slayers or the slain.
Your deeds are with the deeds of glory flown,
The lyres are hush'd that swell'd your fame afar
The halls that echoed to their sounds are gone,
Perish'd the conquering weapons of your
 war; (21)
And if a massy stone your names retain,
'T is but to tell your sons, for them ye died in vain

#### XLIV.

Yet, where some lone sepulchral relic stands,
That with those names tradition hallows yet,
Oft shall the wandering son of other lands
Linger in solemn thought and hush'd regret.
And still have legends mark'd the lonely spot
Where low the dust of Agamemnon lies;
And shades of kings and leaders unforgot,
Hovering around, to fancy's vision rise.
Souls of the heroes! seek your rest again,
Nor mark how changed the realms that saw your
 glories reign.

#### XLV.

Lo, where th' Albanian spreads his despot sway
O'er Thessaly's rich vales and glowing plains
Whose sons in sullen abjectness obey,
Nor lift the hand indignant at its chains;
Oh! doth the land that gave Achilles birth,
And many a chief of old, illustrious line,
Yield not one spirit of unconquer'd worth,
To kindle those that now in bondage pine?
No! on its mountain-air is slavery's breath,
And terror chills the hearts whose utter'd plaints
 were death.

#### XLVI.

Yet if thy light, fair Freedom, rested there,
How rich in charms were that romantic clime,
With streams, and woods, and pastoral valleys
 fair,
And wall'd with mountains, haughtily sublime.
Heights, that might well be deem'd the Muses'
 reign,
Since, claiming proud alliance with the skies,
They lose in loftier spheres their wild domain:
Meet home for those retired divinities
That love, where naught of earth may e'er in-
 trude,
Brightly to dwell on high, in lonely sanctitude.

#### XLVII.

There in rude grandeur, daringly ascends
Stern Pindus, rearing many a pine-clad height;
He with the clouds his bleak dominion blends,
Frowning o'er vales, in woodland verdure bright.
Wild and august in consecrated pride,
There through the deep-blue heaven Olympus
 towers,
Girt'ed with mists, light-floating as to hide
The rock-built palace of immortal powers;
Where far on high the sunbeam finds repose,
Amidst th' eternal pomp of forests and of snows.

#### XLVIII.

Those savage hills and solitudes might seem
The chosen haunts where Freedom's foot would
 roam;
She loves to dwell by glen and torrent-stream,
And make the rocky fastnesses her home.
And in the rushing of the mountain-flood,
In the wild eagle's solitary cry,
In sweeping winds that peal through cave and
 wood,
There is a voice of stern sublimity,
That swells her spirit to a loftier mood
Of solemn joy severe, of power, of fortitude.

#### XLIX.

But from those hills the radiance of her smile
Hath vanish'd long, her step hath fled afar;
O'er Suli's frowning rocks she paused awhile, (22)
Kindling the watch-fires of the mountain-war;
And brightly glow'd her ardent spirit there,
Still brightest 'midst privation: o'er distress
It cast romantic splendour, and despair
But fann'd that beacon of the wilderness:
And rude ravine, and precipice and dell
Sent their deep echoes forth, her rallying voice to
 swell.

#### L.

Dark children of the hills! 't was then ye
 wrought
Deeds of fierce daring, rudely, sternly grand;
As 'midst your craggy citadels ye fought,
And women mingled with your warrior-band.
Then on the cliff the frantic mother stood (23)
High o'er the river's darkly-rolling wave,
And hurl'd, in dread delirium, to the flood,
Her free-born infant, ne'er to be a slave.
For all was lost—all, save the power to die
The wild, indignant death of savage liberty.

#### LI.

Now is that strife a tale of vanish'd days,
With mightier things forgotten soon to lie;
Yet oft hath minstrel sung, in lofty lays,
Deeds less adventurous, energies less high.
And the dread struggle's fearful memory still
O'er each wild rock a wilder aspect throws;
Sheds darker shadows o'er the frowning hill,
More solemn quiet o'er the glen's repose;
Lends to the rustling pines a deeper moan,
And the hoarse river's voice a murmur not its own.

#### LII.

For stillness now—the stillness of the dead,
Hath wrapt that conflict's lone and awful scene,
And man's forsaken homes, in ruin spread,
Tell where the storming of the cliffs hath been.
And there, o'er wastes magnificently rude,
What race may rove, unconscious of the chain?
Those realms have now no desert unsubdued,
Where Freedom's banner may be rear'd again.
Sunk are the ancient dwellings of her fame,
The children of her sons inherit but their name.

#### LIII.

Go, seek proud Sparta's monuments and fanes!
In scatter'd fragments o'er the vale they lie;
Of all they were not e'en enough remains,
To lend their fall a mournful majesty. (24)

Birth-place of those whose names we first re
     vered
In song and story—temple of the free!
Oh thou, the stern, the haughty, and the fear'd,
Are such thy relics, and can this be thee!
Thou shouldst have left a giant-wreck behind,
And e'en in ruin claim'd the wonder of mankind.

### LIV.

For thine were spirits cast in other mould
Than all beside—and proved by ruder test;
They stood alone—the proud, the firm, the bold,
With the same seal indelibly imprest.
Theirs were no bright varieties of mind,
One image stamp'd the rough, colossal race,
In rugged grandeur frowning o'er mankind.
Stern, and disdainful of each milder grace.
As to the sky some mighty rock may tower,
Whose front can brave the storm, but will not
     bear the flower.

### LV.

Such were thy sons—their life a battle-day!
Their youth one lesson how for thee to die!
Closed is t ..it task, and they have pass'd away
Like softer beings train'd to aims less high.
Yet bright on earth *their* fame who proudly fell,
True to their shields, the champion of thy cause,
Whose funeral column bade the stranger tell
How died the brave, obedient to thy laws! (25)
O lofty mother of heroic worth,
How couldst thou live to bring a meaner offspring
     forth!

### LVI.

Hadst thou but perish'd with the free, nor known
A second race, when Glory's noon went by,
Then had thy name in single brightness shone
A watch-word on the helm of liberty!
Thou shouldst have pass'd with all thy light of
     fame,
And proudly sunk in ruins, not in chains
But slowly set thy star 'midst clouds of shame,
And tyrants rose amidst the falling fanes;
And thou, surrounded by thy warriors' graves,
Hast drain'd the bitter cup once mingled for thy
     slaves.

### LVII.

Now all is o'er—for thee alike are flown
Freedom's bright noon, and Slavery's twilight
     cloud;
And in thy fall, as in thy pride, alone,
Deep solitude is round thee, as a shroud.
Home of Leonidas! thy halls are low,
From their cold altars have thy Lares fled,
O'er thee unmark'd the sun-beams fade or glow,
And wild flowers wave, unbent by human tread,
And 'midst thy silence, as the grave's profound,
A voice, a step would seem as some unearthly
     sound.

### LVIII.

Taygetus still lifts his awful brow,
High o'er the mould'ring city of the dead,
Sternly sublime; while o'er his robe of snow
Heaven's floating tints their warm suffusions
     spread.
And yet his rippling wave Eurotas leads
By tombs and ruins o'er the silent plain,
While whispering there, his own wild graceful
     reeds
Rise as of old, when hail'd by classic strain;
There the rose-laurels still in beauty wave, (26)
And a frail shrub survives to bloom o'er Sparta's
     grave.

### LIX.

Oh! thus it is with man—a tree, a flower,
While millions perish, still renews its race,
And o'er the fallen records of his power
Spreads in wild pomp, or smiles in fairy grace.
The laurel shoots when those have pass'd away
Once rivals for its crown, the brave, the free;
The rose is flourishing o'er beauty's clay,
The myrtle blows when love hath ceased to be;
Green waves the bay when song and bard are
     fled,
And all that round us blooms, is blooming o'er the
     dead.

### LX.

And still the olive spreads its foliage round
Morea's fallen sanctuaries and towers,
Once its green boughs Minerva's votaries
     crown'd,
Deem'd a meet offering for celestial powers.
The suppliant's hand its holy branches bore; (27)
They waved around th' Olympic victor's head;
And, sanctified by many a rite of yore,
Its leaves the Spartan's honour'd bier o'erspread:
Those rites have vanish'd—but o'er vale and
     hill
Its fruitful groves arise, revered and hallow'd
     still. (28)

### LXI.

Where now thy shrines, Eleusis! where thy fane
Of fearful visions, mysteries wild and high?
The pomp of rites, the sacrificial train,
The long procession's awful pageantry?
Quench'd is the torch of Ceres (29)—all around
Decay hath spread the stillness of her reign,
There never more shall choral hymns resound,
O'er the hush'd earth and solitary main;
Whose wave from Salamis deserted flows,
To bathe a silent shore of desolate repose.

### LXII.

And oh! ye secret and terrific powers,
Dark oracles! in depth of groves that dwelt,
How are they sunk, the altars of your bowers,
Where superstition trembled as she knelt!
Ye, the unknown, the viewless ones! that made
The elements your voice, the wind and wave;
Spirits! whose influence darken'd many a shade,
Mysterious visitants of fount and cave!
How long your power the awe-struck nation
     sway'd,
How long earth dreamt of you, and shudderingly
     obey'd!

### LXIII.

And say, what marvel, in those early days,
While yet the light of heaven-born truth was
     not,
If man around him cast a fearful gaze,
Peopling with shadowy powers each dell and
     grot?
Awful in Nature in her savage forms,
Her solemn voice commanding in its might,
And mystery then was in the rush of storms,
The gloom of woods, the majesty of night;
And mortals heard fate's language in the blast,
And rear'd your forest-shrines, ye phantoms of the
     past!

### LXIV.

Then through the foliage not a breeze might sigh
But with prophetic sound—a waving tree,
A meteor flashing o'er the summer sky,
A bird's wild flight, reveal'd the things to be.
All spoke of unseen natures and convey'd
Their inspiration; still they hover'd round,
Hallow'd the temple, whisper'd through the
     shade,
Pervaded loneliness, gave soul to sound;
Of them the fount, the forest, murmur'd still,
Their voice was in the stream, their footstep on
     the hill.

### LXV.

Now is the train of Superstition own,
Unearthly Beings walk on earth no more;
The deep wind swells with no portentous tone,
The rustling wood breathes no fatidic lore,
Fled are the phantoms of Livadia's cave,
There dwell no shadows, but of crag and steep!

Fount of Oblivion! in thy gushing wave, (30)
That murmurs nigh, those powers of terror sleep.
Oh! that such dreams alone had fled that clime,
But grace is changed in all that could be changed
    by time!

### LXVI.

Her skies are those whence many a mighty bard
Caught inspiration, glorious as their beams:
Her hills the same that heroes died to guard,
Her vales, that foster'd art's divinest dreams!
But that bright spirit o'er the land that shono,
And all around pervading influence pour'd,
That lent the harp of Æschylus its tone,
And proudly hallow'd Lacedæmon's sword,
And guided Phidias o'er the yielding stone,
With them its ardours lived—with them its light
    is flown.

### LXVII.

Thebes, Corinth, Argos!—ye, renown'd of old,
Where are your chiefs of high romantic name!
How soon the tale of ages may be told!
A page, a verse, records the fall of fame,
The work of centuries—we gaze on you,
Ob cities! once the glorious and the free,
The lofty tales that charm'd our youth renew,
And wondering ask, if these their scenes could
    be?
Search for the classic fane, the regal tomb,
And find the mosque alone—a record of their
    doom!

### LXVIII.

How oft hath war his host of spoilers pour'd,
Fair Elis! o'er thy consecrated vales? (31)
There have the sunbeams glanced on spear and
    sword,
And banners floated on the balmy gales.
Once didst thou smile, secure in sanctitude,
As some enchanted isle 'mid stormy seas;
On thee no hostile footstep might intrude,
And pastoral sounds alone were on thy breeze.
Forsaken home of peace! that spell is broke,
Thou too hast heard the storm and bow'd beneath
    the yoke.

### LXIX.

And through Arcadia's wild and lone retreats
Far other sounds have echo'd than the strain
Of faun and dryad, from their woodland seats,
Or ancient reed of peaceful mountain-swain!
There, though at times Alpheus yet surveys,
On his green banks renew'd, the classic dance,
And nymph-like forms, and wild melodious lays.
Revive the sylvan scenes of old romance;
Yet brooding fear and dark suspicion dwell,
Midst Pan's deserted haunts, by fountain, cave,
    and dell.

### LXX.

But thou, fair Attica! whose rocky bound
All art and nature's richest gifts enshrined,
Thou little sphere, whose soul-illumined round
Concentrated each sunbeam of the mind;
Who, as the summit of some Alpine height
Glows earliest, latest, with the blush of day,
Didst first imbibe the splendours of the light,
And smile the longest in its lingering ray; (32)
Oh! let us gaze on thee, and fondly deem
The past awhile restored, the present but a dream.

### LXXI.

Let Fancy's vivid hues awhile prevail—
Wake at her call—be all thou wert once more!
Hark, hymns of triumph swell on every gale!
Lo, bright processions move along thy shore!
Again thy temples 'midst the olive-shade,
Lovely in chaste simplicity arise;
And graceful monuments, in grove and glade,
Catch the warm tints of thy resplendent skies;
And sculptured forms, of high and heavenly mien,
In their calm beauty smile, around the sun-
    bright scene.

### LXXII.

Again renew'd by thought's creative spells,
In all her pomp thy city, Theseus! towers;
Within, around, the light of glory dwells
On art's fair fabrics, wisdom's holy bowers.
There marble fanes in finish'd grace ascend,
The pencil's world of life and beauty glows;
Shrines, pillars, porticoes, in grandeur blend,
Rich with the trophies of barbaric foes,
And groves of platane wave in verdant pride
The sage's blest retreats, by calm Ilissus' tide.

### LXXIII.

Bright as that fairy vision of the wave,
Raised by the magic of Morgana's wand, (33)
On summer seas, that undulating lave
Romantic Sicily's Arcadian strand;
That pictured scene of airy colonnades,
Light palaces, in shadowy glory drest,
Enchanted groves, and temples, and arcades,
Gleaming and floating on the ocean's breast;
Athens! thus fair the dream of thee appears,
As Fancy's eye pervades the veiling cloud of years

### LXXIV.

Still be that cloud withdrawn—oh! mark on high,
Crowning yon hill, with temples richly graced,
That fane august in perfect symmetry,
The purest model of Athenian taste.
Fair Parthenon! thy Doric pillars rise,
In simple dignity thy marble's hue
Unsullied shines, relieved by brilliant skies,
That round thee spread their deep ethereal blue;
And art o'er all thy light proportions throws
The harmony of grace, the beauty of repose.

### LXXV.

And lovely o'er thee sleeps the sunny glow,
When morn and eve in tranquil splendour reign,
And on thy sculptures, as they smile, bestow
Hues that the pencil emulates in vain.
Then the fair forms by Phidias wrought, unfold
Each latent grace, developing in light,
Catch from soft clouds of purple and of gold,
Each tint that passes, tremulously bright;
And seem indeed whate'er devotion deems,
While so suffused with heaven, so mingling with
    its beams

### LXXVI.

But oh! what words the vision may portray,
The form of sanctitude that guards thy shrine?
There stands thy goddess, robed in war's array,
Supremely glorious, awfully divine!
With spear and helm she stands, and flowing
    vest,
And sculptured ægis, to perfection wrought,
And on each heavenly lineament imprest,
Calmly sublime, the majesty of thought;
The pure intelligence, the chaste repose,—
All that a poet's dream around Minerva throws.

### LXXVII.

Bright age of Pericles! let fancy still
Through Time's deep shadows all thy splendour
    trace,
And in each work of art's consummate skill
Hail the free spirit of thy lofty race.
That spirit, roused by every proud reward,
That hope could picture, glory could bestow,
Foster'd by all the sculptor and the bard
Could give of immortality below.
Thus were thy heroes form'd, and o'er their
    name
Thus did thy genius shed imperishable fame.

### LXXVIII

Mark in the throng'd Ceramicus, the train
Of mourners weeping o'er the martyr'd brave:
Proud be the tears devoted to the slain,

Holy the amaranth strew'd upon their grave! (34)
And hark—unrivall'd eloquence proclaims
Their deeds, their trophies, with triumphant
    voice!
Hark—Pericles records their honour'd names! (35)
Sons of the fallen, in their lot rejoice:
What hath life brighter than so bright a doom?
What power hath fate to soil the garlands of the
    tomb?

### LXXIX.

Praise to the valiant dead! for them doth art
Exhaust her skill, their triumphs bodying forth;
Theirs are enshrined names, and every heart
Shall bear the blazon'd impress of their worth.
Bright on the dreams of youth their fame shall
    rise,
Their fields of fight shall epic song record,
And when the voice of battle rends the skies,
Their name shall be their country's rallying
    word!
While fane and column rise august to tell
How Athens honours those for her who proudly
    fell.

### LXXX.

City of Theseus! bursting on the mind,
Thus dost thou rise, in all thy glory fled!
Thus guarded by the mighty of mankind,
Thus hallow'd by the memory of the dead;
Alone in beauty and renown—a scene
Whose tints are drawn from freedom's loveliest
    ray.
'T is but a vision now—yet thou hast been
More than the brightest vision might portray:
And every stone, with but a vestige fraught
Of thee, hath latent power to wake some lofty
    thought.

### LXXXI.

Fallen are thy fabrics, that so oft have rung
To choral melodies, and tragic lore;
Now is the lyre of Sophocles unstrung,
The song that hail'd Harmodius peals no more.
Thy proud Piræus is a desert strand,
Thy stately shrines are mouldering on their hill,
Closed are the triumphs of the sculptor's hand,
The magic voice of eloquence is still;
Minerva's veil is rent (36)—her image gone,
Silent the sage's bower—the warrior's tomb o'er-
    thrown.

### LXXXII.

Yet in decay thine exquisite remains
Wondering we view, and silently revere
As traces left on earth's forsaken plains
By vanish'd beings of a nobler sphere!
Not all the old magnificence of Rome,
All that dominion there hath left to time,
Proud Coliseum, or commanding dome,
Triumphal arch, or obelisk sublime,
Can bid such reverence o'er the spirit steal
As aught by thee imprest with beauty's plastic seal.

### LXXXIII.

Though still the empress of the sun-burnt waste,
Palmyra rises, desolately grand—
Though with rich gold (37) and massy sculpture
    graced,
Commanding still. Persepolis may stand
In haughty solitude—though sacred Nile
The first-born temples of the world surveys,
And many an awful and stupendous pile
Thebes of the hundred gates e'en yet displays;
City of Pericles! oh, who like thee
Can teach how fair the works of mortal hand may
    be?

### LXXXIV.

Thou led'st the way to that immortal sphere
Where sovereign beauty dwells; and thence
        didst bear
Oh, still triumphant in that high career!
Bright archetypes of all the grand and fair



And still to thee th' enlighten'd mind hath flown,
As to her country;—thou hast been to earth
A cynosure: and e'en from victory's throne,
Imperial Rome gave homage to thy worth;
And nations, rising to their fame afar,
Still to thy model turn, as seamen to their star.

### LXXXV.

Glory to those whose relics thus arrest
The gaze of ages! Glory to the free!
For they, they only, could have thus imprest
Their mighty image on the years to be!
Empires and cities in oblivion lie,
Grandeur may vanish, conquest be forgot;—
To leave on earth renown that cannot die,
Of high-soul'd genius is th' unrivall'd lot.
Honour to thee, O Athens! thou hast shown
What mortals may attain, and seized the palm
    alone.

### LXXXVI.

Oh! live there those who view with scornful eyes
All that attests the brightness of thy prime!
Yes; they who dwell beneath thy lovely skies,
And breathe th' inspiring ether of thy clime!
Their path is o'er the mightiest of the dead,
Their homes are 'midst the works of noblest arts;
Yet all around their gaze, beneath their tread,
Not one proud thrill of loftier thought imparts.
Such are the conquerors of Minerva's land,
Where genius first reveal'd the triumphs of his
    hand!

### LXXXVII.

For them in vain the glowing light may smile
O'er the pale marble, colouring's warmth to
    shed,
And in chaste beauty many a sculptured pile
Still o'er the dust of heroes lift its head.
No patriot feeling binds them to the soil,
Whose tombs and shrines their fathers have
    not rear'd,
Their glance is cold indiff'rence, and their toil
But to destroy what ages have revered,
As if exulting sternly to erase
Whate'er might prove that land had nursed a no-
    bler race.

### LXXXVIII.

And who may grieve that, rescued from their
    hands,
Spoilers of excellence and foes to art,
Thy relics, Athens! borne to other lands,
Claim homage still to thee from every heart?
Though now no more th' exploring stranger's
    sight,
Fix'd in deep reverence on Minerva's fane,
Shall hail, beneath their native heaven of light,
All that remain'd of forms adored in vain;
A few short years—and, vanish'd from the scene,
To blend with classic dust their proudest lot had
    been.

### LXXXIX.

Fair Parthenon! yet still must fancy weep
For thee, thou work of nobler spirits flown.
Bright, as of old, the sunbeams o'er thee sleep
In all their beauty still—and thine is gone!
Empires have sunk since thou wert first revered
And varying rites have sanctified thy shrine.
The dust is round thee of the race that rear'd
Thy walls; and thou—their fate must soon be
    thine!
But when shall earth again exult to see
Visions divine like theirs renew'd in aught like
    thee?

### XC.

Lone are thy pillars now—each passing gale
Sighs o'er them as a spirit's voice, which moan'd
That loneliness, and told the plaintive tale
Of the bright synod once above them throned.
Mourn, graceful ruin! on thy sacred hill,
Thy gods, thy rites, a kindred fate hath shared;

Yet art thou honour'd in each fragment still,
That wasting years and barbarous hands had
    spared ;
Each hallow'd stone, from rapine's fury borne,
Shall wake bright dreams of thee in ages yet un-
    born.

### XCI.

Yes; in those fragments, though by time defaced,
And rude insensate conquerors, yet remains
All that may charm th' enlighten'd eye of taste,
On shores where still inspiring freedom reigns.
As vital fragrance breathes from every part
Of the crush'd myrtle, or the bruised rose,
E'en thus th' essential energy of art,
There in each wreck imperishably glows ! (38)
The soul of Athens lives in every line,
Pervading brightly still the ruins of her shrine.

### XCII.

Mark—on the storied frieze the graceful train,
The holy festival's triumphal throng,
In fair procession, to Minerva's fane,
With many a sacred symbol move along.
There every shade of bright existence trace,
The fire of youth, the dignity of age ;
The matron's calm austerity of grace,
The ardent warrior, the benignant sage ;
The nymph's light symmetry, the chief's proud
    mien,
Each ray of beauty caught and mingled in the
    scene.

### XCIII.

Art unobtrusive there ennobles form, (39)
Each pure, chaste outline exquisitely flows ;
There e'en the steed, with bold expression
    warm, (40)
Is clothed with majesty, with being glows.
One mighty mind hath harmonized the whole ;
Those varied groups the same bright impress
    bear ;
One beam and essence of exalting soul
Lives in the grand, the delicate, the fair ;
And well that pageant of the glorious dead
Blends us with nobler days, and loftier spirits fled.

### XCIV.

O conquering Genius! that couldst thus detain
The subtle graces, fading as they rise,
Eternalize expression's fleeting reign,
Arrest warm life in all its energies,
And fix them on the stone—thy glorious lot
Might wake ambition's envy, and create
Powers half divine ; while nations are forgot,
A thought, a dream of thine hath .vanquish'd
    fate !
And when thy hand first gave its wonders birth,
The realms that hail them now scarce claim'd a
    name on earth.

### XCV.

Wert thou some spirit of a purer sphere
But once beheld, and never to return ?
No—we may hail again thy bright career,
Again on earth a kindred fire shall burn !
Though thy last relics, e'en in ruin, bear
A stamp of heaven, that ne'er hath been re-
    new'd—
A light inherent—let not man despair :
Still be hope ardent, patience unsubdued ;
For still is nature fair, and thought divine,
And art hath won a world in models pure as
    thine. (41)

### XCVI.

Gaze on yon forms, corroded and defaced—
Yet there the germ of future glory lies !
Their virtual grandeur could not be erased,
It clothes them still, though veil'd from common
    eyes.
They once were gods and heroes (42)—and beheld
As the blest guardians of their native scene ;

And hearts of warriors, sages, bards, have swell'd
With awe that own'd their sov'reignty of mien.
—Ages have vanish'd since those hearts were
    cold,
And still those shatter'd forms retain their godlike
    mould.

### XCVII.

'Midst their bright kindred, from their marble
    throne,
They have look'd down on thousand storms of
    time ;
Surviving power and fame and freedom flown,
They still remain'd, still tranquilly sublime !
Till mortal hands the heavenly conclave marr'd,
Th' Olympian groups have sunk, and are forgot ;
Not e'en their dust could weeping Athens guard :
—But these were destined to a nobler lot !
And they have borne, to light another land,
The quenchless ray that soon shall gloriously ex-
    pand.

### XCVIII.

Phidias ! supreme in thought ! what hand but
    thine,
In human works thus blending earth and heaven,
O'er Nature's truth hath shed that grace divine
To mortal form immortal grandeur given ?
What soul but thine, infusing all its power,
In these last monuments of matchless days,
Could from their ruins bid young Genius tower,
And Hope aspire to more exalted praise ?
And guide deep thought to that secluded height,
Where excellence is throned, in purity of light.

### XCIX.

And who can tell how pure, how bright a flame
Caught from these models, may illume the west ?
What British Angelo may rise to fame, (43)
On the free isle what beams of art may rest ?
Deem not, O England ! that by climes confined,
Genius and taste diffuse a partial ray : (44)
Deem not the eternal energies of mind
Sway'd by that sun whose doom is but decay !
Shall thought be foster'd but by skies serene ;
No ! thou hast power to be what Athens e'er hath
    been.

### C.

But thine are treasures oft unprized, unknown,
And cold neglect hath blighted many a mind,
O'er whose young ardours, had thy smile but
    shone,
Their soaring flight had left a world behind !
And many a gifted hand, that might have
    wrought
To Grecian excellence the breathing stone,
Or each pure grace of Raphael's pencil caught
Leaving no record of its power, is gone !
While thou hast fondly sought, on distant coast,
Gems far less rich than those, thus precious, and
    thus lost.

### CI.

Yet rise, O Land in all but Art alone,
Bid the sole wreath that is not thine be won !
Fame dwells around thee—Genius is thine own ;
Call his rich blooms to life—be Thou their Sun !
So should dark ages o'er thy glory sweep,
Should thine e'er be as now are Grecian plains,
Nations unborn shall track thine own blue deep,
To hail thy shore, to worship thy remains ;
Thy mighty monuments with reverence trace,
And cry, " This ancient soil hath nursed a glorious
    race !"

# NOTES.

### NOTE 1.

*Round Doric Pæstum's solitary fanes.*

"The Pæstan rose, from its peculiar fragrance and the singularity of blowing twice a year, is often mentioned by the classic poets. The wild rose, which now shoots up among the ruins, is of the small single damask kind, with a very high perfume; as a farmer assured me on the spot, it flowers both in spring and autumn."—*Swinburne's Travels in the Two Sicilies.*

### NOTE 2.

*Swelled o'er that tide—the sons of battle sleep.*

In the naval engagements of the Greeks, "it was usual for the soldiers before the fight to sing a pæan, or hymn, to Mars, and after the fight another to Apollo."—*See Potter's Antiquities of Greece,* vol. ii, p. 155.

### NOTE 3.

*Her own bright East, thy son, Morea! flies.*

The emigration of the natives of the Morea to different parts of Asia is thus mentioned by Chateaubriand in his "Itinéraire de Paris la Jerusalem."—"Parvenu au dernier degre du malheur, le Moraite s'arrache de son pays, et va chercher en Asie un sort moins rigoureux. Vain espoir! il retrouve des cadis et des pachas jusques dans les sables de Jourdain et dans les deserts de Palmyre."

### NOTE 4.

*Wilt thou receive the wanderer to thine arms.*

In the same work, Chateaubriand also relates his having met with several Greek emigrants who had established themselves in the woods of Florida.

### NOTE 5.

*And isles of flowers, bright-floating o'er the tide.*

"La grace est toujours unie à la magnificence dans les scenes de la nature; et tandis que le courant du milieu entraine vers la mer les cadavres des pins et des chenes, on voit sur les deux courans lateraux remonter le long des rivages des iles flottantes de Pistia et de Nenuphar, dont les roses jaunes s'elevent comme de petits papillons."—*Description of the banks of the Mississippi, Chateaubriand's "Atala."*

### NOTE 6.

*Wild, as when sung by bards of elder time.*

"Looking generally at the narrowness and abruptness of this mountain-channel (Tempe) and contrasting it with the course of the Peneus, through the p'ains of Thessaly, the imagination instantly recurs to the tradition that these plains were once covered with water for which some convulsion of nature had subsequently opened this narrow passage. The term *vale,* in our language, is usually employed to describe scenery in which the predominant features are breadth, beauty, and repose. The reader has already perceived that the term is wholly inapplicable to the scenery at this spot, and that the phrase *vale* of Tempe is one that depends on poetic fiction.——The real character of Tempe, though it perhaps be less beautiful, yet possesses more of magnificence than is implied in the epithet given to it.——To those who have visited St. Vincent's rocks, below Bristol, I cannot convey a more sufficient idea of Tempe, than by saying that its scenery resembles, though on a much larger scale, that of the former place. The Peneus indeed, as it flows through the valley, is not greatly wider than the Avon; and the channel between the cliffs is equally contracted in its dimensions; but these cliffs themselves are much loftier and more precipitous, and project their vast masses of rock with still more extraordinary abruptness over the hollow beneath."—*Holland's Travels in Albania, &c.*

### NOTE 7.

*Years, that have changed thy river's classic name.*

The modern name of the Peneus is Salympria.

### NOTE 8.

*Where the rich arbute's coral berries glow.*

"Towards the lower part of Tempe, these cliffs are peaked in a very singular manner, and form projecting angles on the vast perpendicular faces of the rock which they present towards the chasm; where the surface renders it possible, the summits and ledges of the rocks are for the most part covered with small wood, chiefly oak, with the arbutus and other shrubs. On the banks of the river, wherever there is a small interval between the water and the cliffs, it is covered by the rich and widely spreading foliage of the plane, the oak, and other forest trees, which in these situations have attained a remarkable size, and in various places extend their shadow far over the channel of the stream."——"The rocks on each side the vale of Tempe are evidently the same; what may be called, I believe, a coarse bluish gray marble, with veins and portions of the rock, in which the marble is of finer quality."—*Holland's Travels in Albania, &c.*

### NOTE 9.

*Where Greece her councils held, her Pythian victors crowned.*

The Amphictyonic council was convened in spring and autumn at Delphi or Thermopylæ, and presided at the Pythian games which were celebrated at Delphi every fifth year.

### NOTE 10.

*Blown the wild laurels o'er the warlike dead.*

"This spot (the field of Mantinea) on which so many brave men were laid to rest, is now covered with rosemary and laurels."—*Pouqueville's Travels in the Morea.*

### NOTE 11.

*Where the dark upas taints the gale around.*

For the accounts of the upas or poison-tree of Java, now generally believed to be fabulous, or greatly exaggerated, see the notes to Darwin's Botanic Garden.

### NOTE 12.

*Its sculptured lions, richly wrought arcades.*

"The court most to be admired of the Alhambra is that called the court of the Lions; it is ornamented with sixty elegant pillars of an architecture which bears not the least resemblance to any of the known orders, and might be called the Arabian order. But its principa' ornament, and that from which it took its name, is an alabaster cup, six feet in diameter, supported by twelve lions, which is said to have been made in imitation of the Brazen Sea of Solomon's temple."—*Bourgoanne's Travels in Spain.*

### NOTE 13.

*Bright as that Pleiad sphered in Mecca's fane.*

"Sept des plus fameux parmi les anciens poetes Arabiques, son' designes par les ecrivains orientaux sous le nom de *Pleiade Arabique,* et leurs ouvrages etaient suspendus autour de la Caaba ou Mosque de la Mecque."—*Sismondi, Littérature du Midi.*

### NOTE 14.

*And thou, O last and noblest Constantine!*

"The distress and fall of the last Constantine are more glorious than the long prosperity of the Byzantine Cæsars."—*Gibbon's Decline and Fall, &c.* vol. xii. p. 236.

### NOTE 15

*The closing night of that imperial race!*

See the description of the night previous to the taking of Constantinople by Mahomet II.—*Gibbon,* vol. xii. p. 225.

### NOTE 16.

*And the Seven Towers are scaled, and all is won and lost.*

"This building (the Castle of the Seven Towers) is mentioned as early as the sixth century of the Christian era, as a spot which contributed to the defence of Constantinople, and it was the principal bulwark of the town on the coast of the Propontis, in the last periods of the empire."—*Pouqueville's Travels in the Morea.*

### NOTE 17.

*Preserved inviolate their awful fane*

See the account from Herodotus of the supernatural defence of Delphi.—*Mitford's Greece,* vol. i. p. 396, 7.

### NOTE 18.

*Who from the dead at Marathon arose.*

"In succeeding ages the Athenians honoured Theseus as a demi-god, induced to it as well by other reasons, as because, when they were fighting the Medes at Marathon, a considerable part of the army thought they saw the apparition of Theseus completely armed, and bearing down before them upon the Barbarians."—*Langhorne's Plutarch, Life of Theseus.*

### NOTE 19.

*Or they whose forms, to Alaric's awe-struck eye.*

"From Thermopylæ to Sparta, the leader of the Goths (Alaric) pursued his victorious march without encountering any mortal antagonist: but one of the advocates of expiring paganism has confidently asserted, that the walls of Athens were guarded by the goddess Minerva, with her formidable ægis, and by the angry phantom of Achilles, and that the conqueror was dismayed by the presence of the hostile deities of Greece."—*Gibbon's Decline and Fall, &c.* vol. v. p. 183.

### NOTE 20.

*Ye slept, oh heroes! chief ones of the earth.*

"Even all the chief ones of the earth."—*Isaiah,* 14th chapter.

### NOTE 21.

*Perished the conquering weapons of your war.*

"How are the mighty fallen, and the weapons of war perished!" Samuel, 2d book, 1st chap.

### NOTE 22.

*O'er Suli's frowning rocks she paused awhile.*

For several interesting particulars relative to the Suliote warfare with Ali Pasha, see Holland's Travels in Albania.

### NOTE 23.

*Then on the cliff the frantic mother stood.*

"It is related as an authentic story, that a group of Suliote women assembled on one of the precipices adjoining the modern seraglio, and threw their infants into the chasm below, that they might not become the slaves of the enemy."—*Holland's Travels, &c.*

### NOTE 24.

*To lend their fall a mournful majesty.*

The ruins of Sparta, near the modern town of Mistra, are very inconsiderable, and only sufficient to mark the site of the ancient city. The scenery around them is described by travellers as very striking.

### NOTE 25.

*How died the brave, obedient to thy laws.*

The inscription composed by Simonides for the Spartan monument in the pass of Thermopylæ has been thus translated—"Stranger, go tell the Lacedæmonians that we have obeyed their laws, and that we lie here."

### NOTE 26.

*There the rose-laurels still in beauty wave.*

"In the Eurotas I observed abundance of those famous reeds which were known in the earliest ages, and all the rivers and marshes of Greece are replete with rose-laurels, while the springs and rivulets are covered with lilies, tuberoses, hyacinths, and narcissus orientalis."—*Pouqueville's Travels in the Morea.*

### NOTE 27.

*The suppliant's hand its holy branches bore.*

It was usual for suppliants to carry an olive branch bound with wool.

### NOTE 28.

*Its fruitful groves arise, revered and hallowed still.*

The olive, according to Pouqueville, is still regarded with veneration by the people of the Morea.

### NOTE 29.

*Quenched is the torch of Ceres—all around.*

It was customary at Eleusis on the fifth day of the festival, for men and women to run about with torches in their hands, and also to dedicate torches to Ceres, and to contend who should present the largest. This was done in memory of the journey of Ceres in search of Proserpine, during which she was lighted by a torch kindled in the flames of Etna.—*Potter's Antiquities of Greece,* vol. i. p. 302.

### NOTE 30.

*Fount of Oblivion! in thy gushing wave.*

The Fountains of Oblivion and Memory, with the Herculean fountain, are still to be seen amongst the rocks near Livadia, though the situation of the cave of Trophonius in their vicinity cannot be exactly ascertained.—*See Holland's Travels.*

### NOTE 31.

*Fair Elis, o'er thy consecrated vale.*

Elis was anciently a sacred territory, its inhabitants being considered as consecrated to the service of Jupiter. All armies marching through it delivered up their weapons, and received them again when they had passed its boundary.

### NOTE 32.

*And smile the longest in its lingering ray.*

"We are assured by Thucydides that Attica was the province of Greece in which population first became settled, and where the earliest progress was made toward civilization."—*Mitford's Greece,* vol. i. p. 35.

### NOTE 33.

*Raised by the magic of Morgana's wand.*

Fata Morgana. This remarkable aerial phenomenon, which is thought by the lower orders of Sicilians to be the work of a fairy, is thus described by father Angelucci, whose account is quoted by Swinburne.

"On the 15th August, 1643, I was surprised, as I stood at my window, with a most wonderful spectacle: the sea that washes the Sicilian shore swelled, and became, for ten miles in length, like a chain of dark mountains, while the waters near our Calabrian coast grew quite smooth, and in an instant appeared like one clear polished mirror. On this glass was depicted, in chiaro scuro, a string of several thousands of pilasters all equal in height, distance, and degrees of light and shade. In a moment they bent into arcades, like Roman aqueducts. A long cornice was next formed at the top, and above it rose innumerable castles, all perfectly alike; these again changed into towers, which were shortly after lost in colonnades, then windows, and at last ended in pines, cypresses, and other trees."—*Swinburne's Travels in the Two Sicilies.*

### NOTE 34.

*Holy the amaranth strewed upon their grave.*

All sorts of purple and white flowers were supposed by the Greeks to be acceptable to the dead, and used in adorning tombs; as amaranth, with which the Thessalians decorated the tomb of Achilles.—*Potter's Antiquities of Greece,* vol. ii. p. 232.

### NOTE 35.

*Hush! Pericles records their honoured names.*

Pericles, on his return to Athens after the reduction of Samos, celebrated in a splendid manner the obsequies of his countrymen who fell in that war, and pronounced, himself, the funeral oration usual on such occasions. This gained him great applause; and when he came down from the rostrum, the women paid their respects to him, and presented him with crowns and chaplets, like a champion just returned victorious from the lists.—*Langhorne's Plutarch, Life of Pericles.*

### NOTE 36.

*Minerva's veil is rent—her image gone.*

The peplus, which is supposed to have been suspended as an awning over the statue of Minerva, in the Parthenon, was a principal ornament of the Panathenaic festival; it was embroidered with various colours, representing the battle of the Gods and Titans, and the exploits of Athenian heroes. When the festival was celebrated, the peplus was brought from the Acropolis, and suspended as a sail to the vessel, which on that day was conducted through the Ceramicus and principal streets of Athens, till it had made the circuit of the Acropolis. The peplus was then carried to the Parthenon, and consecrated to Minerva.—*See Chandler's Travels, Stewart's Athens,* &c.

### NOTE 37.

*Though with rich gold and massy sculpture graced.*

The gilding amidst the ruins of Persepolis is still, according to Winckelmann, in high preservation.

### NOTE 38.

*There in each wreck imperishably glows.*

"In the most broken fragment the same great principle of life can be proved to exist, as in the most perfect figure," is one of the observations of Mr. Haydon on the Elgin Marbles.

### NOTE 39.

*Art unobtrusive there ennobles form.*

"Every thing here breathes life, with a veracity, with an exquisite knowledge of art, but without the least ostentation or parade of it, which is concealed by consummate and masterly skill."—*Canova's Letter to the Earl of Elgin.*

### NOTE 40.

*There e'en the steed with bold expression warm.*

Dr. West, after expressing his admiration of the horse's head in Lord Elgin's collection of Athenian sculpture, thus proceeds: "We feel the same when we view the young equestrian Athenians, and in observing them we are insensibly carried on with the impression, that they and their horses actually existed, as we see them, at the instant when they were converted into marble."—*West's Second Letter to Lord Elgin.*

### NOTE 41.

*And art hath won a world in models pure as thine.*

Mr. Flaxman thinks that sculpture has very greatly improved within these last twenty years, and that his opinion is not singular, because works of such prime importance as the Elgin marbles could not remain in any country without a consequent improvement of the public taste, and the talents of the artist.—*See the Evidence given in reply to Interrogatories from the Committee on the Elgin Marbles.*

### NOTE 42.

*They once were gods and heroes—and behold.*

The Theseus and Ilissus, which are considered by Sir T. Lawrence, Mr. Westmacott, and other distinguished artists, to be of a higher class than the Apollo Belvidere; "because there is in them an union of very grand form with a more true and natural expression of the effect of action upon the human frame, than there is in the Apollo, or any of the other more celebrated statues."—*See the Evidence,* &c.

### NOTE 43.

*What British Angelo may rise to fame.*

"Let us suppose a young man at this time in London, endowed with powers such as enabled Michael Angelo to advance the arts, as he did, by the aid of one mutilated specimen of Grecian excellence in sculpture; to what an eminence might not such a genius carry art, by the opportunity of studying those sculptures in the aggregate, which adorned the temple of Minerva at Athens?"—*West's Second Letter to Lord Elgin.*

### NOTE 44.

*Genius and taste diffuse a partial ray.*

In allusion to the theories of Du Bos, Winckelmann, Montesquieu, &c. with regard to the inherent obstacles in the climate of England to the progress of genius and the arts.—*See Moore's Epochs of the Arts,* page 84, &c.

# DARTMOOR.

### A PRIZE POEM.

Come bright Improvement, on the car of Time,
And rule the spacious world from clime to clime!
Thy handmaid, Art, shall every wild explore,
Trace every wave and culture every shore.
　　　　　　　　　　　　*Campbell*

　　　　　　　　　　　　May ne'er
That true succession fail of English hearts,
That can perceive, not less than heretofore
Our ancestors did feelingly perceive,
———————————————— the charm
Of pious sentiment, diffused afar,
And human charity, and social love.
　　　　　　　　　　　　*Wordsworth.*

AMIDST the peopled and the regal Isle,
Whose vales, rejoicing in their beauty, smile;
Whose cities, fearless of the spoiler, tower,
And send on every breeze a voice of power;
Hath Desolation rear'd herself a throne,
And mark'd a pathless region for her own?
Yes! though thy turf no stain of carnage wore,
When bled the noble hearts of many a shore,
Though not a hostile step thy heath-flowers bent,
When empires totter'd, and the earth was rent;
Yet lone, as if some trampler of mankind
Had still'd life's busy murmurs on the wind,
And, flush'd with power, in daring Pride's excess,
Stamp'd on thy soil the curse of barrenness;
For thee in vain descend the dews of heaven,
In vain the sunbeam and the shower are given;
Wild Dartmoor! thou that, 'midst thy mountains
　　rude,
Hast robed thyself with haughty solitude,
As a dark cloud on Summer's clear-blue sky,
A mourner, circled with festivity!
For all beyond is life!—the rolling sea,
The rush, the swell, whose echoes reach not thee.
Yet who shall find a scene so wild and bare,
But man has left his lingering traces there?
E'en on mysterious Afric's boundless plains,
Where noon with attributes of midnight reigns,
In gloom and silence, fearfully profound,
As of a world unwaked to soul or sound;
Though the sad wanderer of the burning zone
Feels, as amidst infinity, alone,
And naught of life be near; his camel's tread
Is o'er the prostrate cities of the dead!
Some column, rear'd by long-forgotten hands,
Just lifts its head above the billowy sands—
Some mouldering shrine still consecrates the scene,
And tells that Glory's footstep there hath been.
There hath the spirit of the mighty pass'd,
Not without record; though the desert-blast,
Borne on the wings of Time, hath swept away
The proud creations, rear'd to brave decay.
But *thou*, lone region! whose unnoticed name
No lofty deeds have mingled with their fame,
Who shall unfold thine annals? Who shall tell
If on thy soil the sons of heroes fell,
In those far ages, which have left no trace,
No sunbeam on the pathway of their race?
Though, haply, in the unrecorded days
Of kings and chiefs, who pass'd without their
　　praise,
Thou might'st have rear'd the valiant and the free,
In history's page there is no tale of thee.—

Yet hast thou thy memorials. On the wild
Still rise the cairns of yore, all rudely piled, (1)
But hallow'd, by that instinct, which reveres
Things fraught with characters of elder years.
And such are these. Long centuries are flown,
Bow'd many a crest, and shatter'd many a throne.

Mingling the urn, the trophy, and the bust,
With that they hide—their shrined and treasured
　　dust;
Men traverse Alps and Oceans, to behold
Earth's glorious works fast mingling with her
　　mould;
But still these nameless chronicles of death,
'Midst the deep silence of the unpeopled heath,
Stand in primeval artlessness, and wear
The same sepulchral mien, and almost share
Th' eternity of nature, with the forms
Of the crown'd hills beyond, the dwellings of the
　　storms.

Yet, what avails it, if each moss grown heap
Still on the waste its lonely vigils keep,
Guarding the dust which slumbers well beneath
(Nor needs such care) from each cold season's
　　breath?
Where is the voice to tell *their* tale who rest,
Thus rudely pillow'd, on the desert's breast?
Doth the sword sleep beside them? Hath there been
A sound of battle 'midst the silent scene,
Where now the flocks repose? did the scythed car
Here reap its harvest in the ranks of war?
And rise these piles in memory of the slain,
And the red combat of the mountain-plain?

It may be thus: the vestiges of strife,
Around yet lingering, mark the steps of life
And the rude arrow's barb remains to tell (2)
How by its stroke perchance the mighty fell
To be forgotten. Vain the warrior's pride,
The chieftain's power—they had no bard, and
　　died. (3)
But other scenes, from their untroubled sphere,
The eternal stars of night have witness'd here.
There stands an altar of unsculptured stone, (4)
Far on the moor, a thing of ages gone,
Propp'd on its granite pillars, whence the rains,
And pure bright dews, have laved the crimson
　　stains
Left by dark rites of blood: for here, of yore,
When the bleak waste a robe of forest wore,
And many a crested oak, which now lies low,
Waved its wild wreath of sacred misletoe;
Here, at dead midnight, through the haunted shade,
On Druid-harps the quivering moon-beam play'd,
And spells were breathed, that fill'd the deepening
　　gloom
With the pale, shadowy people of the tomb.
Or, haply, torches waving through the night,
Bade the red cairn-fires blaze from every height, (5)
Like battle-signals, whose unearthly gleams
Threw o'er the desert's hundred hills and streams,
A savage grandeur; while the starry skies
Rung with the peal of mystic harmonies,
As the loud harp its deep-toned hymns sent forth
To the storm-ruling powers, the war-gods of the
　　North.

But wilder sounds were there; th' imploring cry
That woke the forest's echo in reply,
But not the heart's!—Unmoved, the wizard train
Stood round their human victim, and in vain
His prayer for mercy rose; in vain his glance
Look'd up, appealing to the blue expanse,
Where, in their calm, immortal beauty, shone
Heaven's cloudless orbs. With faint and fainter
　　moan,
Bound on the shrine of sacrifice he lay,
Till, drop by drop, life's current ebb'd away;
Till rock and turf grew deeply, darkly red,
And the pale moon gleam'd paler on the dead.
Have such things been, and here?—where still-
　　ness dwells
'Midst the rude barrows and the moorland swells
Thus undisturb'd?—Oh! long the gulf of time
Hath closed in darkness o'er those days of crime,
And earth no vestige of their path retains,
Save such as these, which strew her loneliest
　　plains
With records of man's conflicts and his doom,
His spirit and his dust—the altar and the tomb.

But ages roll'd away: and England stood,
With her proud banner streaming o'er the flood

And with a lofty calmness in her eye,
And regal in collected majesty,
To breast the storm of battle.  Every breeze
Bore sounds of triumph o'er her own blue seas;
And other lands, redeem'd and joyous, drank
The life-blood of her heroes, as they sank
On the red fields they won; whose wild flowers
    wave
Now in luxuriant beauty, o'er their grave.

'T was then the captives of Britannia's war, (6)
Here for their lovely southern-climes afar,
In bondage pined; the spell-deluded throng
Dragg'd at Ambition's chariot-wheels so long
To die,—because a despot could not clasp
A sceptre, fitted to his boundless grasp!

Yes! they whose march had rock'd the ancient
    thrones
And temples of the world; the deepening tones
Of whose advancing trumpet, from repose
Had startled nations, wakening to their woes,
Were prisoners here.—And there were some whose
    dreams
Were of sweet homes, by chainless mountain-
    streams,
And of the vine-clad hills, and many a strain,
And festal melody of Loire or Seine,
And of those mothers, who had watch'd and wept,
When on the field the unshelter'd conscript slept,
Bathed with the midnight dews.  And some were
    there,
Of sterner spirits, harden'd by despair;
Who in their dark imaginings, again
Fired the rich palace and the stately fane,
Drank in the victim's shriek, as music's breath,
And lived o'er scenes, the festivals of death!

And there was mirth too!—strange and savage
    mirth,
More fearful far than all the woes of earth!
The laughter of cold hearts, and scoffs that spring
From minds for which there is no sacred thing,
And transient bursts of fierce, exulting glee,—
The lightning's flash upon its blasted tree!

But still, howe'er the soul's disguise were worn
If, from wild revelry, or haughty scorn,
Or buoyant hope, it won an outward show,
Slight was the mask, and all beneath it—woe.

Yet was this all?—amidst the dungeon-gloom,
The void, the stillness, of the captive's doom,
Were there no deeper thoughts?—And that dark
    power,
To whom guilt owes one late, but dreadful hour,
The mighty debt through years of crime delay'd,
But, as the grave's, inevitably paid;
Came he not thither, in his burning force,
The lord, the tamer of dark souls—Remorse?

Yes! as the night calls forth from sea and sky
From breeze and wood, a solemn harmony,
Lost, when the swift, triumphant wheels of day,
In light and sound, are hurrying on their way:
Thus, from the deep recesses of the heart,
The voice which sleeps, but never dies, might start
Call'd up by solitude, each nerve to thrill,
With accents heard not, save when all is still!

The voice, inaudible, when Havoc's train
Crush'd the red vintage of devoted Spain;
Mute, when sierras to the war-whoop rung,
And the broad light of conflagration sprung
From the South's marble cities;—hush'd 'midst
    cries
That told the Heavens of mortal agonies;
But gathering silent strength, to wake at last,
In concentrated thunders of the past!

And there, perchance, some long-bewilder'd mind
Torn from its lowly sphere, its path confined
Of village-duties, in the alpine glen,
Where nature cast its lot, 'midst peasant-men;
Drawn to that vortex, whose fierce ruler blent
The earthquake-power of each wild element,

To lend the tide which bore his throne on high,
One impulse more of desperate energy;
Might, when the billow's awful rush was o'er,
Which toss'd its wreck upon the storm-beat shore.
Won from its wanderings past, by suffering tried
Search'd by remorse, by anguish purified,
Have fix'd at length its troubled hopes and fears,
On the far world, seen brightest through our tears,
And in that hour of triumph or despair,
Whose secrets all must learn—but none declare,
When, of the things to come, a deeper sense
Fills the dim eye of trembling penitence,
Have turn'd to him, whose bow is in the cloud,
Around life's limits gathering, as a shroud;—
The fearful mysteries of the heart who knows,
And, by the tempest, calls it to repose!

Who visited that death-bed?—Who can tell
Its brief, sad tale, on which the soul might dwell.
And learn immortal lessons?—who beheld
The struggling hope, by shame, by doubt repell'd—
The agony of prayer—the bursting tears—
The dark remembrances of guilty years,
Crowding upon the spirit in their might?—
He, through the storm who look'd, and there was
    light!

That scene is closed!—that wild, tumultuous
    breast,
With all its pangs and passions, is at rest!
He, too, is fallen, the master-power of strife,
Who woke those passions to delirious life;
And days, prepared a brighter course to run,
Unfold their buoyant pinions to the sun!

It is a glorious hour when Spring goes forth,
O'er the bleak mountains of the shadowy North,
And with one radiant glance, one magic breath,
Wakes all things lovely from the sleep of death;
While the glad voices of a thousand streams,
Bursting their bondage, triumph in her beams!

But *Peace* hath nobler changes!  O'er the mind,
The warm and living spirit of mankind,
*Her* influence breathes, and bids the blighted heart,
To life and hope from desolation start!
She, with a look, dissolves the captive's chain,
Peopling with beauty widow'd homes again;
Around the mother, in her closing years,
Gathering her sons once more, and from the tears
Of the dim past, but winning purer light,
To make the present more serenely bright.

Nor rests that influence here.  From clime to
    clime,
In silence gliding with the stream of time,
Still doth it spread, borne onwards, as a breeze
With healing on its wings, o'er isles and seas:
And, as heaven's breath call'd forth, with genial
    power,
From the dry wand, the almond's living flower;
So doth its deep-felt charm in secret move
The coldest heart to gentle deeds of love;
While round its pathway nature softly glows,
And the wide desert blossoms as the rose.

Yes! let the waste lift up the exulting voice!
Let the far-echoing solitude rejoice!
And thou, lone moor! where no blithe reaper's
    song
E'er lightly sped the summer-hours along,
Bid thy wild rivers, from each mountain-source,
Rushing in joy, make music on their course!
Thou, whose sole record of existence mark
Thy scene of barbarous rites, in ages dark,
And of some nameless combat; Hope's bright eye
Beams o'er thee in the light of prophecy!
Yet shalt thou smile, by busy culture drest,
And the rich harvest wave upon thy breast!
Yet shall thy cottage-smoke, at dewy morn,
Rise, in blue wreaths, above the flowering thorn,
And 'midst thy hamlet-shades, the embosom'd spire
Catch from deep-kindling heavens their earliest
    fire.

Thee too that hour shall bless, the balmy close
Of labour's day, the herald of repose,

Which gathers hearts in peace ; while social mirth
Basks in the blaze of each free village-hearth ;
While peasant-songs are on the joyous gales,
And merry England's voice floats up from all her
    vales.
Yet are there sweeter sounds ; and thou shalt hear
Such as to Heaven's immortal host are dear.
Oh ! if there still be melody on earth,
Worthy the sacred bowers where man drew birth,
When angel-steps their paths rejoicing trod,
And the air trembled with the breath of God ·
It lives in those soft accents, to the sky (7)
Borne from the lips of stainless infancy,
When holy strains, from life's pure fount which
    sprung,
Breathed with deep reverence, falter on its tongue

And such shall be *thy* music, when the cells,
Where Guilt, the child of hopeless Misery, dwells
(And, to wild strength by desperation wrought,
In silence broods o'er many a fearful thought,)
Resound to pity's voice ; and childhood thence,
Ere the cold blight hath reach'd its innocence,
Ere that soft rose-bloom of the soul be fled,
Which vice but breathes on, and its hues are dead,
Shall at the call press forward, to be made
A glorious offering, meet for him, who said,
" Mercy, not sacrifice !" and when, of old,
Clouds of rich incense from his altars roll'd,
Dispersed the smoke of perfumes, and laid bare
The heart's deep folds, to read its homage there !

When some crown'd conqueror, o'er a trampled
    world,
His banner, shadowing nations, hath unfurl'd,
And, like those visitations which deform
Nature for centuries, hath made the storm
His pathway to Dominion's lonely sphere,
Silence behind,—before him, flight and fear ;
When kingdoms rock beneath his rushing wheels
Till each far isle the mighty impulse feels,
And earth is moulded but by one proud will,
And sceptred realms wear fetters, and are still ;
Shall the free soul of song bow down to pay
The earthquake homage on its baleful way ?
Shall the glad harp send up exulting strains,
O'er burning cities and forsaken plains ?
And shall no harmony of softer close,
Attend the stream of mercy as it flows,
And, mingling with the murmur of its wave,
Bless the green shores its gentle currents lave ?

Oh ! there are loftier themes, for him, whose eyes
Have search'd the depths of life's realities,
Than the red battle, or the trophied car,
Wheeling the monarch-victor fast and far ;
There are more noble strains than those which
    swell
The triumphs, Ruin may suffice to tell !

Ye prophet-bards, who sat in elder days
Beneath the palms of Judah ! Ye whose lays
With torrent rapture, from their source on high,
Burst in the strength of immortality !
Oh ! not alone, those haunted groves among,
Of conquering hosts, of empires crush'd, ye sung,
But of that Spirit, destined to explore
With the bright day-spring every distant shore,
To dry the tear, to bind the broken reed,
To make the home of peace in hearts that bleed ;
With beams of hope to pierce the dungeon's gloom,
And pour eternal star-light o'er the tomb.

And bless'd and hallow'd be its haunts ! for there
Hath man's high soul been rescued from despair !—
There hath the immortal spark for Heaven been
    nursed,—
There from the rock the springs of life have burst
Quenchless and pure ! and holy thoughts, that rise
Warm from the source of human sympathies,—
Where'er its path of radiance may be traced,
Shall find their temple in the silent waste.

# NOTES.

### NOTE 1.

*Still rise the cairns of yore, all rudely piled.*

In some parts of Dartmoor, the surface is thickly strewed with stones, which, in many instances, appear to have been collected into piles, on the tops of prominent hillocks, as if in imitation of the natural Tors.  The Stone-barrows of Dartmoor resemble the Cairns of the Cheviot and Grampian hills, and those in Cornwall.—See *Cooke's Topographical Survey of Devonshire.*

### NOTE 2.

*And the rude arrow's barb remain to tell.*

Flint arrow-heads have occasionally been found upon Dartmoor.

### NOTE 3.

*The chieftain's power—they had no bard, and died.*

    Vixere fortes ante Agamemnona
    Multi : Sed omnes illachrymabiles
      Urgentur, ignotique longa
        Nocte, carent quia vate sacro.
                *Horace.*

" They had no Poet, and they died."——*Pope's Translation.*

### NOTE 4.

*There stands an altar of unsculptured stone.*

On the east of Dartmoor are some Druidical remains, one of which is a Cromlech, whose three rough pillars of granite support a ponderous table-stone, and form a kind of large, irregular tripod.

### NOTE 5.

*Bade the red cairn-fires blaze from every height.*

In some of the Druid festivals, fires were lighted on all the cairns and eminences around, by priests, carrying sacred torches.  All the household fires were previously extinguished, and those who were thought worthy of such a privilege, were allowed to relight them with a flaming brand, kindled at the consecrated cairn-fire.

### NOTE 6.

*'Twas then the captives of Britannia's war.*

The French prisoners, taken in the wars with Napoleon, were confined in a depot on Dartmoor.

### NOTE 7.

*It lives in those soft accents, to the sky.*

In allusion to a plan for the erection of a great national school-house on Dartmoor, where it was proposed to educate the children of convicts

---

THE

# MEETING OF WALLACE AND BRUCE

ON THE

## BANKS OF THE CARRON.

A PRIZE POEM.

---

The Scottish historians describe the hero, after the battle of Falkirk, by his military talents and presence of mind, preserving the troops under his own command, and retreating leisurely and in good order, along the banks of the little river Carron, which protected him from the enemy.  They add, that Robert Bruce* appeared on the opposite side of the river, and soon distinguishing the majestic figure of Wallace, he called out to him, and desired a conference.  They represent the Scottish hero as seizing this opportunity to awaken the feelings of patriotism in the youthful mind of Bruce ; as appealing to him in behalf of his country, and describing her oppressed state, as the consequence of being deserted by those whom nature and fortune pointed out, as best fitted by birth and character to maintain the national independence.  The enthusiasm of the speaker is said to have made a deep impression on Bruce, who from that time repented of his engagements with Edward, and secretly determined to seize the first opportunity of aiding the cause of his native country.

---

THE morn rose bright on scenes renown'd,
Wild Caledonia's classic ground,
Where the bold sons of other days
Won their high fame in Ossian's lays,

---

* Not Robert Bruce, afterwards king of Scotland, but his father.

And fell—but not till Carron's tide
With Roman blood was darkly dyed.
—The morn rose bright, and heard the cry
Sent by exulting hosts on high.
And saw the white-cross banner float
(While rang each clansman's gathering note)
O'er the dark plumes and serried spears
Of Scotland's daring mountaineers,
As, all elate with hope, they stood
To buy their freedom with their blood.

The sunset shone, to guide the flying,
And beam a farewell to the dying!
The summer moon, on Falkirk's field,
Streams upon eyes in slumber seal'd:
Deep slumber, not to pass away,
When breaks another morning's ray,
Nor vanish when the trumpet's voice
Bids ardent hearts again rejoice:
What sunbeam's glow, what clarion's breath,
May chase the still, cold, sleep of Death?
Shrouded in Scotland's blood-stain'd plaid
Low are her mountain-warriors laid;
They fell, on that proud soil, whose mould
Was blent with heroes' dust, of old,
And, guarded by the free and brave,
Yielded the Roman but a grave!
Nobly they fell—yet with them died
The warrior's hope, the leader's pride.
Vainly they fell—that martyr host—
All, save the land's high soul, is lost.
Blest are the slain! *they* calmly sleep,
Nor see their bleeding country weep:
The shouts, of England's triumph telling,
Reach not their dark and silent dwelling;
And those, surviving to bequeath
Their sons the choice of chains or death,
May give the slumberer's lowly bier
An envying glance,—but not a tear.
But thou, the fearless and the free,
Devoted Knight of Ellerslie!
No vassal-spirit, form'd to bow
When storms are gathering, clouds thy brow
No shade of fear, or weak despair,
Blends with indignant sorrow there.
The ray which streams on yon red field,
O'er Scotland's cloven helm and shield,
Glitters not *there* alone, to shed
Its cloudless beauty o'er the dead,
But, where smooth Carron's rippling wave
Flows near that death-bed of the brave,
Illuming all the midnight scene,
Sleeps brightly on thy lofty mien.

But other beams, O Patriot! shine
In each commanding glance of thine.
And other light hath fill'd thine eye
With inspiration's majesty.
Caught from the immortal frame divine
Which makes thine inmost heart a shrine
Thy voice a Prophet's tone hath won,
The grandeur Freedom lends her son;
Thy bearing, a resistless power,
The ruling genius of the hour;
And he, yon Chief, with mien of pride,
Whom Carron's waves from thee divide,
Whose haughty gesture fain would seek
To veil the thoughts that blanch his cheek,
Feels his reluctant mind controll'd
By thine, of more heroic mould;
Though, struggling all in vain to war
With that high mind's ascendant star,
He, with a conqueror's scornful eye,
Would mock the name of Liberty.

—Heard ye the Patriot's awful voice?
" Proud victor! in thy fame rejoice!
Hast thou not seen thy brethren slain,
The harvest of thy battle-plain,
And bathed thy sword in blood, whose spot
Eternity shall cancel not?
Rejoice! with sounds of wild lament,
O'er her dark heaths and mountains sent,
With dying moan, and dirge's wail,
Thy ravaged country bids thee hail!

Rejoice!—while yet exulting cries
From England's conquering host arise,
And strains of choral triumph tell
Her royal Slave hath fought too well.
Oh! dark the clouds of woe that rest
Brooding o'er Scotland's mountain-crest;
Her shield is cleft, her banner torn,
O'er martyr'd chiefs her daughters mourn;
And not a breeze, but wafts the sound
Of wailing through the land around.
Yet deem not thou, till life depart,
High hope shall leave the patriot's heart,
Or courage, to the storm inured,
Or stern resolve, by woes matured,
Oppose, to Fate's severest hour,
Less than unconquerable power.
No! though the orbs of heaven expire,
*Thine.* Freedom! is a quenchless fire!
And woe to him whose might would dare
The energies of *thy* despair!
No!—when thy chain, O Bruce! is cast
O'er thy land's charter'd mountain-blast,
Then in my yielding soul shall die
The glorious faith of Liberty!

" Wild hopes! o'er dreamer's mind that rise,"
With haughty laugh, the Conqueror cries,
(Yet his dark cheek is flush'd with shame,
And his eye fill'd with troubled flame;)
" Vain, brief illusions! doom'd to fly
England's red path of victory!
Is not her sword unmatch'd in might?
Her course, a torrent in the fight?
The terror of her name gone forth
Wide o'er the regions of the North?
Far hence, 'midst other heaths and snows,
Must Freedom's footstep now repose.
And thou, in lofty dreams elate,
Enthusiast! strive no more with Fate!
'T is vain—the land is lost and won—
Sheathed be the sword, its task is done.
Where are the chiefs who stood with thee,
First in the battles of the free?
The firm in heart; in spirit high?
—They sought yon fatal field to die.
Each step of Edward's conquering host
Hath left a grave on Scotland's coast."

" Vassal of England! yes, a grave,
Where sleep the faithful and the brave;
And who the glory would resign
Of death like theirs, for life like thine?
They slumber—and the stranger's tread
May spurn thy country's noble dead;
Yet, on the land they loved so well,
Still shall their burning spirit dwell,
Their deeds shall hallow minstrel's theme,
Their image rise on warrior's dream,
Their names be inspiration's breath,
Kindling high hope, and scorn of death,
Till bursts immortal from the tomb,
The flame that shall avenge their doom!
This is no land for chains—away!
O'er softer climes let tyrants sway!
Think'st thou the mountain and the storm
Their hardy sons for bondage form?
Doth our stern wintry blast instil
Submission to a despot's will?
—No! we were cast in other mould
Than theirs, by lawless power controll'd.
The nurture of our bitter sky
Calls forth resisting energy,
And the wild fastnesses are ours,
The rocks with their eternal towers!
The soul to struggle and to dare,
Is mingled with our northern air,
And dust beneath our soil is lying,
Of those who died for fame undying.
Tread'st thou that soil, and can it be
No loftier thought is roused in thee?
Doth no high feeling proudly start
From slumber in thine inmost heart?
No secret voice thy bosom thrill,
For thine own Scotland pleading still?
Oh! wake thee yet!—indignant claim
A nobler fate, a purer fame,

And cast to earth thy fetters riven,
And take thine offer'd crown from Heaven!
Wake! in that high majestic lot,
May the dark past be all forgot,
And Scotland shall forgive the field,
Where with her blood thy shame was seal'd.
E'en I,—though on that fatal plain
Lies my heart's brother with the slain,
Though, reft of his heroic worth,
My spirit dwells alone on earth,
And when all other grief is past,
Must *this* be cherish'd to the last;—
Will lead thy battles, guard thy throne,
With faith unspotted as his own,
Nor in thy noon of fame recall
*Whose* was the guilt that wrought his fall."

Still dost thou hear in stern disdain?
Are Freedom's warning accents vain?
No, royal Bruce! within thy breast,
Wakes each high thought, too long suppress'd
And thy heart's noblest feelings live,
Blent in that suppliant word—" Forgive!
Forgive the wrongs to Scotland done!
Wallace! thy fairest palm is won;
And kindling at my country's shrine,
My soul hath caught a spark from thine.
Oh! deem not, in the proudest hour
Of triumph and exulting power,
Deem not the light of peace could find
A home within my troubled mind.
Conflicts by mortal eye unseen,
Dark, silent, secret, there have been,
Known but to Him, whose glance can trace
Thought to its deepest dwelling-place.
—'T is past, and on my native shore
I tread, a rebel son no more.
Too blest, if yet my lot may be,
In glory's path to follow thee;
If tears, by late repentance pour'd,
May lave the blood-stains from my sword

 —Far other tears, O Wallace! rise
From thy heart's fountain to thine eyes,
Bright, holy, and unchcck'd they spring,
While thy voice falters, " Hail, my King!
Be every wrong by memory traced,
In this full tide of joy, effaced!
Hail! and rejoice! thy race shall claim
An heritage of deathless fame.
And Scotland shall arise at length,
Majestic in triumphant strength,
An eagle of the rock, that won
A way, through tempests, to the sun
Nor scorn the visions, wildly grand,
The prophet-spirit of thy land!
By torrent wave, in desert blast,
Those visions o'er my thoughts have pass'd.
Where mountain-vapours darkly roll,
That spirit hath possess'd my soul,
And shadowy forms have met mine eye
The beings of futurity;
And a deep voice of years to be,
Hath told that Scotland shall be free.

"He comes! exult, thou Sire of Kings!
From thee the Chief, the Avenger springs!
Far o'er the land he comes to save,
His banners in their glory wave,
And Albyn's thousand harps awake
On hill and heath, by stream and lake,
To swell the strains that far around
Bid the proud name of Bruce resound.
And I—but wherefore now recall
The whisper'd omens of my fall?
They come not in mysterious gloom,
—There is no bondage in the tomb!
O'er the soul's world no tyrant reigns,
And earth alone for man hath chains!
What though I perish ere the hour
When Scotland's vengeance wakes in power
If shed for her, my blood shall stain
The field or scaffold not in vain,
Its voice, to efforts more sublime,
Shall rouse the spirit of her clime,

And in the noontide of her lot,
My country shall forget me not!

*Art* thou forgot? and hath thy worth
Without its glory pass'd from Earth?
—Rest with the brave, whose names belong
To the high sanctity of song,
Charter'd our reverence to control,
And traced in sunbeams on the soul
*Thine*, Wallace! while the heart hath still
One pulse a generous thought can thrill,
While Youth's warm tears are yet the meed
Of martyr's death, or hero's deed,
Shall brightly live, from age to age,
Thy country's proudest heritage.
'Midst her green vales thy fame is dwelling,
Thy deeds her mountain-winds are telling,
Thy memory speaks in torrent-wave,
Thy step hath hallow'd rock and cave;
And cold the wanderer's heart must be,
That holds no converse there with thee.

Yet, Scotland! to thy champion's shade,
Still are thy grateful rites delay'd.
From lands of old renown, o'erspread
With proud memorials of the dead,
The trophied urn, the breathing bust,
The pillar, guarding noble dust,
The shrine, where art and genius high
Have labour'd for Eternity;—
The stranger comes —his eye explores
The wilds of thy majestic shores,
Yet vainly seeks one native stone,
Raised to the hero all thine own.

Land of bright deeds and minstrel lore
Withhold the guerdon now no more!
On some bold height of awful form,
Stern eyrie of the cloud and storm,
Sublimely mingling with the skies,
Bid the proud Cenotaph arise!
Not to *record* the name that thrills
Thy soul, the watch-word of thy hills;
Not to assert with needless claim,
The bright *for ever* of its fame;
But in the ages yet untold,
When *ours* shall be the days of old,
To rouse high hearts, and speak thy pride
In him, for thee who lived and died.

---

# The Last Constantine

. . . . . . . . Thou strivest nobly,
When hearts of sterner stuff perhaps had sunk;
And o'er thy fall, if it be so decreed,
Good men will mourn, and brave men will shed tears.

 . . . . . . . . . . . .

. . . . . . . . . Fame I look not for,
But to sustain, in Heaven's all-seeing eye,
Before my fellow-men, in mine own sight,
With graceful virtue and becoming pride,
The dignity and honour of a man.
Thus station'd as I am, I will do all
That man may do.
*Miss Baillie's Constantine Palæologus*

---

### I

THE fires grew pale on Rome's deserted shrines,
In the dim grot the Pythia's voice had died;
—Shout, for the City of the Constantines,
The rising City of the billow-side,
The City of the Cross!—great Ocean's bride,
Crown'd from her birth she sprung!—Long ages
        pass'd,
And still she look'd in glory o'er the tide,
Which at her feet Barbaric riches cast,
Pour'd by the burning East, all joyously and fast.

### II.

Long ages past—they left her porphyry halls
Still trod by kingly footsteps.  Gems and gold
Broider'd her mantle, and her castled walls
Frown'd in their strength; yet there were signs
    which told
The days were full.  The pure high faith of old
Was changed; and on her silken couch of sleep
She lay, and murmur'd if a rose-leaf's fold
Disturb'd her dreams; and call'd her slaves to
    keep
Their watch, that no rude sound might reach her
    o'er the deep.

### III.

But there are sounds that from the regal dwelling
Free hearts and fearless only may exclude;
'Tis not alone the wind at midnight swelling,
Breaks on the soft repose by Luxury woo'd!
There are unbidden footsteps, which intrude
Where the lamps glitter, and the wine-cup flows,
And darker hues have stain'd the marble, strew'd
With the fresh myrtle, and the short-lived rose,
And Parian walls have rung to the dread march
    of foes.

### IV.

A voice of multitudes is on the breeze,
Remote, yet solemn as the night-storm's roar
Through Ida's giant pines!  Across the seas
A murmur comes, like that the deep winds bore
From Tempe's haunted river to the shore
Of the reed-crown'd Eurotas; when, of old,
Dark Asia sent her battle-myriads o'er
Th' indignant wave which would not be con-
    troll'd,
But, past the Persian's chain, in boundless freedom
    roll'd.

### V.

And it is thus again!—Swift oars are dashing
The parted waters, and a light is cast
On their white foam-wreaths, from the sudden
    flashing
Of Tartar spears, whose ranks are thickening
    fast.
There swells a savage trumpet on the blast,
A music of the deserts, wild and deep,
Wakening strange echoes as the shores are past,
Where low 'midst Ilion's dust her conquerors
    sleep,
O'ershadowing with high names each rude sepul-
    chral heap.

### VI.

War from the West!—the snows on Thracian
    hills
Are loosed by Spring's warm breath; yet o'er
    the lands
Which Hæmus girds, the chainless mountain rills
Pour down less swiftly than the Moslem bands.
War from the East!—'midst Araby's lone sands,
More lonely now the few bright founts may be,
While Ishmael's bow is bent in warrior-hands
Against the Golden City of the Sea; (1)
—Oh! for a soul to fire thy dust, Thermopylæ!

### VII.

Here yet again, ye mighty!—where are they,
Who, with their green Olympic garlands crown'd,
Leap'd up in proudly beautiful array,
As to a banquet gathering, at the sound
Of Persia's clarion?—far and joyous round,
From the pine-forests, and the mountain-snows,
And the low sylvan valleys, to the bound
Of the bright waves, at Freedom's voice they
    rose!
—Hath it no thrilling tone to break the tomb's re-
    pose?

### VIII.

They slumber with their swords!—the olive
    shades
In vain are whispering their immortal tale!

In vain the spirit of the past pervades
The soft winds breathing through each Grecian
    vale.
—Yet must *thou* wake, though all unarm'd and
    pale,
Devoted City!—Lo! the Moslem's spear,
Red from its vintage, at thy gates; his sail
Upon thy waves, his trumpet in thine ear!
—Awake and summon those, who yet, perchance,
    may hear!

### IX.

Be hush'd, thou faint and feeble voice of weeping!
Lift ye the banner of the Cross on high,
And call on chiefs whose noble sires are sleeping
In their proud graves of sainted chivalry,
Beneath the palms and cedars, where they sigh
To Syrian gales!—The sons of each brave line,
From their baronial halls shall hear your cry,
And seize the arms which flash'd round Salem's
    shrine,
And wield for you the swords once waved for
    Palestine!

### X.

All still, all voiceless;—and the billow's roar
Alone replies!—Alike *their* soul is gone,
Who shared the funeral feast on Œta's shore,
And *theirs*, that o'er the field of Ascalon
Swell'd the crusader's hymn!—Then gird thou on
Thine armour, Eastern Queen! and meet the
    hour,
Which waits thee ere the day's fierce work is
    done,
With a strong heart; so may thy helmet tower
Unshiver'd through the storm, for generous hope
    is power!

### XI.

But linger not,—array thy men of might!
The shores, the seas are peopled with thy foes.
Arms through thy cypress-groves are gleaming
    bright,
And the dark huntsmen of the wild, repose
Beneath the shadowy marble porticoes
Of thy proud villas.  Nearer and more near,
Around thy walls the sons of battle close;
Each hour, each moment, hath its sound of fear,
Which the deep grave alone is charter'd not to
    hear.

### XII.

Away! bring wine, bring odours to the shade, (2)
Where the tall pine and poplar blend on high!
Bring roses, exquisite, but soon to fade!
Snatch every brief delight,—since we must die!—
Yet is the hour, degenerate Greeks! gone by,
For feast in vine-wreathed bower, or pillar'd
    hall;
Dim gleams the torch beneath yon fiery sky,
And deep and hollow is the tambour's call,
And from the startled hand th' untasted cup will
    fall.

### XIII.

The night, the glorious oriental night,
Hath lost the silence of her purple heaven,
With its clear stars!  The red artillery's light,
Athwart her worlds of tranquil splendour driven,
To the still firmament's expanse hath given
Its own fierce glare, wherein each cliff and
    tower
Starts wildly forth; and now the air is riven
With thunder-bursts, and now dull smoke-clouds
    lower,
Veiling the gentle moon, in her most hallow'd hour

### XIV.

Sounds from the waters, sounds upon the earth,
Sounds in the air, of battle! Yet with these
A voice is mingling, whose deep tones give birth
To Faith and Courage!  From luxurious ease
A gallant few have started!  O'er the seas,
From the Seven Towers, (3) their banner waves
    its sign,
And Hope is whispering in the joyous breeze,

Which plays amidst its folds.  That voice was
*thine;*
*Thy* soul was on that band, devoted Constantine.

### XV.

Was Rome thy parent?  Didst thou catch from
*her*
The fire that lives in thine undaunted eye?
—That city of the throne and sepulchre
Hath given proud lessons how to reign and die!
Heir of the Cæsars! did that lineage high,
Which, as a triumph to the grave, hath pass'd
With its long march of sceptred imagery, (4)
Th' heroic mantle o'er thy spirit cast?
—Thou of an eagle-race the noblest and the last!

### XVI.

Vain dreams! upon that spirit hath descended
Light from the living Fountain, whence each
thought
Springs pure and holy!  In that eye is blended
A spark, with Earth's triumphal memories
fraught,
And far within, a deeper meaning, caught
From worlds unseen.  A hope, a lofty trust,
Whose resting place on buoyant wing is sought,
(Though through its veil, seen darkly from the
dust,)
n realms where Time no more hath power upon
the just.

### XVII.

Those were proud days, when on the battle-plain,
And in the sun's bright face, and 'midst the array
Of awe-struck hosts, and circled by the slain,
The Roman cast his glittering mail away, (5)
And while a silence, as of midnight, lay
O'er breathless thousands, at his voice who
started,
Call'd on the unseen, terrific powers that sway
The heights, the depths, the shades; then fear-
less-hearted,
Girt on his robe of death, and for the grave de-
parted.

### XVIII.

But then, around him as the javelins rush'd,
From earth to heaven swell'd up the loud ac-
claim;
And, ere his heart's last free libation gush'd,
With a bright smile the warrior caught his name,
Far floating on the winds!  And Victory came,
And made the hour of that immortal deed,
A life in fiery feeling!  Valour's aim
Had sought no loftier guerdon.  Thus to bleed,
Was to be Rome's high star!—He died—and had
his meed.

### XIX.

But praise—and dearer, holier praise, be theirs,
Who, in the stillness and the solitude
Uncheer'd by Fame's proud hope, th'ethereal food
Of hearts press'd earthwards by a weight of
cares,
Of restless energies, and only view'd
By Him whose eye, from his eternal throne,
Is on the soul's dark places; have subdued
And vow'd themselves, with strength till then
unknown,
To some high martyr-task, in secret and alone.

### XX.

Theirs be the bright and sacred names enshrined
Far in the bosom! for their deeds belong,
Not to the gorgeous faith which charm'd man-
kind
With its rich pomp of festival and song,
Garland and shrine, and incense-bearing throng;
But to that Spirit, hallowing, as it tries
Man's hidden soul in whispers, yet more strong
Than storm or earthquake's voice; for *thence*
arise
All that mysterious world's unseen sublimities.

### XXI.

Well might *thy* name, brave Constantine! awoke
Such thought, such feeling!—But the scene again
Bursts on my vision, as the day-beams break
Through the red sulphurous mists! the camp,
the plain,
The terraced palaces, the dome-capt fane,
With its bright cross fix'd high in crowning
grace;
Spears on the ramparts, galleys on the main,
And, circling all with arms, that turban'd race,
The sun, the desert, stamp'd in each dark, haughty
face.

### XXII.

Shout, ye seven hills!  Lo!  Christian pennon
streaming
Red o'er the waters! (6)  Hail, deliverers, hail!
Along your billowy wake the radiance gleaming,
Is Hope's own smile!  they crowd the swelling
sail,
On, with the foam, the sun-beam, and the gale,
Borne, as a victor's car!  The batteries pour
Their clouds and thunders; but the rolling veil
Of smoke floats up th' exulting winds before!
And oh! the glorious burst of that bright sea and
shore!

### XXIII.

The rocks, waves, ramparts, Europe's, Asia's
coast,
All throng'd! one theatre for kingly war!
A monarch girt with his Barbaric host,
Points o'er the beach his flashing scymetar!
Dark tribes are tossing javelins from afar,
Hands waving banners o'er each battlement,
Decks, with their serried guns, array'd to bar
The promised aid; but hark! a shout is sent
Up from the noble barks!—the Moslem line is rent!

### XXIV.

On, on through rushing flame, and arrowy
shower,
The welcome prows have cleft their rapid way,
And, with the shadows of the vesper-hour,
Furl'd their white sails, and anchor'd in the bay
Then were the streets with song and torch-fire
gay;
Then the Greek wines flow'd mantling in the
light
Of festal halls;—and there was joy!—the ray
Of dying eyes, a moment wildly bright,
The sunset of the soul ere lost to mortal sight!

### XXV.

For, vain that feeble succour! Day by day
Th' imperial towers are crumbling, and the
sweep
Of the vast engines, in their ceaseless play,
Comes powerful as when Heaven unbinds the
deep!
—Man's heart is mightier than the castled steep,
Yet will it sink when earthly hope is fled;
Man's thoughts work darkly in such hours, and
sleep
Flies far; and in *their* mien, the walls who
tread,
Things by the brave untold, may fearfully be read!

### XXVI.

It was a sad and solemn task to hold
Their midnight-watch on that beleaguer'd wall
As the sea-wave beneath the bastions roll'd,
A sound of fate was in its rise and fall!
The heavy clouds were as an empire's pall,
The giant-shadows of each tower and fane
Lay like the grave's; a low, mysterious call
Breathed in the wind, and from the tented plain
A voice of omens rose, with each wild martial
strain.

### XXVII.

For they might catch the Arab charger's neigh-
    ing,
The Thracian drum, the Tartar's drowsy song,
Might almost hear the soldan's banner swaying,
The watch-word mutter'd in some eastern
    tongue.
Then flash'd the gun's terrific light along
The marble streets, all stillness—not repose:
And boding thoughts came o'er them, dark and
    strong;
For heaven, earth, air, speak auguries to those
Who see their number'd hours fast pressing to the
    close.

### XXVIII.

But strength is from the mightiest! There is one
Still in the breach and on the rampart seen,
Whose cheek grows paler with each morning sun.
And tells in silence how the night hath been,
In kingly halls, a vigil: yet serene,
The ray set deep within his thoughtful eye
And there is that in his collected mien,
To which the hearts of noble men reply,
With fires, partaking not this frame's mortality!

### XXXIX.

Yes! call it not of lofty minds the fate,
To pass o'er earth in brightness, but alone;
High power was made their birthright, to create
A thousand thoughts responsive to their own!
A thousand echoes of their spirit's tone
Start into life, where'er their path may be,
Still following fast; as when the wind hath
    blown
O'er Indian groves, (7) a wanderer wild and free,
Kindling and bearing flames afar from tree to tree!

### XXX.

And it is thus with thee! thy lot is cast
On evil days, thou Cæsar! yet the few
That set their generous bosoms to the blast
Which rocks thy throne—the fearless and the
    true,
Bear hearts wherein thy glance can still renew
The free devotion of the years gone by,
When from bright dreams th' ascendant Roman
    drew
Enduring strength!—states vanish—ages fly—
But leave one task unchanged—to suffer and to
    die!

### XXXI.

These are our nature's heritage. But thou.
The crown'd with Empire! thou wert call'd to
    share
A cup more bitter. On thy fever'd brow
The semblance of that buoyant hope to wear,
Which long had pass'd away; alone to bear
The rush and pressure of dark thoughts, that
    came
As a strong billow in their weight of care;
And, with all this, to smile! for earth-born frame,
These are stern conflicts, yet they pass, unknown
    to fame!

### XXXII.

Her glance is on the triumph, on the field,
On the red scaffold; and where'er, in sight
Of human eyes, the human soul is steel'd
To deeds that seem as of immortal might,
Yet are proud nature's! But her meteor-light
Can pierce no depths, no clouds; it falls not
    where,
In silence, and in secret, and in night,
The noble heart doth wrestle with despair,
And rise more strong than death from its unwit
    ness'd prayer.

### XXXIIL

Men have been firm in battle: they have stood
With a prevailing hope on ravaged plains,
And won the birthright of their hearths with
    blood,
And died rejoicing, 'midst their ancient fanes,

That so their children, undefiled with chains,
Might worship there in peace. But they that
    stand
When not a beacon o'er the wave remains,
Link'd but to perish with a ruin'd land,
Where Freedom dies with them—call *these* a mar-
    tyr-band!

### XXXIV.

But the world heeds them not. Or if, perchance,
Upon their strife it bend a careless eye,
It is but as the Roman's stoic glance
Fell on that stage where man's last agony
Was made *his* sport, who, knowing *one* must die,
Reck'd not *which* champion; but prepared the
    strain,
And bound the bloody wreath of victory,
To greet the conqueror; while, with calm dis
    dain,
The vanquish'd proudly met the doom he met in
    vain.

### XXXV.

The hour of Fate comes on! and it is fraught
With *this* of Liberty, that now the need
Is past to veil the brow of anxious thought,
And clothe the heart, which still beneath must
    bleed,
With Hope's fair-seeming drapery. We are freed
From tasks like these by Misery; one alone
Is left the brave, and rest shall be thy meed,
Prince, watcher, wearied one! when thou hast
    shown
How brief the cloudy space which parts the grave
    and throne.

### XXXVI.

The signs are full. They are not in the sky,
Nor in the many voices of the air,
Nor the swift clouds. No fiery hosts on high
Toss their wild spears; no meteor-banners glare,
No comet fiercely shakes its blazing hair,
And yet the signs are full: too truly seen
In the thinn'd ramparts, in the pale despair
Which lends one language to a people's mien,
And in the ruin'd heaps where walls and towers
    have been!

### XXXVII.

It is a night of beauty; such a night
As, from the sparry grot or laurel-shade,
Or wave in marbled cavern rippling bright,
Might woo the nymphs of Grecian fount and
    glade
To sport beneath its moonbeams, which pervade
Their forest haunts: a night, to rove alone,
Where the young leaves by vernal winds are
    sway'd,
And the reeds whisper, with a dreamy tone
Of melody, that seems to breathe from worlds un-
    known.

### XXXVIII.

A night, to call from green Elysium's bowers
The shades of elder bards: a night, to hold
Unseen communion with th' inspiring powers
That made deep groves their dwelling-place of
    old;
A night for mourners, o'er the hallow'd mould,
To strew sweet flowers; for revellers to fill
And wreath the cup; for sorrows to be told,
Which love hath cherish'd long;—vain thoughts!
    be still!
—It is a night of fate, stamp'd with Almighty
    Will!

### XXXIX.

It *should* come sweeping in the storm, and rend-
    ing
The ancient summits in its dread career!
And with vast billows wrathfully contending,
And with dark clouds o'ershadowing every sphere

—But He, whose footstep shakes the earth with
    fear,
Passing to lay the sovereign cities low
Alike in His omnipotence is near,
When the soft winds o'er spring's green path
    way blow,
And when His thunders cleave the monarch-
    mountain's brow.

### XL.

The heavens in still magnificence look down
On the hush'd Bosphorus, whose ocean-stream
Sleeps, with its paler stars: the snowy crown
Of far Olympus, (8) in the moonlight-gleam
Towers radiantly, as when the Pagan's dream
Throng'd it with gods, and bent the adoring
    knee!
—But that is past—and now the One Supreme
Fills not alone *those* haunts; but earth, air, sea,
And time, which presses on, to finish his decree

### XLI.

Olympus, Ida, Delphi! ye, the thrones
And temples of a visionary might,
Brooding in clouds above your forest-zones,
And mantling thence the realms beneath with
    night:
Ye have look'd down on battles! Fear, and
    Flight,
And arm'd Revenge, all hurrying past below!
But there is yet a more appalling sight
For earth prepared, than e'er, with tranquil
    brow,
Ye gazed on from your world of solitude and snow!

### XLII.

Last night a sound was in the Moslem camp,
And Asia's hills re-echoed to a cry
Of savage mirth!—Wild horn, and war-steeds
    tramp,
Blent with the shout of barbarous revelry.
The clash of desert-spears! Last night the sky
A hue of menace and of wrath put on,
Caught from red watch-fires, blazing far and
    high,
And countless, as the flames, in ages gone,
Streaming to heaven's bright queen from shadowy
    Lebanon!

### XLIII.

But all is stillness now.  May this be sleep
Which wraps those eastern thousands? Yes,
    porchance
Along yon moonlight shore and dark-blue deep,
Bright are their visions with the Houri's glance,
And they behold the sparkling fountains dance
Beneath the bowers of paradise, that shed
Rich odours o'er the faithful; but the lance,
The bow, the spear, now round the slumberers
    spread,
Ere Fate fulfil such dreams, must rest beside the
    dead.

### XLIV.

May this be sleep, this hush?—A sleepless eye
Doth hold its vigil 'midst that dusky race!
One that would scan th' abyss of destiny,
E'en now is gazing on the skies, to trace
In those bright worlds, the burning isles of space,
Fate's mystic pathway: they the while, serene,
Walk in their beauty; but Mohammed's face
Kindles beneath their aspect, (9) and his mien,
All fired with stormy joy, by that soft light is seen.

### XLV.

Oh! wild presumption of a conqueror's dream,
To gaze on those pure altar-fires, enshrined
In depths of blue infinitude, and deem
They shine to guide the spoiler of mankind
O'er fields of blood!—But with the restless mind
It hath been ever thus! and they that veep
For worlds to conquer o'er the bounds assign'd

To human search, in daring pride would sweep,
As o'er the trampled dust wherein they soon must
    sleep.

### XLVI.

But ye! that beam'd on Fate's tremendous night
When the storm burst o'er golden Babylon,
And ye, that sparkled with your wonted light
O'er burning Salem, by the Roman won;
And ye, that calmly view'd the slaughter done
In Rome's own streets, when Alaric's trumpet-
    blast
Rung through the Capitol; bright spheres! roll
    on !
*Still* bright, though empires fall; and bid man
    cast
His humbled eyes to earth, and commune with the
    past.

### XLVII.

For it hath mighty lessons! from the tomb,
And from the ruins of the tomb, and where,
'Midst the wreck'd cities in the desert's gloom,
All tameless creatures make their savage lair,
*There* comes its voice, that shakes the midnight
    air,
And calls up clouds to dim the laughing day,
And thrills the soul;—yet bids us not despair,
But make one rock our shelter and our stay,
Beneath whose shade all else is passing to decay!

### XLVIII.

The hours move on.  I see a wavering gleam
O'er the hush'd waters tremulously fall,
Pour'd from the Cæsars' palace: now the beam
Of many lamps is brightening in the hall,
And from its long arcades and pillars tall
Soft, graceful shadows undulating lie
On the wave's heaving bosom, and recall
A thought of Venice, with her moonlight sky,
And festal seas and domes, and fairy pageantry.

### XLIX.

But from that dwelling floats no mirthful sound
The swell of flute and Grecian lyre no more,
Wafting an atmosphere of music round,
Tells the hush'd seaman, gliding past the
    shore,
How monarchs revel there!—Its feasts are o'er—
Why gleam the lights along its colonnade?
—I see a train of guests in silence pour
Through its long avenues of terraced shade,
Whose stately founts and bowers for joy alone
    were made!

### L.

In silence, and in arms! With helm—with
    sword—
These are no marriage-garments!—Yet e'en now
Thy nuptial feast should grace the regal board,
Thy Georgian bride should wreath her lovely
    brow
With an imperial diadem! (10)—but thou,
O fated prince! art call'd, and these with thee,
To darker scenes; and thou hast learn'd to bow
Thine Eastern sceptre to the dread decree,
And count it joy enough to perish—being free!

### LI

On through long vestibules, with solemn tread
As men that in some time of fear and woe,
Bear darkly to their rest the noble dead,
O'er whom by day their sorrows may not flow,
The warriors pass: their measured steps are
    slow,
And hollow echoes fill the marble halls,
Whose long-drawn vistas open as they go,
In desolate pomp; and from the pictured walls,
Sad seems the light itself which on their armour
    falls!

## LII.

And they have reach'd a gorgeous chamber,
    bright
With all we dream of splendour; yet a gloom
Seems gather'd o'er it to the boding sight,
A shadow that anticipates the tomb!
Still from its fretted roof the lamps illume
A purple canopy, a golden throne;
But it is empty!—Hath the stroke of doom
Fallen there already?—Where is He, the One,
Born that high seat to fill, supremely and alone?

## LIII.

Oh! there are times whose pressure doth efface
Earth's vain distinctions!—when the storm
    beats loud,
When the strong towers are tottering to their
    base,
And the streets rock,—who mingle in the crowd?
'—Peasant and chief, the lowly and the proud,
Are in that throng!—Yes, life hath many an hour
Which makes us kindred, by one chastening
    bow'd,
And feeling but, as from the storm we cower,
What shrinking weakness feels before unbounded
    power!

## LIV

Yet then that Power, whose dwelling is on high
Its loftiest marvels doth reveal, and speak
In the deep human heart more gloriously,
Than in the bursting thunder!—Thence the
    weak,
They that seem'd form'd, as flower-stems, but
    to break
With the first wind, have risen to deeds, whose
    name
Still calls up thoughts that mantle to the cheek,
And thrill the pulse!—Ay, strength no pangs
    could tame
Hath look'd from woman's eye upon the sword
    and flame!

## LV.

And this is of such hours!—That throne is void,
And its lord comes, uncrown'd. Behold him
    stand,
With a calm brow, where woes have not destroy'd
The Greek's heroic beauty, 'midst his band,
The gather'd virtue of a sinking land,
Alas! how scanty!—Now is cast aside
All form of princely state? each noble hand
Is prest by turns in his: for earthly pride
There is no room in hearts where earthly hope
    hath died!

## LVI.

A moment's hush—and then he speaks, he speaks!
But not of hope! that dream hath long gone by:
His words are full of memory—as he seeks,
By the strong names of Rome and Liberty,
Which yet are living powers that fire the eye,
And rouse the heart of manhood; and by all
The sad yet grand remembrances that lie
Deep with earth's buried heroes; to recall
The soul of other years, if but to grace their fall!

## LVII.

His words are full of faith!—And thoughts,
    more high
That Rome e'er knew, now fill his glance with
    light;
Thoughts which give nobler lessons how to die
Than e'er were drawn from Nature's haughty
    might!
And to that eye, with all the spirit bright,
Have theirs replied in tears, which may not
    shame
The bravest in such moments!—'Tis a sight
To make all earthly splendours cold and tame,
—That generous burst of soul, with its electric
    flame!

## LVIII.

They weep—those champions of the cross—they
    weep,
Yet vow themselves to death!—Ay, 'midst that
    train
Are martyrs, privileged in tears to steep
Their lofty sacrifice!—The pang is vain,
And yet its gush of sorrow shall not stain
A warrior's sword.—Those men are strangers
    here (11)—
The homes, they never may behold again,
Lie far away, with all things blest and dear,
On laughing shores, to which their barks no more
    shall steer!

## LIX.

Know'st thou the land where bloom the orange
    bowers? (12)
Where through dark foliage gleam the citron's
    dyes?
It is their own. They see their father's towers,
'Midst its Hesperian groves in sunlight rise:
They meet in soul, the bright Italian eyes,
Which long and vainly shall explore the main
For their white sail's return: the melodies
Of that sweet land are floating o'er their brain—
—Oh! what a crowded world one moment may
    contain!

## LX.

Such moments come to thousands!—few may die
Amidst their native shades. The young, the
    brave,
The beautiful, whose gladdening voice and eye
Made summer in a parent's heart, and gave
Light to their peopled homes; o'er land and wave
Are scatter'd fast and far, as rose-leaves fall
From the deserted stem. They find a grave
Far from the shadow of th' ancestral hall,
—A lonely bed is theirs, whose smiles were hope
    to all!

## LXI.

But life flows on, and bears us with its tide,
Nor may we, lingering, by the slumberers dwell,
Though they were those once blooming at our
    side
In youth's gay home!—Away! what sound's
    deep swell
Comes on the wind?—It is an empire's knell,
Slow, sad, majestic, pealing through the night!
For the last time speaks forth the solemn bell,
Which calls the Christians to their holiest rite,
With a funereal voice of solitary might.

## LXII.

Again, and yet again!—A startling power
In sounds like these lives ever; for they bear
Full on remembrance each eventful hour,
Chequering life's crowded path. They fill the air
When conquerors pass, and fearful cities wear
A mien like joy's; and when young brides are
    led
From their paternal homes; and when the glare
Of burning streets, on midnight's cloud, waves
    red,
And when the silent house receives its guest—
    the dead. (13)

## LXIII.

But to those tones what thrilling soul was given
On that last night of empire!—As a spell
Whereby the life-blood to its source is driven,
On the chill'd heart of multitudes they fell.
Each cadence seem'd a prophecy, to tell
Of sceptres passing from their line away,
An angel-watcher's long and sad farewell,
The requiem of a faith's departing sway
A throne's, a nation's dirge, a wail for earth's de
    cay.

### LXIV.

Again, and yet again!—from yon high dome,
Still the slow peal comes awfully; and they
Who never more to rest in mortal home
Shall throw the breastplate off at fall of day,
Th' imperial band in close and arm'd array,
As men that from the sword must part no more,
Take through the midnight streets their silent
    way,
Within their ancient temple to adore,
Ere yet its thousand years of Christian pomp are
    o'er.

### LXV.

It is the hour of sleep: yet few the eyes
O'er which forgetfulness her balm hath shed,
In the beleagur'd city. Stillness lies
With moonlight, o'er the hills and waters spread,
But not the less with signs and sounds of dread,
The time speeds on. No voice is raised to greet
The last brave Constantine; and yet the tread
Of many steps is in the echoing street,
And pressure of pale crowds, scarce conscious why
    they meet.

### LXVI.

Their homes are luxury's yet: why pour they
    thence
With a dim terror in each restless eye?
Hath the dread car, which bears the pestilence,
In darkness, with its heavy wheels, roll'd by,
And rock'd their palaces, as if on high
The whirlwind pass'd?—From couch and joyous
    board
Hath the fierce phantom beckon'd them to die?
—No!— what are these?—for them a cup is
    pour'd (14)
More dark with wrath;—*Man* comes—the spoiler
    and the sword.

### LXVII.

Still as the monarch and his chieftains pass
Through those pale throngs, the streaming torch-
    light throws
On some wild form, amidst the living mass,
Hues deeply red, like lava's, which disclose
What countless shapes are worn by mortal woes!
Lips bloodless, quivering limbs, hands clasp'd in
    prayer,
Starts, tremblings, hurryings, tears; all out-
    ward shows
Betokening inward agonies, were there:
—Greeks! Romans! all but such as image brave
    despair!

### LXVIII.

But high above that scene in bright repose,
And beauty borrowing from the torches' gleams
A mien of life, yet where no life-blood flows,
But all instinct with loftier being seems,
Pale, grand, colossal; lo! th' embodied dreams
Of yore!—Gods, heroes, bards, in marble
    wrought,
Look down, as powers, upon the wild extremes
Of mortal passion!—Yet 't was man that caught,
And in each glorious form enshrined immortal
    thought!

### LXIX.

Stood ye not thus amidst the streets of Rome?
That Rome which witness'd in her sceptred days,
So much of noble death?—When shrine and
    dome,
'Midst clouds of incense, rung with choral lays,
As the long triumph pass'd with all its blaze
Of regal spoil, were ye not proudly borne
Of sovereign forms, concentering all the rays
Of the soul's lightnings?—did ye not adorn
The pomp which earth stood still to gaze on and
    to mourn?

### LXX.

Hath it been thus?—Or did ye grace the halls,
Once peopled by the mighty?—Haply there,
In your still grandeur, from the pillar'd walls
Serene ye smiled on banquets of despair,
Where hopeless courage wrought itself to dare
The stroke of its deliverance, 'midst the glow
Of living wreaths, the sighs of perfumed air,
The sound of lyres, the flower-crown'd goblet's
    flow: (15)
—Behold again!—high hearts make nobler offer-
    ings now!

### LXXI.

The stately fane is reach'd—and at its gate
The warriors pause; on life's tumultuous tide
A stillness falls, while he, whom regal state
Hath mark'd from all, to be more sternly tried
By suffering, speaks;—each ruder voice hath
    died,
While his implores forgiveness!—" If there be
One 'midst your throngs, my people!—whom in
    pride,
Or passion, I have wrong'd; such pardon, free
As mortals hope from Heaven, accord that man to
    me."

### LXXII.

But all is silence; and a gush of tears
Alone replies!—He hath not been of those
Who, fear'd by many, pine in secret fears
Of all; th' environ'd but by slaves and foes,
To whom day brings not safety, night repose,
For they have *heard the voice cry,* "*sleep no
    more!*"
Of them he hath not been, nor such, as close
Their hearts to misery, till the time is o'er,
When it speaks low and kneels th' oppressor's
    throne before!

### LXXIII.

*He* hath been loved—but who may trust the love
Of a degenerate race?—in other moulds
Are cast the free and lofty hearts, that prove
Their faith through fiery trials,—yet behold,
And call him not forsaken,—thoughts untold
Have lent his aspect calmness, and his tread
Moves firmly to the shrine.—What pomps unfold
Within its precincts!—isles and seas have shed
Their gorgeous treasures there, around th' impe-
    rial dead.

### LXXIV.

'T is a proud vision—that most regal pile
Of ancient days!—the lamps are streaming bright
From its rich altar, down each pillar'd isle,
Whose vista fades in dimness; but the sight
Is lost in splendours, as the wavering light
Developes on those walls the thousand dyes
Of the vein'd marbles, which array their height,
And from yon dome, (16) the lode-star of all eyes,
Pour such an iris-glow as emulates the skies.

### LXXV.

But gaze thou not on these; though heaven's
    own hues
In their soft clouds and radiant tracery vie;
Though tints, of sun-burnt glory, may suffuse
Arch, column, rich mosaic: pass thou by
The stately tombs, where eastern Cæsars lie,
Beneath their trophies; pause not here, for
    know,
A deeper source of all sublimity
Lives in man's bosom, than the world can show,
In nature or in art, above, around, below.

### LXXVI.

Turn thou to mark (though tears may dim thy
    gaze)
The steel-clad group before yon altar-stone;
Heed not, though gems and gold around it blaze,
Those heads unhelm'd, those kneeling forms
    alone,

Thus bow'd, look glorious here.  The light is
   thrown
Full from the shrine on one, a nation's lord,
A sufferer!—but his task shall soon be done—
E'en now, as Faith's mysterious cup is pour'd,
See to that noble brow, peace, not of earth, re
   stored!

### LXXVII.

The rite is o'er.  The band of brethren part,
Once—and but once—to meet on earth again!
Each in the strength of a collected heart,
To dare what man may dare — and know 't is
   vain!
The rite is o'er, and thou majestic fane!
The glory is departed from thy brow!
Be clothed with dust!—the Christian's farewell
   strain
Hath died within thy walls; thy Cross must bow;
Thy kingly tombs be spoil'd; thy golden shrines
   laid low!

### LXXVIII.

The streets grow still and lonely—and the star,
The last bright lingerer in the path of morn,
Gleams faint; and in the very lap of war,
As if young Hope with Twilight's rays were
   born,
Awhile the city sleeps;—her throngs, o'erworn
With fears and watchings, to their homes retire:
Nor is the balmy air of day-spring torn
With battle sounds;(17) the winds in sighs ex-
   pire,
And Quiet broods in mists, that veil the sunbeam's
   fire.

### LXXIX.

The city sleeps!—ay! on the combat's eve,
And by the scaffold's brink, and 'midst the swell
Of angry seas, hath Nature'won reprieve
Thus from her cares.  The brave have slumber'd
   well,
And e'en the fearful, in their dungeon-cell,
Chain'd between Life and Death!—Such rest be
   thine,
For conflict waits thee still!—Yet who can tell
In that brief hour, how much of Heaven may
   shine
all on thy spirit's dream!—Sleep, weary Con-
   stantine!

### LXXX.

Doth the blast rise?—the clouded East is red,
As if a storm were gathering; and I hear
What seems like heavy rain-drops, or the tread,
The soft and smother'd step, of those that fear
Surprise from ambush'd foes.  Hark! yet more
   near
It comes, a many-toned and mingled sound,
A rustling, as of winds where boughs are sear,
A rolling as of wheels that shake the ground
From far; a heavy rush, like seas that burst their
   bound!

### LXXXI.

Wake, wake! They come from sea and shore,
   ascending
In hosts your ramparts! Arm ye for the day!
Who now may sleep amidst the thunders rending,
Through tower and wall, a path for their array?
Hark! how the trumpet cheers them to the prey,
With its wild voice to which the seas reply!
And the earth rocks beneath their engine's sway,
And the far hills repeat their battle-cry,
Till that fierce tumult seems to shake the vaulted
   sky!

### LXXXII.

They fail not now, the generous band, that long
Have ranged their swords around a falling
   throne;
Still in those fearless men the walls are strong,
Hearts, such as rescue empires, are their own!
—Shall those high energies be vainly shown?

No! from their towers th' invading tide is driven
Back, like the Red-Sea waves, when God had
   blown
With his strong winds!(18)—the dark-brow'd
   ranks are riven—
Shout, warriors of the cross!—for victory is of
   Heaven!

### LXXXIII.

Stand firm!—Again the crescent host is rushing
And the waves foam, as on the galleys sweep,
With all their fires and darts, though blood is
   gushing
Fast o'er their sides, as rivers to the deep.
Stand firm!—there yet is hope—th' ascent is
   steep,
And from on high no shaft descends in vain;
—But those that fall swell up the mangled heap,
In the red moat, the dying and the slain,
And o'er that fearful bridge th' assailants mount
   again!

### LXXXIV.

Oh! the dread mingling in that awful hour,
Of all terrific sounds!—the savage tone
Of the wild horn, the cannon's peal, the shower
Of hissing darts, the crash of walls o'erthrown,
The deep, dull tambour's beat!—man's voice
   alone
Is there unheard! Ye may not catch the cry
Of trampled thousands—prayer, and shriek, and
   moan,
All drown'd, as that fierce hurricane sweeps by,
But swell the unheeded sum earth pays for victory!

### LXXXV.

War-clouds have wrapt the city!—through their
   dun
O'erloaded canopy, at times a blaze,
As of an angry storm-presaging sun,
From the Greek fire shoots up;(19) and lightning
   rays
Flash, from the shock of sabres, through the
   haze,
And glancing arrows cleave the dusky air!
—Ay! this is in the compass of our gaze,—
But fearful things, unknown, untold, are there,
Workings of Wrath and Death, and Anguish, and
   Despair!

### LXXXVI.

Woe, shame and woe!—A chief, a warrior flies,
A red-cross champion, bleeding, wild, and pale!
—Oh God! that nature's passing agonies
Thus o'er the spark which dies not should pre-
   vail!
Yes! rend the arrow from thy shatter'd mail,
And stanch the blood drops, Genoa's fallen
   son!(20)
Fly swifter yet! the javelins pour as hail!
—But there are tortures which thou canst not
   shun,
The spirit is their prey;—thy pangs are but begun!

### LXXXVII.

Oh! happy in their homes, the noble dead!
The seal is set on their majestic fame;
Earth has drunk deep the generous blood they
   shed,
Fate has no power to dim their stainless name!
They may not, in one bitter moment, shame
Long glorious years; from many a lofty stem
Fall graceful flowers, and eagle-hearts grow
   tame,
And stars drop, fading, from the diadem;
But the bright past is theirs—there is no change
   for them!

### LXXXVIII.

Where art thou, Constantine?—Where Death is
   reaping
His sevenfold harvest! Where the stormy light,
Fast as th' artillery's thunderbolts are sweeping,
Throws meteor-bursts o'er battle's noonday
   night?

Where the towers rock and crumble from their
   height,
As to the earthquake, and the engines ply
Like red Vesuvio; and where human might
Confronts all this, and still brave hearts beat
   high,
While scymetars ring loud on shivering panoply.

### LXXXIX.

Where art thou, Constantine?—Where christian
   blood
Hath bathed the walls in torrents, and in vain!
Where Faith and Valour perish in the flood,
Whose billows, rising o'er their bosoms, gain
Dark strength each moment: where the gallant
   slain
Around the banner of the cross lie strew'd,
Thick as the vine-leaves on the autumnal plain;
Where all, save one high spirit, is subdued,
And through the breach press on the o'erwhelming
   multitude.

### XC.

Now is he battling 'midst a host alone,
As the last cedar stems awhile the sway
Of mountain-storms, whose fury hath o'erthrown
Its forest-brethren in their green array!
And he hath cast his purple robe away,
With its imperial bearings; that his sword
An iron ransom from the chain may pay,
And win, what haply Fate may yet accord,
A soldier's death, the all now left an empire's lord!

### XCI.

Search for him now, where bloodiest lie the files
Which once were men, the faithful and the
   brave!
Search for him now, where loftiest rise the piles
Of shatter'd helms and shields, which could not
   save;
And crests and banners, never more to wave
In the free winds of heaven!—He is of those
O'er whom the host may rush, the tempest rave
And the steeds trample, and the spearmen close
Yet wake them not!—so deep their long and last
   repose!

### XCII.

Woe to the vanquish'd! thus it hath been still,
Since Time's first march!—Hark, hark, a peo-
   ple's cry!
Ay! now the conquerors in the streets fulfil
Their task of wrath! In vain the victims fly;
Hark! now each piercing tone of agony
Blends in the city's shriek!—The lot is cast,
Slaves, 'twas your choice, thus, rather thus, to
   die,
Than where the warrior's blood flows warm and
   fast,
And roused and mighty hearts beat proudly to the
   last!

### XCIII.

Oh! well doth freedom battle!—Men have made,
E'en 'midst their blazing roofs, a noble stand,
And on the floors, where once their children
   play'd,
And by the hearths, round which their house
   hold band
At evening met; ay! struggling hand to hand,
Within the very chambers of their sleep,
There have they taught the spoilers of the land,
In chainless hearts what fiery strength lies deep,
To guard free homes!—but ye! kneel, tremblers!
   kneel and weep!

### XCIV.

'Tis eve—the storm hath died—the valiant rest
Low on their shields; the day's fierce work is
   done,
And blood-stain'd seas and burning towers attest
Its fearful deeds. An empire's race is run!
Sad, 'midst his glory, looks the parting sun
Upon the captive city. Hark! a swell
(Meet to proclaim Barbaric war-fields won)

7

Of fierce triumphal sounds, that wildly tell,
The Soldan comes within the Cæsars' halls to
   dwell!

### XCV.

Yes! with the peal of cymbal and of gong,
He comes, the Moslem treads those ancient halls
But all is stillness there, as Death had long
Been lord alone within those gorgeous walls.
And half that silence of the grave appals
The conqueror's heart. Ay, thus with Triumph's
   hour,
Still comes the boding whisper, which recalls
A thought of those impervious clouds that lower
O'er Grandeur's path, a sense of some far mightier
   Power!

### XCVI.

" The owl upon Afrasiab's towers oath sung
Her watch-song, and around an imperial throne
The spider weaves his web!"(21) Still darkly
   hung
That verse of omen, as a prophet's tone,
O'er his flush'd spirit. Years on years have
   flown
To prove its truth: kings pile their domes in air,
That the coil'd snake may bask on sculptured
   stone,
And nations clear the forest, to prepare
For the wild fox and wolf more stately dwellings
   there!

### XCVII.

But thou! that on thy ramparts proudly dying,
As a crown'd leader in such hours should die,
Upon thy pyre of shiver'd spears art lying,
With the heavens o'er thee for a canopy,
And banners for thy shroud!—No tear, no sigh,
Shall mingle with thy dirge; for thou art now
Beyond vicissitude! Lo! rear'd on high.
The Crescent blazes, while the cross must bow;
But where no change can reach, there, Constan-
   tine, art thou!

### XCVIII.

' After life's fitful fever, thou sleep'st well!"
We may not mourn thee!—Sceptred chiefs, from
   whom
The earth received her destiny, and fell
Before them trembling—to a sterner doom
Have oft been call'd. For them the dungeon's
   gloom,
With its cold starless midnight, hath been made
More fearful darkness, where, as in a tomb,
Without a tomb's repose, the chain hath weigh'd
Their very soul to dust, with each high power de-
   cay'd.

### XCIX.

Or in the eye of thousands they have stood,
To meet the stroke of Death—but not like thee!
From bonds and scaffolds hath appeal'd *their*
   blood,
But thou didst fall unfetter'd, arm'd, and free,
And kingly to the last!—And if it be,
That, from the viewless world, whose marvels
   none
Return to tell, a spirit's eye can see
The things of earth; still may'st thou hail the
   sun,
Which o'er thy land shall dawn, when Freedom's
   fight is won!

### C.

And the hour comes, in storm!—A light is
   glancing
Far through the forest-god's Arcadian shades!
—'Tis not the moonbeam, tremulously dancing,
Where lone Alpheus bathes his haunted glades;
A murmur, gathering power, the air pervades,
Round dark Cithæron, and by Delphi's steep;
—'Tis not the song and lyre of Grecian maids,
Nor pastoral reed that lulls the vales to sleep,
Nor yet the rustling pines, nor yet the sounding
   deep!

98 HEMANS' POETICAL WORKS.

### CL.

Arms glitter on the mountains, which, of old,
Awoke to freedom's first heroic strain,
And by the streams, once crimson as they roll'd
The Persian helm and standard to the main;
And the blue waves of Salamis again
Thrill to the trumpet; and the tombs reply
With their ten thousand echoes, from each plain,
Far as Platæa's, where the mighty lie,
Who crown'd so proudly there the bowl of liber-
    ty! (22)

### CII.

Bright land with glory mantled o'er by song!
Land of the vision-peopled hills and streams,
And fountains, whose deserted banks along,
Still the soft air with inspiration teems;
Land of the graves, whose dwellers shall be
    themes
To verse for ever; and of ruin'd shrines
That scarce look desolate beneath such beams,
As bathe in gold thine ancient rocks and pines!
—When shall thy sons repose in peace beneath
    their vines?

### CIII.

*Thou* wert not made for bonds, nor shame, nor
    fear!
—Do the hoar oaks and dark-green laurels wave
O'er Mantinæa's earth?—doth Pindus rear
His snows, the sunbeam and the storm to brave?
And is there yet on Marathon a grave?
And doth Eurotas lead his silvery line
By Sparta's ruins?—And shall man, a slave,
Bow'd to the dust, amid such scenes repine?
—If e'er a soil was mark'd for Freedom's step—'t is
    thine!

### CIV.

Wash from that soil the stains, with battle-
    showers!
—Beneath Sophia's dome the Moslem prays,
The Crescent gleams amidst the olive-bowers,
In the Comneni's halls (23) the Tartar sways:
But not for long!—the spirit of those days,
When the three hundred made their funeral pale
Of Asia's dead, is kindling, like the rays
Of thy rejoicing sun, when first his smile
Warms the Parnassian rock, and gilds the Delian
    isle.

### CV.

If then 't is given thee to arise in might,
Trampling the scourge, and dashing down the
    chain,
Pure be thy triumphs, as thy name is bright!
The cross of victory should not know a stain!
So may that faith once more supremely reign,
Through which we lift our spirits from the dust!
And deem not, e'en when virtue dies in vain,
She dies forsaken; but repose our trust
On Him whose ways are dark, unsearchable—but
    just.

---

# NOTES

### Note 1.

*While Ishmael's host, &c.*

The army of Mahomet the Second, at the siege of Constantinople, was thronged with fanatics of all sects and nations, who were not enrolled amongst the regular troops. The Sultan himself marched upon the city from Adrianople; but his army must have been principally collected in the Asiatic provinces, which he had previously visited.

### Note 2.

—— *Bring wine, bring odours, &c.*

Huc vina, et unguenta, et nimium breves
Flores amœnæ ferre jube rosæ.

*Hor. lib. ii. od. 3*

### Note 3.

*From the Seven Towers, &c.*

The Castle of the Seven Towers is mentioned in the Byzantine history, as early as the sixth century of the Christian era, as an edifice which contributed materially to the defence of Constantinople, and it was the principal bulwark of the town on the coast of the Propontis, in the latter periods of the empire. For a description of this building, see *Pouqueville's Travels*.

### Note 4.

*With its long march of sceptred imagery.*

An allusion to the Roman custom of carrying in procession, at the funerals of their great men, the images of their ancestors.

### Note 5.

*The Roman cast his glittering mail away.*

The following was the ceremony of consecration with which Decius devoted himself in battle. He was ordered by Valerius, the pontifex maximus, to quit his military habit, and put on the robe he wore in the senate. Valerius then covered his head with a veil; commanded him to put forth his hand under his robe to his chin, and standing with both feet upon a javelin, to repeat these words: "O Janus, Jupiter, Mars, Romulus, Bellona, and ye Lares and Novensiles! All ye heroes who dwell in heaven, and all ye gods who rule over us and our enemies, especially ye gods of hell! I honour you, invoke you, and humbly entreat you to prosper the arms of the Romans, and to transfer all fear and terror from them to their enemies; and I do, for the safety of the Roman people, and their legions, devote myself, and with myself the army and auxiliaries of the enemy, to the infernal gods, and the goddess of the earth." Decius then, girding his robe around him, mounted his horse, and rode full speed into the thickest of the enemy's battalions. The Latins were, for a while, thunderstruck at this spectacle; but at length recovering themselves, they discharged a shower of darts, under which the consul fell.

### Note 6.

—— *Lo! Christian pennons streaming
Red o'er the waters! &c.*

See Gibbon's animated description of the arrival of five Christian ships, with men and provisions, for the succour of the besieged, not many days before the fall of Constantinople.—*Decline and Fall of the Roman Empire*, vol. xii. p. 215.

### Note 7.

—— *As when the wind hath blown
O'er Indian groves, &c.*

The summits of the lofty rocks in the Carnatic, particularly about the Ghauts, are sometimes covered with the bamboo tree, which grows in thick clumps, and is of such uncommon aridity, that in the sultry season of the year the friction occasioned by a strong dry wind will literally produce sparks of fire, which frequently setting the woods in a blaze, exhibit to the spectator stationed in a valley surrounded by rocks, a magnificent, though imperfect circle of fire.—*Notes to Kindersley's Specimens of Hindoo Literature.*

### Note 8.

—— *The snowy crown
Of far Olympus, &c.*

Those who steer their westward course through the middle of the Propontis may at once descry the high lands of Thrace and Bithynia, and never lose sight of the lofty summit of Mount Olympus, covered with eternal snows.—*Decline and Fall, &c.* vol. iii. p. 6.

### Note 9.

—— *Mohammed's face
Kindles beneath their aspect, &c.*

Mahomet II. was greatly addicted to the study of astrology. His calculations in this science led him to fix upon the morning of the 29th of May as the fortunate hour for a general attack upon the city.

### Note 10.

*Thy Georgian bride, &c.*

Constantine Palæologus was betrothed to a Georgian princess; and the very spring which witnessed the fall of Constantinople had been fixed upon as the time for conveying the imperial bride to that city.

### Note 11.

*Those men are strangers here.*

Many of the adherents of Constantine, in his last noble stand for the liberties, or rather the honour, of a falling empire, were foreigners and chiefly Italians.

### Note 12.

*Know'st thou the land, &c.*

This and the next line are an almost literal translation from a beautiful song of Goethe's:

    Kennst du das land, wo die zitronen bluhn
    Mit dunkeln laub die gold orangen gluhn? &c.

### Note 13.

The idea expressed in this stanza is beautifully amplified in Schiller's poem "Das Lied der Glocke."

### Note 14.

*Hath the fierce phantom, &c.*

It is said to be a Greek superstition that the plague is announced by the heavy rolling of an invisible chariot, heard in the streets at midnight; and also by the appearance of a gigantic spectre, who summons the devoted person by name.

### NOTE 15.

*——— Ye smiled on banquets of despair, &c.*

Many instances of such banquets, given and shared by persons resolved upon death, might be adduced from ancient history. That of Vibius Virius, at Capua, is amongst the most memorable.

### NOTE 16.

*——— Yon dome, the lode-star of all eyes.*

For a minute description of the marbles, jaspers, and porphyries, employed in the construction of St. Sophia, see *The Decline and Fall, &c.*, vol. vii. p. 120.

### NOTE 17.

*Nor is the balmy air of day-spring torn*
*With battle-sounds, &c.*

The assault of the city took place at day-break, and the Turks were strictly enjoined to advance in silence, which had also been commanded, on pain of death, during the preceding night. This circumstance is finely alluded to by Miss Baillie, in her tragedy of Constantine Palæologus:

"Silent shall be the march; nor drum, nor trump,
Nor clash of arms, shall to the watchful foe
Our near approach betray; silent and swift,
As the pard's velvet foot on Libya's sands,
Slow stealing with crouch'd shoulders on her prey."
*Constantine Palæologus*, Act iv.

"The march and labour of thousands" must, however, as Gibbon observes, "have inevitably produced a strange confusion of discordant clamours; which reached the ears of the watchmen on the towers."

### NOTE 18.

*——— The dark-browed ranks are riven.*

"After a conflict of two hours, the Greeks still maintained and preserved their advantage," says Gibbon. The strenuous exertions of the Janizaries first turned the fortune of the day.

### NOTE 19.

*From the Greek fire shoots up, &c.*

"A circumstance that distinguishes the siege of Constantinople is the reunion of the ancient and modern artillery. The bullet and the battering-ram were directed against the same wall; nor had the discovery of gunpowder superseded the use of the liquid and inextinguishable fire."—*Decline and Fall, &c.*, vol. xii. p. 213.

### NOTE 20.

*And stanch the blood-drops, Genoa's fallen son!*

"The immediate loss of Constantinople may be ascribed to the bullet, or arrow which pierced the gauntlet of John Justiniana (a Genoese chief.) The sight of his blood, and exquisite pain, appalled the courage of the chief, whose arms and counsels were the firmest rampart of the city."—*Decline and Fall, &c.*, vol. xii. p. 229.

### NOTE 21.

*The owl upon Afrasiab's towers hath sung*
*Her watch-song, &c.*

Mahomet II., on entering, after his victory, the palace of the Byzantine emperors, was strongly impressed with the silence and desolation which reigned within its precincts. "A melancholy reflection on the vicissitudes of human greatness forced itself on his mind, and he repeated an elegant distich of Persian poetry: 'The spider has wove his web in the imperial palace, and the owl hath sung her watch-song on the towers of Afrasiab'"—*Decline and Fall, &c.*, vol. xii. p. 240.

### NOTE 22.

*——— The bowl of liberty.*

One of the ceremonies by which the battle of Platæa was annually commemorated was, to crown with wine a cup called the *Bowl of Liberty*, which was afterwards poured forth in libation.

### NOTE 23.

*In the Comneni's halls, &c.*

The Comneni were amongst the most distinguished of the families who filled the Byzantine throne in the declining years of the eastern empire.

# THE SIEGE OF VALENCIA

## A DRAMATIC POEM.

### DRAMATIS PERSONÆ.

ALVAR GONZALEZ...........................................*Governor of Valencia.*
ALPHONZO }
CARLOS    } ..........................................*His Sons.*
HERNANDEZ...........................................*A Priest.*
ABDULLAH........................................... { *A Moorish Chief, Chief of the Army besieging Valencia.*
GARCIAS,...........................................*A Spanish Knight.*

ELMINA...........................................*Wife to Gonzalez.*
XIMENA...........................................*Her Daughter.*
THERESA...........................................*An Attendant.*

*Citizens, Soldiers, Attendants, &c.*

# ADVERTISEMENT.

The history of Spain records two instances of the severe and self-devoting heroism, which forms the subject of the following dramatic poem. The first of these occurred at the siege of Tarifa, which was defended in 1294, for Sancho, King of Castile, during the rebellion of his brother, Don Juan, by Guzman, surnamed the Good.* The second is related of Alonzo Lopez de Texeda, who, until his garrison had been utterly disabled by pestilence, maintained the city of Zamora for the children of Don Pedro the Cruel, against the forces of Henrique of Trastamara.†

Impressive as were the circumstances which distinguished both these memorable sieges, it appeared to the author of the following pages, that a deeper interest, as well as a stronger colour of nationality, might be imparted to the scenes in which she has feebly attempted "to describe high passions and high actions;" by connecting a religious feeling with the patriotism and high-minded loyalty which had thus been proved "faithful unto death," and by surrounding her ideal *dramatis personæ* with recollections derived from the heroic legends of Spanish chivalry. She has, for this reason, employed the agency of imaginary characters, and fixed upon "*Valencia del Cid*" as the scene to give them

"A local habitation and a name."

---

* See Quintana's 'Vidas de Espanoles celebres,' p. 88.
† See the Preface to Southey's 'Chronicle of the Cid.'

# THE

# SIEGE OF VALENCIA.





*Scene—Room in a Palace of Valencia.*

*Ximena singing to a lute.*

### BALLAD.

' Thou hast not been with a festal throng,
  At the pouring of the wine;
Men bear not from the Hall of Song,
  A mien so dark as thine!
    —There's blood upon thy shield,
    There's dust upon thy plume,
—Thou hast brought from some disastrous field
    That brow of wrath and gloom!"

" And is there blood upon my shield?
  —Maiden! it well may be!
We have sent the streams from our battle-field,
  All darken'd to the sea!
    We have given the founts a stain,
    'Midst their woods of ancient pine;
And the ground is wet—but not with rain,
  Deep-dyed—but not with wine!

" The ground is wet—but not with rain—
  We have been in war array,
And the noblest blood of Christian Spain
  Hath bathed her soil to-day.
    I have seen the strong man die,
    And the stripling meet his fate,
Where the mountain-winds go sounding by,
  In the Roncesvalles' Strait.

" In the gloomy Roncesvalles' Strait
  There are helms and lances cleft;
And they that moved at morn elate
  On a bed of heath are left!
    There's many a fair young face,
    Which the war-steed hath gone o'er;
At many a board there is kept a place
  For those that come no more!"

" Alas! for love, for woman's breast,
  If woe like this must be!
—Hast thou seen a youth with an eagle crest
  And a white plume waving free?
    With his proud quick-flashing eye,
    And his mien of knightly state?
Doth he come from where the swords flash'd high,
  In the Roncesvalles' Strait?"

" In the gloomy Roncesvalles' Strait
  I saw and mark'd him well;
For nobly on his steed he sate,
  When the pride of manhood fell!
    —But it is not *youth* which turns
    From the field of spears again;
For the boy's high heart too wildly burns,
  Till it rests amidst the slain!"

" Thou canst not say that *he* lies low,
  The lovely and the brave;
Oh! none could look on his joyous brow,
  And think upon the grave!
    Dark, dark perchance the day
    Hath been with valour's fate,
But *he* is on his homeward way,
    From the Roncesvalles' Strait."

" There is dust upon his joyous brow,
  And o'er his graceful head;
And the war-horse will not wake him now,
  Though it bruise his greensward bed!
    —I have seen the stripling die,
    And the strong man meet his fate,
Where the mountain-winds go sounding by,
  In the Roncesvalles' Strait!"

*Elmina enters.*

*Elmina.* Your songs are not like those of other
    days,
Mine own Ximena!—Where is now the young
And buoyant spirit of the morn, which once
Breath'd in your spring-like melodies, and woke
Joy's echo from all hearts?
*Ximena.*           My mother, this
Is not the free air of our mountain-wilds;
And these are not the halls, wherein my voice
First pour'd those gladdening strains.
*Elmina.*           Alas! thy heart
(I see it well) doth sicken for the pure
Free-wandering breezes of the joyous hills,
Where thy young brothers, o'er the rock and heath,
Bound in glad boyhood, e'en as torrent-streams
Leap brightly from the heights. Had we not been
Within these walls thus suddenly begirt,
Thou wouldst have track'd ere now, with step as
    light,
Their wild wood-paths.
*Ximena.*        I would not but have shared
These hours of woe and peril, though the deep
And solemn feelings wakening at their voice,
Claim all the wrought-up spirit to themselves,
And will not blend with mirth. The storm doth
    hush
All floating whispery sound, all bird-notes wild
O' th' summer forest, filling earth and heaven
With its own awful music.—And 'tis well!
Should not a hero's child be train'd to hear
The trumpet's blast unstartled, and to look
In the fix'd face of Death without dismay?
*Elmina.* Woe! woe! that aught so gentle and
    so young
Should thus be call'd to stand i' the tempest's path,
And bear the token and the hue of death
On a bright soul so soon! I had not shrunk
From mine own lot, but thou, my child, shouldst
    move
As a light breeze of heaven, through summer
    bowers,

And not o'er foaming billows.  We are fall'n
On dark and evil days!
   *Ximena.*        Ay, days that wake
All to their tasks!—Youth may not loiter now
In the green walks of spring; and womanhood
Is summon'd unto conflicts, heretofore
The lot of warrior souls.  But we will take
Our toils upon us nobly!  Strength is born
In the deep silence of long-suffering hearts;
Not amidst joy.
   *Elmina.*     Hast thou some secret woe,
That thus thou speak'st?
   *Ximena.*      What sorrow should be mine
Unknown to thee?
   *Elmina.*      Alas! the baleful air
Wherewith the pestilence in darkness walks
Through the devoted city, like a blight
Amidst the rose-tints of thy cheek hath fall'n,
And wrought an early withering!—Thou has
    cross'd
The paths of Death, and minister'd to those
O'er whom his shadow rested, till thine eye
Hath changed its glancing sunbeam for a still,
Deep, solemn radiance, and thy brow hath caugh
A wild and high expression, which at times
Fades unto desolate calmness, most unlike
What youth's bright mien should wear.  My gentle
    child!
I look on thee in fear!
   *Ximena.*      Thou hast no cause
To fear for me.  When the wild clash of steel,
And the deep tambour, and the heavy step
Of armed men, break on our morning dreams;
When, hour by hour, the noble and the brave
Are falling round us, and we deem it much
To give them funeral rites, and call them blest
If the good sword, in its own stormy hour,
Hath done its work upon them, ere disease
Had chill'd their fiery blood;—it is no time
For the light mien wherewith, in happier hours,
We trod the woodland mazes, when young leaves
Were whispering in the gale.—My Father comes—
Oh! speak of me no more.  I would not shade
His princely aspect with a thought less high
Than his proud duties claim.

        GONZALEZ *enters.*

   *Elmina.*       My noble lord!
Welcome from this day's toil!—It is the hour
Whose shadows, as they deepen, bring repose
Unto all weary men; and wilt not thou
Free thy mail'd bosom from the corselet's weight,
To rest at fall of eve?
   *Gonzalez.*     There may be rest
For the tired peasant when the vesper-bell
Doth send him to his cabin, and beneath
His vine and olive he may sit at eve,
Watching his children's sport: but unto *him*
Who keeps the watch-place on the mountain
    height,
When Heaven lets loose the storms that chasten
    realms
—Who speaks of rest?
   *Ximena.*      My father, shall I fill
The wine-cup for thy lips, or bring the lute
Whose sounds thou loved?
   *Gonzalez.*     If there be strains of power
To rouse a spirit, which in triumphant scorn
May cast off nature's feebleness, and hold
Its proud career unshackled, dashing down
Tears and fond thoughts to earth; give voice to
    those!
I have need of such, Ximena! we must hear
No melting music now.
   *Ximena.*      I know all high
Heroic ditties of the elder time,
Sung by the mountain-Christians,(1) In the bo..ds
Of th' everlasting hills. whose snows yet hear
The print of Freedom's step; and all wild strains
Wherein the dark serranos* teach the rocks
And the pine forests deeply to resound
The praise of later champions.  Wouldstthou hear
The war-song of thine ancestor, the Cid?
   *Gonzalez.* Ay, speak of him, for in that name is
    power

------

    * "Serranos," mountaineers.

Such as might rescue kingdoms! Speak of him!
We are his children! They that can look back
I' th' annals of their house on such a name,
How should *they* take dishonour by the hand,
And o'er the threshold of their fathers' halls
First lead her as a guest?
   *Elmina.*      Oh, why this?
How my heart sinks!
   *Gonzalez.*    It must not fail thee yet,
Daughter of heroes!—thine inheritance
Is strength to meet all conflicts.  Thou canst
    number
In thy long line of glorious ancestry
Men, the bright offering of whose blood hath made
The ground it bathed e'en as an altar whence
High thoughts shall rise for ever.  Bore they not,
'Midst flame and sword, their witness of the Cross,
With its victorious inspiration girt
As with a conqueror's robe, till th' infidel
O'erawed, shrank back beforethem?—Ay, the earth
Doth call them martyrs, but *their* agonies
Were of a moment, tortures whose brief aim
Was to destroy, within whose powers and scope
Lay naught but dust—And earth doth call them.
    martyrs!
Why, Heaven but claim'd their blood, their lives,
    and not
The things which grow as tendrils round their
    hearts;
No, not their children!
   *Elmina.*   Mean'st thou?—know'st thou aught?
I cannot utter it—My sons! my sons!
Is it of them?—Oh! wouldst thou speak of them?
   *Gonzalez.* A mother's heart divineth but too well!
   *Elmina.* Speak, I adjure thee!—I can bear it all.
—Where are my children?
   *Gonzalez.*     In the Moorish camp
Whose lines have girt the city.
   *Ximena.*      But they live?
—All is not lost my mother!
   *Elmina.*      Say, they live,
   *Gonzalez.*  Elmina, still they live.
   *Elmina.*      But captives!—They
Whom my fond heart had imaged to itself
Bounding from cliff to cliff amidst the wilds
Where the rock-eagle seem'd not more secure
In its rejoicing freedom!—And my boys
Are captives with the Moor!—Oh! how was this!
   *Gonzalez.* Alas! our brave Alphonso, in the pride
Of boyish daring, left our mountain-halls,
With his young brother, eager to behold
The face of noble war.  Thence on their way
Were the rash wanderers captured.
   *Elmina.*      'Tis enough.
—And when shall they be ransomed?
   *Gonzalez.*     There is ask'd
A ransom far too high.
   *Elmina.*     What! have we wealth
Which might redeem a monarch, and our sons
The while wear fetters?—Take thou all for them
And we will cast our worthless grandeur from us
As 'twere a cumbrous robe!—Why, *thou* art one
To whose high nature pomp hath ever been
But as the plumage to a warrior's helm,
Worn or thrown off as lightly.  And for me,
Thou know'st not how serenely I could take
The peasant's lot upon me, so my heart,
Amidst its deep affections undisturb'd,
May dwell in silence.
   *Ximena.*    Father! doubt thou not
But we will bind ourselves to poverty,
With glad devotedness, if this, but this,
May win them back.—Distrust us not, my father
We can bear all things.
   *Gonzalez.*    Can ye bear disgrace?
   *Ximena.*  We were not born for this.
   *Gonzalez.*     No, thou sayest well!
Hold to that lofty faith.—My wife, my child!
Hath earth no treasures richer than the gems
Torn from her secret caverns?—If by them
Chains may be riven, then let the captive spring
Rejoicing to the light!—But he, for whom
Freedom and life may but be worn with shame,
Hath naught to do, save fearlessly to fix
His steadfast look on the majestic heavens,
And proudly die!

*Elmina.*          Gonzalez, *who* must die?
*Gonzalez (hurriedly).* They on whose lives a fear-
ful price is set,
But to be paid by treason!—Is 't enough?
Or must I yet seek words?
*Elmina.*              That look saith more!
Thou canst not mean——
*Gonzalez.*          I do: why dwells there not
Power in a glance to speak it?—They must die!
They—must their names be told—*Our sons* must die
Unless I yield the city!
*Ximena.*          Oh! look up!
My mother, sink not thus!—Until the grave
Shut from our sight its victims, there is hope.
*Elmina (in a low voice.)* Whose knell was in the
breeze!
          —No, no, not *theirs!*
Whose was the blessed voice that spoke of hope?
—And there *is* hope!—I will not be subdued—
I will not hear a whisper of despair!
For Nature is all-powerful, and her breath
Moves like a quickening spirit o'er the depths
Within a father's heart.—Thou too, Gonzalez,
Wilt tell me there is hope!
*Gonzalez (solemnly.)*       Hope but in him
Who bade the patriarch lay his fair young son
Bound on the shrine of sacrifice, and when
The bright steel quiver'd in the father's hand
Just raised to strike, sent forth his awful voice
Through the still clouds, and on the breathless air,
Commanding to withhold!—Earth has no hope:
It rests with him.
*Elmina.*          *Thou* canst not tell me this!
Thou father of my sons, within whose hands
Doth lie thy children's fate.
*Gonzalez.*          If there have been
Men in whose bosoms Nature's voice hath made
Its accents as the solitary sound
Of an o'erpowering torrent, silencing
Th' austere and yet divine remonstrances
Whispered by faith and honour, lift thy hands,
And, to that Heaven, which arms the brave with
strength.
Pray that the father of thy sons may ne'er
Be thus found wanting!
*Elmina.*          Then their doom is sealed!
Thou wilt not save thy children?
*Gonzalez.*          Hast thou cause
Wife of my youth, to deem it lies within
The bounds of possible things, that I should link
My name to that word—*traitor?* They that sleep
On their proud battle-fields, thy sires and mine,
Died not for this!
*Elmina.*          Oh, cold and hard of heart!
Thou shouldst be born for empire, since thy soul
Thus lightly from all human bonds can free
Its haughty flight!—Men! men! too much is yours
Of vantage; ye, that with a sound, a breath,
A shadow, thus can fill the desolate space
Of rooted-up affections, o'er whose void
Our yearning hearts must wither!—So it is,
Dominion must be won!—Nay, leave me not—
My heart is bursting, and I *must* be heard!
Heaven hath given power to mortal agony,
As to the elements in their hour of might
And mastery o'er creation!—Who shall dare
To mock that fearful strength?—I *must* be heard!
Give me my sons!
*Gonzalez.*          That they may live to hide
With covering hands th' indignant flush of shame
On their young brows, when men shall speak of
him
They called their father!—Was the oath, whereby,
On th' altar o' my faith, I bound myself,
With an unswerving spirit to maintain
This free and Christian city for my God
And for my king, a writing traced on sand?
That passionate tears should wash it from the
earth,
Or e'en the life-drops of a bleeding heart
Efface it, as a billow sweeps away
The last light vessel's wake?—Then never more
Let man's deep vows be trusted!—though enforced
By all th' appeals of high remembrances,
And silent claims o' th' sepulchres. wherein
His fathers with their stainless glory sleep,

On their good swords! Think'st thou I feel no
pangs?
He that hath given me sons, doth know the heart
Whose treasures he recalls.—Of this no more.
'Tis vain. I tell thee that th' inviolate cross
Still, from our ancient temples, must look up
Through the blue heavens of Spain, though at its
foot
I perish, with my race. Thou *darest* not ask
That I, the son of warriors—men who died
To fix it on that proud supremacy—
Should tear the sign of our victorious faith
From its high place of sunbeams, for the Moor
In impious joy to trample!
*Elmina.*          Scorn me not!
In mine extreme of misery!—Thou art strong—
Thy heart is not as mine. My brain grows wild
I know not what I ask!—And yet 'twere but
Anticipating fate—since it must fall,
That cross *must* fall at last! There is no power,
No hope within this city of the grave,
To keep its place on high. Her sultry air
Breathes heavily of death, her warriors sink
Beneath their ancient banners, ere the Moor
Hath bent his bow against them; for the shaft
Of pestilence flies more swiftly to its mark,
Than the arrow of the desert. Ev'n the skies
O'erhang the desolate splendour of her domes
With an ill omen's aspect, shaping forth,
From the dull clouds, wild menacing forms and
signs
Foreboding ruin. *Man* might be withstood,
But who shall cope with famine and disease,
When leagued with armed foes!—Where now the
aid,
Where the long-promised lances of Castile?
—We are forsaken, in our utmost need,
By heaven and earth forsaken!
*Gonzalez.*          If this be,
(And yet I will not deem it) we must fall
As men that in severe devotedness
Have chosen their part and bound themselves to
death.
Through high conviction that their suffering land,
By the free blood of martyrdom alone,
Shall call deliverance down.
*Elmina.*          Oh! I have stood
Beside thee through the beating storms of life,
With the true heart of unrepining love,
As the poor peasant's mate doth cheerily
In the parch'd vineyard, or the harvest-field,
Bearing her part, sustain with him the heat
And burden of the day. But now the hour,
The heavy hour is come, when human strength
Sinks down, a toil-worn pilgrim, in the dust,
Owning that woe is mightier!—Spare me yet
This bitter cup, my husband!—Let not her,
The mother of the lovely, sit and mourn
In her unpeopled home, a broken stem,
O'er its fallen roses dying!
*Gonzalez.*          Urge me not,
Thou that through all sharp conflicts hast been
found
Worthy a brave man's love, oh! urge me not
To guilt, which, through the mist of blinding
tears,
In its own hues thou seest not!—Death may scarce
Bring aught like this!
*Elmina.*          All, all thy gentle race,
The beautiful beings that around thee grew,
Creatures of sunshine! Wilt thou doom them all?
—She, too, thy daughter—doth her smile unmark'd
Pass from thee, with its radiance, day by day?
Shadows are gathering round her—seest thou not?
The misty dimness of the spoiler's breath
Hangs o'er her beauty, and the face which made
The summer of our hearts, now doth but send,
With every glance, deep bodings through the soul.
Telling of early fate.
*Gonzalez.*          I see a change
Far nobler on her brow!—She is as one,
Who, at the trumpet's sudden call, hath risen
From the gay banquet, and in scorn cast down
The wine-cup, and the garland, and the lute,
Of festal hours, for the good spear and helm,
Beseeming sterner tasks.—Her eye hath lost

The beam which laughed upon th' awakening
    heart,
E'en as morn breaks o'er earth.  But far within
Its full dark orb, a light hath sprung, whose source
Lies deeper in the soul.—And let the torch
Which but illumed the glittering pageant, fade!
The altar-flame, i' th' sanctuary's recess,
Burns quenchless, being of heaven!—She hath
    put on
Courage, and faith, and generous constancy.
Ev'n as a breastplate.—Ay, men look on her,
As she goes forth serenely to her tasks,
Binding the warrior's wounds, and bearing fresh
Cool draughts to fevered lips; they look on her,
Thus moving in her beautiful array
Of gentle fortitude, and bless the fair
Majestic vision, and unmurmuring turn
Unto their heavy toils.
    *Elmina.*                And seest thou not
In that high faith and strong collectedness,
A fearful inspiration ?—*They* have cause
To tremble, who behold th' unearthly light
Of high, and, it may be, prophetic thought,
Investing youth with grandeur!—From the grave
It rises, on whose shadowy brink thy child
Waits but a father's hand to snatch her back
Into the laughing sunshine.—Kneel with me,
Ximena, kneel beside me, and implore
That which a deeper, more prevailing voice
Than ours doth ask, and will not be denied;
—His children's lives!
    *Ximena.*        Alas! this may not be,
Mother!—I cannot.            [*Exit* XIMENA.
    *Gonzalez.*        My heroic child!
—A terrible sacrifice thou claim'st, O God!
From creatures in whose agonizing hearts
Nature is strong as death.
    *Elmina.*                Is't thus in thine?
Away!—what time is given thee to resolve
On ?—what I cannot utter!—Speak! thou know'st
Too well what I would say.
    *Gonzalez.*                Until—ask not!
The time is brief.
    *Elmina.*        Thou said'st—I heard not right—
    *Gonzalez.*  The time is brief.
    *Elmina.*                What! must we burst all ties
Wherewith the thrilling chords of life are twined;
And, for this task's fulfilment, can it be
That man, in his cold heartlessness, hath dared
To number and to mete us forth the sands
Of hours, nay, moments?—Why, the sentenced
    wretch,
He on whose soul there rests a brother's blood
Poured forth in slumber, is allowed more time
To wean his turbulent passions from the world
His presence doth pollute!—It is not thus!
We must have time to school us.
    *Gonzalez.*                We have but
To bow the head in silence, when Heaven's voice
Calls back the things we love.
    *Elmina.*  Love! Love!—there are soft smiles
    and gentle words,
And there are faces skilful to put on
The look we trust in—and 'tis mockery all!
—A faithless mist, a desert-vapour, wearing
The brightness of clear waters, thus to cheat
The thirst that semblance kindled!—There is none
In all this cold and hollow world, no fount
Of deep, strong, deathless love, save that within
A mother's heart.—It is but pride, wherewith
To his fair son the father's eye doth turn
Watching his growth.  Ay, on the boy he looks,
The bright glad creature springing in his path,
But as the heir of his great name, the young
And stately tree, whose rising strength ere long
Shall bear his trophies well.—And this is love!
This is *man's* love!—What marvel?—*you* ne'er
    made
Your breast the pillow of his infancy,
While to the fullness of your heart's glad heavings
'Tis fair cheek rose and fell; and his bright hair
Waved softly to your breast!—*You* ne'er kept
    watch
Beside him, till the last pale star had set,
And morn, all dazzling, as in triumph broke
On your dim weary eye; not *yours* the face

Which early faded through fond care for him,
Hung o'er his sleep, and duly as Heaven's light,
Was there to greet his wakening!  *You* ne'er
    smoothed
His couch, ne'er sung him to his rosy rest,
Caught his least whisper, when his voice *from* yours
Had learned soft utterance; pressed your lips to his
When fever parched it; hushed his wayward cries,
With patient, vigilant, never-wearied love!
No! these are *woman's* tasks!—In these her youth,
And bloom of cheek, and buoyancy of heart,
Steal from her all unmarked!—My boys! my boys!
Hath vain affection borne with all for this?
—Why were ye given me ?
    *Gonzalez.*                Is there strength in man
Thus to endure ?—That thou couldst read, thro' all
Its depths of silent agony, the heart
Thy voice of woe doth read!
    *Elmina.* Thy heart!—*thy* heart!—Away! it feels
    not *now!*
But an hour comes to tame the mighty man
Unto the infant's weakness; nor shall Heaven
Spare you that bitter chastening!—May you live
To be alone, when loneliness doth seem
Most heavy to sustain!—For me, my voice
Of prayer and fruitless weeping shall be soon
With all forgotten sounds; my quiet place
Low with my lovely ones, and we shall sleep,
Though kings lead armies o'er us; we shall sleep,
Wrapt in earth's covering mantle! you the while
Shall sit within your vast, forsaken halls,
And hear the wild and melancholy winds
Moan through their drooping banners, never more
To wave above your race.  Ay, then call up
Shadows—dim phantoms from ancestral tombs,
But all—all *glorious*—conquerors, chieftains, kings
—To people that cold void!—And when the
    strength
From your right arm hath melted, when the blast
Of the shrill clarion gives your heart no more
A fiery wakening; if at last you pine
For the glad voices, and the bounding steps,
Once through your home re-echoing, and the clasp
Of twining arms, and all the joyous light
Of eyes that laugh'd with youth, and made your
    board
A place of sunshine;—When those days are come,
Then, in your utter desolation, turn
To the cold world, the smiling, faithless world,
Which hath swept past you long, and bid it quench
Your soul's deep thirst with *fame?* immortal *fame.*
Fame to the sick of heart!—a gorgeous robe,
A crown of victory, unto him that dies
I' th' burning waste, for water!
    *Gonzalez.*                This from *thee.*
Now the last drop of bitterness is pour'd.
Elmina—I forgive thee!            [*Exit* ELMINA.
                Aid me, Heaven !
From whom alone is power!—Oh! thou hast set
Duties, so stern of aspect, in my path,
They almost, to my startled gaze, assume
The hue of things less hallow'd!  Men have sunk
Unblamed beneath such trials!—Doth not He
Who made us, know the limits of our strength?
My wife! my sons!—Away! I must not pause
To give my heart one moment's mastery thus!
                [*Exit* GONZALEZ.

————

*Scene—The Aisle of a Gothic Church.*

HERNANDEZ, GARCIAS, *and others.*

*Hernandez.*  The rites are closed.  Now, valiant
    men, depart,
Each to his place—I may not say, of rest;
Your faithful vigils for your sons may win
What must not be your own.  Ye are as those
Who sow, in peril and in care, the seed
Of the fair tree, beneath whose stately shade
They may not sit.  But bless'd be they who toil
For after-days!—All high and holy thoughts
Be with yon, warriors, thro' the lingering hours
Of the night-watch!
    *Garcias.*                Ay, father! we have need
Of high and holy thoughts, wherewith to fence
Our hearts against despair.  Yet have I been

From youth a son of war.  The stars have look'd
A thousand times upon my couch of health,
Spread 'midst the wild sierras, hy some stream
Whose dark-red waves look'd e'en as though their
      source
Lay not in rocky caverns, but the veins
Of noble hearts; while many a nightly crest
Roll'd with them to the deep.  And in the years
Of my long exile and captivity,
With the fierce Arab, I have watch'd beneath
The still pale shadow of some lonely palm,
At midnight, in the desert; while the wind
Swell'd with the lion's roar, and heavily
The fearfulness and might of solitude
Press'd on my weary heart.
    *Hernandez (thoughtfully.)*  Thou little know'st
Of what is solitude!—I tell thee, those·
For whom—in earth's remotest nook—howe'er
Divided from their path by chain on chain
Of mighty mountains, and the amplitude
Of rolling seas—there beats one human heart,
There breathes one being unto whom their name
Comes with a thrilling and a gladdening sound,
Heard o'er the din of life! are not alone!
Not on the deep, nor in the wild, alone;
For there is that on earth with which they hold
A brotherhood of soul!—Call *him* alone,
Who stands shut out from this!—And let not those
Whose homes are bright with sunshine and with
      love,
Put on the insolence of happiness,
Glorying in that proud lot!—A lonely hour
Is on its way to each, to all; for Death
Knows no companionship.
    *Garcias.*                    I have look'd on Death
In field, and storm, and flood.  But never yet
Hath aught weigh'd down·my spirit to a mood
Of sadness, dreaming o'er dark auguries,
Like this, our watch by midnight.  Fearful things
Are gathering round us.  Death upon the earth,
Omens in Heaven!—The summer-skies put forth
No clear bright stars above us, but at times,
Catching some comet's fiery hue of wrath,
Marshal their clouds to armies, traversing
Heaven with the rush of meteor steeds, the array
Of spears and banners, tossing like the pines
Of Pyrenean forests, when the storm
Doth sweep the mountains.
    *Hernandez.*                Ay, last night, I too
Kept vigil, gazing on the angry heavens;
And I beheld the meeting and the shock
Of those wild hosts i' th' air, when as they closed,
A red and sultry mist, like that which mantles
The thunder's path, fell o'er them.  Then were
      flung
Through the dull glare, broad cloudy banners forth,
And chariots seem'd to whirl, and steeds to sink,
Bearing down crested warriors.  But all this
Was dim and shadowy;—then swift darkness
      rush'd
Down on th' unearthly battle, as the deep
Swept o'er the Egyptian's armament.—I look'd—
And all that fiery field of plumes and spears
Was blotted from heaven's face!—I look'd again
—And from the brooding mass of clouds leap'd
      forth
One meteor sword, which o'er the reddening sea
Shook with strange motion, such as earthquakes
      give
Unto a rocking citadel!—I beheld,
And yet my spirit sunk not.
    *Garcias.*                Neither deem
That mine hath blench'd.—But these are sights
      and sounds
To awe the firmest.—Know'st thou what we hear
At midnight from the walls?—Were 't but the deep
Barbaric horn or Moorish tambour's peal,
Thence might the warrior's heart catch impulses,
Quickening its fiery currents.  But our ears
Are pierced by other tones.  We hear the knell
For brave men in their noon of strength cut down,
And the shrill wail of woman, and the dirge
Faint swelling through the streets.  Then e'en the
      air
Hath strange and fitful murmurs of lament,
As if the viewless watchers of the land

Sigh'd on its hollow breezes!—To my soul,
The torrent-rush of battle, with its din
Of trampling steeds and ringing panoply
Were, after these faint sounds of drooping woe,
As the free sky's glad music unto him
Who leaves a couch of sickness.
    *Hernandez (with solemnity.)*  If to plunge
In the mid-waves of combat, as they bear
Chargers and spearmen onwards; and to make
A reckless bosom's front the buoyant mark
On that wild current, for ten thousand arrows;
If *thus* to dare were valour's noblest aim,
Lightly might fame be won!—but there are things
Which ask a spirit of more exalted pitch,
And courage temper'd with a holier fire!
Well may'st thou say, that these are fearful times
Therefore be firm, be patient!—There is strength
And a fierce instinct, e'en in common souls,
To bear up manhood with a stormy joy,
When red swords meet in lightning!—but our task
Is more, and nobler!—We have to endure,
And to keep watch, and to arouse a land,
And to defend an altar!—If we fall,
So that our blood make but the millionth part
Of Spain's great ransom, we may count it joy
To die upon her bosom, and beneath
The banner of her faith!—Think but on this,
And gird your hearts with silent fortitude,
Suffering, yet hoping all things—Fare ye well.
    *Garcias.*  Father, farewell.    [*Exeunt* GARCIAS
        *and his followers.*
    *Hernandez.*                These men have earthly ties
And bondage on their natures!—To the cause
Of God, and Spain's revenge, they bring but half
Their energies and hopes.  But he whom Heaven
Hath called to be th' awakener of a land,
Should have his soul's affections all absorb'd
In that majestic purpose, and press on
To its fulfilment, as a mountain-born
And mighty stream, with all its vassal rills
Sweeps proudly to the ocean, pausing not
To dally with the flowers.
                        Hark! what quick step
Comes hurrying through the gloom at this dead
      hour?

            ELMINA *enters*

    *Elmina.*  Are not all hours as one to misery?—
      Why
Should *she* take note of time, for whom the day
And night have lost their blessed attributes
Of sunshine and repose?
    *Hernandez.*                I know thy griefs;
But there are trials for the noble heart
Wherein its own deep fountains must supply
All it can hope of comfort.  Pity's voice
Comes with vain sweetness to th' unheeding ear
Of anguish, e'en as music heard afar
On the green shore, by him who perishes
'Midst rocks and eddying waters.
    *Elmina.*                Think thou not
I sought thee but for pity.  I am come
For that which grief is privileged to demand
With an imperious claim, from all whose form,
Whose human form, doth seal them unto suffering.
Father!  I ask thine aid.
    *Hernandez.*                There is no aid
For thee or for thy children, but with Him
Whose presence is around us in the cloud,
As in the shining and the glorious light.
    *Elmina.*  There is no aid!—Art thou a man of
      God?
Art thou a man of sorrow, (for the world
Doth call thee such) and hast thou not been taught
By God and sorrow—mighty as they are,
To own the claims of misery?
    *Hernandez.*                Is there power
With me to save thy sons?—Implore of Heaven!
    *Elmina.*  Doth not Heaven work its purposes by
      man?
I tell thee *thou* canst save them!—Art thou not
Gonzalez' counsellor?—Unto him thy words
Are e'en as oracles——
    *Hernandez.*                And therefore?—Speak
The noble daughter of Pelayo's line

Hath naught to ask, unworthy of the name
Which is a nation's heritage.—Dost thou shrink?
   *Elmina.* Have pity on me, father!—I must speak
That, from the thought of which, but yesterday,
I had recoil'd in scorn!—But this is past.
Oh! we grow humble in our agonies,
And to the dust—their birth-place—bow the heads
That wore the crown of glory!—I am weak—
My chastening is far more than I can bear.
   *Hernandez.* These are no times for weakness.
      On our hills,
The ancient cedars, in their gather'd might,
Are battling with the tempest; and the flower
Which cannot meet its driving blast must die.
—But thou hast drawn thy nurture from a stem
Unwont to bend or break—Lift thy proud head,
Daughter of Spain!—What wouldst thou with thy
   lord?
   *Elmina.* Look not upon me thus!—I have no
   power
To tell thee.  Take thy keen disdainful eye
Off from my soul!—What! am I sunk to this?
I, whose blood sprung from heroes!—How my
   sons
Will scorn the mother that would bring disgrace
On their majestic line!—My sons! my sons!
—Now is all else forgotten!—I had once
A babe that in the early spring-time lay
Sickening upon my bosom, till at last,
When earth's young flowers were opening to the
   sun,
Death sunk on his meek eyelid, and I deem'd
All sorrow light to mine!—But now the fate
Of all my children seems to brood above me
In the dark thunder-clouds!—Oh! I have power
And voice unfaltering now to speak my prayer,
And my last lingering hope that thou shouldst win
The father to relent, to save his sons!
   *Hernandez.* By yielding up the city?
   *Elmina.* Rather say,
By meeting that which gathers close upon us
Perchance one day the sooner!—Is't not so?
Must we not yield at last?—How long shall man
Array his single breast against disease,
And famine, and the sword?
   *Hernandez.* How long?—While he,
Who shadows forth his power more gloriously
In the high deeds and suff'rings of the soul,
Than in the circling heavens, with all their stars,
Or the far-sounding deep, doth send abroad
A spirit, which takes affliction for its mate,
In the good cause, with solemn joy!—How long?
—And who art *thou*, that, in the littleness
Of thine own selfish purpose, would'st set bounds
To the free current of all noble thought
And generous action, bidding its bright waves
Be stay'd, and flow no further?—But the Power
Whose interdict is laid on seas and orbs,
To chain them in from wandering, hath assign'd
No limits unto that which man's high strength
Shall, through its aid, achieve!
   *Elmina.* Oh! there are times,
When *all* that hopeless courage can achieve
But sheds a mournful beauty o'er the fate
Of those who die in vain.
   *Hernandez.* *Who* dies in vain
Upon his country's war-fields, and within
The shadow of her altars?—Feeble heart!
I tell thee that the voice of noble blood,
Thus pour'd for faith and freedom, hath a tone
Which from the night of ages, from the gulf
Of death shall burst, and make its high appeal
Sound unto earth and heaven!  Ay, let the land,
Whose sons through centuries of woe have striven
And perish'd by her temples, sink awhile,
Borne down in conflict!—But Immortal seed
Deep, by heroic suffering, hath been sown
On all her ancient hills; and generous hope
Knows that the soil, in its good time, shall yet
Bring forth a glorious harvest!—Earth receives
Not one red drop from faithful hearts in vain.
   *Elmina.* Then it must be!  And ye will make
   those lives,
Those young bright lives, an offering, to retard
Our doom one day!

   *Hernandez.* The mantle of that day
May wrap the fate of Spain!
   *Elmina.* What led me here?
Why did I turn to *thee* in my despair?
Love hath no ties upon thee; what had I
To hope from *thee*, thou lone and childless man?
Go to thy silent home!—there no young voice
Shall bid thee welcome, no light footstep spring
Forth at the sound of thine!—What knows thy
   heart?
   *Hernandez.* Woman! how dar'st thou taunt me
   with my woes?
*Thy* children too shall perish, and I say
It shall be well!—Why tak'st thou thought for
   them?
Wearing thy heart, and wasting down thy life
Unto its dregs, and making night thy time
Of care yet more intense, and casting health,
Unpriz'd to melt away, i' th' bitter cup
Thou minglest for thyself!—Why, what hath earth
To pay thee back for this?—Shall they not live,
(If the sword spare them now) to prove how soon
All love may be forgotten?  Years of thought,
Long faithful watchings, looks of tenderness,
That changed not, though to change be this world's
   law?
Shall they not flush thy cheeks with shame, whose
   blood
Marks, e'en like branding iron?—to thy sick heart
Make death a want, as sleep to weariness?
Doth not all hope end thus?—or e'en at best,
Will they not leave thee?—far from thee seek
   room
For th' overflowings of their fiery souls,
On life's wide ocean?—Give the bounding steed,
Or the wing'd bark to youth, that his free course
May be o'er hills and seas; and weep thou not
In thy forsaken home, for the bright world
Lies all before him, and be sure he wastes
No thought on thee?
   *Elmina.* Not so! it is not so!
Thou dost but torture me!—*My* sons are kind,
And brave, and gentle.
   *Hernandez.* Others too have worn
The semblance of all good.  Nay, stay thee yet:
I will be calm, and thou shalt learn how earth,
The fruitful in all agonies, hath woes
Which far outweigh thine own.
   *Elmina.* It may not be—
*Whose* grief is like a mother's for her sons?
   *Hernandez.* *My* son lay stretch'd upon his bat-
   tle-bier,
And there were hands wrung o'er him, which had
   caught
Their hue from his young blood!
   *Elmina.* What tale is this?
   *Hernandez.* Read you no records in this mien,
   of things
Whose traces on man's aspect are not such
As the breeze leaves on water?—Lofty birth,
War, peril, power?—Affliction's hand is strong,
If it erase the haughty characters
They grave so deep!—I have not always been
That which I am.  The name I bore is not
Of those which perish!—I was once a chief,
A warrior!—nor, as now, a lonely man!
I was a father!
   *Elmina.* Then thy heart can *feel!*
Thou wilt have pity!
   *Hernandez.* Should I pity *thee?*
*Thy* sons will perish gloriously—their blood——
   *Elmina.* Their blood! my children's blood!—
   Thou speak'st as 'twere
Of casting down a wine-cup, in the mirth
And wantonness of feasting!—My fair boys!
—Man! hast *thou* been a father?
   *Hernandez.* Let them die!
Let them die *now*, thy children! so thy heart
Shall wear their beautiful image all undimm'd,
Within it, to the last!  Nor shalt thou learn
The bitter lesson, of what worthless dust
Are framed the idols, whose false glory binds
Earth's fetters on our souls!—Thou think'st I much
To mourn the early dead; but there are tears
Heavy with deeper anguish! We endow

Those whom we love, in our fond passionate
    blindness,
With power upon our souls, too absolute
To be a mortal's trust! Within their hands
We lay the flaming sword, whose stroke alone
Can reach our hearts, and *they* are merciful,
As they are strong. that wield it not to pierce us!
—Ay, fear them, fear the loved!—Had I but wept
O'er my son's grave, as o'er a babe's, where tears
Are as spring dew-drops, glittering in the sun,
And brightening the young. verdure, *I* might still
Have loved and trusted!
    *Elmina (disdainfully.)* But he fell in war!
And hath not glory medicine in her cup
For the brief pangs of nature?
    *Hernandez.* Glory!—Peace,
And listen!—By my side the stripling grew,
Last of my line. I rear'd him to take joy
I' th' blaze of arms, as eagles train their young
To look upon the day-king—His quick blood
E'en to his boyish cheek would mantle up,
When the heavens rang with trumpets, and his eye
Flash with the spirit of a race whose deeds—
But this availeth not!—Yet he *was* brave.
I've seen him clear himself a path in fight
As lightning through a forest, and his plume
Waved like a torch, above the battle-storm.
The soldier's guide, when princely crests had sunk,
And banners were struck down—Around my steps
Floated his fame, like music, and I lived
But in the lofty sound. But when my heart
In one frail ark had ventured all, when most
He seem'd to stand between my soul and heaven
—Then came the thunder-stroke!
    *Elmina.* 'Tis ever thus!
And the unquiet and foreboding sense
That thus 'twill ever be, doth link itself
Darkly with all deep love!—He died?
    *Hernandez.* Not so!
—Death! Death!—Why, earth should be a para-
    dise,
To make that name so fearful! Had he died,
With his young fame about him for a shroud,
    had not learn'd the might of agony,
To bring proud natures low!—No! he fell off—
—Why do I tell thee this?—What right hast *thou*
To learn how pass'd the glory from my house?
Yet listen!—He forsook me!—He, that was
As mine own soul, forsook me!—trampled o'er
The ashes of his sires!—Ay, leagued himself
E'en with the infidel, the curse of Spain,
And, for the dark eye of a Moorish maid,
Abjured his faith, his God!—Now, talk of death!
    *Elmina.* Oh! I can pity thee——
    *Hernandez.* There's more to hear
braced the corselet o'er my heart's deep wound,
And cast my troubled spirit on the tide
Of war and high events, whose stormy waves
Might bear it up from sinking;——
    *Elmina.* And ye met
No more?
    *Hernandez.* Be still!—We did!—we met *once*
    more.
God had his own high purpose to fulfil,
Or think'st thou that the sun in his bright heaven
Had look'd upon such things?—We met *once more.*
—That was an hour to leave its lightning-mark
Seared upon brain and bosom!—there had been
Combat on Ebro's banks, and when the day
Sank in red clouds, it faded from a field
Still held by Moorish lances. Night closed round,
A night of sultry, darkness, in the shadow
Of whose broad wing, e'en unto death I strove
Long with a turban'd champion; but my sword
Was heavy with God's vengeance—and prevail'd.
He fell—my heart exulted—and I stood
In gloomy triumph o'er him—Nature gave
No sign of horror, for 'twas Heaven's decree!
He strove to speak—but I had done the work
Of wrath too well—yet in his last deep moan
A dreadful something of familiar sound
Came o'er my shuddering sense—The moon look'd
    forth,
And I beheld—speak not!—'twas he—my son!
My boy lay dying there! He raised one glance,
And knew me—for he sought with feeble hand

To cover his glazed eyes. A darker veil
Sank o'er them soon—I will not have thy look
Fixed on me thus!—away!
    *Elmina.* Thou hast seen this,
Thou hast *done* this—and yet thou liv'st?
    *Hernandez.* I live!
And know'st thou wherefore?—On my soul there
    fell
A horror of great darkness, which shut out
All earth, and heaven, and hope. I cast away
The spear and helm, and made the cloister's shade
The home of my despair. But a deep voice
Came to me through the gloom, and sent its tones
Far through my bosom's depths. And I awoke,
Ay, as the mountain cedar doth shake off
Its weight of wintry snow, e'en so I shook
Despondence from my soul, and knew myself
Seal'd by that blood wherewith my hands were
    dyed,
And set apart, and fearfully mark'd out
Unto a mighty task!—To rouse the soul
Of Spain, as from the dead; and to lift up
The cross, her sign of victory, on the hills,
Gathering her sons to battle!—And my voice
Must be as freedom's trumpet on the winds,
From Roncesvalles to the blue sea-waves
Where Calpe looks on Afric; till the land
Have fill'd her cup of vengeance!—Ask me *now*
To yield the Christian city, that its fanes
May rear the minaret in the face of heaven!
—But death shall have a bloodier vintage-feast
Ere that day come!
    *Elmina.* I ask thee this no more,
For I am hopeless now—But yet one boon—
Hear me, by all thy woes!—Thy voice hath power
Through the wide city—here I cannot rest:—
Aid me to pass the gates!
    *Hernandez.* And wherefore?
    *Elmina.* Thou,
That *wert* a father, and art now—alone!
Canst *thou* ask 'wherefore?'—Ask the wretch
    whose sands
Have not an hour to run. whose failing limbs
Have but one earthly journey to perform,
Why, on his pathway to the place of death,
Ay, when the very axe is glistening cold
Upon his dizzy sight, his pale, parched lip
Implores a cup of water?—Why, the stroke
Which trembles o'er him in itself shall bring
Oblivion of all wants, yet who denies
Nature's last prayer?—I tell thee that the thirst
Which burns my spirit up is agony
To be endured no more!—And I *must* look
Upon my children's faces, I must hear
Their voices, ere they perish!—But hath Heaven
Decreed that they *must* perish?—Who shall say
If in yon Moslem camp there beats no heart
Which prayers and tears may melt?
    *Hernandez.* There!—with the Moor.
Let him fill up the measure of his guilt!
—'Tis madness all!—How would'st thou pass the
    array
Of armed foes?
    *Elmina.* Oh! free doth sorrow pass,
Free and unquestion'd, through a suffering
    world! (2)
    *Hernandez.* This must not be. Enough of woe
    is laid
E'en now, upon thy lord's heroic soul,
For man to bear, unsinking. Press thou not
Too heavily th' o'erburthen'd heart—Away!
Bow down the knee, and send thy prayers for
    strength
Up to Heaven's gate—Farewell! [*Exit* HERNANDEZ.
    *Elmina.* Are all men thus?
—Why, wer't not better they should fall e'en now
Than live to shut their hearts, in haughty scorn,
Against the sufferer's pleadings?—But no, no!
Who can be like *this* man, that slew his son,
Yet wears his life still proudly, and a soul
Untamed upon his brow? (*After a pause*)
    There's one, whose arms
Have borne my children in their infancy,
And on whose knees they sported, and whose hard
Hath led them oft—a vassal of their sire's:
And I will seek him: he may lend me aid,
When all beside pass on.

### DIRGE HEARD WITHOUT.

Thou to thy rest art gone,
　High heart! and what are we,
While o'er our heads the storm sweeps on,
　That we should mourn for thee?

Free grave and peaceful bier
　To the buried son of Spain!
To those that live, the lance and spear,
　And well if not the chain!

Be *theirs* to weep the dead
　As they sit beneath their vines,
Whose flowery land hath borne no tread
　Of spoilers o'er its shrines!

Thou hast thrown off the load
　Which we must yet sustain,
And pour our blood where *thine* hath flow'd.
　Too blest if not in vain!

We give thee holy rite,
　Slow knell, and chanted strain!
—For those that fall to-morrow night
　May be left no funeral train.

Again, when trumpets wake,
　We must brace our armour on;
But a deeper note *thy* sleep must break—
　—Thou to thy rest art gone!

Happier in *this* than all
　That, now thy race is run,
Upon thy name no stain may fall,
　Thy work hath well been done

---

### Scene—*A Street in the City.*

#### HERNANDEZ, GONZALEZ.

*Hernandez.*　Would they not hear?
*Gonzalez.*　　　　They heard, as one that stands
By the cold grave which hath but newly closed
O'er his last friend, doth hear some passer-by
Bid him be comforted!—Their hearts have died
Within them:—We must perish, not as those
That fall when battle's voice doth shake the hills,
And peal through Heaven's great arch, but silently,
And with a wasting of the spirit down,
A quenching, day by day, of some bright spark,
Which lit us on our toils!—Reproach me not;
My soul is darken'd with a heavy cloud—
—Yet fear not I shall yield!
*Hernandez.*　　　　Breathe not the word,
Save in proud scorn:—Each bitter day, o'erpass'd
By slow endurance, is a triumph won
For Spain's red cross. And be of trusting heart!
A few brief hours, and those that turn'd away
In cold despondence, shrinking from your voice,
May crowd around their leader, and demand
To be array'd for battle. We must watch
For the swift impulse, and await its time,
As the bark waits the ocean's. You have chosen
To kindle up their souls, an hour, perchance,
When they were weary. They had cast aside
Their arms to slumber; or a knell, just then
With its deep hollow tone, had made the blood
Creep shuddering through their veins; or they
　　had caught
A glimpse of some new meteor, and shaped forth
Strange omens from its blaze.
*Gonzalez.*　　　　Alas! the cause
Lies deeper in their misery!—I have seen,
In my night's course through this beleaguer'd city,
Things, whose remembrance doth not pass away
As vapours from the mountains.—There were
　　some,
That sat beside their dead, with eyes wherein
Grief had ta'en place of sight, and shut out all
But its own ghastly object. To my voice
Some answer'd with a fierce and bitter laugh,
As men whose agonies were made to pass
The bounds of sufferance, by some reckless word,
Dropt from the light of spirit.—Others lay—
Why should I tell thee, father! how despair
Can bring the lofty brow of manhood down
Unto the very dust?—And yet for this,

Fear not that I embrace my doom—Oh God!
That 'twere my doom alone!—with less of fix'd
And solemn fortitude.—Lead on, prepare
The holiest rites of faith, that I by them
Once more may consecrate my sword, my life,
—But what are these?—Who hath not dearer lives
Twined with his own?—I shall be lonely soon—
Childless!—Heaven wills it so. Let us begone.
Perchance before the shrine my heart may beat
With a less troubled motion.
　　　　[*Exeunt* GONZALEZ *and* HERNANDEZ.

---

### Scene—*A tent in the Moorish Camp.*

#### ABDULLAH, ALPHONSO, CARLOS.

*Abdullah.*　These are bold words: but hast thou
　　look'd on death,
Fair stripling!—On thy cheek and sunny brow
Scarce fifteen summers of their laughing course
Have left light traces. If thy shaft hath pierc'd
The ibex of the mountains, if thy step
Hath climb'd some eagle's nest, and thou hast made
His nest thy spoil, 't is much:—And fear'st thou not
The leader of the mighty?
*Alphonso.*　　　　I have been
Rear'd among fearless men, and 'midst the rocks
And the wild hills, whereon my fathers fought
And won their battles. There are glorious tales
Told of their deeds, and I have learn'd them all.
How should I fear thee, Moor?
*Abdullah.*　　　　So, thou hast seen
Fields, where the combat's roar hath died away
Into the whispering breeze, and where wild flowers
Bloom o'er forgotten graves!—But know'st thou
　　aught
Of those, where sword from crossing sword strikes
　　fire,
And leaders are borne down, and rushing steeds
Trample the life from out the mighty hearts
That ruled the storm so late?—Speak not of death,
Till thou hast look'd on such.
*Alphonso.*　　　　I was not born
A shepherd's son, to dwell with pipe and crook,
And peasant-men, amidst the lowly vales;
Instead of ringing clarions, and bright spears,
And crested knights!—I am of princely race,
And, if my father would have heard my suit,
I tell thee, infidel! that long ere now,
I should have seen how lances meet, and swords
Do the field's work.
*Abdullah.*　Boy! know'st thou there are sights
A thousand times more fearful!—Men may die
Full proudly, when the skies and mountains ring
To battle-horn and tecbir.*—But not all
So pass away in glory. There are those,
'Midst the dead silence of pale multitudes,
Led forth in fetters—dost thou mark me, boy?—
To take their last look of th' all-gladdening sun,
And bow, perchance, the stately head of youth,
Unto the death of shame!—Hast thou seen this?—
*Alphonso (to Carlos.)* Sweet brother, God is with
　　us—fear thou not!
We have had heroes for our sires—This man
Should not behold us tremble.
*Abdullah.*　　　　There are means
To tame the loftiest natures. Yet again
I ask thee, wilt thou, from beneath the walls,
Sue to thy sire for life; or wouldst thou die,
With this, thy brother?
*Alphonso.*　　　　Moslem! on the hills,
Around my father's castle, I have heard
The mountain-peasants, as they dress'd the vines,
Or drove the goats, by rock and torrent, home,
Singing their ancient songs; and these were all
Of the Cid Campeador; and how his sword
Tizona (3) clear'd its way through turban'd hosts
And captured Afric's kings, and how he won
Valencia from the Moor. (4)—I will not shame
The blood we draw from him!
　　　　(*A Moorish Soldier enters.*)
*Soldier.*　　　　Valencia's lord
Sends messengers, my chief.
*Abdullah.*　　　. Conduct them hither.

---

* "Tecbir," the war-cry of the Moors and Arabs.

[*The Soldier goes out, and re-enters with* ELMINA,
  *disguised, and an Attendant.*]

*Carlos* (*springing forward to the Attendant.*) Oh!
      take me hence, Diego! take me hence
With thee, that I may see my mother's face
At morning, when I wake.  Here dark-brow'd
      men
Frown strangely, with their cruel eyes, upon us.
Take me with thee, for thou art good and kind,
And well I know thou lov'st me, my Diego!
  *Abdullah.* Peace, boy.—What tidings, Christian,
      from thy lord ?
Is he grown humbler ?—doth he set the lives
Of these fair nurslings at a city's worth ?
  *Alphonso* (*rushing forward impatiently.*) Say not,
      he doth !—Yet wherefore art thou here ?
If it be so—I could weep with burning tears
For very shame !—If this *can* be, return !
Tell him, of all his wealth, his battle-spoils,
I will but ask a war-horse and a sword,
And that beside him in the mountain-chase,
And in his halls, and at his stately feasts,
My place shall be no more !—But no !—I wrong,
I wrong my father !—Moor! believe it not!
He is a Champion of the Cross and Spain,
Sprung from the Cid ; and I too, I can die
As a warrior's high-born child !
  *Elmina.*                      Alas ! alas !
And wouldst thou die, thus early die, fair boy ?
What hath life done to thee, that thou shouldst
      cast
Its flower away, in very scorn of heart,
Ere yet the blight be come ?
  *Alphonso.*              That voice doth sound——
  *Abdullah.* Stranger, who art thou ?—this is
      mockery—speak !
  *Elmina* (*throwing off a mantle and a helmet, and
embracing her sons.*)  My boys ! whom I have
      rear'd through many hours
Of silent joys and sorrows, and deep thoughts
Untold and unimagined ; let me die
With you, now I have held you to my heart,
And seen once more the faces, in whose light
My soul hath lived for years !
  *Carlos.*                    Sweet mother ! now
Thou shalt not leave us more.
  *Abdullah.*                 Enough of this !
Woman ! what seek'st thou here ?—How hast thou
      dared
To front the mighty thus amidst his hosts ?
  *Elmina.*  Think'st thou there dwells no courage
      but in breasts
That set their mail against the ringing spears,
When helmets are struck down ?—Thou little
      know'st
Of nature's marvels !—Chief! my heart is nerved
To make its way through things which warrior
      men,
—Ay, they that master death by field or flood,
Would look on, ere they braved !—I have no
      thought,
No sense of fear !—Thou'rt mighty ; but a soul
Wound up like mine, is mightier, in the power
Of that one feeling, pour'd through all its depths,
Than monarchs with their hosts !—Am I not come
To die with these, my children ?
  *Abdullah.*              Doth thy faith
Bid thee do this, fond Christian ?—Hast thou not
The means to save them ?
  *Elmina.*              I have prayers and tears,
And agonies !—and he—my God—the God
Whose hand, or soon or late, doth find its hour
To bow the crested head—hath made these things
Most powerful in a world where all must learn
That one deep language, by the storm call'd forth
From the bruis'd reeds of earth !—For thee, per-
      chance,
Affliction's chastening lesson hath not yet
Been laid upon thy heart, and thou may'st love
To see the creatures, by its might brought low,
Humbled before thee.
                    [*She throws herself at his feet*
                    Conqueror ! I can kneel !
I, that drew birth from princes, bow myself
E'en to thy feet !  Call in thy chiefs, thy slaves.

If this will swell thy triumph, to behold
The blood of kings, of heroes, thus debased !
Do this, but spare my sons !
  *Alphonso* (*attempting to raise her.*)  Thou shouldst
      not kneel
Unto this infidel !—Rise, rise, my mother !
This sight doth shame our house.
  *Abdullah.*                    Thou daring boy !
They that in arms have taught thy father's land
How chains are worn, shall school that haughty
      mien
Unto another language.
  *Elmina.*              Peace, my son ;
Have pity on my heart —Oh, pardon, Chie'—
He is of noble blood.—Hear, hear me yet !
Are there no lives through which the shalt  .f
      Heaven
May reach your soul ?—He that loves aught on
      earth,
Dares far too much, if he be merciless !
Is it for those, whose frail mortality
Must one day strive alone with God and death,
To shut their souls against th' appealing voice
Of nature in her anguish ?—Warrior ! man !
To you too, ay, and haply with your hosts,
By thousands and ten thousands marshall'd round,'
And your strong armour on, shall come that stroke
Which the lance wards not.—Where shall your
      high heart
Find refuge then, if in the day of might
Woe hath laid prostrate, bleeding at your feet,
And you have pitied not ?
  *Abdullah.*              These are vain words.
  *Elmina.*  Have you no children ?—fear you not
      to bring
The lightning on their heads ?—In your own land
Doth no fond mother, from the tents, beneath
Your native palms, look o'er the deserts out,
To greet your homeward step ?—You have not yet
Forgot so utterly her patient love—
—For is not woman's, in all climes, the same !—
That you should scorn my prayer !—Oh Heaven !
      his eye
Doth wear no mercy !
  *Abdullah.*          Then it mocks you not.
I have swept o'er the mountains of your land,
Leaving my traces, as the visitings
Of storms, upon them !—Shall I now be stay'd ?
Know, unto me it were as light a thing,
In this, my course, to quench your children's lives,
As, journeying through a forest, to break off
The young wild branches that obstruct the way
With their green sprays and leaves.
  *Elmina.*              Are there such hearts
Among thy works, oh God ?
  *Abdullah.*              Kneel not to me.
Kneel to your lord ; on his resolves doth hang
His children's doom.  He may be lightly won
By a few bursts of passionate tears and words.
  *Elmina* (*rising indignantly.*)  Speak not of noble
      men !—he bears a soul
Stronger than love or death.
  *Alphonso* (*with exultation.*)  I knew 't was thus—
He could not fail !
  *Elmina.*          There is no mercy, none,
On this cold earth !—To strive with such a world,
Hearts should be void of love.  We will go hence
My children, we are summon'd.  Lay your heads
In their young radiant beauty, once again
To rest upon this bosom.  He that dwells
Beyond the clouds which press us darkly round,
Will yet have pity, and before his face
We three will stand together !  Moslem ! now
Let the stroke fall at once.
  *Abdullah.*              'Tis thine own will.
These might e'en yet be spared.
  *Elmina.*              Thou wilt not spare
And he beneath whose eye their childhood grew,
And in whose paths they sported, and whose ear
From their first lisping accents caught the sound
Of that word—*Father*—once a name of love—
Is——Men shall call him *steadfast.*
  *Abdullah.*              Hath the blast
Of sudden trumpets ne'er at dead of night,
When the land's watchers fear'd no hostile step,
Startled the slumberers from their dreamy world,

In cities, whose heroic lords have been
Steadfast as thine?
  *Elmina.*    There's meaning in thine eye,
More than thy words.
  *Abdullah* (*pointing to the city.*) Look to yon
    towers and walls!
Think you no hearts within their limits pine,
Weary of hopeless warfare, and prepared
To burst the feeble links which bind them still
Unto endurance?
  *Elmina*    Thou hast said too well.
But what of this?
  *Abdullah.*    Then there are those, to whom
The Prophet's armies not as foes would pass
Your gates, but as deliverers. Might they not,
'n some still hour, when weariness takes rest,
Be won to welcome us? Your children's steps
May yet bound lightly through their father's halls.
  *Alphonso* (*indignantly.*) Thou treacherous Moor!
  *Elmina.* Let me not thus be tried
Beyond all strength, oh Heaven!
  *Abdullah.*    Now, 'tis for *thee*,
Thou Christian mother, on thy sons to pass
The sentence—life or death—the price is set
On their young blood, and rests within thy hands.
  *Alphonso.* Mother, thou tremblest!
  *Abdullah.* Hath thy heart resolved?
  *Elmina* (*covering her face with her hands.*)
My boy's proud eye is on me, and the things
Which rush, in stormy darkness, through my soul,
Shrink from his glance. I cannot answer *here*.
  *Abdullah.* Come forth. We'll commune else-
    where.
  *Carlos* (*to his mother.*) Wilt thou go?
Oh, let me follow thee!
  *Elmina.*    Mine own fair child!
—Now that thine eyes have pour'd once more on
    mine
The light of their young smile, and thy sweet voice
Hath sent its gentle music through my soul,
And I have felt the twining of thine arms—
—How shall I leave thee?
  *Abdullah.*    Leave him, as 'twere bu
For a brief slumber, to behold his face
At morning, with the sun's.
  *Alphonso.*    Thou hast no look
For me, my mother?
  *Elmina.*    Oh, that I should live
To say, I dare not look on thee!—Farewell,
My first-born, fare thee well.
  *Alphonso*    Yet, yet beware!
It were a grief more heavy on thy soul,
That I should blush for thee, than o'er my grave
That thou shouldst proudly weep.
  *Abdullah.* Away! we trifle here. The night
    wanes fast.
Come forth.
  *Elmina.* One more embrace—My sons, farewell.
[*Exeunt* ABDULLAH *with* ELMINA *and her Attendant.*
  *Alphonso.* Hear me yet once, my mother!
    Art thou gone?
But one word more.
    [*He rushes out, followed by* CARLOS

---

*Scene—The Garden of a Palace in Valencia.*

XIMENA, THERESA.

  *Theresa.* Stay yet awhile. A purer air doth rove
Here through the myrtles whispering, and the
    limes,
And shaking sweetness from the orange boughs,
Than waits you in the city.
  *Ximena.*    There are those
In their last need, and on their bed of death,
At which no hand doth minister but mine,
That wait me in the city. Let us hence.
  *Theresa.* You have been wont to love the music
    made
By founts, and rustling foliage, and soft winds,
Breathing of citron-groves. And will you turn
From these to scenes of death?
  *Ximena.*    To me the voice
Of summer, whispering through young flowers
    and leaves,

Now speaks too deep a language; and of all
Its dreamy and mysterious melodies,
The breathing soul is sadness.—I have felt
That summons through my spirit, after which
The hues of earth are changed, and all her sounds
Seem fraught with secret warnings. There is
    cause
That I should bend my footsteps to the scenes
Where death is busy, taming warrior-hearts,
And pouring winter through the fiery blood,
And fettering the strong arm.—For now no sigh
In the dull air, nor floating cloud in heaven,
No, not the lightest murmur of a leaf,
But of his angel's silent coming bears
Some token to my soul. But naught of this
Unto my mother.—These are awful hours!
And on their heavy steps, afflictions crowd
With such dark pressure, there is left no room
For one grief more.
  *Theresa.*    Sweet lady, talk not thus!
Your eye this morn doth wear a calmer light.
There's more of life in its clear tremulous ray
Than I have mark'd of late. Nay, go not yet;
Rest by this fountain, where the laurels dip
Their glossy leaves. A fresher gale doth spring
From the transparent waters, dashing round
Their silvery spray, with a sweet voice of cool-
    ness,
O'er the pale glistening marble. 'Twill call up
Faint bloom, if but a moment's, to your cheek.
Rest here, ere you go forth, and I will sing
The melody you love.

THERESA *sings.*

Why is the Spanish maiden's grave
  So far from her own bright land?
The sunny flowers that o'er it wave
  Were sown by no kindred hand.

'Tis not the orange-bough that sends
  Its breath on the sultry air,
'Tis not the myrtle-stem that bends
  To the breeze of evening there!

But the Rose of Sharon's eastern bloom
  By the silent dwelling fades,
And none but strangers pass the tomb
  Which the Palm of Judah shades.

The lowly cross, with flowers o'ergrown,
  Marks well that place of rest;
But who hath graved, on its mossy stones,
  A sword, a helm, a crest?

These are the trophies of a chief,
  A lord of the axe and spear!
—Some blossom pluck'd, some faded leaf,
  Should grace a maiden's bier!

Scorn not her tomb—deny not her
  The honours of the brave!
O'er that forsaken sepulchre,
  Banner and plume might wave.

She bound the steel, in battle tried,
  Her fearless heart above,
And stood with brave men, side by side,
  In the strength and faith of love!

That strength prevail'd—that faith was bless'd
  True was the javelin thrown,
Yet pierced it not her warrior's breast,
  She met it with her own!

And nobly won, where heroes fell
  In arms for the holy shrine,
A death which saved what she loved so well,
  And a grave in Palestine.

Then let the Rose of Sharon spread
  Its breast to the glowing air,
And the Palm of Judah lift its head,
  Green and immortal there!

And let yon gray stone, undefaced,
  With its trophy mark the scene,
Telling the pilgrim of the waste,
  Where Love and Death have been.

...men.. These notes were wont to make my
heart beat quick,
As a voice of victory: but to-day
The spirit of the song is changed, and seems
All mournful  Oh! that ere my early grave
Shuts out the sun-beam, I might hear one peal
Of the Castilian trumpet, ringing forth
Beneath my father's banner!—In that sound
Were life to you, sweet brothers!—But for me—
Come on—our tasks await us.  They who know
Their hours are number'd out, have little time
To give the vague and slumberous languor way,
Which doth steal o'er them in the breath of flowers
And whisper of soft winds.

ELMINA *enters hurriedly.*

*Elmina.* This air will calm my spirit, ere yet I
meet
His eye, which must be met.  Thou here, Ximena!
[*She starts back, on seeing* XIMENA.

*Ximena.* Alas! my mother! in that hurrying step
And troubled glance I read——
*Elmina (wildly.)*        Thou read'st it not!
Why, who would live, if unto mortal eye
The things lay glaring, which within our hearts
We treasure up for God's?—Thou read'st it not!
I say, thou canst not!—There's not one on earth
Shall know the thoughts, which for themselves
have made
And kept dark places in the very breast
Whereon he hath laid his slumber, till the hour
When the graves open!
*Ximena.*        Mother! what is this?
Alas! your eye is wandering, and your cheek
Flush'd, as with fever!  To your woes the night ·
Hath brought no rest.
*Elmina.*    Rest!—who should rest?—not he
That holds one earthly blessing to his heart
Nearer than life!—No! if this world have aught
Of bright or precious, let not him who calls
Such things his own, take rest!—Dark spirits keep
watch
And they to whom fair honour, chivalrous fame,
Were as heaven's air, the vital element
Wherein they breathed, may wake, and find their
souls
Made marks for human scorn!—Will they bear on
With life struck down, and thus disrobed of all
Its glorious drapery?—Who shall tell us this?
—Will *he* so bear it?
*Ximena.*        Mother! let us kneel,
And blend our hearts in prayer!—What else is left
To mortals when the dark hour's might is on
them?
—Leave us, Theresa.—Grief like this doth find'
Its balm in solitude.        [*Exit* THERESA.
My mothe ! peace
Is heaven's benignant answer to the cry
Of wounded spirits.  Wilt thou kneel with me?
*Elmina.*  Away! 'tis but for souls unstain'd to
wear
Heaven's tranquil image on their depths.—The
stream
Of my dark thoughts, all broken by the storm,
Reflects but clouds and lightnings!—Didst thou
speak
Of peace?—'Tis fled from earth!—but there is joy.
Wild, troubled joy!—And who shall know, my
child!
It is not happiness?—Why, our own hearts
Will keep the secret close!—Joy, joy! if but
To leave this desolate city, with its dull
Slow knells and dirges, and to breathe again
Th' untainted mountain air!—But hush! the
trees,
The flowers, the waters, must hear naught of this!
They are full of voices, and will whisper things—
—We'll speak of it no more.
*Ximena.*        Oh! pitying Heaven!
This grief doth shake her reason!
*Elmina (starting.)*        Hark! a step!
'Tis—'tis thy father's—come away—not now—
He must not see us now!
*Ximena.*        Why should this be?

GONZALEZ *enters and detains* ELMINA.

*Gonzalez.* Elmina, dost thou shun me?—Have
we not
E'en from the hopeful and the sunny time
When youth was as a glory round our brows,
Held on through life together?—And is this,
When eve is gathering round us, with the gloom
Of stormy clouds, a time to part our steps
Upon the darkening wild?
*Elmina (coldly.)*        There needs not this.
Why shouldst thou think I shunn'd thee?
*Gonzalez.*        Should the love
That shone o'er many years, th' unfading love,
Whose only change hath been from gladdening
smiles
To mingling sorrows and sustaining strength,
Thus lightly be forgotten?
*Elmina.*        Speak'st thou thus!
—I have knelt before thee with that very plea,
When it avail'd me not!—But there are things
Whose very breathings on the soul erase
All record of past love, save the chill sense,
Th' unquiet memory of its wasted faith,
And vain devotedness!—Ay, they that fix
Affection's perfect trust on aught of earth
Have many a dream to start from!
*Gonzalez.*        This is but
The wildness and the bitterness of grief,
Ere yet th' unsettled heart hath closed its long
Impatient conflicts with a mightier power,
Which makes all conflicts vain.
        ——Hark! was there not
A sound of distant trumpets, far beyond
The Moorish tents, and of another tone
Than th' Afric horn, Ximena?
*Ximena.*        Oh, my father!
I know that horn too well.—'Tis but the wind,
Which, with a sudden rising, bears its deep
And savage war-note from us, wafting it
O'er the far hills.
*Gonzalez.*        Alas! this woe must be
I do but shake my spirit from its height  ·
So startling it with hope!—But the dread no ,
Shall be met bravely still.  I can keep down
Yet for a little while—and Heaven will ask
No more—the passionate workings of my heart;
—And thine—Elmina!
*Elmina.*        'Tis—I am prepared.
I *have* prepared for all.
*Gonzalez.*        Oh, well I knew
Thou wouldst not fail me!—Not in vain my soul,
Upon thy faith and courage, hath built up
Unshaken trust.
*Elmina (wildly.)* Away!—thou know'st me not!
Man dares too far: his rashness would invest
This our mortality with an attribute
Too high and awful, boasting that he knows
One human heart!
*Gonzalez.*        These are wild words, but yet
I will not doubt thee!—Hast thou not been found
Noble in all things, pouring thy soul's light
Undimin'd o'er every trial?—And, as our fates,
So must our names be, undivided!—Thine,
I' th' record of a warrior's life, shall find
Its place of stainless honour.  By his side——
*Elmina.* May this be borne!—How much of
agony
Hath the heart room for?—Speak to me in wrath—
I can endure it!—But no gentle words!
No words of love! no praise!—Thy sword might
slay,
And be more merciful!
*Gonzalez.*        Wherefore art thou thus?
Elmina, my beloved!
*Elmina.*        No more of love!
—Have I not said there's that within my heart,
Whereon it falls as living fire would fall
Upon an unclosed wound?
*Gonzalez.*        Nay, lift thine eyes
That I may read *their* meaning!
*Elmina.*        Never more
With a free soul—What have I said?—'twas
naught!
Take thou no heed! The words of wretchedness
Admit not scrutiny.  Wouldst thou mark the speech
Of troubled dreams?

*Gonzalez.*                    I have seen thee in the hour
Of thy deep spirit's joy, and when the breath
Of grief hung chilling round thee; in all change,
Bright health and drooping sickness; hope and
      fear;
Youth and decline; but never yet, Elmina,
Ne'er hath thine eye till now shrunk back per-
      turb'd
With shame or dread, from mine!
    *Elmina.*                    Thy glance doth search
A wounded heart too deeply.
    *Gonzalez.*                    Hast thou there
Aught to conceal?
    *Elmina.*              Who hath not?
    *Gonzalez.*                    Till this hour
*Thou* never hadst!—Yet hear me!—by the free
And unattainted fame which wraps the dust
Of thine heroic fathers——
    *Elmina.*                    This to me!
—Bring your inspiring war-notes, and your sounds
Of festal music, round a dying man!
Will his heart echo them?—But if thy words
Were spells, to call up with each lofty tone,
Th' grave's most awful spirits, they would stand
Powerless, before my anguish!
    *Gonzalez.*                    Then, by her,
Who there looks on thee in the purity
Of her devoted youth, and o'er whose name
No blight must fall, and whose pale cheek must
      ne'er
Burn with that deeper tinge, caught painfully
From the quick feeling of dishonour—Speak!
Unfold this mystery!—By thy sons——
    *Elmina.*                    My sons!
And canst *thou* name them?
    *Gonzalez.*              ·Proudly!—Better far
They died with all the promise of their youth,
And the fair honour of their house upon them,
Than that with manhood's high and passionate
      soul
To fearful strength unfolded, they should live,
Barr'd from the lists of crested chivalry,
And pining in the silence of a woe,
Which from the heart shuts daylight:—o'er the
      shame
Of those who gave them birth!—but *thou* couldst
      ne'er
Forget their lofty claims!
    *Elmina (wildly.)*          'Twas but for them!
'Twas for them only!—Who shall dare arraign
Madness of crime?—And he who made us, knows
There are dark moments of all hearts and lives,
Which bear down reason!
    *Gonzalez.*              Thou, whom I have loved
With such high trust, as o'er our nature threw
A glory, scarce allow'd;—what hast thou done?
——Ximena, go thou hence!
    *Elmina.*                    No, no! my child!
There's pity in thy look!—All other eyes
Are full of wrath and scorn!—Oh! leave me not!
    *Gonzalez.*          That I should live to see thee thus
      abased!
—Yet speak!—What hast thou done?
    *Elmina.*                    Look to the gate!
Thou'rt worn with toil—But take no rest to-night!
The western gate!—Its watchers have been won—
The Christian city hath been bought and sold!
They will admit the Moor!
    *Gonzalez.*              They have been won!
Brave men and tried so long!—Whose work was
      this?
    *Elmina.* Think'st thou all hearts like thine?—
      Can mothers stand
To see their children perish?
    *Gonzalez.*              Then the guilt
Was thine!
    *Elmina.* —Shall mortal dare to call it guilt?
  I tell thee, Heaven, which made all holy things,
Made naught more holy than the boundless love
Which fills a mother's heart!—I say, 'tis woe
Enough with such an aching tenderness,
To love aught earthly!—and in vain! in vain!
—We are press'd down too sorely!
    *Gonzalez (in a low desponding voice.)* Now my life
Is struck to worthless ashes!—In my soul
Suspicion hath ta'en root. The nobleness

Henceforth is blotted from all human brows,
And fearful power, a dark and troublous gift,
Almost like prophecy, is pour'd upon me,
To read the guilty secrets in each eye
That once look'd bright with truth!
                    —Why then I have gain'd
What men call wisdom!—A new sense, to which
All tales that speak of high fidelity,
And holy courage, and proud honour, tried,
Search'd, and found steadfast, even to martyrdom,
Are food for mockery!—Why should I not cast
From my thinn'd locks the wearing helm at once,
And in the heavy sickness of my soul
Throw the sword down for ever?—Is there aught
In all this world of gilded hollowness,
Now the bright hues drop off its loveliest things,
Worth striving for again?
    *Ximena.*              Father! look up!
Turn unto me, thy child!
    *Gonzalez.*                    Thy face is fair;
And hath been unto me, in other days,
As morning to the journeyer of the deep;
But now—'tis too like here!
    *Elmina (falling at his feet.)* Woe, shame and woe
Are on me in their might!—forgive, forgive!
    *Gonzalez (starting up.)* Doth the Moor deem
      that *I* have part, or share,
Or counsel in this vileness?—Stay me not!
Let go thy hold—'tis powerless on me now—
I linger here, while treason is at work!
                    [*Exit* Gonzalez.
    *Elmina.* Ximena, dost *thou* scorn me?
    *Ximena.*              I have found
In mine own heart too much of feebleness,
Hid, beneath many foldings, from all eyes
But *His* whom naught can blind;—to dare do aught
But pity thee, dear mother!
    *Elmina.*              Blessings light
On thy fair head, my gentle child, for this!
Thou kind and merciful!—My soul is faint—
Worn with long strife!—Is there aught else to do,
Or suffer, ere we die?—Oh God! my sons!
—I have betray'd them!—All their innocent blood
Is on my soul!
    *Ximena.*          How shall I comfort thee?
—Oh! hark! what sounds come deepening on the
      wind,
So full of solemn hope!

(*A procession of Nuns passing across the Scene, bear-
      ing relics, and chanting.*)

    *Chant.*    A sword is on the land!
He that bears down young tree and glorious flower,
Death is gone forth, he walks the wind in power!
      —Where is the warrior's hand?
Our steps are in the shadows of the grave,
Hear us, we perish! Father, hear, and save!

      If, in the days of song,
The days of gladness, we have call'd on thee,
When mirthful voices rang from sea to sea,
      And joyous hearts were strong;
Now, that alike the feeble and the brave
Must cry, "We perish!"—Father! hear, and save!

      The days of song are fled!
The winds come loaded, wafting dirge-notes by,
But they that linger, soon unmourn'd must die;
      —The dead weep not the dead!
—Wilt thou forsake us 'midst the stormy wave?
We sink, we perish!—Father, hear, and save!

      Helmet and lance are dust!
Is not the strong man wither'd from our eye?
The arm struck down that held our banners high?
      —Thine is our spirit's trust!
Look through the gathering shadows of the grave!
Do we not perish?—Father, hear, and save!

    Hernandez *enters.*

    *Elmina.* Why comest thou, man of vengeance?—
      What have I
To do with thee?—Am I not bow'd enough?
Thou art no mourner's comforter!
    *Hernandez*                    Thy lord
Hath sent me unto thee. Till this day's task
He closed, thou daughter of the feeble heart!
He bids thee seek him not, but lay thy woes

Before Heaven's altar, and in penitence
Make thy soul's peace with God.
   *Elmina.*          Till this day's task
Be closed!—there is strange triumph in thine eyes.
Is it that I have fallen from that high place
Whereon I stood in fame?—But I can feel
A wild and bitter pride in thus being past
The power of thy dark glance!—My spirit now
Is wound about by one sole mighty grief;
Thy scorn hath lost its sting.—Thou may'st re-
    proach—
   *Hernandez.* I come not to reproach thee. Heaven
    doth work
By many agencies; and in its hour
There is no insect which the summer breeze
From the green leaf shakes trembling, but may
    serve
Its deep unsearchable purposes, as well
As the great ocean, or th' eternal fires,
Pent in earth's caves!—Thou hast but speeded that
Which, in th' infatuate blindness of thy heart,
Thou wouldst have trampled o'er all holy ties,
But to avert one day!
   *Elmina.*         My senses fail—
Thou saidst—speak yet again!—I could not catch
The meaning of thy words.
   *Hernandez.*        E'en now thy lord
Hath sent our foes defiance. On the walls
He stands in conference with the boastful Moor,
And awful strength is with him. Through the
    blood
Which, this day, must be pour'd in sacrifice,
Shall Spain be free. On all her olive-hills
Shall men set up the battle-sign of fire,
And round its blaze, at midnight, keep the sense
Of vengeance wakeful in each other's hearts
E'en with thy children's tale!
   *Ximena.*      Peace, father! peace!
Behold, she sinks!—the storm hath done its work
Upon the broken reed. Oh! lend thine aid
To bear her hence.      [*They lead her away*

*Scene—A Street in Valencia. Several Groups of
Citizens and Soldiers, many of them lying on the
steps of a Church. Arms scattered on the ground
around them.*

   *An old Citizen.* The air is sultry, as with thun
    der-clouds.
I left my desolate home, that I might breathe
More freely in heaven's face, but my heart feels
With this hot gloom o'erburthen'd. I have now
No sons to tend me. Which of you, kind friends,
Will bring the old man water from the fount,
To moisten his parch'd lip?    [*A Citizen goes out.*
   *Second Citizen.*      This wasting siege,
Good Father Lopez, hath gone hard with you!
'Tis sad to hear no voices through the house,
Once peopled with fair sons!
   *Third Citizen.*      Why, better thus,
Than to be haunted with their famish'd cries,
E'en in your very dreams!
   *Old Citizen.*     Heaven's will be done!
These are dark times! I have not been alone
In my affliction.
   *Third Citizen (with bitterness,)* Why, we have but
    this thought
Left for our gloomy comfort!—And 'tis well!
Ay, let the balance be awhile struck even
Between the noble's palace and the hut,
Where the worn peasant sickens!—They that bear
The humble dead unhonour'd to their homes,
Pass now i' th' street no lordly bridal train,
With its exulting music; and the wretch
Who on the marble steps of some proud hall
Flings himself down to die, in his last need
And agony of famine, doth behold
No scornful guests, with their long purple robes,
To the banquet sweeping by. Why, this is just!
These are the days when pomp is made to feel
Its human mould!
   *Fourth Citizen.* Heard you last night the sound
Of Saint Iago's bell?—How sullenly
From the great tower it peal'd!
   *Fifth Citizen.*      Ay, and 'tis said

No mortal hand was near when so it seem'd
To shake the midnight streets.
   *Old Citizen.*      Too well I know
The sound of coming fate!—'Tis ever thus
When death is on his way to make it night
In the Cid's ancient house. (5)—Oh! there are
    things
In this strange world of which we have all to learn
When its dark bounds are pass'd.—Yon bell, un-
    touch'd
(Save by hands we see not) still doth speak—
—When of that line some stately head is mark'd—
With a wild hollow peal, at dead of night,
Rocking Valencia's towers. I have heard it oft,
Nor known its warning false.
   *Fourth Citizen.*     And will our chief
Buy, at the price of his fair children's blood,
A few more days of pining wretchedness
For this forsaken city?
   *Old Citizen.*      Doubt it not!
—But with that ransom he may purchase still
Deliverance for the land?—And yet 'tis sad
To think that such a race, with all its fame,
Should pass away!—For she, his daughter too,
Moves upon earth as some bright thing whose time
To sojourn there is short.
   *Fifth Citizen.*     Then woe for us
When she is gone!—Her voice—the very sound
Of her soft step was comfort as she moved
Through the still house of mourning!—Who like
    her
Shall give us hope again?
   *Old Citizen.*     Be still! she comes,
And with a mien how changed!—A hurrying step,
And a flush'd cheek!—What may this bode?—Be
    still!

*Ximena enters, with Attendants carrying a Banner.*

   *Ximena.* Men of Valencia! in an hour like this,
What do ye here?
   *A Citizen.*     We die!
   *Ximena.*      Brave men die now
Girt for the toil, as travellers suddenly
By the dark night o'ertaken on their way!
These days require such death!—It is too much
Of luxury for our wild and angry times,
To fold the mantle round us and to sink
From life, as flowers that shut up silently,
When the sun's heat doth scorch them!—Hear ye
    not?
   *A Citizen.* Lady! what wouldst thou with us?
   *Ximena.* Rise and arm!
E'en now the children of your chief are led
Forth by the Moor to perish!—Shall this be?
Shall the high sound of such a name be hush'd,
I' th' land to which for ages it hath been
A battle-word, as 'twere some passing note
Of shepherd music?—Must this work be done,
And ye lie pining here, as men in whom
The pulse which God hath made for noble thought
Can so be thrill'd no longer?
   *Citizens.*     'Tis even so!
Sickness, and toil, and grief, have breathed upon us.
Our hearts beat faint and low.
   *Ximena.*     Are ye so poor
Of soul, my countrymen! that ye can draw
Strength from no deeper source than that which
    sends
The red blood mantling through the joyous veins
And gives the fleet step wings?—Why, how have
    age
And sensitive womanhood ere now endured,
Through pangs of searching fire, in some proud
    cause,
Blessing that agony?—Think ye the Power
Which bore them nobly up, as if to teach
The torturer where eternal Heaven had set
Bounds to his sway, was earthly, of this earth,
This dull mortality?—Nay, then look on me!
Death's touch hath mark'd me, and I stand among
    you,
As one whose place, i' th' sunshine of your world,
Shall soon be left to fill!—I say the breath
Of th' incense, floating through yon fane, shall
    scarce
Pass from your path before me! But even now,

I have that within me, kindling through the dust,
Which from all time hath made high deeds its
     voice
And token to the nations!—Look on me!
Why hath Heaven pour'd forth courage, as a flame
Wasting the womanish heart, which must be still'd
Yet sooner for its swift consuming brightness,
If not to shame your doubt, and your despair,
And your soul's torpor?—Yet, arise and arm!
It may not be too late.
     *A Citizen.*               Why, what are we,
To cope with hosts?—Thus faint, and worn, and
     few,
O'ernumber'd and forsaken, is't for us
To stand against the mighty?
     *Ximena.*               And for whom
Hath He, who shakes the mighty with a breath
From their high places, made the fearfulness,
And ever-wakeful presence of his power,
To the pale startled earth most manifest,
But for the weak?—Was't for the helm'd and
     crown'd
That suns were stay'd at noonday?—Stormy seas
As a rill parted?—Mail'd archangels sent
To wither up the strength of kings with death?
—I tell you, if these marvels have been done,
'Twas for the wearied and the oppress'd of men,
They needed such!—And generous faith hath
     power
By her prevailing spirit, e'en yet to work
Deliverances, whose tale shall live with those
Of the great elder time!—Be of good heart!
*Who is forsaken?*—He that gives the thought
A place within his breast!—'Tis not for you.
—Know ye this banner?
     *Citizens (murmuring to each other.)*  Is she not
          inspired?
Doth not Heaven call us by her fervent voice?
     *Ximena.*  Know ye this banner?
     *Citizens.*               'Tis the Cid's.
     *Ximena.*  The Cid's!
Who breathes that name but in th' exulting tone
Which the heart rings to?—Why, the very wind,
As it swells out the noble standard's fold,
Hath a triumphant sound!—The Cid's!—it moved
Even as a sign of victory through the land,
From the free skies ne'er stooping to a foe!
     *Old Citizen.*  Can ye still pause, my brethren?—
          Oh! that youth
Through this worn frame were kindling once
     again!
     *Ximena.*  Ye linger still!—Upon this very air,
He that was born in happy hour for Spain, (6)
Pour'd forth his conquering spirit!—'Twas the
     breeze
From your own mountains which came down to
     wave
This banner of his battles, as it droop'd
Above the champion's death-bed.  Nor even then
Its tale of glory closed.—They made no moan
O'er the dead hero, and no dirge was sung, (7)
But the deep tambour and shrill horn of war
Told when the mighty pass'd!—They wrapt him
     not
With the pale shroud, but braced the warrior's
     form
In war array, and on his barbed steed,
As for a triumph, rear'd him; marching forth
In the hush'd midnight from Valencia's walls,
Beleaguer'd then as now.  All silently
The stately funeral moved:—but who was he
That follow'd, charging on the tall white horse,
And with the solemn standard, 'rond and pale,
Waving in sheets of snow-light?—And the cross,
The bloody cross, far-blazing from his shield,
And the fierce meteor-sword?  They fled, they fled
The kings of Afric, with their countless hosts,
Were dust in his red path!—The scimetar
Was shiver'd as a reed.—For in that hour
The warrior saint that keeps the watch for Spain,
Was arm'd betimes!—And o'er that fiery field
The Cid's high banner stream'd all joyously,
For still its lord was there!
     *Citizens (rising tumultuously.)*  Even unto death
Again it shall be follow'd!
     *Ximena.*               Will he see

'The noble stem hewn down, the beacon-light
Which his high house for ages o'er the land
Hath shone through cloud and storm, thus
     quench'd at once?
Will he not aid his children in the hour
Of this their uttermost peril?—Awful power
Is with the holy dead, and there are times
When the tomb hath no chain they cannot burst
—Is it a thing forgotten, how he woke
From its deep rest of old, remembering Spain
In her great danger?—At the night's mid-watch
How Leon started, when the sound was heard
That shook her dark and hollow-echoing streets,
As with the heavy tramp of steel clad men,
By thousands marching through!—For he had
     risen!
The Campeador was on his march again,
And in his arms, and follow'd by his hosts
Of shadowy spearmen!—He had lef. the world
From which we are dimly parted, and gone forth
And call'd his buried warriors from their sleep,
Gathering them round him to deliver Spain;
For Afric was upon her!—Morning broke—
Day rush'd through clouds of battle;—but at eve
Our God had triumph'd, and the rescued land
Sent up a shout of victory from the field,
That rock'd her ancient mountains.
     *The Citizens.*               Arm! to arms
On to our chief!  We have strength within us yet
To die with our blood roused!  Now, be the word
For the Cid's house!  [*They begin to arm themselves*
     *Ximena.*               Ye know his battle-song,
The old rude strain wherewith his bands went
     forth
To strike down Paynim swords!   (*She sings.*)


               THE CID'S BATTLE SONG.

     The Moor is on his way!
With the tambour-peal and the techir-shout,
And the horn o'er the blue seas ringing out,
     He hath marshall'd his dark array!

     Shout through the vine-clad land!
That her sons on all their hills may hear,
And sharpen the point of the red wolf-spear,
     And the sword for the brave man's hand!

(*The Citizens join in the song, while they continue
     arming themselves.*)

     Banners are in the field!
The chief must rise from his joyous board,
And turn from the feast ere the wine be pour'd,
     And take up his father's shield!

     The Moor is on his way!
Let the peasant leave his olive-ground,
And the goats roam wild through the pine-woods
     round!
     —There is nobler work to-day!

     Send forth the trumpet's call!
Till the bridegroom cast the goblet down,
And the marriage-robe and the flowery crown,
     And arm in the banquet-hall!

     And stay the funeral-train!
Bid the chaunted mass be hush'd awhile,
And the bier laid down in the holy aisle,
     And the mourners girt for Spain!

(*They take up the banner and follow* XIMENA *out
     Their voices are heard gradually dying away at a
     distance.*)

     Ere night, must swords be red!
It is not an hour for knells and tears,
But for helmets braced, and serried spears!
     To-morrow for the dead!

     The Cid is in array!
His steed is barb'd, his plume waves high,
His banner is up in the sunny sky,
     Now, joy for the Cross to-day!

*Scene—The Walls of the City. The Plain beneath, with the Moorish Camp and Army.*

GONZALEZ, GARCIAS, HERNANDEZ.

*(A wild sound of Moorish Music heard from below.)*

*Hernandez.* What notes are these, in their deep mournfulness
So strangely wild?
  *Garcias.*       'Tis the shrill melody
Of the Moor's ancient death-song. Well I know
The rude barbaric sound; but, till this hour,
It seem'd not fearful. Now, a shuddering chill
Comes o'er me with its tones.—Lo! from yon tent
They lead the noble boys!
  *Hernandez.*       The young, and pure,
And beautiful victims!—'Tis on things like these
We cast our hearts in wild idolatry,
Sowing the winds with hope!—Yet this is well.
Thus brightly crown'd with life's most gorgeous
    flowers,
And all unblemish'd, earth should offer up
Her treasures unto Heaven!
  *Garcias (to Gonzalez.)* My chief, the Moor
Hath led your children forth.
  *Gonzalez (starting.)*     Are my sons there?
I knew they could not perish; for you Heaven
Would ne'er behold it!—Where is he that said
I was no more a father?—They look changed—
Pallid and worn, as from a prison-house!
Or is't mine eye sees dimly?—But their steps
Seem heavy, as with pain—I hear the clank—
Oh God! their limbs are fetter'd!
  *Abdullah (coming forward beneath the walls.)*
                  Christian, look
Once more upon thy children. There is yet
One moment for the trembling of the sword.
Their doom is still with thee.
  *Gonzalez.*       Why should this man
So mock us with the semblance of our kind?
—Moor! Moor! thou dost too daringly provoke,
In thy bold cruelty, th' all-judging One,
Who visits for such things!—Hast thou no sense
Of thy frail nature?—'Twill be taught thee yet,
And darkly shall the anguish of my soul,
Darkly and heavily, pour itself on thine,
When thou shalt cry for mercy from the dust,
And be denied!
  *Abdullah.*     Nay, is it not thyself
That hast no mercy and no love within thee?
These are thy sons, the nurslings of thy house;
Speak! must they live or die?
  *Gonzalez (in violent emotion.)* Is it Heaven's will
To try the dust it kindles for a day,
With infinite agony!—How have I drawn
This chastening on my head!—They bloom'd
    around me,
And my heart grew too fearless in its joy,
Glorying in their bright promise!—If we fall,
Is there no pardon for our feebleness?

  *(Hernandez, without speaking, holds up a Cross before him.)*

*Abdullah.*         Speak!
  *Gonzalez (snatching the Cross, and lifting it up.)*
Let the earth be shaken through its depths,
But this must triumph!
  *Abdullah (coldly.)* Be it as thou wilt.
—Unsheathe the scimetar!     [To his Guards.
  *Garcias (to Gonzalez.)* Away, my chief!
This is your place no longer. There are things
No human heart, though battle-proof as yours,
Unmadden'd may sustain.
  *Gonzalez.*     Be still! I have now
No place on earth but this!
  *Alphonso (from beneath.)* Men! give me way,
That I may speak forth once before I die!
  *Garcias.* The princely boy!—How gallantly his
    brow
Wears its high nature in the face of death!
  *Alphonso.*         Father!
  *Gonzalez.* My son! my son!—mine eldest-born!
  *Alphonso.* Stay but upon the ramparts!—Fear
    thou not—
There is good courage in me: oh! my father!
I will not shame thee!—only let me fall

Knowing thine eye looks proudly on thy child,
So shall my heart have strength.
  *Gonzalez.*     Would, would to God,
That I might die for thee, my noble boy!
Alphonso, my fair son!
  *Alphonso.*       Could I have lived,
I might have been a warrior!—Now, farewell!
But look upon me still!—I will not blench
When the keen sabre flashes.—Mark me well!
Mine eyelid shall not quiver as it falls,
So thou wilt look upon me!
  *Garcias (to Gonzalez.)*   Nay, my lord!
We must be gone!—thou *canst* not bear it!
  *Gonzalez.*         Peace!
—Who hath told *thee* how much man's heart can
    bear?
—Lend me thine arm—my brain whirls fearfully—
How thick the shades close round!—my boy! my
    boy!
Where art thou in this gloom?
  *Garcias.*       Let us go hence.
This is a dreadful moment!
  *Gonzalez.*     Hush!—what saidst thou?
Now let me look on him!—Dost *thou* see aught
Through the dull mist that wraps us?
  *Garcias.*       I behold—
Oh! for a thousand Spaniards to rush down—
  *Gonzalez.* Thou seest—My heart stands still to
    hear thee speak!
—There seems a fearful hush upon the air,
As 't were the dead of night!
  *Garcias.*     The hosts have closed
Around the spot in stillness. Through the spears,
Ranged thick and motionless, I see him not;
—But now——
  *Gonzalez.* He bade me keep mine eye upon him,
And all is darkness round me!—Now?
  *Garcias.*       A sword,
A sword, springs upward, like a lightning burst,
Through the dark serried mass!—Its cold blue
    glare
Is wavering to and fro—'t is vanish'd—hark!
  *Gonzalez.* I heard it, yes!—I heard the dull dead
    sound
That heavily broke the silence!—Didst thou speak?
—I lost thy words—come nearer!
  *Garcias.*       'Twas—'t is past!—
The sword fell then!
  *Hernandez (with exultation.)* Flow forth, thou
    noble blood!
Fount of Spain's ransom and deliverance, flow
Uncheck'd and brightly forth!—Thou kingly
    stream!
Blood of our heroes! blood of martyrdom!
Which through so many warrior-hearts hast pour'd
Thy fiery currents, and hast made our hills
Free, by thine own free offering!—Bathe the land,
But there thou shalt not sink!—Our very air
Shall take thy colouring, and our loaded skies
O'er th' infidel hang dark and ominous,
With battle-hues of thee!—And thy deep voice
Rising above them to the judgment-seat
Shall call a burst of gather'd vengeance down,
To sweep th' oppressor from us!—For thy wave
Hath made his guilt run o'er!
  *Gonzalez (endeavouring to rouse himself.)* 'Tis all
    a dream!
There is not one—no hand on earth could harm
That fair boy's graceful head!—Why look you
    thus!
  *Abdullah (pointing to Carlos.)* Christian e'en
    yet thou hast a son!
  *Gonzalez.*       E'en yet!
  *Carlos.* My father! take me from these fearful
    men!
Wilt thou not save me, father?
  *Gonzalez (attempting to unsheathe his sword.)* Is
    the strength
From mine arm shiver'd? Garcias, follow me!
  *Garcias.* Whither, my chief?
  *Gonzalez.*     Why, we can die as well
On yonder plain,—ay, a spear's thrust will do
The little that our misery doth require.
Sooner than e'er this anguish! Life is best
Thrown from us in such moments.
            [*Voices heard at a distance.*

*Hernandez.*                    Hush! what strain
Floats on the wind?
*Garcias.*                'Tis the Cid's battle-song!
What marvel hath been wrought?
          [*Voices approaching heard in chorus.*
          The Moor is on his way!
With the tambour peal and the tecbir-shout,
And the horn o'er the blue seas ringing out,
          He hath marshall'd his dark array!

XIMENA *enters, followed by the* CITIZENS, *with the*
          BANNER.

  *Ximena.*  Is it too late?—My father, these are
          men
Through life and death prepared to follow thee
Beneath this banner!—Is their zeal too late.'
—Oh! there's a fearful history on thy brow!
What hast thou seen?
  *Garcias.*                It is not *all* too late
  *Ximena.*  My brothers!
  *Hernandez.*                All is well.
(*To* GARCIAS.)  Hush! would'st thou chill
That which hath sprung within them, as a flame
From th' altar-embers mounts in sudden bright-
          ness?
I say, 'tis not too late. ye men of Spain!
On to the rescue!
  *Ximena.*          Bless me, oh, my father!
And I will hence, to aid thee with my prayers,
Sending my spirit with thee through the storm,
Lit up by flashing swords!
  *Gonzalez* (*falling on her neck.*)  Hath aught been
          spared?
Am I not all bereft?—Thou 'rt left me still!
Mine own, my loveliest one, thou 'rt left me still!
Farewell!—thy father's blessing, and thy God's,
Be with thee, my Ximena.
  *Ximena.*                Fare thee well!
If, ere thy steps turn homeward from the field,
The voice is hush'd that still hath welcomed thee,
Think of me in thy victory!
  *Hernandez.*                Peace! no more!
This is no time to melt our nature down
To a soft stream of tears.—Be of strong heart!
Give me the banner!  Swell the song again!

THE CITIZENS.

Ere night, must swords be red!
It is not an hour for knells and tears,
But for helmets braced and serried spears!
          To-morrow for the dead!  [*Exeunt omnes.*

———

*Scene—Before the Altar of a Church.*

ELMINA *rises from the steps of the Altar.*

  *Elmina.*  The clouds are fearful that o'erhang
          thy ways,
Oh, thou mysterious Heaven!—It cannot be
That I have drawn the vials of thy wrath,
To burst upon me through the lifting up
Of a proud heart, elate in happiness!
No! in my day's full noon, for me life's flowers
But wreathed a cup of trembling; and the love,
The boundless love, my spirit was form'd to bear,
Hath ever, in its place of silence, been
A trouble and a shadow, tinging thought
With hues too deep for joy!—I never look'd
On my fair children, in their buoyant mirth,
Or sunny sleep, when all the gentle air
Seem'd glowing with their quiet blessedness,
But o'er my soul there came a shuddering sense
Of earth, and its pale changes; even like that
Which vaguely mingles with our glorious dreams,
A restless and disturbing consciousness
That the bright things must fade!—How have I
          shrunk
From the dull murmur of th' unquiet voice,
With its low tokens of mortality,
Till my heart fainted 'midst their smiles!—their
          smiles!
—Where are those glad looks now?—Could they
          go down
With all their joyous light, that seem'd not earth's

To the cold grave?— My children!—Righteous
          Heaven!
There floats a dark remembrance o'er my brain
Of one who told me, with relentless eye,
That *this* should be the hour!

XIMENA *enters.*

  *Ximena.*                They are gone forth
Unto the rescue—strong in heart and hope,
Faithful, though few!—My mother, let thy prayers
Call on the land's good saints to lift once more
The sword and cross that sweep the field for Spain,
As in old battle; so thine arms e'en yet
May clasp thy sons!—For me, my part is done!
The flame, which dimly might have lingered yet
A little while, hath gather'd all its rays
Brightly to sink at once! and it is well!
The shadows are around me; to thy heart
Fold me, that I may die.
  *Elmina.*                My child!—What dream
Is on thy soul?—E'en now thine aspect wears
Life's brightest inspiration!
  *Ximena.*                Death's!
  *Elmina.*                Away!
Thine eye hath starry clearness, and thy cheek
Doth glow beneath it with a richer hue
Than ting'd its earliest flower!
  *Ximena.*                It well may be!
There are far deeper and far warmer hues
Than those which draw their colouring from the
          founts
Of youth, or health, or hope.
  *Elmina.*                Nay, speak not thus!
There's that about thee shining which would send
E'en through my heart a sunny glow of joy,
Wer't not for these sad words.  The dim cold air
And solemn light, which wrap these tombs and
          shrines
As a pale gleaming shroud, seem kindled up
With a young spirit of ethereal hope
Caught from thy mien!—Oh no! this is not death!
  *Ximena.*  Why should not He, whose touch dis
          solves our chain.
Put on his robes of beauty when he comes
As a deliverer?—He hath many forms,
They should not all be fearful!—If his call
Be but our gathering to that distant land
For whose sweet waters we have pined with
          thirst,
Why should not its prophetic sense be borne
Into the heart's deep stillness, with a breath
Of summer-winds, a voice of melody,
Solemn, yet lovely?—Mother! I depart!
—Be it thy comfort, in the after-days,
That thou hast seen me thus!
  *Elmina.*                Distract me not
With such wild fears! Can I bear on with life
When thou art gone?—Thy voice, thy step, thy
          smile,
Pass'd from my path?—Alas! even now thine eye
Is changed—thy cheek is fading!
  *Ximena.*                Ay, the clouds
Of the dim hour are gathering o'er my sight,
And yet I fear not, for the God of Help
Comes in that quiet darkness!—It may soothe
Thy woes, my mother, if I tell thee now,
With what glad calmness I behold the veil
Falling between me and the world, wherein
My heart so ill hath rested.
  *Elmina.*                Thine!
  *Ximena.*                Rejoice
For her, that, when the garland of her life
Was blighted, and the springs of hope were dried
Received her summons hence; and had no time,
Bearing the canker at th' impatient heart,
To wither, sorrowing for that gift of Heaven,
Which lent one moment of existence light,
That dimm'd the rest for ever!
  *Elmina.*                How is this?
My child, what mean'st thou?
  *Ximena.*                Mother! I have loved
And been beloved!—the sunbeam of an hour,
Which gave life's hidden treasures to mine eye,
As they lay shining in their secret founts,
Went out, and left them colourless.—'Tis past—
And what remains on earth?—the rainbow mist

Through which I gazed, hath melted, and my sight
Is clear'd to look on all things as they are!
—But this is far too mournful!—Life's dark gift
Hath fallen too early and too cold upon me!
—Therefore I would go hence!
   *Elmina.*        And thou hast loved
Unknown——
   *Ximena.*     Oh! pardon, pardon that I veil'd
My thoughts from thee!—But thou hadst woes
     enough,
And mine came o'er me when thy soul had need
Of more than mortal strength!—For I had scarce
Given the deep consciousness that I was loved
A treasure's place within my secret heart,
When earth's brief joy went from me!
                 'Twas at morn
I saw the warriors to their field go forth,
And he—my chosen—was there among the rest,
With his young, glorious brow!—I look'd again—
The strife grew dark beneath me—but his plume
Waved free above the lances.—Yet again—
It had gone down! and steeds were trampling o'er
The spot to which mine eyes were riveted
Till blinded by th' intenseness of their gaze!
—And then—at last—I hurried to the gate,
And met him there!—I met him!—on his shield,
And with his cloven helm, and shiver'd sword,
And dark hair steep'd in blood!—They bore him
     past—
Mother! I saw his face!—Oh! such a death
Works fearful changes on the fair of earth,
The pride of woman's eye!
   *Elmina.*      Sweet daughter, peace!
Wake not the dark remembrance; for thy frame—
   *Ximena.*  There *will* be peace ere long.  I shut
     my heart
E'en as a tomb, o'er that lone silent grief,
That I might spare it thee!—But now the hour
Is come when that which would have pierced thy
     soul
Shall be its healing balm.  Oh! weep thou not,
Save with a gentle sorrow!
   *Elmina.*        Must it be?
Art thou indeed to leave me?
   *Ximena (exultingly.)*    Be thou glad!
I say, rejoice above thy favour'd child!
Joy for the soldier, when his field is fought;
Joy for the peasant, when his vintage-task
Is closed at eve!—But most of all for her,
Who, when her life changed its glittering robes
For the dull garb of sorrow, which doth cling
So heavily around the journeyers on,
Cast down its weight—and slept!
   *Elmina.*       Alas! thine eye
Is wandering—yet how brightly!—Is this death,
Or some high wondrous vision?—Speak, my child!
How is it with thee now?
   *Ximena (wildly.)*     I see it still!
'Tis floating, like a glorious cloud on high,
My father's banner!—Hear'st thou not a sound?
The trumpet of Castile?—Praise, praise to Hea-
     ven!
—Now may the weary rest!—Be still!—Who calls
The night so fearful?——       [*She dies.*
   *Elmina.*      No! she is not dead!
—Ximena! speak to me!—Oh! yet a tone
From that sweet voice, that I may gather in
One more remembrance of its lovely sound,
Ere the deep silence fall!—What! is all hush'd?
—No, no!—it cannot be!—How should we bear
The dark misgivings of our souls, if Heaven
Left not such beings with us?—But is this
Her wonted look?—too sad a quiet lies
On its dim fearful beauty!—Speak, Ximena!
Speak!—my heart dies within me!—She is gone,
With all her blessed smiles!—My child! my child!
Where art thou?—Where is that which answer'd
     me,
From thy soft-shining eyes!—Hush! doth she
     move?
—One light lock seem'd to tremble on her brow,
As a pulse throbb'd beneath;—'twas but the voice
Of my despair that stirr'd it!—She is gone!
     [*She throws herself on the body. Gonzalez enters
     alone, and wounded.*

   *Elmina (rising as he approaches.)* I must not *now*
     be scorn'd!—No, not a look,
A whisper of reproach!—Behold my woe!
Thou canst not scorn me now!
   *Gonzalez.*        Hast thou heard *all?*
   *Elmina.* Thy daughter on my bosom laid her
     head,
And pass'd away to rest.—Behold her there,
Even such as death hath made her! (8)
   *Gonzalez (bending over Ximena's body.)* Thou
     art gone
A little while before me, oh, my child!
Why should the traveller weep to part with those
That scarce an hour will reach their promised
     land
Ere he too cast his pilgrim staff away,
And spread his couch beside them?
   *Elmina.*        Must it be
Henceforth enough that *once* a thing so fair
Had its bright place among us?—Is this all,
Left for the years to come?—We will not stay!
Earth's chain each hour grows weaker.
   *Gonzalez (still gazing upon Ximena.)* And thou'rt
     laid
To slumber in the shadow, blessed child!
Of a yet stainless altar, and beside
A sainted warrior's tomb!—Oh, fitting place
For thee to yield thy pure heroic soul
Back unto him that gave it!—And thy cheek
Yet smiles in its bright paleness!
   *Elmina.*      Hadst thou seen
The look with which she pass'd!
   *Gonzalez (still bending over her.)*  Why, 'tis
     almost
Like joy to view thy beautiful repose!
The faded image of that perfect calm
Floats, e'en as long-forgotten music, back
Into my weary heart!—No dark wild spot
On *thy* clear brow doth tell of bloody hands
That quench'd young life by violence!—We have
     seen
Too much of horror, in one crowded hour,
To weep for aught, so gently gather'd hence!
—Oh! *man* leaves other traces!
   *Elmina (starting suddenly.)*  It returns
On my bewilder'd soul!—Went ye not forth
Unto the rescue?—And thou'rt here alone!
—Where are my sons?
   *Gonzalez (solemnly)*    We were too late!
   *Elmina.*         Too late!
Hast thou naught else to tell me?
   *Gonzalez.*      I brought back
From that last field the banner of my sires,
And my own death-wound.
   *Elmina.*        Thine!
   *Gonzalez.*         Another hour
Shall hush its throbs for ever.  I go hence,
And with me——
   *Elmina.*   No!—Man *could* not lift his hands—
Where hast thou left thy sons?
   *Gonzalez.*      I *have* no sons.
   *Elmina.* What hast thou said?
   *Gonzalez.*     That now there lives not one
To wear the glory of mine ancient house,
When I am gone to rest.
   *Elmina (throwing herself on the ground, and
speaking in a low hurried voice.)* In one brief hour,
     all gone!—and such a death!
—I see their blood gush forth!—their graceful
     heads——
Take the dark vision from me, oh my God!
And such a death for *them!*—I was not there!—
They were but mine in beauty and in joy,
Not in that mortal anguish!—Ah, all gone!
—Why should I struggle more?—What *is* this
     Power
Against whose might, on all sides pressing us,
We strive with fierce impatience, which but lays
Our own frail spirit prostrate?
   *(After a long pause.)*     Now I know
Thy hand, my God!—and they are soonest crush'd
That most withstand it!—I resist no more.
*(She rises.)*—A light, a light springs up from grief
     and death,

Which with its solemn radiance doth reveal
Why we have thus been tried!
   *Gonzalez.*         Then I may still
Fix my last look on thee, in holy love,
Parting, but yet with hope.
   *Elmina (falling at his feet.)*  Canst thou forgive?
—Oh, I have driven the arrow to thy heart,
That should have buried it within mine own,
And borne the pang in silence!—I have cast
Thy life's fair honour, in my wild despair,
As an unvalued gem upon the waves,
Whence thou hast snatch'd it back, to bear from
earth,
All stainless, on thy breast—Well hast thou done—
But I—canst thou forgive?
   *Gonzalez.*         Within this hour
I have stood upon that verge whence mortals fall,
And learn'd how 't is with one whose sight grows
dim,
And whose foot trembles on the gulf's dark side,
—Death purifies all feeling—We will part
In pity and in love.
   *Elmina.*         Death!—And thou too
Art on thy way!—Oh, joy for thee, high heart!
Glory and joy for thee!—The day is closed,
And well and nobly hast thou borne thyself
Through its long battle-toils, though many swords
Have enter'd thine own soul!—But on my head
Recoil the fierce invokings of despair,
And I am left far distanced in the race,
The lonely one of earth?—Ay, this is just.
I am not worthy that upon my breast
In this, thine hour of victory, thou shouldst yield
Thy spirit unto God.
   *Gonzalez.*         Thou art! thou art!
Oh! a life's love, a heart's long faithfulness,
E'en in the presence of eternal things,
Wearing their chasten'd beauty all undimm'd,
Assert their lofty claims; and these are not
For one dark hour to cancel!—We are here
Before that altar which received the vows
Of our unbroken youth, and meet it is
For such a witness in the sight of Heaven,
And in the face of death, whose shadowy arm
Comes dim between us, to regard th' exchange
Of our tried hearts' forgiveness,—Who are they,
That in one path have journey'd, needing not
Forgiveness at its close?

        *(A Citizen enters hastily.)*

   *Citizen.* The Moors! the Moors!
   *Gonzalez.*         How! is the city storm'd?
Oh! righteous Heaven!—for this I look'd not yet!
Hath all been done in vain?—Why, then 't is time
For prayer, and then to rest!
   *Citizen.*         The sun shall set,
And not a Christian voice be left for prayer,
To-night, within Valencia!—Round our walls
The paynim host is gathering for th' assault,
And we have none to guard them.
   *Gonzalez.*         Then my place
Is here no longer,—I had hoped to die
Ev'n by the altar and the sepulchre
Of my brave sires—but this was not to be!
Give me my sword again, and lead me hence
Back to the ramparts. I have yet an hour,
And it hath still high duties.—Now my wife
Thou mother of my children—of the dead—
Whom I name unto thee, in steadfast hope—
Farewell!
   *Elmina.* No, not farewell!—My soul hath risen
To mate itself with thine; and by thy side,
Amidst the hurtling lances, I will stand,
As one on whom a brave man's love hath been
Wasted not utterly.
   *Gonzalez.*         I thank thee, Heaven,
That I have tasted of the awful joy
Which thou hast given to temper hours like this,
With a deep sense of thee, and of thine ends
In these dread visitings!
   *(To Elmina.)*         We will not part
But with the spirit's parting!
   *Elmina.*         One farewell
To her, that, mantled with fair loveliness,
Doth slumber at our feet!—My blessed child!
Oh! in thy heart's affliction thou wert strong,

And holy courage did pervade thy woe,
As light the troubled waters!—Be at peace!
Thou whose bright spirit made itself the soul
Of all that were around thee!—And thy life
E'en then was struck, and withering at the core
—Farewell!—Thy parting look hath on me fall'n
E'en as a gleam of heaven, and I am now
More like what thou hast been!—My soul is
hush'd,
For a still sense of purer worlds has sunk
And settled on its depths with that last smile
Which from thine shone forth.—Thou hast not
lived
In vain—my child, farewell!
   *Gonzalez.*         Surely for thee
Death had no sting, Ximena!—We are blest,
To learn one secret of the shadowy pass,
From such an aspect's calmness. Yet once more
I kiss thy pale young cheek, my broken flower.
In token of th' undying love and hope,
Whose land is far away.

--------

      *Scene.—The walls of the City.*

  *Hernandez.—A few Citizens gathered round him*

   *Hernandez.* Why, men have cast the treasures,
      which their lives
Had been worn down in gathering, on the pyre,
Ay, at their household hearths have lit the brand
Ev'n from that shrine of quiet love to bear
The flame which gave their temples and their
      homes,
In ashes, to the winds!—They have done this,
Making a blasted void, where once the sun
Look'd upon lovely dwellings; and from earth
Razing all record that on such a spot
Childhood hath sprung, age faded, misery wept,
And frail Humanity knelt before her God;
—They have done *this*, in their free nobleness,
Rather than see the spoiler's tread pollute
Their holy places!—Praise, high praise be theirs,
Who have left man such lessons!—And these
      things,
Made your own hills their witnesses!—The sky,
Whose arch bends o'er you, and the seas, wherein
Your rivers pour their gold, rejoicing saw
The altar, and the birth-place, and the tomb,
And all memorials of man's heart and faith,
Th' us proudly honour'd.—Be ye not outdone
By the departed!—Though the godless foe
Be close upon us, we have power to snatch
The spoils of victory from him. Be but strong!
A few bright torches and brief moments yet
Shall baffle his flush'd hope, and we may die,
Laughing him unto scorn.—Rise, follow me,
And thou, Valencia! triumph in thy fate.
The ruin, not the yoke, and make thy towers
A beacon unto Spain!
   *Citizen.*         We'll follow thee!
—Alas! for our fair city, and the homes,
Wherein we rear'd our children!—But away!
The Moor shall plant no crescent o'er our fanes!
   *Voice (from a tower on the walls.)* Succours!—
      Castile! Castile!
   *Citizens (rushing to the spot.)* It is even so!
Now blessing be to Heaven, for we are saved!
Castile, Castile!
   *Voice (from the tower.)* Line after line of spears,
Lance after lance, upon the horizon's verge,
Like festal lights from cities bursting up,
Doth skirt the plains!—in faith, a noble host!
   *Another Voice.* The Moor hath turn'd him from
      our walls, to front
Th' advancing might of Spain!
   *Citizens (shouting.)*     Castile! Castile!

   *(Gonzalez enters, supported by Elmina and a
      Citizen.)*

   *Gonzalez.* What shouts of joy are these?
   *Hernandez.*      Hail, chieftain! hail!
Thus ev'n in death 't is given thee to receive
The conqueror's crown!—Behold our God hath
      heard,
And arm'd himself with vengeance!—Lo! they
      come!
The lances of Castile!

*Gonzalez.*                    I knew, I knew
Thou wouldst not utterly, my God, forsake
Thy servant in his need!—My blood and tears
Have not sunk vainly to th' attesting earth!
Praise to thee, thanks and praise, that I have lived
To see this hour!
      *Elmina.*            And I too bless thy name,
Though thou hast proved me unto agony!
Oh God!—thou God of chastening!
      *Voice from the tower.*)          They move on!
I see the royal banner in the air,
With its emblazon'd towers!
      *Gonzalez.*            Go, bring ye forth
The banner of the Cid, and plant it here,
To stream above me for an answering sign
That the good cross doth hold its lofty place
Within Valencia still!—What see ye now?
      *Hernandez.* I see a kingdom's might upon its
            path,
Moving in terrible magnificence,
Unto revenge and victory!—With the flush
Of knightly swords, up-springing from the ranks,
As meteors from a still and gloomy deep,
And with the waving of ten thousand plumes,
Like a land's harvest in the autumn wind,
And with fierce light, which is not of the sun,
But flung from sheets of steel—it comes, it comes,
The vengeance of our God!
      *Gonzalez.*            I hear it now,
The heavy tread of mail-clad multitudes,
Like thunder-showers upon the forest paths.
      *Hernandez.* Ay, earth knows well the omen of
            that sound,
And she hath echoes, like a sepulchre's,
Pent in her secret hollows, to respond
Unto the step of death!
      *Gonzalez.*            Hark! how the wind
Swells proudly with the battle-march of Spain!
Now the heart feels its power!—A little while
Grant me to live, my God!—What pause is this?
      *Hernandez.* A deep and dreadful one!—the ser-
            ried files
Level their spears for combat; now the hosts
Look on each other in their brooding wrath,
Silent, and face to face.

            VOICES HEARD WITHOUT, CHANTING.

      Calm on the bosom of thy God,
         Fair spirit! rest thee now!
      E'en while with ours thy footsteps trod,
         His seal was on thy brow.

      Dust, to its narrow house beneath!
         Soul, to its place on high!
      They that have seen thy look in death,
         No more may fear to die.

      *Elmina (to Gonzalez).* It is the death-hymn
         o'er thy daughter's bier!
—But I am calm, and e'en like gentle winds,
That music, through the stillness of my heart,
Sends mournful peace.
      *Gonzalez.*         Oh! well those solemn tones
Accord with such an hour, for all her life
Breathed of a hero's soul!

[*A sound of trumpets and shouting from the plain.*]

      *Hernandez.* Now, now they close!—Hark! what
         a dull dead sound
Is in the Moorish war-shout!—I have known
Such tones prophetic oft.—The shock is given—
Lo! they have placed their shields before their
         hearts,
And lower'd their lances with the streamers on,
And on their steeds bent forward!—God for
         Spain!
The first bright sparks of battle have been struck
From spear to spear, across the gleaming field!
—There is no sight on which the blue sky looks
To match with this!—'T is not the gallant crests,
Nor banners with their glorious blazonry;
The very nature and high soul of man
Doth now reveal itself!
      *Gonzalez.*         Oh, raise me up,
That I may look upon the noble scene!
—It will not be!—That this dull mist would pass

A moment from my sight!—Whence rose that
      shout,
As in fierce triumph?
      *Hernandez (clasping his hands.)* Must I look on
         this?
The banner sinks—'tis taken!
      *Gonzalez.*            Whose?
      *Hernandez.*                  Castile's!
      *Gonzalez.* Oh, God of battles!
      *Elmina.*            Calm thy noble heart!
Thou wilt not pass away without thy meed.
Nay, rest thee on my bosom.
      *Hernandez.*            Cheer thee yet!
Our knights have spurr'd to rescue.—There is now
A whirl, a mingling of all terrible things,
Yet more appalling than the fierce distinctness
Wherewith they moved before!—I see tall plumes
All wildly tossing o'er the battle's tide,
Sway'd by the wrathful motion, and the press
Of desperate men, as cedar-boughs by storms.
Many a white streamer there is dyed with blood,
Many a false corselet broken, many a shield
Pierced through!—Now, shout for Santiago, shout!
Lo! javelins with a moment's brightness cleave
The thickening dust, and barbed steeds go down
With their helm'd riders!—Who, but One, can tell
How spirits part amidst that fearful rush
And trampling on of furious multitudes?
      *Gonzalez.* Thou'rt silent!—See'st thou more?—
         My soul grows dark.
      *Hernandez.* And dark and troubled, as an angry
         sea,
Dashing some gallant armament in scorn
Against its rocks, is all on which I gaze!
—I can but tell thee how tall spears are cross'd,
And lances seem to shiver, and proud helms
To lighten with the stroke!—But round the spot,
Where, like a storm-fell'd mast, our standard
         sank,
The heart of battle burns.
      *Gonzalez.*            Where is that spot?
      *Hernandez.* It is beneath the lonely tuft of
         palms,
That lift their green heads o'er the tumult still,
In calm and stately grace.
      *Gonzalez.*            There, didst thou say?
Then God is with us, and we *must* prevail!
For on that spot they died!—My children's blood
Calls on th' avenger thence!
      *Elmina.*            They perish'd there!
—And the bright locks that waved so joyously
To the free winds, lay trampled and defiled
Ev'n on that place of death!—Oh, Merciful!
Hush the dark thought within me!
      *Hernandez (with sudden exultation.)* Who is he,
On the white steed, and with the castled helm,
And the gold broider'd mantle, which doth float
E'en like a sunny cloud above the fight;
And the pale cross, which from his breast-plate
         gleams
With star-like radiance?
      *Gonzalez (eagerly.)* Didst thou say the cross?
      *Hernandez.* On his mail'd bosom shines a broad
         white cross,
And his long plumage through the darkening air
Streams like a snow-wreath.
      *Gonzalez.*            That should be—
      *Hernandez.*                  The king!
—Was it not told us how he sent, of late,
To the Cid's tomb, e'en for the silver cross,
Which he who slumbers there was wont to bind
O'er his brave heart in fight? (9)
      *Gonzalez (springing up joyfully.)* My king! my
         king!
Now all good saints for Spain!—My noble king!
And thou art there!—That I might look once more
Upon thy face!—But yet I thank thee, Heaven!
That thou hast sent him, from my dying hands
Thus to receive his city!
            [*He sinks back into* Elmina's *arms.*
      *Hernandez.*            He hath clear'd
A pathway 'midst the combat, and the light
Follows his charge through yon close living mass,
E'en as the gleam on some proud vessel's wake
Along the stormy waters!—'T is redeem'd—
The castled banner!—It is flung once more

In joy and glory, to the sweeping winds!
—There seems a wavering through the paynim
      boats—
Castile doth press them sore—Now, now rejoice!
   *Gonzalez.* What hast thou seen?
   *Hernandez.*        Abdullah falls! He falls!
The man of blood!—the spoiler!—he hath sunk
In our king's path!—Well hath that royal sword
Avenged thy cause, Gonzalez.
                     They give way,
The Crescent's van is broken!—On the hills
And the dark pine-woods may the infidel
Call vainly in his agony of fear,
To cover him from vengeance!—Lo! they fly!
They of the forest and the wilderness
Are scatter'd e'en as leaves upon the wind!
Woe to the sons of Afric!—Let the plains,
And the vine-mountains, and Hesperian seas,
Take their dead unto them!—that blood shall wash
Our soil from stains of bondage.
   *Gonzalez (attempting to raise himself.)* Set me
     free!
Come with me forth, for I must greet my king,
After his battle-field!
   *Hernandez.*       Oh, blest in death!
Chosen of Heaven, farewell!—Look on the Cross,
And part from earth in peace!
   *Gonzalez.*      Now charge once more!
God is with Spain, and Santiago's sword
Is reddening all the air!—Shout forth 'Castile!'
The day is ours!—I go!—but fear ye not!
For Afric's lance is broken, and my sons
Have won their first good field!    [*He dies.*
   *Elmina.*        Look on me yet!
Speak one farewell, my husband!—must thy voice
Enter my soul no more?—Thine eye is fix'd—
Now is my life uprooted,—and 'tis well.

  *(A Sound of triumphant music is heard, and many*
     *Castilian Knights and Soldiers enter.)*

  *A Citizen.* Hush your triumphal sounds, al-
    though ye come
E'en as deliverers!—But the noble dead,
And those that mourn them, claim from human
    hearts
Deep silent reverence.
   *Elmina (rising proudly.)* No, swell forth, Castile!
Thy trumpet-music, till the seas and heavens,
And the deep hills, give every stormy note
Echoes to ring through Spain!—How, know ye not
That all array'd for triumph, crown'd and robed
With the strong spirit which hath saved the land,
Ev'n now a conqueror to his rest is gone?
—Fear not to break that sleep, but let the wind
Swell on with victory's shout!—He will not hear—
Hath earth a sound more sad?
   *Hernandez.*      Lift ye the dead,
And bear him with the banner of his race
Waving above him proudly, as it waved
O'er the Cid's battles, to the tomb, wherein

His warrior-sires are gather'd  [*They raise the body*
   *Elmina.*          Ay, 'tis thus
Thou shouldst be honour'd!—And I follow thee
With an unfaltering and a lofty step,
To the last home of glory. She that wears
In her deep heart the memory of thy love
Shall thence draw strength for all things, till the
    God,
Whose hand around her hath unpeopled earth,
Looking upon her still and chasten'd soul,
Call it once more to thine!
            *(To the Castilians.)*
              Awake, I say
Tambour and trumpet, wake!—and let the land
Through all her mountains hear your funeral peal
—So should a hero pass to his repose.
                 *[Exeunt omnes*

# NOTES.

### Note 1.

Mountain Christians, those natives of Spain, who, under their
prince, Pelayo, took refuge among the mountains of the northern
provinces, where they maintained their religion and liberty, while
the rest of their country was overrun by the Moors.

### Note 2.

*Oh free doth sorrow pass, &c.*
*Frey geht das Unglock durch die ganze Erde.*
    *Schiller's Death of Wallenstein*, Act iv. sc. 2.

### Note 3.

Tizona, the fire-brand. The name of the Cid's favourite sword,
taken in battle from the Moorish king Bucar.

### Note 4.

*How he won Valencia from the Moor, &c.*
Valencia, which has been repeatedly besieged, and taken by the
armies of different nations, remained in the possession of the Moors
for an hundred and seventy years after the Cid's death. It was re-
gained from them by King Don Jayme, of Aragon, surnamed the
Conqueror; after whose success I have ventured to suppose it go-
verned by a descendant of the Campeador.

### Note 5.

It was a Spanish tradition, that the great bell of the Cathedral of
Saragossa always tolled spontaneously before a king of Spain died.

### Note 6.

" El que en buen hora nasco;" he that was born in happy hour.
An appellation given to the Cid in the ancient chronicles.

### Note 7.

For this, and the subsequent allusions to Spanish legends, see Romances and *Chronicles of the Cid.*

### Note 8.

" La volla, la lla que la mort nous l's faits!"—*Bossuet, Oraisons
Funebres*

### Note 9.

This circumstance is recorded of King Don Alphonso, the last of
that name. He sent to the Cid's tomb for the cross which that warrior was accustomed to wear upon his breast when he went to battle, and had it made into one for himself; " because of the faith
which he had, that through it he should obtain the victory."
*Southey's Chronicle of the Cid.*

# THE

# VESPERS OF PALERMO.

## A TRAGEDY, IN FIVE ACTS.

# VESPERS OF PALERMO.



| | |
|---|---|
| Count di Procida. | Alberti. |
| Raimond di Procida, *his Son.* | Anselmo, *a Monk.* |
| Eribert, *Viceroy.* | |
| De Couci. | Vittoria. |
| Montalba. | Constance, *Sister to Eribert.* |
| Guido. | |

*Nobles, Soldiers, Messengers, Vassals, Peasants, &c., &c.*

Scene—*Palermo.*

# VESPERS OF PALERMO.

---

## ACT THE FIRST.



*Scene I.—A Valley, with Vineyards and Cottages.*

*Groups of Peasants—*Procida, *disguised as a Pilgrim, among them.*

  *First Peasant.* Ay, this was wont to be a festal'
time
In days gone by! I can remember well
The old familiar melodies that rose
At break of morn, from all our purple hills,
To welcome in the vintage. Never since
Hath music seem'd so sweet. But the light hearts
Which to those measures beat so joyously,
Are tamed to stillness now. There is no voice
Of joy through all the land.
  *Second Peasant.*        Yes! there are sounds
Of revelry within the palaces,
And the fair castles of our ancient lords,
Where now the stranger banquets. Ye may hear,
From *thence* the peals of song and laughter rise
At midnight's deepest hour.
  *Third Peasant.*       Alas! we sat,
In happier days, so peacefully beneath
The olives and the vines our fathers rear'd,
Encircled by our children, whose quick steps
Flew by us in the dance! The time hath been
When peace was in the hamlet, wheresoe'er
The storm might gather. But this yoke of France
Falls on the peasant's neck as heavily
As on the crested chieftain's. We are bow'd
E'en to the earth.
  *Peasant's Child.* My father, tell me when
Shall the gay dance and song again resound
Amidst our chestnut-woods, as in those days
Of which thou 'rt wont to tell the joyous tale?
  *First Peasant.* When there are light and reck
    less hearts once more
In Sicily's green vales. Alas! my boy,
Men meet not now to quaff the flowing bowl,
To hear the mirthful song, and cast aside
The weight of work-day care:—they meet to speak
Of wrongs and sorrows, and to whisper thoughts
They dare not breathe aloud.
  *Procida (from the back ground.)* Ay, it is well
So to relieve th' o'erburthen'd heart, which pants
Beneath its weight of wrong; but better far
In silence to avenge them!
  *An old Peasant.*      What deep voice
Came with that startling tone?
  *First Peasant.*       It was our guest's,
The stranger pilgrim, who hath sojourn'd here
Since yester-morn. Good neighbours, mark him
    well:
He hath a stately bearing, and an eye
Whose glance looks through the heart. His mien
    accords
Ill with such vestments. How he folds round him
His pilgrim-cloak, e'en as it were a robe

Of knightly ermine. That commanding step
Should have been used in courts and camps to
    move.
Mark him!
  *Old Peasant.* Nay, rather, mark him not; the
    times
Are fearful, and they teach the boldest hearts
A cautious lesson. What should bring him here?
  *A Youth.* He spoke of vengeance!
  *Old Peasant.*      Peace! we are beset
By snares on every side, and we must learn
In silence and in patience to endure
Talk not of vengeance, for the word is death.
  *Procida (coming forward indignantly.)* The word
Is death! And what hath life for *thee*,
That thou shouldst cling to it thus? thou abject
    thing!
Whose very soul is moulded to the yoke,
And stamp'd with servitude. What! is it life
Thus at a breeze to start, to school thy voice
Into low fearful whispers, and to cast
Pale jealous looks around thee, lest, e'en then,
Strangers should catch its echo?—Is there aught
In *this* so precious, that thy furrow'd cheek
Is blanch'd with terror at the passing thought
Of hazarding some few and evil days,
Which drag thus poorly on?
  *Some of the Peasants.*     Away, away!
Leave us, for there is danger in thy presence.
  *Procida.* Why, what is danger?—Are there deep-
    er ills
Than those ye bear thus calmly? Ye have drain'd
The cup of bitterness, till naught remains
To fear or shrink from—therefore, be ye strong!
Power dwelleth with despair.—Why start ye thus
At words which are but echoes of the thoughts
Lock'd in your secret souls?—Full well I know,
There is not one among you, but hath nursed
Some proud indignant feeling, which doth make
One conflict of his life. I know *thy* wrongs,
And thine—and thine,—but if within your breasts
There is no chord that vibrates to *my* voice,
Then fare ye well.
  *A Youth (coming forward.)* No, no! say on, say
    on!
There are still free and fiery hearts e'en here,
That kindle at thy words.
  *Peasant.*      If that indeed
Thou hast a hope to give us——
  *Procida.*      There is hope
For all who suffer with indignant thoughts
Which work in silent strength. What! think ye
    Heaven
O'erlooks th' oppressor, if he bear awhile
His crested head on high?—I tell you, no!
Th' avenger will not sleep. It was an hour
Of triumph to the conqueror, when our king,
Our young brave Conradin, in life's fair morn,
On the red scaffold died. Yet not the less
Is Justice throned above; and her good time

Comes rushing on in storms: that royal blood
Hath lifted an accusing voice from earth,
And hath been heard.  The traces of the past
Fade in man's heart, but ne'er doth Heaven forget.
    *Peasant.*  Had we but arms and leaders, we are
        men
Who might earn vengeance yet; but wanting
        these,
What wouldst thou have us do?
    *Procida.*                    Be vigilant
And when the signal wakes the land, arise!
The peasant's arm is strong, and there shall be
A rich and noble harvest.  Fare ye well.
                        [*Exit* PROCIDA.
    *First Peasant.*  This man should be a prophet:
        how he seem'd
To read our hearts with his dark searching glance
And aspect of command!  And yet his garb
Is mean as ours.
    *Second Peasant.*  Speak low; I know him well.
At first his voice disturb'd me, like a dream
Of other days: but I remember now
His form, seen oft when in my youth I served
Beneath the banners of our kings!  'Tis he
Who hath been exiled and proscribed so long,
The Count di Procida.
    *Peasant.*              And is this he?
Then Heaven protect him! for around his steps
Will many snares be set.
    *First Peasant.*          He comes not thus
But with some mighty purpose; doubt it not;
Perchance to bring us freedom.  He is one,
Whose faith, through many a trial, hath been
        proved
True to our native princes.  But away!
The noontide heat is past, and from the seas
Light gales are wandering through the vineyards;
        now
We may resume our toil.        [*Exeunt Peasants.*

SCENE II.—*The Terrace of a Castle.*

ERIBERT, VITTORIA.

    *Vittoria.*  Have I not told thee, that I bear a
        heart
Blighted and cold?—Th' affections of my youth
Lie slumbering in the grave; their fount is closed,
And all the soft and playful tenderness
Which hath its home in woman's breast, ere yet
Deep wrongs have sear'd it; all is fled from mine.
Urge me no more.
    *Eribert.*          O lady! doth the flower
That sleeps entomb'd through the long wintry
        storms
Unfold its beauty to the breath of spring;
And shall not woman's heart, from chill despair,
Wake at love's voice?
    *Vittoria.*          Love!—make *love's* name thy spell,
And I am strong!—the very word calls up
From the dark past, thoughts, feelings, powers,
        array'd
In arms against thee!—Know'st thou *whom* I loved,
While my soul's dwelling-place was still on earth?
One who was born for empire, and endow'd
With such high gifts of princely majesty,
As bow'd all hearts before him!—Was *he* not
Brave, royal, beautiful?—And such he died;
He died!—hast thou forgotten?—And thou 'rt here,
Thou meet'st my glance, with eyes which coldly
        look'd,
—Coldly!—nay, rather with triumphant gaze,
Upon his murder!—Desolate as I am,
Yet in the mien of *thine* affianced bride,
Oh, my lost Conradin! there should be still
Somewhat of loftiness, which might o'erawe
The hearts of thine assassins.
    *Eribert.*                Haughty dame!
If thy proud heart to tenderness be closed,
Know, danger is around thee · thou hast foes
That seek thy ruin, and my power alone
Can shield thee from their arts.

    *Vittoria.*                    Provençal, tell
Thy tale of danger to some happy heart,
Which hath its little world of loved ones round,
For whom to tremble; and its tranquil joys
That make earth, Paradise.  I stand alone;
—They that are blest, may fear.
    *Eribert.*                    Is there not one
Who ne'er commands in vain?—proud lady, bend
Thy spirit to thy fate; for know that he,
Whose car of triumph in its earthquake path
O'er the bow'd neck of prostrate Sicily,
Hath borne him to dominion; he, my king,
Charles of Anjou, decrees thy hand the boon
My deeds have well deserved; and who hath power
Against his mandates?
    *Vittoria.*            Viceroy, tell thy lord,
That e'en where chains lie heaviest on the land,
Souls may not all be fetter'd.  Oft, ere now,
Conquerors have rock'd the earth, yet fail'd to
        tame
Unto their purposes, that restless fire,
Inhabiting man's breast.—A spark bursts forth,
And so they perish!—'t is the fate of those
Who sport with lightning—and it may be his.
—Tell him I fear him not, and thus am free.
    *Eribert.*  'Tis well.  Then nerve that lofty heart
        to bear
The wrath which is not powerless.  Yet again
Bethink thee, lady!—Love may change—*hath*
        changed
To vigilant hatred oft, whose sleepless eye
Still finds what most it seeks for.  Fare thee well.
—Look to it yet!—To-morrow I return.
                        [*Exit* ERIBERT.
    *Vittoria.*  To-morrow!—Some ere now have slept
        and dreamt
Of morrows which ne'er dawn'd—or ne'er for them,
So silently their deep and still repose
Hath melted into death!—Are there not balms
In nature's boundless realm, to pour out sleep
Like this, on me?—Yet should my spirit still
Endure its earthly bonds, till it could bear
To *his* a glorious tale of his own isle,
Free and avenged.—*Thou* shouldst be now at
        work,
In wrath, my native Etna! who dost lift
Thy spiry pillar of dark smoke so high,
Through the red heaven of sunset!—sleep'st thou
        still,
With all thy founts of fire, while spoilers tread
The glowing vales beneath?
                [PROCIDA *enters, disguised.*
                        Ha! who art thou,
Unbidden guest, that with so mute a step
Dost steal upon me?
    *Procida.*          One, o'er whom hath pass'd
All that can change man's aspect!—Yet not long
Shalt thou find safety in forgetfulness.
—I am he, to breathe whose name is perilous,
Unless thy wealth could bribe the winds to silence.
—Know'st thou *this*, lady?        [*He shows a ring.*
    *Vittoria.*            Righteous Heaven! the pledge
Amidst his people from the scaffold thrown
By him who perish'd, and whose kingly blood
E'en yet is unatoned.—My heart beats high—
—Oh, welcome, welcome! thou art Procida,
Th' Avenger, the Deliverer!
    *Procida.*                Call me so,
When my great task is done.  Yet who can tell
If the return'd *be* welcome?—Many a heart
Is changed since last we met.
    *Vittoria.*                Why dost thou gaze
With such a still and solemn earnestness,
Upon my alter'd mien?
    *Procida.*            That I may read
If to the widow'd love of Conradin,
Or the proud Eribert's triumphant bride,
I now intrust my fate.
    *Vittoria.*            Thou, Procida!
That *thou* shou'dst wrong me thus!—Prolong thy
        gaze
Till it hath found an answer.
    *Procida.*                'Tis enough.
I find it in thy cheek, whose rapid change
Is from death's hue to fever's: in the wild
Unsettled brightness of thy proud dark eye,

And in thy wasted form.   Ay, 't is a deep
And solemn joy, thus in thy looks to trace,
Instead of youth's gay bloom, the characte's
Of noble suffering;—on thy brow the same
Commanding spirit holds its native state
Which could not stoop to vileness.   Yet th' voice
Of Fame hath told afar, that thou shoulds. wed
This tyrant Eribert.
    *Vittoria.*            And told it not
A tale of insolent love repell'd with scorn,
Of stern commands and fearful menaces
Met with indignant courage?—Procida!
It was but now that haughtily I braved
His sovereign's mandate, which decrees my hand,
With its fair appanage of wide domains
And wealthy vassals, a most fitting boon,
To recompense his crimes.—I smiled—ay, smiled—
In proud security! for the high of heart
Have still a pathway to escape disgrace,
Though it be dark and lone.
    *Procida.*         Thou shalt not need
To tread its shadowy mazes.   Trust my words:
I tell thee, that a spirit is abroad,
Which will not slumber till its path be traced
By deeds of fearful fame.   Vittoria, live!
It is most meet that thou *shouldst* live, to see
The mighty expiation; for thy heart
(Forgive me that I wrong'd its faith) hath nursed
A high, majestic grief, whose seal is set
Deep on thy marble brow.
    *Vittoria.*        Then thou *canst* tell,
By gazing on the wither'd rose, that there
Time, or the blight, hath work'd!—Ay, this is in
Thy. vision's scope: but oh! the things unseen,
Untold, undreamt of, which like shadows pass
Hourly o'er that mysterious world, a mind
To ruin struck by grief!—Yet doth my soul,
Far 'midst its darkness, nurse one soaring hope,
Wherein is bright vitality.—'T is to see
*His* blood avenged, and his fair heritage,
My beautiful native land, in glory risen,
Like a warrior from his slumbers!
    *Procida.*        Hear'st thou not
With what a deep and ominous moan, the voice
Of our great mountain swells?—There will be
    soon
A fearful burst!—Vittoria! brood no more
In silence o'er thy sorrows, but go forth
Amidst thy vassals (yet be secret still)
And let thy breath give nurture to the spark
Thou'lt find already kindled.   I move on
In shadow, yet awakening in my path
That which shall startle nations.   Fare thee well.
    *Vittoria.*  When shall we meet again?—Are we
    not those
Whom most he loved on earth, and think'st thou
    not
*That* love e'en yet shall bring his spirit near
While thus we hold communion?
    *Procida.*        Yes, I feel
Its breathing influence whilst I look on thee,
Who wert its light in life.   Yet will we not
Make womanish tears our offering on his tomb;
He shall have nobler tribute!—I must hence,
But thou shalt soon hear more.   Await the time.
    *[Exeunt separately.*

------

SCENE III.—*The Sea-Shore.*

RAIMOND DI PROCIDA, CONSTANCE.

    *Constance.*   There is a shadow far within your
    eye
Which hath of late been deepening.   You were
    wont
Upon the clearness of your open brow
To wear a brighter spirit, shedding round
Joy like our southern sun.   It is not wel..
If some dark thought be gathering o'er your soul,
To hide it from affection   Why is this,
My Raimond, why is this?
    *Raimond.*        Oh! from the dreams
Of youth, sweet Constance, hath not manhood still
A wild and stormy wakening?—They depart,
Light after light, our glorious visions fade,
The vaguely beautiful! till earth, unveil'd,

Lies pale around; and life's realities
Press on the soul, from its unfathom'd depth
Rousing the fiery feelings, and proud thoughts,
In all their fearful strength!—'T is ever thus,
And doubly so with me; for I awoke
With high aspirings, making it a curse
To breathe where noble minds are bow'd, as here.
—To breathe!—It is not breath!
    *Constance.*        I know thy grief,
—And is 't not mine?—for those devoted men
Doom'd with their life to expiate some wild word,
Born of the social hour.   Oh! I have knelt,
E'en at my brother's feet, with fruitless tears,
Imploring him to spare.   His heart is shut
Against my voice; yet will I not forsake
The cause of mercy.
    *Raimond.*  Waste not thou thy prayers,
Oh, gentle love, for them.   There's little need
For Pity, though the galling chain be worn
By some few slaves the less.   Let them depart!
There is a world beyond the oppressor's reach,
And thither lies their way.
    *Constance.*       Alas! I see
That some new wrong hath pierced you to the soul.
    *Raimond.*   Pardon, beloved Constance, if my
    words,
From feelings hourly stung, have caught, per-
    chance,
A tone of bitterness.—Oh! when thine eyes,
With their sweet eloquent thoughtfulness, are
    fix'd
Thus tenderly on mine, I should forget
All else in their soft beams; and yet I came
To tell thee——
    *Constance.*    What?   What wouldst thou say?
    O speak!—
Thou wouldst not leave me!
    *Raimond.*       I have cast a cloud,
The shadow of dark thoughts and ruin'd fortunes,
O'er thy bright spirit.   Haply, were I gone,
Thou wouldst resume thyself, and dwell once more
In the clear sunny light of youth and joy,
E'en as before we met—before we loved!
    *Constance.*   This is but mockery.—Well thou
    know'st thy love
Hath given me nobler being; made my heart
A home for all the deep sublimities
Of strong affection; and I would not change
Th' exalted life I draw from that pure source,
With all its chequer'd hues of hope and fear,
Ev'n for the brightest calm.   Thou most unkind'
Have I deserved this?
    *Raimond.*      Oh! thou hast deserved
A love less fatal to thy peace than mine.
Think not 't is mockery:—But I cannot rest
To be the scorn'd and trampled thing I am
In this degraded land.   Its very skies,
That smile as if but festivals were held
Beneath their cloudless azure, weigh me down
With a dull sense of bondage, and I pine
For freedom's charter'd air.   I would go forth
To seek my noble father; he hath been
Too long a lonely exile, and his name
Seems fading in the dim obscurity
Which gathers round my fortunes.
    *Constance.*      Must we part?
And is it come to this?   Oh! I have still
Deem'd it enough of joy with *thee* to share
E'en grief itself—and now—but this is vain;
Alas! too deep, too fond, is woman's love.
Too full of hope, she casts on troubled waves
The treasures of her soul!
    *Raimond.*      Oh, speak not thus!
Thy gentle and desponding tones fall cold
Upon my inmost heart.—I leave thee but
To be more worthy of a love like thine.
For I have dreamt of fame!—A few short years
And we may yet be blest.
    *Constance.*      A few short years!
Less time may well suffice for death and fate
To work all change on earth!—To break the ties
Which early love had form'd; and to bow down
Th' elastic spirit, and to blight each flower
Strewn in life's crowded path!—But be it so!
Be it enough to know that happiness
Meets thee on other shores.

*Raimond.*                    Where'er I roam,
Thou shalt be with my soul!—Thy soft low voice
Shall rise upon remembrance, like a strain
Of music heard in boyhood, bringing back
Life's morning freshness.—Oh! that there should be
Things, which we love with such deep tenderness,
But, through that love, to learn how much of woe
Dwells in one hour like this!—Yet weep thou not!
We shall meet soon; and many days, dear love,
Ere I depart.
   *Constance.*       Then there's a respite still.
Days!—not a day but in its course may bring
Some strange vicissitude to turn aside
Th' impending blow we shrink from.—Fare thee
    well.                              (*returning*)
—Oh, Raimond! this is not our *last* farewell!
Thou wouldst not so deceive me?
   *Raimond.*                    Doubt me not,
Gentlest and best beloved! we meet again.
                   [*Exit* CONSTANCE.
   *Raimond* (*after a pause.*)  When shall I breathe
    in freedom, and give scope
To those untameable and burning thoughts,
And restless aspirations, which consume
My heart i' th' land of bondage?—Oh! with you,
Ye everlasting images of power,
And of infinity! thou blue-rolling deep,
And you, ye stars! whose beams are characters
Wherewith the oracles of fate are traced;
With you my soul finds room, and casts aside
The weight that doth oppress her.—But my
    thoughts
Are wandering far; there should be one to share
This awful and majestic solitude
Of sea and heaven with me.
           [PROCIDA *enters unobserved.*
           It is the hour
He named, and yet he comes not.
   *Procida* (*coming forward.*)       He is here.
   *Raimond.* Now, thou mysterious stranger, thou,
    whose glance
Doth fix itself on memory, and pursue
Thought, like a spirit, haunting its lone hours;
Reveal thyself; what art thou?
   *Procida.*                    One, whose life
Hath been a troubled stream, and made its way
Through rocks and darkness, and a thousand
    storms,
With still a mighty aim. But now the shades
Of eve are gathering round me, and I come
To this, my native land, that I may rest
Beneath its vines in peace.
   *Raimond.*                    Seek'st thou for peace?
This is no land of peace: unless that deep
And voiceless terror, which doth freeze men's
    thoughts
Back to their source, and mantle its pale mien
With a dull hollow semblance of repose,
May so be called.
   *Procida.*       There are such calms full oft
Preceding earthquakes. But I have not been
So vainly school'd by fortune, and inured
To shape my course on peril's dizzy brink,
That it should irk my spirit to put on
Such guise of hush'd submissiveness as best
May suit the troubled aspect of the times.
   *Raimond.* Why, then, thou art welcome, stran-
    ger, to the land
Where most disguise is needful.—He were bold
Who now should wear his thoughts upon his brow
Beneath Sicilian skies. The brother's eye
Doth search distrustfully the brother's face;
And friends, whose undivided lives have drawn
From the same past their long remembrances,
Now meet in terror, or no more; lest hearts
Full to o'erflowing, in their social hour,
Should pour out some rash word, which roving
    winds
Might whisper to our conquerors.—This it is,
To wear a foreign yoke.
   *Procida.*       It matters not
To him who holds the mastery o'er his spirit,
And can suppress its workings, till endurance
Becomes as nature. We can tame ourselves
To all extremes, and there is that in life

To which we cling with most tenacious grasp,
Ev'n when its lofty claims are all reduced
To the poor common privilege of breathing.—
Why dost thou turn away?
   *Raimond.*       What wouldst thou with me?
I deem'd thee, by th' ascendant soul which lived,
And made its throne on thy commanding brow,
One of a sovereign nature, which would scorn
So to abase its high capacities
For aught on earth. But thou art like the rest.
What wouldst thou with me?
   *Procida.*                    I would counsel thee.
Thou must do that which men—ay, valiant men,—
Hourly submit to do; in the proud court,
And in the stately camp and at the board
Of midnight revellers, whose flush'd mirth is all
A strife, won hardly.—Where is he whose heart
Lies bare, through all its foldings, to the gaze
Of mortal eye?—If vengeance wait the foe,
Or fate th' oppressor, 't is in depths conceal'd
Beneath a smiling surface.—Youth! I say,
Keep thy soul down!—Put on a mask!—'t is worn
Alike by power and weakness, and the smooth
And specious intercourse of life requires
Its aid in every scene.
   *Raimond.*                    Away, dissembler!
Life hath its high and its ignoble tasks,
Fitted to every nature. Will the free
And royal eagle stoop to learn the arts
By which the serpent wins his spell-bound prey?
It is because I *will* not clothe myself
In a vile garb of coward semblances,
That now, e'en now, I struggle with my heart,
To bid what most I love a long farewell,
And seek my country on some distant shore,
Where such things are unknown!
   *Procida* (*exultingly.*)       Why, this is joy:
After a long conflict with the doubts and fears,
And the poor subtleties of meaner minds,
To meet a spirit, whose bold elastic wing
Oppression hath not crush'd.—High-hearted youth!
Thy father, should his footsteps ere again
Visit these shores——
   *Raimond.*       My father! what of him?
Speak! was he known to thee?
   *Procida.*       In distant lands
With him I've traversed many a wild, and look'd
On many a danger; and the thought that thou
Wert smiling then in peace, a happy boy,
Oft through the storm hath cheer'd him.
   *Raimond.*                    Dost thou deem
That still he lives?—Oh! if it be in chains,
In woe, in poverty's obscurest cell,
Say but he lives—and I will track his steps
E'en to earth's verge!
   *Procida.*       It may be that he lives,
Though long his name hath ceased to be a word
Familiar in man's dwellings. But its sound
May yet be heard!—Raimond di Procida,
Rememberest thou thy father?
   *Raimond.*                    From my mind
His form hath faded long, for years have pass'd
Since he went forth to exile: but a vague,
Yet powerful image of deep majesty,
Still dimly gathering round each thought of him,
Doth claim instinctive reverence; and my love
For his inspiring name hath long become
Part of my being.
   *Procida.*       Raimond! doth no voice
Speak to thy soul, and tell thee whose the arms
That would enfold thee now?—My son! my son!
   *Raimond.* Father!—Oh God!—my father! Now
    I know
Why my heart woke before thee!
   *Procida.*                    Oh! this hour
Makes hope reality; for thou art all
My dreams had pictured thee!
   *Raimond.*                    Yet why so long,
E'en as a stranger hast thou cross'd my paths,
One nameless and unknown?—and yet I felt
Each pulse within me thrilling to thy voice.
   *Procida.* Because I would not link thy fate with
    mine,
Till I could hail the day-spring of that hope
Which now is gathering round us.—Listen, youth!
*Thou* hast told me of a subdued and scorn'd,

And trampled land, whose very soul is bow'd
And fashion'd to her chains—but *I* tell *thee*
Of a most generous and devoted land,
A land of kindling energies; a land
Of glorious recollections!—proudly true
To the high memory of her ancient kings,
And rising, in majestic scorn, to cast
Her alien bondage off!
 *Raimond.*   And where is this?
 *Procida.* Here, in our isle, our own fair Sicily!
Her spirit is awake, and moving on,
In its deep silence mightier, to regain
Her place amongst the nations; and the hour
Of that tremendous effort is at hand.
 *Raimond.* Can it be thus indeed?—Thou pour'st
  new life
Through all my burning veins!—I am as one
Awakening from a chill and death-like sleep
To the full glorious day.
 *Procida.*   Thou shalt hear more!
Thou shalt hear things which would—which *will*
  arouse
The proud, free spirits of our ancestors
E'en from their marble rest. Yet mark me well!
Be secret!—for along my destined path
I yet must darkly move.—Now, follow me;
And join a band of men, in whose high hearts
There lies a nation's strength.
 *Raimond.*   My noble father!
Thy words have given me all for which I pined—
An aim, a hope, a purpose!—And the blood
Doth rush in warmer currents through my veins,
As a bright fountain from its icy bonds
By the quick sun-stroke freed.
 *Procida.*   Ay, this is well!
Such natures' burst men's chains!—Now, follow
 me.        [*Exeunt*

### ACT THE SECOND.

#### Scene I.—*Apartment in a Palace.*

#### Eribert, Constance.

 *Constance.* Will you not hear me?—Oh! that
  they who need
Hourly forgiveness, they who do but live,
While mercy's voice, beyond th' eternal stars,
Wins the great Judge to listen, should be thus,
In their vain exercise of pageant power.
Hard and relentless!—Gentle brother, yet
'Tis in your choice to imitate that heaven
Whose noblest joy is pardon.
 *Eribert.*   'Tis too late.
You have a soft and moving voice, which pleads
With eloquent melody—but they must die.
 *Constance.* What!—die!—for words?—for breath,
  which leaves no trace
To sully the pure air, wherewith it blends,
And is, being utter'd, gone?—Why, 't were enough
For such a venial fault to be deprived
One little day of man's free heritage,
Heaven's warm and sunny light!—Oh! if you
  deem
That evil harbours in their souls, at least
Delay the stroke, till guilt, made manifest,
Shall bid stern Justice wake.
 *Eribert.*   I am not one
Of those weak spirits, that timorously keep watch
For fair occasions, thence to borrow hues
Of virtue for their deeds. My school hath been
Where power sits crown'd and arm'd.—And, mark
 me, sister!
To a distrustful nature it might seem
Strange, that your lips thus earnestly should plead
For these Sicilian rebels. O'er *my* being
Suspicion holds no power.—And yet, take note
—I have said, and they must die.
 *Constance.*   Have you no fear?
 *Eribert.* Of what?—that heaven should fall?
 *Constance.* No!—But that earth
Should arm in madness.—Brother! I have seen

Dark eyes bent on you, e'en midst festal throngs,
With such deep hatred settled in their glance,
My heart hath died within me.
 *Eribert.*   Am I then
To pause, and doubt, and shrink, because a girl,
A dreaming girl, hath trembled at a look?
 *Constance.* Oh! looks are no illusions, when the
  soul,
Which may not speak in words, can find no way
But theirs, to liberty!—Have not these men
Brave sons, or noble brothers?
 *Eribert.*   Yes! whose name
It rests with me to make a word of fear,
A sound forbidden 'midst the haunts of men.
 *Constance.* But not forgotten!—Ah! beware,
  beware!
—Nay, look not sternly on me.—There is one
Of that devoted band, who yet will need
Years to be ripe for death.—He is a youth,
A very boy, on whose unshaded cheek
The spring-time glow is lingering. 'Twas but now
His mother left me, with a timid hope
Just dawning in her breast; and I—I dared
To foster its faint spark.—You smile!—Oh! then
He will be saved!
 *Eribert.*  Nay, I but smiled to think
What a fond fool is Hope!—She may be taught
To deem that the great sun will change his course
To work her pleasure; or the tomb give back
Its inmates to her arms. In sooth, 'tis strange!
Yet, with your pitying heart, you should not thus
Have mock'd the boy's sad mother—I have said,
You should not thus have *mock'd* her!—Now, fare-
  well!      [*Exit* Eribert.
 *Constance.* Oh, brother! hard of heart!—for
  deeds like these
There must be fearful chastening, if on high
Justice doth hold her state.—And I must tell
Yon desolate mother that her fair young son
Is thus to perish!—Haply the dread tale
May slay *her* too;—for heaven is merciful.
—'Twill be a bitter task!  [*Exit* Constance.

#### Scene II.—*A ruined Tower, surrounded by Woods*

#### Procida, Vittoria.

 *Procida.* Thy vassals are prepared then?
 *Vittoria.*   Yes, they wait
Thy summons to their task.
 *Procida.*  Keep the flame bright,
But hidden, till this hour.—Wouldst thou dare,
  lady,
To join our councils at the night's mid watch,
In the lone cavern by the rock-hewn cross?
 *Vittoria.* What should I shrink from?
 *Procida.*  Oh! the forest paths
Are dim and wild, e'en when the sunshine streams
Through their high arches: but when powerful
  night
Comes, with her cloudy phantoms, and her pale
Uncertain moonbeams, and the hollow sounds
Of her mysterious winds; their aspect *then*
Is of another and more fearful world;
A realm of indistinct and shadowy forms,
Waking strange thoughts, almost too much for
  this,
Our frail terrestrial nature.
 *Vittoria.*  Well I know
All this, and more. Such scenes have been th'
  abodes
Where through the silence of my soul have pass'd
Voices, and visions from the sphere of those
That have to die no more!—Nay, doubt it not!
If such unearthly intercourse hath e'er
Been granted to our nature, 'tis to hearts
Whose love is with the dead. They, they alone,
Unmadden'd could sustain the fearful joy
And glory of its trances!—at the hour
Which makes guilt tremulous, and peoples earth
And air with infinite, viewless multitudes,
I will be with thee, Procida.
 *Procida.*   Thy presence
Will kindle nobler thoughts, and, in the souls
Of suffering and indignant men, arouse

That which may strengthen our majestic cause
With yet a deeper power.—Know'st thou the spot?
  *Vittoria.*                Full well.   There is no scene so wild
    and lone
In these dim woods, but I have visited
I s tangled shades.
  *Procida.*                At midnight, then, we meet.
                                    [*Exit* Procida.
  *Vittoria.*   Why should I fear?—Thou wilt be
    with me, thou
Th' immortal dream and shadow of my soul,
Spirit of him I love! that meet'st me still
In loneliness and silence; in the noon
Of the wild night, and in the forest depths,
Known but to me; for whom thou giv'st the winds
And sighing leaves a cadence of thy voice,
Till my heart faints with that o'erthrilling joy!
—Thou wilt be with me there, and lend my lips
Words, fiery words, to flush dark cheeks with
    shame,
That thou art unavenged!            [*Exit* Vittoria.

------

Scene III.—*A Chapel, with a Monument, on which
    is laid a Sword.—Moonlight.*

Procida, Raimond, Montalba.

  *Montalba.*   And know you not my story?
  *Procida.*                In the lands
Where I have been a wanderer, your deep wrongs
Were number'd with our country's; but their tale
Came only in faint echoes to mine ear.
I would fain hear it now.
  *Montalba.*                Hark! while you spoke,
There was a voice like murmur in the breeze,
Which ev'n like death came o'er me;—'t was a
    night
Like this, of clouds contending with the moon,
A night of sweeping winds, of rustling leaves,
And swift wild shadows floating o'er the earth,
Clothed with a phantom life; when, after years
Of battle and captivity, I spurr'd
My good steed homewards. — Oh! what lovely
    dreams
Rose on my spirit!—There were tears and smiles,
But all of joy!—And there were bounding steps,
And clinging arms, whose passionate clasp of love
Doth twine so fondly round the warrior's neck,
When his plumed helm is doff'd. —Hence, feeble
    thoughts!
—I am sterner now, yet once such dreams were
    mine!
  *Raimond.*   And were they realized?
  *Montalba.*                Youth! Ask me not,
But listen!—I drew near my own fair home;
There was no light along its walls, no sound
Of bugle, pealing from the watch-tower's height
At my approach, although my trampling steed
Made the earth ring; yet the wide gates were
    thrown
All open.—Then my heart misgave me first,
And on the threshold of my silent hall
I paused a moment, and the wind swept by
With the same deep and dirge-like tone, which
    pierced
My soul e'en now.—I call'd—my struggling voice
Gave utterance to my wife's, my children's names;
They answer'd not—I roused my failing strength,
And wildly rush'd within.—And they were there.
  *Raimond.*   And was all well?
  *Montalba.*                Ay, well!—for death is well,
And they were all at rest!—I see them yet,
Pale in their innocent beauty, which had fail'd
To stay th' assassin's arm!
  *Raimond.*                Oh, righteous Heaven!
Who had done this?
  *Montalba.*                Who!
  *Procida.*                Canst thou question, *who?*
Whom hath the earth to perpetrate such deeds,
In the cold-blooded revelry of crime,
 -But those whose yoke is on us?
  *Raimond.*                Man of woe!
What words hath pity for despair like thine?
  *Montalba.*   Pity!—fond youth!—My soul disdains
    the grief

Which doth club some its deep secrecies,
To ask a vain companionship of tears,
And so to be relieved!
  *Procida.*                For woes like these,
There is no sympathy but vengeance.
  *Montalba.*                None!
Therefore I brought you hither, that your hearts
Might catch the spirit of the scene!—Look round!
We are in the awful presence of the dead;
Within yon tomb *they* sleep, whose gentle blood
Weighs down the murderer's soul.—*They* sleep!—
    but I
Am wakeful o'er their dust!—I laid my sword,
Without its sheath, on their sepulchral stone,
As on an altar; and the eternal stars,
And heaven, and night, bore witness to my vow,
No more to wield it, save in one great cause,
The vengeance of the grave!—And now the hour
Of that atonement comes!
                [*He takes the sword from the tomb.*
  *Raimond.*   My spirit burns!
And my full heart almost to bursting swells.
—Oh! for the day of battle!
  *Procida.*                Raimond, they
Whose souls are dark with guiltless blood must
    die;
—But not in battle.
  *Raimond.*                How, my father?
  *Procida.*                No!
Look on that sepulchre, and it will teach
Another lesson.—But th' appointed hour
Advances.—Thou wilt join our chosen band,
Noble Montalba?
  *Montalba.*                Leave me for a time,
That I may calm my soul by intercourse
With the still dead, before I mix with men,
And with their passions.  I have nursed for years
In silence and in solitude, the flame
Which doth consume me; and it is not used
Thus to be look'd or breathed on.—Procida!
I would be tranquil—or appear so—ere
I join your brave confederates.  Through my heart
There struck a pang—but it will soon have pass'd
  *Procida.*   Remember!—in the cavern by the cross
Now, follow me, my son.
                [*Exeunt* Procida *and* Raimond
  *Montalba* (*after a pause, leaning on the tomb.*)
                                    Said he,
" *My son?*"—Now, why should this man's life
Go down in hope, thus resting on a son,
And I be desolate?—How strange a sound
Was that—" *my son!*"—I had a boy, who might
Have worn as free a soul upon his brow
As doth this youth.—Why should the thought of
    *him*
Thus haunt me?—when I tread the peopled ways
Of life again, I shall be pass'd each hour
By fathers with their children, and I must
Learn calmly to look on.—Methinks 't were now
A gloomy consolation to behold
All men bereft, as I am!—But away,
Vain thoughts!—One task is left for blighted
    hearts,
And it shall be fulfill'd.            [*Exit* Montalba.

------

Scene IV.—*Entrance of a Cave, surrounded by
    Rocks and Forests.  A rude Cross seen among
    the Rocks.*

Procida, Raimond.

  *Procida.*   And is it thus, beneath the solemn skies
Of midnight, and in solitary caves,
Where the wild forest creatures make their lair,—
Is 't thus the chiefs of Sicily must hold
The councils of their country?
  *Raimond.*                Why, such scenes
In their primeval majesty, beheld
Thus by faint starlight, and the partial glare
Of the red-streaming lava, will inspire
Far deeper thoughts than pillar'd halls, wherein
Statesmen hold weary vigils.—Are we not
O'ershadow'd by that Etna, which of old
With its dread prophecies, hath struck dismay
Through tyrants' hearts, and bade them seek a
    home

In other climes ?—Hark ! from its depths e'en now
What hollow moans are sent !

*Enter* MONTALBA, GUIDO, *and other* SICILIANS.

*Procida.* Welcome, my brave associates !—We
    can share
The wolf's wild freedom here !—Th' oppressor's
    haunt
Is not 'midst rocks and caves. Are we all met ?
*Sicilians.* All, all !
*Procida.* The torch-light, sway'd by every gust,
But dimly shows your features.—Where is he
Who from his battles had return'd to breathe
Once more without a corselet, and to meet
The voices, and the footsteps, and the smiles,
Blent with his dreams of home ?—Of that dark tale
The rest is known to vengeance !—Art thou here,
With thy deep wrongs, and resolute despair,
Childless Montalba ?
    *Montalba (advancing.)* He is at thy side.
Call on that desolate father, in the hour
When his revenge is nigh.
    *Procida.* Thou, too, come forth,
From thine own halls an exile !—Dost thou make
The mountain-fastnesses thy dwelling still,
While hostile banners, o'er thy rampart walls,
Wave their proud bluzonry ?
    *First Sicilian.* Even so. I stood,
Last night, before my own ancestral towers
An unknown outcast, while the tempest beat
On my bare head—what reck'd it ?—There was joy
Within, and revelry ; the festive lamps
Were streaming from each turret, and gay songs,
I' th' stranger's tongue, made mirth. They little
    deem'd
Who heard their melodies !—but there are thoughts
Best nurtured in the wild ; there are dread vows
Known to the mountain echoes.—Procida !
Call on the outcast, when revenge is nigh.
    *Procida.* I knew a young Sicilian, one whose
    heart
Should be all fire. On that most guilty day,
When, with our martyr'd Conradin, the flower
Of the land's knighthood perish'd ; he, of whom
I speak, a weeping boy, whose innocent tears
Melted a thousand hearts that dared not aid,
Stood by the scaffold with extended arms,
Calling upon his father, whose last look
Turn'd full on him its parting agony.
The father's blood gush'd o'er him !—and the boy
Then dried his tears, and with a kindling eye,
And a proud flush on his young cheek, look'd up
To the bright heaven.—Doth he remember still
That bitter hour ?
    *Second Sicilian.* He bears a sheathless sword !
—Call on the orphan when revenge is nigh.
    *Procida.* Our band shows gallantly—but there
    are men
Who should be with us now, had they not dared
In some wild moment of festivity
To give their full hearts way, and breathe a wish
For freedom !—and some traitor—it might be
A breeze perchance—bore the forbidden sound
To Eribert :—so they must die—unless
Fate (who at times is wayward) should select
Some other victim first !—But have they not
Brothers or sons among us ?
    *Guido.* Look on me !
I have a brother, a young high-soul'd boy,
And beautiful as a sculptor's dream, with brow
That wears, amidst its dark rich curls, the stamp
Of inborn nobleness. In truth, he is
A glorious creature !—But his doom is seal'd
With their's of whom you spoke ; and I have
    knelt—
—Ay, scorn me not ! 't was for his life—I knelt
E'en at the viceroy's feet, and he put on
That heartless laugh of cold malignity
We know so well, and spurn'd me.—But the stain
Of shame like this, takes blood to wash it off,
And thus it shall be cancell'd !—Call on me,
When the stern moment of revenge is nigh.
    *Procida.* I call upon thee *now* ! The land's high
    soul
Is roused, and moving onward, like a breeze
Or a swift sunbeam, kindling nature's hues

To deeper life before it. In his chains,
The peasant dreams of freedom !—Ay, 'tis thus
Oppression fans th' imperishable flame
With most unconscious hands.—No praise be her's
For what she blindly works !—When slavery's cup
O'erflows its bounds, the creeping poison, meant
To dull our senses, through each burning vein
Pours fever, lending a delirious strength
To burst man's fetters—and they *shall* be burst
I have hoped, when hope seem'd frenzy ; but a
    power
Abides in human will, when bent with strong
Unswerving energy on one great aim,
To make and rule its fortunes !—I have been
A wanderer in the fullness of my years,
A restless pilgrim of the earth and seas,
Gathering the generous thoughts of other lands,
To aid our holy cause. And aid is near :
But we must give the signal. Now, before
The majesty of yon pure Heaven, whose eye
Is on our hearts, whose righteous arm befriends
The arm that strikes for freedom ; speak ! decree
The fate of our oppressors.
    *Montalba.* Let them fall
When dreaming least of peril !—When the heart,
Basking in sunny pleasure, doth forget
That hate may smile, but sleeps not.—Hide th
    sword
With a thick veil of myrtle, and in halls
Of banqueting, where the full wine-cup shines
Red in the festal torch-light ; meet we there,
And bid them welcome to the feast of death.
    *Procida.* Thy voice is low and broken, and thy
    words
Scarce meet our ears.
    *Montalba.* Why, then, I thus repeat
Their import. Let th' avenging sword burst forth
In some free festal hour—and woe to him
Who first shall spare !
    *Raimond.* Must innocence and guilt
Perish alike ?
    *Montalba.* Who talks of innocence ?
When hath *their* hand been stay'd for innocence ?
Let them all perish !—Heaven will choose its own
Why should *their* children live ?—The earthquake
    whelms
Its undistinguish'd thousands, making graves
Of peopled cities in its path—and this
Is Heaven's dread justice—ay, and it is well !
Why then should *we* be tender, when the skies
Deal thus with man ?—What, if the infant bleed ?
Is there not power to hush the mother's pangs ?
What, if the youthful bride perchance should fall
In her triumphant beauty ?—Should we pause ?
As if death were not mercy to the pangs
Which make our lives the records of our woes ?
Let them all perish !—And if one be found
Amidst our band to stay th' avenging steel
For pity, or remorse, or boyish love,
Then be his doom as theirs !     [*A pause.*
    Why gaze ye thus !
Brethren, what means your silence !
    *Sicilians.* Be it so !
If one among us stay th' avenging steel
For love or pity, be his doom as theirs ?
Pledge we our faith to this !
    *Raimond (rushing forward indignantly.)* Our
    faith to *this* !
No ! I but *dreamt* I heard it :—Can it be ?
My countrymen ! my father !—Is it thus
That freedom should be won ?—Awake ! Awake
To loftier thoughts !—Lift up, exultingly,
On the crown'd heights and to the sweeping winds,
Your glorious banner !—Let your trumpet's blast
Make the tombs thrill with echoes ! Call aloud,
Proclaim from all your hills, the land shall bear
The stranger's yoke no longer !—What is he
Who carries on his practised lip a smile,
Beneath his vest a dagger, which but waits
Till the heart bounds with joy, to still its beatings ?
That which our nature's instinct doth recoil from,
And our blood curdle at—Ay, yours and mine—
A murderer !—Heard ye ?—Shall that name with
    ours
Go down to after days ?—Oh, friends ! a cause

Like that for which we rise, hath made bright
      names
Of the elder time as rallying words to men,
Sounds full of might and immortality!
And shall not ours be such?
  *Montalba.*      Fond dreamer, peace!
Fame! What is fame?—Will our unconscious dust
Start into thrilling rapture from the grave,
At the vain breath of praise?—I tell ye, youth,
Our souls are parch'd with agonizing thirst,
Which must be quench'd though death were in the
      draught:
We must have vengeance, for our foes have left
No other joy unblighted.
  *Procida.*      Oh! my son,
The time is past for such high dreams as thine,
Thou know'st not whom we deal with. Knightly
      faith
And chivalrous honour, are but things whereon
They cast disdainful pity. We must meet
Falsehood with wiles, and insult with revenge.
And for our names—whate'er the deeds, by which
We burst our bondage—is it not enough
That in the chronicle of days to come,
We, through a bright ' For Ever,' shall be call'd
The men who saved their country?
  *Raimond.*      Many a land
Hath bow'd beneath the yoke, and then arisen,
As a strong lion rending silken bonds,
And on the open field, before high Heaven,
Won such majestic vengeance, as hath made
Its name a power on earth.—Ay, nations own
It is enough of glory to be call'd
The children of the mighty, who redeem'd
Their native soil—but not by means like these.
  *Montalba.* I have no children.—Of Montalba's
      blood
Not one red drop doth circle through the veins
Of aught that breathes?—Why, what have *I* to do
With far futurity?—My spirit lives
But in the past.—Away! when thou dost stand
On this fair earth, as doth a blasted tree
Which the warm sun revives not, *then* return,
Strong in thy desolation; but till then,
Thou art not for our purpose; we have need
Of more unshrinking hearts.
  *Raimond.*      Montalba! know,
I shrink from crime alone. Oh! if my voice
Might yet have power among you, I would say,
Associates, leaders, *be* avenged! but yet
As knights, as warriors!
  *Montalba.*      Peace! have we not borne
Th' indelible taint of contumely and chains?
We *are not* knights and warriors.—Our bright crests
Have been defiled and trampled to the earth,
Boy! we are slaves—and our revenge shall be
Deep as a slave's disgrace.
  *Raimond.*      Why, then, farewell:
I leave you to your counsels. He that still
Would hold his lofty nature undebased,
And his name pure, were but a loiterer here.
  *Procida.* And is it thus indeed?—dost *thou*
      forsake
Our cause, my son!
  *Raimond.*      Oh, father! what proud hopes
This hour hath blighted!—yet, whate'er betide,
It is a noble privilege to look up
Fearless in heaven's bright face—and this is mine,
And shall be still.      [*Exit* RAIMOND.
  *Procida.*      He's gone!—Why, let it be!
I trust our Sicily hath many a son
Valiant as mine. Associates! 't is decreed
Our foes shall perish. We have but to name
The hour, the scene, the signal.
  *Montalba.*      It should be
In the full city, when some festival
Hath gather'd throngs, and lull'd infatuate hearts
To brief security. Hark! is there not
A sound of hurrying footsteps on the breeze?
We are betray'd.—Who art thou?

      VITTORIA *enters.*

  *Procida.*      One alone
Should be thus daring. Lady, lift the veil
That shades thy noble brow

(*She raises her veil, the Sicilians draw back with
      respect.*)
  *Sicilians.*      Th' affianced bride
Of our lost king!
  *Procida.*      And more, Montalba; know
Within this form there dwells a soul as high
As warriors in their battles e'er have proved,
Or patriots on the scaffold.
  *Vittoria.*      Valiant men!
I come to ask your aid. You see me, one
Whose widow'd youth hath all been consecrate
To a proud sorrow, and whose life is held
In token and memorial of the dead.
Say, is it meet that lingering thus on earth,
But to behold one great atonement made,
And keep one name from fading in men's hearts,
A tyrant's will should force me to profane
Heaven's altar with unhallow'd vows—and live
Stung by the keen unutterable scorn
Of my own bosom, live—another's bride?
  *Sicilians.* Never, oh, never!—fear not, noble
      lady!
Worthy of Conradin!
  *Vittoria.*      Yet hear me still.
*His* bride, that Eribert's, who notes our tears
With his insulting eye of cold derision,
And, could he pierce the depths where feeling
      works,
Would number e'en our agonies as crimes.
—Say, is this meet?
  *Guido.*      We deem'd these nuptials, lady.
Thy willing choice; but 't is a joy to find
Thou art noble still. Fear not; by all our wrongs,
This shall not be.
  *Procida.*      Vittoria, thou art come
To ask our aid, but we have need of thine.
Know, the completion of our high designs
Requires—a festival: and it must be
Thy bridal!
  *Vittoria.* Procida!
  *Procida.*      Nay, start not thus,
'T is no hard task to bind your raven hair
With festal garlands, and to bid the song
Rise, and the wine-cup mantle. No—nor yet
To meet your suitor at the glitt'ring shrine,
Where death, not love, awaits him!
  *Vittoria.*      Can my soul
Dissemble thus?
  *Procida.*      We have no other means
Of winning our great birthright back from those
Who have usurp'd it, than so lulling them
Into vain confidence, that they may deem
All wrongs forgot; and this may be best done
By what I ask of thee.
  *Montalba.*      Then we will mix
With the flush'd revellers, making their gay feast
The harvest of the grave.
  *Vittoria.*      A bridal day!
—Must it be so?—Then, chiefs of Sicily,
I bid you to my nuptials! but be there
With your bright swords unsheathed, for thus alone
My guests should be adorn'd.
  *Procida.*      And let thy banquet
Be soon announced, for there are noble men
Sentenced to die, for whom we fain would purchase
Reprieve with other blood.
  *Vittoria.*      Be it then the day
Preceding that appointed for their doom.
  *Guido.* My brother, thou shalt live!—Oppression
      boasts
No gift of prophecy!—It but remains
To name our signal, chiefs!
  *Montalba.*      The Vesper-bell.
  *Procida.* Even so, the Vesper-bell, whose deep-
      toned peal
Is heard o'er land and wave. Part of our band,
Wearing the guise of antic revelry,
Shall enter, as in some fantastic pageant,
The halls of Eribert; and at the hour
Devoted to the sword's tremendous task,
I follow with the rest.—The Vesper-bell!
That sound shall wake th' avenger; for 't is come
The time when power is in a voice, a breath,
To burst the spell which bound us. But the night
Is waning, with her stars, which, one by one,

Warn us to part.  Friends, to your homes!—your,
    homes?
That name is yet to win.—Away, prepare
For our next meeting in Palermo's walls.
The Vesper-bell!  Remember!
    Sicilians.                          Fear us not.
The Vesper-bell!                    [Exeunt omnes.

ACT THE THIRD.

Scene I.—Apartment in a Palace.

Eribert, Vittoria.

Vittoria.  Speak not of love—it is a word with
    deep,
Strange magic in its melancholy sound,
To summon up the dead; and they should rest,
At such an hour, forgotten.  There are things
We must throw from us, when the heart would
    gather
Strength to fulfil its settled purposes;
Therefore, no more of love!—But, if to robe
This form in bridal ornaments, to smile,
(I can smile yet,) at thy gay feast, and stand
At th' altar by thy side; if this be deem'd
Enough, it shall be done.
    Eribert.                          My fortune's star
Doth rule th' ascendant still!  (Apart.)—If not of
    love,
Then pardon, lady, that I speak of joy,
And with exulting heart——
    Vittoria.                          There is no joy!
—Who shall look through the far futurity,
And, as the shadowy visions of events
Develop on his gaze, 'midst their dim throng,
Dare, with oracular mien, to point, and say,
" This will bring happiness?"—Who shall do this?
—Who, thou and I, and all!—There 's One, who
    sits
In His own bright tranquillity enthroned,
High o'er all storms, and looking far beyond
Their thickest clouds; but we, from whose dull
    eyes
A grain of dust hides the great sun, e'en as
Usurp his attributes, and talk, as seers,
Of future joy and grief!
    Eribert.                          Thy words are strange.
Yet will I hope that peace at length shall settle
Upon thy troubled heart, and add soft grace
To thy majestic beauty.—Fair Vittoria!
Oh! if my cares——
    Vittoria.                          I know a day shall come
Of peace to all.  Ev'n from my darken'd spirit
Soon shall each restless wish be exorcised,
Which haunts it now, and I shall then lie down
Serenely to repose.  Of this no more.
—I have a boon to ask.
    Eribert.                          Command my power,
And deem it thus most honour'd.
    Vittoria.                          Have I then
Soar'd such an eagle-pitch, as to command
The mighty Eribert?—And yet 'tis meet;
For I bethink me now, I should have worn
A crown upon this forehead.—Generous lord!
Since thus you give me freedom, know, there is
An hour I have loved from childhood, and a sound
Whose tones, o'er earth and ocean sweetly bearing
A sense of deep repose, have lull'd me oft
To peace—which is forgetfulness; I mean
The Vesper-bell.  I pray you let it be
The summons to our bridal—Hear you not?
To our fair bridal!
    Eribert.                          Lady, let your will
Appoint each circumstance.  I am too bless'd,
Proving my homage thus.
    Vittoria.                          Why, then, 'tis mine
To rule the glorious fortunes of the day,
And I may be content.  Yet much remains
For thought to brood on, and I would be left
Alone with my resolves.  Kind Eribert!
(Whom I command so absolutely,) now
Part we a few brief hours; and doubt not, when
I am at thy side once more, but I shall stand
There—to the last.

    Eribert.                          Your smiles are troubled, lady;
May they ere long be brighter!—Time will seem
Slow till the Vesper-bell.
    Vittoria.                          'Tis lover's phrase
To say—Time lags; and therefore meet for you:
But with an equal pace the hour moves on,
Whether they bear, on their swift silent wing,
Pleasure or—fate.
    Eribert.                          Be not so full of thought
On such a day.—Behold, the skies themselves
Look on my joy with a triumphant smile,
Unshadow'd by a cloud.
    Vittoria.                          'Tis very meet
That Heaven (which loves the just) should wear a
    smile
In honour of his fortunes.—Now, my lord,
Forgive me if I say, farewell, until
Th' appointed hour.
    Eribert.                          Lady, a brief farewell.
                          [Exeunt separately

Scene II.—The Sea-Shore

Procida, Raimond.

Procida.  And dost thou still refuse to share the
    glory
Of this, our daring enterprise?
    Raimond.                          Oh, father!
I, too, have dreamt of glory, and the word
Hath to my soul been as a trumpet's voice,
Making my nature sleepless.—But the deeds
Whereby 't was won, the high exploits, whose tale
Bids the heart burn, were of another cast
Than such as thou requirest.
    Procida.                          Every deed
Hath sanctity, if bearing for its aim
The Freedom of our country; and the sword
Alike is honour'd in the patriot's hand,
Searching 'midst warrior-hosts, the heart which
    gave
Oppression birth: or flashing through the gloom
Of the still chamber, o'er its troubled couch,
At dead of night.
    Raimond (turning away.)  There is no path but
    one
For noble natures.
    Procida.                          Wouldst thou ask the man
Who to the earth hath dash'd a nation's chains,
Rent as with Heaven's own lightning, by what
    means
The glorious end was won?—Go, swell with th'
    acclaim;
Bid the deliverer, hail! and if his path
To that most bright and sovereign destiny
Hath led o'er trampled thousands, be it call'd
A stern necessity, but not a crime!
    Raimond.  Father! my soul yet kindles at the
    thought
Of nobler lessons, in my boyhood learn'd
Ev'n from thy voice.—The high remembrances
Of other days are stirring in the heart
Where thou didst plant them; and they speak of
    men
Who needed no vain sophistry to gild
Acts, that would bear Heaven's light.—And such
    be mine!
Oh, father! is it yet too late to draw
The praise and blessing of all valiant hearts
On our most righteous cause?
    Procida.                          What wouldst thou do?
    Raimond.  I would go forth, and rouse th' indig-
    nant land
To generous combat.  Why should Freedom strike
Mantled with darkness?—Is there not more
    strength
Ev'n in the waving of her single arm
Than hosts can wield against her?—I would rouse
That spirit, whose fire doth press resistless on
To its proud sphere, the stormy field of fight!
    Procida.  Ay! and give time and warning to the
    foe
To gather all his might:—It is too late.
There is a work to be this eve begun,
When rings the Vesper-bell; and, long before

To-morrow's sun hath reach'd i' th' noonday
    heaven
His throne of burning glory, every sound
Of the Provençal tongue within our walls,
As by one thunderstroke—(you are pale, my son)—
Shall be for ever silenced.
    *Raimond.*          What! such sounds
As falter on the lip of infancy,
In its imperfect utterance? or are breathed
By the fond mother, as she lulls her babe?
Or in sweet hymns, upon the twilight air
Pour'd by the timid maid?—Must all alike
Be still'd in death; and wouldst thou tell my heart
There is no crime in *this*?
    *Procida.*        Since thou dost feel
Such horror of our purpose, in thy power
Are means that might avert it.
    *Raimond.*        Speak! Oh speak!
    *Procida.* How would those rescued thousands
      bless thy name,
Shouldst thou betray us!
    *Raimond.*        Father! I can hear—
Ay, proudly woo—the keenest questioning
Of thy soul-gifted eye; which almost seems
To claim a part of Heaven's dread royalty,
—The power that searches thought!
    *Procida (after a pause.)*    Thou hast a brow
Clear as the day—and yet I doubt thee, Raimond!
Whether it be that I have learn'd distrust
From a long look through man's deep-folded heart;
Whether my paths have been so seldom cross'd
By honour and fair mercy, that they seem
But beautiful deceptions, meeting thus
My unaccustom'd gaze;—howe'er it be—
I doubt thee!—See thou waver not—take heed.
Time lifts the veil from all things!
                [*Exit* PROCIDA.
    *Raimond.*        And 'tis thus
Youth fades from off our spirit; and the robes
Of beauty and of majesty, wherewith
We clothed our idols, drop!—Oh! bitter day,
When at the crushing of our glorious world,
We start, and find men thus! Yet be it so!
Is not my soul still powerful, in *itself*
To realize its dreams?—Ay, shrinking not
From the pure eye of heaven, my brow may well
Undaunted meet my father's.—But, away!
*Thou* shalt be saved, sweet Constance!—Love is
    yet
Mightier than vengeance.      [*Exit* RAIMOND.

---

SCENE III.—*Gardens of a Palace*

CONSTANCE, *alone.*

    *Constance.* There was a time when my thoughts
      wander'd not
Beyond these fairy scenes! when but to catch
The languid fragrance of the southern breeze
From the rich flowering citrons, or to rest,
Dreaming of some wild legend, in the shade
Of the dark laurel-foliage, was enough
Of happiness.—How have these calm delights
Fled from before one passion, as the dews,
The delicate gems of morning, are exhaled
By the great sun!

(RAIMOND *enters.*)
        Raimond! oh! now thou 'rt come
I read it in thy look, to say farewell
For the last time—the last!
    *Raimond.*        No, best beloved!
I come to tell thee there is now no power
To part us but in death.
    *Constance.*       I have dreamt of joy,
But never aught like this.—Speak yet again!
Say, we shall part no more!
    *Raimond.*        No more, if love
Can strive with darker spirits, and he is strong
In his immortal nature! all is changed
Since last we met. My father—keep the tale
Secret from all, and most of all, my Constance,
From Eribert—my father is return'd:
I leave thee not.
    *Constance.*    Thy father! blessed sound!

Good angels be his guard!—Oh! if he knew
How my soul clings to thine, he could no hate
Even a Provençal maid!—Thy father!—now
Thy soul will be at peace, and I shall see
The sunny happiness of earlier days
Look from thy brow once more!—But how is this
Thine eye reflects not the glad soul of mine;
And in thy look is that which ill befits
A tale of joy.
    *Raimond.*    A dream is on my soul.
I see a slumberer, crown'd with flowers, and
    smiling
As in delighted visions, on the brink
Of a dread chasm; and this strange phantasy
Hath cast so deep a shadow o'er my thoughts,
I cannot but be sad.
    *Constance.*      Why, let me sing
One of the sweet wild strains you love so well,
And this will banish it.
    *Raimond.*       It may not be.
Oh! gentle Constance, go not forth to-day:
Such dreams are ominous.
    *Constance.*      Have you then forgot
My brother's nuptial feast?—I must be one
Of the gay train attending to the shrine
His stately bride. In sooth, my step of joy
Will print earth lightly now.—What fear'st thou,
    love?
Look all around! the blue transparent skies,
And sunbeams pouring a more buoyant life
Through each glad thrilling vein, will brightly
    chase
All thought of evil.—Why, the very air
Breathes of delight!—Through all its glowing
    realms
Doth music blend with fragrance, and e'en here
The city's voice of jubilee is heard,
Till each light leaf seems trembling unto sounds
Of human joy!
    *Raimond.*      There lie far deeper things,—
Things that may darken thought for life, beneath
That city's festive semblance—I have pass'd
Through the glad multitudes, and I have mark'd
A stern intelligence in meeting eyes,
Which deem'd their flash unnoticed, and a quick,
Suspicious vigilance, too intent to clothe
Its mien with carelessness; and now and then,
A hurrying start, a whisper, or a hand
Pointing by stealth to some one, singled out
Amidst the reckless throng. O'er all is spread
A mantling flush of revelry, which may hide
Much from unpractised eyes; but lighter signs
Have been prophetic oft.
    *Constance.*     I tremble!—Raimond!
What may these things portend?
    *Raimond.*       It was a day
Of festival, like this; the city sent
Up through her sunny firmament a voice
Joyous as now; when, scarcely heralded
By one deep moan, forth from his cavernous depths
The earthquake burst; and the wide splendid
    scene
Became one chaos of all fearful things,
Till the brain whirl'd, partaking the sick motion
Of rocking palaces.
    *Constance.*     And then didst thou,
My noble Raimond! through the dreadful paths
Laid open by destruction, past the chasms,
Whose fathomless clefts, a moment's work, had
    given
One burial unto thousands, rush to save
Thy trembling Constance! she who lives to bless
Thy generous love, that still the breath of Heaven
Wafts gladness to her soul!
    *Raimond.*      Heaven!—Heaven is just.
And being so, must guard thee, sweet one, still.
Trust none beside.—Oh! the omnipotent skies
Make their wrath manifest, but insidious man
Doth compass those he hates with secret snares,
Wherein lies fate. Know, danger walks abroad,
Mask'd as a reveller. Constance! oh! by all
Our tried affection, all the vows which bind
Our hearts together, meet me in these bowers,
Here, I adjure thee, meet me, when the bell
Doth sound for vesper-prayer!

*Constance.*                      And know'st thou not
'Twill be the bridal hour ?
*Raimond.*                              It will not, love !
That hour will bring no bridal !—Naught of this
To human ear ; but speed thou hither, fly,
When evening brings that signal.—Dost thou
  heed !
This is no meeting, by a lover sought
To breathe fond tales, and make the twilight
  groves
And stars attest his vows ; deem thou not so,
Therefore denying it !—I tell thee, Constance !
If thou wouldst save me from such fierce despair
As falls on man, beholding all he loves
Perish before him, while his strength can but
Strive with his agony—thou'lt meet me then ?
Look on me, love !—I am not oft so moved—
Thou'lt meet me ?
  *Constance.* Oh ! what mean thy words ?—If then
My steps are free,—I will. Be thou but calm.
  *Raimond.* Be calm !—there is a cold and sullen
    calm,
And, were my wild fears made realities,
It might be mine ; but, in this dread suspense,
This conflict of all terrible phantasies,
There is no calm.—Yet fear thou not, dear love !
I will watch o'er thee still. And now, farewell
Until that hour !
  *Constance.* My Raimond, fare thee well.
                             [*Exeunt.*

---

### Scene IV.—*Room in the Citadel of Palermo.*

#### Alberti, De Couci.

*De Couci.* Said'st thou this night ?
  *Alberti.*                    This very night—and lo !
E'en now the sun declines.
  *De Couci.*              What ! are they arm'd ?
  *Alberti.* All arm'd and strong in vengeance and
    despair.
  *De Couci.* Doubtful and strange the tale ! Why
    was not this reveal'd before ?
  *Alberti.*            Mistrust me not, my lord !
That stern and jealous Procida hath kept
O'er all my steps, (as though he did suspect
The purposes, which oft his eye hath sought
To read in mine,) a watch so vigilant,
I knew not how to warn thee, though for this
A one I mingled with his bands, to learn
Their projects and their strength. Thou know'st
  my faith
To Anjou's house full well.
  *De Couci.*              How may we now
Avert the gathering storm ?—The viceroy holds
His bridal feast, and all is revelry.
—'Twas a true-boding heaviness of heart
Which kept me from these nuptials.
  *Alberti.*                      Thou thyself
May'st yet escape, and, haply of thy hands
Rescue a part, ere long to wreak full vengeance
Upon these rebels. 'Tis too late to dream
Of saving Eribert. E'en shouldst thou rush
Before him with the tidings, in his pride
And confidence of soul, he would but laugh
Thy tale to scorn.
  *De Couci.*       He must not die unwarn'd,
Though it be all in vain. But thou, Alberti,
Rejoin thy comrades, lest thine absence wake
Suspicion in their hearts. Thou hast done well,
And shalt not pass unguerdon'd, should I live
Through the deep horrors of th' approaching night.
  *Alberti.* Noble De Couci, trust me still. Anjou
Commands no heart more faithful than Alberti's.
                     [*Exit Alberti.*
  *De Couci.* The grovelling slave !—And yet he
    spoke too true !
For Eribert, in blind elated joy,
Will scorn the warning voice.—The day wanes
  fast,
And through the city, recklessly dispersed,
Unarm'd and unprepared, my soldiers revel,
E'en on the brink of fate.—I must away.
                    [*Exit De Couci*

### Scene V.—*A Banqueting Hall.*

#### Provençal Nobles *assembled.*

*First Noble.* Joy be to this fair meeting !—Who
  hath seen
The viceroy's bride ?
  *Second Noble.*      I saw her, as she pass'd
The gazing throngs assembled in the city.
'Tis said she hath not left for years, till now,
Her castle's wood-girt solitude. 'Twill gall
These proud Sicilians, that her wide domains
Should be the conqueror's guerdon.
  *Third Noble.*              'Twas their boast
With what fond faith she worshipp'd still the name
Of the boy, Conradin. How will the slaves
Brook this new triumph of their lords ?
  *Second Noble.*                      In sooth,
It stings them to the quick. In the full streets
They mix with our Provençals, and assume
A guise of mirth, but it sits hardly on them.
'Twere worth a thousand festivals, to see
With what a bitter and unnatural effort
They strive to smile !
  *First Noble.*            Is this Vittoria fair ?
  *Second Noble.* Of a most noble mien ; but yet
    her beauty
Is wild and awful, and her large dark eye,
In its unsettled glances, hath strange power,
From which thou'lt shrink, as I did.
  *First Noble.*                      Hush ! they come.

*Enter* Eribert, Vittoria, Constance, *and others.*

  *Eribert.* Welcome, my noble friends !—there
    must not lower
One clouded brow to-day in Sicily !
Behold my bride !
  *Nobles.*            Receive our homage, lady
  *Vittoria.* I bid all welcome. May the feast we
    offer
Prove worthy of such guests !
  *Eribert.* Look on her, friends !
And say, if that majestic brow is not
Meet for a diadem ?
  *Vittoria.*          'Tis well, my lord !
When memory's pictures fade, 'tis kindly done
To brighten their dimm'd hues !
  *First Noble (apart.)*      Mark'd you her glance ?
  *Second Noble (apart.)* What eloquent scorn was
    there ? Yet he, th' elate
Of heart, perceives it not.
  *Eribert.*              Now to the feast !
Constance, you look not joyous. I have said
That all should smile to-day.
  *Constance.*            Forgive me, brother
The heart is wayward, and its garb of pomp
At times oppresses it.
  *Eribert.*            Why, how is this ?
  *Constance.* Voices of woe, and prayers of agony
Unto my soul have risen, and left sad sounds
There echoing still. Yet would I fain be gay,
Since 'tis your wish.—In truth, I should have been
A village-maid !
  *Eribert.*            But, being as you are,
Not thus ignobly free, command your looks
(They may be taught obedience) to reflect
The aspect of the time.
  *Vittoria.*            And know, fair maid !
That if in this unskill'd, you stand alone
Amidst our court of pleasure.
  *Eribert.*            To the feast !
Now let the red wine foam !—There should be
  mirth
When conquerors revel !—Lords of this fair isle !
Your good swords' heritage, crown each bowl, and
  pledge
The present and the future ! for they both
Look brightly on us. Dost thou smile, my bride ?
  *Vittoria.* Yes, Eribert !—thy prophecies of joy
Have taught e'en me to smile.
  *Eribert.*            'Tis well. To-day
I have won a fair and almost *royal* bride ;
To-morrow—let the bright sun spread his course,
To waft me happiness !—my proudest foes
Must die—and then my slumber shall be laid

On rose-leaves, with no envious fold, to mar
The luxury of its visions!—Fair Vittoria,
Your looks are troubled!
*Vittoria.*                      It is strange, but oft,
'Midst festal songs and garlands, o'er my soul
Death comes, with some dull image! as you spoke
Of those whose blood is claim'd, I thought for them
Who, in a darkness thicker than the night
E'er wove with all her clouds, have pined so long.
How bless'd were the stroke which makes them
          things
Of that invisible world, wherein, we trust,
There is at least no bondage!—But should we
    roin such a scene as this, where all earth's joys
    ontend for mastery, and the very sense
    f life is rapture; should we pass, I say,
At once from such excitements to the void
And silent gloom of that which doth await us—
—Were it not dreadful?
*Eribert.*                    Banish such dark thoughts!
They ill beseem the hour.
*Vittoria.*                         There is no hour
Of this mysterious world, in joy or woe,
But they beseem it well!—Why, what a slight,
Impalpable bound is that, th' unseen, which severs
Being from death!—And who can tell how near
Its misty brink he stands?
*First Noble (aside.)*        What mean her words?
*Second Noble.* There's some dark mystery here.
*Eribert.*                          No more of this!
Pour the bright juice which Etna's glowing vines
Yield to the conquerors! And let music's voice
Dispel these ominous dreams!—Wake, harp and
          song!
Swell out your triumph!

    *A Messenger enters, bearing a letter*

*Messenger.* Pardon, my good lord!
But this demands——
*Eribert.* What means thy breathless haste?
And that ill-boding mien?—Away! such looks
Befit not hours like these.
*Messenger.*                       The Lord De Couci
Made me bear this, and say, 'tis fraught with
          tidings
Of life and death.
*Vittoria (hurriedly.)*  Is this a time for aught
But revelry?—My lord, these dull intrusions
Mar the bright spirit of the festal scene!
*Eribert (to the Messenger.)* Hence! tell the Lord
    de Couci, we will talk
Of life and death to-morrow.  [*Exit* MESSENGER
                              Let there be
Around me none but joyous looks to-day,
And strains whose very echoes wake to mirth!

(*A band of the conspirators enter, to the sound of
music, disguised as shepherds, bacchanals, &c.*)

*Eribert.* What forms are these?—What means
          this antic triumph?
*Vittoria.* 'Tis but a rustic pageant, by my vassals
Prepared to grace our bridal.  Will you not
Hear their wild music? Our Sicilian vales
Have many a sweet and mirthful melody,
To which the glad heart bounds.—Breathe ye some
          strain
Meet for the time, ye sons of Sicily!

    (*One of the Masquers sings.*)

The festal eve, o'er earth and sky,
   In her sunset robe, looks bright.
And the purple hills of Sicily,
   With their vineyards, laugh in light,
From the marble cities of her plains,
   Glad voices mingling swell;
—But with yet more loud and lofty strains,
   They shall hail the Vesper-bell!

Oh! sweet its tones, when the summer-breeze
   Their cadence wafts afar,
To float o'er the blue Sicilian seas,
   As they gleam to the first pale star!
The shepherd greets them on his height,
   The hermit in his cell;
—But a deeper voice shall breathe, to-night,
   In the sound of the Vesper-bell!

    [*The Bell rings.*

*Eribert.* It is the hour!—Hark, hark!—my bride
          our summons!
The altar is prepared and crown'd with flowers
That wait——
*Vittoria.*      The victim!

    (*A tumult heard without.*)

PROCIDA and MONTALBA *enter, with others, armed.*

*Procida.*              Strike! the hour is come
*Vittoria.*  Welcome, avengers, welcome!  Now
          be strong!

(*The Conspirators throw off their disguise, and rush,
with their swords drawn, upon the Provençals.
ERIBERT is wounded, and falls.*)

*Procida.* Now hath fate reach'd thee in thy mid
          career,
Thou reveller in a nation's agonies!

(*The Provençals are driven off, and pursued by the
          Sicilians.*)

*Constance (supporting Eribert.)* My brother! oh
          my brother!
*Eribert.*              Have I stood
A leader in the battle-fields of kings,
To perish thus at last?—Ay, by these pangs,
And this strange chill, that heavily doth creep,
Like a slow poison, through my curdling veins,
    his should be—death!—In sooth, a dull exchange
For the gay bridal feast!
*Voices (without.)* Remember Conradin!—spare
          none, spare none.
*Vittoria (throwing off her bridal wreath and orna-
          ments.)*
This is proud freedom! Now my soul may cast,
In generous scorn, her mantle of dissembling
To earth for ever!—And it is such joy,
As if a captive from his dull, cold cell,
Might soar at once, on charter'd wing, to range
The realms of starr'd infinity!—Away!
Vain mockery of a bridal wreath! The hour
For which stern patience ne'er kept watch in vain
Is come: and I may give my bursting heart
Full and indignant scope.—Now, Eribert!
Believe in retribution! What, proud man!
Prince, ruler, conqueror! didst thou deem Heaven
          slept?
" Or that the unseen, immortal ministers,
" Ranging the world, to note e'en purposed crime
" In burning characters, had laid aside
" Their everlasting attributes for *thee?*"
—Oh! blind security!—He, in whose dread hand
The lightnings vibrate, holds them back, until
The trampler of this goodly earth hath reach'd
His pyramid-height of power; that so his fall
May, with more fearful oracles, make pale
Man's crown'd oppressors!
*Constance.*              Oh! reproach him not!
His soul is trembling on the dizzy brink
Of that dim world where passion may not enter.
Leave him in peace.
*Voices (without.)* Anjou. Anjou!—De Couci, to
          the rescue!
*Eribert (half raising himself.)* My brave Pro-
          vençals! do ye combat still?
And I, your chief, am here!—Now, now I feel
That death, indeed, is bitter!
*Vittoria.*                    Fare thee well!
Thine eyes so oft, with their insulting smile,
Have look'd on man's last pangs, thou shouldst,
          by this,
Be perfect how to die!         [*Exit* VITTORIA.

    RAIMOND *enters.*

*Raimond.*              Away, my Constance!
Now is the time for flight.  Our slaughtering bands
Are scatter'd far and wide.  A little while
And thou shalt be in safety.  Know'st thou not
That low sweet vale, where dwells the holy man
Anselmo?  He whose hermitage is rear'd
'Mid some old temple's ruins?—Round the spot
His name hath spread so pure and deep a charm,
'Tis hallow'd as a sanctuary, wherein
Thou shalt securely bide, till this wild storm
Have spent its fury.  Haste!

*Constance.*                    I will not fly!
While in his heart there is one throb of life,
One spark in his dim eyes, I will not leave
The brother of my youth to perish thus,
Without one kindly bosom to sustain
His dying head.
   *Eribert.*          The clouds are darkening round.
There are strange voices ringing in mine ear
That summon me—to what?—But I have been
Used to command!—Away! I will not die
But on the field——                    [*He dies.*
   *Constance (kneeling by him.)* Oh Heaven! be
     merciful.
As thou art just!—for he is now where naught
But mercy can avail him.—It is past!

     Guido *enters, with his sword drawn.*

   *Guido (to* Raimond.) I've sought thee long—
     Why art thou lingering here?
Haste, follow me!—Suspicion with thy name
Joins that word—*Traitor!*
   *Raimond.*                    Traitor!——Guido?
   *Guido.*                              Yes
Hast thou not heard, that, with his men-at-arms,
After vain conflict with a people's wrath,
De Couci hath escaped?—And there are those
Who murmur that from *thee* the warning came
Which saved him from our vengeance. But e'en
     yet,
In the red current of Provencal blood,
That doubt may be effaced. Draw thy good sword,
And follow me!
   *Raimond.* And *thou* couldst doubt me, Guido!
'Tis come to this!—Away! mistrust me still.
I will not stain my sword with deeds like thine.
Thou know'st me not!
   *Guido.*          Raimond di Procida!
If thou art he whom once I deem'd so noble—
Call me thy friend no more!          [*Exit* Guido.
   *Raimond (after a pause.)* Rise, dearest, rise!
Thy duty's task hath nobly been fulfill'd,
E'en in the face of death; but all is o'er,
And this is now no place where nature's tears
In quiet sanctity may freely flow.
—Hark! the wild sounds that wait on fearful
     deeds
Are swelling on the wind as the deep roar
Of fast-advancing billows, and for *thee*
I shame not thus to tremble.—Speed! oh, speed!
                     [*Exeunt.*

------

### ACT THE FOURTH

#### Scene I.—*A Street in Palermo*

#### Procida *enters.*

   *Procida.* How strange and deep a stillness loads
     the air,
As with the power of midnight!—Ay, where death
Hath pass'd, there should be silence.—But this hush
Of nature's heart, this breathlessness of all things,
Doth press on thought too heavily, and the sky,
With its dark robe of purple thunder-clouds
Brooding in sullen masses, o'er my spirit
Weighs like an omen!—Wherefore should this be?
s not our task achieved, the mighty work
Of our deliverance?—Yes; I should be joyous:
But this our feeble nature, with its quick
Instinctive superstitious, will drag down
Th' ascending soul.—And I have fearful bodings
That treachery lurks amongst us. — Raimond!
     Raimond!
Oh! Guilt ne'er made a mien like his its garb!
It cannot be!

   Montalba, Guido, *and other Sicilians, enter.*

   *Procida.* Welcome! we meet in joy!
Now may we bear ourselves erect, resuming
The kingly port of freemen! Who shall dare,
After this proof of slavery's dread recoil,
To weave us chains again?—Ye have done well.
   *Montalba.* We *have* done well. There need no
     choral song,
No shouting multitudes, to blazon forth
Our stern exploits.—The *silence* of our foes

Doth vouch enough, and they are laid to rest
Deep as the sword could make it. Yet our task
Is still but half achieved, since, with his bands,
De Couci hath escaped, and, doubtless, leads
Their footsteps to Messina, where our foes
Will gather all their strength. Determined hearts
And deeds to startle earth, are yet required,
To make the mighty sacrifice complete.—
Where is thy son?
   *Procida.*          I know not. Once last night
He cross'd my path, and with one stroke beat down
A sword just raised to smite me, and restored
My own, which in that deadly strife had been
Wrench'd from my grasp: but when I would have
     press'd him
To my exulting bosom, he drew back,
And with a sad, and yet a scornful smile,
Full of strange meaning, left me. Since that hour
I have not seen him. Wherefore didst thou ask?
   *Montalba.* It matters not. We have deep things
     to speak of.—
Know'st thou that we have traitors in our coun-
     cils?
   *Procida.* I know some voice in secret must have
     warn'd
De Couci; or his scatter'd bands had ne'er
So soon been marshall'd, and in close array
Led hence as from the field.—Hast thou heard
     aught
That may develop this?
   *Montalba.*          The guards we set
To watch the city gates, have seized, this morn,
One whose quick fearful glance, and hurried step,
Betray'd his guilty purpose. Mark! he bore
(Amidst the tumult deeming that his flight
Might all unnoticed pass,) these scrolls to him,
The fugitive Provencal. Read and judge!
   *Procida.* Where is this messenger?
   *Montalba.*                    Where *should* he be?—
They slew him in their wrath.
   *Procida.*                    Unwisely done!
Give me the scrolls.
                   [*He reads.*
     Now, if there be such things
As may to death add sharpness, yet delay
The pang which gives release; if there be power
In execration, to call down the fires
Of you avenging heaven, whose rapid shafts
But for such guilt were aimless; be they heap'd
Upon the traitor's head!—Scorn make his name
Her mark for ever!
   *Montalba.*          In our passionate blindness,
We send forth curses, whose deep stings recoil
Oft on ourselves.
   *Procida.*          Whate'er fate hath of ruin
Fall on his house!—What! to resign again
That freedom for whose sake our souls have now
Engrain'd themselves in blood!—Why, who is he
That hath devised this treachery?—To the scroll
Why fix'd he not his name, so stamping it
With an immortal infamy, whose brand
Might warn men from him?—Who should be so
     vile?
Alberti?—In his eye is that which ever
Shrinks from encountering mine!—But no! his
     race
Is of our noblest—Oh! he could not shame
That high descent!—Urbino?—Conti?—No!
They are too deeply pledged.—There's one name
     more!
—I cannot utter it!—Now shall I read
Each face with cold suspicion, which doth blot
From man's high mien its native royalty,
And seal his noble forehead with the impress
Of its own vile imaginings!—Speak your thoughts,
Montalba! Guido!—Who should this man be?
   *Montalba.* Why, what Sicilian youth unsheathed
     last night
His sword to aid our foes, and turn'd its edge
Against his country's chiefs—He that did *this*,
May well be deem'd for guiltier treason ripe.
   *Procida.* And who is he?
   *Montalba.*                    Nay, ask thy son.
   *Procida.*                              My son
What should *he* know of such a recreant be it?
Speak, Guido! thou'rt his friend!

*Guido.*                          I would not wear
The brand of such a name!
  *Procida.*                      How? what means this?
A flash of light breaks in upon my soul!
Is it to blast me?—Yet the fearful doubt
Hath crept in darkness through my thoughts before,
And been flung from them.—Silence!—Speak not
          yet!
I would be calm, and meet the thunder-burst
With a strong heart.                  [*A pause.*
                      Now, what have I to hear?
Your tidings?
  *Guido.*        Briefly, 'twas your son did thus:
He hath disgraced your name.
  *Procida.*                    My son did thus!
Are thy words oracles, that I should search
Their hidden meaning out?—*What* did my son?
I have forgot the tale.—Repeat it, quick!
  *Guido.*   'Twill burst upon thee all too soon.
          While we
Were busy at the dark and solemn rites
Of retribution; while we bathed the earth
In red libations, which will consecrate
The soil they mingled with to freedom's step
Through the long march of ages; 'twas his task
To shield from danger a Provençal maid,
Sister of him whose cold oppression stung
Our hearts to madness.
  *Montalba.*              What! should she be spared
To keep that name from perishing on earth?
—I cross'd them in their path, and raised my sword
To smite her in her champion's arms.—We fought.
The boy disarm'd me!—And I live to tell
My shame, and wreak my vengeance!
  *Guido.*                            Who but he
Could warn De Couci, or devise the guilt
These scrolls reveal?—Hath not the traitor still
Sought, with his fair and specious eloquence,
To win us from our purpose?—All things seem
Leagued to unmask him.
  *Montalba.*            Know you not there came
E'en in the banquet's hour, from this De Couci,
One, bearing unto Eribert the tidings
Of all our purposed deeds?—And have we not
Proof, as the noon-day clear, that Raimond loves
The sister of that tyrant?
  *Procida.*                  There was one
Who mourn'd for being childless!—Let him now
Feast o'er his children's graves, and I will join
The revelry!
  *Montalba* (*apart.*) You shall be childless too!
  *Procida.*   Was't you, Montalba?—Now rejoice,
          I say!
There is no name so near you, that its stains
Should call the fever'd and indignant blood
To your dark cheek!—But I will dash to earth
The weight that presses on my heart, and then
Be glad as thou art.
  *Montalba.*         What means this, my lord?
Who hath seen gladness on Montalba's mien?
  *Procida.*  Why, should not all be glad who have
          no *sons*
To tarnish their bright name?
  *Montalba.*                    I am not used
To bear with mockery.
  *Procida.*         Friend! By yon high Heaven,
I mock thee not!—'Tis a proud fate, to live
Alone and unallied.—Why, what's alone?
A word whose sense is—*free!*—Ay, free from all
The venom'd stings implanted in the heart
By those it loves.—Oh! I could laugh to think
O' th' joy that riots in baronial halls,
When the word comes—" A son is born!"—A *son!*
—They should say thus—" He that shall knit your
          brow
To furrows, not of years; and bid your eye
Quail its proud glance, to tell the earth its shame,
Is born, and so rejoice!"—*then* might we feast,
And know the cause!—Were it not excellent?
  *Montalba.* This is all idle.  There are deeds to do ·
Arouse thee, Procida!
  *Procida.*          Why, am I not
Calm as immortal Justice?—She can strike,
And yet be passionless—and thus will I.
I know thy meaning.—Deeds to do!—'t is well.
They shall be done ere thought on.—Go ye forth,

There is a youth who calls himself my son.
His name is—Raimond—in his eye is light
That shows like truth—but be not ye deceived!
Bear him in chains before us.  We will sit
To-day in judgment, and the skies shall see
The strength which girds our nature.—Will not
          this
Be glorious, brave Montalba?—Linger not,
Ye tardy messengers! for there are things
Which ask the speed of storms.
                [*Exeunt* Guido *and others.*
                          Is not this well?
  *Montalba.* 'T is noble.  Keep thy spirit to this
          proud height,
(*aside.*) And then—be desolate like me!—my woes
Will at the thought grow light.
  *Procida.*                  What now remains
To be prepared?—There should be solemn pomp
To grace a day like this.—Ay, breaking hearts
Require a drapery to conceal their throbs
From cold inquiring eyes; and it must be
Ample and rich, that so their gaze may not
Explore what lies beneath.            [*Exit* Procida
  *Montalba.*                  Now this is well!
—I hate this Procida; for he hath won
In all our councils that ascendency
And mastery o'er bold hearts, which should have
          been
Mine by a thousand claims.—Had *he* the strength
Of wrongs like mine?—No! for that name—his
          country—
*He* strikes—*my* vengeance hath a deeper fount:
But there's dark joy in this!—And fate hath barr'd
My soul from every other.        [*Exit* Montalba.

---

Scene II.—*A Hermitage surrounded by the Ruins
          of an Ancient Temple.*

Constance, Anselmo.

  *Constance.* 'Tis strange he comes not!—Is not
          this the still
And sultry hour of noon?—He should have been
Here by the day-break.—Was there not a voice?
—" No! 't is the shrill Cicala, with glad life
Peopling these marble ruins, as it sports
Amidst them, in the sun."—Hark! yet again!
No! no!—Forgive me, father! that I bring
Earth's restless griefs and passions, to disturb
The stillness of thy holy solitude:
My heart is full of care.
  *Anselmo.*              There is no place
So hallow'd, as to be unvisited
By mortal cares.  Nay, whither should we go,
With our deep griefs and passions, but to scenes
Lonely and still; where he that made our hearts
Will speak to them in whispers?  I have known
Affliction too, my daughter.
  *Constance.*              Hark! his step!
I know it well—he comes—my Raimond, welcome

Vittoria *enters,* Constance *shrinks back on per-
          ceiving her.*

Oh, Heaven! that aspect tells a fearful tale.
  *Vittoria* (*not observing her.*) There is a cloud of
          horror on my soul;
And on thy words, Anselmo, peace doth wait,
Even as an echo, following the sweet close
Of some divine and solemn harmony:
Therefore I sought thee now.  Oh! speak to me
Of holy things and names, in whose deep sound
Is power to hid the tempests of the heart
Sink, like a storm rebuked.
  *Anselmo.*                  What recent grief
Darkens thy spirit thus?
  *Vittoria.*              I said not grief.
We should rejoice to-day, but joy is not
That which it hath been.  In the flowers which
          wreathe
Its mantling cup, there is a scent unknown,
Fraught with strange delirium.  All things now
Have changed their nature: still, I say rejoice!
There is a cause, Anselmo!—We are free,
Free and avenged!—Yet on my soul there hangs
A darkness, heavy as th' oppressive gloom

Of midnight phantasies.—Ay, for this, too,
There is a cause.

*Anselmo.*     How say'st thou, we are free?
There may have raged, within Palermo's walls,
Some brief wild tumult, but too well I know
They call the stranger lord.

*Vittoria.*     Who calls the *dead*
Conqueror or lord?—Hush! breathe it not aloud,
The wild winds must not hear it!—Yet, again,
I tell thee, we are free!

*Anselmo.*     Thine eye hath look'd
On fearful deeds, for still their shadows hang
O'er its dark orb.—Speak! I adjure thee, say,
How hath this work been wrought?

*Vittoria.*     Peace! ask me not!
Why shouldst *thou* hear a tale to send thy blood
Back on its fount?—We cannot wake them now!
The storm is in my soul, but *they* are all
At rest!—Ay, sweetly may the slaughter'd babe
By its dead mother sleep; and warlike men
Who 'midst the slain have slumber'd oft before,
Making the shield their pillow, may repose
Well, now their toils are done.—Is't not enough?

*Constance.*     Merciful Heaven! have such things
    been? And yet
There is no shade come o'er the laughing sky!
—I am an outcast now.

*Anselmo.*     O thou, whose ways
Clouds mantle fearfully; of all the blind,
But terrible ministers that work thy wrath,
How much is *man* the fiercest!—Others know
Their limits—Yes! the earthquakes, and the
    storms,
And the volcanoes!—He alone o'erleaps
The bounds of retribution!—Couldst thou gaze,
Vittoria! with thy woman's heart and eye,
On such dread scenes unmoved?

*Vittoria.*     Was it for *me*
To stay th' avenging sword?—No, though it pierced
My very soul!—Hark! hark! what thrilling shrieks
Ring through the air around me!—Canst thou not
Bid them be hush'd?—Oh! look not on me thus!

*Anselmo.*     Lady! thy thoughts lend sternness to
    the looks
Which are but sad!—Have all then perish'd? all?
Was there no mercy!

*Vittoria.*     Mercy! it hath been
A word forbidden as th' unhallow'd names
Of evil powers.—Yet one there was who dared
To own the guilt of pity, and to aid
The victims! but in vain.—Of him no more!
He is a traitor, and a traitor's death
Will be his meed.

*Constance (coming forward.)*     Oh, Heaven!—his
    name, his name!
Is it—it cannot be!

*Vittoria (starting.)*     *Thou* here, pale girl!
I deem'd thee with the dead!—How hast thou
    'scaped
The snare!—Who saved thee, last of all thy race!
Was it not he of whom I spake e'en now,
Raimond di Procida?

*Constance.*     It is enough.
Now the storm breaks upon me, and I sink.
Must he too die?

*Vittoria.*     Is it e'en so?—Why then,
Live on—thou hast the arrow at thy heart!
" Fix not on me thy sad reproachful eyes,"
I mean not to betray thee. Thou may'st live!
Why should death bring thee his oblivious balms!
*He* visits but the happy.—Didst thou ask
If Raimond too must die?—It is as sure
As that his blood is on *thy* head, for thou
Didst win him to this treason.

*Constance.*     When did men
Call mercy, *treason?*—Take my life, but save
My noble Raimond!

*Vittoria.*     Maiden! he must die.
E'en now the youth before his judges stands,
And they are men, who, to the voice of prayer,
Are as the rock is to the murmur'd sigh
Of summer-waves! ay, though a father sit
On their tribunal. Bend thou not to me.
What wouldst thou?

*Constance.*     Mercy!—Oh! wert thou to plead

But with a look, e'en yet he might be saved!
If thou hast ever loved——

*Vittoria.*     If I have loved?
It is *that* love forbids me to relent;
I am what it hath made me.—O'er my soul
Lightning hath pass'd, and sear'd it. Could I weep
I then might pity—but it will not be.

*Constance.*     Oh! thou wilt yet relent, for wo-
    man's heart
Was form'd to suffer and to melt.

*Vittoria.*     Away!
Why should I pity thee?—Thou wilt but prove
What I have known before—and yet I live!
Nature is strong, and it may all be borne—
The sick impatient yearning of the heart
For that which is not; and the weary sense
Of the dull void, wherewith our homes have been
Circled by death; yes, all things may be borne!
All, save remorse.—But I will *not* bow down
My spirit to that dark power:—there *was* no guilt
Anselmo! wherefore didst thou talk of guilt?

*Anselmo.*     Ay, thus doth sensitive conscience
    quicken thought,
Lending reproachful voices to a breeze,
Keen lightning to a look.

*Vittoria.*     Leave me in peace!
Is't not enough that I should have a sense
Of things thou canst not see, all wild and dark,
And of unearthly whispers, haunting me
With dread suggestions, but that *thy* cold words,
Old man, should gall me, too?—Must all conspire
Against me?—Oh! thou beautiful spirit! wont
To shine upon my dreams with looks of love,
Where art *thou* vanish'd?—Was it not the thought
Of thee which urged me to the fearful task,
And wilt thou now forsake me?—I must seek
The shadowy woods again, for there, perchance,
Still may thy voice be in my twilight-paths;
—Here I but meet despair!     [*Exit* VITTORIA

*Anselmo (to Constance.)*     Despair not *thou*,
My daughter!—he that purifies the heart
With grief, will lend it strength.

*Constance (endeavouring to rouse herself.)*     Did
    she not say
That some one was to die?

*Anselmo.*     I tell thee not.
Thy pangs are vain—for nature will have way.
Earth must have tears; yet in a heart like thine,
Faith may not yield its place.

*Constance.*     Have I not heard
Some fearful tale?—Who said, that there should
    rest
Blood on my soul?—What blood?—I never bore
Hatred, kind father, unto aught that breathes;
Raimond doth know it well.—Raimond!— High
    Heaven,
It bursts upon me now!—and he must die!
For my sake—e'en for mine!

*Anselmo.*     Her words were strange,
And her proud mind seem'd half to frenzy wrought
—Perchance this may not be.

*Constance.*     It *must* not be.
Why do I linger here?     (*She rises to depart.*

*Anselmo.*     Where wouldst thou go?

*Constance.*     To give their stern and unrelenting
    hearts
A victim in his stead.

*Anselmo.*     Stay! wouldst thou rush
On certain death?

*Constance.*     I may not falter now.
—Is not the life of woman all bound up
In her affections?—What hath *she* to do
In this bleak world alone?—It may be well
For *man* on his triumphal course to move,
Uncumber'd by soft bonds; but *we* were born
For love and grief.

*Anselmo.*     Thou fair and gentle thing,
Unused to meet a glance which doth not speak
Of tenderness or homage! how shouldst *thou*
Bear the hard aspect of unpitying men,
Or face the king of terrors?

*Constance.*     There is strength
Deep bedded in our hearts, of which we reck
But little, till the shafts of heaven have pierced
Its fragile dwelling.—Must not earth be rent

Before her gems are found ?—Oh ! now I feel
Worthy the generous love which hath not shunn'd
To look on death for me!—My heart hath given
Birth to as deep a courage, and a faith
As high in its devotion.   [*Exit* Constance.
  *Anselmo.*         She is gone !
Is it to perish ?—God of mercy! lend
Power to my voice, that so its prayer may save
This pure and lofty creature!—I will follow—
But her young footstep and heroic heart
Will bear her to destruction faster far
Than I can track her path.   [*Exit* Anselmo.

---

Scene III.—*Hall of a Public Building.*

Procida, Montalba, Guido, *and others, seated as
on a Tribunal.*

  *Procida.*   The morn lower'd darkly, but the sun
hath now
With fierce and angry splendour, through the clouds
Burst forth, as if impatient to behold
This, our high triumph.—Lead the prisoner in.

  (Raimond *is brought in, fettered and guarded.*)

Why, what a bright and fearless brow is here !
—Is this man guilty ?—Look on him, Montalba !
  *Montalba.*   Be firm. Should justice falter at a
  look ?
  *Procida.*   No, thou say'st well. Her eyes are
  filleted,
Or should be so. Thou, that dost call thyself—
—But no! I will not breathe a traitor's name—
Speak ! thou art arraign'd of treason.
  *Raimond.*              I arraign
You, before whom I stand, of darker guilt,
In the bright face of Heaven ; and your own hearts
Give echo to the charge. Your very looks
Have ta'en the stamp of crime, and seem to shrink,
With a perturb'd and haggard wildness, back
From the too-searching light.— Why, what hath
  wrought
This change on noble brows ?—There is a voice
With a deep answer, rising from the blood
Your hands have coldly shed !—Ye are of those
From whom just men recoil, with curdling veins,
All thrill'd by life's abhorrent consciousness,
And sensitive feeling of a *murderer's* presence.
—Away ! come down from your tribunal-seat,
Put off your robes of state, and let your mien
Be pale and humbled ; for ye bear about you
That which repugnant earth doth sicken at,
More than the pestilence.—That I should live
To see my father shrink !
  *Procida.*         Montalba, speak!
There's something chokes my voice—but fear me
  not.
  *Montalba.*   If we must plead to vindicate our acts,
Be it when thou hast made thine own look clear ;
Most eloquent youth ! What answer canst thou
  make
To this our charge of treason ?
  *Raimond.*         I will plead
*That* cause before a mightier judgment-throne,
Where mercy is not guilt. But here, I *feel*
Too buoyantly the glory and the joy
Of my free spirit's whiteness ; for e'en now
Th' embodied hideousness of crime doth seem
Before me glaring out.—Why, I saw *thee,*
Thy foot upon an aged warrior's breast,
Trampling out nature's last convulsive heavings.
—And thou—*thy* sword—Oh, valiant chief!—is yet
Red from the noble stroke which pierced, at once,
A mother and the babe, whose little life
Was from her bosom drawn !—Immortal deeds
For bards to hymn !
  *Guido (aside.)*   I look upon his mien,
And waver.—Can it be ?—My boyish heart
Deem'd him so noble once !— Away, weak
  thoughts !
Why should I shrink, as if the guilt were *mine,*
From his proud glance ?
  *Procida.*       Oh, thou dissembler! thou
So skill'd to clothe with virtue's generous flush
The hollow cheek of cold hypocrisy,

That, with thy guilt made manifest, I can scarce
Believe thee guilty !—look on me, and say
Whose was the secret warning voice, that saved
De Couci with his bands, to join our foes,
And forge new fetters for th' indignant land ?
Whose was *this* treachery ?   (*Shows him papers.*)
             Who hath promised here
(Belike to appease the manes of the dead,)
At midnight to unfold Palermo's gates,
And welcome in the foe ?—Who hath done this,
But thou, a tyrant's friend ?
  *Raimond.*         Who hath done this?
Father !—if I may call thee by that name—
Look, with thy piercing eye, on those whose smiles
Were masks that hid their daggers.—*There,* per-
  chance,
May lurk what loves not light too strong. For me,
I know but this—there needs no deep research
To prove the truth—that murderers may be traitors
Ev'n to each other.
  *Procida (to Montalba.)*   His unaltering cheek
Still vividly doth hold its natural hue,
And his eye quails not !—Is this innocence ?
  *Montalba.*   No ! 't is th' unshrinking hardihood
  of crime.
—Thou bear'st a gallant mien !—But where is she
Whom thou hast barter'd fame and life to save,
The fair Provençal maid ?—What ! know'st thou
  not
That this alone were guilt, to death allied ?
Was 't not our law that he who spared a foe,
(And is she not of that detested race ?)
Should thenceforth be amongst us *as* a foe ?
  —Where hast thou borne her?—speak !
  *Raimond.*         That Heaven, whose eye
Burns up thy soul with its far-searching glance,
Is with her: she is safe.
  *Procida.*         And by that word
Thy doom is seal'd.—Oh God ! that I had died
Before this bitter hour, in the full strength
And glory of my heart !

  Constance *enters, and rushes to* Raimond.

  *Constance.*       Oh ! art thou found ?
—But yet, to find thee thus !—Chains, chains for
  thee !
My brave, my noble love!—Off with these bonds ;
Let him be free as air :—for I am come
To be your victim now,
  *Raimond.*        Death has no pang
More keen than this.—Oh! wherefore art thou
  here ?
I could have died so calmly, deeming thee
Saved, and at peace.
  *Constance.*   At peace !—And thou hast thought
Thus poorly of my love !—But woman's breast
Hath strength to suffer too.—Thy father sits
On this tribunal ; Raimond, which is he ?
  *Raimond.* My father ! who hath lull'd thy gentle
  heart
With that false hope ?—Beloved ! gaze around—
See, if thine eye can trace a father's soul
In the dark looks bent on us.
  *Constance (after earnestly examining the counte-
  nances of the judges, falls at the feet of Procida.*)
            Thou art he !
Nay, turn thou not away ! for I beheld
Thy proud lip quiver, and a watery mist
Pass o'er thy troubled eye ; and then I knew
Thou wert his father!—Spare him  take my life !
In truth a worthless sacrifice for his,
But yet mine all.—Oh ! *he* hath still to run
A long bright race of glory.
  *Raimond.*         Constance, peace !
I look upon thee, and my failing heart
Is as a broken reed.
  *Constance (still addressing Procida.)*   Oh, yet
  relent.
If 't was his crime to rescue *me,* behold
I come to be the atonement ! Let him live
To crown thine age with honour.—In thy heart
There's a deep conflict ; but great Nature pleads
With an o'ermastering voice, and thou wilt yield !
—Thou *art* his father !

*Procida (after a pause.)* Maiden, thou'rt deceived!
I am as calm as that dead pause of nature
Ere the full thunder bursts.—A judge is not
Father or friend.  Who calls this man my son ?
—*My* son !—Ay ! thus his mother proudly smiled—
But she was noble !—Traitors stand alone,
Loosed from all ties.—Why should I trifle thus ?
—Bear her away !
 *Raimond (starting forward.)*  And whither ?
 *Montalba.*         Unto death.
Why should she live when all her race have
  perish'd ?
 *Constance (sinking into the arms of Raimond.)*
Raimond, farewell !—Oh! when thy star hath risen
To its bright noon, forget not, best beloved,
I died for thee !
 *Raimond.* High Heaven ! thou seest these things,
And yet endur'st them !—Shalt thou die for me,
Purest and loveliest being ?—but our fate
May not divide us long.—Her cheek is cold—
Her deep blue eyes are closed—Should this be death!
—If thus, there yet were mercy !—Father, father !
Is thy heart human ?
 *Procida.*       Bear her hence, I say !
Why must my soul be torn ?

   Anselmo *enters, holding a Crucifix.*

 *Anselmo.*        Now, by this sign
Of Heaven's prevailing love, ye shall not harm
One ringlet of her head.—How! is there not
Enough of blood upon your burthen'd souls ?
Will not the visions of your midnight couch
Be wild and dark enough, but ye must heap
Crime upon crime ?—Be ye content : your dreams,
Your councils, and your banquetings, will yet
Be haunted by the voice which doth not sleep,
E'en though this maid be spared !—Constance,
  look up!
Thou shalt not die.
 *Raimond.*   Oh ! death e'en now hath veil'd
The light of her soft beauty.—Wake, my love !
Wake at my voice !
 *Procida.*      Anselmo, lead her hence,
And let her live, but never meet my sight.
—Begone !—my heart will burst.
 *Raimond.*        One last embrace !
—Again life's rose is opening on her cheek ;
Yet must we part.—So love is crush'd on earth !
But there are brighter worlds !—Farewell, farewell !
   (*He gives her to the care of* Anselmo.)
 *Constance (slowly recovering.)* There was a voice
  which call'd me.—Am I not
A spirit freed from earth ?—Have I not pass'd
The bitterness of death ?
 *Anselmo.*       Oh, haste away!
 *Constance.* Yes ! Raimond calls me.—He too is
  released
From his cold bondage.—We are free at last,
And all is well.—Away !
    (*She is led out by* Anselmo.
 *Raimond.*       The pang is o'er,
And I have but to die.
 *Montalba.*       Now, Procida,
Comes thy great task. Wake! summon to thine aid
All thy deep soul's commanding energies ;
For thou—a chief among us—must pronounce
The sentence of thy son.  It rests with thee.
 *Procida.* Ha ! ha !—Men's hearts should be of
  softer mould
Than in the elder time.—Fathers could doom
Their children *then* with an unfaltering voice,
And we must tremble thus !—Is it not said
That nature grows degenerate, earth being now
So full of days ?
 *Montalba.*    Rouse up thy mighty heart.
 *Procida.* Ay, thou say'st right.  There yet are
  souls which tower
As landmarks to mankind.—Well, what's the task ?
—There is a man to be condemn'd, you say ?
Is he then guilty ?
 *All.*        Thus we deem of him
With one accord.
 *Procida.*      And hath he naught to plead ?
 *Raimond.* Naught but a soul unstain'd.
 *Procida*        Why that is little

Stains on the soul are but as conscience deems
  them,
And conscience—may be sear'd.—But, for this
  sentence !
—Was't not the penalty imposed on man,
E'en from creation's dawn, that he must die ?
—It was : thus making guilt a sacrifice
Unto eternal justice ; and we but
Obey Heaven's mandate, when we cast dark souls
To th' elements from among us.—Be it so !
Such be *his* doom !—I have said.  Ay, now my
  heart
Is girt with adamant, whose cold weight doth press
Its gaspings down.—Off ! let me breathe in freedom !
—Mountains are on my breast !  (*He sinks back.*)
 *Montalba.*     Guards, bear the prisoner
Back to his dungeon.
 *Raimond.*      Father ! oh, look up ;
Thou art my father still !
 *Guido (leaving the tribunal, throws himself on the
  neck of Raimond.)* Oh ! Raimond, Raimond !
If it should be that I have wrong'd thee, say
Thou dost forgive me.
 *Raimond.*      Friend of my young days,
So may all-pitying Heaven !  (*Raimond is led out.*)
 *Procida.*       Whose voice was that ?
Where is he ?—gone ?—now I may breathe once
  more
In the free air of heaven.  Let us away.
          [ *Exeunt omnes.*

---

## ACT THE FIFTH.

### Scene I.—*A Prison, dimly lighted.*

Raimond *sleeping.* Procida *enters.*

 *Procida (gazing upon him earnestly.)*  Can he
  then sleep ?—Th' o'ershadowing night hath
  wrapt
Earth, at her stated hours—the stars have set
Their burning watch ; and all things hold their
  course
Of wakefulness and rest ; yet hath not sleep
Sat on mine eyelids since—but this avails not !
—And thus *he* slumbers !—" Why, this mien doth
  seem
As if its soul were but one lofty thought
Of an immortal destiny !"—his brow
Is calm as waves whereon the midnight heavens
Are imaged silently.—Wake, Raimond, wake !
Thy rest is deep.
 *Raimond (starting up.)*  My father !—Wherefore
  here ?
I am prepared to die, yet would I not
Fall by *thy* hand.
 *Procida.*    'Twas not for *this* I came.
 *Raimond.* Then wherefore ?—and upon thy lofty
  brow
Why burns the troubled flush ?
 *Procida.*      Perchance 't is shame.
Yes, it may well be shame !—for I have striven
With nature's feebleness, and been o'erpower'd.
—Howe'er it be, 't is not for *thee* to gaze,
Noting it thus.  Rise, let me loose thy chains.
Arise, and follow me ; but let thy step
Fall without sound on earth : I have prepared
The means for thy escape.
 *Raimond.*      What ! *thou* ! the austere,
The inflexible Procida ! hast *thou* done this,
Deeming me guilty still !
 *Procida.*      Upbraid me not !
It is even so.  There have been nobler deeds
By Roman fathers done,—but I am weak.
Therefore, again I say, arise ! and haste,
For the night wanes.  Thy fugitive course must be
To realms beyond the deep ; so let us part
In silence, and for ever.
 *Raimond.*      Let him fly
Who holds no deep asylum in his breast,
Wherein to shelter from the scoffs of men !
—I can sleep calmly here.
 *Procida*       Art thou in love

With death and infamy, that so thy choice
Is made, lost boy ! when freedom courts thy grasp?
   *Raimond.* Father ! to set th' irrevocable seal
Upon that shame wherewith ye have branded me,
There needs but flight.—What should I bear from
   this,
My native land ?—A blighted name, to rise
And part me, with its dark remembrances,
For ever from the sunshine !—O'er my soul
Bright shadowings of a nobler destiny
Float in dim beauty through the gloom ; but here,
On earth, my hopes are closed.
   *Procida.*          *Thy* hopes are closed !
And what were they to mine ?—Thou wilt not fly !
Why, let all traitors flock to thee, and learn
How proudly guilt can talk !—Let fathers rear
Their offspring henceforth, as the free wild birds
Foster their young ; when these can mount alone,
Dissolving nature's bonds—why should it not
Be so with us ?
   *Raimond.*      Oh, father !—Now I feel
What high prerogatives belong to death.
He hath a deep though voiceless eloquence,
To which I leave my cause. " His solemn veil
Doth with mysterious beauty clothe our virtues,
And in its vast oblivious folds, for ever
Give shelter to our faults."—When I am gone,
The mists of passion which have dimm'd my name
Will melt like day-dreams ; and my memory then
Will be—not what it should have been—for I
Must pass without my fame—but yet, unstain'd
As a clear morning dew-drop. Oh ! the grave
Hath rights inviolate as a sanctuary's,
And they should be my own !
   *Procida.*         Now, by just Heaven,
I will not thus be tortured !—Were my heart
But of thy guilt or innocence assured,
I could be calm again. " But, in this wild
Suspense—this conflict and vicissitude
Of opposite feelings and convictions—What !
Hath it been mine to temper and to bend
All spirits to my purpose ; have I raised
With a severe and passionless energy,
From the dread mingling of their elements,
Storms which have rock'd the earth ?—And shall I
   now
Thus fluctuate, as a feeble reed, the scorn
And plaything of the winds ?"—Look on me, boy !
Guilt never dared to meet these eyes, and keep
Its heart's dark secret close.—Oh, pitying Heaven,
Speak to my soul with some dread oracle,
And tell me which is truth.
   *Raimond.*        I will not plead.
I will not call th' Omnipotent to attest
My innocence. No, father, in thy heart
I know my birthright shall be soon restored ;
Therefore I look to death, and bid thee speed
The great absolver.
   *Procida.*        Oh ! my son, my son !
We will not part in wrath !—The sternest hearts,
Within their proud and guarded fastnesses,
Hide something still, round which their tendrils
   cling
With a close grasp, unknown to those who dress
Their love in smiles. And such wert thou to me !
The all which taught me that my soul was cast
In nature's mould.—And I must now hold on
My desolate course alone !—Why, be it thus !
He that doth guide a nation's star, should dwell
High o'er the clouds in regal solitude,
Sufficient to himself.
   *Raimond.*       Yet, on the summit,
When with her bright wings glory shadows thee,
Forget not him who coldly sleeps beneath,
Yet might have soar'd as high !
   *Procida.*        No, fear thou not !
Thou 'lt be remember'd long. The canker-worm
O' th' heart is ne'er forgotten.
   *Raimond.*       " Oh ! not thus—
I would not *thus* be thought of."
   *Procida.*        Let me deem
Again that thou art base !—for thy bright looks,
Thy glorious mien of fearlessness and truth,
Then would not haunt me as th' avenging powers
Follow'd the parricide.—Farewell, farewell !
I have no tears.—Oh ! thus thy mother look'd,

When, with a sad, yet half-triumphant smile,
All radiant with deep meaning, from her death-bed
She gave thee to my arms.
   *Raimond.*       Now death has lost
His sting, since thou believ'st me innocent.
   *Procida* (*wildly.*)   *Thou* innocent !—Am I thy
   murderer, then ?
Away ! I tell thee thou hast made my name
A scorn to men !—No ! I will *not* forgive thee ;
A traitor !—What ! the blood of Procida
Filling a traitor's veins ?—Let the earth drink it ;
*Thou* wouldst receive our foes !—but they shall
   meet
From thy perfidious lips a welcome, cold
As death can make it.—Go, prepare thy soul !
   *Raimond.* Father ! yet hear me !
   *Procida.*       No ! thou 'rt skill'd to make
E'en shame look fair.—Why should I linger thus ?
   (*Going to leave the prison, he turns back for a
        moment.*)
If there be aught—if aught—for which thou need'st
Forgiveness—not of me, but that dread power
From whom no heart is veil'd—delay thou not
Thy prayer.—Time hurries on.
   *Raimond.*       I am prepared.
   *Procida.* 'T is well.     [*Exit* PROCIDA.
   *Raimond.* Men talk of torture !—Can they wreak
Upon the sensitive and shrinking frame,
Half the mind bears and lives ?—My spirit feels
Bewilder'd ; on its powers this twilight gloom
Hangs like a weight of earth.—It should be morn,
Why, then, perchance, a beam of Heaven's bright
   sun
Hath pierced, ere now, the grating of my dungeon,
Telling of hope and mercy !
                 [*Exit into an inner cell.*

---

SCENE II.—A street of Palermo.

*Many* CITIZENS *assembled.*

   *First Citizen.* The morning breaks ; his time is
   almost come :
Will he be led this way ?
   *Second Citizen.*     Ay, so 't is said,
To die before that gate through which he purposed
The foe should enter in.
   *Third Citizen.*     'T was a vile plot !
And yet I would my hands were pure as his
From the deep stain of blood. Didst hear the sounds
I' th' air last night ?
   *Second Citizen.* Since the great work of slaughter,
Who hath not heard them duly at those hours
Which should be silent ?
   *Third Citizen.*     Oh ! the fearful mingling,
The terrible mimicry of human voices,
In every sound which to the heart doth speak
Of woe and death.
   *Second Citizen.* Ay, there was woman's shrill
And piercing cry ; and the low feeble wail
Of dying infants ; and the half-suppress'd
Deep groan of man in his last agonies !
And now and then there swell'd upon the breeze
Strange, savage bursts of laughter, wilder far
Than all the rest.
   *First Citizen.* Of our own fate, perchance,
These awful midnight wailings may be deem'd
An ominous prophecy.—Should France regain
Her power among us, doubt not, we shall have
Stern reckoners to account with.—Hark !
   (*The sound of trumpets heard at a distance.*)
   *Second Citizen.*     'T was but
A rushing of the breeze.
   *Third Citizen.*    E'en now, 't is said,
The hostile bands approach.
   (*The sound is heard gradually drawing nearer.*)
   *Second Citizen.*     Again ! that sound
Was no illusion. Nearer yet it swells—
They come, they come !

PROCIDA *enters.*

   *Procida.* The foe is at your gates ;
But hearts and hands prepared shall meet his onset
Why are ye loitering here ?
   *Citizens.*      My lord, we came——
   *Procida.* Think ye I know not wherefore ?—
   't was to see

A fellow-being die!—Ay, 'tis a sight
Man loves to look on, and the tenderest hearts
Recoil, and yet withdraw not from the scene.
For *this* ye came.—What! is our nature fierce,
Or is there that in mortal agony,
From which the soul, exulting in its strength,
Doth learn immortal lessons?—Hence, and arm!
Ere the night dews descend, ye will have seen
Enough of death; for this must be a day
Of battle!—'Tis the hour which troubled souls
Delight in, for its rushing storms are wings
Which bear them up!—Arm, arm! 'tis for your homes,
And all that lends them loveliness—Away!
　　　　　　　　　　　　　　　[*Exeunt.*

---

SCENE III.—*Prison of* RAIMOND.

RAIMOND, ANSELMO.

*Raimond.* And Constance then is safe!—Heaven
　　bless thee, father!
Good angels bear such comfort.
　*Anselmo.*　　　　　　　I have found
A safe asylum for thine honour'd love,
Where she may dwell until serener days,
With Saint Rosalia's gentlest daughters; those
Whose hallow'd office is to tend the bed
Of pain and death, and soothe the parting soul
With their soft hymns: and therefore are they
　call'd
" Sisters of Mercy."
　*Raimond.*　　　　Oh! that name, my Constance,
Befits thee well! E'en in our happiest days,
There was a depth of tender pensiveness,
Far in thine eyes' dark azure, speaking ever
Of pity and mild grief.—Is she at peace?
　*Anselmo.* Alas! what should I say?
　*Raimond.*　　　　　　　Why did I ask?
Knowing the deep and full devotedness
Of her young heart's affections?—Oh! the thought
Of my untimely fate will haunt her dreams,
Which should have been so tranquil!—And her
　soul,
Whose strength was but the lofty gift of love,
Even unto death will sicken.
　*Anselmo.*　　　　　　All that faith
Can yield of comfort, shall assuage her woes;
And still, whate'er betide, the light of Heaven
Rests on her gentle heart. But thou, my son!
Is thy young spirit master'd and prepared
For nature's fearful and mysterious change?
　*Raimond.* Ay, father! of my brief remaining
　　task
The least part is to die!—And yet the cup
Of life still mantled brightly to my lips,
Crown'd with that sparkling bubble, whose proud
　name
Is—glory!—Oh! my soul, from boyhood's morn,
Hath nursed such mighty dreams!—It was my hope
To leave a name, whose echo, from the abyss
Of time should rise, and float upon the winds,
Into the far hereafter; there to be
A trumpet-sound, a voice from the deep tomb,
Murmuring—Awake!—Arise!—But this is past!
Erewhile, and it had seem'd enough of shame,
To sleep *forgotten* in the dust—but now
—Oh God!—the undying record of my grave
Will be—Here sleeps a traitor!—One, whose crime
Was—to deem brave men might find nobler wea-
　pons
Than the cold murderer's dagger!
　*Anselmo.*　　　　　　Oh, my son,
Subdue these troubled thoughts! Thou wouldst
　not change
Thy lot for theirs, o'er whose dark dreams will
　hang
The avenging shadows, which the blood-stain'd
　soul
Doth conjure from the dead!
　*Raimond.*　　　　Thou 'rt right. I would not.
Yet 'tis a weary task to school the heart,
Ere years or griefs have tamed its fiery spirit
Into that still and passive fortitude,
Which is but learn'd from suffering.—Would the
　hour
To hush these passionate throbbings were at hand!

*Anselmo.* It will not be to-day. Hast thou not
　heard—
—But no—the rush, the trampling, and the stir
Of this great city, arming in her haste,
Pierce not these dungeon-depths.—The foe hath
　reach'd
Our gates, and all Palermo's youth, and all
Her warrior-men, are marshall'd, and gone forth
In that high hope which makes realities,
To the red field. Thy father leads them on.
　*Raimond* (*starting up.*) They are gone forth! my
　　father leads them on!
All, all Palermo's youth!—No! *one* is left,
Shut out from glory's race!—They are gone forth!
—Ay! now the soul of battle is abroad,
It burns upon the air!—The joyous winds
Are tossing warrior-plumes, the proud white foam
Of battle's roaring billows!—On my sight
The vision bursts—it maddens! 'tis the flash,
The lightning-shock of lances, and the cloud
Of rushing arrows, and the broad full blaze
Of helmets in the sun!—The very steed
With his majestic rider glorying shares
The hour's stern joy, and waves his floating mane
As a triumphant banner!—Such things are
Even now—and I am here!
　*Anselmo.*　　　　　　Alas, be calm!
To the same grave ye press,—thou that dost pine
Beneath a weight of chains, and they that rule
The fortunes of the fight.
　*Raimond.*　　　　　Ay! *Thou* canst feel
The calm thou wouldst impart, for unto thee
All men alike, the warrior and the slave,
Seem as thou say'st, but pilgrims, pressing on
To the same bourne.—Yet call it not the same;
*Their* graves who fall in this day's fight, will be
As altars to their country, visited
By fathers with their children, bearing wreaths,
And chanting hymns in honour of the dead:
Will mine be such?

　VITTORIA *rushes in wildly, as if pursued.*

　*Vittoria.*　　　　Anselmo! art thou found?
Haste, haste, or all is lost! Perchance thy voice
Whereby they deem Heaven speaks, thy lifted
　cross,
And prophet mien, may stay the fugitives,
Or shame them back to die.
　*Anselmo.*　　　　　　The fugitives!
What words are these?—the sons of Sicily
Fly not before the foe?
　*Vittoria.*　　　　　　That I should say
It is too true!
　*Anselmo.*　　　And thou—thou bleedest, lady!
　*Vittoria.* Peace! heed not me, when Sicily is
　　lost!
I stood upon the walls, and watch'd our bands,
As, with their ancient, royal banner spread,
Onward they march'd. The combat was begun,
The fiery impulse given, and valiant men
Had seal'd their freedom with their blood—when, lo,
That false Alberti led his recreant vassals
To join th' invader's host.
　*Raimond.*　　　　　His country's curse
Rest on the slave for ever!
　*Vittoria.*　　　　　Then distrust
E'en of their noble leaders, and dismay,
That swift contagion, on Palermo's bands
Came, like a deadly blight. They fled!—Oh shame
E'en now they fly!—Ay, through the city gates
They rush, as if all Etna's burning streams
Pursued their winged steps!
　*Raimond.*　　　　　Thou hast not named
Their chief—Di Procida—*He* doth not fly?
　*Vittoria.* No! like a kingly lion in the toils,
Daring the hunters yet, he proudly strives;
But all in vain! The few that breast the storm,
With Guido and Montalba, by his side,
Fight but for graves upon the battle-field.
　*Raimond.* And I am *here!* Shall there be power
　　Oh God!
In the roused energies of fierce despair,
To burst my heart—and not to rend my chains?

Oh, for one moment of the thunderbolt
To set the strong man free!
  *Vittoria (after gazing upon him earnestly.)* Why,
    't were a deed
Worthy the fame and blessing of all time,
To loose thy bonds, thou son of Procida!
Thou art no traitor!—from thy kindled brow
Looks out thy lofty soul!—rise! go forth!
And rouse the noble heart of Sicily
Unto high deeds again. Anselmo, haste;
Unbind him! Let my spirit still prevail,
Ere I depart—for the strong hand of death
Is on me now.   *(She sinks back against a pillar.)*
  *Anselmo.*   Oh Heaven! the life-blood streams
Fast from thy heart—thy troubled eyes grow dim
Who hath done this?
  *Vittoria.*   Before the gates I stood,
And in the name of him, the loved and lost,
With whom I soon shall be, all vainly strove
To stay the shameful flight. Then from the foe,
Fraught with my summons, to his viewless home,
Came the fleet shaft which pierced me.
  *Anselmo.*   Yet, oh yet,
It may not be too late. Help, help!
  *Vittoria.*   Away!
Bright is the hour which brings me liberty!

*ATTENDANTS enter.*

Haste, be those fetters riven!—Unbar the gates,
And set the captive free!
  *(The Attendants seem to hesitate.)* Know ye not *her*
Who should have worn your country's diadem?
  *Attendants.*. Oh, lady, we obey.

*(They take off* RAIMOND's *chains. He springs up,
exultingly.)*

  *Raimond.*   Is this no dream?
—Mount, eagle! thou art free!—Shall I then die,
Not 'midst the mockery of insulting crowds,
But on the field of banners, where the brave
Are striving for an immortality?
—It is e'en so!—Now for bright arms of proof,
A helm, a keen-edged falchion, and e'en yet
My father may be saved!
  *Vittoria.*   Away, be strong!
And let thy battle-word, to rule the storm,
Be—Conradin.   *(He rushes out.)*
    Oh! for one hour of life,
To hear that name blent with th' exulting shout
Of victory!—It will not be!—A mightier power
Doth summon me away.
  *Anselmo.*   To purer worlds
Raise thy last thoughts in hope.
  *Vittoria.*   Yes! he is there,
All glorious in his beauty!—Conradin!
Death parted us—and death shall reunite!
—He will not stay—it is all darkness now!
Night gathers o'er my spirit.   *(She dies.)*
  *Anselmo.*   She is gone!
It is an awful hour which stills the heart
That beat so proudly once.—Have mercy, Heaven!
    *(He kneels beside her.)*

SCENE IV.—*Before the Gates of Palermo.*

*Sicilians flying tumultuously towards the Gates.*

  *Voices (without.)* Montjoy! Montjoy! St. Dennis
    for Anjou!
Provençals, on!
  *Sicilians.*   Fly, fly, or all is lost!

*(*RAIMOND *appears in the gateway, armed, and carrying a banner.)*

  *Raimond.* Back, back, I say! ye men of Sicily!
All is not lost! Oh shame!—A few brave hearts
In such a cause, ere now, have set their breasts
Against the rush of thousands, and sustain'd,
And made the shock recoil.—Ay, man, free man,
Still to be call'd so, hath achieved such deeds
As heaven and earth have marvell'd at; and souls,
Whose spark yet slumbers with the days to come,
Shall burn to hear; transmitting brightly thus
Freedom from race to race!—Back! or prepare
Amidst your hearths, your bowers, your very
  shrines

To bleed and die in vain!—Turn, follow me!
Conradin, Conradin!—for Sicily
His spirit fights!—Remember Conradin!
    *(They begin to rally round him.)*
Ay, this is well!—Now follow me, and charge!

*The Provençals rush in, but are repulsed by the
  Sicilians.*

      *[Exeunt*

SCENE V.—*Part of the Field of Battle.*

MONTALBA *enters wounded, and supported by* RAI-
MOND, *whose face is concealed by his helmet.*

  *Raimond.* Here rest thee, warrior.
  *Montalba.*   Rest! ay, death is rest,
And such will soon be mine—But thanks to *thee,*
I shall not die a captive. Brave Sicilian!
These lips are all unused to soothing words,
Or I should bless the valour which hath won,
For my last hour, the proud free solitude
Wherewith my soul would gird itself.—Thy name?
  *Raimond.* 'T will be no music to thine ear, Mon-
  talba.
Gaze—read it thus! *(He lifts the visor of his helmet.)*
  *Montalba.*   Raimond di Procida!
  *Raimond.* Thou hast pursued me with a bitter
  hate:
But fare thee well! Heaven's peace be with thy
  soul!
I must away—One glorious effort more,
And this proud field is won!   *[Exit* RAIMOND.
  *Montalba.*   Am I thus humbled?
How my heart sinks within me! But 'tis death
(And he can tame the mightiest) hath subdued
My towering nature thus!—Yet is he welcome!
That youth—'t was in his pride he rescued me!
I was his deadliest foe, and thus he proved
His fearless scorn. Ha! ha! but he shall fail
To melt me into womanish feebleness.
*There* I still baffle him—the grave shall seal
My lips for ever—mortal shall not hear
Montalba say—"*forgive!*"   *[He dies.*

SCENE VI.—*Another part of the Field.*

PROCIDA, GUIDO, *and other Sicilians.*

  *Procida.* The day is ours; but he, the brave
  unknown,
Who turn'd the tide of battle; he whose path
Was victory—who hath seen him?

ALBERTI *is brought in, wounded and fettered.*

  *Alberti.*   Procida!
  *Procida.* Be silent, traitor!—Bear him from my
  sight
Unto your deepest dungeons.
  *Alberti.*   In the grave
A nearer home awaits me.—Yet one word
Ere my voice fail—thy son——
  *Procida.*   Speak, speak!
  *Alberti.*   Thy son
Knows not a thought of guilt. That trait'rous plot
Was mine alone.   *(He is led away.)*
  *Procida.*   Attest it, earth and Heaven!
My son is guiltless!—Hear it, Sicily!
The blood of Procida is noble still!—
My son!—He lives, he lives!—His voice shall speak
Forgiveness to his sire!—His name shall cast
Its brightness o'er my soul!
  *Guido.*   Oh, day of joy!
The brother of my heart is worthy still
The lofty name he bears.

ANSELMO *enters.*

  *Procida.*   Anselmo, welcome!
In a glad hour we meet; for know, my son
Is guiltless.
  *Anselmo.* And victorious! by his arm
All hath been rescued.
  *Procida.*   How!—the unknown——
  *Anselmo*   Was he
Thy noble Raimond! By Vittoria's band
Freed from his bondage, in that awful hour
When all was flight and terror.
  *Procida.*   Now my cup
Of joy too brightly mantles!—Let me press

My warrior to a father's heart—and die;
For life hath naught beyond—Why comes he not?
*Anselmo*, lead me to my valiant boy!
   *Anselmo.* Temper this proud delight.
   *Procida.*        What means that look?
He hath not fallen?
   *Anselmo.*      He lives.
   *Procida.*        Away, away!
Bid the wide city with triumphal pomp
Prepare to greet her victor.　Let this hour
Atone for all his wrongs!—     [*Exeunt.*

---

SCENE VII.—*Garden of a Convent.*

RAIMOND *is led in wounded, leaning on Attendants.*

   *Raimond.* Bear me to no dull couch, but let me die
In the bright face of nature!—Lift my helm,
That I may look on Heaven.
   *First Attendant (to second Attendant.)* Lay him
     to rest
On this green sunny bank, and I will call
Some holy sister to his aid: but thou
Return unto the field, for high-born men
There need the peasant's aid.
     [*Exit second Attendant.*
   (*To Raimond.*)    Here gentle hands
Shall tend thee, warrior; for in these retreats
*They* dwell, whose vows devote them to the care
Of all that suffer. May'st thou live to bless them!
     [*Exit first Attendant.*
   *Raimond.* Thus have I wish'd to die!—'Twas a
     proud strife!
My father bless'd th' unknown who rescued him,
(Bless'd him, alas! because unknown!) and Guido,
Beside me bravely struggling, call'd aloud,
" Noble Sicilian, on!"　Oh! had they deem'd
'Twas I who led that rescue, they had spurn'd
Mine aid, though 'twas deliverance; and their looks
Had fallen, like blights, upon me.—There is one,
Whose eye ne'er turn'd on mine, but its blue light
Grew softer, trembling through the dewy mist
Raised by deep tenderness!—Oh, might the soul
Set in that eye, shine on me ere I perish!
—Is't not her voice?

CONSTANCE *enters, speaking to a Nun, who turns
into another path.*

   *Constance.*   Oh! happy they, kind sister,
Whom thus ye tend; for it is theirs to fall
With brave men side by side, when the roused heart
Beats proudly to the last!—There are high souls
Whose hope was such a death, and 'tis denied!
     (*She approaches* RAIMOND.)
Young warrior, is there aught—*thou* here, my
     Raimond!
*Thou* here—and thus!—Oh! is this joy or woe?
   *Raimond.* Joy, be it joy, my own, my blessed love,
E'en on the grave's dim verge!—yes! it *is* joy!
My Constance! victors have been crown'd, ere now,
With the green shining laurel, when their brows
Wore death's own impress—and it may be thus
E'en yet, with me!—They freed me, when the foe
Had half prevail'd, and I have proudly earn'd,
With my heart's dearest blood, the meed to die
Within thine arms.
   *Constance.*   Oh! speak not thus—to die!
These wounds may yet be closed.
     (*She attempts to bind his wounds.*)
     Look on me, love!
Why, there is more than life in thy glad mien.
'Tis full of hope! and from thy kindled eye
Breaks e'en unwonted light, whose ardent ray
Seems born to be immortal!
   *Raimond.*     'Tis e'en so!
The parting soul doth gather all her fires
Around her; all her glorious hopes, and dreams,
And burning aspirations, to illume
The shadowy dimness of the untrodden path
Which lies before her; and, encircled thus,
Awhile she sits in dying eyes, and thence
Sends forth her bright farewell.　Thy gentle cares
Are vain, and yet I bless them.
   *Constance.*   Say not vain;
The dying look not thus　We shall not part!

   *Raimond.* I have seen death ere now, and know
     him wear
Full many a changeful aspect.
   *Constance.*     Oh! but none
Radiant as thine, my warrior!—Thou wilt live
Look round thee!—all is sunshine—is not this
A smiling world?
   *Raimond.*     Ay, gentlest love, a world
Of joyous beauty and magnificence,
Almost too fair to leave!—Yet must we tame
Our ardent hearts to this!—Oh, weep thou not!
There is no home for liberty, or love,
Beneath these festal skies!—Be not deceived;
My way lies far beyond!—I shall be soon
That viewless thing, which, with its mortal weeds
Casting off meaner passions, yet, we trust,
Forgets not how to love!
   *Constance.*   And must this be?
Heaven, thou art merciful!—Oh! bid our souls
Depart together!
   *Raimond.*   Constance! there is strength
Within thy gentle heart, which hath been proved
Nobly, for me :—Arouse it once again!
Thy grief unmans me—and I fain would meet
That which approaches, as a brave man yields
With proud submission to a mightier foe.
—It is upon me now!
   *Constance.*   I will be calm.
Let thy head rest upon my bosom, Raimond,
And I will so suppress its quick deep sobs,
They shall but rock thee to thy rest.　There is
A world, (ay, let us seek it!) where no blight
Falls on the beautiful rose of youth, and there
I shall be with thee soon!

PROCIDA *and* ANSELMO *enter.* PROCIDA, *on seeing*
   RAIMOND, *starts back.*

   *Anselmo.*     Lift up thy head,
Brave youth, exultingly! for lo! thine hour
Of glory comes!—Oh! doth it come too late?
E'en now the false Alberti hath confess'd
   hat guilty plot, for which thy life was doom'd
To be th' atonement.
   *Raimond.*   'Tis enough! Rejoice,
Rejoice, my Constance! for I leave a name
O'er which thou may'st weep proudly!
     (*He sinks back.*)
     To thy breast
Fold me yet closer, for an icy dart
Hath touch'd my veins.
   *Constance.* And must thou leave me, Raimond?
Alas! thine eye grows dim—its wandering glance
Is full of dreams.
   *Raimond.*   Haste, haste, and tell my father
I was no traitor!
   *Procida (rushing forward.)* To that father's heart
Return, forgiving all thy wrongs, return!
Speak to me, Raimond!—Thou wert ever kind,
And brave, and gentle! Say that all the past
Shall be forgiven! That word from none but thee
My lips e'er ask'd.—Speak to me once, my boy,
My pride, my hope!—And is it with thee thus?
Look on me yet!—Oh! must this woe be borne?
   *Raimond.* Off with this weight of chains! it is
     not meet
For a crown'd conqueror!—Hark! the trumpet's
     voice!

     (*A sound of triumphant music is hear
     gradually approaching.*)

Is't not a thrilling call?—What drowsy spell
Benumbs me thus?—Hence! I am free again!
Now swell your festal strains, the field is won!
Sing me to glorious dreams.    (*He dies.*)
   *Anselmo.*     The strife is past.
There fled a noble spirit
   *Constance.*     Hush! he sleeps—
Disturb him not!
   *Anselmo.*     Alas! this is no sleep
From which the eye doth radiantly unclose:
Bow down thy soul, for earthly hope is o'er!

     (*The music continues approaching.　*GUIDO
     *enters, with Citizens and Soldiers.*)

   *Guido.* The shrines are deck'd, the festive torches
     blaze—

Where is our brave deliverer ?—We are come
To crown Palermo's victor !
  *Anselmo.*                Ye come too late.
The voice of human praise doth send no echo
Into the world of spirits.     (*The music ceases.*)
  *Procida* (*after a pause.*) Is this dust
I look on—Raimond ?—'t is but sleep—a smile
On his pale cheek sits proudly. Raimond, wake !
Oh, God ! and this was his triumphant day !
My son, my injured son !
  *Constance* (*starting.*)   Art *thou* his father ?
I know thee now.—Hence ! with thy dark stern eye,
And thy cold heart ! Thou canst not wake him
    now .
Away ! he will not answer but to me,
For none like me hath loved him ! He is mine !
Ye shall not rend him from me.
  *Procida.*               Oh ! he knew

Thy love,. poor maid !—Shrink from me now no
    more !
He knew *thy* heart—but who shall tell him now
The depth, th' intenseness, and the agony,
Of my suppress'd affection ?—I have learn'd
All his high worth in time to deck his grave !
Is there not power in the strong spirit's woe
To force an answer from the viewless world
Of the departed ?—Raimond !—Speak ! forgive !
Raimond ! my victor, my deliverer, hear !
Why, what a world is this !—Truth ever bursts
On the dark soul too late ; and glory crowns
Th' unconscious dead ! An hour comes to break
The mightiest hearts !—My son ! my son ! is this
A day of triumph !—Ay, for thee alone !
    (*He throws himself upon the body of* RAIMOND.)
                [*Curtain falls*

# THE

# LEAGUE OF THE ALPS;

OR,

## THE MEETING ON THE FIELD OF GRUTLI.

# ADVERTISEMENT.

It was in the year 1304, that the Swiss rose against the tyranny of the Bailiffs appointed over them by Albert of Austria. The field called the Grutli, at the foot of the Seelisberg, and near the boundaries of Uri and Unterwalden, was fixed upon by three spirited yeomen, Walter Furst, (the father-in-law of William Tell,) Werner Stauffacher, and Erni (or Arnold) Melchthal, as their place of meeting to deliberate on the accomplishment of their projects.

"Hither came Furst and Melchthal, along secret paths over the heights, and Stauffacher in his boat across the Lake of the Four Cantons. On the night preceding the 11th of November, 1307, they met here, each with ten associates, men of approved worth; and while at this solemn hour they were wrapt in the contemplation that on their success depended the fate of their whole posterity, Werner, Walter, and Arnold, held up their hands to heaven, and in the name of the Almighty, who has created man to an inalienable degree of freedom, swore jointly and strenuously to defend that freedom. The thirty associates heard the oath with awe; and with uplifted hands attested the same God, and all his saints, that they were firmly bent on offering up their lives for the defence of their injured liberty. They then calmly agreed on their future proceedings, and for the present, each returned to his hamlet."—*Planta's History of the Helvetic Confederacy.*

On the first day of the year 1308, they succeeded in throwing off the Austrian yoke, and "it is well attested," says the same author, "that not one drop of blood was shed on this memorable occasion, nor had one proprietor to lament the loss of a claim, a privilege, or an inch of land. The Swiss met on the succeeding Sabbath, and once more confirmed by oath their ancient, and (as they fondly named it) their perpetual league."

# THE

# LEAGUE OF THE ALPS.

### I.

'Twas night upon the Alps.—The Senn's (1) wild
   horn,
Like a wind's voice, had pour'd its last long tone,
Whose pealing echoes through the larch-woods
   borne,
To the low cabins of the glens made known
That welcome steps were nigh. The flocks had
   gone,
By cliff and pine-bridge, to their place of rest;
The chamois slumber'd, for the chase was done;
His cavern-bed of moss the hunter press'd,
And the rock-eagle couch'd high on his cloudy nest.

### II.

Did the land sleep?—the woodman's axe had
   ceased
Its ringing notes upon the beech and plane;
The grapes were gather'd in; the vintage feast
Was closed upon the hills, the reaper's strain
Hush'd by the streams; the year was in its wane,
The night in its mid-watch; it was a time
E'en mark'd and hallow'd unto slumber's reign.
But thoughts were stirring, restless and sublime,
And o'er his white Alps moved the spirit of the
   clime.

### III.

For there, where snows, in crowning glory
   spread,
High and unmark'd by mortal footstep lay;
And there, where torrents, 'mid the ice-caves fed,
Burst in their joy of light and sound away;
And there, where freedom, as in scornful play,
Had hung man's dwellings 'midst the realms of
   air,
O'er cliffs the very birth-place of the day—
Oh! who would dream that tyranny could dare
To lay her withering hand on God's bright works
   e'en there?

### IV.

Yet thus it was—amidst the fleet streams gush-
   ing
To bring down rainbows o'er their sparry cell,
And the glad heights, through mist and tempest
   rushing
Up where the sun's red fire-glance earliest fell,
And the fresh pastures where the herd's sweet
   bell
Recall'd such life as Eastern patriarchs led:
*There* peasant-men their free thoughts might not
   tell
Save in the hour of shadows and of dread,
And hollow sounds that wake to Guilt's dull
   stealthy tread.

### V.

But in a land of happy shepherd homes,
On its green hills in quiet joy reclining
With their bright hearth-fires 'midst the twilight
   glooms,
From bowery lattice through the fir-woods shin-
   ing;
A land of legends and wild songs, entwining
Their memory with all memories loved and
   blest—
In such a land there dwells a power, combining
The strength of many a calm, but fearless breast;
—And woe to him who breaks the Sabbath of its
   rest!

### VI.

A sound went up—the wave's dark sleep was
   broken—
On Uri's lake was heard a midnight oar—
Of man's brief course a troubled moment's token
Th' eternal waters to their barriers bore;
And then their gloom a flashing image wore
Of torch-fires streaming out o'er crag and wood,
And the wild falcon's wing was heard to soar
In startled haste—and by that moonlight flood,
A band of patriot-men on Grutli's verdure stood.

### VII.

They stood in arms—the wolf-spear and the bow
Had waged their war on things of mountain
   race;
Might not their swift stroke reach a mail-clad
   foe?
—Strong hands in harvest, daring feet in chase,
True hearts in fight, were gather'd on that place
Of secret council.—Not for fame or spoil
So met those men in Heaven's majestic face;—
To guard free hearths they rose, the sons of toil,
The hunter of the rocks, the tiller of the soil.

### VIII.

O'er their low pastoral valleys might the tide
Of years have flow'd, and still, from sire to son,
Their names and records on the green earth died,
As cottage-lamps, expiring one by one,
In the dim glades, when midnight hath begun
To hush all sound.—But silent on its height,
The snow-mass, full of death, while ages run
Their course, may slumber, bathed in rosy light,
Till some rash voice or step disturb its brooding
   might.

### IX.

So were *they* roused—th' invading step had past
Their cabin thresholds, and the lowly door,
Which well had stood against the Fohnwind's (2)
   blast,
Could bar Oppression from their home no more.

Why, what had *she* to do where all things wore
Wild grandeur's impress?—In the storm's free way,
How dared *she* lift her pageant crest before
Th' enduring and magnificent array
Of sovereign Alps, that wing'd their eagles with
the day?

### X.

This might not long be borne—the tameless hills
Have voices from the cave and cataract swelling,
Fraught with His name, whose awful presence fills
Their deep lone places, and for ever telling
That He hath made man free! and they whose dwelling
Was in those ancient fastnesses, gave ear;—
The weight of sufferance from their hearts repelling,
They rose—the forester—the mountaineer—
Oh! what hath earth more strong than the good peasant-spear?

### XI.

Sacred be Grutli's field—their vigil keeping
Through many a blue and starry summer-night,
There while the sons of happier lands were sleeping,
Had those brave Switzers met; and in the sight
Of the just God, who pours forth burning might
To gird the oppress'd, had given their deep thoughts way,
And braced their spirits for the patriot fight,
With lovely images of homes that lay
Bower'd 'midst the rustling pines, or by the torrent spray.

### XII.

Now had endurance reach'd its bounds!—They came
With courage set in each bright earnest eye,
The day, the signal, and the hour to name,
When they should gather on their hills to die,
Or shake the Glaciers with their joyous cry
For the land's freedom.—'Twas a scene, combining
All glory in itself—the solemn sky,
The stars, the waves their soften'd light enshrining,
And man's high soul supreme o'er mighty Nature shining.

### XIII.

Calmly they stood, and with collected mien,
Breathing their souls in voices firm but low,
As if the spirit of the hour and scene,
With the woods' whisper and the waves' sweet flow,
Had temper'd in their thoughtful hearts the glow
Of all indignant feeling. To the breath
Of Dorian flute, and lyre-note soft and slow,
E'en thus, of old, the Spartan from its sheath
Drew his devoted sword, and girt himself for death.

### XIV.

And three, that seem'd as chieftains of the band,
Were gather'd in the midst on that lone shore
By Uri's lake—a father of the land, (3)
One on his brow the silent record wore
Of many days whose shadows had pass'd o'er
His path among the hills, and quench'd the dreams
Of youth with sorrow.—Yet from memory's lore
Still his life's evening drew its loveliest gleams,
For he had walk'd with God, beside the mountain streams.

### XV,

And his gray hairs, in happier times, might well
To their last pillow silently have gone,
As melts a wreath of snow.—But who shall tell
How life may task the spirit?—He was one,
Who from its morn a freeman's work had done,
And reap'd his harvest, and his vintage press'd,
Fearless of wrong; and now, at set of sun,
He bow'd not to his years, for on the breast
Of a still chainless land he deem'd it much to rest.

### XVI.

But for such holy rest strong hands must toil,
Strong hearts endure!—By that pale elder's side,
Stood one that seem'd a monarch of the soil,
Serene and stately in his manhood's pride,
Werner, (4) the brave and true!—If men have died,
Their hearths and shrines inviolate to keep,
He was a mate for such.—The voice, that cried
Within his breast, " Arise !" came still and deep
From his far home, that smiled e'en then in moonlight sleep.

### XVII.

It was a home to die for!—As it rose
Through its vine-foliage, sending forth a sound
Of mirthful childhood, o'er the green repose
And laughing sunshine of the pastures round;
And, he whose life to that sweet spot was bound,
Raised unto Heaven a glad yet thoughtful eye,
And set his free step firmer on the ground,
When o'er his soul its melodies went by
As through some Alpine pass, a breeze of Italy.

### XVIII.

But who was he, that on his hunting-spear
Lean'd with a prouder and more fiery bearing?
—His was a brow for tyrant hearts to fear,
Within the shadow of its dark locks wearing
That which they may not tame—a soul declaring
War against earth's oppressors.—'Midst the throng,
Of other mould he seem'd, and loftier daring,
One whose blood swept high impulses along,
One that should pass, and leave a name for warlike song.

### XIX.

A memory on the mountains!—one to stand,
When the hills echoed with the deepening swell
Of hostile trumpets, foremost for the land,
And in some rock defile, or savage dell,
Array her peasant-children to repel
Th' invader, sending arrows for his chains!
Ay, one to fold around him, as he fell,
Her banner with a smile—for through his veins
The joy of danger flow'd, as torrents to the plains.

### XX.

There was at times a wildness in the light
Of his quick-flashing eye; a something, born
Of the free Alps, and beautifully bright,
And proud, and tameless, laughing Fear to scorn!
It well might be!—Young Erni's (5) step had worn
The mantling snows on their most regal steeps,
And track'd the lynx above the clouds of morn,
And follow'd where the flying chamois leaps
Across the dark-blue rifts, th' unfathom'd glacier deeps.

### XXI.

He was a creature of the Alpine sky,
A being whose bright spirit had been fed
'Midst the crown'd heights of joy and liberty,
And thoughts of power.—He knew each path which led
To the rock's treasure-caves, whose crystals shed
Soft light o'er secret fountains.—At the tone
Of his loud horn, the Lammer-Geyer (6) had spread
A startled wing; for oft that peal had blown
Where the free cataract's voice was wont to sound alone.

### XXII.

His step had track'd the waste, his soul had stirr'd
The ancient solitudes—his voice had told
Of wrongs to call down Heaven. (7) That tale was heard
In Hasli's dales, and where the shepherd's fold
Their flocks in dark ravine and craggy hold
On the bleak Oberland; and where the light
Of Day's last footstep bathes in burning gold

Great Righi's cliffs; and where Mount Pilate's
  height
Casts o'er his glassy lake the darkness of his might.

### XXIII.

Nor was it heard in vain.—There all things press
High thoughts on man. The fearless hunter
  pass'd,
And, from the bosom of the wilderness,
There leapt a spirit and a power to cast
The weight of bondage down—and bright and
  fast,
As the clear waters, joyously and free,
Burst from the desert-rock, it rush'd at last,
Through the far valleys; till the patriot three
Thus with their brethren stood, beside the Forest
  Sea.(8)

### XXIV.

They link'd their hands,—they pledged their
  stainless faith,
In the dread presence of attesting Heaven—
They bound their hearts to suffering and to
  death,
With the severe and solemn transport given
To bless such vows.—How man had striven,
How man *might* strive, and vainly strive, they
  knew,
And call'd upon their God, whose arm had riven
The crest of many a tyrant, since He blew
The foaming sea-wave on, and 'Egypt's might
  o'erthrew.

### XXV.

They knelt, and rose in strength.—The valleys
  lay
Still in their dimness, but the peaks which darted
Into the bright mid-air, had caught from day
A flush of fire, when those true Switzers parted
Each to his glen or forest, steadfast-hearted,
And full of hope. Not many suns had worn
Their setting glory, ere from slumber started
Ten thousand voices, of the mountains born—
So far was heard the blast of Freedom's echoing
  horn !

### XXVI.

The ice-vaults trembled, when that peal came
  rending
The frozen stillness which around them hung ;
From cliff to cliff the avalanche descending,
Gave answer, till the sky's blue hollows rung:
And the flame-signals through the midnight
  sprung,
From the Surennen rocks like banners streaming
To the far Seelisberg ; whence light was flung
On Grutli's field, till all the red lake gleaming
Shone out, a meteor-heaven in its wild splendour
  seeming.

### XXVII.

And the winds toss'd each summit's blazing crest,
As a host's plumage ; and the giant pines,
Fell'd where they waved o'er crag and eagle's
  nest,
Heap'd up the flames. The clouds grew fiery
  signs,

As o'er a city's burning towers and shrines
Reddening the distance. Wine-cups, crown'd
  and bright,
In Werner's dwelling flow'd; through leafless
  vines
From Walter's hearth stream'd forth the festive
  light,
And Erni's blind old sire gave thanks to Heaven
  that night.

### XXVIII.

Then on the silence of the snows there lay
A Sabbath's quiet sunshine,—and its bell
Fill'd the hush'd air awhile, with lonely sway
For the stream's voice was chain'd by Winter's
  spell,
The deep wood-sounds had ceased.—But rock and
  dell
Rung forth, ere long, when strains of jubilee
Peal'd from the mountain-churches, with a swell
Of praise to Him who stills the raging sea,—
For now the strife was closed, the glorious Alps
  were free !

## NOTES.

#### NOTE 1.

*————The Senn's wild horn.*

Senn, the name given to a herdsman among the Swiss Alps.

#### NOTE 2.

*————Against the Fohnwind's blast.*

Fohnwind, the South-east wind, which frequently lays waste the country before it.

#### NOTE 3.

*————A father of the land.*

Walter Furst, the father-in-law of Tell.

#### NOTE 4.

*Warner, the brave and true ! &c.*

Werner Stauffacher, who had been urged by his wife to rouse and unite his countrymen for the deliverance of Switzerland.

#### NOTE 5.

*————Young Erni's step had worn, &c.*

Erni, Arnold Melchthal.

#### NOTE 6.

*————The Lammer-Geyer had spread, &c.*

The Lammer-Geyer, the largest kind of Alpine eagle.

#### NOTE 7.

*Of wrongs to call down Heaven, &c.*

The eyes of his aged father had been put out, by the orders of the Austrian Governor.

#### NOTE 8.

*————Beside the Forest-Sea.*

Forest-Sea. The Lake of the Four Cantons is frequently so called.

# RECORDS OF WOMAN.

Mightier far
Than strength of nerve or sinew, or the sway
Of magic, potent over sun and star,
Is love, though oft to agony distrest,
And though his favourite seat be feeble woman's breast.
*Wordsworth.*

Das ist das Loos des Schonen auf der Erde!
*Schiller.*

## ARABELLA STUART.

"The Lady Arabella," as she has been frequently entitled, was descended from Margaret, eldest daughter of Henry VII., and consequently allied, by birth, to Elizabeth, as well as James I. This affinity to the throne proved the misfortune of her life, as the jealousies which it constantly excited in her royal relatives, who were anxious to prevent her marrying, shut her out from the enjoyment of that domestic happiness which her heart appears to have so fervently desired. By a secret, but early discovered union, with William Seymour, son of Lord Beauchamp, she alarmed the cabinet of James, and the wedded lovers were immediately placed in separate confinement. From this they found means to concert a romantic plan of escape; and having won over a female attendant, by whose assistance she was disguised in male attire, Arabella, though faint from recent sickness and suffering, stole out in the night, and at last reached an appointed spot, where a boat and servants were in waiting. She embarked; and, at break of day, a French vessel, engaged to receive her, was discovered and gained. As Seymour, however, had not yet arrived, she was desirous that the vessel should lie at anchor for him; but this wish was overruled by her companions, who, contrary to her entreaties, hoisted sail, "which," says D'Israeli, "occasioned so fatal a termination to this romantic adventure. Seymour, indeed, had escaped from the Tower:—he reached the wharf, and found his confidential man waiting with a boat, and arrived at Lee. The time passed; the waves were rising; Arabella was not there; but in the distance he descried a vessel. Hiring a fisherman to take him on board, he discovered, to his grief, on hailing it, that it was not the French ship charged with his Arabella; in despair and confusion he found another ship from Newcastle, which, for a large sum, altered its course, and landed him in Flanders."— Arabella, meantime, while imploring her attendants to linger, and earnestly looking out for the expected boat of her husband, was overtaken in Calais Roads by a vessel in the King's service, and brought back to a captivity, under the suffering of which her mind and constitution gradually sunk——"What passed in that dreadful imprisonment, cannot, perhaps, be recovered for authentic history,—but enough is known; that her mind grew impaired, that she finally lost her reason, and, if the duration of her imprisonment was short, that it was only terminated by her death. Some effusions, often begun and never ended, written and erased, incoherent and rational, yet remain among her papers."—*D'Israeli's Curiosities of Literature.*—The following poem, meant as some record of her fate, and the imagined fluctuations of her thoughts and feelings, is supposed to commence during the time of her first imprisonment, while her mind was yet buoyed up by the consciousness of Seymour's affection, and the cherished hope of eventual deliverance.

---

And is not love in vain,
Torture enough without a living tomb?
*Byron.*

Fermossi al fin il cor che balzo tanto.
*Pindemonte.*

'T was but a dream!—I saw the stag leap free,
  Under the boughs where early birds were singing
I stood, o'ershadow'd by the greenwood tree,
  And heard, it seem'd, a sudden bugle ringing
Far thro' a royal forest: then the fawn
Shot, like a gleam of light, from grassy lawn
To secret covert;—and the smooth turf shook,
And lilies quiver'd by the glade's lone brook,
And young leaves trembled, as, in fleet career,
A princely band, with horn. and hound, and spear,
Like a rich masque swept forth. I saw the dance
Of their white plumes, that bore a silvery glance
Into the deep wood's heart; and all pass'd by,
Save one—I met the smile of *one* clear eye,
Flashing out joy to mine.—Yes, *thou* wert there,
Seymour! a soft wind blew the clustering hair
Back from thy gallant brow, as thou didst rein
Thy courser, turning from that gorgeous train,
And fling, methought, thy hunting-spear away,
And, lightly graceful in thy green array,
Bound to my side; and we, that met and parted,
  Ever in dread of some dark watchful power,
Won back to childhood's trust, and, fearless-hearted,
  Blent the glad fullness of our thoughts that hour
Ev'n like the mingling of sweet streams, beneath
Dim woven leaves, and midst the floating breath
Of hidden forest flowers.

### II.

            'T is past!—I wake,
  A captive, and alone, and far from thee,
My love and friend! Yet fostering, for thy sake,
  A quenchless hope of happiness to be;
And feeling still my woman's spirit strong,
In the deep faith which lifts from earthly wrong,
A heavenward glance. I know, I know our love
Shall yet call gentle angels from above,
By its undying fervour; and prevail,
Sending a breath, as of the spring's first gale,
Thro' hearts now cold; and, raising its bright face
With a free gush of sunny tears erase
The characters of anguish; in this trust,
I bear, I strive, I bow not to the dust,
That I may bring thee back no faded form,
No bosom chill'd and blighted by the storm,
But all my youth's first treasures, when we meet
Making past sorrow, by communion, sweet.

### III.

And thou too art in bonds!—yet droop thou not,
Oh, my beloved!—there is *one* hopeless lot,
But one, and that not ours. Beside the dead
*There* sits the grief that mantles up its head,
Loathing the laughter and proud pomp of light,
When darkness, from the vainly-doting sight,
Covers its beautiful! (1) If thou wert gone
  To the grave's bosom, with thy radiant brow,—
If thy deep-thrilling voice, with that low tone
  Of earnest tenderness, which now, ev'n now,
Seems floating thro' my soul, were music taken
For ever from this world,—oh! thus forsaken,
Could I bear on?—thou liv'st, thou liv'st, thou 'rt
            mine!
With this glad thought I make my heart a shrine,
And by the lamp which quenchless there shall burn,
Sit, a lone watcher for the day's return.

### IV.

And lo! the joy that cometh with the morning,
  Brightly victorious o'er the hours of care!
I have not watch'd in vain, serenely scorning
  The wild and busy whispers of despair!

Thou hast sent tidings, as of heaven.—I wait
　The hour, the sign, for blessed flight to thee.
Oh! for the skylark's wing that seeks its mate
　As a star shoots!—but on the breezy sea
We shall meet soon.—To think of such an hour
　Will not my heart, o'erburden'd by its bliss,
Faint and give way within me, as a flower
　Borne down and perishing by noontide's kiss?
Yet shall I *fear* that lot?—the perfect rest,
The full deep joy of dying on thy breast,
After long-suffering won! So rich a close
Too seldom crowns with peace affection's woes.
Sunset!—I tell each moment—from the skies
　The last red splendour floats along my wall,
Like a king's banner!—Now it melts, it dies!
I see one star—I hear—'t was not the call,
Th' expected voice; my quick heart throbb'd too
　soon.
I must keep vigil till yon rising moon
Shower down less golden light. Beneath her beam
Thro' my lone lattice pour'd, I sit and dream
Of summer lands afar, where holy love,
Under the vine, or in the citron-grove,
May breathe from terror.
　　　　Now the night grows deep,
And silent as its clouds, and full of sleep.
I hear my veins beat.—Hark! a bell's slow chime.
My heart strikes with it.—Yet again—'t is time!
A step!—a voice!—or but a rising breeze?
Hark!—haste!—I come, to meet thee on the seas.

### VI.

Now never more, oh! never, in the worth
Of its pure cause, let sorrowing love on earth
Trust fondly—never more!—the hope is crush'd
That lit my life, the voice within me hush'd
That spoke sweet oracles; and I return
To lay my youth, as in a burial-urn,
Where sunshine may not find it.—All is lost!
No tempest met o r barks—no billow toss'd;
Yet were they sever'd, ev'n as we must be,
That so have loved, so striven our hearts to free
From their close-coiling fate! In vain—in vain!
The dark links meet, and clasp themselves again,
And press out life.—Upon the deck I stood,
And a white sail came gliding o'er the flood,
Like some proud bird of ocean; then mine eye
Strain'd out, one moment earlier to descry
The form it ached for, and the bark's career
Seem'd slow to that fond yearning: It drew near
Fraught with our foes!—What boots it to recall
The strife, the tears? Once more a prison-wall
Shuts the green hills and woodlands from my sight
And joyous glance of waters to the light,
And thee, my Seymour, thee!
　　　　　　　I will not sink!
　Thou, *thou* hast rent the heavy chain that bound
　　thee;
And this shall be my strength—the joy to think
　That thou may'st wander with heaven's breath
　　around thee;
And all the laughing sky! This thought shall yet
Shine o'er my heart, a radiant amulet,
Guarding it from despair. Thy bonds are broken,
And unto me, I know, thy true love's token
Shall one day be deliverance, though the years
ie dim between, o'erhung with mists of tears.

### VII.

My friend, my friend! where art thou? Day by
　　day,
Gliding, like some dark mournful stream, away,
My silent youth flows from me. Spring, the while,
　Comes and rains beauty on the kindling boughs
Round hall and hamlet; Summer, with her smile,
　Fills the green forest;—young hearts breathe
　　their vows;
Brothers, long parted, meet; fair children rise
Round the glad board: Hope laughs from loving
　　eyes;
All this is in the world!—These joys lie sown,
The dew of every path—On *one* alo.)

Their freshness may not fall—the stricken deer
Dying of thirst with all the waters near.

### VIII.

Ye are from dingle and fresh glade, ye flowers
　By some kind hand to cheer my dungeon sent;
O'er you the oak shed down the summer showers,
　And the lark's nest was where your bright cups
　　bent,
Quivering to breeze and rain-drop, like the sheen
Of twilight stars. On you Heaven's eye hath been,
Thro' the leaves, pouring its dark sultry blue
Into your glowing hearts; the bee to you
Hath murmur'd, and the rill.—My soul grows faint
With passionate yearning, as its quick dreams
　　paint
Your haunts by dell and stream,—the green, the
　　free,
The full of all sweet sound,—the shut from me!

### IX.

There went a swift bird singing past my cell—
　O Love and Freedom! ye are lovely things!
With you the peasant on the hills may dwell,
　And by the streams; but I—the blood of kings,
A proud, unmingling river, thro' my veins
Flows in lone brightness,—and its gifts are chains!
Kings!—I had silent visions of deep bliss,
Leaving their thrones far distant, and for this
I am cast under their triumphal car,
An insect to be crush'd.—Oh! Heaven is far,—
Earth pitiless!

Dost thou forget me, Seymour? I am proved
So long, so sternly! Seymour, my beloved!
There are such tales of holy marvels done
By strong affection, of deliverance won
Thro' its prevailing power! Are these things told
Till the young weep with rapture, and the old
Wonder, yet dare not doubt,—and thou, oh! thou,
　Dost thou forget me in my hope's decay?—
Thou canst not!—thro' the silent night, ev'n now
　I, that need prayer so much, wake and pray
Still first for thee.—Oh! gentle, gentle friend!
How shall I bear this anguish to the end?

Aid!—comes there yet no aid?—the voice of blood
Passes Heaven's gate, ev'n ere the crimson flood
Sinks thro' the greensward!—is there not a cry
From the wrung heart, of power, thro' agony,
To pierce the clouds? Hear, Mercy! hear me
　　None
That bleed and weep beneath the smiling sun,
Have heavier cause!—yet hear!—my soul grows
　　dark—
Who bears the last shriek from the sinking bark,
On the mid seas, and with the storm alone,
And bearing to th' abyss, unseen, unknown,
Its freight of human hearts?—th' o'ermastering
　　wave!
Who shall tell how it rush'd—and none to save?

Thou hast forsaken me! I feel, I know,
There would be rescue if this were not so.
Thou 'rt at the chase, thou 'rt at the festive board,
Thou 'rt where the red wine free and high is pour'd,
Thou 'rt where the dancers meet!—a magic glass
Is set within my soul, and proud shapes pass,
Flushing it o'er with pomp from bower and hall;—
I see one shadow, stateliest there of all,—
*Thine!*—What dost *thou* amidst the bright and fair,
Whispering light words, and mocking my despair?
It is not well of thee!—my love was more
Than fiery song may breathe, deep thought explore,
And there thou smilest, while my heart is dying,
With all its blighted hopes around it lying;
Ev'n thou, on whom they hung their last green
　　leaf—
Yet smile, smile on! too bright art thou for grief.

Death!—what, is death a lock'd and treasured thing
Guarded by swords of fire?(2) a hidden spring,
A fabled fruit, that I should thus endure,
As if the world within me held no cure?

Wherefore not spread free wings—Heaven, Hea-
ven I con.rol
These thoughts—they rush—I look into my soul
As down a gulf, and tremble at th' array
Of fierce forms crowding it! Give strength to pray,
So shall their dark host pass.

               The storm is still'd.
Father in Heaven! Thou, only thou, canst sound
The heart's great deep, with floods of anguish fill'd,
  For human line too fearfully profound.
Therefore, forgive, my Father! if Thy child,
Rock'd on its heaving darkness, hath grown wild,
And sinn'd in her despair! It well may be,
That Thou wouldst lead my spirit back to Thee,
By the crush'd hope too long on this world pour'd,
The stricken love which hath perchance ador'd
A mortal in Thy place! Now let me strive
With Thy strong arm no more! Forgive, forgive!
Take me to peace!

            And peace at last is nigh.
A sign is on my brow, a token sent
Th' o'erwearied dust, from home: no breeze flits by,
  But calls me with a strange sweet whisper, blent
Of many mysteries.

           Hark! the warning tone
Deepens—its word is *Death*. Alone, alone,
And sad in youth, but chasten'd, I depart,
Bowing to heaven. Yet, yet my woman's heart
Shall wake a spirit and a power to bless,
Ev'n in this hour's o'ershadowing fearfulness,
Thee, its first love!—oh! tender still, and true!
Be it forgotten if mine anguish threw
Drops from its bitter fountain on thy name,
Though but a moment.

           Now, with fainting frame
With soul just lingering on the flight begun,
To bind for thee its last dim thoughts in one,
I bless thee! Peace be on thy noble head,
Years of bright fame, when I am with the dead!
I bid this prayer survive me, and retain
Its might, again to bless thee, and again!
Thou hast been gather'd into my dark fate
Too much; too long, for my sake, desolate
Hath been thine exiled youth; but now take back,
From dying hands, thy freedom, and re-track
(After a few kind tears for her whose days
Went out in dreams of thee) the sunny ways
Of hope, and find thou happiness! Yet send,
Ev'n then, in silent hours, a thought, dear friend!
Down to my voiceless chamber; for thy love
Hath been to me all gifts of earth above,
Though bought with burning tears! It is the sting
Of death to leave that vainly-precious thing
In this cold world! What were it then, if thou,
With thy fond eyes, wert gazing on me now?
Too keen a pang!—Farewell! and yet once more,
Farewell!—the passion of long years I pour
Into that word: thou hear'st not,—but the woe
And fervour of its tones may one day flow
To thy heart's holy place; there let them dwell—
We shall o'ersweep the grave to meet—Farewell!

---

THE

## BRIDE OF THE GREEK ISLE.[*]

*Fear!—I'm a Greek, and how should I fear death?*
*A slave, and wherefore should I dread my freedom?*
    *      *      *      *      *
*I will not live degraded.*
                          *Sardanapalus.*

---

Come from the woods with the citron-flowers,
Come with your lyres for the festal hours,
Maids of bright Scio! They came, and the breeze
Bore their sweet songs o'er the Grecian seas;—
They came, and Eudora stood robed and crown'd,
The bride of the morn, with her train around.

[*] Founded on a circumstance related in the Second Series of the
Curiosities of Literature, and forming part of a picture in the
"*Painted Biography*" there described.

Jewels flash'd out from her braided hair,
Like starry dews 'midst the roses there;
Pearls on her bosom quivering shone,
Heaved by her heart through its golden zone;
But a brow, as those gems of the ocean pale,
Gleam'd from beneath her transparent veil;
Changeful and faint was her fair cheek's hue,
Though clear as a flower which the light looks
    through;
And the glance of her dark resplendent eye,
For the aspect of woman at times too high,
Lay floating in mists, which the troubled stream
Of the soul sent up o'er its fervid beam.

She look'd on the vine at her father's door,
Like one that is leaving his native shore;
She hung o'er the myrtle once call'd her own,
As it greenly waved by the threshold stone;
She turn'd—and her mother's gaze brought back
Each hue of her childhood's faded track.
Oh! hush the song, and let her tears
Flow to the dream of her early years!
Holy and pure are the drops that fall
When the young bride goes from her father's hall:
She goes unto love yet untried and new,
She parts from love which hath still been true
Mute be the song and the choral strain,
Till her heart's deep well-spring is clear again!
She wept on her mother's faithful breast,
Like a babe that sobs itself to rest;
She wept—yet laid her hand awhile
In *his* that waited her dawning smile,
Her soul's affianced, nor cherish'd less
For the gush of nature's tenderness!
She lifted her graceful head at last—
The choking swell of her heart was past;
And her lovely thoughts from their cells found way
In the sudden flow of a plaintive lay.(3)

THE BRIDE'S FAREWELL.

Why do I weep?—to leave the vine
  Whose clusters o'er me bend,—
The myrtle—yet, oh! call it mine!—
  The flowers I loved to tend.
A thousand thoughts of all things dear,
  Like shadows o'er me sweep,
I leave my sunny childhood here,
  Oh, therefore let me weep!

I leave thee, sister! we have play'd
  Through many a joyous hour,
Where the silvery green of the olive shade
  Hung dim over fount and bower.
Yes, thou and I, by stream, by shore,
  In song, in prayer, in sleep,
Have been as we may be no more—
  Kind sister, let me weep!

I leave thee father! Eve's bright moon
  Must now light other feet,
With the gather'd grapes, and the lyre in tune,
  Thy homeward step to greet.
Thou in whose voice, to bless thy child
  Lay tones of love so deep,
Whose eye o'er all my youth hath smiled—
  I leave thee! let me weep!

Mother! I leave thee! on thy breast,
  Pouring out joy and woe,
I have found that holy place of rest
  Still changeless,—yet I go!
Lips, that have lull'd me with your strain,
  Eyes, that have watch'd my sleep!
Will earth give love like *yours* again?
  Sweet mother! let me weep!

---

And like a slight young tree, that throws
The weight of rain from its drooping boughs,

Once more she wept.  But a changeful thing
Is the human heart, as a mountain spring,
That works its way, through the torrent's foam,
To the bright pool near it, the lily's home!
It is well!—the cloud, on her soul that lay,
Hath melted in glittering drops away.
Wake again, mingle, sweet flute and lyre!
She turns to her lover, she leaves her sire.
Mother! on earth it must still be so,
Thou rearest the lovely to see them go!

They are moving onward, the bridal throng,
Ye may track their way by the swells of song;
Ye may catch thro' the foliage their white robes'
        gleam,
Like a swan 'midst the reeds of a shadowy stream.
Their arms bear up garlands, their gliding tread
Is over the deep-vein'd violet's bed;
They have light leaves around them, blue skies
        above,
An arch for the triumph of youth and love!

### II.

Still and sweet was the home that stood
In the flowering depths of a Grecian wood,
With the soft green light o'er its low roof spread,
As if from the glow of an emerald shed,
Pouring through lime-leaves that mingled on high,
Asleep in the silence of noon's clear sky
Citrons amidst their dark foliage glow'd,
Making a gleam round the lone abode;
Laurels o'erhung it, whose faintest shiver
Scatter'd out rays like a glancing river;
Stars of the jasmine its pillars crown'd,
Vine-stalks its lattice and walls had bound,
And brightly before it a fountain's play
Flung showers through a thicket of glossy bay,
To a cypress which rose in that flashing rain,
Like one tall shaft of some fallen fane.

And thither Ianthis had brought his bride,
And the guests were met by that fountain-side;
They lifted the veil from Eudora's face,
It smiled out softly in pensive grace,
With lips of love, and a brow serene,
Meet for the soul of the deep wood-scene.——
Bring wine, bring odours!—the board is spread—
Bring roses! a chaplet for every head!
The wine-cups foam'd, and the rose was shower'd
On the young and fair from the world embower'd,
The sun look'd not on them in that sweet shade,
The winds amid scented boughs were laid;
But there came by fits, through some wavy tree,
A sound and a gleam of the moaning sea.

        Hush! be still!—was that no more
        Than the murmur from the shore?
        Silence!—did thick rain-drops beat
        On the grass like trampling feet?—
        Fling down the goblet, and draw the sword!
        The groves are fill'd with a pirate-horde!
        Through the dim olives their sabres shine;—
        Now must the red blood stream for wine!

The youths from the banquet to battle sprang,
The woods with the shriek of the maidens rang;
Under the golden-fruited boughs
There were flashing poniards, and darkening
        brows,
Footsteps, o'er garland and lyre that fled;
And the dying soon on a greensward bed.

Eudora, Eudora! thou dost not fly!—
She saw but Ianthis before her lie,
With the blood from his breast in a gushing flow,
Like a child's large tears in its hour of woe,
And a gathering film in his lifted eye,
That sought his young bride out mournfully.—
She knelt down beside him, her arms she wound,
Like tendrils, his drooping neck around,
As if the passion of that fond grasp
Might chain in life with its ivy-clasp.

But they tore her thence in her wild despair,
The sea's fierce rovers—they left him there;
They left to the fountain a dark-red vein,
And on the wet violets a pile of slain,
And a hush of fear through the summer-grove—
So closed the triumph of youth and love!

### III.

        Gloomy lay the shore that night,
        When the moon, with sleeping light,
        Bathed each purple Sciote hill,—
        Gloomy lay the shore, and still.
        O'er the wave no gay guitar
        Sent its floating music far;
        No glad sound of dancing feet
        Woke, the starry hours to greet
        But a voice of mortal woe,
        In its changes wild or low,
        Through the midnight's blue repose,
        From the sea-beat rocks arose,
        As Eudora's mother stood
        Gazing o'er th' Egean flood,
        With a fix'd and straining eye—
        Oh! was the spoilers' vessel nigh?
        Yes! there, becalm'd in silent sleep,
        Dark and alone on a breathless deep,
        On a sea of molten silver dark,
        Brooding it frown'd, that evil bark!
        There its broad pennon a shadow cast,
        Moveless and black from the tall still mast,
        And the heavy sound of its flapping sail,
        Idly and vainly woo'd the gale.
        Hush'd was all else—had ocean's breast
        Rock'd e'en Eudora that hour to rest?

To rest?—the waves tremble!—what piercing cry
Bursts from the heart of the ship on high?
What light through the heavens, in a sudden spire
Shoots from the deck up?  Fire! 'tis fire!
There are wild forms hurrying to and fro,
Seen darkly clear on that lurid glow;
There are shout, and signal-gun, and call,
And the dashing of water,—but fruitless all!
Man may not fetter, nor ocean tame
The might and wrath of the rushing flame!
It hath twined the mast like a glittering snake,
That coils up a tree from a dusky brake;
It hath touch'd the sails, and their canvas rolls
Away from its breath into shrivell'd scrolls;
It hath taken a flag's high place in air,
And redden'd the stars with its wavy glare,
And sent out bright arrows, and soar'd in glee,
To a burning mount 'midst the moonlit sea.
The swimmers are plunging from stern and prow—
Eudora, Eudora! where, where art thou?
The slave and his master alike are gone.—
Mother! who stands on the deck alone?
The child of thy bosom!—and lo! a brand
Blazing up high in her lifted hand!
And her veil flung back, and her free dark hair
Sway'd by the flames as they rock and flare,
And her fragile form to its loftiest height
Dilated, as if by the spirit's might,
And her eye with an eagle-gladness fraught,—
Oh! could this work be of woman wrought?
Yes! 'twas her deed!—by that haughty smile,
It was her's!—She hath kindled her funeral pile!
Never might shame on that bright head be,
Her blood was the Greek's, and hath made her free.

Proudly she stands, like an Indian bride
On the pyre with the holy dead beside;
But a shriek from her mother hath caught her ear,
As the flames to her marriage-robe draw near,
And starting, she spreads her pale arms in vain,
To the form they must never enfold again.

One moment more, and her hands are clasp'd,
Fallen is the torch they had wildly grasp'd,
Her sinking knee unto Heaven is bow'd,
And her last look raised through the smoke's dim
        shroud,
And her lips as in prayer for her pardon move—
Now the night gathers o'er youth and love!*

* Originally published, as well as several other of these Records
in the *New Monthly Magazine.*

## THE SWITZER'S WIFE.

Werner Stauffacher, one of the three confederates of the field of Grutli, had been alarmed by the eavy with which the Austrian Bailiff, Landenberg, had noticed the appearance of wealth and comfort which distinguished his dwelling. It was not, however, until roused by the entreaties of his wife, a woman who seems to have been of an heroic spirit, that he was induced to deliberate with his friends upon the measures by which Switzerland was finally delivered.

Nor look nor tone revealeth aught
Save woman's quietness of thought
And yet around her is a light
Of inward majesty and might.    M. J. J.

*    *    *    *    *    *

Wer solch ein herz an seinen Busen druckt,
Der kann für herd und hof mit freuden fechten.
*Wilhelm Tell.*

It was the time when children bound to meet
  Their father's homeward step from field or hill,
And when the herd's returning bells are sweet
  In the Swiss valleys, and the lakes grow still,
And the last note of that wild horn swells by,
Which haunts the exile's heart with melody.

And lovely smiled full many an Alpine home,
  Touch'd with the crimson of the dying hour,
Which lit its low roof by the torrent's foam,
  And pierced its lattice through the vine-hung
    bower;
But one, the loveliest o'er the land that rose,
Then first look'd mournful in its green repose.

For Werner sat beneath the linden-tree,
  That sent its lulling whispers through his door
Ev'n as a man sits whose heart alone would be
  With some deep care, and thus can find no more
Th' accustom'd joy in all which evening brings,
Gathering a household with her quiet wings.

His wife stood hush'd before him,—sad, yet mild
  In her beseeching mien;—he mark'd it not.
The silvery laughter of his bright-hair'd child
  Rang from the greensward round the shelter'd
    spot,
But seem'd unheard; until at last the boy
Raised from his heap'd-up flowers a glance of joy,

And met his father's face: but then a change
  Pass'd swiftly o'er the brow of infant glee,
And a quick sense of something dimly strange
  Brought him from play to stand beside the knee
So often climb'd, and lift his loving eyes
That shone through clouds of sorrowful surprise.

Then the proud bosom of the strong man shook;
  But tenderly his babe's fair mother laid
Her hand on his, and with a pleading look,
  Thro' tears half quivering, o'er him bent, and
    said,
' What grief, dear friend, hath made thy heart its
    prey,
That thou shouldst turn thee from our love away?

" It is too sad to see thee thus, my friend!
  Mark'st thou the wonder on thy boy's fair brow,
Missing the smile from thine? Oh! cheer thee!
    bend
  To his soft arms, unseal thy thoughts e'en now!
Thou dost not kindly to withhold the share
Of tried affection in thy secret care."

He look'd up into that sweet earnest face,
  But sternly, mournfully: not yet the band
Was loosen'd from his soul; its inmost place

Not yet unveil'd by love's o'ermastering hand.
"Speak low!" he cried, and pointed where on high
The white Alps glitter'd through the solemn sky:

" We must speak low amidst our ancient hills
  And their free torrents; for the days are come
When tyranny lies couch'd by forest-rills,
  And meets the shepherd in his mountain-home
Go, pour the wine of our own grapes in fear,
Keep silence by the hearth! its foes are near.

" The envy of the oppressor's eye hath been
  Upon my heritage. I sit to-night
Under my household tree, if not serene,
  Yet with the faces best-beloved in sight:
To-morrow eve may find me chain'd, and thee—
How can I bear the boy's young smiles to see?"

The bright blood left that youthful mother's cheek;
  Back on the linden-stem she lean'd her form,
And her lip trembled, as it strove to speak,
  Like a frail harp-string, shaken by the storm.
'Twas but a moment, and the faintness pass'd,
And the free Alpine spirit woke at last.

And she, that ever through her home had moved
  With the meek thoughtfulness and quiet smile
Of woman, calmly loving and beloved,
  And timid in her happiness the while,
Stood brightly forth, and steadfastly, that hour,
Her clear glance kindling into sudden power

Ay, pale she stood, but with an eye of light,
  And took her fair child to her holy breast,
And lifted her soft voice, that gather'd might
  As it found language:—"Are we thus oppress'd?
Then must we rise upon our mountain-sod,
And man must arm, and woman call on God!

" I know what thou wouldst do,—and be it done!
  Thy soul is darken'd with its fears for me.
Trust me to Heaven, my husband!—this, thy son,
  The babe whom I have borne thee, must be free!
And the sweet memory of our pleasant hearth
May well give strength—if aught be strong on
    earth.
" Thou hast been brooding o'er the silent dread
  Of my desponding tears; now lift once more,
My hunter of the hills! thy stately head,
  And let thine eagle glance my joy restore!
I can bear all, but seeing thee subdued,—
Take to thee back thine own undaunted mood.

" Go forth beside the waters, and along
  The chamois-paths, and through the forests go;
And tell, in burning words, thy tale of wrong
  To the brave hearts that 'midst the hamlets glow
God shall be with thee, my beloved!—Away!
less but thy child, and leave me,—I can pray!"

He sprang up like a warrior-youth awaking
  To clarion-sounds upon the ringing air;
He caught her to his breast, while proud tears
    breaking
  From his dark eyes, fell o'er her braided hair,—
And "Worthy art thou," was his joyous cry,
" That man for thee should gird himself to die.

" My bride, my wife, the mother of my child!
  Now shall thy name be armour to my heart;
And this our land, by chains no more defiled,
  Be taught of thee to choose the better part!
I go—thy spirit on my words shall dwell,
Thy gentle voice shall stir the Alps—Farewell!

And thus they parted, by the quiet lake,
  In the clear starlight: he, the strength to rouse
Of the free hills; she, thoughtful for his sake,
  To rock her child beneath the whispering boughs
Singing its blue, half-curtain'd eyes to sleep,
With a low hymn, amidst the stillness deep.

# PROPERZIA ROSSI.

Properzia Rossi, a celebrated female sculptor of Bo-
ogna, possessed also of talents for poetry and music,
died in consequence of an unrequited attachment.—A
painting by Ducis, represents her showing her last work,
basso-relievo of Ariadne, to a Roman Knight, the ob-
ect of her affection, who regards it with indifference.

> ——————— Tell me no more, no more
> Of my soul's lofty gifts !  Are they not vain
> To quench its haunting thirst for happiness ?
> Have I not loved, and striven, and fail'd to bind
> One true heart unto me, whereon my own
> Might find a resting-place, a home for all
> Its burden of affections ?  I depart,
> Unknown, tho' Fame goes with me ; I must leave
> The earth unknown.  Yet it may be that death
> Shall give my name a power to win such tears
> As would have made life precious.

### I.

One dream of passion and of beauty more !
And in its bright fulfilment let me pour
My soul away !  Let earth retain a trace
Of that which lit my being, tho' its race
Might have been loftier far.—Yet one more dream !
From my deep spirit one victorious gleam
Ere I depart !  For thee alone, for thee !
May this last work, this farewell triumph be,
Thou, loved so vainly !  I would leave enshrined
Something immortal of my heart and mind,
That yet may speak to thee when I am gone,
Shaking thine inmost bosom with a tone
Of lost affection ;—something that may prove
What she hath been, whose melancholy love
On thee was lavish'd ; silent pang and tear,
And fervent song, that gush'd when none were
        near,
And dream by night, and weary thought by day,
Stealing the brightness from her life away,—
While thou————Awake ! not yet within me die,
Under the burden and the agony
Of this vain tenderness,—my spirit, wake !
Ev'n for thy sorrowful affection's sake,
Live ! in thy work breathe out !—that he may yet
Feeling sad mastery there, perchance regret
Thine unrequited gift.

### II.

            It comes,—the power
Within me born, flows back ; my fruitless dower
That could not win me love.  Yet once again
I greet it proudly, with its rushing train
Of glorious images :—they throng—they press—
A sudden joy lights up my loneliness,—
I shall not perish all !
            The bright work grows
Beneath my hand, unfolding, as a rose,
Leaf after leaf, to beauty ; line by line,
I fix my thought, heart, soul, to burn, to shine,
Thro' the pale marble's veins.  It grows—and now
I give my own life's history to thy brow,
Forsaken Ariadne ! thou shalt wear
My form, my lineaments ; but oh ! more fair,
Touch'd into lovelier being by the glow
    Which in me dwells, as by the summer-light
All things are glorified.  From thee my woe
    Shall yet look beautiful to meet his sight,
When I am pass'd away.  Thou art the mould
Wherein I pour the fervent thoughts, th' untold,
The self-consuming !  Speak to him of me,
Thou, the deserted by the lonely sea,
With the soft sadness of thine earnest eye,
Speak to him, lorn one ! deeply, mournfully,
Of all my love and grief ! Oh ! could I throw
Into thy frame a voice, a sweet, and low,

And thrilling voice of song ! when he came nigh,
To send the passion of its melody
Through his pierced bosom—on its tones to bear
My life's deep feeling, as the southern air
Wafts the faint myrtle's breath,—to rise, to swell,
To sink away in accents of farewell,
Winning but one, one gush of tears, whose flow
Surely my parted spirit yet might know,
If love be strong as death.

### III.

            Now fair thou art,
Thou form, whose life is of my burning heart !
Yet all the vision that within me wrought,
    I cannot make thee !  Oh ! I might have given
Birth to creations of far nobler thought,
    I might have kindled, with the fire of heaven,
Things not of such as die !  But I have been
Too much alone ; a heart whereon to lean,
With all these deep affections, that o'erflow
My aching soul, and find no shore below ;
An eye to be my star, a voice to bring
Hope o'er my path, like sounds that breathe of
        spring,
These are denied me—dreamt of still in vain,—
Therefore my brief aspirings from the chain,
Are ever but as some wild fitful song,
Rising triumphantly, to die ere long
In dirge-like echoes.

### IV.

            Yet the world will see
Little of this, my parting work, in thee,
    Thou shalt have fame ! Oh, mockery ! give the
        reed
From storms a shelter,—give the drooping vine
Something round which its tendrils may entwine,—
    Give the parch'd flower a rain-drop, and the
        meed
Of love's kind words to woman ! Worthless fame !
That in *his* bosom wins not for my name
Th' abiding-place it ask'd !  Yet how my heart,
In its own fairy world of song and art,
Once beat for praise !—Are those high longings
        o'er ?
That which I have been can I be no more ?—
Never, oh ! never more ; though still thy sky
Be blue as then, my glorious Italy !
And tho' the music, whose rich breathings fill
Thine air with soul, be wandering past me still,
And tho' the mantle of thy sunlight streams,
Unchanged on forms, instinct with poet-dreams ;
Never, oh ! never more !  Where'er I move,
The shadow of this broken-hearted love
Is on me and around !  Too well *they* know,
    Whose life is all within, too soon and well,
When there the blight hath settled ;—but I go
    Under the silent wings of peace to dwell ;
From the slow wasting, from the lonely pain,
The inward burning of those words—"*in vain*,"
Sear'd on the heart—I go.  'Twill soon be past.
Sunshine, and song, and bright Italian heaven,
    And thou, oh ! thou, on whom my spirit cast
Unvalued wealth,—who know'st not what was
        given
In that devotedness,—the sad, and deep,
And unrepaid—farewell !  If I could weep
Once, only once, belov'd one ! on thy breast,
Pouring my heart forth ere I sink to rest !
But that were happiness, and unto me
Earth's gift is *fame*.  Yet I was form'd to be
So richly blest !  With thee to watch the sky,
Speaking not, feeling but that thou wert nigh ;
With thee to listen, while the tones of song
Swept ev'n as part of our sweet air along,
To listen silently ;—with th' eye to gaze
On forms, the deified of olden days,
This had been joy enough ;—and hour by hour,
From its glad well-springs drinking life and power
How had my spirit soar'd, and made its fame
    A glory for thy brow !—Dreams, dreams !—the fire
Burns faint within me.  Yet I leave my name—
    As a deep thrill may linger on the lyre
When its full chords are hush'd—awhile to live
And one day haply in thy heart revive

sad thoughts of me:—I leave it, with a sound,
A spell o'er memory, mournfully profound,
I leave it, on my country's air to dwell,—
Say proudly yet—"'*Twas her's who loved me well!*"

---

## GERTRUDE,

### OR

## FIDELITY TILL DEATH.

The Baron Von der Wart, accused, though it is believed unjustly, as an accomplice in the assassination of the Emperor Albert, was bound alive on the wheel, and attended by his wife Gertrude, throughout his last agonizing hours, with the most heroic devotedness. Her own sufferings, with those of her unfortunate husband, are most affectingly described in a letter which she afterwards addressed to a female friend, and which was published some years ago, at Haarlem, in a book entitled Gertrude Von der Wart, or Fidelity unto Death.

Dark lowers our fate,
And terrible the storm that gathers o'er us;
But nothing, till that latest agony
Which severs thee from nature, shall unloose
This fix'd and sacred hold. In thy dark prison-house,
In the terrific face of armed law,
Yes, on the scaffold, if it needs must be,
I never will forsake thee.
                    *Joanna Baillie.*

HER hands were clasp'd, her dark eyes raised,
The breeze threw back her hair;
Up to the fearful wheel she gazed—
All that she loved was there.
The night was round her clear and cold,
The holy heaven above,
Its pale stars watching to behold
The might of earthly love.

" And bid me not depart," she cried,
" My Rudolph, say not so!
This is no time to quit thy side,
Peace, peace! I cannot go.
Hath the world aught for me to fear,
When death is on thy brow?
The world! what means it?—*mine is here*—
I will not leave thee now.

" I have been with thee in thine hour
Of glory and of bliss;
Doubt not its memory's living power
To strengthen me through *this!*
And thou, mine honour'd love and true,
Bear on, bear nobly on!
We have the blessed heaven in view,
Whose rest shall soon be won."

And were not these high words to flow
From woman's breaking heart?
Through all that night of bitterest woe,
She bore her lofty part;
But oh! with such a glazing eye,
With such a curdling cheek—
Love, love! of mortal agony,
Thou, only *thou* shouldst speak!

The wind rose high,—but with it rose
Her voice, that he might hear:
Perchance that dark hour brought repose
To happy bosoms near;
While she sat striving with despair
Beside his tortured form,
And pouring her deep soul in prayer
Forth on the rushing storm.

**11**

She wiped the death-damps from his brow,
With her pale hands and soft,
Whose touch upon the lute-chords low,
Had still'd his heart so oft.
She spread her mantle o'er his breast,
She bathed his lips with dew,
And on his cheeks such kisses press'd
As hope and joy ne'er knew.

Oh! lovely are ye, Love and Faith,
Enduring to the last!
She had her meed—one smile in death—
And his worn spirit pass'd.
While ev'n as o'er a martyr's grave
She knelt on that sad spot,
And, weeping, bless'd the God who gave
Strength to forsake it not!

---

## IMELDA.

————Sometimes
The young forgot the lessons they had learnt,
And loved when they should hate,—like thee, Imelda! (4)
                    *Italy, a Poem.*

Passa la bella Donna, e par che dorma.
                    *Tasso.*

We have the myrtle's breath around us here,
Amidst the fallen pillars;—this hath been
Some Naiad's fane of old. How brightly clear,
Flinging a vein of silver o'er the scene,
Up through the shadowy grass, the fountain wells
And music with it, gushing from beneath
The ivied altar!—that sweet murmur tells
The rich wild flowers no tale of woe or death;
Yet once the wave was darken'd, and a stain
Lay deep, and heavy drops—but not of rain—
On the dim violets by its marble bed,
And the pale shining water-lily's head.
Sad is that legend's truth.—A fair girl met
One whom she loved, by this lone temple's spring,
Just as the sun behind the pine-grove set,
And eve's low voice in whispers woke, to bring
All wanderers home. They stood, that gentle pair,
With the blue heaven of Italy above,
And citron-odours dying on the air,
And light leaves trembling round, and early love
Deep in each breast.—What reck'd *their* souls of
        strife
Between their fathers? Unto them young life
Spread out the treasures of its vernal years;
And if they wept, they wept far other tears
Than the cold world wrings forth. They stood,
        that hour,
Speaking of hope, while tree, and fount, and flower,
And star, just gleaming thro' the cypress boughs,
Seem'd holy things, as records of their vows.

But change came o'er the scene. A hurrying tread
Broke on the whispery shades. Imelda knew
The footstep of her brother's wrath, and fled
Up where the cedars make yon avenue
Dim with green twilight: pausing there, she caught,
Was it the clash of sword?'—a swift dark thought
Struck down her lip's rich crimson as it pass'd,
And from her eye the sunny sparkle took
One moment with its fearfulness, and shook
Her slight frame fiercely, as a stormy blast
Might rock the rose. Once more, and yet once
        more,
She still'd her heart to listen,—all was o'er;
Sweet summer winds alone were heard to sigh,
Bearing the nightingale's deep spirit by.

That night Imelda's voice was in the song,
Lovely it floated through the festive throng,
Peopling her father's halls. That fatal night
Her eye look'd starry in its dazzling light,
And her cheek glow'd with beauty's flushing dyes,
Like a rich cloud of eve in southern skies,
A burning, ruby cloud. There were, whose gaze
Follow'd her form beneath the clear lamp's blaze,

And marvell'd at its radiance.  But a few
Beheld the brightness of that feverish hue,
With something of dim fear; and in that glance
Found strange and sudden tokens of unrest,
Startling to meet amidst the mazy dance,
Where thought, if present, an unbidden guest,
Comes not unmask'd.  Howe'er this were, the time
Sped as it speeds with joy, and grief, and crime
Alike: and when the banquet's hall was left
Unto its garlands of their bloom bereft,
When trembling stars look'd silvery in their wane,
And heavy flowers yet slumber'd, once again
There stole a footstep, fleet, and light, and lone,
  through the dim cedar shade; the step of one
hat started at a leaf, of one that fled,
  f one that panted with some secret dread:—
What did Imelda there?  She sought the scene
Where love so late with youth and hope had been;
Bodings were on her soul—a shuddering thrill
Ran through each vein, when first the Naiad's rill
Met her with melody—sweet sounds and low;
We hear them yet, they live along its flow—
Her voice is music lost!  The fountain-side
She gain'd—the wave flash'd forth—'t was darkly
            dyed
Ev'n as from warrior-hearts; and on its edge,
  Amidst the fern, and flowers, and moss-tufts deep,
There lay, as lull'd by stream and rustling sedge,
  A youth, a graceful youth.  "Oh! dost thou sleep?
Azzo!" she cried, "my Azzo! is this rest?"
But then her low tones falter'd:—"On thy breast
Is the stain,—yes, 't is blood!—and that cold cheek,
That moveless lip!—thou dost not slumber?—speak,
Speak, Azzo, my beloved!—no sound—no breath—
What hath come thus between our spirits?—Death!
Death?—I but dream—I dream!"—and there she
            stood,
A faint, frail trembler, gazing first on blood,
With her fair arm around yon cypress thrown,
Her form sustain'd by that dark stem alone,
And fading fast, like spell-struck maid of old,
'nto white waves dissolving, clear and cold;
When from the grass her dimm'd eye caught a
            gleam—
'Twas where a sword lay shiver'd by the stream,—
Her brother's sword!—she knew it; and she knew
'T was with a venom'd point that weapon slow!
Woe for young love!  But love is strong.  There
            came
Strength upon woman's fragile heart and frame,
There came swift courage!  On the dewy ground
She knelt, with all her dark hair floating round,
Like a long silken stole; she knelt, and press'd
Her lips of glowing life to Azzo's breast,
Drawing the poison forth.  A strange, sad sight!
Pale death, and fearless love, and solemn night!—
So the moon saw them last.

                The morn came singing
Through the green forests of the Apennines,
With all her joyous birds their free flight winging,
  And steps and voices out among the vines.
What found that day-spring *here*?  Two fair forms
            laid
Like sculptured sleepers; from the myrtle shade
Casting a gleam of beauty o'er the wave,
Still, mournful, sweet.  Were such things for the
            grave?
Could it be so indeed?  That radiant girl,
Deck'd as for bridal hours!—long braids of pearl
Amidst her shadowy locks were faintly shining,
  As tears might shine, with melancholy light;
And there was gold her slender waist entwining;
  And her pale graceful arms—how sadly bright!
And fiery gems upon her breast were lying,
And round her marble brow red roses dying.—
But she died first!—the violets hue had spread
  O'er her sweet eyelids with repose oppress'd,
She had bow'd heavily her gentle head,
  And, on the youth's hush'd bosom, sunk to rest.
So slept they well!—the poison's work was done;
Love with true heart had striven—but Death had
            won

---

# EDITH;

## A TALE OF THE WOODS.*

Da Heilige! rufe dein Kind zurück!
Ich habe genossen das irdische Glück,
Ich habe gelebt und geliebet.
                        *Wallenstein.*

The woods—oh solemn are the boundless woods
  Of the great Western World, when day declines
And louder sounds the roll of distant floods,
  More deep the rustling of the ancient pines·
When dimness gathers on the stilly air,
  And mystery seems o'er every leaf to brood
Awful it is for human heart to bear
  The might and burden of the solitude!
Yet, in that hour, 'midst those green wastes, there
            sate
One young and fair; and oh! how desolate!
But undismay'd; while sank the crimson light,
And the high cedars darken'd with the night.
Alone she sate: though many lay around,
They, pale and silent on the bloody ground,
Were sever'd from her need and from her woe,
  Far as Death severs Life.  O'er that wild spot
Combat had raged, and brought the valiant low,
  And left them, with the history of their lot,
Unto the forest oaks.  A fearful scene
For her whose home of other days had been
'Midst the fair halls of England! but the love
  Which fill'd her soul was strong to cast out fear,
And by its might upborne all else above,
  She shrank not—mark'd not that the dead were
            near.
Of him alone she thought, whose languid head
  Faintly upon her wedded bosom fell;
Memory of aught but him on earth was fled,
  While heavily she felt his life-blood well
Fast o'er her garments forth, and vainly bound
With her torn robe and hair the streaming wound,
Yet hoped, still hoped!—Oh! from such hope how
            long
Affection wooes the whispers that deceive,
Ev'n when the pressure of dismay grows strong,
  And we, that weep, watch, tremble, ne'er believe
The blow indeed can fall!  So bow'd she there,
Over the dying, while unconscious prayer
Fill'd all her soul.  Now pour'd the moonlight
            down,
Veining the pine-stems through the foliage brown,
And fire-flies, kindling up the leafy place,
Cast fitful radiance o'er the warrior's face,
Whereby she caught its changes: to her eye,
  The eye that faded look'd through gathering
            haze,
Whence love, o'ermastering mortal agony,
  Lifted a long deep melancholy gaze,
When voice was not: that fond sad meaning
            pass'd—
She knew the fullness of her woe at last!
One shriek the forests heard,—and mute she lay,
And cold; yet clasping still the precious clay
To her scarce-heaving breast.  O Love and Death
Ye have sad meetings on this changeful earth,
Many and sad! but airs of heavenly breath
Shall melt the links which bind you, for your birth
Is far apart.

                Now light, of richer hue
Than the moon sheds, came flushing mist and dew
The pines grew red with morning; fresh winds
            play'd,
Bright-colour'd birds with splendour cross'd the
            shade,
Flitting on flower-like wings; glad murmurs broke
  From reed, and spray, and leaf, the living strings
Of earth's Eolian lyre, whose music woke
  Into young life and joy all happy things.
And she too woke from that long dreamless trance,
The widow'd Edith: fearfully her glance

---

* Founded on incidents related in an American work, "Sketches
of Connecticut."

Fell, as in doubt, on faces dark and strange,
And dusky forms.  A sudden sense of change
Flash'd o'er her spirit, ev'n ere memory swept
The tide of anguish back with thoughts that slept:
Yet half instinctively she rose, and spread
Her arms, as 't were for something lost or fled,
Then faintly sank again.  The forest-bough,
With all its whispers, waved not o'er her now,—
Where was she ?  'Midst the people of the wild,
    By the red hunter's fire: an aged chief,
Whose home look'd sad—for therein play'd no
        child—
    Had borne her, in the stillness of her grief,
To that lone cabin of the woods; and there,
Won by a form so desolately fair,
Or touch'd with thoughts from some past sorrow
        sprung,
O'er her low couch an Indian matron hung,
While in grave silence, yet with earnest eye,
The ancient warrior of the waste stood by,
Bending in watchfulness his proud gray head,
    And leaning on his bow,
                    And life return'd,
Life, but with all its memories of the dead,
    To Edith's heart; and well the sufferer learn'd
Her task of meek endurance, well she wore
The chasten'd grief that humbly can adore,
'Midst blinding tears.  But unto that old pair,
Ev'n as a breath of spring's awakening air,
Her presence was; or as a sweet wild tune
Bringing back tender thoughts, which all too soon
Depart with childhood.  Sadly they had seen
    A daughter to the land of spirits go,
And ever from that time her fading mien,
    And voice, like winds of summer, soft and low,
Had haunted their dim years; but Edith's face
Now look'd in holy sweetness from her place,
And they again seem'd parents.  Oh! the joy,
The rich, deep blessedness—though earth's alloy,
Fear that still bodes, be there—of pouring forth
The heart's whole power of love, its wealth and
        worth
Of strong affection, in one healthful flow,
On something all its own!—that kindly glow,
Which to shut inward is consuming pain,
Gives the glad soul its flowering time again,
When, like the sunshine, freed.—And gentle cares
Th' adopted Edith meekly gave for theirs
Who loved her thus:—her spirit dwelt, the while,
With the departed, and her patient smile
Spoke of farewells to earth;—yet still she pray'd,
Ev'n o'er her soldier's lowly grave, for aid
One purpose to fulfil, to leave one trace
Brightly recording that her dwelling-place
Had been among the wilds; for well she knew
The secret whisper of her bosom true,
Which warn'd her hence.
                    And now, by many a word
Link'd unto moments when the heart was stirr'd,
By the sweet mournfulness of many a hymn,
Sung when the woods at eve grew hush'd and dim,
By the persuasion of her fervent eye,
All eloquent with child-like piety,
By the still beauty of her life, she strove
To win for heaven, and heaven-born truth, the
        love
Pour'd out on her so freely.—Nor in vain
Was that soft-breathing influence to enchain
The soul in gentle bonds: by slow degrees
Light follow'd on, as when a summer breeze
Parts the deep masses of the forest shade
And lets the sunbeam through:—her voice was
        made
Ev'n such a breeze; and she, a lowly guide,
By faith and sorrow raised and purified,
So to the Cross her Indian fosterers led,
Until their prayers were one.  When morning
        spread
O'er the blue lake, and when the sunset's glow
Touch'd into golden bronze the cypress-bough,
And when the quiet of the Sabbath time
Sank on her heart, though no melodious chime
Waken'd the wilderness, their prayers were one.
—Now might she pass in hope, her work was done.

And she *was* passing from the woods away,
The broken flower of England might not stay
Amidst those alien shades: her eye was bright
Ev'n yet with something of a starry light,
But her form wasted, and her fair young cheek
Wore oft and patiently a fatal streak,
A rose whose root was death.  The parting sigh
Of autumn through the forests had gone by,
And the rich maple o'er her wanderings lone
Its crimson leaves in many a shower had strown
Flushing the air; and winter's blast had been
Amidst the pines; and now a softer green
Fringed their dark boughs; for spring again had
        come,
The sunny spring! but Edith to her home
Was journeying fast.  Alas! we think it sad
To part with life, when all the earth looks glad
In her young lovely things, when voices break
Into sweet sounds, and leaves and blossoms wake.
Is it not brighter then, in that far clime
Where graves are not, nor blights of changeful time,
If *here* such glory dwell with passing blooms,
Such golden sunshine rest around the tombs?
So thought the dying one.  'Twas early day,
And sounds and odours with the breezes' play,
Whispering of spring-time, through the cabin-door,
Unto her couch life's farewell sweetness bore;
Then with a look where all her hope awoke,
"My father!"—to the gray-hair'd chief she spoke—
"Know'st thou that I depart?"—"I know, I
        know,"
He answer'd mournfully, "that thou must go
To thy beloved, my daughter!"—"Sorrow not
    For me, kind mother!" with meek smiles once
        more
She murmur'd in low tones; "one happy lot
    Awaits, us, friends! upon the better shore;
For we have pray'd together in one trust,
And lifted our frail spirits from the dust,
To God, who gave them.  Lay me by mine own,
Under the cedar-shade: where he is gone
Thither I go.  There will my sisters be,
And the dead parents, lisping at whose knee
My childhood's prayer was learn'd,—the Saviour's
        prayer
Which now ye know,—and I shall meet you there,
Father, and gentle mother!—ye have bound
The bruised reed, and mercy shall be found
By Mercy's children."—From the matron's eye
Dropp'd tears, her sole and passionate reply;
But Edith felt them not; for now a sleep,
Solemnly beautiful, a stillness deep,
Fell on her settled face.  Then, sad and slow,
And mantling up his stately head in woe,
"Thou'rt passing hence," he sang, that warrior old,
In sounds like those by plaintive waters roll'd.

------

"Thou'rt passing from the lake's green side,
    And the hunter's hearth away;
For the time of flowers, for the summer's pride,
    Daughter! thou canst not stay.

Thou'rt journeying to thy spirit's home,
    Where the skies are ever clear;
The corn-month's golden hours will come,
    But they shall not find thee here.

And we shall miss thy voice, my bird!
    Under our whispering pine;
Music shall 'midst the leaves be heard,
    But not a song like thine.

A breeze that roves o'er stream and hill,
    Telling of winter gone,
Hath such sweet falls—yet caught we still
    A farewell in its tone.

But thou, my bright one! thou shalt be
    Where farewell sounds are o'er;
Thou, in the eyes thou lov'st, shalt see
    No fear of parting more.

The mossy grave thy tears have wet,
    And the wind's wild moanings by,
Thou with thy kindred shalt forget,
    'Midst flowers—not such as die."

The shadow from thy brow shall melt,
  The sorrow from thy strain,
But where thine earthly smile hath dwelt,
  Our hearts shall thirst in vain.

Dim will our cabin be, and lone,
  When thou, its light, art fled;
Yet hath thy step the pathway shown
  Unto the happy dead.

And we will follow thee, our guide!
  And join that shining band;
Thou'rt passing from the lake's green side—
  Go to the better land!"

The song had ceased—the listeners caught no
  breath.
That lovely sleep had melted into death.

## THE INDIAN CITY.[*]

What deep wounds ever closed without a scar?
The heart's bleed longest, and but heal to wear
That which disfigures it.
                                    *Childe Harold.*

### I.

ROYAL in splendour went down the day
On the plain where an Indian city lay,
With its crown of domes o'er the forest high,
Red as if fused in the burning sky,
And its deep groves pierced by the rays which made
A bright stream's way through each long arcade,
Till the pillar'd vaults of the Banian stood,
Like torch-lit aisles 'midst the solemn wood,
And the plantain glitter'd with leaves of gold,
As a tree 'midst the genii-gardens old,
And the cypress lifted a blazing spire,
And the stems of the cocoas were shafts of fire.
Many a white pagoda's gleam
Slept lovely round upon lake and stream,
Broken alone by the lotus-flowers,
As they caught the glow of the sun's last hours,
Like rosy wine in their cups, and shed
Its glory forth on their crystal bed.
Many a graceful Hindoo maid,
With the water-vase from the palmy shade,
Came gliding light as the desert's roe,
Down marble steps to the tanks below;
And a cool sweet plashing was ever heard,
As the molten glass of the wave was stirr'd;
And a murmur, thrilling the scented air,
Told where the Bramin bow'd in prayer.

There wander'd a noble Moslem boy
Through the scene of beauty in breathless joy,
He gazed where the stately city rose
Like a pageant of clouds in its red repose;
He turn'd where birds through the gorgeous gloom
Of the woods went glancing on starry plume;
He track'd the brink of the shining lake,
By the tall canes feather'd in tuft and brake,
Till the path he chose, in its mazes wound
To the very heart of the holy ground.

And there lay the water, as if enshrined
In a rocky urn from the sun and wind,
Bearing the hues of the grove on high,
Far down through its dark still purity.
The flood beyond, to the fiery west
Spread out like a metal-mirror's breast,
But that lone bay, in its dimness deep,
Seem'd made for the swimmer's joyous leap,
For the stag athirst from the noontide chase,
For all free things of the wild-wood's race.

Like a falcon's glance on the wide blue sky,
Was the kindling flush of the boy's glad eye.

[*] From a tale in Forbes' Oriental Memoirs.

Like a sea-bird's flight to the foaming wave,
From the shadowy bank was the bound he gave;
Dashing the spray-drops, cold and white,
O'er the glossy leaves in his young delight,
And bowing his locks to the waters clear—
Alas! he dreamt not that fate was near.

His mother look'd from her tent the while,
O'er heaven and earth with a quiet smile:
She, on her way unto Mecca's fane,
Had stay'd the march of her pilgrim-train,
Calmly to linger a few brief hours,
In the Bramin city's glorious bowers;
For the pomp of the forest, the wave's bright fall,
The red gold of sunset—she loved them all.

### II.

The moon rose clear in the splendour given
To the deep-blue night of an Indian heaven;
The boy from the high-arch'd woods came back—
Oh! what had he met in his lonely track?
The serpent's glance, thro' the long reeds bright?
The arrowy spring of the tiger's might?
No!—yet as one by a conflict worn,
With his graceful hair all soil'd and torn,
And a gloom on the lids of his darken'd eye,
And a gash on his bosom—he came to die!
He look'd for the face to his young heart sweet,
And found it, and sank at his mother's feet.

"Speak to me!—whence doth the swift blood run?
What hath befall'n thee, my child, my son?"
The mist of death on his brow lay pale,
But his voice just linger'd to breathe the tale,
Murmuring faintly of wrongs and scorn,
And wounds from the children of Brahma borne:
This was the doom for a Moslem found
With foot profane on their holy ground,
This was for sullying the pure waves free
Unto them alone—'t was their God's decree.

A change came over his wandering look—
The mother shriek'd not then, nor shook:
Breathless she knelt in her son's young blood,
Rending her mantle to staunch its flood;
But it rush'd like a river which none may stay,
Bearing a flower to the deep away.
That which our love to the earth would chain,
Fearfully striving with Heaven in vain,
That which fades from us, while yet we hold,
Clasp'd to our bosoms, its mortal mould,
Was fleeting before her, afar and fast;
One moment—the soul from the face had pass'd!

Are there no words for that common woe?
—Ask of the thousands, its depth that know!
The boy had breathed, in his dreaming rest,
Like a low-voiced dove, on her gentle breast,
He had stood, when she sorrow'd, beside her knee,
Painfully stilling his quick heart's glee;
He had kiss'd from her cheek the widow's tears,
With the loving lip of his infant years;
He had smiled o'er her path like a bright spring
  day—
Now in his blood on the earth he lay!
*Murder'd!*—Alas! and we love so well
In a world where anguish like this can dwell!

She bow'd down mutely o'er her dead—
They that stood round her watch'd in dread;
They watch'd—she knew not they were by—
Her soul sat veil'd in its agony.
On the silent lip she press'd no kiss,
Too stern was the grasp of her pangs for this;
She shed no tear as her face bent low,
O'er the shining hair of the lifeless brow;
She look'd but into the half-shut eye,
With a gaze that found there no reply,
And shrieking, mantled her head from sight,
And fell, struck down by her sorrow's might!

And what deep change, what work of power,
Was wrought on her secret soul that hour?
How rose the lonely one?—She rose
Like a prophetess from dark repose!
And proudly flung from her face the veil,
And shook the hair from her forehead pale,

And 'midst her wondering handmaids stood,
With the sudden glance of a dauntless mood.
Ay, lifting up to the midnight sky
A brow in its regal passion high,
With a close and rigid grasp she press'd
The blood-stain'd robe to her heaving breast,
And said—" Not yet—not yet I weep,
Not yet my spirit shall sink or sleep,
Not till yon city, in ruins rent,
Be piled for its victim's monument.
—Cover his dust! bear it on before!
It shall visit those temple-gates once more."

And away in the train of the dead she turn'd,
The strength of her step was the heart that burn'd;
And the Bramin groves in the starlight smiled,
As the mother pass'd with her slaughter'd child.

### III.

Hark! a wild sound of the desert's horn
Through the woods round the Indian city borne,
A peal of the cymbal and tambour afar—
War! 't is the gathering of Moslem war!
The Bramin look'd from the leaguer'd towers—
He saw the wild archer amidst his bowers;
And the lake that flash'd thro' the plantain shade,
As the light of the lances along it play'd;
And the canes that shook as if winds were high,
When the fiery steed of the waste swept by;
And the camp as it lay, like a billowy sea,
Wide round the sheltering Banian tree.

There stood one tent from the rest apart—
That was the place of a wounded heart.
—Oh! deep is a wounded heart, and strong
A voice that cries against mighty wrong;
And full of death, as a hot wind's blight,
Doth the ire of a crush'd affection light.

Maimuna from realm to realm had pass'd,
And her tale had rung like a trumpet's blast.
There had been words from her pale lips pour'd,
Each one a spell to unsheathe the sword.
The Tartar had sprung from his steed to hear,
And the dark chief of Araby grasp'd his spear,
Till a chain of long lances begirt the wall,
And a vow was recorded that doom'd its fall.

Back with the dust of her son she came,
When her voice had kindled that lightning flame
She came in the might of a queenly foe,
Banner, and javelin, and bended bow;
But a deeper power on her forehead sate—
*There* sought the warrior his star of fate;
Her eye's wild flash through the tented line
Was hail'd as a spirit and a sign,
And the faintest tone from her lip was caught,
As a Sibyl's breath of prophetic thought.

Vain, bitter glory!—the gift of grief,
That lights up vengeance to find relief,
Transient and faithless!—it cannot fill
So the deep void of the heart, nor still
The yearning left by a broken tie,
That haunted fever of which we die!

Sickening she turn'd from her sad renown,
As a king in death might reject his crown;
Slowly the strength of the walls gave way—
*She* wither'd faster from day to day.
All the proud sounds of that banner'd plain,
To stay the flight of her soul were vain;
Like an eagle caged, it had striven, and worn
The frail dust ne'er for such conflicts born,
Till the bars were rent, and the hour was come
For its fearful rushing through darkness home.

The bright sun set in his pomp and pride,
As on that eve when the fair boy died;
She gazed from her couch, and a softness fell

O'er her weary heart with the day's farewell;
She spoke, and her voice in its dying tone
Had an echo of feelings that long seem'd flown.
She murmur'd a low sweet cradle song,
Strange 'midst the din of a warrior throng,

A song of the time when her boy's young cheek
Had glow'd on her breast in its slumber meek;
But something which breathed from that mournful
      strain
Sent a fitful gust o'er her soul again,
And starting as if from a dream, she cried—
" Give him proud burial at my side!
There, by yon lake, where the palm-boughs wave,
When the temples are fallen, make there our
      grave."

And the temples fell, though the spirit pass'd,
That stay'd not for victory's voice at last;
When the day was won for the martyr-dead,
For the broken heart, and the bright blood shed.

Thro' the gates of the vanquish'd the Tartar steed
Bore in the avenger with foaming speed;
Free swept the flame through the idol-fanes,
And the streams glow'd red, as from warrior-veins
And the sword of the Moslem, let loose to slay,
Like the panther leapt on its flying prey,
Till a city of ruin begirt the shade,
Where the boy and his mother at rest were laid.

Palace and tower on that plain were left,
Like fallen trees by the lightning cleft;
The wild vine mantled the stately square,
The Rajah's throne was the serpent's lair,
And the jungle grass o'er the altar sprung—
This was the work of one deep heart wrung!

---

THE

## PEASANT GIRL OF THE RHONE.

---

————There is but one place in the world.
Thither where he lies buried !

*　　*　　*　　*　　*　　*

There, there is all that still remains of him,
That single spot is the whole earth to me.
                              *Coleridge's Wallenstein*

Alas! our young affections run to waste,
Or water but the desert.
                              *Childe Harold.*

---

THERE went a warrior's funeral through the night
A waving of tall plumes, a ruddy light
Of torches, fitfully and wildly thrown
From the high woods, along the sweeping Rhone,
Far down the waters.   Heavily and dead,
Under the moaning trees the horse-hoof's tread
In muffled sounds upon the greensward fell,
As chieftains pass'd; and solemnly the swell
Of the deep requiem, o'er the gleaming river
Borne with the gale, and with the leaves' low
      shiver,
Floated and died.  Proud mourners there, yet pale,
  Wore man's mute anguish sternly;—but of *one*
Oh! who shall speak? What *words his* brow
      unveil?
  A father following to the grave his son!
That is no grief to picture! Sad and slow,
  Through the wood-shadows moved the knightly
      train,
With youth's fair form upon the bier laid low,
  Fair even when found, amidst the bloody slain,
Stretch'd by its broken lance.  They reach'd the
      lone
  Baronial chapel, where the forest gloom
Fell heaviest, for the massy boughs had grown
  Into thick archways, as to vault the tomb.

Stately they trod the hollow-ringing aisle,
A strange deep echo shudder'd through the pile,
Till crested heads at last, in silence bent
Round the De Coucis' antique monument,
When dust to dust was given :—and Aymer slept
　Beneath the drooping banners of his line,
Whose broider'd folds the Syrian wind had swept
　Proudly and oft o'er fields of Palestine :
So the sad rite was closed.—The sculptor gave
Trophies, ere long, to deck that lordly grave,
And the pale image of a youth, array'd
As warriors are for fight, but calmly laid
　In slumber.on his shield.—Then all was done,
All still, around the dead.—His name was heard
Perchance when wine-cups flow'd, and hearts were
　　　stirr'd
By some old song, or tale of battle won,
Told round the hearth : but in his father's breast
Manhood's high passions woke again, and press'd
On to their mark ; and in his friend's clear eye
There dwelt no shadow of a dream gone by ;
And with the brethren of his fields, the feast
Was gay as when the voice whose sounds had
　　　ceased
Mingled with theirs.—Ev'n thus life's rushing tide
Bears back affection from the grave's dark side :
Alas ! to think of this !—the heart's void place
　Fill'd up so soon !—so like a summer-cloud,
All that we loved to pass and leave no trace !—
　He lay forgotten in his early shroud.
Forgotten ?—not of all !—the sunny smile
Glancing in play o'er that proud lip erewhile,
And the dark locks whose breezy waving threw
A gladness round, whene'er their shade withdrew
From the bright brow ; and all the sweetness lying
　Within that eagle-eye's jet radiance deep,
And all the music with that young voice dying,
　Whose joyous echoes made the quick heart leap
As at a hunter's bugle—these things lived
Still in one breast. whose silent love survived
The pomps of kindred sorrow.—Day by day,
On Aymer's tomb fresh flowers in garlands lay,
Thro' the dim fane soft summer-odours breathing,
And all the pale sepulchral trophies wreathing,
And with a flush of deeper brilliance glowing
In the rich light, like molten rubies flowing
Through storied windows down. The violet there
Might speak of love—a secret love and lowly,
And the rose image all things fleet and fair,
And the faint passion-flower, the sad and holy,
Tell of diviner hopes. But whose light hand,
As for an altar, wove the radiant band?
Whose gentle nurture brought, from hidden dells,
That gem-like wealth of blossoms and sweet bells,
To blush through every season ?—Blight and chill
Might touch the changing woods, but duly still,
For years, those gorgeous coronals renew'd,
　And brightly clasping marble spear and helm,
Even through mid-winter, fill'd the solitude
　With a strange smile, a glow of summer's realm
Surely some fond and fervent heart was pouring
Its youth's vain worship on the dust, adoring
In lone devotedness !
　　　　　One spring-morn rose,
And found, within that tomb's proud shadow
　　　laid—
Oh ! not as 'midst the vineyards, to repose
　From the fierce noon —a dark-hair'd peasant
　　　maid :
Who could reveal her story ?—That still face
　Had once been fair ; for on the clear arch'd brow,
And the curved lip, there linger'd yet such grace
　As sculpture gives its dreams ; and long and low
The deep black lashes, o'er the half-shut eye—
For death was on its lids—fell mournfully.
But the cold cheek was sunk. the raven hair
Dimm'd the slight form all wasted, as by care.
Whence came that early blight ?—*Her* kindred's
　　　place
Was not amidst the high De Couci race ;
Yet there her shrine had been !—She grasp'd a
　　　wreath—
The tomb's last garland !—This was love in death!

## INDIAN WOMAN'S DEATH-SONG.

An Indian woman, driven to despair by her husband
desertion of her for another wife, entered a canoe with
her children, and rowed it down the Mississippi toward
a cataract. Her voice was heard from the shore singing
a mournful death-song, until overpowered by the sound
of the waters in which she perished. The tale is related
in Long's Expedition to the source of St. Peter's River.

Non, je ne puis vivre avec un cœur brisé. Il faut que je retrouve
la joie, et que je m'unisse aux esprits libres de l'air.
　　　*Bride of Messina*, Translated by Madame de Staël.

Let not my child be a girl, for very sad is the life of a woman.
　　　　　　*The Prairie.*

Down a broad river of the western wilds,
Piercing thick forest glooms, a light canoe
Swept with the current : fearful was the speed
Of the frail bark, as by a tempest's wing
Borne leaf-like on to where the mist of spray
Rose with the cataract's thunder.—Yet within,
Proudly, and dauntlessly, and all alone,
Save that a babe lay sleeping at her breast,
A woman stood : upon her Indian brow
Sat a strange gladness, and her dark hair waved
As if triumphantly. She press'd her child,
In its bright slumber, to her beating heart,
And lifted her sweet voice, that rose awhile
Above the sound of waters, high and clear,
Wafting a wild proud strain, her song of death.

Roll swiftly to the Spirit's land, thou mighty stream
　and free !
Father of ancient waters, (5) roll ! and bear our
　lives with thee !
The weary bird that storms have toss'd, would
　seek the sunshine's calm,
And the deer that hath the arrow's hurt, flies to
　the woods of balm.

Roll on !—my warrior's eye hath look'd upon an-
　other's face,
And mine hath faded from his soul, as fades a
　moonbeam's trace ;
My shadow comes not o'er his path, my whisper
　to his dream,
He flings away the broken reed—roll swifter yet,
　thou stream !

The voice that spoke of other days is hush'd with-
　in *his* breast,
But *mine* its lonely music haunts, and will not let
　me rest ;
It sings a low and mournful song of gladness that
　is gone,
I cannot live without that light—Father of waves !
　roll on !

Will he not miss the bounding step that met him
　from the chase ?
The heart of love that made his home an ever
　sunny place ?
The hand that spread the hunter's board, and deck'
　his couch of yore ?—
He will not !—roll, dark foaming stream, on to the
　better shore !

Some blessed fount amidst the woods of that bright
　land must flow,
Whose waters from my soul may lave the memory
　of this woe ;
Some gentle wind must whisper there, whose
　breath may waft away
The burden of the heavy night, the sadness of the
　day.

And thou, my babe ! though born, like me, for
　woman's weary lot,
Smile !—to that wasting of the heart, my own ! I
　leave thee not ;

Too bright a thing art *thou* to pine in aching love
    away,
Thy mother bears thee far, young Fawn! from
    sorrow and decay.

She bears thee to the glorious bowers where none
    are heard to weep,
And where th' unkind one hath no power again
    to trouble sleep;
And where the soul shall find its youth, as waken-
    ing from a dream,—
One moment, and that realm is ours—On, on, dark
    rolling stream!

---

## JOAN OF ARC, IN RHEIMS.

Jeanne d'Arc avait eu la joie de voir a Chalons quelques amis de son enfance. Une joie plus ineffable encore
l'attendait a Rheims, au sein de son triomphe : Jaques
d'Arc, son pere y se trouva, aussitot que le troupes de
Charles VII. y furent entrees ; et comme les deux freres
de notre Heroine l'avaient accompagnes, elle se vit, pour
un instant au milieu de sa famille, dans les bras d'un
pere vertueux.       *Vie de Jeanne d'Arc*

---

> Thou hast a charmed cup, O Fame!
>   A draught that mantles high,
> And seems to lift this earth-born frame
>   Above mortality :
> Away! to me—a woman—bring
> Sweet waters from affection's spring.

---

THAT was a joyous day in Rheims of old,
When peal on peal of mighty music roll'd
Forth from her throng'd cathedral ; while around,
A multitude, whose billows made no sound,
Chain'd to a hush of wonder, though elate
With victory, listen'd at their temple's gate.
And what was done within ?—within, the light
  Thro' the rich gloom of pictured windows flowing
Tinged with soft awfulness a stately sight,
  The chivalry of France, their proud heads bow-
    ing
In martial vassalage!—while 'midst that ring,
And shadow'd by ancestral tombs, a king
Received his birthright's crown. For this, the hymn
  Swell'd out like rushing waters, and the day
With the sweet censer's misty breath grew dim,
  As through long aisles it floated o'er th' array
Of arms and sweeping stoles. But who, alone
And unapproach'd, beside the altar-stone,
With the white banner, forth like sunshine
    streaming,
And the gold helm, through clouds of fragrance
    gleaming,
Silent and radiant stood ?—the helm was raised,
And the fair face reveal'd that upward gazed,
  Intensely worshipping :—a still, clear face,
Youthful, but brightly solemn !—Woman's cheek
And brow were there, in deep devotion meek,
  Yet glorified with inspiration's trace
On its pure paleness ; while, enthroned above,
The pictured virgin, with her smile of love,
Seem'd bending o'er her votaress.—That slight
    form !
Was that the leader through the battle storm ?
Had the soft light in that adoring eye,
Guided the warrior where the swords flash'd high ?
'T was so, even so !—and thou the shepherd's child,
Joanne, the lowly dreamer of the wild !
Never before, and never since that hour,
Hath woman, mantled with victorious power,
Stood forth as *thou* beside the shrine didst stand,
Holy amidst the knighthood of the land ;
And beautiful with joy and with renown,
Lift thy white banner o'er the olden crown,
Ransom'd for France by thee !
             The rites are done.
Now let the dome with trumpet-notes be shaken,
And bid the echoes of the tombs awaken,
  And come thou forth, that Heaven's rejoicing sun
May give thee welcome from thine own blue skies,
  Daughter of victory!—a triumphant strain,
A proud rich stream of warlike melodies,
  Gush'd through the portals of the antique fane,
And forth she came.—Then rose a nation's sound !
Oh! what a power to bid the quick heart bound,
The wind bears onward with the stormy cheer
Man gives to glory on her high career !
Is there indeed such power ?—far deeper dwells
In one kind household voice, to reach the cells
Whence happiness flow'd forth !—The shouts that
    fill'd
The hollow heaven tempestuously, were still'd
One moment ; and in that brief pause, the tone,
As of a breeze that o'er her home had blown,
Sank on the bright maid's heart,—"Joanne !"—
    who spoke
  Like those whose childhood with *her* childhood
    grew
Under one roof ?—"Joanne !"—*that* murmur broke
  With sounds of weeping forth !—She turn'd—
    she knew
Beside her, mark'd from all the thousands there,
In the calm beauty of his silver hair,
The stately shepherd ; and the youth, whose joy
From his dark eye flash'd proudly ; and the boy,
The youngest-born, that ever loved her best ;
"Father! and ye, my brothers !"—On the breast
Of that gray sire she sank—and swiftly back,
Ev'n in an instant, to their native track
Her free thoughts flow'd.—She saw the pomp no
    more—
The plumes, the banners :—to her cabin-door,
And to the Fairy's fountain in the glade, (fil
Where her young sisters by her side had play'd,
And to her hamlet's chapel, where it rose
Hallowing the forest unto deep repose,
Her spirit turn'd.—The very wood-note, sung
  In early spring-time by the bird, which dwelt
Where o'er her father's roof the beech-leaves hung,
  Was in her heart ; a music heard and felt,
Winning her back to nature.—She unbound
  The helm of many battles from her head,
And, with her bright locks bow'd to sweep the
    ground,
  Lifting her voice up, wept for joy, and said,—
"Bless me, my father, bless me! and with thee,
To the still cabin and the beechen-tree,
Let me return !"

             Oh! never did thine eye
Through the green haunts of happy infancy
Wander again, Joanne!—too much of fame
Had shed its radiance on thy peasant name ;
And bought alone by gifts beyond all price,
The trusting heart's repose, the paradise
Of home with all its loves, doth fate allow
The crown of glory unto woman's brow.

---

## PAULINE.

> To die for what we love!—Oh! there is power
>   In the true heart, and pride, and joy, for *this ;*
> It is to live without the vanish'd light
> That strength is needed.  
>
> Cosi trapassa al trapassar d'un Giorno
> Della vita mortal il fiore e'l verde.
>                   *Tasso.*

---

ALONG the star-lit Seine went music swelling
  Till the air thrill'd with its exulting mirth ;
Proudly it floated, even as if no dwelling
  For cares or stricken hearts were found on earth
And a glad sound the measure lightly beat,
A happy chime of many dancing feet.
For in a palace of the land that night,
  Lamps, and fresh roses, and green leaves were
    hung,
And from the painted walls a stream of light
  On flying forms beneath soft splendour flung !

But loveliest far amidst the revel's pride
Was one, the lady from the Danube-side? (7)

Pauline, the meekly bright!—though now no more
  Her clear eye flash'd with youth's all tameless
    glee,
Yet something holier than its dayspring wore,
  There in soft rest lay beautiful to see;
A charm with graver, tenderer, sweetness fraught—
The blending of deep love and matron thought.

Through the gay throng she moved, serenely fair,
  And such calm joy as fills a moonlight sky,
Sate on her brow beneath its graceful hair,
  As her young daughter in the dance went by,
With the fleet step of one that yet hath known
Smiles and kind voices in this world alone.

Lurk'd there no secret boding in her breast?
  Did no faint whisper warn of evil nigh?
Such oft awake when most the heart seems blest
  'Midst the light laughter of festivity:
Whence come those tones!—Alas! enough we
    know,
To mingle fear with all triumphal show!

Who spoke of evil, when young feet were flying
  In fairy rings around the echoing hall?
Soft airs through braided locks in perfume sighing,
  Glad pulses beating unto music's call?
Silence!—the minstrels pause—and hark! a sound,
A strange quick rustling which their notes had
    drown'd!

And lo! a light upon the dancers breaking—
  Not such their clear and silvery lamps had shed!
From the gay dream of revelry awaking,
  One moment holds them still in breathless dread;
The wild fierce lustre grows—then bursts a cry—
Fire! through the hall and round it gathering—fly!

And forth they r n—as chased by sword and
    spear—
  To th green coverts of the garden-bowers;
A gorgeous masque of pageantry and fear,
  Startling the birds and trampling down the
    flowers:
While from the dome behind, red sparkles driven
Pierce the dark stillness of the midnight heaven.

And where is she, Pauline?—the hurrying throng
  Have swept her onward, as a stormy blast
Might sweep some faint o'erwearied bird along—
  Till now the threshold of that death is past,
And free she stands beneath the starry skies,
Calling her child—but no sweet voice replies.

" Bertha! where art thou?—Speak, oh! speak, my
    own!"
  Alas! unconscious of her pangs the while,
The gentle girl, in fear's cold grasp alone,
  Powerless hath sunk within the blazing pile;
A young bright form, deck'd gloriously for death,
With flowers all shrinking from the flame's fierce
    breath!

But oh! thy strength, deep love!—there is no power
  To stay the mother from that rolling grave,
Though fast on high the fiery volumes tower,
  And forth, like banners, from each lattice wave;
Back, back she rushes through a host combined—
Mighty is anguish, with affection twined!

And what bold step may follow, 'midst the roar
  Of the red billows, o'er their prey that rise?
None!—Courage there stood still—and never more
  Did those fair forms emerge on human eyes!
Was one brief meeting theirs, one wild farewell?
And died they heart to heart?—Oh! who can tell?

Freshly and cloudlessly the morning broke
  On that sad palace, 'midst its pleasure-shades,
Its painted roofs had sunk—yet black with smoke
  And lonely stood its marble colonnades:
But yester-eve their shafts with wreaths were
    bound!—
Now lay the scene one shrivell'd scroll around!

And bore the ruins no recording trace
  Of all that woman's heart had dared and done?
Yes! there were gems to mark its mortal place,
  That forth from dust and ashes dimly shone!
Those had the mother on her gentle breast,
Worn round her child's fair image, there at rest

And they were all—the tender and the true
  Left this alone her sacrifice to prove,
Hallowing the spot where mirth once lightly flew,
  To deep, lone, chasten'd thoughts of grief and
    love.
Oh! we have need of patient faith below,
To clear away the mysteries of such woe!

---

# JUANA.

Juana, mother of the Emperor Charles V., upon the
death of her husband, Philip the Handsome of Austria,
who had treated her with uniform neglect, had his body
laid upon a bed of state in a magnificent dress, and being
possessed with the idea that it would revive, watched it
for a length of time incessantly, waiting for the moment
of returning life.

It is but dust thou look'st upon,  This love,
This wild and passionate idolatry,
What doth it in the shadow of the grave
Gather it back within thy lonely heart;
So must it ever end: too much we give
Unto the things that perish.

The night-wind shook the tapestry round an an-
    cient palace-room,
And torches, as it rose and fell, waved through the
    gorgeous gloom,
And o'er a shadowy regal couch threw fitful gleams
    and red,
Where a woman with long raven hair sat watch-
    ing by the dead

Pale shone the features of the dead, yet glorious
    still to see,
Like a hunter or a chief struck down while his
    heart and step were free;
No shroud he wore, no robe of death, but there
    majestic lay,
Proudly and sadly glittering in royalty's array.

But she that with the dark hair watch'd by the
    cold slumberer's side,
On her wan cheek no beauty dwelt, and in her
    garb no pride;
Only her full impassion'd eyes as o'er that clay
    she bent,
A wildness and a tenderness in strange resplen-
    dence blent.

And as the swift thoughts cross'd her soul, like
    shadows of a cloud,
Amidst the silent room of death, the dreamer
    spoke aloud;
She spoke to him who could not hear, and cried,
    " Thou yet wilt wake,
And learn my watchings and my tears, beloved
    one! for thy sake.

" They told me this was death, but well I knew it
    could not be;
Fairest and stateliest of the earth! who spoke of
    death for thee?
They would have wrapt the funeral shroud thy
    gallant form around,
But I forbade—and there thou art, a monarch,
    robed and crown'd!

" With all thy bright locks gleaming still, their
    coronal beneath,
And thy brow so proudly beautiful—who said that
    this was death?

Silence hath been upon thy lips, and stillness round
   thee long,
But the hopeful spirit in my breast is all undimm'd
   and strong.

"I know thou hast not loved me yet; I am not
   fair like thee,
The very glance of whose clear eye threw round a
   light of glee!
A frail and drooping form is mine—a cold un-
   smiling cheek,
Oh! I have but a woman's heart, wherewith *thy*
   heart to seek.

"But when thou wak'st, my prince, my lord! and
   hear'st how I have kept
A lonely vigil by thy side, and o'er thee pray'd and
   wept;
How in one long deep dream of thee my nights
   and days have past,
Surely that humble, patient love *must* win back
   love at last!

"And thou wilt smile—my own, my own, shall be
   the sunny smile,
Which brightly fell, and joyously, on all *but me*
   erewhile!
No more in vain affection's thirst my weary soul
   shall pine—
Oh! years of hope deferr'd were paid by one fond
   glance of thine!

'Thou'lt meet me with that radiant look when
   thou comest from the chase,
For me, for me, in festal halls it shall kindle o'er
   thy face!
Thou'lt reck no more though beauty's gift mine
   aspect may not bless;
In thy kind eyes this deep, deep love, shall give
   me loveliness.

"But wake! my heart within me burns, yet once
   more to rejoice
In the sound to which it ever leap'd, the music of
   thy voice:
Awake! I sit in solitude, that thy first look and
   tone,
And the gladness of thine opening eyes, may all
   be mine alone."

In the still chambers of the dust, thus pour'd forth
   day by day,
The passion of that loving dream from a troubled
   soul found way,
Until the shadows of the grave had swept o'er
   every grace,
Left 'midst the awfulness of death on the princely
   form and face.

And slowly broke the fearful truth upon the
   watcher's breast,
And they bore away the royal dead with requiems
   to his rest,
With banners and with knightly plumes all waving
   in the wind—
But a woman's broken heart was left in its lone
   despair behind.

---

## THE AMERICAN FOREST GIRL.

A fearful gift upon thy heart is laid,
Woman!—a power to suffer and to love,
Therefore thou so canst pity.

---

WILDLY and mournfully the Indian drum
   On the deep hush of moonlight forests broke;—
"Sing us a death-song, for thine hour is come,"—
   So the red warriors to their captive spoke.
Still, and amidst those dusky forms alone,
   A youth, a fair-hair'd youth of England stood,
Like a king's son; tho' from his cheek had flown
   The mantling crimson of the island-blood,
And his press'd lips look'd marble.—Fiercely bright,
And high around him, blazed the fires of night,

Rocking beneath the cedars to and fro,
As the wind pass'd, and with a fitful glow
Lighting the victim's face:—But who could tell
Of what within his secret heart befell,
Known but to heaven that hour?—Perchance a
   thought
Of his far home then so intensely wrought,
That its full image, pictured to his eye
On the dark ground of mortal agony,
Rose clear as day!—and he might *see* the band,
Of his young sisters wandering hand in hand,
Where the laburnums droop'd; or haply binding
The jasmine, up the door's low pillars winding;
Or, as day closed upon their gentle mirth,
Gathering, with braided hair, around the hearth
Where sat their mother;—and that mother's face
Its grave sweet smile yet wearing in the place
Where so it ever smiled!—Perchance the prayer
Learn'd at her knee came back on his despair;
The blessing from her voice, the very tone
Of her "*Good-night*" might breathe from boyhood
   gone!—

He started and look'd up:—thick cypress boughs
   Full of strange sound, waved o'er him, darkly
   red
In the broad stormy firelight;—savage brows,
   With tall plumes crested and wild hues o'er
   spread,
Girt him like feverish phantoms; and pale stars
Look'd thro' the branches as thro' dungeon bars,
Shedding no hope.—He knew, he felt his doom—
Oh! what a tale to shadow with its gloom
That happy hall in England!—Idle fear!
Would the winds tell it?—Who might dream or
   hear
The secret of the forests?—To the stake
   They bound him; and that proud young soldier
   strove
His father's spirit in his breast to wake,
   Trusting to die in silence! He, the love
Of many hearts!—the fondly rear'd,—the fair
Gladdening all eyes to see!—And fetter'd there
He stood beside his death-pyre, and the brand
Flamed up to light it, in the chieftain's hand.
He thought upon his God.—Hush! hark!—a cry
Breaks on the stern and dread solemnity,—
A step hath pierced the ring!—Who dares intrude
On the dark hunters in their vengeful mood?—
A girl—a young slight girl—a fawn-like child
Of green Savannas and the leafy wild,
Springing unmark'd till then, as some lone flower,
Happy because the sunshine is its dower;
Yet one that knew how early tears are shed,—
For *hers* had mourn'd a playmate brother dead.

She had sat gazing on the victim long,
Until the pity of her soul grew strong;
And, by its passion's deepening fervour sway'd,
Ev'n to the stake she rush'd, and gently laid
His bright head on her bosom, and around
His form her slender arms to shield it wound
Like close Liannes; then raised her glittering eye
And clear-toned voice that said, "He shall not
   die!"

"He shall not die!"—the gloomy forest thrill'd
   To that sweet sound. A sudden wonder fell
On the fierce throng; and heart and hand were
   still'd,
   Struck down, as by the whisper of a spell.
They gazed,—their dark souls bow'd before the
   maid,
She of the dancing step in wood and glade!
And, as her cheek flush'd through its olive hue,
As her black tresses to the night-wind flew,
Something o'ermaster'd them from that young
   mien—
Something of heaven, in silence felt and seen;
And seeming, to their child-like faith, a token
That the Great Spirit by her voice had spoken.

They loosed the bonds that held their captive's
   breath;
From his pale lips they took the cup of death;
They quench'd the brand beneath the cypress tree;
"Away," they cried, "young stranger, thou art
   free!"

## COSTANZA.

*——————Art thou then desolate?*
*Of friends, of hopes forsaken?—Come to me!*
*I am thine own.—Have trusted hearts proved false?*
*Flatterers deceived thee?  Wanderer, come to me!*
*Why didst thou ever leave me?  Know'st thou all*
*I would have borne, and call'd it joy to bear,*
*For thy sake?  Know'st thou that thy voice had power*
*To shake me with a thrill of happiness*
*By one kind tone?—to fill mine eyes with tears*
*Of yearning love?  And thou—oh! thou didst throw*
*That crush'd affection back upon my heart;—*
*Yet come to me!—It died not.*

She knelt in prayer.  A stream of sunset fell
Through the stain'd window of her lonely cell,
And with its rich, deep, melancholy glow
Flushing her cheek and pale Madonna-brow,
While o'er her long hair's flowing jet it threw
Bright waves of gold—the autumn forest's hue—
Seem'd all a vision's mist of glory, spread
By painting's touch around some holy head,
Virgin's or fairest martyr's.  In her eye,
Which glanced as dark clear water to the sky,
What solemn fervour lived! And yet what woe,
Lay like some buried thing, still seen below
The glassy tide! Oh! he that could reveal
What life had taught that chasten'd heart to feel,
Might speak indeed of woman's blighted years,
And wasted love, and vainly bitter tears!
But she had told her griefs to heaven alone,
And of the gentle saint no more was known,
Than that she fled the world's cold breath, and made
    made
A temple of the pine and chestnut shade,
Filling its depths with soul, whene'er her hymn
Rose through each murmur of the green, and dim,
And ancient solitude; where hidden streams
Went moaning through the grass, like sounds in
    dreams,
Music for weary hearts! 'Midst leaves and flowers
She dwelt, and knew all secrets of their powers,
All nature's balms, wherewith her gliding tread
To the sick peasant on his lowly bed,
Came, and brought hope; while scarce of mortal
    birth
He deem'd the pale fair form, that held on earth
Communion but with grief.

                    Ere long a cell,
A rock-hewn chapel rose, a cross of stone
Gleam'd thro' the dark trees o'er a sparkling well,
    And a sweet voice, of rich, yet mournful tone,
Told the Calabrian wilds, that duly there
Costanza lifted her sad heart in prayer.
And now 't was prayer's own hour.  That voice
    again
Through the dim foliage sent its heavenly strain,
That made the cypress quiver where it stood
In day's last crimson soaring from the wood
Like spiry flame.  But as the bright sun set,
Other and wilder sounds in tumult met
The floating song. Strange sounds!—the trumpet's
    peal,
Made hollow by the rocks; the clash of steel,
The rallying war-cry,—In the mountain-pass,
There had been combat; blood was on the grass,
Banners had strewn the waters; chiefs lay dying,
And the pine-branches crash'd before the flying.

And all was changed within the still retreat,
Costanza's home:—there enter'd hurrying feet,
Dark looks of shame and sorrow; mail-clad men,
Stern fugitives from that wild battle-glen,
Scaring the ringdoves from the porch-roof, bore
A wounded warrior in: the rocky floor
Gave back deep echoes to his clanging sword,
As there they laid their leader, and implored
The sweet saint's prayers to heal him; then to
    flight,
Through the wide forest and the mantling night,
Sped breathlessly again.—They pass'd—but he,
The stateliest of a host—alas! to see
What mother's eyes have watch'd in rosy sleep
Till joy, for very fullness, turn'd to weep,
Thus changed!—a fearful thing! His golden crest
Was shiver'd, and the bright scarf on his breast—
Some costly love-gift—rent:—but what of these?
There were the clustering raven-locks—the breeze
As it came in through lime and myrtle flowers,
Might scarcely lift them—steep'd in bloody showers
So heavily upon the pallid clay
Of the damp cheek they hung! the eye's dark ray—
Where was it?—and the lips!—they gasp'd apart,
With their light curve, as from the chisel's art,
Still proudly beautiful! but that white hue—
Was it not death's?—that stillness—that cold dew
On the scarr'd forehead? No! his spirit broke
From its deep trance ere long, yet but awoke
To wander in wild dreams; and there he lay,
By the fierce fever as a green reed shaken,
The haughty chief of thousands—the forsaken
Of all save one!—She fled not.  Day by day—
Such hours are woman's birthright—she, unknown,
Kept watch beside him, fearless and alone;
Binding his wounds, and oft in silence laving
His brow with tears that mourn'd the strong man's
    raving.
He felt them not, nor mark'd the light veil'd form
Still hovering nigh; yet sometimes, when that
    storm
    Of frenzy sank, her voice, in tones as low
As a young mother's by the cradle singing,
Would soothe him with sweet *aves*, gently bringing
    Moments of slumber, when the fiery glow
Ebb'd from his hollow cheek.

                    At last, faint gleams
Of memory dawn'd upon the cloud of dreams,
And feebly lifting, as a child, his head,
And gazing round him from his leafy bed,
He murmur'd forth, "Where am I? What soft
    strain
Pass'd, like a breeze, across my burning brain?
Back from my youth it floated, with a tone
Of life's first music, and a thought of one—
Where is she now? and where the gauds of pride
Whose hollow splendour lured me from her side?
All lost!—and this is death!—I *cannot* die
Without forgiveness from that mournful eye!
Away! the earth hath lost her.  Was *she* born
To brook abandonment, to strive with scorn?
My first, my holiest love!—her broken heart
Lies low, and I—unpardon'd I depart."

But then Costanza raised the shadowy veil
From her dark locks and features brightly pale,
And stood before him with a smile—oh! ne'er
Did aught that *smiled* so much of sadness wear—
And said, "Cesario! look on me; I live
To say my heart hath bled, and can forgive.
I loved thee with such worship, such deep trust
As should be Heaven's alone—and Heaven is just
I bless thee—be at peace!"

                    But o'er his frame
Too fast the strong tide rush'd—the sudden shame,
The joy, th' amaze!—he bow'd his head—it fell
On the wrong'd bosom which had loved so well;
And love, still perfect, gave him refuge there,—
His last faint breath just waved her floating hair

## MADELINE.

### A DOMESTIC TALE.*

Who should it be !—Where shouldst thou look for kindness?
When we are sick, where can we turn for succour,
When we are wretched, where can we complain;
And when the world looks cold and surly on us,
Where can we go to meet a warmer eye
With such sure confidence as to a mother?

*Joanna Baillie.*

"My child, my child, thou leav'st me !—I shall hear
The gentle voice no more that blest mine ear
With its first utterance; I shall miss the sound
Of thy light step amidst the flowers around,
And thy soft breathing hymn at twilight's close,
And thy "Good-night" at parting for repose:
Under the vine-leaves I shall sit alone,
And the low breeze will have a mournful tone
Amidst their tendrils, while I think of thee,
My child ! and thou, along the moonlight sea,
With a soft sadness haply in thy glance,
Shalt watch thine own, thy pleasant land of France,
Fading to air.—Yet blessings with thee go !
Love guard thee, gentlest ! and the exile's woe
From thy young heart be far !—And sorrow not
For me, sweet daughter ! in my lonely lot,
God shall be with me.—Now farewell, farewell !
Thou that hast been what words may never tell
Unto thy mother's bosom, since the days
When thou wert pillow'd there, and wont to raise
In sudden laughter thence thy loving eye
That still sought mine :—these moments are gone
      by,
Thou too must go, my flower !—Yet with thee dwell
The peace of God !—One, one more gaze—farewell!"

This was a mother's parting with her child,
A young meek Bride on whom fair fortune smiled,
And woo'd her with a voice of love away
From childhood's home ; yet there, with fond delay
She linger'd on the threshold, heard the note
Of her caged bird thro' trellis'd rose-leaves float,
And fell upon her mother's neck, and wept,
Whilst old remembrances, that long had slept,
Gush'd o'er her soul, and many a vanish'd day,
As in one picture traced, before her lay.

But the farewell was said ; and on the deep,
When its breast heaved in sunset's golden sleep
With a calm'd heart, young Madeline ere long
Pour'd forth her own sweet solemn vesper-song,
Breathing of home : through stillness heard afar,
And duly rising with the first pale star,
That voice was on the waters ; till at last
The sounding ocean-solitudes were pass'd,
And the bright land was reach'd, the youthful world
That glows along the West : the sails were furl'd
In its clear sunshine, and the gentle bride
Look'd on the home that promised hearts untried
A bower of bliss to come.—Alas ! we trace
The map of our own paths, and long ere years
With their dull steps the brilliant lines efface,
On sweeps the storm, and blots them out with tears.
That home was darken'd soon : the summer breeze
Welcomed with death the wanderers from the seas,
Death unto one, and anguish how forlorn !
To her, that widow'd in her marriage-morn,
Sat in her voiceless dwelling, whence with him,
  Her bosom's first beloved, her friend and guide,
Joy had gone forth, and left the green earth dim,
  As from the sun shut out on every side.
By the close veil of misery !—Oh ! but ill,
  When with rich hopes o'erfraught, the young
      high heart
  Bears its first blow !—it knows not yet the part
Which life will teach—to suffer and be still,

---

* Originally published in the Literary Souvenir for 1828

And with submissive love to count the flowers
Which yet are spared, and thro' the future hours
To send no busy dream !—*She* had not learn'd
Of sorrow till that hour, and therefore turn'd,
In weariness, from life : then came th' unrest,
The heart-sick yearning of the exile's breast,
The haunting sounds of voices far away,
And household steps ; until at last she lay
On her lone couch of sickness, lost in dreams
Of the gay vineyards and blue-rushing streams
In her own sunny land, and murmuring oft
Familiar names, in accents wild, yet soft,
To strangers round that bed, who knew not aught
Of the deep spells wherewith each word was fraught.
To strangers ?—Oh ! could strangers raise the head
Gently as *hers* was raised ?—did strangers shed
The kindly tears which bathed that feverish brow
And wasted cheek with half unconscious flow ?
Something was there, that thro' the lingering night
Outwatches patiently the taper's light,
Something that faints not thro' the day's distress,
That fears not toil, that knows not weariness ;
Love, true and perfect love !—Whence came that
      power,
Uprearing through the storm the drooping flower ?
Whence ?—who can ask ?—the wild delirium pass'd,
And from her eyes the spirit look'd at last
Into her *mother's* face, and wakening knew
The brow's calm grace, the hair's dear silvery hue,
The kind sweet smile of old !—and had *she* come,
Thus in life's evening, from her distant home,
To save her child ?—Ev'n so—nor yet in vain :
In that young heart a light sprung up again,
And lovely still, with so much love to give,
Seem'd this fair world, though faded ; still to live
Was not to pine forsaken.  On the breast
That rock'd her childhood, sinking in soft rest,
"Sweet mother, gentlest mother ! can it be ?"
The lorn one cried, "and do I look on thee ?
Take back thy wanderer from this fatal shore,
Peace shall be ours beneath our vines once more."

---

### THE

## QUEEN OF PRUSSIA'S TOMB.

"'This tomb is in the garden of Charlottenburgh, near
Berlin. It was not without surprise that I came sudden
ly, among trees, upon a fair white Doric temple. I might,
and should have deemed it a mere adornment of the
grounds, but the cypress and the willow declare it a habitation of the dead. Upon a sarcophagus of white
marble lay a sheet, and the outline of the human form
was plainly visible beneath its folds. The person with
me reverently turned it back, and displayed the statue of
his Queen. It is a portrait-statue recumbent, said to be
a perfect resemblance—not as in death, but when she
lived to bless and be blessed. Nothing can be more calm
and kind than the expression of her features. The hands
are folded on the bosom ; the limbs are sufficiently cross
ed to show the repose of life.—Here the King brings her
children annually, to offer garlands at her grave. These
hang in withered mournfulness above this living image
of their departed mother."—*Sherer's Notes and Reflections during a Ramble in Germany.*

---

In sweet pride upon that insult keen
She smiled ; then drooping mute and broken-hearted
To the cold comfort of the grave departed.

*Milman*

---

It stands where northern willows weep,
  A temple fair and lone ;
Soft shadows o'er its marble sweep,
  From cypress-branches thrown ;
While silently around it spread,
Thou feal'st the presence of the dead.

And what within is richly shrined?
    A sculptured woman's form,
Lovely in perfect rest reclined,
    As one beyond the storm.
Yet not of death, but slumber, lies
The solemn sweetness on those eyes.

The folded hands, the calm pure face,
    The mantle's quiet flow,
The gentle, yet majestic grace,
    Throned on the matron brow;
These, in that scene of tender gloom,
With a still glory robe the tomb.

There stands an eagle, at the feet
    Of the fair image wrought;
A kingly emblem—nor unmeet
    To wake yet deeper thought:
She whose high heart finds rest below
Was royal in her birth and woe.

There are pale garlands hung above,
    Of dying scent and hue;—
She was a mother—in her love
    How sorrowfully true!
Oh! hallow'd long he every leaf,
The record of her children's grief!

She saw their birthright's warrior crown
    Of olden glory spoil'd,
The standard of their sires borne down,
    The shield's bright blazon soil'd:
She met the tempest meekly brave,
Then turn'd, o'erwearied, to the grave.

She slumber'd; but it came—it came,
    Her land's redeeming hour,
With the glad shout, and signal-flame,
    Sent on from tower to tower!
Fast through the realm a spirit moved—
'Twas hers, the lofty and the loved.

Then was her name a note that rung
    To rouse bold hearts from sleep,
Her memory, as a banner flung
    Forth by the Baltic deep;
Her grief, a bitter vial pour'd
To sanctify th' avenger's sword.

And the crown'd eagle spread again
    His pinion to the sun;
And the strong land shook off its chain—
    So was the triumph won!
But woe for earth, where sorrow's tone
Still blends with victory's—*She* was gone!

## THE MEMORIAL PILLAR.

On the road-side between Penrith and Appleby, stands
a small pillar, with this inscription:—"This pillar was
erected in the year 1656, by Ann, Countess Dowager of
Pembroke, for a memorial of her last parting, in this
place, with her good and pious mother, Margaret,
Countess Dowager of Cumberland, on the 2d April,
1616."—See Notes to the "*Pleasures of Memory*"

Hast thou, through Eden's wild-wood vales pursued
Each mountain-scene, magnificently rude,
Nor with attention's lifted eye, revered
That modest stone, by pious Pembroke rear'd,
Which still records, beyond the pencil's power,
The silent sorrows of a parting hour?
                                        *Rogers.*

MOTHER and child! whose blending tears
    Have sanctified the place,
Where, to the love of many years,
    Was given one last embrace;
Oh! ye have shrined a spell of power,
Deep in your record of that hour!

A spell to waken solemn thought,
    A still, small under-tone,
That calls back days of childhood, fraught
    With many a treasure gone;
And smites, perchance, the hidden source,
Though long untroubled—of remorse.

For who, that gazes on the stone
    Which marks your parting spot,
Who but a mother's love hath known
    The *one* love changing not?
Alas! and haply learn'd its worth
First with the sound of "Earth to earth?"

But thou, high-hearted daughter! thou,
    O'er whose bright, honour'd head,
Blessings and tears of holiest flow,
    Ev'n here were fondly shed,
Thou from the passion of thy grief,
In its full burst, couldst draw relief.

For oh! though painful be th' excess,
    The might wherewith it swells,
In nature's fount no bitterness
    Of nature's mingling, dwells;
And thou hadst not, by wrong or pride,
Poison'd the free and healthful tide.

But didst thou meet the face no more
    Which thy young heart first knew?
And all—was all in this world o'er,
    With ties thus close and true?
It was!—On earth no other eye
Could give thee back thine infancy.

No other voice could pierce the maze
    Where deep within thy breast,
The sounds and dreams of other days,
    With memory lay at rest;
No other smile to thee could bring
A gladd'ning, like the breath of spring.

Yet, while thy place of weeping still
    Its lone memorial keeps,
While on thy name, 'midst wood and hill,
    The quiet sunshine sleeps,
And touches, in each graven line,
Of reverential thought a sign;

Can I, while yet these tokens wear
    The impress of the dead,
Think of the love embodied there,
    As of a vision fled?
A perish'd thing, the joy and flower
And glory of one earthly hour?

Not so!—I will not bow me so,
    To thoughts that breathe despair!
A loftier faith we need below,
    Life's farewell words to bear.
Mother and child!—Your tears are past—
Surely your hearts have met at last!

## THE GRAVE OF A POETESS.*

"Ne me plaignez pas—si vous saviez
Combien de peines ce tombeau m'a épargnées!"

I STOOD beside thy lowly grave;—
    Spring-odours breathed around,
And music, in the river-wave,
    Pass'd with a lulling sound.

All happy things that love the sun
    In the bright air glanced by,
And a glad murmur seem'd to run
    Through the soft azure sky.

Fresh leaves were on the ivy-bough
    That fringed the ruins near;

* Extrinsic interest has lately attached to the fine scenery of
Woodstock, near Kilkenny, on account of its having been the last
residence of the author of Psyche. Her grave is one of many in the
church-yard of the village. The river runs smoothly by. The ruins
of an ancient abbey that has been partially converted into a church,
reverently throw their mantle of tender shadow over it.—*Tales by
the O'Hara Family.*

Young voices were abroad—but thou
  Their sweetness couldst not hear.

And mournful grew my heart for thee,
  Thou in whose woman's mind,
The ray that brightens earth and sea,
  The light of song was shrined.

Mournful, that thou wert slumbering low,
  With a dread curtain drawn
Between thee and the golden glow
  Of this world's vernal dawn.

Parted from all the song and bloom
  Thou wouldst have loved so well,
To thee the sunshine round thy tomb
  Was but a broken spell.

The bird, the insect on the wing,
  In their bright reckless play,
Might feel the flush and life of spring,—
  And thou wert pass'd away !

But then, ev'n then, a nobler thought
  O'er my vain sadness came ;
Th' immortal spirit woke, and wrought
  Within my thrilling frame.

Surely on lovelier things, I said,
  Thou must have look'd ere now,
Than all that round our pathway shed
  Odours and hues below.

The shadows of the tomb are here,
  Yet beautiful is earth !
What seest thou then where no dim fear,
  No haunting dream, hath birth ?

Here a vain love to passing flowers
  Thou gav'st—but where thou art,
The sway is not with changeful hours,
  There love and death must part.

Thou hast left sorrow in thy song,
  A voice not loud, but deep !
The glorious bowers of earth among,
  How often didst thou weep !

Where couldst thou fix on mortal ground
  Thy tender thoughts and high ?—
Now peace the woman's heart hath found,
  And joy the poet's eye.

---

## NOTES TO RECORDS OF WOMAN.

### NOTE 1.

*When darkness from the vainly-doting sight,*
*  Covers its beautiful !*

" Wheresoever you are, or in what state soever you be, it sufficeth me you are mine. *Rachel wept, and would not be comforted, because her children were no more.* And that, indeed, is the remediless sorrow, and none else !"—From a letter of Arabella Stuart's to her husband.—See Curiosities of Literature.

### NOTE 2.

*Death !—what, is death a lock'd and treasured thing,*
*  Guarded by swords of fire ?*

" And if you remember of old, *I dare die.*—Consider what the world would conceive, if I should be violently enforced to do it."—*Fragments of her Letters.*

### NOTE 3.

*And her lovely thoughts from their cells found way,*
*  In the sudden flow of a plaintive lay.*

A Greek Bride, on leaving her father's house, takes leave of her friends and relatives frequently in extemporaneous verse. — See Fauriel's Chants Populaires de la Grece Moderne.

### NOTE 4.

*And loved when they should hate—like thee, Imelda.*

The tale of Imelda is related in Sismondi's Histoire des Republiques Italiennes. Vol. iii. p. 443.

### NOTE 5.

*Father of ancient waters roll !*

" Father of waters," the Indian name for the Mississippi.

### NOTE 6.

*And to the Fairy's fountain in the glade.*

A beautiful fountain near Domremi, believed to be haunted by fairies, and a favourite resort of Jeanne d'Arc in her childhood.

### NOTE 7.

*But loveliest far amidst the revel's pride,*
*Was she, the Lady from the Danube-side.*

The Princess Pauline Schwartzenberg. The story of her fate is beautifully related in L'Allemagne. Vol. iii. p. 336.

# SONGS

## OF

# THE AFFECTIONS.

---

They tell but dreams—a lonely spirit's dreams—
Yet ever through their fleeting imagery
Wanders a vein of melancholy love,
An aimless thought of home:—as in the song
Of the caged skylark ye may deem there dwells
A passionate memory of blue skies and flowers,
And living streams—far off!

## A SPIRIT'S RETURN.

This is to be a mortal,
And seek the things beyond mortality !

*Manfred.*

Thy voice prevails; dear Friend, my gentle Friend
This long shut heart for thee shall be unseal'd,
And though thy soft eye mournfully will bend
Over the troubled stream, yet once reveal'd
Shall its freed waters flow; then rocks must close
For evermore, above their dark repose.

Come while the gorgeous mysteries of the sky
Fused in the crimson sea of sunset lie;
Come to the woods, where all strange wandering
      sound
Is mingled into harmony profound;
Where the leaves thrill with spirit, while the wind
Fills with a viewless being, unconfined,
The trembling reeds and fountains;—Our own dell,
With its green dimness and Æolian breath,
Shall suit th' unveiling of dark records well—
Hear me in tenderness and silent faith!

Thou knew'st me not in life's fresh vernal noon—
I would thou hadst!—for then my heart on thine
Had pour'd a worthier love; now, all o'erworn
By its deep thirst for something too divine,
It hath but fitful music to bestow,
Echoes of harp-strings, broken long ago.

Yet even in youth companionless I stood,
As a lone forest-bird midst ocean's foam;
For me the silver cords of brotherhood
Were early loosed; the voices from my home
Pass'd one by one, and Melody and Mirth
Left me a dreamer by a silent hearth.

But with the fullness of a heart that burn'd
For the deep sympathies of mind, I turn'd
From that unanswering spot, and fondly sought
In all wild scenes with thrilling memories fraught,
In every still small voice and sound of power,
And flute-note of the wind through cave and
      bower,
A perilous delight !—for then first woke
My life's lone passion, the mysterious quest
Of secret knowledge; and each tone that broke
From the wood-arches or the fountain's breast,
Making my quick soul vibrate as a lyre,
But minister'd to that strange inborn fire.

'Midst the bright silence of the mountain-dells,
In noontide hours or golden summer-eves,
My thoughts have burst forth as a gale that swells
Into a rushing blast, and from the leaves
Shakes out response --O thou rich world unseen!
Thou curtain'd realm of spirits !—Thus my cry
Hath troubled air and silence—dost thou lie
Spread all around, yet by some filmy screen



Shut from us ever ?—The resounding woods,
Do their depths teem with marvels ? — and the
      floods,
And the pure fountains, leading secret veins
Of quenchless melody through rock and hill,
Have they bright dwellers ? — are their lone do
      mains
Peopled with beauty, which may never still
Our weary thirst of soul ?—Cold, weak and cold
Is Earth's vain language, piercing not one fold
Of our deep being !—Oh, for gifts more high !
For a seer's glance to rend mortality !
For a charm'd rod, to call from each dark shrine,
The oracles divine !

I woke from those high fantasies, to know
My kindred with the Earth—I woke to love;
O, gentle Friend ! to love in doubt and woe,
Shutting the heart the worshipp'd name above,
Is to love deeply—and *my* spirit's dower
Was a sad gift, a melancholy power
Of so adoring;—with a buried care,
And with the o'erflowing of a voiceless prayer
And with a deepening dream, that day by day,
In the still shadow of its lonely sway,
Folded me closer;—till the world held naught
Save the *one* Being to my centred thought.
There was no music but his voice to hear,
No joy but such as with *his* step drew near;
Light was but where he look'd—life where he
      moved—
Silently, fervently, thus, thus I loved.
Oh! but such love is fearful !—and I knew
Its gathering doom:—the soul's prophetic sight
Even then unfolded in my breast, and threw
O'er all things round, a full, strong, vivid light,
Too sorrowfully clear !—an under-tone
Was given to Nature's harp, for me alone
Whispering of grief.—Of grief ?—be strong, awake!
Hath not thy love been victory, O, my soul ?
Hath not its conflict won a voice to shake
Death's fastnesses ?—a magic to control
Worlds far removed ?—from o'er the grave to thee
Love hath made answer; and *thy* tale should be
Sung like a lay of triumph !—Now return,
And take thy treasure from its bosom'd urn,
And lift it once to light !

                    In fear, in pain,
I said I loved—but yet a heavenly strain
Of sweetness floated down the tearful stream,
A joy flash'd through the trouble of my dream !
I knew myself beloved !—we breathed no vow,
No mingling visions might our fate allow,
As unto happy hearts; but still and deep,
Like a rich jewel gleaming in a grave,
Like golden sand in some dark river's wave,
So did my soul that costly knowledge keep
So jealously !—a thing o'er which to shed,
When stars alone beheld the drooping head,
Lone tears! yet ofttimes burden'd with th' excess
Of our strange nature's quivering happiness.

But, oh! sweet Friend! we dream not of love's might
Till Death has robed with soft and solemn light
The image we enshrine!—Before that hour,
We have but glimpses of the o'ermastering power
Within us laid!—then doth the spirit-flame
With sword-like lightning rend its mortal frame;
The wings of that which pants to follow fast,
Shake their clay-bars, as with a prison'd blast,—
The sea is in our souls!

He died, he died,
On whom my lone devotedness was cast,
I might not keep one vigil by his side,
I, whose wrung heart watch'd with him to the last!
I might not once his fainting head sustain,
Nor bathe his parch'd lips in the hour of pain,
Nor say to him. "Farewell!"—He pass'd away—
O! had my love been there, its conquering sway
Had won him back from death!—but thus removed,
Borne o'er the abyss no sounding-line hath proved,
Join'd with the unknown, the viewless,—he became
Unto my thoughts another, yet the same—
Changed—hallow'd—glorified!—and his low grave
Seem'd a bright mournful altar—mine, all mine:—
Brother and Friend soon left me that sole shrine,
The birthright of the Faithful!—their world's wave
Soon swept them from its brink.—Oh! deem thou not
That on the sad and consecrated spot
My soul grew weak!—I tell thee that a power
There kindled heart and lip;—a fiery shower
My words were made;—a might was given to prayer,
And a strong grasp to passionate despair,
And a dread triumph!—Know'st thou what I sought?
For what high boon my struggling spirit wrought?
—Communion with the dead!—I sent a cry
Through the veil'd empires of eternity,
A voice to cleave them! By the mournful truth,
By the lost promise of my blighted youth.
By the strong chain a mighty love can bind
On the beloved, the spell of mind o'er mind;
By words, which in themselves are magic high,
Arm'd, and inspired, and wing'd with agony;
By tears, which comfort not, but burn, and seem
To bear the heart's blood in their passion-stream;
I summon'd, I adjured!—with quicken'd sense,
With the keen vigil of a life intense,
I watch'd, an answer from the winds to wring,
I listen'd, if perchance the stream might bring
Token from worlds afar: I taught one sound
Unto a thousand echoes: one profound
Imploring accent to the tomb, the sky;
One prayer to night,—"Awake, appear, reply!"

Hast thou been told that from the viewless bourne,
The dark way never hath allow'd return?
That all, which tears can move, with life is fled,
That earthly love is powerless on the dead?
Believe it not!—there is a large lone star,
Now burning o'er yon western hill afar,
And under its clear light there lies a spot,
Which well might utter forth—Believe it not!

I sat beneath that planet,—I had wept
My woe to stillness; every night-wind slept;
A hush was on the hills; the very streams
Went by like clouds, or noiseless founts in dreams
And the dark tree o'ershadowing me that hour,
Stood motionless, even as the gray church-tower
Whereon I gazed unconsciously:—there came
A low sound, like the tremour of a flame,
Or like the light quick shiver of a wing
Flitting through twilight woods, across the air;
And I look'd up!—Oh! for strong words to bring
Conviction o'er thy thought!—Before me there,
He, the Departed, stood!—Aye, face to face—
So near, and yet how far!—his form, his mien,
Gave to remembrance back each burning trace
Within:—Yet something awfully serene,
Pure,—sculpture-like,—on the pale brow that wore
Of the once beating heart no token more;

And stillness on the lip—and o'er the hair
A gleam, that trembled through the breathless air
And an unfathom'd calm, that seem'd to lie
In the grave sweetness of the illumined eye
Told of the gulfs between our being set,
And, as that unsheathed spirit-glance I met,
Made my soul faint:—with fear?—Oh! not with fear!
With the sick feeling that in his far sphere
My love could be as nothing!—But he spoke—
How shall I tell thee of the startling thrill
In that low voice, whose breezy tones could fill
My bosom's infinite?—O Friend, I woke
Then first to heavenly life!—Soft, solemn, clear,
Breathed the mysterious accents on mine ear,
Yet strangely seem'd as if the while they rose
From depths of distance, o'er the wide repose
Of slumbering waters wafted, or the dells
Of mountains, hollow with sweet echo-cells,
But, as they murmur'd on, the mortal chill
Pass'd from me, like a mist before the morn,
And, to that glorious intercourse upborne,
By slow degrees, a calm, divinely still,
Possess'd my frame:—I sought that lighted eye,—
From its intense and searching purity
I drank in soul!—I question'd of the dead—
Of the hush'd, starry shores their footsteps tread—
And I was answer'd:—if remembrance there,
With dreamy whispers fill the immortal air;
If Thought, here piled from many a jewel-heap,
Be treasure in that pensive land to keep;
If Love, o'ersweeping change, and blight, and blast,
Find there the music of his home at last;
I ask'd, and I was answer'd:—Full and high
Was that communion with eternity,
Too rich for aught so fleeting!—Like a knell
Swept o'er my sense its closing words,—"Farewell,
On earth we meet no more!"—and all was gone—
The pale bright settled brow—the thrilling tone—
The still and shining eye!—and never more
May twilight gloom or midnight hush restore
That radiant guest!—One full-fraught hour of Heaven,
To earthly passion's wild implorings given,
Was made my own—the ethereal fire hath shiver'd
The fragile censer in whose mould it quiver'd,
Brightly, consumingly!—What now is left?—
A faded world, of glory's hues bereft,
A void, a chain!—I dwell 'midst throngs, apart,
In the cold silence of the stranger's heart;
A fix'd, immortal shadow stands between
My spirit and life's fast-receding scene;
A gift hath sever'd me from human ties,
A power is gone from all earth's melodies,
Which never may return:—their chords are broken—
The music of another land hath spoken,—
No after-sound is sweet!—this weary thirst!—
And I have heard celestial fountains burst!—
What here shall quench it?
                    Dost thou not rejoice,
When the spring sends forth an awakening voice
Through the young woods?—Thou dost!—And in that birth
Of early leaves, and flowers, and songs of mirth,
Thousands, like thee, find gladness!—Couldst thou know
How every breeze then summons me to go!
How all the light of love and beauty shed
By those rich hours, but wooes me to the Dead!
The only beautiful that change no more,
The only loved!—the dwellers on the shore
Of spring fulfill'd!—The Dead!—whom call we so?
They that breathe purer air, that feel, that know
Things wrapt from us!—Away!—within me pent,
That which is barr'd from its own element
Still droops or struggles!—But the day will come—
Over the deep the free bird finds its home,
And the stream lingers 'midst the rocks, yet greets
The sea at last; and the wing'd flower-seed meets
A soil to rest in:—shall not I, too, be,
My spirit-love! upborne to dwell with thee?
Yea, by the power whose conquering anguish stirr'd
The tomb, whose cry beyond the stars was heard,

Whose agony of triumph won thee back
Through the dim pass no mortal step may track.
Yet shall we meet!—that glimpse of joy divine,
Proved thee for ever and for ever mine!

## THE LADY OF PROVENCE.*

Courage was cast about her like a dress
  Of solemn comeliness,
A gather'd mind and an untroubled face
  Did give her dangers grace.
                              DONNE.

The war-note of the Saracen
  Was on the winds of France;
It had still'd the harp of the Troubadour,
  And the clash of the tourney's lance.

The sounds of the sea, and the sounds of the night
And the hollow echoes of charge and flight,
Were around Clotilde, as she knelt to pray
In a chapel where the mighty lay,
    On the old Provençal shore;
Many a Chatillon beneath,
Unstirr'd by the ringing trumpet's breath,
  His shroud of armour wore.
And the glimpses of moonlight that went and
    came
Through the clouds, like bursts of a dying flame,
Gave quivering life to the slumber pale
Of stern forms couch'd in their marble mail,
At rest on the tombs of the knightly race,
The silent throngs of that burial-place.

They were imaged there with helm and spear,
As leaders in many a bold career,
And haughty their stillness look'd and high,
Like a sleep whose dreams were of victory;
But meekly the voice of the lady rose
Through the trophies of their proud repose;
Meekly, yet fervently, calling down aid,
Under their banners of battle she pray'd;
With her pale fair brow, and her eyes of love,
Upraised to the Virgin's pourtray'd above,
And her hair flung back, till it swept the grave
Of a Chatillon with its gloomy wave,
And her fragile frame, at every blast,
That full of the savage war-horn pass'd,
Trembling, as trembles a bird's quick heart,
When it vainly strives from its cage to part,—
    So knelt she in her woe;
A weeper alone with the tearless dead—
Oh! they reck not of tears o'er their quiet shed,
    Or the dust had stirr'd below!

Hark! a swift step! she hath caught its tone,
Through the dash of the sea, through the wild
    wind's moan;—
Is her lord return'd with his conquering bands?
No! a breathless vassal before her stands!
—"Hast thou been on the field?—Art thou come
    from the host?"
—"From the slaughter, lady!—All, all is lost!
Our banners are taken, our knights laid low,
Our spearmen chased by the Paynim foe,
And thy Lord," his voice took a sadder sound—
"Thy Lord—he is not on the bloody ground!
There are those who tell that the leader's plume
Was seen on the flight through the gathering
    gloom."

—A change o'er her mien and her spirit past;
She ruled the heart which had beat so fast,
She dash'd the tears from her kindling eye,
With a glance, as of sudden royalty:
The proud blood sprang in a fiery flow,
Quick o'er bosom, and cheek, and brow,
And her young voice rose till the peasant shook
At the thrilling tone and the falcon-look:
—"Dost thou stand by the tombs of the glorious
    dead,
And fear not to say, that their son hath fled?

_________
* Founded on an incident in the early French history

—Away! he is lying by lance and shield,—
Point me the path to his battle-field!"

  The shadows of the forest
    Are about the lady now;
  She is hurrying through the midnight on,
    Beneath the dark pine bough.

There's a murmur of omens in every leaf,
There's a wail in the stream like the dirge of a
    chief;
The branches that rock to the tempest-strife,
Are groaning like things of troubled life;
The wind from the battle seems rushing by
With a funeral march through the gloomy sky;
The pathway is rugged, and wild, and long,
But her frame in the daring of love is strong,
And her soul as on swelling seas upborne,
And girded all fearful things to scorn.

And fearful things were around her spread,
When she reach'd the field of the warrior-dead,
There lay the noble, the valiant, low—
Ay! but _one_ word speaks of deeper woe;
There lay the _loved_—on each fallen head
Mothers vain blessings and tears had shed,
Sisters were watching in many a home
For the fetter'd footstep, no more to come;
Names in the prayer of that night were spoken
Whose claim unto kindred prayer was broken;
And the fire was heap'd, and the bright wine
    pour'd,
For those, now needing nor hearth nor board:
Only a requiem, a shroud, a knell,
And oh! ye beloved of woman, farewell!

    Silently, with lips compress'd,
    Pale hands clasp'd above her breast,
    Stately brow of anguish high,
    Death-like cheek, but dauntless eye;
    Silently, o'er that red plain,
    Moved the lady 'midst the slain.

Sometimes it seem'd as a charging cry,
Or the ringing tramp of a steed, came nigh
Sometimes a blast of the Paynim horn,
Sudden and shrill from the mountains borne,
And her maidens trembled;—but on _her_ ear
No meaning fell with those sounds of fear;
They had less of mastery to shake her now,
Than the quivering, erewhile, of an aspen bough
She search'd into many an unclosed eye,
That look'd, without soul, to the starry sky;
She bow'd down o'er many a shatter'd breast,
She lifted up helmet and cloven crest—
    Not there, not there he lay!
"Lead where the most hath been dared and done,
Where the heart of the battle hath bled,—lead on!"
    And the vassal took the way.

    He turn'd to a dark and lonely tree
      That waved o'er a fountain red;
    Oh! swiftest _there_ had the currents free,
      From noble veins been shed.

    Thickest there the spear-heads gleam'd,
    And the scatter'd plumage stream'd,
    And the broken shields were toss'd,
    And the shiver'd lances cross'd,
    And the mail-clad sleepers round
    Made the harvest of that ground.

He was there! the leader amidst his band,
Where the faithful had made their last vain
He was there! but affection's glance alone
The darkly-changed in that hour had known
With the falchion yet in his cold hand grasp;
And a banner of France to his bosom clasp
And the form that of conflict bore fearful t
And the face—oh! speak not of that dead
As it lay to answer love's look no more,
Yet never so proudly loved before!
She quell'd in her soul the deep floods of w
The time was not yet for their waves to flo
She felt the full presence, the might of des
Yet there came no sob with her struggling
And a proud smile shone o'er her pale despair,
As she turn'd to his followers—"Your Lord is
    there!

Look on him! know him by scarf and crest!—
Bear him away with his sires to rest!"

    Another day—another night—
      And the sailor on the deep
    Hears the low chant of a funeral rite
      From the lordly chapel sweep;

It comes with a broken and muffled tone,
As if that rite were in terror done;
Yet the songs 'midst the seas hath a thrilling
    power,
And he knows 't is a chieftain's burial hour.

    Hurriedly, in fear and woe,
    Through the aisle the mourners go;
    With a hush'd and stealthy tread,
    Bearing on the noble dead,
    Sheathed in armour of the field—
    Only his wan face reveal'd,
    Whence the still and solemn gleam
    Doth a strange sad contrast seem
    To the anxious eyes of that pale band,
    With torches wavering in every hand,
    For they dread each moment the shout of war,
    And the burst of the Moslem scimitar.

There is no plumed head o'er the bier to bend,
No brother of battle, no princely friend,
No sound comes back like the sounds of yore,
Unto sweeping swords from the marble floor;
By the red fountain the valiant lie,
The flower of Provençal chivalry,
But *one* free step, and one lofty heart,
Bear through that scene, to the last, their part

She hath led the death-train of the brave
To the verge of his own ancestral grave;
She hath held o'er her spirit long rigid sway,
But the struggling passion must now have way.
In the cheek, half seen through her mourning veil,
By turns does the swift blood flush and fail;
The pride on the lip is lingering still,
But it shakes as a flame to the blast might thrill;
Anguish and Triumph are met at strife,.
Rending the chords of her frail young life;
And she sinks at last on her warrior's bier,
Lifting her voice, as if Death might hear.—

" I have won thy fame from the breath of wrong,
My soul hath risen for thy glory strong!
Now call me hence, by thy side to be,
The world thou leavest has no place for me.
The light goes with thee, the joy, the worth—
Faithful and tender! Oh! call me forth!
Give me my home on thy noble heart,—
Well have we loved, let us both depart!"

And pale on the breast of the Dead she lay,
The living cheek to the cheek of clay;
The *living* cheek!—Oh! it was not vain,
That strife of the spirit to rend its chain;
She is there at rest in her place of pride,
In death how queen-like—a glorious bride!

Joy for the freed One!—she might not stay
When the crown had fallen from her life away;
She might not linger—a weary thing,
A dove, with no home for its broken wing,
Thrown on the harshness of alien skies,
That know not its own land's melodies.
From the long heart-withering early gone;
She hath lived—she hath loved—her task is done!

---

## THE CORONATION OF INEZ DE CASTRO.

Tableau, ou l'Amour fait alliance avec la Tombe; union redou
table de la mort et de la vie!—*Madame de Stael.*

Therz was music on the midnight;—
    From a royal fane it roll'd,
And a mighty bell, each pause between,
    Sternly and slowly toll'd

Strange was their mingling in the sky,
    It hush'd the listener's breath;
For the music spoke of triumph high,
    The lonely bell, of death.

There was hurrying through the midnight—
    A sound of many feet·
But they fell with a muffled fearfulness,
    Along the shadowy street:
And softer, fainter, grew their tread,
    As it near'd the minster-gate,
Whence a broad and solemn light was shed
    From a scene of royal state.

Full glow'd the strong red radiance,
    In the centre of the nave,
Where the folds of a purple canopy
    Swept down in many a wave;
Loading the marble pavement old
    With a weight of gorgeous gloom,
For something lay 'midst their fretted gold,
    Like a shadow of the tomb.

And within that rich pavilion,
    High on a glittering throne,
A woman's form sat silently,
    'Midst the glare of light alone
Her jewell'd robes fell strangely still—
    The drapery on her breast
Seem'd with no pulse beneath to thrill,
    So stonelike was its rest!

But a peal of lordly music
    Shook e'en the dust below,
When the burning gold of the diadem
    Was set on her pallid brow!
Then died away that haughty sound,
    And from the encircling band
Stept Prince and Chief, 'midst the hush profound,
    With homage to her hand.

Why pass'd a faint, cold shuddering
    Over each martial frame,
As one by one, to touch that hand,
    Noble and leader came?
Was not the settled aspect fair?
    Did not a queenly grace,
Under the parted ebon hair,
    Sit on the pale still face?

Death! Death! canst *thou* be lovely
    Unto the eye of Life?
Is not each pulse of the quick high breast
    With thy cold mien at strife?
—It was a strange and fearful sight.
    The crown upon that head,
The glorious robes, and the blaze of light,
    All gather'd round the Dead!

And beside her stood in silence
    One with a brow as pale,
And white lips rigidly compress'd,
    Lest the strong heart should fail·
King Pedro, with a jealous eye,
    Watching the homage done,
By the land's flower and chivalry,
    To her, his martyr'd one.

But on the face he look'd not,
    Which once his star had been;
To every form his glance was turn'd,
    Save of the breathless queen:
Tho' something, won from the grave's embrace
    Of her beauty still was there,
Its hues were all of that shadowy place,
    It was not for *him* to bear.

Alas! the crown, the sceptre,
    The treasures of the earth,
And the priceless love that pour'd those gifts,
    Alike of wasted worth!
The rites are closed:—bear back the Dead
    Unto the chamber deep!
Lay down again the royal head,
    Dust with the dust to sleep!

There is music on the midnight—
    A requiem sad and slow,
As the mourners through the sounding aisle
    In dark procession go;

And the ring of state, and the starry crown,
  And all the rich array,
Are borne to the house of silence down,
  With her, that queen of clay!

And tearlessly and firmly
  King Pedro led the train,—
But his face was wrapt in his folding robe,
  When they lower'd the dust again.
'Tis hush'd at last the tomb above,
  Hymns die, and steps depart:
Who call'd thee strong as Death, O Love?
  *Mightier* thou wast and art.

## ITALIAN GIRL'S HYMN TO THE VIRGIN

O sanctissima, o purissima!
Dulcis Virgo Maria,
Mater amata, intemerata,
Ora, ora pro nobis.
    *Sicilian Mariner's Hymn.*

In the deep hour of dreams,
Through the dark woods, and past the moaning sea,
  And by the star-light gleams,
Mother of Sorrows! lo, I come to thee.

  Unto thy shrine I bear
Night-blowing flowers, like my own heart, to lie
  All, all unfolded there,
Beneath the meekness of thy pitying eye.

  For thou, that once didst move,
In thy still beauty, through an early home,
  Thou know'st the grief, the love,
The fear of woman's soul; to thee I come!

  Many, and sad, and deep,
Were the thoughts folded in thy silent breast;
  Thou, too, couldst watch and weep—
Hear, gentlest mother! hear a heart oppress'd!

  There is a wandering bark
Bearing one from me o'er the restless waves;
  Oh! let thy soft eye mark
His course;—be with him, Holiest, guide and save!

  My soul is on that way;
My thoughts are travellers o'er the waters dim,
  Through the long weary day,
I walk, o'ershadow'd by vain dreams of him.

  Aid him, and me, too, aid!
Oh! 'tis not well, this earthly love's excess
  On thy weak child is laid
The burden of too deep a tenderness.

  Too much o'er *him* is pour'd
My being's hope—scarce leaving Heaven a part;
  Too fearfully adored,
Oh! make not him the chastener of my heart!

  I tremble with a sense
Of grief to be; I hear a warning low—
  Sweet mother! call me hence!
This wild idolatry must end in woe.

  The troubled joy of life,
Love's lightning happiness, my soul hath known;
  And, worn with feverish strife,
Would fold its wings'—take back, take back thine own!

  Hark! how the wind swept by!
The tempest's voice comes rolling o'er the wave—
  Hope of the sailor's eye,
And maiden's heart, blest mother, guide and save!

## TO A DEPARTED SPIRIT.

From the bright stars, or from the viewless air,
Or from some world unreach'd by human thought,
Spirit, sweet spirit! if thy home be there,

And if thy visions with the past be fraught,
    Answer me, answer me!

Have we not communed here with life and death?
Have we not said that love, such love as ours,
Was not to perish as a rose's breath,
To melt away, like song from festal bowers?
    Answer, oh! answer me!

Thine eye's last light was mine—The soul that
  shone
Intensely, mournfully, through gathering haze—
Didst thou bear with thee to the shore unknown,
Naught of what lived in that long earnest gaze?
    Hear, hear, and answer me!

Thy voice—its low, soft, fervent, farewell tone
Thrill'd through the tempest of the parting strife,
Like a faint breeze:—oh! from that music flown,
Send back *one* sound, if love's be quenchless life,
    But once, oh! answer me!

In the still noontide, in the sunset's hush,
In the dead hour of night, when thought grows
  deep,
When the heart's phantoms from the darkness rush,
Fearfully beautiful, to strive with sleep—
    Spirit! then answer me!

By the remembrance of our blended prayer;
By all our tears, whose mingling made them sweet;
By our last hope, the victor o'er despair;—
Speak! if our souls in deathless yearnings meet;
    Answer me, answer me!

The grave is silent:—and the far-off sky,
And the deep midnight—silent all, and lone!
Oh! if thy buried love make no reply,
What voice has Earth?—Hear, pity, speak, mine
  own!
    Answer me, answer me!

## THE CHAMOIS HUNTER'S LOVE.

For all his wildness and proud fantasies,
I love him!
    *Croly.*

Thy heart is in the upper world, where fleet the
  Chamois bounds,
Thy heart is where the mountain-fir shakes to the
  torrent-sounds;
And where the snow-peaks gleam like stars, through
  the stillness of the air,
And where the Lauwine's* peal is heard—Hunter!
  thy heart is there!
I know thou lov'st me well, dear Friend! but bet-
  ter, better far,
Thou lov'st that high and haughty life, with rocks
  and storms at war;
In the green sunny vales with me, thy spirit would
  but pine—
And yet I will be thine, my Love! and yet I will
  be thine!

And I will not seek to woo thee down from those
  thy native heights,
With the sweet song, our land's own song, of pastoral delights;
For thou must live as eagles live, thy path is not
  as mine—
And yet I will be thine, my Love! and yet I will
  be thine.

And I will leave my blessed home, my Father's
  joyous hearth,
With all the voices meeting there in tenderness
  and mirth,
With all the kind and laughing eyes, that in its
  fire-light shine,
To sit forsaken in thy hut,—yet know that thou
  art mine!

---

*Lauwine,* the avalanche.

t is my youth, it is my bloom, it is my glad free
      heart,
That I cast away for thee—for thee—all reckless
      as thou art !
With tremblings and with vigils lone, I bind my-
      self to dwell ;
Yet, yet I would not change that lot,—oh no! I
      love too well !

A mournful thing is love which grows to one so
      wild as thou,
With that bright restlessness of eye, that tameless
      fire of brow !
Mournful!—but dearer far I call its mingled fear
      and pride,
And the trouble of its happiness, than aught on
      earth beside.

To listen for thy step in vain, to start at every
      breath,
To watch through long, long nights of storm, to
      sleep and dream of death,
To wake in doubt and loneliness—this doom I
      know is mine,—
And yet I will be thine, my Love ! and yet I will
      be thine !

That I may greet thee from thine Alps, when
      thence thou com'st at last,
That I may hear thy thrilling voice tell o'er each
      danger past,
That I may kneel and pray for thee, and win thee
      aid divine,—
For this I will be thine, my Love ! for this I will
      be thine !

---

### SONG OF EMIGRATION

There was heard a song on the chiming sea,
A mingled breathing of grief and glee ;
Man's voice, unbroken by sighs, was there,
Filling with triumph the sunny air ;
Of fresh green lands, and of pastures new,
It sang, while the bark through the surges flew.

      But ever and anon
      A murmur of farewell
      Told, by its plaintive tone,
      That from woman's lip it fell.

"Away, away, o'er the foaming main !"
—This was the free and the joyous strain—
"There are clearer skies than ours, afar,
We will shape our course by a brighter star ;
There are plains whose verdure no foot hath press'd,
And whose wealth is all for the first brave guest."

      " But alas ! that we should go"
      —Sang the farewell voices then—
      " From the homesteads, warm and low,
      By the brook and in the glen !"

"We will rear new homes under trees that glow
As if gems were the fruitage of every bough ;
O'er our white walls we will train the vine,
And sit in its shadow at day's decline ;
And watch our herds, as they range at will
Through the green savannas, all bright and still."

      " But woe for that sweet shade
      Of the flowering orchard-trees,
      Where first our children play'd
      'Midst the birds and honey-bees !"

" All, all our own shall the forests be,
As to the bound of the roebuck free !
None shall say, ' Hither, no further pass !'
We will track each step through the wavy grass ;
We will chase the elk in his speed and might,
And bring proud spoils to the hearth at night."

      "But, oh ! the gray church-tower,
      And the sound of Sabbath-bell,
      And the shelter'd garden-bower,—
      We have bid them all farewell !"

" We will give the names of our fearless race
To each bright river whose course we trace ;
We will leave our memory with mounts and floods
And the path of our daring in boundless woods !
And our works unto many a lake's green shore,
Where the Indian's graves lay, alone, before."

      " But who shall teach the flowers,
      Which our children loved, to dwell
      In a soil that is not ours?
      —Home, home and friends, farewell !"

---

### THE INDIAN WITH HIS DEAD CHILD

      In the silence of the midnight
      I journey with my dead ;
      In the darkness of the forest-boughs,
      A lonely path I tread.

      But my heart is high and fearless,
      As by mighty wings upborne ;
      The mountain eagle hath not plumes
      So strong as Love and Scorn.

      I have raised thee from the grave-sod
      By the white man's path defiled ;
      On to th' ancestral wilderness,
      I bear thy dust, my child !

      I have ask'd the ancient deserts
      To give my dead a place,
      Where the stately footsteps of the free
      Alone should leave a trace.

      And the tossing pines made answer—
      "Go, bring us back thine own !"
      And the streams from all the hunters' hills,
      Rush'd with an echoing tone.

      Thou shalt rest by sounding waters
      That yet untamed may roll ;
      The voices of that chainless host
      With joy shall fill thy soul.

      In the silence of the midnight
      I journey with the dead,
      Where the arrows of my father's bow
      Their falcon flight have sped.

      I have left the spoiler's dwellings,
      For evermore, behind ;
      Unmingled with their household sounds,
      For me shall sweep the wind.

      Alone, amidst their hearth-fires,
      I watch'd my child's decay,
      Uncheer'd, I saw the spirit-light
      From his young eyes fade away.

      When his head sank on my bosom,
      When the death-sleep o'er him fell,
      Was there one to say, "A friend is near ?"
      There was none !—pale race, farewell !

      To the forests, to the cedars,
      To the warrior and his bow,
      Back, back !—I bore thee laughing thence
      I bear thee slumbering now !

      I bear thee unto burial
      With the mighty hunters gone ;
      I shall hear thee in the forest-breeze,
      Thou wilt speak of joy, my son !

      In the silence of the midnight
      I journey with the dead ;
      But my heart is strong, my step is fleet,
      My father's path I tread.

---

* An Indian, who had established himself in a township of
Maine, feeling indignantly the want of sympathy evinced towards
him by the white inhabitants, particularly on the death of his only
child, gave up his farm soon afterwards, dug up the body of his
child, and carried it with him two hundred miles through the
forests to join the Canadian Indians. See *Tudor's Letters on the
Eastern States of America.*

## THE KING OF ARRAGON'S LAMENT FOR HIS BROTHER.*

' If I could see him, it were well with me?
*Coleridge's Wallenstein.*

THERE were lights and sounds of revelling in the
 vanquish'd city's halls,
As by night the feast of victory was held within
 its walls;
And the conquerors fill'd the wine-cup high, after
 years of bright blood shed;
But their Lord, the King of Arragon, 'midst the
 triumph, wail'd the dead.

He look'd down from the fortress won, on the tents
 and towers below,
The moon-lit sea, the torch-lit streets,—and a
 gloom came o'er his brow:
The voice of thousands floated up, with the horn
 and cymbal's tone;
But his heart, 'midst that proud music, felt more
 utterly alone.

And he cried, "Thou art mine, fair city! thou city
 of the sea!
But, oh! what portion of delight is mine at last
 in thee?
—I am lonely 'midst thy palaces, while the glad
 waves past them roll,
And the soft breath of thine orange-bowers is
 mournful to my soul.

"My brother! oh! my brother! thou art gone,—
 the true and brave,
And the haughty joy of victory hath died upon thy
 grave;
There are many round my throne to stand, and to
 march where I lead on;
There was *one* to *love* me in the world,—my brother! thou art gone!

'In the desert, in the battle, in the ocean-tempest's
 wrath,
We stood together, side by side; one hope was
 ours,—one path;
Thou hast wrapt me in the soldier's cloak, thou
 hast fenced me with thy breast;
Thou hast watch'd beside my couch of pain—oh!
 bravest heart, and best!

"I see the festive lights around;—o'er a dull sad
 world they shine;
I hear the voice of victory—my Pedro! where is
 *thine?*
The only voice in whose kind tone my spirit found
 reply!—
Oh brother! I have bought too dear this hollow
 pageantry!

"I have hosts, and gallant fleets, to spread my
 glory and my sway,
And chiefs to lead them fearlessly;—my *friend*
 hath pass'd away!
For the kindly look, the word of cheer, my heart
 may thirst in vain,
And the face that was as light to mine—it cannot
 come again!

"I have made thy blood, thy faithful blood, the
 offering for a crown;
With love, which earth bestows not twice, I have
 purchased cold renown;
How often will my weary heart 'midst the sounds
 of triumph die,
When I think of thee, my brother! thou flower of
 chivalry!

"I am lonely—I am lonely! this rest is even as
 death!
Let me hear again the ringing spears, and the bat-
 tle-trumpet's breath;

---

* The grief of Ferdinand, King of Arragon, for the loss of his
brother, Don Pedro, who was killed during the siege of Naples, is
affectingly described by the historian, Mariana. It is also the subject of one of the old Spanish ballads in Lockhart's beautiful collection.

Let me see the fiery charger foam, and the royal
 banner wave—
But where art thou, my brother? where?—in thy
 low and early grave!"

And louder swell'd the songs of joy through that
 victorious night,
And faster flow'd the red wine forth, by the stars'
 and torches' light;
But low and deep, amidst the mirth, was heard
 the conqueror's moan—
"My brother! oh! my brother! best and bravest
 thou art gone!"

---

## THE RETURN.

"HAST thou come with the heart of thy childhood
 back?
 The free, the pure, the kind?"
—So murmur'd the trees in my homeward track,
 As they play'd to the mountain-wind.

"Hath thy soul been true to its early love?"
 Whisper'd my native streams;
"Hath the spirit nursed amidst hill and grove,
 Still revered its first high dreams?"

"Hast thou borne in thy bosom the holy prayer
 Of the child in his parent-halls?"
—Thus breathed a voice on the thrilling air
 From the old ancestral walls.

"Hast thou kept thy faith with the faithful dead
 Whose place of rest is nigh?
With the father's blessing o'er thee shed,
 With the mother's trusting eye?"

—Then my tears gush'd forth in sudden rain,
 As I answer'd—"O, ye shades!
I bring not my childhood's heart again
 To the freedom of your glades.

"I have turn'd from my first pure love aside,
 O bright and happy streams!
Light after light, in my soul have died
 The day-spring's glorious dreams.

"And the holy prayer from my thoughts hath
 pass'd—
 The prayer at my mother's knee!
Darken'd and troubled I come at last,
 Home of my boyish glee!

"But I bear from my childhood a gift of tears
 To soften and atone;
And oh! ye scenes of those blessed years,
 They shall make me again your own."

---

## THE VAUDOIS' WIFE.*

Clasp me a little longer, on the brink
 Of fate! while I can feel thy dear caress:
And when this heart hath ceased to beat, oh! think—
 And let it mitigate thy woe's excess—
 That thou to me hast been all tenderness,
And friend, to more than human friendship just.
 Oh! by that retrospect of happiness,
And by the hopes of an immortal trust,
God shall assuage thy pangs, when I am laid in dust.
 *Gertrude of Wyoming.*

---

THY voice is in mine ear, beloved!
 Thy look is in my heart,
Thy bosom is my resting-place,
 And yet I must depart.
Earth on my soul is strong—too strong—
 Too precious is its chain,
All woven of thy love, dear friend,
 Yet vain—though mighty—vain!

---

* The wife of a Vaudois leader, in one of the attacks made on the
Protestant hamlets, received a mortal wound, and died in her husband's arms, exhorting him to courage and endurance.

Thou see'st mine eye grow dim, beloved;
  Thou see'st my life-blood flow.—
Bow to the chastener silently,
  And calmly let me go!
A little while between our hearts
  The shadowy gulf must lie,
Yet have we for their communing
  Still, still Eternity!

Alas! thy tears are on my cheek
  My spirit they detain;
I know that from thine agony
  Is wrung that burning rain.
Best, kindest, weep not;—make the pang
  The bitter conflict, less—
Oh! sad it is, and yet a joy,
  To feel thy love's excess!

But calm thee! Let the thought of death
  A solemn peace restore!
The voice that must be silent soon,
  Would speak to thee once more.
That thou may'st bear its blessing on
  Through years of after life—
A token of consoling love,
  Even from this hour of strife.

I bless thee for the noble heart,
  The tender, and the true,
Where mine hath found the happiest rest
  That e'er fond woman's knew;
I bless thee, faithful friend and guide,
  For my own, my treasured share,
In the mournful secrets of thy soul,
  In thy sorrow, in thy prayer.

I bless thee for kind looks and words
  Shower'd on my path like dew,
For all the love in those deep eyes
  A gladness ever new!
For the voice which ne'er to mine replied
  But in kindly tones of cheer;
For every spring of happiness
  My soul hath tasted here!

I bless thee for the last rich boon
  Won from affection tried,
The right to gaze on death with thee,
  To perish by thy side!
And yet more for the glorious hope
  Even to *these* moments given—
Did not *thy* spirit ever lift
  The trust of *mine* to Heaven.

Now be *thou* strong! Oh! knew we not
  Our path must lead to this?
A shadow and a trembling still
  Were mingled with our bliss!
We plighted our young hearts when storms
  Were dark upon the sky,
In full, deep knowledge of their task
  To suffer and to die!

Be strong! I leave the living voice
  Of this, my martyr'd blood,
With the thousand echoes of the hills,
  With the torrent's foaming flood,—
A spirit 'midst the caves to dwell,
  A token on the air,
To rouse the valiant from repose,
  The fainting from despair.

Hear it, and bear thou on, my love!
  Ay, joyously endure!
Our mountains must be altars yet,
  Inviolate and pure;
There must our God be worshipp'd still
  With the worship of the free—
Farewell! there's but *one* pang in death,
  One only,—leaving thee!

# THE GUERILLA LEADER'S VOW.

Did you say all?     All my pretty ones!
*     *     *     *
Let us make medicine of this great revenge,
To cure this deadly grief!
*Macbeth.*

My battle-vow!—no minster walls
  Gave back the burning word,
Nor cross nor shrine the low deep tone
  Of smother'd vengeance heard;
But the ashes of a ruin'd home
  Thrill'd, as it sternly rose,
With the mingling voice of blood that shook
  The midnight's dark repose.

I breathed it not o'er kingly tombs,
  But where my children lay,
And the startled vulture, at my step,
  Soar'd from their precious clay.
I stood amidst my dead alone—
  I kiss'd their lips—I pour'd,
In the strong silence of that hour,
  My spirit on my sword.

The roof-tree fall'n, the smouldering floor,
  The blacken'd threshold-stone,
The bright hair torn, and soil'd with blood,
  Whose fountain was my own;
These, and the everlasting hills,
  Bore witness that wild night;
Before them rose th' avenger's soul,
  In crush'd affection's might.

The stars, the searching stars of heaven,
  With keen looks would upbraid,
If from my heart the fiery vow,
  Sear'd on it then, could fade.
They have no cause!—Go, ask the streams
  That by my paths have swept,
The red waves that unstain'd were born—
  How hath my faith been kept?

And other eyes are on my soul,
  That never, never close,
The sad, sweet glances of the lost—
  They leave me no repose.
Haunting my night-watch 'midst the rocks,
  And by the torrent's foam,
Through the dark-rolling mists they shine,
  Full, full of love and home!

Alas! the mountain eagle's heart,
  When wrong'd, may yet find rest;
Scorning the place made desolate,
  He seeks another nest.
But I—your soft looks wake the thirst
  That wins no quenching rain;
Ye drive me back, my beautiful!
  To the stormy fight again!

---

# THEKLA AT HER LOVER'S GRAVE.*

Thither where he lies buried!
That single spot is the whole world to me.
*Coleridge's Wallenstein.*

Thy voice was in my soul! it call'd me on;
  O my lost friend! thy voice was in my soul!
From the cold faded world, whence thou art gone,
  To hear no more life's troubled billows roll,
      I come, I come!

Now speak to me again! we loved so well—
  We *loved!* oh! still, I know that still we love!
I have left all things with thy dust to dwell,
  Through these dim aisles in dreams of *thee* to
  rove:
      This is my home!

Speak to me in the thrilling minster's gloom!
　Speak! thou hast died, and sent me no farewell!
I will not shrink;—oh, mighty is the tomb,
　But one thing mightier, which it cannot quell,
　　　This woman's heart

This lone, full, fragile heart!—the strong alone
　In love and grief—of both the burning shrine!
Thou, my soul's friend! with grief hast surely done,
　But with the love which made thy spirit mine,
　　　Say, couldst thou part?

hear the rustling banners; and I hear
　The wind's low singing through the fretted
　　stone;
I hear not thee; and yet I feel thee near—
　What is this sound that keeps thee from thine
　　own?
　　　Breathe it away!

I wait thee—I adjure thee! hast thou known
　How I have loved thee? couldst thou dream it
　　all?
Am I not here, with night and death alone,
　And fearing not? and hath my spirit's call
　　　O'er thine no sway?

Thou canst not come! or thus I should not weep!
　Thy love is deathless—but no longer free!
Soon would its wing triumphantly o'ersweep
　The viewless barrier, if such power might be,
　　　Soon, soon, and fast!

But I shall come to thee! our souls' deep dreams,
　Our young affections, have not gush'd in vain;
Soon in one tide shall blend the sever'd streams,
　The worn heart break its bonds—and death and
　　pain
　　　Be with the past!

## THE SISTERS OF SCIO

As are our hearts, our way is one,
And cannot be divided. Strong affliction
Contends with all things, and o'ercometh all things.
Wilt I not live with thee? will I not cheer thee?
Wouldst thou be lonely then? wouldst thou be sad?
　　　　　　　　　*Joanna Baillie.*

"Sister, sweet Sister! let me weep awhile!
　Bear with me—give the sudden passion way!
Thoughts of our own lost home, our sunny isle,
　Come, as a wind that o'er a reed hath sway;
Till my heart dies with yearnings and sick fears;—
Oh! could my life melt from me in these tears!

"Our father's voice, our mother's gentle eye,
　Our brother's bounding step—where are they,
　　where?
Desolate, desolate our chambers lie!
　—How hast thou won thy spirit from despair?
O'er mine swift shadows, gusts of terror, sweep;—
I sink away—bear with me—let me weep!"

"Yes! weep, my Sister! weep, till from thy heart
　The weight flow forth in tears; yet sink thou
　　not!
I bind my sorrow to a lofty part,
　For thee, my gentle one! our orphan lot
To meet in quenchless trust; my soul is strong—
Thou, too, wilt rise in holy might ere long.

"A breath of our free heavens and noble sires,
　A memory of our old victorious dead,—
These mantle me with power! and though their
　　fires
In a frail censer briefly may be shed,
Yet shall they light us onward, side by side;—
Have the wild birds, and have not we, a guide?

"Cheer, then, beloved, on whose meek brow is set
　Our mother's image—in whose voice a tone,
A faint sweet sound of hers is lingering yet,
　An echo of our childhood's music gone;—
Cheer thee! thy Sister's heart and faith are high
Our path is one—with thee I live and die!"

## BERNARDO DEL CARPIO.

The celebrated Spanish champion, Bernardo del Carpio, having made many ineffectual efforts to procure the release of his father, the Count Saldana, who had been imprisoned by King Alfonso of Asturias, almost from the time of Bernardo's birth, at last took up arms in despair. The war which he maintained proved so destructive, that the men of the land gathered round the King, and united in demanding Saldana's liberty. Alfonso, accordingly, offered Bernardo immediate possession of his father's person, in exchange for his castle of Carpio. Bernardo, with ut hesitation, gave up his strong hold, with all his captives; and being assured that his father was then on his way from prison, rode forth with the King to meet him. "And when he saw his father approaching, he exclaimed," says the ancient chronicle, "'Oh, God! is the Count of Saldana indeed coming?'—'Look where he is,' replied the cruel King, 'and now go and greet him whom you have so long desired to see.'" The remainder of the story will be found related in the ballad. The chronicles and romances leave us nearly in the dark as to Bernardo's history after this event.

The warrior bow'd his crested head, and tamed
　　his heart of fire,
And sued the haughty king to free his long-impri-
　　son'd sire;
"I bring thee here my fortress keys, I bring my
　　captive train,
I pledge thee faith, my liege, my lord!—oh, break
　　my father's chain!"

"Rise, rise! even now thy father comes, a ran-
　　som'd man this day;
Mount thy good horse, and thou and I will meet
　　him on his way."
Then lightly rose that loyal son, and bounded on
　　his steed,
And urged, as if with lance in rest, the charger's
　　foamy speed.

And lo! from far, as on they press'd, there came a
　　glittering band,
With one that 'midst them stately rode, as a leader
　　in the land;
"Now haste, Bernardo, haste! for there, in very
　　truth, is he,
The father whom thy faithful heart hath yearn'd
　　so long to see."

His dark eye flash'd, his proud breast heaved, his
　　cheek's blood came and went,
He reach'd that gray-hair'd chieftain's side, and
　　there, dismounting, bent;
A lowly knee to earth he bent, his father's hand
　　he took,—
What was there in its touch that all his fiery spi-
　　rit shook?

That hand was cold—a frozen thing—it dropp'd
　　from his like lead,—
He look'd up to the face above—the face was of
　　the dead!
A plume waved o'er the noble brow—the brow was
　　fix'd and white;—
He met at last his father's eyes—but in them was
　　no sight!

Up from the ground he sprung, and gazed, but who
　　could paint that gaze?
They hush'd their very hearts, that saw its horror
　　and amaze;
They might have chain'd him, as before that stony
　　form he stood,
For the power was stricken from his arm, and
　　from his lip the blood.

"Father!" at length he murmur'd low—and wept
　　like childhood then,—
Talk not of grief till thou hast seen the tears of
　　warlike men!—
He thought on all his glorious hopes, and all his
　　young renown,—
He flung the falchion from his side, and in the dust
　　sate down.

Then covering with his steel-gloved hands his
    darkly mournful brow,
" No more, there is no more," he said, " to lift the
    sword for now.—
My king is false, my hope betray'd, my Father—
    oh! the worth,
The glory, and the loveliness, are pass'd away
    from earth!

' I thought to stand where banners waved, my sire
    beside thee yet,
I would that *there* our kindred blood on Spain's
    free soil had met,—
Thou wouldst have known my spirit then,—for
    thee my fields were won,—
And thou hast perish'd in thy chains, as though
    thou hadst no son!"

Then, starting from the ground once more, he
    seized the monarch's rein,
Amidst the pale and wilder'd looks of all the cour-
    tier train;
And with a fierce, o'ermastering grasp, the rearing
    war-horse led,
And sternly set them face to face,—the king before
    the dead!—

' Came I not forth upon thy pledge, my father's
    hand to kiss?—
Be still, and gaze thou on, false king! and tell me
    what is this!
The voice, the glance, the heart I sought—give an-
    swer, where are they?—
If thou wouldst clear thy perjured soul, send life
    through this cold clay!

" Into these glassy eyes put light,—be still! keep
    down thine ire,—
Bid these white lips a blessing speak—this earth is
    not my sire!
Give me back him for whom I strove, for whom my
    blood was shed,—
Thou canst not—and a king?—His dust be moun-
    tains on thy head!"

He loosed the steed; his slack hand fell,—upon the
    silent face
He cast one long, deep, troubled look,—then turn'd
    from that sad place:
His hope was crush'd, his after-fate untold in mar-
    tial strain,—
His banner led the spears no more amidst the hills
    of Spain.

## THE TOMB OF MADAME LANGHANS.*

To a mysteriously consorted pair
This place is consecrate; to death and life
And to the best affections that proceed
From this conjunction.
                        *Wordsworth.*

How many hopes were borne upon thy bier,
O bride of stricken love! in anguish hither!
Like flowers, the first and fairest of the year
Pluck'd on the bosom of the dead to wither;
Hopes, from their source all holy, though of earth,
All brightly gathering round affection's hearth.

Of mingled prayer they told; of Sabbath hours;
Of morn's farewell, and evening's blessed meeting;
Of childhood's voice, amidst the household bowers;
And bounding step, and smile of joyous greeting;—
But thou, young mother! to thy gentle heart
Didst take thy babe, and meekly so depart.

How many hopes have sprung in radiance hence!
Their trace yet lights the dust where thou art
    sleeping!
A solemn joy comes o'er me, and a sense
Of triumph, blent with nature's gush of weeping,
As, kindling up the silent stone, I see
The glorious vision, caught by faith, of thee.

---

* At Hindelbank, near Berne, she is represented as bursting from the sepulchre, with her infant in her arms, at the sound of the last trumpet. An inscription on the tomb concludes thus:—" Here am I, O God! with the child whom thou hast given me."

Slumberer! love calls thee, for the night is past;
Put on the immortal beauty of thy waking!
Captive! and hear'st thou not the trumpet's blast,
The long, victorious note, thy bondage breaking?
Thou hear'st, thou answer'st, "God of earth and
    Heaven!
Here am I, with the child whom thou hast given!"

## THE EXILE'S DIRGE.

Fear no more the heat o' the sun,
Nor the furious Winter's rages,
Thou thy worldly task hast done,
Home art gone, and ta'en thy wages.
                        *Cymbeline.*

I attended a funeral where there were a number of the German settlers present. After I had performed such service as is usual on similar occasions, a most venerable-looking old man came forward, and asked me if I were willing that they should perform some of their peculiar rites. He opened a very ancient version of Luther's Hymns, and they all began to sing, in German, so loud that the woods echoed the strain. There was something affecting in the singing of these ancient people, carrying one of their brethren to his last home, and using the language and rites which they had brought with them over the sea, from the *Vaterland*, a word which often occurred in this hymn. It was a long, slow and mournful air, which they sung as they bore the body along; the words " *mein Gott*," " *mein Bruder*" and " *Vaterland*," died away in distant echoes amongst the woods. I shall long remember that funeral hymn.—*Flint's Recollections of the Valley of the Mississippi.*

---

There went a dirge through the forest's gloom
—An exile was borne to a lonely tomb.

    " Brother!" (so the chant was sung
    In the slumberer's native tongue,)
    " Friend and brother! not for thee
    Shall the sound of weeping be:—
    Long the Exile's woe hath lain
    On thy life a withering chain;
    Music from thine own blue streams,
    Wander'd through thy fever-dreams;
    Voices from thy country's vines,
    Met thee 'midst the alien pines,
    And thy true heart died away;
    And thy spirit would not stay."

So swell'd the chant; and the deep wind's moan
Seem'd through the cedars to murmur—" *Gone!*"

    " Brother! by the rolling Rhine,
    Stands the home that once was thine—
    Brother! now thy dwelling lies
    Where the Indian arrow flies!
    He that blest thine infant head,
    Fills a distant greensward bed;
    She that heard thy lisping prayer,
    Slumbers low beside him there;
    They that earliest with thee play'd,
    Rest beneath their own oak shade,
    Far, far hence!—yet sea nor shore
    Haply, brother! part ye more;
    God hath call'd thee to that band
    In the immortal Fatherland!"

' The *Fatherland!*"—with that sweet word
A burst of tears 'midst the strain was heard.

    " Brother! were we there with thee
    Rich would many a meeting be!
    Many a broken garland bound,
    Many a mourn'd and lost one found!
    But our task is still to bear,
    Still to breathe in changeful air;
    Loved and bright things to resign,
    As even now this dust of thine;

Yet to hope!—to hope in Heaven,
Though flowers fall, and ties be riven—
Yet to pray! and wait the hand
Beckoning to the Fatherland!"

And the requiem died in the forest's gloom;—
They had reach'd the Exile's lonely tomb.

## THE DREAMING CHILD.

Alas! what kind of grief should thy years know?
Thy brow and cheek are smooth as waters be
When no breath troubles them.
*Beaumont and Fletcher.*

AND is there sadness in *thy* dreams, my boy?
What should the cloud be made of?—blessed child!
Thy spirit, borne upon a breeze of joy,
All day hath ranged through sunshine, clear, yet
   mild:

And now thou tremblest!—wherefore?—in *thy* soul
There lies no past, no future.—Thou hast heard
No sound of presage from the distance roll,
Thy heart bears traces of no arrowy word.

From thee no love hath gone; thy mind's young
   eye
Hath look'd not into Death's, and thence become
A questioner of mute Eternity,
A weary searcher for a viewless home:

Nor hath thy sense been quicken'd unto pain,
By feverish watching for some step beloved;
Free are thy thoughts, an ever-changeful train,
Glancing like dewdrops, and as lightly moved.

Yet now, on billows of strange passion toss'd,
How art thou wilder'd in the cave of sleep!
My gentle child! 'midst what dim phantoms lost,
Thus in mysterious anguish dost thou weep?

Awake! they sadden me—those early tears,
First gushings of the strong dark river's flow,
That must o'ersweep thy soul with coming years,
Th' unfathomable flood of human woe!

Awful to watch, ev'n rolling through a dream,
Forcing wild spray-drops but from childhood's eyes!
Wake, wake! as yet *thy* life's transparent stream
Should wear the tinge of none but summer skies.

Come from the shadow of those realms unknown,
Where now thy thoughts dismay'd and darkling
   rove;
Come to the kindly region all thine own,
Thy home, still bright for thee with guardian love

Happy, fair child! that yet a mother's voice
Can win thee back from visionary strife!—
Oh! shall my soul, thus waken'd to rejoice,
Start from the dreamlike wilderness of life?

## THE CHARMED PICTURE.

Oh! that those lips had language!—Life hath pass'd
With me but roughly since I saw thee last.
*Cowper.*

THINE eyes are charm'd—thine earnest eyes—
   Thou image of the dead!
A spell within their sweetness lies,
   A virtue thence is shed.

Oft in their meek blue light enshrined,
   A blessing seems to be,
And sometimes there my wayward mind
   A still reproach can see:

And sometimes Pity—soft and deep,
   And quivering through a tear;
Even as if Love in Heaven could weep,
   For Grief left drooping here.

And oh! my spirit needs that balm,
   Needs it 'midst fitful mirth;
And in the night-hour's haunted calm,
   And by the lonely hearth.

Look on me *thus*, when hollow praise
   Hath made the weary pine
For one true tone of other days,
   One glance of love like thine!

Look on me *thus*, when sudden glee
   Bears my quick heart along,
On wings that struggle to be free,
   As bursts of skylark song.

In vain, in vain!—too soon are felt
   The wounds they cannot flee;
Better in childlike tears to melt,
   Pouring my soul on thee!

Sweet face, that o'er my childhood shone,
   Whence is thy power of change,
Thus ever shadowing back my own,
   The rapid and the strange?

Whence are they charm'd—those earnest eyes?
   —I know the mystery well!
In mine own trembling bosom lies
   The spirit of the spell!

Of Memory, Conscience, Love, 't is born—
   Oh! change no longer, thou!
For ever be the blessing worn
   On thy pure thoughtful brow!

## PARTING WORDS

One struggle more, and I am free.——*Byron.*

LEAVE me, oh! leave me!—unto all below
Thy presence binds me with too deep a spell;
Thou makest those mortal regions, whence I go,
Too mighty in their loveliness—farewell,
     That I may part in peace!

Leave me!—thy footstep, with its lightest sound,
The very shadow of thy waving hair,
Wakes in my soul a feeling too profound,
Too strong for aught that loves and dies, to bear—
     Oh! bid the conflict cease!

I hear thy whisper—and the warm tears gush
Into mine eyes, the quick pulse thrills my heart;
Thou bid'st the peace, the reverential hush,
The still submission, from my thoughts depart;
     Dear one! this must not be.

The past looks on me from thy mournful eye,
The beauty of our free and vernal days;
Our communings with sea, and hill, and sky—
Oh! take that bright world from my spirit's gaze
     Thou art all earth to me!

Shut out the sunshine from my dying room,
The jasmine's breath, the murmur of the bee;
Let not the joy of bird-notes pierce the gloom!
They speak of love, of summer, and of thee,
     Too much—and death is here!

Doth our own spring make happy music now,
From the old beech-roots flashing into day?
Are the pure lilies imaged in its flow?
Alas! vain thoughts! that fondly thus can stray
     From the dread hour so near!

If I could but draw courage from the light
Of thy clear eye, that ever shone to bless!
—Not now! 't will not be now!—my aching sight
Drinks from that fount a flood of tenderness,
     Bearing all strength away!

Leave me!—thou com'st between my heart and
   Heaven!
I would be still, in voiceless prayer to die!
—Why must our souls thus love, and then be riven?
—Return! thy parting wakes mine agony!
     —Oh, yet awhile delay!

## THE MESSAGE TO THE DEAD.[*]

Thou'rt passing hence, my brother!
  Oh! my earliest friend, farewell!
Thou'rt leaving me, without thy voice,
  In a lonely home to dwell;
And from the hills, and from the hearth,
  And from the household-tree,
With thee departs the lingering mirth,
  The brightness goes with thee.

But thou, my friend, my brother!
  Thou'rt speeding to the shore
Where the dirge-like tone of parting words
  Shall smite the soul no more!
And thou wilt see our holy dead,
  The lost on earth and main;
Into the sheaf of kindred hearts,
  Thou wilt be bound again!

Tell, then, our friend of boyhood,
  That yet his name is heard
On the blue mountains, whence his youth
  Pass'd like a swift bright bird.
The light of his exulting brow,
  The vision of his glee,
Are on me still—Oh! still I trust
  That smile again to see.

And tell our fair young sister,
  The rose cut down in spring,
That yet my gushing soul is fill'd
  With lays she loved to sing.
Her soft, deep eyes look through my dreams
  Tender and sadly sweet;—
Tell her my heart within me burns
  Once more that gaze to meet!

And tell our white-hair'd father,
  That in the paths he trode,
The child he loved, the last on earth,
  Yet walks and worships God.
Say, that his last fond blessing yet
  Rests on my soul like dew,
And by its hallowing might I trust
  Once more his face to view.

And tell our gentle mother,
  That on her grave I pour
The sorrows of my spirit forth,
  As on her breast of yore.
Happy thou art that soon, how soon,
  Our good and bright will see!—
Oh! brother, brother! may I dwell,
  Ere long, with them and thee!

---

## THE TWO HOMES.

---

Oh! if the soul immortal be,
Is not its love immortal too?

---

Seest thou my home?—'t is where yon woods are
    waving,
In their dark richness, to the summer air;
Where yon blue stream, a thousand flower-banks
    laving,
Leads down the hills a vein of light,—'t is there!

'Midst those green wilds how many a fount lies
    gleaming,
Fringed with the violet, colour'd with the skies!
My boyhood's haunt, through days of summer
    dreaming,
Under young leaves that shook with melodies.

My home! the spirit of its love is breathing
In every wind that plays across my track;



---

From its white walls the very tendrils wreathing
Seem with soft links to draw the wanderer back.

There am I loved—there pray'd for—there my mo-
    ther
Sits by the hearth with meekly thoughtful eye;
There my young sisters watch to greet their brother
—Soon their glad footsteps down the path will fly.

There, in sweet strains of kindred music blending,
All the home-voices meet at day's decline;
One are those tones, as from one heart ascending,—
There laughs my home—sad stranger! where is
    thine?

Ask'st thou of mine?—In solemn peace 't is lying,
Far o'er the deserts and the tombs away;
'Tis where I, too, am loved with love undying,
And fond hearts wait my step—But where are
    they?

Ask where the earth's departed have their dwel
    ing;
Ask of the clouds, the stars, the trackless air!
I know it not, yet trust the whisper, telling
My lonely heart, that love unchanged is there.

And what is home, and where, but with the loving?
Happy thou art, that so canst gaze on thine!
My spirit feels but, in its weary roving,
That with the dead, where'er they be, is mine.

Go to thy home, rejoicing son and brother!
Bear in fresh gladness to the household scene!
For me, too, watch the sister and the mother,
I well believe—but dark seas roll between.

---

## THE SOLDIER'S DEATH-BED

---

Wie herrlich die Sonne dort untergeht! da ich noch ein Bube war
—war's mein Lieblingsgedanke, wie sie zu leben, wie sie zu sterben!
                                        *Die Räuber.*

---

*Like thee to die, thou sun!*—My boyhood's dream
Was this; and now my spirit, with thy beam,
Ebbs from a field of victory!—yet the hour
Bears back upon me, with a torrent's power,
Nature's deep longings:—Oh! for some kind eye,
Wherein to meet love's fervent farewell gaze;
Some breast to pillow life's last agony,
Some voice, to speak of hope and brighter days,
Beyond the pass of shadows!— But I go,
I, that have been so loved, go hence alone;
And ye, now gathering round my own hearth'
    glow,
Sweet friends! if it may be that a softer tone,
Even in this moment, with your laughing glee,
Mingles its cadence while you speak of me:
Of me, your soldier, 'midst the mountains lying,
On the red banner of his battles dying.
Far, far away!—and oh! your parting prayer—
Will not his name be fondly murmur'd there?
It will!—A blessing on that holy hearth!
Though clouds are darkening to o'ercast its mirth
Mother! I may not hear thy voice again;
Sisters! ye watch to greet my step in vain;
Young brother, fare thee well!—on each dear head
Blessing and love a thousandfold be shed,
My soul's last earthly breathings!—May your home
Smile for you ever!—May no winter come,
No *world*, between your hearts!—May even your
    tears,
For my sake, full of long-remember'd years,
Quicken the true affections that entwine
Your lives in one bright bond!—I may not sleep
Amidst our fathers, where those tears might shine
Over my slumbers; yet your love will keep
My memory living in the ancestral halls,
Where shame hath never trod:—the dark night
    falls,
And I depart.—The brave are gone to rest,
The brothers of my combats, on the breast
Of the red field they reap'd:—their work is done—
*Thou*, too, art set!—farewell, farewell, thou sun!
The last lone watcher of the bloody sod,
Offers a trusting spirit up to God.

---

[*] "Messages from the living to the dead are not uncommon in the Highlands. The Gael have such a ceaseless consciousness of immortality, that their departed friends are considered as merely absent for a time, and permitted to relieve the hours of separation by occasional intercourse with the objects of their earliest affections."—See the Notes to Mrs. Brunton's Works

## THE IMAGE IN THE HEART.

### TO * * *

> True, indeed, it is,
> That they whom death has hidden from our sight,
> Are worthiest of the mind's regard; with them
> The future cannot contradict the past—
> Mortality's last exercise and proof
> Is undergone.                    *Wordsworth.*

> The love where death has set his seal,
> Nor age can chill, nor rival steal,
>     Nor falsehood disavow
>                     *Byron.*

I CALL thee blest,—though now the voice be fled,
Which, to thy soul, brought day-spring with its
        tone,
And o'er the gentle eyes though dust be spread,
Eyes that ne'er look'd on thine but light was
        thrown
        Far through thy breast:

And though the music of thy life be broken,
Or changed in every chord, since he is gone,
Feeling all this, even yet, by many a token,
O thou, the deeply, but the brightly lone!
        I call thee blest!

For in thy heart there is a holy spot,
As 'mid the waste an Isle of fount and palm,
For ever green!—the world's breath enters not,
The passion-tempests may not break its calm;
        'Tis thine, all thine!

Thither, in trust unbaffled, may'st thou turn,
From bitter words, cold greetings, heartless eyes,
Quenching thy soul's thirst at the hidden urn,
That, fill'd with waters of sweet memory, lies
        In its own shrine.

Thou hast thy *home!*—there is no power in change
To reach that temple of the past;—no sway,
In all time brings of sudden, dark, or strange,
To sweep the still transparent peace away
        From its hush'd air!

And oh, that glorious image of the dead!
Sole thing whereon a deathless love may rest,
And in deep faith and dreamy worship shed
Its high gifts fearlessly!—I call thee blest,
        If only *there!*

Blest, for the beautiful within me dwelling,
Never to fade!—a refuge from distrust,
A spring of purer life, still freshly welling,
To clothe the barrenness of earthly dust
        With flowers divine.

And thou hast been beloved!—It is no dream,
No false mirage for *thee,* the fervent love,
The rainbow still unreach'd, the ideal gleam,
That ever seems before, beyond, above,
        Far off to shine.

But thou, from all the daughters of the earth
Singled and mark'd, hast *known* its home and place;
And the high memory of its holy worth,
To this our life a glory and a grace
        For thee hath given.

And art thou not *still* fondly, truly loved?
Thou art!—the love his spirit bore away,
Was not for death!—a treasure but removed,
A bright bird parted for a clearer day,—
        Thine still in Heaven!

## WOMAN ON THE FIELD OF BATTLE.

> Where hath not woman stood,
> Strong in affection's might? a reed upborn
> By an o'ermastering current!

GENTLE and lovely form,
    What didst thou here,
When the fierce battle-storm
    Bore down the spear?

Banner and shiver'd crest,
    Beside thee strown,
Tell, that amidst the best,
    Thy work was done!

Yet strangely, sadly fair,
    O'er the wild scene,
Gleams, through its golden hair
    That brow serene.

Low lies the stately head,—
    Earth-bound the free;
How gave those haughty dead
    A place to thee?

Slumberer! *thine* early bier
    Friends should have crown'd
Many a flower and tear
    Shedding around.

Soft voices, clear and young,
    Mingling their swell,
Should o'er thy dust have sung
    Earth's last farewell.

Sisters, above the grave
    Of thy repose,
Should have bid violets wave
    With the white rose.

Now must the trumpet's note
    Savage and shrill,
For requiem o'er thee float,
    Thou fair and still!

And the swift charger sweep
    In full career,
Trampling thy place of sleep,—
    Why camest thou here?

Why?—ask the true heart why
    Woman hath been
Ever, where brave men die,
    Unshrinking seen?

Unto this harvest ground
    Proud reapers came,—
Some, for that stirring sound,
    A warrior's name;

Some, for the stormy play
    And joy of strife;
And some, to fling away
    A weary life;—

But thou, pale sleeper, thou,
    With the slight frame,
And the rich locks, whose glow
    Death cannot tame;

Only one thought, one power,
    *Thee* could have led,
So, through the tempest's hour,
    To lift thy head!

Only the true, the strong,
    The love, whose trust
Woman's deep soul too long
    Pours on the dust!

## THE LAND OF DREAMS.

And dreams, in their developement, have breath,
And tears, and tortures, and the touch of joy;
They leave a weight upon our waking thoughts,
They make us what we were not—what they will,
And shake us with the vision that 's gone by.
*Byron.*

O SPIRIT-LAND! thou land of dreams!
A world thou art of mysterious gleams,
Of startling voices, and sounds at strife,—
A world of the dead in the hues of life.

Like a wizard's magic glass thou art,
When the wavy shadows float by, and part:
Visions of aspects, now loved, now strange,
Glimmering and mingling in ceaseless change.

Thou art like a city of the past,
With its gorgeous halls into fragments cast,
Amidst whose ruins there glide and play
Familiar forms of the world's to-day.

Thou art like the depths where the seas have birth,
Rich with the wealth that is lost from earth,—
All the sere flowers of our days gone by,
And the buried gems in thy bosom lie.

Yes! thou art like those dim sea-caves,
A realm of treasures, a realm of graves!
And the shapes through thy mysteries that come
        and go,
Are of beauty and terror, of power and woe.

But for me, O thou picture-land of sleep!
Thou art all one world of affections deep,—
And wrung from my heart is each flushing dye,
That sweeps o'er thy chambers of imagery.

And thy bowers are fair—even as Eden fair;
All the beloved of my soul are there!
The forms my spirit most pines to see,
The eyes, whose love hath been life to me:

They are there,—and each blessed voice I hear,
Kindly, and joyous, and silvery clear;
But under-tones are in each, that say,—
" It is but a dream; it will melt away!"

I walk with sweet friends in the sunset's glow;
I listen to music of long ago;
But one thought, like an omen, breathes faint
        through the lay,—
" It is but a dream; it will melt away!"

I sit by the hearth of my early days;
All the home-faces are met by the blaze,—
And the eyes of the mother shine soft, yet say,
" It is but a dream; it will melt away!"

And away, like a flower's passing breath, 't is gone,
And I wake more sadly, more deeply lone!
Oh! a haunted heart is a weight to bear,—
Bright faces, kind voices! where are ye, where?

Shadow not forth, O thou land of dreams,
The past, as it fled by my own blue streams!
Make not my spirit within me burn
For the scenes and the hours that may ne'er return!

Call out from the *future* thy visions bright,
From the world o'er the grave, take thy solemn
        light,
And oh! with the loved, whom no more I see,
Show me my home, as it yet may be!

As it yet may be in some purer sphere,
No cloud, no parting, no sleepless fear;
So my soul may bear on through the long, long day,
Till I go where the beautiful melts not away!

## THE DESERTED HOUSE.

GLOOM is upon thy silent hearth,
O silent house! once fill'd with mirth;
Sorrow is in the breezy sound
Of thy tall poplars whispering round.

The shadow of departed hours
Hangs dim upon thy early flowers;
Even in thy sunshine seems to brood
Something more deep than solitude.

Fair art thou, fair to a stranger's gaze,
Mine own sweet home of other days,
My children's birth-place! yet for me,
It is too much to look on thee.

Too much! for all about thee spread,
I feel the memory of the dead,
And almost linger for the feet
That never more my step shall meet.

The looks, the smiles, all vanish'd now,
Follow me where thy roses blow;
The echoes of kind household-words
Are with me 'midst thy singing birds.

Till my heart dies, it dies away
In yearnings for what might not stay;
For love which ne'er deceived my trust,
For all which went with " dust to dust."

What now is left me, but to raise
From thee, lorn spot! my spirit's gaze,
To lift through tears, my straining eye
Up to my Father's house on high?

Oh! many are the mansions there,*
But not in one hath grief a share!
No haunting shade from things gone by,
May there o'ersweep the unchanging sky.

And *they* are there, whose long-loved mien
In earthly home no more is seen;
Whose places, where they smiling sate,
Are left unto us desolate.

We miss them when the board is spread;
We miss them when the prayer is said;
Upon our dreams their dying eyes
In still and mournful fondness rise.

But they are where those longings vain
Trouble no more the heart and brain;
The sadness of this aching love
Dims not our Father's house above.

Ye are at rest, and I in tears,†
Ye dwellers of immortal spheres!
Under the poplar boughs I stand,
And mourn the broken household band.

But by your life of lowly faith,
And by your joyful hope in death,
Guide me, till on some brighter shore,
The sever'd wreath is bound once more!

Holy ye were, and good, and true!
No change can cloud my thoughts of you;
Guide me like you to live and die,
And reach my Father's house on high!

----

## THE STRANGER'S HEART.

THE stranger's heart! Oh! wound it not!
A yearning anguish is its lot;
In the green shadow of thy tree,
The stranger finds no rest with thee.

----

* In my Father's house there are many mansions.—*John,* chap. xiv.

† From an ancient Hebrew dirge:
    " Mourn for the mourner, and not for the dead
    For he is at rest, and we in tears!"

Thou think'st the vine's low rustling leaves
Glad music round thy household eaves;
To him that sound hath sorrow's tone—
The stranger's heart is with his own.

Thou think'st thy children's laughing play
A lovely sight at fall of day;—
Then are the stranger's thoughts oppress'd—
His mother's voice comes o'er his breast.

Thou think'st it sweet when friend with friend
Beneath one roof in prayer may blend;
Then doth the stranger's eye grow dim—
Far far are those who pray'd with him.

Thy hearth, thy home, thy vintage land—
The voices of thy kindred band—
Oh! 'midst them all when blest thou art,
Deal gently with the stranger's heart!

———

## COME HOME!

———

Come home!—there is a sorrowing breath
　In music since ye went,
And the early flower-scents wander by,
　With mournful memories blent.
The tones in every household voice
　Are grown more sad and deep,
And the sweet word—*brother*—wakes a wish
　To turn aside and weep.

O ye Beloved! come home;—the hour
　Of many a greeting tone,
The time of hearth-light and of song,
　Returns—and ye are gone!
And darkly, heavily it falls
　On the forsaken room,
Burdening the heart with tenderness,
　That deepens 'midst the gloom.

Where finds it *you*, ye wandering ones?
　With all your boyhood's glee
Untamed, beneath the desert's palm,
　Or on the lone mid-sea?
By stormy hills of battles old?
　Or where dark rivers foam?
—Oh! life is dim where ye are not—
　Back, ye beloved, come home!

Come with the leaves and winds of spring,
　And swift birds, o'er the main!
Our love is grown too sorrowful—
　Bring us its youth again!
Bring the glad tones to music back!
　Still, still your home is fair,
The spirit of your sunny life
　Alone is wanting there!

———

## THE FOUNTAIN OF OBLIVION.

———

"*Implora pace!*"*

One draught, kind Fairy! from that fountain deep,
To lay the phantoms of a haunted breast,
And lone affections, which are griefs, to steep
In the cool honey-dews of dreamless rest;
And from the soul the lightning-marks to lave—
　　One draught of that sweet wave!

Yet, mortal, pause!—within thy mind is laid
Wealth, gather'd long and slowly; thoughts divine
Heap that full treasure-house; and thou hast made
The gems of many a spirit's ocean thine;

———

* Quoted from a letter of Lord Byron's. He describes the impression produced upon him by some tombs at Bologna, bearing this simple inscription and adds, "When I die, I could wish that some friend would see these words, and no other, placed above my grave.—"*Implora pace.*"

—Shall the dark waters to oblivion bear
　　A pyramid so fair?

Pour from the fount! and let the draught efface
All the vain lore by memory's pride amass'd,
So it but sweep along the torrent's trace,
And fill the hollow channels of the past;
And from the bosom's inmost folded leaf,
　　Rase the one master-grief!

Yet pause once more!—all, *all* thy soul hath
　　known,
Loved, felt, rejoiced in, from its grasp must fade!
Is there no voice whose kind awakening tone
A sense of spring-time in thy heart hath made?
No eye whose glance thy day-dreams would recall?
　　—Think—wouldst thou part with all?

Fill with forgetfulness!—there are, there *are*
Voices whose music I have loved too well;
Eyes of deep gentleness—but they are far—
Never! oh—never, in my home to dwell!
Take their soft looks from off my yearning soul—
　　Fill high th' oblivious bowl!

Yet pause again!—with memory wilt thou cast
The undying hope away, of memory born?
Hope of reunion, heart to heart at last,
No restless doubt between, no rankling thorn?
Wouldst thou erase all records of delight
　　That make such visions bright?

Fill with forgetfulness, fill high!—yet stay—
—'Tis from the past we shadow forth the land
Where smiles, long lost, again shall light our way,
And the soul's friends be wreath'd in one bright
　　band:
—Pour the sweet waters back on their own rill,
　　I *must* remember still.

For their sake, for the dead—whose image naught
May dim within the temple of my breast—
For their love's sake, which now no earthly thought
May shake or trouble with its own unrest,
Though the past haunt me as a spirit,—yet
　　I ask not to forget.

———

## THE THEMES OF SONG.

———

Of truth, of grandeur, beauty, love, and hope,
And melancholy fear subdued by faith.
　　　　　　　　　　　*Wordsworth.*

———

Where shall the minstrel find a theme?
　—Where'er, for freedom shed,
Brave blood hath dyed some ancient stream,
　Amidst the mountains, red.

Where'er a rock, a fount, a grove,
　Bears record to the faith
Of love, deep, holy, fervent love,
　Victor o'er fear and death.

Where'er a chieftain's crested brow
　Too soon hath been struck down,
Or a bright virgin head laid low,
　Wearing its youth's first crown.

Where'er a spire points up to heaven,
　Through storm and summer air,
Telling, that all around have striven
　Man's heart, and hope, and prayer.

Where'er a blessed Home hath been
　That now is Home no more;
A place of ivy, darkly green,
　Where laughter's light is o'er.

Where'er, by some forsaken grave,
　Some nameless greensward heap,
A bird may sing, a wild-flower wave,
　A star its vigil keep.

Or where a yearning heart of old,
  A dream of shepherd men,
With forms of more than earthly mould
  Hath peopled grot or glen.

*There* may the bard's high themes be found—
  —We die, we pass away:
But faith, love, pity—these are bound
  To earth without decay.

The heart that burns, the cheek that glows,
  The tear from hidden springs,
The thorn and glory of the rose—
  *These* are undying things.

Wave after wave of mighty stream
  To the deep sea hath gone:
Yet not the less, like youth's bright dream,
  The exhaustless flood rolls on.

## RHINE SONG

### OF THE GERMAN SOLDIERS AFTER VICTORY.

"I wish you could have heard Sir Walter Scott describe a glorious sight, which had been witnessed by a friend of his!—the crossing of the Rhine, at Ehrenbreitstein, by the German army of Liberators on their victorious return from France. 'At the first gleam of the river,' he said, 'they all burst forth into the national chaunt, 'Am Rhein! Am Rhein!' They were two days passing over; and the rocks and the castle were ringing to the song the whole time;—for each band renewed it while crossing; and even the Cossacks, with the clash and the clang, and the roll of their stormy war-music, catching the enthusiasm of the scene, swelled forth the chorus, '*Am Rhein! Am Rhein!*'"—*Manuscript Letter.*

#### TO THE AIR OF—"AM RHEIN, AM RHEIN."

#### SINGLE VOICE.

IT is the Rhine! our mountain vineyards laving,
  I see the bright flood shine, I see the bright flood
  shine!
Sing on the march, with every banner waving—
  Sing, brothers, 'tis the Rhine! Sing, brothers,
  'tis the Rhine!

#### CHORUS.

The Rhine! the Rhine! our own imperial River!
  Be glory on thy track, be glory on thy track!
We left thy shores, to die or to deliver ;—
  We bear thee Freedom back, we bear thee Free-
  dom back!

#### SINGLE VOICE.

Hail!, Hail! my childhood knew thy rush of water,
  Ev'n as my mother's song; ev'n as my mother's
  song;
That sound went past me on the field of slaughter,
  And heart and arm grew strong! And heart
  and arm grew strong!

#### CHORUS.

Roll proudly on!—brave blood is with thee sweeping,
  Pour'd out by sons of thine, pour'd out by sons
  of thine,
Where sword and spirit forth in joy were leaping,
  Like thee, victorious Rhine! Like thee, victorious Rhine!

#### SINGLE VOICE.

Home!—Home!—thy glad wave hath a tone of
  greeting,
  Thy path is by my home, thy path is by my home:
Even now my children count the hours till meeting,
  O ransom'd ones, I come! O ransom'd ones, I
  come!

#### CHORUS.

Go, tell the seas, that chain shall bind thee never,
  Sound on by hearth and shrine, sound on by
  hearth and shrine!
Sing through the hills, that thou art free for ever—
  Lift up thy voice, O Rhine! Lift up thy voice,
  O Rhine!

## A SONG OF DELOS.

The Island of Delos was considered of such peculiar sanctity by the ancients, that they did not allow it to be desecrated by the events of birth or death. In the following poem, a young priestess of Apollo is supposed to be conveyed from its shores during the last hours of a mortal sickness, and to bid the scenes of her youth farewell in a sudden flow of unpremeditated song.

> Terre, soleil, vallons, belle et douce Nature,
> Je vous dois une larme aux bords de mon tombeau ;
> L'air est si parfume ! la lumiere est si pure !
> Aux regards d' un Mourant le soliel est si beau !
>
>            *Lamartine.*

A song was heard of old—a low, sweet song,
On the blue seas by Delos: from that isle,
The Sun-God's own domain, a gentle girl
Gentle—yet all inspired of soul, of mien,
Lit with a life too perilously bright
Was borne away to die. How beautiful
Seems this world to the dying!—but for *her*,
The child of beauty and of poesy,
And of soft Grecian skies—oh! who may dream
Of all that from *her* changeful eye flash'd forth.
Or glanced more quiveringly through starry tears.
As on her land's rich vision, fane o'er fane
Colour'd with loving light—she gazed her last,
Her young life's last, that hour! From her pale
  brow
And burning cheek she threw the ringlets back,
And bending forward—as the spirit sway'd
The reed-like form still to the shore beloved,
Breathed the swan-music of her wild farewell
O'er dancing waves :—" Oh! linger yet," she cried

" Oh! linger, linger on the oar,
  Oh! pause upon the deep!
That I may gaze yet once, once more,
Where floats the golden day o'er fane and steep,
Never so brightly smiled mine own sweet shore
—Oh! linger, linger on the parting oar!

" I see the laurels fling back showers
  Of soft light still on many a shrine;
I see the path to haunts of flowers
Through the dim olives lead its gleaming line;
I hear a sound of flutes—a swell of song—
*Mine* is too low to reach that joyous throng!

" Oh! linger, linger on the oar
  Beneath my native sky!
Let my life part from that bright shore
With Day's last crimson—gazing let me die!
Thou bark, glide slowly!—slowly should be borne
The voyager that never shall return.

" A fatal gift hath been thy dower,
  Lord of the Lyre! to me;
With song and wreath from bower to bower,
Sisters went bounding like young Oreads free;
While I, through long, lone, voiceless hours apart,
Have lain and listen'd to my beating heart.

"Now, wasted by the inborn fire.
  I sink to early rest ;
The ray that lit the incense-pyre,
Leaves unto death its temple in my breast.
—O sunshine, skies, rich flowers ! too soon I go,
While round me thus triumphantly ye glow !

  "Bright Isle ! might but thine echoes keep
    A tone of my farewell,
  One tender accent, low and deep,
Shrined 'midst thy founts and haunted rocks to
    dwell !
Might my last breath send music to thy shore !
—Oh ! linger, seamen, linger on the oar !"

---

## ANCIENT GREEK CHAUNT OF VICTORY

Fill high the bowl with Samian wine,
Our virgins dance beneath the shade.

*Byron.*

---

Io ! they come, they come !
  Garlands for every shrine !
Strike lyres to greet them home ;
  Bring roses, pour ye wine !

Swell, swell the Dorian flute
  Through the blue, triumphant sky !
Let the Cittern's tone salute
  The sons of victory.

With the offering of bright blood
  They have ransom'd hearth and tomb,
Vineyard, and field, and flood ;—
  Io ! they come, they come !

Sing it where olives wave,
  And by the glittering sea,
And o'er each hero's grave,—
  Sing, sing, the land is free !

Mark ye the flashing oars,
  And the spears that light the deep ?
How the festal sunshine pours
  Where the lords of battle sweep !

Each hath brought back his shield ;—
  Maid, greet thy lover home !
Mother, from that proud field,
  Io ! thy son is come !

Who murmur'd of the dead ?
  Hush, boding voice ! We know
That many a shining head
  Lies in its glory low.

Breathe not those names to-day !
  They shall have their praise ere long,
And a power all hearts to sway,
  In ever-burning song.

But now shed flowers, pour wine,
  To hail the conquerors home !
Bring wreaths for every shrine—
  Io ! they come, they come !

---

## NAPLES.

### A SONG OF THE SYREN.

Then gentle winds arose,
With many a mingled close,
Of wild Æolian sound and mountain odour keen ;
Where the clear Baian ocean
Welters with air-like motion
Within, above, around its bowers of starry green.

*Shelley.*

---

STILL is the Syren warbling on thy shore,
Bright City of the Waves !—her magic song
Still, with a dreamy sense of ecstasy,
Fills thy soft summer air :—and while my glance

13

Dwells on thy pictured loveliness, that lay
Floats thus o'er Fancy's ear ; and thus to thee,
Daughter of Sunshine ! doth the Syren sing.

  "Thine is the glad wave's flashing play,
  Thine is the laugh of the golden day,
  The golden day, and the glorious night,
And the vine with its clusters all bathed in light !
—Forget, forget, that thou art not free !
      Queen of the summer sea.

  "Favour'd and crown'd of the earth and sky !
Thine are all voices of melody,
Wandering in moonlight through fane and tower,
Floating o'er fountain and myrtle bower ;
Hark ! how they melt o'er thy glittering sea ;
      —Forget that thou art not free !

  "Let the wine flow in thy marble halls !
Let the lute answer thy fountain falls !
And deck thy feasts with the myrtle bough,
And cover with roses thy glowing brow !
Queen of the day and the summer sea,
      Forget that thou art not free !"

*　　　*　　　*　　　*　　　*

So doth the Syren sing, while sparkling waves
Dance to her chaunt.  But sternly, mournfully,
O city of the deep ! from Sybil grots
And Roman tombs, the echoes of thy shore
Take up the cadence of her strain alone.
Murmuring—" *Thou art not free !*"

---

## THE DEATH-SONG OF ALCESTIS.

SHE came forth in her bridal robes array'd,
And 'midst the graceful statues, round the hall
Shedding the calm of their celestial mien,
Stood pale, yet proudly beautiful, as they :
Flowers in her bosom, and the star-like gleam
Of jewels trembling from her braided hair,
And *death* upon her brow !—but glorious death !
Her own heart's choice, the token and the seal
Of love, o'ermastering love ; which, till that hour,
Almost an anguish in the brooding weight
Of its unutterable tenderness,
Had burden'd her full soul.  But now, oh ! now,
Its time was come—and from the spirit's depths,
The passion and the mighty melody
Of its immortal voice, in triumph broke,
Like a strong rushing wind !

              The soft pure air,
Came floating through that hall ;—the Grecian air
Laden with music—flute-notes from the vales,
Echoes of song—the last sweet sounds of life ;
And the glad sunshine of the golden clime
Stream'd, as a royal mantle, round her form,
The glorified of love !  But she—she look'd
Only on *him* for whom 't was joy to die,
Deep—deepest, holiest joy !—or if a thought
Of the warm sunlight, and the scented breeze,
And the sweet Dorian songs, o'erswept the tide
Of her unswerving soul—'t was but a thought
That own'd the summer-loveliness of life
For *him* a worthy offering !—So she stood,
Wrapt in bright silence, as entranced awhile,
Till her eye kindled, and her quivering frame
With the swift breeze of inspiration shook,
As the pale priestess trembles to the breath
Of inborn oracles !—then flush'd her cheek,
And all the triumph, all the agony,
Borne on the battling waves of love and death,
All from her woman's heart, in sudden song,
Burst like a fount of fire.

              "I go, I go !
  Thou Sun, thou golden Sun. I go,
    Far from thy light to dwell ;
  Thou shalt not find my place below,
Dim is that world—bright Sun of Greece, farewell !"

  The Laurel and the glorious Rose
    Thy glad beam yet may see,
  But where no purple summer glows,
O'er the dark wave *I* haste from them and thee.

Yet doth my spirit faint to part?
—I mourn thee not, O Sun!
Joy, solemn joy, o'erflows my heart,
Sing me triumphal songs!—my crown is won!

Let not a voice of weeping rise!
My heart is girt with power!
Let the green earth and festal skies
Laugh as to grace a conqueror's closing hour!

For thee, for *thee*, my bosom's lord!
Thee, my soul's loved! I die;
Thine is the torch of life restored,
Mine, mine the rapture, mine the victory!

Now may the boundless love, that lay
Unfathom'd still before,
In one consuming burst find way,
In one bright flood all, all its riches pour!

Thou know'st, thou know'st what love is *now*!
Its glory and its might—
Are they not written on my brow?
And will that image ever quit thy sight?

No! deathless in thy faithful breast,
There shall my memory keep
Its own bright altar-place of rest,
While o'er my grave the cypress-branches weep.

—Oh! the glad light!—the light is fair,
The soft breeze warm and free,
And rich notes fill the scented air,
And all are gifts—my love's last gifts to thee!

Take me to thy warm heart once more!
Night falls—my pulse beats low—
Seek not to quicken, to restore,
Joy is in every pang—I go, I go!

I feel thy tears, I feel thy breath,
I meet thy fond look still;
Keen is the strife of love and death;
Faint and yet fainter grows my bosom's thrill!

Yet swells the tide of rapture strong,
Though mists o'ershade mine eye;
—Sing, Pæan! sing a conqueror's song!
For thee, for *thee*, my spirit's lord, I die!"

## THE FALL OF D'ASSAS.

### A BALLAD OF FRANCE.

The Chevalier D'Assas, called the French Decius, fell
nobly whilst reconnoitring a wood, near Closterkamp,
by night. He had left his regiment, that of Auvergne,
at a short distance, and was suddenly surrounded by an
ambuscade of the enemy, who threatened him with instant death if he made the least sign of their vicinity.
With their bayonets at his breast, he raised his voice,
and calling aloud " A moi, Avergne! ce sont les enne-
mis!" fell, pierced with mortal blows.

ALONE through gloomy forest shades
A soldier went by night;
No moonbeam pierced the dusky glades,
No star shed guiding light.

Yet on his vigil's midnight round,
The youth all cheerly pass'd;
Uncheck'd by aught of boding sound
That mutter'd in the blast.

Where were his thoughts that lonely hour?
—In his far home; perchance;
His father's hall, his mother's bower,
'Midst the gay vines of France:

Wandering from battles lost and won,
To hear and bless again
The rolling of the wild Garonne,
Or murmur of the Seine.

—Hush! Hark!—did stealing steps go by?
Came not faint whispers near?
No! the wild wind hath many a sigh
Amidst the foliage sere.

Hark, yet again!—and from his hand,
What grasp hath wrench'd the blade?
—Oh! single 'midst a hostile band,
Young soldier! thou'rt betray'd!

" Silence!" in under-tones they cry—
" No whisper—not a breath!
The sound that warns thy comrades nigh
Shall sentence thee to death."

—Still, at the bayonet's point he stood,
And strong to meet the blow;
And shouted, 'midst his rushing blood,
" Arm, arm, Auvergne! the foe!"

The stir, the tramp, the bugle-call—
He heard their tumults grow;
And sent his dying voice through all—
"*Auvergne, Auvergne! the foe!*"

## THE

# BURIAL OF WILLIAM THE CONQUEROR,

### AT CAEN, IN NORMANDY.—1087.

"At the day appointed for the king's interment, Prince
Henry, his third son, the Norman prelates, and a multitude of clergy and people, assembled in the Church of
St. Stephen, which the Conqueror had founded. The
mass had been performed, the corse was placed on the
bier, and the Bishop of Evreux had pronounced the
panegyric on the deceased, when a voice from the crowd
exclaimed,—' He whom you have praised, was a robber.
The very land on which you stand is mine. By violence
he took it from my father; and, in the name of God, I
forbid y  to bury him in it.' The speaker was Asce-
line Fitz Arthur, who had often, but fruitlessly, sought
reparation from the justice of William. After some de-
bate, the prelates called him to them, paid him sixty shil-
lings for the grave, and promised that he should receive
the full value of his land. The ceremony was then continued, and the body of the king deposited in a coffin o.
stone."—*Lingard*, Vol. II. p. 98.

LOWLY upon his bier
The royal Conqueror lay;
Baron and chief stood near,
Silent in war-array.

Down the long minster's aisle
Crowds mutely gazing stream'd,
Altar and tomb the while
Through mists of incense gleam'd.

And by the torches' blaze,
The stately priest had said
High words of power and praise
To the glory of the dead.

They lower'd him, with the sound
Of requiems, to repose;
When from the throngs around
A solemn voice arose:—

" Forbear! forbear!" it cried,
" In the holiest name, forbear!
He hath conquer'd regions wide,
But he shall not slumber *there!*

" By the violated hearth
Which made way for yon proud shrine;
By the harvests which this earth
Hath borne for me and mine;

" By the house e'en here o'erthrown,
On my brethren's native spot;
Hence! with his dark renown,
Cumber our birth-place not!

"Will my sire's unransom'd field,
  O'er which your censers wave,
'To the buried spoiler yield
  Soft slumbers in the grave?

"The tree before him fell,
  Which we cherish'd many a year,
But its deep root yet shall swell,
  And heave against his bier.

"The land that I have till'd
  Hath yet its brooding breast
With my home's white ashes fill'd,
  And it shall not give him rest!

"Each pillar's massy bed
  Hath been wet by weeping eyes—
Away! bestow your dead
  Where no wrong against him cries."

Shame glow'd on each dark face
  Of those proud and steel-girt men,
And they bought with gold a place
  For their leader's dust e'en then.

A little earth for him
  Whose banner flew so far!
And a peasant's tale could dim
  The name, a nation's star!

*One* deep voice thus arose
  From a heart which wrongs had riven,
Oh! who shall number those
  That were but heard in heaven?

---

## CHORUS.

### TRANSLATED FROM THE ALCESTIS OF ALFIERI.

---

(In the scene where the dying Alcestis has bid farewell
to her husband and children.)

#### (ATTENDANTS OF ALCESTIS.)

PEACE, mourners, peace!
Be hush'd, be silent, in this hour of dread!
  Our cries would but increase
The sufferer's pangs; let tears unheard be shed,
  Cease, voice of weeping, cease!

Sustain, O friend!
  Upon thy faithful breast,
The head that sinks, with mortal pain opprest!
  And thou, assistance lend
  To close the languid eye,
Still beautiful, in life's last agony,

Alas! how long a strife!
What anguish struggles in the parting breath,
  Ere yet immortal life
  Be won by death!
Death! Death! thy work complete!
Let thy sad hour be fleet,
Speed, in thy mercy, the releasing sigh!
  No more keen pangs impart
  To her, the high in heart,
The adored Alcestis, worthy ne'er to die.

#### (ATTENDANTS OF ADMETUS.)

'Tis not enough, ah! no!
To hide the scene of anguish from his eyes;
  Still must our silent band
  Around him watchful stand,
And on the mourner ceaseless care bestow,
That his ear catch not grief's funereal cries

Yet, yet hope is not dead,
  All is not lost below,
While yet the gods have pity on our woe.

Oft when all joy is fled,
  Heaven lends support to those
Who on its care in pious hope repose.
  Then to the blessed skies
Let our submissive prayers in chorus rise.

Pray! pray! pray!
What other task have mortals, born to tears,
Whom fate controls, with adamantine sway?
  O ruler of the spheres!
Jove! Jove! enthroned immortally on high,
  Our supplication hear!
  Nor plunge in bitterest woes,
Him, who nor footstep moves, nor lifts his eye,
  But as a child, which only knows
  Its father to revere.

---

## SONGS OF A GUARDIAN SPIRIT.
### I.

---

#### NEAR THEE, STILL NEAR THEE![*]

NEAR thee, still near thee!—o'er thy path-way
    gliding,
Unseen I pass thee with the wind's low sigh;
Life's veil enfolds thee still, our eyes dividing,
Yet viewless love floats round thee silently!

    Not 'midst the festal throng,
    In halls of mirth and song;
    But when thy thoughts are deepest,
    When holy tears thou weepest,
        Know then *that* love is nigh!

When the night's whisper o'er thy harp-strings
    creeping,
Or the sea-music on the sounding shore,
Or breezy anthems through the forest sweeping,
Shall move thy trembling spirit to adore;

    When every thought and prayer
    We loved to breathe and share,
    On thy full heart returning,
    Shall wake its voiceless yearning;
        Then feel me near once more!

Near thee, still near thee!—trust thy soul's deep
    dreaming!
—Oh! love is not an earthly Rose to die!
Ev'n when I soar where fiery stars are beaming,
Thine image wanders with me through the sky.

    The fields of air are free,
    Yet lonely, wanting thee;
    But when thy chains are falling,
    When heaven its own is calling,
        Know  then, thy guide is nigh!

---

## THE SISTERS.†

### A BALLAD.

"I go, sweet sister; yet, my heart would linger
    with thee fain,
And unto every parting gift some deep remem-
    brance chain;
Take then the braid of Eastern pearls which once
    I loved to wear,
And with it bind for festal scenes the dark waves
    of thy hair!

---

* This piece has been set to music of most impressive beauty by John Lodge, Esq., for whose compositions several of the author's songs were written.

† This ballad was composed for a kind of dramatic recitative, relieved by music. It was thus performed by two graceful and highly accomplished sisters.

Its pale pure brightness will beseem those raven
   tresses well,
And I shall need such pomp no more in my lone
   convent cell."

"Oh speak not thus, my Leonor! why part from
   kindred love?
Through festive scenes when thou art gone—my
   steps no more shall move!
How could I bear a lonely heart amid a reckless
   throng?
I should but miss earth's dearest voice in every
   tone of song;
Keep, keep the braid of Eastern pearls, or let me
   proudly twine
Its wreath once more around that brow, that
   queenly brow of thine."

"Oh wouldst thou strive a wounded bird from
   shelter to detain?
Or wouldst thou call a spirit freed, to weary life
   again?
Sweet sister, take the golden cross that I have
   worn so long,
And bathed with many a burning tear for secret
   woe and wrong.
It could not still my beating heart! but may it be
   a sign
Of peace and hope, my gentle one! when meekly
   press'd to thine!"

"Take back, take back the cross of gold, our
   mother's gift to thee,
I would but of this parting hour, a bitter token be;
With funeral splendour to mine eye, it would but
   sadly shine,
And tell of early treasures lost, of joy no longer
   mine!
Oh sister! if thy heart be thus with buried grief
   oppress'd,
Where wouldst thou pour it forth so well, as on
   my faithful breast?"

"Urge me no more! a blight hath fallen upon my
   summer years!
I should but darken thy young life with fruitless
   pangs and fears;
But take at least the lute I loved, and guard it for
   my sake,
And sometimes, from its silvery strings one tone
   of memory wake!
Sing to those chords by starlight's gleam our own
   sweet vesper hymn,
And think that I too chant it then, far in my
   cloister dim."

'Yes, I *will* take the silvery lute—and I will sing
   to thee
A song we heard in childhood's days, ev'n from
   our father's knee.
Oh sister! sister! are these notes amid forgotten
   things?
Do they not linger as in love, on the familiar
   strings?
Seems not our sainted mother's voice to murmur
   in the strain?
Kind sister! gentlest Leonor! say, shall it plead in
   vain?

### SONG.

"Leave us not, leave us not!
   Say not adieu!
Have we not been to thee
   Tender and true?

"Take not thy sunny smile
   Far from our hearth!
With that sweet light will fade
   Summer and mirth.

"Leave us not, leave us not!
   Can thy heart roam?
Wilt thou not pine to hear
   Voices from home?

"Too sad our love would be,
   If thou wert gone!
Turn to us, leave us not!
   Thou art our own!"

"Oh sister, hush that thrilling lute, oh cease that
   haunting lay,
Too deeply pierce those wild sweet notes; yet, yet
   I cannot stay,
For weary—weary is my heart! I hear a whisper'd
   call
In every breeze that stirs the leaf and bids the
   blossom fall.
I cannot breathe in freedom here, my spirit pines
   to dwell
Where the world's voice can reach no more!—oh
   calm thee! Fare thee well!"

## SONGS OF A GUARDIAN SPIRIT.
### II.

#### OH! DROOP THOU NOT!

They sin who tell us love can die,
With life all other passions fly;
All others are but vanity,
In heaven ambition cannot dwell,
Nor avarice in the vaults of hell.
Earthly these passions, as of earth—
They perish where they drew their birth.
But love is indestructible!
Its holy flame for ever burneth,
From heaven it came, to heaven returneth.
                *Southey.*

Oh! droop thou not, my gentle earthly love!
   Mine still to be!
I bore through death, to brighter lands above
   My thoughts of thee.

Yes! the deep memory of our holy tears,
   Our mingled prayer,
Our suffering love, through long devoted years,
   Went with me there.

It was not vain, the hallow'd and the tried—
   It was not vain!
Still, though unseen, still hovering at thy side,
   I watch again!

From our own paths, our love's attesting bowers,
   I am not gone;
In the deep calm of midnight's whispering hours,
   Thou art not lone:

Not lone, when by the haunted stream thou weepest,
   That stream, whose tone
Murmurs of thoughts, the richest and the deepest,
   We two have known:

Not lone, when mournfully some strain awaking
   Of days long past,
From thy soft eyes the sudden tears are breaking,
   Silent and fast:

Not lone, when upwards, in fond visions turning
   Thy dreamy glance,
Thou seek'st my home, where solemn stars are
   burning,
   O'er night's expanse.

My home is near thee, loved one! and around thee,
   Where'er thou art;
Tho' still mortality's thick cloud hath bound thee,
   Doubt not thy heart!

Hear its low voice, nor deem thyself forsaken—
   Let faith be given
To the still tones which oft our being waken—
   They are of heaven!

## MIGNON'S SONG.

### TRANSLATED FROM GOETHE.

Mignon, a young and enthusiastic girl, (the character
in one of Goethe's romances, from which Sir Walter
Scott's Fenella is partially imitated,) has been stolen
away, in early childhood, from Italy. Her vague reco-
lections of that land, and of her early home, with its
graceful sculptures and pictured saloons, are perpetually
haunting her, and at times break forth into the following
song. The original has been set to exquisite music, by
Zelter, the friend of Goethe.

*Kennst du das Land wo die Citronen bluhn?*

KNOW'ST thou the land where bloom the Citron
    bowers,
Where the gold-orange lights the dusky grove?
High waves the laurel there, the myrtle flowers,
And thro' a still blue heaven the sweet winds rove
Know'st thou it well?
        —There, there, with thee,
O friend, O loved one! fain my steps would flee.

Know'st thou the dwelling?—there the pillars rise,
Soft shines the hall, the painted chambers glow;
And forms of marble seem with pitying eyes
To say—" Poor child! what thus hath wrought thee
      woe?"
Know'st thou it well?
        There, there with thee,
O my protector! homewards might I flee!

Know'st thou the mountain?—high its bridge is
    hung,
Where the mule seeks thro'mist and cloud his way;
There lurk the dragon-race, deep caves among,
O'er beetling rocks there foams the torrent spray
Know'st thou it well?
        With thee, with thee,
There lies my path, O father! let us flee!

## THE LAST SONG OF SAPPHO.

Suggested by a beautiful sketch, the design of the
younger Westmacott. It represents Sappho sitting on a
rock above the sea, with her lyre cast at her feet. There
is a desolate grace about the whole figure, which seems
penetrated with the feeling of utter abandonment.

SOUND on, thou dark unslumbering sea!
   My dirge is in thy moan:
My spirit finds response in thee,
To its own ceaseless cry—" Alone, alone!"

Yet send me back one other word,
   Ye tones that never cease!
Oh! let your secret caves be stirr'd,
And say, dark waters! will ye give me *peace?*

Away! my weary soul hath sought
   In vain one echoing sigh,
One answer to consuming thought
In human hearts—and will the *wave* reply?

Sound on, thou dark unslumbering sea!
   Sound in thy scorn and pride!
I ask not, alien world, from thee,
What my own kindred earth hath still denied.

And yet I loved that earth so well,
   With all its lovely things!
—Was it for this the death-wind fell
On my rich lyre, and quench'd its living strings?

   —Let them lie silent at my feet!
   Since broken even as they,
The heart whose music made them sweet,
Hath pour'd on desert-sands its wealth away.

Yet glory's light hath touch'd my name,
   The laurel-wreath is n ne—
—With a lone heart, a weary frame—
O restless deep! I come to make them thine!

Give to that crown, that burning crown,
   Place in thy darkest hold!
Bury my anguish, my renown,
With hidden wrecks, lost gems, and wasted gold

Thou sea-hird on the billow's crest,
   *Thou* hast thy love, thy home;
They wait thee in the quiet nest,
And I, th' unsought, unwatch'd-for—I too come!

I, with this winged nature fraught,
   These visions wildly free,
This houndless love, this fiery thought—
—*Alone* I come -oh! give me peace, dark sea

## DIRGE.

WHERE shall we make her grave?
—Oh! where the wild-flowers wave
   In the free air!
Where shower and singing-bird
'Midst the young leaves are heard—
   There—lay her there!

Harsh was the world to her—
Now may sleep minister
   Balm for each ill:
Low on sweet nature's breast,
Let the meek heart find rest,
   Deep, deep and still!

Murmur, glad waters, by!
Faint gales, with happy sigh,
   Come wandering o'er
That green and mossy bed,
Where, on a gentle head,
   Storms beat no more!

What though for her in vain
Falls now the bright spring-rain,
   Plays the soft wind;
Yet still, from where she lies,
Should blessed breathings rise,
   Gracious and kind.

Therefore let song and dew
Thence, in the heart renew
   Life's vernal glow!
And, o'er that holy earth,
Scents of the violet's birth
   Still come and go!

Oh! then where wild-flowers wave,
Make ye her mossy grave
   In the free air!
Where shower and singing-bird
'Midst the young leaves are heard—
   There, lay her there!

## A SONG OF THE ROSE.

*Così fior diverrai che non soggiace
All' acqua, al gelo, al vento ed alto scherno,
D' una stagion volubile e fugace;
E a più fido Cultor posto in governo,
Unir potrai nella tranquilla pace,
Ad eterna Bellezza odore eterno.*
                *Pietro Metastasio.*

ROSE! what dost thou here?
   Bridal, royal rose?
How, 'midst grief and fear,
   Canst thou thus disclose
That fervid hue of love, which to thy heart-leaf
   glows?

Rose! too much array'd
   For triumphal hours,
Look'st thou through the shade
   Of these mortal bowers,
Not to disturb my soul, thou crown'd one of all
   flowers!

As an eagle soaring
  Through a sunny sky,
As a clarion pouring
  Notes of victory,
So dost *thou* kindle thoughts, for earthly life too
    high.

Thoughts of rapture, flushing
  Youthful poet's cheek;
Thoughts of glory, rushing
  Forth in song to break,
But finding the spring-tide of rapid song too weak.

Yet, oh! festal rose,
  I have seen thee lying
In thy bright repose
  Pillow'd with the dying,
*Thy* crimson by the lip whence life's quick blood
    was flying.

Summer, hope, and love
  O'er that bed of pain,
Met in thee, yet wove
  Too, too frail a chain
In its embracing links the lovely to detain.

Smil'st thou, gorgeous flower?
  —Oh! within the spells
Of thy beauty's power,
  Something dimly dwells,
At variance with a world of sorrows and fare
    wells.

All the soul forth flowing
  In that rich perfume,
All the proud life glowing
  In that radiant bloom,—
Have they no place but *here*, beneath th' o'ersha
    dowing tomb?

Crown'st thou but the daughters
  Of our tearful race?
—Heaven's own purest waters
  Well might wear the trace
Of thy consummate form, melting to softer grace

Will that clime enfold thee
  With immortal air?
Shall we not behold thee
  Bright and deathless there?
In spirit-lustre cloth'd, transcendantly more fair?

Yes! my fancy sees thee
  In that light disclose,
And its dream thus frees thee
  From the mist of woes,
Darkening thine earthly bowers, O bridal, royal
    rose!

---

## NIGHT-BLOWING FLOWERS,

CHILDREN of night! unfolding meekly, slowly
To the sweet breathings of the shadowy hours,
When dark-blue heavens look softest and most
    holy,
And glow-worm light is in the forest bowers;
  To solemn things and deep,
  To spirit-haunted sleep,
  To thoughts, all purified
  From earth, ye seem allied;
    O dedicated flowers!

Ye, from the gaze of crowds your beauty veiling,
Keep in dim vestal urns the sweetness shrined;
Till the mild moon, on high serenely sailing,
Looks on you tenderly and sadly kind.
  —So doth love's dreaming heart
  Dwell from the throng apart,
  And but to shades disclose
  The inmost thought which glows
    With its pure life entwined.

Shut from the sounds wherein the day rejoices,
To no triumphant song your petals thrill,
But send forth odours with the faint soft voices
Rising from hidden streams, when all is still.

So doth lone prayer arise,
  Mingling with secret sighs,
When grief unfolds, like you,
  Her breast, for heavenly dew
    In silent hours to fill.

---

## THE
## WANDERER AND THE NIGHT-FLOWERS

CALL back your odours, lovely flowers,
  From the night-winds call them back,
And fold your leaves till the laughing hours
  Come forth in the sunbeam's track.

The lark lies couch'd in her grassy nest,
  And the honey-bee is gone,
And all bright things are away to rest,
  Why watch ye here alone?

Is not your world a mournful one,
  When your sisters close their eyes,
And your soft breath meets not a lingering tone
  Of song in the starry skies?

Take ye no joy in the day-spring's birth,
  When it kindles the sparks of dew?
And the thousand strains of the forest's mirth,
  Shall they gladden all but you?

Shut your sweet bells till the fawn comes out
  On the sunny turf to play,
And the woodland child with a fairy shout
  Goes dancing on its way!

"Nay, let our shadowy beauty bloom
  When the stars give quiet light,
And let us offer our faint perfume
  On the silent shrine of night.

"Call it not wasted, the scent we lend
  To the breeze, when no step is nigh:
Oh thus for ever the earth should send
  Her grateful breath on high!

"And love us as emblems, night's dewy flowers
  Of hopes unto sorrow given,
That spring through the gloom of the darkest
    hours,
  Looking alone to heaven!"

---

## ECHO-SONG.

IN thy cavern-hall,
  Echo! art thou sleeping?
By the fountain's fall
  Dreamy silence keeping?
    Yet one soft note borne
    From the shepherd's horn,
Wakes thee, Echo! into music leaping!
—Strange sweet Echo! into music leaping.

Then the woods rejoice,
  Then glad sounds are swelling
From each sister-voice
  Round thy rocky dwelling;
    And their sweetness fills
    All the hollow hills,
With a thousand notes, of *one* life telling!
—Softly mingled notes, of one life telling.

Echo! in my heart
  Thus deep thoughts are lying,
Silent and apart,
  Buried, yet undying.
    Till some gentle tone
    Wakening haply one,
Calls a thousand forth like thee replying!
—Strange sweet Echo! even like thee replying.[*]

[*] This song is in the possession of M. Power

## THE MUFFLED DRUM.*

THE muffled drum was heard
In the Pyrenees by night,
With a dull deep rolling sound
Which told the hamlets round
Of a soldier's burial rite.

But it told them not how dear
In a home beyond the main,
Was the warrior youth laid low that hour,
By a mountain stream of Spain.

The oaks of England waved
O'er the slumbers of his race,
But a pine of the Ronceval made moan
Above *his* last lone place:

When the muffled drum was heard
In the Pyrenees by night,
With a dull deep rolling sound
Which call'd strange echoes round
To the soldier's burial rite.

Brief was the sorrowing *there*,
By the stream from battle red,
And tossing on its wave the plumes
Of many a stately head;

But a mother—soon to die,
And a sister—long to weep,
Ev'n then were breathing prayer for him,
In that home beyond the deep:

While the muffled drum was heard
In the Pyrenees by night,
With a dull deep rolling sound,
And the dark pines mourn'd around,
O'er the soldier's burial rite.

---

## THE SWAN AND THE SKY-LARK.

Adieu, adieu! my plaintive anthem fades
　Past the near meadows, over the still stream,
Up the hill-side; and now 't is buried deep
　In the next valley-glades.
　　　　　　　　　　　　*Keats.*

Higher still and higher
　From the earth thou springest
Like a cloud of fire;
　The blue deep thou wingest,
And singing still dost soar, and soaring ever singest.
　　　　　　　　　　　　*Shelley.*

---

'MIDST the long reeds that o'er a Grecian stream
Unto the faint wind sigh'd melodiously,
And where the sculpture of a broken shrine
Sent out, through shadowy grass and thick wild
　flowers,
Dim alabaster gleams—a lonely Swan
Warbled his death-chaunt; and a poet stood
Listening to that strange music, as it shook
The lilies on the wave; and made the pines
And all the laurels of the haunted shore
Thrill to its passion. Oh! the tones were sweet,
Ev'n painfully—as with the sweetness rung
From parting love; and to the Poet's thought
*This* was their language.

　　"Summer, I depart!
O light and laughing summer, fare thee well!
No song the less thro' thy rich woods will swell,
　For one, one broken heart.

　　And fare ye well, young flowers!
Ye will not mourn! ye will shed odour still,
And wave in glory, colouring every rill,
　Known to my youth's fresh hours.

---

* Set to beautiful music by John Lodge, Esq.

And ye, bright founts, that lie
Far in the whispering forests, lone and deep,
My wing no more shall stir your shadowy sleep—
　—Sweet waters! I must die.

　　Will ye not send one tone
Of sorrow thro' the pines?—one murmur low?
Shall not the green leaves from your voices know
　That I, your child, am gone?

　　No, ever glad and free!
Ye have no sounds a tale of death to tell,
Waves, joyous waves, flow on, and fare ye well!
　Ye will not mourn for me.

　　But *thou*, sweet boon, too late
Pour'd on my parting breath, vain gift of song!
Why com'st thou thus, o'ermastering, rich and
　　strong,
　In the dark hour of fate?

　　Only to wake the sighs
Of echo-voices from their sparry cell;
Only to say—" O sunshine and blue skies!
　O life and love, farewell!"

Thus flow'd the death-chaunt on; while mournfully
Low winds and waves made answer, and the tones
Buried in rocks along the Grecian stream,
Rocks and dim caverns of old Prophecy,
Woke to respond: and all the air was fill'd
With that one sighing sound—" Farewell, Fare-
　well!"
—Fill'd with *that* sound? high in the calm blue
　heaven
Ev'n then a Sky-lark hung; soft summer clouds
Were floating round him, all transpierced with
　light,
And 'midst that pearly radiance his dark wings
Quiver'd with song:—such free triumphant song,
As if tears were not,—as if breaking hearts
Had not a place below—and thus that strain
Spoke to the Poet's ear exultingly.

" The summer is come; she hath said, ' Rejoice!'
The wild woods thrill to her merry voice;
Her sweet breath is wandering around, on high;
　—Sing, sing thro' the echoing sky!

" There is joy in the mountains; the bright waves
　leap,
Like the bounding stag when he breaks from sleep;
Mirthfully, wildly, they flash along—
　—Let the heavens ring with song!

" There is joy in the forests; the bird of night
Hath made the leaves tremble with deep delight;
But *mine* is the glory to sunshine given—
　Sing, sing thro' the echoing heav'n!

" Mine are the wings of the soaring morn,
Mine are the fresh gales with day-spring born:
Only young rapture can mount so high—
　—Sing, sing thro' the echoing sky!"

So those two voices met; so Joy and Death
Mingled their accents; and amidst the rush
Of many thoughts, the listening Poet cried,
—" Oh! thou art mighty, thou art wonderful.
Mysterious Nature! Not in thy free range
Of woods and wilds alone, thou blendest thus
The dirge-note and the song of festival;
But in one *heart*, one changeful human heart
—Ay, and within one hour of that strange world—
Thou call'st their music forth, with all its tones
To startle and to pierce!—the dying Swan's,
And the glad Sky-Lark's—Triumph and Despair."

## SONGS OF SPAIN.*

### No. I.
### ANCIENT BATTLE SONG.

Fling forth the proud banner of Leon again!
Let the high word "*Castile*" go resounding thro'
    Spain!
And thou, free Asturias, encamp'd on the height,
Pour down thy dark sons to the vintage of fight!
Wake, wake! the old soil where thy children re-
    pose,
Sounds hollow and deep to the trampling of foes.
The voices are mighty that swell from the past,
With Arragon's cry on the shrill mountain-blast:
The ancient Sierras give strength to our tread,
Their pines murmur song where bright blood hath
    been shed.
—Fling forth the proud banner of Leon again,
And shout ye "Castile! to the rescue for Spain!"

### II.
### THE ZEGRI MAID.

The Zegris were one of the most illustrious Moorish
tribes. Their exploits, and feuds with their celebrated
rivals the Abencerrages, form the subject of many ancient Spanish romances.

The summer leaves were sighing,
    Around the Zegri maid,
To her low sad song replying
    As it fill'd the olive shade.

" Alas! for her that loveth
    Her land's, her kindred's foe!
Where a Christian Spaniard roveth,
    Should a Zegri's spirit go?

" From thy glance, my gentle mother!
    I sink, with shame oppress'd,
And the dark eye of my brother
    Is an arrow to my breast."
—Where summer leaves were sighing,
    Thus sang the Zegri maid,
While the crimson day was dying
    In the whispery olive shade.

" And for all this heart's wealth wasted,
    This woe, in secret borne,
This flower of young life blasted,
    Should I win back aught but scorn?
By aught but daily dying
    Would my lone truth be repaid?"
—Where the olive leaves were sighing,
    Thus sang the Zegri maid.

### III.
### THE RIO VERDE SONG.

The Rio Verde, a small river of Spain, is celebrated
in the old ballad romances of that country for the frequent combats on its banks, between Moor and Christian. The ballad referring to this stream, in Percy's
Reliques,

    " Gentle river, gentle river,
      Lo! thy streams are stain'd with gore,"

will be remembered by many readers.

Flow, Rio Verde!
    In melody flow;
Win her that weepeth
    To slumber from woe:

Bid thy wave's music
    Roll through her dreams,
Grief ever loveth
    The kind voice of streams.

Bear her lone spirit
    Afar on the sound,
Back to her childhood,
    Her life's fairy ground;
Pass like the whisper
    Of love that is gone—
Flow, Rio Verde!
    Softly flow on!

Dark glassy water,
    So crimson'd of yore!
Love, death, and sorrow
    Know thy green shore.
Thou shouldst have echoes
    For grief's deepest tone—
—Flow, Rio Verde,
    Softly flow on!

### IV.
### SEEK BY THE SILVERY DARRO.

Seek by the silvery Darro,
    Where jasmine flowers have blown;
There hath she left no footsteps?
    —Weep, weep, the maid is gone

Seek where our Lady's image
    Smiles o'er the pine-hung steep;
Hear ye not there her vespers?
    —Weep for the parted, weep!

Seek in the porch where vine-leaves
    O'ershade her father's head?
—Are *his* gray hairs left lonely?
    Weep! her bright soul is fled

### V.
### SPANISH EVENING HYMN.

Ave! now let prayer and music
    Meet in love on earth and sea!
Now, sweet Mother! may the weary
    Turn from this cold world to thee!

From the wide and restless waters
    Hear the sailor's hymn arise!
From his watch-fire 'midst the mountains,
    Lo! to thee the shepherd cries!

Yet, when thus full hearts find voices,
    If o'erburden'd souls there be,
Dark and silent in their anguish,
    Aid those captives! set them free!

Touch them, every fount unsealing,
    Where the frozen tears lie deep;
Thou, the Mother of all Sorrows,
    Aid, oh! aid to pray and weep!

### VI.
### BIRD, THAT ART SINGING ON EBRO'S SIDE

Bird, that art singing on Ebro's side,
Where myrtle shadows make dim the tide,
Doth sorrow dwell 'midst the leaves with thee?
Doth song avail thy full heart to free?
—Bird of the midnight's purple sky!
Teach me the spell of thy melody.

Bird! is it blighted affection's pain,
Whence the sad sweetness flows thro' thy strain?
And is the wound of that arrow still'd,
When thy lone music the leaves have fill'd?
—Bird of the midnight's purple sky!
Teach me the spell of thy melody.

* Written for a set of airs, entitled " Peninsular Melodies,"
selected by Colonel Hodges, and published by Messrs. Goulding and
D'Almaine, who have permitted the reappearance of the words in
this volume.

### VII.

### MOORISH GATHERING SONG.
#### ZORZICO.*

CHAINS on the cities! gloom in the air!
—Come to the hills! fresh breezes are there.
Silence and fear in the rich orange bowers!
—Come to the rocks where freedom hath towers.

Come from the Darro!—changed is its tone;
Come where the streams no bondage have known,
Wildly and proudly foaming they leap,
Singing of freedom from steep to steep.

Come from Alhambra! garden and grove
Now may not shelter beauty or love.
Blood on the waters, death 'midst the flowers!
—Only the spear and the rock are ours.

### VIII.

### THE SONG OF MINA'S SOLDIERS

WE heard thy name, O Mina!
　Far through our hills it rang;
A sound more strong than tempests,
　More keen than armour's clang.
The peasant left his vintage,
　The shepherd grasp'd the spear—
—We heard thy name. O Mina!
　The mountain bands are here.

As eagles to the day-spring,
　As torrents to the sea,
From every dark Sierra
　So rush'd our hearts to thee.

Thy spirit is our banner,
　Thine eye our beacon-sign,
Thy name our trumpet, Mina!
　—The mountain bands are thine.

### IX.

### MOTHER, OH! SING ME TO REST.
#### A CANCION.

MOTHER! oh, sing me to rest
　As in my bright days departed:
Sing to thy child, the sick-hearted,
Songs for a spirit oppress'd

Lay this tired head on thy breast!
　Flowers from the night-dew are closing,
　Pilgrims and mourners reposing—
—Mother, oh! sing me to rest!

Take back thy bird to its nest!
　Weary is young life when blighted,
　Heavy this love unrequited;—
Mother, oh! sing me to rest!

### X.

### THERE ARE SOUNDS IN THE DARK RONCESVALLES.

THERE are sounds in the dark Roncesvalles,
　There are echoes on Biscay's wild shore;
There are murmurs—but not of the torrent,
　Nor the wind, nor the pine-forest's roar.

---

* The Zorico is an extremely wild and singular antique Moorish melody.

'T is a day of the spear and the banner,
　Of armings and hurried farewells;
Rise, rise on your mountains, ye Spaniards!
　Or start from your old battle-dells.

There are streams of unconquer'd Asturias,
　That have roll'd with your fathers' free blood;
Oh! leave on the graves of the mighty,
　Proud marks where their children have stood!

### THE CURFEW-SONG OF ENGLAND.

HARK! from the dim church-tower,
　The deep slow curfew's chime!
—A heavy sound unto hall and bower,
　In England's olden time!
Sadly 't was heard by him who came
　From the fields of his toil at night,
And who might not see his own hearth-flame
　In his children's eyes make light.

Sternly and sadly heard,
　As it quench'd the wood-fire's glow,
Which had cheered the board with the mirthful
　　word,
　And the red wine's foaming flow!
Until that sullen boding knell
　Flung out from every fane,
On harp and lip, and spirit, fell,
　With a weight and with a chain.

Woe for the pilgrim then,
　In the wild deer's forest far!
No cottage-lamp, to the haunts of men,
　Might guide him, as a star.
And woe for him whose wakeful soul,
　With lone aspirings fill'd,
Would have lived o'er some immortal scroll,
　While the sounds of earth were still'd!

And yet a deeper woe
　For the watcher by the bed,
Where the fondly loved in pain lay low,
　In pain and sleepless dread!
For the mother, doom'd unseen to keep
　By the dying babe, her place,
And to feel its flitting pulse, and weep,
　Yet not behold its face!

Darkness in chieftain's hall!
　Darkness in peasant's cot!
While freedom, under that shadowy pall,
　Sat mourning o'er her lot.
Oh! the fireside's peace we well may prize!
　For blood hath flow'd like rain,
Pour'd forth to make sweet sanctuaries
　Of England's homes again.

Heap the yule-fagots high,
　Till the red light fills the room!
It is home's own hour when the stormy sky
　Grows thick with evening-gloom.
Gather ye round the holy hearth,
　And by its gladdening blaze,
Unto thankful bliss we will change our mirth,
　With a thought of the olden days!

### THE CALL TO BATTLE.

Ah! there and there was hurrying to and fro,
And gathering tears, and tremblings of distress,
And there were sudden partings, such as press
The life from out young hearts, and choking sighs
Which ne'er might be repeated.
　　　　　　　　　　　　　　　　*Byron.*

THE vesper-bell, from church and tower,
　Had sent its dying sound;
And the household, in the hush of eve,
　Where met, their porch around.

A voice rang through the olive-wood, with a sud-
    den trumpet's power—
"We rise on all our hills! come forth! 'tis thy
    country's gathering hour—
There's a gleam of spears by every stream, in each
    old battle-dell—
Come forth, young Juan! bid thy home a brief and
    proud farewell!"

    Then the father gave his son the sword,
      Which a hundred fights had seen—
    "Away! and bear it back, my boy!
      All that it still hath been!

"Haste, haste! the hunters of the foe are up, and
    who shall stand
The lion-like awakening of the roused indignant
    land ?
Our chase shall sound through each defile where
    swept the clarion's blast,
With the flying footsteps of the Moor in stormy
    ages past."

    Then the mother kiss'd her son, with tears
      That o'er his dark locks fell:
    "I bless, I bless thee o'er and o'er,
      Yet I stay thee not—Farewell!"

"One moment! but one moment give to parting
    thought or word!
It is no time for woman's tears when manhood's
    heart is stirr'd.
Bear but the memory of thy love about thee in the
    fight,
To breathe upon th' avenging sword a spell of
    keener might."

    And a maiden's fond adieu was heard,
      Though deep, yet brief and low:
    "In the vigil, in the conflict, love!
      My prayer shall with thee go!"

"Come forth! come as the torrent comes when
    the winter's chain is burst!
So rushes on the land's revenge, in night and
    silence nursed—
The night is past, the silence o'er—on all our hills
    we rise—
We wait thee, youth! sleep, dream no more! the
    voice of battle cries."

    There were sad hearts in a darken'd home,
      When the brave had left their bower;
    But the strength of prayer and sacrifice
      Was with them in that hour.

---

# SONGS FOR SUMMER HOURS.*

## I.

### AND I TOO IN ARCADIA.

A celebrated picture of Poussin represents a band of
shepherd youths and maidens suddenly checked in their
wanderings, and affected with various emotions by the
sight of a tomb which bears this inscription—"*Et in
Arcadia ego.*"

They have wander'd in their glee
With the butterfly and bee;
They have climb'd o'er heathery swells,
They have wound thro' forest dells;
Mountain moss hath felt their tread,
Woodland streams their way have led;
Flowers, in deepest shadowy nooks,
Nurslings of the loneliest brooks,
Unto them have yielded up
Fragrant bell and starry cup:

* Of these songs, the ones entitled "Ye are not miss'd, fair Flowers," the "Willow Song," "Leave me not yet," and the "Orange
bough," are in the possession of Mr. Willis, by whom they will be
published with music.

Chaplets are on every brow—
—What hath stay'd the wanderers now ?
Lo! a gray and rustic tomb,
Bower'd amidst the rich wood-gloom;
Whence these words their stricken spirits melt,
—"I too, Shepherds! in Arcadia dwelt."

There is many a summer sound
That pale sepulchre around;
Thro' the shade young birds are glancing,
Insect-wings in sun-streaks dancing;
Glimpses of blue festal skies
Pouring in when soft winds rise;
Violets o'er the turf below
Shedding out their warmest glow;
Yet a spirit not its own
O'er the greenwood now is thrown!
Something of an under-note
Thro' its music seems to float,
Something of a stillness gray
Creeps across the laughing day:
Something, dimly from those old words felt
—"I too, Shepherds! in Arcadia dwelt."

Was some gentle kindred maid
In that grave with dirges laid ?
Some fair creature, with the tone
Of whose voice a joy is gone,
Leaving melody and mirth
Poorer on this alter'd earth ?
Is it thus ? that so they stand,
Dropping flowers from every hand ?
Flowers, and lyres, and gather'd store
Of red wild-fruit prized no more ?
—No! from that bright band of morn,
Not one link hath yet been torn;
'Tis the shadow of the tomb
Falling o'er the summer-bloom,
O'er the flush of love and life
Passing with a sudden strife;
'Tis the low prophetic breath
Murmuring from that house of death,
Whose faint whisper thus their hearts can melt,
"I too, Shepherds! in Arcadia dwelt."

---

## II.

### THE WANDERING WIND

The Wind, the wandering Wind
    Of the golden summer eves—
Whence is the thrilling magic
    Of its tones amongst the leaves ?
Oh! is it from the waters,
    Or from the long, tall grass ?
Or is it from the hollow rocks
    Thro' which its breathings pass ?

Or is it from the voices
    Of all in one combined,
That it wins the tone of mastery ?
    The Wind, the wandering Wind!
No, no! the strange sweet accents
    That with it come and go,
They are not from the osiers,
    Nor the fir-trees whispering low.

They are not of the waters,
    Nor of the cavern'd hill:
'Tis the human love within us
    That gives them power to thrill.
They touch the links of memory
    Around our spirits twined,
And we start, and weep, and tremble,
    To the Wind, the wandering Wind!

---

## III.

### YE ARE NOT MISS'D, FAIR FLOWERS

Ye are not miss'd, fair flowers, that late were
    spreading
    The summer's glow by fount and breezy grot;
There falls the dew, its fairy favours shedding,
    The leaves dance on, the young birds miss you not.

Still plays the sparkle o'er the rippling water,
O lily! whence thy cup of pearl is gone;
The bright wave mourns not for its loveliest daugh-
　ter,
There is no sorrow in the wind's low tone.

And thou, meek hyacinth! afar is roving
　The bee that oft thy trembling bells hath kiss'd;
Cradled ye were, fair flowers! 'midst all things
　loving,
　A joy to all—yet, yet, ye are not miss'd!

Ye, that were born to lend the sunbeam gladness,
　And the winds fragrance, wandering where they
　　list!
—Oh! it were breathing words too deep in sadness,
　To say—earth's *human* flowers not more are
　miss'd.

———

## IV.
### WILLOW-SONG.

Willow! in thy breezy moan,
I can hear a deeper tone;
Thro' thy leaves come whispering low
Faint sweet sounds of long ago.
　　　　　Willow, sighing Willow!

Many a mournful tale of old
Heart-sick love to thee hath told,
Gathering from thy golden bough
Leaves to cool his burning brow.
　　　　　Willow sighing Willow!

Many a swan-like song to thee
Hath been sung, thou gentle tree!
Many a lute its last lament
Down thy moonlight stream hath sent;
　　　　　Willow, sighing Willow!

Therefore, wave and murmur on!
Sigh for sweet affections gone,
And for tuneful voices fled,
And for love, whose heart hath bled,
　　　　　Ever, Willow, Willow!

———

## V.
### LEAVE ME NOT YET!

Leave me not yet—through rosy skies from far,
　But now the song-birds to their nests return;
The quivering image of the first pale star
On the dim lake scarce yet begins to burn:
　　　　　Leave me not yet!

Not yet!—oh hark! low tones from hidden streams,
　Piercing the shivery leaves, ev'n now arise;
Their voices mingle not with daylight dreams,
　They are of vesper's hymns and harmonies:
　　　　　Leave me not yet!

My thoughts are like those gentle sounds, dear
　love!
By day shut up in their own still recess,
They wait for dews on earth, for stars above,
*Then* to breathe out their soul of tenderness:
　　　　　Leave me not yet.

———

## VI.
### THE ORANGE-BOUGH.

Oh! bring me one sweet Orange-bough,
To fan my cheek, to cool my brow;
One bough, with pearly blossoms drest,
And bind it, Mother! on my breast!

Go, seek the grove along the shore,
Whose odours I must breathe no more;
The grove where every scented tree
Thrills to the deep voice of the sea.

Oh! Love's fond sighs, and fervent prayer,
And wild farewell, are lingering there;
Each leaf's light whisper hath a tone,
My faint heart, ev'n in death, would own.

Then bear me thence one bough, to shed
Life's parting sweetness round my head,
And bind it, Mother! on my breast,
When I am laid in lonely rest.

———

## VII.
### THE STREAM SET FREE.

Flow on, rejoice, make music,
　Bright living stream set free!
The troubled haunts of care and strife
　Were not for thee!

The woodland is thy country,
　Thou art all its own again;
The wild birds are thy kindred race,
　That fear no chain.

Flow on, rejoice, make music
　Unto the glistening leaves!
Thou, the beloved of balmy winds
　And golden eves.

Once more the holy starlight
　Sleeps calm upon thy breast,
Whose brightness bears no token more
　Of man's unrest.

Flow, and let free-born music
　Flow with thy wavy line,
While the stock-dove's lingering loving voice
　Comes blent with thine.

And the green reeds quivering o'er thee,
　Strings of the forest-lyre,
All fill'd with answering spirit-sounds,
　In joy respire.

Yet 'midst thy song's glad changes,
　Oh! keep one pitying tone
For gentle hearts, that bear to thee
　Their sadness lone.

One sound, of all the deepest,
　To bring, like healing dew,
A sense that nature ne'er forsakes
　The meek and true.

Then, then, rejoice, make music,
　Thou stream, thou glad and free!
The shadows of all glorious flowers
　Be set in thee.

———

## VIII.
### THE SUMMER'S CALL.

Come away! the sunny hours
Woo thee far to founts and bowers!
O'er the very waters now,
　　In their play,
Flowers are shedding beauty's glow—
　　Come away!
Where the lily's tender gleam
Quivers on the glancing stream—
　　Come away!

All the air is fill'd with sound,
Soft, and sultry, and profound;
Murmurs through the shadowy grass
    Lightly stray;
Faint winds whisper as they pass—
    Come away!
Where the bee's deep music swells
From the trembling fox-glove bells—
    Come away!

In the skies the sapphire blue
Now hath won its richest hue;
In the woods the breath of song
    Night and day
Floats with leafy scents along—
    Come away!
Where the boughs with dewy gloom
Darken each thick bed of bloom—
    Come away!

In the deep heart of the rose
Now the crimson love-hue glows;
Now the glow-worm's lamp by night
    Sheds a ray,
Dreamy, starry, greenly bright—
    Come away!
Where the fairy cup-moss lies,
With the wild-wood strawberries,
    Come away!

Now each tree by summer crown'd
Sheds its own rich twilight round;
Glancing there from sun to shade,
    Bright wings play;
There the deer its couch hath made—
    Come away!
Where the smooth leaves of the lime
Glisten in their honey-time—
    Come away—away!

## GENIUS SINGING TO LOVE.

That voice re-measures
Whatever tones and melancholy pleasures
The things of nature utter; birds or trees,
Or where the tall grass 'mid the heath-plant waves,
Murmur and music thin of sudden breeze.
      *Coleridge.*

I HEARD a song upon the wandering wind,
A song of many tones—though one full soul
Breathed through them all imploringly; and made
All nature as they pass'd, all quivering leaves
And low responsive reeds and waters thrill,
As with the consciousness of human prayer.
—At times the passion-kindled melody
Might seem to gush from Sappho's fervent heart,
Over the wild sea-wave;—at times the strain
Flow'd with more plaintive sweetness, as if born
Of Petrarch's voice, beside the lone Vaucluse;
And sometimes, with its melancholy swell,
A graver sound was mingled, a deep note
Of Tasso's holy lyre;—yet still the tones
Were of a suppliant;—"*Leave me not!*" was still
The burden of their music; and I knew
The lay which Genius, in its loneliness,
Its own still world amidst th' o'erpeopled world,
Hath ever breathed to Love.

They crown me with the glistening crown,
  Borne from a deathless tree;
I hear the pealing music of renown—
  O Love! forsake me not!
  Mine were a lot dark lot,
    Bereft of thee.

They tell me that my soul can throw
  A glory o'er the earth:
From thee, from *thee*, is caught that golden glow!
  Shed by thy gentle eyes
  It gives to flower and skies,
    A bright new birth!

Thence gleams the path of morning,
Over the kindling hills, a sunny zone!
  Thence to its heart of hearts, the rose is burning
    With lustre not its own!
    Thence every wood-recess
    Is fill'd with loveliness,
Each bower, to ring-doves and dim violets known

I see all beauty by the ray
That streameth from thy smile;
  Oh! bear it, bear it not away!
    Can that sweet light beguile?
  Too pure, too spirit-like, it seems,
  To linger long by earthly streams;
  I clasp it with th' alloy
    Of fear 'midst quivering joy,
Yet must I perish if the gift depart—
Leave me not, Love! to mine own beating heart

The music from my lyre
With thy swift step would flee;
  The world's cold breath would quench the starry
    fire
In my deep soul—a temple fill'd with thee!
    Seal'd would the fountains lie,
    The waves of harmony,
Which thou alone canst free!

Like a shrine 'midst rocks forsaken,
  Whence the oracle hath fled;
Like a harp which none might waken
  But a mighty master dead;
Like the vase of a perfume scatter'd,
  Such would my spirit be;
So mute, so void, so shatter'd,
  Bereft of thee!

Leave me not, Love! or if this earth
  Yield not for thee a home,
If the bright summer-land of thy pure birth
  Send thee a silvery voice that whispers—" *Come!*"
Then, with the glory from the rose,
  With the sparkle from the stream,

With the light thy rainbow-presence throws
  Over the poet's dream;
    With all th' Elysian hues
    Thy pathway that suffuse,
With joy, with music, from the fading grove,
Take me, too, heavenward, on thy wing, sweet
    Love!

## XI.

### OH! SKY-LARK FOR THY WING.

Oh! Sky-lark, for thy wing!
  Thou bird of joy and light,
That I might soar and sing
  At heaven's empyreal height!
    With the heathery hills beneath me,
      Whence the streams in glory spring,
    And the pearly clouds to wreathe me
      Oh sky-lark! on thy wing!

Free, free from earth-born fear,
  I would range the blessed skies,
Through the blue divinely clear,
  Where the low mists cannot rise!
    And a thousand joyous measures
      From my chainless heart should spring
    Like the bright rain's vernal treasures,
      As I wander'd on thy wing.

But oh! the silver chords,
  That around the heart are spun,
From gentle tones and words,
  And kind eyes that make our sun!
    To some low sweet nest returning,
      How soon my love would bring,
    There, *there* the dews of morning,
      Oh, sky-lark! on thy wing!

## MUSIC AT A DEATH-BED.

"Music! why thy power employ
Only for the sons of joy?
Only for the smiling guests
At natal, or at nuptial feasts?
Rather thy lenient numbers pour
On those whom secret griefs devour;
And with some softly-whisper'd air
Smooth the brow of dumb despair!"
*Warton, from Euripides.*

Bring music! stir the brooding air
    With an ethereal breath!
Bring sounds my struggling soul to bear
    Up from the couch of death!

A voice, a flute, a dreamy lay,
    Such as the southern breeze
Might waft, at golden fall of day,
    O'er blue transparent seas!

Oh no! not such! that lingering spel.
    Would lure me back to life,
When my wean'd heart hath said farewell,
    And pass'd the gates of strife.

Let not a sight of human love
    Blend with the song its tone!
Let no disturbing echo move
    One that must die alone!

But pour a solemn-breathing strain
    Fill'd with the soul of prayer;
Let a life's conflict, fear, and pain,
    And trembling hope be there.

Deeper, yet deeper! In my thought
    Lies more prevailing sound,
A harmony intensely fraught
    With pleading more profound.

A passion unto music given,
    A sweet, yet piercing cry:
A breaking heart's appeal to heaven,
    A bright faith's victory!

Deeper! Oh! may no richer power
    Be in those notes enshrined!
Can all which crowds on earth's last hour
    No fuller language find?

Away! and hush the feeble song,
    And let the chord be still'd!
Far in another land ere long
    My dream shall be fulfill'd.

## WHERE IS THE SEA?

### SONG OF THE GREEK ISLANDER IN EXILE.

A Greek Islander, being taken to the Vale of Tempe,
and called upon to admire its beauty, only replied—" *The
sea—where is it?*

Where is the sea?—I languish here—
    Where is my own blue sea?
With all its barks in fleet career,
    And flags, and breezes free.

I miss that voice of waves, which first
    Awoke my childhood's glee;
The measured chime—the thundering burst—
    Where is my own blue sea?

Oh! rich your myrtle's breath may rise,
    Soft, soft your winds may be;
Yet my sick heart within me dies—
    Where is my own blue sea?

I hear the shepherd's mountain flute—
    I hear the whispering tree;
The echoes of my soul are mute:
    —Where is my own blue sea?

## MARSHAL SCHWERIN'S GRAVE.

"I came upon the tomb of Marshal Schwerin—a plain
quiet cenotaph, erected in the middle of a wide corn-
field, on the very spot where he closed a long, faithful,
and glorious career in arms. He fell here at eighty
years of age, at the head of his own regiment, the standard of it waving in his hand. His seat was in the
leathern saddle—his foot in the iron stirrup—his fingers
reined the young war-horse to the last."—*Notes and
Reflections during a Ramble in Germany.*

Thou didst fall in the field with thy silver hair,
    And a banner in thy hand;
Thou wert laid to rest from thy battles there,
    By a proudly mournful band.

In the camp, on the steed, to the bugle's blast,
    Thy long bright years had sped;
And a warrior's bier was thine at last,
    When the snows had crown'd thy head.

Many had fallen by thy side, old chief!
    Brothers and friends, perchance;
But thou wert yet as the fadeless leaf,
    And light was in thy glance.

The soldier's heart at thy step leap'd high,
    And thy voice the war-horse knew;
And the first to arm, when the foe was nigh,
    Wert thou, the bold and true.

Now mayest thou slumber—thy work is done—
    Thou of the well-worn sword!
From the stormy fight in thy fame thou'rt gone,
    But not to the festal board.

The corn-sheaves whisper thy grave around,
    Where fiery blood hath flow'd:—
Oh! lover of battle and trumpet-sound!
    Thou art couch'd in a still abode!

A quiet home from the noonday's glare,
    And the breath of the wintry blast—
Didst thou toil thro' the days of thy silvery hair,
    To win thee but *this* at last?

# SONGS OF CAPTIVITY.

These songs (with the exception of the fifth) have all
been set to music by the author's sister, and are in the
possession of Mr. Willis, by whose permission they are
here published.

### INTRODUCTION.

One hour for distant homes to weep
    'Midst Afric's burning sands,
One silent sunset hour was given
    To the slaves of many lands.

They sat beneath a lonely palm,
    In the gardens of their lord;
And mingling with the fountain's tune,
    Their songs of exile pour'd.

And strangely, sadly, did those lays
    Of Alp and Ocean sound,
With Afric's wild red skies above,
    And solemn wastes around.

Broken with tears were oft their tones,
    And most when most they tried
To breathe of hope and liberty,
    From hearts that inly died.

So met the sons of many lands,
    Parted by mount and main;
So did they sing in brotherhood,
    Made kindred by the chain.

## I.

### THE BROTHER'S DIRGE.

In  he proud old fanes of England
　My warrior fathers lie,
Banners hang drooping o'er their dust
　With gorgeous blazonry.
　　But thou, but *thou*, my brother !
　　O'er thee dark billows sweep,
　　The best and bravest heart of all
　　Is shrouded by the deep.

In the old high wars of England
　My noble fathers bled ;
For her lion kings of lance and spear,
　They went down to the dead.
　　But thou, but thou, my brother !
　　*Thy* life-drops flow'd for me—
　　Would I were with thee in thy rest,
　　Young sleeper of the sea.

In a shelter'd home of England
　Our sister dwells alone,
With quick heart listening for the sound
　Of footsteps that are gone.
　　She little dreams, my brother !
　　Of the wild fate we have found
　　I, 'midst the Afric sands a slave,
　　Thou, by the dark seas bound.

## II.

### THE ALPINE HORN.

The Alpine horn ! the Alpine horn !
　Oh ! through my native sky,
Might I but hear its deep notes borne,
　Once more,—but once,—and die !

Yet, no ! 'midst breezy hills thy breath,
　So full of hope and morn,
Would win me from the bed of death—
　O joyous Alpine horn !

But *here* the echo of that blast,
　To many a battle known,
Seems mournfully to wander past,
　A wild, shrill, wailing tone !

Haunt me no more ! for slavery's air
　Thy proud notes were not born ;
The dream but deepens my despair—
　Be hush'd, thou Alpine horn !

## III.

### O YE VOICES.

O ye voices round my own hearth singing !
　As the winds of May to memory sweet,
Might I yet return, a worn heart bringing,
　Would those vernal tones the Wanderer greet,
　　　Once again ?

Never, never ! Spring hath smiled and parted
　Oft since then your fond farewell was said ;
O'er the green turf of the gentle-hearted,
　Summer's hand the rose leaves may have shed,
　　　Oft again.

Or if still around my heart ye linger,
　Yet, sweet voices ! there must change have come.
Years have quell'd the free soul of the singer,
　Vernal tones shall greet the Wanderer home,
　　　Ne'er again !

## IV.

### I DREAM OF ALL THINGS FREE.

I dream of all things free !
　Of a gallant, gallant bark,
That sweeps through storm and sea,
　Like an arrow to its mark !
Of a stag that o'er the hills
　Goes bounding in his glee ;
Of a thousand flashing rills—
　Of all things glad and free !

I dream of some proud bird,
　A bright-eyed mountain king !
In my visions I have heard
　The rushing of his wing.
I follow some wild river,
　On whose breast no sail may be ;
Dark woods around it shiver—
　—I dream of all things free !

Of a happy forest child,
　With the fawns and flowers at play ;
Of an Indian 'midst the wild,
　With the stars to guide his way :
Of a chief his warriors leading,
　Of an archer's greenwood tree :—
—My heart in chains is bleeding,
　And I dream of all things free !

## V.

### FAR O'ER THE SEA.

Where are the vintage songs
　Wandering in glee ?
Where dance the peasant bands
　Joyous and free ?
Under a kind blue sky,
Where doth my birth-place lie ?
　—Far o'er the sea !

Where floats the myrtle-scent
　O'er vale and lea,
When evening calls the dove
　Homewards to flee ?
Where doth the orange gleam
Soft on my native stream ?
　—Far o'er the sea !

Where are sweet eyes of love
　Watching for me ?
Where o'er the cabin roof
　Waves the green tree ?
Where speaks the vesper-chime
Still of a holy time ?
　—Far o'er the sea !

Dance on, ye vintage bands,
　Fearless and free !
Still fresh and greenly wave,
　My father's tree !
Still smile, ye kind blue skies !
Though your son pines and dies
　Far o'er the sea !

## VI.

### THE INVOCATION.

Oh ! art thou still on earth, my love ?
　　My only love !
Or smiling in a brighter home,
　　Far, far above ?

Oh ! is thy sweet voice fled, my love ?
　　Thy light step gone ?
And art thou not, in Earth or Heaven,
　　Still, still my own ?

I see thee with thy gleaming hair,
　　In midnight dreams !
But cold, and clear, and spirit-like,
　　Thy soft eye seems.

Peace in thy saddest hour, my love!
    Dwelt on thy brow;
But something mournfully divine
    There shineth now!

And silent ever is thy lip,
    And pale thy cheek;—
Oh! art thou Earth's, or art thou Heaven's?
    Speak to me, speak!

## VII.

## THE SONG OF HOPE.

Droop not, my brothers! I hear a glad strain—
We shall burst forth like streams from the winter-
    night's chain;
A flag is unfurl'd, a bright star of the sea,
A ransom approaches—we yet shall be free!

Where the pines wave, where the light chamois
    leaps,
Where the lone eagle hath built on the steeps,
Where the snows glisten, the mountain rills foam
Free as the falcon's wing, yet shall we roam.

Where the hearth shines, where the kind looks
    are met,
Where the smiles mingle, our place shall be yet!
Crossing the desert, o'ersweeping the sea,—
Droop not, my brothers! we yet shall be free!

## THE BIRD AT SEA.

Bird of the greenwood!
    Oh! why art thou here!
Leaves dance not o'er thee,
    Flowers bloom not near.

All the sweet waters
    Far hence are at play—
Bird of the greenwood!
    Away, away!

Where the mast quivers
    Thy peace will not be,
As 'midst the waving
    Of wild rose and tree.

How should'st thou battle
    With storm and with spray?
Bird of the greenwood!
    Away, away!

Or art thou seeking
    Some brighter land,
Where by the south-wind
    Vine leaves are fann'd?

'Midst the wild billows
    Why then delay?
Bird of the greenwood!
    Away, away!

" Chide not my lingering
    Where storms are dark,
A hand that hath nursed me
    Is in the bark;

A heart that hath cherish'd
    Through winter's long day,
So I turn from the greenwood.
    Away, away!"

## THE IVY-SONG.

Written on receiving some Ivy-leaves, gathered from
the ruined Castle of Rheinfels on the Rhine.

Oh! how could fancy crown with thee,
    In ancient days, the God of Wine,
And bid thee at the banquet be
    Companion of the vine?

Ivy! thy home is where each sound
    Of revelry hath long been o'er,
Where song and beaker once went round,
    But now are known no more.
      Where long-fallen gods recline,
      There the place is thine.

The Roman on his battle-plains,
    Where Kings before his eagles bent,
With thee, amidst exulting strains,
    Shadow'd the victor's tent:
Though shining there in deathless green,
    Triumphally thy boughs might wave,
Better thou lov'st the silent scene
    Around the victor's grave.
      Urn and sculpture half divine
      Yield their place to thine.

The cold halls of the regal dead,
    Where lone th' Italian sunbeams dwell,
Where hollow sounds the lightest tread—
    Ivy! they know thee well!
And far above the festal vine,
    Thou wav'st where once proud banners hung
Where mouldering turrets crest the Rhine
    —The Rhine, still fresh and young!
      Tower and rampart o'er the Rhine
      —Ivy! all are thine!

High from the fields of air look down
    Those eyries of a vanish'd race,
Where harp, and battle, and renown,
    Have pass'd, and left no trace.
But thou art there!—serenely bright,
    Meeting the mountain storms with bloom,
Thou that wilt climb the loftiest height,
    Or crown the lowliest tomb!
      Ivy, Ivy! all are thine,
      Palace, hearth, and shrine.

'Tis still the same; our pilgrim tread
    O'er classic plains, through deserts free,
On the mute path of ages fled,
    Still meets decay and thee.

And still let man his fabrics rear,
    August in beauty, stern in power;
—Days pass—thou Ivy never sere!*
    And thou shalt have thy dower.
      All are thine, or must be thine—
      —Temple, pillar, shrine!

## THE DYING GIRL AND FLOWERS.

" I desire as I look on these, the ornaments and children
of Earth, to know whether, indeed, such things I shall
see no more?—whether they have no likeness, no arche-
type in the world in which my future home is to be cast?
or whether they *have* their images above, only wrought
in a more wondrous and delightful mould."——*Conver-
sations with an Ambitious Student in ill health.*

Bear them not from grassy dells,
Where wild bees have honey-cells;
Not from where sweet water-sounds
Thrill the greenwood to its bounds;
Not to waste their scented breath
On the silent room of Death!

Kindred to the breeze they are,
And the glow-worm's emerald star,
And the bird, whose song is free,
And the many-whispering tree:
Oh! too deep a love, and vain,
They would win to earth again.

Spread them not before the eyes,
Closing fast on summer skies!

---

* Ye Myrtles brown, and Ivy never sere.—*Lycidas.*

Woo thou not the spirit back,
From its lone and viewless track,
With the bright things which have birth
Wide o'er all the colour'd earth!

With the violet's breath would rise
Thoughts too sad for her who dies;
From the lily's pearl-cup shed,
Dreams too sweet would haunt her bed;
Dreams of youth—of spring-time eves—
Music—beauty—all she leaves!

Hush! 'tis thou that dreaming art,
Calmer is *her* gentle heart.
Yes! o'er fountain, vale, and grove,
Leaf and flower, hath gush'd her love;
But that passion, deep and true,
Knows not of a last adieu.

Types of lovelier forms than these,
In their fragile mould she sees;
Shadows of yet richer things,
Born beside immortal springs,
Into fuller glory wrought,
Kindled by surpassing thought!

Therefore, in the lily's leaf,
She can read no word of grief;
O'er the woodbine she can dwell,
Murmuring not—Farewell! farewell
And her dim, yet speaking eye,
Greets the violet solemnly.

Therefore, once, and yet again,
Strew them o'er her bed of pain;
From her chamber take the gloom,
With a light and flush of bloom:
So should one depart, who goes
Where no Death can touch the rose!

---

## THE MUSIC OF ST. PATRICK'S.

The choral music of St. Patrick's Cathedral, Dublin,
is almost unrivalled in its combined powers of voice,
organ, and scientific skill.—The majestic harmony of
effect thus produced is not a little deepened by the character of the Church itself; which, though small, yet
with its dark rich fretwork, knightly helmets and banners, and old monumental effigies, seems all filled and
overshadowed by the spirit of chivalrous antiquity. The
imagination never fails to recognize it as a fitting scene
for high solemnities of old;—a place to witness the soli
tary vigil of arms, or to resound with the funeral march
at the burial of some warlike King.

All the choir
Sang Hallelujah, as the sound of seas.
*Milton.*

Again, oh! send that anthem peal again
Thro' the arch'd roof in triumph to the sky!
Bid the old tombs ring proudly to the strain,
The banners thrill as if with victory!

Such sounds the warrior awe-struck might have
heard,
While arm'd for fields of chivalrous renown;
Such the high hearts of Kings might well have
stirr'd,
While throbbing still beneath the recent crown.

Those notes once more!—they bear my soul away
They lend the wings of morning to its flight;
No earthly passion, in th' exulting lay,
Whispers one tone to win me from that height.

All is of Heaven!—Yet wherefore to mine eye
Gush the vain tears unbidden from their source?
Ev'n while the waves of that strong harmony
Roll with my spirit on their sounding course!

Wherefore must rapture its full heart reveal
Thus by the burst of sorrow's token-shower?
—Oh! is it not, that humbly we may feel
Our nature's limit in its proudest hour?

---

## KEENE, OR LAMENT OF AN IRISH MO-
## THER OVER HER SON.

This lament is intended to imitate the peculiar style of
the Irish Keenes, many of which are distinguished by a
wild and deep pathos, and other characteristics analo-
gous to those of the national music.

Darkly the cloud of night comes rolling on
Darker is thy repose, my fair-haired son!
               Silent and dark.

There is blood upon the threshold
   Whence thy step went forth at morn
Like a dancer's in its fleetness,
   O my bright first-born!

At the glad sound of that footstep,
   My heart within me smiled;
—Thou wert brought me back all silent
   On thy bier, my child!

Darkly the cloud of night comes rolling on;
Darker is thy repose, my fair-haired son!
               Silent and dark.

I thought to see thy children
   Laugh on me with thine eyes;
But my sorrow's voice is lonely
   Where my life's flower lies.

I shall go to sit beside thee,
   Thy kindred's graves among;
I shall hear the tall grass whisper—
   I shall hear it not long!

Darkly the cloud of night comes rolling on;
Darker is thy repose, my fair-haired son!
               Silent and dark

And I too shall find slumber
   With my lost one, in the earth;
—Let none light up the ashes
   Again on our hearth!

Let the roof go down!—let silence
   On the home for ever fall,
Where my boy lay cold, and heard not,
   His lone Mother's call!

Darkly the cloud of night comes rolling on;
Darker is thy repose, my fair-haired son!
               Silent and dark.

---

## ENGLAND'S DEAD

Son of the Ocean Isle!
   Where sleep your mighty dead?
Show me what high and stately pile
   Is rear'd o'er Glory's bed.

Go, Stranger! track the deep,
   Free, free, the white sail spread!
Wave may not foam, nor wild wind sweep
   Where rest not England's dead.

On Egypt's burning plains,
   By the Pyramid o'ersway'd,
With fearful power the noon-day reigns,
   And the Palm-trees yield no shade.

But let the angry sun
   From heaven look fiercely red,
Unfelt by those whose task is done!
   *There* slumber England's dead.

The hurricane hath might
Along the Indian shore,
And far, by Ganges' banks, at night
Is heard the tiger's roar.

But let the sound roll on!
It hath no tone of dread,
For those that from their toils are gone—
—*There* slumber England's dead!

Loud rush the torrent floods
The western wilds among,
And free, in green Columbia's woods,
The hunter's bow is strung.

But let the floods rush on!
Let the arrow's flight be sped!
Why should *they* reck whose task is done?
—*There* slumber England's dead.

The mountain storms rise high
In the snowy Pyrenees,
And toss the pine-boughs through the sky,
Like rose-leaves on the breeze.

But let the storm rage on!
Let the fresh wreaths be shed!
For the Roncesvalles' field is won—
—*There* slumber England's dead.

On the frozen deep's repose,
'T is a dark and dreadful hour
When round the ship the ice-fields close
And the northern night-clouds lower.

But let the ice drift on!
Let the cold blue desert spread!
*Their* course with mast and flag is done—
—Ev'n there sleep England's dead!

The warlike of the Isles,
The men of field and wave!
Are not the rocks their funeral piles?
The seas and shores their grave?

Go, Stranger! track the deep!
Free, free the white sail spread!
Wave may not foam, nor wild wind sweep,
Where rest not England's dead!*

---

## FAR AWAY.†

Far away!—my home is far away,
Where the blue sea laves a mountain shore;
In the woods I hear my brothers play,
'Midst the flowers my sister sings once more,
Far away!

Far away! my dreams are far away,
When at midnight, stars and shadows reign;
"Gentle child," my mother seems to say,
" Follow me where home shall smile again!"
Far away!

Far away! my hope is far away,
Where love's voice young gladness may restore;
—O thou dove! now soaring through the day,
Lend me wings to reach that better shore,
Far away

---

## THE LYRE AND FLOWER.

A lyre its plaintive sweetness pour'd
Forth on the wild wind's track;
The stormy wanderer jarr'd the chord,
But gave no music back.

* Set to music by the Author's sister.

† This, and the five following songs, have been set to music of great merit, by J. Zaugheer Herrmann, and H. F. C., and are publish ed in a set by Mr. Power, who has given permission for the appearance of the words in this Volume.

14

—Oh! child of song!
Bear hence to heaven thy fire!
What hop'st thou from the reckless throng?
Be not like that lost lyre!
Not like that lyre!

A flower its leaves and odours cast
On a swift-rolling wave;
Th' unheeding torrent darkly pass'd,
And back no treasure gave.
—Oh! heart of love!
Waste not thy precious dower!
Turn to thine only home above,
Be not like that lost flower!
Not like that flower.

---

## SISTER! SINCE I MET THEE LAST

Sister! since I met thee last,
O'er thy brow a change hath past.
In the softness of thine eyes
Deep and still a shadow lies;
From thy voice there thrills a tone,
Never to thy childhood known;
Through thy soul a storm hath moved,
Gentle sister, thou hast loved!

Yes! thy varying cheek hath caught
Hues too bright from troubled thought
Far along the wandering stream,
Thou art followed by a dream;
In the woods and valleys lone,
Music haunts thee not thine own:
Wherefore fall thy tears like rain?
Sister, thou hast loved in vain!

Tell me not the tale, my flower!
On my bosom pour that shower!
Tell me not of kind thoughts wasted
Tell me not of young hopes blasted;

Wring not forth one burning word,
Let thy heart no more be stirr'd!
Home alone can give thee rest.
—Weep, sweet sister, on my breast!

---

## THE LONELY BIRD.

From a ruin thou art singing,
Oh! lonely, lonely bird!
The soft blue air is ringing,
By thy summer music stirr'd;
But all is dark and cold beneath,
Where harps no more are heard:
Whence winn'st thou that exulting breath,
Oh! lonely, lonely bird?

Thy song flows richly swelling,
To a triumph of glad sounds,
As from its cavern dwelling
A stream in glory bounds!
Though the castle echoes catch no tone
Of human step or word,
Tho' the fires be quench'd and the feasting done
Oh! lonely, lonely bird!

How can that flood of gladness
Rush through thy fiery lay,
From the haunted place of sadness,
From the bosom of decay?
While dirge-notes in the breeze's moan,
Through the ivy garlands heard,
Come blent with thy rejoicing tone,
Oh! lonely, lonely bird!

There's many a heart, wild singer,
Like thy forsaken tower,
Where joy no more may linger,
Where love hath left his bower!
And there's many a spirit e'en like thee,
To mirth as lightly stirr'd,
Though it soar from ruins in its glee,
Oh! lonely, lonely bird!

## DIRGE AT SEA.

Sleep!—we give thee to the wave,
Red with life-blood from the brave,
Thou shalt find a noble grave.
    Fare thee well!

Sleep! thy billowy field is won.
Proudly may the funeral gun,
'Midst the hush at set of sun,
    Boom thy knell!

Lonely, lonely is thy bed,
Never there may flower be shed,
Marble rear'd, or brother's head
    Bow'd to weep.

Yet thy record on the sea,
Borne through battle high and free,
Long the red cross flag shall be.
    Sleep! O sleep!

## PILGRIM'S SONG TO THE EVENING STAR

O soft star of the west!
    Gleaming far,
Thou 'rt guiding all things home,
    Gentle star!
Thou bring'st from rock and wave,
    The sea-bird to her nest,
The hunter from the hills,
    The fisher back to rest.
Light of a thousand streams,
    Gleaming far!
O soft star of the west,
    Blessed star!

No bowery roof is mine,
    No hearth of love and rest,
Yet guide me to my shrine,
    O soft star of the west!
There, there, my home shall be,
    Heaven's dew shall cool my breast,
When prayer and tear gush free,
    —O soft star of the west!

O soft star of the west,
    Gleaming far!
Thou 'rt guiding all things home,
    Gentle star!
Shine from thy rosy heaven,
    Pour joy on earth and sea!
Shine on, though no sweet eyes
    Look forth to watch for me!
Light of a thousand streams,
    Gleaming far!
O soft star of the west!
    Blessed star!

## THE SPARTAN'S MARCH.

' The Spartans used not the trumpet in their march into battle," says Thucydides, because they wished not to excite the rage of their warriors. Their charging-step was made " to the Dorian mood of flutes and soft recorders." The valour of a Spartan was too highly tempered to require a stunning or rousing impulse. His spirit was like a steed too proud for the spur."—*Campbell on the Elegiac Poetry of the Greeks.*

'Twas morn upon the Grecian hills,
    Where peasants dress'd the vines,
Sunlight was on Cithæron's rills,
    Arcadia's rocks and pines.

And brightly, through his reeds and flowers
    Eurotas wander'd by,
When a sound arose from Sparta's towers
    Of solemn harmony.

Was it the hunter's choral strain
    To the woodland-goddess pour'd?
Did virgin hands in Pallas' fane
    Strike the full-sounding chord?

But helms were glancing on the stream,
    Spears ranged in close array,
And shields flung back a glorious beam
    To the morn of a fearful day!

And the mountain echoes of the land
    Swell'd through the deep-blue sky,
While to soft strains moved forth a band
    Of men that moved to die.

They march'd not with the trumpet's blast,
    Nor bade the horn peal out,
And the laurel-groves, as on they pass'd,
    Rung with no battle-shout!

They ask'd no clarion's voice to fire
    Their souls with an impulse high;
But the Dorian reed, and the Spartan lyre,
    For the sons of liberty!

And still sweet flutes, their path around,
    Sent forth Æolian breath:
They needed not a sterner sound
    To marshal them for death!

So moved they calmly to their field,
    Thence never to return,
Save bringing back the Spartan shield,
    Or on it proudly borne!

## THE MEETING OF THE SHIPS.

"We take each other by the hand, and we exchange a few words and looks of kindness, and we rejoice together for a few short moments;—and then days, months, years intervene—and we see and know nothing of each other."——*Washington Irving.*

Two barks met on the deep mid-sea,
    When calms had still'd the tide;
A few bright days of summer glee
    There found them side by side.

And voices of the fair and brave
    Rose mingling thence in mirth;
And sweetly floated o'er the wave
    The melodies of earth.

Moonlight on that lone Indian main
    Cloudless and lovely slept;—
While dancing step, and festive strain
    Each deck in triumph swept.

And bands were link'd, and answering eyes
    With kindly meaning shone;
—Oh! brief and passing sympathies,
    Like leaves together blown!

A little while such joy was cast
    Over the deep's repose,
Till the loud singing winds at last
    Like trumpet music rose.

And proudly, freely on their way
    The parting vessels bore;
—In calm or storm, by rock or bay
    To meet—Oh! never more!

Never to blend in victory's cheer,
    To aid in hours of woe:—
And thus bright spirits mingle here,
    Such ties are form'd below!

## THE ROCK OF CADER IDRIS.

### A LEGEND OF WALES.

It is an old tradition of the Welsh Bards, that on the summit of the mountain Cader Idris, is an excavation resembling a couch; and that whoever should pass a night in that hollow, would be found in the morning either dead, in a state of frenzy, or endowed with the highest poetical inspiration. This song is one of a "Selection of Welsh Melodies, arranged by John Parry, and published by Mr. Power."

I lay on that rock where the storms have their dwelling,
The birth-place of phantoms, the home of the cloud;
Around it for ever deep music is swelling,
The voice of the mountain-wind, solemn and loud.
'Twas a midnight of shadows all fitfully streaming,
Of wild waves and breezes, that mingled their moan;
Of dim shrouded stars, as from gulphs faintly gleaming,
And I met the dread gloom of its grandeur alone.

I lay there in silence—a Spirit came o'er me;
Man's tongue hath no language to speak what I saw;
Things glorious, unearthly, pass'd floating before me,
And my heart almost fainted with rapture and awe!
I view'd the dread beings, around us that hover,
Though veil'd by the mists of mortality's breath;
And I call'd upon darkness the vision to cover,
For a strife was within me of madness and death.

I saw them—the powers of the wind and the ocean,
The rush of whose pinion bears onward the storms;
Like the sweep of the white-rolling wave was their motion,
I *felt* their dim presence,—but knew not their forms!
I saw them—the mighty of ages departed—
The dead were around me that night on the hill:
From their eyes, as they pass'd, a cold radiance they darted,
—There was light on my soul, but my heart's blood was chill.

I saw what man looks on, and dies—but my spirit
Was strong, and triumphantly lived thro' that hour!
And as from the grave, I awoke to inherit
A flame all immortal, a voice, and a power!
Day burst on that rock with the purple cloud crested,
And high Cader Idris rejoiced in the sun;
—But oh! what new glory all nature invested,
When the sense which gives soul to her beauty was won!

## A FAREWELL TO WALES.

### FOR THE MELODY CALLED "THE ASH GROVE."

### ON LEAVING THAT COUNTRY WITH MY CHILDREN.

The sound of thy streams in my spirit I bear—
—Farewell! and a blessing be with thee, green land!
On thy hearths, on thy halls, on thy pure mountain-air,
On the chords of the harp, and the minstrel's free hand!
From the love of my soul with my tears it is shed,
As I leave thee, green land of my home and my dead!

I bless thee!—yet not for the beauty which dwells
In the heart of thy hills, on the rocks of thy shore;
And not for the memory set deep in thy dells,
Of the bard and the hero, the mighty of yore;
And not for thy songs of those proud ages fled,
Green land, Poet-land of my home and my dead!

I bless thee for all the true bosoms that beat,
Where'er a low hamlet smiles up to thy skies,
For thy cottage hearths, burning the stranger to greet,
For the soul that shines forth from thy children's kind eyes!
May the blessing, like sunshine, about thee be spread,
Green land of my childhood, my home, and my dead!

## THE DYING BARD'S PROPHECY.[*]

> "All is not lost—the unconquerable will
> And courage never to submit or yield."
> *Milton.*

The Hall of Harps is lone to-night,
And cold the chieftain's hearth;
It hath no mead, it hath no light,
No voice of melody, no sound of mirth.

The bow lies broken on the floor
Whence the free step is gone;
The pilgrim turns him from the door
Where minstrel-blood hath stain'd the threshol'd stone.

And I too go—my wound is deep,
My brethren long have died—
Yet ere my soul grow dark with sleep,
Winds! bear the spoiler one more tone of pride

Bear it, where on his battle plain,
Beneath the setting sun,
He counts my country's noble slain—
Say to him—Saxon! think not *all* is won.

Thou hast laid low the warrior's head,
The minstrel's chainless hand;
—Dreamer! that number'st with the dead,
The burning spirit of the mountain land!

Think'st thou because the song hath ceased,
The soul of song is flown?
Think'st thou it woke to crown the feast,
It lived beside the ruddy hearth alone?

No! by our wrongs, and by our blood,
We leave it pure and free—
Though hush'd awhile, that sounding flood
Shall roll in joy through ages yet to be.

We leave it 'midst our country's woe,
The birth-right of her breast—
We leave it as we leave the snow
Bright and eternal on †Eryri's crest.

We leave it with our fame to dwell
Upon our children's breath.
Our voice in theirs through time shall swell—
The Bard hath gifts of prophecy from death.

He dies—but yet the mountains stand,
Yet sweeps the torrent's tide;
And this is yet ‡Aneurin's land—
Winds! bear the spoiler one more tone of pride!

---

* At the time of the supposed massacre of the Welsh bards by Edward the First.

† Eryri, Welsh name for the Snowdon mountains.

‡ Aneurin, one of the noblest of the Welsh bards.

## COME AWAY!*

Come away!—the child, where flowers are spring-
ing
　Round its footsteps on the mountain slope,
Hears a glad voice from the upland singing,
　Like the sky-lark's with its tone of hope:
　　　　Come away!

Bounding on, with sunny lands before him,
　All the wealth of glowing life outspread,
Ere the shadow of a cloud comes o'er him,
　By that strain the youth in joy is led:
　　　　Come away!

Slowly, sadly, heavy change is falling
　O'er the sweetness of the voice within;
Yet its tones, on restless manhood calling,
　Urge the hunter still to chase, to win:
　　　　Come away!

Come away!—the heart, at last forsaken,
　Smile by smile, hath proved each hope untrue;
Yet a breath can still those words awaken,
　Though to other shores far hence they woo:
　　　　Come away!

In the light leaves, in the reed's faint sighing,
　In the low sweet sounds of early spring,
Still their music wanders—till the dying
　Hears them pass, as on a spirit's wing:
　　　　Come away!

## MUSIC FROM SHORE.

A sound comes on the rising breeze,
　A sweet and lovely sound!
Piercing the tumult of the seas
　That wildly dash around.

From land, from sunny land it comes,
　From hills with murmuring trees,
From paths by still and happy homes—
　That sweet sound on the breeze.

Why should its faint and passing sigh
　Thus bid my quick pulse leap?
No part in earth's glad melody
　Is mine upon the deep.

Yet blessing, blessing on the spot,
　Whence those rich breathings flow!
Kind hearts, although they know me not,
　Like mine there beat and glow.

And blessing, from the bark that roams
　O'er solitary seas,
To those that far in happy homes
　Give sweet sounds to the breeze!

## FAIR HELEN OF KIRCONNEL.

"Fair Helen of Kirconnel," as she is called in the
Scottish Minstrelsy, throwing herself between her betrothed lover and a rival by whom his life was assailed,
received a mortal wound, and died in the arms of the
former.

Hold me upon thy faithful heart,
　Keep back my flitting breath;
'Tis early, early to depart,
　Beloved!—yet this is death!

Look on me still:—let that kind eye
　Be the last light I see!
Oh! sad it is in spring to die,
　But yet I die for thee!



For thee, my own! thy stately head
　Was never thus to bow!—
Give tears when with me love hath fled,
　True love, thou know'st it now!

Oh! the free streams lock'd bright, where'er
　We in our gladness roved;
And the blue skies were very fair—
　O friend! because we loved.

Farewell!—I bless thee—live thou on,
　When this young heart is low!
Surely my blood thy life hath won—
　Clasp me once more—I go!

## ‡ LOOK ON ME WITH THY CLOUDLESS EYES.

Look on me with thy cloudless eyes,
　Truth in their dark transparence lies;
Their sweetness gives me back the tears,
　And the free trust of early years;
　　　　My gentle child!

The spirit of my infant prayer
　Shines in the depths of quiet there;
And home and love once more are mine,
　Found in that dewy calm divine,
　　　　My gentle child!

Oh! heaven is with thee in thy dreams,
　Its light by day around thee gleams;
Thy smile hath gifts from vernal skies;
　—Look on me with thy cloudless eyes,
　　　　My gentle child!

## I GO, SWEET FRIENDS.

I go, sweet friends! yet think of me
　When Spring's young voice awakes the flowers
For we have wander'd far and free,
　In those bright hours, the violet's hours.

I go—but when you pause to hear,
　From distant hills, the Sabbath bell
On summer winds float silvery clear,
　Think on me then—I loved it well!

Forget me not around your hearth,
　When cheerly smiles the ruddy blaze,
For dear hath been its evening mirth
　To me, sweet friends! in other days.

And oh! when music's voice is heard
　To melt in strains of parting woe,
When hearts to love and grief are stirr'd—
　—Think of me then! I go, I go!

## IF THOU HAST CRUSHED A FLOWER.

　　　Oh cast thou not
　Affection from thee! In this bitter world
　Hold to thy heart that only treasure fast;
　Watch—guard it—suffer not a breath to dim
　　The bright gem's purity!

If thou hast crush'd a flower,
　The root may not be blighted;
If thou hast quench'd a lamp,
　Once more it may be lighted:

But on thy harp or on thy lute,
  The string which thou hast broken,
Shall never in sweet sound again
  Give to thy touch a token !

If thou hast loosed a bird,
  Whose voice of song could cheer thee,
Still, still he may be won
  From the skies to warble near thee :
But if upon the troubled sea
  Thou hast thrown a gem unheeded,
Hope not that wind or wave will bring
  The treasure back when needed.

If thou hast bruised a vine,
  The summer's breath is healing,
And its clusters yet may glow,
  Through the leaves their bloom revealing
But if thou hast a cup o'erthrown
  With a bright draught fill'd—oh ! never
Shall earth give back that lavish'd wealth,
  To cool thy parch'd lip's fever !

The heart is like that cup,
  If thou waste the love it bore thee ;
And like that jewel gone,
  Which the deep will not restore thee .
And like that strain of harp or lute
  Whence the sweet sound is scatter'd ;—
Gently, oh ! gently touch the chords,
  So soon for ever shatter'd !

---

## BRIGHTLY HAST THOU FLED.

BRIGHTLY, brightly hast thou fled,
Like one grief had bow'd thy head,
      Brightly didst thou part !
With thy young thoughts pure from spot,
With thy fond love wasted not,
      With thy bounding heart.

Ne'er by sorrow to be wet,
Calmly smiles thy pale cheek yet,
      Ere with dust o'erspread.
Lilies ne'er by tempest blown,
White-rose which no stain hath known,
      Be about thee shed !

So we give thee to the earth,
And the primrose shall have birth
      O'er thy gentle head ;
Thou that like a dew-drop, borne
On a sudden breeze of morn,
      Brightly thus hast fled !

---

## ‡SING TO ME, GONDOLIER !

SING to me, Gondolier !
  Sing words from Tasso's lay ;
While blue, and still, and clear,
  Night seems but softer day :
The gale is gently falling
  As if it paused to hear
Some strain the past recalling ;
  Sing to me, Gondolier !

Oh, ask me not to wake
  The memory of the brave ;
Bid no high numbers break
  The silence of the wave.
Gone are the noble-hearted,
  Closed the bright pageants here ;
And the glad song is departed
  From the mournful Gondolier !

---

## O'ER THE FAR BLUE MOUNTAINS.*

O'ER the far blue mountains,
  O'er the white sea foam,
Come, thou long parted one !
  Back to thine home !

When the bright fire shineth,
  Sad looks thy place,
While the true heart pineth
  Missing thy face.

Music is sorrowful
  Since thou art gone,
Sisters are mourning thee,
  Come to thine own !

Hark ! the home voices call
  Back to thy rest ;
Come to thy father's hall,
  Thy mother's breast !

O'er the far blue mountains,
  O'er the white sea foam,
Come, thou long parted one !
  Back to thine home !

---

## O THOU BREEZE OF SPRING.†

O THOU breeze of spring !
  Gladdening sea and shore,
Wake the woods to sing,
  Wake my heart no more
Streams have felt the sighing
  Of thy scented wing,
Let each fount replying
  Hail thee, breeze of spring,
      Once more !

O'er long buried flowers
  Passing, not in vain,
Odours in soft showers
  Thou hast brought again.
—Let the primrose greet thee,
  Let the violet pour
Incense forth to meet thee—
  Wake my heart no more !
      No more !

From a funeral urn
  Bower'd in leafy gloom,
Ev'n thy soft return
  Calls not song or bloom.
Leave my spirit sleeping
  Like that silent thing ;
Stir the founts of weeping
  There, O breeze of spring,
      No more !

---

## COME TO ME, DREAMS OF HEAVEN.

COME to me, dreams of heaven !
  My fainting spirit bear
On your bright wings, by morning given,
  Up to celestial air.
Away, far, far away,
  From bowers by tempests riven.
Fold me in blue, still, cloudless day,
  O blessed dreams of heaven !

Come but for one brief hour,
  Sweet dreams ! and yet again,
O'er burning thought and memory shower
  Your soft effacing rain !

---

Waft me where gales divine,
  With dark clouds ne'er have striven,
Where living founts for ever shine—
  O blessed dreams of heaven!*

---

## GOOD NIGHT.†

DAY is past!
Stars have set their watch at last,
Founts that through the deep woods flow
Make sweet sounds, unheard till now,
Flowers have shut with fading light—
        Good night!

Go to rest!
Sleep sit dove-like on thy breast!
If within that secret cell
One dark form of memory dwell,
Be it mantled from thy sight—
        Good night!

Joy be thine!
Kind looks o'er thy slumbers shine!
Go, and in the spirit-land
Meet thy home's long parted band,
Be their eyes all love and light—
        Good night!

Peace to all!
Dreams of heaven on mourners fall!
Exile! o'er thy couch may gleams
Pass from thine own mountain streams;
Bard! away to worlds more bright—
        Good night!

---

## LET HER DEPART.

HER home is far, oh! far away!
  The clear light in her eyes
Hath naught to do with earthly day,
  'T is kindled from the skies.
        Let her depart!

She looks upon the things of earth,
  Ev'n as some gentle star
Seems gazing down on grief or mirth,
  How softly, yet how far!
        Let her depart!

Her spirit's hope—her bosom's love—
  Oh! could they mount and fly!
She never sees a wandering dove,
  But for its wings to sigh.
        Let her depart!

She never hears a soft wind bear
  Low music on its way,
But deems it sent from heavenly air,
  For her who cannot stay.
        Let her depart.

Wrapt in a cloud of glorious dreams,
  She breathes and moves alone,
Pining for those bright bowers and streams
  Where her beloved is gone.
        Let her depart!

---

## ‡ I WOULD WE HAD NOT MET AGAIN

I WOULD we had not met again!
  —I had a dream of thee,
Lovely, though sad, on desert plain,
  Mournful on midnight sea.

* Set to music by Miss Graves.
† For a melody of Eisenhofer's.

---

What though it haunted me by night
  And troubled through the day?
It touch'd all earth with spirit-light,
  It glorified my way!

Oh! what shall now my faith restore
  In holy things and fair?
We met—I saw thy soul once more—
  —The world's breath had been there!

Yes! it was sad on desert-plain,
  Mournful on midnight sea,
Yet would I buy with life again
  That one deep dream of thee!

---

## WATER-LILIES.
### A FAIRY-SONG.

COME away, Elves! while the dew is sweet,
Come to the dingles where fairies meet;
Know that the lilies have spread their bells
O'er all the pools in our forest-dells;
Stilly and lightly their vases rest
On the quivering sleep of the water's breast,
Catching the sunshine through leaves that throw
To their scented bosoms an emerald glow;
And a star from the depth of each pearly cup,
A golden star unto heaven looks up,
As if seeking its kindred where bright they lie,
Set in the blue of the summer sky.
—Come away! under arching boughs we'll float,
Making those urns each a fairy boat;
We'll row them with reeds o'er the fountains free
And a tall flag leaf shall our streamer be,
And we'll send out wild music so sweet and low,
It shall seem from the bright flower's heart to flow
As if 't were a breeze with a flute's low sigh,
Or water-drops train'd into melody.
—Come away! for the midsummer sun grows strong,
And the life of the lily may not be long.

---

## ‡ THE BROKEN FLOWER.

OH! wear it on thy heart, my love!
  Still, still a little while!
Sweetness is lingering in its leaves,
  Though faded be their smile.
Yet, for the sake of what hath been,
  Oh! cast it not away!
'T was born to grace a summer scene,
  A long, bright, golden day,
        My love!
  A long, bright, golden day!

A little while around thee, love!
  Its fragrance yet shall cling,
Telling, that on thy heart hath lain,
  A fair, though faded thing.
But not ev'n that warm heart hath power
  To win it back from fate:
—Oh! *I* am like thy broken flower,
  Cherish'd too late, too late,
        My love!
  Cherish'd, alas! too late!

---

## FAIRIES' RECALL.

WHILE the blue is richest
  In the starry sky,
While the softest shadows
  On the greensward lie,
While the moonlight slumbers
  In the lily's urn,
Bright elves of the wild wood!
  Oh! return, return!

Round the forest fountain,
  On the river shore,
Let your silvery laughter
  Echo yet once more

While the joyous bounding
Of your dewy feet
Rings to that old chorus:
"The daisy is so sweet!"*

Oberon, Titania,
Did your starlight mirth,
With the song of Avon,
Quit this work-day earth?
Yet while green leaves glisten,
And while bright stars burn,
By that magic memory,
Oh, return, return!

## BY A MOUNTAIN STREAM AT REST.

By a mountain stream at rest,
We found the warrior lying,
And around his noble breast
A banner, clasp'd in dying:
Dark and still
Was every hill,
And the winds of night were sighing.

Last of his noble race,
To a lonely bed we bore him;
'Twas a green, still, solemn place
Where the mountain heath waves o'er him.
Woods alone
Seem to moan,
Wild streams to deplore him.

Yet, from festive hall and lay
Our sad thoughts oft are flying,
To those dark hills far away,
Where in death we found him lying;
On his breast
A banner press'd,
And the night-wind o'er him sighing.

## THE ROCK BESIDE THE SEA.

Oh! tell me not the woods are fair,
Now Spring is on her way;
Well, well I know how brightly there
In joy the young leaves play;
How sweet on winds of morn or eve
The violet's breath may be;—
—Yet ask me, woo me not to leave
My lone rock by the sea.

The wild wave's thunder on the shore,
The curlew's restless cries,
Unto my watching heart are more
Than all earth's melodies.
—Come back, my ocean rover! come!
There 's but one place for me,
Till I can greet thy swift sail home—
—My lone rock by the sea!

## O YE VOICES GONE.†

Oh! ye voices gone,
Sounds of other years!
Hush that haunting tone,
Melt me not to tears!
All around forget,
All who loved you well,
Yet, sweet voices, yet
O'er my soul ye swell.

With the winds of spring,
With the breath of flowers,
Floating back, ye bring
Thoughts of vanish'd hours.
Hence your music take,
Oh! ye voices gone!
This lone heart ye make
But more deeply lone.

---

* See the chorus of Fairies, in the "Flower and the Leaf" of Chaucer.

† Set to music by Miss H. Corbett.

## ‡ IS THERE SOME SPIRIT SIGHING.

Is there some spirit sighing
With sorrow in the air,
Can weary hearts be dying,
Vain love repining *there?*
If not, then how can that wild wail,
O sad Æolian lyre!
Be drawn forth by the wandering gale,
From thy deep thrilling wire?

No, no!—thou dost not borrow
That sadness from the wind,
Nor are those tones of sorrow
In thee, O harp! enshrined;
But in our own hearts deeply set
Lies the true quivering lyre,
Whence love, and memory, and regret,
Wake answers from thy wire.

## THE NAME OF ENGLAND.

The trumpet of the battle
Hath a high and thrilling tone;
And the first deep gun of an ocean fight
Dread music all its own.

But a mightier power, my England!
Is in that name of thine,
To strike the fire from every heart
Along the banner'd line.

Proudly it woke the spirits
Of yore, the brave and true,
When the bow was bent on Cressy's field,
And the yeoman's arrow flew.

And proudly hath it floated
Through the battles of the sea,
When the red-cross flag o'er smoke-wreaths
play'd
Like the lightning in its glee.

On rock, on wave, on bastion,
Its echoes have been known,
By a thousand streams the hearts lie low,
That have answer'd to its tone.

A thousand ancient mountains
Its pealing note hath stirr'd;
—Sound on, and on, for evermore,
O thou victorious word!

## COME TO ME, GENTLE SLEEP.

Come to me, gentle sleep!
I pine, I pine for thee;
Come with thy spells, the soft, the deep,
And set my spirit free!
Each lonely, burning thought,
In twilight languor steep—
Come to the full heart, long o'erwrought,
O gentle, gentle sleep!

Come with thine urn of dew,
Sleep, gentle sleep! yet bring
No voice, love's yearning to renew,
No vision on thy wing!
Come, as to folding flowers,
To birds in forests deep;
—Long, dark, and dreamless be thine hours,
O gentle, gentle sleep!

## OLD NORWAY*

### A MOUNTAIN WAR-SONG.

"To a Norwegian the words *Gamle Norge* (Old Norway) have a spell in them immediate and powerful: they cannot be resisted. *Gamle Norge* is heard, in an instant repeated by every voice: the glasses are filled, raised, and drained, not a drop is left: and then bursts forth the simultaneous chorus "*For Norge!*" the national song of Norway. Here, (at Christiansand) and in a hundred other instances in Norway, I have seen the character of a company entirely changed by the chance introduction of the expression *Gamle Norge* The gravest discussion is instantly interrupted: and one might suppose for the moment, that the party was a party of patriots, assembled to commemorate some national anniversary of freedom."—*Derwent Conway's Personal Narrative of a Journey through Norway and Sweden.*

The following words were written to the national air, as contained in the work above cited.

Arise! old Norway sends the word
  Of battle on the blast;
Her voice the forest pines have stirr'd,
  As if a storm went past;
Her thousand hills the call have heard,
  And forth their fire-flags cast.

Arm, arm, free hunters! for the chase,
  The kingly chase of foes;
'T is not the bear or wild wolf's race,
  Whose trampling shakes the snows;
Arm, arm! 't is on a nobler trace
  The northern spearman goes.

Our hills have dark and strong defiles,
  With many an icy bed;
Heap there the rocks for funeral piles,
  Above the invader's head!
Or let the seas, that guard our Isles,
  Give burial to his dead!

---

## ENGLISH SOLDIER'S SONG OF MEMORY.

### TO THE AIR OF "AM RHEIN, AM RHEIN!"

Sing, sing in memory of the brave departed,
  Let song and wine be pour'd!
Pledge to their fame, the free and fearless hearted,
  Our brethren of the sword!

Oft at the feast, and in the fight, their voices
  Have mingled with our own;
Fill high the cup, but when the soul rejoices,
  Forget not who are gone!

They that stood with us, 'midst the dead and dying,
  On Albuera's plain;
They that beside us cheerly track'd the flying,
  Far o'er the hills of Spain:

They that amidst us, when the shells were showering,
  From old Rodrigo's wall,
The rampart scaled, through clouds of battle towering,
  First, first at victory's call!

They that upheld the banners, proudly waving,
  In Roncesvalles' dell;
—With England's blood the southern vineyards laving,
  Forget not how they fell!

Sing, sing in memory of the brave departed,
  Let song and wine be pour'd!
Pledge to their fame, the free and fearless hearted,
  Our brethren of the sword!

* These words have been published, as arranged to the spirited national air of Norway, by Charles Graves, Esq.

## Miscellaneous Poems.

### THE HOME OF LOVE

Thou movest in visions, Love!—Around thy way
E'en through this world's rough path and changeful day,
  For ever floats a gleam,
Not from the realms of moonlight or the morn,
But thine own soul's illumined chambers born—
  The colouring of a dream!

Love, shall I read thy dream?—oh! is it not
All of some sheltering, wood-embosom'd spot—
  A bower for thee and thine?
Yes! lone and lowly is that home; yet there
Something of heaven in the transparent air
  Makes every flower divine.

Something that mellows and that glorifies,
Breathes o'er it ever from the tender skies,
  As o'er some blessed isle;
E'en like the soft and spiritual glow,
Kindling rich woods, whereon th' ethereal bow
  Sleeps lovingly awhile.

The very whispers of the wind have there
A flute-like harmony that seems to bear
  Greeting from some bright shore,
Where none have said *Farewell!*—Where no decay
Lends the faint crimson to the dying day;
  Where the storm's might is o'er

And there thou dreamest of Elysian rest,
In the deep sanctuary of one true breast
  Hidden from earthly ill:
There wouldst thou watch the homeward step, whose sound
Wakening all nature to sweet echoes round,
  Thine inmost soul can thrill.

There by the hearth should many a glorious page,
From mind to mind th' immortal heritage,
  For thee its treasures pour;
Or music's voice at vesper hours be heard,
Or dearer interchange of playful word,
  Affection's household lore.

And the rich unison of mingled prayer,
The melody of hearts in heavenly air,
  Thence duly should arise;
Lifting th' eternal hope, th' adoring breath,
Of spirits, not to be disjoin'd by death,
  Up to the starry skies.

There, dost thou well believe, no storm should come
To mar the stillness of that angel-home;—
  There should thy slumbers be
Weigh'd down with honey-dew, serenely bless'd,
Like theirs who first in Eden's grove took rest
  Under some balmy tree.

Love, Love! thou passionate in joy and woe!
And canst *thou* hope for cloudless peace below—
  *Here*, where bright things must die?
Oh, thou! that wildly worshipping, dost shed
On the frail altar of a mortal head
  Gifts of infinity!

Thou must be still a trembler, fearful Love!
Danger seems gathering from beneath, above,
  Still round thy precious things;
Thy stately pine-tree, or thy gracious rose,
In their sweet shade can yield thee no repose,
  Here, where the blight hath wings.

And, as a flower with some fine sense imbued
To shrink before the wind's vicissitude,
  So in thy prescient breast
Are lyre-strings quivering with prophetic thrill
To the low footstep of each coming ill;
  —Oh! canst *Thou* dream of rest?

Bear up thy dream! thou mighty and thou weak!
Heart, strong as death, yet as a reed to break,
  As a flame, tempest-sway'd!

He that sits calm on high is yet the source
Whence thy soul's current hath its troubled course.
He that great deep hath made!

Will He not pity?—He whose searching eye
Reads all the secrets of thine agony?—
Oh! pray to be forgiven
Thy fond idolatry, thy blind excess,
And seek with *Him* that bower of blessedness—
Love! *thy* sole home is heaven!

## BOOKS AND FLOWERS.

La vue d'une fleur caresse mon imagination, et flatte
mes sens a un point inexprimable. Sous le tranquille
abri du toit paternel, j'etais nourrie des l'enfance avec
des fleurs et des livres;—dans l'etroite enceinte d'une prison, au milieu des fers imposies par la tyrannie, j'oublie
l'injustice des hommes, leurs sottises et mes maux avec
des livres et des fleurs.——*Madame Roland.*

Come, let me make a sunny realm around thee,
Of thought and beauty! Here are books and
flowers,
With spells to loose the fetter which hath bound
thee,
The ravell'd coil of this world's feverish hours.

The soul of song is in these deathless pages,
Even as the odour in the flower enshrined!
Here the crown'd spirits of departed ages
Have left the silent melodies of mind.

Their thoughts, that strove with time, and change,
and anguish,
For some high place where faith her wing might
rest,
Are burning here; a flame that may not languish,
Still pointing upward to that bright hill's crest!

Their grief, the veil'd infinity exploring
For treasures lost, is here;—their boundless love
Its mighty streams of gentleness outpouring
On all things round, and clasping all above.

And the bright beings, their own heart's creations,
Bright, yet all human, here are breathing still;
Conflicts, and agonies, and exultations
Are here, and victories of prevailing will!

Listen, oh! listen, let their high words cheer thee!
Their swan-like music ringing through all woes,
Let my voice bring their holy influence near thee,
The Elysian air of their divine repose!

Or wouldst thou turn to earth? *Not* earth all fur-
row'd
By the old traces of man's toil and care,
But the green peaceful world that never sorrow'd,
The world of leaves, and dews, and summer air!

Look on these flowers! As o'er an altar shedding
O'er Milton's page, soft light from colour'd urns!
They are the links, man's heart to nature wedding,
When to her breast the prodigal returns.

They are from lone wild places, forest dingles,
Fresh banks of many a low-voiced hidden stream,
Where the sweet star of eve looks down and min-
gles
Faint lustre with the water-lily's gleam.

They are from where the soft winds play in glad-
ness,
Covering the turf with flowery blossom-showers'
—Too richly dower'd, O friend! are *we* for sadness,
Look on an empire—mind and nature—ours!

## FOR A PICTURE OF ST. CECILIA ATTENDED BY ANGELS.

How rich that forehead's calm expanse!
How bright that heaven-directed glance!
—Waft her to glory, winged powers,
Ere sorrow be renew'd,
And intercourse with mortal hours
Bring back an humbler mood!

*Wordsworth.*

How can that eye, with inspiration beaming,
Wear yet so deep a calm?—Oh, child of song!
Is not the music-land a world of dreaming,
Where forms of sad bewildering beauty throng?

Hath it not sounds from voices long departed?
Echoes of tones that rung in childhood's ear?
Low haunting whispers, which the weary-hearted,
Stealing 'midst crowds away, have wept to hear?

No, not to thee!—thy spirit, meek, yet queenly,
On its own starry height, beyond all this,
Floating triumphantly and yet serenely,
Breathes no faint under-tone through songs of
bliss!

Say by what strain, through cloudless ether swelling,
Thou hast drawn down those wanderers from
the skies?
Bright guests! even such as left of yore their
dwelling,
For the deep cedar shades of Paradise!

What strain?—oh! not the Nightingale's when
showering
Her own heart's life drops on the burning lay,
She stirs the young woods in the days of flowering,
And pours her strength, but not her grief away;

And not the Exile's—when 'midst lonely billows
He wakes the Alpine notes his mother sung,
Or blends them with the sigh of alien willows,
Where, murmuring to the wind, his harp is hung.

And not the Pilgrim's—though his thoughts be holy,
And sweet his Ave song, when day grows dim,
Yet as he journeys, pensively and slowly,
Something of sadness floats thro' that low hymn.

But thou!—the spirit which at eve is filling
All the hush'd air and reverential sky,
Founts, leaves, and flowers, with solemn rapture
thrilling,
This is the soul of thy rich harmony.

This bears up high those breathings of devotion
Wherein the currents of thy heart gush free
Therefore no world of sad and vain emotion
Is the dream-haunted music land for *thee.*

## THE VOICE OF THE WAVES.

WRITTEN NEAR THE SCENE OF A RECENT SHIPWRECK.

How perfect was the calm! It seem'd no sleep,
No mood, which season takes away or brings
I could have fancied that the mighty deep
Was even the gentlest of all gentle things.
* * * * * * * *
But welcome fortitude and patient cheer,
And frequent sights of what is to be borne!

*Wordsworth.*

Answer, ye chiming waves!
That now in sunshine sweep;
Speak to me from thy hidden caves,
Voice of the solemn deep!

Hath man's lone spirit here
  With storms in battle striven?
Where all is now so calmly clear,
  Hath anguish cried to heaven?

—Then the sea's voice arose,
  Like an earthquake's under-tone:
" Mortal, the strife of human woes
  *Where* hath *not* nature known?

" Here to the quivering mast
  Despair hath wildly clung,
The shriek upon the wind hath past,
  The midnight sky hath rung.

" And the youthful and the brave
  With their beauty and renown,
To the hollow chambers of the wave
  In darkness have gone down.

" They are vanish'd from their place—
  Let their homes and hearths make moan
But the rolling waters keep no trace
  Of pang or conflict gone."

—Alas! thou haughty deep!
  The strong, the sounding far!
My heart before thee dies,—I weep
  To think on what we are!

To think that so we pass,
  High hope, and thought, and mind,
Ev'n as the breath-stain from the glass,
  Leaving no sign behind!

Saw'st thou naught else, thou main?
  Thou and the midnight sky?
Naught save the struggle, brief and vain,
  The parting agony?

—And the sea's voice replied,
  " Here nobler things have been!
Power with the valiant when they died,
  To sanctify the scene:

" Courage, in fragile form,
  Faith, trusting to the last,
Prayer, breathing heavenwards thro' the storm,
  But all alike have pass'd."

Sound on, thou haughty sea!
  *These* have not pass'd in vain;
My soul awakes, my hope springs free
  On victor wings again.

*Thou*, from thine empire driven,
  May'st vanish with thy powers;
But, by the hearts that here have striven,
  A loftier doom is ours!

---

### THE HAUNTED HOUSE.

---

> I seem like one
> Who treads alone
>     Some banquet-hall deserted,
> Whose lights are fled,
> Whose garlands dead,
>     And all but me departed.
>
>                         *Moore.*

---

Seest thou yon gray gleaming hall,
Where the deep elm-shadows fall?
Voices that have left the earth
      Long ago,
Still are murmuring round its hearth,
      Soft and low;
Ever there; yet one alone
Hath the gift to hear their tone.

Guests come thither, and depart,
Free of step, and light of heart;
Children with sweet visions bless'd,
In the haunted chambers rest;

One alone unslumbering lies
When the night hath seal'd all eyes,
One quick heart and watchful ear,
Listening for those whispers clear.

Seest thou where the woodbine flowers
O'er yon low porch hang in showers?
Startling faces of the dead,
      Pale, yet sweet,
One lone woman's entering tread
      There still meet!
Some with young smooth foreheads fair,
Faintly shining through bright hair;
Some with reverend locks of snow—
All, all buried long ago!

All, from under deep sea-waves,
Or the flowers of foreign graves,
Or the old and banner'd aisle,
Where their high tombs gleam the while
Rising, wandering, floating by,
Suddenly and silently,
Through their earthly home and place,
But amidst another race.

Wherefore, unto one alone,
Are those sounds and visions known?
Wherefore hath that spell of power
      Dark and dread,
On *her* soul, a baleful dower,
      Thus been shed?
Oh! in those deep-seeing eyes,
No strange gift of mystery lies
She is lone where once she moved,
Fair, and happy, and beloved!

Sunny smiles were glancing round her,
Tendrils of kind hearts had bound her;
Now those silver chords are broken,
Those bright looks have left no token;
Not one trace on all the earth,
Save her memory of their mirth.

She is lone and lingering now,
Dreams have gather'd o'er her brow,
'Midst gay songs and children's play,
She is dwelling far away;
Seeing what none else may see—
Haunted still her place must be!

---

### O'CONNOR'S CHILD.

---

This piece was suggested by a picture in the possession of Mrs. Lawrence, of Wavertree Hall.—It represents the " Hero's Child" of Campbell's Poem, seated beside a solitary tomb of rock, marked with a cross, in a wild and desert place. A tempest seems gathering in the angry skies above her, but the attitude of the drooping figure expresses the utter carelessness of desolation, and the countenance speaks of entire abstraction from all external objects.—A bow and quiver lie beside her amongst the weeds and wild flowers of the desert.

---

> I fled the home of grief
> At Connoeh' Moran's tomb to fall,
> I found the helmet of my Chief,
>   His bow still hanging on our wall,
> And took it down, and vow'd to rove
>   This desert place, a huntress bold;
> Nor would I change my buried love
>   For any heart of living mould.
>
>                         *Campbell.*

---

The sleep of storms is dark upon the skies,
  The weight of omens heavy in the cloud:—
Bid the lorn huntress of the desert rise,
  And gird the form whose beauty grief hath bow'd,
And leave the tomb, as tombs are left—alone,
To the star's vigil, and the wind's wild moan.

Tell her of revelries in bower and hall,
  Where gems are glittering, and bright wine is
      pour'd ;
Where to glad measures chiming footsteps fall,
  And soul seems gushing from the harp's full
      chord ;
And richer flowers amid fair tresses wave,
Than the sad "*Love lies bleeding*" of the grave.

Oh ! little know'st thou of the o'ermastering spell,
  Wherewith love binds the spirit strong in pain,
To the spot hallow'd by a wild farewell,
  A parting agony,—intense, yet vain,
A look—and darkness when its gleam hath flown,
A voice—and silence when its words are gone !

She hears thee not ; her full, deep, fervent heart
  Is set in her dark eyes ;—and *they* are bound
Unto that cross, that shrine, that world apart,
  Where faithful love hath sanctified the ground ;
And love with death striven long by tear and
      prayer,
And anguish frozen into still despair.

Yet on her spirit hath arisen at last
  A light, a joy, of its own wanderings born ;
Around her path a vision's glow is cast,
  Back, back, her lost one comes, in hues of morn !
For her the gulf is fill'd—the dark night fled ;
Whose mystery parts the living and the dead.

And she can pour forth in such converse high,
  All her soul's tide of love, the deep, the strong,
Oh ! lonelier far, perchance, *thy* destiny,
  And more forlorn, amidst the world's gay throng
Than her's—the queen of that majestic gloom,
The tempest, and the desert, and the tomb !

THE

# BRIGAND LEADER AND HIS WIFE.

SUGGESTED BY A PICTURE OF EASTLAKE'S

Dark chieftain of the heath and height !
Wild feaster on the hills by night !
Seest thou the stormy sunset's glow
Flung back by glancing spears below ?
Now for one strife of stern despair !
The foe hath track'd thee to thy lair.

Thou, against whom the voice of blood
Hath risen from rock and lonely wood ;
And in whose dreams a moan should be,
Not of the water, nor the tree ;
Haply thine own last hour is nigh,—
Yet shalt thou not forsaken die.

There 's one that pale beside thee stands,
More true than all thy mountain bands !
She will not shrink in doubt and dread,
When the balls whistle round thy head :
Nor leave thee, though thy closing eye
No longer may to her's reply

Oh ! many a soft and quiet grace
Hath faded from her form and face ;
And many a thought, the fitting guest
Of woman's meek religious breast,
Hath perish'd in her wanderings wide,
Through the deep forests, by thy side.

Yet, mournfully surviving all,
A flower upon a ruin's wall,
A friendless thing whose lot is cast,
Of lovely ones to be the last ;
Sad, but unchanged through good and ill,
Thine is her lone devotion still.

---

* "A son of light, a lovely form,
    He comes, and makes her glad."
                              *Campbell.*

And oh ! not wholly lost the heart
Where that undying love hath part ;
Not worthless all, though far and long
From home estranged, and guided wrong ;
Yet may its depths by heaven be stirr'd,
Its prayer for thee be pour'd and heard !

THE

# CHILD'S RETURN FROM THE WOODLANDS.

All good and guiltless as thou art,
Some transient griefs will touch thy heart—
Griefs that along thy alter'd face
Will breathe a more subduing grace,
Than even those looks of joy that lie
On the soft cheek of infancy.
                              *Wilson.*

---

Hast thou been in the woods with the honey-bee ?
Hast thou been with the lamb in the pastures free ?
With the hare thro' the copses and dingles wild ?
With the butterfly over the heath, fair child ?
Yea : the light fall of thy bounding feet
Hath not startled the wren from her mossy seat ;
Yet hast thou ranged the green forest-dells
And brought back a treasure of buds and bells.

Thou know'st not the sweetness, by antique song
Breathed o'er the names of that flowery throng ;
The woodbine, the primrose, the violet dim,
The lily that gleams by the fountain's brim ;
These are old words, that have made each grove
A dreaming haunt for romance and love ;
Each sunny bank, where faint odours lie,
A place for the gushings of poesy.

Thou know'st not the light wherewith fairy lore
Sprinkles the turf and the daisies o'er ;
Enough for thee are the dews that sleep,
Like hidden gems, in the flower-urns deep ;
Enough the rich crimson spots that dwell
'Midst the gold of the cowslip's perfumed cell ;
And the scent by the blossoming sweet-briers shed,
And the beauty that bows the wood-hyacinth's
      head.

Oh ! happy child, in thy fawn-like glee !
What is remembrance or thought to thee ?
Fill thy bright locks with those gifts of spring,
O'er thy green pathway their colours fling '
Bind them in chaplet and wild festoon—
What if to droop and to perish soon ?
Nature hath mines of such wealth—and thou
Never wilt prize its delights as now !

For a day is coming to quell the tone
That rings in thy laughter, thou joyous one !
And to dim thy brow with a touch of care,
Under the gloss of its clustering hair ;
And to tame the flash of thy cloudless eyes
Into the stillness of autumn skies ;
And to teach thee that grief hath her needful part,
'Midst the hidden things of each human heart.

Yet shall we mourn, gentle child ! for this ?
Life hath enough of yet holier bliss !
Such be thy portion !—the bliss to look,
With a reverent spirit, through nature's book
By fount, by forest, by river's line,
To track the paths of a love divine ;
To read its deep meanings—to see and hear
God in earth's garden—and not to fear !

---

## THE FAITH OF LOVE.

Thou hast watch'd beside the bed of death,
  Oh fearless human love !
Thy lip received the last faint breath
  Ere the spirit fled above.

Thy prayer was heard by the parting bier,
　In a low and a farewell tone,
Thou hast given the grave both flower and tear—
　—Oh love! thy task is done.

Then turn thee from each pleasant spot
　Where thou wert wont to rove,
For there the friend of thy soul is not,
　Nor the joy of thy youth, oh love!

Thou wilt meet but mournful memory there,
　Her dreams in the grove she weaves,
With echoes filling the summer air,
　With sighs the trembling leaves.

Then turn thee to the world again,
　From those dim haunted bowers,
And shut thine ear to the wild sweet strain
　That tells of vanish'd hours.

And wear not on thine aching heart
　The image of the dead,
For the tie is rent that gave thee part
　In the gladness its beauty shed.

And gaze on the pictured smile no more
　That thus can life outlast,
All between parted souls is o'er;—
　—Love! love! forget the past!

" Voice of vain boding! away, be still!
　Strive not against the faith
That yet my bosom with light can fill,
　Unquench'd, and undimm'd by death:

" From the pictured smile I will not turn,
　Though sadly now it shine;
Nor quit the shades that in whispers mourn
　For the step once link'd with mine:

" Nor shut mine ear to the song of old
　Though its notes the pang renew,
—Such memories deep in my heart I hold,
　To keep it pure and true.

" By the holy instinct of my heart,
　By the hope that bears me on,
I have still my own undying part
　In the deep affection gone.

" By the presence that about me seems
　Through night and day to dwell,
Voice of vain bodings and fearful dreams!
　—I have breathed no *last* farewell !"

---

### THE SISTER'S DREAM.

Suggested by a picture, in which a young girl is represented as sleeping, and visited during her slumbers by
the spirits of her departed sisters

---

She sleeps!—but not the free and sunny sleep
　That lightly on the brow of childhood lies:
Though happy be her rest, and soft, and deep,
　Yet, ere it sunk upon her shadow'd eyes,
Thoughts of past scenes and kindred graves o'er-
　　swept
Her soul's meek stillness:—she had pray'd and
　　wept.

And now in visions to her couch they come,
　The early lost—the beautiful—the dead—
That unto her bequeath'd a mournful home,
　Whence with their voices all sweet laughter fled;
They rise—the sisters of her youth arise,
As from the world where no frail blossom dies.

And well the sleeper knows them not of earth—
　Not as they were when binding up the flowers,
Telling wild legends round the winter-hearth,
　Braiding their long fair hair for festal hours;
These things are past;—a spiritual gleam,
A solemn glory, robes them in that dream.

Yet, if the glee of life's fresh budding years
　In those pure aspects may no more be read,
Thence, too, hath sorrow melted,—and the tears
　Which o'er their mother's holy dust they shed,
　re all effaced; there earth hath left no sign
Save its deep love, still touching every line.

But oh! more soft, more tender, breathing more
　A thought of pity, than in vanish'd days:
While hovering silently and brightly o'er
　The lone one's head, they meet her spirit's gaze
With their immortal eyes, that seem to say,
" Yet, sister, yet we love thee, come away!"

'Twill fade, the radiant dream! and will she not
　Wake with more painful yearning at her heart?
Will not her home seem yet a lonelier spot,
　Her task more sad, when those bright shadows
　　part?
And the green summer after them look dim,
And sorrow's tone be in the bird's wild hymn?

But let her hope be strong, and let the dead
　Visit her soul in heaven's calm beauty still,
Be their names utter'd, be their memory spread
　Yet round the place they never more may fill!
All is not over with earth's broken tie—
Where, where should sisters love, if not on high?

---

### WRITTEN AFTER VISITING A TOMB,

*Near Woodstock, in the County of Kilkenny.*

---

Yes! bide beneath the mouldering heap,<br>
The undelighting, slighted thing;<br>
There, in the cold earth, buried deep,<br>
In silence let it wait the spring.<br>
Mrs. Tighe's Poem on the Lily.

---

I STOOD where the lip of song lay low,
Where the dust had gather'd on beauty's brow;
Where stillness hung on the heart of love,
And a marble weeper kept watch above.

I stood in the silence of lonely thought,
Of deep affections that inly wrought,
Troubled, and dreamy, and dim with fear—
—They knew themselves exiled spirits here!

Then didst *thou* pass me in radiance by,
Child of the sunbeam, bright butterfly!
　thou that dost bear on thy fairy wings,
No burden of mortal sufferings!

Thou wert flitting past that solemn tomb,
Over a bright world of joy and bloom,
And strangely I felt, as I saw thee shine,
The all that sever'd *thy* life and *mine.*

*Mine,* with its inborn mysterious things,
Of love and grief, its unfathom'd springs,
And quick thoughts wandering o'er earth and sky,
With voices to question eternity!

*Thine,* in its reckless and joyous way,
Like an embodied breeze at play!
Child of the sunlight!—thou winged and free!
One moment, *one* moment, I envied thee!

Thou art not lonely, though born to roam,
Thou hast no longings that pine for home,
Thou seek'st not the haunts of the bee and bird,
To fly from the sickness of hope deferr'd:

In thy brief being, no strife of mind,
No boundless passion is deeply shrined;
While I—as I gazed on thy swift flight by,
One hour of my soul seem'd infinity!

And she, that voiceless below me slept,
Flow'd not her song from a heart that wept?
—O love and song, though of heaven your powers,
Dark is your fate in this world of ours!

Yet, ere I turn'd from that silent place,
Or ceased from watching thy sunny race,
Thou, even thou, on those glancing wings,
Didst waft me visions of brighter things!

Thou, that dost image the freed soul's birth,
And its flight away o'er the mists of earth,
Oh! fitly thy path is through flowers that rise
Round the dark chamber where genius lies!

---

## PROLOGUE TO THE TRAGEDY OF FIESCO.

As translated from the German of Schiller, by Colonel
D'Aguilar, and performed at the Theatre Royal, Dublin,
December, 1832.

---

Too long apart, a bright but sever'd band,
The mighty minstrels of the Rhine's fair land,
Majestic strains, but not for us, had sung,—
Moulding to melody a stranger tongue.
Brave hearts leap'd proudly to their words of
   power,
As a true sword bounds forth in battle's hour!
Fair eyes rain'd homage o'er the impassion'd lays,
In loving tears, more eloquent than praise;
While we, far distant, knew not, dream'd not
   aught
Of the high marvels by that magic wrought.
But let the barriers of the sea give way,
When mind sweeps onward with a conqueror's
   sway!
And let the Rhine divide high souls no more
From mingling on its old heroic shore,
Which, e'en like ours, brave deeds through many
   an age,
Have made the Poet's own free heritage!

To us, though faintly, may a wandering tone
Of the far minstrelsy at last be known;
Sounds which the thrilling pulse, the burning tear,
Have sprung to greet, must not be strangers here,
And if by one, more used, on march and heath
To the shrill bugle, than the muse's breath,
With a warm heart the offering hath been brought,
And in a trusting loyalty of thought,—
So let it be received!—a Soldier's hand
Bears to the breast of no ungenerous land
A seed of foreign shores. O'er this fair clime,
Since Tara heard the harp of ancient time,
Hath song held empire; then if not with Fame,
Let the green isle with kindness bless his aim,
The joy, the power, of kindred song to spread,
Where once that harp "the soul of music shed!"

---

## A FAREWELL TO ABBOTSFORD.

These lines were given to Sir Walter Scott, at the
gate of Abbotsford, in the summer of 1829. He was
then apparently in the vigour of an existence whose
energies promised long continuance; and the glance of
his quick, smiling eye, and the very sound of his kindly
voice, seemed to kindle the gladness of his own sunny
and benignant spirit in all who had the happiness of approaching him.

---

Home of the gifted! fare thee well,
  And a blessing on thee rest;
While the heather waves its purple bell
  O'er moor and mountain crest;
While stream to stream around thee calls,
  And braes with broom are drest,
Glad be the harping in thy halls—
  A blessing on thee rest!

While the high voice from thee sent forth,
  Bids rock and cairn reply,
Wakening the spirits of the North,
  Like a chieftain's gathering cry;
While its deep master-tones hold sway,
  As a king's o'er every breast,
Home of the Legend and the Lay!
  A blessing on thee rest.

Joy to thy hearth, and board, and bower!
  Long honours to thy line!
And hearts of proof, and hands of power,
  And bright names worthy thine!
By the merry step of childhood still
  May thy free sward be prest!
—While one proud pulse in the land can thrill,
  A blessing on thee rest!

---

## SCENE IN A DALECARLIAN MINE.

"Oh! fondly, fervently, those two had loved,
  Had mingled minds in Love's own perfect trust;
  Had watch'd bright sunsets, dreamt of blissful years;
  ——And thus they met.

"Haste, with your torches, haste! make firelight
  round!"
—They speed, they press—what hath the miner
  found?
Relic or treasure, giant sword of old?
Gems bedded deep, rich veins of burning gold?
—Not so—the dead, the dead! An awe-struck
  band,
In silence gathering round the silent stand,
Chain'd by one feeling, hushing e'en their breath
Before the thing that, in the might of death,
Fearful, yet beautiful, amidst them lay—
A sleeper, dreaming not!—a youth with hair
Making a sunny gleam (how sadly fair!)
O'er his cold brow: no shadow of decay
Had touch'd those pale bright features—yet he
  wore
A mien of other days, a garb of yore.
Who could unfold that mystery? From the throng
A woman wildly broke; her eye was dim,
As if through many tears, through vigils long,
Through weary strainings:—all had been for him
Those two had loved! And there he lay, the dead,
In his youth's flower—and she, the living, stood
With her gray hair, whence hue and gloss had
  fled—
And wasted form, and cheek, whose flushing blood
Had long since ebb'd—a meeting sad and strange
—Oh! are not meetings in this world of change
Sadder than partings oft? She stood there, still
And mute, and gazing, all her soul to fill
With the loved face once more—the young, fair
  face,
'Midst that rude cavern touch'd with sculpture's
  grace,
By torchlight and by death:—until at last
From her deep heart the spirit of the past
Gush'd in low broken tones:—"And there thou
  art!
And thus we meet, that loved, and did but part
As for a few brief hours!—My friend, my friend!
First love, and only one! Is this the end
Of hope deferr'd, youth blighted? Yet thy brow
Still wears its own proud beauty, and thy cheek
Smiles—how unchanged!—while I, the worn, and
  weak,
And faded—oh! thou wouldst but scorn me now,
If thou couldst look on me!—a wither'd leaf,
Sear'd—though for thy sake—by the blast of grief!
Better to see thee thus! For thou didst go,
Bearing my image on thy heart, I know,
Unto the dead. My Ulric! through the night
How have I call'd thee! With the morning light
How have I watch'd for thee!—wept, wander'd,
  pray'd,
Met the fierce mountain tempest, undismay'd,
In search of thee! Bound my worn life to one,
One torturing hope! Now let me die! 'Tis gone.
Take thy betroth'd!"—And on his breast she fell—
—Oh! since their youth's last passionate farewell,
How changed in all but love!—the true, the strong,
Joining in death whom life had parted long
—They had one grave—one lonely bridal bed—
No friend, no kinsman, there a tear to shed!
His name had ceased—her heart outlived each tie,
Once more to look on that dead face—and die!

## THE VICTOR.

*"De tout ce qui t'aimoit n'est-il plus rien qui t'aime?"*
*Lamartine.*

MIGHTY ones, Love and Death!
Ye are the strong in this world of ours,
Ye meet at the banquets, ye dwell 'midst the
    flowers,
  —Which hath the conqueror's wreath?

*Thou* art the victor, Love!
*Thou* art the fearless, the crown'd, the free,
The strength of the battle is given to thee,
  The spirit from above!

Thou hast look'd on Death, and smiled!
Thou hast borne up the reed-like and fragile form,
Through the waves of the fight, through the rush
    of the storm,
  On field, and flood, and wild!

No!—*Thou* art the victor, Death!
Thou comest, and where is that which spoke,
From the depths of the eye, when the spirit woke?
  —Gone with the fleeting breath!

Thou comest—and what is left
Of all that loved us, to say if aught
*Yet loves*—yet answers the burning thought
  Of the spirit lone and reft?

Silence is where thou art!
Silently there must kindred meet,
No smile to cheer, and no voice to greet,
  No bounding of heart to heart!

Boast not thy victory, Death!
It is but as the cloud's o'er the sunbeam's power,
It is but as the winter's o'er leaf and flower,
  That slumber, the snow beneath.

It is but as a Tyrant's reign
O'er the voice and the lip which he bids be still:
But the fiery thought, and the lofty will,
  Are not for him to chain!

They shall soar his might above!
And thus with the root whence affection springs
Though buried, it is not of mortal things—
  *Thou* art the victor, Love!

---

# GREEK SONGS.

### I.

### THE STORM OF DELPHI.[*]

FAR through the Delphian shades
  An Eastern trumpet rung!
And the startled eagle rush'd on high,
With a sounding flight through the fiery sky
And banners o'er the shadowy glades
  To the sweeping winds were flung.

Banners, with deep-red gold
  All waving, as a flame,
And a fitful g'ance from the bright spear-head
On the dim wood paths of the mountain shed,
And a peal of Asia's war-notes, told
  That in arms the Persian came.

He came with starry gems
  On his quiver and his crest;
With starry gems, at whose heart the day
Of the cloudless orient burning lay,
And they cast a gleam on the laurel-stems,
  As onward his thousands press'd.

---

[*] See the account cited from Herodotus, in Mitford's Greece.

But a gloom fell o'er their way,
  And a heavy moan went by!
A moan, yet not like the wind's low swell,
When its voice grows wild 'midst cave and dell
But a mortal murmur of dismay,
  Or a warrior's dying sigh!

A gloom fell o'er their way!
  'Twas not the shadow cast
By the dark pine-boughs, as they cross'd the blue
Of the Grecian heavens with their solemn hue;
  —The air was fill'd with a mightier sway,
  —But on the spearmen pass'd!

And hollow, to their tread,
  Came the echoes of the ground,
And banners droop'd as with dews o'erborne,
And the wailing blast of the battle-horn
Had an alter'd cadence, dull and dead,
  Of strange foreboding sound.

—But they blew a louder strain,
  When the steep defiles were pass'd!
And afar the crown'd Parnassus rose,
To shine through heaven with his radiant snows
And in golden light the Delphian fane
  Before them stood at last!

In golden light it stood,
  'Midst the laurels gleaming lone,
For the Sun God, yet, with a lovely smile,
O'er its graceful pillars look'd awhile,
Though the stormy shade on cliff and wood
  Grew deep, round its mountain-throne.

And the Persians gave a shout!
  But the marble walls replied
With a clash of steel, and a sullen roar
Like heavy wheels on the ocean-shore,
And a savage trumpet's note peal'd out,
  Till their hearts for terror died!

On the armour of the God,
  Then a viewless hand was laid;
There was helm and spear, with a clanging din
And corslet brought from the shrine within,
From the inmost shrine of the dread abode,
  And before its front array'd.

And a sudden silence fell
  Through the dim and loaded air!
On the wild bird's wing, and the myrtle-spray,
And the very founts in their silvery way,
With a weight of sleep came down the spell,
  Till man grew breathless there.

But the pause was broken soon!
  'Twas not by song or lyre;
For the Delphian maids had left their bowers,
And the hearths were lone in the city towers,
But there burst a sound through the misty noon,
  That battle-noon of fire!

It burst from earth and heaven!
  It roll'd from crag and cloud!
For a moment of the mountain-blast,
With a thousand stormy voices pass'd,
And the purple gloom of the sky was riven,
  When the thunder peal'd aloud.

And the lightnings in their play
  Flash'd forth, like javelins thrown;
Like sun-darts wing'd from the silver bow,
They smote the spear and the turban'd brow
And the bright gems flew from the crests like spray,
  And the banners were struck down!

And the massy oak-boughs crash'd
  To the fire-bolt from on high,
And the forest lent its billowy roar,
While the glorious tempest onward bore,
And lit the streams, as they foam'd and dash'd
  With the fierce rain sweeping by.

Then rush'd the Delphian men
On the pale and scatter'd host;
Like the joyous burst of a flashing wave,
They rush'd from the dim Corycian cave,
And the singing blast o'er wood and glen
   Roll'd on, with the spears they tost.

There were cries of wild dismay,
There were shouts of warrior-glee,
There were savage sounds of the tempest's mirth,
That shook the realm of their eagle-birth;
But the mount of song, when they died away,
   Still rose, with its temple, free!

And the Pæan swell'd ere long,
Io Pæan! from the fane;
Io Pæan! for the war array,
On the crown'd Parnassus, riven that day!
—Thou shalt rise as free, thou mount of song!
   With thy bounding streams again.

---

## II.
## THE BOWL OF LIBERTY.

BEFORE the fiery sun,
The sun that looks on Greece with cloudless eye,
In the free air, and on the war-field won,
Our fathers crown'd the Bowl of Liberty.

Amidst the tombs they stood,
The tombs of heroes! with the solemn skies,
And the wide plain around where patriot-blood
Had steep'd the soil in hues of sacrifice.

They call'd the glorious dead,
In the strong faith which brings the viewless nigh,
And pour'd rich odours o'er their battle-bed,
And bade them to the rite of Liberty.

They call'd them from the shades,
The golden-fruited shades, where minstrels tell
How softer light th' immortal clime pervades,
And music floats o'er meads of Asphodel.

Then fast the bright-red wine*
Flow'd to their manes who taught the world to die,
And made the land's green turf a living shrine,
Meet for the wreath and Bowl of Liberty.

So the rejoicing earth
Took from her vines again the blood she gave,
And richer flowers to deck the tomb drew birth
From the free soil thus hallow'd to the brave.

*We* have the battle-fields,
The tombs, the names, the blue majestic sky,
We have the founts the purple vintage yields;
—When shall *we* crown the Bowl of Liberty!

---

## III.
## THE VOICE OF SCIO.

A voice from Scio's isle,
A voice of song, a voice of old,
Swept far as cloud or billow roll'd,
   And earth was hush'd the while.

The souls of nations woke!
Where lies the land whose hills among,
That voice of Victory hath not rung,
   As if a trumpet spoke?

To sky, and sea, and shore
Of those whose blood, on Ilion's plain,
Swept from the rivers to the main,
   A glorious tale it bore.

Still by our sun-bright deep,
With all the fame that fiery lay
Threw round them, in its rushing way,
   The sons of battle sleep.

And kings their turf have crown'd!
And pilgrims o'er the foaming wave
Brought garlands there: so rest the brave,
   Who thus their bard have found!

A voice from Scio's isle,
A voice as deep hath risen again!
As far shall peal its thrilling strain,
   Where'er our sun may smile!

Let not its tones expire!
Such power to waken earth and heaven,
And might and vengeance ne'er was given
   To mortal song or lyre!

Know ye not whence it comes?
—From ruin'd hearths, from burning fanes,
From kindred blood on you red plains,
   From desolated homes!

'Tis with us through the night!
'Tis on our hills, 'tis in our sky—
Hear it, ye heavens! when swords flash high,
   O'er the mid-waves of fight!

---

## IV.
## THE URN AND SWORD.

THEY sought for treasures in the tomb,
Where gentler hands were wont to spread
Fresh boughs and flowers of purple bloom,
And sunny ringlets, for the dead.*

They scatter'd far the greensward-heap,
Where once those hands the bright wine pour'd
—What found they in the home of sleep?
—A mouldering urn, a shiver'd sword!

An urn, which held the dust of one
Who died when hearths and shrines were free;
A sword, whose work was proudly done,
Between our mountains and the sea.

And these are treasures!—undismay'd,
Still for the suffering land we trust,
Wherein the past its fame hath laid,
With freedom's sword, and valour's dust.

---

## V.
## THE MYRTLE-BOUGH.

STILL green along our sunny shore
   The flowering myrtle waves,
As when its fragrant boughs of yore
   Were offer'd on the graves;
The graves, wherein our mighty men
Had rest, unviolated then.

Still green it waves! as when the hearth
   Was sacred through the land;
And fearless was the banquet's mirth,
   And free the minstrel's hand;
And guests, with shining myrtle crown'd,
Sent the wreath'd lyre and wine-cup round

Still green! as when on holy ground
   The tyrant's blood was pour'd:
—Forget ye not what garlands bound
   The young deliverer's sword!
Though earth may shroud Harmodius now,
We still have sword and myrtle-bough!

---

* For an account of this ceremony, anciently performed in commemoration of the battle of Platæa, see *Potter's Antiquities of Greece*, vol. I. p. 349.

* See *Potter's Grecian Antiquities*, vol. II. p. 234.

## SONGS OF THE CID.

The following ballads are not translations from the
Spanish, but are founded upon some of the 'wild and
wonderful' traditions preserved in the romances of that
language, and the ancient poem of the Cid.

### THE
### CID'S DEPARTURE INTO EXILE.

With sixty knights in his gallant train,
Went forth the Campeador of Spain;
For wild sierras and plains afar,
He left the lands of his own Bivar. (1)

To march o'er field, and to watch in tent,
From his home in good Castile he went;
To the wasting siege and the battle's van,
—For the noble Cid was a banish'd man!

Through his olive-woods the morn-breeze play'd,
And his native streams wild music made,
And clear in the sunshine his vineyards lay,
When for march and combat he took his way.

With a thoughtful spirit his way he took,
And he turn'd his steed for a parting look,
For a parting look at his own fair towers;
—Oh! the Exile's heart hath weary hours!

The pennons were spread, and the band array'd,
But the Cid at the threshold a moment stay'd;
It was but a moment—the halls were lone,
And the gates of his dwelling all open thrown.

There was not a steed in the empty stall,
Nor a spear nor a cloak on the naked wall,
Nor a hawk on the perch, nor a seat at the door,
Nor the sound of a step on the hollow floor. (2)

Then a dim tear swell'd to the warrior's eye,
As the voice of his native groves went by;
And he said—"My foemen their wish have won—
—Now the will of God be in all things done!"

But the trumpet blew, with its note of cheer,
And the winds of the morning swept off the tear,
And the fields of his glory lay distant far,
—He is gone from the towers of his own Bivar!

---

### THE CID'S DEATH-BED

It was an hour of grief and fear
   Within Valencia's walls,
When the blue spring-heaven lay still and clear
   Above her marble halls.

There were pale cheeks and troubled eyes,
   And steps of hurrying feet,
Where the Zambra's (3) notes were wont to rise
   Along the sunny street.

It was an hour of fear and grief
   On bright Valencia's shore,
For death was busy with her chief,
   The noble Campeador.

The Moor-king's barks were on the deep,
   With sounds and signs of war,
For the Cid was passing to his sleep,
   In the silent Alcazar.

No moan was heard through the towers of state,
   No weeper's aspect seen,
But by the couch Ximena sate,
   With pale yet steadfast mien. (4)

Stillness was round the leader's bed,
   Warriors stood mournful nigh,
And banners, o'er his glorious head,
   Were drooping heavily.

And feeble grew the conquering hand,
   And cold the valiant breast;
—He had fought the battles of the land,
   And his hour was come to rest.

What said the Ruler of the field?
   —His voice is faint and low;
The breeze that creeps o'er his lance and shield
   Hath louder accents now.

" Raise ye no cry, and let no moan
   Be made when I depart;
The Moor must hear no dirge's tone,
   Be ye of mighty heart!

" Let the cymbal-clash and the trumpet-strain
   From your walls ring far and shrill,
And fear ye not, for the saints of Spain
   Shall grant you victory still.

' And gird my form with mail-array,
   And set me on my steed,
So go ye forth on your funeral-way,
   And God shall give you speed.

" Go with the dead in the front of war
   All arm'd with sword and helm,
And march by the camp of King Bucar
   For the good Castilian realm.

" And let me slumber in the soil
   Which gave my fathers birth;
I have closed my day of battle-toil,
   And my course is done on earth."

—Now wave, ye glorious banners, wave! (5)
   Through the lattice a wind sweeps by,
And the arms, o'er the death-bed of the brave
   Send forth a hollow sigh

Now wave, ye banners of many a fight!
   As the fresh wind o'er you sweeps;
The wind and the banners fall hush'd as night
   The Campeador—he sleeps!

Sound the battle-horn on the breeze of morn,
   And swell out the trumpet's blast,
Till the notes prevail o'er the voice of wail,
   For the noble Cid hath pass'd!

---

### THE CID'S FUNERAL PROCESSION.

The Moor had beleaguer'd Valencia's towers,
And lances gleam'd up through her citron-bowers,
And the tents of the desert had girt her plain,
And camels were trampling the vines of Spain;
         For the Cid was gone to rest.

There were men from wilds where the death-wind
      sweeps,
There were spears from hills where the lion sleeps,
There were bows from the sands where the ostrich
      runs,
For the shrill horn of Afric had call'd her sons
         To the battles of the West.

The midnight bell, o'er the dim seas heard
Like the roar of waters, the air had stirr'd;
The stars were shining o'er tower and wave,
And the camp lay hush'd like a wizard's cave;
         But the Christians woke that night.

They rear'd the Cid on his barbed steed,
Like a warrior mail'd for the hour of need,
And they fix'd the sword in the cold right hand
Which had fought so well for his fathers' land,
         And the shield from his neck hung bright

There was arming heard in Valencia's halls,
There was vigil kept on the rampart walls;
Stars had not faded, nor clouds turn'd red,
When the knights had girded the noble dead,
         And the burial-train moved out.

With a measured pace, as the pace of one,
Was the still death-march of the host begun;
With a silent step went the cuirass'd bands,
Like a lion's tread on the burning sands,
    And they gave no battle-shout.

When the first went forth it was midnight deep,
In heaven was the moon, in the camp was sleep,
When the last through the city's gates had gone,
O'er tent and rampart the bright day shone,
    With a sun-burst from the sea.

There were knights five hundred went arm'd before,
And Bermudez the Cid's green standard bore; (6)
To its last fair field, with the break of morn,
Was the glorious banner in silence borne,
    On the glad wind streaming free.

And the Campeador came stately then,
Like a leader circled with steel clad men!
The helmet was down o'er the face of the dead
But his steed went proud, by a warrior led,
    For he knew that the Cid was there.

He was there, the Cid, with his own good sword,
And Ximena following her noble lord;
Her eye was solemn her step was slow,
But there rose not a sound of war or woe,
    Not a whisper on the air.

The halls in Valencia were still and lone,
The churches were empty, the masses done;
There was not a voice through the wide streets far,
Nor a foot-fall heard in the Alcazar,
    —So the burial-train moved out.

With a measured pace, as the pace of one,
Was the still death-march of the host begun;
With a silent step went the cuirass'd bands,
Like a lion's tread on the burning sands;
    —And they gave no battle-shout.

But the deep hills peal'd with a cry ere long,
When the Christians burst on the Paynim throng!
With a sudden flash of the lance and spear,
And a charge of the war-steed in full career,
    It was Alvar Fañez came! (7)

He that was wrapt with no funeral shroud,
Had pass'd before, like a threatening cloud!
And the storm rush'd down on the tented plain,
And the Archer-Queen (8) with her hands lay slain,
    For the Cid upheld his fame.

Then a terror fell on the King Bucar,
And the Libyan kings who had join'd his war;
And their hearts grew heavy, and died away,
And their hands could not wield an assagay,
    For the dreadful things they saw!

For it seem'd where Minaya his onset made,
There were seventy thousand knights array'd,
All white as the snow on Neyada's steep,
And they came like the foam of a roaring deep;
    —'Twas a sight of fear and awe!

And the crested form of a warrior tall,
With a sword of fire, went before them all;
With a sword of fire, and a banner pale,
And a blood-red cross on his shadowy mail,
    He rode in the battle's van!

There was fear in the path of his dim white horse,
There was death in the Giant-warrior's course!
Where his banner stream'd with its ghostly light,
Where his sword blazed out, there was hurrying
flight.
    For it seem'd not the sword of man!

The field and the river grew darkly red,
As the kings and leaders of Afric fled;
There was work for the men of the Cid that day!
—They were weary at eve, when they ceased to
slay,
    As reapers whose task is done!

The kings and the leaders of Afric fled!
The sails of their galleys in haste were spread;



But the sea had its share of the Paynim-slain,
And the bow of the desert was broke in Spain;
    —So the Cid to his grave pass'd on!

## THE CID'S RISING.

'Twas the deep mid-watch of the silent night,
    And Leon in slumber lay,
When a sound went forth, in rushing might,
    Like an army on its way! (9)
    In the stillness of the hour,
    When the dreams of sleep have power,
    And men forget the day.

Through the dark and lonely streets it went,
    Till the slumberers woke in dread;
The sound of a passing armament,
    With the charger's stony tread.
    There was heard no trumpet's peal,
    But the heavy tramp of steel,
    As a host's, to combat led.

Through the dark and lonely streets it pass'd,
    And the hollow pavement rang,
And the towers, as with a sweeping blast,
    Rock'd to the stormy clang!
    But the march of the viewless train
    Went on to a royal fane,
    Where a priest his night-hymn sang.

There was knocking that shook the marble floor,
    And a voice at the gate, which said—
" That the Cid Ruy Diez, the Campeador,
    Was there in his arms array'd;
    And that with him, from the tomb,
    Had the Count Gonzalez come,
    With a host, uprisen to aid!

" And they came for the buried king that lay
    At rest in that ancient fane;
For he must be arm'd on the battle-day,
    With them to deliver Spain!"
    —Then the march went sounding on,
    And the Moors, by noontide sun,
    Were dust on Tolosa's plain.

## NOTES

### NOTE 1.

Bivar, the supposed birth-place of the Cid, was a castle, about two leagues from Burgos.

### NOTE 2.

Tornaba la cabeza, estabalos catando:
Vio puertas abiertas, e uzos sin canados,
Alcnodaras vacias, sin pielles e sin mantns;
E sin falcones, e sin adtores mudados.
Sospiro mio Cid.        *Poem of the Cid.*

### NOTE 3.

The zambra, a Moorish dance. When Valencia was taken by the Cid, many of the Moorish families chose to remain there, and reside under his government.

### NOTE 4.

The calm fortitude of Ximena is frequently alluded to, in the romances.

### NOTE 5.

Banderas antiguas, tristes
De victorias en tiempo amadas,
Tremolando estan al viento
Y lloran aunque no hablan, &c.

Herder's translation of these romances (Der Cid, nach Spanischen Romanzen besungen) are remarkable for their spirit and scrupulous fidelity.

### NOTE 6.

" And while they stood there, they saw the Cid Ruy Diez coming up with three hundred knights; for he had not been in the battle, and they knew his green pennon."—*Southey's Chronicle of the Cid.*

### NOTE 7.

Alvar Fanez Minaya, one of the Cid's most distinguished warriors.

Note 8.
———— *The archer-queen.*

A Moorish Amazon, who, with a band of female warriors, accompanied King Bucar from Africa. Her arrows were so unerring, that she obtained the name of the Star of archers.

Una Mora muy gallarda,
Gran maestra en el tirar
Con saetas del Aljava,
De los arcos de Turquia
Estrella era nombrada,
Por la destreza que avia
En el herir de la Xara.

Note 9.
See Southey's Chronicle of the Cid, p. 368

---

# THE HEART OF BRUCE

IN

## MELROSE ABBEY.

Heart! that didst press forward still,*
Where the trumpet's note rang shrill,
Where the knightly swords were crossing,
And the plumes like sea-foam tossing,
Leader of the charging spear,
Fiery heart!—and liest thou *here?*
May this narrow spot inurn
Aught that so could beat and burn?

Heart! that lovedst the clarion's blast,
Silent is thy place at last;
Silent,—save when early bird
Sings where once the mass was heard;
Silent,—save when breeze's moan
Comes through flowers or fretted stone;
And the wild-rose waves around thee,
And the long dark grass hath bound thee,—
—Sleep'st thou, as the swain might sleep,
In his nameless valley deep?

No! brave heart!—though cold and lone,
Kingly power is yet thine own!
Feel I not thy spirit brood
O'er the whispering solitude?
Lo! at one high thought of thee,
Fast they rise, the bold, the free,
Sweeping past thy lowly bed,
With a mute, yet stately tread,
Shedding their pale armour's light
Forth upon the breathless night,
Bending every warlike plume
In the prayer o'er saintly tomb.

Is the noble Douglas nigh,
Arm'd to follow thee, or die?
Now, true heart, as thou wert wont,
Pass thou to the peril's front!
Where the banner-spear is gleaming,
And the battle's red wine streaming,
Till the Paynim quail before thee,
Till the cross wave proudly o'er thee;—
—Dreams! the falling of a leaf
Wins me from their splendours brief;
Dreams, yet bright ones! scorn them not,
Thou that seek'st the holy spot;
Nor, amidst its lone domain,
Call the faith in relics vain!

---

## NATURE'S FAREWELL.

The beautiful is vanished, and returns not.
*Coleridge's Wallenstein.*

A youth rode forth from his childhood's home,
Through the crowded paths of the world to roam,
And the green leaves whisper'd, as he pass'd,
"Wherefore, thou dreamer, away so fast?

* "Now pass thou forward, as thou wert wont, and Douglas will follow thee or die!" With these words Douglas threw from him the heart of Bruce, into mid-battle against the Moors of Spain.

"Knew'st thou with what thou art parting here
Long wouldst thou linger in doubt and fear;
Thy heart's light laughter, thy sunny hours,
Thou hast left in our shades with the spring's wild flowers.

"Under the arch by our mingling made,
Thou and thy brother have gaily play'd;
Ye may meet again where ye roved of yore,
But as ye *have* met there—oh! never more!"

On rode the youth—and the boughs among
Thus the free birds o'er his pathway sung:
"Wherefore so fast unto life away?
Thou art leaving for ever thy joy in our lay!

"Thou mayst come to the summer woods again,
And thy heart have no echo to greet their strain;
Afar from the foliage its love will dwell—
A change must pass o'er thee—farewell, farewell!"

On rode the youth;—and the founts and streams
Thus mingled a voice with his joyous dreams:
—"We have been thy playmates through many a day,
Wherefore thus leave us?—oh! yet delay!

"Listen but once to the sound of our mirth!
For thee 'tis a melody passing from earth.
Never again wilt thou find in its flow,
The peace it could once on thy heart bestow.

"Thou wilt visit the scenes of thy childhood's glee,
With the breath of the world on thy spirit free;
Passion and sorrow its depths will have stirr'd,
And the singing of waters be vainly heard.

"Thou wilt bear in our gladsome laugh no part—
What should it do for a burning heart?
Thou wilt bring to the banks of our freshest rill,
Thirst which no fountain on earth may still.

"Farewell!—when thou comest again to thine own,
Thou wilt miss from our music its loveliest tone;
Mournfully true is the tale we tell—
Yet on, fiery dreamer! farewell, farewell!"

And a something of gloom on his spirit weigh'd,
As he caught the last sounds of his native shade;
But he knew not, till many a bright spell broke,
How deep were the oracles Nature spoke!

---

## THE LYRE'S LAMENT.

A large lyre hung in an opening of the rock, and gave forth a melancholy music to the wind—but no human being was to be seen.
*Salathiel.*

A deep toned Lyre hung murmuring
  To the wild wind of the sea:
"O melancholy wind," it sigh'd,
  "What would thy breath with me?

"Thou canst not wake the spirit
  That in me slumbering lies,
Thou strikest not forth th' electric fire
  Of buried melodies.

"Wind of the dark sea-waters!
  Thou dost but sweep my strings
Into wild gusts of mournfulness,
  With the rushing of thy wings.

"But the spell—the gift—the lightning—
  Within my frame conceal'd,
Must I moulder on the rock away,
  With their triumphs unreveal'd?

"I have power, high power, for freedom
  To wake the burning soul!
I have sounds that through the ancient hills
  Like a torrent's voice might roll

"I have pealing notes of victory
  That might welcome kings from war;
I have rich deep tones to send the wail
  For a hero's death afar.

"I have chords to lift the pæan
  From the temple to the sky,
Full as the forest-unisons
  When sweeping winds are high.

'And Love—for Love's lone sorrow
  I have accents that might swell
Through the summer-air with the rose's breath
  Or the violet's faint farewell:

"Soft—spiritual—mournful—
  Sighs in each note enshrined—
But who shall call that sweetness forth?
  *Thou* canst not, ocean-wind!

"I pass without my glory,
  Forgotten I decay—
Where is the touch to give me life?
  —Wild fitful wind, away!"

So sigh'd the broken music
  That in gladness had no part—
How like art thou, neglected Lyre,
  To many a human heart!

## THE WOUNDED EAGLE.

Eagle! this is not thy sphere:
Warrior bird! what seek'st thou here?
Wherefore by the fountain's brink
Doth thy royal pinion sink?
Wherefore on the violet's bed
Lay'st thou thus thy drooping head?
Thou, that hold'st the blast in scorn,
Thou that wear'st the wings of morn

Eagle! wilt thou not arise?
Look upon thine own bright skies?
Lift thy glance! the fiery sun
There his pride of place hath won!
And the mountain-lark is there,
And sweet sound hath fill'd the air;
Hast thou left that realm on high?
—Oh! it can be but to die!

Eagle, Eagle! thou hast bow'd
From thine empire o'er the cloud!
Thou, that hadst ethereal birth,
Thou hast stoop'd too near the earth,
And the hunter's shaft hath found thee,
And the toils of death have bound thee!
—Wherefore didst thou leave thy place,
Creature of a kingly race?

Wert thou weary of thy throne?
Was thy sky's dominion lone?
Chill and lone it well might be,
Yet that mighty wing was free!

Now the chain is o'er it cast,
From thy heart the blood flows fast,
—Woe for gifted souls and high!
Is not such *their* destiny?

## THE NIGHTINGALE'S DEATH-SONG.

Willst du nach den Nachtigallen fragen,
Die mit seelenvollen Melodie
Dich entzückten in des Lenzes Tagen?
—Nur so lang sie liebten, waren sie.

*Schiller.*

Mournfully, sing mournfully,
  And die away, my heart!
The rose, the glorious rose is gone,
  And I, too, will depart.

The skies have lost their splendour,
  The waters changed their tone,
And wherefore, in the faded world,
  Should music linger on?

Where is the golden sunshine,
  And where the flower-cup's glow?
And where the joy of the dancing leaves,
  And the fountain's laughing flow?

A voice, in every whisper
  Of the wave, the bough, the air,
Comes asking for the beautiful,
  And moaning, "Where, oh! where?"

Tell of the brightness parted,
  Thou bee, thou lamb at play!
Thou lark, in thy victorious mirth
  —Are ye, too, pass'd away?

Mournfully, sing mournfully!
  The royal rose is gone.
Melt from the woods, my spirit, melt
  In one deep farewell tone!

Not so!—swell forth triumphantly,
  The full, rich, fervent strain!
Hence with young love and life I go,
  In the summer's joyous train.

With sunshine, with sweet odour,
  With every precious thing,
Upon the last warm southern breeze
  My soul its flight shall wing.

Alone I shall not linger,
  When the days of hope are past,
To watch the fall of leaf by leaf,
  To wait the rushing blast.

Triumphantly, triumphantly!
  Sing to the woods, I go!
For me, perchance, in other lands,
  The glorious rose may blow.

The sky's transparent azure,
  And the greensward's violet breath,
And the dance of light leaves in the wind,
  May there know naught of death.

No more, no more sing mournfully!
  Swell high, then break, my heart!
With love, the spirit of the woods,
  With summer I depart!

## THE DIVER.

They learn in suffering what they teach in song.

Thou hast been where the rocks of coral grow,
  Thou hast fought with eddying waves;—
Thy cheek is pale, and thy heart beats low,
  Thou searcher of ocean's caves!

Thou hast look'd on the gleaming wealth of old,
  And wrecks where the brave have striven;
The deep is a strong and a fearful hold,
  But thou its bar hast riven!

A wild and weary life is thine,
  A wasting task and lone;
Though treasure-grots for thee may shine,
  To all besides unknown!

A weary life! but a swift decay
  Soon, soon shall set thee free;
Thou'rt passing fast from thy toils away,
  Thou wrestler with the sea!

In thy dim eye, on thy hollow cheek,
  Well are the death-signs read—
Go! for the pearl in its cavern seek,
  Ere hope and power be fled!

And bright in beauty's coronal
  That glistening gem shall be;
A star to all in the festive hall—
  But who will think on *thee?*

None!—as it gleams from the queen-like head,
  Not one 'midst throngs will say
" A life hath been like a rain-drop shed,
  For that pale quivering ray."

Woe for the wealth thus dearly bought!
  —And are not those like thee,
Who win for earth the gems of thought?
  O wrestler with the sea!

Down to the gulfs of the soul they go,
  Where the passion-fountains burn,
Gathering the jewels far below
  From many a buried urn:

Wringing from lava-veins the fire,
  That o'er bright words is pour'd;
Learning deep sounds, to make the lyre
  A spirit in each chord.

But, oh! the price of bitter tears,
  Paid for the lonely power
That throws at last, o'er desert years,
  A darkly-glorious dower!

Like flower-seeds, by the wild wind spread,
  So radiant thoughts are strew'd;
—The soul whence those high gifts are shed,
  May faint in solitude!

And who will think, when the strain is sung,
  Till a thousand hearts are stirr'd,
What life-drops, from the minstrel wrung,
  Have gush'd with every word?

None, none!—his treasures live like thine,
  *He* strives and dies like thee;
—Thou, that hast been to the pearl's dark shrine
  O wrestler with the sea!

---

## TRIUMPHANT MUSIC.

Tacete, tacete, O vocal trionfanti!
Risvegliate in vano 'l cor che non puo liberarsi.

WHEREFORE and whither bear'st thou up my spirit,
  On eagle wings, through every plume that thrill?
It hath no crown of victory to inherit—
  Be still, triumphant harmony! be still!

Thine are no sounds for earth, thus proudly swell-
    ing
  Into rich floods of joy;—it is but pain
To mount so high, yet find on high no dwelling,
  To sink so fast, so heavily again!

No sounds for earth?—Yes, to young chieftain
    dying
  On his own battle-field, at set of sun,
With his freed country's banner o'er him flying,
  Well mightst thou speak of fame's high guerdon
    won.

No sounds for earth?—Yes, for the martyr leading
  Unto victorious death serenely on,
For patriot by his rescued altars bleeding,
  Thou hast a voice in each majestic tone.

But speak not thus to one whose heart is beating
  Against life's narrow bound, in conflict vain!
For power, for joy, high hope, and rapturous greet-
    ing,
    Thou wakest lone thirst—be hush'd, exulting
    strain!

Be hush'd, or breathe of grief!—of exile yearnings
  Under the willows of the stranger-shore;
Breathe of the soul's untold and restless burnings,
  For looks, tones, footsteps, that return no more.

Breathe of deep love—a lonely vigil keeping
  Through the night-hours, o'er wasted wealth to
    pine;
Rich thoughts and sad, like faded rose-leaves
    heaping,
  In the shut heart, at once a tomb and shrine.

Or pass as if thy spirit-notes came sighing
  From worlds beneath some blue Elysian sky;
Breathe of repose, the pure, the bright, th' undy-
    ing—
    Of joy no more—bewildering harmony!

---

## THE SOUND OF THE SEA.

THOU art sounding on, thou mighty sea,
  For ever and the same!
The ancient rocks yet ring to thee,
  Those thunders naught can tame.

Oh! many a glorious voice is gone
  From the rich bowers of earth,
And hush'd is many a lovely one
  Of mournfulness or mirth.

The Dorian flute, that sigh'd of yore
  Along the wave, is still;
The harp of Judah peals no more
  On Zion's awful hill.

And Memnon's lyre hath lost the chord
  That breathed the mystic tone,
And the songs at Rome's high triumphs pour'd,
  Are with her eagles flown.

And mute the Moorish horn, that rang
  O'er stream and mountain free,
And the hymn the leagued Crusaders sang,
  Hath died in Galilee.

But thou art swelling on, thou deep,
  Through many an olden clime,
Thy billowy anthem, ne'er to sleep
  Until the close of time.

Thou liftest up thy solemn voice
  To every wind and sky,
And all our earth's green shores rejoice
  In that one harmony.

It fills the noontide's calm profound,
  The sunset's heaven of gold;
And the still midnight hears the sound
  Even as first it roll'd.

Let there be silence, deep and strange
  Where sceptred cities rose!
*Thou* speak'st of one who doth not change—
  —So may our hearts repose.

---

## THE FUNERAL GENIUS.

### AN ANCIENT STATUE.

THOU should'st be look'd on when the starlight
  falls
Through the blue stillness of the summer air,
Not by the torch-fire wavering on the walls;
It has too fitful and too wild a glare!
And thou!—thy rest, the soft, the lovely, seems
To ask light steps, that will not break its dreams.

Flowers are upon thy brow; for so the dead
Were crown'd of old, with pale spring flowers like
  these:
Sleep on thine eye hath sunk; yet softly shed,
As from the wing of some faint southern breeze;
And the pine-boughs o'ershadow thee with gloom,
Which of the grove seems breathing—not the
  tomb.

They fear'd not death, whose calm and gracious
    thought
Of the last hour, hath settled thus in thee !
They who thy wreath of pallid roses wrought,
And laid thy head against the forest-tree,
As that of one by music's dreamy close,
On the wood-violets lull'd to deep repose.

They fear'd not death !—yet who shall say his
    touch
Thus lightly falls on gentle things and fair ?
Doth he bestow, or will he leave so much
Of tender beauty as thy features wear !
Thou sleeper of the bower ! on whose young eyes
So still a night, a night ot summer, lies !

Had they seen aught like thee ?—Did some fair
    boy
Thus, with his graceful hair, before them rest ?
—His graceful hair no more to wave in joy,
But drooping as with heavy dews oppress'd !
And his eye veil'd so softly by its fringe,
And his lip faded to the white-rose tinge !

Oh ! happy, if to them the one dread hour
Made known its lessons from a brow like thine !
If all their knowledge of the spoiler's power
Came by a look, so tranquilly divine !
—Let him, who *thus* hath seen the lovely part,
Hold well that image to his thoughtful heart !

But thou, fair slumberer ! was there less of woe,
Or love, or terror, in the days of old,
That men pour'd out their gladdening spirit's
    flow,
Like sunshine, on the desolate and cold,
And gave thy semblance to the shadowy king
Who for deep souls had then a deeper sting ?

In the dark bosom of the earth they laid
Far more than we—for loftier faith is ours !
*Their* gems were lost in ashes—yet they made
The grave a place of beauty and of flowers
With fragrant wreaths, and summer boughs ar-
    ray'd,
And lovely sculpture gleaming through the shade.

Is it for *us* a darker gloom to shed
O'er its dim precincts ?—do we not intrust
But for a time its chambers with our dead,
And strew immortal seed upon the dust ?
—Why should *we* dwell on that which lies be-
    neath,
When living light hath touch'd the brow of death ?

---

## TROUBADOUR SONG.

The warrior cross'd the ocean's foam,
  For the stormy fields of war—
The maid was left in a smiling home,
  ·And a sunny land afar.

*His* voice was heard where javelin showers
  Pour'd on the steel-clad line ;
*Her* step was 'midst the summer flowers,
  Her seat beneath the vine.

His shield was cleft, his lance was riven,
  And the red blood stain'd his crest ;
While she—the gentlest wind of heaven
  Might scarcely fan her breast.

Yet a thousand arrows pass'd him by,
  And again he cross'd the seas ;
But she frail died, as roses die
  That perish with a breeze.

As roses die, when the blast is come,
  For all things bright and fair—
There was death within the smiling home,
  How had death found her there ?

---

## OWEN GLENDWYER'S WAR-SONG.

Saw ye the blazing star ?
The heavens look down on freedom's war,
  And light her torch on high :
Bright on the dragon crest
It tells that glory's wing shall rest,
  When warriors meet to die !
Let earth's pale tyrants read despair
  And vengeance in its flame,
Hail ye, my bards ! the omen fair
  Of conquest and of fame,
And swell the rushing mountain air,
  With songs to Glendwyer's name

At the dead hour of night,
Mark'd ye how each majestic height
  Burn'd in its awful beams !
Red shone th' eternal snows,
And all the land, as bright it rose,
  Was full of glorious dreams.
Oh ! eagles of the battles, rise !
  The hope of Gwynedd wakes—
It is your banner in the skies,
  Through each dark cloud that breaks
And mantles with triumphant dyes,
  Your thousand hills and lakes !

A sound is on the breeze,
A murmur, as of swelling seas !
  The Saxon's on his way !
Lo ! spear, and shield, and lance,
From Deva's waves with lightning glance
  Reflected to the day.
But who the torrent-wave compels
  A conqueror's chains to bear ?
Let those who wake the soul that dwells
  On our free winds, beware !
The greenest and the loveliest dells
  May be the lion's lair.

Of us *they* told the seers
And monarch-bards of elder years,
  Who walk'd on earth as powers ;
And in their burning strains,
A spell of might and mystery reigns,
  To guard our mountain-towers.
—In Snowdon's caves a prophet lay,
  Before his gifted sight
The march of ages pass'd away,
  With hero-footsteps bright,
But proudest, in that long array
  Was Glendwyer's path of light.

---

## THE PENITENT'S OFFERING.

[St. Luke, vii. 37, 38.]

---

Thou that with pallid cheek,
  And eyes in sadness meek,
And faded locks that humbly swept the ground,
  From their long wanderings won,
  Before the all-healing Son,
Didst bow thee to the earth, oh, lost and found !

  When thou would'st bathe his feet,
  With odours richly sweet,
And many a shower of woman's burning tear,
  And dry them with that hair,
  Brought low the dust to wear
From the crowded beauty of its festal year.

  Did he reject thee then,
  While the sharp scorn of men
On thy once bright and stately head was cast
  No, from the Saviour's mien,
  A solemn light serene,
Bore to thy soul the peace of God at last.

  For thee, their smiles no more
  Familiar faces wore,

Voices, once kind, had learn'd the stranger's tone,
    Who raised thee up and bound
    Thy silent spirit's wound?
He, from all guilt the stainless, He alone!

    But which, oh, erring child!
    From home so long beguiled,
Which of thine offerings won those words of
    Heaven,
    That o'er the bruised reed,
    Condemn'd of earth to bleed,
In music pass'd, "Thy sins are all forgiven?"

    Was it that perfume fraught
    With balm and incense, brought
From the sweet woods of Araby the blest?
    Or that fast flowing rain
    Of tears, which not in vain
To Him who scorn'd not tears, thy woes confess'd?

    No, not by these restored
    Unto thy Father's board,
Thy peace, that kindled joy in Heaven, was made;
    But costlier in his eyes,
    By that blest sacrifice,
Thy heart, thy full deep heart, before Him laid.

---

## THE WISH

"Holy hath been our converse, gentle friend!
Full of high thoughts breathing of heavenward
    hope,
Deepen'd by tenderest memories of the dead;
Therefore, beyond the grave, I surely deem
That we shall meet again."

    Come to me, when my soul
Hath but a few dim hours to linger here;
When earthly chains are as a shrivell'd scroll,
Oh! let me feel thy presence! be but near!

    That I may look once more
Into thine eyes, which never changed for me;
That I may speak to thee of that bright shore,
Where, with our treasure, we have yearn'd to be.

    Thou friend of many days!
Of sadness and of joy, of home and hearth!
Will not thy spirit aid me then to r. ise
The trembling pinion of my hope from earth?

    By every solemn thought
Which on our hearts hath sunk, in years gone by,
From the deep voices of the mountains caught,
O'er all the adoring silence of the sky;

    By every lofty theme,
Wherein, in low-toned reverence, we have spoken!
By our communion in each fervent dream
That sought from realms beyond the grave, a to-
    ken;

    And by our tears for those
Whose loss had touch'd our world with hues of
    death;
And by the hopes that with their dust repose,
As flowers await the south wind's vernal breath:

    Come to me in that day—
The one—the sever'd from all days!—O Friend!
Even then, if human thought may then have sway
My soul with thine shall yet rejoice to blend.

    Nor then, nor *there* alone:
I ask my heart if all indeed must die;
All that of holiest feelings it hath known?
And my heart's voice replies—*Eternity!*

## THE WELCOME TO DEATH

    "Shall I abide
In this dull world?
    I have
Immortal longings in me!"
    *Antony and Cleopatra.*

Thou art welcome, O thou warning voice,
    My soul hath pined for thee;
Thou art welcome as sweet sounds from shore,
    To wanderer on the sea.
I hear thee in the rustling woods,
    In the sighing vernal airs;
Thou call'st me from the lonely earth,
    With a deeper tone than theirs.

The lonely earth! since kindred steps
    From its green paths are fled,
A dimness and a hush have fall'n
    O'er all its beauty spread.
The silence of the unanswering soul
    Is on me and around;
My heart hath echoes but for *thee*,
    Thou still small warning sound!

Voice after voice hath died away,
    Once in my dwelling heard,
Sweet household name by name hath changed
    To grief's forbidden word!
From dreams of night on each I call,
    Each of the far removed;
And waken to my own wild cry,
    Where are ye, my beloved?

Ye left me! and earth's flowers grew fill'd
    With records of the past,
And stars pour'd down another light
    Than o'er my youth they cast:
The skylark sings not as he sang
    When ye were by my side,
And mournful tones are in the wind,
    Unheard before ye died!

Thou art welcome, O thou summons!
    Why should the last remain?
What eye can reach my heart of hearts,
    Bearing in light again?
Even could this be—too much of fear
    O'er love would *now* be thrown—
Away, away! from time, from change,
    To dwell amidst mine own!

---

## THE VOICE OF MUSIC

"Striking the electric chain wherewith we are darkly bound."
    *Childe Harold*

Whence is the might of thy master spell?
    Speak to me, voice of sweet sound, and tell
How canst thou wake, by one gentle breath,
    Passionate visions of love and death!

How call'st thou back, with a note, a sigh,
    Words and low tones from the days gone by—
A sunny glance, or a fond farewell?
    Speak to me, voice of sweet sound, and tell.

What is thy power, from the soul's deep spring
    In sudden gushes the tears to bring;
Even 'midst the swells of thy festal glee,
    Fountains of sorrow are stirr'd by thee!

Vain are those tears!—vain and fruitless all—
    Showers that refresh not, yet still must fall
For a purer bliss while the full heart burns,
    For a brighter home while the spirit yearns.

Something of mystery there surely dwells,
  Waiting thy touch, in our bosom-cells;
Something that finds not its answer here—
  A chain to be clasp'd in another sphere.

Therefore a current of sadness deep,
  Through the stream of thy triumphs is heard to
      sweep,
Like a moan of the breeze through a summer sky—
  Like a name of the dead when the wine foams
      high!

Yet speak to me still, though thy tones be fraught
  With vain remembrance and troubled thought ;—
Speak ! for thou tellest my soul that its birth
  Links it with regions more bright than earth

----

## SWISS HOME-SICKNESS.

TRANSLATED FROM THE LAST OF THE MELODIES
SUNG BY THE TYROLESE FAMILY.

"Hers mein Herz, warum so traurig," &c.

WHEREFORE so sad and faint, my heart ?
  The stranger's land is fair ;
Yet weary, weary still thou art—
  What find'st thou wanting there ?

What wanting ?—all, oh ! all I love !
  Am I not lonely here ?
Through a fair land in sooth I rove
  Yet what like home is dear?

My home ! oh ! thither would I fly
  Where the free air is sweet,
My father's voice, my mother's eye
  My own wild hills to greet.

My hills with all their soaring steeps,
  With all their glaciers bright,
Where in his joy the chamois leaps,
  Mocking the hunter's might.

Oh ! but to hear the herd-bell's sound,
  When shepherds lead the way
Up the high Alps, and children bound,
  And not a lamb will stay !

Oh ! but to climb the uplands free,
  And, where the pure streams foam,
By the blue shining lake, to see,
  Once more, my hamlet-home !

Here, no familiar look I trace ;
  I touch no friendly hand ;
No child laughs kindly in my face—
  As in my own bright land !—

----

## MONUMENTAL INSCRIPTION

Elle etait du monde, ou les plus belles choses
  Ont le pire destin ;
Et Rose, elle a dure, ce que durent les roses,
  L'espace d'un matin.

EARTH ! guard what here we lay in holy trust ;
  That which hath left our home a darken'd place,
Wanting the form, the smile, now veil'd with dust,
  The light departed with our loveliest face.
Yet from thy bonds undying hope springs free—
We have but *lent* our beautiful to thee.

But thou, oh Heaven ! keep ! keep what *Thou* hast
    taken,
  And with our treasure keep our hearts on high,
The spirit meek, and yet by pain unshaken,
  The faith, the love, the lofty constancy,
Guide us where *these* are with our sister flown—
They were of Thee, and thou hast claim'd thine
    own !

----



## A THOUGHT OF THE ROSE.

Rosa, Rosa ! per che sulla tua belta
Sempre e scritta questa parola.
                              *Morte.*

How much of memory dwells amidst thy bloom,
  *Rose !* ever wearing beauty for thy dower !
The bridal day—the festival—the tomb— ,
  Thou hast thy part in each, thou stateliest
      flower !

Therefore with thy soft breath come floating by
  A thousand images of love and grief,
Dreams, fill'd with tokens of mortality,
  Deep thoughts of all things beautiful and brief.

Not such thy spells o'er those that hail'd thee first
  In the clear light of Eden's golden day !
*There* thy rich leaves to crimson glory burst,
  Link'd with no dim remembrance of decay.

Rose ! for the banquet gather'd, and the bier ;
  Rose ! colour'd now by human hope or pain ;
Surely where death is not—nor change, nor fear,
  Yet may we meet thee, Joy's own flower, again

----

## STANZAS.

CROWN ye the brave ! crown ye the brave !
  As through your streets they ride,
And the sunbeams dance on the polish'd arms
  Of the warriors, side by side ;
Shower on them your sweetest flowers,
  Let the air ring with their praise,
For they come from a far and foreign land,
  The standard of war to raise !

Crown ye the brave ! crown ye the brave !
  They have heard with proud disdain,
That a tyrant seeks your beautiful land
  To bind in his iron chain ;
And now they come with hearts and arms,
  To the land that will be free,
With their blood to give in the cause of those
  Who fight for their liberty !

Crown ye the brave ! crown ye the brave !
  As they wend them from the shore,
For many of those who ride gaily now,
  Ye never shall look on more ;
Amid the battle's fiercest rage,
  Unnoticed and unblest ;
Woe for the forms on the bloody field,
  That will sink to endless rest.

----

## TO THE SEA.

THOU glorious sea ! more pleasing far
  When all thy waters are at rest,
And noonday sun, or midnight star
  Is shining on thy waveless breast.

More pleasing far, than when the wings
  Of stormy winds are o'er thee spread,
And every billowy mountain flings
  Aloft to heaven its foaming head.

Yet is the very tempest dear,
  Whose mighty voice but tells of thee
For, wild, or calm, or far or near,
  I love thee still, thou glorious sea !

## THE VOICE OF SPRING.

I come! I come! ye have call'd me long,
I come o'er the mountains with light and song!
Ye may trace my step o'er the wakening earth,
By the winds which tell of the violet's birth
By the primrose stars in the shadowy grass,
By the green leaves opening as I pass.

I have breathed on the south, and the chestnut
　　flowers
By thousands have burst from the forest-bowers,
And the ancient graves, and the fallen fanes,
Are veil'd with wreaths on Italian plains;
— But it is not for me, in my hour of bloom,
To speak of the ruin or the tomb!

I have look'd o'er the hills of the stormy north,
And the larch has hung all his tassels forth,
The fisher is out on the sunny sea,
And the reindeer bounds o'er the pastures free,
And the pine has a fringe of softer green,
And the moss looks bright, where my foot hath
　　been.

I have sent through the wood-paths a glowing
　　sigh,
And call'd out each voice of the deep-blue sky;
From the night-bird's lay through the starry time,
In the groves of the soft Hesperian clime,
To the swan's wild note by the Iceland lakes,
When the dark fir-branch into verdure breaks.

From the streams and founts I have loosed the
　　chain,
They are sweeping on to the silvery main,
They are flashing down from the mountain brows,
They are flinging spray o'er the forest-boughs,
They are bursting fresh from their sparry caves,
And the earth resounds with the joy of waves!

Come forth, O ye children of gladness, come!
Where the violets lie may be now your home.
Ye of the rose lip and the dew-bright eye,
And the boundless footsteps to meet me, fly!
With the lyre, and the wreath, and the joyous
　　lay,
Come forth to the sunshine, I may not stay.

Away from the dwellings of care-worn men,
The waters are sparkling in grove and glen!
Away from the chamber and sullen hearth,
The young leaves are dancing in breezy mirth!
Their light stems thrill to the wild-wood strains,
And youth is abroad in my green domains.

But ye—ye are changed since ye met me last!
There is something bright from your features
　　pass'd!
There is that come over your brow and eye,
Which speaks of a world where the flowers must
　　die!
—Ye smile! but your smile hath a dimness yet—
Oh! what have ye look'd on since last we met?

Ye are changed, ye are changed!—and I see not
　　here
All whom I saw in the vanish'd year;
There were graceful heads with their ringlets
　　bright,
Which toss'd in the breeze with a play of light,
There were eyes in whose glistening laughter
　　lay
No faint remembrance of dull decay!

There were steps that flew o'er the cowslip's
　　head,
As if for a banquet all earth was spread;
There were voices that rang through the sapphire
　　sky,
And had not a sound of mortality!
Are they gone? is their mirth from the mountains
　　pass'd?
—Ye have look'd on death since ye met me last!

I know whence the shadow comes o'er you now,
Ye have strewn the dust on the sunny brow!
Ye have given the lovely to earth's embrace,
She hath taken the fairest of beauty's race,
With their laughing eyes and their festal crown,
They are gone from among you in silence down.

They are gone from among you, the young and
　　fair,
Ye have lost the gleam of their shining hair!
—But I know of a land where there falls no
　　blight,
I shall find them there, with their eyes of light!
Where Death 'midst the blooms of the morn may
　　dwell,
I tarry no longer—farewell, farewell!

The summer is coming, on soft winds borne,
Ye may press the grape, ye may bind the corn!
For me I depart to a brighter shore,
Ye are mark'd by care, ye are mine no more.
I go where the loved who have left you dwell,
And the flowers are not Death's—fare ye well,
　　farewell!

---

## THE CHILD AND DOVE



Thou art a thing on our dreams to rise,
'Midst the echoes of long-lost melodies,
And to fling bright dew from the morning back,
Fair form on each image of childhood's track.

Thou art a thing to recall the hours,
When the love of our souls was on leaves and
　　flowers,
When a world was our own in some dim sweet
　　grove,
And treasure untold in one captive dove.

Are they gone? can we think it, while thou art
　　there,
Thou joyous child with the clustering hair?
Is it not Spring that indeed breathes free
And fresh o'er each thought, while we gaze on
　　thee?

No! never more may we smile as thou
Sheddest round smiles from thy sunny brow;
Yet something it is, in our hearts to shrine
A memory of beauty undimm'd as thine.

To have met the joy of thy speaking face,
To have felt the spell of thy breezy grace,
To have linger'd before thee, and turn'd and
　　borne
One vision away of the cloudless morn.

---

## THE VAUDOIS VALLEYS.

Yes, thou hast met the sun's last smile,
　　From the haunted hills of Rome;
By many a bright Ægean isle,
　　Thou hast seen the billows foam;

From the silence of the Pyramid
　　Thou hast watch'd the solemn flow
Of the Nile, that with its waters hid
　　The ancient realm below.

Thy heart hath burn'd as shepherds sung
　　Some wild and warlike strain,
Where the Moorish horn once proudly rung
　　Through the pealing hills of Spain:

And o'er the lonely Grecian streams
　　Thou hast heard the laurels moan,
With a sound yet murmuring in thy dreams
　　Of the glory that is gone.

But go thou to the pastoral vales
    Of the Alpine mountains old,
If thou wouldst hear immortal tales,
    By the wind's deep whispers told!

Go, if thou lovest the soil to tread,
    Where man hath nobly striven,
And life, like incense, hath been shed,
    An offering unto heaven.

For o'er the snows, and round the pines,
    Hath swept a noble flood;
The nurture of the peasant's vines
    Hath been the martyr's blood!

A spirit, stronger than the sword,
    And loftier than despair,
Through all the heroic region pour'd,
    Breathes in the generous air.

A memory clings to every steep
    Of long-enduring faith,
And the sounding streams glad record keep
    Of courage unto death.

Ask of the peasant *where his sires*
    For truth and freedom bled,
Ask, where were lit the torturing fires,
    Where lay the holy dead;

And he will tell thee, all around,
    On fount, and turf, and stone,
Far as the chamois' foot can bound,
    Their ashes have been sown!

Go, when the sabbath bell is heard *
    Up through the wilds to float,
When the dark old woods and caves are stirr'd
    To gladness by the note;

When forth, along their thousand rills,
    The mountain people come,
Join thou their worship on those hills
    Of glorious martyrdom.

And while the song of praise ascends,
    And while the torrent's voice
Like the swell of many an organ blends,
    Then let thy soul rejoice!

Rejoice, that human heart, through scorn,
    Through shame, through death, made strong,
Before the rocks and heavens have borne
    Witness of God so long!

---

## CHRIST'S AGONY IN THE GARDEN

He knelt—the Saviour knelt and pray'd,
    When but His Father's eye
Look'd through the lonely garden's shade,
    On that dread agony!
The Lord of all, above, beneath,
Was bow'd with sorrow unto death.

The sun set in a fearful hour
    The skies might well grow dim,
When this mortality had power
    So to o'ershadow *Him!*
When He who gave man's breath must know
The very depth of human woe.

He knew them all—the doubt, the strife,
    The faint perplexing dread,
The mists that hang o'er parting life,
    All darken'd round his head!
And the Deliverer knelt to pray—
Yet pass'd it not, that cup, away.

* See 'Gilley's Researches among the mountains of Piedmont,' for an interesting description of a sabbath day in the upper regions of the Vaudois. The inhabitants of those Protestant valleys, who, like the Swiss, repair with their flocks and herds to the summits of the hills, during the summer, are followed thither by their pastors, and at that season of the year, assemble on that sacred day, to worship in the open air.

It pass'd not—though the stormy wave
    Had sunk beneath his tread;
It pass'd not—though to Him the grave
    Had yielded up its dead,
But there was sent him, from on high
A gift of strength, for man to die.*

And was *His* mortal hour beset
    With anguish and dismay?
—How may *we* meet our conflict yet,
    In the dark narrow way?
How, but through Him, that path who trod?
Save, or we perish, Son of God!

---

## ON A LEAF FROM THE TOMB OF VIRGIL

And was thy home, pale wither'd thing,
    Beneath the rich blue southern sky?
Wert thou a nursling of the spring,
The winds and suns of glorious Italy?

Those suns in golden light, e'en now,
    Look'd o'er the poet's lovely grave,
Those winds are breathing soft, but thou,
Answering their whisper, there no more shalt
    wave.

The flowers, o'er Posilippo's brow,
    May cluster in their purple bloom,
But on the o'ershadowing ilex-bough,
Thy breezy place is void, by Virgil's tomb.

Thy place is void—oh! none on earth,
    This crowded earth, may so remain,
Save that which souls of loftiest birth
Leave when they part, their brighter home to
    gain.

Another leaf, ere now, hath sprung
    On the green stem which once was thine—
When shall another strain be sung
Like his whose dust hath made that spot a
    shrine?

---

## THE ANGELS' CALL

"Hark! they whisper! angels say
Sister spirit, come away!"

Come to the land of peace!
Come where the tempest hath no longer sway,
The shadow passes from the soul away,
    The sounds of weeping cease!

Fear hath no dwelling there!
Come to the mingling of repose and love,
Breathed by the silent spirit of the dove
    Through the celestial air!

Come to the bright and blest
And crown'd for ever!—'midst that shining band,
Gather'd to heaven's own wreath from every land,
    Thy spirit shall find rest!

Thou hast been long alone;
Come to thy mother!—on the sabbath shore,
The heart that rock'd thy childhood, back, once
    more
    Shall take its wearied one.

In silence wert thou left!
Come to thy sisters!—joyously again
All the home-voices, blest in one sweet strain,
    Shall greet their long-bereft.

Over thine orphan head
The storm hath swept as o'er a willow's bough;
Come to thy father!—it is finish'd now;
    *Thy tears have all been shed.*

* "And there appeared an angel unto him from Heaven, strengthening him."—*St. Luke,* xxii. 43.

In thy divine abode
Change finds no pathway, mem'ry no dark trace,
And, oh! bright victory—death by love no place:
    Come, Spirit, to thy God!

## THE VOICE OF GOD

"I heard thy voice in the garden, and I was afraid."

AMIDST the thrilling leaves, thy voice
    At evening's fall drew near;
Father! and did not man rejoice
    That blessed sound to hear?

Did not his heart within him burn,
    Touch'd by the solemn tone?
Not so! for, never to return,
    Its purity was gone.

Therefore, 'midst holy stream and bower,
    His spirit shook with dread,
And call'd the cedars, in that hour,
    To veil his conscious head.

Oh! in each wind, each fountain flow,
    Each whisper of the shade,
Grant me, my God, thy voice to know,
    And not to be afraid!

## THE SPELL

THERE 's such a glory on thy cheek,
    And such a magic power around thee
That, if I would, I could not break
    The spell with which thine eyes have bound me.

Though all my stubborn heart rebel
    Against the thraldom of thy frown,
The tameless spirit thou canst quell,
    And keep the bursting madness down.

vainly struggle to be free;
    I rouse that withering pride in vain,
Whose blight might change my love for thee
    To fiery hate or cold disdain.

loathe my very soul, that bears
    To drink thy poisonous love-draughts up,
Until my frenzied spirit swears
    To dash to earth the dazzling cup.

Yet every effort of my heart
    To cast thee off but draws thee nearer,
And rage and agony impart
    A venom-charm, that makes thee dearer.

## THE SHEPHERD POET OF THE ALPS.

"God gave him reverence of laws,
Yet stirring blood in freedom's cause—
A spirit to his rocks akin,
The eye of the hawk, and the fire therein!"
                                        *Coleridge.*

SINGING of the free blue sky,
And the wild flower glens that lie
Far amidst the ancient hills,
Which the fountain music fills;
Singing of the snow-peaks bright,
And the royal eagle's flight,
And the courage and the grace
Foster'd by the chamois-chase;
In his fetters day by day,
So the shepherd-poet lay.

Wherefore, from a dungeon-cell
Did those notes of freedom swell,
Breathing sadness not their own,
Forth with every Alpine tone?
Wherefore can a tyrant ear
Brook the mountain winds to bear,
When each blast goes pealing by
With a song of Liberty!

Darkly hung the oppressor's hand
O'er the shepherd-poet's land,
Sounding there the waters gush'd,
While the lip of man was hush'd;
There the falcon pierced the cloud,
While the fiery heart was bow'd;
But this might not long endure,
Where the mountain-homes were pure,
And a valiant voice arose,
Thrilling all the silent snows;
*His*—now singing far and lone.
Where the young breeze ne'er was known;
Singing of the glad blue sky,
Wildly—and how mournfully!

Are none but the wind and the lammer-geyer,
To be free where the hills unto heaven aspire?
Is the soul of song from the deep glens past,
Now that their poet is chain'd at last?
Think of the mountains, and deem not so!
Soon shall each blast like a clarion blow!
Yes! though forbidden be every word,
Wherewith that spirit the Alps hath stirr'd,
Yet e'en as a buried stream through earth
Rolls on to another and brighter birth,
So shall the voice that hath seem'd to die,
Burst forth with the anthem of Liberty!

And another power is moving
In a bosom fondly loving;
Oh! a sister's heart is deep,
And her spirit 's strong to keep
Each light link of early hours,
All sweet scents of childhood's flowers!

Thus each lay by Erni sung,
Rocks and crystal caves among,
Or beneath the linden-leaves,
Or the cabin's vine-hung eaves,
Rapid though as bird-notes gushing,
Transient as a wan cheek's flushing.
Each in young Teresa's breast
Left its fiery words impress'd;
Treasured there lay every line
As a rich book on a hidden shrine;
Fair was that lone girl, and meek,
With a pale transparent cheek
And a deep-fringed violet eye,
Seeking in sweet shade to lie;
Or, if raised to glance above,
Dim with its own dews of love;
And a pure Madonna brow,
And a silver voice, and low,
Like the echo of a flute.
E'en the last though all be mute.
But a loftier soul was seen
In the orphan sister's mien.
From that hour when chains defiled
Him, the high Alps' noble child;
Tones in her quivering voice awoke,
As if a harp of battle spoke;
Light, that seem'd born of an eagle's nest,
Flash'd from her soft eyes unrepress'd;
And her form, like a spreading water flower,
When its frail cup swells with a sudden
        shower,
Seem'd all dilated with love and pride,
And grief for that brother, her young heart's
        guide.
Well might they love!—those two had grown,
Orphans together and alone;
The silence of the Alpine sky
Had hush'd their hearts to piety;
The turf, o'er their dead mother laid,
Had been their altar when they pray'd;
There, more in tenderness than woe,
The stars had seen their young tears flow

The clouds, a spirit-like descent,
Their deep thoughts by one touch had blent,
And the wild storms link'd them to each other
How dear can peril make a brother!

Now is their hearth a forsaken spot,
The vine waves unpruned o'er their mountain cot,
Away, in that holy affection's might,
The maiden is gone, like a breeze of the night;
She is gone forth alone, but her lighted face,
Filling with soul ev'ry secret place,
Hath a dower from heaven, and a gift of sway,
To arouse brave hearts in its hidden way
Like the sudden flinging forth on high,
Of a banner that starteth silently!
She hath wander'd through a hamlet-vale,
Telling its children her brother's tale;
And the strains, by his spirit pour'd away,
Freely as fountains might shower their spray,
From her fervent lip a new life have caught
And a power to kindle yet bolder thought:
Whi e sometimes, a melody all her own,
Like a gush of tears in its plaintive tone,
May be heard 'midst the lonely rocks to flow,
Clear through the water-chimes—clear, yet low

" Thou 'rt not where wild flowers wave,
O'er crag and sparry cave;
Thou'rt not where pines are sounding,
Or joyous torrents bounding.
        Alas, my brother!

" Thou 'rt not where green, on high,
The brighter pastures lie;
E'en those thine own wild places,
Bear of our chain dark traces;
        Alas, my brother!

" Far hath the sunbeam spread,
Nor found thy lonely bed;
Long hath the fresh wind sought thee,
Nor one sweet whisper brought thee—
        Alas, my brother!

" Thou, that for joy wert born,
Free as the winds of morn,
Will aught thy young life cherish,
Where the Alpine rose would perish?
        Alas! my brother!

" Canst thou be singing still,
As once on every hill?
Is not thy soul forsaken,
And the bright gift from thee taken?
        Alas, alas, my brother!"

And was the bright gift from the captive fled?
Like the fire on his hearth, was his spirit dead?
Not so!—but as rooted in stillness deep,
The pure stream-lily its place will keep,
Though its tearful urns to the blast may quiver,
While the red waves rush down the foaming river,
So freedom's faith in his bosom lay,
Trembling, yet not to be borne away!
He thought of the Alps and their breezy air,
And felt that his country no chains might bear;
He thought of the hunter's haughty life,
And knew there must yet be noble strife;
But, oh! when he thought of that orphan maid,
His high heart melted—he wept and pray'd!
For he saw her not as she moved e'en then,
A wakener of heroes in every glen,
With a glance inspired, which no grief could tame
Bearing on Hope like a torch's flame,
While the strengthening voice of mighty wrongs
Gave echoes back to her thrilling songs;
But his dreams were fill'd by a haunting tone,
Sad as a sleeping infant's moan;
And his soul was pierced by a mournful eye,
Which look'd on it—oh! how beseechingly!
And there floated past him a fragile form,
With a willowy droop, as beneath the storm.
Till wakening in anguish, his faint heart strove
In vain with its burden of helpless love!
—Thus woke the dreamer one weary night—
There flash'd through his dungeon a swift strong
    light:

He sprang up—he climb'd to the grating bars,
—It was not the rising of moon or stars,
But a signal flame from a peak of snow,
Rock'd through the dark skies to and fro!
There shot forth another—another still,
A hundred answers of hill to hill!
Tossing like pines in the tempest's way,
Joyously, wildly, the bright spires play,
And each is hail'd with a pealing shout,
For the high Alps waving their banners out!
Erni, young Erni! the land has risen!
—Alas! to be lone in thy narrow prison!
Those free streamers glancing, and thou not there,
—Is the moment of rapture, or fierce despair?
—Hark! there 's a tumult that shakes his cell!
At the gates of the mountain citadel!
Hark! a clear voice through the rude sounds
    ringing,
—Doth he know the strain, and the wild sweet
    singing?

" There may not long be fetters,
Where the cloud is in earth's array,
And the bright floods leap from cave and steep,
Like a hunter on the prey!

" There may not long he fetters
Where the white Alps have their towers;
Unto eagle homes, if the arrow comes,
The chain is not for ours!"

It is she!—She is come like a day-spring beam,
She that so mournfully shadow'd his dream!
With her shining eyes and her buoyant form,
She is come! her tears on his check are warm.
And oh! the thrill in that weeping voice!
" My brother, my brother! come forth, rejoice."

—Poet! the land of thy love is free,
—Sister! thy brother is won by thee!

## THE RELEASE OF TASSO.

There came a bard to Rome; he brought a lyre
Of sounds to peal through Rome's triumphant sky,
To mourn a hero on his funeral pyre,
Or greet a conqueror with its war-notes high.
For on each chord had fallen the gift of fire,
The living breath of power and victory—
Yet he, its lord, the sovereign city's guest,
Sigh'd but to flee away, and be at rest.

He brought a spirit, whose ethereal birth
Was of the loftiest, and whose haunts had been
Amidst the marvels and the pomps of earth,
Wild fairy bowers, and groves of deathless green,
And fields where mail-clad bosoms prove their
    worth,
When flashing swords lift up the stormy scene—
He brought a weary heart, a wasted frame,—
The child of visions from a dungeon came.

On the blue waters, as in joy they sweep,
With starlight floating o'er their swells and falls,
On the blue waters of the Adrian deep,
His numbers had been sung—and in the halls,
Where, through the rich foliage, if a sunbeam
    peep,
It seems Heaven's wakening to the sculptured
    walls,—
Had princes listened to those lofty strains,
While the high soul they burst from pined in
    chains.

And in the summer gardens, where the spray
Of founts, far glancing from their marble bed,
Rains on the flowery myrtles in its play,
And the sweet limes, and glassy leaves that spread
Round the deep golden citrons—o'er his lay
Dark eyes, dark, soft, Italian eyes, had shed
Warm tears, fast glittering in that sun, whose
    light
Was a forbidden glory to his sight.

Oh ! if it be that wizard sign and spell,
And talisman, had power of old to bind,
In the dark chambers of some cavern-cell,
Or knotted oak, the spirits of the wind,
Things of the lightning-pinion, wont to dwell
High o'er the reach of eagles, and to find
Joy in the rush of storms—even such a doom
Was that high minstrel's, in his dungeon-gloom.

But he was free at last !—the glorious land
Of the white Alps and pine-crown'd Apennines,
Along whose shore the sapphire seas expand,
And the wastes teem with myrtle, and the shrines
Of long-forgotten gods, from nature's hand
Receive bright offerings still ; with all its vines,
And rocks, and ruins, clear before him lay—
The seal was taken from the founts of day.

The winds came o'er his cheek ; the soft winds,
    blending
All summer-sounds and odours in their sigh ;
The orange groves waved round, the hills were
    sending
Their bright streams down, the free birds darting
    by,
And the blue festal heavens above him bending,
As if to fold a world where none could die !
And who was he that look'd upon these things ?
—If but of earth, yet one whose thoughts were
    wings

To bear him o'er creation ! and whose mind
Was as an air-harp, wakening to the sway
Of sunny nature's breathings unconfined,
With all the mystic harmonies that lay
Far in the slumber of its chords enshrined,
Till the light breeze went thrilling on its way,
—There was no sound that wander'd through the
    sky,
But told him secrets in its melody.

Was the deep forest lonely unto him,
With all its whispering leaves ?  Each dell and
    glade
Teem'd with such forms as on the moss-clad brim
Of fountains, in their starry grottoes play'd,
Seen, by the Greek of yore, through twilight dim,
Or misty noontide in the laurel shade.
—There is no solitude on earth so deep
As that where man decrees that man should
    weep !

But, oh ! the life in nature's green domains,
The breathing sense of joy ! where flowers are
    springing
By starry thousands, on the slopes and plains,
And the gray rocks—and all the arch'd woods ring-
    ing,
And the young branches trembling to the strains
Of wild born creatures, through the sunshine
    winging
Their fearless flight—and sylvan echoes round,
Mingling all tones to one Eolian sound.

And the glad voice, the laughing voice of streams,
And the low cadence of the silvery sea,
And reed-notes from the mountains, and the
    beams
Of the warm sun—all these are for the free !
And they were *his* once more, the bard whose
    dreams
Their spirit still had haunted—Could it be
That he had borne the chain ?—oh ! who shall
    dare
To say how much man's heart uncrush'd may
    bear ?

So deep a root hath hope ! but woe for this,
Our frail mortality, that aught so bright,
So almost burthen'd with excess of bliss,
As the rich hour which back to summer's light
Calls the worn captive, with the gentle kiss
Of winds, and gush of waters, and the sight
Of the green earth, must so be bought with years
Of the heart's fever, parching up its tears·

And feeding a slow fire on all its powers,
Until the boon for which we gasp in vain,
If hardly won at length, too late made ours,
When the soul's wing is broken, comes like rain
Withheld till evening, on the stately flowers
Which wither'd in the noontide, ne'er again
To lift their heads in glory.—So doth Earth
Breathe on her gifts and melt away their worth.

The sailor dies in sight of that green shore
Whose fields, in slumbering beauty, seem'd to lie
On the deep's foam, amidst its hollow roar
Call'd up to sunlight by his fantasy—
And when the shining desert-mists, that wore
The lake's bright semblance, have been all pass'd
    by,
The pilgrim sinks beside the fountain wave,
Which flashes from its rock, too late to save.

Or if we live, if that, too dearly bought,
And made too precious by long hopes and fears,
Remains our own—love, darken'd and o'er·
    wrought
By memory of privation, love which wears
And casts o'er life a troubled hue of thought,
Becomes the shadow of our closing years,
Making it almost misery to possess
Aught watch'd with such unquiet tenderness.

Such unto him, the bard, the worn and wild,
And sick with hope deferr'd, from whom the sky,
With all its clouds in burning glory piled,
Had been shut out by long captivity ;
Such freedom was to Tasso.—As a child
Is to the mother, whose foreboding eye,
In its too radiant glance from day to day,
Reads that which calls the brightest first away.

And he became a wanderer—in whose breast
Wild fear, which, e'en when every sense doth
    sleep,
Clings to the burning heart, a wakeful guest,
Sat brooding as a spirit, raised to keep
Its gloomy vigil of intense unrest
O'er treasures, burthening life, and buried deep
In cavern tomb, and sought, through shades and
    stealth,
By some pale mortal, trembling at his wealth.

But woe for those who trample o'er a mind !
A deathless thing.—They know not what they do,
Or what they deal with !—Man perchance may
    bind
The flower his step hath bruised ; or light anew
The torch he quenches ; or to music wind
Again the lyre-string from his touch that flew—
But for the soul !—oh ! tremble, and beware
To lay rude hands upon God's mysteries *there !*

For blindness wraps that world—our touch may
    turn
Some balance, fearfully and darkly hung,
Or put out some bright spark, whose ray should
    burn
To point the way a thousand rocks among—
Or break some subtle chain, which none discern,
Though binding down the terrible, the strong,
Th' o'ersweeping passions—which to loose on life,
Is to set free the elements for strife !

Who then to power and glory shall restore
That which our evil rashness hath undone ?
Who unto mystic harmony once more
Attune those viewless chords ?—There is but One !
He that through dust the stream of life can pour,
The mighty and the merciful alone !
—Yet oft His paths have midnight for their
    shade—
He leaves to man the ruin man hath made !—

## THE PRAYER FOR LIFE.

O sunshine and fair earth
Sweet is your kindly mirth
Angel of death! yet, yet awhile delay—
Too sad it is to part,
Thus in my spring of heart,
With all the light and laughter of the day.

For me the falling leaf
Touches no chord of grief,
No dark worm in the rose's bosom lies:
Not one triumphal tone,
One hue of hope is gone
From song or bloom beneath the summer skies

Call me not hence away,
Death, death! ere yet decay
Over the golden hours one shade has thrown;
The poesy that dwells
Deep in green woods and dells,
Still to my spirit speaks of joy alone.

Yet not for this, O death!
Not for the vernal breath
Of winds, that shake forth music from the trees;
Not for the splendour given
To night's dark regal heaven,
Spoiler! I ask thee not reprieve for *these*.

But for the happy love
Whose light, where'er I rove,
Kindles all nature to a sudden smile,
Shedding on branch and flower
A rainbow-tinted shower
Of richer life—spare, spare me yet awhile.

Too soon, too fast thou 'rt come!
Too beautiful is home,
A home of gentle voices and kind eyes!
And I the loved of all,
On whom fond blessings fall,
From every lip—oh! wilt thou rend such ties?

Sweet sisters! weave a chain
My spirit to detain;
Hold me to earth with strong affection back!
Bind me with mighty love
Unto the stream, the grove,
Our daily paths—our life's familiar track!

Stay with me—gird me round!
Your voices hear a sound
Of hope—a light comes with you and departs:
Hush my soul's boding knell,
That murmurs of farewell!
How can I leave this ring of kindest hearts!

Death! grave! and are there those
That woo your dark repose
Midst the rich beauty of the glowing earth?
Surely about them lies
No world of loving eyes—
Leave me, oh leave me unto home and hearth!

## THE BATTLE-FIELD.

I look'd on the field where the battle was spread,
When thousands stood forth in their glancing array,
And the beam from the steel of the valiant was shed
Through the dun rolling clouds that o'ershadow'd the fray.

I saw the dark forest of lances appear,
As the ears of the harvest unnumber'd they stood,
I heard the stern shout as the foemen drew near,
Like the storm, that lays low the proud pines of the wood.

Afar, the harsh notes of the war-drum were roll'd,
Uprousing the wolf from the depth of his lair;
On high to the gust stream'd the banner's red fold,
O'er the death-close of hate, and the scowl of despair.

I look'd on the field of contention again,
When the sabre was sheathed and the tempest had past;
The wild weed and thistle grew rank on the plain,
And the fern softly sigh'd in the low wailing blast

Unmoved lay the lake in its hour of repose,
And bright shone the stars through the sky's deep en'd blue;
And sweetly the song of the night-bird arose,
Where the foxglove lay gemm'd with its pearl-drops of dew.

But where swept the ranks of that dark frowning host,
As the ocean in might—as the storm-cloud in speed!
Where now were the thunders of victory's boast—
The slayer's dead wrath and the strength of the steed!

Not a time-wasted cross, not a mouldering stone,
To mark the lone scene of their shame or their pride;
One grass-cover'd mound told the traveller alone,
Where thousands lay down in their anguish and died!

Oh! Glory! behold thy famed guerdon's extent,
For this toil thy slaves through their earth-wasting lot;
A name like the mist, when night-beams are spent—
A grave with its tenants unwept and forgot!

## THINGS THAT CHANGE.

Know'st thou that seas are sweeping
Where cities once have been?
When the calm wave is sleeping,
Their towers may yet be seen;
Far down below the glassy tide
Man's dwelling 's where his voice hath died!

Know'st thou that flocks are feeding
Above the tombs of old,
Which kings, their armies leading,
Have linger'd to behold?
A short, smooth greensward o'er them spread
Is all that marks where heroes bled.

Know'st thou that now the token
Of temples once renown'd,
Is but a pillar, broken,
With grass and wall-flowers crown'd?
And the lone serpent rears her young
Where the triumphant lyre hath sung?

Well, well, I know the story
Of ages pass'd away,
And the mournful wrecks that glory
Has left to dull decay.
But thou hast yet a tale to learn
More full of warnings sad and stern.

Thy pensive eye but ranges
O'er ruin'd fane and hall,
Oh! the deep *soul* has changes
More sorrowful than all.
Talk not, while these before thee throng,
Of silence in the place of song.

See scorn—where love has perish'd;
Distrust—where friendship grew!
Pride—where once nature cherish'd
All tender thoughts and true!
And shadows of oblivion thrown
O'er every trace of idols gone.

Weep not for tombs far scatter'd,
  For temples prostrate laid—
In thine own heart lie shatter'd
  The altars it had made.
Go, sound its depths in doubt and fear!
Heap up no more its treasures *here.*

---

## A THOUGHT OF THE FUTURE.

DREAMER! and wouldst thou know
If love goes with us to the viewless bourne?
Wouldst *thou* bear hence th' unfathom'd source of
    woe
  In thy heart's lonely urn?

What hath it been to thee,
That power, the dweller of thy secret breast?
A dove, sent forth across a stormy sea,
  Finding no place of rest:

A precious odour cast
On a wild stream, that recklessly swept by;
A voice of music utter'd to the blast,
  And winning no reply.

Even were such answer thine,
Wouldst thou be blest?—too sleepless, too pro-
    found,
Are thy soul's hidden springs; there is no line
  Their depth of love to sound.

Do not words faint and fall,
When thou wouldst fill them with that ocean's
    power?
As thine own cheek before high thoughts grows
    pale
  In some o'erwhelming power?

Doth not thy frail form sink
Beneath the chain that binds thee to one spot,
When thy heart strives, held down by many a link,
  Where thy beloved are not?

Is not thy very soul
Oft in the gush of powerless blessing shed,
Till a vain tenderness, beyond control,
  Bows down thy weary head?

And wouldst thou bear all *this,*
The burden and the shadow of thy life,
To trouble the blue skies of cloudless bliss,
  With earthly feelings' strife?

Not thus, not thus—oh no!
Not veil'd and mantled with dim clouds of care,
That spirit of my soul should with me go,
  To breathe celestial air:

But as the sky-lark springs
To its own sphere, where night afar is driven,
As to its place the flower-seed findeth wings,
  So must love mount to Heaven!

Vainly it shall not strive
There on weak words to pour a stream of fire;
Thought unto thought shall kindling impulse give,
  As light might wake a lyre.

And, oh! its blessings *there*
Shower'd like rich balsam forth on some dear head,
Powerless no more, a gift shall surely bear
  A joy of sunlight shed!

Let me, then, let me dream
That love goes with us to the shore unknown;
So o'er its burning tears a heavenly gleam
  In mercy shall be thrown!

## A FAREWELL SONG.

I go, sweet friends! yet think of me
  When spring's low voice awakes the flowers,
For we have wander'd far and free
  In those bright hours—the violet's hours!

I go—but when you pause to hear
  From distant hills, the sabbath-bell
On summer's wind float silvery clear,
  Think of me then—I loved it well!

Forget me not around your hearth,
  When clearly shines the ruddy blaze;
For dear hath been its hour of mirth
  To me, sweet friends! in other days.

And, oh! when music's voice is heard
  To melt in strains of parting woe!
When hearts to tender thought are stirr'd,
  Think on me then! I go, I go!

---

## THE BELL AT SEA.

The dangerous islet called the Bell Rock, on the coast
of Fife, used formerly to be marked only by a bell
which was so placed as to be swung by the motion of
the waves, when the tide rose above the rock. A light-
house has since been erected there.

---

WHEN the tide's billowy swell
  Had reach'd its height,
Then toll'd the rock's lone bell,
  Sternly by night.

Far over cliff and surge
  Swept the deep sound,
Making each wild wind's dirge
  Still more profound.

Yet that funereal tone
  The sailor bless'd,
Steering through darkness on,
  With fearless breast.

E'en so may we, that float
  On life's wide sea,
Welcome each warning note,
  Stern though it be!

---

## A THOUGHT OF HOME AT SEA.

'Tis lone on the waters,
  When eve's mournful bell
Sends forth to the sunset
  A note of farewell!

When, borne with the shadows,
  And winds as they sweep,
There comes a fond memory
  Of Home o'er the deep!

When the wing of the sea-bird
  Is turn'd to her nest,
And the heart of the sailor
  To all he loves best.

'Tis lone on the waters—
  That hour hath a spell
To bring back sweet voices,
  And words of farewell!

---

## THE COTTAGE GIRL

A CHILD beside a hamlet's fount at play,
Her fair face laughing at the sunny day;
The cheerful girl her labour leaves awhile,
To gaze on Heaven's and Earth's unsullied smile

Her happy dog looks on her dimpled cheeks,
And of his joy in his own language speaks.
A gush of waters tremulously bright,
Kindling the air to gladness with their light;
And a soft gloom beyond, of summer trees,
Darkening the turf, and shadow'd o'er by these,
A low, dim, woodland cottage:—this was all!

What had the scene for memory to recall,
With a fond look of love? What secret spell
With the heart's pictures made its image dwell?
What but the spirit of the joyous child,
That freshly forth o'er stream and verdure smiled
Casting upon the common things of earth
A brightness, born and gone with infant mirth!

------

## DEATH OF AN INFANT

DEATH found strange beauty on that cherub brow
And dash'd it out.—There was a tint of rose
On cheek and lip,—he touch'd the veins with ice,
And the rose faded;—forth from those blue eyes
There spoke a wishful tenderness,—a doubt
Whether to grieve or sleep, which innocence
Alone can wear. With ruthless haste he bound
The silken fringes of their curtaining lids

For ever; there had been a murmuring sound,
With which the babe would claim its mother's ear,
Charming her even to tears. The spoiler set
His seal of silence,—but there beam'd a smile

So fix'd and holy from that marble brow
Death gazed, and left it there;—he dared not steal
The signet-ring of Heaven.

## MAN AND WOMAN

*"———— Women act their parts*
*When they do make their order'd houses know them.*
*Men must be busy out of doors, must stir*
*The city; yea, make the great world aware*
*That they are in it; for the mastery*
*Of which they race and wrestle."*
*Knowles.*

WARRIOR! whose image on thy tomb,
With shield and crested head,
Sleeps proudly in the purple gloom
By the stain'd window shed;
The records of thy name and race
Have faded from the stone,
Yet through a cloud of years I trace
What thou hast been and done.

A banner from its flashing spear
Flung out o'er many a fight;
A war-cry ringing far and clear,
And strong to turn the flight;
An arm that bravely bore the lance
On for the holy shrine,
A haughty heart and kingly glance—
Chief! were not these things thine?

A lofty place where leaders sate
Around the council board;
In festive halls a chair of state,
When the blood-red wine was pour'd;
A name that drew a prouder tone
From herald, harp, and bard;
—Surely these things were all thine own,
So hadst thou thy reward!

Woman! whose sculptured form at rest
By the arm'd knight is laid,
With meek hands folded o'er thy breast,
In matron robes array'd;

What was thy tale?—Oh, gentle mate
Of him the bold and free,
Bound unto his victorious fate,
What bard hath sung of thee?

He woo'd a bright and burning star;
Thine was the void, the gloom,
The straining eye that follow'd far
His oft-receding plume;
The heart-sick listening while his steed
Sent echoes on the breeze;
The pang—but when did fame take heed
Of griefs obscure as these?

Thy silent and secluded hours,
Through many a lonely day
While bending o'er thy broider'd flowers,
With spirit far away;
Thy weeping midnight prayers for him
Who fought on Syrian plains;
Thy watchings till the torch grew dim,—
These fill no minstrel strains.

A still sad life was thine!—long years,
With tasks unguerdon'd fraught,
Deep, quiet love, submissive tears,
Vigils of anxious thought;
Prayers at the cross in fervour pour'd
Alms to the pilgrims given;
O happy, happier than thy lord,
In that lone path to heaven!

------

## THE RUINED HOUSE.

No dower of storied song is thine,
O desolate abode!
Forth from thy gates no glittering line
Of lance and spear hath flow'd:
Banners of knighthood have not flung
Proud drapery o'er thy walls,
Nor bugle-notes to battle rung
Through thy resounding halls.

Nor have rich bowers of *Pleasaunce* here
By courtly hands been dress'd,
For princes, from the chase of deer,
Under green leaves to rest:
Only some rose, yet lingering bright
Beside thy casements lone,
Tells where the spirit of delight
Hath dwelt, and now is gone.

Yet minstrel tale of harp and sword,
And sovereign beauty's lot,
House of quench'd light and silent board!
For me thou needest not:
It is enough to know that here,
Where thoughtfully I stand,
Sorrow and love, and hope and fear
Have link'd one kindred band.

Thou bindest me with mighty spells!
—A solemnizing breath,
A presence all around thee dwells
Of human life and death.
I need but pluck yon garden-flower
From where the wild weeds rise,
To wake, with strange and sudden power
A thousand sympathies!

Thou hast heard many sounds, thou hearth
Deserted now by all!
Voices at eve here met in mirth,
Which eve may ne'er recall.
Youth's buoyant step, and woman's tone,
And childhood's language glee,
And song and prayer have well been known
Hearth of the dead! to thee.

Thou hast heard blessings fondly pour'd
    Upon the infant head,
As if in every fervent word
    The living soul were shed:
Thou hast seen partings—such as bear
    The bloom from life away—
Alas! for love in changeful air,
    Where naught beloved can stay!

Here, by the restless bed of pain,
    The vigil hath been kept,
Till sunrise, bright with hope in vain,
    Burst forth on eyes that wept:
Here hath been felt the hush, the gloom,
    The breathless influence shed
Through the dim dwelling, from the room
    Wherein reposed the dead.

The seat left void, the missing face,
    Have here been mark'd and mourn'd;
And time hath fill'd the vacant place,
    And gladness hath return'd:
Till from the narrowing household chain
    The links dropp'd, one by one;
And homeward hither o'er the main
    Came the spring-birds alone.

Is there not cause then—cause for thought,
    Fix'd eye, and lingering tread,
Where, with their thousand mysteries fraught
    E'en lowliest hearts have bled!
Where, in its ever haunting thirst
    For draughts of purer day,
Man's soul with fitful strength hath burst
    The clouds that wrapt its way?

Holy to human nature seems
    The long-forsaken spot!
To deep affections, tender dreams,
    Hopes of a brighter lot!
Therefore in silent reverence here,
    Hearth of the dead! I stand,
Where joy and sorrow, smile and tear,
    Have link'd one kindred band.

---

### SONG.

"Oh, cast thou not
Affection from thee! in this bitter world
Hold to thy heart that only treasure fast,
Watch—guard it—suffer not a breath to dim
The bright gem's purity!"

If thou hast crush'd a flower,
    The root may not be blighted;
If thou hast quench'd a lamp,
    Once more it may be lighted:
But on thy harp or on thy lute,
    The string which thou hast broken
Shall never in sweet sound again
    Give to thy touch a token!

If thou hast loosed a bird,
    Whose voice of song could cheer thee,
Still, still he may be won
    From the skies to warble near thee;
But if upon the troubled sea
    Thou hast thrown a gem unheeded,
Hope not that wind or wave shall bring
    The treasure back when needed.

If thou hast bruised a vine,
    The summer's breath is healing,
And its cluster yet may glow
    Through the leaves their bloom revealing
But if thou hast a cup o'erthrown,
    With a bright draught fill'd—oh! never
Shall earth give back that lavish'd wealth
    To cool thy parch'd lip's fever!

The heart is like that cup,
    If thou waste the love it bore thee,
And like that jewel gone,
    Which the deep will not restore thee;
And like that string of harp or lute
    Whence the sweet sound is scatter'd;—
—Gently, oh! gently touch the chords
    So soon for ever shatter'd!

---

### THE RECALL.

"Alas! the kind, the playful, and the gay,
They who have gladdened their domestic board,
And cheer'd the winter hearth, do they return?"
                    *Joanna Baillie.*

Come home!—there is a sorrowing breath
    In music since we went;
And the early flower-scents wander by,
    With mournful memories blent:
The sounds of every household voice
    Are grown more sad and deep,
And the sweet word—*brother*—wakes a wish
    To turn aside and weep.

O ye beloved, come home!—the hour
    Of many a greeting tone,
The time of hearth-light and of song,
    Returns—and ye are gone!
And darkly, heavily it falls
    On the forsaken room,
Burdening the heart with tenderness
    That deepens 'midst the gloom.

Where finds it you, our wandering ones
    With all your boyhood's glee
Untamed, beneath the desert's palm,
    Or on the lone mid sea?
'Mid stormy hills of battles old,
    Or where dark rivers foam?
Oh! life is dim where ye are not—
    Back, ye beloved! come home!

Come with the leaves and winds of spring,
    And swift birds o'er the main!
Our love is grown too sorrowful,
    Bring us its youth again!
Bring the glad tones to music back—
    —Still, still your home is fair;
The spirit of your sunny life
    Alone is wanting there!

---

### THE SUMMONS.

The vesper-bell, from church and tower,
    Had sent its dying sound;
And the household, in the hush of eve,
    Were met, their porch around.

A voice rang through the olive-wood, with a sud-
    den triumph's power—
"We rise on all our hills! come forth! 'tis thy
    country's gathering hour!
There's a gleam of spears by every stream, in each
    old battle dell—
Come forth, young Juan! bid thy home a brief and
    proud farewell."

Then the father gave his son the sword
    Which a hundred fights had seen—
"Away! and bear it back, my boy!
    All that it still hath been!"

"Haste, haste! the hunters of the foe are up, and
    who shall stand
The lion-like awakening of the roused indignant
    land?
Our chase shall sound through each defile where
    swept the clarion's blast,
With the flying footsteps of the Moor in stormy
    ages past"

Then the mother kiss'd her son, with tears
    That o'er his dark locks fell:
"I bless, I bless thee o'er and o'er
    Yet stay thee not—farewell!"

"One moment! but one moment give to parting
    thought or word!
It is no time for woman's tears when manhood's
    heart is stirr'd.
Bear but the memory of thy love about thee in
    the fight,
To breathe upon the avenging sword a spell of
    keener might."

And a maiden's fond adieu was heard,
  Though deep, yet brief and low:
" In the vigil, in the conflict, love!
  My prayer shall with thee go!"

"Come forth! come as the torrent comes when
    the winter's chain is burst!
So rushes on the land's revenge, in night and
    silence nursed—
The night is pass'd, the silence o'er—on all our
    hills we rise—
We wait thee, youth! sleep, dream no more! the
    voice of battle cries."

There were sad hearts in a darken'd home,
  When the brave had left their bower!
But the strength of prayer and sacrifice
  Was with them in that hour.

---

## TO THE MEMORY OF A FRIEND AND RELATIVE.

"Blessed are the pure in heart, for they shall see
God."

We miss thy voice while early flowers are blow-
    ing,
  And the first flush of blossom clothes each
    bough,
And the spring sunshine round our home is glow-
    ing,
  Soft as thy smile—thou would'st be with us
    now!

*With us!—we wrong thee by the earthly thought—*
Could our fond gaze but follow where thou art,
Well might the glories of this world seem naught
  To the one promise given the pure in heart.

Yet wert thou blest e en here—oh! ever blest
  In thine own sunny thoughts and tranquil
    faith;
The silent joy that still o'erflow'd thy breast,
  Needed but guarding from all change, by death.

So is it seal'd to peace!—on thy clear brow
  Never was care one fleeting shade to cast,
And thy calm days in brightness were to flow,
  A holy stream untroubled to the last!

Farewell! thy life hath left surviving love
  A wealth of records and sweet " feelings given."
From sorrow's heart the faintness to remove,
  By whispers breathing " less of earth than
    heaven."

Thus rests thy spirit still on those with whom
  Thy step the path of joyous duty trod,
Bidding them make an altar of thy tomb,
  Where chasten'd thought may offer praise to
    God!

---

## EVENING SONG OF THE TYROLESE PEASANTS.*

Come to the sunset tree!
  The day is past and gone,
The woodman's axe lies free,
  And the reaper's work is done.

The twilight star to heaven,
  And the summer dew to flowers,
And rest to us is given
  By the cool soft evening hours.

---

* " The loved hour of repose is striking. Let us come to the sunset tree."—See Captain Sherer's interesting " Notes and Reflections
during a Ramble in Germany."



Sweet is the hour of rest!
  Pleasant the wind's low sigh,
And the gleaming of the west,
  And the turf whereon we lie.

When the burden and the heat
  Of labour's task are o'er,
And kindly voices greet
  The tired one at his door.

Come to the sunset tree!
  The day is past and gone;
The woodman's axe lies free,
  And the reaper's work is done.

Yes; tuneful is the sound
  That dwells in whispering boughs;
Welcome the freshness round,
  And the gale that fans our brows.

But rest more sweet and still
  Than ever night-fall gave,
Our longing hearts shall fill
  In the world beyond the grave.

There shall no tempest blow,
  No scorching noontide heat;
There shall be no more snow,
  No weary wandering feet.

And we lift our trusting eyes,
  From the hills our fathers trod,
To the quiet of the skies,
  To the Sabbath of our God.

Come to the sunset tree!
  The day is past and gone;
The woodman's axe lies free,
  And the reaper's work is done!

---

## FRAGMENT.

Oh, what is Nature's strength? the vacant eye
By mind deserted hath a dread reply;
The wild delirious laughter of despair,
The mirth of frenzy—seek an answer *there*.
—Weep not, sad moralist, o'er desert plains,
Strew'd with the wrecks of grandeur, mouldering
    fanes,
Arches of triumphs long with weeds o'ergrown,
And regal cities—now the serpent's own;—
Earth has more dreadful ruins—one lost mind
Whose star is quench'd, hath lessons for mankind
Of deeper import than each prostrate dome
Mingling its marble with the dust of Rome.

---

## THE FOUNTAIN OF MARAH.

"And when they came to Marah, they could not drink
of the waters of Marah, for they were bitter

" And the people murmured against Moses, saying,
What shall we drink?

"And he cried unto the Lord; and the Lord showed
him a tree, which when he had cast into the waters, the
waters were made sweet."——*Exod.* xv. 23—25.

---

Where is the tree the prophet threw
  Into the bitter wave?
Left it no scion where it grew,
  The thirsting soul to save?

Hath nature lost the hidden power
  Its precious foliage shed?
Is there no distant eastern bower
  With such sweet leaves o'erspread?

Nay, wherefore ask ?—since gifts are ours,
    Which yet may well imbue
Earth's many troubled founts with showers
    Of Heaven's own balmy dew.

Oh! mingled with the cup of grief,
    Let faith's deep spirit be;
And every prayer shall win a leaf
    From that blest healing tree !

---

## HAUNTED GROUND.

" And slight, withal, may be the things which bring
Back on the heart the weight which it would fling
Aside for ever:—it may be a sound,
A tone of music—summer's breath, or spring,
A flower—a leaf—the ocean—which may wound,
Striking the electric chain wherewith we 're darkly bound."
                                        BYRON.

---

Yes, it is haunted—this quiet scene,
Fair as it looks, and all softly green;
Yet fear thou not—for the spell is thrown,
And the might of the shadow on me alone.

Are thy thoughts wandering to elves and fays,
And spirits that dwell where the water plays?
Oh! in the heart there are stronger powers,
That sway, though viewless, this world of ours!

Have I not lived 'midst these lonely dells,
And loved, and sorrow'd, and heard farewells,
And learn'd in my own deep soul to look,
And tremble before that mysterious book?

Have I not, under these whispering leaves,
Woven such dreams as the young heart weaves?
Shadows—yet unto which life seem'd bound,
And is it not—is it not haunted ground?

Must I not hear what thou hearest not,
Trembling the air of the sunny spot?
Is there not something, to none but me,
Told by the rustling of every tree?

Song hath been here, with its flow of thought;
Love—with its passionate visions fraught;
Death—breathing stillness and sadness round—
And is it not—is it not haunted ground?

Are there no phantoms, but such as come
By night from the darkness that wraps the tomb?
—A sound, a scent, or a whispering breeze,
Can summon up mightier far than these!

But I may not linger amidst them here,
Lovely they are, and yet things to fear,
Passing and leaving a weight behind,
And a thrill on the chords of the stricken mind.

Away, away! that my soul may soar
As a free bird of blue skies once more!
Here from its wing it may never cast
The chain by those spirits brought back from the
    past.

Doubt it not—smile not—but go thou too,
Look on the scenes where thy childhood grew,
Where thou hast pray'd at thy mother's knee,
Where thou hast roved with thy brethren free;

Go thou when life unto thee is changed,
Friends thou hast loved as thy soul estranged,
When from the idols thy heart hath made,
Thou hast seen the colours of glory fade;

Oh! painfully then, by the wind's low sigh
By the voice of the stream, by the flower-cup's dye,
By a thousand tokens of sight and sound,
Thou wilt feel thou art treading on haunted
    ground.

## THE IVY OF KENILWORTH.

HEARD'ST thou what the ivy sigh'd,
Waving where all else hath died,
In the place of regal mirth,
Now the silent Kenilworth ?

With its many glistening leaves,
There a solemn robe it weaves;
And a voice is in each fold,
Like an oracle's of old.

Heard'st thou, while with dews of night,
Shone its berries darkly bright,
Yes! the whisperer seem'd to say,
"All things—all things pass away!

" Where I am, the harp hath rung
Banners and proud fields among,
And the blood-red wine flow'd free,
And the fire shot sparks of glee.

" Where I am, now lost and lone,
(Leafly steps have come and gone;
Gorgeous masques have glided by,
Unto rolling harmony.

" Flung from these illumined towers,
Light hath pierced the forest bowers,
Lake, and pool, and fount have been
Kindled by their midnight sheen.

" Where is now the feasting high?
Where the lordly minstrelsy?
Where the tourney's ringing spear?
—I am sole and silent here.

" In my home no hearth is crown'd,
Through my hall no wine foams round,
By my gates hath ceased the lay—
All things—all things pass away!"

Yes! thy warning voice I knew,
Ivy! and its tale is true:
All is passing, or hath pass'd—
Thou thyself must perish last !

Yet my secret soul replied,
" Surely one thing shall abide,
'Midst the wreck of ages, one,—
Heaven's eternal Word alone !"

---

## THE CHILDE'S DESTINY.

" And none did love him,—not his leman dear,—
But pomp and power alone are woman's care;
And where these are, light Eros finds a feere."
                                        BYRON.

---

No mistress of the hidden skill,
    No wizard gaunt and grim,
Went up by night to heath or hill,
    To read the stars for him;
The merriest girl in all the land
    Of vine-encircled France,
Bestow'd upon his brow and hand
    Her philosophic glance:
" I bind thee with a spell," said she
    " I sign thee with a sign;
No woman's love shall light on thee,
    No woman's heart be thine !

" And trust me, 't is not that thy cheek
    Is colourless and cold,
Nor that thine eye is slow to speak
    What only eyes have told;
For many a cheek of paler white
    Hath blush'd with passion's kiss;
And many an eye of lesser light
    Hath caught its fire from bliss;

Yet while the rivers seek the sea,
  And while the young stars shine,
No woman's love shall light on thee,
  No woman's heart be thine!

" And 't is not that thy spirit, awed
  By beauty's numbing spell,
Shrinks from the force, or from the fraud
  Which beauty loves so well;
For thou hast learn'd to watch and wake,
  And swear by earth and sky;
And thou art very bold to take
  What we must still deny;
I cannot tell; the charm was wrought
  By other threads than mine,
The lips are lightly begg'd or bought,
  The heart may not be thine!

' Yet thine the brightest smile shall be
  That ever beauty wore,
And confidence from two or three,
  And compliments from more:
And one shall give—perchance hath given,
  What only is not love;
Friendship,—oh! such as saints in heaven
  Rain on us from above.
If she shall meet thee in the bower,
  Or name thee in the shrine,
Oh! wear the ring, and guard the flower
  Her heart may not be thine!

" Go, set thy boat before the blast,
  Thy breast before the gun:—
The haven shall be reach'd at last,
  The battle shall be won:
Or muse upon thy country's laws,
  Or strike thy country's lute;—
And patriot hands shall sound applause,
  And lovely lips be mute:
Go, dig the diamond from the wave,
  The treasure from the mine;
Enjoy the wreath, the gold, the grave,—
  No woman's heart is thine!

" I charm thee from the agony
  Which others feel or feign;
From anger, and from jealousy,
  From doubt, and from disdain:
I bid thee wear the scorn of years
  Upon the cheek of youth,
And curl the lip at passion's tears,
  And shake the head at truth;
While there is bliss in revelry,
  Forgetfulness in wine,
Be thou from woman's love as free
  As woman is from thine!"

---

## THE SUBTERRANEAN STREAM.

" Thou stream,
Whose source is inaccessibly profound,
Whither do thy mysterious waters tend?
—Thou imagest my life."

Darkly thou glidest onward,
  Thou deep and hidden wave!
The laughing sunshine hath not 'ook'd
  Into thy secret cave.

Thy current makes no music—
  A hollow sound we hear,
A muffled voice of mystery,
  And know that thou art near.

No brighter line of verdure
  Follows thy lonely way;
No fairy moss, or lily's cup,
  Is freshen'd by thy play.

The halcyon doth not seek thee,
  Her glorious wings to lave;
Thou know'st no tint of the summer sky,
  Thou dark and hidden wave!

Yet once will day behold thee,
  When to the mighty sun,
Fresh bursting from their cavern'd veins,
  Leap thy lone waters free.

There wilt thou greet the sunshine
  For a moment, and be lost,
With all thy melancholy sounds
  In the ocean's billowy host.

Oh! art thou not, dark river,
  Like the fearful thoughts untold,
Which haply in the hush of night
  O'er many a soul have roll'd?

Those earth-born strange misgivings—
  Who hath not felt their power?
Yet who hath breathed them to his friend,
  E'en in his fondest hour?

They hold no heart-communion,
  They find no voice in song,
They dimly follow far from earth
  The grave's departed throng.

Wild is their course, and lonely,
  And fruitless in man's breast;
They come and go, and leave no trace
  Of their mysterious quest.

Yet surely must their wanderings
  At length be like thy way;
Their shadows, as thy waters lost,
  In one bright flood of day!

---

## WOMAN AND FAME.

Happy—happier far than thou,
  With the laurel on thy brow;
She that makes the humblest hearth
  Lovely but to one on earth.

Thou hast a charmed cup, O Fame,
  A draught that mantles high,
And seems to lift this earthly frame
  Above mortality.
Away! to me—a woman—bring
Sweet water from affection's spring.

Thou hast green laurel leaves that twine
  Into so proud a wreath;
For that resplendent gift of thine,
  Heroes have smiled in death.
Give me from some kind hand a flower,
The record of one happy hour!

Thou hast a voice, whose thrilling tone
  Can bid each life-pulse beat,
As when a trumpet's note hath blown,
  Calling the brave to meet:
But mine, let mine—a woman's breast,
By words of home-born love be bless'd.

A hollow sound is in thy song,
  A mockery in thine eye,
To the sick heart that doth but long
  For aid, for sympathy,
For kindly looks to cheer it on,
For tender accents that are gone.

Fame, Fame! thou canst not be the stay
  Unto the drooping reed,
The cool fresh fountain in the day
  Of the soul's feverish need:
Where must the lone one turn or flee?—
Not unto thee, oh! not to thee!

---

## THE SLEEPER OF MARATHON.

I lay upon the solemn plain
  And by the funeral mound,
Where those who died not there in vain,
  Their place of sleep had found.

'T was silent where the free blood gush'd,
  When Persia came array'd—
So many a voice had there been hush'd,
  So many a footstep stay'd.

I slumber'd on the lonely spot,
  So sanctified by Death—
I slumber'd—but my rest was not
  As theirs who lay beneath.
For on my dreams, that shadowy hour,
  They rose—the chainless dead—
All arm'd they sprang, in joy in power,
  Up from their grassy bed.

I saw their spears, on that red field,
  Flash as in time gone by—
Chased to the seas without his shield
  I saw the Persian fly.
I woke—the sudden trumpet's blast
  Call'd to another fight—
From visions of our glorious past,
  Who doth not wake in might ?

---

## WE RETURN NO MORE!*

" When I stood beneath the fresh green tree,
And saw around me the wide field revive
With fruits and fertile promise, and the spring
Come forth her work of gladness to contrive,
With all her reckless birds upon the wing,
I turn'd from all she brought to all she could not bring."
                         *Childe Harold.*

' We return—we return—we return no more."
—So comes the song to the mountain shore,
From those that are leaving their Highland home,
For a world far over the blue sea's foam :
" We return no more !" and through cave and dell
Mournfully wanders that wild farewell.

" We return—we return—we return no more."
—So breathe sad voices our spirits o'er:
Murmuring up from the depths of the heart,
Where lovely things with their light depart;
And the inborn sound hath a prophet's tone,
And we feel that a joy is for ever gone.

" We return—we return—we return no more."
—Is it heard when the days of flowers are o'er ?
When the passionate soul of the night-bird's lay
Hath died from the summer woods away ?
When the glory from sunset's robe hath pass'd,
Or the leaves are borne on the rushing blast ?

No ! it is not the rose that returns no more;
A breath of spring shall its bloom restore;
And it is not the voice that o'erflows the bowers
With a stream of love through the starry hours ;
Nor is it the crimson of sunset hues,
Nor the frail flush'd leaves which the wild wind
    strews.

" We return—we return—we return no more."
—Doth the Lord sing thus from a brighter shore ?
Those wings that follow the southern breeze,
Float they not homeward o'er vernal seas?
Yes ! from the lands of the vine and palm,
They come, with the sunshine, when waves grow
    calm.

' But we—we return—we return no more !"
The heart's young dreams when their spring is
    o'er;
The love it hath pour'd so freely forth,
The boundless trust in ideal worth;
The faith in affection—deep, fond, yet vain—
—*These* are the lost that return not again !

* " Ha til—ha til—ha til mi tulidle"—we return—we return—we
return no more,—the burden of the Highland song of emigration.

## THE CHIEFTAIN'S SON.

Yes, it is ours !—the field is won,
  A dark and evil field !
Lift from the ground my noble son,
And bear him homewards on his bloody shield !

Let me not hear your trumpets ring,
  Swell not the battle-horn !
Thoughts far too sad those notes will bring,
When to the grave my glorious flower is borne!

Speak not of victory !—in the name
  There is too much of woe!
Hush'd be the empty voice of Fame—
Call me back *his* whose graceful head is low

Speak not of victory !—from my halls
  The sunny hour is gone !
The ancient banner on my walls
Must sink ere long—I had but him—but one!

Within the dwelling of my sires
  The hearths will soon be cold,
With me must die the beacon-fires
That stream'd at midnight from the mountain
    hold.

And let them fade, since *this* must be,
  My lovely and my brave !
Was thy bright blood pour'd forth for me,
And is there but for stately youth a grave ?

Speak to me once again, my boy !
  Wilt thou not hear my call?
Thou wert so full of life and joy,
I had not dreamt of *this*—that thou couldst fall !

Thy mother watches from the steep
  For thy returning plume ;
How shall I tell her that thy sleep
Is of the silent house, th' untimely tomb ?

Thou didst not seem as one to die,
  With all thy young renown !
—Ye saw his falchion's flash on high,
In the mid-fight, when spears and crests went
    down !

Slow be your march!—the field is won
  A dark and evil field !
Lift from the ground my noble son,
And bear him homewards on his bloody shield

---

## THE TOMBS OF PLATÆA

From a Painting by Williams.

And there they sleep !—the men who stood
In arms before th' exulting sun,
And bathed their spears in Persian blood,
And taught the earth how freedom might be won.

They sleep !—th' Olympic wreaths are dead,
Th' Athenian lyres are hush'd and gone;
  The Dorian voice of song is fled—
—Slumber, ye mighty! slumber deeply on !

They sleep, and seems not all around
As hallow'd unto glory's tomb?
  Silence is on the battle ground,
The heavens are loaded with a breathless gloom.

And stars are watching on their height,
But dimly seen through mist and cloud,
  And still and solemn is the light
Which folds the plain, as with a glimmering
    shroud.

And thou, pale night-queen ! here thy beams
Are not as those the shepherd loves,
  Nor look they down on shining streams,
By Naiads haunted, in their laurel groves:

Thou seest no pastoral hamlet sleep,
In shadowy quiet, 'midst its vines;
No temple gleaming from the steep,
'Midst the gray olives, or the mountain pines!

But o'er a dim and boundless waste,
Thy rays, e'en like a tomb-lamp's, brood,
Where man's departed steps are traced
But by his dust, amidst the solitude.

And be it thus!—What slave shall tread
O'er freedom's ancient battle-plains?
Let deserts wrap the glorious dead,
When their bright land sits weeping o'er her
    chains:

Here, where the Persian clarion rung,
And where the Spartan sword flash'd high,
And where the Pæan strains were sung,
From year to year swell'd on by liberty!

Here should no voice, no sound, be heard,
Until the bonds of Greece be riven,
Save of the leader's charging word,
Or the shrill trumpet, pealing up through heaven!

Rest in your silent homes, ye brave!
No vines festoon your lonely tree!*
No harvest o'er your war-field wave,
Till rushing winds proclaim—the land is free!

---

## LOVE AND DEATH.

By thy birth, so oft renew'd
From the embers long subdued;
By the life-gift in thy chain,
Broken link to weave again;

By thine infinite of woe,
All we know not, all we know;
If there be what dieth not,
*Thine* affection is its lot!

Mighty ones, Love and Death
Ye are strong in this world of ours;
Ye meet at the banquets, ye strive 'midst the
    flowers—
Which hath the conqueror's wreath?

*Thou* art the victor, Love!
Thou art the peerless, the crown'd, the free—
The strength of the battle is given to thee,
The spirit from above.

Thou hast look'd on death and smiled!
Thou hast buoy'd up the fragile and reed-like form
Through the tide of the fight, through the rush of
    the storm,
On field, and flood, and wild.

Thou hast stood on the scaffold alone:
Thou hast watch'd by the wheel through the tor-
    turer's hour,
And girt thy soul with a martyr's power
Till the conflict hath been won.

No—*thou* art the victor, Death!
Thou comest—and where is that which spoke
From the depths of the eye, when the bright soul
    woke!
—Gone with the flitting breath!

Thou comest—and what is left
Of all that loved us, to say if aught
*Yet loves*, yet answers the burning thought
Of the spirit lorn and reft?

---

* A single tree appears in Mr. Williams's impressive picture

Silence is where thou art!
Silently thou must kindred meet;
No glance to cheer, and no voice to greet,
No bounding of heart to heart!

Boast not of thy victory, Death!
It is but as the cloud's o'er the sunbeam's power—
It is but as the winter's o'er leaf and flower,
That slumber, the snow beneath.

It is but as a tyrant's reign
O'er the look and the voice, which he bids be still,
—But the sleepless thought and the fiery will
Are not for him to chain.

They shall soar his might above!
And so with the reed whence affection springs,
Though buried, it is not of mortal things—
*Thou* art the victor, Love!

---

## LIGHTS AND SHADES.

The gloomiest day hath gleams of light,
The darkest wave hath bright foam near it,
And twinkles through the cloudiest night
Some solitary star to cheer it.

The gloomiest soul is not *all* gloom;
The saddest heart is not *all* sadness;
And sweetly o'er the darkest doom
There shines some lingering beam of gladness.

Despair is never quite despair:
Nor life, nor death, the future closes;
And round the shadowy brow of care
Will hope and fancy twine their roses.

---

## THE MEETING OF THE BROTHERS.*

"———His early days
Were with him in his heart."
            *Wordsworth.*

The voices of two forest boys,
In years when hearts entwine,
Had fill'd with childhood's merry noise
A valley of the Rhine.
To rock and stream that sound was known
Gladsome as hunter's bugle tone.

The sunny laughter of their eyes
There had each vineyard seen;
Up every cliff whence eagles rise,
Their bounding step had been;
Ay! their bright youth a glory threw
O'er the wild place wherein they grew.

But this, as day-spring's flush, was brief
As early bloom or dew;
Alas! 't is but the wither'd leaf
That wears th' enduring hue;
Those rocks along the Rhine's fair shore,
Might girdle in their world no more.

For now on manhood's verge they stood,
And heard life's thrilling call,
As if a silver clarion woo'd
To some high festival;
And parted as young brothers part,
With love in each unsullied heart.

They parted—soon the paths divide
Wherein our steps were one,
Like river-branches, far and wide
Dissevering as they run,

---

* For the tale on which this little poem is founded, see "L'Italie sous Italie."

And making strangers in their course
Of waves that had the same bright source.

Met they no more?—once more they met,
　Those kindred hearts and true!
'T was on a field of death, where yet
　The battle-thunders flew,
Though the fierce day was well-nigh past,
And the red sunset smiled its last.

But as the combat closed, they found
　For tender thoughts a space,
And e'en upon that bloody ground
　Room for one bright embrace,
And pour'd forth on each other's neck
Such tears as warriors need not check.

The mists o'er boyhood's memory spread
　All melted with those tears;
The faces of the holy dead
　Rose as in vanish'd years;
The Rhine, the Rhine, the ever blest,
Lifted its voice in each full breast!

Oh! was it then a time to die!
　It was!—that not in vain
The soul of childhood's purity
　And peace might turn again,
A ball swept forth—'t was guided well—
Heart unto heart those brothers fell.

Happy, yes, happy thus to go!
　Bearing from earth away
Affections, gifted ne'er to know
　A shadow—a decay,
A passing touch of change or chill,
A breath of aught whose breath can kill

And they, between whose sever'd souls,
　Once in close union tied,
A gulf is set, a current rolls
　For ever to divide.
Well may they envy such a lot,
Whose hearts yearn on—but mingle not

## THE VIEW FROM CASTRI

### From a Painting by Williams.

THERE have been bright and glorious pageants
　here,
Where now gray stones and moss-grown columns
　lie;
There have been words, which earth grew pale
　to bear,
Breathed from the cavern's misty chambers
　nigh:
There have been voices, through the sunny sky,
And the pine-woods, their choral hymn-notes
　sending,
And reeds and lyres, their Dorian melody,
With incense-clouds around the temple blend-
　ing,
And throngs, with laurel-boughs, before the altar
　bending.

There have been treasures of the seas and isles
Brought to the day-god's now forsaken throne:
Thunders have peal'd along the rock-defiles,
When the far-echoing battle-horn made known
That foes were on their way!—the deep wind's
　moan
Hath chill'd the invader's heart with secret fear
And from the Sibyl-grottoes, wild and lone,
Storms have gone forth, which, in their fierce
　career,
From his bold hand have struck the banner and
　the spear.

The shrine hath sunk!—but thou unchanged art
　there!
Mount of the voice and vision, robed with
　dreams!
Unchanged, and rushing through the radiant
　air,
With thy dark-waving pines, and flashing
　streams,

And all thy founts of song! their bright course
　teems
With inspiration yet; and each dim haze,
Or golden cloud which floats around thee, seems
As with its mantle, veiling from our gaze
The mysteries of the past, the gods of elder days!

Away, vain phantasies!—doth less of power
Dwell round thy summit, or thy cliffs invest,
Though in deep stillness now, the ruin's flower
Wave o'er the pillars mouldering on thy breast?
—Lift through the free blue heavens thine ar-
　rowy crest!
Let the great rocks their solitude regain!
No Delphian lyres now break thy noontide rest
With their full chords:—but silent be the strain!
Thou hast a mightier voice to speak th' Eternal's
　reign!

## THE FESTAL HOUR.

WHEN are the lessons given
That shake the startled earth?—When wakes the
　foe,
While the friend sleeps!—When falls the traitor's
　blow?
When are proud sceptres riven,
High hopes o'erthrown!—It is, when lands rejoice,
When cities blaze, and lift th' exulting voice,
And wave their banners to the kindling heaven!

Fear ye the festal hour!
When mirth o'erflows, then tremble!—'T was a
　night
Of gorgeous revel, wreaths, and dance, and light
　When through the regal bower
The trumpet peal'd ere yet the song was done,
And there were shrieks in golden Babylon,
And trampling armies ruthless in their power.

The marble shrines were crown'd:
Young voices, through the blue Athenian sky,
And Dorian reeds, made summer-melody,
　And censers waved around;
And lyres were strung, and bright libations pour'd,
When through the streets, flash'd out the avenging
　sword,
Fearless and free, the sword with myrtles bound.[*]

Through Rome a triumph pass'd,
Rich in her sun-god's mantling beams went by
That long array of glorious pageantry,
　With shout and trumpet-blast.
An empire's gems their starry splendour shed
O'er the proud march; a king in chains was led,
A stately victor, crown'd and robed, came last.[†]

And many a Dryad's bower
Had lent the laurels, which, in waving play,
Stirr'd the warm air, and glisten'd round his way
　As a quick-flashing shower.
—O'er his own porch, meantime the cypress hung
Through his fair halls a cry of anguish rung—
Woe for the dead!—the father's broken flower!

A sound of lyre and song,
In the still night went floating o'er the Nile,
Whose waves, by many an old mysterious pile,
　Swept with that voice along;
And lamps were shining o'er the red wine's foam,
Where a chief revell'd in a monarch's dome,
And fresh rose-garlands deck'd a glittering throng

'T was Antony that bade
The joyous chords ring out!—but strains arose
Of wilder omen at the banquet's close!
　Sounds by no mortal made!

---

[*] The sword of Harmodius.

[†] Paulus Æmilius, one of whose sons died a few days before, and another shortly after, his triumph on the conquest of Macedon, when Perseus, king of that country, was led in chains.

[‡] See the description given by Plutarch, in his life of Antony, of the supernatural sounds heard in the streets of Alexandria, the night before Antony's death

Shook Alexandria through her streets that night,
And pass'd—and with another sunset's light,
The kingly Roman on his bier was laid.

Bright 'midst its vineyards lay
The fair Campanian city,* with its towers
And temples gleaming through dark olive-bowers
    Clear in the golden day;
Joy was around it as the glowing sky
And crowds had fill'd its halls of revelry,
And all the sunny air was music's way.

A cloud came o'er the face
Of Italy's rich heaven!—its crystal blue
Was changed and deepen'd to a wrathful hue
    Of night, o'ershadowing space,
As with the wings of death!—in all his power
Vesuvius woke, and hurl'd the burning shower,
And who could tell the buried city's place?

Such things have been of yore,
In the gay regions where the citrons blow,
And purple summers all their sleepy glow
    On the grape-clusters pour;
And where the palms to spicy winds are waving,
Along clear seas of melted sapphire, laving,
As with a flood of light, their southern shore.

Turn we to other climes!
Far in the Druid-Isle a feast was spread,
'Midst the rock-altars of the warrior-dead,†
    And ancient battle rhymes
Were chanted to the harp; and yellow mead
Went flowing round, and tales of martial deed,
And lofty songs of Britain's elder time.

But ere the giant-fane
Cast its broad shadows on the robe of even,
Hush'd were the bards, and, in the face of Heaven,
    O'er that old burial-plain
Flash'd the keen Saxon dagger!—Blood was
    streaming,
Where late the mead-cup to the sun was gleaming,
And Britain's hearths were heaped that night in
    vain.

For they return'd no more!
They that went forth at morn, with reckless heart
In that fierce banquet's mirth to bear their part;
    And, on the rushy floor,
And the bright spears and bucklers of the walls,
The high wood-fires were blazing in their halls;
But not for them—they slept—their feast was
    o'er!

Fear ye the festal hour!
Ay, tremble when the cup of joy o'erflows!
Tame down the swelling heart!—the bridal rose,
    And the rich myrtle's flower
Have veil'd the sword!—Red wines have sparkled
    fast
From venom'd goblets, and soft breezes pass'd,
With fatal perfume, through the revel's bower.

Twine the young glowing wreath!
But pour not all your spirit in the song,
Which through the sky's deep azure floats along,
    Like summer's quickening breath!
The ground is hollow in the path of mirth,
Oh! far too daring seems the joy of earth,
So darkly press'd and girdled in by death!

* Herculaneum, of which it is related, that all the inhabitants were assembled in the theatres, when the shower of ashes, which covered the city, descended.

† Stonehenge, said by some traditions to have been erected to the memory of Ambrosius, an early British king; and by others mentioned as a monumental record of the massacre of British chiefs here alluded to.

---

# SONG
## OF
## THE BATTLE OF MORGARTEN.

"In the year 1315, Switzerland was invaded by Duke Leopold of Austria, with a formidable army. It is well attested, that this prince repeatedly declared he 'would trample the audacious rustics under his feet;' and that he had procured a large stock of cordage, for the purpose of binding their chiefs, and putting them to death.

"The 15th October, 1315, dawned. The sun darted its first rays on the shields and armour of the advancing host; and this being the first army ever known to have attempted the frontiers of the cantons, the Swiss viewed its long line with various emotions. Monfort de Tettnang led the cavalry into the narrow pass, and soon filled the whole space between the mountain (Mount Sattel) and the lake. The fifty men on the eminence (above Morgarten) raised a sudden shout, and rolled down heaps of rocks and stones among the crowded ranks. The confederates on the mountain, perceiving the impression made by this attack, rushed down in close array, and fell upon the flank of the disordered column. With many clubs they dashed in pieces the armour of the enemy, and dealt their blows and thrusts with long pikes. The narrowness of the defile admitted of no evolutions, and a slight frost having injured the road, the horses were impeded in all their motions; many leaped into the lake; all were startled; and at last the whole column gave way, and fell suddenly back on the infantry; and these last, as the nature of the country did not allow them to open their files, were run over by the fugitives, and many of them trampled to death. A general rout ensued, and Duke Leopold was, with much difficulty, rescued by a peasant, who led him to Winerthur, where the historian of the times saw him arrive in the evening, pale, sullen, and dismayed."—*Planta's History of the Helvetic Confederacy.*

---

The wine-month* shone in its golden prime,
    And the red grapes clustering hung,
But a deeper sound through the Switzer's clime,
    Than the vintage music, rung.
        A sound, through vaulted cave,
        A sound, through echoing glen,
    Like the hollow swell of a rushing wave;
        —'Twas the tread of steel-girt men.

And a trumpet, pealing wild and far,
    'Midst the ancient rocks was blown,
Till the Alps replied to that voice of war,
    With a thousand of their own.
        And through the forest glooms
        Flash'd helmets to the day,
    And the winds were tossing knightly plumes,
        Like the larch-boughs in their play.

In Hasli's† wilds there was gleaming steel,
    As the host of the Austrian pass'd;
And the Schreckhorn's‡ rocks, with a savage peal,
    Made mirth of his clarion's blast.
        Up 'midst the Rigi's§ snows
        The stormy march was heard,
    With the charger's tramp, whence fire-sparks rose,
        And the leader's gathering word

But a band, the noblest band of all,
    Through the rude Morgarten strait,
With blazon'd streamers and lances tall,
    Moved onwards, in princely state.

---

* Wine-month, the German name for October.

† Hasli, a wild district in the canton of Berne.

‡ Schreckhorn, *the peak of terror*, a mountain in the canton of Berne.

§ Rigi, a mountain in the canton of Schwytz.

They came with heavy chains
For the race despised so long -
—But amidst his Alp-domains,
The herdsman's arm is strong !

The sun was reddening the clouds of morn
When they enter'd the rock-defile,
And shrill as a joyous hunter's horn
Their bugles rang the while,
But on the misty height,
Where the mountain-people stood,
There was stillness, as of night,
When storms at distance brood.

There was stillness, as of deep dead night,
And a pause—but not of fear,
While the Switzers gazed on the gathering might
Of the hostile shield and spear,
On wound those columns bright
Between the lake and wood,
But they look'd not to the height
Where the mountain-people stood.

The pass was fill'd with their serried power,
All helm'd and mail-array'd,
And their steps had sounds like a thunder-shower
In the rustling forest-shade,
There were prince and crested knight,
Hemm'd in by cliff and flood,
When a shout arose from the misty height,
Where the mountain-people stood.

And the mighty rocks came bounding down,
Their startled foes among,
With a joyous whirl from the summit thrown—
—Oh! the herdsman's arm is strong !
They came, like lauwine* hurl'd
From Alp to Alp in play,
When the echoes shout through the snowy
    world,
And the pines are borne away.

The fir-woods crash'd on the mountain-side,
And the Switzers rush'd from high,
With a sudden charge on the flower and pride
Of the Austrian chivalry :
Like hunters of the deer,
They storm'd the narrow dell,
And the first in the shock, with Uri's spear,
Was the arm of William Tell.†

There was tumult in the crowded strait,
And a cry of wild dismay,
And many a warrior met his fate
From a peasant's hand that day !
And the empire's banner then,
From its place of waving free,
Went down before the shepherd-men
The men of the Forest-sea ‡

With their pikes and massy clubs they brake
The cuirass and the shield,
And the war-horse dash'd to the reddening lake,
From the reapers of the field !
The field—but not of sheaves—
Proud crests and pennons lay
Strewn o'er it thick as the birch-wood leaves
In the autumn-tempest's way.

Oh! the sun in heaven fierce havoc view'd,
When the Austrian turn'd to fly,
And the brave, in the trampling multitude,
Had a fearful death to die !
And the leader of the war
At eve unhelm'd was seen,
With a hurrying step on the wilds afar,
And a pale and troubled mien.

But the sons of the land which the freemen tills,
Went back from the battle-toil,
To their cabin homes 'midst the deep green hills,
All burden'd with royal spoil.

---

* *Lauwine*, the Swiss name for avalanche.

† William Tell's name is particularly mentioned amongst the confederates at Morgarten.

‡ *Forest-sea*, the lake of the four cantons is also so called.

There were songs and festal fires
On the soaring Alps that night,
When children sprung to greet their sires,
From the wild Morgarten fight.

---

## CHORUS.

Translated from Manzoni's " Conte di Carmagnola."

HARK! from the right bursts forth a trumpet's
    sound !
A loud shrill trumpet from the left replies !
On every side, hoarse echoes from the ground,
To the quick tramp of steeds and warriors rise,
Hollow and deep :—and banners all around,
Meet hostile banners waving through the skies,
Here steel-clad bands in marshall'd order shine,
And there a host confronts their glittering line.

Lo ! half the field already from the sight
Hath vanish'd, hid by closing groups of foes !
Swords crossing swords, flash lightning o'er the
    fight,
And the strife deepens, and the life-blood flows !
—Oh! who are these ? what stranger in his might
Comes bursting on the lovely land's repose ?
What patriot hearts have nobly vow'd to save
Their native soil, and make its dust their grave ?

One race, alas ! these foes, one kindred race,
Were born and rear'd the same bright scenes among!
The stranger calls them brothers—and each face
That brotherhood reveals ; one common tongue
Dwells on their lips ;—the earth, on which ye trace
Their heart's blood, is the soil from whence they
    sprung,
One mother gave them birth—this chosen land,
Girdled with Alps and seas, by Nature's guardian
    hand.

Oh, grief and horror !—Who the first could dare
Against a brother's breast the sword to wield ?
What cause unhallow'd and accursed, declare !
Hath bathed with carnage this ignoble field ?
—Think'st thou they know ?—they but inflict and
    share
Misery and death, the motive unreveal'd !
Sold to a leader, sold *himself* to die,
With him they strive, they fall—and ask not why.

But are there none who love them ?—Have they
    none,
No wives, no mothers, who might rush between,
And win with tears the husband and the son,
Back to their homes from this polluted scene ?
And they, whose hearts when life's bright day is
    done,
Unfold to thoughts more solemn and serene,
Thoughts of the tomb ; why cannot *they* assuage
The storms of passion with the voice of age ?

Ask not ! the peasant at his cabin door
Sits, calmly pointing to the distant cloud
Which skirts th' horizon, menacing to pour
Destruction down o'er fields he hath not plough'd.
Thus, where no echo of the battle's roar
Is heard afar, e'en thus the reckless crowd
In tranquil safety number o'er the slain,
Or tell of cities burning on the plain.

There may'st thou mark the boy, with earnest
    gaze,
Fix'd on his mother's lips intent to know,
By names of insult, those, whom future days
Shall see him meet in arms, their deadliest foe !
There proudly many a glittering dame displays
Bracelet and zone, with radiant gems that glow,
By husbands, lovers, home in triumph borne,
From the sad brides of fallen warriors torn.

Woe to the victors and the vanquish'd ! Woe !
The earth is heap'd, is loaded with the slain,
Loud and more loud the cries of fury grow,
A sea of blood is swelling o'er the plain !

But from the embattled front, already, lo!
A band recoils—it flies—all hope is vain,
And venal hearts, despairing of the strife,
Wake to the love, the clinging love of life

As the light grain disperses in the air,
Borne from the winnowing by the gales around.
Thus fly the vanquish'd, in their wild despair,
Chased—sever'd—scatter'd—o'er the ample ground.
But mightier bands, that lay in ambush there,
Burst on their flight—and hark! the deepening
    sound
Of fierce pursuit!—still nearer and more near,
The rush of war-steeds trampling in the rear!

The day is won;—they fall—disarm'd they yield,
Low at the conqueror's feet all suppliant lying!
'Midst shouts of victory pealing o'er the field,
Oh! who may hear the murmurs of the dying?
—Haste! let the tale of triumph be reveal'd!
E'en now the courier to his steed is flying;
He spurs—he speeds—with tidings of the day,
To rouse up cities in his lightning way.

Why pour ye thus from your deserted homes,
Oh, eager multitudes! around him pressing?
Each hurrying where his breathless courser foams,
Each tongue, each eye, infatuate hope confessing!
Know ye not whence th' ill-omen'd herald comes,
And dare ye dream he comes with words of bless-
    ing?
—Brothers, by brothers slain, lie low and cold—
Be ye content! the glorious tale is told.

I hear the voice of joy, th' exulting cry!
They deck the shrine, they swell the choral
    strains;
E'en now the homicides assail the sky
With pæans, which indignant Heaven disdains!
But, from the soaring Alps, the stranger's eye
Looks watchful down on our ensanguined plains,
And with the cruel rapture of a foe,
Numbers the mighty, stretch'd in death below.

Haste! form your lines again, ye brave and true!
Haste, haste! your triumphs and your joys sus-
    pending!
Th' invader comes; your banners raise anew,
Rush to the strife, your country's cause defending!
Victors! why pause ye?—Are ye weak and few?
Ay, such he deem'd you! and for this descending,
He waits you on the field ye know too well,
The same red war-field where your brethren fell.

Oh! thou devoted land! that canst not rear
In peace thine offspring; thou, the lost and won,
The fair and fatal soil, that dost appear
Too narrow still for each contending son;
Receive the stranger, in his fierce career,
Parting thy spoils!—thy chastening is begun!
And, wresting from thy chiefs the guardian sword,
Foes whom thou ne'er hadst wrong'd, sit proudly
    at thy board.

Are these infatuate too? Oh! who hath known
A people e'er by guilt's vain triumph blest?
The wrong'd, the vanquish'd, suffer not alone,
Brief is the joy that swells th' oppressor's breast.
What though not yet his day of pride be flown,
Though yet Heaven's vengeance spare his tower-
    ing crest,
Well hath it mark'd him—and ordain'd the hour
When his last sigh shall own its mightier power.

Are we not creatures of one hand divine?
Form'd in one mould, to one redemption born?
Kindred alike, where'er our skies may shine,
Where'er our sight first drank the vital morn?
Brothers! one bond around our souls should twine,
And woe to him by whom that bond is torn!
Who mounts by trampling broken hearts to earth,
Who bears down spirits of immortal birth!

## THE MEETING OF THE BARDS.

### WRITTEN FOR AN EISTEDDVOD, OR MEETING OF WELSH BARDS,

*Held in London, May 22d, 1822.*

The *Gorseddau*, or meetings of the British bards, were anciently ordained to be held in the open air, on some conspicuous situation, whilst the sun was above the horizon: or, according to the expression employed on these occasions, "in the face of the sun, and in the eye of light." The places set apart for this purpose were marked out by a circle of stones, called the circle of federation. The presiding bard stood on a large stone (Maen Gorsedd or the stone of assembly,) in the centre. The sheathing of a sword upon this stone was the ceremony which announced the opening of a *Gorsedd*, or meeting. The bards always stood in their uni-coloured robes, with their heads and feet uncovered within the circle of federation.—See *Owen's Translation of the Heroic Elegies of Llywarc Hen.*

Where met our bards of old?—the glorious
    throng,
They of the mountain and the battle song?
They met—oh! not in kingly hall or bower,
But where wild nature girt herself with power:
They met—where streams flash'd bright from rocky
    caves,
They met—where woods made moan o'er warriors'
    graves,
And where the torrent's rainbow spray was cast,
And where dark lakes were heaving to the blast,
And 'midst th' eternal cliffs, whose strength de-
    fied
The crested Roman in his hour of pride;

And where the Carnedd,* on its lonely hill,
Bore silent record of the mighty still;
And where the Druid's ancient Cromlech† frown'd,
And the oaks breathed mysterious murmurs round.
There throng'd th' inspired of yore!—on plain or
    height,
*In the sun's face, beneath the eye of light,*
And, baring unto heaven each noble head,
Stood in the circle, where none else might tread.

Well might their lays be lofty!—soaring thought
From Nature's presence tenfold grandeur caught:
Well might bold Freedom's soul pervade the
    strains,
Which startled eagles from their lone domains,
And, like a breeze, in chainless triumph, went
Up through the blue resounding firmament!

Whence came the echoes to those numbers high?
—'T was from the battle-fields of days gone by!
And from the tombs of heroes, laid to rest
With their good swords, upon the mountain's
    breast;
And from the watch-towers on the heights of
    snow,
Sever'd by cloud and storm, from all below;
And the turf-mounds,‡ once girt by ruddy spears,
And the rock-altars of departed years.

Thence, deeply mingling with the torrent's roar,
The winds a thousand wild responses bore;
And the green land, whose every vale and glen
Doth shrine the memory of heroic men,
On all her hills awakening to rejoice,
Sent forth proud answers to her children's voice.
For us, not ours the festival to hold,
'Midst the stone-circles, hallow'd thus of old;

* *Carnedd*, a stone-barrow, or cairn.

† *Cromlech*, a Druidical monument, or altar. The word means a stone of covenant.

‡ The ancient British chiefs frequently harangued their followers from small artificial mounts of turf.—See *Pennant.*

Not where great Nature's majesty and might
First broke, all-glorious, on our infant sight;
Not near the tombs, where sleep our free and
    brave,
Not by the mountain-llyn,* the ocean wave,
In these late days we meet!—dark Mona's shore,
Eryri's† cliffs resound with harps no more!
But, as the stream (though time or art may turn
The current, bursting from its cavern'd urn,
To bathe soft vales of pastures and of flowers,
From Alpine glens, or ancient forest-bowers,)
Alike, in rushing strength or sunny sleep,
Holds on its course, to mingle with the deep;
Thus, though our paths be changed, still warm
    and free,
Land of the bard! our spirit flies to thee!
To thee our thoughts, our hopes, our hearts be-
    long,
Our dreams are haunted by thy voice of song!
Nor yield our souls one patriot-feeling less,
To the green memory of thy loveliness,
Than theirs, whose harp-notes peal'd from every
    height,
*In the sun's face, beneath the eye of light!*

---

## O, YE HOURS!

O ye hours, ye sunny hours!
    Floating lightly by,
Are ye come with birds and flowers,
    Odours and blue sky?

Yes, we come, again we come,
    Through the wood-paths free
Bringing many a wanderer home,
    With the bird and bee.

O ye hours, ye sunny hours!
    Are ye wafting song?
Doth mild music stream in showers
    All the groves among?

Yes, the nightingale is there,
    While the starlight reigns,
Making young leaves and sweet air
    Tremble with her strains.

O ye hours, ye sunny hours!
    In your silent flow,
Ye are mighty, mighty powers!
    Bring ye bliss or woe!

Ask not this—oh! seek not this:
    Yield your hearts awhile
To the soft wind's balmy kiss,
    And the heaven's bright smile!

Throw not shades of anxious thought
    O'er the glowing flowers!
We are come with sunshine fraught,
    Question not the hours!

---

## THE SONG OF THE GIFTED.

> "That voice remeasures
> Whatever tones and melancholy pleasures,
> The things of nature utter: birds or trees,
> Or where the tall grass 'mid the heath-plant waves,
> Murmur and music this of sudden breeze."
>
> *Coleridge.*

---

I HEARD a song upon the wandering wind,
A song of many tones—though one full soul
Breathed through them all imploringly; and made
All nature as they pass'd, all quivering leaves
And low responsive reeds and waters thrill,
As with the consciousness of human prayer.

—At times the passion-kindled melody
Might seem to gush from Sappho's fervent heart,
Over the wild sea-wave;—at times the strain
Flow'd with more plaintive sweetness, as if born
Of Petrarch's voice, beside the lone Vaucluse;
And sometimes, with its melancholy swell,
A graver sound was mingled, a deep note
Of Tasso's holy lyre; yet still the tones
Were of a suppliant;—"*Leave me not!*" was still
The burden of their music; and I knew
The lay which genius, in its loneliness,
Its own still world amidst th' o'erpeopled world,
Hath ever breathed to Love.

They crown me with the glistening crown,
    Borne from a deathless tree;
I hear the pealing music of renown—
    O Love! forsake me not!
    Mine were a lone dark lot,
        Bereft of thee!

They tell me that my soul can throw
    A glory o'er the earth!
From thee, from *thee*, is caught that golden glow!
    Shed by thy gentle eyes
    It gives to flower and skies,
        A bright, new birth!
    Thence gleams the path of morning,
    Over the kindling hills, a sunny zone!
        Thence to its heart of hearts, the rose is
            burning
            With lustre not its own!
            Thence every wood-recess
            Is fill'd with loveliness,
    Each bower, to ringdoves, and dim violets
        known.

I see all beauty by thy ray
    That streameth from thy smile;
Oh! bear it, bear it not away,
    Can that sweet light beguile?
    Too pure, too spirit-like, it seems,
    To linger long by earthly streams;

I clasp it with th' alloy
    Of fear 'midst quivering joy;
Yet must I perish if the gift depart—
Leave me not, Love! to mine own beating
    heart!

The music from my lyre
With thy swift step would flee;
    The world's cold breath would quench the starry
        fire
In my deep soul—a temple fill'd with thee!
    Seal'd would the fountains lie,
    The waves of harmony,
Which thou alone canst free?

Like a shrine 'midst rocks forsaken,
    Whence the oracle hath fled;
Like a harp which none might waken
    But a mighty master dead;
Like the vase of perfume scatter'd,
    Such would my spirit be;
So mute, so void, so shatter'd,
    Bereft of thee!

Leave me not, Love! or if this earth
    Yield not for thee a home,
If the bright summer-land of thy pure birth
    Send thee a silvery voice that whispers—
        "Come!"
Then, with the glory from the rose,
    With the sparkle from the stream,
With the light thy rainbow-presence throws
    Over the poet's dream;
    With all th' Elysian hues
    Thy pathway that suffuse,
With joy, with music, from the fading grove,
Take me, too, heavenward, on thy wing, sweet
    Love!

---

## MARGUERITE OF FRANCE.*

Thou falcon-hearted dove.
*Coleridge.*

THE Moslem spears were gleaming
  Round Damietta's towers,
Though a Christian banner from her wall,
  Waved free its Lily-flowers.
Ay, proudly did the banner wave,
  As Queen of Earth and Air;
But faint hearts throbb'd beneath its folds,
  In anguish and despair.

Deep, deep in Paynim dungeon,
  Their kingly chieftain lay,
And low on many an Eastern field
  Their knighthood's best array.
'T was mournful, when at feasts they met,
  The wine-cup round to send,
For each that touch'd it silently,
  Then miss'd a gallant friend!

And mournful was their vigil
  On the beleaguer'd wall,
And dark their slumber, dark with dreams
  Of slow defeat and fall.
Yet a few hearts of Chivalry
  Rose high to breast the storm,
And one—of all the loftiest there—
  Thrill'd in a woman's form.

A woman, meekly bending
  O'er the slumber of her child,
With her soft sad eyes of weeping love,
  As the Virgin Mother's mild.
Oh! roughly cradled was thy Babe,
  'Midst the clash of spear and lance,
And a strange, wild bower was thine, young
      Queen:
  Fair Marguerite of France!

A dark and vaulted chamber,
  Like a scene for wizard-spell,
Deep in the Saracenic gloom
  Of the warrior citadel;
And there 'midst arms the couch was spread,
  And with banners curtain'd o'er,
For the Daughter of the Minstrel-land,
  The gay Provençal shore!

For the bright Queen of St. Louis,
  The star of court and hall!—
But the deep strength of the gentle heart,
  Wakes to the tempest's call!
Her Lord was in the Paynim's hold,
  His soul with grief oppress'd,
Yet calmly lay the Desolate,
  With her young babe on her breast!

There were voices in the city,
  Voices of wrath and fear—
" The walls grow weak, the strife is vain,
  We will not perish here!
Yield! yield! and let the crescent gleam
  O'er tower and bastion high!
Our distant homes are beautiful—
  We stay not here to die!"

They bore those fearful tidings
  To the sad Queen where she lay—
They told a tale of wavering hearts,
  Of treason and dismay:

The blood rush'd through her pearly cheek,
  The sparkle to her eye—
" Now call me hither those recreant knights,
  From the bands of Italy!"*

Then through the vaulted chambers
  Stern iron footsteps rang;
And heavily the sounding floor
  Gave back the sabre's clang.
They stood around her—steel-clad men,
  Moulded for storm and fight,
But they quail'd before the loftier soul
  In that pale aspect bright.

Yes—as before the Falcon shrinks
  The Bird of meaner wing,
So shrank they from th' imperial glance
  Of Her—that fragile thing!
And her flute-like voice rose clear and high,
  Through the din of arms around,
Sweet, and yet stirring to the soul,
  As a silver clarion's sound.

" The honour of the Lily
  Is in your hands to keep,
And the Banner of the Cross, for Him
  Who died on Calvary's steep:
And the city which for Christian prayer
  Hath heard the holy bell—
And is it *these* your hearts would yield
  To the godless Infidel?

" Then bring me here a breastplate,
  And a helm, before ye fly,
And I will gird my woman's form,
  And on the ramparts die!
And the Boy whom I have borne for woe,
  But never for disgrace,
Shall go within mine arms to death
  Meet for his royal race.

" Look on him as he slumbers
  In the shadow of the Lance!
Then go, and with the Cross forsake
  The princely Babe of France!
But tell your homes ye left one heart
  To perish undefiled;
A Woman and a Queen, to guard
  Her Honour and her Child!"

Before her words they thrill'd, like leaves,
  When winds are in the wood;
And a deepening murmur told of men
  Roused to a loftier mood.
And her Babe awoke to flushing swords,
  Unsheathed in many a hand,
As they gather'd round the helpless One,
  Again a noble band!

" We are thy warriors, Lady!
  True to the Cross and thee!
The spirit of thy kindling words
  On every sword shall be!
Rest, with thy fair child on thy breast,
  Rest—we will guard thee well:
St. Dennis for the Lily-flower,
  And the Christian citadel!"

---

## THE FALLEN LIME-TREE.

OH, joy of the peasant! O stately lime!
Thou art fallen in thy golden honey-time
      Thou whose wavy shadows,
        Long and long ago,
      Screen'd our gray forefathers
        From the noontide's glow;
      Thou, beneath whose branches,
        Touch'd with moonlight gleams,
      Lay our early poets
        Wrapt in fairy dreams.
O tree of our fathers! O hallow'd tree!
A glory is gone from our home with thee

* Queen of St. Louis. Whilst besieged by the Turks in Damietta, during the captivity of the king, her husband, she there gave birth to a son, whom she named Tristan, in commemoration of her misfortunes. Information being conveyed to her that the knights intrusted with the defence of the city had resolved on capitulation, she had them summoned to her apartment, and, by her heroic words, so wrought upon their spirits, that they vowed to defend her and the Cross to the last extremity

* The proposal to capitulate is attributed by the French historide to the Knights of Pisa.

Where shall now the weary
    Rest through summer eves?
Or the bee find honey,
    As on thy sweet leaves?
Where shall now the ring-dove
    Build again her nest?
She so long the inmate
    Of thy fragrant breast?
But the sons of the peasant have lost in thee
Far more than the ring-dove, far more than the
    bee!

These may yet find coverts,
    Leafy and profound,
Full of dewy dimness,
    Odour and soft sound:
But the gentle memories
    Clinging all to thee,
When shall they be gather'd
    Round another tree?
O pride of our fathers; O, hallow'd tree!
The crown of the hamlet is fallen in thee!

## THE FREED BIRD.

Swifter far than summer's flight,
Swifter far than youth's delight,
Swifter far than happy night,
            Thou art come and gone!

As the earth when leaves are dead,
As the night when sleep is sped,
As the heart when joy is fled,
            I am left here, alone!
                                *Shelley.*

Return, return, my Bird!
    I have dress'd thy cage with flowers,
'T is lovely as a violet bank
    In the heart of forest bowers.

" I am free, I am free, I return no more!
The weary time of the cage is o'er!
Through the rolling clouds I can soar on high,
The sky is around me, the blue bright sky!

" The hills lie beneath me, spread far and clear,
With their glowing heath-flowers and bounding
        deer—
I see the waves flash on the sunny shore—
I am free, I am free—I return no more!"

Alas, alas, my Bird!
    Why seek'st thou to be free?
Wert thou not blest in thy little bower,
    When thy song breathed naught but glee?

" Did my song of summer breathe naught but
        glee?
Did the voice of the captive seem sweet to thee?
—Oh! hadst thou known its deep meaning well!
It had tales of a burning heart to tell!

" From a dream of the forest that music sprang,
Through its notes the peal of a torrent rang;
And its dying fall, when it soothed thee best,
Sigh'd, for wild flowers and a leafy nest."

Was it with thee thus, my Bird?
    Yet thine eye flash'd clear and bright!
I have seen the glance of sudden joy
    In its quick and dewy light!

" It flash'd with the fire of a tameless race,
With the soul of the wild wood, my native place!
With the spirit that panted through heaven to
        soar—
Woo me not back—I return no more!

" My home is high, amidst rocking trees,
My kindred things are the star and breeze,
And the fount uncheck'd in its lonely play,
And the odours that wander afar, away!"

Farewell, farewell, then, Bird!
    I have call'd on spirits gone,
And it may be they joy'd like *thee* to part,
    Like thee, that wert all my own!

' If they were captives, and pined like me,
Though Love might guard them, they joy'd to be
        free!
They sprang from the earth with a burst of power,
To the strength of their wings, to their triumph's
        hour!

" Call them not back when the chain is riven,
When the way of the pinion is all through heaven!
Farewell!—With my song through the clouds I
        soar,
I pierce the blue skies—I am Earth's no more!"

## THE FLOWER OF THE DESERT.

" Who does not recollect the exultation of Valliant
over a flower in the torrid wastes of Africa?—The affecting mention of the influence of a flower upon the
mind, by Mungo Park, in a time of suffering and despondency, in the heart of the same savage country, is
familiar to every one."—*Howitt's Book of the Seasons.*

Why art thou thus in thy beauty cast,
    O lonely, loneliest flower!
Where the sound of song hath never pass'd
    From human hearth or bower?

I pity thee, for thy heart of love,
    For thy glowing heart, that fain
Would breathe out joy with each wind to rove—
    In vain, lost thing! in vain!

I pity thee for thy wasted bloom,
    For thy glory's fleeting hour,
For the desert place, thy living tomb—
    O lonely, loneliest flower!

I said—but a low voice made reply,
    " Lament not for the flower!
Though its blossoms all unmark'd must die,
    They have had a glorious dower.

" Though it bloom afar from the minstrel's way,
    And the paths where lovers tread,
Yet strength and hope, like an inborn day,
    By its odours hath been shed.

" Yes! dews more sweet than ever fell
    O'er island of the blest,
Were shaken forth, from its perfumed bell,
    On a suffering human breast.

" A wanderer came, as a stricken deer,
    O'er the waste of burning sand,
He bore the wound of an Arab spear,
    He fled from a ruthless band.

" And dreams of home, in a troubled tide,
    Swept o'er his darkening eye,
As he lay down by the fountain side,
    In his mute despair to die.

" But his glance was caught by the desert's flower,
    The precious boon of heaven!
And sudden hope, like a vernal shower,
    To his fainting heart was given.

" For the bright flower spoke of One above;
    Of the Presence, felt to brood,
With a Spirit of pervading love,
    O'er the wildest solitude.

" Oh! the seed was thrown these wastes among,
    In a blest and gracious hour!
For the lorn one rose, in heart made strong,
    By the lonely loneliest flower!"

## THE HUGUENOT'S FAREWELL.

I stand upon the threshold stone
  Of mine ancestral hall;
I hear my native river moan;
  I see the night o'er my old forests fall.

I look round on the darkening vale,
  That saw my childhood's plays:
The low wind in its rising wail
  Hath a strange tone, a sound of other days.

But I must rule my swelling breath:
  A sign is in the sky;
Bright o'er yon gray rock's eagle nest
  Shines forth a warning star—it bids me fly

My father's sword is in my hand,
  His deep voice haunts mine ear;
He tells me of the noble band,
  Whose lives have left a brooding glory here.

He bids their offspring guard from stain
  Their pure and lofty faith;
And yield up all things to maintain
  The cause, for which they girt themselves to
    death.

And I obey.—I leave their towers
  Unto the stranger's tread;
Unto the creeping grass and flowers;
  Unto the fading pictures of the dead.

I leave their shields to slow decay,
  Their banners to the dust;
I go, and only bear away
  Their old majestic name,—a solemn trust!

I go up to the ancient hills,
  Where chains may never be,
Where leap in joy the torrent rills,
  Where man may worship God, alone and free.

There shall an altar and a camp
  Impregnably arise;
There shall be lit a quenchless lamp,
  To shine unwavering through the open skies.

And song shall 'midst the rocks be heard,
  And fearless prayer ascend;
While thrilling to God's holy word,
  The mountain pines in adoration bend.

And there the burning heart no more
  Its deep thought shall suppress,
But the long-buried truth shall pour
  Free currents thence, amidst the wilderness.

Then fare thee well, my mother's bower,
  Farewell, my father's hearth;
Perish, my home! where lawless power
  Hath rent the tie of love to native earth.

Perish! let deathlike silence fall
  Upon the lone abode:
Spread fast, dark ivy, spread thy pall:—
  I go up to the mountains with my God.

## THE WANDERER.

From the German of Schmidt Von Lubeck.[*]

I come down from the hills alone,
Mist wraps the vale, the billows moan;
I wander on in thoughtful care,
For ever asking, sighing—*Where?*

The sunshine round seems dim and cold,
And flowers are pale, and life is old,
And words fall soulless on my ear,
Oh! I am still a stranger here.

[*] See the original in the Dublin University Magazine for February, 1831.

---

Where art thou, land, sweet land, mine own?
Still sought for, longed for, never known!
The land, the land of hope, of light,
Where glow my roses, freshly bright;—

And where my friends the green paths tread
And where in beauty rise my dead;
The land that speaks my native speech,
The blessed land I may not reach!

I wander on in thoughtful care,
For ever asking, sighing—*Where?*
And spirit-sounds come answering this,
*"There, where thou art not, there is bliss."*

## THE SILENT MULTITUDE.

*For we are many in our Solitude.*
*Lament of Tasso.*

A mighty and a mingled throng
  Were gather'd in one spot;
The Dwellers of a thousand Homes—
  Yet 'midst them Voice was not.

The Soldier and his Chief were there—
  The Mother and her Child;
The friends, the Sisters of one hearth—
  None spoke—none moved, none smiled.

There lovers met, between whose lives
  Years had swept darkly by;
After that heart-sick hope deferr'd—
  They met—but silently.

You might have heard the rustling leaf,
  The breeze's faintest sound,
The shiver of an insect's wing
  On that thick-peopled ground.

Your voice to whispers would have died,
  For the deep quiet's sake;
Your tread the softest moss have sought,
  Such stillness not to break.

What held the countless Multitude
  Bound in that spell of peace?
How could the ever-sounding life
  Amid so many cease?

Was it some pageant of the air—
  Some glory high above,
That link'd and hush'd those human souls
  In reverential love?

Or did some burdening passion's weight
  Hang on their indrawn breath?
Awe—the pale awe that freezes words?
  Fear—the strong fear of Death?

A mightier thing—Death, Death himself
  Lay on each lonely heart!
Kindred were there—yet hermits all—
  Thousands—but each apart

## WASHINGTON'S STATUE.

Sent from England to America.

Yes! rear thy guardian Hero's form
On thy proud soil, thou Western World
A watcher through each sign of storm,
  O'er Freedom's flag unfurl'd.

There, as before a shrine to bow,
Bid thy true sons their children lead;
The language of that noble brow
  For all things good shall plead.

The spirit rear'd in patriot fight,
The Virtue born of Home and Hearth,
There calmly throned, a holy light
    Shall pour o'er chainless earth.

And let that work of England's hand,
Sent through the blast and surge's roar,
So girt with tranquil glory, stand
    For ages on thy shore!

Such through all time the greetings be,
That with the Atlantic billow sweep!
Telling the Mighty and the Free
    Of Brothers o'er the Deep!

## THE BROKEN LUTE

She dwelt in proud Venetian halls,
  Midst forms that breathed from the pictured
    walls;
But in a glow of beauty like her own,
There had no dream of the painter thrown.
Lit from within was her noble brow,
As an urn, whence rays from a lamp may flow;
Her young, clear cheek had a changeful hue,
As if ye might see how the soul wrought through;
And every flash of her fervent eye
Seem'd the bright wakening of Poesy.

Even thus it was!—from her childhood's years,—
A being of sudden smiles and tears,—
Passionate visions, quick light and shade,—
Such was tha. high-born Italian maid!
And the spirit of song in her bosom-cell,
Dwelt as the odours in violets dwell,—
Or as the sounds in Eolian strings,
Or in aspen-leaves the quiverings;
There, ever there, with the life enshrined,
And waiting the call of the faintest wind.

Oft, on the wave of the Adrian sea,
In the city's hour of moonlight glee,—
Oft would that gift of the southern sky,
O'erflow from her lip in melody;—
Oft amid festal halls it came,
Like the springing forth of a sudden flame,—
Till the dance was hush'd, and the silvery tone
Of her inspiration was heard alone.
And Fame went with her, the bright, the crown'd,
And Music floated her steps around;
And every lay of her soul was borne
Through the sunny land, as on wings of morn.

And was the daughter of Venice blest,
With a power so deep in her youthful breast?
Could she be happy, o'er whose dark eye
So many changes and dreams went by?
And in whose cheek the swift crimson wrought,
As if but born from the rush of thought?
—Yes! in the brightness of joy awhile
She moved, as a bark in the sunbeam's smile;
For her spirit, as over her lyre's full chord,
All, all on a happy love was pour'd.
How loves a heart, whence the stream of song
Flows like the life-blood, quick, bright, and
    strong?
How loves a heart which hath ever proved
One breath of the world?—Even so she loved!
Blest, though the lord of her soul afar,
Was charging the foremost in Moslem war,—
Bearing the flag of St. Mark's on high,
As a ruling star in the Grecian sky.
Proud music breathed in her song, when Fame
Gave a tone more thrilling to his name;
And her trust in his love was a woman's faith—
Perfect, and fearing no change but death.

But the fields are won from the Ottoman host,
In the land that quell'd the Persian's boast;
And a thousand hearts in Venice burn,
For the day of triumph and return!
—The day is come! the flashing deep
Foams where the galleys of victory sweep;

And the sceptred city of the wave,
With her festal splendour, greets the brave;
Cymbal and clarion, and voice, around,
Make the air one stream of exulting sound,
While the beautiful, with their sunny smiles,
Look from each hall of the hundred isles.

But happiest and brightest that day of all,
Robed for her warrior's festival,
Moving a queen 'midst the radiant throng,
Was she, th' inspired one, the maid of song!
The lute he loved on her arm she bore,
As she rush'd in her joy to the crowded shore;
With a hue on her cheek like the damask glow
By the sunset given unto mountain snow,
And her eye all fill'd with the spirit's play,
Like the flash of a gem to the changeful day,
And her long hair waving in ringlets bright—
So came that being of hope and light!
—One moment, Erminia! one moment more,
And life, all the beauty of life, is o'er!
The bark of her lover hath touch'd the strand—
Whom leads he forth with a gentle hand?
—A young, fair form, whose nymph-like grace
Accorded well with the Grecian face,
And the eye, in its clear soft darkness meek,
And the lashes that droop'd o'er a pale rose
    cheek;
And he look'd on that beauty with tender pride—
The warrior hath brought back an eastern bride!

But how stood she, the forsaken, there,
Struck by the lightning of swift despair?
Still, as amazed with grief, she stood,
And her cheek to her heart sent back the blood
And there came from her quivering lip no word—
Only the fall of her lute was heard,
As it dropt from her hand at her rival's feet,
Into fragments, whose dying thrill was sweet!

What more remaineth? Her day was done;
Her fate and the Broken Lute's were one!
The light, the vision, the gift of power,
Pass'd from her soul in that mortal hour,
Like the rich sound from the shatter'd string,
Whence the gush of sweetness no more might
    spring!

As an eagle struck in his upward flight,
So was her hope from its radiant height,
And her song went with it for ever more,
A gladness taken from sea and shore!
She had moved to the echoing sound of fame—
Silently, silently, died her name!
Silently melted her life away,
As ye have seen a young flower decay,
Or a lamp that hath swiftly burn'd, expire,
Or a bright stream shrink from the Summer's fire,
Leaving its channel all dry and mute—
Woe for the Broken Heart and Lute!

## SABBATH SONNET

How many blessed groups this hour are bending
Through England's primrose meadow paths their
    way
Toward spire and tower, 'midst shadowy elms
    ascending,
Whence the sweet chimes proclaim the hallow'd
    day!
The halls from old heroic ages gray
Pour their fair children forth; and hamlets low,
With those thick orchard blooms the soft winds
    play,
Sent out their inmates in a happy flow,
Like a free vernal stream.   I may not tread
With them those pathways,—to the feverish bed
Of sickness bound:—yet, oh my God! I bless
Thy mercy, that with Sabbath peace hath fill'd
My chasten'd heart, and all its throbbings still'd
To one deep calm of lowliest thankfulness

## THE CROSS OF THE SOUTH.

The beautiful constellation of the Cross is seen only in the Southern Hemisphere. The following lines are supposed to be addressed to it by a Spanish Traveller in South America.

In the silence and grandeur of midnight I tread,
Where savannahs, in boundless magnificence,
    spread;
And bearing sublimely their snow-wreaths on
    high,
The far Cordilleras unite with the sky.

The fern-tree waves o'er me, the fire-fly's red light
With its quick-glancing splendour illumines the
    night,
And I read in each tint of the skies and the earth,
How distant my steps from the land of my birth.

But to thee, as thy load-stars resplendently burn
In their clear depths of blue, with devotion I turn,
Bright Cross of the South!—and beholding thee
    shine,
Scarce regret the loved land of the olive and vine.

Thou recallest the ages when first o'er the main
My fathers unfolded the ensign of Spain,
And planted their faith in the regions that see
Its unperishing symbol emblazon'd in thee.

How oft in their course o'er the ocean's unknown,
Where all was mysterious and awful and lone,
Hath their spirit been cheer'd by thy light, when
    the deep
Reflected its brilliance in tremulous sleep!

As the vision that rose to the lord of the world,*
When first his bright banner of faith was unfurl'd;
Even such to the heroes of Spain, when their
    prow
Made the billows the path of their glory, wert
    thou!

* Constantine.

And to me as I traversed the world of the west,
Through deserts of beauty in stillness that rest;
By forests and rivers untamed in their pride,
Thy beams have a language, thy course is a
    guide.

Shine on—my own land is a far distant spot,
And the stars of thy sphere can enlighten it not,
And the eyes that I know, though e'en now they
    may be
O'er the firmament wandering, can gaze not on
    thee!

But thou to my thoughts art a pure-blazing
    shrine,
A fount of bright hopes, and of visions divine;
And my soul, as an eagle exulting and free,
Soars high o'er the Andes to mingle with thee.

## THE POETRY OF THE PSALMS.

Nobly thy song, O minstrel! rush'd to meet
    Th' Eternal on the pathway of the blast,
    With darkness round him as a mantle cast
And cherubim to waft his flying seat,
Amidst the hills that smoked beneath his feet,
    With trumpet voice thy spirit call'd aloud,
And bade the trembling rocks his name repeat,
    And the bent cedars, and the bursting cloud.
But far more gloriously to earth made known
By that high strain, than by the thunder's tone,
    Than flashing torrents, or the ocean's roll;
Jehovah spoke through the inbreathing fire,
Nature's vast realms for ever to inspire
    With the deep worship of a living soul.

Dublin, April, 1836.

## MOORISH BRIDAL SONG.

*It is a custom among the Moors, that a female who dies unmarried is clothed for interment in wedding apparel, and the bridal song is sung over her remains before they are borne from her home.— See the Narrative of a Ten Years' Residence in Tripoli, by the sister-in-law of Mr. Tully.*

THE citron groves their fruit and flowers were
    strewing
Around a Moorish palace, while the sigh
Of low sweet summer-winds, the branches woo
    ing,
With music through their shadowy bowers went
    by;
Music and voices, from the marble halls,
Through the leaves gleaming, and the fountain-
    falls.

A song of joy, a bridal song came swelling,
To blend with fragrance in those southern shades,
And told of feasts within the stately dwelling,
Bright lamps, and dancing steps, and gem-
    crown'd maids;
And thus it flow'd;—yet something in the lay
Belong'd to sadness, as it died away.

"The bride comes forth! her tears no more are
    falling
To leave the chamber of her infant years;
Kind voices from a distant home are calling;
She comes like day-spring—she hath done with
    tears;
Now must her dark eye shine on other flowers,
Her soft smile gladden other hearts than ours!—
    Pour the rich odours round!

"We haste! the chosen and the lovely bringing,
Love still goes with her from her place of birth,
Deep, silent joy within her soul is springing,
Though in her glance the light no more is mirth!
Her beauty leaves us in its rosy years;
Her sisters weep—but she hath done with tears!—
    Now may the timbrel sound!"

Know'st thou for *whom* they sang the bridal
    numbers?
—One, whose rich tresses were to wave no more!
One, whose pale cheek soft winds, nor gentle
    slumbers,
Nor Love's own sigh, to rose-tints might restore!
Her graceful ringlets o'er a bier were spread.—
Weep for the young, the beautiful,—the dead!

## THE SWORD OF THE TOMB.

### A NORTHERN LEGEND.

The idea of this ballad is taken from a scene in "Star-kother," a tragedy by the Danish poet Oehlenschlager.



A sepulchral fire here alluded to, and supposed to guard the ashes of deceased heroes, is frequently mentioned in the Northern Sagas. Severe sufferings to the departed spirit were supposed by the Scandinavian mythologists to be the consequence of any profanation of the sepulchre.——*See Oehlenschlager's Plays.*

"Voice of the gifted elder time!
Voice of the charm and the Rune rhyme!
Speak! from the shades and the depths disclose,
How Sigurd may vanquish his mortal foes;
    Voice of the buried past!

"Voice of the grave! 't is the mighty hour,
When Night with her stars and dreams hath power,
And my step hath been soundless on the snows,
And the spell I have sung hath laid repose
    On the billow and the blast."

    Then the torrents of the North,
    And the forest pines were still,
    While a hollow chant came forth
    From the dark sepulchral hill.

"There shines no sun 'midst the hidden dead,
But where the day looks not, the brave may tread;
There is heard no song, and no mead is pour'd,
But the warrior may come to the silent board,
    In the shadow of the night.

"There is laid a sword in thy father's tomb,
And its edge is fraught with thy foeman's doom;
But soft be thy step through the silence deep,
And move not the urn in the house of sleep,
    For the viewless have fearful might!"

    Then died the solemn lay,
    As a trumpet's music dies,
    By the night-wind borne away
    Through the wild and stormy skies.

The fir-trees rock'd to the wailing blast,
As on through the forest the warrior pass'd,—
Through the forest of Odin, the dim and old
The dark place of visions and legends, told
    By the fires of northern pine.

The fir-trees rock'd, and the frozen ground
Gave back to his footstep a hollow sound;
And it seem'd that the depths of those awful shades
From the dreary gloom of their long arcades,
    Gave warning, with voice and sign.

    But the wind strange magic knows,
    To call wild shape and tone
    From the gray wood's tossing boughs,
    When Night is on her throne.

The pines closed o'er him with deeper gloom,
As he took the path to the monarch's tomb;
The Pole-star shone, and the heavens were bright
With the arrowy streams of the Northern light,
    But his road through dimness lay!

He pass'd, in the heart of that ancient wood,
The dark shrine stain'd with the victim's blood,
Nor paused, till the rock where a vaulted bed
Had been hewn of old for the kingly dead,
    Arose on his midnight way.

    Then first a moment's chill
    Went shuddering through his breast,
    And th' steel-clad man stood still
    Before that place of rest.

But he cross'd at length with a deep-drawn breath
The threshold-floor of the hall of Death,
And look'd on the pale mysterious fire
Which gleam'd from the urn of his warrior-sire,
    With a strange and solemn light.

Then darkly the words of the boding strain
Like an omen rose on his soul again,
—"Soft be thy step through the silence deep,
And move not the urn in the house of sleep,
    For the viewless have fearful might!"

    But the gleaming sword and shield
    Of many a battle-day
    Hung o'er that urn, reveal'd
    By the tomb-fire's waveless ray

With a faded wreath of oak-leaves bound,
They hung o'er the dust of the far-renown'd,
Whom the bright Valkyriur's warning voice
Had call'd to the banquet where gods rejoice,
    And the rich mead flows in light.

With a beating heart his son drew near
And still rang the verse in his thrilling ear,
—"Soft be thy step through the silence deep,
And move not the urn in the house of sleep,
    For the viewless have fearful might!"

    And many a Saga's rhyme,
    And legend of the grave,
    That shadowy scene and time
    Call'd back to daunt the brave.

But he raised his arm—and the flame grew dim,
And the sword in its light seem'd to wave and
    swim,
And his faltering hand could not grasp it well—
From the pale oak-wreath, with a clash it fell
    Through the chamber of the dead!

The deep tomb rang with the heavy sound,
And the urn lay shiver'd in fragments round;
And a rush, as of tempests, quench'd the fire,
And the scatter'd dust of his war-like sire
    Was strewn on the champion's head.

    One moment—and all was still
    In the slumberer's ancient hall,
    When the rock had ceased to thrill
    With the mighty weapon's fall.

The stars were just fading, one by one,
The clouds were just tinged by the early sun,
When there stream'd through the cavern a torch's
    flame,
And the brother of Sigurd the valiant came
    To seek him in the tomb.

Stretch'd on his shield, like the steel-girt slain,
By moonlight seen on the battle-plain,
In a speechless trance lay the warrior there,
But he wildly woke when the torch's glare
    Burst on him through the gloom.

    " The morning wind blows free,
    And the hour of chase is near;
    Come forth, come forth, with me!
    What dost thou, Sigurd, here?"'

" I have put out the holy sepulchral fire,
I have scatter'd the dust of my warrior-sire!
It burns on my head, and it weighs down my
    heart:
But the winds shall not wander without their part
    To strew o'er the restless deep!

17

" In the mantle of death he was here with me
    now,
There was wrath in his eye, there was gloom on
    his brow;
And his cold, still glance on my spirit fell
With an icy ray and a withering spell—
    Oh! chill is the house of sleep!"

    " The morning wind blows free,
    And the reddening sun shines clear;
    Come forth, come forth, with me!
    It is dark and fearful here!"

" He is there, he is there, with his shadowy frown
But gone from his head is the kingly crown,—
The crown from his head, and the spear from his
    hand,—
They have chased him far from the glorious land
    Where the feast of the gods is spread!

" He must go forth alone on his phantom steed,
He must ride o'er the grave-hills with stormy speed;
His place is no longer at Odin's board,
He is driven from Valhalla without his sword!
    But the slayer shall avenge the dead!"

    That sword its fame had won
    By the fall of many a crest,
    But its fiercest work was done
    In the tomb, on Sigurd's breast!

---

## THE BIRD'S RELEASE.

The Indians of Bengal and of the Coast of Malabar
bring cages filled with birds to the graves of their friends,
over which they set the birds at liberty. This custom is
alluded to in the description of Virginia's funeral.—*See
Paul and Virginia.*

---

    Go forth, for she is gone!
With the golden light of her wavy hair,
She is gone to the fields of the viewless air;
    She hath left her dwelling lone!

    Her voice hath pass'd away!
It hath pass'd away like a summer breeze,
When it leaves the hills for the far blue seas,
    Where we may not trace its way.

    Go forth, and like her be free!
With thy radiant wing, and thy glancing eye
'Thou hast all the range of the sunny sky
    And what is our grief to thee?

    Is it aught ev'n to her we mourn?
Doth she look on the tears by her kindred shed?
Doth she rest with the flowers o'er her gentle head
    Or float on the light wind borne?

    We know not—but she is gone!
Her step from the dance, her voice from the song,
And the smile of her eye from the festal throng;—
    She hath left her dwelling lone!

    When the waves at sunset shine,
We may hear thy voice, amidst thousands more,
In the scented woods of our glowing shore,
    But we shall not know 't is thine!

    Ev'n so with the loved one flown!
Her smile in the starlight may wander by,
Her breath may be near in the wind's low sigh,
    Around us—but all unknown.

Go forth, we have loosed thy chain!
We may deck thy cage with the richest flowers,
Which the bright day rears in our eastern bowers,
    But thou wilt not be lured again.

Ev'n thus may the summer pour
All fragrant things on the land's green breast,
And the glorious earth like a bride be dress'd,
    But it wins *her* back no more!

## VALKYRIUR SONG.

The Valkyriur, or Fatal Sisters of Northern mythology, were supposed to single out the warriors who were
to die in battle, and be received into the halls of Odin.

When a Northern chief fell gloriously in war, his obsequies were honoured with all possible magnificence
His arms, gold and silver, war-horse, domestic attendants, and whatever else he held most dear, were placed
with him on the pile. His dependents and friends frequently made it a point of honour to die with their leader, in order to attend on his shade in Valhalla, or the
Palace of Odin. And lastly, his wife was generally
consumed with him on the same pile.——*See Mallet's
Northern Antiquities, Herbert's Helga, &c.*

Tremblingly flash'd th' inconstant meteor light,
Showing thin forms like virgins of this earth,
Save that all signs of human joy or grief,
The flush of passion smile or tear, had seem'd
On the fix'd brightness of each dazzling cheek
Strange and unnatural.        *Milman.*

THE Sea-king woke from the troubled sleep
  Of a vision-haunted night,
And he look'd from his bark o'er the gloomy deep
  And counted the streaks of light;
    For the red sun's earliest ray
    Was to rouse his bands that day,
  To the stormy joy of fight!

But the dreams of rest were still on earth,
  And the silent stars on high,
And there waved not the smoke of one cabin hearth
  'Midst the quiet of the sky;
    And along the twilight bay,
    In their sleep the hamlets lay,
  For they knew not the Norse were nigh!

The Sea-king look'd o'er the brooding wave,
  He turn'd to the dusky shore,
And there seem'd, through the arch of a tide-worn
    cave,
    A gleam, as of snow, to pour;
    And forth, in watery light,
    Moved phantoms, dimly white,
  Which the garb of woman bore.

Slowly they moved to the billow side;
  And the forms, as they grew more clear,
Seem'd each on a tall, pale steed to ride,
  And a shadowy crest to rear,
    And to beckon with faint hand
    From the dark and rocky strand,
  And to point a gleaming spear.

Then a stillness on his spirit fell,
  Before th' unearthly train,
For he knew Valhalla's daughters well,
  The Choosers of the slain!
    And a sudden rising breeze
    Bore, across the moaning seas,
  To his ear their thrilling strain.

"There are songs in Odin's Hall,
  For the brave, ere night to fall!
Doth the great sun hide his ray?—
  He must bring a wrathful day!
Sleeps the falchion in its sheath?—
  Swords must do the work of death!
Regner!—Sea-king!—*thee* we call!—
  There is joy in Odin's Hall.

' At the feast and in the song,
  Thou shalt be remember'd long!
By the green isles of the fiord
  Thou hast left thy track in blood!
On the earth and on the sea,
  There are those will speak of thee!
'Tis enough,—the war-gods call,—
  There is mead in Odin's Hall!

"Regner! tell thy fair-hair'd bride
  She must slumber at thy side!
Tell the brother of thy breast,
  E'en for him thy grave hath rest!
Tell the raven steed which bore thee,
  When the wild wolf fled before thee,
He, too, with his lord must fall,—
  There is room in Odin's Hall!

"Lo! the mighty sun looks forth—
  Arm! thou leader of the north!
Lo! the mists of twilight fly,—
  We must vanish, thou must die!
    By the sword and by the spear,
    By the hand that knows not fear,
  Sea-king! nobly shalt thou fall!—
  There is joy in Odin's Hall!"

There was arming heard on land and wave,
  When afar the sunlight spread,
And the phantom forms of the tide-worn cave
  With the mists of morning fled.
    But at eve, the kingly hand
    Of the battle-axe and brand,
  Lay cold on a pile of dead!

## SWISS SONG,

### ON THE ANNIVERSARY OF AN ANCIENT BATTLE.

The Swiss, even to our days, have continued to celebrate the anniversaries of their ancient battles with much
solemnity; assembling in the open air on the fields where
their ancestors fought, to hear thanksgivings offered up
by the priests, and the names of all who shared in the
glory of the day enumerated. They afterwards walk in
procession to chapels, always erected in the vicinity of
such scenes, where masses are sung for the souls of the
departed.——*See Planta's History of the Helvetic
Confederacy.*

Look on the white Alps round!
  If yet they gird a land
Where freedom's voice and step are found,
  Forget ye not the band,
The faithful band, our sires, who fell
Here, in the narrow battle dell!

If yet, the wilds among,
  Our silent hearts may burn,
When the deep mountain-horn hath rung,
  And home our steps may turn,—
Home!—home!—if still that name be dear,
Praise to the men who perish'd here!

Look on the white Alps round!
  Up to their shining snows
That day the stormy rolling sound,
  The sound of battle, rose!
Their caves prolong'd the trumpet's blast,
Their dark pines trembled as it pass'd!

They saw the princely crest,
  They saw the knightly spear,
The banner and the mail-clad breast,
  Borne down, and trampled here!
They saw—and glorying there they stand,
Eternal records to the land!

Praise to the mountain-born,
  The brethren of the glen!
By them no steel array was worn,
  They stood as peasant-men!
They left the vineyard and the field
To break an empire's lance and shield!

Look on the white Alps round!
  If yet, along their steeps,
Our children's fearless feet may bound,
  Free as the chamois leaps:
Teach them in song to bless the band
Amidst whose mossy graves we stand!

If, by the wood-fire's blaze,
  When winter stars gleam cold,
The glorious tales of elder days
  May proudly yet be told,
Forget not then the shepherd race,
Who made the hearth a holy place!

Look on the white Alps round!
If yet the Sabbath-bell
Comes o'er them with a gladdening sound,
Think of the battle dell!
For blood first bathed its flowery sod,
That chainless hearts might worship God!

---

## THE CAVERN OF THE THREE TELLS.
### SWISS TRADITION.

The three founders of the Helvetic Confederacy are
thought to sleep in a cavern near the Lake of Lucerne.
The herdsmen call them the Three Tells; and say that
they lie there in their antique garb, in quiet slumber;
and when Switzerland is in her utmost need, they will
awaken and regain the liberties of the land.——*See
Quarterly Review,* No. 44.

The Grutli, where the confederates held their nightly
meetings, is a meadow on the shore of the Lake of Lucerne, or Lake of the Forest-cantons, here called the
Forest-sea.

---

Oh! enter not yon shadowy cave,
Seek not the bright spars there,
Though the whispering pines that o'er it wave
With freshness fill the air:
For there the Patriot Three,
In the garb of old array'd,
By their native Forest-sea
On a rocky couch are laid.

The Patriot Three that met of yore,
Beneath the midnight sky,
And leagued their hearts on the Grütli shore,
In the name of liberty!
Now silently they sleep
Amidst the hills they freed;
But their rest is only deep,
Till their country's hour of need.

They start not at the hunter's call,
Nor the Lämmer-geyer's cry,
Nor the rush of a sudden torrent's fall,
Nor the Lauwine thundering by!
And the Alpine herdsman's lay,
To a Switzer's heart so dear!
On the wild wind floats away,
No more for them to hear

But when the battle-horn is blown
Till the Schreckhorn's peaks reply,
When the Jungfrau's cliffs send back the tone
Through their eagles' lonely sky;
When spear-heads light the lakes,
When trumpets loose the snows,
When the rushing war-steed shakes
The glacier's mute repose;

When Uri's beechen woods wave red
In the burning hamlet's light;—
Then from the cavern of the dead,
Shall the sleepers wake in might!
With a leap, like Tell's proud leap,
When away the helm he flung,*
And boldly up the steep
From the flashing billow sprung!

They shall wake beside their Forest-sea,
In the ancient garb they wore
When they link'd the hands that made us free
On the Grütli's moonlight shore:
And their voices shall be heard,
And be answer'd with a shout,
Till the echoing Alps are stirr'd,
And the signal-fires blaze out.

And the land shall see such deeds again
As those of that proud day,
When Winkelried, on Sempach's plain,
Through the serried spears made way;

---

* The point of rock on which Tell leaped from the boat of Ges-
ler is marked by a chapel, and called the *Tellensprung.*

And when the rocks came-down
On the dark Morgarten dell,
And the crown'd casques,* o'erthrown,
Before our fathers fell!

For the Kühreihen's† notes must never sound
In a land that wears the chain,
And the vines on freedom's holy ground
Untrampled must remain!
And the yellow harvests wave
For no stranger's hand to reap,
While within their silent cave
The men of Grütli sleep!

---

## THE MESSENGER BIRD.

Some of the Brazilians pay great attention to a certain bird that sings mournfully in the night-time. They
say it is a messenger which their deceased friends and
relations have sent, and that it brings them news from
the other world.——*See Picart's Ceremonies and Religious Customs.*

---

Thou art come from the spirit's land, thou bird!
Thou art come from the spirit's land!
Through the dark pine-grove let thy voice be heard,
And tell of the shadowy band!

We know that the bowers are green and fair
In the light of that summer shore,
And we know that the friends we have lost are
there,
They are there—and they weep no more!

And we know they have quench'd their fever's
thirst,
From the Fountain of Youth ere now,‡
For *there* must the stream in its freshness burst,
Which none may find below!

And we know that they will not be lured to earth
From the land of deathless flowers,
By the feast, or the dance, or the song of mirth,
Though their hearts were once with ours:

Though they sat with us by the night-fire's blaze,
And bent with us the bow,
And heard the tales of our father's days,
Which are told to others now!

But tell us, thou bird of the solemn strain!
Can those who have loved forget?
We call—and they answer not again—
Do they love—do they love us yet?

Doth the warrior think of his brother *there,*
And the father of his child?
And the chief, of those that were wont to share
His wanderings through the wild?

We call them far through the silent night,
And they speak not from cave or hill;
We know, thou bird! that their land is bright,
But say, do they love there still?

---

* *Crowned Helmets,* as a distinction of rank, are mentioned in
Simond's *Switzerland.*

† The *Kühreihen,* the celebrated *Rans des Vaches.*

‡ An expedition was actually undertaken by Juan Ponce de Leon,
in the 16th century, with the view of discovering a wonderful fountain, believed by the natives of Puerto Rico to spring in one of the
Lucayo Isles, and to possess the virtue of restoring youth to all who
bathed in its waters.——*See Robertson's History of America.*

## THE STRANGER IN LOUISIANA.

An early traveller mentions a people on the banks of
the Mississippi who burst into tears at the sight of a
stranger. The reason of this is, that they fancy their
deceased friends and relations to be gone on a journey
and being in constant expectation of their return, look
for them vainly amongst these foreign travellers.—*Picart's Ceremonies and Religious Customs.*

"J'ai passe moi-meme," says Chateaubriand in his
Souvenirs d'Amerique, "chez une peuplade Indienne
qui se prenait a pleurer a la vue d'un voyageur, parce
qu'il lui rappelait des amis partis pour la Contree des
Ames, et depuis long-tems *en voyage.*"

We saw thee, O stranger, and wept!
We look'd for the youth of the sunny glance,
Whose step was the fleetest in chase or dance,
The light of his eye was a joy to see,
The path of his arrows a storm to flee!
But there came a voice from a distant shore,
He was call'd—he is found 'midst his tribe no more!
He is not in his place when the night-fires burn,
But we look for him still—he will yet return!—
His brother sat with a drooping brow
In the gloom of the shadowing cypress bough;
We roused him—we bade him no longer pine,
For we heard a step—but the step was thine.

We saw thee, O stranger, and wept!
We look'd for the maid of the mournful song—
Mournful, though sweet—she hath left us long!
We told her the youth of her love was gone,
And she went forth to seek him—she pass'd alone
We hear not her voice when the woods are still,
From the bower where it sang, like a silvery rill.
The joy of her sire with her smile is fled,
The winter is white on his lonely head,
He hath none by his side when the wilds we track,
He hath none when we rest—yet she comes not
    back!
We look'd for her eye on the feast to shine,
For her breezy step—but the step was thine!

We saw thee, O stranger, and wept!
We look'd for the chief who hath left the spear
And the bow of his battles forgotten here!
We look'd for the hunter, whose bride's lament
On the wind of the forest at eve is sent;
We look'd for the first-born, whose mother's cry
Sounds wild and shrill through the midnight sky!—
Where are they?—thou'rt seeking some distant
    coast—
Oh, ask of them, stranger!—send back the lost!
Tell them we mourn by the dark blue streams,
Tell them our lives but of them are dreams!
Tell, how we sat in the gloom to pine,
And to watch for a step—but the step was thine!

---

## THE BENDED BOW.

It is supposed that war was anciently proclaimed in
Britain by sending messengers in different directions
through the land, each bearing a *bended bow;* and that
peace was in like manner announced by a bow unstrung,
and therefore straight.—*See the Cambrian Antiquities*

There was heard the sound of a coming foe,
There was sent through Britain a Bended Bow,
And a voice was pour'd on the free winds far,
As the land rose up at the sign of war.

"Heard ye not the battle-horn?—
Reaper! leave thy golden corn!
Leave it for the birds of Heaven,
Swords must flash, and spears be riven!
Leave it for the winds to shed—
Arm! ere Britain's turf grow red!"

And the reaper arm'd, like a freeman's son,
And the Bended Bow and the voice pass'd on.

"Hunter! leave the mountain-chase!
Take the falchion from its place!
Let the wolf go free to-day,
Leave him for a nobler prey!
Let the deer ungall'd sweep by,—
Arm thee! Britain's foes are nigh!"

And the hunter arm'd ere the chase was done,
And the Bended Bow and the voice pass'd on.

"Chieftain! quit the joyous feast!
Stay not till the song hath ceas'd:
Though the mead be foaming bright,
Though the fires give ruddy light,
Leave the hearth, and leave the hall—
Arm thee! Britain's foes must fall."

And the chieftain arm'd, and the horn was blown
And the Bended Bow and the voice pass'd on.

"Prince! thy father's deeds are told,
In the bower and in the hold!
Where the goatherd's lay is sung,
Where the minstrel's harp is strung!—
Foes are on thy native sea—
Give our bards a tale of thee!"

And the prince came arm'd, like a leader's son,
And the Bended Bow and the voice pass'd on.

"Mother! stay thou not thy boy!
He must learn the battle's joy.
Sister! bring the sword and spear,
Give thy brother words of cheer!
Maiden! bid thy lover part,
Britain calls the strong in heart!"

And the Bended Bow and the voice pass'd on,
And the bards made song for a battle won.

---

## THE ISLE OF FOUNTS.

### AN INDIAN TRADITION.

"The river St. Mary has its source from a vast lake
or marsh, which lies between Flint and Oakmulge rivers,
and occupies a space of near three hundred miles in circuit. This vast accumulation of waters, in the wet season, appears as a lake, and contains some large islands
or knolls of rich high land; one of which the present
generation of the Creek Indians represent to be a most
blissful spot of earth: they say it is inhabited by a peculiar race of Indians, whose women are incomparably
beautiful. They also tell you that this terrestrial paradise has been seen by some of their enterprising hunters,
when in pursuit of game; but that in their endeavours
to approach it, they were involved in perpetual labyrinths, and, like enchanted land, still as they imagined
they had just gained it, it seemed to fly before them, alternately appearing and disappearing. They resolved
at length, to leave the delusive pursuit, and to return,
which, after a number of difficulties, they effected.
When they reported their adventures to their countrymen, the young warriors were inflamed with an irre
sistible desire to invade, and make a conquest of so
charming a country; but all their attempts have hitherto
proved abortive, never having been able to find that enchanting spot."—*Bartram's Travels through North
and South Carolina, &c.*

The additional circumstances in the "Isle of Founts"
are merely imaginary.

---

Son of the stranger! wouldst thou take
    O'er yon blue hills thy lonely way,
To reach the still and shining lake
    Along whose banks the west winds play?—
Let no vain dreams thy heart beguile,
Oh! seek thou not the Fountain Isle!

I see the pines there waving yet, I see the rills
  descend,
I see thy bounding step no more—my brother and
  my friend!

'I come with flowers—for Spring is come!—Ianthis! art thou *here?*
I bring the garlands she hath brought, I cast them
  on thy bier!
Thou shouldst be crown'd with victory's crown—
  but oh! more meet *they* seem,
The first faint violets of the wood, and lilies of the
  stream!
More meet for one so fondly loved, and laid thus
  early low—
Alas! how sadly sleeps thy face amidst the sunshine's glow:
The golden glow that through thy heart was wont
  such joy to send,—
Woe! that it smiles, and not for thee!—my brother
  and my friend!"

## THE PARTING SONG.

This piece is founded on a tale related by Fauriel, in
his "Chansons Populaires de la Grece Moderne," and
accompanied by some very interesting particulars respecting the extempore parting songs, or songs of expa-
triation, as he informs us they are called, in which the
modern Greeks are accustomed to pour forth their feelings on bidding farewell to their country and friends.

A YOUTH went forth to exile, from a home
Such as to early thought gives images,
The longest treasured, and most oft recall'd,
And brightest kept, of love;—a mountain home,
That, with the murmur of its rocking pines
And sounding waters, first in childhood's heart
Wakes the deep sense of nature unto joy,
And half unconscious prayer;—a Grecian home,
With the transparence of blue skies o'erhung,
And, through the dimness of its olive shades,
Catching the flash of fountains, and the gleam
Of shining pillars from the fanes of old.

And this was what he left!—Yet many leave
Far more:—the glistening eye, that first from theirs
Call'd out the soul's bright smile; the gentle hand,
Which through the sunshine led forth infant steps
To where the violets lay; the tender voice
That earliest taught them what deep melody
Lives in affection's tones.—*He* left not these.
Happy the weeper, that but weeps to part
With all a mother's love!—A bitterer grief
Was his—To part *unloved!*—of her unloved,
That should have breathed upon his heart, like
  spring
Fostering its young faint flowers!

            Yet had he friends,
And they went forth to cheer him on his way
Unto the parting spot;—and she too went,
That mother, tearless for her youngest-born.
The parting spot was reach'd:—a lone deep glen,
Holy, perchance, of yore, for cave and fount
Were there, and sweet-voiced echoes; and above,
The silence of the blue, still, upper Heaven
Hung round the crags of Pindus, where they wore
Their crowning snows.—Upon a rock he sprung,
The unbeloved one, for his home to gaze
Through the wild laurels back; but then a light
Broke on the stern, proud sadness of his eye,
A sudden quivering light, and from his lips
A burst of passionate song.

         "Farewell, farewell!
"I hear thee, O thou rushing stream!—thou'rt
  from my native dell,
Thou'rt bearing thence a mournful sound—a murmur of farewell!

And fare *thee* well—flow on, my stream! flow on,
  thou bright and free!
I do but dream that in thy voice one tone laments
  for me:
But I have been a thing unloved, from childhood's
  loving years,
And therefore turns my soul to thee, for thou hast
  known my tears;
The mountains, and the caves, and thou, my secret tears have known;
The woods can tell where *he* hath wept, that ever
  wept alone!

"I see thee once again, my home! thou'rt there
  amidst thy vines,
And clear upon thy gleaming roof the light of summer shines.
It is a joyous hour when eve comes whispering
  through thy groves,
The hour that brings the son from toil, the hour
  the mother loves!—
The hour *the mother* loves!—for *me* beloved it hath
  not been;
Yet ever in its purple smile, *thou* smil'st, a blessed
  scene!
Whose quiet beauty o'er my soul through distant
  years will come—
Yet what but as the dead to thee, shall I be then,
  my home?

"Not as the dead!—no, not the dead!—We speak
  of *them*—we keep
*Their* names, like light that must not fade, within
  our bosoms deep!
We hallow ev'n the lyre they touch'd, we love the
  lay they sung,
We pass with softer step the place *they* fill'd our
  band among!
But I depart like sound, like dew, like aught that
  leaves on earth
No trace of sorrow or delight, no memory of its
  birth!
I go!—the echo of the rock a thousand songs may
  swell
When mine is a forgotten voice.—Woods, mountains, home, farewell!

"And farewell, mother!—I have borne in lonely
  silence long,
But now the current of my soul grows passionate
  and strong!
And I will speak! though but the wind that wanders through the sky,
And but the dark, deep-rustling pines and rolling
  streams reply.
Yes! I will speak!—within my breast whate'er
  hath seem'd to be,
There lay a hidden fount of love, that would have
  gush'd for thee!
Brightly it would have gush'd, but thou, my mother! thou hast thrown
Back on the forests and the wilds what should
  have been thine own!

"Then fare thee well! I leave thee not in loneliness to pine,
Since thou hast sons of statelier mien and fairer
  brow than mine!
Forgive me that thou couldst not love!—it may be
  that a tone
Yet from my burning heart may pierce through
  thine, when I am gone!
And thou, perchance, may'st weep for him on
  whom thou ne'er hast smiled,
And the grave give his birthright back to thy neglected child!
Might but my spirit *then* return, and 'midst its kindred dwell,
And quench its thirst with love's free tears!—'T is
  all a dream—farewell!"

"Farewell!—the echo died with that deep word
Yet died not so the late repentant pang
By the strain quicken'd in the mother's breast
There had pass'd many changes o'er her brow,
And cheek, and eye; but into one bright flood

And solemn were the strains they pour'd
  Through the stillness of the night,
With the cross above, and the crown and sword,
  And the silent king in sight.

There was heard a heavy clang,
  As of steel-girt men the tread,
And the tombs and the hollow pavement rang
  With a sounding thrill of dread;
And the holy chant was hush'd awhile,
  As by the torch's flame,
A gleam of arms, up the sweeping aisle,
  With a mail-clad leader came.

He came with haughty look,
  An eagle-glance and clear,
But his proud heart through its breastplate shook
  When he stood beside the bier!
He stood there still with a drooping brow,
  And clasp'd hands o'er it raised;—
For his father lay before him low,
  It was Cœur Lion gazed!

And silently he strove
  With the workings of his breast,—
But there's more in late repentant love
  Than steel may keep suppress'd!
And his tears brake forth, at last, like rain,—
  Men held their breath in awe,
For his face was seen by his warrior-train,
  And he reck'd not that they saw.

He look'd upon the dead,
  And sorrow seem'd to lie,
A weight of sorrow, ev'n like lead,
  Pale on the fast-shut eye.
He stoop'd—and kiss'd the frozen cheek,
  And the heavy hand of clay,
Till bursting words—yet all too weak—
  Gave his soul's passion way.

"Oh, father! is it vain,
  This late remorse and deep?
Speak to me, father! once again,
  I weep—behold, I weep!
Alas! my guilty pride and ire!
  Were but this work undone,
I would give England's crown, my sire
  To hear thee bless thy son.

"Speak to me! mighty grief
  Ere now the dust hath stirr'd!
Hear me, but hear me!—father, chief,
  My king! I must be heard!—
Hush'd, hush'd—how is it that I call,
  And that thou answerest not?
When was it thus?—woe, woe for all
  The love my soul forgot!

"Thy silver hairs I see,
  So still, so sadly bright!
And father, father! but for me
  They had not been so white!
I bore thee down, high heart! at last,
  No longer couldst thou strive;—
Oh! for one moment of the past,
  To kneel and say—'forgive!'

"Thou wert the noblest king,
  On royal throne e'er seen;
And thou didst wear, in knightly ring,
  Of all, the stateliest mien;
And thou didst prove, where spears are proved
  In war, the bravest heart—
Oh! ever the renown'd and loved
  Thou wert—and there thou art!

"Thou that my boyhood's guide
  Didst take fond joy to be!—
The times I've sported at thy side,
  And climb'd thy parent knee!
And there before the blessed shrine,
  My sire! I see thee lie,—
How will that sad, still face of thine
  Look on me till I die?"

## THE VASSAL'S LAMENT FOR THE FALLEN TREE.

"Here (at Cape Brereton in Cheshire) is one thing in credibly strange, but attested, as I myself have heard by many persons, and commonly believed. Before any heir of this family dies, there are seen, in a lake adjoining, the bodies of trees swimming on the water for several days."——*Camden's Britannia.*

Yes! I have seen the ancient oak,
  On the dark, deep water cast,
And it was not fell'd by the woodman's stroke,
  Or the rush of the sweeping blast;
For the axe might never touch that tree,
And the air was still as a summer sea.

I saw it fall, as falls a chief
  By an arrow in the fight,
And the old woods shook to their loftiest leaf,
  At the crashing of its might!
And the startled deer to their coverts drew,
And the spray of the lake as a fountain's flew!

'T is fall'n! but think thou not I weep
  For the forest's pride o'erthrown;
An old man's tears lie far too deep,
  To be pour'd for this alone!
But by that sign too well I know,
That a youthful head must soon be low!

A youthful head, with its shining hair,
  And its bright, quick-flashing eye—
Well may I weep! for the boy is fair,
  Too fair a thing to die!
But on his brow the mark is set—
Oh! could my life redeem him yet!

He bounded by me as I gazed
  Alone on the fatal sign,
And it seem'd like sunshine when he raised
  His joyous glance to mine!
With a stag's fleet step he bounded by,
So full of life—but he must die!

He must, he must! in that deep dell,
  By that dark water's side,
'T is known that ne'er a proud tree fell,
  But an heir of his fathers died.
And he—there's laughter in his eye,
Joy in his voice—yet he must die!

I've borne him in these arms, that now
  Are nerveless and unstrung;
And must I see on that fair brow,
  The dust untimely flung?
I must!—yon green oak, branch and crest,
Lies floating on the dark lake's breast!

The noble boy!—how proudly sprung
  The falcon from his hand!
It seem'd like youth to see him young,
  A flower in his father's land!
But the hour of the knell and the dirge is nigh,
For the tree hath fall'n, and the flower must die

Say not 'tis vain!—I tell thee, some
  Are warn'd by a meteor's light,
Or a pale bird, flitting, calls them home,
  Or a voice on the winds by night;
And they must go!—and he too, he—
Woe for the fall of the glorious Tree!

## THE WILD HUNTSMAN.

It is a popular belief in the Odenwald, that the passing of the Wild Huntsman announces the approach of war. He is supposed to issue with his train from the ruined castle of Rodenstein, and traverse the air to the opposite castle of Schnellerts. It is confidently asserted that the sound of his phantom horses and hounds was heard by the Duke of Baden before the commencement of the last war in Germany.

Thy rest was deep at the slumberer's hour,
If thou didst not hear the blast
Of the savage horn, from the mountain tower,
As the Wild Night-Huntsman pass'd,
And the roar of the stormy chase went by,
Through the dark unquiet sky!

The stag sprung up from his mossy bed
When he caught the piercing sounds,
And the oak-boughs crash'd to his antler'd head,
As he flew from the viewless hounds;
And the falcon soar'd from her craggy height,
Away through the rushing night!

The banner shook on its ancient hold,
And the pine in its desert place,
As the cloud and tempest onward roll'd
With the din of the trampling race;
And the glens were fill'd with the laugh and shout
And the bugle, ringing out!

From the chieftain's hand the wine-cup fell,
At the castle's festive board,
And a sudden pause came o'er the swell
Of the harp's triumphant chord;
And the Minnesinger's* thrilling lay
In the hall died fast away.

The convent's chanted rite was stay'd,
And the hermit dropp'd his beads,
And a trembling ran through the forest-shade,
At the neigh of phantom steeds,
And the church-bells peal'd to the rocking blast
As the Wild Night-Huntsman pass'd.

The storm hath swept with the chase away,
There is stillness in the sky,
But the mother looks on her son to-day,
With a troubled heart and eye,
And the maiden's brow hath a shade of care
'Midst the gleam of her golden hair;

The Rhine flows bright, but its waves ere long
Must hear a voice of war,
And a clash of spears our hills among.
And a trumpet from afar:
And the brave on a bloody turf must lie,
For the Huntsman hath gone by!

---

## BRANDENBURGH HARVEST-SONG.†

From the German of La Motte Fouqué.

The corn, in golden light,
Waves o'er the plain;
The sickle's gleam is bright;
Full swells the grain.

Now send we far around
Our harvest lay!—
Alas! a heavier sound
Comes o'er the day!

Earth shrouds with burial sod
Her soft eye's blue,—
Now o'er the gifts of God
Fall tears like dew!

---

* Minnesinger, love-singer,—the wandering minstrels of Germany were so called in the middle ages.

† For the year of the Queen of Prussia's death.

On every breeze a knell
The hamlets pour,—
We know its cause too well,
*She is no more!*

---

## THE SHADE OF THESEUS.
### ANCIENT GREEK TRADITION.

Know ye not when our dead
From sleep to battle sprung?—
When the Persian charger's tread
On their covering greensward rung!
When the trampling march of foes
Had crush'd our vines and flowers,
When jewell'd crests arose
Through the holy laurel bowers,

When banners caught the breeze,
When helms in sunlight shone,
When masts were on the seas.
And spears on Marathon.

There was one, a leader crown'd,
And arm'd for Greece that day
But the falchions made no sound
On his gleaming war-array.
In the battle's front he stood,
With his tall and shadowy crest;
But the arrows drew no blood
Though their path was through his breast.

When banners caught the breeze,
When helms in sunlight shone,
When masts were on the seas,
And spears on Marathon.

His sword was seen to flash
Where the boldest deeds were done;
But it smote without a clash;
The stroke was heard by none!

His voice was not of those
That swell'd the rolling blast,
And his steps fell hush'd like snows—
'Twas the Shade of Theseus pass'd!

When banners caught the breeze,
When helms in sunlight shone,
When masts were on the seas,
And spears on Marathon.

Far sweeping through the foe,
With a fiery charge he bore;
And the Mede left many a bow
On the sounding ocean-shore.
And the foaming waves grew red,
And the sails were crowded fast,
When the sons of Asia fled,
As the Shade of Theseus pass'd!

When banners caught the breeze,
When helms in sunlight shone,
When masts were on the seas,
And spears on Marathon.

---

## ANCIENT GREEK SONG OF EXILE.

Where is the summer, with her golden sun?—
That festal glory hath not pass'd from earth:
For me alone the laughing day is done!
Where is the summer with her voice of mirth?
—Far in my own bright land!

Where are the Fauns, whose flute-notes breathe
and die
On the green hills?—the founts, from sparry caves
Through the wild places bearing melody?
The reeds, low whispering o'er the river waves?
—Far in my own bright land!

Where are the temples, through the dim wood
    shining,
  The virgin-dances, and the choral strains?
Where the sweet sisters of my youth, entwining
  The spring's first roses for their sylvan fanes?
    —Far in my own bright land!

Where are the vineyards, with their joyous throngs,
  The red grapes pressing when the foliage fades?
The lyres, the wreaths, the lovely Dorian songs,
  And the pine forests, and the olive shades?
    —Far in my own bright land!

Where the deep haunted grots, the laurel bowers,
  The Dryad's footsteps, and the minstrel's
    dreams?—
Oh! that my life were as a southern flower's!
  I might not languish then by these chill streams,
    Far from my own bright land!

## GREEK FUNERAL CHANT OR MYRIOLOGUE.

"Les Chants Funebres par lesquels on deplore en
Grece la mort de ses proches, prennent le nom particu-
lier de Myriologia, comme qui dirait, Discours de lamen-
tation, complaintes. Un malade vient-il de rendre le
dernier soupir, sa femme, sa mere, ses filles, ses sœurs,
celles, en un mot, de ses plus proches parentes qui sont
là, lui ferment les yeux et la bouche, en epanchant libre-
ment, chacune selon son naturel et sa mesure de ten-
dresse pour le defunt, la douleur qu'elle ressent de sa
perte. Ce premier devoir rempli, elles se retirent toutes
chez une de leurs parentes ou de leurs amies. La elles
changent de vetemens, s'habillent de blanc, comme pour
la ceremonie nuptiale, avec cette difference, qu'elles
gardent la tete nue, les cheveux epars et pendants. Ces
apprets termines, les parentes reviennent dans leur parure
de deuil; toutes se rangent en circle autour du mort, et
leur douleur s'exhale de nouveau, et, comme la pre-
miere fois, sans regle et sans contrainte. A ces plaintes
spontanees succedent bientot des lamentations d'une
autre espece; ce sont les *Myriologues.* Ordinairement
c'est la plus proche parente qui prononce le sien la pre-
miere; apres elle les autres parentes. les amies, les
simples voisines. Les Myriologues sont toujours com-
poses et chantes par les femmes. Ils sont toujours im-
provises, toujours en vers, et toujours chantes sur un air
qui differe d'un lieu a un autre, mais qui, dans un lieu
donne, reste invariablement consacre a ce genre de
poesie."——*Chants Populaires de la Grece Moderne,
par C. Fauriel.*

A wail was heard around the bed, the death-bed
    of the young,
Amidst her tears the Funeral Chant a mournful
    mother sung.—
" Ianthis! dost thou sleep?—Thou sleep'st!—but
    this is not the rest,
The breathing and the rosy calm, I have pillow'd
    on my breast!
I lull'd thee not to *this* repose, Ianthis! my sweet
    son!
As in thy glowing childhood's time by twilight I
    have done!—
How is it that I bear to stand and look upon thee
    now?
And that I die not, seeing death on thy pale glo-
    rious brow?

" I look upon thee, thou that wert of all most fair
    and brave!
I see thee wearing still too much of beauty for the
    grave!
Though mournfully thy smile is fix'd, and heavily
    thine eye
Hath shut above the falcon-glance that in it loved
    to lie;
And fast is bound the springing step, that seem'd
    on breezes borne,
When to thy couch I came and said,—' Wake,
    hunter, wake! 'tis morn!'

'Yet art thou lovely still, my flower! untouch'd by
    slow decay,—
And I, the wither'd stem, remain—I would that
    grief might slay!

" Oh! ever when I met thy look, I knew that *this*
    would be!
I knew too well that length of days was not a
    gift for thee!
I saw it in thy kindling cheek, and in thy bearing
    high;—
A voice came whispering to my soul, and told me
    thou must die!
That thou must die, my fearless one! where swords
    were flashing red.—
Why doth a mother live to say—My first-born and
    my dead?
They tell me of thy youthful fame, they talk of
    victory won—
Speak *thou,* and I will hear! my child, Ianthis!
    my sweet son!"

A wail was heard around the bed, the death-bed
    of the young,
A fair-hair'd bride the Funeral Chant amidst her
    weeping sung.—
" Ianthis! look'st thou not on *me?*—Can love in-
    deed be fled?
When was it woe before to gaze upon thy stately
    head?
I would that I had follow'd thee, Ianthis, my be-
    loved!
And stood as woman oft hath stood where faith-
    ful hearts are proved!
That I had bound a breastplate on, and battled at
    thy side—
It would have been a blessed thing together had
    we died!

" But where was I when thou didst fall beneath
    the fatal sword?
Was I beside the sparkling fount, or at the peace-
    ful board?
Or singing some sweet song of old, in the shadow
    of the vine,
Or praying to the saints for thee, before the holy
    shrine?
And thou wert lying low the while, the life-drops
    from thy heart
Fast gushing like a mountain-spring!—and couldst
    thou thus depart?
Couldst thou depart, nor on my lips pour out thy
    fleeting breath?—
Oh! I was with thee but in joy, that should have
    been in death!

" Yes! I was with thee when the dance through
    mazy rings was led,
And when the lyre and voice were tuned, and
    when the feast was spread!
But not where noble blood flow'd forth, where
    sounding javelins flew.—
Why did I hear love's first sweet words, and not
    its last adieu?
What now can breathe of gladness more, what
    scene, what hour, what tone?
The blue skies fade with all their lights, they fade,
    since thou art gone!
Ev'n *that* must leave me, that still face, by all my
    tears unmoved—
Take me from this dark world with thee, Ianthis!
    my beloved!"

A wail was heard around the bed, the death-bed
    of the young,
Amidst her tears the Funeral Chant a mournful
    sister sung.
" Ianthis! brother of my soul!—oh! where are now
    the days
That laugh'd among the deep green hills, on all
    our infant plays?
When we two sported by the streams, or track'd
    them to their source,
And like a stag's, the rocks along, was thy fleet
    fearless course!—

Lull but the mighty Serpent King,*
  'Midst the gray rocks, his old domain;
Ward but the cougar's deadly spring,—
  Thy step that lake's green shores may gain;
And the bright Isle, when all is pass'd,
Shall vainly meet thine eye at last!

Yea! there, with all its rainbow streams
  Clear as within thine arrow's flight,
The Isle of Founts, the Isle of dreams,
  Floats on the wave in golden light;
And lovely will the shadows be
Of groves whose fruit is not for thee!

And breathings from their sunny flowers,
  Which are not of the things that die,
And singing voices from their bowers,
  Shall greet thee in the purple sky;
Soft voices, e'en like those that dwell
Far in the green reed's hollow cell.

Or hast thou heard the sounds that rise
  From the deep chambers of the earth?
The wild and wondrous melodies
  To which the ancient rocks gave birth?†
Like that sweet song of hidden caves
Shall swell those wood-notes o'er the waves.

The emerald waves!—they take their hue
  And image from that sunbright shore;
But wouldst thou launch thy light canoe,
  And wouldst thou ply thy rapid oar,
Before thee, hadst thou morning's speed,
The dreamy land should still recede!

Yet on the breeze thou still wouldst hear
  The music of its flowering shades,
And ever should the sound be near
  Of founts that ripple through its glades;
The sound, and sight, and flashing ray
Of joyous waters in their play!

But wo for him who sees them burst
  With their bright spray-showers to the lake
Earth has no spring to quench the thirst
  That semblance in his soul shall wake,
For ever pouring through his dreams,
The gush of those untasted streams!

Bright, bright in many a rocky urn,
  The waters of our deserts lie,
Yet at their source his lip shall burn,
  Parch'd with the fever's agony!
From the blue mountains to the main,
Our thousand floods may roll in vain.

E'en thus our hunters came of yore
  Back from their long and weary quest;—
Had they not seen th' untrodden shore,
  And could they 'midst our wilds find rest?
The lightning of their glance was fled,
They dwelt amongst us as the dead!

They lay beside our glittering rills,
  With visions in their darken'd eye,
Their joy was not amidst the hills,
  Where elk and deer before us fly;
Their spears upon the cedar hung,
Their javelins to the wind were flung.

They bent no more the forest-bow,
  They arm'd not with the warrior-band,
The moons waned o'er them dim and slow—
  They left us for the spirits' land!
Beneath our pines yon greensward heap
Shows where the restless found their sleep.

---

* The Cherokees believe that the recesses of their mountains, overgrown with lofty pines and cedars, and covered with old mossy rocks, are inhabited by the kings or chiefs of the rattle-snakes, whom they denominate the "bright old inhabitants." They represent them as snakes of an enormous size, and which possess the power of drawing to them every living creature that comes within the reach of their eyes. Their heads are said to be crowned with a carbuncle of dazzling brightness.—*See Notes to Leyden's "Scenes of Infancy."*

† The stones on the banks of the Oronoco, called by the South American miss'onaries *Lazas de Musica,* and alluded to in a former note.

Son of the stranger! if at eve
  Silence be 'midst us in thy place,
Yet go not where the mighty leave
  The strength of battle and of chase!
Let no vain dreams thy heart beguile,
Oh! seek thou not the Fountain Isle!

---

## HE NEVER SMILED AGAIN

It is recorded of Henry the First, that after the death of his son, Prince William, who perished in a shipwreck off the coast of Normandy, he was never seen to smile.

The bark that held a prince went down,
  The sweeping waves roll'd on;
And what was England's glorious crown
  To him that wept a son?
He lived—for life may long be borne
  Ere sorrow break its chain;—
Why comes not death to those who mourn?—
  He never smiled again!

There stood proud forms around his throne,
  The stately and the brave,
But which could fill the place of one,
  That one beneath the wave?
Before him pass'd the young and fair,
  In pleasure's reckless train,
But seas dash'd o'er his son's bright hair—
  He never smiled again!

He sat where festal bowls went round;
  He heard the minstrel sing,
He saw the tourney's victor crown'd,
  Amidst the knightly ring:
A murmur of the restless deep
  Was blent with every strain,
A voice of winds that would not sleep—
  He never smiled again!

Hearts, in that time, closed o'er the trace
  Of vows once fondly pour'd,
And strangers took the kinsman's place
  At many a joyous board;
Graves, which true love had bathed with
  Were left to Heaven's bright rain,
Fresh hopes were born for other years—
  *He* never smiled again!

---

## CŒUR DE LION AT THE BIER OF HIS FATHER.

The body of Henry the Second lay in state in the abbey church of Fontevraud, where it was visited by Richard Cœur de Lion, who on beholding it, was struck with horror and remorse, and bitterly reproached himself for that rebellious conduct which had been the means of bringing his father to an untimely grave.

Torches were blazing clear,
  Hymns pealing deep and slow,
Where a king lay stately on his bier,
  In the church of Fontevraud.
Banners of battle o'er him hung,
  And warriors slept beneath,
And light, as Noon's broad light, was flung
  On the settled face of death.

On the settled face of death
  A strong and ruddy glare,
Though dimm'd at times by the censer's breath,
  Yet it fell still brightest there:
As if each deeply-furrow'd trace
  Of earthly years to show,—
Alas! that sceptred mortal's race
  Had surely closed in woe!

The marble floor was swept
  By many a long dark stole,
As the kneeling priests round him that slept,
  Sang mass for the parted soul;

Of tears at last all melted; and she fell
On the glad bosom of her child, and cried,
" Return, return, my son !"—The echo caught
A lovelier sound than song, and woke again,
Murmuring—" Return, my son !"————

## THE SULIOTE MOTHER.

It is related, in a French Life of Ali Pacha, that several of the Suliote women, on the advance of the Turkish troops into their mountain fastnesses, assembled on a lofty summit, and after chanting a wild song, precipitated themselves, with their children, into the chasm below, to avoid becoming the slaves of the enemy.

She stood upon the loftiest peak,
    Amidst the clear blue sky,
A bitter smile was on her cheek,
    And a dark flash in her eye.

" Dost thou see them, boy ?— through the dusky
    pines
Dost thou see where the foeman's armour shines ?
Hast thou caught the gleam of the conqueror's
    crest ?
My babe, that I cradled on my breast !
Wouldst thou spring from thy mother's arms with
    joy ?
—That sight hath cost thee a father, my boy !"

For in the rocky strait beneath
    Lay Suliote sire and son ;
They had heap'd high the piles of death
    Before the pass was won.

" They have cross'd the torrent, and on they come !
Woe for the mountain hearth and home !
There, where the hunter laid by his spear,
There, where the lyre hath been sweet to hear,
There, where I sang thee, fair babe ! to sleep,
Caught but the blood-stain our trace shall keep !"

And now the horn's loud blast was heard,
    And now the cymbal's clang,
Till ev'n the upper air was stirr'd,
    As cliff and hollow rang.

'Hark ! they bring music, my joyous child !
What saith the trumpet to Suli's wild !
Doth it light thine eye with so quick a fire,
As if at a glance of thine armed sire ?—
Still !—be thou still !—there are brave men low—
Thou wouldst not smile couldst thou see him now !"

But nearer came the clash of steel,
    And louder swell'd the horn,
And farther yet the tambour's peal
    Through the dark pass was borne.

" Hear'st thou the sound of their savage mirth ?—
Boy ! thou wert free when I gave thee birth,—
Free, and how cherish'd, my warrior's son !
He too hath bless'd thee, as I have done !
Ay, and unchain'd must his loved ones be—
Freedom, young Suliote ! for thee and me !"

And from the arrowy peak she sprung,
    And fast the fair child bore :—
A veil upon the wind was flung,
    A cry—and all was o'er !

## THE FAREWELL TO THE DEAD.

The following piece is founded on a beautiful part of the Greek funeral service, in which relatives and friends are invited to embrace the deceased (whose face is uncovered) and to bid their final adieu.——*See Christian Researches in the Mediterranean.*

————'T is hard to lay into the earth
A countenance so benign ! a form that walk'd
But yesterday so stately o'er the earth !

                            *Wilson.*

Come near !—ere yet the dust
Soil the bright paleness of the settled brow,
Look on your brother, and embrace him now,
    In still and solemn trust !
Come near !—once more let kindred lips be press'd
On his cold cheek ; then bear him to his rest !

Look yet on this young face !
What shall the beauty, from amongst us gone,
Leave of its image, ev'n where most it shone,
    Gladdening its hearth and race ?
Dim grows the semblance on man's heart im-
        press'd—
Come near, and bear the beautiful to rest !

Ye weep, and it is well !
For tears befit earth's partings !—Yesterday,
Song was upon the lips of this pale clay,
    And sunshine seem'd to dwell
Where'er he moved—the welcome and the bless'd !—
Now gaze ! and bear the silent unto rest !

Look yet on him, whose eye
Meets yours no more, in sadness or in mirth !
Was he not fair amidst the sons of earth,
    The beings born to die ?—
But not where death has power may love be
        bless'd—
Come near ! and bear ye the beloved to rest !

How may the mother's heart
Dwell on her son, and dare to hope again ?
The spring's rich promise hath been given in vain,
    The lovely must depart !
Is he not gone, our brightest and our best ?
Come near ! and bear the early-call'd to rest !

Look on him ! is he laid
To slumber from the harvest or the chase ?—
Too still and sad the smile upon his face,
    Yet that, ev'n that, must fade !
Death holds not long unchanged his fairest guest,—
Come near ! and bear the mortal to his rest !

His voice of mirth hath ceased
Amidst the vineyards ! there is left no place
For him whose dust receives your vain embrace.
    At the gay bridal feast !
Earth must take earth to moulder on her breast ;
Come near ! weep o'er him ! bear him to his rest !

Yet mourn ye not as they
Whose spirit's light is quench'd !—for him the past
Is seal'd.  He may not fall, he may not cast
    His birthright's hope away !
All is not here of our beloved and bless'd—
Leave ye the sleeper with his God to rest !

# MISCELLANEOUS POEMS.

## THE BRIDAL DAY.

On a monument in a Venetian church is an epitaph, recording that the remains beneath are those of a noble lady, who expired suddenly while standing as a bride at the altar.

> We bear her home! we bear her home!
> Over the murmuring salt sea's foam;
> One who has fled from the war of life,
> From sorrow, pale, and the fever strife.
> *Barry Cornwall.*

BRIDE! upon thy marriage-day,
When thy gems in rich array
Made the glistening mirror seem
As a star-reflecting stream;
When the clustering pearls lay fair
'Midst thy braids of sunny hair,
And the white veil o'er thee streaming,
Like a silvery halo gleaming,
Mellow'd all that pomp and light
Into something meekly bright;
Did the fluttering of thy breath
Speak of joy or woe beneath?
And the hue that went and came
O'er thy cheek, like wavering flame,
Flow'd that crimson from th' unrest,
Or the gladness of thy breast?
—Who shall tell us?—from thy bower,
Brightly didst thou pass that hour;
With the many-glancing oar,
And the cheer along the shore,
And the wealth of summer flowers
On thy fair head cast in showers,
And the breath of song and flute,
And the clarion's glad salute,
Swiftly o'er the Adrian tide
Wert thou borne in pomp, young bride!
Mirth and music, sun and sky,
Welcomed thee triumphantly!
Yet, perchance, a chastening thought,
In some deeper spirit wrought,
Whispering, as untold it blent
With the sounds of merriment,—
" From the home of childhood's glee,
From the days of laughter free,
From the love of many years,
Thou art gone to cares and fears;
To another path and guide,
To a bosom yet untried!
Bright one! oh! there well may be
Trembling 'midst our joy for thee."

Bride! when through the stately fane,
Circled with thy nuptial train,
'Midst the banners hung on high
By thy warrior-ancestry,
'Midst those mighty fathers dead,
In soft beauty thou wast led;
When before the shrine thy form
Quiver'd to some bosom storm,

When, like harp-strings with a sigh
Breaking in mid-harmony,
On thy lip the murmurs low
Died with love's unfinish'd vow;
When, like scatter'd rose leaves, fled
From thy cheek each tint of red,
And the light forsook thine eye,
And thy head sank heavily;
Was that drooping but th' excess
Of thy spirit's blessedness?
Or did some deep feeling's might,
Folded in thy heart from sight,
With a sudden tempest-shower,
Earthward bear thy life's young flower?
—Who shall tell us?—on *thy* tongue
Silence, and for ever, hung!
Never to thy lip and cheek
Rush'd again the crimson streak.
Never to thine eye return'd
That which there had beam'd and burn'd!
With the secret none might know,
With thy rapture or thy woe,
With thy marriage-robe and wreath,
Thou wert fled, young bride of death!
One, one lightning moment there
Struck down triumph to despair,
Beauty, splendour, hope, and trust,
Into darkness—terror—dust!

There were sounds of weeping o'er thee,
Bride! as forth thy kindred bore thee,
Shrouded in thy gleaming veil,
Deaf to that wild funeral wail.
Yet perchance a chastening thought,
In some deeper spirit wrought,
Whispering, while the stern sad knell
On the air's bright stillness fell;
—" From the power of chill and change
Souls to sever and estrange;
From love's wane—a death in life
But to watch—a mortal strife
From the secret fevers known
To the burning heart alone,
Thou art fled—afar, away—
Where these blights no more have sway!
Bright one! oh! there well may be
Comfort 'midst our tears for thee!"

## THE ANCESTRAL SONG.

> A long war disturb'd your mind—
> Here your perfect peace is sign'd;
> 'T is now full tide 'twixt night and day,
> End your moan, and come away!
> *Webster—Duchess of Malfy*

THERE were faint sounds of weeping;—fear and
  gloom
And midnight vigil in a stately room
Of Lusignan's old halls:—rich odours there
Fill'd the proud chamber as with Indian air.

And soft light fell, from lamps of silver thrown,
On jewels that with rainbow lustre shone
Over a gorgeous couch:—there emeralds gleam'd,
And deeper crimson from the ruby stream'd
Than in the heart-leaf of the rose is set,
Hiding from sunshine.—Many a carcanet
Starry with diamonds, many a burning chain
Of the red gold, sent forth a radiance vain,
And sad, and strange, the canopy beneath
Whose shadowy curtains, round a bed of death,
Hung drooping solemnly;—for there one lay,
Passing from all Earth's glories fast away,
Amidst those queenly treasures: They had been
Gifts of her lord, from far-off Paynim lands,
And for *his* sake, upon their orient sheen
She had gazed fondly, and with faint, cold hands
Had press'd them to her languid heart once more,
Melting in childlike tears.   But this was o'er—
Love's last vain clinging unto life; and now—
A mist of dreams was hovering o'er her brow,
Her eye was fix'd, her spirit seem'd removed,
Though not from Earth, from all it knew or loved,
Far, far away! her handmaids watch'd around,
In awe, that lent to each low midnight sound
A might, a mystery; and the quivering light
Of wind-sway'd lamps, made spectral in their sight
The forms of buried beauty, sad, yet fair,
Gleaming along the walls with braided hair,
Long in the dust grown dim; and she, too, saw,
But with the spirit's eye of raptured awe,
Those pictured shapes!—a bright, yet solemn train,
Beckoning, they floated o'er her dreamy brain,
Clothed in diviner hues; while on her ear
Strange voices fell, which none besides might hear,
Sweet, yet profoundly mournful, as the sigh
Of winds o'er harp-strings through a midnight sky:
And thus it seem'd, in that low thrilling tone,
Th' ancestral shadows call'd away their own.

> Come, come, come!
> Long thy fainting soul hath yearn'd
> For the step that ne'er return'd!
> Long thine anxious ear hath listen'd,
> And thy watchful eye hath glisten'd
> With the hope, whose parting strife
> Shook the flower-leaves from thy life—
> Now the heavy day is done,
> Home awaits thee, wearied one!
> Come, come, come!

> From the quenchless thoughts that burn
> In the seal'd heart's lonely urn;
> From the coil of memory's chain
> Wound about the throbbing brain;
> From the veins of sorrow deep,
> Winding through the world of sleep;
> From the haunted halls and bowers,
> Throng'd with ghosts of happier hours!
> Come, come, come!

> On our dim and distant shore
> 'Aching love is felt no more!
> *We* have loved with earth's excess—
> Past is now that weariness!
> *We* have wept, that weep not now—
> Calm is each once beating brow!
> We have known the dreamer's woes—
> All is now one bright repose!
> Come, come, come!

> Weary heart that long hast bled,
> Languid spirit, drooping head,
> Restless memory, vain regret,
> Pining love whose light is set,
> Come away!—'tis hush'd, 'tis well!
> Where by shadowy founts we dwell,
> All the fever-thirst is still'd,
> All the air with peace is fill'd,—
> Come, come, come!

And with her spirit rapt in that wild lay,
She pass'd, as twilight melts to night, away!


## THE MAGIC GLASS.

How lived, how loved, how died they?
                                        *Byron.*

"The Dead! the glorious Dead!—And shall they
      rise?
Shall they look on thee with their proud bright
      eyes?
                  Thou ask'st a fearful spell!
Yet say, from shrine or dim sepulchral hall,
What kingly vision shall obey my call?
                  The deep grave knows it well!

"Wouldst thou behold earth's conquerors? shall
      they pass
Before thee, flushing all the Magic Glass
                  With triumph's long array?
Speak! and those dwellers of the marble urn,
Robed for the feast of victory, shall return,
                  As on their proudest day.

"Or wouldst thou look upon the lords of song?—
O'er the dark mirror that immortal throng
                  Shall waft a solemn gleam!
Passing, with lighted eyes and radiant brows,
Under the foliage of green laurel-boughs,
                  But silent as a dream."

"Not these, O mighty master!—Though their lays
Be unto man's free heart, and tears, and praise,
                  Hallow'd for evermore!
And not the buried conquerors! Let them sleep
And let the flowery earth her Sabbaths keep
                  In joy, from shore to shore!

"But, if the narrow house may so be moved,
Call the bright shadows of the most beloved,
                  Back from their couch of rest
That I may learn if *their* meek eyes be fill'd
With peace, if human love hath ever still'd
                  The yearning human breast."

'Away, fond youth!—An idle quest is thine;
*These* have no trophy, no memorial shrine;
                  I know not of their place!
'Midst the dim valleys, with a secret flow,
Their lives, like shepherd reed-notes, faint and low
                  Have pass'd, and left no trace.

"Haply, begirt with shadowy woods and hills,
And the wild sounds of melancholy rills,
                  Their covering turf may bloom
But ne'er hath Fame made relics of its flowers,—
Never hath pilgrim sought their household bowers,
                  Or poet hail'd their tomb."

"Adieu, then, master of the midnight spell!
Some voice, perchance, by those lone graves may
      tell
                  That which I pine to know!
I haste to seek, from woods and valleys deep,
Where the beloved are laid in lowly sleep,
                  Records of joy and woe."


## CORINNE AT THE CAPITOL.

*Les femmes doivent penser qu'il est dans cette carrière bien peu de sort qui puissent valoir la plus obscure vie d'une femme aimée et d'une mère heureuse.——Madame de Staël.*

Daughter of th' Italian heaven!
Thou, to whom its fires are given,
Joyously thy car hath roll'd
Where the conquerors pass'd of old;
And the festal sun, that shone
O'er three * hundred triumphs gone,
Makes thy day of glory bright,
With a shower of golden light.
Now thou tread'st th' ascending road,
Freedom's foot so proudly trode;
While, from tombs of heroes borne,
From the dust of empire shorn,

---

* The trebly hundred triumphs.     *Byron.*

Flowers upon thy graceful head,
Chaplets of all hues, are shed,
In a soft and rosy rain,
Touch'd with many a gem-like stain.

Thou hast gain'd the summit now !
Music hails thee from below ;—
Music, whose rich notes might stir
Ashes of the sepulchre ;
Shaking with victorious notes
All the bright air as it floats.
Well may woman's heart beat high
Unto that proud harmony !

Now afar it rolls— it dies—
And thy voice is heard to rise
With a low and lovely tone
In its thrilling power alone ;
And thy lyre's deep silvery string,
Touch'd as by a breeze's wing,
Murmurs tremblingly at first,
Ere the tide of rapture burst.

All the spirit of thy sky
Now hath lit thy large dark eye,
And thy cheek a flush hath caught
From the joy of kindled thought ;
And the burning words of song
From thy lip flow fast and strong,
With a rushing stream's delight
In the freedom of its might.

Radiant daughter of the sun !
Now thy living wreath is won.
Crown'd of Rome !—Oh ! art thou not
Happy in that glorious lot ?—
Happier, happier far than thou,
With the laurel on thy brow,
She that makes the humblest hearth
Lovely but to one on earth !

---

## THE RUIN

Oh ! 't is the heart that magnifies this life,
Making a truth and beauty of its own.
*Wordsworth.*

Birth has gladden'd it : Death has sanctified it.
*Guesses at Truth.*

---

No dower of storied song is thine,
O desolate abode !
Forth from thy gates no glittering line
Of lance and spear hath flow'd.
Banners of knighthood have not flung
Proud drapery o'er thy walls,
Nor bugle-notes to battle rung
Through thy resounding halls.

Nor have rich bowers of *pleasaunce* here
By courtly hands been dress'd.
For Princes, from the chase of deer,
Under green leaves to rest :
Only some rose, yet lingering bright
Beside thy casement lone,
Tells where the spirit of delight
Hath dwelt, and now is gone.

Yet minstrel tale of harp and sword,
And sovereign beauty's lot,
House of quench'd light and silent board !
For me thou needest not.
It is enough to know that *hers*,
Where thoughtfully I stand,
Sorrow and love and hope and fear,
Have link'd one kindred band.

Thou bindest me with mighty spells !
—A solemnizing breath,
A presence all around thee dwells,
Of human life and death.
I need but pluck yon garden flower
From where the wild weeds rise,
To wake, with strange and sudden power,
A thousand sympathies.

Thou hast heard many sounds, thou hearth !
Deserted now by all !
Voices at eve here met in mirth,
Which eve may ne'er recall.
Youth's buoyant step, and woman's tone,
And childhood's laughing glee,
And song and prayer, have all been known,
Hearth of the dead ! to thee.

Thou hast heard blessings fondly pour'd
Upon the infant head,
As if in every fervent word
The living soul were shed ;
Thou hast seen partings, such as bear
The bloom of life away—
Alas ! for love in changeful air,
Where naught beloved can stay !

Here, by the restless bed of pain,
The vigil hath been kept,
Till sunrise, bright with hope in vain,
Burst forth on eyes that wept :
Here hath been felt the hush, the gloom,
The breathless influence, shed
Through the dim dwelling, from the room
Wherein reposed the dead.

The seat left void, the missing face,
Have here been mark'd and mourn'd,
And time hath fill'd the vacant place,
And gladness hath return'd ;
Till from the narrowing household chain
The links dropp'd one by one !
And homewards hither, o'er the main,
Came the spring-birds alone.

Is there not cause, then—cause for thought,
Fix'd eye and lingering tread,
Where, with their thousand mysteries fraught,
Ev'n lowliest hearts have bled ?
Where, in its ever-haunting thirst
For draughts of purer day,
Man's soul, with fitful strength, hath burst
The clouds that wrapt its way ?

Holy to human nature seems
The long-forsaken spot ;
To deep affections, tender dreams,
Hopes of a brighter lot ;
Therefore in silent reverence here,
Hearth of the dead ! I stand,
Where joy and sorrow, smile and tear,
Have link'd one household band.

---

## THE MINSTER.

A fit abode, wherein appear enshrined
Our hopes of immortality.           *Byron.*

Speak low !—the place is holy to the breath
Of awful harmonies, of whisper'd prayer ;
Tread lightly !—for the sanctity of death
Broods with a voiceless influence on the air
Stern, yet serene !—a reconciling spell,
Each troubled billow of the soul to quell.

Leave me to linger silently awhile !
—Not for the light that pours its fervid streams
Of rainbow glory down through arch and aisle,
Kindling old banners into haughty gleams,
Flushing proud shrines, or by some warrior's tomb
Dying away in clouds of gorgeous gloom :

Not for rich music, though in triumph pealing,
Mighty as forest sounds when winds are high ;
Nor yet for torch, and cross, and stole, revealing
Through incense-mists their sainted pageantry ;—
Though o'er the spirit each hath charm and power,
Yet not for *these* I ask one lingering hour.

But by strong sympathies, whose silver cord
Links me to mortal weal, my soul is bound
Thoughts of the human hearts, that here have
         pour'd
Their anguish forth, are with me and around ;—
I look back on the pangs, the burning tears,
Known to these altars of a thousand years.

Send up a murmur from the dust, Remorse!
  That here hast bow'd with ashes on thy head;
And thou, still battling with the tempest's force—
  Thou, whose bright spirit through all time has
        blind—
Speak, wounded Love! if penance here, or prayer,
Hath laid one haunting shadow of despair?

No voice, no breath!—of conflicts past, no trace!
  —Doth not this hush give answer to my quest?
Surely the dread religion of the place
  By every grief hath made its might confest!
—Oh! that within my heart I could but keep
Holy to Heaven, a spot thus pure, and still, and
    deep!

## THE SONG OF NIGHT.

O night,
And storm, and darkness! ye are wondrous strong,
Yet lovely in your strength!
                                *Byron.*

I come to thee, O Earth!
With all my gifts!—for every flower sweet dew,
In bell, and urn, and chalice, to renew
      The glory of its birth.

Not one which glimmering lies
Far amidst folding hills, or forest leaves,
But, through its veins of beauty, so receives
      A spirit of fresh dyes.

I come with every star;
Making thy streams, that on their noon-day track
Give but the moss, the reed, the lily back,
      Mirrors of worlds afar.

I come with peace;—I shed
Sleep through thy wood-walks, o'er the honey-bee.
The lark's triumphant voice, the fawn's young
        glee,
      The hyacinth's meek head.

On my own heart I lay
The weary babe; and sealing with a breath
Its eyes of love, send fairy dreams, beneath
      The shadowing lids to play.

I come with mightier things!
Who calls me silent? I have many tones—
The dark skies thrill with low, mysterious moans,
      Borne on my sweeping wings.

I waft them not alone
From the deep organ of the forest shades,
Or buried streams, unheard amidst their glades,
      Till the bright day is done;

But in the human breast
A thousand still small voices I awake,
Strong, in their sweetness, from the soul to shake
      The mantle of its rest.

I bring them from the past:
From true hearts broken, gentle spirits torn,
From crush'd affections, which, though long o'er-
        borne,
      Make their tones heard at last.

I bring them from the tomb:
O'er the sad couch of late repentant love
They pass—though low as murmurs of a dove—
      Like trumpets through the gloom.

I come with all my train
Who calls me lonely?—Hosts around me tread,
The intensely bright, the beautiful,—the dead,—
      Phantoms of heart and brain!

Looks from departed eyes—
These are my lightnings!—fill'd with anguish vain
Or tenderness too piercing to sustain,
      They smite with agonies.

I, that with soft control
Shut the dim violet, hush the woodland song,
I am the avenging one! the arm'd—the strong.
      The searcher of the soul!

I, that shower dewy light
Through slumbering leaves, bring storms!—the
        tempest-birth
Of memory, thought, remorse:—Be holy, earth!
      I am the solemn night!

## THE STORM PAINTER* IN HIS DUNGEON.

Where of ye, O tempests! is the goal?
Are ye like those that shake the human breast?
Or do ye find at length, like eagles, some high nest?
                              *Childe Harold.*

Midnight, and silence deep!
  —The air is fill'd with sleep,
With the stream's whisper, and the citron's breath;
    The fix'd and solemn stars
    Gleam through my dungeon bars—
Wake, rushing winds! this breezeless calm is
      death!

Ye watch-fires of the skies!
  The stillness of your eyes
Looks too intensely through my troubled soul:
    I feel this weight of rest
    An earth-load on my breast—
Wake, rushing winds, awake! and, dark clouds
      roll!

I am your own, your child,
  O ye, the fierce and wild
And kingly tempests!—will ye not arise?
    Hear the bold spirit's voice,
    That knows not to rejoice
But in the peal of your strong harmonies.

By sounding ocean-waves,
  And dim Calabrian caves,
And flashing torrents, I have been your mate
    And with the rocking pines
    Of the olden Apennines,
In your dark path stood fearless and elate

Your lightnings were as rods,
  That smote the dark abodes
Of thought and vision—and the stream gush'd free
    Come, that my soul again
    May swell to burst its chain—
Bring me the music of the sweeping sea!

Within me dwells a flame,
  An eagle caged and tame,
Till call'd forth by the harping of the blast;
    Then in its triumph's hour,
    It springs to sudden power,
As mounts the billow o'er the quivering mast.

Then, then, the canvas o'er,
  With hurried hand I pour
The lava-waves and gusts of my own soul!
    Kindling to fiery life
    Dreams, worlds, of pictured strife;
Wake, rushing winds, awake! and, dark clouds,
      roll!

Wake, rise! the reed may bend,
  The shivering leaf descend,
The forest branch give way before your might;
    But I, your strong compeer,
    Call, summon, wait you here,—
Answer, my spirit!—answer, storm and night

## DEATH AND THE WARRIOR.

"Ay, Warrior, arm! and wear thy plume
  On a proud and fearless brow!
I am the lord of the lonely tomb,
  And a mightier one than thou!

---

* Pietro Mulier, called Il Tempesta, from his surprising pictures of storms. "His compositions," says Lanzi, "inspire a real horror, presenting to our eyes death-devoted ships overtaken by tempests and darkness; fired by lightning; now rising on the mountain wave, and again submerged in the abyss of ocean." During an imprisonment of five years in Genoa, the pictures which he painted in his dungeon were marked by additional power and gloom.—See *Lanzi's History of Painting.*

' Bid thy soul's love farewell, young chief,
  Bid her a long farewell!
Like the morning's dew shall pass that grief—
  Thou comest with me to dwell!

" Thy bark may rush through the foaming deep,
  Thy steed o'er the breezy hill;
But they bear thee on to a place of sleep,
  Narrow, and cold, and chill!"

" Was the voice I heard, thy voice, oh Death?
  And is thy day so near?
Then on the field shall my life's last breath
  Mingle with victory's cheer!

" Banners shall float, with the trumpet's note,
  Above me as I die!
And the palm-tree wave o'er my noble grave,
  Under the Syrian sky.

" High hearts shall burn in the royal hall,
  When the minstrel names that spot;
And the eyes I love shall weep my fall,—
  Death, Death! I fear thee not!"

" Warrior! thou bearest a haughty heart!
  But I can bend its pride!
How shouldst thou know that thy soul will part
  In the hour of victory's tide?

" It may be far from thy steel-clad bands,
  That I shall make thee mine;
It may be lone on the desert sands,
  Where men for fountains pine!

' It may be deep amidst heavy chains,
  In some strong Paynim hold;—
I have slow dull steps and lingering pains,
  Wherewith to tame the bold!"

" Death, Death! I go to a doom unblest,
  If this indeed must be;
But the cross is bound upon my breast,
  And I may not shrink for thee!

Sound, clarion, sound!—for my vows are given
  To the cause of the holy shrine:
I bow my soul to the will of Heaven,
  O Death! and not to thine!"

---

## THE TWO VOICES.

Two solemn Voices in a funeral strain,
Met as rich sunbeams and dark bursts of rain
        Meet in the sky:
" Thou art gone hence!" one sang; " Our light is
  flown,
Our beautiful, that seem'd too much our own,
        Ever to die!

" Thou art gone hence!—our joyous hills among
Never again to pour thy soul in song,
      When spring-flowers rise!
Never the friend's familiar step to meet
With loving laughter, and the welcome sweet
        Of thy glad eyes."

" Thou art gone home, gone home!" then, high and
  clear,
Warbled that other Voice. " Thou hast no tear
        Again to shed.
Never to fold the robe o'er secret pain,
Never, weigh'd down by Memory's clouds, again
    To bow thy head.

" Thou art gone home! oh! early crown'd and
  blest!
Where could the love of that deep heart find rest
        With aught below!
Thou must have seen rich dream by dream decay,
All the bright rose-leaves drop from life away—
        Thrice blest to go!"

Yet sigh'd again that breeze-like Voice of grief—
" Thou art gone hence! alas! that aught so brief,
        So loved should be!

Thou tak our summer hence!—the flower, the
  tone,
The music of our being, all in one,
        Depart with thee!

" Fair form, young spirit, morning vision fled!
Canst thou be of the dead, the awful dead!
        The dark unknown?
Yes! to the dwelling where no footsteps fall,
Never again to light up hearth or hall,
        Thy smile is gone!"

" Home! home!" "once more th' exulting voice arose.
" Thou art gone home! from that divine repose
        Never to roam!
Never to say farewell, to weep in vain,
To read of change in eyes beloved, again—
        Thou art gone home!

" By the bright waters now thy lot is cast,—
Joy for thee, happy friend! thy bark hath past
        The rough sea's foam!
Now the long yearnings of thy soul are still'd,—
Home! home!—thy peace is won, thy heart is fill'd.
      —Thou art gone home!"

---

## THE PARTING SHIP.

*A glittering ship that hath the plain*
*Of ocean for her own domain.*
         *Wordsworth.*

---

Go, in thy glory, o'er the ancient sea,
  Take with thee gentle winds thy sails to swell!
Sunshine and joy upon thy streamers be,—
  Fare thee well, bark! farewell!

Proudly the flashing billow thou hast cleft,
  The breeze yet follows thee with cheer and song
Who now of storms hath dream or memory left?
  And yet the deep is strong!

But go thou triumphing, while still the smiles
  Of summer tremble on the water's breast!
Thou shalt be greeted by a thousand isles,
  In lone, wild beauty drest.

To thee a welcome, breathing o'er the tide,
  The genii groves of Araby shall pour;
Waves that enfold the pearl shall bathe thy side
  On the old Indian shore.

Oft shall the shadow of the palm-tree lie
  O'er glassy bays wherein thy sails are furl'd,
And its leaves whisper, as the wind sweeps by,
  Tales of the elder world.

Oft shall the burning stars of Southern skies,
  On the mid-ocean see thee chain'd in sleep,
A lonely home for human thoughts and ties,
  Between the heavens and deep.

Blue seas that roll on gorgeous coasts renown'd,
  By night shall sparkle where thy prow makes
    way;
Strange creatures of the abyss that none may
    sound,
  In thy broad wake shall play.

From hills unknown, in mingled joy and fear,
  Free dusky tribes shall pour, thy flag to mark;—
Blessings go with thee on thy lone career!
  Hail, and farewell, thou bark!

A long farewell!—Thou wilt not bring us back
  All whom thou bearest far from home and hearth
Many are thine, whose steps no more shall track
  Their own sweet native earth!

Some wilt thou leave beneath the plantain's shade,
  Where through the foliage Indian suns look
    bright:
Some, in the snows of wintry regions laid,
  By the cold northern light.

And some, far down below the sounding wave,—
  Still shall they lie, though tempests o'er them
    sweep;
Never may flower be strewn above their grave,
  Never may sister weep!

And thou—the billow's queen—even thy proud
    form
  On our glad sight no more perchance may swell;
Yet God alike is in the calm and storm—
  Fare thee well, bark! farewell!

---

## THE LAST TREE OF THE FOREST.

Whisper, thou Tree, thou lonely Tree,
  One, where a thousand stood!
Well might proud tales be told by thee,
  Last of the solemn wood!

Dwells there no voice amidst thy boughs,
  With leaves yet darkly green?
Stillness is round, and noontide glows—
  Tell us what thou hast seen.

'I have seen the forest shadows lie
  Where men now reap the corn;
I have seen the kingly chase rush by,
  Through the deep glades at morn.

"With the glance of many a gallant spear,
  And the wave of many a plume,
And the bounding of a hundred deer,
  It hath lit the woodland's gloom.

"I have seen the knight and his train ride past,
  With his banner borne on high;
O'er all my leaves there was brightness cast
  From his gleaming panoply.

"The pilgrim at my feet hath laid
  His palm-branch 'midst the flowers,
And told his deeds, and meekly pray'd,
  Kneeling, at vesper-hours.

'And the merry-men of wild and glen,
  In the green array they wore,
Have feasted here with the red wine's cheer,
  And the hunter's song of yore.

"And the minstrel, resting in my shade,
  Hath made the forest ring
With the lordly tales of the high Crusade,
  Once loved by chief and king.

"But now the noble forms are gone,
  That walk'd the earth of old;
The soft wind hath a mournful tone,
  The sunny light looks cold.

"There is no glory left us now,
  Like the glory with the dead:—
I would that where they slumber low
  My latest leaves were shed!"

Oh! thou dark Tree, thou lonely tree,
  That mournest for the past!
A peasant's home in thy shades I see,
  Embower'd from every blast.

A lovely and a mirthful sound
  Of laughter meets mine ear;
For the poor man's children sport around
  On the turf, with naught to fear.

And roses lend that cabin's wall
  A happy summer-glow;
And the open door stands free to all,
  For it recks not of a foe.

And the village bells are on the breeze
  That stirs thy leaf, dark Tree!
How can I mourn, 'midst things like these,
  For the stormy past, with thee?

## THE STREAMS.

The power, the beauty, and the majesty,
That had their haunts in dale or piny mountain,
Or forest by slow stream, or pebbly spring,
Or chasms and watery depths; all these have vanish'd!
They live no longer in the faith of heaven,
But still the heart doth need a language!
Coleridge's Wallenstein.

Ye have been holy, O founts and floods!
Ye of the ancient and solemn woods,
Ye that are born of the valleys deep,
With the water-flowers on your breast asleep,
And ye that gush from the sounding caves—
    Hallow'd have been your waves.

Hallow'd by man, in his dreams of old,
Unto beings not of this mortal mould,
Viewless, and deathless, and wondrous powers,
Whose voice he heard in his lonely hours,
And sought with its fancied sound to still
    The heart earth could not fill.

Therefore the flowers of bright summers gone,
O'er your sweet waters, ye streams! were thrown
Thousand of gifts, to the sunny sea
Have ye swept along in your wanderings free,
And thrill'd to the murmur of many a vow—
    Where all is silent now!

Nor seems it strange that the heart hath been
So link'd in love to your margins green;
That still, though ruin'd, your early shrines
In beauty gleam through the southern vines,
And the ivied chapels of colder skies,
    On your wild banks arise.

For the loveliest scenes of the glowing earth,
Are those, bright streams! where your springs
    have birth:
Whether their cavern'd murmur fills,
With a tone of plaint, the hollow hills,
Or the glad sweet laugh of their healthful flow
    Is heard 'midst the hamlets low.

Or whether ye gladden the desert-sands,
With a joyous music to Pilgrim bands,
And a flash from under some ancient rock,
Where a shepherd-king might have watch'd his
    flock,
Where a few lone palm-trees lift their heads,
    And a green Acacia spreads.

Or whether, in bright old lands renown'd,
The laurels thrill to your first-born sound,
And the shadow, flung from the Grecian pine,
Sweeps with the breeze o'er your gleaming line,
And the tall reeds whisper to your waves,
    Beside heroic graves.

Voices and lights of the lonely place!
By the freshest fern your path we trace;
By the brightest cups on the emerald moss,
Whose fairy goblets the turf emboss,
By the rainbow-glancing of insect wings,
    In a thousand mazy rings.

There sucks the bee, for the richest flowers
Are all your own through the summer-hours;
There the proud stag his fair image knows,
Traced on your glass beneath alder-boughs,
And the Halcyon's breast, like the skies array'd,
    Gleams through the willow-shade.

But the wild sweet tales, that with elves and fay
Peopled your banks in the elden days,
And the memory left by departed love,
To your antique founts in glen and grove,
And the glory born of the poet's dreams—
    These are your charms, bright streams!

Now is the time of your flowery rites,
Gone by with its dances and young delights:

From your marble urns ye have burst away
From your chapel-cells to the laughing day
Low lie your altars with moss o'ergrown,
   —And the woods again are lone.

Yet holy still be your living springs,
Haunts of all gentle and gladsome things!
Holy, to converse with nature's lore,
That gives the worn spirit its youth once more,
And to silent thoughts of the love divine,
   Making the heart a shrine.

## THE VOICE OF THE WIND.

*There is nothing in the wide world so like the voice of a spirit.*
*Gray's Letters.*

Oh! many a voice is thine, thou Wind! full many
   a voice is thine,
From every scene thy wing o'ersweeps thou bear'st
   a sound and sign;
A minstrel wild and strong thou art, with a mas
   tery all thine own,
And the spirit is thy harp, O Wind! that gives the
   answering tone.

Thou hast been across red fields of war, where
   shiver'd helmets lie,
And thou bringest thence the thrilling note of a
   clarion in the sky;
A rustling of proud banner-folds, a peal of stormy
   drums,—
All these are in thy music met, as when a leader
   comes.

Thou hast been o'er solitary seas, and from their
   wastes brought back
Each noise of waters that awoke in the mystery
   of thy track;
The chime of low soft southern waves on some
   green palmy shore,
The hollow roll of distant surge, the gather'd bil·
   lows' roar.

Thou art come from forests dark and deep, thou
   mighty rushing Wind!
And thou bearest all their unisons in one full
   swell combined;
The restless pines, the moaning stream, all hidden
   things and free,
Of the dim old sounding wilderness, have lent
   their soul to thee.

Thou art come from cities lighted up for the con·
   queror passing by,
Thou art wafting from their streets a sound of
   haughty revelry;
The rolling of triumphant wheels, the harpings in
   the hall,
The far-off shout of multitudes, are in thy rise
   and fall.

Thou art come from kingly tombs and shrines,
   from ancient minsters vast,
Through the dark aisles of a thousand years thy
   lonely wing hath pass'd;
Thou hast caught the anthem's billowy swell, the
   stately dirge's tone,
For a chief, with sword, and shield, and helm, to
   his place of slumber gone.

Thou art come from long-forsaken homes, wherein
   our young days flew,
Thou hast found sweet voices lingering there, the
   loved, the kind, the true;
Thou callest back those melodies, though now all
   changed and fled,—
Be still, be still, and haunt us not with music from
   the dead!

Are all these notes in *thee*, wild Wind? these many
   notes in *thee*?
For in our own unfathom'd souls their fount must
   surely be;

18

Yes! buried, but unsleeping, *there* Thought watch·
   es, Memory lies,
From whose deep urn the tones are pour'd through
   all Earth's harmonies.

## THE VIGIL OF ARMS.[*]

A sounding step was heard by night
   In a church where the mighty slept,
As a mail-clad youth, till morning's light,
   'Midst the tombs his vigil kept.
He walk'd in dreams of power and fame,
   He lifted a proud, bright eye,
For the hours were few that withheld his name
   From the roll of chivalry.

Down the moon-lit aisles he paced alone,
   With a free and stately tread;
And the floor gave back a muffled tone
   From the couches of the dead:
The silent many that round him lay,
   The crown'd and helm'd that were,
   The haughty chiefs of the war-array—
   Each in his sepulchre!

But no dim warning of time or fate
   That youth's flush'd hopes could chill,
He moved through the trophies of buried state
   With each proud pulse throbbing still.
He heard, as the wind through the chancel sung
   A swell of the trumpet's breath;
He look'd to the banners on high that hung,
   And not to the dust beneath.

And a royal masque of splendour seem'd
   Before him to unfold;
Through the solemn arches on it stream'd,
   With many a gleam of gold:

There were crested knight, and gorgeous dame,
   Glittering athwart the gloom.
And he follow'd, till his bold step came
   To his warrior-father's tomb.

But there the still and shadowy might
   Of the monumental stone,
And the holy sleep of the soft lamp's light,
   That over its quiet shone.
And th' image of that sire, who died
   In his noonday of renown—
*These* had a power unto which the pride
   Of fiery life bow'd down.

And a spirit from his early years
   Came back o'er his thoughts to move,
Till his eye was fill'd with memory's tears,
   And his heart with childhood's love!
And he look'd, with a change in his softening
   glance,
   To the armour o'er the grave,—
For there they hung, the shield and lance,
   And the gauntlet of the brave.

And the sword of many a field was there,
   With its cross for the hour of need,
When the knight's bold war-cry hath sunk in
   prayer,
   And the spear is a broken reed!
—Hush! did a breeze through the armour sigh?
   Did the fold of the banner shake?
Not so!—from the tomb's dark mystery
   There seem'd a voice to break!

He had heard that voice bid clarions blow,
   He had caught its last blessing's breath,—
'Twas the same—but its awful sweetness now
   Had an under-tone of death!
And it said,—"The sword hath conquer'd kings,
   And the spear through realms hath pass'd;
But the cross, alone, of all these things,
   Might aid me at the last.

[*] The candidate for knighthood was under the necessity of keep·
ing watch, the night before his inauguration, in a church, and com·
pletely armed. This was called "the Vigil of Arms."

## THE BEINGS OF THE MIND

The beings of the mind are not of clay;
Essentially immortal, they create
And multiply in us a brighter ray,
And more beloved existence; that which Fate
Prohibits to dull life, in this our state
Of mortal bondage.
                                        *Byron.*

Come to me with your triumphs and your woes,
  Ye forms, to life by glorious poets brought!
I sit alone with flowers and vernal boughs,
  In the deep shadow of a voiceless thought:
'Midst the glad music of the spring alone,
And sorrowful for visions that are gone!

Come to me! make your thrilling whispers heard,
  Ye, by those masters of the soul endow'd
With life, and love, and many a burning word,
  That bursts from grief, like lightning from a
        cloud,
And smites the heart, till all its chords reply,
As leaves make answer when the wind sweeps by.

Come to me! visit my dim haunt!—the sound
  Of hidden springs is in the grass beneath;
The stock-dove's note above; and all around,
  The poesy that with the violet's breath
Floats through the air, in rich and sudden streams,
Mingling, like music, with the soul's deep dreams

Friends, friends!—for such to my lone heart ye
        are—
Unchanging ones! from whose immortal eyes
The glory melts not as a waning star.
  And the sweet kindness never, never dies;
Bright children of the bard! o'er this green dell
Pass once again, and light it with your spell!

Imogen! fair Fidele! meekly blending
  In patient grief, a "smiling with a sigh;"*
And thou, Cordelia! faithful daughter, tending
  That sire, an outcast to the bitter sky;
Thou of the soft low voice!—thou art not gone!
Still breathes for me its faint and flute-like tone.

And come to me! sing me thy willow-strain,
  Sweet Desdemona! with the sad surprise
In thy beseeching glance, where still, though vain,
  Undimm'd, unquenchable affection lies;
Come, bowing thy young head to wrong and scorn,
As a frail hyacinth, by showers o'erborne.

And thou, too, fair Ophelia! flowers are here
  That well might win thy footstep to the spot—
Pale cowslips, meet for maiden's early bier,
  And pansies for sad thoughts,†—but needed not!
Come with thy wreaths, and all the love and light
In that wild eye still tremulously bright.

And Juliet, vision of the south! enshrining
  All gifts that unto its rich heaven belong;
The glow, the sweetness, in its rose combining,
  The soul its nightingales pour forth in song!
Thou, making death deep joy!—but *couldst* thou
        die?
No!—thy young love hath immortality!

From earth's bright faces fades the light of morn,
  From earth's glad voices drops the joyous tone;
But ye, the children of the soul, were born
  Deathless, and for undying love alone;
And, oh! ye beautiful! 'tis well, how well,
In the soul's world, with you, where change is not,
        to dwell!

* Nobly he yokes
A smiling with a sigh.
                        *Cymbeline.*
† Here's pansies for you—that's for thoughts.
                        *Hamlet.*

## TASSO'S CORONATION.*

A crown of victory! a triumphal song!
Oh! call some friend, upon whose pitying heart
The weary one may calmly sink to rest;
Let some kind voice, beside his lowly couch,
Pour the last prayer for mortal agony!

A trumpet's note is in the sky, in the glorious
        Roman sky,
Whose dome hath rung, so many an age, to the
        voice of victory;
There is crowding to the capitol, the imperial
        streets along,
For again a conqueror must be crown'd,—a kingly
        child of song:

        Yet his chariot lingers,
        Yet around his home
        Broods a shadow silently,
        'Midst the joy of Rome.

A thousand thousand laurel-boughs are waving
        wide and far,
To shed out their triumphal gleams around his
        rolling car;
A thousand haunts of olden gods have given their
        wealth of flowers,
To scatter o'er his path of fame bright hues in
        gem-like showers.

        Peace! within his chamber
        Low the mighty lies;
        With a cloud of dreams on his noble brow,
        And a wandering in his eyes.

Sing, sing for him, the lord of song, for him, whose
        rushing strain
In mastery o'er the spirit sweeps, like a strong
        wind o'er the main!

Whose voice lives deep in burning hearts, for ever
        there to dwell,
As full-toned oracles are shrined in a temple's ho-
        liest cell.

        Yes! for him, the victor,
        Sing,—but low, sing low!
        A soft sad *miserere* chant
        For a soul about to go!

The sun, the sun of Italy is pouring o'er his way,
Where the old three hundred triumphs moved, a
        flood of golden day;
Streaming through every haughty arch of the Cæ-
        sars' past renown—
Bring forth, in that exulting light, the conqueror
        for his crown!

        Shut the proud bright sunshine
        From the fading sight!
        There needs no ray by the bed of death,
        Save the holy taper's light.

The wreath is twined,—the way is strewn—the
        lordly train are met—
The streets are hung with coronals—why stays
        the minstrel yet?
Shout! as an army shouts in joy around a royal
        chief—
Bring forth the bard of chivalry, the bard of love
        and grief!

        Silence! forth we bring him,
        In his last array;
        From love and grief the freed, the flown—
        Way for the bier—make way!

## THE BETTER LAND.

"I hear thee speak of the better land,
Thou callest its children a happy band;
Mother! oh where is that radiant shore?
Shall we not seek it, and weep no more?

* Tasso died at Rome on the day before the appointed for his
Coronation in the Capitol.

Is it where the flower of the orange blows,
And the fire-flies glance through the myrtle boughs?
   —" Not there, not there, my child!"

' Is it where the feathery palm-trees rise,
And the date grows ripe under sunny skies?
Or 'midst the green islands of glittering seas,
Where fragrant forests perfume the breeze,
And strange, bright birds, on their starry wings
Bear the rich hues of all glorious things?"
   —" Not there, not there, my child!"

" Is it far away, in some region old,
Where the rivers wander o'er sands of gold?—
Where the burning rays of the ruby shine,
And the diamond lights up the secret mine,
And the pearl gleams forth from the coral strand?
Is it there, sweet mother, that better land?"
   —" Not there, not there, my child!

" Eye hath not seen it, my gentle boy!
Ear hath not heard its deep songs of joy;
Dreams cannot picture a world so fair—
Sorrow and death may not enter there;—
Time doth not breathe on its fadeless bloom,
For beyond the clouds, and beyond the tomb,
   —It is there, it is there, my child!"

## THE REQUIEM OF GENIUS.

*Les poètes dont l'imagination tient à la puissance d'aimer et de souffrir, ne sont-ils pas les bannis d'une autre region?*
    *Madame De Staël. De L'Allemagne.*

No tears for thee!—though light be from us gone
With thy soul's radiance, bright, yet restless one!
   No tears for thee!
They that have loved an exile, must not mourn
To see him parting for his native bourne
   O'er the dark sea.

All the high music of thy spirit here,
Breathed but the language of another sphere,
   Unechoed round;
And strange, though sweet, as 'midst our weeping skies
Some half-remember'd strain of paradise
   Might sadly sound.

Hast thou been answer'd? thou, that from the night
And from the voices of the tempest's might,
   And from the past,
Wert seeking still some oracle's reply,
To pour the secrets of man's destiny
   Forth on the blast!

Hast thou been answer'd?—thou, that through the gloom,
And shadow, and stern silence of the tomb,
   A cry didst send,
So passionate and deep? to pierce, to move,
To win back token of unburied love
   From buried friend!

And hast thou found where living waters burst?
Thou, that didst pine amidst us, in the thirst
   Of fever-dreams!
Are the true fountains thine for evermore?
Oh! lured so long by shining mists, that wore
   The light of streams!

Speak! is it well with thee?—We call, as thou,
With thy lit eye, deep voice, and kindled brow,
   Wert wont to call
On the departed! Art thou blest and free?
—Alas! the lips earth covers, even to thee,
   Were silent all!

Yet shall our hope rise, fann'd by quenchless faith,
As a flame, foster'd by some warm wind's breath,
   In light upsprings:
Freed soul of song! yes, thou hast found the sought;
Borne to thy home of beauty and of thought,
   On morn'ng's wings.

And we will dream it is thy joy we hear,
When life's young music, ringing far and clear,
   O'erflows the sky:
—No tears for thee! the lingering gloom is ours—
Thou art for converse with all glorious powers,
   Never to die!

## SADNESS AND MIRTH.

Nay, these wild fits of uncurb'd laughter
Athwart the gloomy tenor of your mind,
As it has lower'd of late, so keenly cast,
Unsuited seem, and strange.
   Oh! nothing strange!
Didst thou ne'er see the swallow's veering breast,
Winging the air beneath some murky cloud,
In the sunn'd glimpses of a troubled day,
Shiver in silvery brightness?
Or boatman's oar, as vivid lightning flash
In the faint gleam, that like a spirit's path,
Tracks the still waters of some sullen lake?
   O, gentle friend!
Chide not *her* mirth, who yesterday was sad,
And may be so to-morrow!
    *Joanna Baillie.*

Ye met at the stately feasts of old,
Where the bright wine foam'd over sculptured gold,
Sadness and Mirth!—ye were mingled there
With the sound of the lyre in the scented air;
As the cloud and the lightning are blent on high,
Ye mix'd in the gorgeous revelry.

For there hung o'er those banquets of yore a gloom,
A thought and a shadow of the tomb;
It gave to the flute-notes an under-tone,
To the rose a colouring not its own,
To the breath of the myrtle a mournful power—
Sadness and Mirth! ye had each your dower!

Ye met when the triumph swept proudly by,
With the Roman eagles through the sky!
I know that ev'n then, in his hour of pride,
The soul of the mighty within him died;
That a void in his bosom lay darkly still,
Which the music of victory might never fill!

Thou wert there, oh! Mirth! swelling on the shout,
Till the temples, like echo-caves, rang out;
Thine were the garlands, the songs, the wine,
All the rich voices in air were thine,
The incense, the sunshine—but, Sadness! thy part,
Deepest of all, was the victor's heart!

Ye meet at the bridal with flower and tear;
Strangely and wildly ye meet by the bier!
As the gleam from a sea-bird's white wing shed,
Crosses the storm in its path of dread;
As a dirge meets the breeze of a summer sky—
Sadness and Mirth! so ye come and fly!

Ye meet in the poet's haunted breast,
Darkness and rainbow, alike its guest!
When the breath of the violet is out in spring,
When the woods with the wakening of music ring,
O'er his dreamy spirit your currents pass,
Like shadow and sunlight o'er mountain grass.

When will your parting be, Sadness and Mirth?
Bright stream and dark one!—oh! never on earth;
Never while triumphs and tombs are so near,
While Death and Love walk the same dim sphere,
While flowers unfold where the storm may sweep,
While the heart of man is a soundless deep!

But there smiles a land, oh! ye troubled pair!
Where ye have no part in the summer air,
Far from the breathings of changeful skies,
Over the seas and the graves it lies;
Where the day of the lightning and cloud is done
And joy reigns alone, as the lonely sun!

## SECOND SIGHT.

Ne'er err'd the prophet heart that grief inspired,
Though joy's illusions mock their votarist.
*Maturin.*

A MOURNFUL gift is mine, O friends!
  A mournful gift is mine!
A murmur of the soul which blends
  With the flow of song and wine.

An eye that through the triumph's hour,
  Beholds the coming woe,
And dwells upon the faded flower
  'Midst the rich summer's glow.

Ye smile to view fair faces bloom
  Where the father's board is spread;
I see the stillness and the gloom
  Of a home whence all are fled.

I see the wither'd garlands lie
  Forsaken on the earth,
While the lamps yet burn, and the dancers fly
  Through the ringing hall of mirth.

I see the blood-red future stain
  On the warrior's gorgeous crest;
And the bier amidst the bridal train
  When they come with roses drest.

I hear the still small moan of Time,
  Through the ivy branches made,
Where the palace, in its glory's prime,
  With the sunshine stands array'd.

The thunder of the seas I hear,
  The shriek along the wave,
When the bark sweeps forth, and song and cheer
  Salute the parting brave

With every breeze a spirit sends
  To me some warning sign:—
A mournful gift is mine, O friends!
  A mournful gift is mine!

Oh! prophet heart! thy grief, thy power,
  To all deep souls belong;
The shadow in the sunny hour,
  The wail in the mirthful song.

There sight is all too sadly clear—
  For them a veil is riven;
Their piercing thoughts repose not here,
  Their home is but in Heaven.


## THE SEA-BIRD FLYING INLAND.

Thy path is not as mine:—where thou art blest,
My spirit would but wither: mine own grief
Is in mine eyes a richer, holier thing
Than all thy happiness.

HATH the summer's breath, on the south-wind
    borne,
Met the dark seas in their sweeping scorn?
Hath it lured thee, Bird! from their sounding caves,
To the river-shores, where the osier waves?

Or art thou come on the hills to dwell,
Where the sweet-voiced echoes have many a cell?
Where the moss bears print of the wild-deer's
    tread,
And the heath like a royal robe is spread?

Thou hast done well, O thou bright sea-bird!
There is joy where the song of the lark is heard,
With the dancing of waters through copse and dell
And the bee's low tune in the foxglove's bell.

Thou hast done well:—Oh! the seas are lone,
And the voice they send up hath a mournful tone;
A mingling of dirges and wild farewells,
Fitfully breathed through its anthem-swells.

—The proud bird rose as the words were said—
The rush of his pinion swept o'er my head,
And the glance of his eye, in its bright disdain,
Spoke him a child of the haughty main.


He hath flown from the woods to the ocean's breast
To his throne of pride on the billow's crest!
—Oh! who shall say, to a spirit free,
" *There* lies the pathway of bliss for thee?"


## THE SLEEPER.

For sleep is awful.——*Byron.*

OH! lightly, lightly tread!
  A holy thing is sleep,
On the worn spirit shed,
  And eyes that wake to weep.

A holy thing from Heaven,
  A gracious dewy cloud,
A covering mantle given
  The weary to enshroud.

Oh! lightly, lightly tread!
  Revere the pale still brow,
The meekly-drooping head,
  The long hair's willowy flow.

Ye know not what ye do,
  That call the slumberer back,
From the world unseen by you,
  Unto life's dim faded track.

Her soul is far away,
  In her childhood's land, perchance,
Where her young sisters play,
  Where shines her mother's glance.

Some old sweet native sound
  Her spirit haply weaves;
A harmony profound
  Of woods with all their leaves;

A murmur of the sea,
  A laughing tone of streams:—
Long may her sojourn be
  In the music-land of dreams!

Each voice of love is there,
  Each gleam of beauty fled,
Each lost one still more fair—
  Oh! lightly, lightly tread!


## THE MIRROR IN THE DESERTED HALL

O, DIM, forsaken mirror!
  How many a stately throng
Hath o'er thee gleam'd, in vanish'd hours
  Of the wine-cup and the song!

The song hath left no echo;
  The bright wine hath been quaff'd;
And hush'd is every silvery voice
  That lightly here hath laugh'd.

Oh! mirror, lonely mirror,
  Thou of the silent hall!
Thou hast been flush'd with beauty's bloom
  Is this, too, vanish'd all?

It is, with the scatter'd garlands
  Of triumphs long ago;
With the melodies of buried lyres;
  With the faded rainbow's glow.

And for all the gorgeous pageants,
  For the glance of gem and plume,
For lamp, and harp, and rosy wreath,
  And vase of rich perfume.

Now, dim, forsaken mirror,
  Thou givest but faintly back
The quiet stars, and the smiling moon,
  On her solitary track.

And thus with man's proud spirit
  Thou tellest me 't will be,
When the forms and hues of this world fade
  From his memory, as from thee:

And his heart's long-troubled waters
  At last in stillness lie,
Reflecting but the images
  Of the solemn world on high.

# THE FOREST SANCTUARY.

The voices of my home!—I hear them still!
They have been with me through the dreamy
    night—
The blessed household voices, wont to fill
My heart's clear depths with unalloy'd delight!
I hear them still unchanged:—though some from
    earth
Are music parted, and the tones of mirth—
Wild, silvery tones, that rang through days
    more bright!
Have died in others,—yet to me they come,
Singing of boyhood back—the voices of my home!

### II.

They call me through this hush of woods, re
    posing
In the gray stillness of the summer morn,
They wander by when heavy flowers are closing,
And thoughts grow deep, and winds and stars
    are born;
E'en as a fount's remember'd gushings burst
On the parch'd traveller in his hour of thirst,
E'en thus they haunt me with sweet sounds, till
    worn
By quenchless longings, to my soul I say—
Oh! for the dove's swift wings, that I might flee
    away,

### III.

And find mine ark!—yet whither?—I must bear
A yearning heart within me to the grave.
I am of those o'er whom a breath o. air—
Just darkening in its course the lake's bright
    wave,
And sighing through the feathery canes(I)—
    hath power
To call up shadows, in the silent hour,
From the dim past, as from a wizard's cave!
So must it be!—These skies above me spread,
Are they my own soft skies?—Ye rest not here,
    my dead!

### IV

Ye far amidst the southern flowers lie sleeping.
Your graves all smiling in the sunshine clear,
Save one!—a blue, lone, distant main is sweep
    ing
High o'er *one* gentle head—ye rest not here!—
'Tis not the olive, with a whisper swaying,
Not thy low ripplings, glassy water, playing
Through my own chestnut groves, which fill
    mine ear;
But the faint echoes in my breast that dwell,
And for their birth-place moan, as moans the
    ocean-shell. (2)

### V.

Peace!—I will dash these fond regrets to earth,
Ev'n as an eagle shakes the cumbering rain

From his strong pinion. Thou that gav'st me
    birth,
And lineage, and once home, my native Spain.
My own bright land—my father's land—my
    child's!
What hath thy son brought from thee to the
    wilds?
He hath brought marks of torture and the chain,
Traces of things which pass not as a breeze,
A blighted name, dark thoughts, wrath, woe—thy
    gifts are these.

### VI.

A blighted name!—I hear the winds of morn—
Their sounds are not of this!—I hear the shiver
Of the green reeds, and all the rustlings, borne
From the high forest, when the light leaves
    quiver:
Their sounds are not of this!—the cedars, waving,
Lend it no tone: His wide savannahs laving,
It is not murmur'd by the joyous river!
What part hath mortal name, where God alone
Speaks to the mighty waste, and through its heart
    is known?

### VII.

Is it not much that I may worship Him,
With naught my spirit's breathings to control,
And feel His presence in the vast and dim,
And whispery woods, where dying thunders roll
From the far cataracts?—Shall I not rejoice
That I have learn'd at last to know *His* voice
From man's?—I will rejoice!—my soaring soul
Now hath redeem'd her birth-right of the day,
And won, through clouds, to Him, her own unfet-
    ter'd way!

### VIII.

And thou, my boy! that silent at my knee
Dost lift to mine thy soft, dark, earnest eyes,
Fill'd with the love of childhood, which I see
Pure through its depths, a thing without disguise,
Thou that hast breath'd in slumber on my breast,
When I have check'd its throbs to give thee rest,
Mine own! whose young thoughts fresh before
    me rise!
Is it not much that I may guide thy prayer,
And circle thy glad soul with free and healthful air?

### IX.

Why should I weep on thy bright head, my boy?
Within thy father's halls thou wilt not dwell,
Nor lift their banner, with a warrior's joy,
Amidst the sons of mountain chiefs, who fell
For Spain of old.—Yet what if rolling waves
Have borne us far from our ancestral graves!
Thou shalt not feel thy bursting heart rebel,
As mine hath done; nor bear what I have borne,
Casting in falsehood's mould th' indignant brow
    of scorn.

#### X.

This shall not be thy lot, my blessed child!
I have not sorrow'd, struggled, lived in vain—
Hear me! magnificent and ancient wild;
And mighty rivers, ye that meet the main,
As deep meets deep; and forests, whose dim
   shade
The flood's voice, and the wind's, by swells per-
   vade;
Hear me!—'t is well to die and not complain,
Yet there are hours when the charged heart must
   speak,
Ev'n in the desert's ear to pour itself, or break!

#### XI.

I see an oak before me, (3) it had been
The crown'd one of the woods; and might have
   flung
Its hundred arms to Heaven, still freshly green,
But a wild vine around the stem hath clung,
From branch to branch close wreaths of bondage
   throwing,
Till the proud tree, before no tempest bowing,
Hath shrunk and died, those serpent folds among.
Alas! alas!—what is it that I see?
An image of man's mind, land of my sires, with
   thee!

#### XII.

Yet art thou lovely!—Song is on thy hills—
Oh sweet and mournful melodies of Spain,
That lull'd my boyhood, how your memory
   thrills
The exile's heart with sudden-wakening pain!—
Your sounds are on the rocks—that I might hear
Once more the music of the mountaineer!—
And from the sunny vales the shepherd's strain
Floats out, and fills the solitary place
With the old tuneful names of Spain's heroic race.

#### XIII.

But there was silence one bright, golden day,
Through my own pine-hung mountains.  Clear,
   yet lone,
In the rich autumn light the vineyards lay,
And from the fields the peasant's voice was gone;
And the red grapes untrodden strew'd the ground,
And the free flocks untended roam'd around:
Where was the pastor?—where the pipe's wild
   tone?
Music and mirth were hush'd the hills among,
While to the city's gates each hamlet pour'd its
   throng.

#### XIV.

Silence upon the mountains!—But within
The city's gates a rush—a press—a swell
Of multitudes their torrent way to win;
And heavy boomings of a dull deep bell,
A dead pause following each—like that which
   parts
The dash of billows, holding breathless hearts
Fast in the hush of fear—knell after knell;
And sounds of thickening steps, like thunder-
   rain,
That plashes on the roof of some vast echoing fane!

#### XV.

What pageant's hour approach'd?—The sullen
   gate
Of a strong ancient prison-house was thrown
Back to the day.  And who, in mournful state,
Came forth, led slowly o'er its threshold stone?
They that had learn'd, in cells of secret gloom,
How sunshine is forgotten!—They, to whom
The very features of mankind were grown
Things that bewilder'd!—O'er their dazzled sight
They lifted their wan hands, and cower'd before
   the light!

#### XVI.

To this man brings his brother!—Some were
   there,
Who with their desolation had entwined
Fierce strength, and girt the sternness of despair
Fast round their bosoms, ev'n as warriors bind
The breast-plate on for fight: but brow and cheek
Seem in theirs a torturing panoply to speak!
And there were some, from whom the very mind
Had been wrung out: they smiled—oh! startling
   smile,
Whence man's high soul is fled!—where doth it
   sleep the while?

#### XVII.

But onward moved the melancholy train,
For their false creeds in fiery pangs to die.
This was the solemn sacrifice of Spain—
Heaven's offering from the land of chivalry!
Through thousands, thousands of their race they
   moved
—Oh! how unlike all others!—the beloved,
The free, the proud, the beautiful! whose eye
Grew fix'd before them, while a people's breath
Was hush'd, and its one soul bound in the thought
   of death!

#### XVIII.

It might be that amidst the countless throng,
There swell'd some heart, with pity's weight op-
   press'd—
For the wide stream of human love is strong,
And woman, on whose fond and faithful breast
Childhood is rear'd, and at whose knee the sigh
Of its first prayer is breathed, she, too, was nigh.
But life is dear, and the free footstep bless'd,
And home a sunny place, where each may fill
Some eye with glistening smiles,—and therefore all
   were still—

#### XIX.

All still—youth, courage, strength!—a winter
   laid,
A chain of palsy, cast on might and mind!
Still, as at noon a southern forest's shade,
They stood, those breathless masses of mankind;
Still, as a frozen torrent!—but the wave
Soon leaps to foaming freedom—they, the brave,
Endured—they saw the martyr's place assign'd
In the red flames—whence is the withering spell
That numbs each human pulse?—they saw, and
   thought it well.

#### XX.

And I, too, thought it well! That very morn
From a far land I came, yet round me clung
The spirit of my own.  No hand had torn
With a strong grasp away the veil which hung
Between mine eyes and truth.  I gazed, I saw,
Dimly, as through a glass.  In silent awe
I watch'd the fearful rites; and if there sprung
One rebel feeling from its deep founts up,
Shuddering, I flung it back as guilt's own poison-
   cup.

#### XXI.

But I was waken'd as the dreamers waken,
Whom the shrill trumpet and the shriek of dread
Rouse up at midnight, when their walls are ta-
   ken,
And they must battle till their blood is shed
On their own threshold floor. A path for light
Through my torn breast was shatter'd by the
   might
Of the swift thunder-stroke—and Freedom's tread
Came in through ruins, late, yet not in vain,
Making the blighted place all green with life again.

#### XXII.

Still darkly, slowly, as a sullen mass
Of cloud o'ersweeping, without wind, the sky,
Dream-like I saw the sad procession pass,
And mark'd its victims with a tearless eye.

They moved before me but as pictures, wrought
Each to reveal some secret of man's thought,
On the sharp edge of sad mortality,
Till in his place came one—oh! could it be?
—My friend, my heart's first friend!—and did I
    gaze on thee?

### XXIII.

On thee! with whom in boyhood I had play'd,
At the grape-gatherings, by my native streams;
And to whose eye my youthful soul had laid
Bare, as to Heaven's, its glowing world of dreams;
And by whose side 'midst warriors I had stood,
And in whose helm was brought—oh! earn'd
    with blood!—
The fresh wave to my lips, when tropic beams
Smote on my fever'd brow!—Ay, years had pass'd,
Severing our paths, brave friend! and _thus_ we met
    at last!

### XXIV.

I see it still—the lofty mien thou borest—
On thy pale forehead sat a sense of power!
The very look that once thou brightly worest
Cheering me onward through a fearful hour,
When we were girt by Indian bow and spear,
'Midst the white Andes—ev'n as mountain dee
Hemm'd in our camp—but through the javelin
    shower
We rent our way, a tempest of despair!
—And thou—hadst thou but died with thy true
    brethren there!

### XXV.

I call the fond wish back—for thou hast perish'd
More nobly far, my Alvar!—making known
The might of truth; (4) and be thy memory cher-
    ish'd
With theirs, the thousands, that around her
    throne
Have pour'd their lives out smiling, in that
    doom
Finding a triumph, if denied a tomb!
—Ay, with their ashes hath the wind been sown,
And with the wind their spirit shall be spread,
Filling man's heart and home with records of the
    dead.

### XXVI.

Thou Searcher of the Soul! in whose dread sight
Not the bold guilt alone, that mocks the skies,
But the scarce own'd, unwhisper'd thought of
    night,
As a thing written with the sunbeam lies;
_Thou_ know'st—whose eye through shade and
    depth can see,
That this man's crime was but to worship thee,
Like those that made their hearts thy sacrifice,
The call'd of yore; wont by the Saviour's side,
On the dim Olive-Mount to pray at eventide.

### XXVII.

For the strong spirit will at times awake,
Piercing the mists that wrap her clay-abode;
And, born of thee, she may not always take
Earth's accents for the oracles of God;
And ev'n for this—O dust, whose mask is power!
Reed, that wouldst be a scourge thy little hour!
Spark, whereon yet the mighty hath not trod,
And therefore thou destroyest!—where were
    flown
Our hope, if man were left to man's decree alone?

### XXVIII.

But this I felt not yet. I could but gaze
On him, my friend; while that swift moment
    threw
A sudden freshness back on vanish'd days,
Like water-drops on some dim picture's hue;
Calling the proud time up, when first I stood
Where banners floated, and my heart's quick
    blood
Sprang to a torrent as the clarion blew,
And he—his sword was like a brother's worn,
That watches through the field his mother's young-
    est born.

### XXIX.

But a lance met me in that day's career,
Senseless I lay amidst th' o'erweeping fight,
Wakening at last—how full, how strangely clear,
That scene on memory flash'd!—the shivery light,
Moonlight, on broken shields—the plain of
    slaughter,
The fountain-side—the low sweet sound of water,
And Alvar bending o'er me—from the night
Covering me with his mantle!—all the past
Flow'd back—my soul's far chords all answer'd to
    the blast.

### XXX.

Till, in that rush of visions, I became
As one that, by the bands of slumber wound,
Lies with a powerless, but all-thrilling frame,
Intense in consciousness of sight and sound,
Yet buried in a wildering dream which brings
Loved faces round him, girt with fearful things!
Troubled ev'n thus I stood, but chain'd and bound
On that familiar form mine eye to keep—
—Alas! I might not fall upon his neck and weep!

### XXXI.

He pass'd me—and what next?—I look'd on two,
Following his footsteps to the same dread place,
For the same guilt—his sisters! (5)—Well I knew
The beauty on those brows, though each young
    face
Was changed—so deeply changed!—a dungeon's
    air
Is hard for loved and lovely things to bear.
And ye, O daughters of a lofty race,
Queen-like Theresa! radiant Inez!—flowers
So cherish'd! were ye then but rear'd for those
    dark hours?

### XXXII.

A mournful home, young sisters! had ye left,
With your lutes hanging hush'd upon the wall,
And silence round the aged man, bereft
Of each glad voice, once answering to his call.
Alas, that lonely father! doom'd to pine
For sounds departed in his life's decline,
And, 'midst the shadowing banners of his hall,
With his white hair to sit, and deem the name
A hundred chiefs had borne, cast down by you to
    shame! (6)

### XXXIII.

And woe for you, 'midst looks and words of love,
And gentle hearts and faces, nursed so long!
How had I seen you in your beauty move,
Wearing the wreath, and listening to the song
—Yet sat, ev'n then, what seem'd the crowd to
    shun,
Half veiled upon the clear pale brow of one,
And deeper thoughts than oft to youth belong,
Thoughts, such as wake to evening's whispery
    sway,
Within the drooping shade of her sweet eyelids lay

### XXXIV.

And if she mingled with the festive train,
It was but as a melancholy star
Beholds the dance of shepherds on the plain,
In its bright stillness present, though afar.
Yet would she smile—and that, too, hath its
    smile—
Circled with joy which reach'd her not the while
And bearing a lone spirit, not at war
With earthly things, but o'er their form and hue
Shedding too clear a light, too sorrowfully true.

### XXXV.

But the dark hours wring forth the hidden might
Which hath lain bedded in the silent soul,
A treasure all undreamt of;—as the night
Calls out the harmonies of streams that roll
Unheard by day. It seem'd as if her breast
Had hoarded energies, till then suppress'd
Almost with pain, and bursting from control,

And finding first that hour their pathway free:
Could a rose brave the storm, such might her em-
    blem be.

#### XXXVI.

For the soft gloom whose shadow still had hung
On her fair brow, beneath its garlands worn,
Was fled; and fire, like prophecy's, had sprung,
Clear to her kindled eye.  It might be scorn—
Pride—sense of wrong—ay, the frail heart is
    bound
By these at times, ev'n as with adamant around,
Kept so from breaking!—yet not *thus* upborne
She moved, though some sustaining passion's
    wave
Lifted her fervent soul—a sister for the brave!

#### XXXVII.

And yet, alas! to see the strength which clings
Round woman in such hours!—a mournful sight,
Though lovely!—an o'erflowing of the springs,
The full springs of affection, deep as bright!
And she, because her life is ever twined
With other lives, and by no stormy wind
May thence be shaken, and because the light
Of tenderness is round her, and her eye
Doth weep such passionate tears—therefore she
    thus can die.

#### XXXVIII.

Therefore didst *thou*, through that heart-shaking
    scene,
As through a triumph move; and cast aside
Thine own sweet thoughtfulness for victory's
    mien,
O faithful sister! cheering thus the guide,
And friend, and brother of thy sainted youth,
Whose hand had led thee to the source of truth,
Where thy glad soul from earth was purified;
Nor wouldst thou, following him through all the
    past,
That he should see thy step grow tremulous at last

#### XXXIX.

For thou hast made no deeper love a guest
'Midst thy young spirit's dreams, than that
    which grows
Between the nurtured of the same fond breast,
The shelter'd of one roof; and thus it rose
Twined in with life.—How is it, that the hours
Of the same sport, the gathering early flowers
Round the same tree, the sharing one repose,
And mingling one first prayer in murmurs soft,
From the heart's memory fade, in this world's
    breath, so oft?

#### XL.

But thee that breath had touch'd not; thee, nor
    him,
The true in all things found!—and thou wert
    blest
Ev'n then, that no remember'd change could dim
The perfect image of affection, press'd
Like armour to thy bosom!—thou hadst kept
Watch by that brother's couch of pain, and
    wept,
Thy sweet face covering with thy robe, when rest
Fled from the sufferer; thou hadst bound his faith
Upon thy soul—one light, one hope ye chose—one
    death.

#### XLI.

So didst thou pass on brightly!—but for her,
Next in that path, how may *her* doom be spoken?
—All-merciful! to think that such things were,
And *are*, and seen by men with hearts unbroken!
To think of that fair girl, whose path had been
So strew'd with rose-leaves, all one fairy scene!
And whose quick glance came ever as a token
Of hope to drooping thought, and her glad voice
As a free bird's in spring, that makes the woods
    rejoice!

#### XLII.

And she to die!—she loved the laughing earth
With such deep joy in its fresh leaves and
    flowers!

—Was not her smile ev'n as the sudden birth
Of a young rainbow, colouring vernal showers?
Yes! but to meet her fawn-like step, to hear
The gushes of wild song, so silvery clear,
Which, oft unconsciously, in happier hours
Flow'd from her lips, was to forget the sway
Of Time and Death below,—blight, shadow, dull
    decay.

#### XLIII.

Could this change be?—the hour, the scene,
    where last
I saw that form, came floating o'er my mind:
—A golden vintage-eve;—the heats were pass'd,
And, in the freshness of the fanning wind,
Her father sat, where gleam'd the first faint star
Through the lime-boughs; and with her light
    guitar,
She, on the greensward at his feet reclined,
In his calm face laugh'd up; some shepherd-lay
Singing, as childhood sings on the lone hills at play.

#### XLIV.

And now—oh God!—the bitter fear of death,
The sore amaze, the faint o'ershadowing dread,
Had grasp'd her!—panting in her quick-drawn
    breath,
And in her white lips quivering;—onward led,
She look'd up with her dim bewilder'd eyes,
And there smiled out her own soft brilliant skies,
Far in their sultry southern azure spread,
Glowing with joy, but silent!—still they smiled,
Yet sent down no reprieve for earth's poor trem-
    bling child.

#### XLV.

Alas!—that earth had all too strong a hold,
Too fast, sweet Inez! on thy heart, whose bloom
Was given to early love, nor know how cold
The hours which follow.  There was one, with
    whom,
Young as thou wert, and gentle, and untried,
Thou might'st, perchance, unshrinkingly have
    died;
But he was far away;—and with thy doom
Thus gathering, life grew so intensely dear,
That all thy slight frame shook with its cold mor-
    tal fear!

#### XLVI.

No aid!—thou too didst pass!—and all had pass'd,
The fearful—and the desperate—and the strong!
Some like the bark that rushes with the blast,
Some like the leaf swept shiveringly along,
And some as men that have but one more field
To fight, and then may slumber on their shield,
Therefore they arm in hope. But now the throng
Roll'd on, and bore me with their living tide,
Ev'n as a bark wherein is left no power to guide.

#### XLVII.

Wave swept on wave.  We reach'd a stately
    square,
Deck'd for the rites.  An altar stood on high,
And gorgeous, in the midst, a place for prayer,
And praise, and offering.  Could the earth supply
No fruits, no flowers for sacrifice, of all
Which on her sunny lap unheeded fall?
No fair young firstling of the flock to die,
As when before their God the Patriarchs stood?
—Look down! man brings thee, Heaven! his bro-
    ther's guiltless blood!

#### XLVIII.

Hear its voice, hear!—a cry goes up to thee,
From the stain'd sod;—make thou thy judgment
    known
On him, the shedder!—let his portion be
The fear that walks at midnight—give the moan
In the wind haunting him a power to say,
"Where is thy brother?"—and the stars a ray
To search and shake his spirit, when alone,
With the dread splendour of their burning eyes
—So shall earth own thy will—mercy, not sacrifice.

#### XLIX.

Sounds of triumphant praise!—the mass was
    sung—
—Voices that die not might have pour'd such
    strains!

Through Salem's towers might that proud chant
   have rung,
When the Most High, on Syria's palmy plains,
Had quell'd her foes!—so full it swept, a sea
Of loud waves jubilant, and rolling free!
Oft, when the wind, as through resounding fanes,
Hath fill'd the choral forests with its power,
Some deep tone brings me back the music of that
   hour.

### L.

It died away;—the incense-cloud was driven
Before the breeze—the words of doom were said;
And the sun faded mournfully from heaven,
—He faded mournfully! and dimly red,
Parting in clouds from those that look'd their
   last,
And sigh'd—"Farewell, thou sun!"—Eve glow'd
   and pass'd—
Night—midnight and the moon—came forth and
   shed
Sleep, even as dew, on glen, wood, peopled spot—
Save one—a place of death—and there men slum
   ber'd not.

### LI.

'Twas not within the city (7)—but in sight
Of the snow-crown'd sierras, freely sweeping,
With many an eagle's eyrie on the height,
And hunter's cabin, by the torrent peeping
Far off: and vales between, and vineyards lay,
With sound and gleam of waters on their way,
And chestnut-woods, that girt the happy sleeping,
In many a peasant's home!—The midnight sky
Brought softly that rich world round those who
   came to die.

### LII.

The darkly-glorious midnight sky of Spain,
Burning with stars!—What had the torches'
   glare
To do beneath that temple, and profane
Its holy radiance?—By their wavering flare,
I saw beside the pyres—I see thee now,
O bright Theresa! with thy lifted brow,
And thy clasp'd hands, and dark eyes fill'd with
   prayer!
And thee, sad Inez! bowing thy fair head,
And mantling up thy face, all colourless with dread!

### LIII.

And Alvar, Alvar!—I beheld thee too,
Pale, steadfast, kingly, till thy clear glance fell
On that young sister; then perturb'd it grew,
And all thy labouring bosom seem'd to swell
With painful tenderness. Why came I there,
That troubled image of my friend to bear
Thence, for my after-years?—a thing to dwell
In my heart's core, and on the darkness rise,
Disquieting my dreams with its bright mournful
   eyes!

### LIV.

Why came I? oh! the heart's deep mystery!—
   Why
In man's last hour doth vain affection's gaze
Fix itself down on struggling agony,
To the dimm'd eye-balls freezing, as they glaze?
It might be—yet the power to will seem'd o'er—
That my soul yearn'd to hear his voice once more!
But mine was fetter'd—mute in strong amaze,
I watch'd his features as the night-wind blew,
And torch-light or the moon's pass'd o'er their
   marble hue.

### LV.

The trampling of a steed!—a tall white steed,
Rending his fiery way the crowds among—
A storm's way through a forest—came at speed,
And a wild voice cried "Inez!" Swift she flung
The mantle from her face, and gazed around,
With a faint shriek at that familiar sound,
And from his seat a breathless rider sprung,
And dash'd off fiercely those who came to part,
And rush'd to that pale girl, and clasp'd her to his
   heart.

### LVI.

And for a moment all around gave way
To that full burst of passion!—on his breast,
Like a bird panting yet from fear she lay,
But blest—in misery's very lap—yet blest!—
Oh love, love, strong as death!—from such an
   hour
Pressing out joy by thine immortal power,
Holy and fervent love! had earth but rest
For thee and thine, this world were all too fair!
How could we thence be wean'd to die without
   despair?

### LVII.

But she—as falls a willow from the storm,
O'er its own river streaming—thus reclined
On the youth's bosom hung her fragile form,
And clasping arms, so passionately twined
Around his neck—with such a trusting fold,
A full deep sense of safety in their hold,
As if naught earthly might th' embrace unbind!
Alas! a child's fond faith, believing still
Its mother's breast beyond the lightning's reach
   to kill!

### LVIII.

Brief rest! upon the turning billow's height,
A strange sweet moment of some heavenly
   strain,
Floating between the savage gusts of night,
That sweep the seas to foam! Soon dark again
The hour—the scene—th' intensely present,
   rush'd
Back on her spirit, and her large tears gush'd
Like blood-drops from a victim; with swift rain
Bathing the bosom where she lean'd that hour,
As if her life would melt into th' o'erswelling
   shower.

### LIX.

But he, whose arm sustain'd her!—oh! I knew
'Twas vain, and yet he hoped!—he fondly strove
Back from her faith her sinking soul to woo,
As life might yet be hers!—A dream of love
Which could not look upon so fair a thing,
Remembering how like hope, like joy, like spring,
Her smile was wont to glance, her step to move,
And deem that men indeed, in very truth,
Could mean the sting of death for her soft flower
   ing youth.

### LX.

He woo'd her back to life.—"Sweet Inez, live!
My blessed Inez!—visions have beguiled
Thy heart—abjure them!—thou wert form'd to
   give,
And to find, joy; and hath not sunshine smiled
Around thee ever? Leave me not, mine own!
Or earth will grow too dark!—for thee alone,
Thee have I loved, thou gentlest! from a child,
And borne thy image with me o'er the sea,
Thy soft voice in my soul!—Speak! Oh! yet live
   for me!"

### LXI.

She look'd up wildly; there were anxious eyes
Waiting that look—sad eyes of troubled thought,
Alvar's—Theresa's!—Did her childhood rise,
With all its pure and home affections fraught,
In the brief glance?—She clasp'd her hands—the
   strife
Of love, faith, fear, and that vain dream of life
Within her woman's breast so deeply wrought,
It seem'd as if a reed so slight and weak
Must in the rending storm not quiver only—break!

### LXII.

And thus it was—the young cheek flush'd and
   faded,
As the swift blood in currents came and went,
And hues of death the marble brow o'ershaded,
And the sunk eye a watery lustre sent

Through its white fluttering lids.  Then trem-
  blings pass'd
O'er the frail form, that shook it, as the blast
Shakes the sere leaf, until the spirit rent
Its way to peace—the fearful way unknown—
Pale in love's arms she lay—she!—what had loved
  was gone!

### LXIII.

Joy for thee, trembler!—thou redeem'd one, joy!
Young dove set free! earth, ashes, soulless clay,
Remain'd for baffled vengeance to destroy;
—Thy chain was riven!—nor hadst thou cast
  away
Thy hope in thy last hour!—though love was
  there
Striving to wring thy troubled soul from prayer,
And life seem'd robed in beautiful array,
Too fair to leave!—but this might be forgiven,
Thou wert so richly crown'd with precious gifts of
  Heaven.

### LXIV.

But woe for him who felt the heart grow still,
Which, with its weight of agony, had lain
Breaking on his!—Scarce could the mortal chill
Of the hush'd bosom, ne'er to heave again,
And all the silence curdling round the eye,
Bring home the stern belief that she could die,
That she indeed could die!—for wild and vain
As hope might be—his soul had hoped—'t was
  o'er—
Slowly his falling arms dropp'd from the form they
  bore:

### LXV.

They forced him from that spot.—It might be well,
That the fierce, reckless words by anguish wrung
From his torn breast, all aimless as they fell,
Like spray-drops from the strife of torrents
  flung,
Were mark'd as guilt.—There are, who no°
  these things
Against the smitten heart; its breaking strings
—On whose low thrills once gentle music hung—
With a rude hand of touch unholy trying,
And numbering them as crimes, the deep, strange
  tones replying.

### LXVI.

But ye in solemn joy, O faithful pair!
Stood gazing on your parted sister's dust;
I saw your features by the torch's glare,
And they were brightening with a heavenward
  trust!
I saw the doubt, the anguish, the dismay,
Melt from my Alvar's glorious mien away:
And peace was there—the calmness of the just.
And, bending down the slumberer's brow to kiss,
"Thy rest is won," he said;—"sweet sister! praise
  for this!"

### LXVII.

I started as from sleep;—yes, he had spoken—
A breeze had troubled memory's hidden source
At once the torpor of my soul was broken—
Thought, feeling, passion, woke in tenfold force
—There are soft breathings in the southern wind
That so your ice-chains, O ye streams! unbind
And free the foaming swiftness of your course
—I burst from those that held me back, and ran
Fen on his neck, and cried—"Friend, brother
  fare thee well!"

### LXVIII.

Did he not say "Farewell?"—Alas! no breath
Came to mine ear.  Hoarse murmurs from the
  throng
Told that the mysteries in the face of death
Had from their eager sight been veil'd too long,
And we were parted as the surge might part
Those that would die together, true of heart.
—His hour was come—but in mine anguish
  strong,
Like a fierce swimmer through the midnight sea,
Blindly I rush'd away from that which was to be

### LXIX.

Away—away I rush'd!—but swift and high
The arrowy pillars of the firelight grew,
Till the transparent darkness of the sky
Flush'd to a blood-red mantle in their hue;
And phantom-like, the kindling city seem'd
To spread, float, wave, as on the wind they
  stream'd,
With their wild splendour chasing me!—I knew
The death-work was begun—I veil'd mine eyes,
Yet stopp'd in spell-bound fear to catch the victims'
  cries.

### LXX.

What heard I then?—a ringing shriek of pain,
Such as for ever haunts the tortured ear?
I heard a sweet and solemn-breathing strain
Piercing the flames, untremulous and clear!
—The rich, triumphal tones!—I knew them well,
As they came floating with a breezy swell!
Man's voice was there—a clarion voice to cheer
In the mid-battle—ay, to turn the flying—
Woman's—that might have sung of Heaven beside
  the dying!

### LXXI

It was a fearful, yet a glorious thing,
To hear that hymn of martyrdom, and know
That its glad stream of melody could spring
Up from th' unsounded gulfs of human woe!
Alvar! Theresa!—what is deep? what strong?
God's breath within the soul!—It fill'd that song
From your victorious voices!—but the glow
On the hot air and lurid skies increased—
Faint grew the sounds—more faint—I listen'd—
  they had ceased!

### LXXII.

And thou indeed hadst perish'd, my soul's friend!
I might form other ties—but thou alone
Couldst with a glance the veil of dimness rend,
By other years o'er boyhood's memory thrown!
Others might aid me onward:—Thou and I
Had mingled the fresh thoughts that early die,
Once flowering—never more!—And thou wert
  gone!
Who could give back my youth, my spirit free,
Or be in aught again what thou hadst been to me?

### LXXIII.

And yet I wept thee not, thou true and brave!
I could not weep!—there gather'd round thy
  name
Too deep a passion!—thou denied a grave!
Thou, with the blight flung on thy soldier's fame!
Had I not known thy heart from childhood's
  time?
Thy heart of hearts?—and couldst thou die for
  crime?
—No! had all earth decreed that death of shame,
I would have set, against all earth's decree,
Th' unalienable trust of my firm soul in thee!

### LXXIV.

There are swift hours in life—strong, rushing
  hours,
That do the work of tempests in their might!
They shake down things that stood as rocks and
  towers,
Unto th' undoubting mind;—they pour in light
Where all is startles—like a burst of day
For which th' uprooting of an oak makes way;—
They sweep the colouring mists from off our sight,
They touch with fire thought's graven page, the
  roll
Stamp'd with past years—and lo! it shrivels as a
  scroll.

### LXXV.

And this was of such hours!—the sudden flow
Of my soul's tide seem'd whelming me: the glare
Of the red flames, yet rocking to and fro,
Scorch'd up my heart with breathless thirst for
  air

And solitude, and freedom.  It had been
Well with me then, in some vast desert scene,
To pour my voice out, for the winds to bear
On with them, wildly questioning the sky,
Fiercely th' untroubled stars, of man's dim destiny.

### LXXVI.

I would have call'd, adjuring the dark cloud ;
To the most ancient Heavens I would have said
—" Speak to me ! show me truth !" (8)—through
    night aloud
I would have cried to him, the newly dead,
" Come back ! and show me truth !"—My spirit
    seem'd
Gasping for some free burst, its darkness teem'd
With such pent storms of thought !—again I fled—
I fled, a refuge from man's face to gain,
Scarce conscious when I paused, entering a lonely
    fane.

### LXXVII.

A mighty minster, dim, and proud, and vast !
Silence was round the sleepers, whom its floor
Shut in the grave ; a shadow of the past,
A memory of the sainted steps that wore
Erewhile its gorgeous pavement, seem'd to brood
Like mist upon the stately solitude,
A halo of sad fame to mantle o'er
Its white sepulchral forms of mail-clad men,
And all was hush'd as night in some deep Alpine
    glen.

### LXXVIII.

More hush'd, far more !—for there the wind
    sweeps by,
Or the woods tremble to the streams' loud play !
Here a strange echo made my very sigh
Seem for the place too much a sound of day !
Too much my footsteps broke the moonlight,
    fading,
Yet arch thro' arch in one soft flow pervading ;
And I stood still :—prayer, chant, had died away.
Yet past me floated a funereal breath
Of 'ncense.—I stood still—as before God and death

### LXXIX.

For thick ye girt me round, ye long-departed ! (9)
Dust—imaged form—with cross, and shield, and
    crest ;
It seem'd as if your ashes would have started,
Had a wild voice burst forth above your rest !
Yet ne'er, perchance, did worshipper of yore
Bear to your thrilling presence what *I* bore
Of wrath — doubt — anguish—battling in the
    breast !
I could have pour'd out words, on that pale air,
To make your proud tombs ring :—no, no ! I could
    not *there* !

### LXXX.

Not 'midst those aisles, through which a thou-
    sand years
Mutely as clouds and reverently had swept ;
Not by those shrines, which yet the trace of tears
And kneeling votaries on their marble kept !
Ye were too mighty in your pomp of gloom
And trophied age, O temple, altar, tomb !
And you, ye dead !—for in that faith ye slept,
Whose weight had grown a mountain's on my
    heart,
Which could not *there* be loosed.—I turn'd me to
    depart.

### LXXXI.

I turn'd—what glimmer'd faintly on my sight,
Faintly, yet brightening, as a wreath of snow
Seen thro' dissolving haze !—The moon, the night,
Had waned, and dawn poured in ; gray, shadowy,
    slow,
Yet dayspring still !—a solemn hue it caught,
Piercing the storied windows, darkly fraught
With stoles and draperies of imperial glow ;
And soft and sad, that colouring gleam was
    thrown,
Where, pale, a pictured form above the altar shone.

### LXXXII.

Thy form, thou Son of God !—a wrathful deep,
With foam, and cloud, and tempest round thee
    spread,
And such a weight of night !—a night, when sleep
From the fierce rocking of the billows fled.
A bark show'd dim beyond thee, with its mast
Bow'd, and its rent sail shivering to the blast ;
But like a spirit in thy gliding tread,
Thou, as o'er glass, didst walk that stormy sea
Through rushing winds, which left a silent path for
    thee !

### LXXXIII.

So still thy white robes fell !—no breath of air
Within their long and slumberous folds had sway
So still the waves of parted, shadowy hair
From thy clear brow flow'd droopingly away !
Dark were the heavens above thee, Saviour !—
    dark
The gulfs, Deliverer ! round the straining bark
But thou !—o'er all thine aspect and array
Was pour'd one stream of pale, broad, silvery
    light—
Thou wert the single star of that all-shrouding
    night !

### LXXXIV.

Aid for one sinking !—Thy lone brightness
    gleam'd
On his wild face, just lifted o'er the wave,
With its worn, fearful, *human* look, that seem'd
To cry thro' surge and blast—" I perish—save !"
Not to the winds—not vainly !—thou wert nigh.
Thy hand was stretch'd to fainting agony,
Even in the portals of th' unquiet grave !
O thou that art the life ! and yet didst bear
Too much of mortal woe to turn from mortal prayer !

### LXXXV.

But was it not a thing to rise on death,
With its remember'd light, that face of thine,
Redeemer ! dimm'd by this world's misty breath,
Yet mournfully, mysteriously divine ?
—Oh ! that calm, sorrowful, prophetic eye,
With its dark depths of grief, love, majesty !
And the pale glory of the brow !—a shrine
Where power sat veil'd, yet shedding softly round
What told that *thou* couldst be but for a time un-
    crown'd !

### LXXXVI.

And more than all, the Heaven of that sad smile
The lip of mercy, our immortal trust !
Did not that look, that very look, erewhile,
Pour its o'ershadow'd beauty on the dust ?
Wert thou not such when earth's dark cloud
    hung o'er thee !
Surely thou wert !—my heart grew hush'd before
    thee,
Sinking with all its passions, as the gust
Sank at thy voice, along its billowy way :
—What had I there to do, but kneel, and weep,
    and pray ?

### LXXXVII.

Amidst the stillness rose my spirit's cry,
Amidst the dead—" But that full cup of woe,
Press'd from the fruitage of mortality,
Saviour !—for thee—give light ! that I may know
If by *thy* will, in thine all-healing name,
Men cast down human hearts to blighting shame.
And early death—and say, if this be so,
Where then is mercy ?—whither shall we flee,
So unallied to hope, save by our hold on thee ?

### LXXXVIII.

" But didst thou not, the deep sea brightly tread-
    ing,
Lift from despair that struggler with the wave ?
And wert thou not, sad tears, yet awful, shedding,
Beheld, a weeper at a mortal's grave ?
And is this weight of anguish, which they bind
On life, this searing to the quick of mind,
That but to God its own free path would crave
This crushing out of hope, and love, and youth,
Thy will indeed ?—Give light, that I may know the
    truth !

#### LXXXIX.

" For my sick soul is darken'd unto death,
With shadows, from the suffering it hath seen ;
The strong foundations of mine ancient faith
Sink from beneath me—whereon shall I lean ?
—Oh ! if from thy pure lips was wrung the sigh
Of the dust's anguish ! if like man to die,
—And earth round *him* shuts heavily—hath been
Even to *thee* bitter, aid me !—guide me !—turn
My wild and wandering thoughts back from their
    starless bourn !"

#### XC.

And calm'd I rose ;—but how the while had risen
Morn's orient sun, dissolving mist and shade !
—Could there indeed be wrong, or chain, or prison,
In the bright world such radiance might pervade ?
It fill'd the fane, it mantled the pale form
Which rose before me thro' the pictured storm,
Even the gray tombs it kindled and array'd
With life ?—how hard to see thy race begun,
And think man wakes to grief, wakening to *thee*,
    O sun !

#### XCI

I sought my home again :—and thou, my child,
There at thy play beneath yon ancient pine,
With eyes, whose lightning laughter (10) hath
    beguiled
A thousand pangs, thence flashing joy to mine ;
Thou in thy mother's arms, a babe, didst meet
My coming with young smiles, which yet, though
    sweet,
Seem'd on my soul all mournfully to shine,
And ask a happier heritage for thee,
Than but in turn the blight of human hope to see.

#### XCII.

Now sport, for thou art free—the bright birds
    chasing,
Whose wings waft star-like gleams from tree to
    tree ;
Or with the fawn, thy swift wood-playmate
    racing,
Sport on, my joyous child ! for thou art free !
Yes, on that day I took thee to my heart,
And inly vow'd, for thee, a better part
To choose ; that so thy sunny bursts of glee
Should wake no more dim thoughts of far-seen
    woe,
But, gladdening fearless eyes, flow on—as now
    they flow.

#### XCIII.

Thou hast a rich world round thee :—Mighty
    shades
Weaving their gorgeous tracery o'er thy head,
With the light melting through their high arcades
As through a pillar'd cloister's : (11) but the dead
Sleep not beneath ; nor doth the sunbeam pass
To marble shrines through rainbow-tinted glass ;
Yet thou, by fount and forest-murmur led
To wors'<sub>i</sub>p, thou art blest !—to thee is shown
Earth in her holy pomp, deck'd for her God alone


### THE

# FOREST SANCTUARY.

#### PART SECOND.

Wie diese treue liebe Seele
Von ihrem Glauben voll,
Der ganz allein
Ihr selig machend ist, sich heilig quale,
Dass sie den liebsten Mann verloren halten soll !
        *Faust*

I never smile more—but all my days
Walk with still footsteps and with humble eyes,
An everlasting hymn within my soul.
        *Wilson.*

#### I.

Bring me the sounding of the torrent-water
With yet a nearer swell—fresh breeze, awake ! (12)
And river dark'ning ne'er with hues of slaughter
Thy wave's pure silvery green,—and shining lake,
Spread far before my cabin, with thy zone
Of ancient woods, ye chainless things and lone !
Send voices through the forest aisles, and make
Glad music round me, that my soul may dare,
Cheer'd by such tones, to look back on a dun-
    geon's air !

#### II.

Oh, Indian hunter of the desert's race !
That with the spear at times, or bended bow,
Dost cross my footsteps in the fiery chase
Of the swift elk or blue hill's flying roe ;
Thou that beside the red night-fire thou heapest,
Beneath the cedars and the star-light sleepest,
Thou know'st not, wanderer—never may'st thou
    know !
Of the dark holds wherewith man cumbers earth,
To shut from human eyes the dancing season's
    mirth.

#### III.

There, fetter'd down from day, to think the
    while
How bright in Heaven the festal sun is glowing,
Making earth's loneliest places, with his smile,
Flush like the rose ; and how the streams are
    flowing
With sudden sparkles thro' the shadowy grass,
And water-flowers, all trembling as they pass ;
And how the rich dark summer-trees are bowing
With their full foliage ;—this to know, and pine,
Bound unto midnight's heart, seems a stern lot -
    't was mine.

#### IV.

Wherefore was this ?—Because my soul had
    drawn
Light from the book whose words are graved in
    light !
There at its well-head had I found the dawn,
And day, and noon of freedom :—but too bright
It shines on that which man to man hath given,
And call'd the truth—the very truth, from
    Heaven !
And therefore seeks he, in his brother's sight,
To cast the mote ; and therefore strives to bind
With his strong chains to earth, what is not
    earth's—the mind

#### V.

It is a weary and a bitter task
Back from the lip the burning word to keep,
And to shut out Heaven's air with falsehood's
    mask,
And in the dark urn of the soul to heap

Indignant feelings—making even of thought
A buried treasure, which may but be sought
When shadows are abroad—and night—and
   sleep.
I might not brook it long—and thus was thrown
Into that grave-like cell, to wither there alone.

### VI.

And I, a child of danger, whose delights
Were on dark hills and many-sounding seas—
I, that amidst the Cordillera heights
Had given Castilian banners to the breeze,
And the full circle of the rainbow seen
There, on the snows; (13) and in my country
   been
A mountain wanderer, from the Pyrenees
To the Morena crags—how left I not
Life, or the soul's life, quench'd, on that sepulchral
   spot ?

### VII.

Because *Thou* didst not leave me, oh my God !
Thou wert with those that bore the truth of old
Into the deserts from the oppressor's rod,
And made the caverns of the rock their fold,
And in the hidden chambers of the dead,
Our guiding lamp with fire immortal fed,
And met when stars met, by their beams to hold
The free heart's communing with Thee,—and
   Thou
Wert in the midst, felt, own'd—the strengthener
   then as now !

### VIII.

Yet once I sank. Alas ! man's wavering mind !
Wherefore and whence the gusts that o'er it
   blow ?
How they bear with them, floating uncombined,
The shadows of the past, that come and go,
As o'er the deep the old long-buried things,
Which a storm's working to the surface brings
Is the reed shaken, and must *we* be so,
With every wind ?—So, Father ! must we be,
Till we can fix undimm'd our steadfast eyes on
   Thee.

### IX.

Once my soul died within me. What had thrown
That sickness o'er it ?—Even a passing thought
Of a clear spring, whose side, with flowers o'er-
   grown,
Fondly and oft my boyish steps had sought !
Perchance the damp roof's water-drops that fell
Just then, low tinkling through my vaulted cell,
Intensely heard amidst the stillness, caught
Some tone from memory, of the music, swelling
Ever with that fresh rill, from its deep rocky
   dwelling.

### X.

But so my spirit's fever'd longings wrought,
Wakening, it might be, to the faint sad sound
That from the darkness of the walls they brought
A loved scene round me, visibly around. (14)
Yes ! kindling, spreading, brightening, hue by
   hue,
Like stars from midnight, through the gloom it
   grew,
That haunt of youth, hope, manhood !—till the
   bound
Of my shut cavern seem'd dissolved, and I
Girt by the solemn hills and burning pomp of sky.

### XI.

I look'd—and lo ! the clear broad river flowing,
Past the old Moorish ruin on the steep,
The lone tower dark against a heaven all glow-
   ing,
Like seas of glass and fire !—I saw the sweep
Of glorious woods far down the mountain side,
And their still shadows in the gleaming tide,
And the red evening on its waves asleep;
And 'midst the scene—oh ! more than all—there
   smiled
My child's fair face and her's, the mother of my
   child.

### XII.

With their soft eyes of love and gladness raised
Up to the flushing sky, as when we stood
Last by that river, and in silence gazed
On the rich world of sunset :—but a flood
Of sudden tenderness my soul oppress'd,
And I rush'd forward with a yearning breast,
To clasp—alas ! a vision ! Wave and wood,
And gentle faces lifted in the light
Of day's last hectic blush, all melted from my sight.

### XIII.

Then darkness ! oh ! th' unutterable gloom
That seem'd as narrowing round me, making less
And less my dungeon, when, with all its bloom,
That bright dream vanish'd from my loneliness !
It floated off, the beautiful !—yet left
Such deep thirst in my soul, that thus bereft,
I lay down, sick with passion's vain excess,
And pray'd to die.—How oft would sorrow weep
Her weariness to death, if he might come like sleep !

### XIV.

But I was roused—and how ?—It is no tale
Even 'midst *thy* shades, thou wilderness, to tell !
I would not have my boy's young cheek made
   pale
Nor haunt his sunny rest with what befell
In that drear prison-house.—His eye must grow
More dark with thought, more earnest his fair
   brow,
More high his heart in youthful strength must
   swell ;
So shall it fitly burn when all is told :—
Let childhood's radiant mist the free child yet en-
   fold !

### XV.

It is enough that through such heavy hours,
As wring us by our fellowship of clay,
I lived, and undegraded. We have powers
To snatch th' oppressor's bitter joy away !
Shall the wild Indian, for his savage fame,
Laugh and expire, and shall not Truth's high
   name
Bear up her martyrs with all-conquering sway ?
It is enough that Torture may be vain—
I had seen Alvar die—the strife was won from
   pain.

### XVI.

And faint not, heart of man ! though years wane
   slow !
There have been those that from the deepest
   caves,
And cells of night, and fastnesses below
The stormy dashing of the ocean-waves,
Down, farther down than gold lies hid, have
   nursed
A quenchless hope, and watch'd their time, and
   burst
On the bright day, like wakeners from the graves !
I was of such at last !—unchain'd I trod
This green earth, taking back my freedom from
   my God !

### XVII.

That was an hour to send its fadeless trace
Down life's far sweeping tide !—A dim, wild
   night,
Like sorrow hung upon the soft moon's face,
Yet how my heart leap'd in her blessed light !
The shepherd's light—the sailor's on the sea—
The hunter's homeward from the mountain free,
Where its lone smile makes tremulously bright
The thousand streams ! I could but gaze through
   tears—
Oh ! what a sight is heaven, thus first beheld for
   years !

### XVIII.

The rolling clouds !—they have the whole blue
   space
Above to sail in—all the dome of sky !

My soul shot with them in their breezy race
O'er star and gloom !—but   had yet to fly,
As flies the hunted wolf.  A secret spot,
And strange, I knew—the sunbeam knew it not;
Wildest of all the savage glens that lie
In far sierras, hiding their deep springs,
And traversed but by storms, or sounding eagles'
    wings.

### XIX.

Ay, and I met the storm there !—I had gain'd
The covert's heart with swift and stealthy tread ;
A moan went past me, and the dark trees rain'd
Their autumn foliage rustling on my head ;
A moan—a hollow gust—and there I stood
Girt with majestic night, and ancient wood,
And foaming water.—Thither might have fled
The mountain Christian with his faith of yore,
When Afric's tambour shook the ringing western
    shore !

### XX.

But through the black ravine the storm cam
    swelling—
Mighty thou art amidst the hills, thou blast !
In thy lone course the kingly cedars felling,
Like plumes upon the path of battle cast !
A rent oak thunder'd down beside my cave—
Booming it rush'd, as booms a deep sea-wave ;
A falcon soar'd ; a startled wild-deer pass'd ;
A far-off bell toll'd faintly through the roar—
How my glad spirit swept forth with the winds
    once more !

### XXI.

And with the arrowy lightnings !—for they flash'd
Smiting the branches in their fitful play,
And brightly shivering where the torrents dash'd
Up, even to crag and eagle's nest their spray !
And there to stand amidst the pealing strife,
The strong pines groaning with tempestuous life,
And all the mountain voices on their way,—
Was it not joy ?—'t was joy in rushing might,
After those years that wove but one long dead of
    night !

### XXII.

There came a softer hour, a lovelier moon,
And lit me to my home of youth again,
Through the dim chestnut shade, where oft at
    noon,
By the fount's flashing burst, my head had lain,
In gentle sleep: but now I pass'd as one
That may not pause where wood-streams whis-
    pering run,
Or light sprays tremble to a bird's wild strain,
Because th' avenger's voice is in the wind,
The foe's quick rustling step close on the leaves
    behind.

### XXIII.

My home of youth !—oh ! if indeed to part
With the soul's loved ones be a mournful thing,
When we go forth in buoyancy of heart,
And bearing all the glories of our spring
For life to breathe on,—is it less to meet,
When these are faded ?—Who shall call it sweet ?
Even though love's mingling tears may haply
    bring
Balm as they fall, too well their heavy showers
Teach us how much is lost of all that once was
    ours !

### XXIV.

Not by the sunshine, with its golden glow,
Nor the green earth, nor yet the laughing sky,
Nor the faint flower-scents, (15) as they come
    and go
In the soft air, like music wandering by ;
—Oh ! not by these, th' unfailing, are we taught
How time  and  sorrow on  our frames  have
    wrought ;
But by the sadden'd eye, the darken'd brow,
Of kindred aspects, and the long dim gaze,
Which tells us we are changed,—how changed from
    other days !

### XXV.

Before my father—in my place of birth,
I stood an alien.  On the very floor
Which oft had trembled to my boyish mirth,
The love that rear'd me, knew my face no more !
There hung the antique armour, helm and crest,
Whose every stain woke childhood in my breast,
There droop'd the banner, with the marks it bore
Of Paynim spears ; and I, the worn in frame
And heart, what there was I ?—another and the
    same !

### XXVI.

Then bounded in a boy, with clear dark eye—
—How should he know his father ?—when we
    parted,
From the soft cloud which mantles infancy,
His soul, just wakening into wonder, darted
Its first looks round.  Him follow'd one, the bride
Of my young days, the wife how loved and tried !
Her glance met mine—I could not speak—she
    started
With a bewilder'd gaze ;—until there came
Tears to my burning eyes, and from my lips her
    name.

### XXVII.

She knew me then !—I murmur'd "*Leonor !*"
And her heart answer'd !—oh ! the voice is known
First from all else, and swiftest to restore
Love's buried images with one low tone,
That strikes like lightning, when the cheek is
    faded,
And the brow heavily with thought o'ershaded,
And all the brightness from the aspect gone !
—Upon my breast she sunk, when doubt was fled,
Weeping as those may weep, that meet in woe
    and dread.

### XXVIII.

For there we might not rest.  Alas ! to leave
Those native towers and know that they must
    fall
By slow decay, and none remain to grieve
When the weeds cluster'd on the lonely wall !
We were the last—my boy and I—the last
Of a long line which brightly thence had pass'd !
My father bless'd me as I left his hall—
With his deep tones and sweet, tho' full of years,
He bless'd me there, and bathed my child's young
    head with tears.

### XXIX.

I had brought sorrow on his gray hairs down,
And cast the darkness of my branded name
(For so he deem'd it) on the clear renown,
My own ancestral heritage of fame.
And yet he bless'd me !—Father ! if the dust
Lie on those lips benign, my spirit's trust
Is to behold thee yet, where grief and shame
Dim the bright day no more ; and thou wilt know
That not through guilt thy son thus bow'd thine
    age with woe !

### XXX.

And thou, my Leonor ! that unrepining,
If sad in soul, didst quit all else for me,
When stars—the stars that earliest rise—are
    shining,
How their soft glance unseals each thought of
    thee !
For on our flight they smiled ; their dewy rays,
Through the last olives, lit thy tearful gaze
Back to the home we never more might see ;
So pass'd we on, like earth's first exiles, turning
Fond looks where hung the sword above their Eden
    burning.

### XXXI.

It was a woe to say—" Farewell, my Spain !
The sunny and the vintage land, farewell !"
—I could have died upon the battle-plain
For thee, my country ! but I might not dwell
In thy sweet vales, at peace.—The voice of song
Breathes with the myrtle scent, thy hills along ;
The citron's glow is caught from shade and dell ;

But what are these ?—upon thy flowery sod
I might not kneel, and pour my free thoughts out
   to God !

### XXXII.

O'er the blue deep I fled, the chainless deep !
Strange heart of man ! that ev'n 'midst woe
   swells high,
When through the foam he sees his proud bark
   sweep,
Flinging out joyous gleams to wave and sky !
Yes ! it swells high, whate'er he leaves behind ;
His spirit rises with the rising wind ;
For, wedded to the far futurity,
On, on, it bears him ever, and the main
Seems rushing like his hope, some happier shore
   to gain.

### XXXIII.

Not thus is woman. Closely *her* still heart
Doth twine itself with ev'n each lifeless thing,
Which, long remember'd, seem'd to bear its part
In her calm joys. For ever would she cling,
A brooding dove, to that sole spot of earth
Where she hath loved, and given her children
   birth,
And heard their first sweet voices. There may
   Spring
Array no path, renew no flower, no leaf,
But hath its breath of home, its claim to farewell
   grief.

### XXXIV.

I look'd on Leonor, and if there seem'd
A cloud of more than pensiveness to rise,
In the faint smiles that o'er her features gleam'd,
And the soft darkness of her serious eyes,
Misty with tender gloom, I call'd it naught
But the fond exile's pang, a lingering thought
Of her own vale, with all its melodies
And living light of streams. Her soul would rest
Beneath your shades, I said, bowers of the gor-
   geous west !

### XXXV.

Oh could we live in visions ! could we hold
Delusion faster, longer to our breast,
When it shuts from us, with its mantle's fold,
That which we see not, and are therefore blest !
But they our loved and loving, they to whom
We have spread out our souls in joy and gloom,
*Their* looks and accents, unto ours address'd,
Have been a language of familiar tone
Too long to breathe at last dark sayings and un-
   known.

### XXXVI.

I told my heart 'twas but the exile's woe
Which press'd on that sweet bosom ;—I deceived
My heart but half:—a whisper faint and low,
Haunting it ever, and at times believed,
Spoke of some deeper cause. How oft we seem
Like those that dream, and *know* the while they
   dream,
'Midst the soft falls of airy voices, grieved
And troubled, while bright phantoms round them
   play,
By a dim sense that all will float and fade away !

### XXXVII.

Yet, as if chasing joy, I woo'd the breeze,
To speed me onward with the wings of morn.
—Oh ! far amidst the solitary seas,
Which were not made for man, what man hath
   borne,
Answering their moan with his !—what *thou*
   didst bear,
My lost and loveliest ! while that secret care
Grew terror, and thy gentle spirit, worn
By its dull brooding weight, gave way at last,
   holding me as one from hope for ever cast !

### XXXVIII.

For unto thee, as through all change, reveal'd
Mine inward being lay. In other eyes
I had to bow me yet, and make a shield,
To fence my burning bosom, of disguise ;

But the still hope sustain'd, ere long to win
Some sanctuary, whose green retreats within,
My thoughts unfetter'd to their source might rise,
Like songs and scents of morn.—But thou didst
   look
Through all my soul, and thine even unto fainting
   shook.

### XXXIX.

Fall'n, fall'n, I seem'd—yet, oh ! not less be
   loved,
Tho' from thy love was pluck'd the early pride,
And harshly, by a gloomy faith, reproved
And sear'd with shame !—though each young
   flower had died,
There was the root,—strong, living, not the less
That all it yielded now was bitterness ;
Yet still such love as quits not misery's side,
Nor drops from guilt its ivy-like embrace,
Nor turns away from death its pale heroic face.

### XL.

Yes ! thou hadst follow'd me through fear and
   flight ;
Thou wouldst have follow'd, had my pathway led
Even to the scaffold ; had the flashing light
Of the raised axe made strong men shrink with
   dread,
Thou, 'midst the hush of thousands, wouldst
   have been
With thy clasp'd hands beside me kneeling seen,
And meekly bowing to the shame thy head—
—The shame !—oh ! making beautiful to view
The might of human love—fair thing ! so bravely
   true !

### XLI.

There was thine agony—to love so well
Where fear made love life's chastener.—Hereto-
   fore
Whate'er of earth's disquiet round thee fell,
Thy soul, o'erpassing its dim bounds, could soar
Away to sunshine, and thy clear eye speak
Most of the skies when grief most touch'd thy
   cheek.
Now, that far brightness faded ! never more
Couldst thou lift heavenwards for its hope thy
   heart,
Since at Heaven's gate it seem'd that thou and I
   must part.

### XLII.

Alas ! and life hath moments when a glance
(If thought to sudden watchfulness be stirr'd,)
A flush—a fading of the cheek perchance,
A word—less, less—the *cadence* of a word,
Lets in our gaze the mind's dim veil beneath,
Thence to bring haply knowledge fraught with
   death !
—Even thus, what never from thy lip was heard
Broke on my soul.—I knew that in thy sight
I stood—howe'er beloved—a recreant from the
   light !

### XLIII.

Thy sad sweet hymn, at eve, the seas along,—
—Oh ! the deep soul it breathed !—the love, the
   woe,
The fervour, pour'd in that full gush of song,
As it went floating through the fiery glow
Of the rich sunset !—bringing thoughts of Spain,
With all her vesper-voices o'er the main,
Which seem'd responsive in its murmuring flow,
—" *Ave sanctissima !*"—how oft that lay
Hath melted from my heart the martyr-strength
   away !

Ave sanctissima !
'T is night-fall on the sea ;
  Ora pro nobis !
Our souls rise to thee !

Watch us while shadows lie
  O'er the dim water spread ;
Hear the heart's lonely sigh,
  —*Thine*, too, hath bled !

Thou that hast look'd on death,
  Aid us when death is near!
Whisper of Heaven to faith;
  Sweet mother, hear!

Ora pro nobis!
The wave must rock our sleep,
  Ora, mater, ora!
Thou star of the deep!

### XLIV.

'Ora pro nobis, mater!'—What a spell
Was in those notes with day's last glory dying
On the flush'd waters!—seem'd they not to swell
From the far dust, wherein my sires were lying
With crucifix and sword?—Oh! yet how clear
Comes their reproachful sweetness to mine ear!
"Ora!"—with all the purple waves replying,
All my youth's visions rising in the strain—
—And I had thought it much to bear the rack and
    chain!

### XLV.

Torture!—the sorrow of affection's eye,
Fixing its meekness on the spirit's core,
Deeper, and teaching more of agony,
May pierce than many swords!—and this I bore
With a mute pang. Since I had vainly striven
From its free springs to pour the truth of Heaven
Into thy trembling soul, my Leonor!
Silence rose up where hearts no more could share:
—Alas! for those that love, and may not blend in
    prayer!

### XLVI.

We could not pray together 'midst the deep,
Which, like a floor of sapphire, round us lay,
Through days of splendour, nights too bright for
    sleep,
Soft, solemn, holy!—We were on our way
Unto the mighty Cordillera-land,
With men whom tales of that world's golden
    strand
Had lured to leave their vines.—Oh! who shall say
What thoughts rose in us, when the tropic sky
Touch'd all its molten seas with sunset's alchemy?

### XLVII.

Thoughts no more mingled!—Then came night
    —th' intense
Dark blue—the burning stars!—I saw thee shine
Once more, in thy serene magnificence,
O Southern Cross! (16) as when thy radiant sign
First drew my gaze of youth.—No, not as then;
I had been stricken by the darts of men
Since those fresh days, and now thy light divine
Look'd on mine anguish, while within me strove
The still small voice against the might of suffering
    love.

### XLVIII.

But thou, the clear, the glorious! thou wert
    pouring
Brilliance and joy upon the crystal wave,
While she, that met thy ray with eyes adoring,
Stood in the lengthening shadow of the grave!
—Alas! I watch'd her dark religious glance,
As it still sought thee thro' the Heaven's expanse,
Bright Cross!—and knew not that I watch'd what
    gave
But passing lustre—shrouded soon to be—
A soft light found no more—no more on earth or sea!

### XLIX.

I knew not all—yet something of unrest
Sat on my heart. Wake, ocean-wind! I said;
Waft us to land, in leafy freshness drest,
Where thro' rich clouds of foliage o'er her head,
Sweet day may steal, and rills unseen go by,
Like singing voices, and the green earth lie,
Starry with flowers, beneath her graceful tread!
—But the calm bound us 'midst the glassy main;
Ne'er was her step to bend earth's living flower
    again.

### L.

Yes! as if heaven upon the waves were sleeping,
Vexing my soul with quiet, there they lay
All moveless through their blue transparence
    keeping,
The shadows of our sails from day to day;
While she—oh! strongest in the strong heart's
    woe—
And yet I live! I feel the sunshine's glow—
And I am he that look'd, and saw decay
Steal o'er the fair of earth, the adored too much!
—It is a fearful thing to love what death may touch.

### LI.

A fearful thing that love and death may dwell
In the same world!—She faded on—and I—
Blind to the last, there needed death to tell
My trusting soul that she could fade to die!
Yet, ere she parted, I had mark'd a change,
But it breathed hope—'twas beautiful, though
    strange:
Something of gladness in the melody
Of her low voice, and in her words a flight
Of airy thought—alas! too perilously bright!

### LII.

And a clear sparkle in her glance, yet wild,
And quick, and eager, like the flashing gaze
Of some all-wondering and awakening child,
That first the glories of the earth surveys.
—How could it thus deceive me?—she had worn
Around her, like the dewy mists of morn,
A pensive tenderness through happiest days,
And a soft world of dreams had seem'd to lie
Still in her dark, and deep, and spiritual eye.

### LIII

And I could hope in that strange fire!—she died,
She died with all its lustre on her mien!
—The day was melting from the waters wide,
And through its long bright hours her thoughts
    had been,
It seem'd, with restless and unwonted yearning,
To Spain's blue skies and dark sierras turning:
For her fond words were all of vintage-scene,
And flowering myrtle, and sweet citron's breath—
Oh! with what vivid hues life comes back oft on
    death!

### LIV.

And from her lips the mountain-songs of old,
In wild faint snatches, fitfully had sprung;
Songs of the orange bower, the Moorish hold,
The "Rio verde," (17) on her soul that hung,
And thence flow'd forth.—But now the sun was
    low,
And watching by my side its last red glow,
That ever stills the heart, once more she sung
Her own soft "Ora, mater!"—and the sound
Was ev'n like love's farewell—so mournfully pro-
    found

### LV.

The boy had dropp'd to slumber at our feet;—
"And I have lull'd him to his smiling rest
Once more!" she said:—I raised him—it was
    sweet,
Yet sad, to see the perfect calm which bless'd
His look that hour;—for now her voice grew
    weak:
And on the flowery crimson of his cheek,
With her white lips a long, long kiss she press'd,
Yet light, to wake him not.—Then sank her head
Against my bursting heart.—What did I clasp?—
    the dead!

### LVI.

I call'd—to call what answers not our cries—
By that we loved to stand unseen, unheard,
With the loud passion of our tears and sighs
To see but some cold glistering ringlet stirr'd,
And in the quench'd eye's fixedness to gaze,
All vainly searching for the parted rays;
This is what waits us!—Dead!—with that chill
    word
To link our bosom-names!—For this we pour
Our souls upon the dust—nor tremble to adore!

### LVII.

But the true parting came!—I look'd my last
On the sad beauty of that slumb'ring face;
How could I think the lovely spirit pass'd,
Which there had left so tenderly its trace?
Yet a dim awfulness' was on the brow—
No! not like sleep to look upon art Thou,
Death, death!—she lay, a thing for earth's em
    brace,
To cover with spring-wreaths.—For earth's?—
    the wave
That gives the bier no flowers—makes moan above
    her grave!

### LVIII.

On the mid-seas a knell!—for man was there,
Anguish and love—the mourner with his dead!
A long low-rolling knell—a voice of prayer—
Dark glassy waters, like a desert spread,—
And the pale shining Southern Cross on high,
Its faint stars fading from a solemn sky,
Where mighty clouds before the dawn grew red;—
Were these things round me? such o'er memory
    sweep
Wildly, when aught brings back that burial of the
    deep.

### LIX.

Then the broad lonely sunrise!—and the plash
Into the sounding waves! (18)—around her head
They parted, with a glancing moment's flash,
Then shut—and all was still. And now thy bed
Is of their secrets, gentlest Leonor!
Once fairest of young brides!—and never more,
Loved as thou wert, may human tear be shed
Above thy rest!—No mark the proud seas keep,
To show where he that wept may pause again to
    weep.

### LX.

So the depths took thee!—Oh! the sullen sense
Of desolation in that hour compress'd!
Dust going down, a speck, amidst th' immense
And gloomy waters, leaving on their breast
The trace a weed might leave there!—Dust!—
    the thing
Which to the heart was as a living spring
Of joy, with fearfulness of love possess'd,
Thus sinking!—Love, joy, fear, all crush'd to
    this—
And the wide Heaven so far—so fathomless th'
    abyss!

### LXI.

Where the line sounds not, where the wrecks
    lie low,
What shall wake thence the dead?—Blest, blest
    are they
That earth to earth intrust; for they may know
And tend the dwelling whence the slumberer's
    clay
Shall rise at last, and bid the young flowers
    bloom,
That waft a breath of hope around the tomb,
And kneel upon the dewy turf to pray!
But thou, what cave hath dimly chamber'd *thee?*
Vain dreams!—oh! art thou not where there is no
    more sea? (19)

### LXII.

The wind rose free and singing:—when for ever,
O'er that sole spot of all the watery plain,
I could have bent my sight with fond endeavour
Down, where its treasure was, its glance to strain;
Then rose the reckless wind!—Before our prow
The white foam flash'd—ay, joyously—and thou
Wert left with all the solitary main
Around thee—and thy beauty in my heart,
And thy meek sorrowing love! oh, where could
    *that* depart?

### LXIII.

I will not speak of woe; I may not tell—
Friend tells not such to friend—the thoughts
    which rent
My fainting spirit, when its wild farewell
Across the billows to thy grave was sent,

19

Thou, there most lonely!—He that sits above,
In his calm glory, will forgive the love
His creatures bear each other, ev'n if blent
With a vain worship; for its close is dim
Ever with grief, which lends the wrung soul back
    to Him!

### LXIV

And with a milder pang if now I bear
To think of thee in thy forsaken rest,
If from my heart be lifted the despair,
The sharp remorse with healing influence press'd
If the soft eyes that visit me in sleep
Look not reproach, tho' still they seem to weep
It is that He my sacrifice hath bless'd,
And fill'd my bosom, through its inmost cell,
With a deep chastening sense that all at last is
    well.

### LXV.

Yes! thou art now—Oh! wherefore does the
    thought
Of the wave dashing o'er thy long bright hair,
The sea-weed into its dark tresses wrought,
The sand thy pillow—thou that wert so fair;
Come o'er me still?—Earth, earth!—it is the hold
Earth ever keeps on that of earthy mould!
But *thou* art breathing now in purer air,
I well believe, and freed from all of error,
Which blighted here the root of thy sweet life with
    terror.

### LXVI.

And if the love which here was passing light,
Went with what died not—Oh! that *this* we
    knew,
But this!—that through the silence of the night
Some voice of all the lost ones and the true,
Would speak, and say, if in their far repose,
We are yet aught of what we were to those
We call the dead!—their passionate adieu,
Was it but breath, to perish!—Holier trust
Be mine!—thy love *is* there, but purified from dust

### LXVII.

A thing all heavenly!—clear'd from that which
    hung
As a dim cloud between us, heart and mind!
Loosed from the fear, the grief, whose tendrils
    flung
A chain so darkly, with its growth entwined.
This is my hope!—though when the sunset fades
When forests rock the midnight on their shades
When tones of wail are in the rising wind,
Across my spirit some faint doubt may sigh;
For the strong hours *will* sway this frail mortality

### LXVIII.

We have been wanderers since those days of woe
Thy boy and I!—As wild birds tend their young
So have I tended him—my bounding roe!
The high Peruvian solitudes among;
And o'er the Andes torrents borne his form,
Where our frail bridge hath quiver'd 'midst the
    storm.—(20)
—But there the war-notes of my country rung,
And, smitten deep of Heaven and man, I fled
To hide in shades unpierced a mark'd and weary
    head.

### LXIX.

But he went on in gladness—that fair child!
Save when at times his bright eye seem'd to
    dream,
And his young lips, which then no longer smiled,
Ask'd of his mother!—that was but a gleam
Of Memory, fleeting fast; and then his play
Thro' the wide Llanos (21) cheer'd again our way
And by the mighty Orinoco stream,
On whose lone margin we have heard at morn,
From the mysterious rocks, the sunrise-music
    borne. (22)

### LXX.

So like a spirit's voice! a harping tone,
Lovely, yet ominous to mortal ear,
Such as might reach us from a world unknown,
Troubling man's heart with thrills of joy and
    fear!

'Twas sweet!—yet those deep southern shades
   oppress'd
My soul with stillness, like the calms that rest
On melancholy waves: (23) I sigh'd to hear
Once more earth's breezy sounds, her foliage
   fann'd,
And turn'd to seek the wilds of the red hunter's land.

#### LXXI.

And we have won a bower of refuge now,
In this fresh waste, the breath of whose repose
Hath cool'd, like dew, the fever of my brow,
And whose green oaks and cedars round me close,
As temple-walls, and pillars, that exclude
Earth's haunted dreams from their free solitude;
All, save the image and the thought of those
Before us gone; our loved of early years,
Gone where affection's cup hath lost the taste of
   tears.

#### LXXII.

I see a star—eve's first born!—in whose train
Past scenes, words, looks, come back. The ar
   rowy spire
Of the lone cypress, as of wood-girt fane,
Rest dark and still amidst a heaven of fire;
The pine gives forth its odours, and the lake
Gleams like one ruby, and the soft winds wake,
'Till every string of nature's solemn lyre
Is touch'd to answer; its most secret tone
Drawn from each tree, for each hath whispers all
   its own.

#### LXXIII.

And hark! another murmur on the air,
Not of the hidden rills, nor quivering shades!
—That is the cataract's, which the breezes bear,
Filling the leafy twilight of the glades
With hollow surge-like sounds, as from the bed
Of the blue mournful seas, that keep the dead!
But they are far!—the low sun here pervades
Dim forest-arches, bathing with red gold
Their stems, till each is made a marvel to behold.

#### LXXIV.

Gorgeous, yet full of gloom!—In such an hour,
The vesper-melody of dying bells
Wanders through Spain, from each gray con-
   vent's tower
O'er shining rivers pour'd, and olive-dells,
By every peasant heard, and muleteer,
And hamlet, round my home:—and I am here,
Living again through all my life's farewells,
In these vast woods, where farewell ne'er was
   spoken,
And sole I lift to Heaven a sad heart—yet un-
   broken!

#### LXXV.

In such an hour are told the hermit's beads;
With the white sail the seaman's hymn floats by;
Peace be with all! whate'er their varying creeds,
With all that send up holy thoughts on high!
Come to me, boy!—by Guadalquivir's vines,
By every stream of Spain, as day declines,
Man's prayers are mingled in the rosy sky.
—We, too, will pray; nor yet unheard, my child!
Of Him whose voice we hear at eve amidst the wild.

#### LXXVI.

At eve?—oh! through all hours!—from dark
   dreams oft
Awakening, I look forth, and learn the might
Of solitude, while thou art breathing soft,
And low, my loved one! on the breast of night:
I look forth on the stars—the shadowy sleep
Of forests—and the lake, whose gloomy deep
Sends up red sparkles to the fire-flies' light.
A lonely world!—ev'n fearful to man's thought,
But for His presence felt, whom here my soul hath
   sought.

## NOTES.

### NOTE 1.

*And sighing through the feathery canes, &c.*

The canes in some parts of the American forests form a thick
undergrowth for many hundred miles.—See *Hodgson's letters from
North America,* vol. i. p 242.

### NOTE 2.

*And for their birth-place moan, as moans the ocean-shell.*

Such a shell as Wordsworth has beautifully described

    " I have seen
A curious child, who dwelt upon a tract
Of inland ground, applying to his ear
The convolutions of a smooth-lipp'd shell;
To which, in silence hush'd, his very soul
Listen'd intently, and his countenance soon
Brighten'd with joy; for murmuring from within
Were heard—sonorous cadences! whereby,
To his belief, the monitor express'd
Mysterious union with its native sea.
—Even such a shell the universe itself
Is to the ear of Faith."—*The Excursion.*

### NOTE 3.

*I see an oak before me, &c.*

" I recollect hearing a traveller, of poetical temperament, expressing the kind of horror he felt on beholding on the banks of the
Missouri, an oak of prodigious size, which had been in a manner
overpowered by an enormous wild grape vine. The vine had
clasped its huge folds round the trunk, and from thence had wound
about every branch and twig, until the mighty tree had withered in
its embrace. It seemed like Laocoon struggling ineffectually in the
coils of the monster Python."—*Bracebridge Hall. Chapter on Forest Trees.*

### NOTE 4.

*Thou hast perish'd*
*More nobly far, my Alvar!—making known*
*The might of truth.*

For a more interesting account of the Spanish Protestants, and the
heroic devotion with which they met the spirit of persecution in
the sixteenth century, see the *Quarterly Review,* No. 67, art. *Quin's
Visit to Spain.*

### NOTE 5.

*I look'd on two*
*Following his footsteps to the same dread place,*
*For the same guilt—his sisters!—*

" A priest, named Gonzalez, had, among other proselytes, gained
over two young females, his sisters, to the protestant faith. All
three were confined in the dungeons of the Inquisition. The torture,
repeatedly applied, could not draw from them the least evidence
against their religious associates. Every artifice was employed to
obtain a recantation from the two sisters, since the constancy and
learning of Gonzalez precluded all hopes of a theological victory.
Their answer, if not exactly logical, is wonderfully simple, and
affecting. ' We will die in the faith of our brother: he is too wise
to be wrong, and too good to deceive us.'—The three stakes on which
they died were near each other. The priest had been gagged till the
moment of lighting up the wood. The few minutes that he was
allowed to speak he employed in comforting his sisters, with whom
he sung the 109th Psalm, till the flames smothered their voices."—
*Ibid.*

### NOTE 6.

*And dim the name*
*A hundred chiefs had borne, cast down by you to shame.*

The names, not only of the immediate victims of the Inquisition,
were devoted to infamy, but those of all their relations were branded
with the same indelible stain, which was likewise to descend as an
inheritance to their latest posterity.

### NOTE 7.

*'Twas not within the city—but in sight*
*Of the snow-crown'd sierras.*

The piles erected for these executions were without the towns,
and the final scene of an Auto da Fe was sometimes, from the length
of the preceding ceremonies, delayed till midnight.

### NOTE 8.

*I would have call'd, adjuring the dark cloud,*
*To the most ancient Heavens I would have said—*
*" Speak to me! show me truth!"*

For one of the most powerful and impressive pictures perhaps
ever drawn, of a young mind struggling against habit and superstition in its first aspirations after truth, see the admirable *Letters from
Spain by Don Leucadio Doblado.*

### NOTE 9.

*For thick ye girt me round, ye long-departed!*
*Dust—image form—with cross, and shield, and crest.*

" You walk from end to end over a floor of tomb-stones, inlaid in
brass with the forms of the departed, mitres, and crosiers, and

spears, and shields, and helmets, all mingled together—all worn into glass-like smoothness by the feet and the knees of long-departed worshippers. Around, on every side, each in their separate chapel, sleep undisturbed from age to age the venerable ashes of the holiest or the loftiest that of old came thither to worship—their images and their dying prayers sculptured among the resting places of their remains."—From a beautiful description of ancient Spanish Cathedrals, in *Peter's Letters to his Kinsfolk*.

### NOTE 10.

*With eyes, whose lightning laughter hath beguiled*
*A thousand pangs.*

"El' lampeggiar de l' angelico riso."—*Petrarch*.

### NOTE 11.

*Mighty shades*
*Waving their gorgeous tracery o'er thy head,*
*With the light melting through their high arcades,*
*As through a pillar'd cloister's*

"Sometimes their discourse was held in the deep shades of mossgrown forests, whose gloom and interlaced boughs first suggested that Gothic architecture, beneath whose pointed arches, where they had studied and prayed, the parti-coloured windows shed a tinged light: scenes which the gleams of sunshine, penetrating the deep foliage, and flickering on the variegated turf below, might have recalled to their memory."—*Webster's Oration on the Landing of the Pilgrim Fathers in New England.—See Hodgson's Letters from North America,* vol. ii. p. 305.

### NOTE 12.

*Bring me the sounding of the torrent-water,*
*With yet a nearer swell—fresh breeze, awake!*

The varying sounds of waterfalls are thus alluded to in an interesting work of Mrs. Grant's. "On the opposite side the view was bounded by steep hills, covered with lofty pines, from which a waterfall descended, which not only gave animation to the sylvan scene, but was the best barometer imaginable; foretelling by its varied and intelligible sounds every approaching change, not only of the weather, but of the wind."—*Memoirs of an American Lady,* vol. i. p. 143.

### NOTE 13.

*And the full circle of the rainbow seen*
*There on the snows.*

The circular rainbows, occasionally seen among the Andes, are described by Ulloa.

### NOTE 14.

*But to my spirit's fever'd longings wrought,*
*Wakening, it might be, to the faint sad sound,*
*That from the darkness of the walls they brought*
*A word some round me, visibly around.*

Many striking instances of the vividness with which the mind, when strongly excited, has been known to renovate past impressions, and embody them into visible imagery, are noticed and accounted for in Dr. Hibbert's *Philosophy of Apparitions*. The following illustrative passage is quoted in the same work, from the writings of the late Dr. Ferriar. "I remember that, about the age of fourteen, it was a source of great amusement to myself, if I had been viewing any interesting object in the course of the day, such as a romantic ruin, a fine seat, or a review of a body of troops, as soon as evening came on, if I had occasion to go into a dark room, the whole scene was brought before my eyes with a brilliancy equal to what it had possessed in daylight, and remained visible for several minutes. I have no doubt that dismal and frightful images have been thus presented to young persons after scenes of domestic affliction or public horror."

The following passage from the "Alcazar of Seville," a tale, or historical sketch, by the author of Ikobladn's letters, affords a further illustration of this subject:—"When descending fast into the vale of years, I strongly fix my mind's eye on those narrow, shady, silent streets, where I breathed the scented air which came rustling through the surrounding groves; where the footsteps re-echoed from the clean watered porches of the houses, and where every object spoke of quiet and contentment;...... the objects around me begin to fade into a mere delusion and not only the thoughts, but the external sensations, which I then experienced, revive with a reality that almost makes me shudder—it has so much the character of a trance, or vision."

### NOTE 15.

*Nor the faint flower-scents, as they come and go*
*In the soft air, like music wandering by.*

"For because the breath of flowers is farre sweeter in the aire (where it comes and goes like the warbling of music) than in the hand, therefore nothing is more fit for that delight than to know what be the flowers and plants which doe best perfume the aire."—*Lord Bacon's Essay on Gardens*.

### NOTE 16.

*I saw thee shine*
*Once more, in thy serene magnificence,*
*O Southern Cross!*

"The pleasure we felt on discovering the Southern Cross was warmly shared by such of the crew as had lived in the colonies. In the solitude of the seas, we hail a star as a friend from whom we have long been separated. Among the Portuguese and the Spaniards, peculiar motives seem to increase this feeling; a religious sentiment attaches them to a constellation, the form of which recalls the sign of the faith planted by their ancestors in the deserts of the New World. . . . . . . It has been observed at what hour of the night, in different seasons, the Cross of the South is erect or inclined. It is a time-piece that advances very regularly near four minutes a day, and no other group of stars exhibits to the naked eye an observation of time so easily made. How often have we heard our guides exclaim, in the savannas of Venezuela, or in the desert extending from Lima to Truxillo, "Midnight is past, the cross begins to bend!" How often these words reminded us of that affecting scene where Paul and Virginia, seated near the source of the river Lataniers, conversed together for the last time, and where the old man, at the sight of the Southern Cross, warns them that it is time to separate."—*De Humboldt's Travels*.

### NOTE 17.

*Songs of the orange bower, the Moorish hold,*
*The "Rio Verde."*

"Rio verde, rio verde," the popular Spanish romance, known to the English reader in Percy's translation.

"Gentle river, gentle river,
Lo, thy streams are stain'd with gore,
Many a brave and noble captain
Floats along thy willow'd shore," &c. &c.

### NOTE 18.

*Then the broad lonely sunrise!—and the plash*
*Into the sounding waves!—*

De Humboldt, in describing the burial of a young Asturian at sea, mentions the entreaty of the officiating priest, that the body, which had been brought upon deck during the night, might not be committed to the waves until after sunrise, in order to pay it the last rites according to the usage of the Romish church.

### NOTE 19.

*Oh! art thou not where there is no more sea?*
"And there was no more sea."—*Rev.* chap. xxi. v. 1.

### NOTE 20.

*And o'er the Andes-torrents borne his form,*
*Where our frail bridge hath quiver'd 'midst the storm.*

The bridges over many deep chasms among the Andes are pendulous, and formed only of the fibres of equinoctial plants. That tremulous motion has afforded a striking image to one of the poems in 'Gertrude of Wyoming.'

"Anon some wilder portraiture he draws,
Of nature's savage glories he would speak;
The loneliness of earth, that overawes,
Where, resting by the tomb of old Cacique,

The lama-driver, on Peruvia's peak,
Nor voice, nor living motion marks around,
But storks that to the boundless forest shriek,
Or wild-cane arch, high flung o'er gulf profound,
That fluctuates when the storms of El Dorado sound."

### NOTE 21.

*And then his play*
*Through the wide Llanos cheer'd again our way.*
Llanos, or savannas, the great plains in South America.

### NOTE 22.

*And by the mighty Orinoco stream,*
*On whose lone margin we have heard at morn*
*From the mysterious rocks, the sunrise music borne.*

De Humboldt speaks of these rocks on the shores of the Orinoco. Travellers have heard from time to time subterraneous sounds proceeding from them at sun-rise, resembling those of an organ. He believes in the existence of this mysterious music, although not certain enough to have heard it himself, and thinks that it may be produced by currents of air issuing through the crevices.

### NOTE 23.

*Yet those deep southern shades oppress'd*
*My soul with stillness.*

The same distinguished traveller frequently alludes to the extreme stillness of the air in the equatorial regions of the new continent, and particularly on the thickly wooded shores of the Orinoco. "In this neighbourhood," he says, "no breath of wind ever agitates the foliage."

## The English Martyrs.

### A SCENE OF THE DAYS OF QUEEN MARY.

Thy face
Is all at once spread over with a calm
More beautiful than sleep, or mirth, or joy,
I am no more disconsolate.——*Wilson.*

*Scene in a Prison.*

EDITH *alone.*

*Edith.* Morn once again! Morn in the lone dim
    cell,
The cavern of the prisoner's fever dream,
And morn on all the green rejoicing hills,
And the bright waters round the prisoner's home
Far, far away! Now wakes the early bird
That in the lime's transparent foliage sings,
Close to my cottage lattice—he awakes,
To stir the young leaves with his gushing soul,
And to call forth rich answers of delight
From voices buried in a thousand trees,
Through the dim starry hours. Now doth the lake
Darken and flash in rapid interchange
Unto the matin breeze; and the blue mist
Rolls, like a furling banner, from the brows
Of the forth-gleaming hills and woods that rise
As if new-born. Bright world! and I am here!
And thou, O thou! th' awakening thought of whom
Was more than day-spring, dearer than the sun,
Herbert! the very glance of whose clear eye
Made my soul melt away to one pure fount
Of living, bounding gladness!—where art *thou?*
My friend! my only and my blessed love!
Herbert, my soul's companion!

    [GOMEZ, *a Spanish priest, enters*

*Gomez.*                     Daughter, hail!
I bring thee tidings.

*Edith.*                  Heaven will aid my soul
Calmly to meet whate'er thy lips announce.

*Gomez.* Nay, lift a song of thanksgiving to
    Heaven,
And bow thy knee down for deliverance won!
Hast thou not pray'd for life? and wouldst thou not
Once more be free?

*Edith.*                 Have I not pray'd for life!
I, that am so beloved! that love again
With such a heart of tendrils? Heaven! thou
    know'st
The gushings of my prayer! And would I not
Once more be free? I, that have been a child
Of breezy hills, a playmate of the fawn
In ancient woodlands, from mine infancy!
A watcher of the clouds and of the stars,
Beneath the adoring silence of the night;
And a glad wanderer with the happy streams,
Whose laughter fills the mountains! Oh! to hear
Their blessed sounds again!

*Gomez.*                  Rejoice! rejoice!
Our Queen hath pity, maiden, on thy youth;
She wills not thou shouldst perish.—I am come



To loose thy bonds.

*Edith.*              And shall I see *his* face,
And shall I listen to *his* voice again,
And lay my head upon his faithful breast,
Weeping there in my gladness? *Will* this be?—
Blessings upon thee, father! my quick heart
Hath deem'd thee stern—say, will thou not forgive
The wayward child, too long in sunshine rear'd,
Too long unused to chastening? Wilt thou not?—
But Herbert, Herbert! Oh, my soul hath rush'd
On a swift gust of sudden joy away,
Forgetting all beside? Speak, father, speak!
Herbert—is he too free?

*Gomez.*                 His freedom lies
In his own choice—a boon like thine.

*Edith.*                      Thy words
Fall changed and cold upon my boiling heart.
Leave not this dim suspense o'ershadowing me.
Let all be told.

*Gomez.*         The monarchs of the earth
Shower not their mighty gifts without a claim
Unto some token of true vassalage,
Some mark of homage.

*Edith.*              Oh! unlike to *Him,*
Who freely pours the joy of sunshine forth,
And the bright quickening rain, on those who
    serve
And those who heed him not!

*Gomez,* (*laying a paper before her.*) Is it so much
That thine own hand should set the crowning seal
To thy deliverance? Look, thy task is here!
Sign but these words for liberty and life.

*Edith,* (*examining and then throwing it from her.*)
Sign but these words! and wherefore saidst thou
    not,
" Be but a traitor to God's light within?"—
Cruel, oh, cruel! thy dark sport hath been
With a young bosom's hope! Farewell, glad life!
Bright opening path to love and home, farewell!
And thou—now leave me with my God alone!

*Gomez.* Dost thou reject Heaven's mercy?

*Edith.*                Heaven's! doth *Heaven*
Woo the free spirit for dishonour'd breath
To sell its birthright? doth *Heaven* set a price
On the clear jewel of unsullied faith,
And the bright calm of conscience? Priest, away.
God hath been with me 'midst the holiness
Of England's mountains—not in sport alone
I trod their heath-flowers — but high thoughts
    rose up
From the broad shadow of the enduring rocks,
And wander'd with me into solemn glens,
Where my soul felt the beauty of His word.
I have heard voices of immortal truth,
Blent with the everlasting torrent-sounds
That make the deep hills tremble.—Shall I quail?
Shall England's daughter sink? — No! He who
    there
Spoke to my heart in silence and in storm,
Will not forsake his child!

*Gomez,* (*turning from her.*) Then perish! lost
In thine own blindness.

*Edith,* (*suddenly throwing herself at his feet.*)
               Father! hear me yet!

Oh! if the kindly touch of human love
Hath ever warm'd thy breast——
   *Gomez.*                 Away—away!
I know not love.
   *Edith.*   Yet hear! if thou hast known
The tender sweetness of a mother's voice—
If the true vigil of affection's eye
Hath watch'd thy childhood —if fond tears have e'er
Been shower'd upon thy head—if parting words
E'er pierced thy spirit with their tenderness—
Let me but look upon *his* face once more.
Let me but say—Farewell, my soul's beloved!
And I will bless thee still!
   *Gomez.* (*aside.*)        Her soul may yield,
Beholding him in fetters; woman's faith
Will bend to woman's love—
                Thy prayer is heard
Follow, and I will guide thee to his cell.
   *Edith.* Oh! stormy hour of agony and joy!
But I shall see him—I shall hear his voice!
                  [*They go out.*

---

### SCENE II.

*Another Part of the Prison.*

HERBERT—EDITH.

  *Edith.* Herbert, my Herbert! is it thus we meet?
  *Herbert.* The voice of my own Edith! Can such joy
Light up this place of death? And do I feel
Thy breath of love once more upon my cheek,
And the soft floating of thy gleamy hair.
My blessed Edith! Oh! so pale! so changed!
My flower, my blighted flower! thou that wert made
For the kind fostering of sweet summer airs,
How hath the storm been with thee!—Lay thy head
On this true breast again, my gentle one!
And tell me all.
   *Edith.*         Yes, take me to thy heart,
For I am weary, weary! Oh! that heart!
The kind, the brave, the tender!—how my soul
Hath sicken'd in vain yearnings for the balm
Of rest on that warm heart!—full, deep repose!
One draught of dewy stillness after storm!
And God hath pitied me, and I am here—
Yet once before I die!
   *Herbert.*        They cannot slay
One, young and meek, and beautiful as thou!
My broken lily! Surely the long days
Of the dark cell have been enough for thee!
Oh! thou shalt live, and raise thy gracious head
Yet in calm sunshine.
   *Edith.*       Herbert! I have cast
The snare of proffer'd mercy from my soul,
This very hour. God to the weak hath given
Victory o'er life and death!—The tempter's price
Hath been rejected—Herbert, I must die.
   *Herbert.* O Edith! Edith! I, that led thee first
From the old path wherein thy fathers trod—
I, that received it as an angel's task,
To pour the fresh light on thine ardent soul,
Which drank it as a sun-flower—*I* have been
Thy guide to death!
   *Edith.*     To Heaven! my guide to Heaven
My noble and my blessed! Oh! look up.
Be strong, rejoice, my Herbert! But for *thee*
How could my spirit have sprung up to God,
Through the dark cloud which o'er its vision hung,
The night of fear and error? thy dear hand
First raised that veil, and show'd the glorious world
My heritage beyond—Friend! love and friend!
It was as if thou gavest me mine own soul
In those bright days! Yes! a new earth and heaven,
And a new sense for all their splendours born,
There were thy gifts! and shall I not rejoice
To die, upholding their immortal worth.
Even for *thy* sake? Yes, fill'd with nobler life
By thy pure love, made holy to the truth,
Lay me upon the altar of thy God,
The first fruits of thy ministry below;
Thy work, thine own!
   *Herbert.*       My love, my sainted love
Oh! I can almost yield thee unto heaven;
Earth would but sully thee! Thou must depart,
With the rich crown of thy celestial gifts
Untainted by a breath! And yet, alas!
Edith! what dreams of holy happiness,
Even for *this* world, were ours! the low, sweet home—
The pastoral dwelling, with its ivied porch,
And lattice gleaming through the leaves—and thou,
My life's companion!—Thou, beside my hearth,
Sitting with thy meek eyes, or greeting me
Back from brief absence with thy bounding step,
In the green meadow path, or by my side
Kneeling—thy calm uplifted face to mine,
In the sweet hush of prayer! and now—oh! now—
How have we loved—how fervently, how long!
And *this* to be the close!
   *Edith.*       Oh! bear me up
Against the unutterable tenderness
Of earthly love, my God! in the sick hour
Of dying human hope, forsake me not!
Herbert, my Herbert! even from that sweet home
Where it had been too much of Paradise
To dwell with thee—even thence the oppressor's hand
Might soon have torn us; or the touch of death
Might one day there have left a widow'd heart,
Pining alone. We will go hence, beloved!
To the bright country, where the wicked cease
From troubling, where the spoiler hath no sway:
Where no harsh voice of worldliness disturbs
The Sabbath-peace of love. We will go hence,
Together with our wedded souls, to Heaven
No solitary lingering, no cold void.
No dying of the heart! Our lives have been
Lovely through faithful love, and in our deaths
We will not be divided.
   *Herbert.*       Oh! the peace
Of God is lying far within thine eyes,
Far underneath the mist of human tears.
Lighting those blue still depths, and sinking thence
On my worn heart. Now am I girt with strength,
Now I can bless thee, my true bride for Heaven!
   *Edith.* And let me bless *thee*, Herbert! in this hour
Let my soul bless thee with prevailing might!
Oh! thou hast loved me nobly! thou didst take
An orphan to thy heart, a thing unprized
And desolate; and thou didst guard her there,
That lone and lowly creature, as a pearl
Of richest price; and thou didst fill her soul
With the high gifts of an immortal wealth.—
I bless, I bless thee! Never did thine eye
Look on me but in glistening tenderness,
My gentle Herbert! Never did thy voice
But in affection's deepest music speak
To thy poor Edith! Never was thy heart
Aught but the kindliest sheltering home to mine,
My faithful, generous Herbert! Woman's peace
Ne'er on a breast so tender and so true
Reposed before.—Alas! thy showering tears
Fall fast upon my cheek—forgive, forgive!
I should not melt thy noble strength away
In such an hour.
   *Herbert.*       Sweet Edith, no! my heart
Will fail no more; God bears me up through thee,
And, by thy words, and by the heavenly light
Shining around thee, through thy very tears,
Will yet sustain me! Let us call on him!
Let us kneel down, as we have knelt so oft,
Thy pure cheek touching mine, and call on Him,
Th' all-pitying One, to aid.
                  [*They kneel.*
             O, look on us,
Father above! In tender mercy look
On us, thy children! through th' o'ershadowing cloud
Of sorrow and mortality, send aid,
Save or we perish! we would pour our lives
Forth as a joyous offering to thy truth,
But we are weak—we, the bruised reeds of earth,
Are sway'd by every gust. Forgive, O God!
The blindness of our passionate desires,

The fainting of our hearts, the lingering thoughts,
Which cleave to dust! Forgive the strife; accept
The sacrifice, though dim with mortal tears,
From mortal pangs wrung forth! And if our souls,
In all the fervent dreams, the fond excess,
Of their long-clasping love, have wander'd not,
Holiest! from thee; oh! take them to thyself,
After the fiery trial, take them home
To dwell, in that imperishable bond
Before thee link'd, for ever. Hear, through Him
Who meekly drank the cup of agony,
Who pass'd through death to victory, hear and
        save!
Pity us, Father! we are girt with snares;
Father in Heaven! we have no help but thee.
                    [*They rise.*

Is thy soul strengthen'd, my beloved one?
O Edith! couldst thou lift up thy sweet voice,
And sing me that old solemn-breathing hymn
We loved in happier days—the strain which tells
Of the dread conflict in the olive shade?
                    [*She sings.*

He knelt, the Saviour knelt and pray'd,
  When but his Father's eye
Look'd through the lonely garden's shade
  On that dread agony;
The Lord of All above, beneath,
Was bow'd with sorrow unto death.

The sun set in a fearful hour,
  The stars might well grow dim,
When this mortality had power
  So to o'ershadow Him!
That He who gave man's breath, might know
The very depths of human woe.

He proved them all! the doubt, the strife,
  The faint perplexing dread,
The mists that hang o'er parting life,
  All gather'd round his head;
And the Deliverer knelt to pray—
Yet pass'd it not, that cup, away!

It pass'd not—though the stormy wave
  Had sunk beneath his tread;
It pass'd not—though to him the grave
  Had yielded up its dead.
But there was sent him from on high
A gift of strength for man to die.

And was the sinless thus beset
  With anguish and dismay?
How may *we* meet our conflict yet,
  In the dark narrow way?
Thro' Him—Thro' Him, that path who trod—
Save, or we perish, Son of God!

Hark! hark! the parting signal.
            [*Prison attendants enter*
                    Fare-thee-well!
O thou unutterably loved, farewell!
Let our hearts bow to God!
    *Herbert.*            One last embrace—
On earth the last!—We have eternity
For love's communion yet!—Farewell—farewell!—
                    [*She is led out.*
'T is o'er—the bitterness of death is past!

------

## FLOWERS AND MUSIC IN A ROOM OF SICKNESS.

*Once, when I look'd along the laughing earth,*
*Up the blue heavens, and through the middle air,*
*Joyfully ringing with the sky-lark's song,*
*I wept! and thought how sad for one so young,*
*To bid farewell to so much happiness.*
*But Christ hath call'd me from this lower world,*
*Delightful though it be.——Wilson.*

------

*Apartment in an English Country-House.—*LILIAN *reclining, as sleeping on a couch. Her Mother watching beside her. Her Sister enters with flowers.*

    *Mother.* Hush, lightly tread! still tranquilly she
        sleeps,
As, when a babe, I rock'd her on my heart,
I've watch'd, suspending e'en my breath, in fear
To break the heavenly spell. Move silently!
And oh! these flowers! dear Jessy, bear them
        hence—
Dost thou forget the passion of quick tears
That shook her trembling frame, when last we
        brought
The roses to her couch? Dost thou not know
What sudden longings for the woods and hills,
Where once her free steps moved so buoyantly,
These leaves and odours with strange influence
        wake
In her fast-kindled soul?
    *Jessy.*            Oh! she would pine,
Were the wild scents and glowing hues withheld,
Mother! far more than *now* her spirit yearns
For the blue sky, the singing birds and brooks,
And swell of breathing turf, whose lightsome
        spring
Their blooms recall.
    *Lilian, (raising herself.)* Is that my Jessy's voice?
It woke me not, sweet mother! I had lain
Silently, visited by waking dreams,
Yet conscious of thy brooding watchfulness,
Long ere I heard the sound. Hath she brought
        flowers?
Nay, fear not now thy fond child's waywardness,
My thoughtful mother!—in her chasten'd soul
The passion-colour'd images of life,
Which, with their sudden startling flush, awoke
So oft those burning tears, have died away:
And night is there—still solemn, holy night,
With all her stars, and with the gentle tune
Of many fountains, low and musical,
By day unheard
    *Mother.*            And wherefore *night,* my child?
Thou art a creature all of life and dawn,
And from thy couch of sickness yet shalt rise,
And walk forth with the day-spring.
    *Lilian.*            Hope it not!
Dream it no more, my mother! there are things
  nown but to God, and in the parting soul,
Which feels his thrilling summons.
                    But my words
Too much o'ershadow those kind loving eyes.
Bring me thy flowers, dear Jessy! Ah! thy step,
Well do I see, hath not alone explored
The garden bowers, but freely visited
Our wilder haunts. This foam-like meadow sweet
Is from the cool green shadowy river nook,
Where the stream chimes around th' old mossy
        stones
With sounds like childhood's laughter. Is that spot
Lovely as when our glad eyes hail'd it first?
Still doth the golden willow bend, and sweep
The clear brown wave with every passing wind?
And thro' the shallower waters, where they lie
Dimpling in light, do the vein'd pebbles gleam
Like bedded gems? And the white butterflies,
From shade to sun-streak are they glancing still
Among the poplar-boughs?
    *Jessy.*            All, all is there
Which glad midsummer's wealthiest hours can
        bring:
All, save the *soul* of all, thy lightening smile!
Therefore I stood in sadness, 'midst the leaves,
And caught an under-music of lament
In the stream's voice; but Nature waits thee still,
And for thy coming piles a fairy throne
Of richest moss.
    *Lilian.*            Alas! it may not be!
My soul hath sent her farewell voicelessly,
To all these blessed haunts of song and thought;
Yet not the less I love to look on these,
Their dear memorials: strew them o'er my couch,
Till it grow like a forest-bank in spring,
All flush'd with violets and anemones.
Ah! the pale brier rose! touch'd so tenderly,
As a pure ocean-shell, with faintest red,
Melting away to pearliness!—I know
How its long light festoons o'erarching hung
From the gray rock, that rises altar-like,
With its high waving crown of mountain ash,
'Midst the lone grassy dell. And this rich bough
Of honey'd woodbine, tells me of the oak

Whose deep midsummer gloom sleeps heavily,
Shedding a verdurous twilight o'er the face
Of the glade's pool. Methinks I see it now:
I look up through the stirring of its leaves
Unto the intense blue crystal firmament.
The ring-dove's wing is flitting o'er my head,
Casting at times a silvery shadow down
'Midst the large water-lilies. Beautiful!
How beautiful is all this fair free world
Under God's open sky!
    *Mother.*          Thou art o'erwrought
Once more, my child! The dewy trembling light
Presaging tears, again is in thine eye.
O, hush, dear Lilian! turn thee to repose.
    *Lilian.*    Mother, I cannot. In my soul the
         thoughts
Burn with too subtle and too swift a fire;
Importunately to my lips they throng,
And with their earthly kindred seek to blend
Ere the veil drop between. When I am gone—
(For I *must* go)—then the remember'd words
Wherein these wild imaginings flow forth,
Will to thy fond heart be as amulets
Held there with life and love. And weep not thus!
Mother—dear sister! kindest, gentlest ones!
Be comforted that now *I* weep no more
For the glad earth and all the golden light
Whence I depart.
No! God hath purified my spirit's eye,
And in the folds of this consummate rose
I read bright prophecies. I see not there,
Dimly and mournfully, the word "*farewell*"
On the rich petals traced:—No—in soft veins
And characters of beauty, I can read—
"*Look up, look heavenward!*"
         Blessed God of Love!
I thank thee for these gifts, the precious links
Whereby my spirit unto thee is drawn!
I thank thee that the loveliness of earth
Higher than earth can raise me! Are not these
But germs of things unperishing, that bloom
Beside th' immortal streams? Shall I not find
The lily of the field, the Saviour's flower,
In the serene and never-moaning air,
And the clear starry light of angel eyes,
A thousand-fold more glorious? Richer far
Will not the violet's dusky purple glow,
When it hath ne'er been press'd to broken hearts,
A record of lost love?
    *Mother.*         My Lilian! thou
Surely in *thy* bright life hast little known
Of lost things or of changed!
    *Lilian.*         Oh! little yet,
For *thou* hast been my shield! But had it been
My lot on this world's billows to be thrown
Without thy love—O mother! there are hearts
So perilously fashion'd, that for them
God's touch alone hath gentleness enough
To waken, and not break, their thrilling strings!—
We will not speak of this!
         By what strange spell
Is it, that ever, when I gaze on flowers,
  dream of music? Something in their hues
All melting into colour'd harmonies,
Wafts a swift thought of interwoven chords,
Of blended singing-tones, that swell and die
In tenderest falls away.—O, bring thy harp,
sister! a gentle heaviness at last
Hath touch'd mine eyelids: sing to me, and sleep
Will come again.
    *Jessy.*    What wouldst thou hear? Th' Italian
         Peasant's Lay,
Which makes the desolate Campagna ring
With "*Roma, Roma?*" or the Madrigal
Warbled on moonlight seas of Sicily?
Or the old ditty left by Troubadours
To girls of Languedoc?
    *Lilian.*         Oh, no! not these.
    *Jessy.*    What then? the Moorish melody still
         known
Within the Alhambra city? or those notes
Born of the Alps, which pierce the exile's heart
Even unto death?

    *Lilian.*         No, sister, nor yet those.—
Too much of dreamy love, of faint regret,
Of passionately fond remembrance, breathes
In the caressing sweetness of their tones,
For one who dies:—They would but woo me back
To glowing life with those Arcadian sounds—
And vainly, vainly—No! a loftier strain,
A deeper music!—Something that may bear
The spirit up on slow yet mighty wings,
Unsway'd by gusts of earth: something, all fill'd
With solemn adoration, tearful prayer.—
Sing me that antique strain which once I deem'd
Almost too sternly simple, too austere
In its grave majesty! I love it now—
*Now* it seems fraught with holiest power, to hush
All billows of the soul, e'en like His voice
That said of old—"Be still!" Sing me that strain—
"The Saviour's dying hour."

         [Jessy *sings to the Harp*

        O Son of Man!
      In thy last mortal hour
Shadows of earth closed round thee fearfully!
        All that on us is laid,
        All the deep gloom,
The desolation and th' abandonment,
        The dark amaze of death;
        All upon *thee* too fell,
        Redeemer! Son of Man!

        But the keen pang
        Wherewith the silver cord
Of earth's affection from the soul is wrung;
Th' uptearing of those tendrils which have grown
        Into the quick strong heart;
This, *this*, the passion and the agony
        Of battling love and death,
        Surely was not for *thee*,
        Holy One! Son of God!

        Yes, my Redeemer!
        E'en this cup was thine!
Fond wailing voices call'd thy spirit back;
        E'en 'midst the mighty thoughts
        Of that last crowning hour;
E'en on thine awful way to victory,

        Wildly they call'd thee back!
        And weeping eyes of love
        Unto thy heart's deep core,
Pierced thro' the folds of death's mysterious veil—
        Sufferer! thou Son of Man!

        Mother-tears were mingled
        With thy costly blood-drops,
In the shadow of th' atoning cross;
        And the friend, the faithful,
        He that on thy bosom,
Thence imbibing heavenly love, had lain—
        He, a pale sad watcher—
        Met with looks of anguish,
All the anguish in *thy* last meek glance—
        Dying Son of Man!

        Oh! therefore unto thee,
        Thou that hast known all woes
Bound in the girdle of mortality!
        Thou that wilt lift the reed
        Which storms have bruised,
To thee may sorrow through each conflict cry,
And, in that tempest-hour when love and life
        Mysteriously must part,
        When tearful eyes
        Are passionately bent
To drink earth's last fond meaning from our gaze,
        Then, then forsake us not!
        Shed on our spirits then
The faith and deep submissiveness of thine!
        Thou that didst love,
        Thou that didst weep and die—
Thou that didst rise, a victor glorified!
        Conqueror! thou Son of God!

## CATHEDRAL HYMN.

*"They dream not of a perishable home*
*Who thus could build. Be mine, in hours of fear*
*Or grovelling thought, to seek a refuge here."*
*Wordsworth.*

A DIM and mighty minster of old time!
A temple shadowy with remembrances
Of the majestic past!—the very light
Streams with a colouring of heroic days
In every ray, which leads through arch and aisle
A path of dreamy lustre, wandering back
To other years;—and the rich fretted roof,
And the wrought coronals of summer leaves,
Ivy and vine, and many a sculptured rose—
The tenderest image of mortality—
Binding the slender columns, whose light shafts
Cluster like stems in corn-sheaves—all these things
Tell of a race that nobly, fearlessly,
On their heart's worship pour'd a wealth of love!
Honour be with the dead!—The people kneel
Under the helms of antique chivalry,
And in the crimson gloom from banners thrown,
And 'midst the forms, in pale proud slumber carved
Of warriors on their tombs.—The people kneel
Where mail-clad chiefs have knelt; where jewell'd
   crowns
On the flush'd brows of conquerors have been set;
Where the high anthems of old victories
Have made the dust give echoes.—Hence, vain
   thoughts!
Memories of power and pride, which, long ago,
Like dim processions of a dream, have sunk
In twilight depths away.—Return, my soul!
The cross recalls thee—Lo! the blessed cross!
High o'er the banners and the crests of earth,
Fix'd in its meek and still supremacy!
And lo! the throng of beating human hearts,
With all their secret scrolls of buried grief,
All their full treasures of immortal hope,
Gather'd before their God!—Hark! how the flood
Of the rich organ harmony bears up
Their voice on its high waves!—a mighty burst!
A forest-sounding music!—every tone
Which the blasts call forth with their harping
   wings
From gulfs of tossing foliage there is blent·
And the old minster—forest-like itself—
With its long avenues of pillar'd shade,
Seems quivering all with spirit, as that strain
O'erflows its dim recesses, leaving not
One tomb unthrill'd by the strong sympathy
Answering the electric notes.—Join, join, my soul!
In thine own lowly, trembling consciousness,
And thine own solitude, the glorious hymn.

Rise like an altar-fire!
   In solemn joy aspire,
Deepening thy passion still, O choral strain!
   On thy strong rushing wind
   Bear up from human kind
Thanks and implorings—be they not in vain!

   Father, which art on high!
   Weak is the melody
Of harp or song to reach thine awful ear,
   Unless the heart be there,
   Winging the words of prayer,
With its own fervent faith or suppliant fear.

   Let, then, thy spirit brood
   Over the multitude—
Be thou amidst them through that heavenly Guest!
   So shall their cry have power
   To win from thee a shower
Of healing gifts for every wounded breast.

   What griefs that make no sign,
   That ask no aid but thine,
Father of Mercies! here before thee swell,
   As to the open sky,
   All their dark waters lie
To thee reveal'd, in each close bosom cell

   The sorrow for the dead,
   Mantling its lonely head
From the world's glare, is, in thy sight, set free!
   And the fond, aching love,
   Thy minister, to move
All the wrung spirit, softening it for thee.

   And doth not thy dread eye
   Behold the agony
In that most hidden chamber of the heart,
   Where darkly sits remorse,
   Beside the secret source
Of fearful visions, keeping watch apart?

   Yes! here before thy throne
   Many—yet each alone—
To thee that terrible unveiling make;
   And still small whispers clear
   Are startling many an ear,
As if a trumpet bade the dead awake.

   How dreadful is this place!
   The glory of thy face
Fills it too searchingly for mortal sight:
   Where shall the guilty flee?
   Over what far-off sea?
What hills, what woods, may shroud him from
   that light?

   Not to the cedar shade
   Let his vain flight be made;
Nor the old mountains, nor the desert sea;
   What, but the cross, can yield
   The hope—the stay—the shield?
*Thence* may the Atoner lead him up to Thee!

   Be thou, be thou his aid!
   Oh! let thy love pervade
The haunted caves of self-accusing thought!
   There let the living stone
   Be cleft—the seed be sown—
The song of fountains from the silence brought!

   So shall thy breath once more
   Within the soul restore
Thine own first image—Holiest and most High!
   As a clear lake is fill'd
   With hues of Heaven, instill'd
Down to the depths of its calm purity.

   And if, amidst the throng
   Link'd by the ascending song,
There are, whose thoughts in trembling rapture
   soar;
   Thanks, Father! that the power
   Of joy, man's early dower,
Thus, e'en 'midst tears, can fervently adore!

   Thanks for each gift divine!
   Eternal praise be thine,
Blessing and love, O Thou that hearest prayer!
   Let the hymn pierce the sky,
   And let the tombs reply!
For seed that waits thy harvest-time, is there.

---

## WOOD WALK AND HYMN

*Move along these shades*
*In gentleness of heart, with gentle hand*
*Touch—for there is a spirit in the woods*
*Wordsworth.*

---

### FATHER—CHILD.

*Child.* There are the aspens, with their silvery
   leaves
Trembling, for ever trembling! though the lime
And chestnut boughs, and those long arching sprays
Of eglantine, hang still, as if the wood
Were all one picture!
   *Father.*          Hast thou heard, my boy,
The peasant's legend of that quivering tree!

*Child.* No, father; doth he say the fairies dance
Amidst the branches?
    *Father.*         Oh! a cause more deep,
More solemn far, the rustic doth assign
To the strange restlessness of those wan leaves!
The cross, he deems, the blessed cross, whereon
The meek Redeemer bow'd his head to death,
Was framed of aspen wood; and since that hour,
Through all its race the pale tree hath sent down
A thrilling consciousness, a secret awe.
Making them tremulous, when not a breeze
Disturbs the airy thistle-down, or shakes
The light lines of the shining gossamer.
    *Child,* (*after a pause.*) Dost thou believe it, father?
    *Father.*         Nay, my child.
We walk in clearer light. But yet, even now,
With something of a lingering love, I read
The characters by that mysterious hour,
Stamp'd on the reverential soul of man
In visionary days; and thence thrown back
On the fair forms of nature. Many a sign
Of the great sacrifice which won us Heaven,
The woodman and the mountaineer can trace
On rock, on herb, and flower. And be it so!
*They* do not wisely that, with hurried hand,
Would pluck these salutary fancies forth
From their strong soil within the peasant's breast,
And scatter them—far, far too fast!—away
'As worthless weeds:—Oh! little do we know
*When* they have soothed, when saved!
              But come, dear boy!
My words grow tinged with thought too deep for
    thee.
Come—let us search for violets.
    *Child.*         Know you not
More of the legends which the woodmen tell
Amidst the trees and flowers?
    *Father.*     Wilt thou know more?
Bring then the folding leaf, with dark brown stains,
There—by the mossy roots of yon old beech,
Midst the rich tuft of cowslips—see'st thou not?
There is a spray of woodbine from the tree
Just bending o'er it, with a wild bee's weight.
    *Child.* The Arum leaf?
    *Father.*     Yes, these deep inwrought marks,
The villager will tell thee (and with voice
Lower'd in his true heart's reverent earnestness)
Are the flower's portion from th' atoning blood
On Calvary shed. Beneath the cross it grew;
And, in the vase-like hollow of its leaf,
Catching from that dread shower of agony
A few mysterious drops, transmitted thus
Unto the groves and hills, their sealing stains,
A heritage, for storm or vernal wind
Never to waft away!
           And hast thou seen
The passion-flower?—It grows not in the woods,
But 'midst the bright things brought from other
    climes.
    *Child.* What, the pale star-shaped flower, with
    purple streaks
And light green tendrils?
    *Father.*     Thou hast mark'd it well.
Yes, a pale, starry, dreamy-looking flower,
As from a land of spirits!—To mine eye
Those faint wan petals—colourless—and yet
Not white, but shadowy—with the mystic lines
(As letters of some wizard language gone)
Into their vapour-like transparence wrought.
Bear something of a strange solemnity,
Awfully lovely!—and the Christian's thought,
Loves, in their cloudy pencilling, to find
Dread symbols of his Lord's last mournful pangs,
Set by God's hand—The coronal of thorns—
The cross—the wounds—with other meanings deep,
Which I will teach thee when we meet again
That flower, the chosen for the martyr's wreath,
The Saviour's holy flower.
           But let us pause:
Now have we reach'd the very inmost heart
Of the old wood.—How the green shadows close
Into a rich, clear, summer darkness round,
A luxury of gloom!—Scarce doth one ray,
Even when a soft wind parts the foliage, steal
O'er the bronzed pillars of these deep arcades;

Or if it doth, 'tis with a mellow'd hue
Of glow-worm colour'd light.
           Here, in the days
Of pagan visions, would have been a place
For worship of the wood nymphs! Through these
    oaks
A small, fair gleaming temple might have thrown
The quivering image of its Dorian shafts
On the stream's bosom; or a sculptured form,
Dryad, or fountain-goddess of the gloom,
Have bow'd its head o'er that dark crystal down,
Drooping with beauty, as a lily droops
Under bright rain:—but we, my child, are here
With God, our God, a Spirit; who requires
Heart-worship, given in spirit and in truth;
And this high knowledge—deep, rich, vast enough
To fill and hallow all the solitude,
Makes consecrated earth where'er we move,
Without the aid of shrines.
           What! dost thou feel
The solemn whispering influence of the scene
Oppressing thy young heart, that thou dost draw
More closely to my side, and clasp my hand
Faster in thine? Nay, fear not, gentle child!
'Tis love, not fear, whose vernal breath pervades
The stillness round. Come, sit beside me here,
Where brooding violets mantle this green slope
With dark exuberance—and beneath these plumes
Of wavy fern, look where the cup-moss holds
In its pure crimson goblets, fresh and bright,
The starry dews of morning. Rest awhile
And let me hear once more the woodland verse
I taught thee late—'twas made for such a scene.
               *Child speaks*


### WOOD HYMN.

  Broods there some spirit here?
The summer leaves hang silent as a cloud;
And o'er the pools, all still and darkly clear,
The wild wood-hyacinth with awe seems bow'd;
And something of a tender cloistral gloom
  Deepens the violet's bloom.

  The very light that streams
Through the dim dewy veil of foliage round,
Comes tremulous with emerald-tinted gleams,
As if it knew the place were holy ground,
And would not startle with too bright a burst,
  Flowers, all divinely nursed.

  *Wakes* there some spirit here?
A swift wind, fraught with change, comes rush-
    ing by,
And leaves and waters, in its wild career,
Shed forth sweet voices—each a mystery!
Surely some awful influence must pervade
  These depths of trembling shade!

  Yes, lightly, softly move!
There *is* a power, a presence in the woods;
A viewless being, that, with life and love,
Informs the reverential solitudes;
The rich air knows it, and the mossy sod—
  Thou, *thou* art here, my God!

  And if with awe we tread
The minster floor, beneath the storied pane,
And 'midst the mouldering banners of the dead,
Shall the green voiceful wild seem *less* thy fane,
Where thou alone hast built?—where arch and
    roof
  Are of thy living woof?

  The silence and the sound,
In the lone places, breathe alike of thee;
The temple twilight of the gloom profound,
The dew-cup of the frail anemone,
The reed by every wandering whisper thrill'd—
  All, all with thee are fill'd!

  Oh! purify mine eyes,
More and yet more, by love and lowly thought,
Thy presence, holiest One! to recognize,
In these majestic aisles which thou hast wrought!
And 'midst their sea-like murmurs, teach mine ear
  Ever thy voice to hear!

And sanctify my heart
To meet the awful sweetness of that tone
With no faint thrill or self-accusing start,
But a deep joy the heavenly guest to own—
Joy, such as dwelt in Eden's glorious bowers
Ere sin had dimm'd the flowers.

Let me not know the change
O'er nature thrown by guilt!—the boding sky,
The hollow leaf-sounds ominous and strange,
The weight wherewith the dark tree shadows lie
Father, oh! keep my footsteps pure and free,
To walk the woods with thee!

---

## PRAYER OF THE LONELY STUDENT

Sov. of our souls, and safeguard of the world!
Sustain—*Thou* only canst—the sick at heart,
Restore their languid spirits, and recall
Their lost affections unto thee and thine.
                              *Wordsworth*

---

Night—holy night!—the time
For mind's free breathings in a purer clime!
Night! when in happier hour the unveiling sky
Woke all my kindled soul,
To meet its revelations, clear and high,
With the strong joy of immortality:

Now hath strange sadness wrapt me—strange and
deep—
And my thoughts faint, and shadows o'er them roll,
E'en when I deem'd them seraph-plumed, to sweep
Far beyond earth's control.

Wherefore is this?—I see the stars returning,
Fire after fire in Heaven's rich temple burning—
Fast shine they forth—my spirit friends, my guides,
Bright rulers of my being's inmost tides;

They shine — but faintly, through a quivering
haze—
Oh! is the dimness mine which clouds those rays?
They from whose glance my childhood drank de-
light!
A joy unquestioning—a love intense—
They, that unfolding to more thoughtful sight,
The harmony of their magnificence,
Drew silently the worship of my youth
To the grave sweetness on the brow of truth:
Shall they shower blessings, with their beams di-
vine,
Down to the watcher on the stormy sea,
And to the pilgrim toiling for his shrine
Through some wild pass of rocky Apennine,
And to the wanderer lone
On wastes of Afric thrown,
And not to me?
Am I a thing forsaken,
And is the gladness taken
From the bright-plmion'd nature which hath soar'd
Through realms by royal eagle ne'er explored,
And, bathing there in streams of fiery light,
Found strength to gaze upon the Infinite?

And now an alien!—Wherefore must this be?
How shall I rend the chain!
How drink rich life again
From those pure urns of radiance, swelling free?
Father of Spirits! let me turn to thee!

Oh! if too much exulting in her dower,
My soul not yet to lowly thought subdued,
Hath stood without thee on her hill of power—
A fearful and a dazzling solitude!
And therefore from that haughty summit's crown,
To dim desertion is by thee cast down;
Behold! thy child submissively hath bow'd—
Shine on him through the cloud!

At the now darken'd earth and curtain'd heaven
Back to his vision with thy face be given!
Bear him on high once more,
But in thy strength to soar,

And wrapt and still by that o'ershadowing might
Forth on the empyreal blaze to look with chasten-
ed sight.

Or if it be, that like the ark's lone dove,
My thoughts go forth, and find no resting-place,
No sheltering home of sympathy and love,
In the responsive bosoms of my race,
And back return, a darkness and a weight,
Till my unanswer'd heart grows desolate—
Yet, yet sustain me, Holiest!—I am vow'd
To solemn service high;
And shall the spirit, for thy tasks endow'd,
Sink on the threshold of the sanctuary,
Fainting beneath the burden of the day,
Because no human tone,
Unto the altar-stone,
Of that pure spousal fane inviolate,
Where it should make eternal truth its mate,
May cheer the sacred solitary way?

Oh! be the whisper of thy voice within
Enough to strengthen! Be the hope to win
A more deep-seeing homage for thy name,
Far, far beyond the burning dream of fame!
Make me thine only! Let me add but one
To those refulgent steps all undefiled,
Which glorious minds have piled
Thro' bright self-offering, earnest, child-like, lone
For mounting to thy throne!
And let my soul, upborne
On wings of inner morn,
Find, in illumined secrecy, the sense
Of that blest work, its own high recompense.

The dimness melts away,
That on your glory lay,
O ye majestic watchers of the skies!
Through the dissolving veil,
Which made each aspect pale,
Your gladd'ning fires once more I recognize;
And once again a shower
Of hope, and joy, and power,
Streams on my soul from your immortal eyes.

And, if that splendour to my sober'd sight
Come tremulous, with more of pensive light—
Something, though beautiful, yet deeply fraught,
With more that pierces thro' each fold of thought
Than I was wont to trace
On Heaven's unshadow'd face—
Be it e'en so!—be mine, though set apart
Unto a radiant ministry, yet still
A lowly, fearful, self-distrusting heart;
Bow'd before thee, O Mightiest! whose blest will
All the pure stars rejoicingly fulfil.

---

## THE TRAVELLER'S EVENING SONG.

---

Father, guide me! Day declines,
Hollow winds are in the pines;
Darkly waves each giant bough
O'er the sky's last crimson glow;
Hush'd is now the convent's bell,
Which erewhile with breezy swell
From the purple mountains bore
Greeting to the sunset-shore.
Now the sailor's vesper-hymn
Dies away.
Father! in the forest dim,
Be my stay!

In the low and shivering thrill
Of the leaves that late hung still;
In the dull and muffled tone
Of the sea-wave's distant moan;
In the deep tints of the sky,
There are signs of tempest nigh.
Ominous, with sullen sound,
Falls the closing dusk around.
Father! through the storm and shade
O'er the wild,
Oh! be Thou the lone one's aid—
Save thy child!

Many a swift and sounding plume
Homewards, through the healing gloom,
O'er my way hath flitted fast,
Since the farewell sunbeam pass'd
From the chestnut's ruddy bark,
And the pools, now lone and dark,
Where the wakening night-winds sigh
Through the long reeds mournfully.
Homeward, homeward, all things haste—
 God of might!
Shield the homeless 'midst the waste,
 Be his light!

In his distant cradle nest,
Now my babe is laid to rest;
Beautiful his slumber seems
With a glow of heavenly dreams,
Beautiful, o'er that bright sleep,
Hang soft eyes of fondness deep,
Where his mother bends to pray,
For the loved and far away.—
Father! guard that household bower,
 Hear that prayer!
Back, through thine all-guiding power,
 Lead me there!

Darker, wilder, grows the night—
Not a star sends quivering light
Through the massy arch of shade
By the stern old forest made.
Thou! to whose unslumbering eyes
All my pathway open lies,
By thy Son, who knew distress
In the lonely wilderness,
Where no roof to that blest head
Shelter gave—
Father! through the time of dread,
 Save, oh! save!

---

## BURIAL OF AN EMIGRANT'S CHILD
## IN THE FORESTS

SCENE.—*The banks of a solitary river in an American Forest. A tent under pine-trees in the foreground. AGNES sitting before the tent with a child in her arms, apparently sleeping.*

*Agnes.* Surely 'tis all a dream—a fever-dream!
The desolation and the agony—
The strange red sunrise—and the gloomy woods,
So terrible with their dark giant boughs,
And the broad lonely river! all a dream!
And my boy's voice will wake me, with its clear,
Wild, singing tones, as they were wont to come,
Through the wreath'd sweet-brier at my lattice
 panes,
In happy, happy England! Speak to me!
Speak to thy mother, bright one! she hath watch'd
All the dread night beside thee, till her brain
Is darken'd by swift waves of fantasies,
And her soul faint with longing for thy voice.
Oh! I *must* wake him with one gentle kiss
On his fair brow!
 (*Shudderingly*) The strange damp thrilling
 touch!
The marble chill! Now, now it rushes back—
Now I know all!—dead—*dead!*—a fearful word!
My boy hath left me in the wilderness,
To journey on without the blessed light
In his deep loving eyes—he's gone—he's gone!
 [*Her* HUSBAND *enters.*

*Husband.* Agnes, my Agnes! hast thou look'd
 thy last
On our sweet slumberer's face? The hour is come—
The couch made ready for his last repose.
*Agnes.* Not yet, thou canst not take him from
 me yet!

If he but left me for a few short days,
This were too brief a gazing time, to draw
His angel image into my fond heart,
And fix its beauty there. And now—oh! now,
Never again the laughter of his eye
Shall send its gladd'ning summer through my soul,
Never on earth again. Yet, yet delay!
Thou canst not take him from me.
 *Husband.*    My beloved,
Is it not God hath taken him? the God
That took our first-born, o'er whose early grave
Thou didst bow down thy saint-like head, and say,
'His will be done!"
 *Agnes.*   Oh! that near household grave,
Under the turf of England, seem'd not half,
Not half so much to part me from my child
As these dark woods. It lay beside our home,
And I could watch the sunshine, through all hours
Loving and clinging to the grassy spot,
And I could dress its greensward with fresh flow-
 ers—
Familiar, meadow flowers. O'er *thee*, my babe,
The primrose will not blossom! Oh! that now,
Together, by thy fair young sister's side,
We lay 'midst England's valleys!
 *Husband.*   Dost thou grieve,
Agnes! that thou hast follow'd o'er the deep
An exile's fortunes? If it *thus* can be,
Then, after many a conflict cheerily met,
My spirit sinks at last.
 *Agnes.*   Forgive, forgive!
My Edmund, pardon me! Oh! grief is wild—
Forget its words, quick spray-drops from a fount
Of unknown bitterness! Thou art my home!
Mine only and my blessed one! Where'er
Thy warm heart beats in its true nobleness,
*There* is my country! *there* my head shall rest,
And throb no more. Oh! still, by thy strong love,
Bear up the feeble reed!
 [*Kneeling with the child in her arms*
  And thou, my God!
Hear my soul's cry from this dread wilderness,
Oh! hear, and pardon me! If I have made
This treasure, sent from thee, too much the ark
Fraught with mine earthward-clinging happiness,
Forgetting Him who gave, and might resume,
Oh, pardon me!
  If nature hath rebell'd,
And from thy light turn'd wilfully away,
Making a midnight of her agony,
When the despairing passion of her clasp
Was from its idol stricken at one touch
Of thine Almighty hand—oh, pardon me!
By thy Son's anguish, pardon! In the soul
The tempests and the waves will know thy voice—
Father, say " Peace, be still!"
 [*Giving the child to her husband*
  Farewell, my babe!
Go from my bosom now to other rest!
With this last kiss on thine unsullied brow,
And on thy pale calm cheek these contrite tears,
I yield thee to thy Maker!
 *Husband.*   Now, my wife,
Thine own meek holiness beams forth once more
A light upon my path. Now shall I bear,
From thy dear arms, the slumberer to repose—
With a calm, trustful heart.
 *Agnes.*   My Edmund! where—
Where wilt thou lay him?
 *Husband.*   Seest thou where the spire
Of yon dark cypress reddens in the sun
To burning gold?—there—o'er yon willow-tuft!
Under that native desert monument
Lies his lone bed. Our Hubert, since the dawn,
With the grey mosses of the wilderness
Hath lined it closely through; and there breathed
 forth,
E'en from the fullness of his own pure heart,
A wild, sad forest hymn—a song of tears,
Which thou wilt learn to love. I heard the boy
Chanting it o'er his solitary task,
As wails a wood-bird to the thrilling leaves,
Perchance unconsciously.
 *Agnes.*   My gentle son!
Th' affectionate, the gifted!—With what joy—

Edmund, rememberest thou?—with what bright
      joy
His baby brother ever to his arms
Would spring from rosy sleep, and playfully
Hide the rich clusters of his gleaming hair
In that kind youthful breast!—Oh! now no more—
But strengthen me, my God! and melt my heart,
Even to a well-spring of adoring tears,
For many a blessing left.
 (*Bending over the Child.*) Once more farewell!
Oh! the pale piercing sweetness of that look!
How can it be sustain'd? Away, away!
     [*After a short pause*
Edmund, my woman's nature still is weak—
I cannot see thee render dust to dust!
Go thou, my husband, to thy solemn task;
I will rest here, and still my soul with prayer
Till thy return.
 *Husband.*  Then strength be with thy prayer
Peace on thy bosom! Faith and heavenly hope
Unto thy spirit! Fare thee well awhile!
We must be pilgrims of the woods again,
After this mournful hour.

  [*He goes out with the child. Agnes kneels in
  prayer. After a time, voices without are heard
  singing*

THE FUNERAL HYMN.

  Where the long reeds quiver,
   Where the pines make moan,
  By the forest river,
   Sleeps our babe alone.
England's field flowers may not deck his grave,
Cypress shadows o'er him darkly wave.

  Woods unknown receive him,
   'Midst the mighty wild;
  Yet with God we leave him,
   Blessed, blessed child!
And our tears gush o'er his lovely dust,
Mournfully, yet still from hearts of trust.

  Though his eye hath brighten'd
   Oft our weary way,
  And his clear laugh lighten'd
   Half our heart's dismay;
Still in hope we give back what was given,
Yielding up the beautiful to Heaven.

  And to her who bore him,
   Her who long must weep,
  Yet shall Heaven restore him
   From his pale, sweet sleep!
Those blue eyes of love and peace again
Through her soul will shine, undimm'd by pain.

  Where the long reeds quiver,
   Where the pines make moan,
  Leave we by the river,
   Earth to earth alone!
God and Father! may our journeyings on
Lead to where the blessed boy is gone!

  From the exile's sorrow,
   From the wanderer's dread
  Of the night and morrow,
   Early, brightly fled;
Thou hast call'd him to a sweeter home
Than our lost one o'er the ocean's foam.

  Now let thought behold him
   With his angel look,
  Where those arms enfold him,
   Which benignly took
Israel's babes to their Good Shepherd's breast,
When his voice their tender meekness blest.

  Turn thee now, fond mother
   From thy dead, oh, turn!
  Linger not, young brother,
   Here to dream and mourn:
Only kneel once more around the sod,
Knee, and bow submitted hearts to God!

EASTER-DAY

IN A MOUNTAIN CHURCH-YARD.

There is a wakening on the mighty hills,
 A kindling with the spirit of the morn!
Bright gleams are scatter'd from the thousand rills
 And a soft visionary hue is born
   On the young foliage, worn
By all the embosom'd woods—a silvery green,
Made up of spring and dew, harmoniously serene

And lo! where floating through a glory, sings
 The lark, alone amidst a crystal sky!
Lo! where the darkness of his buoyant wings,
 Against a soft and rosy cloud on high,
   Trembles with melody!
While the far-echoing solitudes rejoice
To the rich laugh of music in that voice.

But purer light than of the early sun
 Is on you cast, O mountains of the earth,
And for your dwellers nobler joy is won
 Than the sweet echoes of the skylark's mirth,
   By this glad morning's birth!
And gifts more precious by its breath are shed
Than music on the breeze, dew on the violet's
 head.

Gifts for the *soul*, from whose illumin'd eye,
 O'er nature's face the colouring glory flows;
Gifts from the fount of immortality,
 Which, fill'd with balm, unknown to human woes,
   Lay hush'd in dark repose,
Till thou, bright day-spring! mad'st its waves our
 own,
By thine unsealing of the burial-stone.

Sing, then, with all your choral strains, ye hills!
 And let a full victorious tone be given,
By rock and cavern, to the wind which fills
 Your urn like depths with sound! The tomb is
 riven,
   The radiant gate of Heaven
Unfolded—and the stern, dark shadow cast
By death's o'ersweeping wing, from the earth's
 bosom past.

And you, ye graves! upon whose turf I stand,
 Girt with the slumber of the hamlet's dead,
Time with a soft and reconciling hand
 The covering mantle of bright moss hath spread
   O'er every narrow bed:
But not by time, and not by nature sown
Was the celestial seed, whence round you peace
 hath grown.

Christ hath arisen! oh! not one cherish'd head
 Hath, 'midst the flowery sods, been pillow'd here
Without a hope, (howe'er the heart hath bled
 In its vain yearnings o'er the unconscious bier,)
   A hope, upspringing clear
From those majestic tidings of the morn,
Which lit the living way to all of woman born.

Thou hast wept mournfully, O human love!
 E'en on this greensward; night hath heard thy cry
Heart-stricken one! thy precious dust above,
 Night, and the hills, which sent forth no reply
   Unto thine agony!
But He who wept like thee, thy Lord, thy guide,
Christ hath arisen, O love! thy tears shall all be
 dried.

Dark must have been the gushing of those tears.
 Heavy the unsleeping phantom of the tomb
On thine impassion'd soul, in elder years
 When, burden'd with the mystery of its doom,
   Mortality's thick gloom
Hung o'er the sunny world, and with the breath
Of the triumphant rose came blending thoughts of
 death.

By thee, sad Love, and by thy sister, Fear,
 Then, was the ideal robe of beauty wrought
To veil that haunting shadow, still too near,
 Still ruling secretly the conqueror's thought,

And where the board was fraught
With wine and myrtles in the summer-bower,
Felt, e'en when disavow'd, a presence and a power.

But that dark night is closed : and o'er the dead,
*Here*, where the gleamy primrose tufts have blown,
And where the mountain heath a couch has
    spread,
And, settling oft on some gray-letter'd stone ;
    The red-breast warbles lone ;
And the wild bee's deep, drowsy murmurs pass
Like a low thrill of harp-strings through the grass.

Here, 'midst the chambers of the Christian's sleep,
*We* o'er death's gulf may look with trusting eye,
For hope sits, dove-like, on the gloomy deep,
And the green hills wherein these valleys lie
    Seem all one sanctuary
Of holiest thought — nor needs their fresh bright
    sod,
Urn, wreath or shrine, for tombs all dedicate to
    God.

Christ hath arisen !—O mountain peaks ! attest,
Witness, resounding glen and torrent-wave,
The immortal courage in the human breast
Sprung from that victory—tell how oft the brave
    To camp 'midst rock and cave,
Nerved by those words, their struggling faith have
    borne,
Planting the cross on high above the clouds of
    morn.

The Alps have heard sweet hymnings for to-day—
Ay, and wild sounds of sterner, deeper tone,
Have thrill'd their pines, when those that knelt
    to pray
Rose up to arm ! the pure, high snows have known
    A colouring not their own,
But from true hearts which by that crimson stain
Gave token of a trust that call'd no suffering vain

Those days are past — the mountains wear no
    more
The solemn splendour of the martyr's blood,
And may that awful record, as of yore,
Never again be known to field or flood !
    E'en though the faithful stood,
A noble army, in the exulting sight
Of earth and heaven, which blest their battle for
    the right

But many a martyrdom by hearts unshaken
Is yet borne silently in homes obscure ;
And many a bitter cup is meekly taken ;
And, for the strength whereby the just and pure
    Thus steadfastly endure,
Glory to Him whose victory won that dower,
Him, from whose rising stream'd that robe of spirit
    power.

Glory to Him ! Hope to the suffering breast !
Light to the nations ! He hath roll'd away
The mists, which, gathering into deathlike rest,
Between the soul and Heaven's calm ether lay—
    His love hath made it day
With those that sat in darkness.—Earth and sea !
Lift up glad strains for man by truth divine made
    free !

---

## THE CHILD READING THE BIBLE

"A dancing shape, an image gay,
To haunt, to startle, to waylay.
    *    *    *    *
A being breathing thoughtful breath,
A traveller between life and death."
                  *Wordsworth.*

---

I saw him at his sport erewhile,
    The bright exulting boy,
Like summer's lightning came the smile
    Of his young spirit's joy ;
A flash that whereso'er it broke,
To life undreamt-of beauty woke.

His fair locks waved in sunny play,
    By a clear fountain's side,
Where jewel-colour'd pebbles lay
    Beneath the shallow tide ;
And pearly spray at times would meet
The glancing of his fairy feet.

He twined him wreaths of all spring-flowers,
    Which drank that streamlet's dew ;
He flung them o'er the wave in showers,
    Till, gazing, scarce I knew
Which seem'd more pure, or bright, or wild,
The singing fount or laughing child.

To look on all that joy and bloom
    Made earth one festal scene,
Where the dull shadow of the tomb
    Seem'd as it ne'er had been.
How could one image of decay,
Steal o'er the dawn of such clear day ?

I saw once more that aspect bright—
    The boy's meek head was bow'd
In silence o'er the Book of Light,
    And like a golden cloud,
The still cloud of a pictured sky—
His locks droop'd round it lovingly

And if my heart had deem'd him fair,
    When in the fountain glade,
A creature of the sky and air,
    Almost on wings he play'd ;
Oh ! how much holier beauty now
Lit the young human being's brow

The being born to toil, to die,
    To break forth from the tomb,
Unto far nobler destiny
    Than waits the sky-lark's plume !
I saw him, in that thoughtful hour,
Win the first knowledge of his dower.

The *soul*, the awakening *soul* I saw,
    My watching eye could trace
The shadows of its new-born awe,
    Sweeping o'er that fair face :
As o'er a flower might pass the shade
By some dread angel's pinion made !

The soul, the mother of deep fears,
    Of high hopes infinite,
Of glorious dreams, mysterious tears,
    Of sleepless inner sight ;
Lovely, but solemn, it arose,
Unfolding what no more might close

The red-leaved tablets,* undefiled,
    As yet, by evil thought—
Oh ! little dream'd the brooding child,
    Of what within me wrought,
While *his* young heart first burn'd and stirr'd
And quiver'd to the eternal word.

And reverently my spirit caught
    The reverence of *his* gaze,
A sight with dew of blessing fraught
    To hallow after-days ;
To make the proud heart meekly wise,
By the sweet faith in those calm eyes.

It seem'd as if a temple rose
    Before me brightly there,
And in the depths of its repose
    My soul o'erflow'd with prayer,
Feeling a solemn presence nigh—
The power of infant sanctity !

O Father ! mould my heart once more,
    By thy prevailing breath !
Teach me, oh ! teach me to adore
    E'en with that pure one's faith ;
A faith, all made of love and light,
Child-like, and, therefore, full of might

---

* "All this, and more than this, is now engraved upon the red sacred tablets of my heart."—*Harwood.*

## A POET'S DYING HYMN.

*Be mute who will, who can,*
*Yet I will praise thee with impassion'd voice!*
*Me didst thou constitute a priest of thine*
*In such a temple as we now behold,*
*Rear'd for thy presence; therefore am I bound*
*To worship, here and everywhere.*

*Wordsworth.*

THE blue, deep, glorious heavens!—I lift mine eye,
  And bless thee, O my God! that I have met
And own'd thine image in the majesty
  Of their calm temple still!—that never yet
There hath thy face been shrouded from my sight
By noontide blaze, or sweeping storm of night:
      I bless thee, O my God!

That now still clearer, from their pure expanse,
  I see the mercy of thine aspect shine,
Touching death's features with a lovely glance
  Of light, serenely, solemnly divine,
And lending to each holy star a ray
As of kind eyes, that woo my soul away:
      I bless thee, O my God!

That I have heard thy voice, nor been afraid,
  In the earth's garden—'midst the mountains old,
And the low thrillings of the forest shade,
  And the wild sounds of waters uncontroll'd,
And upon many a desert plain and shore—
No solitude—for there I felt *thee* more:
      I bless thee, O my God!

And if thy spirit on thy child hath shed
  The gift, the vision of the unseal'd eye,
To pierce the mist o'er life's deep meanings spread,
  To reach the hidden fountain-urns that lie
Far in man's heart—if I have kept it free
And pure—a consecration unto thee:
      I bless thee, O my God!

If my soul's utterance hath by thee been fraught
  With an awakening power—if thou hast made,
Like the wing'd seed, the breathings of my thought
  And by the swift winds bid them be convey'd
To lands of other lays, and there become
Native as early melodies of home:
      I bless thee, O my God!

Not for the brightness of a mortal wreath,
  Not for a place 'midst kingly minstrels dead,
But that perchance, a faint gale of thy breath,
  A still small whisper in my song hath led
One struggling spirit upwards to thy throne,
Or but one hope, one prayer:—for this alone
      I bless thee, O my God!

That I have loved—that I have known the love
  Which troubles in the soul the tearful springs,
Yet, with a colouring halo from above,
  Tinges and glorifies all earthly things,
Whate'er its anguish or its woe may be,
Still weaving links for intercourse with thee:
      I bless thee, O my God!

That by the passion of its deep distress,
  And by the o'erflowing of its mighty prayer,
And by the yearning of its tenderness,
  Too full for words upon their stream to bear,
I have been drawn still closer to thy shrine,
Well-spring of love, the unfathom'd, the divine:
      I bless thee, O my God!

That hope hath ne'er my heart or song forsaken,
  High hope, which even from mystery, doubt, or
      dread,
Calmly, rejoicingly, the things hath taken,
  Whereby its torchlight for the race was fed,
That passing storms have only fann'd the fire,
Which pierced them still with its triumphal spire,
      I bless thee, O my God!

Now art thou calling me in every gale,
  Each sound and token of the dying day:
Thou leav'st me not, though early life grows pale.
  I am not darkly sinking to decay:
But, hour by hour, my soul's dissolving shroud
Melts off to radiance, as a silvery cloud.
      I bless thee, O my God!

And if this earth, with all its choral streams,
  And crowning woods, and soft or solemn sky,
And mountain sanctuaries for poet's dreams,
  Be lovely still in my departing eyes—
'Tis not that fondly I would linger here,
But that thy foot-prints on its dust appear:
      I bless thee, O my God!

And that the tender shadowing I behold,
  The tracery veining every leaf and flower,
Of glories cast in more consummate mould,
  No longer vassals to the changeful hour;
That life's last roses to my thoughts can bring
Rich visions of imperishable spring:
      I bless thee, O my God!

Yes! the young vernal voices in the skies
  Woo me not back, but, wandering past mine ear
Seem heralds of th' eternal melodies,
  The spirit-music, imperturb'd and clear;
The full of soul, yet passionate no more—
Let me too, joining those pure strains, adore!
      I bless thee, O my God!

Now aid, sustain me still!—to thee I come,
  Make thou my dwelling where thy children are
And for the hope of that immortal home,
  And for thy Son, the bright and morning star,
The sufferer and the victor-king of death,
I bless thee with my glad song's dying breath!
      I bless thee, O my God!

THE

## FUNERAL DAY OF SIR WALTER SCOTT

*Many an eye*
*May wail the dimming of our shining star.*
*Shakspeare.*

A glorious voice hath ceased!—
Mournfully, reverently—the funeral chant
Breathe reverently!—There is a dreamy sound,
A hollow murmur of the dying year,
In the deep woods:—let it be wild and sad!
A more Æolian melancholy tone
Than ever wail'd o'er bright things perishing!
For *that* is passing from the darken'd land,
Which the green summer will not bring us back—
Though all her songs return—The funeral chant
Breathe reverently!—They bear the mighty forth,
The kingly ruler in the realms of mind—
They bear him through the household paths, the
    groves,
Where every tree had music of its own
To his quick ear of knowledge taught by love—
And he is silent!—Past the living stream
They bear him now; the stream, whose kindly
    voice
On alien shores his true heart burn'd to hear—
And he is silent. O'er the heathery hills,
Which his own soul had mantled with a light
Richer than autumn's purple, now they move—
And he is silent!—he, whose flexile lips
Were but unseal'd, and, lo! a thousand forms,
From every pastoral glen and fern-clad height,
In glowing life upsprang:—Vassal and chief,
Rider and steed, with shout and bugle-peal,
Fast rushing through the brightly troubled air,
Like the wild huntsman's band. And still they
    live,
To those fair scenes imperishably bound,
And, from the mountain mist still flashing by.

Startle the wanderer who hath listen'd there
To the seer's voice: phantoms of colour'd thought
Surviving him who raised.—O eloquence!
O power, whose breathings thus could wake th
    dead!
Who shall wake *thee?* lord of the buried past!
And art thou *there*—to those dim nations join'd,
Thy subject host so long?—The wand is dropp'd,
The bright lamp broken which the gifted hand
Touch'd and the genii came!—Sing reverently
The funeral chant!—The mighty is borne home—
And who shall be his mourners?—Youth and age
For each hath felt his magic—love and grief,
For he hath communed with the heart of each;
Yes—the free spirit of humanity
May join the august procession, for to him
Its mysteries have been tributary things,
And all its accents known:—from field or wave,
Never was conqueror on his battle bier,
By the vail'd banner and the muffled drum,
And the proud drooping of the crested head,
More nobly follow'd home.—The last abode,
The voiceless dwelling of the bard is reach'd:
A still majestic spot! girt solemnly
With all th' imploring beauty of decay;
A stately couch 'midst ruins! meet for him
With his bright fame to rest in, as a king
Of other days, laid lonely with his sword
Beneath his head.   Sing reverently the chant
O'er the honour'd grave!—the *grave!*—oh, say
Rather the shrine!—An altar for the love,
The light, soft pilgrim steps, the votive wreaths
Of years unborn—a place where leaf and flower
By that which dies not of the sovereign dead,
Shall be made holy things—where every weed
Shall have its portion of th' inspiring gift
From buried glory breathed.  And now, what strain
Making victorious melody ascend
High above sorrow's dirge, befits the tomb
Where he that sway'd the nations thus is laid—
The crown'd of men?

     A lowly, lowly song

   Lowly and solemn be
   Thy children's cry to thee,
     Father divine!
   A hymn of suppliant breath,
   Owning that life and death
     Alike are thine!

   A spirit on its way,
   Sceptred the earth to sway,
     From thee was sent:
   Now call'st thou back thine own—
   Hence is that radiance flown—
     To earth but lent.

   Watching in breathless awe,
   The bright head bow'd we saw,
     Beneath thy hand!
   Fill'd by one hope, one fear,
   Now o'er a brother's bier,
     Weeping we stand.

   How hath he pass'd!—the lord
   Of each deep bosom chord,
     To meet thy sight,
   Unmantled and alone,
   On thy blest mercy thrown,
     O Infinite!

   So, from his harvest home,
   Must the tired peasant come;
     So, in one trust,
   Leader and king must yield
   The naked soul, reveal'd
     To thee, All Just!

   The sword of many a fight—
   What *then* shall be its might?
     The lofty lay,
   That rush'd on eagle wing—
   What shall its memory bring?
     What hope, what stay?

   O Father! in that hour,
   When earth all succouring power
     Shall disavow;
   When spear, and shield, and crown,
   In faintness are cast down—
     Sustain us, Thou!

   By Him who bow'd to take
   The death-cup for our sake,
     The thorn, the rod;
   From whom the last dismay
   Was not to pass away—
     Aid us, O God!

   Tremblers beside the grave,
   We call on thee to save,
     Father, divine!
   Hear, hear our suppliant breath,
   Keep us, in life and death,
     Thine, only thine!

---

## THE PRAYER IN THE WILDERNESS.

#### Suggested by a Picture of Correggio's.

In the deep wilderness unseen she pray'd,
The daughter of Jerusalem; alone,
With all the still small whispers of the night,
And with the searching glances of the stars,
And with her God. alone:—she lifted up
Her sweet, sad voice, and, trembling o'er her head
The dark leaves thrill'd with prayer—the tearfu
    prayer
Of woman's quenchless, yet repentant love.

   Father of Spirits, hear!
Look on the inmost heart to thee reveal'd,
Look on the fountain of the burning tear,
Before thy sight in solitude unseal'd!

   Hear, Father! hear, and aid!
If I have loved too well, if I have shed,
In my vain fondness, o'er a mortal head,
Gifts, on thy shrine, my God! more fitly laid.

   If I have sought to live
But in *one* light, and made a human eye
The lonely star of mine idolatry,
Thou that art Love! oh, pity and forgive!

   Chasten'd and school'd at last,
No more, no more my struggling spirit burns,
But fix'd on thee, from that wild worship turns—
What have I said?—the deep dream is not past!

   Yet hear!—if *still* I love,
Oh! still too fondly—if, for ever seen,
An earthly image comes, my heart between,
And thy calm glory, Father! throned above!

   If still a voice is near,
(E'en while I strive these wanderings to contro',)
An earthly voice, disquieting my soul
With its deep music, too intensely dear.

   O Father draw to thee
My lost affections back!—the dreaming eyes
Clear from their mist—sustain the heart that dies,
Give the worn soul once more its pinions free!

   I must love on, O God!
This bosom must love on! but let thy breath
Touch and make pure the flame that knows no
    death,
Bearing it up to Heaven!—Love's own abode!

Ages and ages past, the wilderness,
With its dark cedars, and the thrilling night,
With her clear stars, and the mysterious winds,
That waft all sound, were conscious of those
    prayers.
How many such hath woman's bursting heart
*Since then*, in silence and in darkness breathed,
Like the dim night-flower's odour, up to God?

## PRISONERS' EVENING SERVICE

### A SCENE OF THE FRENCH REVOLUTION.*

From their spheres
The stars of human glory are cast down ;
Perish the roses and the flowers of kings,
Princes and emperors, and the crown and palms
Of all the mighty, wither'd and consumed !
Nor is power given to lowliest innocence
Long to protect her own.

*Wordsworth.*

Scene—*Prison of the Luxembourg, in Paris, during
the Reign of Terror.*

D'AUBIGNÉ, an *aged Royalist—* BLANCHE, *his
Daughter, a young girl.*

*Blanche.*   What was our doom, my father?—In
    thine arms
I lay unconsciously through that dread hour.
Tell me the sentence !—Could our judges look,
Without relenting, on thy silvery hair ?
Was there not mercy, father ?—Will they not
Restore us to our home.
*D'Aubigné.*         Yes, my poor child !
They send us home.
*Blanche.*         Oh ! shall we gaze again
On the bright Loire ?—Will the old hamlet spire,
And the gray turret of our own château,
Look forth to greet us through the dusky elms ?
Will the kind voices of our villagers,
The loving laughter in their children's eyes,
Welcome us back at last ?—But how is this ?—
Father ! thy glance is clouded—on thy brow,
There sits no joy !
*D'Aubigné.*      Upon my brow, dear girl,
There sits, I trust, such deep and solemn peace
As may befit the Christian, who receives
And recognizes, in submissive awe,
The summons of his God.
*Blanche.*         Thou dost not mean—
No, no ! it cannot be !—Didst thou not say
They sent us *home ?*
*D'Aubigné.*      Where is the spirit's home ?—
Oh ! most of all, in these dark evil days,
Where should it be—but in that world serene,
Beyond the sword's reach, and the tempest's pow-
    er—
Where, but in Heaven?
*Blanche.*         My father !
*D'Aubigné.*            *We must die.*
We must look up to God, and calmly die.—
Come to my heart, and weep there !—for awhile
Give Nature's passion way, then brightly rise
In the still courage of a woman's heart !
Do I not know thee ?—Do I ask too much
From mine own noble Blanche ?
*Blanche.* (*falling on his bosom.*) Oh ! clasp me
    fast !
Thy trembling child !—Hide, hide me in thine
    arms—
Father !
*D'Aubigné.*  Alas ! my flower, thou'rt young to
    go—
Young, and so fair !—Yet were it worse methinks,
To leave thee where the gentle and the brave,
The loyal-hearted and the chivalrous,
And they that loved their God, have all been swept,
Like the sere leaves, away.—For them no hearth
Through the wide land was left inviolate,
No altar holy ; therefore did they fall,
Rejoicing to depart.—The soil is steep'd
In noble blood ! the temples are gone down ;
The voice of prayer is hush'd, or fearfully
Mutter'd, like sounds of guilt.—Why, who would
    live ?

Who hath not panted, as a dove, to flee,
To quit for ever the dishonour'd soil,
The burden'd air ?—Our God upon the cross—
Our king upon the scaffold*—let us think
Of *these*—and fold endurance to our hearts,
And bravely die !
*Blanche.*         A dark and fearful way !
An evil doom for thy dear honour'd head !
Oh ! thou, the kind, the gracious !—whom all eyes
Bless'd as they look'd upon !—Speak yet again—
Say, will they part us ?
*D'Aubigné.*         No, my Blanche ; in death
We shall not be divided.
*Blanche.*            Thanks to God !
He, by thy glance, will aid me—I shall see
His light before me to the last.—And when—
Oh ! pardon these weak shrinkings of thy child !—
When shall the hour befall ?
*D'Aubigné.*            Oh ! swiftly now,
And suddenly, with brief dread interval,
Comes down the mortal stroke.—But of that hour
As yet I know not.—Each low throbbing pulse
Of the quick pendulum may usher in
Eternity !
*Blanche,* (*kneeling before him.*) My father ! lay
    thy hand
On thy poor Blanche's head, and once again
Bless her with thy deep voice of tenderness,
Thus breathing saintly courage through her soul,
Ere we are call'd.
*D'Aubigné.*   If I may speak through tears !—
Well may I bless thee, fondly, fervently,
Child of my heart !—thou who dost look on me
With thy lost mother's angel eyes of love !
Thou that hast been a brightness in my path,
A guest of Heaven unto my lonely soul,
A stainless lily in my widow'd house,
There springing up — with soft light round thee
    shed—
For immortality !—Meek child of God !
I bless thee—He will bless thee !—In his love
He calls thee now from this rude stormy world
To thy Redeemer's breast.—And thou wilt die !
As thou hast lived—my duteous, holy Blanche !
In trusting and serene submissiveness,
Humble, yet full of Heaven.
*Blanche,* (*rising.*)      Now is there strength
Infused through all my spirit.—I can rise
And say, "Thy will be done !"
*D'Aubigné,* (*pointing upwards.*) See'st thou, my
    child,
Yon faint light in the west ?  The signal star
Of our due vesper service, gleaming in
Through the close dungeon grating ! Mournfully
It seems to quiver ; yet shall this night pass,
*This* night alone, without the lifted voice
Of adoration in our narrow cell,
As if unworthy Fear or wavering Faith
Silenced the strain ?—No ! let it waft to Heaven
The prayer, the hope of poor mortality,
In its dark hour once more !—And we will sleep—
Yes—calmly sleep, when our last rite is closed.

[*They sing together.*

PRISONERS' EVENING HYMN.

We see no more in thy pure skies,
How soft, O God ! the sunset dies ;
How every colour'd hill and wood
Seems melting in the golden flood :
Yet, by the precious memories won
From bright hours now for ever gone,
Father ! o'er all thy works, we know,
Thou still art shedding beauty's glow ;
Still touching every cloud and tree
With glory, eloquent of Thee ;
Still feeding all thy flowers with light,
Though man hath barr'd it from our sight.

* The last days of two prisoners in the Luxembourg, Sillery and La Source, so affectingly described by Helen Maria Williams, in her Letters from France, gave rise to this little scene. These two victims had composed a simple hymn, which they every night sung together in a low and restrained voice.

* A French royalist officer, dying upon a field of battle, and hearing some one near him ut'ering the most plaintive lamentations, turned towards the sufferer, and thus addressed him. "My friend, whoever you may be, remember that your God expired upon the cross—your king upon the scaffold—and he who now speaks to you has had his limbs shot from under him.  Meet your fate as becomes thee . . ."

We know Thou reign'st, the Unchanging One, th'
     All Just!
And bless thee still with free and boundless trust!

We read no more, O God! thy ways
On earth, in these wild evil days,
The red sword in th' oppressor's hand
Is ruler of the weeping land;
Fallen are the faithful and the pure,
No shrine is spared, no hearth secure.
Yet, by the deep voice from the past,
Which tells us these things cannot last—
And by the hope which finds no a.k.
Save in thy breast, when storms grow dark—
We trust thee!—As the sailor knows
That in its place of bright repose
His pole-star burns, though mist and cloud
May veil it with a midnight shroud.
We know thou reign'st!—All Holy One, All Just!
And bless thee still with love's own boundless trust.

We feel no more that aid is nigh,
When our faint hearts within us die.
We suffer—and we know our doom
Must be one suffering till the tomb.
Yet, by the anguish of thy Son
When his last hour came darkly on—
By his dread cry, the air which rent
In terror of abandonment—
And by his parting word, which rose
Through faith victorious o'er all woes—
We know that Thou mayst wound, mayst break
The spirit, but wilt ne'er forsake!
Sad suppliants whom our brethren spurn,
In our deep need to Thee we turn!
To whom but Thee?—All Merciful, All Just!
In life, in death, we yield thee boundless trust.

HYMN OF THE VAUDOIS MOUNTAINEERS
IN TIMES OF PERSECUTION.

"Thanks be to God for the mountains!"
                    *Howitt's Book of the Seasons.*

For the strength of the hills we bless thee,
     Our God, our fathers' God!
Thou hast made thy children mighty,
     By the touch of the mountain sod.
Thou hast fix'd our ark of refuge
     Where the spoiler's foot ne'er trod;
For the strength of the hills we bless thee,
     Our God, our fathers' God!

We are watchers of a beacon
     Whose light must never die;
We are guardians of an altar
     'Midst the silence of the sky:
The rocks yield founts of courage,
     Struck forth as by thy rod;
For the strength of the hills we bless thee,
     Our God, our fathers' God!

For the dark resounding caverns,
     Where thy still, small voice is heard;
For the strong pines of the forests,
     That by thy breath are stirr'd;
For the storms, on whose free pinions
     Thy spirit walks abroad;
For the strength of the hills we bless thee,
     Our God, our fathers' God!

The royal eagle darteth
     On his quarry from the heights,
And the stag that knows no master,
     Seeks there his wild delights;
But we, for thy communion,
     Have sought the mountain sod;
For the strength of the hills we bless thee,
     Our God, our fathers' God!

The banner of the chieftain,
     Far far below us waves;
The war-horse of the spearman
     Cannot reach our lofty caves:
Thy dark clouds wrap the threshold
     Of freedom's last abode;
For the strength of the hills we bless thee,
     Our God, our fathers' God!

For the shadow of thy presence,
     Round our camp of rock outspread;
For the stern defiles of battle,
     Bearing record of our dead;
For the snows and for the torrents,
     For the free heart's burial sod;
For the strength of the hills we bless thee,
     Our God, our fathers' God!

THE INDIAN'S REVENGE.

SCENE IN THE LIFE OF A MORAVIAN MISSIONARY.[*]

But by my wrongs and by my wrath,
To-morrow Areouski's breath
That fires yon Heaven with storms of death,
Shall guide me to the foe!
                    *Indian Song in "Gertrude of Wyoming."*

SCENE—*The shore of a Lake surrounded by deep
woods. A solitary cabin on its banks, overshadowed
by maple and sycamore trees. HERRMANN, the
missionary, seated alone before the cabin. The
hour is evening twilight.*

*Herrmann.* . . Was that the light from some lone
                         swift canoe
Shooting across the waters?—No, a flash
From the night's first quick fire-fly, lost again
In the deep bay of cedars. Not a bark
Is on the wave; no rustle of a breeze
Comes through the forest. In this new, strange
     world,
Oh how mysterious, how eternal, seems
The mighty melancholy of the woods!
The desert's own great spirit, infinite!
Little they know, in mine own father-land,
Along the castled Rhine, or e'en amidst
The wild Harz mountains, or the sylvan glades
Deep in the Odenwald, they little know
Of what is solitude! In hours like this,
There, from a thousand nooks, the cottage hearths
Pour forth red light through vine-hung lattices,
To guide the peasant, singing cheerily,
On the home path; while round his lowly porch,
With eager eyes awaiting his return,
The cluster'd faces of his children shine
To the clear harvest moon. Be still, fond thoughts!
Melting my spirit's grasp from heavenly hope
By your vain earthward yearnings. O my God!
Draw me still nearer, closer unto thee,
Till all the hollow of these deep desires
May with thyself be fill'd!—Be it enough
At once to gladden and to solemnize
My lonely life, if for thine altar here
In this dread temple of the wilderness,
By prayer, and toil, and watching, I may win
The offering of one heart, one human heart
Bleeding, repenting, loving!
                              Hark! a step,
An Indian tread! I know the stealthy sound—
'Tis on some quest of evil, through the grass
Gliding so serpent-like.

          [*He comes forward and meets an Indian
               warrior armed.*

               Enonio, is it thou? I see thy form
Tower stately through the dusk, yet scarce mine eye
Discerns thy face.
     *Enonio.* .          My father speaks my name.
     *Herrmann.* Are not the hunters from the chase
          return'd?
The night-fires lit? Why is my son abroad?

---

[*] Circumstances similar to those on which this scene is founded,
are recorded in Crantz's Narrative of the Moravian Missions in Green-
land, and gave rise to the dramatic sketch.

*Enonio.*     The warrior's arrow knows of
   nobler prey
Than elk or deer. Now let my father leave
The lone path free
   *Herrmann.*     The forest way is long
From the red chieftain's home. Rest thee awile
Beneath my sycamore, and we will speak
Of these things further.
   *Enonio.*     Tell me not of rest !
My heart is sleepless, and the dark night swift.—
I must begone.
   *Herrmann,* (*solemnly*) No, warrior, thou
    must stay !
The Mighty One hath given me power to search
Thy soul with piercing words—and thou must stay,
And hear me, and give answer! If thy heart
Be grown thus restless, is it not because
Within its dark folds thou hast mantled up
Some burning thought of ill ?—
*Enonio* (*with sudden impetuosity.*) How should
   I rest ?—
Last night the spirit of my brother came,
An angry shadow in the moonlight streak,
And said, "*Avenge me!*"—In the clouds this morn
I saw the frowning color of his blood—
And that, too, had a voice.—I lay at noon
Alone beside the sounding waterfall,
And through its thunder music spake a tone—
A low tone piercing all the roll of waves—
And said,"*Avenge me*"!—Therefore have I raised
The tomahawk, and strung the bow again
That I may send the shadow from my couch,
And take the strange sound from the cataract,
And sleep once more.
   *Herrmann.*     A better path, my son,
Unto the still and dewy land of sleep,
My hand in peace can guide thee—e'en the way
Thy dying brother trod.—Say, dist thou love
That lost one well ?
   *Enonio.*     Know'st thou not we grew up
Even as twin roes amidst the wilderness?
Unto the chase we journey'd in one path;
We stemmed the lake in one canoe; we lay
Beneath one oak to rest.—When fever hung
Upon my burning lips, my brother's hand
Was still beneath my head; my brother's robe
Cover'd my bosom from the chill night air.
Our lives were girdled by one belt of love,
Until he turn'd him from his fathers' gods,
And then my soul fell from him—then the grass
Grew in the way between our parted homes,
And wheresoe'er I wander'd, then it seem'd
That all the woods were silent.—I went forth—
I journeyed, with my lonely heart, afar
And so return'd—and where was he?—the earth
Owned him no more.
   *Herrmann.*     But thou thyself, since then,
Hast turned thee from the idols of thy tribe,
And like thy brother, bow'd the suppliant knee
To the one God.
   *Enonio.*     Yes, I have learn'd to pray
With my white father's words, yet all the more
My heart, that shut against my brther's love,
Hath been within me as an arrowy fire.
Burning my sleep away—In the night hush,
'Midst the strange whispers and dim shadowy
    things
Of the great forests I have call'd aloud,
" Brother! forgive, forgive!"—He answered not—
His deep voice, rising from the land of souls,
Cries but "*Avenge me !*"—and I go forth now
To slay his murderer, that when next his eyes
Gleam on me mournfully from that pale shore,
I may look up and meet their glance, and say,
" I have avenged thee."
   *Herrmann*     Oh! that human love
Should be the root of this dread bitterness,
Till heaven through all the fever'd being pours
Transmitting balsam!—Stay, Enonio, stay!
Thy brother calls thee not!—The spirit world
Where the departed go, sends back to earth
No visitants for evil.—'Tis the might
Of the strong passion, the remorseful grief
At work in thine own breast, which lends the voice
Unto the forest and the cataract.
The angry colour to the clouds of morn.

The shadow to the moonlight.—Stay, my son!
Thy brother is at peace —Beside his couch,
When of the murderer's poison'd shaft he died,
I knelt and pray'd; he named his Saviour's name
Meekly, beseechingly he spoke of thee
In pity and in love.
   *Enonio,* (*hurriedly.*) Did he not say
My arrow should avenge him ?
   *Herrmann.*     His last words
Were all forgiveness
   *Enonio.*     What! and shall the man
Who pierced him with the shaft of treachery,
Walk fearless forth in joy ?
   *Herrmann.*     Was he not once
Thy brother's friend?—Oh! trust me, not in *joy*
He walks the frowning forest. Did keen love,
Too late repentant of its heart estranged,
Wake in *thy* haunted bosom, with its train
Of sounds and shadows—and shall *he* escape?
Enonio, dream it not!—Our God, the All Just,
Unto himself reserves this royalty—
The secret chastening of the guilty heart,
The fiery touch, the scourge that purifies,
Leave it with him!—Yet make it not thy *hope*—
For that strong heart of thine—oh! listen yet—
Must, in its depths, o'ercome the very wish
For death or torture to the guilty one,
Ere it can sleep again.
   *Enonio.*     My father speaks
Of change, for man too mighty.
   *Herrmann.*     I but speak
Of that which hath been, and again must be,
If thou wouldst join thy brother, in the life
Of the bright country, where, I well believe,
His soul rejoices. *He* had known such change,
He died in peace. He, whom his tribe once named
The Avenging Eagle, took to his meek heart,
In its last pangs, the spirit of those words
Which, from the Saviour's cross, went up to
    heaven—
"*Forgive them, for they know not what they do,
Father, forgive!*"— and o'er the eternal bounds
Of that celestial kingdom, undefiled,
Where evil may not enter, he, I deem,
Hath to his Master pass'd —He waits thee there—
For love, we trust, springs heavenward from
    the grave,
Immortal in its holiness —He calls
His brother to the land of golden light
And ever-living fountains—couldst thou hear
His voice o'er those bright waters, it would say,
" My brother! oh! be pure, be merciful!
That we may meet again."
   *Enonio.* (*hesitating* ) Can I return
Unto my tribe, and unavenged ?
   *Herrmann.*     To him,
To him return, from whom thine erring steps
Have wander'd far and long!—Return, my son,
To thy Redeemer!—died he not in love—
The sinless, the divine, The Son of God—
Breathing forgiveness 'midst all agonies,
And *we*, dare *we* be ruthless?—By his aid
Shalt thou be guided to thy brother's place
'Midst the pure spirits.—Oh! retrace the way
Back to thy Saviour! he rejects no heart
E'en with the dark stains on it, if true tears
Be o'er them shower'd.—Ay, weep, thou In-
    dian chief !
For by the kindling moonlight, I behold
Thy proud lips working—weep, relieve thy soul,
Tears will not shame thy manhood, in the hour
Of its great conflict.
   *Enonio,* (*giving up his weapons to Herrmann.*)
    Father, take the bow,
Keep the sharp arrows till the hunters call
Forth to the chase once more.—And let me dwell
A little while, my father! by thy side,
That I may hear the blessed words again—
Like water brooks amidst the summer hills—
From thy true lips flow forth; for in my heart
The music and the memory of their sound
Too long have died away.
   *Herrmann.*     O, welcome back,
Friend, rescued one!—Yes, thou shalt be my guest,
And we will pray beneath my sycamore
Together, morn and eve ; and I will spread

Thy couch beside my fire, and sleep at last—
After the visiting of holy thoughts—
With dewy wing shall sink upon thine eyes—
Enter my home, and welcome, welcome back
To peace, to God, thou lost and found again!

[*They go into the cabin together—*HERMANN,
*lingering for a moment on the threshold,
looks up to the starry skies.*]

Father! that from amidst yon glorious worlds
Now look'st on us, thy children! make this hour
Blessed for ever!  May it see the birth
Of thine own image in the unfathom'd deep
Of an immortal soul;—a thing to name
With reverential thought, a solemn world!
To Thee more precious than those thousand stars
Burning on high in thy majestic Heaven!

## PRAYER AT SEA AFTER VICTORY.

The land shall never rue
So England to herself do prove but true.
*Shakspeare.*

Through evening's bright repose
A voice of prayer arose,
    When the sea-fight was done:
The sons of England knelt,
With hearts that now could melt
For on the wave her battle had been won.

Round their tall ship, the main
Heaved with a dark red stain,
    Caught not from sunset's cloud:
While with the tide swept past
Pennon and shiver'd mast,
Which to the Ocean-Queen that day had bow'd.

But free and fair on high,
A native of the sky,
    *Her* streamer met the breeze;
It flow'd o'er fearless men,
'Though hush'd and child-like then,
Before their God they gather'd on the seas.

Oh! did not thoughts of home
O'er each bold spirit come
    As from the land, sweet gales?
In every word of prayer
Had not some hearth a share,
Some bower, inviolate 'midst England's vales?

Yes! bright green spots that lay
In beauty far away,
    Hearing no billows roar;
Safer from touch of spoil,
For that day's fiery toil,
Rose on high hearts that now with love gush'd o'er.

A solemn scene, and dread!
The victors and the dead,
    The breathless burning sky!
And, passing with the race
Of waves, that keep no trace,
The wild, brief signs of human victory!

A stern, yet holy scene!
Billows where strife hath been,
    Sinking to mournful sleep:
And words that breathe the sense
Of God's omnipotence,
Making a minster of that silent deep.

Borne through such hours afar,
Thy flag hath been a star,
    Where eagle's wing ne'er flew:—
England! the unprofaned,
Those of the hearths unstain'd,
Be to the banner and the shrine be true!

## THE DAY OF FLOWERS.

### A MOTHER'S WALK WITH HER CHILD.

One spirit—His
Who wore the platted thorn with bleeding brows,
Rules universal nature.—Not a flower
But shows some touch, in freckle, freak, or stain,
Of his unrivall'd pencil.  He inspires
Their balmy odours, and imparts their hues,
And bathes their eyes with nectar.—
Happy who walks with him.
*Cowper.*

        Come to the woods, my boy!
Come to the streams and bowery dingles forth,
My happy child!  The spirit of bright hours
Wooes us in every wind; fresh wild-leaf scents
From thickets where the lonely stock-dove broods,
Enter our lattice; fitful songs of joy
Float in with each soft current of the air;
And we will hear their summons; we will give
One day to flowers, and sunshine, and glad
        thoughts,
And thou shalt revel 'midst free nature's wealth,
And, for thy mother, twine wild wreaths; while
        she
From thy delight, wins to her own fond heart
The vernal ecstasy of childhood back:—
Come to the woods, my boy!
What! wouldst thou lead already to the path
Along the copsewood brook?  Come, then I in truth
Meet playmate for a child, a blessed child,
Is a glad singing stream, heard, or unheard,
Singing its melody of happiness
Amidst the reeds, and bounding in free grace;
To that sweet chime.—With what a sparkling life
It fills the shadowy dingle! now the wing
Of some low-skimming swallow shakes bright
        spray
Forth to the sunshine from its dimpled wave;
Now, from some pool of crystal darkness deep,
The trout springs upward, with a showery gleam
And plashing sound of waters.  What swift rings
Of mazy insects o'er the shallow tide
Seem, as they glance, to scatter sparks of light
From burnish'd films!  And mark yon silvery line
Of gossamer, so tremulously hung
Across the narrow current, from the tuft
Of hazels to the hoary poplar's bough!
See, in the air's transparence, how it waves,
Quivering and glistening with each faintest gale,
Yet breaking not—a bridge for fairy shapes,
How delicate, how wondrous!
                Yes, my boy!
Well may we make the stream's bright winding
        vein
Our woodland guide, for He who made the stream
Made it a clue to haunts of loveliness,
For ever deepening.  O, forget him not,
Dear child! that airy gladness which thou feel'st
Wafting thee after bird and butterfly,
As 'twere a breeze within thee is not less
*His* gift, his blessing on thy spring-time hours,
Than this rich outward sunshine, mantling all
The leaves, and grass, and mossy tinted stones
With summer glory.  Stay thy bounding step,
My merry wanderer! let us rest awhile
By this clear pool, where, in the shadow flung
From alder boughs and osiers o'er its breast,
The soft red of the flowering willow herb
So vividly is pictured.  Seems it not
E'en melting to a more transparent glow
In that pure glass?  Oh! beautiful are streams!
And, through all ages, human hearts have loved
Their music, still accordant with each mood
Of sadness or of joy.  And love hath grown
Into vain worship, which hath left its trace
On sculptured urn and altar, gleaming still
Beneath dim olive boughs, by many a fount
Of Italy and Greece.  But we will take
Our lesson e'en from erring hearts, which bless'd
The river Deities or fountain Nymphs,
For the cool breeze, and for the freshening shade

And the sweet water's tune.  The One supreme,
The all-sustaining, ever-present God,
Who dower'd the soul with immortality,
Gave also these delights, to cheer on earth
Its fleeting passage; therefore let us greet
Each wandering flower scent as a boon from Him,
Each bird-note, quivering 'midst light summer
    leaves,
And every rich celestial tint unnamed,
Wherewith transpierced, the clouds of morn and
    eve
Kindle and melt away!
            And now, in love,
In grateful thoughts rejoicing, let us bend
Our footsteps onward to the dell of flowers
Around the ruin'd mansion.  Thou, my boy,
Not yet, I deem, hast visited that lorn
But lovely spot, whose loveliness for thee
Will wear no shadow of subduing thought—
No colouring from the past.  This way our path
Winds through the hazels;—mark how brightly
    shoots
The dragon-fly along the sunbeam's line,
Crossing the leafy gloom.  How full of life,
The life of song, and breezes, and free wings,
Is all the murmuring shade! and thine, O thine!
Of all the brightest and the happiest here,
My blessed child! my gift of God! that mak'st
My heart o'erflow with summer!
                Hast thou twined
Thy wreath so soon! yet will we loiter not,
Though here the blue-bell wave, and gorgeously
Round the brown twisted roots of yon scathed oak
The heath-flower spread its purple.  We must
    leave
The copse, and through yon broken avenue,
Shadow'd by drooping walnut foliage, reach
The ruin's glade.
         And, lo! before us, fair,
Yet desolate, amidst the golden day,
It stands, that house of silence! wedded now
To verdant nature by the o'ermantling growth
Of leaf and tendril, which fond woman's hands
Once loved to train.  How the rich wall-flower
    scent
From every niche and mossy cornice floats,
Embalming its decay!  The bee alone
Is murmuring from its casement, whence no more
Shall the sweet eyes of laughing children shine,
Watching some homeward footstep. See! unbound
From the old fretted stone-work, what thick
    wreaths
Of jasmine, borne by waste exuberance down,
Trail through the grass their gleaming stars, and
    load
The air with mournful fragrance, for it speaks
Of life gone hence; and the faint southern breath
Of myrtle leaves from yon forsaken porch,
Startles the soul with sweetness! Yet rich knots
Of garden flowers, for wandering, and self-sown
Through all the sunny hollow, spread around
A flush of youth and joy, free nature's joy,
Undimm'd by human change.  How kindly here,
With the low thyme and daisies they have blent!
And, under arches of wild eglantine,
Drooping from this tall elm, how strangely seems
The frail gumcistus o'er the turf to snow
Its pearly flower-leaves down!—Go, happy boy!
Rove thou at will amidst these roving sweets,
Whilst I, beside this fallen dial-stone,
Under the tall moss ross-tree, long unpruned,
Rest where thick clustering pansies weave around
Their many tinged mosaic, 'midst dark grass,
Budded like jewels.
         He hath bounded on,
Wild with delight!—The crimson on his cheek
richer and richer e'en than that which lies
In this deep-hearted rose-cup!—Bright moss-rose!
Though not so lorn, yet surely, gracious tree!
Once thou wert cherish'd! and, by human love,
Through many a summer daily visited
For thy bloom-offerings, which, o'er festal board,
And youthful brow, and e'en the shaded couch
Of long secluded sickness, may have shed
A joy, now lost.

            Yet shall there still be joy,
Where God hath pour'd forth beauty, and the
    voice
Of human love shall still be heard in praise
Over his glorious gifts!—O Father, Lord!
The All Beneficent! I bless thy name,
That thou hast mantled the green earth with
    flowers,
Linking our hearts to nature! By the love
Of their wild blossoms, our young footsteps first
Into her deep recesses are beguiled,
Her minster cells; dark glen and forest bower,
Where, thrilling with its earliest sense of thee
Amidst the low religious whisperings
And shivery leaf-sounds of the solitude,
The spirit wakes to worship, and is made
Thy living temple.  By the breath of flowers,
Thou callest us, from city throngs and cares,
Back to the woods, the birds, the mountain
    streams,
That sing of Thee! back to free childhood's heart.
Fresh with the dews of tenderness!—Thou bidd'st
The lilies of the field with placid smile
Reprove man's feverish strivings, and infuse
Through his worn soul a more unworldly life,
With their soft holy breath.  Thou hast not left
His purer nature, with its fine desires,
Uncared for in this universe of thine!
The glowing rose attests it, the beloved
Of poet hearts, touch'd by their fervent dreams
With spiritual light, and made a source
Of heaven-ascending thoughts.  E'en to faint age
Thou lend'st the vernal bliss:—The old man's eye
Falls on the kindling blossoms, and his soul
Remembers youth and love, and hopefully
Turns unto thee, who call'st earth's buried germs
From dust to splendour; as the mortal seed
Shall, at thy summons, from the grave spring up
To put on glory, to be girt with power,
And fill'd with immortality.  Receive
Thanks, blessings, love, for these, thy lavish boons
And, most of all, their heavenward influences,
    Thou that gav'st us flowers!
              Return, my boy,
With all thy chaplets and bright hands, return!
See, with how deep a crimson eve hath touch'd
And glorified the ruin! glow-worm light
Will twinkle on the dew-drops, ere we reach
Our home again.  Come, with thy last sweet
    prayer
At thy bless'd mother's knee, to-night shall thanks
Unto our Father in his Heaven arise,
For all the gladness, all the beauty shed
O'er one rich day of flowers!

---

## EVENING SONG OF THE WEARY.

    FATHER of Heaven and Earth!
      I bless thee for the night,
        The soft, still night!
The holy pause of care and mirth,
      Of sound and light!

    Now far in glade and dell,
      Flower-cup, and bud, and bell,
Have shut around the sleeping woodlark's nest—
      The bee's long murmuring toils are done,
      And I, the o'erwearied one,
      O'erwearied and o'erwrought,
Bless thee, O God, O Father of the oppress'd,
      With my last waking thought,
        In the still night!

    Yes, ere I sink to rest,
      By the fire's dying light,
      Thou Lord of Earth and Heaven!
      I bless thee, who hast given
Unto life's fainting travellers, the night.
    The soft, still, holy night!

## HYMN OF THE TRAVELLER'S HOUSE-HOLD ON HIS RETURN.

### IN THE OLDEN TIME.

Joy! the lost one is restored!
Sunshine comes to hearth and board.
From the far-off countries old
Of the diamond and red gold;
From the dusky archer bands,
Roamers of the fiery sands;
From the desert winds, whose breath
Smites with sudden silent death;
He hath reach'd his home again,
　　Where we sing
In thy praise a fervent strain,
　　God our King!

Mightiest! unto Thee be turn'd,
When the noon-day fiercest burn'd;
When the fountain springs were far,
And the sounds of Arab war
Swell'd upon the sultry blast,
And the sandy columns past,
Unto Thee he cried! and Thou,
Merciful! didst hear his vow!
Therefore unto Thee again
　　Joy shall sing,
Many a sweet and thankful strain,
　　God our King!

Thou wert with him on the main,
And the snowy mountain-chain,
And the rivers, dark and wide,
Which through Indian forests glide,
Thou didst guard him from the wrath
Of the lion in his path,
And the arrows on the breeze,
And the dropping poison-trees:
Therefore from our household train
　　Oft shall spring
Unto Thee a blessing strain
　　God our King!

Thou to his lone watching wife
Hast brought back the light of life!
Thou hast spared his loving child
Home to greet him from the wild.
Though the sons of eastern skies
On his cheek have set their dyes,
Though long toils and sleepless cares
On his brow have blanch'd the hairs,
Yet the night of fear is flown,
He is living and our own!—
Brethren! spread his festal board,
Hung his mantle and his sword
With the armour on the wall
While this long, long silent hall
Joyfully doth hear again
　　Voice and string
Swell to Thee the exulting strain,
　　God our King!

---

## A PRAYER OF AFFECTION.

Blessings, O Father, shower!
Father of mercies! round his precious head!
On his lone walks and on his thoughtful hour,
And the pure visions of his midnight bed,
　　Blessings be shed!

Father! I pray Thee not
For earthly treasure to that most beloved,
Fame, fortune, power;—oh be his spirit proved
By these, or by their absence, at Thy will!
But let Thy peace be wedded to his lot,
Guarding his inner life from touch of ill,
　　With its dove-pinion still!

Let such a sense of Thee,
Thy watching presence, thy sustaining love,
His bosom guest inalienably be,
　　That wheresoe'er he move.

A heavenly light serene
Upon his heart and mien
May sit undimm'd! a gladness rest his own,
Unspeakable, and to the world unknown!
Such as from childhood's morning land of dreams,
　　Remember'd faintly, gleams,
Faintly remember'd, and too swiftly flown!

So let him walk with Thee,
Made by Thy spirit free;
And when Thou call'st him from his mortal place,
To his last hour be still that sweetness given,
That joyful trust! and brightly let him part,
With lamp clear burning, and unlingering heart,
　　Mature to meet in heaven
　　His Saviour's face!

---

## THE PAINTER'S LAST WORK.*

Clasp me a little longer on the brink
Of life, while I can feel thy dear caress;
And when this heart hath ceased to beat, oh! think,
And let it mitigate thy woe's excess,
That thou hast been to me all tenderness,
　　And friend to more than human friendship just—
Oh! by that retrospect of happiness,
And by the hope of an immortal trust,
God shall assuage thy pangs when I am laid in dust!
　　　　　　　　　　*Campbell*

---

*The scene is in an English cottage. The lattice opens upon a landscape at sunset.*

### EUGENE—TERESA.

*Teresa.* The fever's hue hath left thy cheek, beloved!
Thine eyes, that make the day-spring in my heart,
Are clear and still once more!—Wilt thou look forth?
Now, while the sunset with low streaming light—
The light thou lovest—hath made the elm-wood stems
All burning bronze, the river molten gold!
Wilt thou be raised upon thy couch, to meet
The rich air fill'd with wandering scents and sounds?
Or shall I lay thy dear, dear head once more
On this true bosom, lulling thee to rest
With our own evening hymn?
　*Eugene.* 　　　　　　Not now, dear love,
My soul is wakeful—lingering to look forth,
Not on the sun, but thee!—Doth the light sleep
On the stream tenderly? and are the stems
Of our own elm trees, ey its alchemy,
So richly changed? and is the sweet-brier scent
Floating around?—But I have said farewell,
Farewell to earth, Teresa!—not to thee,
Nor yet to our deep love, nor yet awhile
Unto the spirit of mine art, which flows
Back on my soul in mastery,—One last work!
And I will shrine my wealth of glowing thoughts
Clinging affections, and undying hopes,
All, all in that memorial!
　*Teresa.* 　　　　　　O, what dream
Is this, mine own Eugene?—Waste thou not thus
Thy scarce returning strength; keep thy rich
　　thoughts
For happier days! they will not melt away
Like passing music from the lute—dear friend!
Dearest of friends! thou canst win back at will
The glorious visions.
　*Eugene.* 　　　　　Yes! the unseen land
Of glorious visions hath sent forth a voice
To call me hence.—Oh! be thou not deceived!
Bind to thy heart no *earthly* hope, Teresa!
I must, *must* leave thee!—Yet be strong, my love
As thou hast still been gentle.
　*Teresa.* 　　　　O Eugene!
What will this dim world be to me, Eugene,
When wanting thy bright soul, the life of all?

---

* Suggested by the closing scene in the life of the painter Blake, which is beautifully related by Allan Cunningham.

My only sunshine!—How can I bear on?
How can we part? We that have loved so well,
With clasping spirits link'd so long by grief,
By tears, by prayer?
　　*Eugene.*　　E'en *therefore* we can part,
With an immortal trust, that such high love
Is not of things to perish.
　　　　　　　Let me leave
One record still of its ethereal flame
Brightening through death's cold shadow.　Once
　　again.
Stand with thy meek hands folded on thy breast,
And eyes half veil'd, in thine own soul absorb'd
As in thy watchings, e'er I sink to sleep;
And I will give the bending flower-like grace
Of that soft form, and the still sweetness throned
On that pale brow, and in that quivering smile
Of voiceless love, a life that shall outlast
Their delicate earthly being.　There! thy head
Bow'd down with beauty, and with tenderness,
And lowly thought—even thus—my own Teresa!
Oh! the quick glancing radiance and bright bloom
That once around thee hung, have melted now
Into more solemn light—but holier far,
And dearer, and yet lovelier in mine eyes.
Than all that summer flush!　For by my couch,
In patient and serene devotedness,
Thou hast made those rich hues and sunny smiles
Thine offering unto me.　Oh! I may give
Those pensive lips, that clear Madonna brow,
And the sweet earnestness of that dark eye,
Unto the canvas;—I may catch the flow
Of all those drooping locks, and glorify
With a soft halo what is imaged thus—
But how much rests unbreathed! my faithful one
What thou hast been to me!　This bitter world,
This cold unanswering world, that hath no voice
To greet the gentle spirit, that drives back
All birds of Eden, which would sojourn here
A little while—how have I turn'd away
From its keen soulless air, and in thy heart,
Found ever the sweet fountain of response,
To quench my thirst for home!
　　　　　　　The dear work grows
Beneath my hand,—the last!
　　*Teresa, (falling on his neck in tears.)*
　　　　　　　Eugene, Eugene!
Break not my heart with thine excess of love!—
Oh! must I lose thee—thou that hast been still
The tenderest—best—
　　*Eugene.*　　　　Weep, weep not thus, beloved!
Let my true heart o'er thine retain its power
Of soothing to the last!—Mine own Teresa!
Take strength from strong affection!—Let our
　　souls,
Ere this brief parting, mingle in one strain
Of deep, full thanksgiving, for God's rich boon—
Our perfect love!—Oh! blessed have we been
In that high gift!　Thousands o'er earth may pass
With hearts unfreshen'd by the heavenly dew,
Which hath kept *ours* from withering.—Kneel, true
　　wife!
And lay thy hands in mine.—
　　　*[She kneels beside the couch; he prays.*
　　　　　　　O, thus receive
Thy children's thanks, Creator! for the love
Which thou hast granted, through all earthly woes,
To spread heaven's peace around them; which
　　hath bound
Their spirits to each other and to thee,
With links whereon unkindness ne'er hath
　　breathed,
Nor wandering thought.　We thank thee, gracious
　　God!
For all its treasured memories! tender cares,
Fond words, bright, bright sustaining looks un-
　　changed
Through tears and joy.　O Father! most of all
We thank, we bless Thee, for the priceless trust,
Through Thy redeeming Son vouchsafed, to those
That love in Thee, of union, in Thy sight,
And in Thy heavens, immortal!—Hear our prayer!
Take home our fond affections, purified
To spirit-radiance from all earthly stain;
Exalted, solemnized, made fit to dwell,

Father! where all things that are lovely meet
And all things that are pure—for evermore,
With Thee and Thine!

## MOTHER'S LITANY BY THE SICK-BE
## OF A CHILD.

Saviour that of woman born,
Mother-sorrow didst not scorn,
Thou, with whose last anguish strove
One dear thought of earthly love;
　　　　　　Hear and aid!

Low he lies, my precious child,
With his spirit wandering wild
From its gladsome tasks and play,
And its bright thoughts far away:—
　　　　　　Saviour, aid!

Pain sits heavy on his brow,
E'en though slumber seal it now;
Round his lip is quivering strife,
In his hand unquiet life;
　　　　　　Aid, oh! aid

Saviour! loose the burning chain
From his fever'd heart and brain,
Give, oh! give his young soul back
Into its own cloudless track!
　　　　　　Hear and aid!

Thou that said'st, " *awake, arise!*"
E'en when death had quench'd the eyes,
In this hour of grief's deep sighing,
When o'erwearied hope is dying!
　　　　　　Hear and aid!

Yet, oh! make him thine, all thine,
Saviour! whether Death's or mine
Yet, oh! pour on human love,
Strength, trust, patience, from above!
　　　　　　Hear and aid!

## NIGHT HYMN AT SEA.

THE WORDS WRITTEN FOR A MELODY BY FELTON.

Night sinks on the wave,
　Hollow gusts are sighing,
Sea-birds to their cave
　Through the gloom are flying.
Oh! should storms come sweeping,
Thou, in Heaven unsleeping,
O'er thy children vigil keeping,
　　Hear, hear, and save!

Stars look o'er the sea,
　Few, and sad, and shrouded!
Faith our light must be,
　When all else is clouded.
Thou, whose voice came thrilling,
Wind and billow stilling,
Speak once more! our prayer fulfilling—
　　Power dwells with Thee!

## FEMALE CHARACTERS OF SCRIPTURE.

### A SERIES OF SONNETS.

Your tents are desolate; your stately steps,
Of all their choral dances, have not left
One trace beside the fountains; your full cup
Of gladness and of trembling, each alike
Is broken: yet, amidst undying things,
The mind still keeps your loveliness, and still
All the fresh glories of the early world
Hang round you in the spirit's pictured halls,
Never to change!

### I.

#### INVOCATION.

As the tired voyager on stormy seas
　Invokes the coming of bright birds from shore,
To waft him tidings with the gentler breeze,
　Of dim sweet woods that hear no billows' roar

So from the depth of days, when earth yet wore
Her solemn beauty and primeval dew,
I call you, gracious Forms! Oh! come, restore
Awhile that holy freshness, and renew
Life's morning dreams. Come with the voice, the
    lyre,
Daughters of Judah! with the timbrel rise!
Ye of the dark prophetic eastern eyes,
Imperial in their visionary fire;
Oh! steep my soul in that old glorious time,
When God's own whisper shook the cedars of your
    clime!

## II.

### INVOCATION CONTINUED.

And come, ye faithful! round Messiah seen,
    With a soft harmony of tears and light
Streaming through all your spiritual mien,
    As in calm clouds of pearly stillness bright,
    Showers weave with sunshine, and transpierce
        their slight
Ethereal cradle.—From your heart subdued
    All haughty dreams of power had wing'd their
        flight,
And left high place for martyr fortitude,
True faith, long suffering love.—Come to me, come!
    And, as the seas beneath your master's tread
    Fell into crystal smoothness, round him spread
Like the clear pavement of his heavenly home;
    So in your presence, let the soul's great deep
    Sink to the gentleness of infant sleep.

## III.

### THE SONG OF MIRIAM.

A song for Israel's God!—Spear, crest, and helm,
    Lay by the billows of the old Red Sea,
When Miriam's voice o'er that sepulchral realm
    Sent on the blast a hymn of jubilee;
With her lit eye, and long hair floating free,
    Queen-like she stood, and glorious was the strain,
E'en as instinct with the tempestuous glee
    Of the dark waters, tossing o'er the slain.
A song for God's own victory!— O, thy lays,
    Bright Poesy! were holy in their birth:—
How hath it died, thy seraph note of praise,
    In the bewildering melodies of earth!
Return from troubling bitter founts—return,
Back to the life-springs of thy native urn!

## IV.

### RUTH.

The plume-like swaying of the auburn corn,
    By soft winds to a dreamy motion fann'd,
Still brings me back thine image—Oh! forlorn,
    Yet not forsaken, Ruth!—I see thee stand
    Lone, 'midst the gladness of the harvest band—
Lone as a wood-bird on the ocean's foam,
    Fall'n in its weariness. Thy father-land
Smiles far away! yet to the sense of home,
    That finest, purest, which can recognize
    Home in affection's glance, for ever true
Beats thy calm heart; and if thy gentle eyes
    Gleam tremulous through tears, 'tis not to rue
Those words, immortal in their deep Love's tone,
"Thy people and thy God shall be mine own!"

## V.

### THE VIGIL OF RIZPAH.

"And Rizpah, the daughter of Aiah, took sackcloth,
and spread it for her upon the rock, from the beginning
of harvest until water dropped upon them out of heaven; and suffered neither the birds of the air to rest on
them by day, nor the beasts of the field by night."—2
Sam. xxi. 10.

Who watches on the mountain with the dead,
    Alone before the awfulness of night?—
    A seer awaiting the deep spirit's might?
A warrior guarding some dark pass of dread?
No, a lorn woman!—On her drooping head,
    Once proudly graceful, heavy beats the rain,
    She recks not—living for the unburied slain,
Only to scare the vulture from their bed.

So, night by night, her vigil hath she kept
With the pale stars, and with the dews hath
    wept;—
    Oh! surely some bright Presence from above
On those wild rocks the lonely one must aid!—
E'en so; a strengthener through all storm and
    shade,
    Th' unconquerable Angel, mightiest Love!

## VI

### THE REPLY OF THE SHUNAMITE WOMAN.

"And she answered, I dwell among mine own people."
—2 Kings, iv. 13.

"I dwell among mine own,"—Oh! happy thou!
    Not for the sunny clusters of the vine,
Nor for the olives on the mountain's brow;
    Nor the flocks wandering by the flowery line
    Of streams, that make the green land where
        they shine
Laugh to the light of waters—not for these,
Nor the soft shadow of ancestral trees,
    Whose kindly whisper floats o'er thee and thine—
Oh! not for these I call thee richly blest,
But for the meekness of thy woman's breast,
        Where that sweet depth of still contentment
        lies;
    And for thy holy household love, which clings
    Unto all ancient and familiar things,
Weaving from each some link for home's dear
        charities.

## VII.

### THE ANNUNCIATION.

Lowliest of women, and most glorified!
    In thy still beauty sitting calm and lone,
A brightness round thee grew—and by thy side
    Kindling the air, a form ethereal shone,
    Solemn, yet breathing gladness.—From her
        throne
A queen had risen with more imperial eye,
A stately prophetess of victory
    From her proud lyre had struck a tempest's tone,
For such high tidings as to thee were brought,
    Chosen of Heaven! that hour;—but thou, O
        thou!
E'en as a flower with gracious rains o'erfraught,
    Thy virgin head beneath its crown didst bow,
And take to thy meek breast th' all holy word,
And own thyself the handmaid of the Lord.

## VIII.

### THE SONG OF THE VIRGIN.

Yet as a sun-burst flushing mountain snow,
    Fell the celestial touch of fire ere long
On the pale stillness of thy thoughtful brow,
    And thy calm spirit lighten'd into song.
    Unconsciously perchance, yet free and strong
Flow'd the majestic joy of tuneful words,
    Which living harps the quires of Heaven among
Might well have link'd with their divinest chords.
Full many a strain, borne far on glory's blast,
Shall leave, where once its haughty music pass'd,
    No more to memory than a reed's faint sigh;
While thine, O childlike virgin! through all time
Shall send its fervent breath o'er every clime,
    Being of God, and therefore not to die.

## IX.

### THE PENITENT ANOINTING CHRIST'S FEET.

There was a mournfulness in angel eyes,
    That saw thee, woman! bright in this world's
        train,
Moving to pleasure's airy melodies,
    Thyself the idol of the enchanted strain.
    But from thy beauty's garland, brief and vain,
When one by one the rose-leaves had been torn,
    When thy heart's core had quiver'd to the pain
Through every life-nerve sent by arrowy scorn;
When thou didst kneel to pour sweet odours forth
    On the Redeemer's feet, with many a sigh,
And showering tear-drop, of yet richer worth
    Than all those costly balms of Araby;
Then was there joy, a song of joy in Heaven
For thee, the child won back, the penitent for
        given!

## X.

### MARY AT THE FEET OF CHRIST.

Oh! blest beyond all daughters of the earth!
  What were the Orient's thrones to that low seat.
Where thy hush'd spirit drew celestial birth?
  Mary! meek listener at the Saviour's feet!
  No feverish cares to that divine retreat
Thy woman's heart of silent worship brought,
  But a fresh childhood, heavenly truth to meet,
With love, and wonder, and submissive thought.
Oh! for the holy quiet of thy breast,
  'Midst the world's eager tones and footsteps
    flying!
  Thou, whose calm soul was like a well-spring,
    lying
So deep and still in its transparent rest,
That e'en when noontide burns upon the hills,
Some one bright solemn star all its lone mirror
  fills.

## XI.

### THE SISTERS OF BETHANY AFTER THE DEATH OF LAZARUS.

One grief, one faith, O sisters of the dead!
  Was in your bosoms—thou, whose steps, made
    fleet
By keen hope fluttering in the heart which bled,
  Bore thee, as wings, the Lord of Life to greet;
  And thou, that duteous in thy still retreat
Didst wait his summons—then with reverent love
  Fell weeping at the blest Deliverer's feet,
Whom e'en to heavenly tears thy woe could move,
And which to Him, the All Seeing and All Just
Was loveliest, that quick zeal, or lowly trust?
Oh! question not, and let no law be given
  To those unveilings of its deepest shrine,
  By the wrong spirit made in outward sign:
Free service from the heart is all in all to Heaven

## XII.

### THE MEMORIAL OF MARY.

"Verily I say unto you, wheresoever this gospel shall
be preached in the whole world, there shall also this, that
this woman hath done, be told for a memorial of her."—
*Matthew*, xxvi. 13.—See also *John*, xii. 3.

Thou hast thy record in the monarch's hall,
  And on the waters of the far mid sea;
And where the mighty mountain-shadows fall,
  The Alpine hamlet keeps a thought of thee:
  Where'er beneath some Oriental tree,
The Christian traveller rests—where'er the child
  Looks upward from the English mother's knee,
With earnest eyes in wondering reverence mild,
There art thou known — where'er the Book of
  Light
Bears hope and healing, there, beyond all blight,
  Is borne thy memory, and all praise above;
Oh! say what deed so lifted thy sweet name,
Mary! to that pure silent place of fame?
  One lowly offering of exceeding love.

## XIII.

### THE WOMEN OF JERUSALEM AT THE CROSS.

Like those pale stars of tempest hours, whose
  gleam
  Waves calm and constant on the rocking mast,
Such by the Cross doth your bright lingering seem,
  Daughters of Zion! faithful to the last!
  Ye, through the darkness o'er the wide earth cast
By the death-cloud within the Saviour's eye,
  E'en till away the heavenly spirit pass'd,
Stood in the shadow of his agony.
O blessed faith; a guiding lamp, that hour,
Was lit for woman's heart; to her, whose dower
  Is all of love and suffering from her birth;
Still hath your act a voice—through fear, through
    strife,
  Bidding her bind each tendril of her life,
To that which her deep soul hath proved of holiest
  worth.

## XIV.

### MARY MAGDALENE AT THE SEPULCHRE.

Weeper! to thee how bright a morn was given
  After thy long, long vigil of despair,
When that high voice which burial rocks had
    riven,
  Thrill'd with immortal tones the silent air!
Never did clarion's royal blast declare
Such tale of victory to a breathless crowd,
  As the deep sweetness of one word could bear
Into thy heart of hearts, O woman! bow'd
By strong affection's anguish!—one low word—
  "*Mary!*"—and all the triumph wrung from
    death
Was thus reveal'd! and thou, that so hadst err'd,
  So wept, and been forgiven, in trembling faith
  Didst cast thee down before th' all conquering
    Son,
Awed by the mighty gift thy tears and love had
  won!

## XV.

### MARY MAGDALENE BEARING TIDINGS OF THE RESURRECTION.

Then was a task of glory all thine own,
  Nobler than e'er the still small voice assign'd
To lips in awful music making known
  The stormy splendours of some prophet's mind.
  "Christ is arisen!" by thee, to wake mankind,
First from the sepulchre those words were brought!
  Thou wert to send the mighty rushing wind
First on its way, with those high tidings fraught—
"*Christ is arisen!*"—Thou, *thou*, the sin enthrall'd,
Earth's outcast, Heaven's own ransom'd one, wert
  call'd
  In human hearts to give that rapture birth:
  Oh! raised from shame to brightness!—there
    doth lie
The tenderest meaning of *His* ministry,
Whose undespairing love still own'd the spirit's
  worth.

---

## THE TWO MONUMENTS.

Oh! blest are they who live and die like "him,"
Loved with such love, and with such sorrow mourn'd!
                      *Wordsworth*

Banners hung drooping from on high
  In a dim cathedral's nave,
Making a gorgeous canopy
  O'er a noble, noble grave!

And a marble warrior's form beneath,
  With helm and crest array'd,
As on his battle bed of death,
  Lay in their crimson shade.

Triumph yet linger'd in his eye,
  Ere by the dark night seal'd,
And his head was pillow'd haughtily
  On standard and on shield.

And shadowing that proud trophy pile
  With the glory of his wing,
An eagle sat;—yet seem'd the while
  Panting through Heaven to spring

He sat upon a shiver'd lance,
  There by the sculptor bound;
But in the light of his lifted glance
  Was *that* which scorn'd the ground.

And a burning flood of gem-like hues
  From a storied window pour'd,
There fell, there centred, to suffuse
  The conqueror and his sword.

A flood of hues!—but one rich dye
  O'er all supremely spread,
With a purple robe of royalty
  Mantling the mighty dead.

Meet was that robe for him whose name
  Was a trumpet note in war,
His pathway still the march of fame,
  His eye the battle star.

But faintly, tenderly was thrown
    From the colour'd light one ray,
Where a low and pale memorial stone
    By the couch of glory lay.

Few were the fond words chisell'd *there*,
    Mourning for parted worth;
But the very heart of love and prayer
    Had given their sweetness forth.

They spoke of one whose life had been
    As a hidden streamlet's course,
Bearing on health and joy unseen,
    From its clear mountain source:

Whose young pure memory, lying deep
    'Midst rock, and wood, and hill,
Dwelt in the homes where poor men sleep,*
    A soft light meek and still:

Whose gentle voice, too early call'd
    Unto Music's land away,
Had won for God the earth's enthrall'd
    By words of silvery sway.

These were *his* victories—yet enroll'd
    In no high song of fame,
The pastor of the mountain-fold
    Left but to Heaven his name.

To Heaven and to the peasant's hearth,
    A blessed household sound—
And finding lowly love on earth,
    Enough, enough, he found!

Bright and more bright before me gleam'd
    That sainted image still;
Till one sweet moonlight memory seem'd
    The regal fane to fill.

Oh! how my silent sp.rit turn'd
    From those proud trophies nigh;
How my full heart within me burn'd
    Like *Him* to live and die!

---

## THE MEMORY OF THE DEAD.

Forget them not! though now their name
    Be but a mournful sound,
Though by the hearth its utterance claim
    A stillness round:

Though for their sake this earth no more
    As it hath been, may be,
And shadows, never mark'd before,
    Brood o'er each tree:

And though their image dim the sky,
    Yet, yet, forget them not!
Nor, where their love and life went by,
    Forsake the spot!

They have a breathing influence there,
    A charm not elsewhere found;
Sad—yet it sanctifies the air,
    The stream, the ground.

Then, though the wind an alter'd tone
    Through the young foliage bear,
Though every flower, of something gone,
    A tinge may wear:

Oh, fly it not!—no *fruitless* grief
    Thus in their presence felt,
A record links to every leaf,
    There, where they dwelt.

Still trace the path which knew their tread,
    Still tend their garden bower,
Still commune with the holy dead,
    In each lone hour.

The *holy* dead!—oh! blest we are,
    That we may call them so,
And to their image look afar,
    Through all our woe!

* Love had he seen in huts where poor men lie.<br>
*Wordsworth.*

Blest that the things they loved on earth
    As relics we may hold,
That wake sweet thoughts of parted worth
    By springs untold!

Blest, that a deep and chastening power
    Thus o'er our souls is given,
If but to bird, or song, or flower,
    Yet, all for Heaven.

---

## ANGEL VISITS.

No more of talk where God or angel guest
With man, as with his friend, familiar used
To sit indulgent, and with him partake
Rural repast.
            *Milton.*

---

Are ye for ever to your skies departed?
    Oh! will ye visit this dim world no more?
Ye, whose bright wings a solemn splendour darted
    Through Eden's fresh and flowering shades of
        yore?
Now are the fountains dried on that sweet spot,
And ye—our faded earth beholds you not!

Yet, by your shining eyes not all forsaken,
    Man wander'd from his Paradise away;
Ye, from forgetfulness his heart to waken,
    Came down, high guests! in many a later day,
And with the Patriarchs, under vine or oak,
'Midst noontide calm or hush of evening, spoke.

From you, the veil of midnight-darkness rending,
    Came the rich mysteries to the Sleeper's eye,
That saw your hosts ascending and descending
    On those bright steps between the earth and sky:
Trembling he woke, and bow'd o'er glory's trace,
And worshipp'd, awe-struck, in that fearful place

By Chebar's* brook ye pass'd, such radiance wear
        ing
    As mortal vision might but ill endure;
Along the stream the living chariot bearing,
    With its high crystal arch, intensely pure!
And the dread rushing of your wings that hour
Was like the noise of waters in their power.

But in the Olive-mount, by night appearing,
    'Midst the dim leaves, your holiest work was
        done!
Whose was the voice that came divinely cheering
    Fraught with the breath of God, to aid his Son?—
Haply of those that, on the moon lit plains,
Wafted good tidings unto Syrian swains.

Yet one more task was yours! your hea venly
        dwelling
    Ye left, and by th' unseal'd sepulchral stone,
In glorious raiment, sat; the weepers telling,
    That *He* they sought had triumph'd, and was
        gone!
Now have ye left us for the brighter shore,
Your presence lights the lonely groves no more.

But may ye not, unseen, around us hover,
    With gentle promptings and sweet influence yet,
Though the fresh glory of those days be over,
    When, 'midst the palm-trees, man your footsteps
        met?
Are ye not near when faith and hope rise high,
When love, by strength, o'ermasters agony?

Are ye not near when sorrow, unrepining,
    Yields up life's treasures unto Him who gave?
When martyrs, all things for His sake resigning,
    Lead on the march of death, serenely brave?
Dreams!—but a deeper thought our souls may fill—
One, One *is* near—a Spirit holier still!

---

* Ezekiel, chap. x.

## A PENITENT'S RETURN.

Can guilt or misery ever enter here?
Ah! no, the spirit of domestic peace,
Though calm and gentle as the brooding dove
And ever murmuring forth a quiet song,
Guards, powerful as the sword of Cherubim,
The hallow'd Porch.   She hath a heavenly smile,
That sinks into the sullen soul of vice,
And wins him o'er to virtue.

                                        *Wilson.*

My father's house once more,
In its own moonlight beauty! Yet around,
Something amidst the dewy calm profound,
    Broods, never mark'd before!

Is it the brooding night,
Is it the shivery creeping on the air,
That makes the home, so tranquil and so fair,
    O'erwhelming to my sight?

All solemnized it seems,
And still, and darken'd in each time-worn hue,
Since the rich clustering roses met my view,
    As now, by starry gleams.

And this high elm, where last
I stood and linger'd—where my sisters made
Our mother's bower—I deem'd not that it cast
    So far and dark a shade!

How spirit-like a tone
Sighs through yon tree! My father's place was
        there
At evening hours, while soft winds waved his hair!
    Now those gray locks are gone!

My soul grows faint with fear;
Even as if angel steps had mark'd the sod.
I tremble where I move—the voice of God
    Is in the foliage here!

Is it indeed the night
That makes my home so awful? Faithless-
        hearted!
'Tis that from thine own bosom hath departed
    The inborn gladd'ning light!

No outward thing is changed;
Only the joy of purity is fled,
And, long from nature's melodies estranged,
    Thou hear'st their tones with dread

Therefore, the calm abode,
By thy dark spirit, is o'erhung with shade;
And, therefore, in the leaves, the voice of God
    Makes thy sick heart afraid!

The night-flowers round that door,
Still breathe pure fragrance on the untainted air;
Thou, thou alone art worthy now no more
    To pass, and rest thee there.

And must I turn away?—
Hark, hark!—it is my mother's voice I hear—
Sadder than once it seem'd—yet soft and clear—
    Doth she not seem to pray?

My name!—I caught the sound!
Oh! blessed tone of love—the deep, the mild—
Mother, my mother! Now receive thy child,
    Take back the lost and found!

## A THOUGHT OF PARADISE.

We receive but what we give,
And in our life alone does nature live:

Ours is her wedding-garment, ours her shroud
And would we aught behold of higher worth
Than that inanimate cold world allow'd
To the poor, loveless, ever-anxious crowd;
Ah! from the soul itself must issue forth
A light, a glory, a fair luminous cloud,
        Enveloping the earth—
And from the soul itself must there be sent
A sweet and potent voice of its own birth,
Of all sweet sounds the life and element.

                                        *Coleridge.*

Green spot of holy ground!
    If thou couldst yet be found,
Far in deep woods, with all thy starry flowers;
    If not one sullying breath
    Of time, or change, or death,
Had touch'd the vernal glory of thy bowers·

    Might our tired pilgrim-feet,
    Worn by the desert's heat,
On the bright freshness of thy turf repose?
    Might our eyes wander there
    Through heaven's transparent air,
And rest on colours of the immortal rose?

    Say, would thy balmy skies
    And fountain-melodies
Our heritage of lost delight restore?
    Could thy soft honey-dews
    Through all our veins diffuse
The early, child-like, trustful sleep once more?

    And might we, in the shade
    By thy tall cedars made,
With angel voices high communion hold?
    Would their sweet solemn tone
    Give back the music gone,
Our Being's harmony, so jarr'd of old?

    Oh! no—thy sunny hours
    Might come with blossom showers,
All thy young leaves to spirit lyres might thrill;
    But *we*—should we not bring
    Into thy realms of spring
The shadows of our souls to haunt us still?

    What could thy flowers and airs
    Do for our earth-born cares?
Would the world's chain melt off and leave us free?
    No!—past each living stream,
    Still would some fever dream
Track the lorn wanderers, meet no more for thee

    Should we not shrink with fear,
    If angel steps were near,
Feeling our burden'd souls within us die?
    How might our passions brook
    The still and searching look,
The star-like glance of seraph purity?

    Thy golden-fruited grove
    Was not for pining love;
Vain sadness would but dim thy crystal skies!
    Oh! *Thou* wert but a part
    Of what man's exiled heart
Hath lost—the dower of *inborn* Paradise!

## LET US DEPART.

It is mentioned by Josephus, that, a short time previously to the destruction of Jerusalem by the Romans, the priests, going by night into the inner court of the temple to perform their sacred ministrations at the feast of Pentecost, felt a quaking, and heard a rushing noise, and, after that, a sound as of a great multitude saying "Let us depart hence."

Night hung on Salem's towers,
    And a brooding hush profound
Lay where the Roman eagle shone,
    High o'er the tents around,

The tents that rose by thousands,
  In the moonlight glimmering pale;
Like white waves of a frozen sea,
  Filling an Alpine vale.

And the temple's massy shadow
  Fell broad, and dark, and still,
In peace, as if the Holy One
  Yet watch'd his chosen hill.

But a fearful sound was heard
  In that old fane's deepest heart,
As if mighty wings rush'd by,
  And a dread voice raised the cry,
    " Let us depart!"

Within the fated city
  E'en then fierce discord raved,
Though o'er night's heaven the comet sword
  Its vengeful token waved.

There were shouts of kindred warfare
  Through the dark streets ringing high,
Though every sign was full which told
  Of the bloody vintage nigh.

Though the wild red spears and arrows
  Of many a meteor host,
Went flashing o'er the holy stars,
  In the sky now seen, now lost.

And that fearful sound was heard
  In the Temple's deepest heart,
As if mighty wings rush'd by,
  And a voice cried mournfully,
    " Let us depart!"

But within the fated city
  There was revelry that night;
The wine-cup and the timbrel note,
  And the blaze of banquet light.

The footsteps of the dancer
  Went bounding through the hall,
And the music of the dulcimer
  Summon'd to festival.

While the clash of brother weapons
  Made lightning in the air,
And the dying at the palace gates
  Lay down in their despair.

And that fearful sound was heard
  At the Temple's thrilling heart,
As if mighty wings rush'd by,
  And a dread voice raised the cry,
    *" Let us depart!"*

## ON A PICTURE OF CHRIST BEARING THE CROSS.

### PAINTED BY VELASQUEZ.*

By the dark stillness brooding in the sky,
  Holiest of sufferers! round thy path of woe,
And by the weight of mortal agony
  Laid on thy drooping form and pale meek
    brow,
My heart was awed: the burden of thy pain
Sank on me with a mystery and a chain.

I look'd once more, and, as the virtue shed
  Forth from thy robe of old, so fell a ray
Of victory from thy mien! and round thy beau,
  The halo, melting spirit-like away,
Seem'd of the very soul's bright rising morn,
To glorify all sorrow, shame, and scorn.

And upwards, through transparent darkness
    gleaming,
  Gazed, in mute reverence, woman's earnest eye,

* This picture is in the possession of the Viscount Harberton, Merrion Square, Dublin.

Lit, as a vase whence inward light is streaming,
  With quenchless faith, and deep love's fervency;
Gathering, like incense round some dim-veil'd
    shrine,
About the Form, so mournfully divine!

Oh! let thine image, as e'en then it rose,
  Live in my soul for ever, calm and clear,
Making itself a temple of repose,
  Beyond the breath of human hope or fear!
A holy place, where through all storms may lie
One living beam of day-spring from on high

## COMMUNINGS WITH THOUGHT.

  Could we but keep our spirits to that height,
  We might be happy; but this clay will sink
  Its spark immortal.
                    *Byron.*

RETURN, my thoughts, come home!
Ye wild and wing'd! what do ye o'er the deep?
And wherefore thus th' abyss of time o'ersweep
  As birds the ocean foam?

Swifter than shooting star,
Swifter than glances of the northern light,
Upspringing through the purple heaven of night,
  Hath been your course afar!

Through the bright battle-clime,
Where laurel boughs make dim the Grecian
  streams,
And reeds are whispering of heroic theme,
  By temples of old time:

Through the north's ancient halls,
Where banners thrill'd of yore, where harp-strings
  rung,
But grass waves now o'er those that fought and
  sung—
  Hearth-light hath left their walls

Through forests old and dim,
Where o'er the leaves dread magic seems to
  brood,
And sometimes on the haunted solitude
  Rises the pilgrim's hymn:

Or where some fountain lies,
With lotus-cups through orient spice-woods gleam-
  ing!
There have ye been, ye wanderers! idly dreaming
  Of man's lost paradise!

Return, my thoughts, return!
Cares wait your presence in life's daily track,
And voices, not of music, call you back—
  Harsh voices, cold and stern!

Oh! no, return ye not!
Still farther, loftier, let your soarings be
Go, bring me strength from journeyings bright
  and free
  O'er many a haunted spot.

Go, seek the martyr's grave,
'Midst the old mountains, and the deserts vast;
Or, through the ruin'd cities of the past,
  Follow the wise and brave!

Go, visit cell and shrine!
Where woman hath endured!—through wrong
  through scorn,
Uncheer'd by fame, yet silently upborne
  By promptings more divine!

Go, shoot the gulf of death!
Track the pure spirit where no chain can bind,
Where the heart's boundless love its rest may find,
  Where the storm sends no breath!

Higher, and yet more high!
Shake off the cumbering chain which earth would
  lay
On your victorious wings—mount, mount!—Your
  way
  Is through eternity!

## SONNETS,

### DEVOTIONAL AND MEMORIAL.

---

#### I.

##### THE SACRED HARP.

How shall the Harp of poesy regain
  That old victorious tone of prophet-years,
  A spell divine o'er guilt's perturbing fears,
And all the hovering shadows of the brain?
Dark evil wings took flight before the strain,
  And showers of holy quiet, with its fall,
  Sank on the soul:—Oh! who may now recall
The mighty music's consecrated reign?—
Spirit of God! whose glory once o'erhung
  A throne, the Ark's dread cherubim between,
  So let thy presence brood, though now unseen,
O'er those two powers by whom the harp is
   strung—
Feeling and Thought!—till the rekindled chords
Give the long-buried tone back to immortal words!

#### II.

##### TO A FAMILY BIBLE.

What household thoughts around thee, as their
   shrine,
Cling reverently!—of anxious looks beguiled
My mother's eyes, upon thy page divine,
Each day were bent;—her accents, gravely mild,
Breathed out thy lore: whilst I, a dreamy child,
Wander'd on breeze-like fancies oft away,
To some lone tuft of gleaming spring-flowers wild,
Some fresh discover'd nook for woodland play,
Some secret nest:—yet would the solemn Word
At times, with kindlings of young wonder heard
  Fall on my waken'd spirit, there to be
A seed not lost;—for which, in darker years,
O Book of Heaven! I pour, with grateful tears,
  Heart blessings on the holy dead and thee!

#### III.

##### REPOSE OF A HOLY FAMILY.

##### From an Old Italian Picture.

Under a palm tree, by the green old Nile,
  Lull'd on his mother's breast, the fair Child lies,
With dove-like breathings, and a tender smile,
  Brooding above the slumber of his eyes.
While, through the stillness of the burning skies,
  Lo! the dread works of Egypt's buried kings,
Temple and pyramid, beyond him rise,
  Regal and still as everlasting things!—
Vain pomps! from Him, with that pure flowery
   cheek,
  Soft shadow'd by his mother's drooping head,
A new-born Spirit, mighty, and yet meek,
  O'er the whole world-like vernal air shall spread!
And bid all earthly Grandeurs cast the crown,
Before the suffering and the lowly, down.

#### IV.

##### PICTURE OF THE INFANT CHRIST WITH FLOWERS.

All the bright hues from eastern garlands glowing,
Round the young Child luxuriantly are spread;
Gifts fairer far than Magian kings, bestowing
In adoration, o'er his cradle shed.
Roses, deep-fill'd with rich midsummer's red,
 ircle his hands; but, in his grave sweet eye,
Thought seems e'en now to wake, and prophecy
Of ruder coronals for that meek head.
And thus it was! a diadem of thorn
  Earth gave to Him who mantled her with flow-
   ers,
  To him who pour'd forth blessings in soft showers
O'er all her paths, a cup of bitter scorn!
And we repine, for whom that cup He took,
O'er blooms that mock'd our hope, o'er idols that
   forsook!

#### V.

##### ON A REMEMBERED PICTURE OF CHRIST.

##### An Ecce Homo, by Leonardo da Vinci.

I met that image on a mirthful day
  Of youth; and, sinking with a still'd surprise,
  The pride of life, before those holy eyes,
In my quick heart died thoughtfully away,
Abash'd to mute confession of a sway,
  Awful, though meek; and now, that from the
   strings
Of my soul's lyre, the tempest's mighty wings
Have struck forth tones which then awaken'd lay;
Now, that around the deep life of my mind,
Affections, deathless as itself, have twined,
  Oft does the pale bright vision still float by;
But more divinely sweet, and speaking *now*
Of One whose pity, throned on that sad brow,
  Sounded all depths of love, grief, death, huma
   nity!

#### VI.

##### THE CHILDREN WHOM JESUS BLEST.

Happy were they, the mothers, in whose sight
  Ye grew, fair children! hallow'd from that hour
  By your Lord's blessing! surely thence a shower
Of heavenly beauty, a transmitted light
Hung on your brows and eyelids, meekly bright,
  Through all the after years, which saw ye move
Lowly, yet still majestic, in the might,
  The conscious glory of the Saviour's love!
And honour'd be all childhood, for the sake
  Of that high love! Let reverential care
Watch to behold the immortal spirit wake,
  And shield its first bloom from unholy air;
Owning, in each young suppliant glance, the sign
Of claims upon a heritage divine.

#### VII.

##### MOUNTAIN SANCTUARIES.

" He went up to a mountain apart to pray."

A child 'midst ancient mountains I have stood,
  Where the wild falcons make their lordly nest
On high. The spirit of the solitude
  Fell solemnly upon my infant breast,
Though then I pray'd not; but deep thoughts have
   press'd
Into my being since it breathed that air,
Nor could I *now* one moment live the guest
  Of such dread scenes, without the springs of
   prayer
O'erflowing all my soul. No minsters rise
Like them in pure communion with the skies,
Vast, silent, open unto night and day;
  So might the o'erburden'd Son of man have felt,
  When, turning where inviolate stillness dwelt
He sought high mountains, there apart to pray.

#### VIII.

##### THE LILIES OF THE FIELD.

" Consider the lilies of the field."

Flowers! when the Saviour's calm benignant eye
  Fell on your gentle beauty—when *from you*
  That heavenly lesson from all hearts he drew,
Eternal, universal, as the sky—
Then, in the bosom of your purity,
  A voice He set, as in a temple-shrine,
That life's quick travellers ne'er might pass you by
  Unwarn'd of that sweet oracle divine,
And though too oft its low, celestial sound,
By the harsh notes of work-day Care is drown'd,
And the loud steps of vain unlistening Haste,
  Yet, the great ocean hath no tone of power
  Mightier to reach the soul, in thought's hush'd
   hour,
Than yours, ye Lilies! chosen thus and graced!

### IX.

#### THE BIRDS OF THE AIR.

*" And behold the birds of the air."*

Ye too, the free and fearless Birds of air,
  Were charged that hour, on missionary wing,
The same bright lesson o'er the seas to bear,
  Heaven-guided wanderers with the winds of
    spring!
Sing on, before the storm and after, sing!
  And call us to your echoing woods away,
From worldly cares; and bid our spirits bring
  Faith to imbibe deep wisdom from your lay.
So may those blessed vernal strains renew
Childhood, a childhood yet more pure and true
  E'en than the first, within th' awaken'd mind;
While sweetly, joyously, they tell of life,
That knows no doubts, no questionings, no strife,
  But hangs upon its God, unconsciously resign'd.

### X.

#### THE RAISING OF THE WIDOW'S SON.

*" And he that was dead sat up and began to speak."*

*He that was dead rose up and spoke*—He spoke!
  Was it of that majestic world unknown?
Those words, which first the bier's dread silence
    broke,
  Came they with revelation in each tone?
Were the far cities of the nations gone,
  The solemn halls of consciousness or sleep,
For man uncurtain'd by that spirit lone,
  Back from their portal summon'd o'er the deep?
Be hush'd, my soul! the veil of darkness lay
Still drawn:—thy Lord call'd back the voice de-
    parted,
To spread his truth, to comfort his weak-hearted,
  Not to reveal the mysteries of its way.
Oh! take that lesson home in silent faith,
Put on submissive strength to *meet*, not *question*
    death!

### XI.

#### THE OLIVE TREE.

The Palm—the Vine—the Cedar—each hath
    power
To bid fair Oriental shapes glance by,
And each quick glistening of the Laurel bower
Wafts Grecian images o'er fancy's eye.
But thou, pale Olive!—in *thy* branches lie
Far deeper spells than prophet-grove of old
Might e'er enshrine:—I could not hear thee sigh
To the wind's faintest whisper, nor behold
One shiver of thy leaves' dim silvery green,
Without high thoughts and solemn, of that scene
When, in the garden, the Redeemer pray'd—
When pale stars look'd upon his fainting head,
And angels, ministering in silent dread,
Trembled, perchance, within *thy* trembling shade.

### XII.

#### THE DARKNESS OF THE CRUCIFIXION.

On Judah's hills a weight of darkness hung,
Felt shudderingly at noon:—the land had driven
A Guest divine back to the gates of Heaven,
A life, whence all pure founts of healing sprung,
All grace, all truth:—and, when to anguish wrung,
From the sharp cross th' enlightening spirit fled,
O'er the forsaken earth a pall of dread
By the great shadow of that death was flung.
O Saviour! O Atoner! thou that fain
Wouldst make thy temple in each human breast,
Leave not such darkness in my soul to reign,
Ne'er may thy presence from its depths depart,
Chased thence by guilt!—Oh! turn not *thou* away,
The bright and morning star, my guide to perfect
    day!

### XIII.

#### PLACES OF WORSHIP.

*"God is a Spirit."*

Spirit! whose life-sustaining presence fills
Air, ocean, central depths, by man untried,
Thou for thy worshippers hast sanctified
All place, all time! The silence of the hills
Breathes veneration:—founts and choral rills
Of thee are murmuring:—to its inmost glade
The living forest with thy whisper thrills,
And there is holiness on every shade.
Yet must the thoughtful soul of man invest
With dearer consecration those pure fanes,
Which, sever'd from all sound of earth's unrest,
Hear naught but suppliant or adoring strains
Rise heavenward.—Ne'er may rock or cave possess
*Their* claim on human hearts to solemn tender
    ness.

### XIV.

#### OLD CHURCH IN AN ENGLISH PARK.

Crowning a flowery slope, it stood alone
In gracious sanctity. A bright rill wound,
Caressingly, about the holy ground;
And warbled, with a never-dying tone,
Amidst the tombs. A hue of ages gone
Seem'd, from that ivied porch, that solemn gleam
Of tower and cross, pale quivering on the stream,
O'er all th' ancestral woodlands to be thrown,
And something yet more deep. The air was fraught
With noble memories, whispering many a thought
Of England's fathers; loftily serene,
They that had toil'd, watch'd, struggled, to secure,
Within such fabrics, worship free and pure,
Reign'd there, the o'ershadowing spirits of the
    scene.

### XV.

#### A CHURCH IN NORTH WALES.

Blessings be round it still! that gleaming fane,
Low in its mountain-glen! old mossy trees
Mellow the sunshine through the untinted pane,
And oft, borne in upon some fitful breeze,
The deep sound of the ever-pealing seas,
Filling the hollows with its anthem-tone,
There meets the voice of psalms!—yet not alone,
For memories lulling to the heart as these,
I bless thee, 'midst thy rocks, gray house of prayer!
But for *their* sakes who unto thee repair
From the hill-cabins and the ocean-shore,
Oh! may the fisher and the mountaineer,
Words to sustain earth's toiling children hear,
Within thy lowly walls for evermore!

### XVI.

#### LOUISE SCHEPLER.

Louise Schepler was the faithful servant and friend of
  the pastor Oberlin. The last letter addressed by him
  to his children for their perusal after his decease, affectingly commemorates her unwearied zeal in visiting
  and instructing the children of the mountain hamlets
  through all seasons, and in all circumstances of difficulty and danger.

A fearless journeyer o'er the mountain snow
Wert thou, Louise! the sun's decaying light,
Oft, with its latest melancholy glow,
Redden'd thy steep wild way: the starry night
Oft met thee, crossing some lone eagle's height,
Piercing some dark ravine; and many a dell
Knew, through its ancient rock-recesses well,
Thy gentle presence, which hath made them bright
Oft in mid-storms; oh! not with beauty's eye,
Nor the proud glance of genius keenly burning;
No! pilgrim of unwearying charity!
Thy spell was *love*—the mountain deserts turning
To blessed realms, where stream and rock rejoice,
When the glad human soul lifts a thanksgiving
    voice!

### XVII.

#### TO THE SAME.

For thou, a holy shepherdess and kind,
Through the pine forests, by the upland rills,
Didst roam to seek the children of the hills,
A wild neglected flock! to seek, and find,
And meekly win! there feeding each young mind
With balms of heavenly eloquence: not *thine*,
Daughter of Christ! but his, whose love divine,
Its own clear spirit in thy breast had shrined,

A burning light! Oh! beautiful, in truth,
Upon the mountains are the feet of those
Who bear his tidings!  From thy morn of youth,
For this were all thy journeyings, and the close
Of that long path, Heaven's own bright sabbath-
    rest,
Must wait thee, wanderer! on thy Saviour's breast.

## LINES

### TO A BUTTERFLY RESTING ON A SKULL.

CREATURE of air and light!
Emblem of that which will not fade or die!
    Wilt thou not speed thy flight,
To chase the south wind through the glowing sky?
    What lures thee thus to stay,
    With silence and decay,
Fix'd on the wreck of cold mortality?

    The thoughts, once chamber'd there,
Have gather'd up their treasures, and are gone;—
    Will the dust tell thee where
That which hath burst the prison-house is flown?
    Rise, nursling of the day!
    If thou would'st trace its way—
Earth has no voice to make the secret known

    Who seeks the vanish'd bird,
Near the deserted nest and broken shell?
    Far thence, by us unheard,
He sings, rejoicing in the woods to dwell;
    Thou of the sunshine born,
    Take the bright wings of morn!
Thy hope springs heavenward from yon ruin'd cell.

## THE PALMER

The faded palm-branch in his hand,
Shew'd pilgrim from the Holy Land.
*Scott.*

ART thou come from the far-off land at last?
    Thou that hast wander'd long!
Thou art come to a home whence the smile hath
    pass'd,
    With the merry voice of song.

For the sunny glance and the bounding heart
    Thou wilt seek— but all are gone;
They are parted e'en as waters part,
    To meet in the deep alone!

And thou—from thy lip is fled the glow,
    From thine eye the light of morn;
And the shades of thought o'erhang thy brow,
    And thy cheek with life is worn.

Say what hast thou brought from the distant shore
    For thy wasted youth to pay?
Hast thou treasure to win thee joys once more?
    Hast thou vassals to smooth thy way?

'I have brought but the palm branch in my hand,
    Yet I call not my bright youth lost!
I have won but high thought in the Holy Land,
    Yet I count not too dear the cost!

"I look on the leaves of the deathless tree—
    These records of my track;
And better than youth in its flush of glee,
    Are the memories they give me back!

"They speak of toil, and of high emprise,
    As in words of solemn cheer,
They speak of lonely victories
    O'er pain, and doubt, and fear.

"They speak of scenes which have now become
    Bright pictures in my breast;
Where my spirit finds a glorious home,
    And the love of my heart can rest.

"The colours pass not from *these* away,
    Like tints of shower or sun;
Oh! beyond all treasures that know decay,
    Is the wealth my soul hath won!

"A rich light thence o'er my life's decline,
    An inborn light is cast;
For the sake of the palm from the holy shrine,
    I bewail not my bright days past!"

## THE WATER-LILY.

The Water-Lilies, that are serene in the calm clear
water, but no less serene among the black and scowling
waves.—*Lights and Shadows of Scottish Life.*

    Oh! beautiful thou art,
Thou sculpture-like and stately River-Queen!
Crowning the depths, as with the light serene
    Of a pure heart.

    Bright lily of the wave!
Rising in fearless grace with every swell,
Thou seem'st as if a spirit meekly brave
    Dwelt in thy cell:

    Lifting alike thy head
Of placid beauty, feminine yet free,
Whether with foam or pictured azure spread
    The waters be.

    What is like thee, fair flower,
The gentle and the firm? thus bearing up
To the blue sky that alabaster cup,
    As to the shower?

    Oh! Love is most like thee,
The love of woman; quivering to the blast
Through every nerve, yet rooted deep and fast,
    'Midst Life's dark sea.

    And Faith—O, is not faith
Like thee too, Lily, springing into light,
Still buoyantly, above the billows' might,
    Through the storm's breath?

    Yes, link'd with such high thought,
Flower, let thine image in my bosom lie!
Till something there of its own puri'y
    And peace be wrought:

    Something yet more divine
Than the clear, pearly virgin lustre shed
Forth from thy breast upon the river's bed,
    As from a shrine.

## THOUGHT FROM AN ITALIAN POET.

WHERE shall I find, in all this fleeting earth,
    This world of changes and farewells, a friend
That will not fail me in his love and worth,
    Tender, and firm, and faithful to the end?

Far hath my spirit sought a place of rest—
    Long on vain idols its devotion shed;
Some have forsaken whom I loved the best,
    And some deceived, and some are with the dead

But thou, my Saviour! thou, my hope and trust,
    Faithful art thou when friends and joys depart
each me to lift these yearnings from the dust,
    And fix on thee, th' Unchanging One, my heart

## ELYSIUM.

In the Elysium of the ancients, we find none but heroes and persons who had either been fortunate or
distinguished on earth; the children, and apparently
the slaves and lower classes, that is to say, Poverty,
Misfortune, and Innocence, were banished to the infernal regions."
*Chateaubriand, Genie du Christianisme.*

FAIR wert thou in the dreams
Of elder time, thou land of glorious flowers,
And summer winds, and low-toned silvery streams
Dim with the shadows of thy laurel-bowers!
Where, as they pass'd, bright hours
Left no faint sense of parting, such as clings
To earthly love, and joy in loveliest things!

Fair wert thou, with the light
On thy blue hills and sleepy waters cast,
From purple skies ne'er deepening into night,
Yet soft, as if each moment were their last
Of glory, fading fast
Along the mountains!—but *thy* golden day
Was not as those that warn us of decay.

And ever, through thy shades,
A swell of deep Æolian sound went by,
From fountain-voices in their secret glades,
And low reed-whispers, making sweet reply
To summer's breezy sigh!
And young leaves trembling to the wind's light
breath
Which ne'er had touch'd them with a hue of death!

And the transparent sky
Rang as a dome, all thrilling to the strain
Of harps that, 'midst the woods, made harmony
Solemn and sweet; yet troubling not the brain
With dreams and yearnings vain,
And dim remembrances, that still draw birth
From the bewildering music of the earth.

And who, with silent tread,
Moved o'er the plains of waving Asphodel?
Call'd from the dim procession of the Dead,
Who, 'midst the shadowy amaranth-bowers might
dwell,
And listen to the swell
Of those majestic hymn-notes, and inhale
The spirit wandering in the immortal gale?

They of the sword, whose praise,
With the bright wine at nations' feasts, went
round!
They of the lyre, whose unforgotten lays
Forth on the winds had sent their mighty sound,
And in all regions found
Their echoes 'midst the mountains!—and become
In man's deep heart as voices of his home!

They of the daring thought!
Daring and powerful, yet to dust allied—
Whose flight through stars, and seas, and depths
had sought
The soul's far birth-place—but without a guide!
Sages and seers, who died,
And left the world their high mysterious dreams,
Born 'midst the olive-woods, by Grecian streams.

But the most *loved* are they
Of whom Fame speaks not with her clarion voice
In regal halls! the shades o'erhang their way,
The vale, with its deep fountains, is their choice,
And gentle hearts rejoice
Around their steps; till, silently, they die,
As a stream shrinks from summer's burning eye.

And these—of whose abode,
Midst her green valleys, earth retain'd no trace,
Save a flower springing from their burial-sod,
A shade of sadness on some kindred face,
A dim and vacant place
In some sweet home;—thou hadst no wreath for
*these,*
Thou sunny land! with all thy deathless trees!

The peasant at his door
Might sink to die when vintage feasts were spread,
And songs on every wind! From *thy* bright shore
No lovelier vision floated round his head—
Thou wert for nobler dead!
He heard the bounding steps which round him fell,
And sigh'd to bid the festal Sun farewell!

The slave, whose very tears
Were a forbidden luxury, and whose breast
Kept the mute woes and burning thoughts of
years,
As embers in a burial urn compress'd;
*He* might not be thy guest!
No gentle breathings from thy distant sky
Came o'er *his* path, and whisper'd " Liberty!"

Calm, on its leaf-strewn bier,
Unlike a gift of nature to decay,
Too rose-like still, too beautiful, too dear,
The child at rest before the mother lay,
E'en so to pass away,
With its bright smile! what wert *thou*
To her, who wept o'er that young slumberer's brow?

Thou hadst no home, green land
For the fair creature from her bosom gone,
With life's fresh flowers just opening in its hand,
And all the lovely thoughts and dreams unknown,
Which, in its clear eye, shone
Like spring's first wakening! but that light was
past—
Where went the dew-drop swept before the blast?

Not where *thy* soft winds play'd,
Not where thy waters lay in glassy sleep!
Fade with thy bowers, thou land of visions, fade!
From thee no voice came o'er the gloomy deep,
And bade man cease to weep!
Fade, with the amaranth-plain, the myrtle grove,
Which could not yield one hope to sorrowing love!

## BELSHAZZAR'S FEAST.

'TWAS night in Babylon: yet many a beam
Of lamps far-glittering from her domes on high,
Shone, brightly mingling in Euphrates' stream,
With the clear stars of that Chaldean sky,
Whose azure knows no cloud:—each whisper'd
sigh
Of the soft night-breeze through her terrace-
bowers
Bore deepening tones of joy and melody,
O'er an illumined wilderness of flowers;
And the glad city's voice went up from all her
towers.

But prouder mirth was in the kingly hall,
Where, 'midst adoring slaves, a gorgeous band
High at the stately midnight festival,
Belshazzar sat enthroned.—There Luxury's hand
Had shower'd around all treasures that expand
Beneath the burning East!—all gems that pour
The sunbeams back;—all sweets of many a land
Whose gales waft incense from their spicy shore
—But mortal pride look'd on, and still demanded
more.

With richer zest the banquet may be fraught,
A loftier theme may swell th' exulting strain!
The Lord of nations spoke,—and forth were
brought
The spoils of Salem's devastated fane
Thrice holy vessels!—pure from earthly stain,
And set apart, and sanctified to Him,
Who deign'd within the oracle to reign,
Reveal'd, yet shadow'd; making noon-day dim,
To that most glorious cloud between the Cherubim.

They came, and louder peal'd the voice of song,
And pride flash'd brighter from the kindling eye,
And He who sleeps not heard th' elated throng,
In mirth that plays with thunderbolts, defy
The Rock of Zion!—Fill the nectar high.

High in the cups of consecrated gold!
And crown the bowl with garlands, ere they die,
Aud bid the censers of the Temple hold
Offerings to Babel's gods, the mighty ones of old!

Peace!—is it but a phantom of the brain,
Thus shadow'd forth the senses to appal,
Yon fearful vision?—Who shall gaze again
To search its cause?—Along the illumined wall,
Startling, yet riveting the eyes of all,
Darkly it moves,—a hand, a human hand,
O'er the bright lamps of that resplendent hall
In silence tracing, as a mystic wand,
Words all unknown, the tongue of some far dis
   tant land.

There are pale cheeks around the regal board,
And quivering lips and whispers deep and low,
And fitful starts!—the wine in triumph pour'd,
Untasted foams, the song hath ceased to flow.
The waving censer drops to earth—and lo!
The King of Men, the Ruler, girt with might,
Trembles before a shadow!—Say not so!
—The child of dust, with guilt's foreboding sight,
Shrinks from the Dread Unknown, th' avenging
   Infinite!

But haste ye!—bring Chaldea's gifted seers,
The men of prescience!—haply to *their* eyes,
Which track the future through the rolling
   spheres,
Yon mystic sign may speak in prophecies.
They come—the readers of the midnight skies,
They that give voice to visions—but in vain!
Still wrapt in clouds the awful secret lies,
It hath no language 'midst the starry train,
Earth has no gifted tongue Heaven's mysteries to
   explain.

Then stood forth one, a child of other sires,
And other inspiration!—One of those
Who on the willows hung their captive lyres,
And sat, and wept, where Babel's river flows.
His eye was bright, and yet the deep repose
Of his pale features half o'erawed the mind,
And imaged forth a soul, whose joys and woes
Were of a loftier stamp than aught assign'd
To earth; a being seal'd and sever'd from man-
   kind.

Yes!—what was earth to him, whose spirit pass'd
Time's utmost bounds?—on whose unshrinking
   sight
Ten thousand shapes of burning glory cast
Their full resplendence?—Majesty and might
Were in his dreams;—for him the veil of light
Shrouding heaven's inmost sanctuary and
   throne,
The curtain of th' unutterably bright
Was raised!—to him, in fearful splendour shown,
Ancient of days! e'en thou mad'st thy dread pre-
   sence known.

He spoke;—the shadows of the things to come
Pass'd o'er his soul:—" O King, elate in pride!
God hath sent forth the writing of thy doom,
The one, the living God, by thee defied!
He in whose balance earthly lords are tried,
Hath weigh'd, and found thee wanting.  'T is
   decreed
The conqueror's hands thy kingdom shall divide,
The stranger to thy throne of power succeed!
The days are full, they come;—the Persian and
   the Mede!"

There fell a moment's thrilling silence round,
A breathless pause! the hush of hearts that beat
And limbs that quiver:—is there not a sound,
A gathering cry, a tread of hurrying feet?
—'T was but some echo in the crowded street,
Of far-heard revelry; the shout, the song.
The measured dance to music wildly sweet,
That speeds the stars their joyous course along;—
Away! nor let a dream disturb the festal throng!

Peace yet aga'n!—Hark! steps in tumult flying,
Steeds rushing on as o'er a battle-field!
The shout of hosts exulting or defying,
The press of multitudes that strive or yield!
And the loud, startling clash of spear and shield,
Sudden as earthquake's burst!—and, blent with
   these,
The last wild shriek of those whose doom is
   seal'd
In their full mirth!—all deepening on the breeze,
As the long stormy roar of far advancing seas!

And nearer yet the trumpet's blast is swelling,
Loud, shrill, and savage, drowning every cry!
And lo! the spoiler in the regal dwelling,
Death bursting on the halls of revelry!
Ere one bright star be faded from the sky,
Red flames, like banners, wave from dome and
   fane,
Empire is lost and won, Belshazzar with the slain.

Fallen is the golden city! in the dust
Spoil'd of her crown, dismantled of her state,
She that hath made the Strength of Towers her
   trust,
Weeps by her dead, supremely desolate!
She that beheld the nations at her gate,
Thronging in homage, shall be call'd no more
Lady of kingdoms!—Who shall mourn her fate?
Her guilt is full, her march of triumph o'er;—
—What widow'd land shall now *her* widowhood
   deplore?

Sit thou in silence!  Thou that wert enthroned
On many waters! thou, whose augurs read
The language of the planets, and disown'd
The mighty name it blazons!—Veil thy head,
Daughter of Babylon! the sword is red
From thy destroyers' harvest, and the yoke
Is on thee, O most proud!—for thou hast said,
" I am, and none beside!"—Th' Eternal spoke,
Thy glory was a spoil, thine idol-gods were broke.

But go thou forth, O Israel! wake! rejoice!
Be clothed with strength, as in thine ancient day.
Renew the sound of harps, th' exulting voice,
The mirth of timbrels!—loose the chain, and say
God hath redeem'd his people!—from decay
The silent and the trampled shall arise;
—Awake; put on thy beautiful array,
Oh long-forsaken Zion! to the skies
Send up on every wind thy choral melodies!

And lift thy head!—Behold thy sons returning,
Redeem'd from exile, ransom'd from the chain!
Light hath revisited the house of mourning;
She that on Judah's mountain wept in vain
Because her children were not—dwells again
Girt with the lovely!—through thy streets once
   more,
City of God! shall pass the bridal train
And the bright lamps their festive radiance pour
And the triumphal hymns the joy of youth restore

# HYMNS

## FOR

# CHILDHOOD.

# PREFACE.

THE following very simple compositions were written a few years ago, exclusively for the Author's family circle, and without the remotest idea of their publication. It is now her wish to render them more extensively, however humbly, useful. The Hymns were intended to associate the first devotional thoughts of childhood with the loveliness and solemnity diffused over the outward creation. Should they prove acceptable, they may perhaps be followed by a series, of a character more entirely scriptural.

# HYMNS FOR CHILDHOOD.

## INTRODUCTORY VERSES.

On! blest art thou, whose steps may rove
Through the green paths of vale and grove,
Or leaving all their charms below,
Climb the wild mountain's airy brow;

And gaze afar o'er cultured plains,
And cities with their stately fanes,
And forests, that beneath thee lie,
And ocean mingling with the sky.

For man can show thee naught so fair,
As Nature's vari'd marvels there;
And if thy pure and artless breast
Can feel their grandeur, thou art blest

For thee the stream in beauty flows,
For thee the gale of summer blows,
And, in deep glen and wood-walk free,
Voices of joy still breathe for thee.

But happier far, if then thy soul
Can soar to Him who made the whole,
If to thine eye the simplest flower
Portray His bounty and His power.

If, in whate'er is bright or grand,
Thy mind can trace His viewless hand,
If Nature's music bid thee raise
Thy song of gratitude and praise;

If heaven and earth with beauty fraught,
Lead to His throne thy raptured thought,
If there thou lov'st His love to read,
Then wanderer, thou art blest indeed.

## THE RAINBOW.

*I do set my bow in the cloud, and it shall be for a to
ken of a covenant between me and the earth.*
*Genesis* ix. 13

Sort falls the mild, reviving show-er
From April's changeful skies,
And rain-drops bend each trembling flower
They tinge with richer dyes.

Soon shall their genial influence call
A thousand buds to day,
Which, waiting but that balmy fall,
In hidden beauty lay.

E'en now full many a blossom's bell
With fragrance fills the shade!
And verdure clothes each grassy dell,
In brighter tints array'd.

But mark! what arch of varied hue
From Heaven to earth is bow'd!
Haste, ere it vanish, haste to view
The Rainbow in the cloud.

How bright its glory! there behold
The emerald's verdant rays,
The topaz blends its hue of gold
With the deep ruby's blaze.

Yet not alone to charm thy sight
Was given the vision fair;—
Gaze on that arch of colour'd light,
And read God's mercy there.

It tells us that the mighty deep,
Fast by th' Eternal chain'd,
No more o'er earth's domains shall sweep,
Awful and unrestrain'd.

It tells that seasons, heat and cold,
Fix'd by his sovereign will,
Shall, in their course, bid man behold
Seed-time and harvest still;

That still the flower shall deck the field
When vernal zephyrs blow;
That still the vine its fruit shall yield,
When autumn sun-beams glow.

Then, child of that fair earth! which yet
Smiles with each charm endow'd,
Bless thou *His* name, whose mercy set
The Rainbow in the cloud!

## THE SUN.

The Sun comes forth;—each mountain height
Glows with a tinge of rosy light,
And flowers that slumber'd through the night
Their dewy leaves unfold;
A flood of splendour bursts on high,
And ocean's breast reflects a sky
Of crimson and of gold.

Oh! thou art glorious, orb of day!
Exulting nations hail thy ray,
Creation swells a choral lay,
To welcome thy return;
From thee all nature draws her hues,
Thy beams the insect's wings suffuse,
And in the diamond burn.

Yet must thou fade;—when earth and heaven
By fire and tempest shall be riven,
Thou, from thy sphere of radiance driven,
Oh Sun! must fall at last;
Another heaven, another earth,
Far other glory shall have birth,
When all we see is past.

But He, who gave the word of might,
"Let there be light"—and there was light,
Who bade thee chase the gloom of night,

And beam, the world to bless ;—
For ever bright, for ever pure,
Alone, unchanging, shall endure
The Sun of Righteousness !


## THE RIVERS.

Go ! trace th' unnumber'd streams o'er earth
That wind their devious course,
That draw from Alpine heights their birth,
Deep vale, or cavern source.

Some by majestic cities glide,
Proud scenes of man's renown,
Some lead their solitary tide,
Where pathless forests frown.

Some calmly roll in golden sands,
Where Afric's deserts lie !
Or spread, to clothe rejoicing lands
With rich fertility.

These bear the bark, whose stately sail
Exulting seems to swell ;
While these, scarce rippled by a gale,
Sleep in the lonely dell.

Yet on, alike though swift or slow
Their various waves may sweep,
Through cities or through shades they flow
To the same boundless deep.

Oh ! thus, whate'er our path of life,
Through sunshine or through gloom,
Through scenes of quiet or of strife,
Its end is still the tomb.

The chief, whose mighty deeds we hail,
The monarch throned on high,
The peasant in his native vale,
All journey on—to die !

But if *Thy* guardian care, my God !
The pilgrim's course attend,
I will not fear the dark abode,
To which my footsteps bend.

For thence thine all-redeeming Son,
Who died, the world to save,
In light, in triumph, rose, and won
The victory from the grave !


## THE STARS.

The heavens declare the glory of God, and the firma
ment showeth his handy-work.——*Psalm* xix. 1.


No cloud obscures the summer sky,
The moon in brightness walks on high,
And, set in azure, every star
Shines, like a gem of heaven, afar !

Child of the earth ! oh ! lift thy glance
To yon bright firmament's expanse,
The glories of its realm explore,
And gaze, and wonder, and adore !

Doth it not speak to every sense
The marvels of Omnipotence ?
See'st thou not there th' Almighty name
Inscribed in characters of flame ?

Count o'er those lamps of quenchless light,
That sparkle through the shades of night !
Behold them !—can a mortal boast
To number that celestial host ?

Mark well each little star, whose rays
In distant splendour meet thy gaze ;
Each is a world by Him sustain'd,
Who from eternity hath reign'd.

Each, shining not for earth alone,
Hath suns and planets of its own,
And beings, whose existence springs
From Him, th' all-powerful King of kings.

Haply, those glorious beings know
Nor stain of guilt, nor tear of woe !
But raising still th' adoring voice,
For ever in their God rejoice.

What then art *thou*, oh ! child of clay !
Amid creation's grandeur, say ?
—E'en as an insect on the breeze,
E'en as a dew-drop, lost in seas !

Yet fear thou not !—the sovereign hand,
Which spread the ocean and the land,
And hung the rolling spheres in air,
Hath, e'en for thee, a Father's care !

Be thou at peace !—th' all-seeing eye,
Pervading earth, and air, and sky,
The searching glance which none may flee,
Is still, in mercy, turn'd on thee.


## THE OCEAN.

They that go down to the sea in ships, that do busi
ness in great waters, these see the works of the Lord
and his wonders in the deep.——*Psalm* cvii. 23, 24

He that in venturous barks hath been
A wanderer on the deep,
Can tell of many an awful scene,
Where storms for ever sweep.

For many a fair majestic sight
Hath met his wandering eye,
Beneath the streaming northern light,
Or blaze of India's sky.

Go ! ask him of the whirlpool's roar,
Whose echoing thunder peals
Loud, as if rush'd along the shore
An army's chariot-wheels ;

Of icebergs, floating o'er the main
Or fix'd upon the coast,
Like glittering citadel or fane,
'Mid the bright realms of frost ;

Of coral rocks from waves below
In steep ascent that tower,
And, fraught with peril, daily grow,
Form'd by an insect's power ;

Of sea-fires, which at dead of night
Shine o'er the tides afar,
And make th' expanse of ocean bright
As heaven, with many a star.

Oh God ! thy name they well may praise
Who to the deep go down,
And trace the wonders of thy ways
Where rocks and billows frown.

If glorious be that awful deep,
No human power can bind,
What then art Thou, who bid'st it keep
Within its bounds confined !

Let heaven and earth in praise unite,
Eternal praise to Thee,
Whose word can rouse the tempest's might,
Or still the raging sea !


## THE THUNDER-STORM.

Deep, fiery clouds o'ercast the sky,
Dead stillness reigns in air,
There is not e'en a breeze on high,
The gossamer to bear.

The woods are hush'd, the waves at rest,
　The lake is dark and still,
Reflecting on its shadowy breast,
　Each form of rock and hill.

The lime-leaf waves not in the grove
　No rose-tree in the bower;
The birds have ceased their songs of love
　Awed by the threatening hour.

'T is noon;—yet Nature's calm profound
　Seems as at midnight deep;
—But hark! what peal of awful sound
　Breaks on creation's sleep?

The thunder bursts!—its rolling might
　Seems the firm hills to shake;
And in terrific splendour bright,
　The gather'd lightnings break.

Yet fear not, shrink not thou, my child!
　Though by the bolt's descent
Were the tall cliffs in ruins piled,
　And the wide forests rent.

Doth not thy God behold thee still,
　With all-surveying eye?
Doth not his power all nature fill,
　Around, beneath, on high?

Know, hadst thou eagle-pinions free,
　To track the realms of air,
Thou couldst not reach a spot where He
　Would not be with thee there!

In the wide city's peopled towers,
　On the vast ocean's plains,
'Midst the deep woodland's loneliest bowers
　Alike th' Almighty reigns!

Then fear not, though the angry sky
　A thousand darts should cast;—
Why should we tremble e'en to die
　And be with *Him* at last?

---

## THE BIRDS.

Are not five sparrows sold for two farthings, and not
one of them is forgotten before God?——*St. Luke*, xii. 6.

Tribes of the air! whose favour'd race
May wander through the realms of space,
　Free guests of earth and sky;
In form, in plumage, and in song,
What gifts of nature mark your throng
　With bright variety!

Nor differ less your forms, your flight,
Your dwellings hid from hostile sight,
　And the wild haunts ye love;
Birds of the gentle beak!* how dear
Your wood-note, to the wanderer's ear,
　In shadowy vale or grove!

Far other scenes, remote, sublime,
Where swain or hunter may not climb,
　The mountain-eagle seeks;
Alone he reigns, a monarch there,
Scarce will the chamois' footstep dare
　Ascend his Alpine peaks.

Others there are, that make their home
Where the white billows roar and foam,
　Around th' o'erhanging rock;
Fearless they skim the angry wave,
Or, shelter'd in their sea-beat cave,
　The tempest's fury mock.

Where Afric's burning realm expands,
The ostrich haunts the desert sands,
　Parch'd by the blaze of day;
The swan, where northern rivers glide
Through the tall reeds that fringe their tide,
　Floats graceful on her way.

---

* The Italians call all singing-birds, *Birds of the gentle beak.*

The condor, where the Andes tower,
Spreads his broad wing of pride and power
　And many a storm defies:
Bright in the orient realms of morn,
All beauty's richest hues adorn
　The Bird of Paradise.

Some, amidst India's groves of palm,
And spicy forests breathing balm,
　Weave soft their pendent nest;
Some, deep in western wilds, display
Their fairy form and plumage gay,
　In rainbow colours drest.

Others no varied song may pour,
May boast no eagle-plume to soar,
　No tints of light may wear;
Yet, know, our Heavenly Father guides
The least of these, and well provides
　For each, with tenderest care.

Shall He not then thy guardian be?
Will not his aid extend to *thee?*
　Oh! safely may'st thou rest!
Trust in his love, and e'en should pain,
Should sorrow tempt thee to complain,
　Know, what He wills is best!

---

## THE SKY-LARK.

The Sky-lark, when the dews of morn
Hang tremulous on flower and thorn,
And violets round his nest exhale
Their fragrance on the early gale,
To the first sunbeam spreads his wings,
Buoyant with joy, and soars, and sings.

He rests not on the leafy spray,
To warble his exulting lay,
But high above the morning cloud
Mounts, in triumphant freedom proud,
And swells, when nearest to the sky,
His notes of sweetest ecstasy.

Thus, my Creator! thus the more
My spirit's wing to Thee can soar,
The more she triumphs to behold
Thy love in all thy works unfold,
And bids her hymns of rapture be
Most glad, when rising most to Thee.

---

## THE NIGHTINGALE.

When twilight's gray and pensive hour
Brings the low breeze, and shuts the flower
And bids the solitary star
Shine in pale beauty from afar;

When gathering shades the landscape veil,
And peasants seek their village-dale,
And mists from river-wave arise,
And dew in every blossom lies;

When evening's primrose opes, to shed
Soft fragrance round her grassy bed;
When glow-worms in the wood-walk light
Their lamp, to cheer the traveller's sight;

At that calm hour, so still, so pale,
Awakes the lonely nightingale;
And from a hermitage of shade
Fills with her voice the forest-glade.

And sweeter far that melting voice,
Than all which through the day rejoice;
And still shall bard and wanderer love
The twilight music of the grove.

Father in Heaven! oh! thus, when day
With all its cares hath pass'd away,
And silent hours waft peace on earth,
And hush the louder strains of mirth

Thus may sweet songs of praise and prayer
To Thee my spirit's offering bear;
Yon star, my signal, set on high,
For vesper-hymns of piety.

So may thy mercy and thy power
Protect me through the midnight hour;
And balmy sleep and visions blest
Smile on thy servant's bed of rest.

## THE NORTHERN SPRING.

WHEN the soft breath of Spring goes forth
Far o'er the mountains of the North,
How soon those wastes of dazzling snow
With life, and bloom, and beauty glow!

Then bursts the verdure of the plains,
Then break the streams from icy chains;
And the glad rein-deer seeks no more
Amidst deep snows his mossy store.

Then the dark pine-wood's boughs are seen
Array'd in tints of living green;
And roses, in their brightest dyes,
By Lapland's founts and lakes arise.

Thus, in a moment, from the gloom
And the cold fetters of the tomb,
Thus shall the blest Redeemer's voice
Call forth his servants to rejoice.

For He, whose word is truth, hath said,
His power to life shall wake the dead,
And summon those he loves, on high,
To "put on immortality!"

Then, all its transient sufferings o'er,
On wings of light the soul shall soar
Exulting, to that blest abode,
Where tears of sorrow never flow'd.

## PARAPHRASE OF PSALM CXLVIII.

Praise ye the Lord.  Praise ye the Lord from the heavens: praise him in the heights.

PRAISE ye the Lord! on every height
   Songs to his glory raise!
Ye angel-hosts, ye stars of light,
   Join in immortal praise!

Oh! heaven of heavens! let praise far-swelling
   From all your orbs be sent!
Join in the strain, ye waters, dwelling
   Above the firmament!

For His the word which gave you birth,
   And majesty and might;
Praise to the Highest from the earth,
   And let the deeps unite!

Oh! fire and vapour, hail and snow,
   Ye servants of His will;
Oh! stormy winds, that only blow
   His mandates to fulfil;

Mountains and rocks, to heaven that rise;
   Fair cedars of the wood;
Creatures of life, that wing the skies,
   Or track the plains for food;

Judges of nations; kings, whose hand
   Waves the proud sceptre high;
Oh! youths and virgins of the land,
   Oh! age and infancy;

Praise ye *His* name, to whom alone
   All homage should be given;
Whose glory from th' eternal throne
   Spreads wide o'er earth and heaven!

## CHRISTMAS CAROL.

O lovely voices of the sky,
   That hymn'd the Saviour's birth!
Are ye not singing still on high,
   Ye that sang, "Peace on earth?"
      To us yet speak the strains
         Wherewith, in days gone by
      Ye bless'd the Syrian swains,
         O voices of the sky!

O clear and shining light, whose beams
   That hour Heaven's glory shed
Around the palms, and o'er the streams,
   And on the Shepherds' head;
      Be near, through life and death,
         As in that holiest night
      Of Hope, and Joy, and Faith,
         O clear and shining light!

O star which led to Him, whose love
   Brought down man's ransom free;
Where art thou?—'Midst the hosts above,
   May we still gaze on thee?—
      In heaven thou art not set,
         Thy rays earth might not dim—
      Send them to guide us yet!
         O star which led to Him!

## CHRIST WALKING ON THE WATER

FEAR was within the tossing bark,
   When stormy winds grew loud,
And waves came rolling high and dark,
   And the tall mast was bow'd.

And men stood breathless in their dread,
   And baffled in their skill—
But One was there, who rose, and said
   To the wild sea—*be still!*

And the wind ceased—it ceased!—that word
   Pass'd through the gloomy sky;
The troubled billows knew their Lord,
   And fell beneath His eye.

And slumber settled on the deep,
   And silence on the blast;
They sank, as flowers that fold to sleep
   When sultry day is past.

Oh! thou, that in its wildest hour
   Didst rule the tempest's mood,
Send thy meek spirit forth in power
   Soft on our souls to brood.

Thou that didst bow the billow's pride
   Thy mandate to fulfil,
Oh! speak to passion's raging tide,
   Speak, and say, "*Peace, be still!*"

## A FATHER READING THE BIBLE.

'TWAS early Day, and sunlight stream'd
   Soft through a quiet room,
That hush'd, but not forsaken, seem'd,
   Still, but with naught of gloom.
For there, serene in happy age,
   Whose hope is from above,
A Father communed with the page
   Of Heaven's recorded love.

Pure fell the beam, and meekly bright,
   On his gray holy hair,
And touch'd the page with tenderest light
   As if its shrine were there!
But oh! that patriarch's aspect shone
   With something lovelier far,
A radiance all the spirit's own,
   Caught not from sun or star.

Some word of life e'en then had met
  His calm, benignant eye,
Some ancient promise, breathing yet
  Of Immortality :
Some Martyr's prayer, wherein the glow
  Of quenchless faith survives :
For every feature said—"*I knew
  That my Redeemer lives !*"

And silent stood his children by,
  Hushing their very breath,
Before the solemn sanctity
  Of thoughts o'ersweeping death.
Silent—yet did not each young breast
  With love and reverence melt ?
Oh ! blest be those fair girls, and blest
  That home where God is felt !

## A DIRGE

ɔALM on the bosom of thy God,
  Young spirit ! rest thee now !
Ev'n while with us thy footstep trod,
  His seal was on thy brow.

Dust, to its narrow house beneath !
  Soul, to its place on high !
They that have seen thy look in death,
  No more may fear to die.

Lone are the paths, and sad the bowers
  Whence thy meek smile is gone ;
But oh ! a brighter home than ours,
  In heaven, is now thine own.

## THE CHILD'S FIRST GRIEF

" Oh ! call my brother back to me !
  I cannot play alone ;
The summer comes with flower and bee—
  Where is my brother gone ?

The butterfly is glancing bright
  Across the sunbeam's track ;
I care not now to chase its flight—
  Oh ! call my brother back !

The flowers run wild—the flowers we sow'd
  Around our garden tree ;
Our vine is drooping with its load—
  Oh ! call him back to me !"

" He would not hear thy voice, fair child ;
  He may not come to thee ;
The face that once like spring-time smiled
  On earth no more thou'lt see.

" A rose's brief bright life of joy,
  Such unto him was given ;
Go—thou must play alone, my boy !
  Thy brother is in heaven."

" And has he left his birds and flowers ;
  And must I call in vain ?
And through the long, long summer hours,
  Will he not come again ?

And by the brook and in the glade
  Are all our wanderings o'er ?
Oh ! while my brother with me play'd,
  *Would I had loved him more !*"

## EPITAPH

### OVER THE GRAVE OF TWO BROTHERS
#### A CHILD AND A YOUTH.

THOU, that canst gaze upon thine own fair boy,
  And hear his prayer's low murmur at thy knee,
And o'er his slumber bend in breathless joy

Come to this tomb ! it hath a voice for thee !
Pray !—thou art blest—ask strength for sorrow's
  hour,
Love, deep as thine, lays here its broken flower
Thou that art gathering from the smile of youth,
  Thy thousand hopes—rejoicing to behold,
All the heart's depths before thee bright with truth
  All the mind's treasure silently unfold ;
Look on this tomb !—for thee, too, speaks the grave
Where God hath seal'd the fount of hope he gave.

## BIRTH-DAY LINES
### TO A YOUNG CHILD IN AUTUMN.

WHERE sucks the bee now ?—Summer is flying,
Leaves on the grass-plot faded are lying ;
Violets are gone from their grassy dell,
With the cowslip-cups, where the fairies dwell ;
The rose from the garden hath pass'd away—
Yet happy, fair boy ! is thy natal day.

For love bids it welcome, the love which hath
  smiled
Ever around thee, my gentle child !
Watching thy footsteps, and guarding thy bed,
And pouring out joy on thy sunny head.
Roses may vanish, but this will stay—
Happy and bright is thy natal day.

## ON A SIMILAR OCCASION.

THOU wak'st from happy sleep, to play
  With bounding heart, my boy !
Before thee lies a long bright day
  Of summer and of joy.

Thou hast no heavy thought or dream,
  To cloud thy fearless eye ;—
Long be it thus—life's early stream
  Should still reflect the sky.

Yet ere the cares of life lie dim
  On thy young spirit's wings,
Now in thy morn forget not Him
  From whom each pure thought springs !

So in the onward vale of tears,
  Where'er thy path may be,
When strength hath bow'd to evil years—
  *He* will remember thee.

## HYMN BY THE SICK BED OF A MOTHER

FATHER ! that in the olive shade
  When the dark hour came on,
Di'st, with a breath of heavenly aid,
      Strengthen thy Son ;

Oh ! by the anguish of that night,
  Send us down blest relief ;
Or to the chasten'd, let thy might
      Hallow this grief !

And Thou, that when the starry sky
  Saw the dread strife begun,
Didst teach adoring faith to cry,
      " Thy will be done !"

By thy meek spirit, Thou, of all
  That e'er have mourn'd the chief—
Thou Saviour ! if the stroke must fall,
      Hallow this grief !

## THE TREASURES OF THE DEEP

WHAT hidest thou in thy treasure-caves and cells
  Thou hollow-sounding and mysterious main!—
Pale glistening pearls, and rainbow-colour'd shells,
  Bright things which gleam'd unreck'd-of, and in
      vain!—
Keep, keep thy riches, melancholy sea!
      We ask not such from thee

Yet more, the depths have more!—what wealth
      untold,
  Far down, and shining through their stillness
      lies!
Thou hast the starry gems, the burning gold,
  Won from ten thousand royal argosies!—
Sweep o'er thy spoils, thou wild and wrathful
      main!—
      Earth claims not these again.

Yet more, the depths have more!—thy waves have
      roll'd
  Above the cities of a world gone by!
Sand hath fill'd up the palaces of old,
  Sea-weed o'ergrown the halls of revelry.—
Dash o'er them, ocean! in thy scornful play!
      Man yields t 'em to decay.

Yet more! the billows and the depths have more.
  High hearts and brave are gather'd to thy breast!
They hear not now the booming waters roar,
  The battle-thunders will not break their rest.—
Keep thy red gold and gems, thou stormy grave!
      Give back the true and brave!

Give back the lost and lovely!—those for whom
  The place was kept at board and hearth so long!
The prayer went up through midnight's breathless
      gloom,
  And the vain yearning woke 'midst festal song!
Hold fast thy buried isles, thy towers o'erthrown—
      But all is not thine own.

To thee the love of woman hath gone down,
  Dark flow thy tides o'er manhood's noble head,
O'er youth's bright locks, and beauty's flowery
      crown.
  Yet must thou hear a voice—Restore the dead!
Earth shall reclaim her precious things from thee
      Restore the dead, thou sea!

---

### THE CRUSADER'S RETURN

Alas! the mother that him bare,
If she had been in presence there
In his own cheeks and sunburnt hair,
  She had not known her child
      *Marmion.*

---

Rest, pilgrim, rest!—thou'rt from the Syrian land
  Thou'rt from the wild and wondrous east, I know
By the long-wither'd palm-branch in thy hand,
  And by the darkness of thy sunburnt brow.
Alas! the bright, the beautiful, who part,
  So full of hope, for that far country's bourne!
Alas! the weary and the changed in heart,
  And dimm'd in aspect, who like thee return!

Thou'rt faint—stay, rest thee from thy toils at last'
  Through the high chestnuts lightly plays the
      breeze,
The stars gleam out, the *Ave* hour is pass'd,
  The sailor's hymn hath died along the seas.
Thou'rt faint and worn—hear'st thou the fountain
      welling
  By the gray pillars of yon ruin'd shrine?
Seest thou the dewy grapes, before thee swelling?
  —He that hath left me train'd that loaded vine!

He was a child when thus the bower he wove,
  (Oh! hath a day fled since his childhood's time?)
That I might sit and hear the sound I love,
  Beneath its shade—the convent's vesper-chime.
And sit *thou* there!—for he was gentle ever,
  With his glad voice he would have welcomed
      thee,
And brought fresh fruits to cool thy parch'd lips'
      fever—
  There in his place thou'rt resting—where is he?

If I could hear that laughing voice again,
  But once again!—how oft it wanders by,
In the still hours, like some remember'd strain,
  Troubling the heart with its wild melody!—
Thou hast seen much, tired pilgrim! hast thou seen
  In that far land, the chosen land of yore,
A youth—my Guido—with the fiery main,
  And the dark eye of this Italian shore?

The dark, clear, lightning eye!—on Heaven and
      earth
  It smiled—as if man were not dust it smiled!
The very air seem'd kindling with his mirth,
  And I—my heart grew young before my child!
My blessed child!—I had but him—yet he
  Fill'd all my home ev'n with o'erflowing joy,
Sweet laughter, and wild song, and footstep free—
  Where is he now?—my pride, my flower, my boy!

His sunny childhood melted from my sight,
  Like a spring dew-drop—then his forehead wore
A prouder look—his eye a keener light—
  I knew these woods might be his world no more

He loved me—but he left me!—thus they go,
 Whom we have rear'd, watch'd, bless'd, too
 much adored!
He heard the trumpet of the Red-Cross blow,
 And bounded from me with his father's sword!

Thou weep'st—I tremble—thou hast seen the slain
 Pressing a bloody turf; the young and fair,
With their pale beauty strewing o'er the plain
 Where hosts have met—speak! answer!—was
 he there?
Oh! hath his smile departed?—Could the grave
 Shut o'er those bursts of bright and tameless
 glee?—
 No! I shall yet behold his dark locks wave—
 That look gives me hope—I knew it could not be!

Still weep'st thou, wanderer?—some fond mother's
 glance
 O'er thee too brooded in thine early years—
Think'st thou of her, whose gentle eye perchance
 Bathed all thy faded hair with parting tears?
Speak, for thy tears disturb me!—what art thou?
 Why dost thou hide thy face, yet weeping on?
Look up!—oh! is it—that wan cheek and brow!—
 Is it—alas! yet joy!—my son, my son!

---

## BRING FLOWERS

Bring flowers, young flowers, for the festal board,
To wreathe the cup ere the wine is pour'd;
Bring flowers! they are springing in wood and vale
Their breath floats out on the southern gale,
And the touch of the sunbeam hath waked the
 rose,
To deck the hall where the bright wine flows.

Bring flowers to strew in the conqueror's path—
He hath shaken thrones with his stormy wrath!
He comes with the spoils of nations back,
The vines lie crush'd in his chariot's track,
The turf looks red where he won the day—
Bring flowers to die in the conqueror's way!

Bring flowers to the captive's lonely cell,
They have tales of the joyous woods to tell;
Of the free blue streams, and the glowing sky,
And the bright world shut from his languid eye;
They will bear him a thought of the sunny hours,
And a dream of his youth—bring him flowers, wild
 flowers!

Bring flowers, fresh flowers, for the bride to wear!
They were born to blush in her shining hair.
She is leaving the home of her childhood's mirth
She hath bid farewell to her father's hearth,
Her place is now by another's side—
Bring flowers for the locks of the fair young bride!

Bring flowers, pale flowers, o'er the bier to shed,
A crown for the brow of the early dead!
For this through its leaves hath the white rose
 burst,
For this in the woods was the violet nursed!
Though they smile in vain for what once was ours,
They are love's last gift—bring ye flowers, pale
 flowers.

Bring flowers to the shrine where we kneel in
 prayer,
They are nature's offering, their place is there!
They speak of hope to the fainting heart,
With a voice of promise they come and part,
They sleep in dust through the wintry hours,
They break forth in glory—bring flowers, bright
 flowers!

## THEKLA'S SONG; OR THE VOICE OF A SPIRIT.

### FROM THE GERMAN OF SCHILLER.

This song is said to have been composed by Schiller
in answer to the inquiries of his friends respecting the
fate of *Thekla*, whose beautiful character is withdrawn
from the tragedy of "Wallenstein's Death," after her
resolution to visit the grave of her lover is made known.

> ————"'T is not merely
> The human being's *pride* that peoples space
> With life and mystical predominance;
> Since likewise for the stricken heart of *love*
> This visible nature, and this common world,
> Are all too narrow."
> *Coleridge's Translation of Wallenstein.*

Ask'st thou my home?—my pathway wouldst thou
 know,
 When from thine eye my floating shadow pass'd?
Was not my work fulfill'd and closed below?
 Had I not lived and loved?—my lot was cast.

Wouldst thou ask where the nightingale is gone,
 That melting into song her soul away,
Gave the spring-breeze what witch'd thee in its
 tone?—
 But while she loved, she lived, in that deep lay!

Think'st thou my heart its lost one hath not
 found?—
 Yes! we are one, oh! trust me, we have met,
Where naught again may part what love hath
 bound,
 Where falls no tear, and whispers no regret.

There shalt *thou* find us, there with us be blest,
 If as *our* love *thy* love is pure and true!
There dwells my father,* sinless and at rest,
 Where the fierce murderer may no more pursue

And well he feels, no error of the dust
 Drew to the stars of Heaven his mortal ken,
There it is with us, ev'n as is our trust,
 He that believes, is near the holy *then*.

There shall each feeling beautiful and high,
 Keep the sweet promise of its earthly day;—
Oh! fear thou not to dream with waking eye!
 There lies deep meaning oft in childish play.

---

## THE REVELLERS.

Ring, joyous chords!—ring out again!
A swifter still, and a wilder strain!
They are here—the fair face and the careless heart.
And stars shall wane ere the mirthful part.—
But I met a dimly mournful glance,
In a sudden turn of the flying dance;
I heard the tone of a heavy sigh,
In a pause of the thrilling melody!
And it is not well that woe should breathe
On the bright spring-flowers of the festal wreath!—
Ye that to thought or to grief belong,
 Leave, leave the hall of song!

Ring, joyous chords!—but who art *thou*
With the shadowy locks o'er thy pale young brow
And the world of dreamy gloom that lies
In the misty depths of thy soft dark eyes?
Thou hast loved, fair girl! thou hast loved too well!
Thou art mourning now o'er a broken spell,
Thou hast pour'd thy heart's rich treasures forth,
And art unrepaid for their priceless worth!
Mourn on—yet come thou not *here* the while,
It is but a pain to see thee smile!

* Wallenstein.

There is not a tone in our songs for thee—
    Home with thy sorrows flee!

Ring, joyous chords!—ring out again!—
But what dost thou with the Revel's train?
A silvery voice through the soft air floats,
But thou hast no part in the gladdening notes:
There are bright young faces that pass thee by,
But they fix no glance of thy wandering eye!
Away! there's a void in thy yearning breast,
Thou weary man! wilt thou *here* find rest?
Away! for thy thoughts from the scene have fled,
And the love of *thy* spirit is with the dead!
Thou art but more lone 'midst the sounds of
    mirth—
    Back to thy silent hearth!

Ring, joyous chords!—ring forth again!
A swifter still, and a wilder strain!—
But *thou*, though a reckless mien be thine,
And thy cup be crown'd with the foaming wine,
By the fitful bursts of thy laughter loud,
By thine eye's quick flash through its troubled
    cloud,
I know thee!—it is but the wakeful fear
Of a haunted bosom that brings thee here!
I know thee!—thou fearest the solemn night,
With her piercing stars and her deep wind's might!
There's a tone in her voice which thou fain
    would'st shun,
For it asks what the secret soul hath done!
And thou—there's a dark weight on thine—
    away!—
    Back to thy home, and pray!

Ring, joyous chords!—ring out again!
A swifter still, and a wilder strain!
And bring fresh wreaths!—we will banish all
Save the free in heart from our festive hall.
On! through the maze of the fleet dance, on!
But where are the young and the lovely?—gone!
Where are the brows with the red-rose crown'd,
And the floating forms with the bright zone bound?
And the waving locks and the flying feet,
That still should be where the mirthful meet!—
They are gone—they are fled—they are parted all—
    Alas! the forsaken hall!

---

### THE CONQUEROR'S SLEEP

    Sleep, 'midst thy banners furl'd!
Yes! thou art there, upon thy buckler lying,
With the soft wind unfelt around thee sighing,
Thou chief of hosts, whose trumpet shakes the
    world!
Sleep while the babe sleeps on its mother's breast—
Oh! strong is night—for thou too art at rest!

    Stillness hath smooth'd thy brow,
And now might love keep timid vigils by thee,
Now might the foe with stealthy foot draw nigh
    thee,
Alike unconscious and defenceless thou!
Tread lightly, watchers!—now the field is won,
Break not the rest of nature's weary son!

    Perchance some lovely dream
Back from the stormy fight thy soul is bearing,
To the green places of thy boyish daring,
And all the windings of thy native stream;—
Why, this were joy!—upon the tented plain,
Dream on, thou Conqueror!—be a child again!

    But thou wilt wake at morn,
With thy strong passions to the conflict leaping,
And thy dark, troubled thoughts all earth o'er-
    sweeping!
So wilt thou rise, oh! thou of woman born!
And put thy terrors on, till none may dare
Look upon thee—the tired one, slumbering there!

    Why, so the peasant sleeps
Beneath his vine!—and man must kneel before
    thee,

---

And for his birthright vainly still implore thee!—
Shalt thou be stay'd because thy brother weeps?
Wake! and forget that 'midst a dreaming world,
Thou hast lain thus, with all thy banners furl'd!

    Forget that thou, ev'n thou,
Hast feebly shiver'd when the wind pass'd o'er thee,
And sunk to rest upon the earth which bore thee,
And felt the night-dew chill thy fever'd brow!
Wake with the trumpet, with the spear press on!—
Yet shall the dust take home its mortal son.

---

### OUR LADY'S WELL.*

Fount of the woods! thou art hid no more,
From Heaven's clear eye, as in time of yore!
For the roof hath sunk from thy mossy walls,
And the sun's free glance on thy slumber falls;
And the dim tree-shadows across thee pass,
As the boughs are sway'd o'er thy silvery glass;
And the reddening leaves to thy breast are blown,
When the autumn wind hath a stormy tone;
And thy bubbles rise to the flashing rain—
Bright Fount! thou art nature's own again!
Fount of the vale! thou art sought no more
By the pilgrim's foot, as in time of yore,
When he came from afar, his beads to tell,
And to chant his hymn at Our Lady's Well.
There is heard no *Ave* through thy bowers,
Thou art gleaming lone 'midst thy water-flowers.
But the herd may drink from thy gushing wave,
And there may the reaper his forehead lave,
And the woodman seeks thee not in vain—
Bright fount! thou art Nature's own again!

Fount of the Virgin's ruin'd shrine!
A voice that speaks of the past is thine!
It mingles the tone of a thoughtful sigh,
With the notes that ring through the laughing sky,
'Midst the mirthful song of the summer-bird,
And the sound of the breeze, it will yet be heard!
Why is it that thus we may gaze on thee,
To the brilliant sunshine sparkling free?—
'Tis that all on earth is of *Time's* domain—
He hath made thee Nature's own again!

Fount of the chapel with ages gray!
Thou art springing freshly amidst decay!
Thy rites are closed, and thy cross lies low,
And the changeful hours breathe o'er thee now!
Yet if at thine altar one holy thought
In man's deep spirit of old hath wrought;
If peace to the mourner hath here been given,
Or prayer, from a chasten'd heart, to Heaven,
Be the spot still hallow'd while Time shall reign,
Who hath made thee Nature's own again!

---

### THE PARTING OF SUMMER.

Thou'rt bearing hence thy roses,
    Glad Summer, fare thee well!
Thou 'rt singing thy last melodies
    In every wood and dell.

But ere the golden sunset
    Of thy latest lingering day,
Oh! tell me, o'er this chequer'd earth,
    How hast thou pass'd away?

Brightly, sweet Summer! brightly
    Thine hours have floated by,
To the joyous birds of the woodland boughs,
    The rangers of the sky.

And brightly in the forests,
    To the wild deer wandering free;
And brightly, 'midst the garden flowers,
    Is the happy murmuring bee:

---

* A beautiful spring in the woods near St. Asaph, formerly covered in with a chapel, now in ruins. It was dedicated to the Virgin, and, according to Pennant, much the resort of pilgrims.

But how to human bosoms,
  With all their hopes and fears,
And thoughts that make them eagle-wings,
  To pierce the unborn years?

Sweet Summer! to the captive
  Thou hast flown in burning dreams
Of the woods, with all their whispering leaves
  And the blue rejoicing streams!—

To the wasted and the weary
  On the bed of sickness bound,
In swift delirious fantasies,
  That changed with every sound;—

To the sailor on the billows,
  In longings, wild and vain,
For the gushing founts and breezy hills,
  And the homes of earth again!

And unto me, glad Summer!
  How hast thou flown to me?
*My* chainless footstep naught hath kept
  From thy haunts of song and glee.

Thou hast flown in wayward visions,
  In memories of the dead—
In shadows, from a troubled heart,
  O'er thy sunny pathway shed:

In brief and sudden strivings,
  To fling a weight aside—
'Midst these thy melodies have ceased
  And all thy roses died.

But, oh! thou gentle Summer!
  If I greet thy flowers once more,
Bring me again the buoyancy
  Wherewith my soul should soar!

Give me to hail thy sunshine,
  With song and spirit free;
Or in a purer air than this,
  May that next meeting be!

## THE SONGS OF OUR FATHERS.

————Sing aloud
Old Songs, the precious Music of the Heart.
        *Wordsworth.*

Sing them upon the sunny hills,
  When days are long and bright,
And the blue gleam of shining rills
  Is loveliest to the sight!
Sing them along the misty moor,
  Where ancient hunters roved,
And swell them through the torrent's roar,
  The songs our fathers loved!

The songs their souls rejoiced to hear
  When harps were in the hall,
And each proud note made lance and spear
  Thrill on the banner'd wall:
The songs that through our valleys green,
  Sent on from age to age,
Like his own river's voice, have been
  The peasant's heritage.

The reaper sings them when the vale
  Is fill'd with plumy sheaves:
The woodman, by the starlight pale,
  Cheer'd homeward through the leaves:
And unto them the glancing oars
  A joyous measure keep,
Where the dark rocks that crest our shores
  Dash back the foaming deep.

So let it be!—a light they shed
  O'er each old fount and grove,
A memory of the gentle dead,
  A lingering spell of love.
Murmuring the names of mighty men,
  They bid our streams roll on,
And link high thoughts to every glen
  Where valiant deeds were done.

Teach them your children round the hearth.
  When evening-fires burn clear,
And in the fields of harvest-mirth,
  And on the hills of deer:
So shall each unforgotten word,
  When far those loved ones roam,
Call back the hearts which once it stirr'd,
  To childhood's holy home.

The green woods of their native land
  Shall whisper in the strain,
The voices of their household band,
  Shall breathe their names again;
The heathery heights in vision rise
  Where, like the stag, they roved—
Sing to your sons those melodies,
  The songs your fathers loved!

## THE WORLD IN THE OPEN AIR

Come, while in freshness and dew it lies,
To the world that is under the free, blue skies
Leave ye man's home, and forget his care—
There breathes no sigh on the day-spring's air

Come to the woods in whose mossy dells,
A light all made for the poet dwells;
A light, colour'd softly by tender leaves,
Whence the primrose a mellower hue receives

The stock-dove is there in the beechen-tree,
And the lulling tone of the honey-bee;
And the voice of cool waters 'midst feathery fern
Shedding sweet sounds from some hidden urn.

There is life, there is youth, there is tameless
      mirth,
Where the streams, with the lilies they wear, have
      birth;
There is peace where the alders are whispering low;
Come from man's dwellings with all their woe!

Yes! we will come—we will leave behind
The homes and sorrows of human kind;
It is well to rove where the river leads
Its bright, blue vein along sunny meads

It is well through the rich, wild woods to go,
And to pierce the haunts of the fawn and doe;
And to hear the gushing of gentle springs,
When the heart has been fretted by worldly stings

And to watch the colours that flit and pass,
With insect wings through the wavy grass;
And the silvery gleams o'er the ash-tree's bark,
Borne in with a breeze through the foliage dark

Joyous and far shall our wanderings be,
As the flight of birds o'er the glittering sea,
To the woods, to the dingles where violets blow
We will bear no memory of earthly woe.

But if, by the forest-brook, we meet
A line like the pathway of former feet;—
If 'midst the hills, in some lonely spot,
We reach the gray ruins of tower or cot—

If the cell where a hermit of old hath pray'd
Lift up its cross through the solemn shade—
Or if some nook, where the wild-flowers wave
Bear token sad of a mortal grave,—

Doubt not but *there* will our steps be stay'd,
There our quick spirits awhile delay'd;
There will thought fix our impatient eyes,
And win back our hearts to their sympathies.

For what, though the mountains and skies be fair
Steep'd in soft hues of the summer-air,—
'Tis the soul of man, by its hopes and dreams,
That lights up all nature with living gleams

Where it hath suffer'd and nobly striven,
Where it hath pour'd forth its vows to Heaven;
Where to repose it hath brightly past,
O'er this green earth there is glory cast.

And by that soul, amidst groves and rills,
And flocks that feed on a thousand hills,
Birds of the forest, and flowers of the sod.
*We*, only *we*, may be link'd to God!

---

## KINDRED HEARTS.

Oh! ask not, hope thou not too much
　Of sympathy below;
Few are the hearts whence one same touch
　Bids the sweet fountains flow!
Few—and by still conflicting powers
　Forbidden here to meet—
Such ties would make this life of ours
　Too fair for aught so fleet.

It may be that thy brother's eye
　Sees not as thine, which turns
In such deep reverence to the sky,
　Where the rich sunset burns;
It may be that the breath of spring,
　Born amidst violets lone,
A rapture o'er thy soul can bring—
　A dream, to his unknown.

The tune that speaks of other times—
　A sorrowful delight!
The melody of distant chimes,
　The sound of waves by night;
The wind that, with so many a tone,
　Some chord within can thrill,—
These may have language all thine own,
　To *him* a mystery still.

Yet scorn thou not for this, the true
　And steadfast love of years;
The kindly, that from childhood grew,
　The faithful to thy tears!
If there be one that o'er the dead
　Hath in thy grief borne part,
And watch'd through sickness by thy bed,—
　Call *his* a kindred heart!

But for those bonds all perfect made,
　Wherein bright spirits blend,
Like sister flowers of one sweet shade,
　With the same breeze that bend,
For that full bliss of thought allied,
　Never to mortals given,—
Oh! lay thy lovely dreams aside,
　Or lift them unto heaven.

---

## THE TRAVELLER AT THE SOURCE OF THE NILE.

In sunset's light, o'er Afric thrown,
　A wanderer proudly stood
Beside the well-spring, deep and lone,
　Of Egypt's awful flood;
The cradle of that mighty birth,
So long a hidden thing to earth!

He heard its life's first murmuring sound,
　A low mysterious tone;
A music sought, but never found,
　By kings and warriors gone;
He listen'd—and his heart beat high—
That was the song of victory!

The rapture of a conqueror's mood
　Rush'd burning through his frame,—
The depths of that green solitude
　Its torrents could not tame;
Though stillness lay, with eve's last smile—
Round those far fountains of the Nile.

Night came with stars:—across his soul
　There swept a sudden change,
E'en at the pilgrim's glorious goal
　A shadow dark and strange

Breathed from the thought, so swift to fall
O'er triumph's hour—*and is this all?*[*]

No more than this!—what seem'd it now
　First by that spring to stand?
A thousand streams of lovelier flow
　Bathed his own mountain land!
Whence far o'er waste and ocean track,
Their wild sweet voices call'd him back.

They call'd him back to many a glade,
　His childhood's haunt of play,
Where brightly through the beechen shade
　Their waters glanced away;
They call'd him, with their sounding waves,
Back to his fathers' hills and graves.

But darkly mingling with the thought
　Of each familiar scene,
Rose up a fearful vision, fraught
　With all that lay between;
The Arab's lance, the desert's gloom,
The whirling sands, the red simoom!

Where was the glow of power and pride?
　The spirit born to roam?
His alter'd heart within him died
　With yearnings for his home!
All vainly struggling to repress
That gush of painful tenderness.

He wept—the stars of Afric's heaven
　Behold his bursting tears,
E'en on that spot where fate had given
　The meed of toiling years!—
Oh, happiness! how far we flee
Thine own sweet paths in search of thee!

---

## CASABIANCA.[†]

The boy stood on the burning deck
　Whence all but he had fled;
The flame that lit the battle's wreck,
　Shone round him o'er the dead.

Yet beautiful and bright he stood,
　As born to rule the storm;
A creature of heroic blood,
　A proud, though child-like form.

The flames roll'd on—he would not go,
　Without his Father's word;
That Father, faint in death below,
　His voice no longer heard.

He call'd aloud:—"Say, Father, say
　If yet my task is done?"
He knew not that the chieftain lay
　Unconscious of his son.

"Speak, Father!" once again he cried,
　"If I may yet be gone!
And"—but the booming shots replied,
　And fast the flames roll'd on.

Upon his brow he felt their breath,
　And in his waving hair,
And look'd from that lone post of death,
　In still, yet brave despair.

[*] A remarkable description of feelings thus fluctuating from triumph to despondency, is given in Bruce's Abyssinian Travels. The buoyant exultation of his spirits on arriving at the source of the Nile, was almost immediately succeeded by a gloom, which he thus pourtrays: "I was, at that very moment, in possession of what had for many years been the principal object of my ambition and wishes; indifference, which, from the usual infirmity of human nature, follows, at least for a time, complete enjoyment, had taken place of it. The marsh and the fountains of the Nile, upon comparison with the rise of many of our rivers, became now a trifling object in my sight. I remembered that magnificent scene in my own native country, where the Tweed, Clyde, and Annan, rise in one hill. I began, in my sorrow, to treat the inquiry about the source of the Nile as a violent effort of a distempered fancy."

[†] Young Casabianca, a boy about thirteen years old, son to the Admiral of the Orient, remained at his post (in the Battle of the Nile) after the ship had taken fire, and all the guns had been abandoned; and perished in the explosion of the vessel, when the flames had reached the powder.

And shouted but once more aloud,
  "My Father! must I stay?"
While o'er him fast, through sail and shroud,
  The wreathing fires made way.

They wrapt the ship in splendour wild
  They caught the flag on high,
And stream'd above the gallant child,
  Like banners in the sky.

There came a burst of thunder sound—
  The boy—oh! where was he?
Ask of the winds that far around
  With fragments strew'd the sea!—

With mast, and helm, and pennon fair,
  That well had borne their part—
But the noblest thing which perish'd there
  Was that young faithful heart!'

## THE DIAL OF FLOWERS.*

'Twas a lovely thought to mark the hours,
  As they floated in light away,
By the opening and the folding flowers,
  That laugh to the summer's day.

Thus had each moment its own rich hue,
  And its graceful cup and bell,
In whose colour'd vase might sleep the dew,
  Like a pearl in an ocean-shell.

To such sweet signs might the time have flow'd
  In a golden current on,
Ere from the garden, man's first abode,
  The glorious guests were gone.

So might the days have been brightly told—
  Those days of song and dreams—
When shepherds gather'd their flocks of old,
  By the blue Arcadian streams.

So in those isles of delight, that rest
  Far off in a breezeless main,
Which many a bark, with a weary quest,
  Has sought, but still in vain.

Yet is not life, in its real flight,
  Mark'd thus—even thus—on earth,
By the closing of one hope's delight,
  And another's gentle birth?

Oh! let us live, so that flower by flower,
  Shutting in turn, may leave
A lingerer still for the sunset hour,
  A charm for the shaded eve.

## OUR DAILY PATHS.

Naught shall prevail against us, or disturb
Our cheerful faith, that all which we behold
Is full of blessings.
                                    *Wordsworth.*

There's beauty all around our paths, if but our
    watchful eyes
Can trace it 'midst familiar things, and through
    their lowly guise;
We may find it where a hedge-row showers its
    blossoms o'er our way,
Or a cottage window sparkles forth in the last red
    light of day.

We find it where a spring shines clear, beneath an
    aged tree,
With the foxglove o'er the waters' glass borne
    downwards by the bee;

* This dial was, I believe, formed by Linnæus, and marked the
hours by the opening and closing, at regular intervals, of the flowers arranged in it.

Or where a swift and sunny gleam on the birch
    stems is thrown,
As a soft wind playing parts the leaves, in copses
    green and lone.

We may find it in the winter boughs, as they cross
    the cold, blue sky,
While soft on icy pool and stream their pencill'd
    shadows lie,
When we look upon their tracery, by the fairy
    frost-work bound,
Whence the flitting red-breast shakes a shower of
    crystals to the ground.

Yes! beauty dwells in all our paths—but sorrow
    too is there;
How oft some cloud within us dims the bright, still
    summer air!
When we carry our sick hearts abroad amidst the
    joyous things,
That through the leafy places glance on many-co-
    lour'd wings!

With shadows from the past we fill the happy
    woodland shades,
And a mournful memory of the dead is with us in
    the glades;
And our dream-like fancies lend the wind an echo's
    plaintive tone
Of voices, and of melodies, and of silvery laughter
    gone.

But are we free to do ev'n thus—to wander as we
    will—
Bearing sad visions through the grove, and n'er
    the breezy hill?
No! in our daily paths lie cares, that ofttimes bind
    us fast,
While from their narrow round we see the golden
    day fleet past.

They hold us from the woodlark's haunts, and vio-
    let dingles, back.
And from all the lovely sounds and gleams in the
    shining river's track,
They bar us from our heritage of spring-time, hope
    and mirth,
And weigh our burden'd spirits down with the
    cumbering dust of earth.

Yet should this be?—Too much, too soon, despond-
    ingly we yield!
A better lesson we are taught by the lilies of the
    field!
A sweeter by the birds of heaven—which tell us,
    in their flight,
Of One that through the desert air for ever guides
    them right.

Shall not this knowledge calm our hearts, and bid
    vain conflicts cease?
Ay, when they commune with themselves in holy
    hours of peace;
And feel that by the lights and clouds through
    which our pathway lies,
By the beauty and the grief alike, we are training
    for the skies!

## THE CROSS IN THE WILDERNESS.

Silent and mournful sat an Indian chief,
  In the red sunset, by a grassy tomb;
His eyes, that might not weep, were dark with
    grief,
  And his arms folded in majestic gloom,
And his bow lay unstrung beneath the mound
Which sanctified the gorgeous waste around.

For a pale cross above its greensward rose,
  Telling the cedars and the pines that there
Man's heart and hope had struggled with his woes,
  And lifted from the dust a voice of prayer.
Now all was hush'd—and Eve's last splendour
    shone
With a rich sadness on th' attesting stone.

There came a lonely traveller o'er the wild,
  And he, too, paused in reverence by that grave,
Asking the tale of its memorial, piled
  Between the forest and the lake's bright wave;
Till, as a wind might stir a wither'd oak,
On the deep dream of age his accents broke.

And the gray chieftain, slowly rising, said—
  "I listen for the words, which, years ago,
Pass'd o'er these waters: though the voice is fled
  Which made them as a singing fountain's flow,
Yet, when I sit in their long-faded track,
Sometimes the forest's murmur gives them back.

"Ask'st thou of him, whose house is lone beneath?
  I was an eagle in my youthful pride,
When o'er the seas he came, with summer's breath,
  To dwell amidst us, on the lake's green side.
Many the times of flowers have been since then—
Many, but bringing naught like *him* again!

"Not with the hunter's bow and spear he came,
  O'er the blue hills to chase the flying roe;
Not the dark glory of the woods to tame,
  Laying their cedars like the corn-stalks low;
But to spread tidings of all holy things,
Gladdening our souls, as with the morning's wings.

"Doth not yon cypress whisper how we met,
  I and my brethren that from earth are gone,
Under its boughs to hear his voice, which yet
  Seems through their gloom to send a silvery tone?
He told of one, the grave's dark bands who broke
And our hearts burn'd within us as he spoke.

'He told of far and sunny lands, which lie
  Beyond the dust wherein our fathers dwell:
Bright must they be!—for *there* are none that die,
  And none that weep, and none that say 'Fare
    well!'
He came to guide us thither;—but away
The Happy call'd him, and he might not stay.

"We saw him slowly fade,—athirst, perchance,
  For the fresh waters of that lovely clime;
Yet was there still a sunbeam in his glance,
  And on his gleaming hair no touch of time,—
Therefore we hoped:—but now the lake looks dim,
For the green summer comes,—and finds not him!

"We gather'd round him in the dewy hour
  Of one still morn, beneath his chosen tree;
From his clear voice, at first, the words of power
  Came low, like moanings of a distant sea;
But swell'd and shook the wilderness ere long,
As if the spirit of the breeze grew strong.

"And then once more they trembled on his tongue,
  And his white eyelids flutter'd, and his head
Fell back, and mists upon his forehead hung,—
  Know'st thou not how we pass to join the dead?
It is enough!—he sank upon my breast—
Our friend that loved us, he was gone to rest!

"We buried him where he was wont to pray,
  By the calm lake, e'en here, at eventide;
We rear'd this Cross in token where he lay,
  For on the Cross, he said, his Lord had died!
Now hath he surely reach'd, o'er mount and wave,
That flowery land whose green turf hides no grave

"But I am sad!—I mourn the clear light taken
  Back from my people, o'er whose place it shone,
The pathway to the better shore forsaken,
  And the true words forgotten, save by one,
Who hears them faintly sounding from the past,
Mingled with death-songs in each fitful blast."

Then spoke the wanderer forth with kindling
  eye:—
  "Son of the wilderness! despair thou not,
Though the bright hour may seem to thee gone by,
  And the cloud settled o'er thy nation's lot;
Heaven darkly works;—yet where the seed hath
    been
There shall the fruitage, glowing yet, be seen.

"Hope on, hope ever!—by the sudden springing
  Of green leaves which the winter hid so long;
And by the bursts of free, triumphant singing,
  After cold silent months, the woods among;
And by the rending of the frozen chains,
Which bound the glorious rivers on their plains;

"Deem not the words of light that here were
    spoken,
  But as a lovely song to leave no trace,
Yet shall the gloom which wraps thy hills be
    broken,
  And the full day-spring rise upon thy race!
And fading mists the better path disclose,
And the wide desert blossom as the rose."

So by the Cross they parted, in the wild,
  Each fraught with musings for life's after-day,
Memories to visit *one*, the forest's child,
  By many a blue stream in its lonely way;
And upon *one*, 'midst busy throngs to press
Deep thoughts and sad, yet full of holiness.

---

## LAST RITES.

By the mighty minster's bell,
Tolling with a sudden swell;
By the colours half-mast high,
O'er the sea hung mournfully;
    Know, a prince hath died!

By the drum's dull muffled sound,
By the arms that sweep the ground,
By the volleying muskets' tone,
Speak ye of a soldier gone
    In his manhood's pride.

By the chanted psalm that fills
Reverently the ancient hills,[*]
Learn, that from his harvests done,
Peasants bear a brother on
    To his last repose.

By the pall of snowy white
Through the yew-trees gleaming bright
By the garland on the bier,
Weep! a maiden claims thy tear—
    Broken is the rose!

Which is the tenderest rite of all?
Buried virgin's coronal,
Requiem o'er the monarch's head,
Farewell gun for warrior dead,
    Herdsman's funeral hymn?

Tells not each of human woe!
Each of hope and strength brought low?
Number each with holy things,
If one chastening thought it brings,
    Ere life's day grow dim!

---

## THE HEBREW MOTHER.

The rose was in rich bloom on Sharon's plain
When a young mother, with her first-born, thence
Went up to Zion; for the boy was vow'd
Unto the Temple service:—by the hand
She led him, and her silent soul, the while,
Oft as the dewy laughter of his eye
Met her sweet serious glance, rejoiced to think
That aught so pure, so beautiful, was hers,
To bring before her God. So pass'd they on,
O'er Judah's hills; and wheresoe'er the leaves
Of the broad sycamore made sounds at noon,
Like lulling rain-drops, or the olive boughs,
With their cool dimness, cross'd the sultry blue
Of Syria's heaven, she paused, that he might rest
Yet from her own meek eyelids chased the sleep
That weigh'd their dark fringe down, to sit and
    watch

  [*] A custom still retained at rural funerals, in some parts of England and Wales.

The crimson deepening o'er his cheek's repose,
As at a red flower's heart.  And where a fount
Lay like a twilight star 'midst palmy shades,
Making its bank green gems along the wild
There, too, she linger'd, from the diamond wave
Drawing bright water for his rosy lips,
And softly parting clusters of jet curls
To bathe his brow.  At last the Fane was reach'd,
The Earth's One Sanctuary—and rapture hush'd
Her bosom, as before her, through the day,
It rose, a mountain of white marble, steep'd
In light, like floating gold.  But when that hour
Waned to the farewell moment, when the boy
Lifted, through rainbow-gleaming tears, his eye
Beseechingly to hers, and half in fear
Turn'd from the white-robed priest, and round her
            arm
Clung even as joy clings—the deep spring-tide
Of nature then swell'd high, and o'er her child
Bending, her soul broke forth, in mingled sounds
Of weeping and sad song.—"Alas!" she cried,

"Alas! my boy, thy gentle grasp is on me;
The bright tears quiver in thy pleading eyes,
            And now fond thoughts arise,
And silver cords again to earth have won me
And like a vine thou claspest my full heart—
            How shall I hence depart?

"How the lone paths retrace where thou wert
            playing
So late, along the mountains, at my side?
            And I, in joyous pride,
By every place of flowers my course delaying,
Wove, e'en as pearls, the lilies round thy hair,
            Beholding thee so fair!

"And, oh! the home whence thy bright smile hath
            parted,
Will it not seem as if the sunny day
            Turn'd from its door away?
While through its chambers wandering weary-
            hearted,
I languish for thy voice, which past me still,
            Went like a singing rill.

"Under the palm-trees thou no more shalt meet me,
When from the fount at evening I return,
            With the full water-urn;
Nor will thy sleep's low dove-like breathings greet
            me,
As 'midst the silence of the stars I wake,
            And watch for thy dear sake.

"And thou, will slumber's dewy cloud fall round
            thee,
Without thy mother's hand to smooth thy bed?
            Wilt thou not vainly spread
Thine arms, when darkness as a veil hath wound
            thee,
To fold my neck, and lift up, in thy fear,
            A cry which none shall hear?
"What have I said, my child?—Will He not hear
            thee,
Who the young ravens heareth from their nest?
            Shall He not guard thy rest,
And, in the hush of holy midnight near thee,
Breathe o'er thy soul, and fill its dreams with
            joy?—
            Thou shalt sleep soft, my boy.

" I give thee to thy God—the God that gave thee,
A well-spring of deep gladness, to my heart!
            And precious as thou art,
And pure as dew of Hermon, He shall have thee
My own, my beautiful, my undefiled!
            And thou shalt be His child.

"Therefore, farewell!—I go, my soul may fail me,
As the hart panteth for the water-brooks,
            Yearning for thy sweet looks.—
But thou, my first-born, droop not, nor bewail me;
Thou in the Shadow of the Rock shalt dwell,
            The Rock of Strength.—Farewell!"

## THE WRECK.

All night the booming minute gun
      Had peal'd along the deep,
And mournfully the rising sun
      Look'd o'er the tide-worn steep.
A bark from India's coral strand,
      Before the raging blast,
Had vail'd her topsails to the sand,
      And bow'd her noble mast.

The queenly ship!—brave hearts had striven
      And true ones died with her!—
We saw her mighty cable riven,
      Like floating gossamer.
We saw her proud flag struck that morn,
      A star once o'er the seas—
Her anchor gone, her deck uptorn—
      And sadder things than these!

We saw her treasures cast away,—
      The rocks with pearls were sown,
And, strangely sad, the ruby's ray
      Flash'd out o'er fretted stone,
And gold was strewn the wet sands o'er,
      Like ashes by a breeze;
And gorgeous robes—but oh! that shore
      Had sadder things than these!

We saw the strong man still and low,
      A crush'd reed thrown aside!
Yet, by that rigid lip and brow,
      Not without strife he died.
And near him on the sea-weed lay—
      Till then we had not wept—
But well our gushing hearts might say,
      That there a *mother* slept!

For her pale arms a babe had prest,
      With such a wreathing grasp,
Billows had dash'd o'er that fond breast,
      Yet not undone the clasp.
Her very tresses had been flung
      To wrap the fair child's form,
Where still their wet long streamers hung,
      All tangled by the storm.

And beautiful, 'midst that wild scene,
      Gleam'd up the boy's dead face,
Like slumbers, trustingly serene,
      In melancholy grace.
Deep in her bosom lay his head,
      With half-shut violet eye—
*He* had known little of her dread,
      Naught of her agony!

Oh! human love, whose yearning heart
      Through all things vainly true,
So stamps upon thy mortal part
      Its passionate adieu—
Surely thou hast another lot,
      There is some home for thee,
Where thou shalt rest, remembering not
      The moaning of the sea!

## THE TRUMPET.

The trumpet's voice hath roused the land,
      Light up the beacon-pyre!—
A hundred hills have seen the brand,
      And waved the sign of fire.
A hundred banners to the breeze
      Their gorgeous folds have cast—
And, hark! was that the sound of seas?
      —A king to war went past.
The chief is arming in his hall,
      The peasant by his hearth;
The mourner hears the thrilling call,
      And rises from the earth.
The mother on her first-born son,
      Looks with a boding eye—
They come not back, though all be won
      Whose young hearts leap so high.

The bard hath ceased his song, and bound
  The falchion to his side;
E'en for the marriage altar crown'd,
  The lover quits his bride.
And all this haste, and change, and fear,
  By *earthly* clarion spread!—
How will it be, when kingdoms hear
  The blast that wakes the Dead?

---

### EVENING PRAYER AT A GIRL'S SCHOOL.

  Now in thy youth, beseech of Him
    Who giveth, upbraiding not;
  That his light in thy heart become not dim,
    And his love be unforgot;
  And thy God, in the darkest of days, will be
  Greenness, and beauty, and strength to thee.
               *Bernard Barton.*

---

Hush! 'tis a holy hour—the quiet room
  Seems like a temple, while yon soft lamp sheds
A faint and starry radiance, through the gloom
  And the sweet stillness, down on fair young
    heads,
With all their clust'ring locks, untouch'd by care,
And bow'd, as flowers are bow'd with night, in
  prayer.

Gaze on—'tis lovely!—Childhood's lip and cheek,
  Mantling beneath its earnest brow of thought—
Gaze—yet what seest thou in those fair, and meek,
  And fragile things, as but for sunshine wrought?
Thou seest what Grief must nurture for the sky,
What Death must fashion for Eternity!

Oh! joyous creatures! that will sink to rest,
  Lightly, when those pure orisons are done,
As birds with slumber's honey-dew opprest,
  'Midst the dim folded leaves, at set of sun.
Lift up your hearts! though yet no sorrow lies
Dark in the summer-heaven of those clear eyes.

Though fresh within your breasts th' untroubled
    springs
  Of Hope make melody where'er ye tread,
And o'er your sleep bright shadows, from the wings
  Of spirits visiting but youth, be spread—
Yet in those flute-like voices, mingling low,
Is woman's tenderness—how soon her woe!

Her look is on you—silent tears to weep,
  And patient smiles to wear through suffering's
    hour,
And sumless riches, from affection's deep,
  To pour on broken reeds—a wasted shower!
And to make idols, and to find them clay,
And to bewail that worship—therefore pray!

Her lot is on you—to be found untired,
  Watching the stars out by the bed of pain,
With a pale cheek, and yet a brow inspired,
  And a true heart of hope, though hope be vain;
Meekly to bear with wrong, to cheer decay,
And, oh! to love through all things—therefore pray!

And take the thought of this calm vesper time
  With its low murmuring sounds and silvery light,
On through the dark days fading from their prime,
  As a sweet dew to keep your souls from blight!
Earth will forsake—oh! happy to have given
Th' unbroken heart's first fragrance unto Heaven.

---

### THE HOUR OF DEATH.

  Il est dans la Nature d'aimer a se livrer a l'idee meme qu'on se
donte.——*Corinne.*

  Leaves have their time to fall,
And flowers to wither at the north-wind's breath,
  And stars to set—but all,
Thou hast *all* seasons for thine own, oh! Death.

Day is for mortal care,
Eve, for glad meetings round the joyous hearth,
  Night, for the dreams of sleep, the voice of
    prayer—
But all for thee, thou Mightiest of the earth.

  The banquet hath its hour,
Its feverish hour, of mirth, and song, and wine;
  There comes a day for grief's o'erwhelming power
A time for softer tears—but all are thine.

  Youth and the opening rose
May look like things too glorious for decay,
  And smile at thee—but thou art not of those
That wait the ripen'd bloom to seize their prey.

  Leaves have their time to fall,
And flowers to wither at the north-wind's breath
  And stars to set—but all,
Thou hast *all* seasons for thine own, oh! Death.

  We know when moons shall wane,
When summer-birds from far shall cross the sea,
  When autumn's hue shall tinge the golden grain,
But who shall teach us when to look for thee?

  Is it when spring's first gale
Comes forth to whisper where the violets lie?
  Is it when roses in our paths grow pale?—
They have *one* season—*all* are ours to die!

  Thou art where billows foam,
Thou art where music melts upon the air;
  Thou art around us in our peaceful home,
And the world calls us forth—and thou art there.

  Thou art where friend meets friend,
Beneath the shadow of the elm to rest—
  Thou art where foe meets foe, and trumpets rend
The skies, and swords beat down the princely crest.

  Leaves have their time to fall,
And flowers to wither at the north-wind's breath
  And stars to set—but all,
Thou hast *all* seasons for thine own, oh! Death.

---

### THE CLIFFS OF DOVER.

  The inviolate Island of the sage and free.——*Byron.*

Rocks of my country! let the cloud
  Your crested heights array,
And rise ye, like a fortress proud,
  Above the surge and spray!

My spirit greets you as ye stand,
  Breasting the billow's foam:
Oh! thus for ever guard the land,
  The sever'd Land of Home!

I have left rich blue skies behind,
  Lighting up classic shrines,
And music in the southern wind,
  And sunshine on the vines.

The breathings of the myrtle-flowers
  Have floated o'er my way;
The pilgrim's voice, at vesper-hours,
  Hath soothed me with its lay.

The Isles of Greece, the Hills of Spain,
  The purple Heavens of Rome,—
Yes, all are glorious;—yet again,
  I bless thee, Land of Home!

For thine the Sabbath peace, my land!
  And thine the guarded hearth;
And thine the dead, the noble band,
  That make thee holy earth.

Their voices meet me in thy breeze,
  Their steps are on thy plains;
Their names by old majestic trees,
  Are whisper'd round thy fanes.

Their blood hath mingled with the tide
  Of thine exulting sea;
Oh! be it still a joy, a pride,
  To live and die for thee!

## THE LOST PLEIAD.

*"Like the lost Pleiad seen no more below."——Byron.*

And is there glory from the heavens departed?—
Oh! void unmark'd!—thy sisters of the sky
  Still hold their place on high,
Though from its rank thine orb so long hath started,
  Thou, that no more art seen of mortal eye!

Hath the night lost a gem, the regal night?
  She wears her crown of old magnificence,
    Though thou art exiled thence—
No desert seems to part those urns of light,
  'Midst the far depths of purple gloom intense.

They rise in joy, the starry myriads burning—
  The shepherd greets them on his mountains free
    And from the silvery sea
To them the sailor's wakeful eye is turning—
  Unchanged they rise, they have not mourn'd for thee.

Couldst thou be shaken from thy radiant place,
  Ev'n as a dew-drop from the myrtle spray,
    Swept by the wind away?
Wert thou not peopled by some glorious race,
  And was there power to smite them with decay?

Why, who shall talk of thrones, of sceptres riven?
  Bow'd be our hearts to think on what *we* are,
    When from its height afar
A world sinks thus—and yon majestic heaven
  Shines not the less for that one vanish'd star!

---

## THE GRAVES OF MARTYRS.

The kings of old have shrine and tomb,
In many a minster's haughty gloom;
And green, along the ocean-side,
The mounds arise where heroes died;
But show me, on thy flowery breast,
Earth! where thy *nameless* martyrs rest!

The thousands that, uncheer'd by praise,
Have made one offering of their days;
For Truth, for Heaven, for Freedom's sake,
Resign'd the bitter cup to take,
And silently, in fearless faith,
Bowing their noble souls to death.

Where sleep they, Earth?—by no proud stone
Their narrow couch of rest is known;
The still sad glory of their name,
Hallows no mountain unto Fame;
No—not a tree the record bears
Of their deep thoughts and lonely prayers.

Yet haply all around lie strew'd
The ashes of that multitude:
It may be that each day we tread,
Where thus devoted hearts have bled,
And the young flowers our children sow,
Take root in holy dust below.

Oh! that the many-rustling leaves,
Which round our homes the summer weaves
Or that the streams, in whose glad voice
Our own familiar paths rejoice,
Might whisper through the starry sky,
To tell where those blest slumberers lie!

Would not our inmost hearts be still'd,
With knowledge of their presence fill'd
And by its breathings taught to prize
The meekness of self-sacrifice?
—But the old woods and sounding waves
Are silent of those hidden graves.

Yet what if no light footstep there
In pilgrim-love and awe repair,
So let it be!—like him, whose clay
Deep buried by his Maker lay,
They sleep in secret,—but their sod,
Unknown to man, is mark'd of God!

22

## THE VOICE OF HOME TO THE PRODIGAL

Von Baumen, aus Wellen, aus Mauern,
Wie ruft es dir freundlich und lind;
Was hast du zu wandern, zu trauern?
Komm' spielen, du freundliches Kind!
*La Motte Fouqué.*

---

Oh! when wilt thou return
  To thy spirit's early loves?
To the freshness of the morn,
  To the stillness of the groves?

The summer-birds are calling
  Thy household porch around,
And the merry waters falling,
  With sweet laughter in their sound.

And a thousand bright-vein'd flowers
  From their banks of moss and fern,
Breathe of the sunny hours—
  But when wilt thou return?

Oh! thou hast wander'd long
  From thy home without a guide,
And thy native woodland song,
  In thine alter'd heart hath died.

Thou hast flung the wealth away,
  And the glory of thy spring;
And to thee the leaves' light play
  Is a long-forgotten thing.

But when wilt thou return?—
  Sweet dews may freshen soon
The flower, within whose urn
  Too fiercely gazed the noon.

O'er the image of the sky,
  Which the lake's clear bosom wore
Darkly may shadows lie—
  But not for evermore.

Give back thy heart again,
  To the freedom of the woods,
To the birds' triumphant strain,
  To the mountain solitudes!

But when wilt thou return?
  Along thine own pure air,
There are young sweet voices borne—
  Oh! should not thine be there?

Still at thy father's board
  There is kept a place for thee,
And, by thy smile restored,
  Joy round the hearth should be.

Still hath thy mother's eye,
  Thy coming step to greet,
A look of days gone by,
  Tender and gravely sweet.

Still, when the prayer is said,
  For thee kind bosoms yearn,—
For thee fond tears are shed—
  Oh! when wilt thou return?

---

## THE HOUR OF PRAYER.

*Pregar, pregar, pregar,
Ch' altro posso i mortali al pianger na'e?*
*Alfieri.*

---

Child, amidst the flowers at play
While the red light fades away;
Mother, with thine earnest eye,
Ever following silently;
Father, by the breeze of eve
Call'd thy harvest work to leave;
Pray—ere yet the dark hours be,
Lift the heart and bend the knee!

Traveller, in the stranger's land,
Far from thine own household band;
Mourner, haunted by the tone
Of a voice from this world gone;
Captive, in whose narrow cell
Sunshine hath not leave to dwell;
Sailor, on the darkening sea—
Lift the heart and bend the knee!

Warrior, that from battle won
Breathest now at set of sun;
Woman, o'er the lowly slain
Weeping on his burial-plain;
Thou, the weary and o'erworn;
Thou, whose hope hath wings of morn;
Heaven's first star alike ye see
Lift the heart and bend the knee!

---

### THE WAKENING.

How many thousands are wakening now!
Some to the songs from the forest-bough,
To the rustling of leaves at the lattice-pane,
To the chiming fall of the early rain.

And some far out on the deep mid-sea,
To the dash of the waves in their foaming glee,
As they break into spray on the ship's tall side,
That holds through the tumult her path of pride.

And some—oh! well may *their* hearts rejoice—
To the gentle sound of a mother's voice!
Long shall they yearn for that kindly tone,
When from the board and the hearth 'tis gone.

And some in the camp, to the bugle's breath,
And the tramp of the steed on the echoing heath
And the sudden roar of the hostile gun,
Which tells that a field must ere night be won.

And some, in the gloomy convict-cell,
To the dull deep note of the warning bell,
As it heavily calls them forth to die,
When the bright sun mounts in the laughing sky.

And some to the peal of the hunter's horn,
And some to the din from the city borne,
And some to the rolling of torrent-floods,
Far 'midst old mountains and solemn woods.

So are we roused on this chequer'd earth,
Each unto light hath a daily birth,
Though fearful or joyous, though sad or sweet,
Are the voices which first our upspringing meet.

But *one* must the sound be, and *one* the call,
Which from the dust shall awake us all,
One—but to sever'd and distant dooms—
How shall the sleepers arise from the tombs?

---

### THE BREEZE FROM SHORE.

Poetry reveals to us the loveliness of nature, brings back the freshness of youthful feeling, revives the relish of simple pleasures, keeps unquenched the enthusiasm which warmed the spring-time of our being, refines youthful love, strengthens our interest in human nature, by vivid delineations of its tenderest and loftiest feelings, and, through the brightness of its prophetic visions, helps faith to lay hold on the future life.—*Channing.*

---

Joy is upon the lonely seas
  When Indian forests pour
Forth to the billow and the breeze
  Their odours from the shore;
Joy, when the soft air's fanning sigh
Bears on the breath of Araby.

Oh! welcome are the winds that tell
  A wanderer of the deep,
Where, far away, the jasmines dwell,
  And where the myrrh-trees weep!
Blest, on the sounding surge and foam,
Are tidings of the citron's home!

The sailor at the helm they greet,
  And hope his bosom stirs,
Upspringing, 'midst the waves, to greet
  The fair earth's messengers,
That woo him, from the moaning main,
Back to her glorious bowers again.

They woo him, whispering lovely tales
  Of many a flowering glade,
And fount's bright gleam in island vales
  Of golden-fruited shade;
Across his lone ship's wake they bring
A vision and a glow of spring.

And oh! ye masters of the lay,
  Come not ev'n thus your songs
That meet us on life's weary way,
  Amidst her toiling throngs?
Yes! o'er the spirit thus they bear
A current of celestial air.

Their power is from the brighter clime
  That in our birth hath part;
Their tones are of the world, which time
  Sears not within the heart;
They tell us of the living light
In its green places ever bright.

They call us, with a voice divine,
  Back to our early love,—
Our vows of youth at many a shrine,
  Whence far and fast we rove:—
Welcome high thought and holy strain
That make us Truth's and Heaven's again!

---

### THE DYING IMPROVISATORE.[*]

*My heart shall be pour'd over thee—and break.*
Prophecy of Dante.

---

The spirit of my land!
It visits me once more!—though I must die
Far from the myrtles which thy breeze hath fann'd,
  My own bright Italy!

It is, it is thy breath,
Which stirs my soul e'en yet, as wavering flame
Is shaken by the wind;—in life and death
  Still trembling, yet the same!

Oh! that love's quenchless power
Might waft my voice to fill thy summer sky,
And through thy groves its dying music shower,
  Italy! Italy!

The nightingale is there,
The sunbeam's glow, the citron-flower's perfume,
The south-wind's whisper in the scented air—
  It will not pierce the tomb!

Never, oh! never more,
On thy Rome's purple heaven mine eye shall dwell,
Or watch the bright waves melt along thy shore—
  My Italy, farewell!

Alas!—thy hills among,
Had I but left a memory of my name,
Of love and grief, one deep, true, fervent song,
  Unto immortal fame!

But like a lute's brief tone,
Like a rose-odour on the breezes cast,
Like a swift flush of day-spring, seen and gone,
  So hath my spirit pass'd!

---

[*] Sestini, the Roman Improvisatore, when on his death-bed at Paris, is said to have poured forth a Farewell to Italy, in his most impassioned poetry.

Pouring itself away,
As a wild bird amidst the foliage turns
That which within him triumphs, beats, or burns
Into a fleeting lay;

That swells, and floats, and dies,
Leaving no echo to the summer woods
Of the rich breathings and impassion'd sighs,
Which thrill'd their solitudes.

Yet, yet remember me!
Friends! that upon its murmurs oft have hung,
When from my bosom, joyously and free,
The fiery fountain sprung.

Under the dark rich blue
Of midnight heavens, and on the star-lit sea,
And when woods kindle into spring's first hue,
Sweet friends! remember me!

And in the marble halls,
Where life's full glow the dreams of beauty wear
And poet-thoughts embodied light the walls,
Let me be with you there!

Fain would I bind for you
My memory with all glorious things to dwell;
Fain bid all lovely sounds my name renew—
Sweet friends, bright land, farewell!

---

## MUSIC OF YESTERDAY.

O! mein Geist, ich fuhle es in mir, strebt nach etwas Ueberirdischem, das keinem Menschen gegonnt ist.——*Tieck*.

---

The chord, the harp's full chord is hush'd,
    The voice hath died away,
Whence music, like sweet waters, gush'd,
    But yesterday.

'Th' awakening note, the breeze-like swell,
    The full o'ersweeping tone,
The sounds that sigh'd " Farewell, farewell !"
    Are gone—all gone.

The love, whose fervent spirit pass'd
    With the rich measure's flow;
The grief, to which it sank at last—
    Where are they now?

They are with the scents, by summer's breath
    Borne from a rose now shed;
With the words from lips long seal'd in death—
    For ever fled.

The sea-shell of its native deep
    A moaning thrill retains,
But earth and air no record keep
    Of parted strains.

And all the memories, all the dreams,
    They woke in floating by;
The tender thoughts, th' Elysian gleams—
    Could these too die ?

They died—as on the water's breast
    The ripple melts away,
When the breeze that stirr'd it sinks to rest—
    So perish'd they!

Mysterious in their sudden birth,
    And mournful in their close,
Passing, and finding not on earth
    Aim or repose.

Whence were they ?—like the breath of flowers
    Why thus to come and go ?—
A long, long journey must be ours,
    Ere this we know!

Vol. IV.—22

---

## THE FORSAKEN HEARTH.

Was mir fehlt ?—Mir fehlt ja alles,
Bin so ganz verlassen hier !
            *Tyrolese Melody.*

---

The Hearth, the Hearth is desolate, the fire is
    quench'd and gone,
That into happy children's eyes once brightly
    laughing shone;
The place where mirth and music met is hush'd
    through day and night,—
Oh! for one kind, one sunny face, of all that there
    made light !

But scatter'd are those pleasant smiles afar by
    mount and shore,
Like gleaming waters from one spring dispersed
    to meet no more;
Those kindred eyes reflect not now each other's
    joy or mirth,
Unbound is that sweet wreath of home—alas ! the
    lonely Hearth!

The voices that have mingled here now speak
    another tongue,
Or breathe, perchance, to alien ears the songs their
    mother sung;
Sad, strangely sad, in stranger lands, must sound
    each household tone,—
The Hearth, the Hearth is desolate, the bright fire
    quench'd and gone.

But are they speaking, singing yet, as in their days
    of glee ?
Those voices, are they lovely still, still sweet on
    earth or sea ?—
Oh! some are hush'd, and some are changed, and
    never shall one strain
Blend their fraternal cadences triumphantly again

And of the hearts that here were link'd by long
    remember'd years,
Alas! the brother knows not now when fall the
    sister's tears !
One haply revels at the feast, while one may droop
    alone,
For broken is the household chain, the bright fire
    quench'd and gone!

Not so—'t is not a broken chain—thy memory binds
    them still,
Thou holy Hearth of other days, though silent now
    and chill !
The smiles, the tears, the rites beheld by thine
    attesting stone,
Have yet a living power to mark thy children for
    thine own.

The father's voice, the mother's prayer, though
    call'd from earth away,
With music rising from the dead, their spirits yet
    shall sway;
And by the past, and by the grave, the parted yet
    are one,
Though the loved Hearth be desolate, the bright
    fire quench'd and gone!

---

## THE DREAMER.

There is no such thing as *forgetting* possible to the
mind; a thousand accidents may, and will, interpose a
veil between our present consciousness, and the secret
inscription on the mind; but alike, whether veiled or
unveiled, the inscription remains for ever.
            *English Opium-Eater.*

Thou hast been call'd, O Sleep ! the friend of woe,
But 't is the happy who have call'd thee so.
            *Southey.*

---

Peace to thy dreams !—thou art slumbering now,
The moonlight's calm is upon thy brow;

All the deep love that o'erflows thy breast,
Lies 'midst the hush of thy heart at rest,
Like the scent of a flower in its folded bell,
When eve through the woodlands hath sigh'd
        farewell.

Peace!—the sad memories that through the day,
With a weight on thy lonely bosom lay,
The sudden thoughts of the changed and dead,
That bow'd thee, as winds bow the willow's head,
The yearnings for faces and voices gone—
All are forgotten!—Sleep on, sleep on!

*Are* they forgotten?—It is not so!
Slumber divides the heart from its woe,
E'en now o'er thine aspect swift changes pass,
Like lights and shades over wavy grass;
Tremblest thou, Dreamer?—O love and grief!
Ye have storms that shake e'en the closed-up leaf!

On thy parted lips there's a quivering thrill,
As on a lyre ere its chords are still;
On the long silk lashes that fringe thine eye,
There's a large tear gathering heavily;
A rain from the clouds of thy spirit press'd—
Sorrowful Dreamer?—this is not rest!

It is Thought at work amidst buried hours,
It is Love keeping vigil o'er perish'd flowers.—
Oh! we bear within us mysterious things,
Of Memory and Anguish, unfathom'd springs,
And Passion, those gulfs of the heart to fill,
With bitter waves, which it ne'er may still.

Well might we pause ere we gave them away,
Flinging the peace of our couch away!
Well might we look on our souls in fear,
They find no fount of oblivion here!
They forget not, the mantle of sleep beneath—
How know we if under the wings of death?

## THE WINGS OF THE DOVE.

*Oh! that I had the wings of a dove, that I might flee away and
be at rest.*

Oh! for thy wings, thou dove!
Now sailing by with sunshine on thy breast;
        That, borne like thee above,
I too might flee away, and be at rest!

        Where wilt thou fold those plumes,
Bird of the forest shadows, holiest bird?
        In what rich leafy glooms,
By the sweet voice of hidden waters stirr'd?

        Over what blessed home,
What roof with dark, deep, summer foliage crown'd,
        O! fair as ocean's foam!
Shall thy bright bosom shed a gleam around?

        Or seek'st thou some old shrine
Of nymph or saint, no more by votary woo'd,
        Though still, as if divine,
Breathing a spirit o'er the solitude?

        Yet wherefore ask thy way?
Blest, ever blest, whate'er its aim, thou art!
        Unto the greenwood spray,
Bearing no dark remembrance at thy heart!

        No echoes that will blend
A sadness with the whispers of the grove;
        No memory of a friend
Far off, or dead, or changed to thee, thou dove!

        Oh! to some cool recess
Take, take me with thee on the summer wind,
        Leaving the weariness
And all the fever of this life behind:

        The aching and the void
Within the heart, whereunto none reply,
        The young bright hopes destroy'd—
Bird! bear me with thee through the sunny sky!

Wild wish, and longing vain,
And brief upspringing to be glad and free!
        Go to thy woodland reign!
My soul is bound and held—I may not flee

        For even by all the fears
And thoughts that haunt my dreams—untold, un-
                known,
        And burning woman's tears,
Pour'd from mine eyes in silence and alone;

        *Had* I thy wings, thou dove!
High 'midst the gorgeous Isles of Cloud to soar,
        Soon the strong cords of love
Would   draw   me   earthwards—homewards—yet
        once more.

## PSYCHE BORNE BY ZEPHYRS TO THE ISLAND OF PLEASURE.*

Souvent l'ame, fortifiee par la contemplation des
choses divines, voudroit deployer ses ailes vers le ciel
Elle croit qu'au terme de sa carriere un rideau va se
lever pour lui decouvrir des scenes de lumiere: mais
quand la mort touche son corps perissable, elle jette un
regard en arriere vers les plaisirs terrestres et vers ses
compagnes mortelles.—*Schlegel.*

                *Translated by Madame de Stael.*

Fearfully and mournfully
        Thou bidd'st the earth farewell,
And yet thou'rt passing, loveliest one
        In a brighter land to dwell.

Ascend, ascend rejoicing!
        The sunshine of that shore
Around thee, as a glorious robe,
        Shall stream for evermore.

The breezy music wandering
        There through th' Elysian sky,
Hath no deep tone that seems to float
        From a happier time gone by:

And there the day's last crimson
        Gives no sad memories birth,
No thought of dead or distant friends,
        Or partings—as on earth.

Yet fearfully and mournfully
        Thou bidd'st that earth farewell,
Although thou'rt passing, loveliest one!
        In a brighter land to dwell.

A land where all is deathless—
        The sunny wave's repose,
The wood with its rich melodies,
        The summer and its rose.

A land that sees no parting,
        That hears no sound of sighs,
That waits thee with immortal air—
        Lift, lift those anxious eyes!

Oh! how like *thee*, thou trembler!
        Man's spirit fondly clings
With timid love, to this, its world
        Of old familiar things!

We pant, we thirst for fountains
        That gush not here below!
On, on we toil, allured by dreams
        Of the living water's flow:

We pine for kindred natures
        To mingle with our own;
For communings more full and high
        Than aught by mortal known:

We strive with brief aspirings
        Against our bounds in vain;
Yet summon'd to be free at last,
        We shrink—and clasp our chain!

* Written for a picture in which Psyche, on her flight upwards,
is represented looking back sadly and anxiously to the earth.

And fearfully and mournfully
　　We bid the earth farewell,
Though passing from its mists, like thee,
　　In a brighter world to dwell.

## THE BOON OF MEMORY.

*Many things answer'd me.——Manfred.*

I go, I go!—and must mine image fade
From the green spots wherein my childhood play'd,
　　By my own streams?
Must my life part from each familiar place,
As a bird's song, that leaves the woods no trace
　　Of its lone themes?

Will the friend pass my dwelling, and forget
The welcomes there, the hours when we have met
　　In grief or glee?
All the sweet counsel, the communion high,
The kindly words of trust, in days gone by,
　　Pour'd full and free?

A boon, a talisman, O Memory! give,
To shrine my name in hearts where I would live
　　For evermore!
Bid the wind speak of me where I have dwelt,
Bid the stream's voice, of all my soul hath felt,
　　A thought restore!

In the rich rose, whose bloom I loved so well,
In the dim brooding violet of the dell,
　　Set deep that thought!
And let the sunset's melancholy glow,
And let the spring's first whisper, faint and low,
　　With me be fraught:

And Memory answer'd me:—"Wild wish and vain
I have no lines the loveliest to detain
　　In the heart's core.
The place they held in bosoms all their own,
Soon with new shadows fill'd, new flowers o'er-
　　　　grown,
　　Is theirs no more!"

Hast *thou* such power, O Love?—And Love replied,
"It is not mine! Pour out thy soul's full tide
　　Of hope and trust,
Prayer, tear, devotedness, that boon to gain—
'Tis but to write, with the heart's fiery rain,
　　Wild words on dust!"

Song, is the gift with thee?—I ask a lay,
Soft, fervent, deep, that will not pass away
　　From the still breast;
Fill'd with a tone—oh! not for deathless fame,
But a sweet haunting murmur of my name,
　　Where it would rest.

And Song made answer—"It is not in me,
Though call'd immortal; though my gifts may be
　　All but divine.
A place of lonely brightness I can give;—
A changeless one, where thou with Love wouldst
　　　　live—
　　This is not mine!"

Death, Death! wilt *thou* the restless wish fulfil?
And Death, the Strong One, spoke:—"I can but
　　　　still
　　Each vain regret.
What if forgotten?—All thy soul would crave,
Thou too, within the mantle of the grave,
　　Wilt soon forget."

Then did my heart in lone faint sadness die,
As from all nature's voices one reply,
　　But one, was given:—
"Earth has *no* heart, fond dreamer! with a tone
To send thee back the spirit of thine own—
　　Seek it in Heaven."

## THE HOMES OF ENGLAND.



The stately Homes of England,
　　How beautiful they stand!
Amidst their tall ancestral trees,
　　O'er all the pleasant land.
The deer across their greensward bound
　　Through shade and sunny gleam,
And the swan glides past them with the sound
　　Of some rejoicing stream.

The merry Homes of England!
　　Around their hearths by night,
What gladsome looks of household love
　　Meet in the ruddy light!
There woman's voice flows forth in song,
　　Or childhood's tale is told,
Or lips move tunefully along
　　Some glorious page of old.

The blessed Homes of England!
　　How softly on their bowers
Is laid the holy quietness
　　That breathes from Sabbath hours!
Solemn, yet sweet, the church-bell's chime
　　Floats through their woods at morn;
All other sounds, in that still time,
　　Of breeze and leaf are born.

The Cottage Homes of England!
　　By thousands on her plains,
They are smiling o'er the silvery brooks,
　　And round the hamlet fanes,
Through glowing orchards forth they peep,
　　Each from its nook of leaves,
And fearless there the lowly sleep,
　　As the bird beneath their eaves.

The free, fair Homes of England!
　　Long, long, in hut and hall,
May hearts of native proof be rear'd
　　To guard each hallow'd wall!
And green for ever be the groves,
　　And bright the flowery sod,
Where first the child's glad spirit loves,
　　Its country and its God!

## THE SICILIAN CAPTIVE.



The champions had come from their fields of war,
Over the crests of the billows far—
They had brought back the spoils of a hundred
　　　shores,
Where the deep had foam'd to their flashing oars.

They sat at their feast round the Norse king's
　　　board;
By the glare of the torch-light the mead was pour'd;
The hearth was heap'd with the pine-boughs high,
And it flung a red radiance on shields thrown by.

The Scalds had chanted in Runic rhyme
Their songs of the sword and the olden time;
And the solemn thrill, as the harp-chords rung,
Had breathed from the walls where the bright
　　　spears hung.

But the swell was gone from the quivering string
They had summon'd a softer voice to sing,
And a captive girl at the warriors' call,
Stood forth in the midst of that frowning hall

Lonely she stood:—in her mournful eyes
Lay the clear midnight of southern skies;
And the drooping fringe of their lashes low,
Half veil'd a depth of unfathom'd woe

Stately she stood—through her fragile frame
Seem'd struck with the blight of some inward
    flame;
And her proud, pale brow had a shade of scorn,
Under the waves of her dark hair worn.

And a deep flush pass'd, like a crimson haze,
O'er her marble cheek by the pine fire's blaze;
No soft hue caught from the south wind's breath,
But a token of fever, at strife with death.

She had been torn from her home away,
With her long locks crown'd for her bridal day,
And brought to die of the burning dreams
That haunt the exile by foreign streams.

They bade her sing of her distant land—
She held its lyre with a trembling hand,
Till the spirit its blue skies had given her, woke,
And the stream of her voice into music broke.

Faint was the strain, in its first wild flow;
Troubled its murmur, and sad, and low;
But it swell'd into deeper power ere long,
As the breeze that swept o'er her soul grew strong.

———

" They bid me sing of thee, mine own, my sunny
    land! of thee!
Am I not parted from thy shores by the mournful
    sounding sea ?
Doth not thy shadow wrap my soul ?—in silence
    let me die,
In a voiceless dream of thy silvery founts, and thy
    pure, deep sapphire sky;
How should thy lyre give *here* its wealth of buried
    sweetness forth ?
Its tones of summer's breathings born, to the wild
    winds of the north?

Yet thus it shall be once, once more!—my spirit
    shall awake,
And through the mists of death shine out, my
    country, for thy sake!
That I may make *thee* known, with all the beauty
    and the light,
And the glory never more to bless thy daughter's
    yearning sight!
Thy woods shall whisper in my song, thy bright
    streams warble by,
Thy soul flow o'er my lips again—yet once, my
    Sicily !

" There are blue heavens—far hence, far hence !
    but, oh ! their glorious blue !
Its very night is beautiful, with the hyacinth's
    deep hue !
It is above my own fair land, and round my
    laughing home,
And arching o'er my vintage hills, they hang their
    cloudless dome ;
And making all the waves as gems, that melt along
    the shore,
And steeping happy hearts in joy—that now is
    mine no more.

" And there are haunts in that green land—oh !
    who may dream or tell
Of all the shaded loveliness it hides in grot and
    dell ?
By fountains flinging rainbow-spray on dark and
    glossy leaves,
And bowers wherein the forest-dove her nest un-
    troubled weaves;
The myrtle dwells there, sending round the rich-
    ness of its breath,
And the violets gleam like amethysts, from the
    dewy moss beneath.

" And there are floating sounds that fill the skies
    through night and day—

Sweet sounds! the soul to hear them faints in
    dreams of heaven away!
They wander through the olive woods, and o'er
    the shining seas—
They mingle with the orange-scents that load the
    sleepy breeze ;
Lute, voice, and bird, are blending there;—it were
    a bliss to die,
As dies a leaf, thy groves among, my flowery Sicily !

" *I* may not thus depart—farewell! yet no, my
    country ! no !
Is not love stronger than the grave? I feel it
    must be so !
My fleeting spirit shall o'ersweep the mountains
    and the main,
And in thy tender starlight rove, and through thy
    woods again.
Its passion deepens—it prevails!—I break my
    chain—I come
To dwell a viewless thing, yet blest—in thy sweet
    air, my home !"

———

And her pale arms dropp'd the ringing lyre—
There came a mist o'er her eye's wild fire—
And her dark rich tresses, in many a fold,
Loosed from their braids, down her bosom roll'd.

For her head sank back on the rugged wall—
A silence fell o'er the warrior's hall;
She had pour'd out her soul with her song's last
    tone;
The lyre was broken, the minstrel gone !

———

## IVAN THE CZAR

———

" Ivan le Terrible, etant deja devenu vieux, assiegait
Novogorod.   Les Boyards, le voyant affoibli, lui de-
manderent s'il ne voulait pas donner le commandement
de l'assaut a son fils.   Sa fureur fut si grande a cette
proposition, que rien ne put l'appaiser ; son fils se pros-
terna a ses pieds ; il le repoussa avec un coup d'une
telle violence, que deux jours apres le malheureux en
mourut.   Le pere, alors au desespoir, devint indifferent
a la guerre comme au pouvoir, et ne survecut que peu
de mois a son fils."——*Dix Annees d'Exil, par Madame
de Stael.*

    Gieb diesen Todten mir heraus.   Ich muss
    Ihn wieder haben !     *     *     *
    *     *     *     Trostlose allmacht,
    Die nicht einmal in Graber ihren armen
    Verlangern, eine kleine Übereilung
    Mit Menschenleben nicht verbessern kann !
                      *Schiller*

———

He sat in silence on the ground,
    The old and haughty Czar,
Lonely, though princes girt him round,
    And leaders of the war:
He had cast his jewell'd sabre,
    That many a field had won,
To the earth beside his youthful dead—
    His fair and first-born son.

With a robe of ermine for its bed,
    Was laid that form of clay,
Where the light a stormy sunset shed
    Through the rich tent made way ;
And a sad and solemn beauty
    On the pallid face came down,
Which the lord of nations mutely watch'd,
    In the dust, with his renown.

Low tones, at last, of woe and fear
  From his full bosom broke—
A mournful thing it was to hear
  How then the proud man spoke!
The voice that through the combat
  Had shouted far and high,
Came forth in strange, dull, hollow tones,
  Burden'd with agony.

" There is no crimson on thy cheek,
  And on thy lip no breath;
I call thee, and thou dost not speak—
  They tell me this is death!
And fearful things are whispering
  That I the deed have done—
For the honour of thy father's name,
  Look up, look up, my son!

" Well might I know death's hue and mien,
  But on *thine* aspect, boy!
What, till this moment, have I seen
  Save pride and tameless joy?
Swiftest thou wert to battle,
  And bravest there of all—
How could I think a warrior's frame
  Thus like a flower should fall?

" I will not hear that still cold look— .
  Rise up, thou fierce and free!
Wake as the storm wakes! I will brook
  All, save this calm, from thee!
Lift brightly up, and proudly,
  Once more thy kindling eyes!
Hath my word lost its power on earth?
  I say to thee, arise!

" Didst thou not know I loved thee well?
  Thou didst not! and art gone,
In bitterness of soul, to dwell
  Where man must dwell alone.
Come back, young fiery spirit!
  If but one hour, to learn
The secrets of the folded heart
  That seem'd to thee so stern

" Thou wert the first, the first, fair child,
  That in mine arms I press'd·
Thou wert the bright one, that hast smiled
  Like summer on my breast!
I rear'd thee as an eagle
  To the chase thy steps I led,
I bore thee on my battle-horse,
  I look upon thee—dead!

" Lay down my warlike banners here,
  Never again to wave,
And bury my red sword and spear,
  Chiefs! in my first-born's grave!
And leave me!—I have conquer'd,
  I have slain—my work is done!
Whom have I slain?—ye answer not—
  *Thou* too art mute, my son!"

And thus his wild lament was pour'd
  Through the dark resounding night,
And the battle knew no more his sword,
  Nor the foaming steed his might.
He heard strange voices moaning
  In every wind that sigh'd;
From the searching stars of heaven he shrank—
  Humbly the conqueror died.

---

## CAROLAN'S PROPHECY.*

Thy cheek too swiftly flushes, o'er thine eye
The lights and shadows come and go too fast,
Thy tears gush forth too soon, and in thy voice
Are sounds of tenderness too passionate
For peace on earth; oh! therefore, child of song!
'T is well thou shouldst depart.

A sound of music, from amidst the hills,
Came suddenly, and died; a fitful sound
Of mirth, soon lost in wail.—Again it rose,

* Founded on a circumstance related of the Irish Bard, in the
Percy Anecdotes of Imagination.

And sank in mournfulness.—There sat a bard
By a blue stream of Erin, where it swept
Flashing through rock and wood; the sunset's light
Was on his wavy, silver-gleaming hair,
And the wind's whisper in the mountain ash,
Whose clusters droop'd above. His head was bow'd
His hand was on his harp, yet thence its touch
Had drawn but broken strains; and many stood,
Waiting around, in silent earnestness,
Th' unchaining of his soul, the gush of song—
Many and graceful forms!—yet one alone
Seem'd present to his dream; and she, indeed,
With her pale, virgin brow, and changeful cheek,
And the clear starlight of her serious eyes,
Lovely amidst the flowing of dark locks
And pallid braiding flowers, was beautiful,
E'en painfully!—a creature to behold
With trembling 'midst our joy, lest aught unseen
Should waft the vision from us, leaving earth
Too dim without its brightness!—Did such fear
O'ershadow in that hour the gifted one,
By his own rushing stream?—Once more he gazed
Upon the radiant girl, and yet once more
From the deep chords his wandering hand brought
    out
A few short festive notes, an opening strain
Of bridal melody, soon dash'd with grief,
As if some wailing spirit in the strings
Met and o'ermaster'd him; but yielding then
To the strong prophet-impulse, mournfully,
Like moaning waters, o'er the harp he pour'd
The trouble of his haunted soul, and sang—

    Voice of the grave!
  I hear thy thrilling call;
It comes in the dash of the foaming wave,
  In the sere leaf's trembling fall!
In the shiver of the tree,
  I hear thee, O thou voice!
And I would thy warning were but for me,
  That my spirit might rejoice.

    But thou art sent
For the sad earth's young and fair,
For the graceful heads that have not bent
  To the wintry hand of care!
They hear the wind's low sigh,
  And the river sweeping free,
And the green reeds murmuring heavily,
  And the woods—but they hear not thee!

    Long have I striven
With my deep foreboding soul,
But the full tide now its bounds hath riven,
  And darkly on must roll.
There's a young brow smiling near,
  With a bridal white rose wreath—
Unto *me* it smiles from a flowery bier,
  Touch'd solemnly by death!

    Fair art thou, Morna!
The sadness of thine eye
Is beautiful as silvery clouds
  On the dark blue summer sky;
And thy voice comes like the sound
  Of a sweet and hidden rill,
That makes the dim woods tuneful round—
  But soon it must be still!

    Silence and dust
On thy sunny lips must lie—
Make not the strength of love thy trust,
  A stronger yet is nigh!
No strain of festal flow
  That my hand for thee hath tried,
But into dirge notes wild and low
  Its ringing tones have died.

    Young art thou, Morna!
Yet on thy gentle head,
Like heavy dew on the lily's leaves,
  A spirit hath been shed!
And the glance is thine which sees
  Through nature's awful heart—
But bright things go with the summer breeze,
  And thou too must depart!

Yet shall I weep?
I know that in thy breast
There swells a fount of song too deep,
Too powerful for thy rest!
And the bitterness I know,
Go, all undimm'd, in thy glory go!
Young and crown'd bride of death!

Take hence to heaven
Thy holy thoughts and bright,
And soaring hopes, that were not given
For the touch of mortal blight!
Might we follow in thy track,
This parting should not be!
But the spring shall give us violets back,
And every flower but thee!

There was a burst of tears around the bard;
All wept but one, and she serenely stood,
With her clear brow and dark religious eye
Raised to the first faint star above the hills,
And cloudless; though it might be that her cheek
Was paler than before.—So Morna heard
The minstrel's prophecy.
                    And spring return'd,
Bringing the earth her lovely things again,
All, save the loveliest far! A voice, a smile,
A young sweet spirit gone.

------

## THE LADY OF THE CASTLE.

FROM THE "PORTRAIT GALLERY," AN UNFINISHED
POEM.

If there be but one spot upon thy name,
One eye thou fear'st to meet, one human voice
Whose tones thou shrink'st from—Woman! veil thy face,
And bow thy head—and die!

------

THOU see'st her pictured with her shining hair,
  (Famed were those tresses in Provençal song,)
Half braided, half o'er her cheek and bosom fair
  Let loose, and pouring sunny waves along
Her gorgeous vest. A child's light hand is rovin
'Midst the rich curls; and, oh! how meekly loving
Its earnest looks are lifted to the face
Which bends to meet its lip in laughing grace!
Yet that bright lady's eye, methinks, hath less
Of deep, and still, and pensive tenderness,
Than might beseem a mother's;—on her brow
  Something too much there sits of native scorn,
And her smile kindles with a conscious glow,
  As from the thought of sovereign beauty born.
These may be dreams—but how shall woman tell
Of woman's shame, and not with tears?—She fell!
That mother left that child!—went hurrying by
Its cradle—haply not without a sigh,
Haply one moment o'er its rest serene
She hung—but, no! it could not thus have been,
For she went on!—forsook her home, her hearth,
All pure affection, all sweet household mirth,
To live a gaudy and dishonour'd thing,
Sharing in guilt the splendours of a king.

Her lord, in very weariness of life,
Girt on his sword for scenes of distant strife;
He reck'd no more of glory:—grief and shame
Crush'd out his fiery nature, and his name
Died silently. A shadow o'er his halls
Crept year by year; the minstrel pass'd their walls;
The warder's horn hung mute:—meantime the
    child,
On whose first flowering thoughts no parent smiled,
A gentle girl, and yet deep-hearted, grew
Into sad youth; for well, too well, she knew
Her mother's tale! Its memory made the sky
Seem all too joyous for her shrinking eye;
Check'd on her lip the flow of song, which fain
Would there have linger'd; flush'd her cheek to
    pain
If met by sudden glance; and gave a tone
Of sorrow, as for something lovely gone,
E'en to the spring's glad voice. Her own was low
And plaintive.—Oh! there lie such depths of woe
In a young blighted spirit! Manhood rears
A haughty brow, and age has done with tears;

But youth bows down to misery, in amaze
At the dark cloud o'ermantling its fresh days—
And thus it was with her. A mournful sight
In one so fair—for she indeed was fair—
Not with her mother's dazzling eyes of light,
  Hers were more shadowy, full of thought and
    prayer,
And with long lashes o'er a white rose cheek,
Drooping in gloom, yet tender still and meek,
Still that fond child's—and, oh! the brow above
So pale and pure! so form'd for holy love
To gaze upon in silence!—But she felt
That love was not for her, though hearts would
    melt
Where'er she moved, and reverence mutely given
Went with her; and low prayers, that call'd on
    Heaven
To bless the young Isaure.

                        One sunny morn,
  With alms before her castle gate she stood,
'Midst peasant groups; when, breathless and o'er
    worn
  And shrouded in long weeds of widowhood,
A stranger through them broke:—the orphan maid,
With her sweet voice and proffer'd hand of aid,
Turn'd to give welcome; but a wild sad look
Met her—a gaze tha' all her spirit shook;
And that pale woman, suddenly subdued
By some strong passion in its gushing mood,
Knelt at her feet, and bathed them with such tears
As rain the hoarded agonies of years
From the heart's urn; and with her white lips
    press'd
The ground they trod; then, burying in her vest
Her brow's deep flush, sobb'd out—"Oh! undefiled
I am thy mother—spurn me not, my child!"

                    . . . . saure had pray'd for that lost mother; wept
O'er her stain'd memory, while the happy slept
In the hush'd midnight; stood with mournful gaze
Before yon picture's smile of other days.
But never breathed in human ear the name
Which weigh'd her being to the earth with shame.

What marvel if the anguish, the surprise,
The dark remembrances, the alter'd guise,
Awhile o'erpower'd her?—from the weeper's touch
She shrank—'t was but a moment—yet too much
For that all-humbled one; its mortal stroke
Came down like lightning, and her full heart broke
At once in silence. Heavily and prone
She sank, while o'er her castle's threshold stone,
Those long fair tresses—they still brightly wore
Their early pride, though bound with pearls no
    more—
Bursting their fillet, in sad beauty roll'd,
And swept the dust with coils of wavy gold.

Her child bent o'er her—call'd her—'Twas too late ·
Dead lay the wanderer at her own proud gate!
The joy of courts, the star of knight and bard—
How didst thou fall, O bright-hair'd Ermengarde!

------

## THE MOURNER FOR THE BARMECIDES.

A good old man! how well in thee appears
The constant service of the antique world!
Thou art not for the fashion of these times.
                            As You Like It.

------

FALL'N was the House of Giafar; and its name
The high romantic name of Barmecide,
A sound forbidden on its own bright shores,
By the swift Tygris' wave. Stern Haroun's wrath,
Sweeping the mighty with their fame away,
Had so pass'd sentence; but man's chainless heart
Hides that within its depths which never yet
Th' oppressor's thought could reach.

                        'Twas desolate
Where Giafar's halls, beneath the burning sun,
Spread out in ruin lay. The songs had ceased;

The lights, the perfumes, and the genii tales
Had ceased; the guests were gone.  Yet still one
    voice
Was there—the fountain's; through those eastern
    courts,
Over the broken marble and the grass,
Its low clear music shedding mournfully.

And still another voice!—an aged man,
Yet with a dark and fervent eye beneath
His silvery hair, came, day by day, and sate
On a white column's fragment; and drew forth,
From th' forsaken walls and dim arcades,
A tone that shook them with its answering thrill
To his deep accents.  Many a glorious tale
He told that sad yet stately solitude,
Pouring his memory's fulness o'er its gloom,
Like waters in the waste; and calling up,
By song or high recital of their deeds,
Bright solemn shadows of its vanish'd race
To people their own halls: with these alone,
In all this rich and breathing world, his thoughts
Held still unbroken converse.  He had been
Rear'd in this lordly dwelling, and was now
The ivy of its ruins, unto which
His fading life seem'd bound.  Day roll'd on day,
And from that scene the loneliness was fled;
For crowds around the gray-hair'd chronicler
Met as men meet, within whose anxious hearts
Fear with deep feeling strives; till, as a breeze
Wanders through forest branches, and is met
By one quick sound and shiver of the leaves,
The spirit of his passionate lament,
As through their stricken souls it pass'd, awoke
One echoing murmur.—But this might not be
Under a despot's rule, and summon'd thence,
The dreamer stood before the Caliph's throne:
Sentenced to death he stood, and deeply pale,
And with his white lips rigidly compress'd;
Till, in submissive tones, he ask'd to speak
Once more, ere thrust from earth's fair sunshine
    forth.
Was it to sue for grace?—His burning heart
Sprang, with a sudden lightning, to his eye,
And he was changed!—and thus, in rapid words,
Th' o'ermastering thoughts, more strong than death,
    found way.

" And shall I not rejoice to go, when the noble and
    the brave,
With the glory on their brows, are gone before me
    to the grave ?
What is there left to look on now, what bright-
    ness in the land ?
I hold in scorn the faded world, that wants their
    princely band !

" My chiefs! my chiefs! the old man comes that
    in your halls was nursed—
That follow'd you to many a fight, where flash'd
    your sabres first—
That bore your children in his arms, your name
    upon his heart :—
Oh! must the music of that name with him from
    each depart ?

" It shall not be! a thousand tongues, though hu-
    man voice were still,
With that high sound the living air triumphantly
    shall fill;
The wind's free flight shall bear it on, as wander
    ing seeds are sown,
And the starry midnight whisper it, with a deep
    and thrilling tone.

' For it is not as a flower whose scent with the
    dropping leaves expires,
And it is not as a household lamp, that a breath
    should quench its fires;
It is written on our battle-fields with the writing
    of the sword,
It hath left upon our desert sands a light in bless-
    ings pour'd.

' The founts, the many gushing founts, which to
    the wild ye gave,
Or you, my chiefs, shall sing aloud, as they pour a
    joyous wave !

And the groves, with whose deep lovely gloom ye
    hung the pilgrim's way,
Shall send from all their sighing leaves your praises
    on the day.

" The very walls your bounty rear'd for the stran-
    ger's homeless head,
Shall find a murmur to record your tale, my glorious
    dead !
Though the grass be where ye feasted once, where
    lute and cittern rung,
And the serpent in your palaces lie coil'd amidst
    its young.

" It is enough ! mine eye no more of joy or splen-
    dour sees—
I leave your name in lofty faith, to the skies and
    to the breeze !
I go, since earth her flower hath lost, to join the
    bright and fair,
And call the grave a kingly house, for ye, my chiefs,
    are there !"

But while the old man sang, a mist of tears
O'er Haroun's eyes had gather'd, and a thought—
Oh! many a sudden and remorseful thought—
Of his youth's once loved friends, the martyr'd race,
O'erflow'd his softening heart.—" Live! live !" he
    cried,
" Thou faithful unto death ! live on, and still
Speak of thy lords—they *were* a princely band !'

---

## THE CAPTIVE KNIGHT.

The prison'd thrush may brook the cage,
The captive eagle dies for rage.
                                    *Lady of the Lake.*

'Twas a trumpet's pealing sound !
And the knight look'd down from the Paynim's
    tower,
And a Christian host, in its pride and power,
    Through the pass beneath him wound.
Cease awhile, clarion ! Clarion, wild and shrill,
Cease ! let them hear the captive's voice—be still !

" I knew 't was a trumpet's note !
And I see my brethren's lances gleam,
And their pennons wave by the mountain stream,
    And their plumes to the glad wind float !
Cease awhile, clarion ! Clarion, wild and shrill,
Cease ! let them hear the captive's voice—be still !

" I am here, with my heavy chain !
And I look on a torrent sweeping by,
And an eagle rushing to the sky,
    And a host to its battle-plain !
Cease awhile, clarion ! Clarion, wild and shrill,
Cease ! let them hear the captive's voice—be still ?

" Must I pine in my fetters here ?
With the wild wind's foam, and the free bird's
    flight,
And the tall spears glancing on my sight,
    And the trumpet in mine ear ?
Cease awhile, clarion ! Clarion, wild and shrill,
Cease ! let them hear the captive's voice—be still !

" They are gone ! they have all pass'd by !
They in whose wars I had borne my part,
They that I loved with a brother's heart,
    They have left me here to die !
Sound again, clarion ! Clarion, pour thy blast !
Sound ! for the captive's dream of hope is past."

---

## THE SPANISH CHAPEL.[*]

Weep not for those whom the veil of the tomb,
    In life's early morning, hath hid from our eyes,
Ere sin threw a veil o'er the spirit's young bloom,
    Or earth had profaned what was born for the skies.
                                    *Moore.*

---

I MADE a mountain brook my guide,
    Through a wild Spanish glen,

[*] Suggested by a scene beautifully described in the Recollections of
the Peninsula.

And wander'd on its grassy side,
  Far from the homes of men.

It lured me with a singing tone,
  And many a sunny glance,
To a green spot of beauty lone,
  A haunt for old romance.

A dim and deeply bosom'd grove
  Of many an aged tree,
Such as the shadowy violets love,
  The fawn and forest bee.

The darkness of the chestnut bough
  There on the waters lay,
The bright stream reverently below
  Check'd its exulting play;

And bore a music all subdued,
  And led a silvery sheen,
On through the breathing solitude
  Of that rich leafy scene.

For something viewlessly around
  Of solemn influence dwelt,
In the soft gloom and whispery sound,
  Not to be told, but felt:

While sending forth a quiet gleam
  Across the wood's repose,
And o'er the twilight of the stream.
  A lonely chapel rose.

A pathway to that still retreat
  Through many a myrtle wound,
And there a sight—how strangely sweet!
  My steps in wonder bound.

For on a brilliant bed of flowers,
  E'en at the threshold made,
As if to sleep through sultry hours,
  A young fair child was laid.

To sleep!—oh! ne'er on childhood's eye
  And silken lashes press'd,
Did the warm *living* slumber lie
  With such a weight of rest?

Yet still a tender crimson glow
  Its cheek's pure marble dyed—
'Twas but the light's faint streaming flow
  Through roses heap'd beside.

I stoop'd—the smooth round arm was chill,
  The soft lip's breath was fled,
And the bright ringlets hung so still—
  The lovely child was dead!

"Alas!" I cried, "fair faded thing!
  Thou hast wrung bitter tears,
And thou hast left a woe, to cling
  Round yearning hearts for years!"

But then a voice came sweet and low—
  I turn'd, and near me sate
A woman with a mourner's brow,
  Pale, yet not desolate.

And in her still, clear, matron face,
  All solemnly serene,
A shadow'd image I could trace
  Of that young slumberer's mien.

"Stranger! thou pitiest me," she said,
  With lips that faintly smiled,
"As here I watch'd beside my dead,
  My fair and precious child.

"But know the time-worn heart may be
  By pangs in this world riven,
Keener than theirs who yield, like me,
  An angel thus to Heaven!"

## THE KAISER'S FEAST

Louis, Emperor of Germany, having put his brother
the Palsgrave Rodolphus, under the ban of the empire
in the twelfth century, that unfortunate prince fled to
England, where he died in neglect and poverty. "After
his decease, his mother, Matilda, privately invited his
children to return to Germany; and, by her mediation
during a season of festivity, when Louis kept wassail
in the castle of Heidelberg, the family of his brother
presented themselves before him in the garb of suppliants, imploring pity and forgiveness. To this appeal the
victor softened."——*Miss Benger's Memoirs of the
Queen of Bohemia.*

The Kaiser feasted in his hall—
  The red wine mantled high;
Banners were trembling on the wall,
  To the peals of minstrelsy:
And many a gleam and sparkle came
  From the armour hung around,
As it caught the glance of the torch's flame,
  Or the hearth with pine-boughs crown'd.

Why fell there silence on the chord
  Beneath the harper's hand?
And suddenly, from that rich board,
  Why rose the wassail band?
The strings were hush'd—the knights made way
  For the queenly mother's tread,
As up the hall, in dark array,
  Two fair-hair'd boys she led.

She led them e'en to the Kaiser's place,
  And still before him stood;
Till, with strange wonder, o'er his face
  Flush'd the proud warrior blood:
And "Speak, my mother! speak!" he cried,
  "Wherefore this mourning vest?
And the clinging children by thy side,
  In weeds of sadness drest?"

"Well may a mourning vest be mine,
  And theirs, my son, my son!
Look on the features of thy line
  In each fair little one!
Though grief awhile within their eyes
  Hath tamed the dancing glee,
Yet there thine own quick spirit lies—
  Thy brother's children see!

"And where is he, thy brother, where?
  He in thy home that grew,
And smiling, with his sunny hair,
  Ever to greet thee flew?
How would his arms thy neck entwine,
  His fond lips press thy brow!
My son! oh, call these orphans thine—
  Thou hast no brother now!

"What! from their gentle eyes doth naught
  Speak of thy childhood's hours,
And smite thee with a tender thought
  Of thy dead father's towers?
Kind was thy boyish heart and true,
  When rear'd together there,
Through the old woods like fawns ye flew—
  Where is thy brother—where?

"Well didst thou love him then, and he
  Still at thy side was seen!
How is it that such things can be
  As though they ne'er had been?
Evil was this world's breath, which came
  Between the good and brave!
Now must the tears of grief and shame
  Be offer'd to the grave.

"And let them, let them there be pour'd:
  Though all unfelt below—
Thine own wrung heart, to love restored,
  Shall soften as they flow.
Oh! death is mighty to make peace;
  Now bid his work be done!
So many an inward strife shall cease—
  Take, take these babes, my son!"

His eye was dimm'd—the strong man shook
  With feelings long suppress'd;
Up in his arms the boys he took,
  And strain'd them to his breast
And a shout from all in the royal hall
  Burst forth to hail the sight;
And eyes were wet 'midst the brave that met
  At the Kaiser's feast that night.

## TASSO AND HIS SISTER.

"Devant vous est Sorrente; la demeuroit la sœur de
Tasse, quand il vint en pelerin demander a cette obscure
am'a, un asyle contre l'injustice des princes.—Ses longues
douleurs avaient presque egare sa raison; il ne lui
restoit plus que son genie."——*Corinne.*

She sat, where on each wind that sigh'd,
  The citron's breath went by,
While the red gold of eventide
  Burn'd in th' Italian sky.
Her bower was one where daylight's close
  Full oft sweet laughter found,
As thence the voice of childhood rose
  To the high vineyards round.

But still and thoughtful, at her knee
  Her children stood that hour,
Their bursts of song and dancing glee
  Hush'd as by words of power.
With bright, fix'd, wondering eyes, that gazed
  Up to their mother's face,
With brows through parted ringlets raised,
  They stood in silent grace.

While she—yet something o'er her look
  Of mournfulness was spread—
Forth from a poet's magic book
  The glorious numbers read;
The proud undying lay which pour'd
  Its light on evil years;
*His* of the gifted pen and sword,*
  The triumph and the tears.

She read of fair Erminia's flight,
  Which Venice once might hear
Sung on her glittering seas at night
  By many a gondolier;
Of him she read, who broke the charm
  That wrapt the myrtle-grove;
Of Godfrey's deeds, of Tancred's arm,
  That slew his Paynim love.

Young cheeks around that bright page glow'd,
  Young holy hearts were stirr'd;
And the meek tears of woman flow'd
  Fast o'er each burning word,
And sounds of breeze, and fount, and leaf,
  Came sweet, each pause between;
When a strange voice of sudden grief
  Burst on the gentle scene.

The mother turn'd—a way-worn man,
  In pilgrim garb, stood nigh,
Of stately mien, yet wild and wan,
  Of proud yet mournful eye.
But drops which would not stay for pride,
  From that dark eye gush'd free,
As pressing his pale brow, he cried,
  "Forgotten! e'en by thee!

"Am I so changed?—and yet we two
  Oft hand in hand have play'd;—
This brow hath been all bathed in dew,
  From wreaths which thou hast made·
We have knelt down and said one prayer,
  And sung one vesper strain;
My soul is dim with clouds of care—
  Tell me those words again!

* It is scarcely necessary to recall the well-known Italian saying,
that Tasso, with his sword and pen, was superior to all men

"Life hath been heavy on my head,
  I come a stricken deer,
Bearing the heart, 'midst crowds that bled,
  To bleed in stillness here."
She gazed, till thoughts that long had slept
  Shook all her thrilling frame—
She fell upon his neck and wept,
  Murmuring her brother's name.

Her *brother's* name!—and who was he,
  The weary one, th' unknown,
That came, the bitter world to flee,
  A stranger to his own?—
He was the bard of gifts divine
  To sway the souls of men;
He of the song for Salem's shrine,
  He of the sword and pen!

## ULLA, OR THE ADJURATION

Yet speak to me! I have outwatch'd the stars,
And gazed o'er Heaven in vain, in search of thee.
Speak to me! I have wander'd o'er the earth,
And never found thy likeness.  Speak to me!
This once—once more!

  *Manfred*

"Thou'rt gone!—thou'rt slumbering low,
  With the sounding seas above thee;
It is but a restless woe,
  But a haunting dream to love thee?
Thrice the glad swan has sung,
  To greet the spring-time hours,
Since thine oar at parting flung
  The white spray up in showers.

There's a shadow of the grave on thy hearth and
    round thy home;
Come to me from the ocean's dead!—thou'rt surely
    of them—come!"
  'Twas Ulla's voice—alone she stood
    In the Iceland summer night
  Far gazing o'er a glassy flood,
    From a dark rock's beetling height

"I know thou hast thy bed
  Where the sea-weed's coil hath bound thee;
The storm sweeps o'er thy head,
  But the depths are hush'd around thee;
What wind shall point the way
  To the chambers where thou'rt lying?
Come to me thence, and say
  If thou thought'st on me in dying?

I will not shrink to see thee with a bloodless lip
    and cheek—
Come to me from the ocean's dead!—thou'rt surely
    of them—speak!"

  She listen'd—'t was the wind's low moan,
    'T was the ripple of the wave,
  'T was the wakening ospray's cry alone,
    As it started from its cave.

"I know each fearful spell
  Of the ancient Runic lay,
Whose mutter'd words compel
  The tempest to obey.
But I adjure not *thee*
  By magic sign or song—
My voice shall stir the sea
  By love—the deep, the strong!

By the might of woman's tears, by the passion of
    her sighs,
Come to me from the ocean's dead!—by the vows
    we pledged—arise!"

  Again she gazed with an eager glance,
    Wandering and wildly bright;—
  She saw but the sparkling waters dance
    To the arrowy northern light.

" By the slow and struggling death
  Of hope that loathed to part,
By the fierce and withering breath
  Of despair on youth's high heart—
By the weight of gloom which clings
  To the mantle of the night,
By the heavy dawn which brings
  Naught lovely to the sight—

By all that from my weary soul thou hast wrung
    of grief and fear—
Come to me from the ocean's dead—awake, arise,
    appear!"

  Was it her yearning spirit's dream,
    Or did a pale form rise,
  And o'er the hush'd wave glide and gleam,
    With bright, still, mournful eyes?

' Have the depths heard ?—they have !
  My voice prevails—thou'rt there,
Dim from thy watery grave—
  O that thou wert so fair !
Yet take me to thy rest !
  There dwells no fear with love ;
Let me slumber on thy breast,
  While the billow rolls above !

Where the long-lost things lie hid, where the bright
    ones have their home,
We will sleep among the ocean's dead—stay for
    me, stay !—I come !"

  There was a sullen plunge below,
    A flashing on the main,
  And the wave shut o'er that wild heart's woe,
    Shut—and grew still again.

## TO WORDSWORTH.

Thine is a strain to read among the hills,
  The old and full of voices ;—by the source
Of some free stream, whose gladd'ning presence
    fills
  The solitude with sound ; for in its course
Even such is thy deep song, that seems a part
Of those high scenes, a fountain from their heart.

Or its calm spirit fitly may be taken
  To the still breast, in sunny garden bowers,
Where vernal winds each tree's low tones awaken,
  And bud and bell with changes mark the hours,
There let thy thoughts be with me, while the day
Sinks with a golden and serene decay.

Or by some hearth where happy faces meet,
  When night hath hush'd the woods, with all
    their birds,
There, from some gentle voice, that lay were sweet
  As antique music, link'd with household words ;
While, in pleased murmurs, woman's lip might
    move,
And the raised eye of childhood shine in love.

Or where the shadows of dark solemn yews
  Brood silently o'er some lone burial-ground,
Thy verse hath power that brightly might diffuse
  A breath, a kindling, as of spring, around,
From its own glow of hope and courage high,
And steadfast faith's victorious constancy.

True bard and holy !—thou art e'en as one
  Who, by some secret gift of soul or eye,
In every spot beneath the smiling sun,
  Sees where the springs of living waters lie :
Unseen awhile they sleep—till, touch'd by thee,
Bright healthful waves flow forth to each glad
    wanderer free.

## A MONARCH'S DEATH-BED.

The Emperor Albert, of Hapsburgh, who was assassinated by his nephew, afterwards called John the Parricide, was left to die by the way-side, and only supported in his last moments by a female peasant, who happened to be passing.

A monarch on his death-bed lay—
  Did censers waft perfume
And soft lamps pour their silvery ray
  Through his proud chamber's gloom ?
He lay upon a greensward bed,
  Beneath a darkening sky—
A lone tree waving o'er his head,
  A swift stream rolling by.

Had he then fall'n as warriors fall,
  Where spear strikes fire with spear ?
Was there a banner for his pall,
  A buckler for his bier ?
Not so ;—nor cloven shields nor helms
  Had strewn the bloody sod,
Where lie, the helpless lord of realms,
  Yielded his soul to God.

Were there not friends with words of cheer,
  And princely vassals nigh ?
And priests, the crucifix to rear
  Before the glazing eye ?
A peasant girl that royal head
  Upon her bosom laid,
And, shrinking not for woman's dread,
  The face of death survey'd.

Alone she sat :—from hill and wood
  Red sank the mournful sun :
Fast gush'd the fount of noble blood—
  Treason its worst had done.
With her long hair she vainly press'd
  The wounds to stanch their tide—
Unknown, on that meek humble breast,
  Imperial Albert died !

## TO THE MEMORY OF HEBER.

Umile in tanta gloria.—Petrarch.

If it be sad to speak of treasures gone,
  Of sainted genius call'd too soon away,
Of light from this world taken, while it shone
  Yet kindling onward to the perfect day—
How shall our grief, if mournful these things be,
Flow forth, O thou of many gifts ! for thee ?

Hath not thy voice been here amongst us heard ?
  And that deep soul of gentleness and power,
Have we not felt its breath in every word,
  Wont from thy lip, as Hermon's dew, to shower ?
Yes, in our hearts thy fervent thoughts have
    burn'd—
Of heaven they were, and thither have return'd.

How shall we mourn thee ?—With a lofty trust,
  Our life's immortal birthright from above !
With a glad faith, whose eye, to track the just,
  Through shades and mysteries lifts a glance of
    love,
And yet can weep !—for nature thus deplores
The friend that leaves us, though for happier shores.

And one high tone of triumph o'er thy bier,
  One strain of solemn rapture be allow'd !
Thou, that rejoicing on thy mid career,
  Not to decay, but unto death, has bow'd ;
In those bright regions of the rising sun,
Where victory ne'er a crown like thine had won.

Praise ! for yet one more name with power endow'd,
  To cheer and guide us, onward as we press ;
Yet one more image on the heart bestow'd,
  To dwell there, beautiful in holiness !
Thine, Heber, thine ! whose memory from the dead
Shines as the star which to the Saviour led.

## THE ADOPTED CHILD.

"Why wouldst thou leave me, O gentle child?
Thy home on the mountain is bleak and wild,
A straw-roof'd cabin with lowly wall—
Mine is a fair and a pillar'd hall,
Where many an image of marble gleams,
And the sunshine of picture for ever streams."

"Oh! green is the turf where my brothers play,
Through the long bright hours of the summer day;
They find the red cup-moss where they climb,
And they chase the bee o'er the scented thyme,
And the rocks where the heath-flower blooms they
    know—
Lady, kind lady! O, let me go."

"Content thee, boy! in my bower to dwell,
Here are sweet sounds which thou lovest well;
Flutes on the air in the stilly noon,
Harps which the wandering breezes tune,
And the silvery wood-note of many a bird,
Whose voice was ne'er in thy mountains heard."

"Oh! my mother sings, at the twilight's fall,
A song of the hills far more sweet than all;
She sings it under our own green tree,
To the babe half slumbering on her knee;
I dreamt last night of that music low—
Lady, kind lady! O, let me go."

"Thy mother is gone from her cares to rest,
She hath taken the babe on her quiet breast;
Thou wouldst meet her footstep, my boy, no more
Nor hear her song at the cabin door,
Come thou with me to the vineyards nigh,
And we'll pluck the grapes of the richest dye."

"Is my mother gone from her home away?—
But I know that my brothers are there at play—
I know they are gathering the foxglove's bell,
Or the long fern-leaves by the sparkling well;
Or they launch their boats where the bright streams
    flow—
Lady, kind lady! O, let me go."

"Fair child, thy brothers are wanderers now,
They sport no more on the mountain's brow,
They have left the fern by the spring's green side,
And the streams where the fairy barks were tried.
Be thou at peace in thy brighter lot,
For thy cabin home is a lonely spot."

'Are they gone, all gone from the sunny hill?—
But the bird and the blue-fly rove o'er it still;
And the red-deer bound in their gladness free,
And the heath is bent by the singing bee,
And the waters leap, and the fresh winds blow—
Lady kind lady! O, let me go."

## INVOCATION.

I call'd on dreams and visions, to disclose
That which is veil'd from waking thought; conjured
Eternity, as men constrain a ghost,
To appear and answer.

*Wordsworth.*

Answer me, burning stars of night
    Where is the spirit gone,
That past the reach of human sight,
    As a swift breeze hath flown?—
And the stars answer'd me—"We roll
    In light and power on high;
But, of the never-dying soul,
    Ask that which cannot die."

Oh! many-toned and chainless wind
    Thou art a wanderer free;
Tell me if *thou* its place canst find,
    Far over mount and sea?—

And the wind murmur'd in reply—
    "The blue deep I have cross'd,
And met its barks and billows high,
    But not what thou hast lost."

Ye clouds that gorgeously repose
    Around the setting sun,
Answer! have ye a home for those
    Whose earthly race is run?—
The bright clouds answer'd—"We depart,
    We vanish from the sky;
Ask what is deathless in thy heart,
    For that which cannot die."

Speak then, thou voice of God within,
    Thou of the deep, low tone!
Answer me, through life's restless din,
    Where is the spirit flown?—
And the voice answer'd—"Be thou still!
    Enough to know is given;
Clouds, winds, and stars *their* part fulfil,
    *Thine* is to trust in Heaven."

## KORNER AND HIS SISTER.

Charles Theodore Korner, the celebrated young German poet and soldier, was killed in a skirmish with a detachment of French troops, on the 20th of August, 1813, a few hours after the composition of his popular piece, "The Sword Song." He was buried at the village of Wobbelin in Mecklenburgh, under a beautiful oak, in a recess of which he had frequently deposited verses composed by him while campaigning in its vicinity. The monument erected to his memory is of cast iron; and the upper part is wrought into a lyre and sword, a favourite emblem of Korner's, from which one of his works had been entitled. Near the grave of the poet is that of his only sister, who died of grief for his loss, having only survived him long enough to complete his portrait and a drawing of his burial-place. Over the gate of the cemetery is engraved one of his own lines:—

"Vergiss die treuen Todten nicht."
Forget not the faithful dead.

*See Richardson's Translation of Korner's Life and Works, and Downes' Letters from Mecklenburgh.*

### KORNER AND HIS SISTER.

Green wave the oak for ever o'er thy rest,
    Thou that beneath its crowning foliage sleepest,
And, in the stillness of thy country's breast,
    Thy place of memory as an altar keepest;
Brightly thy spirit o'er her hills was pour'd,
    Thou of the Lyre and Sword!

Rest, bard! rest, soldier!—by the father's hand
    Here shall the child of after years be led,
With his wreath-offering silently to stand
    In the hush'd presence of the glorious dead.
Soldier and bard! for thou thy path hast trod
    With freedom and with God.

The oak waved proudly o'er thy burial-rite,
    On thy crown'd bier to slumber warriors bore
        thee,
And with true hearts thy brethren of the fight
    Wept as they vail'd their drooping banners o'er
        thee.
And the deep guns with rolling peal gave token,
    That Lyre and Sword were broken.

Thou hast a hero's tomb;—a lowlier bed
    Is hers, the gentle girl beside thee lying—
The gentle girl, that bow'd her fair young head
    When thou wert gone, in silent sorrow dying.
Brother, true friend! the tender and the brave—
    She pined to share thy grave.

Fame was thy gift from others:—but for *her*,
    To whom the wide world held that only spot,
*She* loved thee!—lovely in your lives ye were,
    And in your early deaths divided not.

Thou hast thine oak, thy trophy:—What hath
  she?—
    Her own blest place by thee!

It was thy spirit, brother, which had made
  The bright earth glorious to her thoughtful eye,
Since first in childhood 'midst the vines ye play'd,
  And sent glad singing through the free blue sky.
Ye were but two—and, when that spirit pass'd,
    Woe to the one, the last!

Woe, yet not long!—She linger'd but to trace
  Thine image from the image in her breast—
Once, once again to see that buried face
  But smile upon her, ere she went to rest.
Too sad a smile! its living light was o'er—
    It answer'd hers no more.

The earth grew silent when thy voice departed,
  The home too lonely whence thy step had fled;
What then was left for her, the faithful-hearted?
  Death, death, to still the yearning for the dead!
Softly she perish'd;—be the Flower deplored
    Here with the Lyre and Sword!

Have ye not met ere now?—so let those trust
  That meet for moments but to part for years—
That weep, watch, pray, to hold back dust from
    dust—
  That love, where love is but a fount of tears.
Brother, sweet sister! peace around ye dwell:—
    Lyre, Sword, and Flower, farewell!"*

---

## THE DEATH-DAY OF KORNER.†

A song for the death-day of the brave—
  A song of pride!
The youth went down to a hero's grave,
  With the Sword, his bride.‡

He went, with his noble heart unworn,
  And pure, and high;
An eagle stooping from clouds of morn,
  Only to die!

He went with the lyre whose lofty tone
  Beneath his hand
Had thrill'd to the name of his God alone
  And his father-land!

And with all his glorious feelings yet
  In their first glow,
Like a southern stream that no frost hath met
  To chain its flow.

A song for the death-day of the brave—
  A song of pride!
For him that went to a hero's grave,
  With the Sword, his bride.

He hath left a voice in his trumpet lays
  To turn the flight,
And a guiding spirit for after-days,
  Like a watch-fire's light.

* The following lines, recently addressed to the author of the
above, by the venerable father of Korner, who, with the mother
still survives the " Lyre, Sword, and Flower," here commemorated,
may not be uninteresting to the German reader.

Wohllaut tont aus der Ferne von freundlichen Lüften getragen,
Schmeichelt mit lindernder Kraft sich in der Trauernden Ohr,
Stärkt den erhebenden Glauben an solcher seelen Verwandschaft,
Die zum Tempel die brust nur fur das Würdige weihn.
Aus dem Lande zu dem sich stets der gefeyerte Jungling
Hingezogen gefuhlt, wird ihm ein glanzender Lohn.
Heil dem Brittischer Volke, wenn ihm das Deutsche nicht fremd ist!
Über Lander und Meer reichen sich beyde die Hand.
               *Theodor Korner's Vater*

† On reading part of a letter from Korner's father, addressed to
Mr. Richardson, the translator of his works, in which he speaks of
" The death-day of his son."

‡ See the Sword Song, composed on the morning of his death.

---

And a grief in his father's soul to rest,
  'Midst all high thought;
And a memory unto his mother's breast,
  With healing fraught.

And a name and fame above the blight
  Of earthly breath,
Beautiful—beautiful and bright,
  In life and death!

A song for the death of the brave—
  A song of pride!
For him that went to a hero's grave,
  With the Sword, his bride!

---

## AN HOUR OF ROMANCE.

            I come
To this sweet place for quiet.  Every tree,
And bush, and fragrant flower, and hilly path,
And thymy mound that flings unto the winds
Its morning incense, is my friend.
              *Barry Cornwall.*

---

THERE were thick leaves above me and around,
  And low sweet sighs, like those of childhood's
    sleep,
Amidst their dimness, and a fitful sound
  As of soft showers on water; dark and deep
Lay the oak shadows o'er the turf, so still
They seem'd but pictured glooms: a hidden rill
Made music, such as haunts us in a dream,
Under the fern tufts; and a tender gleam
Of soft green light, as by the glowworm shed,
  Came pouring through the woven beach boughs
    down,
And steep'd the magic page wherein I read
  Of royal chivalry and old renown,
A tale of Palestine.*—Meanwhile the bee
  Swept past me with a tone of summer hours,
  A drowsy bugle, wafting thoughts of flowers,
Blue skies and amber sunshine: brightly free,
On flung its proud the purple dragon-fly
Shot glancing like a fairy javelin by;
And a sweet voice of sorrow told the dell
  Where sat the lone wood-pigeon.

                  But ere long,
All sense of these things faded, as the spell
  Breathing from that high gorgeous tale grew
    strong
On my chain'd soul.—'t was not the leaves I heard;
A Syrian wind the lion-banner stirr'd,
Through its proud floating folds:—'t was not the
    brook,
  Singing in secret through its grassy glen;—
  A wild shrill trumpet of the Saracen
Peal'd from the desert's lonely heart, and shook
The burning air.—Like clouds when winds are
    high,
O'er glittering sands flew steeds of Araby,
And tents rose up, and sudden lance and spear
Flash'd where a fountain's diamond wave lay clear,
Shadow'd by graceful palm-trees. Then the shout
Of merry England's joy swell'd freely out,
Sent through an eastern heaven, whose glorious
    hue
Made shields dark mirrors to its depths of blue:
And harps were there—I heard their sounding
    strings,
As the waste echo'd to the mirth of kings.—
The bright masque faded.—Unto life's worn track,
What call'd me from its flood of glory back?
A voice of happy childhood!—and they pass'd,
Banner, and harp, and Paynim's trumpet's blast;
Yet might I scarce bewail the splendours gone,
My heart so leap'd to that sweet laughter's tone.

       * Palestine—Tales of the Crusaders.

## A VOYAGER'S DREAM OF LAND.

His very heart athirst
To gaze at Nature in her green array,
Upon the ship's tall side he stands, possess'd
With visions prompted by intense desire;
Fair fields appear below, such as he left
Far distant, such as he would die to find:—
He seeks them headlong, and is seen no more.
*Cowper.*

The hollow dash of waves!—the ceaseless roar!—
Silence, ye billows!—vex my soul no more.

There's a spring in the woods by my sunny home,
Afar from the dark sea's tossing foam;
Oh! the fall of that fountain is sweet to hear,
As a song from the shore to the sailor's ear!
And the sparkle which up to the sun it throws,
Through the feathery fern and the olive boughs,
And the gleam on its path as it steals away
Into deeper shades from the sultry day,
And the large water-lilies that o'er its bed
Their pearly leaves to the soft light spread,
They haunt me! I dream of that bright spring's
     flow,
I thirst for its rills like a wounded roe!

Be still, thou sea-bird, with thy clanging cry,
My spirit sickens, as thy wing sweeps by.

Know ye my home, with the lulling sound
Of leaves from the lime and the chestnut round?
Know ye it, brethren! where bower'd it lies,
Under the purple of southern skies?
With the streamy gold of the sun that shines
In through the cloud of its clustering vines,
And the summer breath of the myrtle flowers,
Borne from the mountains in dewy hours,
And the fire-fly's glance through the dark'ning
     shades,
Like shooting stars in the forest glades,
And the scent of the citron at eve's dim fall—
Speak! have ye known, have ye felt them all?

The heavy rolling surge! the rocking mast!
Hush! give my dream's deep music way, thou blast!

Oh, the glad sounds of the joyous earth!
The notes of the singing cicala's mirth,
The murmurs that live in the mountain pines,
The sighing of reeds as the day declines,
The wings flitting home through the crimson glow
That steeps the wood when the sun is low,
The voice of the night-bird that sends a thrill
To the heart of the leaves when the winds are
     still—
I hear them!—around me they rise, they swell,
They call back my spirit with Hope to dwell—
They come with a breath from the fresh spring-
     time,
And waken my youth in its hour of prime.

The white foam dashes high—away, away!
Shroud my green land no more, thou blinding spray!

It is there!—down the mountains I see the sweep
Of the chestnut forests, the rich and deep,
With the burden and glory of flowers that they
     bear,
Floating upborne on the blue summer air,
And the light pouring through them in tender
     gleams,
And the flashing forth of a thousand streams!
Hold me not, brethren! I go, I go,
To the hills of my youth, where the myrtles blow,
To the depths of the woods, where the shadows
     rest,
Massy and still, on the greensward's breast

To the rocks that resound with the water's play—
I hear the sweet laugh of my fount—give way!

Give way!—the booming surge, the tempest's roar,
The sea-bird's wail, shall vex my soul no more.

## THE EFFIGIES.

Der rasche Kampf verewigt einen Mann:
Er falle gleich, so preiset ihn das Lied.
Allein die Thranen, die unendlichen
Der uberliebnen, der verlass'nen Frau,
Zahlt keine Nachwelt.
*Goethe.*

Warrior! whose image on thy tomb,
     With shield and crested head,
Sleeps proudly in the purple gloom
     By the stain'd window shed
The records of thy name and race
     Have failed from the stone,
Yet, through a cloud of years, I trace
     What thou hast been and done

A banner, from its flashing spear,
     Flung out o'er many a fight;
A war-cry ringing far and clear,
     And strong to turn the flight;
An arm that bravely bore the lance
     On for the holy shrine,
A haughty heart and a kingly glance—
     Chief! were not these things thine?

A lofty place where leaders sate
     Around the council board;
In festive halls a chair of state
     When the blood-red wine was pour'd;
A name that drew a prouder tone
     From herald, harp, and bard;
Surely these things were all thine own—
     So hadst thou thy reward.

Woman! whose sculptured form at rest
     By the arm'd knight is laid,
With meek hands folded o'er a breast
     In matron robes array'd;
What was *thy* tale?—O gentle mate
     Of him, the bold and free,
Bound unto his victorious fate,
     What bard hath sung of *thee?*

*He* woo'd a bright and burning star—
     *Thine* was the void, the gloom,
The straining eye that follow'd far
     His fast receding plume;
The heart-sick listening while his steed
     Sent echoes on the breeze;
The pang—but when did *Fame* take heed
     Of griefs obscure as these?

Thy silent and secluded hours
     Through many a lonely day,
While bending o'er thy broider'd flowers,
     With spirit far away;
Thy weeping midnight prayers for him
     Who fought on Syrian plains,
Thy watchings till the torch grew dim—
     *These* fill no minstrel strains.

A still, sad life was thine!—long years
     With tasks unguerdon'd fraught—
Deep, quiet love, submissive tears,
     Vigils of anxious thought;
Prayer at the cross in fervour pour'd,
     Alms to the pilgrim given—
Oh! happy, happier than thy lord,
     In that lone path to heaven!

## THE LANDING OF THE PILGRIM FATHERS
### IN NEW-ENGLAND.

*Look now abroad—another race has fill'd*
*Those populous borders—wide the wood recedes,*
*And towns shoot up, and fertile realms are till'd;*
*The land is full of harvests and green meads.*
*Bryant.*

The breaking waves dash'd high
  On a stern and rock-bound coast,
And the woods against a stormy sky
  Their giant branches toss'd;

And the heavy night hung dark,
  The hills and waters o'er,
When a band of exiles moor'd their bark
  On the wild New-England shore.

Not as the conqueror comes,
  They, the true-hearted, came;
Not with the roll of the stirring drums,
  And the trumpet that sings of fame:

Not as the flying come,
  In silence and in fear;—
They shook the depths of the desert gloom
  With their hymns of lofty cheer.

Amidst the storm they sang,
  And the stars heard and the sea!
And the sounding aisles of the dim woods rang
  To the anthem of the free.

The ocean eagle soar'd
  From his nest by the white wave's foam,
And the rocking pines of the forest roar'd—
  This was their welcome home!

There were men with hoary hair
  Amidst that pilgrim band;—
Why had *they* come to wither there,
  Away from their childhood's land?

There was woman's fearless eye,
  Lit by her deep love's truth;
There was manhood's brow serenely high,
  And the fiery heart of youth.

What sought they thus afar?
  Bright jewels of the mine?
The wealth of seas, the spoils of war?—
  They sought a faith's pure shrine!

Ay, call it holy ground,
  The soil where first they trod!
They have left unstain'd what there they found—
  Freedom to worship God.

---

## THE SPIRIT'S MYSTERIES.

*And slight, withal, may be the things which bring*
*Back on the heart the weight which it would fling*
*Aside for ever;—it may be a sound—*
*A tone of music—summer's breath, or spring—*
*A flower—a leaf—the ocean—which may wound—*
*Striking th' electric chain wherewith we are darkly bound.*
*Childe Harold.*

The power that dwelleth in sweet sounds to waken
  Vague yearnings, like the sailor's for the shore,
And dim remembrances, whose hue seems taken
  From some bright former state, our own no
    more;
Is not this all a mystery?—Who shall say
Whence are those thoughts, and whither tends
    their way?

The sudden images of vanish'd things,
  That o'er the spirit flash, we know not why;
Tones from some broken harp's deserted strings,
  Warm sunset hues of summers long gone by;
A rippling wave—the dashing of an oar—
A flower-scent floating past our parents' door·

A word—scarce noted in its hour perchance,
  Yet back returning with a plaintive tone;
A smile—a sunny or a mournful glance,
  Full of sweet meanings now from this world
    flown;
Are not these mysteries when to life they start,
And press vain tears in gushes from the heart?

And the far wanderings of the soul in dreams,
  Calling up shrouded faces from the dead,
And with them bringing soft or solemn gleams,
  Familiar objects brightly to o'erspread;
And wakening buried love, or joy, or fear—
These are night's mysteries—who shall make them
    clear?

And the strange inborn sense of coming ill,
  That ofttimes whispers to the haunted breast,
In a low tone which naught can drown or still,
  'Midst feasts and melodies a secret guest;
Whence doth that murmur wake, that shadow
    fall?
Why shakes the spirit thus?—'t is mystery all!

Darkly we move—we press upon the brink
  Haply of viewless worlds, and know it not;
Yes! it may be, that nearer than we think
  Are those whom death has parted from our lot,
Fearfully, wondrously, our souls are made—
Let us walk humbly on, but undismay'd!

Humbly—for knowledge strives in vain to feel
  Her way amidst these marvels of the mind;
Yet undismay'd—for do they not reveal
  Th' immortal being with our dust entwined?—
So let us deem! and e'en the tears they wake
Shall then be blest, for that high nature's sake.

---

## THE DEPARTED.

*Thou shalt lie down*
*With patriarchs of the infant world—with kings,*
*The powerful of the earth—the wise—the good,*
*Fair forms, and hoary seers of ages past,*
*All in one mighty sepulchre.*
*Bryant.*

And shrink ye from the way
  To the spirit's distant shore?—
Earth's mightiest men, in arm'd array,
  Are thither gone before.

The warrior kings, whose banner
  Flew far as eagles fly,
They are gone where swords avail them not,
  From the feast of victory.

And the seers who sat of yore
  By orient palm or wave,
They have pass'd with all their starry lore—
  Can ye still fear the grave?

We fear! we fear!—the sunshine
  Is joyous to behold,
And we reck not of the buried kings,
  Nor the awful seers of old.

Ye shrink!—the bards whose lays
  Have made your deep hearts burn—
They have left the sun, and the voice of praise
  For the land whence none return.

And the beautiful, whose record
  Is the verse that cannot die,
They too are gone, with their glorious bloom,
  From the love of human eye.

Would ye not join that throng
  Of the earth's departed flowers,
And the masters of the mighty song
  In their far and fadeless bowers?

Those songs are high and holy,
　But they vanquish not our fear;
Not from our path those flowers are gone—
　We fain would linger here!

Linger then yet awhile,
　As the last leaves on the bough!—
Ye have loved the light of many a smile,
　That is taken from you now.

There have been sweet singing voices
　In your walks, that now are still;
There are seats left void in your earthly homes,
　Which none again may fill.

Soft eyes are seen no more,
　That made spring-time in your heart;
Kindred and friends are gone before—
　And ye still fear to part?

We fear not now, we fear not!
　Though the way through darkness bends·
Our souls are strong to follow *them*,
　Our own familiar friends!

------

## THE PALM TREE.*

It waved not through an eastern sky,
Beside a fount of Araby:
It was not fann'd by southern breeze
In some green isle of Indian seas;
Nor did its graceful shadow sleep
O'er stream of Afric, lone and deep.

But fair the exiled palm tree grew
'Midst foliage of no kindred hue;
Through the laburnum's dropping gold
Rose the light shaft of orient mould,
And Europe's violets faintly sweet,
Purpled the moss-beds at its feet.

Strange look'd it there !—the willow stream'd,
Where silvery waters near it gleam'd;
The lime bough lured the honey-bee
To murmur by the desert's tree,
And showers of snowy roses made
A lustre in its fan-like shade.

There came an eve of festal hours—
Rich music fill'd that garden's bowers:
Lamps, that from flowering branches hung
On sparks of dew soft colour flung,
And bright forms glanced—a fairy show—
Under the blossoms, to and fro.

But one, a lone one, 'midst the throng,
Seem'd reckless all of dance or song :
He was a youth of dusky mien,
Whereon the Indian sun had been,
Of crested brow, and long black hair—
A stranger, like the palm tree there.

And slowly, sadly moved his plumes,
Glittering athwart the leafy glooms:
He pass'd the pale green olives by,
Nor won the chestnut flowers his eye;
But when to that sole palm he came,
Then shot a rapture through his frame!

To him, to him its rustling spoke,
The silence of his soul it broke!
It whisper'd of his own bright isle,
That lit the ocean with a smile!
Aye, to his ear that native tone
Had something of the sea-wave's moan.

His mother's cabin home, that lay
Where feathery cocoas fringed the bay;
The dashing of his brethren's oar—
The conch-note heard along the shore ;—
All through his wakening bosom swept!
He clasp'd his country's tree, and wept!

* This incident is, I think, recorded by De Lille, in his poem "Les Jardins."

23

Oh, scorn him not !—the strength whereby
The patriot girds himself to die,
Th' unconquerable power which fills
The freeman battling on his hills,
These have one fountain deep and clear—
The same whence gush'd that child-like tear

------

## THE CHILD'S LAST SLEEP,

SUGGESTED BY A MONUMENT OF CHANTREY'S.

------

Thou sleepest—but when wilt thou wake, fair
　　child ?
When the fawn awakes in the forest wild ?
When the lark's wing mounts with the breeze of
　　morn ?
When the first rich breath of the rose is born ?—
Lovely thou sleepest, yet something lies
Too deep and still on thy soft-seal'd eyes;
Mournful, though sweet, is thy rest to see—
When will the hour of thy rising be ?

Not when the fawn wakes, not when the lark
On the crimson cloud of the morn floats dark—
Grief with vain passionate tears hath wet
The hair, shedding gleams from thy pale brow yet
Love, with sad kisses unfelt, hath press'd
Thy meek-dropt eyelids and quiet breast;
And the glad spring, calling out bird and bee,
Shall colour all blossoms, fair child! but thee.

Thou'rt gone from us, bright one !—that *thou*
　　shouldst die,
And life be left to the butterfly !*
Thou'rt gone as a dew-drop is swept from the
　　bough—
Oh! for the world where thy home is now!
How may we love but in doubt and fear,
How may we anchor our fond hearts here,
How should e'en joy but a trembler be,
Beautiful dust ! when we look on thee ?

------

## THE SUNBEAM.

Thou art no lingerer in monarch's hall—
A joy thou art, and a wealth to all!
A bearer of hope unto land and sea :—
Sunbeam ! what gift hath the world like thee ?

Thou art walking the billows, and ocean smiles;
Thou hast touch'd with glory his thousand isles;
Thou hast lit up the ships, and the feathery foam,
And gladden'd the sailor, like words from home.

To the solemn depths of the forest shades,
Thou art streaming on through their green arcades,
And the quivering leaves that have caught thy
　　glow,
Like fire-flies glance to the pools below.

I look'd on the mountains—a vapour lay
Folding their heights in its dark array:
Thou brakest forth, and the mist became
A crown and a mantle of living flame.

I look'd on the peasant's lowly cot—
Something of sadness had wrapt the spot;
But a gleam of *thee* on its lattice fell,
And it laugh'd into beauty at that bright spell.

To the earth's wild places a guest thou art,
Flushing the waste like the rose's heart;
And thou scornest not from thy pomp to shed
A tender smile on the ruin's head.

Thou takest through the dim church aisle thy way
And its pillars from twilight flash forth to day,
And its high, pale tombs, with their trophies old,
Are bathed in a flood as of molten gold.

* A butterfly, as if resting on a flower, is sculptured on the monument

And thou turnest not from the humblest grave,
Where a flower to the sighing winds may wave;
Thou scatterest its gloom like the dreams of rest,
Thou sleepest in love on its grassy breast.

Sunbeam of summer! oh, what is like thee?
Hope of the wilderness, joy of the sea!—
*One* thing is like thee to mortals given,
The faith touching all things with hues of Heaven!

---

## BREATHINGS OF SPRING.

*Thou givest me flowers, thou givest me songs;—bring back*
*The love that I have lost!*

---

What wakest thou, Spring!—sweet voices in the
    woods,
  And reed-like echoes, that have long been mute;
Thou bringest back, to fill the solitudes,
  The lark's clear pipe, the cuckoo's viewless flute,
Whose tone seems breathing mournfulness or glee,
     E'en as our hearts may be.

And the leaves greet thee, Spring!—the joyous
    leaves,
  Whose tremblings gladden many a copse and
    glade,
Where each young spray a rosy flush receives,
  When thy south wind hath pierced the whispery
    shade,
And happy murmurs, running through the grass,
     Tell that thy footsteps pass.

And the bright waters—they too hear thy call,
  Spring, the awakener! thou hast burst their
    sleep!
Amidst the hollows of the rocks their fall
  Makes melody, and in the forests deep,
Where sudden sparkles and blue gleams betray
     Their windings to the day.

And flowers—the fairy-peopled world of flowers!
  Thou from the dust hast set that glory free,
Colouring the cowslip with the sunny hours,
  And pencilling the wood anemone;
Silent they seem—yet each to thoughtful eye
     Glows with mute poesy.

But what awakest thou in the *heart*, O Spring!
  The human heart, with all its dreams and sighs?
Thou that givest back so many a buried thing,
  Restorer of forgotten harmonies!
Fresh songs and scents break forth where'er thou
    art,
     What wakest thou in the heart?

Too much, oh! there too much!—we know not
    well
  Wherefore it should be thus, yet roused by thee,
What fond, strange yearnings, from the soul's deep
    cell,
  Gush for the faces we no more may see!
How are we haunted, in thy wind's low tone,
     By voices that are gone.

Looks of familiar love, that never more,
  Never on earth, our aching eyes shall meet,
Past words of welcome to our household door,
  And vanish'd smiles, and sounds of parted feet—
Spring! 'midst the murmurs of thy flowering trees,
     Why, why revivest thou these?

Vain longings for the dead!—why come they back
  With thy young birds, and leaves, and living
    blooms?
Oh! is it not, that from thine earthly track
  Hope to thy world may look beyond the tombs?
Yes! gentle spring; no sorrow dims thine air
     Breathed by our loved ones *there!*

---

## THE ILLUMINATED CITY.

---

The hills all glow'd with a festive light,
For the royal city rejoiced by night:
There were lamps hung forth upon tower and tree,
Banners were lifted and streaming free;
Every tall pillar was wreath'd with fire,
Like a shooting meteor was every spire;
And the outline of many a dome on high
Was traced, as in stars, on the clear dark sky.

I pass'd through the streets; there were throngs on
    throngs—
Like sounds of the deep were their mingled songs;
There was music forth from each palace borne—
A peal of the cymbal, the harp, and horn;
The forests heard it, the mountains rang,
The hamlets woke to its haughty clang;
Rich and victorious was every tone,
Telling the land of her foes o'erthrown.

Didst thou meet not a mourner for all the slain!
Thousands lie dead on their battle plain!
Gallant and true were the hearts that fell—
Grief in the homes they have left must dwell;
Grief o'er the aspect of childhood spread,
And bowing the beauty of woman's head:
Didst thou hear, 'midst the songs, not one tender
    moan,
For the many brave to their slumbers gone?

I saw not the face of a weeper there—
Too strong, perchance, was the bright lamp's
    glare!—
I heard not a wail 'midst the joyous crowd—
The music of victory was all too loud!
Mighty it roll'd on the winds afar,
Shaking the streets like a conqueror's car;
Through torches and streamers its flood swept by—
How could I listen for moan or sigh?

Turn then away from life's pageants, turn,
If its deep story thy heart would learn!
Ever too bright is that outward show,
Dazzling the eyes till they see not woe.
But lift the proud mantle which hides from thy
    view
The things thou shouldst gaze on, the sad and true
Nor fear to survey what its folds conceal—
So must thy spirit be taught to feel!

---

## THE SPELLS OF HOME.

---

*There blend the ties that strengthen*
  *Our hearts in hours of grief,*
*The silver links that lengthen*
  *Joy's visits when most brief.*
          *Bernard Barton.*

---

By the soft green light in the woody glade,
On the banks of moss where thy childhood play'd
By the household tree through which thine eye
First look'd in love to the summer sky,
By the dewy gleam, by the very breath
Of the primrose tufts in the grass beneath,
Upon thy heart there is laid a spell,
Holy and precious—oh! guard it well!

By the sleepy ripple of the stream,
Which hath lull'd thee into many a dream,
By the shiver of the ivy leaves
To the wind of morn at thy casement eaves,
By the bee's deep murmur in the limes,
By the music of the Sabbath chimes,
By every sound of thy native shade,
Stronger and dearer the spell is made

By the gathering round the winter hearth
When twilight call'd unto household mirth
By the fairy tale or the legend old
In that ring of happy faces told,

By the quiet hour when hearts unite
In the parting prayer and the kind "Good-night!"
By the smiling eye and the loving tone,
Over thy life has the spell been thrown.

And bless that gift!—it hath gentle might,
A guardian power and a guiding light.
It hath led the freeman forth to stand
In the mountain battles of his land;
It hath brought the wanderer o'er the seas
To die on the hills of his own fresh breeze;
And back to the gates of his father's hall
It hath led the weeping prodigal.

Yes! when thy heart, in its pride, would stray
From the pure first loves of its youth away—
When the sullying breath of the world would come
O'er the flowers it brought from its childhood's
    home—
Think thou again of the woody glade,
And the sound by the rustling ivy made,
Think of the tree at thy father's door,
And the kindly spell shall have power once more!

## ROMAN GIRL'S SONG.

*Roma, Roma, Roma!*
*Non e piu come era prima.*

Rome, Rome! thou art no more
    As thou hast been!
On thy seven hills of yore
    Thou satt'st a queen.

Thou hadst thy triumphs then
    Purpling the street,
Leaders and sceptred men
    Bow'd at thy feet.

They that thy mantle wore,
    As gods were seen—
Rome, Rome! thou art no more
    As thou hast been!

Rome! thine imperial brow
    Never shall rise:
What hast thou left thee now?—
    Thou hast thy skies!

Blue, deeply blue, they are,
    Gloriously bright!
Veiling thy wastes afar
    With colour'd light.

Thou hast the sunset's glow,
    Rome, for thy dower,
Flushing tall cypress bough,
    Temple and tower!

And all sweet sounds are thine,
    Lovely to hear,
While night, o'er tomb and shrine,
    Rests darkly clear.

Many a solemn hymn,
    By starlight sung,
Sweeps through the arches dim,
    Thy wrecks among.

Many a flute's low swell,
    On thy soft air
Lingers, and loves to dwell
    With summer there.

Thou hast the south's rich gift
    Of sudden song—
A charmed fountain, swift,
    Joyous, and strong.

Thou hast fair forms that move
    With queenly tread;
Thou hast proud fanes above
    Thy mighty dead.

Yet wears thy Tiber's shore
    A mournful mien :—
Rome, Rome! thou art no more
    As thou hast been!

## THE DISTANT SHIP.

The sea-bird's wing, o'er ocean's breast
    Shoots like a glancing star,
While the red radiance of the west
    Spreads kindling fast and far;
And yet that splendour wins thee not—
    Thy still and thoughtful eye
Dwells but on one dark distant spot
    Of all the main and sky.

Look round thee!—o'er the slumbering deep
    A solemn glory broods;
A fire hath touch'd the beacon-steep,
    And all the golden woods;
A thousand gorgeous clouds on high
    Burn with the amber light!—
What spell, from that rich pageantry,
    Chains down thy gazing sight?

A softening thought of human cares,
    A feeling link'd to earth?
Is not yon speck a bark, which bears
    The loved of many a hearth?
Oh! do not Hope, and Grief, and Fear,
    Crowd her frail world e'en now,
And manhood's prayer, and woman's tear
    Follow her venturous prow?

Bright are the floating clouds above,
    The glittering seas below,
But we are bound by cords of love
    To kindred weal and woe.
Therefore, amidst this wide array
    Of glorious things and fair,
My soul is on that bark's lone way—
    For human hearts are there.

## THE BIRDS OF PASSAGE.

Birds, joyous birds of the wandering wing!
Whence is it ye come with the flowers of spring?—
'We come from the shores of the green old Nile,
From the land where the roses of Sharon smile,
From the palms that wave through the Indian sky
From the myrrh-trees of glowing Araby.

" We have wept o'er cities in song renown'd—
Silent they lie with the deserts round!
We have cross'd proud rivers, whose tide hath
    roll'd
All dark with the warrior-blood of old;
And each worn wing hath regain'd its home,
Under peasant's roof-tree, or monarch's dome."

And what have ye found in the monarch's dome
Since last ye traversed the blue sea's foam?—
" We have found a change, we have found a pall
And a gloom o'ershadowing the banquet's hall,
And a mark on the floor as of life-drops spilt—
Naught looks the same, save the nest we built!"

O joyous birds, it hath still been so;
Through the halls of kings doth the tempest go!
But the huts of the hamlet lie still and deep,
And the hills o'er their quiet a vigil keep,
Say what have ye found in the peasant's cot,
Since last ye parted from that sweet spot?—

" A change we have found there — and many a
    change!
Faces, and footsteps, and all things strange!
Gone are the heads of the silvery hair,
And the young that were have a brow of care,
And the place is hush'd where the children play'd—
Naught looks the same save the nest we made!"

Sad is your tale of the beautiful earth,
Birds that o'ersweep it in power and mirth!

Yet through the wastes of the trackless air
Ye have a guide, and shall we despair?
Ye over desert and deep have pass'd—
So may we reach our bright home at last!

## THE GRAVES OF A HOUSEHOLD

THEY grew in beauty, side by side,
　They fill'd one home with glee;—
Their graves are sever'd, far and wide,
　By mount, and stream, and sea.

The same fond mother bent at night
　O'er each fair sleeping brow;
She had each folded flower in sight—
　Where are those dreamers now?

One, 'midst the forests of the west,
　By a dark stream is laid—
The Indian knows his place of rest,
　Far in the cedar shade.

The sea, the blue lone sea, hath one—
　He lies where pearls lie deep;
He was the loved of all, yet none
　O'er his low bed may weep.

One sleeps where southern vines are drest,
　Above the noble slain:
He wrapt his colours round his breast
　On a blood-red field of Spain.

And one—o'er her the myrtle showers
　Its leaves by soft winds fann'd;
She faded 'midst Italian flowers—
　The last of that bright band.

And parted thus they rest, who play'd
　Beneath the same green tree;
Whose voices mingled as they pray'd
　Around one parent knee!

They that with smiles lit up the hall,
　And cheer'd with song the hearth—
Alas! for love, if thou wert all,
　And naught beyond, O earth!

## MOZART'S REQUIEM.

A short time before the death of Mozart, a stranger
of remarkable appearance, and dressed in deep mourning, called at his house, and requested him to prepare a
Requiem, in his best style, for the funeral of a distinguished person. The sensitive imagination of the com-
poser immediately seized upon the circumstance as an
omen of his own fate; and the nervous anxiety with
which he laboured to fulfil the task, had the effect of
realizing his impression. He died within a few days
after completing this magnificent piece of music, which
was performed at his interment.

> These birds of Paradise but long to see
> Back to their native mansion.
> *Prophecy of Dante.*

A REQUIEM!—and for whom?
　For beauty in its bloom?
For valour fall'n—a broken rose or sword?
　A dirge for king or chief,
　With pomp of stately grief,
Banner, and torch, and waving plume deplored?

Not so, it is not so!
　The warning voice I know,
From other worlds a strange mysterious tone;
　A solemn funeral air
　It call'd me to prepare,
And my heart answer'd secretly—my own!

One more then, one more strain,
　In links of joy and pain,
Mighty the troubled spirit to enthrall!

And let me breathe my dower
　Of passion and of power
Full into that deep lay—the last of all!

　The last!—and I must go
　From this bright world below,
This realm of sunshine, ringing with sweet sounds
　Must leave its festal skies,
　With all their melodies,
That ever in my breast glad echoes found!

　Yet have I known it long:
　Too restless and too strong
Within this clay hath been th' o'ermastering flame;
　Swift thoughts, that came and went,
　Like torrents o'er me sent,
Have shaken, as a reed, my thrilling frame.

　Like perfumes on the wind,
　Which none may stay or bind,
The beautiful comes floating through my soul;
　I strive with yearnings vain
　The spirit to detain
Of the deep harmonies that past me roll!

　Therefore disturbing dreams
　Trouble the secret streams
And founts of music that o'erflow my breast;
　Something far more divine
　Than may on earth be mine,
Haunts my worn heart, and will not let me rest.

　Shall I then fear the tone
　That breathes from worlds unknown?—
Surely these feverish aspirations there
　Shall grasp their full desire,
　And this unsettled fire
Burn calmly, brightly, in immortal air.

　One more then, one more strain,
　To earthly joy and pain
A rich, and deep, and passionate farewell!
　I pour each fervent thought
　With fear, hope, trembling, fraught,
Into the notes that o'er my dust shall swell.

## THE IMAGE IN LAVA.*

THOU thing of years departed!
　What ages have gone by,
Since here the mournful seal was set
　By love and agony!

Temple and tower have moulder'd,
　Empires from earth have pass'd,
And woman's heart hath left a trace
　Those glories to outlast!

And childhood's fragile image
　Thus fearfully enshrined,
Survives the proud memorials rear'd
　By conquerors of mankind.

Babe! wert thou brightly slumbering
　Upon thy mother's breast,
When suddenly the fiery tomb
　Shut round each gentle guest?

A strange, dark fate o'ertook you,
　Fair babe and loving heart!
One moment of a thousand pangs—
　Yet better than to part!

Haply of that fond bosom
　On ashes here impress'd,
Thou wert the only treasure, child!
　Whereon a hope might rest.

Perchance all vainly lavish'd
　Its other love had been,
And where it trusted, naught remain'd
　But thorns on which to lean.

Far better then to perish
　Thy form within its clasp,
Than live and lose thee, precious one!
　From that impassion'd grasp.

---

* The impression of a woman's form, with an infant clasped to
the bosom, found at the uncovering of Herculaneum.

: h ! I could pass all relics
Left by the pomps of old,
To gaze on this rude monument,
Cast in affection's mould.

Love, human love! what art thou,
Thy print upon the dust
Outlives the cities of renown
Wherein the mighty trust;

Immortal, oh! immortal
Thou art, whose earthly glow
Hath given these ashes holiness—
It must, it *must* be so!

## THE LAST WISH.

Well may I weep to leave this world—thee—all these beautiful
w ses, and plains, and hills.——*Lights and Shadows.*

Go to the forest shade,
Seek thou the well-known glade,
Where, heavy with sweet dew, the violets lie,
Gleaming through moss-tufts deep,
Like dark eyes fill'd with sleep,
And bathed in hues of summer's midnight sky.

Bring me their buds, to shed
Around my dying bed,
A breath of May and of the wood's repose;
For I, in sooth, depart
With a reluctant heart,
That fain would linger where the bright sun glows.

Fain would I stay with thee—
Alas! this may not be;
Yet bring me still the gifts of happier hours!
Go where the fountain's breast
Catches, in glassy rest,
The dim green light that pours thro' laurel bowers.

I know how softly bright,
Steep'd in that tender light,
The water-lilies tremble there e'en now;
Go to the pure stream's edge,
And from its whispering sedge
Bring me those flowers to cool my fever'd brow!

Then, as in Hope's young days,
Track thou the antique maze
Of the rich garden to its grassy mound:
There is a lone white rose,
Shedding, in sudden snows,
Its faint leaves o'er the emerald turf around.

Well know'st thou that fair tree—
A murmur of the bee
Dwells ever in the honey'd lime above;
Bring me one pearly flower
Of all its clustering shower—
For on that spot we first reveal'd our love.

Gather one woodbine bough,
Then, from the lattice low
Of the bower'd cottage which I bade thee mark,
When by the hamlet last,
Through dim wood-lanes we pass'd,
While dews were glancing to the glow-worm's
spark.

Haste! to my pillow bear
Those fragrant things and fair;
My hand no more may bind them up at eve—
Yet shall their odour soft
One bright dream round me waft
Of life, youth, summer—all that I must leave!

And, oh! if thou wouldst ask
Wherefore thy steps I task,
The grove, the stream, the hamlet vale to trace—
'T is that some thought of me,
When I am gone, may be
The spirit bound to each familiar place

I bid mine image dwell,
(Oh! break not thou the spell)
In the deep wood and by the fountain side;
Thou must not, my beloved!
Rove where we two have roved,
Forgetting her that in her spring-time died!

## FAIRY FAVOURS.

Give me but
Something whereunto I may bind my heart
Something to love, to rest upon, to clasp
Affection's tendrils round.

WOULDST thou wear the gift of immortal bloom?
Wouldst thou smile in scorn at the shadowy tomb?
Drink of this cup! it is richly fraught
With balm from the gardens of genii brought;
Drink, and the spoiler shall pass thee by,
When the young all scatter'd like rose-leaves lie.

And would not the youth of my soul be gone,
If the loved had left me, one by one?
Take back the cup that may never bless,
The gift that would make me brotherless;
How should I live, with no kindred eye
To reflect mine immortality?

Wouldst thou have empire, by sign or spell,
Over the mighty in air that dwell?
Wouldst thou call the spirits of shore and steep
To fetch thee jewels from ocean's deep?
Wave but this rod, and a viewless band,
Slaves to thy will, shall around thee stand.

And would not fear, at my coming then,
Hush every voice in the homes of men?
Would not bright eyes in my presence quail?
Young checks with a nameless thrill turn pale?
No gift be mine that aside would turn
The human love for whose founts I yearn!

Wouldst thou then read through the hearts of
those
Upon whose faith thou hast sought repose?
Wear this rich gem! it is charm'd to show
When a change comes over affection's glow;
Look on its flushing or fading hue,
And learn if the trusted be false or true!

Keep, keep the gem, that I still may trust,
Though my heart's wealth be but pour'd on dust
Let not a doubt in my soul have place,
To dim the light of a loved one's face;
Leave to the earth its warm sunny smile—
That glory would pass could I look on guile!

Say then what boon of my power shall be,
Favour'd of spirits! pour'd forth on thee?
Thou scornest the treasures of wave and mine,
Thou wilt not drink of the cup divine,
Thou art fain with a mortal's lot to rest—
Answer me! how may I grace it best?

Oh! give me no sway o'er the powers unseen,
But a human heart where my own may lean!
A friend, one tender and faithful friend,
Whose thoughts' free current with mine ma
blend,
And leaving not either on earth alone,
Bid the bright calm close of our lives be one!

## A PARTING SONG.

"Oh! mes Amis, rappelez-vous quelquefois mes vers; mon âme
y est empreinte."

*Corinne.*

WHEN will ye think of me, my friends?
When will ye think of me?—
When the last red light, the farewell of day,
From the rock and the river is passing away—

When the air with a deep'ning hush is fraught,
And the heart grows burden'd with tender thought,
    Then let it be!

When will ye think of me, kind friends?
    When will ye think of me?—
When the rose of the rich mid-summer time
Is fill'd with the hues of its glorious prime—
When ye gather its bloom, as in bright hours fled,
From the walks where my footsteps no more may
    tread—
    Then let it be!

When will ye think of me, sweet friends?
    When will ye think of me?—
When the sudden tears o'erflow your eye
At the sound of some olden melody,
When ye hear the voice of a mountain stream,
When ye feel the charm of a poet's dream,
    Then let it be!

Thus let my memory be with you, friends!
    Thus ever think of me!
Kindly and gently, but as of one
For whom 'tis well to be fled and gone—
As of a bird from a chain unbound,
As of a wanderer whose home is found—
    So let it be.